HENRY JAMES

HENRY JAMES

NOVELS 1896–1899
The Other House
The Spoils of Poynton
What Maisie Knew
The Awkward Age

THE LIBRARY OF AMERICA

James

The paper used in this publication meets the
minimum requirements of the American National Standard for
Information Sciences—Permanence of Paper for Printed
Library Materials, ANSI z39.48—1984.

Distributed to the trade in the United States
by Penguin Putnam Inc.
and in Canada by Penguin Books Canada Ltd.

Library of Congress Catalog Number: 2002030167
For cataloging information, see end of Notes.
ISBN 1–931082–30–8

───────

First Printing
The Library of America—139

Manufactured in the United States of America

Contents

Contents

THE OTHER HOUSE

I

M RS. BEEVER of Eastmead, and of "Beever and Bream,"
was a close, though not a cruel observer of what went
on, as she always said, at the other house. A great deal more
went on there, naturally, than in the great clean, square solitude
in which she had practically lived since the death of Mr. Beever,
who had predeceased by three years his friend and partner, the
late Paul Bream of Bounds, leaving to his only son, the little
godson of that trusted associate, the substantial share of the
business in which his wonderful widow—she knew and rejoiced
that she was wonderful—now had a distinct voice. Paul Beever,
in the bloom of eighteen, had just achieved a scramble from
Winchester to Oxford: it was his mother's design that he
should go into as many things as possible before coming into
the Bank. The Bank, the pride of Wilverley, the high clear arch
of which the two houses were the solid piers, was worth an expensive education. It was, in the talk of town and county, "hun-
dreds of years" old, and as incalculably "good" as a subject of
so much infallible arithmetic could very well be. That it enjoyed
the services of Mrs. Beever herself was at present enough for
her and an ample contentment to Paul, who inclined so little to
the sedentary that she foresaw she should some day be as anxious at putting him into figures as she had in his childhood been
easy about putting him into breeches. Half the ground moreover was held by young Anthony Bream, the actual master of
Bounds, the son and successor of her husband's colleague.

She was a woman indeed of many purposes; another of
which was that on leaving Oxford the boy should travel and inform himself: she belonged to the age that regarded a foreign
tour not as a hasty dip, but as a deliberate plunge. Still another
had for its main feature that on his final return he should
marry the nicest girl she knew: that too would be a deliberate
plunge, a plunge that would besprinkle his mother. It would
do with the question what it was Mrs. Beever's inveterate
household practice to do with all loose and unarranged objects

3

—it would get it out of the way. There would have been difficulty in saying whether it was a feeling for peace or for war, but
her constant habit was to lay the ground bare for complications that as yet at least had never taken place. Her life was like
a room prepared for a dance: the furniture was all against the
walls. About the young lady in question she was perfectly definite; the nicest girl she knew was Jean Martle, whom she had
just sent for at Brighton to come and perform in that character. The performance was to be for the benefit of Paul, whose
midsummer return was at hand and in whom the imagination
of alternatives was to be discouraged from the first. It was on
the whole a comfort to Mrs. Beever that he had little imagination of anything.

Jean Martle, condemned to Brighton by a father who was
Mrs. Beever's second cousin and whom the doctors, the great
men in London, kept there, as this lady opined, because he
was too precious wholly to lose and too boring often to see—
Jean Martle would probably some day have money and would
possibly some day have sense: even as regards a favoured candidate this marked the extent of Mrs. Beever's somewhat dry
expectations. They were addressed in a subordinate degree to
the girl's "playing," which was depended on to become brilliant, and to her hair, which was viewed in the light of a hope
that it would with the lapse of years grow darker. Wilverley, in
truth, would never know if she played ill; but it had an old-
fashioned prejudice against loud shades in the natural covering of the head. One of the things his cousin had been invited
for was that Paul should get used to her eccentric colour—a
colour of which, on a certain bright Sunday of July, Mrs.
Beever noted afresh, with some alarm, the exaggerated pitch.
Her young friend had arrived two days before and now—during the elastic interval from church to luncheon—had been
despatched to Bounds with a message and some preliminary
warnings. Jean knew that she should find there a house in
some confusion, a new-born little girl, the first, a young
mother not yet "up," and an odd visitor, somewhat older
than herself, in the person of Miss Armiger, a school-friend of
Mrs. Bream, who had made her appearance a month before
that of the child and had stayed on, as Mrs. Beever with some
emphasis put it, "right through everything."

This picture of the situation had filled, after the first hour or two, much of the time of the two ladies, but it had originally included for Jean no particular portrait of the head of the family—an omission in some degree repaired, however, by the chance of Mrs. Beever's having on the Saturday morning taken her for a moment into the Bank. They had had errands in the town, and Mrs. Beever had wished to speak to Mr. Bream, a brilliant, joking gentleman, who, instantly succumbing to their invasion and turning out a confidential clerk, had received them in his beautiful private room. "Shall I like him?" Jean, with the sense of a widening circle, had, before this, adventurously asked. "Oh, yes, if you notice him!" Mrs. Beever had replied in obedience to an odd private prompting to mark him as insignificant. Later on, at the Bank, the girl noticed him enough to feel rather afraid of him: that was always with her the foremost result of being noticed herself. If Mrs. Beever passed him over, this was in part to be accounted for by all that at Eastmead was usually taken for granted. The queen-mother, as Anthony Bream kept up the jest of calling her, would not have found it easy to paint off-hand a picture of the allied sovereign whom she was apt to regard as a somewhat restless vassal. Though he was a dozen years older than the happy young prince on whose behalf she exercised her regency, she had known him from his boyhood, and his strong points and his weak were alike an old story to her.

His house was new—he had on his marriage, at a vast expense, made it quite violently so. His wife and his child were new; new also in a marked degree was the young woman who had lately taken up her abode with him and who had the air of intending to remain till she should lose that quality. But Tony himself—this had always been his name to her—was intensely familiar. Never doubting that he was a subject she had mastered, Mrs. Beever had no impulse to clear up her view by distributing her impressions. These impressions were as neatly pigeon-holed as her correspondence and her accounts— neatly, at least, save in so far as they were besprinkled with the dust of time. One of them might have been freely rendered into a hint that her young partner was a possible source of danger to her own sex. Not to her personally, of course; for herself, somehow, Mrs. Beever was not of her own sex. If she

had been a woman—she never thought of herself so loosely—
she would, in spite of her age, have doubtless been conscious
of peril. She now recognised none in life except that of Paul's
marrying wrong, against which she had taken early measures.
It would have been a misfortune therefore to feel a flaw in a
security otherwise so fine. Was not perhaps the fact that she
had a vague sense of exposure for Jean Martle a further motive for her not expatiating to that young lady on Anthony
Bream? If any such sense operated, I hasten to add, it operated without Jean's having mentioned that at the Bank he had
struck her as formidable.

Let me not fail equally to declare that Mrs. Beever's general
suspicion of him, as our sad want of signs for shades and degrees condemns me to call it, rested on nothing in the nature
of evidence. If she had ever really uttered it she might have
been brought up rather short on the question of grounds.
There were certainly, at any rate, no grounds in Tony's having, before church, sent a word over to her on the subject of
their coming to luncheon. "Dear Julia, this morning, is really
grand," he had written. "We've just managed to move to her
downstairs room, where they've put up a lovely bed and
where the sight of all her things cheers and amuses her, to say
nothing of the wide immediate outlook at her garden and her
own corner of the terrace. In short the waves are going down
and we're beginning to have our meals 'regular.' Luncheon
may be rather late, but do bring over your charming little
friend. How she lighted up yesterday my musty den! There
will be another little friend, by the way—not of mine, but of
Rose Armiger's, the young man to whom, as I think you
know, she's engaged to be married. He's just back from
China and comes down till to-morrow. Our Sunday trains are
such a bore that, having wired him to take the other line, I'm
sending to meet him at Plumbury." Mrs. Beever had no need
to reflect on these few lines to be comfortably conscious that
they summarised the nature of her neighbour—down to the
"dashed sociability," as she had heard the poor fellow, in
sharp reactions, himself call it, that had made him scribble
them and that always made him talk too much for a man in
what, more than he, she held to be a "position." He was
there in his premature bustle over his wife's slow recovery; he

was there in his boyish impatience to improvise a feast; he was there in the simplicity with which he exposed himself to the depredations, to the possible avalanche, of Miss Armiger's belongings. He was there moreover in his free-handed way of sending six miles for a young man from China, and he was most of all there in his allusion to the probable lateness of luncheon. Many things in these days were new at the other house, but nothing was so new as the hours of meals. Mrs. Beever had of old repeatedly dined there on the stroke of six. It will be seen that, as I began with declaring, she kept her finger on the pulse of Bounds.

II

WHEN Jean Martle, arriving with her message, was ushered into the hall, it struck her at first as empty, and during the moment that she supposed herself in sole possession she perceived it to be showy and indeed rather splendid. Bright, large and high, richly decorated and freely used, full of "corners" and communications, it evidently played equally the part of a place of reunion and of a place of transit. It contained so many large pictures that if they hadn't looked somehow so recent it might have passed for a museum. The shaded summer was in it now, and the odour of many flowers, as well as the tick from the chimney-piece of a huge French clock which Jean recognised as modern. The colour of the air, the frank floridity, amused and charmed her. It was not till the servant had left her that she became aware she was not alone—a discovery that soon gave her an embarrassed minute. At the other end of the place appeared a young woman in a posture that, with interposing objects, had made her escape notice, a young woman bent low over a table at which she seemed to have been writing. Her chair was pushed back, her face buried in her extended and supported arms, her whole person relaxed and abandoned. She had heard neither the swing of the muffled door nor any footfall on the deep carpet, and her attitude denoted a state of mind that made the messenger from Eastmead hesitate between quickly retreating on tiptoe or still more quickly letting her know that she was observed. Before Jean could decide her companion looked up, then rapidly and confusedly rose. She could only be Miss Armiger, and she had been such a figure of woe that it was a surprise not to see her in tears. She was by no means in tears; but she was for an instant extremely blank, an instant during which Jean remembered, rather to wonder at it, Mrs. Beever's having said of her that one really didn't know whether she was awfully plain or strikingly handsome. Jean felt that one quite did know: she was awfully plain. It may immediately be mentioned that about the charm of the apparition offered meanwhile to her own eyes Rose Armiger had not a particle of doubt: a slim, fair girl who struck her as a light sketch for something larger, a cluster of happy hints with nothing yet quite "put in" but the splendour of the hair and the grace of the clothes—clothes that were not as the clothes of Wilverley. The reflection of these things came back to Jean from a pair of eyes as to which she judged that the extreme lightness of their grey was what made them so strange as to be ugly—a reflection that spread into a sudden smile from a wide, full-lipped mouth, whose regular office, obviously, was to produce the second impression. In a flash of small square white teeth this second impression was produced and the ambiguity that Mrs. Beever had spoken of lighted up—an ambiguity worth all the dull prettiness in the world. Yes, one quite did know: Miss Armiger was strikingly handsome. It thus took her but a few seconds to repudiate every connection with the sombre image Jean had just encountered.

"Excuse my jumping out at you," she said. "I heard a sound—I was expecting a friend." Jean thought her attitude an odd one for the purpose, but hinted a fear of being in that case in the way; on which the young lady protested that she was delighted to see her, that she had already heard of her, that she guessed who she was. "And I daresay you've already heard of *me*."

Jean shyly confessed to this, and getting away from the subject as quickly as possible, produced on the spot her formal credentials.

"Mrs. Beever sent me over to ask if it's really quite right we should come to luncheon. We came out of church before the sermon, because of some people who were to go home with us. They're with Mrs. Beever now, but she told me to come straight across the garden—the short way."

Miss Armiger continued to smile. "No way ever seems short enough for Mrs. Beever!"

There was an intention in this, as Jean faintly felt, that was lost upon her; but while she was wondering her companion went on:

"Did Mrs. Beever direct you to inquire of *me*?"

Jean hesitated. "Of any one, I think, who would be here to tell me in case Mrs. Bream shouldn't be quite so well."

"She isn't quite so well."

The younger girl's face showed the flicker of a fear of losing her entertainment; on perceiving which the elder pursued:

"But we shan't romp or racket—shall we? We shall be very quiet."

"Very, very quiet," Jean eagerly echoed.

Her new friend's smile became a laugh, which was followed by the abrupt question: "Do you mean to be long with Mrs. Beever?"

"Till her son comes home. You know he's at Oxford, and his term soon ends."

"And yours ends with it—you depart as he arrives?"

"Mrs. Beever tells me I positively shan't," said Jean.

"Then you positively won't. Everything is done here exactly as Mrs. Beever tells us. Don't you like her son?" Rose Armiger asked.

"I don't know yet; it's exactly what she wants me to find out."

"Then you'll have to be very clear."

"But if I find out I don't?" Jean risked.

"I shall be very sorry for you!"

"I think then it will be the only thing in this love of an old place that I shan't have liked."

Rose Armiger for a moment rested her eyes on her visitor, who was more and more conscious that she was strange and yet not, as Jean had always supposed strange people to be, disagreeable. "Do you like *me*?" she unexpectedly inquired.

"How can I tell—at the end of three minutes?"

"*I* can tell—at the end of one! You must try to like me—you must be very kind to me," Miss Armiger declared. Then she added: "Do you like Mr. Bream?"

Jean considered; she felt that she must rise to the occasion. "Oh, immensely!" At this her interlocutress laughed again, and it made her continue with more reserve: "Of course I only saw him for five minutes—yesterday at the Bank."

"Oh, we know how long you saw him!" Miss Armiger exclaimed. "He has told us all about your visit."

Jean was slightly awe-stricken: this picture seemed to include so many people. "Whom has he told?"

Her companion had the air of being amused at everything she said; but for Jean it was an air, none the less, with a kind of foreign charm in it. "Why, the very first person was of course his poor little wife."

"But I'm not to see *her*, am I?" Jean rather eagerly asked, puzzled by the manner of the allusion and but half suspecting it to be a part of her informant's general ease.

"You're not to see her, but even if you were she wouldn't hurt you for it," this young lady replied. "She understands his friendly way and likes above all his beautiful frankness."

Jean's bewilderment began to look as if she too now, as she remembered, understood and liked these things. It might have been in confirmation of what was in her mind that she presently said: "He told me I might see the wonderful baby. He told me he would show it to me himself."

"I'm sure he'll be delighted to do that. He's awfully proud of the wonderful baby."

"I suppose it's very lovely," Jean remarked with growing confidence.

"Lovely! Do you think babies are ever lovely?"

Taken aback by this challenge, Jean reflected a little; she found, however, nothing better to say than, rather timidly: "I like dear little children, don't you?"

Miss Armiger in turn considered. "Not a bit!" she then replied. "It would be very sweet and attractive of me to say I adore them; but I never pretend to feelings I can't keep up, don't you know? If you'd like, all the same, to see Effie," she obligingly added, "I'll so far sacrifice myself as to get her for you."

Jean smiled as if this pleasantry were contagious. "You won't sacrifice *her*?"

Rose Armiger stared. "I won't destroy her."

"Then do get her."

"Not yet, not yet!" cried another voice—that of Mrs. Beever, who had just been introduced and who, having heard the last words of the two girls, came, accompanied by the servant, down the hall. "The baby's of no importance. We've come over for the mother. Is it true that Julia has had a bad turn?" she asked of Rose Armiger.

Miss Armiger had a peculiar way of looking at a person before speaking, and she now, with this detachment, delayed so long to answer Mrs. Beever that Jean also rested her eyes, as if for a reason, on the good lady from Eastmead. She greatly admired her, but in that instant, the first of seeing her at Bounds, she perceived once for all how the difference of the setting made another thing of the gem. Short and solid, with rounded corners and full supports, her hair very black and very flat, her eyes very small for the amount of expression they could show, Mrs. Beever was so "early Victorian" as to be almost prehistoric—was constructed to move amid massive mahogany and sit upon banks of Berlin-wool. She was like an odd volume, "sensibly" bound, of some old magazine. Jean knew that the great social event of her younger years had been her going to a fancy-ball in the character of an Andalusian, an incident of which she still carried a memento in the shape of a hideous fan. Jean was so constituted that she also knew, more dimly but at the end of five minutes, that the elegance at Mr. Bream's was slightly provincial. It made none the less a medium in which Mrs. Beever looked superlatively local. That indeed in turn caused Jean to think the old place still more of a "love."

"I believe our poor friend feels rather down," Miss Armiger finally brought out. "But I don't imagine it's of the least consequence," she immediately added.

The contrary of this was, however, in some degree foreshadowed in a speech directed to Jean by the footman who had admitted her. He reported Mr. Bream as having been in his wife's room for nearly an hour, and Dr. Ramage as having arrived some time before and not yet come out. Mrs. Beever decreed, upon this news, that they must drop their idea of lunching and that Jean must go straight back to the friends who had been left at the other house. It was these friends who, on the way from church, had mentioned their having got wind of the rumour—the quick circulation of which testified to the compactness of Wilverley—that there had been a sudden change in Mrs. Bream since the hour at which her husband's note was written. Mrs. Beever dismissed her companion to Eastmead with a message for her visitors. Jean was to entertain them there in her stead and to understand that she might return to luncheon only in case of being sent for. At the door the girl paused and exclaimed rather wistfully to Rose Armiger: "Well, then, give her my love!"

III

Y OUR young friend," Rose commented, "is as affectionate as she's pretty: sending her love to people she has never seen!"

"She only meant the little girl. I think it's rather nice of her," said Mrs. Beever. "My interest in these anxieties is always confined to the mamma. I thought we were going so straight."

"I dare say we are," Miss Armiger replied. "But Nurse told me an hour ago that I'm not to see her at all this morning. It will be the first morning for several days."

Mrs. Beever was silent a little. "You've enjoyed a privilege altogether denied to *me*."

"Ah, you must remember," said Rose, "that I'm Julia's oldest friend. That's always the way she treats me."

Mrs. Beever assented. "Familiarly, of course. Well, you're not mine; but that's the way I treat you too," she went on. "You must wait with me here for more news, and be as still as a mouse."

"Dear Mrs. Beever," the girl protested, "I never made a noise in all my life!"

"You will some day—you're so clever," Mrs. Beever said.

"I'm clever enough to be quiet." Then Rose added, less gaily: "I'm the one thing of her own that dear Julia has ever had."

Mrs. Beever raised her eyebrows. "Don't you count her husband?"

"I count Tony immensely; but in another way."

Again Mrs. Beever considered: she might have been wondering in what way even so expert a young person as this could count Anthony Bream except as a treasure to his wife. But what she presently articulated was: "Do you call him 'Tony' to himself?"

Miss Armiger met her question this time promptly. "He has asked me to—and to do it even to Julia. Don't be afraid!" she exclaimed; "I know my place and I shan't go too far. Of course he's everything to her now," she continued, "and the child is already almost as much; but what I mean is that if he counts for a great deal more, I, at least, go back a good deal further. Though I'm three years older we were brought together as girls by one of the strongest of all ties—the tie of a common aversion."

"Oh, I know your common aversion!" Mrs. Beever spoke with her air of general competence.

"Perhaps then you know that her detestable stepmother was, very little to my credit, my aunt. If her father, that is, was Mrs. Grantham's second husband, my uncle, my mother's brother, had been the first. Julia lost her mother; I lost both my mother and my father. Then Mrs. Grantham took me: she had shortly before made her second marriage. She put me at the horrid school at Weymouth at which she had already put her step-daughter."

"You ought to be obliged to her," Mrs. Beever suggested, "for having made you acquainted."

"We are—we've never ceased to be. It was as if she had made us sisters, with the delightful position for me of the elder, the protecting one. But it's the only good turn she has ever done us."

Mrs. Beever weighed this statement with her alternative, her business manner. "Is she really then such a monster?"

Rose Armiger had a melancholy headshake. "Don't ask me about her—I dislike her too much, perhaps, to be strictly fair. For me, however, I daresay, it didn't matter so much that she was narrow and hard: I wasn't an easy victim—I could take care of myself, I could fight. But Julia bowed her head and suffered. Never was a marriage more of a rescue."

Mrs. Beever took this in with unsuspended criticism. "And yet Mrs. Grantham travelled all the way down from town the other day simply to make her a visit of a couple of hours."

"That wasn't a kindness," the girl returned; "it was an injury, and I believe—certainly Julia believes—that it was a calculated one. Mrs. Grantham knew perfectly the effect she would have, and she triumphantly had it. She came, she said, at the particular crisis, to 'make peace.' Why couldn't she let the poor dear alone? She only stirred up the wretched past and reopened old wounds."

For answer to this Mrs. Beever remarked with some irrelevancy: "She abused *you* a good deal, I think."

Her companion smiled frankly. "Shockingly, I believe; but that's of no importance to me. She doesn't touch me or reach me now."

"Your description of her," said Mrs. Beever, "is a description of a monstrous bad woman. And yet she appears to have got two honourable men to give her the last proof of confidence."

"My poor uncle utterly withdrew his confidence when he saw her as she was. She killed him—he died of his horror of her. As for Julia's father, he's honourable if you like, but he's a muff. He's afraid of his wife."

"And her 'taking' you, as you say, who were no real relation to her—her looking after you and putting you at school: wasn't that," Mrs. Beever propounded, "a kindness?"

"She took me to torment me—or at least to make me feel her hand. She has an absolute necessity to do that—it was what brought her down here the other day."

"You make out a wonderful case," said Mrs. Beever, "and if ever I'm put on my trial for a crime—say for muddling the affairs of the Bank—I hope I shall be defended by some one with your gift and your manner. I don't wonder," she blandly pursued, "that your friends, even the blameless ones, like this dear pair, cling to you as they do."

"If you mean you don't wonder I stay on here so long," said Rose good-humouredly, "I'm greatly obliged to you for your sympathy. Julia's the one thing I have of my own."

"You make light of our husbands and lovers!" laughed Mrs. Beever. "Haven't I had the pleasure of hearing of a gentleman to whom you're soon to be married?"

Rose Armiger opened her eyes—there was perhaps a slight affectation in it. She looked, at any rate, as if she had to make a certain effort to meet the allusion. "Dennis Vidal?" she then asked.

"Lord, are there more than one?" Mrs. Beever cried; after which, as the girl, who had coloured a little, hesitated in a way that almost suggested alternatives, she added: "Isn't it a definite engagement?"

Rose Armiger looked round at the clock. "Mr. Vidal will be here this morning. Ask him how he considers it."

One of the doors of the hall at this moment opened, and

Mrs. Beever exclaimed with some eagerness: "Here he is, perhaps!" Her eagerness was characteristic; it was part of a comprehensive vision in which the pieces had already fallen into
sharp adjustment to each other. The young lady she had been
talking with had in these few minutes, for some reason, struck
her more forcibly than ever before as a possible object of interest to a youth of a candour greater even than any it was in-
cumbent on a respectable mother to cultivate. Miss Armiger
had just given her a glimpse of the way she could handle
honest gentlemen as "muffs." She was decidedly too unusual
to be left out of account. If there was the least danger of
Paul's falling in love with her it ought somehow to be
arranged that her marriage should encounter no difficulty.

The person now appearing, however, proved to be only
Doctor Ramage, who, having a substantial wife of his own, was
peculiarly unfitted to promise relief to Mrs. Beever's anxiety.
He was a little man who moved, with a warning air, on tiptoe,
as if he were playing some drawing-room game of surprises,
and who had a face so candid and circular that it suggested a
large white pill. Mrs. Beever had once said with regard to sending for him: "It isn't to take his medicine, it's to take *him*. I
take him twice a week in a cup of tea." It was his tone that did
her good. He had in his hand a sheet of note-paper, one side
of which was covered with writing and with which he immediately addressed himself to Miss Armiger. It was a prescription
to be made up, and he begged her to see that it was carried on
the spot to the chemist's, mentioning that on leaving Mrs.
Bream's room he had gone straight to the library to think it
out. Rose, who appeared to recognise at a glance its nature,
replied that as she was fidgety and wanted a walk she would
perform the errand herself. Her bonnet and jacket were there;
she had put them on to go to church, and then, on second
thoughts, seeing Mr. Bream give it up, had taken them off.

"Excellent for you to go yourself," said the Doctor. He had
an instruction to add, to which, lucid and prompt, already
equipped, she gave full attention. As she took the paper from
him he subjoined. "You're a very nice, sharp, obliging person."

"She knows what she's about!" said Mrs. Beever with much
expression. "But what in the world is Julia about?"

"I'll tell you when *I* know, my dear lady."

"Is there really anything wrong?"

"I'm waiting to find out."

Miss Armiger, before leaving them, was waiting too. She had been checked on the way to the door by Mrs. Beever's question, and she stood there with her intensely clear eyes on Doctor Ramage's face.

Mrs. Beever continued to study it as earnestly. "Then you're not going yet?"

"By no means, though I've another pressing call. I must have that thing from you first," he said to Rose.

She went to the door, but there again she paused. "Is Mr. Bream still with her?"

"Very much with her—that's why I'm here. She made a particular request to be left for five minutes alone with him."

"So Nurse isn't there either?" Rose asked.

"Nurse has embraced the occasion to pop down for her lunch. Mrs. Bream has taken it into her head that she has something very important to say."

Mrs. Beever firmly seated herself. "And pray what may that be?"

"She turned me out of the room precisely so that I shouldn't learn."

"I think *I* know what it is," their companion, at the door, put in.

"Then what is it?" Mrs. Beever demanded.

"Oh, I wouldn't tell you for the world!" And with this Rose Armiger departed.

IV

L EFT ALONE with the lady of Eastmead, Doctor Ramage
studied his watch a little absently. "Our young friend's
exceedingly nervous."

Mrs. Beever glanced in the direction in which Rose had disappeared. "Do you allude to that girl?"

"I allude to dear Mrs. Tony."

"It's equally true of Miss Armiger; she's as worried as a pea
on a pan. Julia, as far as that goes," Mrs. Beever continued,
"can never have been a person to hold herself together."

"Precisely—she requires to be held. Well, happily she has
Tony to hold her."

"Then he's not himself in one of his states?"

Doctor Ramage hesitated. "I don't quite make him out.
He seems to have fifty things at once in his head."

Mrs. Beever looked at the Doctor hard. "When does he
ever not have? But I had a note from him only this morning—in the highest spirits."

Doctor Ramage's little eyes told nothing but what he
wanted. "Well, whatever happens to him, he'll always have
them!"

Mrs. Beever at this jumped up. "Robert Ramage," she
earnestly demanded, "what *is* to happen to that boy?"

Before he had time to reply there rang out a sudden sound
which had, oddly, much of the effect of an answer and which
caused them both to start. It was the near vibration, from
Mrs. Bream's room, of one of the smart, loud electric bells
which were for Mrs. Beever the very accent of the newness of
Bounds. They waited an instant; then the Doctor said quietly:
"It's for Nurse!"

"It's not for you?" The bell sounded again as she
spoke.

"It's for Nurse," Doctor Ramage repeated, moving nevertheless to the door he had come in by. He paused again to
listen, and the door, the next moment thrown open, gave passage to a tall, good-looking young man, dressed as if, with
much freshness, for church, and wearing a large orchid in his

buttonhole. "You rang for Nurse?" the Doctor immediately said.

The young man stood looking from one of his friends to the other. "She's there—it's all right. But ah, my dear people——!" And he passed his hand, with the vivid gesture of brushing away an image, over a face of which the essential radiance was visible even through perturbation.

"How's Julia now?" Mrs. Beever asked.

"Much relieved, she tells me, at having spoken."

"Spoken of what, Tony?"

"Of everything she can think of that's inconceivable—that's damnable."

"If I hadn't known that she wanted to do exactly that," said the Doctor, "I wouldn't have given her the opportunity."

Mrs. Beever's eyes sounded her colleague of the Bank. "You're upset, my poor boy—you're in one of your greatest states. Something painful to you has taken place."

Tony Bream paid no attention to this remark; all his attention was for his other visitor, who stood with one hand on the door of the hall and an open watch, on which he still placidly gazed, in the other. "Ramage," the young man suddenly broke out, "are you keeping something back? *Isn't* she safe?"

The good Doctor's small, neat face seemed to grow more genially globular. "The dear lady is convinced, you mean, that her very last hour is at hand?"

"So much so," Tony replied, "that if she got you and Nurse away, if she made me kneel down by her bed and take her two hands in mine, what do you suppose it was to say to me?"

Doctor Ramage beamed. "Why, of course, that she's going to perish in her flower. I've been through it so often!" he said to Mrs. Beever.

"Before, but not after," that lady lucidly rejoined.

"She has had her chance of perishing, but now it's too late."

"Doctor," said Tony Bream, "*is* my wife going to die?"

His friend hesitated a moment. "When a lady's only symptom of that tendency is the charming volubility with which she dilates upon it, that's very well as far as it goes. But it's not quite enough."

"She says she *knows* it," Tony returned. "But you surely know more than she, don't you?"

"I know everything that can be known. I know that when, in certain conditions, pretty young mothers have acquitted themselves of that inevitable declaration, they turn over and go comfortably to sleep."

"That's exactly," said Tony, "what Nurse must make her do."

"It's exactly what she's doing." Doctor Ramage had no sooner spoken than Mrs. Bream's bell sounded for the third time. "Excuse me!" he imperturbably added. "Nurse calls me."

"And doesn't she call me?" cried Tony.

"Not in the least." The Doctor raised his hand with instant authority. "Stay where you are!" With this he went off to his patient.

If Mrs. Beever often produced, with promptitude, her theory that the young banker was subject to "states," this habit, of which he was admirably tolerant, was erected on the sense of something in him of which even a passing observer might have caught a glimpse. A woman of still more wit than Mrs. Beever, whom he had met on the threshold of life, once explained some accident to him by the words: "The reason is, you know, that you're so exaggerated." This had not been a manner of saying that he was inclined to overshoot the truth; it had been an attempt to express a certain quality of passive excess which was the note of the whole man and which, for an attentive eye, began with his neckties and ended with his intonations. To look at him was immediately to see that he was a collection of gifts, which presented themselves as such precisely by having in each case slightly overflowed the measure. He could do things—this was all he knew about them; and he was ready-made, as it were—he had not had to put himself together. His dress was just too fine, his colour just too high, his moustache just too long, his voice just too loud, his smile just too gay. His movement, his manner, his tone were respectively just too free, too easy and too familiar; his being a very handsome, happy, clever, active, ambitiously local young man was in short just too obvious. But the result of it all was a presence that was in itself a close contact, the air of immediate, unconscious, unstinted life, and of his doing what he liked and liking to please. One of his "states," for Mrs. Beever, was the state of his being a boy again, and the sign of it was his talking nonsense. It was not an example of that tendency, but she noted almost as if it were that almost as soon as the Doctor had left them he asked if she had not brought over to him that awfully pretty girl.

"She has been here, but I sent her home again." Then his visitor added: "Does she strike you as awfully pretty?"

"As pretty as a pretty song! I took a tremendous notion to her."

"She's only a child—for mercy's sake don't show your notion too much!" Mrs. Beever ejaculated.

Tony Bream gave his bright stare; after which, with his still brighter alacrity, "I see what you mean: of course I won't!" he declared. Then, as if candidly and conscientiously wondering: "Is it showing it too much to hope she'll come back to luncheon?"

"Decidedly—if Julia's so down."

"That's only too much for Julia—not for *her*," Tony said with his flurried smile. "But Julia knows about her, hopes she's coming and wants everything to be natural and pleasant." He passed his hand over his eyes again, and as if at the same time recognising that his tone required explanation, "It's just because Julia's so down, don't you see?" he subjoined. "A fellow can't stand it."

Mrs. Beever spoke after a pause during which her companion roamed rather jerkily about. "It's a mere accidental fluctuation. You may trust Ramage to know."

"Yes, thank God, I may trust Ramage to know!" He had the accent of a man constitutionally accessible to suggestion, and could turn the next instant to a quarter more cheering. "Do you happen to have an idea of what has become of Rose?"

Again Mrs. Beever, making a fresh observation, waited a little before answering. "Do you now call her 'Rose'?"

"Dear, yes—talking with Julia. And with *her*," he went on as if he couldn't quite remember—"do I too? Yes," he recollected, "I think I must."

"What one must one must," said Mrs. Beever dryly. "'Rose,' then, has gone over to the chemist's for the Doctor."

"How jolly of her!" Tony exclaimed. "She's a tremendous comfort."

Mrs. Beever committed herself to no opinion on this point,

but it was doubtless on account of the continuity of the question that she presently asked: "Who's this person who's coming to-day to marry her?"

"A very good fellow, I believe—and 'rising': a clerk in some Eastern house."

"And why hasn't he come sooner?"

"Because he has been at Hong Kong, or some such place, trying hard to pick up an income. "He's 'poor but pushing,' she says. They've no means but her own two hundred."

"Two hundred a year? That's quite enough for them!" Mrs. Beever opined.

"Then you had better tell him so!" laughed Tony.

"I hope you'll back me up!" she returned; after which, before he had time to speak, she broke out with irrelevance: "How is it she knows what Julia wanted to say to you?"

Tony, surprised, looked vague. "Just now? Does she know?—I haven't the least idea." Rose appeared at this moment behind the glass doors of the vestibule, and he added: "Here she is."

"Then you can ask her."

"Easily," said Tony. But when the girl came in he greeted her only with a lively word of thanks for the service she had just rendered; so that the lady of Eastmead, after waiting a minute, took the line of assuming with a certain visible rigour that he might have a reason for making his inquiry without an auditor. Taking temporary leave of him, she mentioned the visitors at home whom she must not forget. "Then you won't come back?" he asked.

"Yes, in an hour or two."

"And bring Miss What's-her-name?"

As Mrs. Beever failed to respond to this, Rose Armiger added her voice. "Yes—do bring Miss What's-her-name." Mrs. Beever, without assenting, reached the door, which Tony had opened for her. Here she paused long enough to be overtaken by the rest of their companion's appeal. "I delight so in her clothes."

"I delight so in her hair!" Tony laughed.

Mrs. Beever looked from one of them to the other.

"Don't you think you've delight enough with what your situation here already offers?" She departed with the private determination to return unaccompanied.

V

THREE MINUTES later Tony Bream put his question to his other visitor. "Is it true that you know what Julia a while ago had the room cleared in order to say to me?"

Rose hesitated. "Mrs. Beever repeated to you that I told her so?—Yes, then; I probably do know." She waited again a little. "The poor darling announced to you her conviction that she's dying." Then at the face with which he greeted her exactitude: "I haven't needed to be a monster of cunning to guess!" she exclaimed.

He had perceptibly paled: it made a difference, a kind of importance for that absurdity that it was already in other ears. "She has said the same to you?"

Rose gave a pitying smile. "She has done me that honour."

"Do you mean to-day?"

"To-day—and once before."

Tony looked simple in his wonder. "Yesterday?"

Rose hesitated again. "No; before your child was born. Soon after I came."

"She had made up her mind then from the first?"

"Yes," said Rose, with the serenity of superior sense; "she had laid out for herself that pleasant little prospect. She called it a presentiment, a fixed idea."

Tony took this in with a frown. "And you never spoke of it?"

"To you? Why in the world should I—when she herself didn't? I took it perfectly for what it was—an inevitable but unimportant result of the nervous depression produced by her stepmother's visit."

Tony had fidgeted away with his hands in the pockets of his trousers. "Damn her stepmother's visit!"

"That's exactly what I did!" Rose laughed.

"Damn her stepmother too!" the young man angrily pursued.

"Hush!" said the girl soothingly: "we mustn't curse our relations before the Doctor!" Doctor Ramage had come back from his patient, and she mentioned to him that the medicine for which she had gone out would immediately be delivered.

23

"Many thanks," he replied: "I'll pick it up myself. I *must* run out—to another case." Then with a friendly hand to Tony and a nod at the room he had quitted: "Things are quiet."

Tony, gratefully grasping his hand, detained him by it. "And what was that loud ring that called you?"

"A stupid flurry of Nurse. I was ashamed of her."

"Then why did you stay so long?"

"To have it out with your wife. She wants you again."

Tony eagerly dropped his hand. "Then I go!"

The Doctor raised his liberated member. "In a quarter of an hour—not before. I'm most reluctant, but I allow her five minutes."

"It may make her easier afterwards," Rose observed.

"That's precisely the ground of my giving in. Take care, you know; Nurse will time you," the Doctor said to Tony.

"So many thanks. And you'll come back?"

"The moment I'm free."

When he had gone Tony stood there sombre. "She wants to say it again—that's what she wants."

"Well," Rose answered, "the more she says it the less it's true. It's not she who decides it."

"No," Tony brooded; "it's not she. But it's not you and I either," he soon went on.

"It's not even the Doctor," Rose remarked with her conscious irony.

Her companion rested his troubled eyes on her. "And yet he's as worried as if it were." She protested against this imputation with a word to which he paid no heed. "If anything should happen"—and his eyes seemed to go as far as his thought—"what on earth do you suppose would become of me?"

The girl looked down, very grave. "Men have borne such things."

"Very badly—the real ones." He seemed to lose himself in the effort to embrace the worst, to think it out. "What should I do? where should I turn?"

She was silent a little. "You ask me too much!" she helplessly sighed.

"Don't say that," replied Tony, "at a moment when I know

so little if I mayn't have to ask you still more!" This exclamation made her meet his eyes with a turn of her own that might have struck him had he not been following another train. "To you I can say it, Rose—she's inexpressibly dear to me."

She showed him a face intensely receptive. "It's for your affection for her that I've really given you mine." Then she shook her head—seemed to shake out, like the overflow of a cup, her generous gaiety. "But be easy. We shan't have loved her so much only to lose her."

"I'll be hanged if we shall!" Tony responded. "And such talk's a vile false note in the midst of a joy like yours."

"Like mine?" Rose exhibited some vagueness.

Her companion was already accessible to the amusement of it. "I hope that's not the way you mean to look at Mr. Vidal!"

"Ah, Mr. Vidal!" she ambiguously murmured.

"Shan't you then be glad to see him?"

"Intensely glad. But how shall I say it?" She thought a moment and then went on as if she found the answer to her question in Tony's exceptional intelligence and their comfortable intimacy. "There's gladness and gladness. It isn't love's young dream; it's rather an old and rather a sad story. We've worried and waited—we've been acquainted with grief. We've come together a weary way."

"I know you've had a horrid grind. But isn't this the end of it?"

Rose hesitated. "That's just what he's to settle."

"Happily, I see! Just look at him."

The glass doors, as Tony spoke, had been thrown open by the butler. The young man from China was there—a short, meagre young man, with a smooth face and a dark blue double-breasted jacket. "Mr. Vidal!" the butler announced, withdrawing again, while the visitor, whose entrance had been rapid, suddenly and shyly faltered at the sight of his host. His pause, however, lasted but just long enough to enable Rose to bridge it over with the frankest maidenly grace; and Tony's quick sense of being out of place at this reunion was not a bar to the impression of her charming, instant action, her soft "Dennis, Dennis!" her light, fluttered arms, her tenderly bent head and the short, bright stillness of her clasp of her lover.

Tony shone down at them with the pleasure of having helped them, and the warmth of it was in his immediate grasp of the traveller's hand. He cut short his embarrassed thanks—he was too delighted; and leaving him with the remark that he would presently come back to show him his room, he went off again to poor Julia.

VI

DENNIS VIDAL, when the door had closed on his host, drew again to his breast the girl to whom he was plighted and pressed her there with silent joy. She softly submitted, then still more softly disengaged herself, though in his flushed firmness he but partly released her. The light of admiration was in his hard young face—a visible tribute to what she showed again his disaccustomed eyes. Holding her yet, he covered her with a smile that produced two strong but relenting lines on either side of his dry, thin lips. "My own dearest," he murmured, "you're still more so than one remembered!"

She opened her clear eyes wider. "Still more what?"

"Still more of a fright!" And he kissed her again.

"It's you that are wonderful, Dennis," she said; "you look so absurdly young."

He felt with his lean, fine brown hand his spare, clean brown chin. "If I looked as old as I feel, dear girl, they'd have my portrait in the illustrated papers."

He had now drawn her down upon the nearest sofa, and while he sat sideways, grasping the wrist of which he remained in possession after she had liberated her fingers, she leaned back and took him in with a deep air of her own. "And yet it's not that you're exactly childish—or so extraordinarily fresh," she went on as if to puzzle out, for her satisfaction, her impression of him.

"'Fresh,' my dear girl!" He gave a little happy jeer; then he raised her wrist to his mouth and held it there as long as she would let him, looking at her hard. "*That's* the freshest thing I've ever been conscious of!" he exclaimed as she drew away her hand and folded her arms.

"You're worn, but you're not wasted," she brought out in her kind but considering way. "You're awfully well, you know."

"Yes, I'm awfully well, I know"—he spoke with just the faintest ring of impatience. Then he added: "Your voice, all the while, has been in my ears. But there's something you put into it that *they*—out there, stupid things!—couldn't. Don't 'size me up' so," he continued smiling; "you make me nervous about what I may seem to come to!"

They had both shown shyness, but Rose's was already gone. She kept her inclined position and her folded arms; supported by the back of the sofa, her head preserved, toward the side on which he sat, its charming contemplative turn. "I'm only thinking," she said, "that you look young just as a steel instrument of the best quality, no matter how much it's handled, often looks new."

"Ah, if you mean I'm kept bright by use——!" the young man laughed.

"You're polished by life."

"'Polished' is delightful of you!"

"I'm not sure you've come back handsomer than you went," said Rose, "and I don't know if you've come back richer."

"Then let me immediately tell you I have!" Dennis broke in.

She received the announcement, for a minute, in silence: a good deal more passed between this pair than they uttered. "What I was going to say," she then quietly resumed, "is that I'm awfully pleased with myself when I see that at any rate you're—what shall I call you?—a made man."

Dennis frowned a little through his happiness. "With 'yourself'? Aren't you a little pleased with me?"

She hesitated. "With myself first, because I was sure of you first."

"Do you mean before I was of you?—I'm somehow not sure of you yet!" the young man declared.

Rose coloured slightly; but she gaily laughed. "Then I'm ahead of you in everything!"

Leaning toward her with all his intensified need of her and holding by his extended arm the top of the sofa-back, he worried with his other hand a piece of her dress, which he had begun to finger for want of something more responsive. "You're as far beyond me still as all the distance I've come." He had dropped his eyes upon the crumple he made in her frock, and her own during that moment, from her superior height, descended upon him with a kind of unseen appeal. When he looked up again it was gone. "What do you mean by a 'made' man?" he asked.

"Oh, not the usual thing, but the real thing. A man one needn't worry about."

"Thank you! The man not worried about is the man who muffs it."

"That's a horrid, selfish speech," said Rose Armiger. "You don't deserve I should tell you what a success I now feel that you'll be."

"Well, darling," Dennis answered, "that matters the less as I know exactly the occasion on which I shall fully feel it for myself."

Rose manifested no further sense of this occasion than to go straight on with her idea. She placed her arm with frank friendship on his shoulder. It drew him closer, and he recovered his grasp of her free hand. With his want of stature and presence, his upward look at her, his small, smooth head, his seasoned sallowness and simple eyes, he might at this instant have struck a spectator as a figure actually younger and slighter than the ample, accomplished girl whose gesture protected and even a little patronised him. But in her vision of him she none the less clearly found full warrant for saying, instead of something he expected, something she wished and had her reasons for wishing, even if they represented but the gain of a minute's time. "You're not splendid, my dear old Dennis—you're not dazzling, nor dangerous, nor even exactly distinguished. But you've a quiet little something that the tiresome time has made perfect, and that—just here where you've come to me at last—makes me immensely proud of you!"

She had with this so far again surrendered herself that he could show her in the ways he preferred how such a declaration touched him. The place in which he had come to her at last was of a nature to cause him to look about at it, just as to begin to inquire was to learn from her that he had dropped upon a crisis. He had seen Mrs. Bream, under Rose's wing, in her maiden days; but in his eagerness to jump at a meeting with the only woman really important to him he had perhaps intruded more than he supposed. Though he expressed again the liveliest sense of the kindness of these good people, he was unable to conceal his disappointment at finding their inmate agitated also by something quite distinct from the joy of his arrival. "Do you really think the poor lady will spoil our fun?" he rather resentfully put it to her.

"It will depend on what our fun may demand of her," said Rose. "If you ask me if she's in danger, I think not quite that: in such a case I must certainly have put you off. I dare say to-day will show the contrary. But she's so much to me—you know how much—that I'm uneasy, quickly upset; and if I seem to you flustered and not myself and not *with* you, I beg you to attribute it simply to the situation in the house."

About this situation they had each more to say, and about many matters besides, for they faced each other over the deep waters of the accumulated and the undiscussed. They could keep no order and for five minutes more they rather helplessly played with the flood. Dennis was rueful at first, for what he seemed to have lighted upon was but half his opportunity; then he had an inspiration which made him say to his companion that they should both, after all, be able to make terms with any awkwardness by simply meeting it with a consciousness that their happiness had already taken form.

"Our happiness?" Rose was all interest.

"Why, the end of our delays."

She smiled with every allowance. "Do you mean we're to go out and be married this minute?"

"Well—almost; as soon as I've read you a letter." He produced, with the words, his pocket-book.

She watched him an instant turn over its contents. "What letter?"

"The best one I ever got. What have I done with it?" On his feet before her, he continued his search.

"From your people?"

"From my people. It met me in town, and it makes everything possible."

She waited while he fumbled in his pockets; with her hands clasped in her lap she sat looking up at him. "Then it's certainly a thing for me to hear."

"But what the dickens have I done with it?" Staring at her, embarrassed, he clapped his hands, on coat and waistcoat, to other receptacles; at the end of a moment of which he had become aware of the proximity of the noiseless butler, upright in the high detachment of the superior servant who has embraced the conception of unpacking.

"Might I ask you for your keys, sir?"

Dennis Vidal had a light—he smote his forehead. "Stupid—it's in my portmanteau!"

"Then go and get it!" said Rose, who perceived as she spoke, by the door that faced her, that Tony Bream was rejoining them. She got up, and Tony, agitated, as she could see, but with complete command of his manners, immediately and sociably said to Dennis that he was ready to guide him upstairs. Rose, at this, interposed. "Do let Walker take him—I want to speak to you."

Tony smiled at the young man. "Will you excuse me then?" Dennis protested against the trouble he was giving, and Walker led him away. Rose meanwhile waited not only till they were out of sight and of earshot, but till the return of Tony, who, his hand on Vidal's shoulder, had gone with them as far as the door.

"Has he brought you good news?" said the master of Bounds.

"Very good. He's very well; he's all right."

Tony's flushed face gave to the laugh with which he greeted this almost the effect of that of a man who had been drinking. "Do you mean he's quite faithful?"

Rose always met a bold joke. "As faithful as I! But your news is the thing."

"Mine?" He closed his eyes a moment, but stood there scratching his head as if to carry off with a touch of comedy his betrayal of emotion.

"Has Julia repeated her declaration?"

Tony looked at her in silence. "She has done something more extraordinary than that," he replied at last.

"What has she done?"

Tony glanced round him, then dropped into a chair. He covered his face with his hands. "I must get over it a little before I tell you!"

VII

S HE WAITED compassionately for his nervousness to pass, dropping again, during the pause, upon the sofa she had just occupied with her visitor. At last as, while she watched him, his silence continued, she put him a question. "Does she at any rate still maintain that she shan't get well?"

Tony removed his hands from his face. "With the utmost assurance—or rather with the utmost serenity. But she treats that now as a mere detail."

Rose wondered. "You mean she's really convinced that she's sinking?"

"So she says."

"But *is* she, good heavens? Such a thing isn't a matter of opinion: it's a fact or it's not a fact."

"It's not a fact," said Tony Bream. "How can it be when one has only to see that her strength hasn't failed? She of course says it has, but she has a remarkable deal of it to show. What's the vehemence with which she expresses herself but a sign of increasing life? It's excitement, of course—partly; but it's also striking energy."

"Excitement?" Rose repeated. "I thought you just said she was 'serene.'"

Tony hesitated, but he was perfectly clear.

"She's calm about what she calls leaving me, bless her heart; she seems to have accepted that prospect with the strangest resignation. What she's uneasy, what she's in fact still more strangely tormented and exalted about, is another matter."

"I see—the thing you just mentioned."

"She takes an interest," Tony went on, "she asks questions, she sends messages, she speaks out with all her voice. She's delighted to know that Mr. Vidal has at last come to you, and she told me to tell you so from her, and to tell *him* so—to tell you both, in fact, how she rejoices that what you've so long waited for is now so close at hand."

Rose took this in with lowered eyes. "How dear of her!" she murmured.

"She asked me particularly about Mr. Vidal," Tony continued—"how he looks, how he strikes me, how you met. She gave me indeed a private message for him."

Rose faintly smiled. "A private one?"

"Oh, only to spare your modesty: a word to the effect that she answers for you."

"In what way?" Rose asked.

"Why, as the charmingest, cleverest, handsomest, in every way most wonderful wife that ever any man will have had."

"She *is* wound up!" Rose laughed. Then she said: "And all the while what does Nurse think?—I don't mean," she added with the same slight irony, "of whether I shall do for Dennis."

"Of Julia's condition? She wants Ramage to come back."

Rose thought a moment. "She's rather a goose, I think—she loses her head."

"So I've taken the liberty of telling her." Tony sat forward, his eyes on the floor, his elbows on his knees and his hands nervously rubbing each other. Presently he rose with a jerk. "What do you suppose she wants me to do?"

Rose tried to suppose. "Nurse wants you——?"

"No—that ridiculous girl." Nodding back at his wife's room, he came and stood before the sofa.

Half reclining again, Rose turned it over, raising her eyes to him. "Do you really mean something ridiculous?"

"Under the circumstances—grotesque."

"Well," Rose suggested, smiling, "she wants you to allow her to name her successor."

"Just the contrary!" Tony seated himself where Dennis Vidal had sat. "She wants me to promise her she shall *have* no successor."

His companion looked at him hard; with her surprise at something in his tone she had just visibly coloured. "I see." She was at a momentary loss. "Do you call that grotesque?"

Tony, for an instant, was evidently struck by her surprise; then seeing the reason of it and blushing too a little, "Not the idea, my dear Rose—God forbid!" he exclaimed. "What I'm speaking of is the mistake of giving that amount of colour to her insistence—meeting her as if one accepted the situation as she represents it and were really taking leave of her."

Rose appeared to understand and even to be impressed. "You think that will make her worse?"

"Why, arranging everything as if she's going to die!" Tony sprang up afresh; his trouble was obvious and he fell into the restless pacing that had been his resource all the morning.

His interlocutress watched his agitation. "Mayn't it be that if you do just that she'll, on the contrary, immediately find herself better?"

Tony wandered, again scratching his head. "From the spirit of contradiction? I'll do anything in life that will make her happy, or just simply make her quiet: I'll treat her demand as intensely reasonable even, if it isn't better to treat it as an ado about nothing. But it stuck in my crop to lend myself, that way, to a death-bed solemnity. Heaven deliver us!" Half irritated and half anxious, suffering from his tenderness a twofold effect, he dropped into another seat with his hands in his pockets and his long legs thrust out.

"Does she wish it very solemn?" Rose asked.

"She's in dead earnest, poor darling. She wants a promise on my sacred honour—a vow of the most portentous kind."

Rose was silent a little. "You didn't give it?"

"I turned it off—I refused to take any such discussion seriously. I said: 'My own darling, how can I meet you on so hateful a basis? Wait till you *are* dying!'" He lost himself an instant; then he was again on his feet. "How in the world can she dream I'm capable——?" He hadn't patience even to finish his phrase.

Rose, however, finished it. "Of taking a second wife? Ah, that's another affair!" she sadly exclaimed. "We've nothing to do with that," she added. "Of course you understand poor Julia's feeling."

"Her feeling?" Tony once more stood in front of her.

"Why, what's at the bottom of her dread of your marrying again."

"Assuredly I do! Mrs. Grantham naturally—*she's* at the bottom. She has filled Julia with the vision of my perhaps giving our child a stepmother."

"Precisely," Rose said, "and if you had known, as I knew it, Julia's girlhood, you would do justice to the force of that horror. It possesses her whole being—she would prefer that the child should die."

Tony Bream, musing, shook his head with dark decision. "Well, I would prefer that they neither of them should!"

"The simplest thing, then, is to give her your word."

"My 'word' isn't enough," Tony said: "she wants mystic rites and spells! The simplest thing, moreover, was exactly what I desired to do. My objection to the performance she demands was that this was just what it seemed to me not to be."

"Try it," said Rose, smiling.

"To bring her round?"

"Before the Doctor returns. When he comes, you know, he won't let you go back to her."

"Then I'll go now," said Tony, already at the door.

Rose had risen from the sofa. "Be very brief—but be very strong."

"I'll swear by all the gods—that or any other nonsense." Rose stood there opposite to him with a fine, rich urgency which operated as a detention. "I see you're right," he declared. "You always are, and I'm always indebted to you." Then as he opened the door: "Is there anything else?"

"Anything else?"

"I mean that you advise."

She thought a moment. "Nothing but that—for you to seem to enter thoroughly into her idea, to show her you understand it as she understands it herself."

Tony looked vague. "As she does?"

"Why, for the lifetime of your daughter." As he appeared still not fully to apprehend, she risked: "If you should lose Effie the reason would fail."

Tony, at this, jerked back his head with a flush. "My dear Rose, you don't imagine that it's as a *needed* vow——"

"That you would give it?" she broke in. "Certainly I don't any more than I suppose the degree of your fidelity to be the ground on which we're talking. But the thing is to convince Julia, and I said that only because she'll be more convinced if you strike her as really looking at what you subscribe to."

Tony gave his nervous laugh. "Don't you know I always 'put down my name'—especially to 'appeals'—in the most reckless way?" Then abruptly, in a different tone, as if with a passionate need to make it plain, "I shall never, never, never," he protested, "so much as look at another woman!"

The girl approved with an eager gesture. "You've got it, my dear Tony. Say it to her *that* way!" But he had already gone, and, turning, she found herself face to face with her lover, who had come back as she spoke.

VIII

WITH his letter in his hand Dennis Vidal stood and smiled at her. "What in the world has your dear Tony 'got,' and what is he to say?"

"To say? Something to his wife, who appears to have lashed herself into an extraordinary state."

The young man's face fell. "What sort of a state?"

"A strange discouragement about herself. She's depressed and frightened—she thinks she's sinking."

Dennis looked grave. "Poor little lady—what a bore for *us*! I remember her perfectly."

"She of course remembers you," Rose said. "She takes the friendliest interest in your being here."

"That's most kind of her in her condition."

"Oh, her condition," Rose returned, "isn't quite so bad as she thinks."

"I see." Dennis hesitated. "And that's what Mr. Bream's to tell her."

"That's a part of it." Rose glanced at the document he had brought to her; it was in its envelope, and he tapped it a little impatiently on his left finger-tips. What she said, however, had no reference to it. "She's haunted with a morbid alarm—on the subject, of all things, of his marrying again."

"If she should die? She wants him not to?" Dennis asked.

"She wants him not to." Rose paused a moment. "She wants to have been the only one."

He reflected, slightly embarrassed with this peep into a situation that but remotely concerned him. "Well, I suppose that's the way women often feel."

"I daresay it is." The girl's gravity gave the gleam of a smile. "I daresay it's the way *I* should."

Dennis Vidal, at this, simply seized her and kissed her. "You needn't be afraid—you'll be the only one!"

His embrace had been the work of a few seconds, and she had made no movement to escape from it; but she looked at him as if to convey that the extreme high spirits it betrayed were perhaps just a trifle mistimed. "That's what I recommended him," she dropped, "to say to Julia."

"Why, I should hope so!" Presently, as if a little struck, Dennis continued: "Doesn't he want to?"

"Absolutely. They're all in all to each other. But he's naturally much upset and bewildered."

"And he came to you for advice?"

"Oh, he comes to me," Rose said, "as he might come to talk of her with the mother that, poor darling, it's her misfortune never to have known."

The young man's vivacity again played up.

"He treats you, you mean, as his mother-in-law?"

"Very much. But I'm thoroughly nice to him. People can do anything to me who are nice to Julia."

Dennis was silent a moment; he had slipped his letter out of its cover. "Well, I hope they're grateful to you for such devotion."

"Grateful to me, Dennis? They quite adore me." Then as if to remind him of something it was important he should feel: "Don't you see what it is for a poor girl to have such an anchorage as this—such honourable countenance, such a place to fall back upon?"

Thus challenged, her visitor, with a moment's thought, did frank justice to her question. "I'm certainly glad you've such jolly friends—one sees they're charming people. It has been a great comfort to me lately to know you were with them." He looked round him, conscientiously, at the bright and beautiful hall. "It *is* a good berth, my dear, and it must be a pleasure to live with such fine things. They've given me a room up there that's full of them—an awfully nice room." He glanced at a picture or two—he took in the scene. "Do they roll in wealth?"

"They're like all bankers, I imagine," said Rose. "Don't bankers always roll?"

"Yes, they seem literally to wallow. What a pity *we* ain't bankers, eh?"

"Ah, with my friends here their money's the least part of them," the girl answered. "The great thing's their personal goodness."

Dennis had stopped before a large photograph, a great picture in a massive frame, supported, on a table, by a small gilded easel. "To say nothing of their personal beauty! He's tremendously good-looking."

Rose glanced with an indulgent sigh at a representation of Tony Bream in all his splendour, in a fine white waistcoat and a high white hat, with a stick and gloves and a cigar, his orchid, his stature and his smile. "Ah, poor Julia's taste!"

"Yes," Dennis exclaimed, "one can see how he must have fetched her!"

"I mean the style of the thing," said Rose.

"It isn't good, eh? Well, *you* know." Then turning away from the picture, the young man added: "They'll be after that fellow!"

Rose faltered. "The people she fears?"

"The women-folk, bless 'em—if he should lose her."

"I daresay," said Rose. "But he'll be proof."

"Has he told you so?" Dennis smiled.

She met his smile with a kind of conscious bravado in her own. "In so many words. But he assures me he'll calm her down."

Dennis was silent a little: he had now unfolded his letter and run his eyes over it. "What a funny subject for him to be talking about!"

"With me, do you mean?"

"Yes, and with his wife."

"My dear man," Rose exclaimed, "you can imagine he didn't begin it!"

"Did *you?*" her companion asked.

She hesitated again, and then, "Yes—idiot!" she replied with a quiet humour that produced, on his part, another demonstration of tenderness. This attempt she arrested, raising her hand, as she appeared to have heard a sound, with a quick injunction to listen.

"What's the matter?"

She bent her ear. "Wasn't there a cry from Julia's room?"

"I heard nothing."

Rose was relieved. "Then it's only my nervousness."

Dennis Vidal held up his letter. "Is your nervousness too great to prevent your giving a moment's attention to this?"

"Ah, your letter!" Rose's eyes rested on it as if she had become conscious of it for the first time.

"It very intimately concerns our future," said her visitor. "I went up for it so that you should do me the favour to read it."

She held out her hand promptly and frankly. "Then give it to me—let me keep it a little."

"Certainly; but kindly remember that I've still to answer it—I mean referring to points. I've waited to see you because it's from the 'governor' himself—practically saying what he'll do for me."

Rose held the letter; her large light eyes widened with her wonder and her sympathy. "Is it something very good?"

Dennis prescribed, with an emphatic but amused nod at the paper, a direction to her curiosity. "Read and you'll see!"

She dropped her eyes, but after a moment, while her left hand patted her heart, she raised them with an odd, strained expression. "I mean is it really good enough?"

"That's exactly what I want you to tell me!" Dennis laughed out. A certain surprise at her manner was in his face.

While she noted it she heard a sound again, a sound this time explained by the opening of the door of the vestibule. Doctor Ramage had come back; Rose put down her letter. "I'll tell you as soon as I have spoken to the Doctor."

IX

THE DOCTOR, eagerly, spoke to her first. "Our friend has not come back?"

"Mine has," said Rose with grace. "Let me introduce Mr. Vidal." Doctor Ramage beamed a greeting, and our young lady, with her discreet gaiety, went on to Dennis: "He too thinks all the world of me."

"Oh, she's a wonder—she knows what to do! But you'll see that for yourself," said the Doctor.

"I'm afraid you won't approve of me," Dennis replied with solicitude. "You'll think me rather in your patient's way."

Doctor Ramage laughed. "No indeed—I'm sure Miss Armiger will keep you out of it." Then looking at his watch, "Bream's not with her still?" he inquired of Rose.

"He came away, but he returned to her."

"He shouldn't have done that."

"It was by my advice, and I'm sure you'll find it's all right," Rose returned. "But you'll send him back to us."

"On the spot." The Doctor picked his way out.

"He's not at all easy," Dennis pronounced when he had gone.

Rose demurred. "How do you know that?"

"By looking at him. I'm not such a fool," her visitor added with some emphasis, "as you strike me as wishing to make of me."

Rose candidly stared. "As I strike you as wishing——?" For a moment this young couple looked at each other hard, and they both changed colour. "My dear Dennis, what do you mean?"

He evidently felt that he had been almost violently abrupt; but it would have been equally evident to a spectator that he was a man of cool courage. "I mean, Rose, that I don't quite know what's the matter with you. It's as if, unexpectedly, on my eager arrival, I find something or other between us."

She appeared immensely relieved. "Why, my dear child, of course you do! Poor Julia's between us—much between us." She faltered again; then she broke out with emotion: "I may as

41

well confess it frankly—I'm miserably anxious. Good heavens," she added with impatience, "don't you see it for yourself?"

"I certainly see that you're agitated and absent—as you warned me so promptly you would be. But remember you've quite denied to me the gravity of Mrs. Bream's condition."

Rose's impatience overflowed into a gesture. "I've been doing that to deceive my own self!"

"I understand," said Dennis kindly. "Still," he went on, considering, "it's either one thing or the other. The poor lady's either dying, you know, or she ain't!"

His friend looked at him with a reproach too fine to be uttered. "My dear Dennis—you're rough!"

He showed a face as conscientious as it was blank. "I'm crude—possibly coarse? Perhaps I *am*—without intention."

"Think what these people are to me," said Rose.

He was silent a little. "Is it anything so very extraordinary? Oh, I know," he went on, as if he feared she might again accuse him of a want of feeling; "I appreciate them perfectly— I do them full justice. Enjoying their hospitality here, I'm conscious of all their merits." The letter she had put down was still on the table, and he took it up and fingered it a moment. "All I mean is that I don't want you quite to sink the fact that I'm something to you too."

She met this appeal with instant indulgence. "Be a little patient with me," she gently said. Before he could make a rejoinder she pursued: "You yourself are impressed with the Doctor's being anxious. I've been trying not to think so, but I daresay you're right. There I've another worry."

"The greater your worry, then, the more pressing our business." Dennis spoke with cordial decision, while Rose, moving away from him, reached the door by which the Doctor had gone out. She stood there as if listening, and he continued: "It's *me*, you know, that you've now to 'fall back' upon."

She had already raised a hand with her clear "Hush!" and she kept her eyes on her companion while she tried to catch a sound. "The Doctor said he would send him out of the room. But he doesn't."

"All the better—for your reading this." Dennis held out the letter to her.

She quitted her place. "If he's allowed to stay, there must be something wrong."

"I'm very sorry for them; but don't you call that a statement?"

"Ah, your letter?" Her attention came back to it, and, taking it from him, she dropped again upon the sofa with it. "*Voyons, voyons* this great affair!"—she had the air of trying to talk herself into calmness.

Dennis stood a moment before her. "It puts us on a footing that really seems to me sound."

She had turned over the leaf to take the measure of the document; there were three, large, close, neat pages. "He's a trifle long-winded, the 'governor'!"

"The longer the better," Dennis laughed, "when it's all in *that* key! Read it, my dear, quietly and carefully; take it in—it's really simple enough." He spoke soothingly and tenderly, turning off to give her time and not oppress her. He moved slowly about the hall, whistling very faintly and looking again at the pictures, and when he had left her she followed him a minute with her eyes. Then she transferred them to the door at which she had just listened; instead of reading she watched as if for a movement of it. If there had been any one at that moment to see her face, such an observer would have found it strangely, tragically convulsed: she had the appearance of holding in with extraordinary force some passionate sob or cry, some smothered impulse of anguish. This appearance vanished miraculously as Dennis turned at the end of the room, and what he saw, while the great showy clock ticked in the scented stillness, was only his friend's study of what he had put before her. She studied it long, she studied it in silence—a silence so unbroken by inquiry or comment that, though he clearly wished not to seem to hurry her, he drew nearer again at last and stood as if waiting for some sign.

"Don't you call that really meeting a fellow?"

"I must read it again," Rose replied without looking up. She turned afresh to the beginning, and he strolled away once more. She went through to the end; after which she said with tranquillity, folding the letter: "Yes; it shows what they think of you." She put it down where she had put it before, getting up as he came back to her. "It's good not only for what he says, but for the way he says it."

"It's a jolly bit more than I expected." Dennis picked the letter up and, restoring it to its envelope, slipped it almost lovingly into a breast-pocket. "It does show, I think, that they don't want to lose me."

"They're not such fools!" Rose had in her turn moved off, but now she faced him, so intensely pale that he was visibly startled; all the more that it marked still more her white grimace. "My dear boy, it's a splendid future."

"I'm glad it strikes you so!" he laughed.

"It's a great joy—you're all right. As I said a while ago, you're a made man."

"Then by the same token, of course, you're a made woman!"

"I'm very, very happy about you," she brightly conceded. "The great thing is that there's more to come."

"Rather—there's more to come!" said Dennis. He stood meeting her singular smile. "I'm only waiting for it."

"I mean there's a lot behind—a general attitude. Read between the lines!"

"Don't you suppose I *have*, miss? I didn't venture, myself, to say that to you."

"Do I have so to be prompted and coached?" asked Rose. "I don't believe you even see all I mean. There are hints and tacit promises—glimpses of what may happen if you'll give them time."

"Oh, I'll give them time!" Dennis declared. "But he's really awfully cautious. You're sharp to have made out so much."

"Naturally—I'm sharp." Then, after an instant, "Let me have the letter again," the girl said, holding out her hand. Dennis promptly drew it forth, and she took it and went over it in silence once more. He turned away as he had done before, to give her a chance; he hummed slowly, to himself, about the room, and once more, at the end of some minutes, it appeared to strike him that she prolonged her perusal. But when he approached her again she was ready with her clear contentment. She folded the letter and handed it back to him. "Oh, you'll do!" she proclaimed.

"You're really quite satisfied?"

She hesitated a moment. "For the present—perfectly." Her eyes were on the precious document as he fingered it, and something in his way of doing so made her break into incongruous gaiety. He had opened it delicately and been caught again by a passage. "You handle it as if it were a thousand-pound note!"

He looked up at her quickly. "It's much more than that. Capitalise his figure."

"'Capitalise' it?"

"Find the invested sum."

Rose thought a moment. "Oh, I'll do everything for you but cipher! But it's millions." Then as he returned the letter to his pocket she added: "You should have that thing mounted in double glass—with a little handle like a hand-screen."

"There's certainly nothing too good for the charter of our liberties—for that's what it really is," Dennis said. "But you *can* face the music?" he went on.

"The music?"—Rose was momentarily blank.

He looked at her hard again. "You have, my dear, the most extraordinary vacancies. The figure we're talking of—the poor, dear little figure. The five-hundred-and-forty," he a trifle sharply explained. "That's about what it makes."

"Why, it seems to me a lovely little figure," said the girl. "To the 'likes' of me, how can that be anything but a duck of an income? Then," she exclaimed, "think also of what's to come!"

"Yes—but I'm not speaking of anything you may bring."

Rose wavered, judicious, as if trying to be as attentive as he desired. "I see—without that. But I wasn't speaking of that either," she added.

"Oh, *you* may count it—I only mean I don't touch it. And the going out—you take that too?" Dennis asked.

Rose looked brave. "Why it's only for two years."

He flushed suddenly, as with a flood of reassurance, putting his arms round her as round the fulfilment of his dream. "Ah, my own old girl!"

She let him clasp her again, but when she disengaged herself they were somehow nearer to the door that led away to Julia Bream. She stood there as she had stood before, while he still held one of her hands; then she brought forth something that betrayed an extraordinary disconnection from all that had just preceded. "I can't make out why he doesn't send him back!"

Dennis Vidal dropped her hand; both his own went into his pockets, and he gave a kick to the turned-up corner of a rug. "Mr. Bream—the Doctor? Oh, they know what they're about!"

"The doctor doesn't at all want him to be there. Something has happened," Rose declared as she left the door.

Her companion said nothing for a moment. "Do you mean the poor lady's gone?" he at last demanded.

"Gone?" Rose echoed.

"Do you mean Mrs. Bream is dead?"

His question rang out so that Rose threw herself back in horror. "Dennis—God forbid!"

"God forbid too, I say. But one doesn't know what you mean—you're too difficult to follow. One thing, at any rate, you clearly have in your head—that we must take it as possibly on the cards. That's enough to make it remarkably to the point to remind you of the great change that would take place in your situation if she *should* die."

"What else in the world but that change am I thinking of?" Rose asked.

"You're not thinking of it perhaps so much in the connection I refer to. If Mrs. Bream goes, your 'anchorage,' as you call it, goes."

"I see what you mean." She spoke with the softest assent; the tears had sprung into her eyes and she looked away to hide them.

"One may have the highest possible opinion of her husband and yet not quite see you staying on here in the same manner with *him*."

Rose was silent, with a certain dignity. "Not quite," she presently said with the same gentleness.

"The way therefore to provide against everything is—as I remarked to you a while ago—to settle with me this minute the day, the nearest one possible, for our union to become a reality."

She slowly brought back her troubled eyes. "The day to marry you?"

"The day to marry me of course!" He gave a short, uneasy laugh. "What else?"

She waited again, and there was a fear deep in her face. "I must settle it this minute?"

Dennis stared. "Why, my dear child, when in the world if not now?"

"You can't give me a little more time?" she asked.

"More time?" His gathered stupefaction broke out. "More time—after giving you years?"

"Ah, but just at the last, here—this news, this rush is sudden."

"Sudden!" Dennis repeated. "Haven't you known I was coming, and haven't you known for what?"

She looked at him now with an effort of resolution in which he could see her white face harden; as if by a play of some inner mechanism something dreadful had taken place in it. Then she said with a painful quaver that no attempt to be natural could keep down: "Let me remind you, Dennis, that your coming was not at my request. You've come—yes; but you've come because you would. You've come in spite of me."

He gasped, and with the mere touch of her tone his own eyes filled. "You haven't wanted me?"

"I'm delighted to see you."

"Then in God's name what do you mean? Where *are* we, and what are you springing on me?"

"I'm only asking you again, as I've asked you already, to be patient with me—to let me, at such a critical hour, turn round. I'm only asking you to bear with me—I'm only asking you to wait."

"To wait for what?" He snatched the words out of her mouth. "It's because I *have* waited that I'm here. What I want of you is three simple words—that you can utter in three simple seconds." He looked about him, in his helpless dismay, as if to call the absent to witness. "And you look at me like a stone. You open up an abyss. You give me nothing, nothing." He paused, as it were, for a contradiction, but she made none; she had lowered her eyes and, supported against a table, stood there rigid and passive. Dennis sank into a chair with his vain hands upon his knees. "What do you mean by my coming in spite of you? You never asked me not to— you've treated me well till now. It was my idea—yes; but you perfectly accepted it." He gave her time to assent to this or to deny it, but she took none, and he continued: "Don't you understand the one feeling that has possessed me and sustained me? Don't you understand that I've thought of nothing else every hour of my way? I arrived here with a longing for you that words can't utter; and now I see—though I couldn't immediately be sure—that I found you from the first constrained and unnatural."

Rose, as he went on, had raised her eyes again; they seemed to follow his words in sombre submission. "Yes, you must have found me strange enough."

"And don't again say it's your being anxious——!" Dennis sprang up warningly. "It's your being anxious that just makes me right."

His companion shook her head slowly and ambiguously. "I *am* glad you've come."

"To have the pleasure of not receiving me?"

"I have received you," Rose replied. "Every word I've spoken to you and every satisfaction I've expressed is true, is deep. I do admire you, I do respect you, I'm proud to have been your friend. Haven't I assured you of my pure joy in your promotion and your prospects?"

"What do you call assuring me? You utterly misled me for some strange moments; you mystified me; I think I may say you trifled with me. The only assurance I'm open to is that of your putting your hand in mine as my wife. In God's name," the young man panted, "what has happened to you and what has changed you?"

"I'll tell you to-morrow," said Rose.

"Tell me what I insist on?"

She cast about her. "Tell you things I can't now."

He sounded her with visible despair. "You're not sincere—you're not straight. You've nothing to tell me, and you're afraid. You're only gaining time, and you've only been doing so from the first. I don't know what it's for—you're beyond me; but if it's to back out I'll be hanged if I give you a moment."

Her wan face, at this, showed a faint flush; it seemed to him five years older than when he came in. "You take, with your cruel accusations, a strange way to keep me!" the girl exclaimed. "But I won't talk to you in bitterness," she pursued in a different tone. "That will drop if we do allow it a day or two." Then on a sharp motion of his impatience she added: "Whether you allow it or not, you know, I must take the time I need."

He was angry now, as if she were not only proved evasion, but almost proved insolence; and his anger deepened at her return to this appeal that offered him no meaning. "No, no, you must choose," he said with passion, "and if you're really honest you will. I'm here for you with all my soul, but I'm here for you now or never."

"Dennis!" she weakly murmured.

"You do back out?"

She put out her hand. "Good-bye."

He looked at her as over a flood; then he thrust his hand behind him and glanced about for his hat. He moved blindly, like a man picking himself up from a violent fall—flung indeed suddenly from a smooth, swift vehicle. "Good-bye."

X

HE QUICKLY remembered that he had not brought in his hat, and also, the next instant, that even to clap it on wouldn't under the circumstances qualify him for immediate departure from Bounds. Just as it came over him that the obligation he had incurred must keep him at least for the day, he found himself in the presence of his host, who, while his back was turned, had precipitately reappeared and whose vision of the place had resulted in an instant question.

"Mrs. Beever has not come back? Julia wants her—Julia must see her!"

Dennis was separated by the width of the hall from the girl with whom he had just enjoyed such an opportunity of reunion, but there was for the moment no indication that Tony Bream, engrossed with a graver accident, found a betrayal in the space between them. He had, however, for Dennis the prompt effect of a reminder to take care: it was a consequence of the very nature of the man that to look at him was to recognise the value of appearances and that he couldn't have dropped upon any scene, however disordered, without, by the simple fact, re-establishing a superficial harmony. His new friend met him with a movement that might have been that of stepping in front of some object to hide it, while Rose, on her side, sounding out like a touched bell, was already alert with her response. "Ah," said Dennis, to himself, "it's for *them* she cares!"

"She has not come back, but if there's a hurry——" Rose was all there.

"There *is* a hurry. Some one must go for her."

Dennis had a point to make that he must make on the spot. He spoke before Rose's rejoinder. "With your increasing anxieties, Mr. Bream, I'm quite ashamed to be quartered on you. Hadn't I really better be at the inn?"

"At the inn—to go from here? My dear fellow, are you mad?" Tony sociably scoffed; he wouldn't hear of it. "Don't be afraid; we've plenty of use for you—if only to keep this young woman quiet."

"He can be of use this instant." Rose looked at her suitor as if there were not the shadow of a cloud between them. "The servants are getting luncheon. Will *you* go over for Mrs. Beever?"

"Ah," Tony demurred, laughing, "we mustn't make him fetch and carry!"

Dennis showed a momentary blankness and then, in his private discomposure, jumped at the idea of escaping from the house and into the air. "Do employ me," he pleaded. "I want to stretch my legs—I'll do anything."

"Since you're so kind, then, and it's so near," Tony replied. "Mrs. Beever's our best friend, and always the friend of our friends, and she's only across the river."

"Just six minutes," said Rose, "by the short way. Bring her back with you."

"The short way," Tony pressingly explained, "is through my garden and out of it by the gate on the river."

"At the river you turn to the right—the little foot-bridge is *her* bridge," Rose went on.

"You pass the gatehouse—empty and closed—at the other side of it, and there you are," said Tony.

"In her garden—it's lovely. Tell her it's for Mrs. Bream and it's important," Rose added.

"My wife's calling aloud for her!" Tony laid his hand, with his flushed laugh, on the young man's shoulder.

Dennis had listened earnestly, looking at his companions in turn. "It doesn't matter if she doesn't know in the least who I am?"

"She knows perfectly—don't be shy!" Rose familiarly exclaimed.

Tony gave him a great pat on the back which sent him off. "She has even something particular to say to you! She takes a great interest in his relations with you," he continued to Rose as the door closed behind their visitor. Then meeting in her face a certain impatience of any supersession of the question of Julia's state, he added, to justify his allusion, a word accompanied by the same excited laugh that had already broken from him. "Mrs. Beever deprecates the idea of any further delay in your marriage and thinks you've got quite enough to 'set up' on. She pronounces your means remarkably adequate."

"What does she know about our means?" Rose coldly asked.

"No more, doubtless, than I! But that needn't prevent her. It's the wish that's father to the thought. That's the result of her general goodwill to you."

"She has no goodwill of any sort to me. She doesn't like me." Rose spoke with marked dryness, in which moreover a certain surprise at the direction of her friend's humour was visible. Tony was now completely out of his groove; they indeed both were, though Rose was for the moment more successful in concealing her emotion. Still vibrating with the immense effort of the morning and particularly of the last hour, she could yet hold herself hard and observe what was taking place in her companion. He had been through something that had made his nerves violently active, so that his measure of security, of reality almost, was merged in the mere sense of the unusual. It was precisely this evidence of what he had been through that helped the girl's curiosity to preserve a waiting attitude—the firm surface she had triumphantly presented to each of the persons whom, from an early hour, she had had to encounter. But Tony had now the air of not intending to reward her patience by a fresh communication; it was as if some new delicacy had operated and he had struck himself as too explicit. He had looked astonished at her judgment of the lady of Eastmead.

"My dear Rose," he said, "I think you're greatly mistaken. Mrs. Beever much appreciates you."

She was silent at first, showing him a face worn with the ingenuity of all that in her interview with Dennis Vidal she had had to keep out of it and put into it. "My dear Tony," she then blandly replied, "I've never known any one like you for not having two grains of observation. I've known people with only a little; but a little's a poor affair. You've absolutely none at all, and that, for your character, is the right thing: it's magnificent and perfect."

Tony greeted this with real hilarity. "I like a good square one between the eyes!"

"You can't like it as much as I like you for being just as you are. Observation's a second-rate thing; it's only a precaution— the refuge of the small and the timid. It protects our own ridicules and props up our defences. You may have ridicules—

XI

TONY turned away from her with a movement which was a confession of incompetence; a sense moreover of the awkwardness of being so close to a grief for which he had no direct remedy. He could only assure her, in his confusion, of his deep regret that she had had a distress. The extremity of her collapse, however, was brief, a gust of passion after which she instantly showed the effort to recover. "Don't mind me," she said through her tears; "I shall pull myself together; I shall be all right in a moment." He wondered whether he oughtn't to leave her; and yet to leave her was scarcely courteous. She was quickly erect again, with her characteristic thought for others flowering out through her pain. "Only don't let Julia know—that's all I ask of you. One's little bothers are one's little bothers—they're all in the day's work. Just give me three minutes, and I shan't show a trace." She straightened herself and even smiled, patting her eyes with her crumpled handkerchief, while Tony marvelled at her courage and good humour.

"Of one thing you must be sure, Rose," he expressively answered, "that whatever happens to you, now or at any time, you've friends here and a home here that are yours for weal and woe."

"Ah, don't say that," she cried; "I can scarcely bear it! Disappointments one can meet; but how in the world is one adequately to meet generosity? Of one thing you, on your side, must be sure: that no trouble in life shall ever make me a bore. It was because I was so awfully afraid to be one that I've been keeping myself in—and that has led, in this ridiculous way, to my making a fool of myself at the last. I knew a hitch was coming—I knew at least something was; but I hoped it would come and go without *this*!" She had stopped before a mirror, still dealing, like an actress in the wing, with her appearance, her make-up. She dabbed at her cheeks and pressed her companion to leave her to herself. "Don't pity me, don't mind me; and, above all, don't ask any questions."

I don't say so; but you've no suspicions and no fears and no doubts; you're natural and generous and easy——"

"And beautifully, exquisitely stupid!" Tony broke in. "'Natural'—thank you! Oh, the horrible people who are natural! What you mean—only you're too charming to say it—is that I'm so utterly taken up with my own interests and feelings that I pipe about them like a canary in a cage. Not to have the things you mention, and above all not to have imagination, is simply not to have tact, than which nothing is more unforgivable and more loathsome. What lovelier proof of my selfishness could I be face to face with than the fact—which I immediately afterwards blushed for—that, coming in to you here a while ago, in the midst of something so important to you, I hadn't the manners to ask you so much as a question about it?"

"Do you mean about Mr. Vidal—after he had gone to his room? You did ask me a question," Rose said; "but you had a subject much more interesting to speak of." She waited an instant before adding: "You spoke of something I haven't ceased to think of." This gave Tony a chance for reference to his discharge of the injunction she had then laid upon him; as a reminder of which Rose further observed: "There's plenty of time for Mr. Vidal."

"I hope indeed he's going to stay. I like his looks immensely," Tony responded. "I like his type; it matches so with what you've told me of him. It's the real thing—I wish we had him here." Rose, at this, gave a small, confused cry, and her host went on: "Upon my honour I do—I know a man when I see him. He's just the sort of fellow I personally should have liked to be."

"You mean *you're* not the real thing?" Rose asked.

It was a question of a kind that Tony's good-nature, shining out almost splendidly even through trouble, could always meet with princely extravagance. "Not a bit! I'm bolstered up with all sorts of little appearances and accidents. Your friend there has his feet on the rock." This picture of her friend's position moved Rose to another vague sound—the effect of which, in turn, was to make Tony look at her more sharply. But he appeared not to impute to her any doubt of his assertion, and after an instant he reverted, with a jump, to a matter that he evidently wished not to drop. "You must really, you know, do justice to Mrs. Beever. When she dislikes one it's not a question of shades or degrees. She's not an underhand enemy—she very soon lets one know it."

"You mean by something she says or does?"

Tony considered a moment. "I mean she gives you her reasons—she's eminently direct. And I'm sure she has never lifted a finger against you."

"Perhaps not. But she will," said Rose. "You yourself just gave me the proof."

Tony wondered. "What proof?"

"Why, in telling Dennis that she had told you she had something special to say to him."

Tony recalled it—it had already passed out of his mind. "What she has to say is only what I myself have already said for the rest of us—that she hopes with all her heart things are now smooth for his marriage."

"Well, what could be more horrid than that?"

"More horrid?" Tony stared.

"What has she to do with his marriage? Her interference is in execrable taste."

The girl's tone was startling, and her companion's surprise augmented, showing itself in his lighted eyes and deepened colour. "My dear Rose, isn't that sort of thing, in a little circle like ours, a permitted joke—a friendly compliment? We're all so *with* you."

She had turned away from him. She went on, as if she had not heard him, with a sudden tremor in her voice—the tremor of a deep upheaval: "Why does she give opinions that nobody wants or asks her for? What does she know of our relations or of what difficulties and mysteries she touches? Why can't she leave us alone—at least for the first hour?"

Embarrassment was in Tony's gasp—the unexpected had sprung up before him. He could only stammer after her as she moved away: "Bless my soul, my dear child—you don't mean to say there *are* difficulties? Of course it's no one's business—but one hoped you were in quiet waters." Across her interval, as he spoke, she suddenly faced round, and his view of her, with this, made him smite his forehead in his penitent, expressive way. "What a brute I am not to have seen you're not quite happy, and not to have noticed that *he*——!" Tony caught

himself up; the face offered him was the convulsed face that had not been offered Dennis Vidal. Rose literally glared at him; she stood there with her two hands on her heaving breast and something in all her aspect that was like the first shock of a great accident. What he saw, without understanding it, was the final snap of her tremendous tension, the end of her wonderful false calm. He misunderstood it in fact, as he saw it give way before him: he sprang at the idea that the poor girl had received a blow—a blow which her self-control up to within a moment only presented as more touchingly borne. Vidal's absence was there as a part of it: the situation flashed into vividness. "His eagerness to leave you surprised me," he exclaimed, "and yours to make him go!" Tony thought again, and before he spoke his thought her eyes seemed to glitter it back. "He has not brought you bad news—he has not failed of what we hoped?" He went to her with compassion and tenderness: "You don't mean to say, my poor girl, that he doesn't meet you as you supposed he would?" Rose dropped, as he came, into a chair; she had burst into passionate tears. She threw herself upon a small table, burying her head in her arms, while Tony, all wonder and pity, stood above her and felt helpless as she sobbed She seemed to have sunk under her wrong and to quiver with her pain. Her host, with his own recurrent pang, could scarcely bear it: he felt a sharp need of making some one pay. "You don't mean to say Mr. Vidal doesn't keep faith?"

"Oh, God! oh, God! oh, God!" Rose Armiger wailed.

"Ah," said Tony in friendly remonstrance, "your bravery makes it too hard to help you!"

"Don't try to help me—don't even want to. And don't tell any tales. Hush!" she went on in a different tone. "Here's Mrs. Beever!"

The lady of Eastmead was preceded by the butler, who, having formally announced her, announced luncheon as invidiously as if it had only been waiting for her. The servants at each house had ways of reminding her they were not the servants at the other.

"Luncheon's all very well," said Tony, "but who in the world's to eat it? Before *you* do," he continued, to Mrs. Beever, "there's something I must ask of you."

"And something I must ask too," Rose added, while the butler retired like a conscientious Minister retiring from untenable office. She addressed herself to their neighbour with a face void, to Tony's astonishment, of every vestige of disorder. "Didn't Mr. Vidal come back with you?"

Mrs. Beever looked incorruptible. "Indeed he did!" she sturdily replied. "Mr. Vidal is in the garden of this house."

"Then I'll call him to luncheon." And Rose floated away, leaving her companions confronted in a silence that ended—as Tony was lost in the wonder of her presence of mind—only when Mrs. Beever had assured herself that she was out of earshot.

"She has broken it off!" this lady then responsibly proclaimed.

Her colleague demurred. "She? How do you know?"

"I know because he has told me so."

"Already—in these few minutes?"

Mrs. Beever hung fire. "Of course I asked him first. I met him at the bridge—I saw he had had a shock."

"It's Rose who has had the shock!" Tony returned. "It's he who has thrown her over."

Mrs. Beever stared. "That's *her* story?"

Tony reflected. "Practically—yes."

Again his visitor hesitated, but only for an instant. "Then one of them lies."

Tony laughed out at her lucidity. "It isn't Rose Armiger!"

"It isn't Dennis Vidal, my dear; I believe in him," said Mrs. Beever.

Her companion's amusement grew. "Your operations are rapid."

"Remarkably. I've asked him to come to me."

Tony raised his eyebrows. "To come to you?"

"Till he can get a train—to-morrow. He can't stay on here."

Tony looked at it. "I see what you mean."

"That's a blessing—you don't always! I like him—he's my sort. And something seems to tell me I'm his!"

"I won't gracefully insult you by saying you're every one's," Tony observed. Then, after an instant, "Is he very much cut up?" he inquired.

"He's utterly staggered. He doesn't understand."

Tony thought again. "No more do I. But you'll console him," he added.

"I'll feed him first," said his neighbour. "I'll take him back with me to luncheon."

"Isn't that scarcely civil?"

"Civil to you?" Mrs. Beever interposed. "That's exactly what he asked me. I told him I would arrange it with you."

"And you're 'arranging' it, I see. But how can you take him if Rose is bringing him in?"

Mrs. Beever was silent a while. "She isn't. She hasn't gone to him. That was for *me*."

Tony looked at her in wonder. "Your operations are rapid," he repeated. "But I found her under the unmistakable effect of a blow."

"I found her exactly as usual."

"Well, that also was for you," said Tony. "Her disappointment's a secret."

"Then I'm much obliged to you for mentioning it."

"I did so to defend her against your bad account of her. But the whole thing's obscure," the young man added with sudden weariness. "I give it up!"

"*I* don't—I shall straighten it out." Mrs. Beever spoke with high decision. "But I must see your wife first."

"Rather!—she's waiting all this while." He had already opened the door.

As she reached it she stopped again. "Shall I find the Doctor with her?"

"Yes, by her request."

"Then how is she?"

"Maddening!" Tony exclaimed; after which, as his visitor echoed the word, he went on: "I mean in her dreadful obsession, to which poor Ramage has had to give way and which is the direct reason of her calling you."

Mrs. Beever's little eyes seemed to see more than he told her, to have indeed the vision of something formidable. "What dreadful obsession?"

"She'll tell you herself." He turned away to leave her to go, and she disappeared; but the next moment he heard her again on the threshold.

"Only a word to say that that child may turn up."

"What child?" He had already forgotten.

"Oh, if you don't remember——!" Mrs. Beever, with feminine inconsequence, almost took it ill.

Tony recovered the agreeable image. "Oh, your niece? Certainly—I remember her hair."

"She's not my niece, and her hair's hideous. But if she does come, send her straight home!"

"Very good," said Tony. This time his visitor vanished.

XII

H E MOVED a minute about the hall; then he dropped upon
a sofa with a sense of exhaustion and a sudden need of
rest; he stretched himself, closing his eyes, glad to be alone,
glad above all to make sure that he could lie still. He wished to
show himself he was not nervous; he took up a position with
the purpose not to budge till Mrs. Beever should come back.
His house was in an odd condition, with luncheon pompously
served and no one able to go to it. Poor Julia was in a predicament, poor Rose in another, and poor Mr. Vidal, fasting in the
garden, in a greater one than either. Tony sighed as he thought
of this dispersal, but he stiffened himself resolutely on his
couch. He wouldn't go in alone, and he couldn't even enjoy
Mrs. Beever. It next occurred to him that he could still less enjoy her little friend, the child he had promised to turn away; on
which he gave a sigh that represented partly privation and
partly resignation—partly also a depressed perception of the
fact that he had never in all his own healthy life been less eager
for a meal. Meanwhile, however, the attempt to stop pacing the
floor was a success: he felt as if in closing his eyes he destroyed
the vision that had scared him. He was cooler, he was easier,
and he liked the smell of flowers in the dusk. What was droll,
when he gave himself up to it, was the sharp sense of lassitude;
it had dropped on him out of the blue and it showed him how
a sudden alarm—such as, after all, he had had—could drain a
fellow in an hour of half his vitality. He wondered whether, if
he might be undisturbed a little, the result of this surrender
wouldn't be to make him delightfully lose consciousness.

He never knew afterwards whether it was in the midst of
his hope or on the inner edge of a doze just achieved that he
became aware of a footfall betraying an uncertain advance. He
raised his lids to it and saw before him the pretty girl from the
other house, whom, for a moment before he moved, he lay
there looking at. He immediately recognised that what had
roused him was the fact that, noiselessly and for a few seconds, her eyes had rested on his face. She uttered a blushing
"Oh!" which deplored this effect of her propinquity and

which brought Tony straight to his feet. "Ah, good morning! How d'ye do?" Everything came back to him but her name. "Excuse my attitude—I didn't hear you come in."

"When I saw you asleep I'm afraid I kept the footman from speaking." Jean Martle was much embarrassed, but it contributed in the happiest way to her animation. "I came in because he told me that Cousin Kate's here."

"Oh yes, she's here—she thought you might arrive. Do sit down," Tony added with his prompt instinct of what, in his own house, was due from a man of some confidence to a girl of none at all. It operated before he could check it, and Jean was as passive to it as if he had tossed her a command; but as soon as she was seated, to obey him, in a high-backed, wide-armed Venetian chair which made a gilded cage for her flutter, and he had again placed himself—not in the same position—on the sofa opposite, he recalled the request just preferred by Mrs. Beever. He was to send her straight home; yes, it was to be invited instantly to retrace her steps that she sat there panting and pink.

Meanwhile she was very upright and very serious; she seemed very anxious to explain. "I thought it better to come, since she wasn't there. I had gone off to walk home with the Marshes—I was gone rather long; and when I came back she had left the house—the servants told me she must be here."

Tony could only meet with the note of hospitality so logical a plea. "Oh, it's all right—Mrs. Beever's with Mrs. Bream." It was apparently all wrong—he must tell her she couldn't stay; but there was a prior complication in his memory of having invited her to luncheon. "I wrote to your cousin—I hoped you'd come. Unfortunately she's not staying herself."

"Ah, then, I mustn't!" Jean spoke with lucidity, but without quitting her chair.

Tony hesitated. "She'll be a little while yet—my wife has something to say to her."

The girl had fixed her eyes on the floor; she might have been reading there the fact that for the first time in her life she was regularly calling on a gentleman. Since this was the singular case she must at least call properly. Her manner revealed an earnest effort to that end, an effort visible even in the fear of a liberty if she should refer too familiarly to Mrs.

Bream. She cast about her with intensity for something that would show sympathy without freedom, and, as a result, presently produced: "I came an hour ago, and I saw Miss Armiger. She told me she would bring down the baby."

"But she didn't?"

"No, Cousin Kate thought it wouldn't do."

Tony was happily struck. "It will do—it shall do. Should you like to see her?"

"I thought I should like it very much. It's very kind of you."

Tony jumped up. "I'll show her to you myself." He went over to ring a bell; then, as he came back, he added: "I delight in showing her. I think she's the wonder of the world."

"That's what babies always seem to me," said Jean. "It's so absorbing to watch them."

These remarks were exchanged with great gravity, with stiffish pauses, while Tony hung about till his ring should be answered.

"Absorbing?" he repeated. "Isn't it, preposterously? Wait till you've watched Effie!"

His visitor preserved for a while a silence which might have indicated that, with this injunction, her waiting had begun; but at last she said with the same simplicity: "I've a sort of original reason for my interest in her."

"Do you mean the illness of her poor mother?" He saw that she meant nothing so patronising, though her countenance fell with the reminder of this misfortune: she heard with awe that the unconscious child was menaced. "That's a very good reason," he declared, to relieve her. "But so much the better if you've got another too. I hope you'll never want for one to be kind to her."

She looked more assured. "I'm just the person always to be."

"Just the person——?" Tony felt that he must draw her out. She was now arrested, however, by the arrival of the footman, to whom he immediately turned. "Please ask Gorham to be as good as to bring down the child."

"Perhaps Gorham will think it won't do," Jean suggested as the servant went off.

"Oh, she's as proud of her as I am! But if she doesn't approve I'll take you upstairs. That'll be because, as you say you're just the person. I haven't the least doubt of it—but you were going to tell me why."

Jean treated it as if it were almost a secret. "Because she was born on *my* day."

"Your birthday?"

"My birthday—the twenty-fourth."

"Oh, I see; that's charming—that's delightful!" The circumstance had not quite all the subtlety she had beguiled him into looking for, but her amusing belief in it, which halved the date like a succulent pear, mingled oddly, to make him quickly feel that it had enough, with his growing sense that Mrs. Beever's judgment of her hair was a libel. "It's a most extraordinary coincidence—it makes a most interesting tie. Do, therefore, I beg you, whenever you keep your anniversary, keep also a little hers."

"That's just what I was thinking," said Jean. Then she added, still shy, yet suddenly almost radiant: "I shall always send her something!"

"She shall do the same to you!" This idea had a charm even for Tony, who determined on the spot, quite sincerely, that he would, for the first years at least, make it his own charge. "You're her very first friend," he smiled.

"Am I?" Jean thought it wonderful news. "Before she has even seen me!"

"Oh, those *are* the first. You're 'handed down,'" said Tony, humouring her.

She evidently deprecated, however, any abatement of her rarity. "Why, I haven't seen her mother, either."

"No, you haven't seen her mother. But you shall. And you have seen her father."

"Yes, I have seen her father." Looking at him as if to make sure of it, Jean gave this assertion the assent of a gaze so unrestricted that, feeling herself after an instant caught, as it were, in it, she turned abruptly away.

It came back to Tony at the same moment with a sort of coarseness that he was to have sent her home; yet now, somehow, as if half through the familiarity it had taken but these minutes to establish, and half through a perception of her extreme juvenility, his reluctance to tell her so had dropped. "Do you know I'm under a sort of dreadful vow to Mrs.

Beever?" Then as she faced him again, wondering: "She told me that if you should turn up I was to pack you off."

Jean stared with a fresh alarm. "Ah, I shouldn't have stayed!"

"You didn't know it, and I couldn't show you the door."

"Then I must go now."

"Not a bit. I wouldn't have mentioned it—to consent to that. I mention it for just the other reason—to keep you here as long as possible. I'll make it right with Cousin Kate," Tony continued. "I'm not afraid of her!" he laughed. "You produce an effect on me for which I'm particularly grateful." She was acutely sensitive; for a few seconds she looked as if she thought he might be amusing himself at her expense. "I mean you soothe me—at a moment when I really want it," he said with a gentleness from which it gave him pleasure to see in her face an immediate impression. "I'm worried, I'm depressed, I've been threshing about in my anxiety. You keep me cool—you're just the right thing." He nodded at her in clear kindness. "Stay with me—stay with me!"

Jean had not taken the flight of expressing a concern for his domestic situation, but in the pity that flooded her eyes at this appeal there was an instant surrender to nature. It was the sweetness of her youth that had calmed him, but in the response his words had evoked she already, on the spot, looked older. "Ah, if I *could* help you!" she timidly murmured.

"Sit down again; sit down!" He turned away. "Here's the wonder of the world!" he exclaimed the next instant, seeing Gorham appear with her charge. His interest in the apparition almost simultaneously dropped, for Mrs. Beever was at the opposite door. She had come back, and Ramage was with her: they stopped short together, and he did the same on catching the direction, as he supposed, of his sharp neighbour's eyes. She had an air of singular intensity; it was peculiarly embodied in a look which, as she drew herself up, she shot straight past him and under the reprobation of which he glanced round to see Jean Martle turn pale. What he saw, however, was not Jean Martle at all, but that very different person Rose Armiger, who, by an odd chance and with Dennis Vidal at her side, presented herself at this very juncture at the door of the vestibule. It was at Rose Mrs. Beever stared—stared with a significance doubtless produced by this young lady's falsification of her denial that Mr. Vidal had been actively pursued. She took no notice of Jean, who, while the rest of them stood about, testified to her prompt compliance with any word of Tony's by being the only member of the company in a chair. The sight of Mrs. Beever's face appeared to have deprived her of the force to rise. Tony observed these things in a flash, and also how far the gaze of the Gorgon was from petrifying Rose Armiger, who, with a bright recovery of zeal by which he himself was wonderstruck, launched without delay a conscientious reminder of luncheon. It was on the table—it was spoiling—it was spoilt! Tony felt that he must gallantly support her. "Let us at last go in then," he said to Mrs. Beever. "Let us go in then," he repeated to Jean and to Dennis Vidal. "Doctor, you'll come too?"

He broke Jean's spell at a touch; she was on her feet; but the Doctor raised, as if for general application, a deterrent, authoritative hand. "If you please, Bream—no banquet." He looked at Jean, at Rose, at Vidal, at Gorham. "I take the house in hand. We immediately subside."

Tony sprang to him. "Julia's worse?"

"No—she's the same."

"Then I may go to her?"

"Absolutely not." Doctor Ramage grasped his arm, linked his own in it and held him. "If you're not a good boy I lock you up in your room. We immediately subside," he said again, addressing the others; "we go our respective ways and we keep very still. The fact is I require a hushed house. But before the hush descends Mrs. Beever has something to say to you."

She was on the other side of Tony, who felt, between them there, like their prisoner. She looked at her little audience, which consisted of Jean and Rose, of Mr. Vidal and the matronly Gorham. Gorham carried in her ample arms a large white sacrifice, a muslin-muffled offering which seemed to lead up to a ceremony. "I have something to say to you because Doctor Ramage allows it, and because we are both under pledges to Mrs. Bream. It's a very peculiar announcement for me to have on my hands, but I've just passed her my promise, in the very strictest manner, to make it, before leaving the house, to every one it may concern, and to repeat it in certain other quarters." She paused again, and Tony, from his closeness to her, could feel the tremor of her solid presence. She disliked the awkwardness and the coercion, and he was sorry for her, because by this time he well knew what was coming. He had guessed his wife's extraordinary precaution, which would have been almost grotesque if it hadn't been so infinitely touching. It seemed to him that he gave the measure of his indulgence for it in overlooking the wound to his delicacy conveyed in the publicity she imposed. He could condone this in a tender sigh, because it meant that in consequence of it she'd now pull round. "She wishes it as generally known as possible," Mrs. Beever brought out, "that Mr. Bream, to gratify her at a crisis which I trust she exaggerates, has assured her on his sacred honour that in the event of her death he will not again marry."

"In the lifetime of her daughter, that is," Doctor Ramage hastened to add.

"In the lifetime of her daughter," Mrs. Beever as clearly echoed.

"In the lifetime of her daughter!" Tony himself took up with an extravagance intended to offer the relief of a humorous treatment, if need be, to the bewildered young people whose embarrassed stare was a prompt criticism of Julia's discretion. It might have been in the spirit of a protest still more vehement that, at this instant, a small shrill pipe rose from the animated parcel with which Gorham, participating in the general awkwardness, had possibly taken a liberty. The comical little sound created a happy diversion; Tony sprang straight to the child. "So it *is*, my own," he cried, "a scandal to be talking of 'lifetimes!'" He caught her from the affrighted nurse— he put his face down to hers with passion. Her wail ceased and he held her close to him; for a minute, in silence, as if something deep went out from him, he laid his cheek to her little cheek, burying his head under her veil. When he gave her up again, turning round, the hall was empty of every one save the Doctor, who signalled peremptorily to Gorham to withdraw. Tony remained there meeting his eyes, in which, after an instant, the young man saw something that led him to exclaim: "How dreadfully ill she must be, Ramage, to have conceived a stroke in such taste!"

His companion drew him down to the sofa, patting, soothing, supporting him. "You must bear it my dear boy—you
must bear everything." Doctor Ramage faltered. "Your wife's
exceedingly ill."

BOOK SECOND

XIII

I T CONTINUED to be for the lady of Eastmead, as the years
went on, a sustaining reflection that if in the matter of up-
holstery she yielded somewhat stiffly to the other house, so
the other house was put out of all countenance by the mere
breath of her garden. Tony could beat her indoors at every
point, but when she took her stand on her lawn she could
defy not only Bounds but Wilverley. Her stand, and still more
her seat, in the summer days, was frequent there, as we easily
gather from the fortified position in which we next encounter
her. From May to October she was out, as she said, at grass,
drawing from it most of the time a comfortable sense that on
such ground as this her young friend's love of newness broke
down. He might make his dinner-service as new as he liked;
she triumphed precisely in the fact that her trees and her
shrubs were old. He could hang nothing on his walls like her
creepers and clusters; there was no velvet in his carpets like
the velvet of her turf. She had everything, or almost everything—she had space and time and the river. No one at Wilverley had the river as she had it; people might say of course
there was little of it to have, but of whatever there was she
was in intimate possession. It skirted her grounds and improved her property and amused her guests; she always held
that her free access made up for being, as people said, on the
wrong side of it. If she had not been on the wrong side she
would not have had the little stone foot-bridge which was her
special pride and the very making of her picture, and which
she had heard compared—she had an off-hand way of bringing it in—to a similar feature, at Cambridge, of one of the celebrated "backs." The other side was the side of the other
house, the side for the view—the view as to which she entertained the merely qualified respect excited in us, after the first
creative flush, by mysteries of our own making. Mrs. Beever
herself formed the view and the other house was welcome to
it, especially to those parts of it enjoyed through the rare gaps

in an interposing leafy lane. Tony had a gate which he called his river-gate, but you didn't so much as suspect the stream till you got well out of it. He had on his further quarter a closer contact with the town; but this was just what on both quarters she had with the country. Her approach to the town was by the "long way" and the big bridge, and by going on, as she liked to do, past the Doctor's square red house. She hated stopping there, hated it as much as she liked his stopping at Eastmead: in the former case she seemed to consult him and in the latter to advise, which was the exercise of her wisdom that she decidedly preferred. Such degrees and dimensions, I hasten to add, had to do altogether with short relations and small things; but it was just the good lady's reduced scale that held her little world together. So true is it that from strong compression the elements of drama spring and that there are conditions in which they seem to invite not so much the opera-glass as the microscope.

Never, perhaps, at any rate, had Mrs. Beever been more conscious of her advantages, or at least more surrounded with her conveniences, than on a beautiful afternoon of June on which we are again concerned with her. These blessings were partly embodied in the paraphernalia of tea, which had cropped up, with promptness and profusion, in a sheltered corner of the lawn and in the midst of which, waiting for custom, she might have been in charge of a refreshment-stall at a fair. Everything at the other house struck her as later and later, and she only regretted that, as the protest of her own tradition, she couldn't move in the opposite direction without also moving from the hour. She waited for it now, at any rate, in the presence of a large red rug and a large white tablecloth, as well as of sundry basket-chairs and of a hammock that swayed in the soft west wind; and she had meanwhile been occupied with a collection of parcels and pasteboard boxes that were heaped together on a bench. Of one of these parcels, enveloped in several layers of tissue-paper, she had just possessed herself, and, seated near her tea-table, was on the point of uncovering it. She became aware, at this instant, of being approached from behind; on which, looking over her shoulder and seeing Doctor Ramage, she straightway stayed her hands. These friends, in a long acquaintance, had dropped

by the way so many preliminaries that absence, in their intercourse, was a mere parenthesis and conversation in general
scarce began with a capital. But on this occasion the Doctor
was floated to a seat not, as usual, on the bosom of the immediately previous.

"Guess whom I've just overtaken on your doorstep. The
young man you befriended four years ago—Mr. Vidal, Miss
Armiger's flame!"

Mrs. Beever fell back in her surprise; it was rare for Mrs.
Beever to fall back. "He has turned up again?" Her eyes had
already asked more than her friend could tell. "For what in
the world——?"

"For the pleasure of seeing you. He has evidently retained
a very grateful sense of what you did for him."

"I did nothing, my dear man—I had to let it alone."

"Tony's condition—of course I remember—again required
you. But you gave him a shelter," said the Doctor, "that
wretched day and that night, and he felt (it was evidently
much to him) that, in his rupture with his young woman, you
had the right instinct of the matter and were somehow on his
side."

"I put him up for a few hours—I saved him, in time, the
embarrassment of finding himself in a house of death. But he
took himself off the next morning early—bidding me good-
bye only in a quiet little note."

"A quiet little note which I remember you afterwards
showed me and which was a model of discretion and good
taste. It seems to me," the Doctor went on, "that he doesn't
violate those virtues in considering that you've given him the
right to reappear."

"At the very time, and the only time, in so long a period
that his young woman, as you call her, happens also to be
again in the field!"

"That's a coincidence," the Doctor replied, "far too singular for Mr. Vidal to have had any forecast of it."

"You didn't then tell him?"

"I told him nothing save that you were probably just where
I find you, and that, as Manning is busy with her tea-things,
I would come straight out for him and announce that he's
there."

Mrs. Beever's sense of complications evidently grew as she thought. "By 'there' do you mean on the doorstep?"

"Far from it. In the safest place in the world—at least when you're not in it."

"In my own room?" Mrs. Beever asked.

"In that austere monument to Domestic Method which you're sometimes pleased to call your boudoir. I took upon myself to show him into it and to close the door on him there. I reflected that you'd perhaps like to see him before any one else."

Mrs. Beever looked at her visitor with appreciation. "You dear, sharp thing!"

"Unless, indeed," the Doctor added, "they have, in so many years, already met."

"She told me only yesterday they haven't."

"I see. However, as I believe you consider that she never speaks the truth, that doesn't particularly count."

"I hold, on the contrary, that a lie counts double," Mrs. Beever replied with decision.

Doctor Ramage laughed. "Then why have you never in your life told one? I haven't even yet quite made out," he pursued, "why—especially with Miss Jean here—you asked Miss Armiger down."

"I asked her for Tony."

"Because he suggested it? Yes, I know that."

"I mean it," said Mrs. Beever, "in a sense I think you don't know." She looked at him a moment; but either her profundity or his caution were too great, and he waited for her to commit herself further. That was a thing she could always do rapidly without doing it recklessly. "I asked her exactly on account of Jean."

The Doctor meditated, but this seemed to deepen her depth. "I give it up. You've mostly struck me as so afraid of every other girl Paul looks at."

Mrs. Beever's face was grave. "Yes, I've always been; but I'm not so afraid of them as of those at whom Tony looks."

Her interlocutor started. "He's looking at Jean?"

Mrs. Beever was silent a little. "Not for the first time!"

Her visitor also hesitated. "And do you think, Miss Armiger——?"

Mrs. Beever took him up. "Miss Armiger's better for him—since he must have somebody!"

"You consider she'd marry him?"

"She's insanely in love with him."

The Doctor tilted up his chin; he uttered an expressive "Euh!—She is indeed, poor thing!" he said. "Since you frankly mention it, I as frankly agree with you, that I've never seen anything like it. And there's monstrous little I've not seen. But if Tony isn't crazy too——?"

"It's a kind of craze that's catching. He must think of that sort of thing."

"I don't know what you mean by 'thinking!' Do you imply that the dear man, on what we know——?" The Doctor couldn't phrase it.

His friend had greater courage. "Would break his vow and marry again?" She turned it over, but at last she brought out: "Never in the world."

"Then how does the chance of his thinking of Rose help her?"

"I don't say it helps her. I simply say it helps poor me."

Doctor Ramage was still mystified. "But if they can't marry——?"

"I don't care whether they marry or not!"

She faced him with the bravery of this, and he broke into a happy laugh. "I don't know whether most to admire your imagination or your morality."

"I protect *my* girl," she serenely declared.

Doctor Ramage made his choice. "Oh, your morality!"

"In doing so," she went on, "I also protect my boy. That's the highest morality I know. I'll see Mr. Vidal out here," she added.

"So as to get rid of him easier?"

"My getting rid of him will depend on what he wants. He must take, after all," Mrs. Beever continued, "his chance of meeting any embarrassment. If he plumps in without feeling his way——"

"It's his own affair—I see," the Doctor said. What he saw was that his friend's diplomacy had suffered a slight disturbance. Mr. Vidal was a new element in her reckoning; for if, of old, she had liked and pitied him, he had since dropped out of her problem. Her companion, who timed his pleasures to the minute, indulged in one of his frequent glances at his watch. "I'll put it then to the young man—more gracefully than you do—that you'll receive him in this place."

"I shall be much obliged to you."

"But before I go," Doctor Ramage inquired, "where are all our friends?"

"I haven't the least idea. The only ones I count on are Effie and Jean."

The Doctor made a motion of remembrance. "To be sure—it's their birthday: that fellow put it out of my head. The child's to come over to you to tea, and just what I stopped for——"

"Was to see if I had got your doll?" Mrs. Beever interrupted him by holding up the muffled parcel in her lap. She pulled away the papers. "Allow me to introduce the young lady."

The young lady was sumptuous and ample; he took her in his hands with reverence. "She's splendid—she's positively human! I feel like a Turkish pasha investing in a beautiful Circassian. I feel too," the Doctor went on, "how right I was to depend, in the absence of Mrs. Ramage, on your infallible taste." Then restoring the effigy: "Kindly mention how much I owe you."

"Pay at the shop," said Mrs. Beever. "They 'trusted' me."

"With the same sense of security that I had!" The Doctor got up. "Please then present the object and accompany it with my love and a kiss."

"You can't come back to give them yourself?"

"What do I ever give 'myself,' dear lady, but medicine?"

"Very good," said Mrs. Beever; "the presentation shall be formal. But I ought to warn you that your beautiful Circassian will have been no less than the fourth." She glanced at the parcels on the bench. "I mean the fourth doll the child's to receive to-day."

The Doctor followed the direction of her eyes. "It's a regular slave-market—a perfect harem!"

"We've each of us given her one. Each, that is, except Rose."

"And what has Rose given her?"

"Nothing at all."

The Doctor thought a moment. "Doesn't she like her?"

"She seems to wish it to be marked that she has nothing to do with her."

Again Doctor Ramage reflected. "I see—that's very clever."

Mrs. Beever, from her chair, looked up at him. "What do you mean by 'clever'?"

"I'll tell you some other time." He still stood before the bench. "There are no gifts for poor Jean?"

"Oh, Jean has had most of hers."

"But nothing from *me*." The Doctor had but just thought of her; he turned sadly away. "I'm quite ashamed!"

"You needn't be," said Mrs. Beever. "She has also had nothing from Tony."

He seemed struck. "Indeed? On Miss Armiger's system?" His friend remained silent, and he went on: "That of wishing it to be marked that he has nothing to do with her?"

Mrs. Beever, for a minute, continued not to reply; but at last she exclaimed: "He doesn't calculate!"

"That's bad—for a banker!" Doctor Ramage laughed. "What then has she had from Paul?"

"Nothing either—as yet. That's to come this evening."

"And what's it to be?"

Mrs. Beever hesitated. "I haven't an idea."

"Ah, you *can* fib!" joked her visitor, taking leave.

XIV

H<small>E</small> CROSSED on his way to the house a tall parlourmaid who had just quitted it with a tray which a moment later she deposited on the table near her mistress. Tony Bream was accustomed to say that since Frederick the Great's grenadiers there had never been anything like the queen-mother's parlourmaids, who indeed on field-days might, in stature, uniform and precision of exercise, have affronted comparison with that formidable phalanx. They were at once more athletic and more reserved than Tony liked to see their sex, and he was always sure that the extreme length of their frocks was determined by that of their feet. The young woman, at any rate, who now presented herself, a young woman with a large nose and a straight back, stiff cap-streamers, stiffer petticoats and stiffest manners, was plainly the corporal of her squad. There was a murmur and a twitter all around her; but she rustled about the tea-table to a tune that quenched the voice of summer. It left undisturbed, however, for awhile, Mrs. Beever's meditations; that lady was thoughtfully occupied in wrapping up Doctor Ramage's doll. "Do you know, Manning, what has become of Miss Armiger?" she at last inquired.

"She went, ma'am, near an hour ago, to the pastrycook's."

"To the pastrycook's?"

"She had heard you wonder, ma'am, she told me, that the young ladies' birthday-cake hadn't yet arrived."

"And she thought she'd see about it? Uncommonly good of her!" Mrs. Beever exclaimed.

"Yes, ma'am, uncommonly good."

"Has it arrived, then, now?"

"Not yet, ma'am."

"And Miss Armiger hasn't returned?"

"I think not, ma'am."

Mrs. Beever considered again. "Perhaps she's waiting to bring it."

Manning indulged in a proportionate pause. "Perhaps, ma'am—in a fly. And when it comes, ma'am, shall I fetch it out?"

"In a fly too? I'm afraid," said Mrs. Beever, "that with such an incubation it will really require one." After a moment she added: "I'll go in and look at it first." And then, as her attendant was about to rustle away, she further detained her. "Mr. Bream hasn't been over?"

"Not yet, ma'am."

Mrs. Beever consulted her watch. "Then he's still at the Bank."

"He must be indeed, ma'am."

Tony's colleague appeared for a little to ponder this prompt concurrence; after which she said: "You haven't seen Miss Jean?"

Manning bethought herself. "I believe, ma'am, Miss Jean is dressing."

"Oh, in honour——" But Mrs. Beever's idea dropped before she finished her sentence.

Manning ventured to take it up. "In honour of her birthday, ma'am."

"I see—of course. And do you happen to have heard if that's what also detains Miss Effie—that she's dressing in honour of hers?"

Manning hesitated. "I heard, ma'am, this morning that Miss Effie had a slight cold."

Her mistress looked surprised. "But not such as to keep her at home?"

"They were taking extra care of her, ma'am—so that she might be all right for coming."

Mrs. Beever was not pleased. "Extra care? Then why didn't they send for the Doctor?"

Again Manning hesitated. "They sent for Miss Jean, ma'am."

"To come and look after her?"

"They often do, ma'am, you know. This morning I took in the message."

"And Miss Jean obeyed it?"

"She was there an hour, ma'am."

Mrs. Beever administered a more than approving pat to the final envelope of her doll. "She said nothing about it."

Again Manning concurred. "Nothing, ma'am." The word sounded six feet high, like the figure she presented. She waited a moment and then, as if to close with as sharp a snap the last open door to the desirable, "Mr. Paul, ma'am," she observed, "if you were wanting to know, is out in his boat on the river."

Mrs. Beever pitched her parcel back to the bench.

"Mr. Paul is never anywhere else!"

"Never, ma'am," said Manning inexorably. She turned the next instant to challenge the stranger who had come down from the house. "A gentleman, ma'am," she announced; and, retiring while Mrs. Beever rose to meet the visitor, drew, with the noise of a lawn-mower, a starched tail along the grass.

Dennis Vidal, with his hat off, showed his hostess a head over which not a year seemed to have passed. He had still his young, sharp, meagre look, and it came to her that the other time as well he had been dressed in double-breasted blue of a cut that made him sailorly. It was only on a longer view that she saw his special signs to be each a trifle intensified. He was browner, leaner, harder, finer; he even struck her as more wanting in height. These facts, however, didn't prevent another fact from striking her still more: what was most distinct in his face was that he was really glad to take her by the hand. That had an instant effect on her: she could glow with pleasure, modest matron as she was, at such an intimation of her having, so many years before, in a few hours, made on a clever young man she liked an impression that could thus abide with him. In the quick light of it she liked him afresh; it was as if their friendship put down on the spot a firm foot that was the result of a single stride across the chasm of time. In this indeed, to her clear sense, there was even something more to pity him for: it was such a dreary little picture of his interval, such an implication of what it had lacked, that there had been so much room in it for an ugly old woman at Wilverley. She motioned him to sit down with her, but she immediately remarked that before she asked him a question she had an important fact to make known. She had delayed too long, while he waited there, to let him understand that Rose Armiger was at Eastmead. She instantly saw at this that he had come in complete ignorance. The range of alarm in his face was narrow, but he coloured, looking grave; and after a brief debate with himself he inquired as to Miss Armiger's actual whereabouts.

"She has gone out, but she may reappear at any moment," said Mrs. Beever.

"And if she does, will she come out here?"

"I've an impression she'll change her dress first. That may take her a little time."

"Then I'm free to sit with you ten minutes?"

"As long as you like, dear Mr. Vidal. It's for you to choose whether you'll avoid her."

"I dislike dodging—I dislike hiding," Dennis returned; "but I daresay that if I had known where she was I wouldn't have come."

"I feel hatefully rude—but you took a leap in the dark. The absurd part of it," Mrs. Beever went on, "is that you've stumbled on her very first visit to me."

The young man showed a surprise which gave her the measure of his need of illumination. "For these four years?"

"For these four years. It's the only time she has been at Eastmead."

Dennis hesitated. "And how often has she been at the other house?"

Mrs. Beever smiled. "Not even once." Then as her smile broadened to a small, dry laugh, "I can quite say *that* for her!" she declared.

Dennis looked at her hard. "To your certain knowledge?"

"To my certain and absolute knowledge." This mutual candour continued, and presently she said: "But you—where do you come from?"

"From far away—I've been out of England. After my visit here I went back to my post."

"And now you've returned with your fortune?"

He gave her a smile from which the friendliness took something of the bitter quality. "Call it my *mis*fortune!" There was nothing in this to deprive Mrs. Beever of the pleasant play of a professional sense that he had probably gathered such an independence as would have made him welcome at the Bank. On the other hand she caught the note of a tired grimness in the way he added: "I've come back with that. It sticks to me!"

For a minute she spared him. "You want her as much as ever?"

His eyes confessed to a full and indeed to a sore acceptance of that expression of the degree. "I want her as much as ever. It's my constitutional obstinacy!"

"Which her treatment of you has done nothing to break down?"

"To break down? It has done everything in life to build it up."

"In spite of the particular circumstance——?" At this point even Mrs. Beever's directness failed.

That of her visitor, however, was equal to the occasion. "The particular circumstance of her chucking me because of the sudden glimpse given her, by Mrs. Bream's danger, of the possibility of a far better match?" He gave a laugh drier than her own had just been, the ring of an irony from which long, hard thought had pressed all the savour. "That 'particular circumstance,' dear madam, is every bit that's the matter with me!"

"You regard it with extraordinary coolness, but I presumed to allude to it——"

"Because," Dennis broke in with lucidity, "I myself made no bones of doing so on the only other occasion on which we've met?"

"The fact that we both equally *saw*, that we both equally judged," said Mrs. Beever, "was on that occasion really the only thing that had time to pass between us. It's a tie, but it's a slender one, and I'm all the more flattered that it should have had any force to make you care to see me again."

"It never ceased to be my purpose to see you, if you would permit it, on the first opportunity. My opportunity," the young man continued, "has been precipitated by an accident. I returned to England only last week, and was obliged two days ago to come on business to Southampton. There I found I should have to go, on the same matter, to Marrington. It then appeared that to get to Marrington I must change at Plumbury——"

"And Plumbury," said Mrs. Beever, "reminded you that you changed there, that it was from there you drove, on that horrible Sunday."

"It brought my opportunity home to me. Without wiring you or writing you, without sounding the ground or doing anything I ought to have done, I simply embraced it. I reached this place an hour ago and went to the inn."

She looked at him wofully. "Poor dear young man!"

He turned it off. "I do very well. Remember the places I've come from."

"I don't care in the least where you've come from! If Rose weren't here I could put you up so beautifully."

"Well, now that I know it," said Dennis after a moment, "I think I'm glad she's here. It's a fact the more to reckon with."

"You mean to see her then?"

He sat with his eyes fixed, weighing it well. "You must tell me two or three things first. Then I'll choose—I'll decide."

She waited for him to mention his requirements, turning to her teapot, which had been drawing, so that she could meanwhile hand him a cup. But for some minutes, taking it and stirring it, he only gazed and mused, as if his curiosities were so numerous that he scarcely knew which to pick out. Mrs. Beever at last, with a woman's sense for this, met him exactly at the right point. "I must tell you frankly that if four years ago she was a girl most people admired——"

He caught straight on. "She's still more wonderful now?"

Mrs. Beever distinguished. "I don't know about 'wonderful,' but she wears really well. She carries the years almost as you do, and her head better than any young woman I've ever seen. Life is somehow becoming to her. Every one's immensely struck with her. She only needs to get what she wants. She has in short a charm that I recognise."

Her visitor stared at her words as if they had been a framed picture; the reflected colour of it made a light in his face. "And you speak as one who, I remember, doesn't like her."

The lady of Eastmead faltered, but there was help in her characteristic courage. "No—I don't like her."

"I see," Dennis considered. "May I ask then why you invited her?"

"For the most definite reason in the world. Mr. Bream asked me to."

Dennis gave his hard smile. "Do you do everything Mr. Bream asks?"

"He asks so little!"

"Yes," Dennis allowed—"if that's a specimen! Does he like her still?" he inquired.

"Just as much as ever."

The young man was silent a few seconds. "Do you mean he's in love with her?"

"He never was—in any degree."

Dennis looked doubtful. "Are you very sure?"

"Well," said his hostess, "I'm sure of the present. That's quite enough. He's not in love with her now—I have the proof."

"The proof?"

Mrs. Beever waited a moment. "His request in itself. If he were in love with her he never would have made it."

There was a momentary appearance on her companion's part of thinking this rather too fine; but he presently said: "You mean because he's completely held by his death-bed vow to his wife?"

"Completely held."

"There's no likelihood of his breaking it?"

"Not the slightest."

Dennis Vidal exhaled a low, long breath which evidently represented a certain sort of relief. "You're very positive; but I've a great respect for your judgment." He thought an instant, then he pursued abruptly: "Why did he wish her invited?"

"For reasons that, as he expressed them to me, struck me as natural enough. For the sake of old acquaintance—for the sake of his wife's memory."

"He doesn't consider, then, that Mrs. Bream's obsession, as you term it, had been in any degree an apprehension of Rose?"

"Why should he?" Mrs. Beever asked. "Rose, for poor Julia, was on the point of becoming your wife."

"Ah! for all that was to prevent!" Dennis ruefully exclaimed.

"It was to prevent little enough, but Julia never knew how little. Tony asked me a month ago if I thought he might without awkwardness propose to Miss Armiger a visit to the other house. I said 'No, silly boy!' and he dropped the question; but a week later he came back to it. He confided to me that he was ashamed for so long to have done so little for her; and she had behaved in a difficult situation with such discretion

and delicacy that to have 'shunted' her, as he said, so completely was a kind of outrage to Julia's affection for her and a
slur upon hers for his wife. I said to him that if it would help
him a bit I would address her a suggestion that she should
honour me with her company. He jumped at that, and I
wrote. *She* jumped, and here she is."

Poor Dennis, at this, gave a spring, as if the young lady had
come into sight. Mrs. Beever reassured him, but he was on his
feet and he stood before her. "This then is their first meeting?"

"Dear, no! they've met in London. He often goes up."

"How often?"

"Oh, irregularly. Sometimes twice a month."

"And he sees her every time?"

Mrs. Beever considered. "Every time? I should think—
hardly."

"Then every other?"

"I haven't the least idea."

Dennis looked round the garden. "You say you're convinced that, in the face of his promise, he has no particular interest in her. You mean, however, of course, but to the extent
of marriage."

"I mean," said Mrs. Beever, "to the extent of anything at
all." She also rose; she brought out her whole story. "He's in
love with another person."

"Ah," Dennis murmured, "that's none of my business!"
He nevertheless closed his eyes an instant with the cool balm
of it. "But it makes a lot of difference."

She laid a kind hand on his arm. "Such a lot, I hope, then,
that you'll join our little party?" He looked about him again,
irresolute, and his eyes fell on the packages gathered hard by,
of which the nature was betrayed by a glimpse of flaxen curls
and waxen legs. She immediately enlightened him. "Preparations for a birthday visit from the little girl at the other house.
She's coming over to receive them."

Again he dropped upon a seat; she stood there and he
looked up at her. "At last we've got to business! It's *she* I've
come to ask about."

"And what do you wish to ask?"

"How she goes on—I mean in health."

"Not very well, I believe, just to-day!" Mrs. Beever laughed.

"Just to-day?"

"She's reported to have a slight cold. But don't be alarmed. In general she's splendid."

He hesitated. "Then you call it a good little life?"

"I call it a beautiful one!"

"I mean she won't pop off?"

"I can't guarantee that," said Mrs. Beever. "But till she does——"

"Till she does?" he asked, as she paused.

She paused a moment longer. "Well, it's a comfort to see her. You'll do that for yourself."

"I shall do that for myself," Dennis repeated. After a moment he went on: "To be utterly frank, it was to do it I came."

"And not to see me? Thank you! But I quite understand," said Mrs. Beever; "you looked to me to introduce you. Sit still where you are, and I will."

"There's one thing more I must ask you. You see; you know; you can tell me." He complied but a minute with her injunction; again, nervously, he was on his feet. "Is Miss Armiger in love with Mr. Bream?"

His hostess turned away. "That's the one question I can't answer." Then she faced him again. "You must find out for yourself."

He stood looking at her. "How shall I find out?"

"By watching her."

"Oh, I didn't come to do *that*!" Dennis, on his side, turned away; he was visibly dissatisfied. But he checked himself; before him rose a young man in boating flannels, who appeared to have come up from the river, who had advanced noiselessly across the lawn and whom Mrs. Beever introduced without ceremony as her "boy." Her boy blinked at Dennis, to whose identity he received no clue; and her visitor decided on a course. "May I think over what you've said to me and come back?"

"I shall be very happy to see you again. But, in this poor place, what will you do?"

Dennis glanced at the river; then he appealed to the young man. "Will you lend me your boat?"

"It's mine," said Mrs. Beever, with decision. "You're welcome to it."

"I'll take a little turn." Raising his hat, Dennis went rapidly down to the stream.

Paul Beever looked after him. "Hadn't I better show him——?" he asked of his mother.

"You had better sit right down there." She pointed with sharpness to the chair Dennis had quitted, and her son submissively took possession of it.

XV

PAUL BEEVER was tall and fat, and his eyes, like his mother's, were very small; but more even than to his mother nature had offered him a compensation for this defect in the extension of the rest of the face. He had large, bare, beardless cheeks and a wide, clean, candid mouth, which the length of the smooth upper lip caused to look as exposed as a bald head. He had a deep fold of flesh round his uncovered young neck, and his white flannels showed his legs to be all the way down of the same thickness. He promised to become massive early in life and even to attain a remarkable girth. His great tastes were for cigarettes and silence; but he was, in spite of his proportions, neither gross nor lazy. If he was indifferent to his figure he was equally so to his food, and he played cricket with his young townsmen and danced hard with their wives and sisters. Wilverley liked him and Tony Bream thought well of him: it was only his mother who had not yet made up her mind. He had done a good deal at Oxford in not doing any harm, and he had subsequently rolled round the globe in the very groove with which she had belted it. But it was exactly in satisfying that he a little disappointed her: she had provided so against dangers that she found it a trifle dull to be so completely safe. It had become with her a question not of how clever he was, but of how stupid. Tony had expressed the view that he was distinctly deep, but that might only have been, in Tony's florid way, to show that he himself was so. She would not have found it convenient to have to give the boy an account of Mr. Vidal; but now that, detached from her purposes and respectful of her privacies, he sat there without making an inquiry, she was disconcerted enough slightly to miss the opportunity to snub him. On this occasion, however, she could steady herself with the possibility that her hour would still come. He began to eat a bun—his row justified that; and meanwhile she helped him to his tea. As she handed him the cup she challenged him with some sharpness. "Pray, when are you going to give it?"

He slowly masticated while he looked at her. "When do you think I had better?"

"Before dinner—distinctly. One doesn't know what may happen."

"Do you think anything at all will?" he placidly asked.

His mother waited before answering. "Nothing, certainly, unless you take some trouble for it." His perception of what she meant by this was clearly wanting, so that after a moment she continued: "You don't seem to grasp that I've done for you all I can do, and that the rest now depends on yourself."

"Oh yes, mother, I grasp it," he said without irritation. He took another bite of his bun and then added: "Miss Armiger has made me quite do that."

"Miss Armiger?" Mrs. Beever stared; she even felt that her opportunity was at hand. "What in the world has she to do with the matter?"

"Why I've talked to her a lot about it."

"You mean she has talked to *you* a lot, I suppose. It's immensely like her."

"It's like my dear mamma—that's whom it's like," said Paul. "She takes just the same view as yourself. I mean the view that I've a great opening and that I must make a great effort."

"And don't you see that for yourself? Do you require a pair of women to tell you?" Mrs. Beever asked.

Paul, looking grave and impartial, turned her question over while he stirred the tea. "No, not exactly. But Miss Armiger puts everything so well."

"She puts some things doubtless beautifully. Still, I should like you to be conscious of some better reason for making yourself acceptable to Jean than that another young woman, however brilliant, recommends it."

The young man continued to ruminate, and it occurred to his mother, as it had occurred before, that his imperturbability was perhaps a strength. "I am," he said at last. "She seems to make clear to me what I feel."

Mrs. Beever wondered. "You mean of course Jean does."

"Dear no—Miss Armiger!"

The lady of Eastmead laughed out in her impatience. "I'm delighted to hear you feel anything. You haven't often seemed to me to feel."

"I feel that Jean's very charming."

She laughed again at the way he made it sound. "Is that the tone in which you think of telling her so?"

"I think she'll take it from me in any tone," Paul replied. "She has always been most kind to me; we're very good friends, and she knows what I want."

"It's more than *I* do, my dear! That's exactly what you said to me six months ago—when she liked you so much that she asked you to let her alone."

"She asked me to give her six months for a definite answer, and she likes me the more for having consented to do that," said Paul. "The time I've waited has improved our relations."

"Well, then, they now must have reached perfection. You'll get her definite answer, therefore, this very afternoon."

"When I present the ornament?"

"When you present the ornament. You've got it safe, I hope?"

Paul hesitated; he took another bun. "I imagine it's all right."

"Do you only 'imagine'—with a thing of that value? What have you done with it?"

Again the young man faltered. "I've given it to Miss Armiger. She was afraid I'd lose it."

"And you were not afraid she would?" his mother cried.

"Not a bit. She's to give it back to me on this spot. She wants me too much to succeed."

Mrs. Beever was silent a little. "And how much do you want her to?"

Paul looked blank. "In what?"

"In making a fool of you." Mrs. Beever gathered herself. "Are you in love with Rose Armiger, Paul?"

He judiciously weighed the question. "Not in the least. I talk with her of nobody and nothing but Jean."

"And do you talk with Jean of nobody and nothing but Rose?"

Paul appeared to make an effort to remember. "I scarcely talk with her at all. We're such old friends that there's almost nothing to say."

"There's this to say, my dear—that you take too much for granted!"

"That's just what Miss Armiger tells me. Give me, please,

some more tea." His mother took his cup, but she looked at him hard and searchingly. He bore it without meeting her eyes, only turning his own pensively to the different dainties on the table. "If I do take a great deal for granted," he went on, "you must remember that you brought me up to it."

Mrs. Beever found only after an instant a reply; then, however, she uttered it with an air of triumph. "I may have brought you up—but I didn't bring up Jean!"

"Well, it's not of her I'm speaking," the young man good-humouredly rejoined; "though I might remind you that she has been here again and again, and month after month, and has always been taught—so far as you could teach her—to regard me as her inevitable fate. Have *you* any real doubt," he went on, "of her recognising in a satisfactory way that the time has come?"

Mrs. Beever transferred her scrutiny to the interior of her teapot. "No!" she said after a moment.

"Then what's the matter?"

"The matter is that I'm nervous, and that your stolidity makes me so. I want you to behave to me as if you cared—and I want you still more to behave so to her." Paul made, in his seat, a movement in which his companion caught, as she supposed, the betrayal of a sense of oppression; and at this her own worst fear broke out. "Oh, don't tell me you *don't* care—for if you do I don't know what I shall do to you!" He looked at her with an air he sometimes had, which always aggravated her impatience, an air of amused surprise, quickened to curiosity, that there should be in the world organisms capable of generating heat. She had thanked God, through life, that she was cold-blooded, but now it seemed to face her as a Nemesis that she was a volcano compared with her son. This transferred to him the advantage she had so long monopolised, that of always seeing, in any relation or discussion, the other party become the spectacle, while, sitting back in her stall, she remained the spectator and even the critic. She hated to perform to Paul as she had made others perform to herself; but she determined on the instant that, since she was condemned to do so, she would do it some purpose. She would have to leap through a hoop, but she would land on her charger's back. The next moment Paul was watching her while she shook her little flags at him. "There's one thing, my dear, that I can give you my word of honour for—the fact that if the influence that congeals, that paralyses you, happens by any chance to be a dream of what may be open to you in any other quarter, the sooner you utterly dismiss that dream the better it will be not only for your happiness, but for your dignity. If you entertain—with no matter how bad a conscience—a vain fancy that you've the smallest real chance of making the smallest real impression on anybody *else*, all I can say is that you prepare for yourself very nearly as much discomfort as you prepare disgust for your mother." She paused a moment; she felt, before her son's mild gape, like a trapezist in pink tights. "How much susceptibility, I should like to know, has Miss Armiger at her command for your great charms?"

Paul showed her a certain respect; he didn't clap her—that is he didn't smile. He felt something, however, which was indicated, as it always was, by the way his eyes grew smaller: they contracted at times, in his big, fair face, to mere little conscious points. These points he now directed to the region of the house. "Well, mother," he quietly replied, "if you would like to know it, hadn't you better ask her directly?" Rose Armiger had come into view; Mrs. Beever, turning, saw her approach, bareheaded, in a fresh white dress, under a showy red parasol. Paul, as she drew near, left his seat and strolled to the hammock, into which he immediately dropped. Extended there, while the great net bulged and its attachments cracked with his weight, he spoke with the same plain patience. "She has come to give me up the ornament."

XVI

"THE GREAT CAKE has at last arrived, dear lady!" Rose gaily announced to Mrs. Beever, who waited, before acknowledging the news, long enough to suggest to her son that she was perhaps about to act on his advice.

"I'm much obliged to you for having gone to see about it" was, however, what, after a moment, Miss Armiger's hostess instructed herself to reply.

"It was an irresistible service. I shouldn't have got over on such a day as this," said Rose, "the least little disappointment to dear little Jean."

"To say nothing, of course, of dear little Effie," Mrs. Beever promptly rejoined.

"It comes to the same thing—the occasion so mixes them up. They're interlaced on the cake—with their initials and their candles. There are plenty of candles for each," Rose laughed, "for their years have been added together. It makes a very pretty number!"

"It must also make a very big cake," said Mrs. Beever.

"Colossal."

"Too big to be brought out?"

The girl considered. "Not so big, you know," she archly replied, "as if the candles had to be yours and mine!" Then holding up the "ornament" to Paul, she said: "I surrender you my trust. Catch!" she added with decision, making a movement to toss him a small case in red morocco, which, the next moment, in its flight through the air, without altering his attitude, he intercepted with one hand.

Mrs. Beever's excited mistrust dropped at the mere audacity of this: there was something perceptibly superior in the girl who could meet half way, so cleverly, a suspicion she was quite conscious of and much desired to dissipate. The lady of Eastmead looked at her hard, reading her desire in the look she gave back. "Trust me, trust me," her eyes seemed to plead; "don't at all events think me capable of any self-seeking that's stupid or poor. I may be dangerous to myself, but I'm not so to others; least of all am I so to you." She had a presence that

90

was, in its way, like Tony Bream's: it made, simply and directly, a difference in any personal question exposed to it. Under its action, at all events, Mrs. Beever found herself suddenly feeling that she could after all trust Rose if she could only trust Paul. She glanced at that young man as he lay in the hammock, and saw that in spite of the familiarity of his posture—which indeed might have been assumed with a misleading purpose—his diminished pupils, fixed upon their visitor, still had the expression imparted to them by her own last address. She hesitated; but while she did so Rose came straight up to her and kissed her. It was the very first time, and Mrs. Beever blushed as if one of her secrets had been surprised. Rose explained her impulse only with a smile; but the smile said vividly: "I'll polish him off!"

This brought a response to his mother's lips. "I'll go and inspect the cake!"

Mrs. Beever took her way to the house, and as soon as her back was turned her son got out of the hammock. An observer of the scene would not have failed to divine that, with some profundity of calculation, he had taken refuge there as a mute protest against any frustration of his interview with Rose. This young lady herself laughed out as she saw him rise, and her laugh would have been, for the same observer, a tribute to the natural art that was mingled with his obvious simplicity. Paul himself recognised its bearing and, as he came and stood at the tea-table, acknowledged her criticism by saying quietly: "I was afraid dear mamma would take me away."

"On the contrary; she has formally surrendered you."

"Then you must let me perform her office and help you to some tea."

He spoke with a rigid courtesy that was not without its grace, and in the rich shade of her umbrella, which she twirled repeatedly on her shoulder, she looked down with detachment at the table. "I'll do it for myself, thank you; and I should like you to return to your hammock."

"I left it on purpose," the young man said. "Flat on my back, that way, I'm at a sort of disadvantage in talking with you."

"That's precisely why I made the request. I wish you to be flat on your back and to have nothing whatever to reply."

Paul immediately retraced his steps, but before again extending himself he asked her, with the same grave consideration, where in this case she would be seated. "I sha'n't be seated at all," she answered; "I'll walk about and stand over you and bully you." He tumbled into his net, sitting up rather more than before; and, coming close to it, she put out her hand. "Let me see that object again." He had in his lap the little box he had received from her, and at this he passed it back. She opened it, pressing on the spring, and, inclining her head to one side, considered afresh the mounted jewel that nestled in the white velvet. Then, closing the case with a loud snap, she restored it to him. "Yes, it's very good; it's a wonderful stone, and she knows. But that alone, my dear, won't do it." She leaned, facing him, against the tense ropes of the hammock, and he looked up at her. "You take too much for granted."

For a moment Paul answered nothing, but at last he brought out: "That's just what I said to my mother you had already said when she said just the same."

Rose stared an instant; then she smiled again. "It's complicated, but I follow you! She has been waking you up."

"She knows," said her companion, "that you advise me in the same sense as herself."

"She believes it at last—her leaving us together was a sign of that. I have at heart perfectly to justify her confidence, for hitherto she has been so blind to her own interest as to suppose that, in these three weeks, you had been so tiresome as to fall in love with me."

"I particularly told her I haven't at all."

Paul's tone had at moments of highest gravity the gift of moving almost any interlocutor to mirth. "I hope you'll be more convincing than that if you ever particularly tell any one you *have* at all!" the girl exclaimed. She gave a slight push to the hammock, turning away, and he swung there gently a minute.

"You mustn't ask too much of me, you know," he finally said, watching her as she went to the table and poured out a cup of tea.

She drank a little and then, putting down the cup, came back to him. "I should be asking too much of you only if you were asking too much of *her*. You're so far from that, and your position's so perfect. It's too beautiful, you know, what you offer."

"I know what I offer and I know what I don't," Paul returned; "and the person we speak of knows exactly as well. All the elements are before her, and if my position's so fine it's there for her to see it quite as well as for you. I agree that I'm a decent sort, and that, as things are going, my business, my prospects, my guarantees of one kind and another, are substantial. But just these things, for years, have been made familiar to her, and nothing, without a risk of greatly boring her, can very well be added to the account. You and my mother say I take too much for granted; but I take only that." This was a long speech for our young man, and his want of accent, his passionless pauses, made it seem a trifle longer. It had a visible effect on Rose Armiger, whom he held there with widening eyes as he talked. There was an intensity in her face, a bright sweetness that, when he stopped, seemed to give itself out to him as if to encourage him to go on. But he went on only to the extent of adding; "All I mean is that if I'm good enough for her she has only to take me."

"You're good enough for the best girl in the world," Rose said with the tremor of sincerity. "You're honest and kind; you're generous and wise." She looked at him with a sort of intelligent pleasure, that of a mind fine enough to be touched by an exhibition of beauty even the most occult. "You're so sound—you're so safe that it makes any relation with you a real luxury and a thing to be grateful for." She shed on him her sociable approval, treating him as a happy product, speaking of him as of another person. "I shall always be glad and proud that you've been, if only for an hour, my friend!"

Paul's response to this demonstration consisted in getting slowly and heavily to his feet. "Do you think I *like* what you do to me?" he abruptly demanded.

It was a sudden new note, but it found her quite ready. "I don't care whether you like it or not! It's my duty, and it's yours—it's the right thing."

He stood there in his tall awkwardness; he spoke as if he had not heard her. "It's too strange to have to take it from you."

"Everything's strange—and the truest things are the strangest. Besides, it isn't so extraordinary as that comes to. It isn't as if you had an objection to her; it isn't as if she weren't beautiful and good—really cultivated and altogether charming. It isn't as if, since I first saw her here, she hadn't developed in the most admirable way, and also hadn't, by her father's death, come into three thousand a year and into an opportunity for looking, with the red gold of her hair, in the deepest, daintiest, freshest mourning, lovelier far, my dear boy, than, with all respect, any girl who can ever have strayed before, or ever will again, into any Wilverley bank. It isn't as if, granting you do care for me, there were the smallest chance, should you try to make too much of it, of my ever doing anything but listen to you with a pained 'Oh, dear!' pat you affectionately on the back and push you promptly out of the room." Paul Beever, when she thus encountered him, quitted his place, moving slowly outside the wide cluster of chairs, while Rose, within it, turned as he turned, pressing him with deeper earnestness. He stopped behind one of the chairs, holding its high back and now meeting her eyes. "If you do care for me," she went on with her warm voice, "there's a magnificent way you can show it. You can show it by putting into your appeal to Miss Martle something that she can't resist."

"And what may she not be able to resist?" Paul inquired, keeping his voice steady, but shaking his chair a little.

"Why, *you*—if you'll only be a bit personal, a bit passionate, have some appearance of really desiring her, some that your happiness really depends on her." Paul looked as if he were taking a lesson, and she gave it with growing assurance. "Show her some tenderness, some eloquence, try some touch of the sort that goes home. Speak to her, for God's sake, the words that women like. We all like them, and we all feel them, and you can do nothing good without them. Keep well in sight that what you must absolutely do is *please* her."

Paul seemed to fix his little eyes on this remote aim. "Please her and please you."

"It sounds odd, yes, lumping us together. But that doesn't matter," said Rose. "The effect of your success will be that you'll unspeakably help and comfort me. It's difficult to talk

about it—my grounds are so deep, deep down." She hesitated, casting about her, asking herself how far she might go.
Then she decided, growing a little pale with the effort. "I've
an idea that has become a passion with me. There's a right I
must see done—there's a wrong I must make impossible.
There's a loyalty I must cherish—there's a memory I must
protect. That's all I can say." She stood there in her vivid
meaning like the priestess of a threatened altar. "If that girl
becomes your wife—why then I'm at last at rest!"

"You get, by my achievement, what you want—I see. And,
please, what do *I* get?" Paul presently asked.

"You?" The blood rushed back to her face with the shock
of this question. "Why, you get Jean Martle!" He turned
away without a word, and at the same moment, in the distance, she saw the person whose name she had just uttered
descend the great square steps. She hereupon slipped through
the circle of chairs and rapidly met her companion, who
stopped short as she approached. Rose looked him straight in
the eyes. "If you give me the peace I pray for, I'll do anything
for you in life!" She left him staring and passed down to the
river, where, on the little bridge, Tony Bream was in sight,
waving his hat to her as he came from the other house.

XVII

ROSE ARMIGER, in a few moments, was joined by Tony, and they came up the lawn together to where Jean Martle stood talking with Paul. Here, at the approach of the master of Bounds, this young lady anxiously inquired if Effie had not been well enough to accompany him. She had expected to find her there; then, failing that, had taken for granted he would bring her.

"I've left the question, my dear Jean, in her nurse's hands," Tony said. "She had been bedizened from top to toe, and then, on some slight appearance of being less well, had been despoiled, denuded and disappointed. She's a poor little lamb of sacrifice. They were at her again, when I came away, with the ribbons and garlands; but there was apparently much more to come, and I couldn't answer for it that a single sneeze wouldn't again lay everything low. It's in the bosom of the gods. I couldn't wait."

"You were too impatient to be with dear, delightful *us*," Rose suggested.

Tony, with a successful air of very light comedy, smiled and inclined himself. "I was too impatient to be with you, Miss Armiger." The lapse of four years still presented him in such familiar mourning as might consort with a country nook on a summer afternoon; but it also allowed undiminished relief to a manner of addressing women which was clearly instinctive and habitual and which, at the same time, by good fortune, had the grace of flattery without phrases and of irony without impertinence. He was a little older, but he was not heavier; he was a little worn, but he was not worn dull. His presence was, anywhere and at any time, as much as ever the clock at the moment it strikes. Paul Beever's little eyes, after he appeared, rested on Rose with an expression which might have been that of a man counting the waves produced on a sheet of water by the plunge of a large object. For any like ripple on the fine surface of the younger girl he appeared to have no attention.

"I'm glad that remark's not addressed to *me*," Jean said

gaily; "for I'm afraid I must immediately withdraw from you the light of my society."

"On whom then do you mean to bestow it?"

"On your daughter, this moment. I must go and judge for myself of her condition."

Tony looked at her more seriously. "If you're at all really troubled about her I'll go back with you. You're too beautifully kind; they told me of your having been with her this morning."

"Ah, you were with her this morning?" Rose asked of Jean in a manner to which there was a clear effort to impart the intonation of the casual, but which had in it something that made the person addressed turn to her with a dim surprise. Jean stood there in her black dress and her fair beauty; but her wonder was not of a sort to cloud the extraordinary radiance of her youth. "For ever so long. Don't you know I've made her my peculiar and exclusive charge?"

"Under the pretext," Tony went on, to Rose, "of saving her from perdition. I'm supposed to be in danger of spoiling her, but Jean treats her quite *as* spoiled; which is much the greater injury of the two."

"Don't go back, at any rate, please," Rose said to him with soft persuasion. "I never see you, you know, and I want just now particularly to speak to you." Tony instantly expressed submission, and Rose, checking Jean, who, at this, in silence, turned to take her way to the bridge, reminded Paul Beever that she had just heard from him of his having, on his side, some special purpose of an interview with Miss Martle.

At this Paul grew very red. "Oh yes, I should rather like to speak to you, please," he said to Jean.

She had paused half way down the little slope; she looked at him frankly and kindly. "Do you mean immediately?"

"As soon as you've time."

"I shall have time as soon as I've been to Effie," Jean replied. "I want to bring her over. There are four dolls waiting for her."

"My dear child," Rose familiarly exclaimed, "at home there are about forty! Don't you give her one every day or two?" she went on to Tony.

Her question didn't reach him; he was too much interested

in Paul's arrangement with Jean, on whom his eyes were fixed. "Go, then—to be the sooner restored to us. And do bring the kid!" He spoke with jollity.

"I'm going in to change—perhaps I shall presently find you here," Paul put in.

"You'll certainly find me, dear Paul. I shall be quick!" the girl called back. And she lightly went her way while Paul walked off to the house and the two others, standing together, watched her a minute. In spite of her black dress, of which the thin, voluminous tissue fluttered in the summer breeze, she seemed to shine in the afternoon light. They saw her reach the bridge, where, in the middle, she turned and tossed back at them a wave of her handkerchief; after which she dipped to the other side and disappeared.

"Mayn't I give you some tea?" Rose said to her companion. She nodded at the bright display of Mrs. Beever's hospitality; Tony gratefully accepted her offer and they strolled on side by side. "Why have you ceased to call me 'Rose'?" she then suddenly demanded.

Tony started so that he practically stopped; on which she promptly halted. "*Have* I, my dear woman? I didn't know——" He looked at her and, looking at her, after a moment flagrantly coloured: he had the air of a man who sees something that operates as a warning. What Tony Bream saw was a circumstance of which he had already had glimpses; but for some reason or other it was now written with a largeness that made it resemble a printed poster on a wall. It might have been, from the way he took it in, a big yellow advertisement to the publicity of whose message no artifice of type was wanting. This message was simply Rose Armiger's whole face, exquisite and tragic in its appeal, stamped with a sensibility that was almost abject, a tenderness that was more than eager. The appeal was there for an instant with rare intensity, and what Tony felt in response to it he felt without fatuity or vanity. He could meet it only with a compassion as unreserved as itself. He looked confused, but he looked kind, and his companion's eyes lighted as with the sense of something that at last even in pure pity had come out to her. It was as if she let him know that since she had been at Eastmead nothing whatever had come out.

"When I was at Bounds four years ago," she said, "you called me Rose and you called our friend there"—she made a movement in the direction Jean had taken—"nothing at all. Now you call her by name and you call me nothing at all."

Tony obligingly turned it over. "Don't I call you Miss Armiger?"

"Is that anything at all?" Rose effectively asked. "You're conscious of some great difference."

Tony hesitated; he walked on. "Between you and Jean?"

"Oh, the difference between me and Jean goes without saying. What I mean is the difference between my having been at Wilverley then and my being here now."

They reached the tea-table, and Tony, dropping into a chair, removed his hat. "What have I called you when we've met in London?"

She stood before him closing her parasol. "Don't you even know? You've called me nothing." She proceeded to pour out tea for him, busying herself delicately with Mrs. Beever's wonderful arrangements for keeping things hot. "Have you by any chance been conscious of what I've called *you*?" she said.

Tony let himself, in his place, be served. "Doesn't every one in the wide world call me the inevitable 'Tony'? The name's dreadful—for a banker; it should have been a bar for me to that career. It's fatal to dignity. But then of course I haven't any dignity."

"I think you haven't much," Rose replied. "But I've never seen any one get on so well without it; and, after all, you've just enough to make Miss Martle recognise it."

Tony wondered. "By calling me 'Mr. Bream'? Oh, for her I'm a greybeard—and I address her as I addressed her as a child. Of course I admit," he added with an intention vaguely pacific, "that she has entirely ceased to be that."

"She's wonderful," said Rose, handing him something buttered and perversely cold.

He assented even to the point of submissively helping himself. "She's a charming creature."

"I mean she's wonderful about your little girl."

"Devoted, isn't she? That dates from long ago. She has a special sentiment about her."

Rose was silent a moment. "It's a little life to preserve and protect," she then said. "Of course!"

"Why, to that degree that she seems scarcely to think the child safe even with its infatuated daddy!"

Still on her feet beyond the table near which he sat, she had put up her parasol again, and she looked across at him from under it. Their eyes met, and he again felt himself in the presence of what, in them, shortly before, had been so deep, so exquisite. It represented something that no lapse could long quench—something that gave out the measureless white ray of a light steadily revolving. She could sometimes turn it away, but it was always somewhere; and now it covered him with a great cold lustre that made everything for the moment look hard and ugly—made him also feel the chill of a complication for which he had not allowed. He had had plenty of complications in life, but he had likewise had ways of dealing with them that were in general clever, easy, masterly—indeed often really pleasant. He got up nervously: there would be nothing pleasant in any way of dealing with this one.

XVIII

Conscious of the importance of not letting his nervousness show, he had no sooner pointlessly risen than he took possession of another chair. He dropped the question of Effie's security, remembering there was a prior one as to which he had still to justify himself. He brought it back with an air of indulgence which scarcely disguised, however, its present air of irrelevance. "I'll gladly call you, my dear Rose, anything you like, but you mustn't think I've been capricious or disloyal. I addressed you of old—at the last—in the way in which it seemed most natural to address so close a friend of my wife's. But I somehow think of you here now rather as a friend of my own."

"And that makes me so much more distant?" Rose asked, twirling her parasol.

Tony, whose plea had been quite extemporised, felt a slight confusion, which his laugh but inadequately covered. "I seem to have uttered a *bêtise*—but I haven't. I only mean that a different title belongs, somehow, to a different character."

"I don't admit my character to be different," Rose said; "save perhaps in the sense of its having become a little intensified. If I was here before as Julia's friend, I'm here still more as Julia's friend now."

Tony meditated, with all his candour; then he gave a highly cordial, even if a slightly illogical assent. "Of course you are—from your own point of view." He evidently only wanted to meet her as far on the way to a quiet life as he could manage. "Dear little Julia!" he exclaimed in a manner which, as soon as he had spoken, he felt to be such a fresh piece of pointlessness that, to carry it off, he got up again.

"Dear little Julia!" Rose echoed, speaking out loud and clear, but with an expression which, unlike Tony's, would have left on the mind of an ignorant auditor no doubt of its conveying a reference to the unforgotten dead.

Tony strolled towards the hammock. "May I smoke a cigarette?" She approved with a gesture that was almost impatient, and while he lighted he pursued with genial gaiety:

"I'm not going to allow you to pretend that you doubt of my having dreamed for years of the pleasure of seeing you here again, or of the diabolical ingenuity that I exercised to enable your visit to take place in the way most convenient to both of us. You used to say the queen-mother disliked you. You see to-day how much!"

"She has ended by finding me useful," said Rose. "That brings me exactly to what I told you just now I wanted to say to you."

Tony had gathered the loose net of the hammock into a single strand, and, while he smoked, had lowered himself upon it, sideways, in a posture which made him sit as in a swing. He looked surprised and even slightly disconcerted, like a man asked to pay twice. "Oh, it isn't then what you did say——?"

"About your use of my name? No, it isn't that—it's something quite different." Rose waited; she stood before him as she had stood before her previous interlocutor. "It's to let you know the interest I take in Paul Beever. I take the very greatest."

"You do?" said Tony approvingly. "Well, you might go in for something worse!"

He spoke with a cheerfulness that covered all the ground; but she repeated the words as if challenging their sense. "I might 'go in'——?"

Her accent struck a light from them, put in an idea that had not been Tony's own. Thus presented, the idea seemed happy, and, in his incontrollable restlessness, his face more vividly brightening, he rose to it with a zeal that brought him for a third time to his feet. He smiled ever so kindly and, before he could measure his words or his manner, broke out: "If you only really would, you know, my dear Rose!"

In a quicker flash he became aware that, as if he had dealt her a blow in the face, her eyes had filled with tears. It made the taste of his joke too bad. "Are you gracefully suggesting that I shall carry Mr. Beever off?" she demanded.

"Not from *me*, my dear—never!" Tony blushed and felt how much there was to rectify in some of his impulses. "I think a lot of him and I want to keep my hand on him. But I speak of him frankly, always, as a prize, and I want something awfully good to happen to him. If you like him," he hastened laughingly to add, "of course it does happen—I see!"

He attenuated his meaning, but he had already exposed it, and he could perceive that Rose, with a kind of tragic perversity, was determined to get the full benefit, whatever it might be, of her impression or her grievance. She quickly did her best to look collected. "You think he's safe then, and solid, and not so stupid as he strikes one at first?"

"Stupid?—not a bit. He's a statue in the block—he's a sort of slumbering giant. The right sort of tact will call him to life, the right sort of hand will work him out of the stone."

"And it escaped you just now, in a moment of unusual expansion, that the right sort are mine?"

Tony puffed away at his cigarette, smiling at her resolutely through its light smoke. "You do injustice to my attitude about you. There isn't an hour of the day that I don't indulge in some tribute or other to your great ability."

Again there came into the girl's face her strange alternative look—the look of being made by her passion so acquainted with pain that even in the midst of it she could flower into charity. Sadly and gently she shook her head. "Poor Tony!" Then she added in quite a different tone: "What do you think of the difference of our ages?"

"Yours and Paul's? It isn't worth speaking of!"

"That's sweet of you—considering that he's only twenty-two. However, I'm not yet thirty," she went on; "and, of course, to gain time, one might press the thing hard." She hesitated again; after which she continued: "It's awfully vulgar, this way, to put the dots on the i's, but as it was you, and not I, who began it, I may ask if you really believe that if one should make a bit of an effort——?" And she invitingly paused, to leave him to complete a question as to which it was natural she should feel a delicacy.

Tony's face, for an initiated observer, would have shown that he was by this time watching for a trap; but it would also have shown that, after a moment's further reflection, he didn't particularly care if the trap should catch him. "If you take such an interest in Paul," he replied with no visible abatement of his preference for the standpoint of pleasantry, "you can calculate better than I the natural results of drawing him out. But what I can assure you is that nothing would give me greater pleasure than to see you so happily 'established,' as they say—so honourably married, so affectionately surrounded and so thoroughly protected."

"And all alongside of you here?" cried Rose.

Tony faltered, but he went on. "It's precisely your being 'alongside' of one that would enable one to see you."

"It would enable one to see *you*—it would have that particular merit," said Rose. "But my interest in Mr. Beever hasn't at all been of a kind to prompt me to turn the possibility over for myself. You can readily imagine how far I should have been in that case from speaking of it to you. The defect of your charming picture," she presently added, "is that an important figure is absent from it."

"An important figure?"

"Jean Martle."

Tony looked at the tip of his cigarette. "You mean because there was at one time so much planning and plotting over the idea that she should make a match with Paul?"

"At one time, my dear Tony?" Rose exclaimed. "There's exactly as much as ever, and I'm already—in these mere three weeks—in the very thick of it! Did you think the question had been quite dropped?" she inquired.

Tony faced her serenely enough—in part because he felt the extreme importance of so doing. "I simply haven't heard much about it. Mrs. Beever used to talk about it. But she hasn't talked of late."

"She talked, my good man, no more than half an hour ago!" Rose replied.

Tony winced; but he stood bravely up; his cigarettes were an extreme resource. "Really? And what did she say to you?"

"She said nothing to *me*—but she said everything to her son. She said to him, I mean, that she'll never forgive him if she doesn't hear from him an hour or two hence that he has at last successfully availed himself, with Miss Martle, of this auspicious day, as well as of the fact that he's giving her, in honour of it, something remarkably beautiful."

Tony listened with marked attention, but without meeting his companion's eyes. He had again seated himself in the hammock, with his feet on the ground and his head thrown back; and he smoked freely, holding it with either hand. "What is he giving her?" he asked after a moment.

Rose turned away; she mechanically did something at the table. "Shouldn't you think she'd show it to you?" she threw over her shoulder.

While this shoulder, sensibly cold for the instant, was presented, he watched her. "I daresay—if she accepts it."

The girl faced him again. "And won't she accept it?"

"Only—I should say—if she accepts *him*."

"And won't she do that?"

Tony made a "ring" with his cigarette. "The thing will be for him to get her to."

"That's exactly," said Rose, "what I want you to do."

"Me?" He now stared at her. "How can I?"

"I won't undertake to tell you how—I'll leave that to your ingenuity. Wouldn't it be a matter—just an easy extension— of existing relations? You saw just now that he appealed to her for his chance and that she consented to give it to him. What I wanted you to hear from me is that I feel how much interested you'll be in learning that this chance is of the highest importance for him and that I know with how good a conscience you'll throw your weight into the scale of his success."

"My weight with the young lady? Don't you rather exaggerate my weight?" Tony asked.

"That question can only be answered by your trying it. It's a situation in which not to take an interest is—well, not your duty, you know," said Rose.

Tony gave a smile which he felt to be a little pale; but there was still good-humour in the tone in which he protestingly and portentously murmured: "Oh, my 'duty'——!"

"Surely; if you see no objection to poor Mrs. Beever's at last gathering the fruit of the tree she long ago so fondly and so carefully planted. Of course if you should frankly tell me you see one that I don't know——!" She looked ingenuous and hard. "*Do* you, by chance, see one?"

"None at all. I've never known a tree of Mrs. Beever's of which the fruit hasn't been sweet."

"Well, in the present case—sweet or bitter!—it's ready to fall. This is the hour the years have pointed to. You think highly of Paul——"

Tony Bream took her up. "And I think highly of Jean, and therefore I must see them through? I catch your meaning. But have you—in a matter composed, after all, of ticklish elements—thought of the danger of one's meddling?"

"A great deal." A troubled vision of this danger dawned even now in Rose's face. "But I've thought still more of one's possible prudence—one's occasional tact." Tony, for a moment, made no reply; he quitted the hammock and began to stroll about. Her anxious eyes followed him, and presently she brought out: "Have you really been supposing that they've given it up?"

Tony remained silent; but at last he stopped short, and there was an effect of returning from an absence in the way he abruptly demanded: "That who have given up what?"

"That Mrs. Beever and Paul have given up what we're talking about—the idea of his union with Jean."

Tony hesitated. "I haven't been supposing anything at all!" Rose recognised the words for the first he had ever uttered to her that expressed even a shade of irritation, and she was unable to conceal that she felt, on the spot, how memorable this fact was to make them. Tony's immediate glance at her showed equally that he had instantly become aware of their so affecting her. He did, however, nothing to modify the impression: he only stood a moment looking across the river; after which he observed quietly: "Here she is—on the bridge."

He had walked nearer to the stream, and Rose had moved back to the tea-table, from which the view of the bridge was obstructed. "Has she brought the child?" she asked.

"I don't make out—she may have her by the hand." He approached again, and as he came he said: "Your idea is really that I should speak to her now?"

"Before she sees Paul?" Rose met his eyes; there was a quick anguish of uncertainty in all her person. "I leave that to you—since you cast a doubt on the safety of your doing so. I leave it," said Rose, "to your judgment—I leave it to your honour."

"To my honour?" Tony wondered with a showy jerk of his head what the deuce his honour had to do with it.

She went on without heeding him. "My idea is only that, whether you speak to her or not, she shall accept him. Gracious heavens, she *must*!" Rose broke out with passion.

"You take an immense interest in it!" Tony laughed.

"Take the same, then, yourself, and the thing will come off." They stood a minute looking at each other, and more passed between them than had ever passed before. The result of it was that Rose had a drop from her strenuous height to sudden and beautiful gentleness. "Tony Bream, I trust you."

She had uttered the word in a way that had the power to make him flush. He answered peaceably, however, laughing again: "I hope so, my dear Rose!" Then in a moment he added: "I *will* speak." He glanced again at the circuitous path from the bridge, but Jean had not yet emerged from the shrubbery by which it was screened. "If she brings Effie will you take her?"

With her ominous face the girl considered. "I'm afraid I can't do that."

Tony gave a gesture of impatience. "Good God, how you stand off from the poor little thing!"

Jean at this moment came into sight without the child. "I shall never take her from *her*!" And Rose Armiger turned away.

XIX

Tony went toward his messenger, who, as she saw Rose apparently leaving the garden, pressingly called out: "Would *you*, Miss Armiger, very kindly go over for Effie? She wasn't even yet ready," she explained as she came back up the slope with her friend, "and I was afraid to wait after promising Paul to meet him."

"He's not here, you see," said Tony; "it's he who, most ungallantly, makes you wait. Never mind; you'll wait with me." He looked at Rose as they overtook her. "Will you go and bring the child, as our friend here asks, or is such an act as that also, and still more, inconsistent with your mysterious principles?"

"You must kindly excuse me," Rose said directly to Jean. "I've a letter to write in the house. Now or never—I must catch the post."

"Don't let us keep you, then," Tony returned. "I'll go over myself—as soon as Paul comes back."

"I'll send him straight out." And Rose Armiger retired in good order.

Tony followed her with his eyes; then he exclaimed: "It's, upon my soul, as if she couldn't trust herself——!" His remark, which he checked, dropped into a snap of his fingers while Jean Martle wondered.

"To do what?" she asked.

Tony hesitated. "To do nothing! The child's all right?"

"Perfectly right. It's only that the great Gorham has decreed that she's to have her usual little supper before she comes, and that, with her ribbons and frills all covered with an enormous bib, Effie had just settled down to that extremely solemn function."

Tony in his turn wondered. "Why shouldn't she have her supper here?"

"Ah, you must ask the great Gorham!"

"And didn't *you* ask her?"

"I did better—I divined her," said Jean. "She doesn't trust our kitchen."

Tony laughed. "Does she apprehend poison?"

"She apprehends what she calls 'sugar and spice.'"

"'And all that's nice?' Well, there's too much that's nice here, certainly! Leave the poor child then, like the little princess you all make of her, to her cook and her 'taster,' to the full rigour of her royalty, and stroll with me here till Paul comes out to you." He looked at his watch and about at the broad garden where the shadows of the trees were still and the long afternoon had grown rich. "This is remarkably peaceful, and there's plenty of time." Jean concurred with a murmur as soft as the stir of the breeze, a "Plenty, plenty," as serene as if, to oblige Tony Bream, so charming a day would be sure to pause in its passage. They went a few steps, but he stopped again with a question. "Do you know what Paul wants of you?"

Jean looked a moment at the grass by her feet. "I think I do." Then raising her eyes without shyness, but with unqualified gravity, "Do *you* know, Mr. Bream?" she asked.

"Yes—I've just now heard."

"From Miss Armiger?"

"From Miss Armiger. She appears to have had if from Paul himself."

The girl gave out her mild surprise. "Why has he told her?"

Tony hesitated. "Because she's such a good person to tell things to."

"Is it her immediately telling them again that makes her so?" Jean inquired with a faint smile.

Faint as this smile was, Tony met it as if he had been struck by it, and as if indeed, in the midst of an acquaintance which four years had now consecrated, he had not quite got used to being struck. That acquaintance had practically begun, on an unforgettable day, with his opening his eyes to it from an effort which had been already then the effort to forget—his suddenly taking her in as he lay on the sofa in his hall. From the way he sometimes looked at her it might have been judged that he had even now not taken her in completely— that the act of slow, charmed apprehension had yet to melt into accepted knowledge. It had in truth been made continuous by the continuous expansion of its object. If the sense of lying there on the sofa still sometimes came back to Tony, it was because he was interested in not interrupting by a rash motion the process taking place in the figure before him, the capricious rotation by which the woman peeped out of the child and the child peeped out of the woman. There was no point at which it had begun and none at which it would end, and it was a thing to gaze at with an attention refreshingly baffled. The frightened child had become a tall, slim nymph on a cloud, and yet there had been no moment of anything so gross as catching her in the act of change. If there had been he would have met it with some punctual change of his own; whereas it was his luxurious idea—unobscured till now—that in the midst of the difference so delightfully ambiguous he was free just *not* to change, free to remain as he was and go on liking her on trivial grounds. It had seemed to him that there was no one he had ever liked whom he could like quite so comfortably: a man of his age had had what he rather loosely called the "usual" flashes of fondness. There had been no worrying question of the light this particular flash might kindle; he had never had to ask himself what his appreciation of Jean Martle might lead to. It would lead to exactly nothing—that had been settled all round in advance. This was a happy, lively provision that kept everything down, made sociability a cool, public, out-of-door affair, without a secret or a mystery—confined it, as one might say, to the breezy, sunny forecourt of the temple of friendship, forbidding it any dream of access to the obscure and comparatively stuffy interior. Tony had acutely remarked to himself that a thing could be led to only when there was a practicable road. As present to him to-day as on that other day was the little hour of violence—so strange and sad and sweet—which in his life had effectually suppressed any thoroughfare, making this expanse so pathless that, had he not been looking for a philosophic rather than a satiric term, he might almost have compared it to a desert. He answered his companion's inquiry about Rose's responsibility as an informant after he had satisfied himself that if she smiled exactly as she did it was only another illustration of a perfect instinct. That instinct, which at any time turned all talk with her away from flatness, told her that the right attitude for her now was the middle course between anxiety and resignation. "If Miss Armiger hadn't spoken," he said, "I shouldn't have known. And of course I'm interested in knowing."

"But why is she interested in your doing so?" Jean asked.

Tony walked on again. "She has several reasons. One of them is that she greatly likes Paul and that, greatly liking him, she wishes the highest happiness conceivable for him. It occurred to her that as I greatly like a certain young lady I might not unnaturally desire for that young lady a corresponding chance, and that with a hint," laughed Tony, "that she really is about to have it, I might perhaps see my way to putting in a word for the dear boy in advance."

The girl strolled beside him, looking quietly before her. "How does she know," she demanded, "whom you 'greatly like'?"

The question pulled him up a little, but he resisted the impulse, constantly strong in him, to stop again and stand face to face with her. He continued to laugh and after an instant he replied: "Why, I suppose I must have told her."

"And how many persons will she have told?"

"I don't care how many," Tony said, "and I don't think you need care either. Every one but she—from lots of observation—knows we're good friends, and it's because that's such a pleasant old story with us all that I feel as if I might frankly say to you what I have on my mind."

"About what Paul may have to say?"

"The first moment you let him."

Tony was going on when she broke in: "How long have you had it on your mind?"

He found himself, at her challenge, just a trifle embarrassed. "How long?"

"As it's only since Miss Armiger has told you that you've known there's anything in the air."

This inquiry gave Tony such pause that he met it first with a laugh and then with a counter-appeal. "You make me feel dreadfully dense! Do you mind my asking how long you yourself have known that what may be in the air is on the point of alighting?"

"Why, since Paul spoke to me."

"Just now—before you went to Bounds?" Tony wondered. "You were immediately sure that that's what he wants?"

"What else can he want? He doesn't want so much," Jean added, "that there would have been many alternatives."

"I don't know what you call 'much'!" Again Tony wondered. "And it produces no more effect upon you——"

"Than I'm showing to you now?" the girl asked. "Do you think me dreadfully stolid?"

"No, because I know that, in general, what you show isn't at all the full measure of what you feel. You're a great little mystery. Still," Tony blandly continued, "you strike me as calm—as quite sublime—for a young lady whose fate's about to be sealed. Unless, of course, you've regarded it," he added, "as sealed from far away back."

They had strolled, in the direction they had followed, as far as they could go, and they necessarily stopped for a turn. Without taking up his last words Jean stood there and looked obscurely happy, as it seemed to him, at his recognition of her having appeared as quiet as she wished. "You haven't answered my question," she simply said. "You haven't told me how long you've had it on your mind that you must say to me whatever it is you wish to say."

"Why is it important I should answer it?"

"Only because you seemed positively to imply that the time of your carrying your idea about had been of the shortest. In the case of advice, if to advise is what you wish——"

"It *is* what I wish," Tony interrupted; "strangely as it may strike you that, in regard to such a matter as we refer to, one should be eager for such a responsibility. The question of time doesn't signify—what signifies is one's sincerity. I had an impression, I confess, that the prospect I a good while ago supposed you have accepted had—what shall I call it?—rather faded away. But at the same time I hoped"—and Tony invited his companion to resume their walk—"that it would charmingly come up again."

Jean moved beside him and spoke with a colourless kindness which suggested no desire to challenge or cross-question, but a thoughtful interest in anything, in the connection in which they were talking, that he would be so good as to tell her and an earnest desire to be clear about it. Perhaps there was also in her manner just the visible tinge of a confidence that he would tell her the absolute truth. "I see. You hoped it would charmingly come up again."

"So that on learning that it *is* charmingly coming up, don't you see?" Tony laughed, "I'm so agreeably agitated that I spill over on the spot. I want, without delay, to be definite to you about the really immense opinion I have of dear Paul. It can't do any harm, and it may do a little good, to mention that it has always seemed to me that we've only got to give him time. I mean, of course, don't you know," he added, "for him quite to distinguish himself."

Jean was silent a little, as if she were thoroughly taking this home. "Distinguish himself in what way?" she asked with all her tranquillity.

"Well—in every way," Tony handsomely replied. "He's full of stuff—there's a great deal of him: too much to come out all at once. Of course you know him—you've known him half your life; but I see him in a strong and special light, a light in which he has scarcely been shown to you and which puts him to a real test. He has ability; he has ideas; he has absolute honesty; and he has moreover a good stiff back of his own. He's a fellow of head; he's a fellow of heart. In short he's a man of gold."

"He's a man of gold," Jean repeated with punctual acceptance, yet as if it mattered much more that Tony should think so than that she should. "It would be odd," she went on, "to be talking with you on a subject so personal to myself if it were not that I've felt Paul's attitude for so long past to be rather publicly taken for granted. He has felt it so, too, I think, poor boy, and for good or for ill there has been in our situation very little mystery and perhaps not much modesty."

"Why *should* there be, of the false kind, when even the true has nothing to do with the matter? You and Paul are great people: he's the heir-apparent and you're the most eligible princess in the Almanach de Gotha. You can't be there and be hiding behind the window-curtain: you must step out on the balcony to be seen of the populace. Your most private affairs are affairs of state. At the smallest hint like the one I just mentioned even an old dunderhead like me catches on—he sees the strong reasons for Paul's attitude. However, it's not of that so much that I wanted to say a word. I thought perhaps you'd just let me touch on your own." Tony hesitated; he felt vaguely disconcerted by the special quality of stillness that, though she moved beside him, her attention, her expectation put forth. It came over him that for the purpose of his plea she was almost too prepared, and this made him speculate. He stopped short again and, uneasily, "May I light one more cigarette?" he asked. She assented with a flicker in her dim smile, and while he lighted he was increasingly conscious that she waited. He met the deep gentleness of her eyes and reflected afresh that if she was always beautiful she was beautiful at different times from different sources. What was the source of the impression she made on him at this moment if not a kind of refinement of patience, in which she seemed actually to hold her breath? "In fact," he said as he threw away his match, "I *have* touched on it—I mean on the great hope we all have that you do see your way to meeting your friend as he deserves."

"You 'all' have it?" Jean softly asked.

Tony hesitated again. "I'm sure I'm quite right in speaking for Wilverley at large. It takes the greatest interest in Paul, and I needn't at this time of day remind you of the interest it takes in yourself. But, I repeat, what I meant more particularly to utter was my own special confidence in your decision. Now that I'm fully enlightened it comes home to me that, as regards such a possibility as your taking your place here as a near neighbour and a permanent friend"—and Tony fixedly smiled—"why, I can only feel the liveliest suspense. I want to make thoroughly sure of you!"

Jean took this in as she had taken the rest; after which she simply said: "Then I think I ought to tell you that I shall not meet Paul in the way that what you're so good as to say seems to point to."

Tony had made many speeches, both in public and in private, and he had naturally been exposed to replies of the incisive no less than of the massive order. But no check of the current had ever made him throw back his head quite so far as this brief and placid announcement. "You'll not meet him——?"

"I shall never marry him."

He undisguisedly gasped. "In spite of all the reasons——?"

"Of course I've thought the reasons over—often and often. But there are reasons on the other side too. I shall never marry him," she repeated.

XX

IT WAS singular that though half an hour before he had not felt the want of the assurance he had just asked of her, yet now that he saw it definitely withheld it took an importance as instantly as a mirror takes a reflection. This importance was so great that he found himself suddenly scared by what he heard. He thought an instant with intensity. "In spite of knowing that you'll disappoint"—he paused a little—"the universal hope?"

"I know whom I shall disappoint; but I must bear that. I shall disappoint Cousin Kate."

"Horribly," said Tony.

"Horribly."

"And poor Paul—to within an inch of his life."

"No, not poor Paul, Mr. Bream; not poor Paul in the least," Jean said. She spoke without a hint of defiance or the faintest ring of bravado, as if for mere veracity and lucidity, since an opportunity quite unsought had been forced upon her. "I know about poor Paul. It's all right about poor Paul," she declared, smiling.

She spoke and she looked at him with a sincerity so distilled, as he felt, from something deep within her that to pretend to gainsay her would be in the worst taste. He turned about, not very brilliantly, as he was aware, to some other resource. "You'll immensely disappoint your own people."

"Yes, my mother and my grandmother—they both would like it. But they've never had any promise from me."

Tony was silent awhile. "And Mrs. Beever—hasn't she had?"

"A promise? Never. I've known how much she has wanted it. But that's all."

"Ah, that's a great deal," said Tony. "If, knowing how much she has wanted it, you've come back again and again, hasn't that been tantamount to giving it?"

Jean considered. "I shall never come back again."

"Ah, my dear child, what a way to treat us!" her friend broke out.

She took no notice of this; she only went on: "Months ago—the last time I was here—an assurance, of a kind, was asked of me. But even then I held off."

"And you've gone on with that intention?"

He had grown so serious now that he cross-questioned her, but she met him with a promptitude that was touching in its indulgence. "I've gone on without an intention. I've only waited to see, to feel, to judge. The great thing seemed to me to be sure I wasn't unfair to Paul. I haven't been—I'm not unfair. He'll never say I've been—I'm sure he won't. I should have liked to be able to become his wife. But I can't."

"You've nevertheless excited hopes," said Tony. "Don't you think you ought to consider that a little more?" His uneasiness, his sense of the unexpected, as sharp as a physical pang, increased so that he began to lose sight of the importance of concealing it; and he went on even while something came into her eyes that showed he had not concealed it. "If you haven't meant not to do it, you've, so far as that goes, meant the opposite. Therefore something has made you change."

Jean hesitated. "Everything has made me change."

"Well," said Tony, with a smile so strained that he felt it almost pitiful, "we've spoken of the disappointment to others, but I suppose there's no use in my attempting to say anything of the disappointment to me. That's not the thing that, in such a case, can have much effect on you."

Again Jean hesitated: he saw how pale she had grown. "Do I understand you tell me that you really *desire* my marriage?"

If the revelation of how he desired it had not already come to him the deep mystery of her beauty at this crisis might have brought it on the spot—a spectacle in which he so lost himself for the minute that he found no words to answer till she spoke again. "Do I understand that you literally ask me for it?"

"I ask you for it—I ask you for it," said Tony Bream.

They stood looking at each other like a pair who, walking on a frozen lake, suddenly have in their ears the great crack of the ice. "And what are your reasons?"

"I'll tell you my reasons when you tell me yours for having changed."

"I've not changed," said Jean.

It was as if their eyes were indissolubly engaged. That was the way he had been looking a while before into another woman's, but he could think at this moment of the exquisite difference of Jean's. He shook his head with all the sadness and all the tenderness he felt he might permit himself to show just this once and never again. "You've changed—you've changed."

Then she gave up. "Wouldn't you much rather I should never come back?"

"Far rather. But you *will* come back," said Tony.

She looked away from him at least—turned her eyes over the place in which she had known none but emotions permitted and avowed, and again seemed to yield to the formidable truth. "So you think I had better come back—so different?"

His tenderness broke out into a smile. "As different as possible. As different as that will be just all the difference," he added.

She appeared, with her averted face, to consider intently how much "all" might in such a case practically amount to. But "Here he comes" was what she presently replied.

Paul Beever was in sight, so freshly dressed that even at a distance his estimate of the requirements of the occasion was visible from his necktie to his boots. Adorned as it unmistakably had never been, his great featureless person moved solemnly over the lawn.

"Take him then—*take* him!" said Tony Bream.

Jean, intensely serious but with agitation held at bay, gave him one more look, a look so infinitely pacific that as, at Paul's nearer approach, he turned away from her, he had the sense of going off with a sign of her acceptance of his solution. The light in her face was the light of the compassion that had come out to him, and what was that compassion but the gage of a relief, of a promise? It made him walk down to the river with a step quickened to exhilaration; all the more that as the girl's eyes followed him he couldn't see in them the tragic intelligence he had kindled, her perception—from the very rhythm of the easy gait she had watched so often— that he really thought such a virtual confession to her would be none too lavishly repaid by the effort for which he had appealed.

Paul Beever had in his hand his little morocco case, but his glance also rested, till it disappeared, on Tony's straight and swinging back. "I've driven him away," he said.

"It was time," Jean replied. "Effie, who wasn't ready for me, must really come at last." Then without the least pretence of unconsciousness she looked straight at the small object Paul carried.

Observing her attention to it he also dropped his eyes on it, while his hands turned it round and round in apparent uncertainty as to whether he had better present it to her open or shut. "I hope you won't be as indifferent as Effie seems to be to the pretty trifle with which I've thought I should like to commemorate your birthday." He decided to open the case and with its lifted lid he held it out to her. "It will give me great pleasure if you'll kindly accept this little ornament."

Jean took it from him—she seemed to study it a moment. "Oh Paul, oh Paul!"—her protest was as sparing as a caress with the back of the hand.

"I thought you might care for the stone," he said.

"It's a rare and perfect one—it's magnificent."

"Well, Miss Armiger told me you would know." There was a hint of relaxed suspense in Paul's tone.

Still holding the case open his companion looked at him a moment. "Did *she* kindly select it?"

He stammered, colouring a little. "No; mother and I did. We went up to London for it; we had the mounting designed and worked out. They took two months. But I showed it to Miss Armiger and she said you'd spot any defect."

"Do you mean," the girl asked, smiling, "that if you had not had her word for that you would have tried me with something inferior?"

Paul continued very grave. "You know well enough what I mean."

Without again noticing the contents of the case she softly closed it and kept it in her hand. "Yes, Paul, I know well enough what you mean." She looked round her; then, as if her old familiarity with him were refreshed and sweetened: "Come and sit down with me." She led the way to a garden

bench that stood at a distance from Mrs. Beever's tea-table,
an old green wooden bench that was a perennial feature of
the spot. "If Miss Armiger knows that I'm a judge," she pursued as they went, "it's, I think, because she knows everything—except one, which I know better than she." She seated
herself, glancing up and putting out her free hand to him
with an air of comradeship and trust. Paul let it take his own,
which he held there a minute. "I know *you.*" She drew him
down, and he dropped her hand; whereupon it returned to
his little box, which, with the aid of the other, it tightly and
nervously clasped. "I can't take your present. It's impossible,"
she said.

He sat leaning forward with his big red fists on his knees.
"Not for your birthday?"

"It's too splendid for that—it's too precious. And how can
I take it for that when it isn't for that you offer it? How can
I take so much, Paul, when I give you so little? It represents
so much more than itself—a thousand more things than I've
any right to let you think I can accept. I can't pretend not to
know—I must meet you half way. I want to do that so
much—to keep our relations happy, happy always, without a
break or a cloud. They will be—they'll be beautiful. We've
only to be frank. They *are* now: I feel it in the kind way you
listen to me. If you hadn't asked to speak to me I should have
asked it myself. Six months ago I promised I would tell you,
and I've known the time was come."

"The time is come, but don't tell me till you've given me a
chance," said Paul. He had listened without looking at her,
his little eyes pricking with their intensity the remotest object
they could reach. "I want so to please you—to make you take
a favourable view. There isn't a condition you may make, you
know, of any sort whatever, that I won't grant you in advance.
And if there's any inducement you can name that I've the
least capacity to offer, please regard it as offered with all my
heart. You know everything—you understand; but just let me
repeat that all I am, all I have, all I can ever be or do——"

She laid her hand on his arm as if to help, not to stop him.
"Paul, Paul—you're beautiful!" She brushed him with the
feather of her tact, but he reddened and continued to avert
his big face, as if he were aware that the moment of such an

assertion was scarcely the moment to venture to show it. "You're such a gentleman!" Jean went on—this time with a tremor in her voice that made him turn.

"That's the sort of fine thing I wanted to say to *you*," he said. And he was so accustomed, in any talk, to see his interlocutor suddenly laugh that his look of benevolence covered even her air of being amused by these words.

She smiled at him; she patted his arm. "You've said to me far more than that comes to. I want you—oh, I want you so to be successful and happy!" And her laugh, with an ambiguous sob, suddenly changed into a burst of tears.

She recovered herself, but she had brought tears into his own eyes. "Oh, that's of no consequence! I'm to understand that you'll never, never——?"

"Never, never."

Paul drew a long, low breath. "Do you know that every one has thought you probably would?"

"Certainly, I've known it, and that's why I'm glad of our talk. It ought to have come sooner. *You* thought I probably would, I think——"

"Oh, yes!" Paul artlessly broke in.

Jean laughed again while she wiped her eyes. "That's why I call you beautiful. You had my possible expectation to meet."

"Oh, yes!" he said again.

"And you were to meet it like a gentleman. I might have—but no matter. You risked your life—you've been magnificent." Jean got up. "And now, to make it perfect, you must take this back."

She put the morocco case into his submissive hand, and he sat staring at it and mechanically turning it round. Unconsciously, musingly he threw it a little way into the air and caught it again. Then he also got up. "They'll be tremendously down on us."

"On 'us'? On me, of course—but why on you?"

"For not having moved you."

"You've moved me immensely. Before *me*—let no one say a word about you!"

"It's of no consequence," Paul repeated.

"Nothing is, if we go on as we are. We're better friends than ever. And we're happy!" Jean announced in her triumph.

He looked at her with deep wistfulness, with patient envy. "*You* are!" Then his eyes took the direction to which her attention at that moment passed: they showed him Tony Bream coming up the slope with his little girl in his hand. Jean went down instantly to welcome the child, and Paul turned away with a grave face, giving at the same time another impulsive toss to the case containing the token she had declined.

XXI

H E DIRECTED his face to the house, however, only to find himself in the presence of his mother, who had come back to her tea-table and whom he saw veritably glare at the small object in his hands. From this object her scrutiny jumped to his own countenance, which, to his great discomfort, was not conscious of very successfully baffling it. He knew therefore a momentary relief when her observation attached itself to Jean Martle, whom Tony, planted on the lawn, was also undisguisedly watching and who was already introducing Effie to the treasure laid up in the shade of the tea-table. The girl had caught up the child on her strong young arm, where she sat robust and radiant, befrilled and besashed, hugging the biggest of the dolls; and in this position—erect, active, laughing, her rosy burden, almost on her shoulder, mingling its brightness with that of her crown of hair, and her other hand grasping, for Effie's further delight, in the form of another puppet from the pile, a still rosier imitation of it—anticipated quickly the challenge, which, as Paul saw, Mrs. Beever was on the point of addressing her.

"Our wonderful cake's not coming out?"

"It's too big to transport," said Mrs. Beever: "it's blazing away in the dining-room."

Jean Martle turned to Tony. "I may carry her in to see it?"

Tony assented. "Only please remember she's not to partake."

Jean smiled at him. "I'll eat her share!" And she passed swiftly over the lawn while the three pair of eyes followed her.

"She looks," said Tony, "like the goddess Diana playing with a baby-nymph."

Mrs. Beever's attention came back to her son. "That's the sort of remark one would expect to hear from *you*! You're not going with her?"

Paul showed vacant and vast. "I'm going in."

"To the dining-room?"

He wavered. "To speak to Miss Armiger."

His mother's gaze, sharpened and scared, had reverted to his morocco case. "To ask her to keep that again?"

At this Paul met her with spirit. "She may keep it for ever!" Giving another toss to his missile, while his companions stared at each other, he took the same direction as Jean.

Mrs. Beever, disconcerted and flushed, broke out on the spot to Tony. "Heaven help us all—she has refused him!"

Tony's face reflected her alarm. "Pray, how do you know?"

"By his having his present to her left on his hands—a jewel a girl would jump at! I came back to hear it was settled——"

"And you haven't heard it's not!"

"What I haven't heard I've seen. That it's 'not' sticks out of them! If she won't accept the gift," Mrs. Beever cried, "how can she accept the giver?"

Tony's appearance, for some seconds, was an echo of her question. "Why, she just promised me she would!"

This only deepened his neighbour's surprise. "Promised *you*——?"

Tony hesitated. "I mean she left me to infer that I had determined her. She was so good as to listen most appreciatively to what I had to say."

"And, pray, what had you to say?" Mrs. Beever asked with austerity.

In the presence of a rigour so immediate he found himself so embarrassed that he considered. "Well—everything. I took the liberty of urging Paul's claim."

Mrs. Beever stared. "Very good of you! What did you think you had to do with it?"

"Why, whatever my great desire that she should accept him gave me."

"Your great desire that she should accept him? This is the first I've heard of it."

Once more Tony pondered. "Did I never speak of it to you?"

"Never that I can remember. From when does it date?" Mrs. Beever demanded.

"From the moment I really understood how much Paul had to hope."

"How 'much'?" the lady of Eastmead derisively repeated. "It wasn't so much that you need have been at such pains to make it less!"

Tony's comprehension of his friend's discomfiture was written in the smile of determined good humour with which he met the asperity of her successive inquiries; but his own uneasiness, which was not the best thing in the world for his temper, showed through this superficial glitter. He looked suddenly as blank as a man can look who looks annoyed. "How in the world could I have supposed I was making it less?"

Mrs. Beever faltered in her turn. "To answer that question I should need to have been present at your appeal."

Tony's eyes put forth a fire. "It seems to me that your answer, as it is, will do very well for a charge of disloyalty. Do you imply that I didn't act in good faith?"

"Not even in my sore disappointment. But I imply that you made a gross mistake."

Tony lifted his shoulders; with his hands in his pockets he had begun to fidget about the lawn—bringing back to her as he did so the worried figure that, in the same attitude, the day of poor Julia's death, she had seen pace the hall at the other house. "But what the deuce then was I to do?"

"You were to let her alone."

"Ah, but I should have had to begin that earlier!" he exclaimed with ingenuous promptitude.

Mrs. Beever gave a laugh of despair. "Years and years earlier!"

"I mean," returned Tony with a blush, "that from the first of her being here I made a point of giving her the impression of all the good I thought of Paul."

His hostess continued sarcastic. "If it was a question of making points and giving impressions, perhaps then you should have begun later still!" She gathered herself a moment; then she brought out: "You should have let her alone, Tony Bream, because you're madly in love with her!"

Tony dropped into the nearest chair; he sat there looking up at the queen-mother. "Your proof of that's my plea for your son?"

She took full in the face his air of pity for her lapse. "Your plea was not for my son—your plea was for your own danger."

"My own 'danger'?" Tony leaped to his feet again in illustration of his security. "Need I inform you at this time of day that I've such a thing as a conscience?"

"Far from it, my dear man. Exactly what I complain of is that you've quite too much of one." And she gave him, before turning away, what might have been her last look and her last word. "Your conscience is as big as your passion, and if both had been smaller you might perhaps have held your tongue!"

She moved off in a manner that added emphasis to her words, and Tony watched her with his hands still in his pockets and his long legs a little apart. He could turn it over that she accused him, after all, only of having been a particularly injurious fool. "I was under the same impression as you," he said "—the impression that Paul was safe."

This arrested and brought her sharply round. "And were you under the impression that Jean was?"

"On my honour—as far as I'm concerned!"

"It's of course of you we're talking," Mrs. Beever replied. "If you weren't her motive are you able to suggest who was?"

"Her motive for refusing Paul?" Tony looked at the sky for an inspiration. "I'm afraid I'm too surprised and distressed to have a theory."

"Have you one by chance as to why, if you thought them both so safe, you interfered?"

"'Interfered' is a hard word," said Tony. "I felt a wish to testify to my great sympathy with Paul from the moment I heard—what I didn't at all know—that this was the occasion on which he was, in more senses than one, to present his case."

"May I go so far as to ask," said Mrs. Beever, "if your sudden revelation proceeded from Paul himself?"

"No—not from Paul himself."

"And scarcely from Jean, I suppose?"

"Not in the remotest degree from Jean."

"Thank you," she replied; "you've told me." She had taken her place in a chair and fixed her eyes on the ground. "I've something to tell you myself, though it may not interest you so much." Then raising her eyes: "Dennis Vidal is here."

Tony almost jumped. "In the house?"

"On the river—paddling about." After which, as his blankness grew, "He turned up an hour ago," she explained.

"And no one has seen him?"

"The Doctor and Paul. But Paul didn't know——"

"And didn't ask?" Tony panted.

"What does Paul ever ask? He's too stupid! Besides, with all my affairs, he sees my people come and go. Mr. Vidal vanished when he heard that Miss Armiger's here."

Tony went from surprise to mystification. "Not to come back?"

"On the contrary, I hope, as he took my boat."

"But he wishes not to see her?"

"He's thinking it over."

Tony wondered. "What, then, did he come for?"

Mrs. Beever hung fire. "He came to see Effie."

"Effie?"

"To judge if you're likely to lose her."

Tony threw back his head. "How the devil does that concern him?"

Again Mrs. Beever faltered; then, as she rose, "Hadn't I better leave you to think it out?" she demanded.

Tony, in spite of his bewildered face, thought it out with such effect that in a moment he exclaimed: "Then he still wants that girl?"

"Very much indeed. That's why he's afraid——"

Tony took her up. "That Effie may die?"

"It's a hideous thing to be talking about," said Mrs. Beever. "But you've perhaps not forgotten who were present——!"

"I've not forgotten who were present! I'm greatly honoured by Mr. Vidal's solicitude," Tony continued; "but I beg you to tell him from me that I think I can take care of my child."

"You must take more care than ever," Mrs. Beever pointedly observed. "But don't mention him to *her*!" she as sharply added. Rose Armiger's white dress and red parasol had reappeared on the steps of the house.

XXII

A T THE SIGHT of the two persons in the garden Rose came straight down to them, and Mrs. Beever, sombre and sharp, still seeking relief in the opportunity for satire, remarked to her companion in a manner at once ominous and indifferent that her guest was evidently in eager pursuit of him. Tony replied with gaiety that he awaited her with fortitude, and Rose, reaching them, let him know that as she had something more to say to him she was glad he had not, as she feared, quitted the garden. Mrs. Beever hereupon signified her own intention of taking this course: she would leave their visitor, as she said, to Rose to deal with.

Rose smiled with her best grace. "That's as I leave Paul to you. I've just been with him."

Mrs. Beever testified not only to interest, but to approval. "In the library?"

"In the drawing-room." Rose the next moment conscientiously showed by a further remark her appreciation of the attitude that, on the part of her hostess, she had succeeded in producing. "Miss Martle's in the library."

"And Effie?" Mrs. Beever asked.

"Effie, of course, is where Miss Martle is."

Tony, during this brief colloquy, had lounged away as restlessly as if, instead of beaming on the lady of Eastmead, Rose were watching the master of the other house. He promptly turned round. "I say, dear lady, you know—be kind to her!"

"To Effie?" Mrs. Beever demanded.

"To poor Jean."

Mrs. Beever, after an instant's reflection, took a humorous view of his request. "I don't know why you call her 'poor'! She has declined an excellent settlement, but she's not in misery yet." Then she said to Rose: "I'll take Paul first."

Rose had put down her parasol, pricking the point of it, as if with a certain shyness, into the close, firm lawn. "If you like, when you take Miss Martle——" She paused in deep contemplation of Tony.

"When I take Miss Martle?" There was a new encouragement in Mrs. Beever's voice.

The apparent effect of this benignity was to make Miss Armiger's eyes widen strangely at their companion. "Why, I'll come back and take the child."

Mrs. Beever met this offer with an alertness not hitherto markedly characteristic of her intercourse with Rose. "I'll send her out to you." Then by way of an obeisance to Tony, directing the words well at him: "It won't indeed be a scene for that poor lamb!" She marched off with her duty emblazoned on her square satin back.

Tony, struck by the massive characters in which it was written there, broke into an indulgent laugh, but even in his mirth he traced the satisfaction she took in letting him see that she measured with some complacency the embarrassment Rose might cause him. "Does she propose to tear Miss Martle limb from limb?" he playfully inquired.

"Do you ask that," said Rose, "partly because you're apprehensive that it's what I propose to do to you?"

"By no means, my dear Rose, after your just giving me so marked a sign of the pacific as your coming round——"

"On the question," Rose broke in, "of one's relation to that little image and echo of her adored mother? That isn't peace, my dear Tony. You give me just the occasion to let you formally know that it's war."

Tony gave another laugh. "War?"

"Not on you—I pity you too much."

"Then on whom?"

Rose hesitated. "On any one, on every one, who may be likely to find that small child—small as she is!—inconvenient. Oh, I know," she went on, "you'll say I come late in the day for this and you'll remind me of how very short a time ago it was that I declined a request of yours to occupy myself with her at all. Only half an hour has elapsed, but what has happened in it has made all the difference."

She spoke without discernible excitement, and Tony had already become aware that the face she actually showed him was not a thing to make him estimate directly the effect wrought in her by the incongruous result of the influence he had put forth under pressure of her ardour. He needed no great imagination to conceive that this consequence might, on the poor girl's part, well be mainly lodged in such depths of her nature as not to find an easy or an immediate way to the surface. That he had her to reckon with he was reminded as soon as he caught across the lawn the sheen of her white dress; but what he most felt was a lively, unreasoning hope that for the hour at least, and until he should have time to turn round and see what his own situation exactly contained for him, her mere incontestable cleverness would achieve a revolution during which he might take breath. This was not a hope that in any way met his difficulties—it was a hope that only avoided them; but he had lately had a vision of something in which it was still obscure to him whether the bitter or the sweet prevailed, and he was ready to make almost any terms to be allowed to surrender himself to these first quick throbs of response to what was at any rate an impression of perfect beauty. He was in bliss with a great chill and in despair with a great lift, and confused and assured and alarmed—divided between the joy and the pain of knowing that what Jean Martle had done she had done for Tony Bream, and done full in the face of all he couldn't do to repay her. That Tony Bream might never marry was a simple enough affair, but that this rare creature mightn't suddenly figured to him as formidable and exquisite. Therefore he found his nerves rather indebted to Rose for her being—if that was the explanation— too proud to be vulgarly vindictive. She knew his secret, as even after seeing it so freely handled by Mrs. Beever he still rather artlessly called the motive of his vain appeal; knew it better than before, since she could now read it in the intenser light of the knowledge of it betrayed by another. If on this advantage he had no reason to look to her generosity, it was at least a comfort that he might look to her for good manners. Poor Tony had the full consciousness of needing to think out a line, but it weighed somewhat against that oppression to feel that Rose also would have it. He was only a little troubled by the idea that, ardent and subtle, she would probably think faster than he. He turned over a moment the revelation of these qualities conveyed in her announcement of a change, as he might call it, of policy.

"What you say is charming," he good-naturedly replied, "so far as it represents an accession to the ranks of my daughter's friends. You will never without touching me remind me how nearly a sister you were to her mother; and I would rather express the pleasure I take in that than the bewilderment I feel at your allusion to any class of persons whose interest in her may not be sincere. The more friends she has, the better—I welcome you all. The only thing I ask of you," he went on, smiling, "is not to quarrel about her among yourselves."

Rose, as she listened, looked almost religiously calm, but as she answered there was a profane quaver in her voice that told him with what an effort she achieved that sacrifice to form for which he was so pusillanimously grateful. "It's very good of you to make the best of me; and it's also very clever of you, let me add, my dear Tony—and add with all deference to your goodness—to succeed in implying that any other course is open to you. You may welcome me as a friend of the child or not. I'm present for her, at any rate, and present as I've never been before."

Tony's gratitude, suddenly contracting, left a little edge for irritation. "You're present, assuredly, my dear Rose, and your presence is to us all an advantage of which, happily, we never become unconscious for an hour. But do I understand that the firm position among us that you allude to is one to which you see your way to attaching any possibility of permanence?"

She waited as if scrupulously to detach from its stem the flower of irony that had sprouted in this speech, and while she inhaled it she gave her visible attention only to the little hole in the lawn that she continued to prick with the point of her parasol. "If that's a graceful way of asking me," she returned at last, "whether the end of my visit here isn't near at hand, perhaps the best satisfaction I can give you is to say that I shall probably stay on at least as long as Miss Martle. What I meant, however, just now," she pursued, "by saying that I'm more on the spot than heretofore, is simply that while I do stay I stay to be vigilant. That's what I hurried out to let you definitely know, in case you should be going home without our meeting again. I told you before I went into the house that I trusted you—I needn't recall to you for what. Mr.

Beever after a while came in and told me that Miss Martle had refused him. Then I felt that, after what had passed between us, it was only fair to say to you———"

"That you've ceased to trust me?" Tony interjected.

"By no means. I don't give and take back." And though his companion's handsome head, with its fixed, pale face, rose high, it became appreciably handsomer and reached considerably higher, while she wore once more the air of looking at his mistake through the enlarging blur of tears. "As I believe you did, in honour, what you could for Mr. Beever, I trust you perfectly still."

Tony smiled as if he apologised, but as if also he couldn't but wonder. "Then it's only fair to say to me———?"

"That I don't trust Miss Martle."

"Oh, my dear woman!" Tony precipitately laughed.

But Rose went on with all deliberation and distinctness. "That's what has made the difference—that's what has brought me, as you say, round to a sense of my possible use, or rather of my clear obligation. Half an hour ago I knew how much you loved her. Now I know how much she loves you."

Tony's laugh suddenly dropped; he showed the face of a man for whom a joke has sharply turned grave. "And what is it that, in possession of this admirable knowledge, you see———?"

Rose faltered; but she had not come so far simply to make a botch of it. "Why, that it's the obvious interest of the person we speak of not to have too stupid a patience with any obstacle to her marrying you."

This speech had a quiet lucidity of which the odd action was for an instant to make him lose breath so violently that, in his quick gasp, he felt sick. In the indignity of the sensation he struck out. "Pray, why is it the person's obvious interest any more than it's yours?"

"Seeing that I love you quite as much as she does? Because you don't love me quite so much as you love *her*. That's exactly 'why,' dear Tony Bream!" said Rose Armiger.

She turned away from him sadly and nobly, as if she had done with him and with the subject, and he stood where she had left him, gazing at the foolish greenness at his feet and

slowly passing his hand over his head. In a few seconds, however, he heard her utter a strange, short cry, and, looking
round, saw her face to face—across the interval of sloping
lawn—with a gentleman whom he had been sufficiently prepared to recognise on the spot as Dennis Vidal.

XXIII

H E HAD, in this preparation, the full advantage of Rose, who, quite thrown for the moment off her balance, was vividly unable to give any account of the apparition which should be profitable to herself. The violence of her surprise made her catch the back of the nearest chair, on which she covertly rested, directing at her old suitor from this position the widest eyes the master of Bounds had ever seen her un- wittingly open. To perceive this, however, was to be almost si- multaneously struck, and even to be not a little charmed, with the clever quickness of her recovery—that of a person consti- tutionally averse to making unmeasured displays. Rose was ca- pable of astonishment, as she was capable of other kinds of emotion; but she was as little capable of giving way to it as she was of giving way to other kinds; so that both of her com- panions immediately saw her moved by the sense that a per- turbing incident could at the worst do her no such evil turn as she might suffer by taking it in the wrong way. Tony be- came aware, in addition, that the fact communicated to him by Mrs. Beever gave him an advantage even over the poor fel- low whose face, as he stood there, showed the traces of an in- sufficient forecast of two things: one of them the influence on all his pulses of the sight again, after such an interval, and in the high insolence of life and strength, of the woman he had lost and still loved; the other the instant effect on his imagi- nation of his finding her intimately engaged with the man who had been, however without fault, the occasion of her perversity. Vidal's marked alertness had momentarily failed him; he paused in his advance long enough to give Tony, after noting and regretting his agitation, time to feel that Rose was already as colourlessly bland as a sensitive woman could wish to be.

All this made the silence, however brief—and it was much briefer than my account of it—vibrate to such a tune as to prompt Tony to speak as soon as possible in the interest of harmony. What directly concerned him was that he had last seen Vidal as his own duly appreciative guest, and he offered him a hand freely charged with reminders of that quality. He was refreshed and even a little surprised to observe that the young man took it, after all, without stiffness; but the strangest thing in the world was that as he cordially brought him up the bank he had a mystic glimpse of the fact that Rose Armiger, with her heart in her throat, was waiting for some sign as to whether she might, for the benefit of her intercourse with himself, safely take the ground of having expected what had happened—having perhaps even brought it about. She naturally took counsel of her fears, and Tony, suddenly more elated than he could have given a reason for being, was ready to concur in any attempt she might make to save her appearance of knowing no reproach. Yet, foreseeing the awkwardness that might arise from her committing herself too rashly, he made haste to say to Dennis that he would have been startled if he had not been forewarned: Mrs. Beever had mentioned to him the visit she had just received.

"Ah, she told you?" Dennis asked.

"Me only—as a great sign of confidence," Tony laughed.

Rose, at this, could be amazed with superiority.

"What?—you've already been here?"

"An hour ago," said Dennis. "I asked Mrs. Beever not to tell you."

That was a chance for positive criticism. "She obeyed your request to the letter. But why in the world such portentous secrecy?" Rose spoke as if there was no shade of a reason for his feeling shy, and now gave him an excellent example of the right tone. She had emulated Tony's own gesture of welcome, and he said to himself that no young woman could have stretched a more elastic arm across a desert of four cold years.

"I can explain to you better," Dennis replied, "why I emerged than why I vanished."

"You emerged, I suppose, because you wanted to see me." Rose spoke to one of her admirers, but she looked, she even laughed, at the other, showing him by this time an aspect completely and inscrutably renewed. "You knew I was here?"

"At Wilverley?" Dennis hesitated. "I took it for granted."

"I'm afraid it was really for Miss Armiger you came," Tony remarked in the spirit of pleasantry. It seemed to him that the spirit of pleasantry would help them on.

It had its result—it proved contagious. "I would still say so—before her—even if it weren't!" Dennis returned.

Rose took up the joke. "Fortunately it's true—so it saves you a fib."

"It saves me a fib!" Dennis said.

In this way the trick was successfully played—they found their feet; with the added amusement for Tony of hearing the necessary falsehood uttered neither by himself nor by Rose, but by a man whose veracity, from the first, on that earlier day, of looking at him, he had felt to be almost incompatible with the flow of conversation. It was more and more distinct while the minutes elapsed that the secondary effect of her old friend's reappearance was to make Rose shine with a more convenient light; and she met her embarrassment, every way, with so happy an art that Tony was moved to deplore afresh the complication that estranged him from a woman of such gifts. It made up indeed a little for this that he was also never so possessed of his own as when there was something to carry off or to put, as the phrase was, through. His light hand, his slightly florid facility were the things that in managing, in presiding, had rendered him so widely popular; and wasn't he, precisely, a little presiding, wasn't he a good deal managing just now? Vidal would be a blessed diversion—especially if he should be pressed into the service as one: Tony was content for the moment to see this with eagerness rather than to see it whole. His eagerness was quite justified by the circumstance that the young man from China did somehow or other—the reasons would appear after the fact—represent relief, relief not made vain by the reflection that it was perhaps only temporary. Rose herself, thank heaven, was, with all her exaltation, only temporary. He could already condone the officiousness of a gentleman too interested in Effie's equilibrium: the grounds of that indiscretion gleamed agreeably through it as soon as he had seen the visitor's fingers draw together over the hand held out by Rose. It was matter to whistle over, to bustle over, that, as had been certified by Mrs. Beever, the passion betrayed by that clasp had survived its shipwreck, and there wasn't a rope's end Tony could throw, or a stray stick he could hold out, for which he didn't immediately cast about him. He saw indeed from this moment his whole comfort in the idea of an organised rescue and of making the struggling swimmer know, as a preliminary, how little any one at the other house was interested in preventing him to land.

Dennis had, for that matter, not been two minutes in touch with him before he really began to see this happy perception descend. It was, in a manner, to haul him ashore to invite him to dine and sleep; which Tony lost as little time as possible in doing; expressing the hope that he had not gone to the inn and that even if he had he would consent to the quick transfer of his effects to Bounds. Dennis showed that he had still some wonder for such an overture, but before he could respond to it the words were taken out of his mouth by Rose, whose recovery from her upset was complete from the moment she could seize a pretext for the extravagance of tranquility.

"Why should you take him away from us and why should he consent to be taken? Won't Mrs. Beever," Rose asked of Dennis—"since you're not snatching the fearful joy of a clandestine visit to her—expect you, if you stay anywhere, to give her the preference?"

"Allow me to remind you, and to remind Mr. Vidal," Tony returned, "that when he was here before he gave her the preference. Mrs. Beever made no scruple of removing him bodily from under my roof. I forfeited—I was obliged to—the pleasure of a visit to him. But that leaves me with my loss to make up and my revenge to take—I repay Mrs. Beever in kind." To find Rose disputing with him the possession of their friend filled him with immediate cheer. "Don't you recognise," he went on to him, "the propriety of what I propose? I take you and deal with Mrs. Beever, as she took you and dealt with me. Besides, your things have not even been brought here as they had of old been brought to Bounds. I promise to share you with these ladies and not to grudge you the time you may wish to spend with Miss Armiger. I understand but too well the number of hours I shall find you putting in. You shall pay me a long visit and come over here as often as you like, and your presence at Bounds may even possibly have the consequence of making them honour me there a little oftener with their own."

Dennis looked from one of his companions to the other; he struck Tony as slightly mystified, but not beyond the point at which curiosity was agreeable. "I think I had better go to Mr. Bream," he after a moment sturdily said to Rose. "There's a matter on which I wish to talk with you, but I don't see that that need prevent."

"It's for you to determine. There's a matter on which I find myself, to you also, particularly glad of the opportunity of saying a word."

Tony glanced promptly at his watch and at Rose, "Your opportunity's before you—say your word now. I've a little job in the town," he explained to Dennis; "I must attend to it quickly and I can easily stop at the hotel and given directions for the removal of your traps. All you will have to do then will be to take the short way, which you know—over the bridge there and through my garden—to my door. We shall dine at an easy eight."

Dennis Vidal assented to this arrangement without qualification and indeed almost without expression: there evidently lingered in him an operative sense that there were compensations Mr. Bream might be allowed the luxurious consciousness of owing him. Rose, however, showed she still had a communication to make to Tony, who had begun to move in the quarter leading straight from Eastmead to the town, so that he would have to pass near the house on going out. She introduced it with a question about his movements. "You'll stop, then, on your way and tell Mrs. Beever——?"

"Of my having appropriated our friend? Not this moment," said Tony—"I've to meet a man on business, and I shall only just have time. I shall if possible come back here, but meanwhile perhaps you'll kindly explain. Come straight over and take possession," he added, to Vidal; "make yourself at home—don't wait for me to return to you." He offered him a hand-shake again, and then, with his native impulse to accommodate and to harmonise making a friendly light in his face, he offered one to Rose herself. She accepted it so frankly that she even for a minute kept his hand—a response that he approved with a smile so encouraging that it scarcely needed even the confirmation of speech. They stood there while Dennis Vidal turned away as if they might have matters between them, and Tony yielded to the impulse to prove to Rose that though there were things he kept from her he kept nothing that was not absolutely necessary. "There's something else I've got to do—I've got to stop at the Doctor's."

Rose raised her eyebrows. "To consult him?"

"To ask him to come over."

"I hope you're not ill."

"Never better in my life. I want him to see Effie."

"She's not ill surely?"

"She's not right—with the fright Gorham had this morning. So I'm not satisfied."

"Let him then by all means see her," Rose said.

Their talk had, through the action of Vidal's presence, dropped from its chilly height to the warmest domestic level, and what now stuck out of Tony was the desire she should understand that on such ground as that he was always glad to meet her. Dennis Vidal faced about again in time to be called, as it were, if only by the tone of his host's voice, to witness this. "*A bientôt.* Let me hear from you—and from him—that in my absence you've been extremely kind to our friend here."

Rose, with a small but vivid fever-spot in her cheek, looked from one of the men to the other, while her kindled eyes showed a gathered purpose that had the prompt and perceptible effect of exciting suspense. "I don't mind letting you know, Mr. Bream, in advance exactly how kind I shall be. It would be affectation on my part to pretend to be unaware of your already knowing something of what has passed between this gentleman and me. He suffered, at my hands, in this place, four years ago, a disappointment—a disappointment into the rights and wrongs, into the good reasons of which I won't attempt to go further than just to say that an inevitable publicity then attached to it." She spoke with slow and deliberate clearness, still looking from Tony to Dennis and back again; after which her strange intensity fixed itself on her old suitor. "People saw, Mr. Vidal," she went on, "the blight that descended on our long relations, and people believed—and I was at the time indifferent to their believing—that it had occurred by my act. I'm not indifferent now—that is to any appearance of having been wanting in consideration for such a man as you. I've often wished I might make you some reparation—some open atonement. I'm sorry for the distress that

I'm afraid I caused you, and here, before the principal witness of the indignity you so magnanimously met, I very sincerely express my regret and very humbly beg your forgiveness." Dennis Vidal, staring at her, had turned dead white as she kept it up, and the elevation, as it were, of her abasement had brought tears into Tony's eyes. She saw them there as she looked at him once more, and she measured the effect she produced upon him. She visibly and excusably enjoyed it and after a moment's pause she handsomely and pathetically completed it. "*That*, Mr. Bream—for your injunction of kindness—is the kindness I'm capable of showing."

Tony turned instantly to their companion, who now stood staring hard at the ground. "I change, then, my appeal—I make it, with confidence, to *you*. Let me hear, Mr. Vidal, when we meet again, that you've not been capable of less!" Dennis, deeply moved, it was plain, but self-conscious and stiff, gave no sign of having heard him; and Rose, on her side, walked a little away like an actress who has launched her great stroke. Tony, between them, hesitated; then he laughed in a manner that showed he felt safe. "Oh, you're both all right!" he declared; and with another glance at his watch he bounded off to his business. He drew, as he went, a long breath—filled his lungs with the sense that he should after all have a margin. She would take Dennis back.

XXIV

"WHY did you do that?" Dennis asked as soon as he was alone with Rose.

She had sunk into a seat at a distance from him, all spent with her great response to her sudden opportunity for justice. His challenge brought her flight to earth; and after waiting a moment she answered him with a question that betrayed her sense of coming down. "Do you really care, after all this time, what I do or don't do?"

His rejoinder to this was in turn only another demand. "What business is it of his that you may have done this or that to me? What has passed between us is still between us: nobody else has anything to do with it."

Rose smiled at him as if to thank him for being again a trifle sharp with her. "He wants me, as he said, to be kind to you."

"You mean he wants you to do *that* sort of thing?" His sharpness brought him step by step across the lawn and nearer to her. "Do you care so very much what he wants?"

Again she hesitated; then, with her pleased, patient smile, she tapped the empty place on the bench. "Come and sit down beside me, and I'll tell you how much I care." He obeyed her, but not precipitately, approaching her with a deliberation which still held her off a little, made her objective to his inspection or his mistrust. He had said to Mrs. Beever that he had not come to watch her, but we are at liberty to wonder what Mrs. Beever might have called the attitude in which, before seating himself, he stopped before her with a silent stare. She met him at any rate with a face that told him there was no scrutiny she was now enough in the wrong to fear, a face that was all the promise of confession and submission and sacrifice. She tapped again upon her bench, and at this he sat down. Then she went on: "When did you come back?"

"To England? The other day—I don't remember which of them. I think you ought to answer my question," Dennis said, "before asking any more of your own."

"No, no," she replied, promptly but gently; "there's an inquiry it seems to me I've a right to make of you before I admit yours to make any at all." She looked at him as if to give him time either to assent or to object; but he only sat rather stiffly back and let her see how fine and firm the added years had hammered him. "What are you really here for? Has it anything to do with *me*?"

Dennis remained profoundly grave. "I didn't know you were here—I had no reason to," he at last replied.

"Then you simply desired the pleasure of renewing your acquaintance with Mrs. Beever?"

"I came to ask her about you."

"How beautiful of you!"—and Rose's tone, untinged with irony, rang out as clear as the impulse it praised. "Fancy your caring!" she added; after which she continued: "As I understand you, then, you've had your chance, you've talked with her?"

"A very short time. I put her a question or two."

"I won't ask you what they were," said Rose, "I'll only say that, since I happen to be here, it may be a comfort to you not to have to content yourself with information at second-hand. Ask *me* what you like. I'll tell you everything."

Her companion considered. "You might then begin by telling me what I've already asked."

She took him up before he could go on. "Oh, why I attached an importance to his hearing what I just now said? Yes, yes; you shall have it." She turned it over as if with the sole thought of giving it to him with the utmost lucidity; then she was visibly struck with the help she should derive from knowing just one thing more. "But first—are you at all jealous of him?"

Dennis Vidal broke into a laugh which might have been a tribute to her rare audacity, yet which somehow, at the same time, made him seem only more serious. "That's a thing for you to find out for yourself!"

"I see—I see." She looked at him with musing, indulgent eyes. "It would be too wonderful. Yet otherwise, after all, why should you care?"

"I don't mind telling you frankly," said Dennis, while, with two fingers softly playing upon her lower lip, she sat estimating the possibility she had named—"I don't mind telling you frankly that I asked Mrs. Beever if you were still in love with him."

She clasped her hands so eagerly that she almost clapped them. "Then you do care?"

He was looking beyond her now—at something at the other end of the garden; and he made no other reply than to say: "She didn't give you away."

"It was very good of her; but I would tell you myself, you know, perfectly, if I were."

"You didn't tell me perfectly four years ago," Dennis returned.

Rose hesitated a minute; but this didn't prevent her speaking with an effect of great promptitude. "Oh, four years ago I was the biggest fool in England!"

Dennis, at this, met her eyes again. "Then what I asked Mrs. Beever——"

"Isn't true?" Rose caught him up. "It's an exquisite position," she said, "for a woman to be questioned as you question me, and to have to answer as a I answer you. But it's your revenge, and you've already seen that to your revenge I minister with a certain amount of resolution." She let him look at her a minute; at last she said without flinching: "I'm not in love with Anthony Bream."

Dennis shook his head sadly. "What does that do for my revenge?"

Rose had another quick flush. "It shows you what I consent to discuss with you," she rather proudly replied.

He turned his eyes back to the quarter to which he had directed them before. "You do consent?"

"Can you ask—after what I've done?"

"Well, then, *he* no longer cares——?"

"For me?" said Rose. "He never cared."

"Never?"

"Never."

"Upon your honour?"

"Upon my honour."

"But you had an idea——?" Dennis bravely pursued.

Rose as dauntlessly met him. "I had an idea."

"And you've had to give it up?"

"I've had to give it up."

Dennis was silent; he slowly got upon his feet. "Well, *that* does something."

"For your revenge?" She sounded a bitter laugh. "I should think it might! What it does is magnificent!"

He stood looking over her head till at last he exclaimed: "So, apparently, is the child!"

"She has come?" Rose sprang up to find that Effie had been borne toward them, across the grass, in the arms of the muscular Manning, who, having stooped to set her down and given her a vigorous impulsion from behind, recovered military stature and posture.

"You're to take her, miss, please—from Mrs. Beever. And you're to keep her."

Rose had already greeted the little visitor. "Please assure Mrs. Beever that I will. She's with Miss Martle?"

"She is indeed, miss."

Manning always spoke without emotion, and the effect of it on this occasion was to give her the air of speaking without pity.

Rose, however, didn't mind that. "She may trust me," she said, while Manning saluted and retired. Then she stood before her old suitor with Effie blooming on her shoulder.

He frankly wondered and admired. "She's magnificent—she's magnificent!" he repeated.

"She's magnificent!" Rose ardently echoed. "Aren't you, my very own?" she demanded of the child, with a sudden passion of tenderness.

"What did he mean about her wanting the Doctor? She'll see us *all* through—every blessed one of us!" Dennis gave himself up to his serious interest, an odd, voracious manner of taking her in from top to toe.

"You look at her like an ogre!" Rose laughed, moving away from him with her burden and pressing to her lips as she went a little plump pink arm. She pretended to munch it; she covered it with kisses; she gave way to the joy of her renounced abstention. "See us all through? I hope so! Why shouldn't you, darling, why shouldn't you? You've got a *real* friend, you have, you duck; and she sees you know what you've got by the wonderful way you look at her!" This was to attribute to the little girl's solemn stare a vividness of meaning which moved Dennis to hilarity; Rose's profession of confidence made her immediately turn her round face over her friend's shoulder to the gentleman who was strolling behind and whose public criticism, as well as his public mirth, appeared to arouse in her only a soft sense of superiority. Rose sat down again where she had sat before, keeping Effie in her lap and smoothing out her fine feathers. Then their companion, after a little more detached contemplation, also took his former place.

"She makes me remember!" he presently observed.

"That extraordinary scene—poor Julia's message? You can fancy whether *I* forget it!"

Dennis was silent a little; after which he said quietly: "You've more to keep it in mind."

"I can assure you I've plenty!" Rose replied.

"And the young lady who was also present—isn't she the Miss Martle——?"

"Whom I spoke of to that woman? She's the Miss Martle. What about her?" Rose asked with her cheek against the child's.

"Does she also remember?"

"Like you and me? I haven't the least idea."

Once more Dennis paused; his pauses were filled with his friendly gaze at their small companion. "She's here again— like you?"

"And like you?" Rose smiled. "No, not like either of us. She's always here."

"And it's from her you're to keep a certain little person?"

"It's from her." Rose spoke with rich brevity.

Dennis hesitated. "Would you trust the little person to another little person?"

"To you—to hold?" Rose looked amused. "Without a pang!" The child, at this, profoundly meditative and imperturbably "good," submitted serenely to the transfer and to the prompt, long kiss which, as he gathered her to him, Dennis, in his turn, imprinted on her arm. "I'll stay with *you*!" she declared with expression; on which he renewed, with finer relish, the freedom she permitted, assuring her that this settled the question and that he was her appointed champion. Rose watched the scene between them, which was charming; then she brought out abruptly: "What I said to Mr. Bream just now I didn't say for Mr. Bream."

Dennis had the little girl close to him; his arms were softly round her and, like Rose's just before, his cheek, as he tenderly bent his head, was pressed against her cheek. His eyes were on their companion. "You said it for Mr. Vidal? He liked it, all the same, better than I," he replied in a moment.

"Of course he liked it! But it doesn't matter what he likes," Rose added. "As for you—I don't know that your 'liking' it was what I wanted."

"What then did you want?"

"That you should see me utterly abased—and all the more utterly that it was in the cruel presence of another."

Dennis had raised his head and sunk back into the angle of the bench, separated from her by such space as it yielded. His face, presented to her over Effie's curls, was a combat of mystifications. "Why in the world should that give me pleasure?"

"Why in the world shouldn't it?" Rose asked. "What's your revenge but pleasure?"

She had got up again in her dire restlessness; she glowed there in the perversity of her sacrifice. If he hadn't come to Wilverley to watch her, his wonder-stricken air much wronged him. He shook his head again with his tired patience. "Oh, damn pleasure!" he exclaimed.

"It's nothing to you?" Rose cried. "Then if it isn't, perhaps you pity me?" She shone at him as if with the glimpse of a new hope.

He took it in, but he only, after a moment, echoed, ambiguously, her word. "Pity you?"

"I think you would, Dennis, if you understood."

He looked at her hard; he hesitated. At last he returned quietly, but relentingly: "Well, Rose, I *don't* understand."

"Then I must go through it all—I must empty the cup. Yes, I must tell you."

She paused so long, however, beautiful, candid and tragic, looking in the face her necessity, but gathering herself for her effort, that, after waiting a while, he spoke. "Tell me what?"

"That I'm simply at your feet. That I'm yours to do what you will with—to take or to cast away. Perhaps you'll care a little for your triumph," she said, "when you see in it the grand opportunity I give you. It's *your* turn to refuse now— you can treat me exactly as you were treated!"

A deep, motionless silence followed, between them, this speech, which left them confronted as if it had rather widened than bridged their separation. Before Dennis found his answer to it the sharp tension snapped in a clear, glad exclamation. The child threw out her arms and her voice: "Auntie Jean, Auntie Jean!"

XXV

THE OTHERS had been so absorbed that they had not seen Jean Martle approach, and she, on her side, was close to them before appearing to perceive a stranger in the gentleman who held Effie in his lap and whom she had the air of having assumed, at a greater distance, to be Anthony Bream. Effie's reach towards her friend was so effective that, with Vidal's obligation to rise, it enabled her to slip from his hands and rush to avail herself of the embrace offered her, in spite of a momentary arrest, by Jean. Rose, however, at the sight of this movement, was quicker than Jean to catch her; she seized her almost with violence, and, holding her as she had held her before, dropped again upon the bench and presented her as a yielding captive. This act of appropriation was confirmed by the flash of a fine glance—a single gleam, but direct—which, however, producing in Jean's fair face no retort, had only the effect of making her look, in gracious recognition, at Dennis. He had evidently, for the moment, nothing but an odd want of words to meet her with; but this, precisely, gave her such a sense of having disturbed a scene of intimacy that, to be doubly courteous, she said: "Perhaps you remember me. We were here together——"

"Four years ago—perfectly," Rose broke in, speaking for him with an amenity that might have been intended as a quick corrective of any impression conveyed by her grab of the child. "Mr. Vidal and I were just talking of you. He has come back, for the first time since then, to pay us a little visit."

"Then he has things to say to you that I've rudely interrupted. Please excuse me—I'm off again," Jean went on to Dennis. "I only came for the little girl." She turned back to Rose. "I'm afraid it's time I should take her home."

Rose sat there like a queen-regent with a baby sovereign on her knee. "Must I give her up to you?"

"I'm responsible for her, you know, to Gorham," Jean returned.

Rose gravely kissed her little ward, who, now that she was

apparently to be offered the entertainment of a debate in which she was so closely concerned, was clearly prepared to contribute to it the calmness of impartial beauty at a joust. She was just old enough to be interested, but she was just young enough to be judicial; the lap of her present friend had the compass of a small child-world, and she perched there in her loveliness as if she had been Helen on the walls of Troy. "It's not to Gorman *I'm* responsible," Rose presently answered.

Jean took it good-humouredly. "Are you to Mr. Bream?"

"I'll tell you presently to whom." And Rose looked intelligently at Dennis Vidal.

Smiled at in alternation by two clever young women, he had yet not sufficiently to achieve a jocose manner shaken off his sense of the strange climax of his conversation with the elder of them. He turned away awkwardly, as he had done four years before, for the hat it was one of the privileges of such a colloquy to make him put down in an odd place. "I'll go over to Bounds," he said to Rose. And then to Jean, to take leave of her: "I'm staying at the other house."

"Really? Mr. Bream didn't tell me. But I must never drive you away. You've more to say to Miss Armiger than I have. I've only come to get Effie," Jean repeated.

Dennis at this, brushing off his recovered hat, gave way to his thin laugh. "That apparently may take you some time!"

Rose generously helped him off. "I've more to say to Miss Martle than I've now to say to you. I think that what I've already said to you is quite enough.

"Thanks, thanks—quite enough. I'll just go over."

"You won't go first to Mrs. Beever?"

"Not yet—I'll come in this evening. Thanks, thanks!" Dennis repeated with a sudden dramatic gaiety that was presumably intended to preserve appearances—to acknowledge Rose's aid and, in a spirit of reciprocity, cover any exposure she might herself have incurred. Raising his hat, he passed down the slope and disappeared, leaving our young ladies face to face.

Their situation might still have been embarrassing had Rose not taken immediate measures to give it a lift. "You must let me have the pleasure of making you the first person to hear of a matter that closely concerns me." She hung fire, watching her companion; then she brought out: "I'm engaged to be married to Mr. Vidal."

"Engaged?"—Jean almost bounded forward, holding up her relief like a torch.

Rose greeted with laughter this natural note. "He arrived half an hour ago, for a supreme appeal—and it has not, you see, taken long. I've just had the honour of accepting him."

Jean's movement had brought her so close to the bench that, though slightly disconnected by its action on her friend, she could only, in consistency, seat herself. "That's very charming—I congratulate you."

"It's charming of you to be so glad," Rose returned. "However, you've the news in all its freshness."

"I appreciate that too," said Jean. "But fancy my dropping on a conversation of such importance!"

"Fortunately you didn't cut it short. We had settled the question. He had got his answer."

"If I had known it I would have congratulated Mr. Vidal," Jean pursued.

"You would have frightened him out of his wits—he's so dreadfully shy," Rose laughed.

"Yes—I could see he was dreadfully shy. But the great thing," Jean candidly observed, "is that he was not too dreadfully shy to come back to you."

Rose continued to be moved to mirth. "Oh, I don't mean with *me*! He's as bold with me as I am—for instance—with you." Jean had not touched the child, but Rose smoothed our her ribbons as if to redress some previous freedom. "You'll think that says everything. I can easily imagine how you judge my frankness," she added. "But of course I'm grossly immodest—I always was."

Jean wistfully watched her light hands play here and there over Effie's adornments. "I think you're a person of great courage—if you'll let me also be frank. There's nothing in the world I admire so much—for I don't consider that I've, myself, a great deal. I daresay, however, that I should let you know just as soon if I were engaged."

"Which, unfortunately, is exactly what you're not!" Rose, having finished her titivation of the child, sank comfortably back on the bench. "Do you object to my speaking to you of that?" she asked.

Jean hesitated; she had only after letting them escape become conscious of the reach of her words, the inadvertence of which showed how few waves of emotion her scene with Paul Beever had left to subside. She coloured as she replied: "I don't know how much you know."

"I know everything," said Rose. "Mr. Beever has already told me."

Jean's flush, at this, deepened. "Mr. Beever already doesn't care!"

"That's fortunate for you, my dear! Will you let me tell you," Rose continued, "how much *I* do?"

Jean again hesitated, looking, however, through her embarrassment, very straight and sweet. "I don't quite see that it's a thing you should tell me or that I'm really obliged to hear. It's very good of you to take an interest——"

"But however good it may be, it's none of my business: is that what you mean?" Rose broke in. "Such an answer is doubtless natural enough. My having hoped you would accept Paul Beever, and above all my having rather publicly expressed that hope, is an apparent stretch of discretion that you're perfectly free to take up. But you must allow me to say that the stretch is more apparent than real. There's discretion and discretion—and it's all a matter of motive. Perhaps you can guess mine for having found a reassurance in the idea of your definitely bestowing your hand. It's a very small and a very pretty hand, but its possible action is out of proportion to its size and even to its beauty. It was not a question of meddling in your affairs—your affairs were only one side of the matter. My interest was wholly in the effect of your marriage on the affairs of others. Let me say, moreover," Rose went smoothly and inexorably on, while Jean, listening intently, drew shorter breaths and looked away, as if in growing pain, from the wonderful white, mobile mask that supplied half the meaning of this speech—"let me say, moreover, that it strikes me you hardly treat me with fairness in forbidding me an allusion that has after all so much in common with the fact, in my own situation, as to which you've no scruple in showing me your exuberant joy. You clap your hands over *my* being—if you'll forgive the vulgarity of my calling things by their names—got out of the way; yet I must suffer in silence to see you rather more in it than ever."

Jean turned again upon her companion a face bewildered and alarmed: unguardedly stepping into water that she had believed shallow, she found herself caught up in a current of fast-moving depths—a cold, full tide that set straight out to sea. "Where *am* I?" her scared silence seemed for the moment to ask. Her quick intelligence indeed, came to her aid, and she spoke in a voice out of which she showed that she tried to keep her heart-beats. "You call things, certainly, by names that are extraordinary; but I, at any rate, follow you far enough to be able to remind you that what I just said about your engagement was provoked by your introducing the subject."

Rose was silent a moment, but without prejudice, clearly, to her firm possession of the ground she stood on—a power to be effectively cool in exact proportion as her interlocutress was troubled. "I introduced the subject for two reasons. One of them was that your eager descent upon us at that particular moment seemed to present you in the light of an inquirer whom it would be really rude not to gratify. The other was just to see if you would succeed in restraining your glee."

"Then your story isn't true?" Jean asked with a promptitude that betrayed the limits of her circumspection.

"There you are again!" Rose laughed. "Do you know your apprehensions are barely decent? I haven't, however, laid a trap with a bait that's all make-believe. It's perfectly true that Mr. Vidal has again pressed me hard—it's not true that I've yet given him an answer completely final. But as I mean to at the earliest moment, you can say so to whomever you like."

"I can surely leave the saying so to *you*!" Jean returned. "But I shall be sorry to appear to have treated you with a want of confidence that may give you a complaint to make on the score of my manners—as to which you set me too high an example by the rare perfection of your own. Let me simply let you know, then, to cover every possibility of that sort, that I intend, under no circumstances—ever—ever—to marry. So far as that knowledge may satisfy you, you're welcome to the satisfaction. Perhaps in consideration of it," Jean wound up, with an effect that must have struck her own ear as the greatest she had ever produced—"perhaps in consideration of it you'll kindly do what I ask you."

The poor girl was destined to see her effect reduced to her mere personal sense of it. Rose made no movement save to lay her hands on Effie's shoulders, while that young lady looked up at the friend of other occasions in round-eyed detachment, following the talk enough for curiosity, but not enough either for comprehension or for agitation. "You take my surrender for granted, I suppose, because you've worked so long to produce the impression, which no one, for your good fortune, has gainsaid, that she's safe only in your hands. But *I* gainsay it at last, for her safety becomes a very different thing from the moment you give such a glimpse of your open field as you must excuse my still continuing to hold that you do give. My 'knowledge'—to use your term—that you'll never marry has exactly as much and as little weight as your word for it. I leave it to your conscience to estimate that wonderful amount. You say too much—both more than I ask you and more than I can oblige you by prescribing to myself to take seriously. You do thereby injustice to what must be always on the cards for you—the possible failure of the great impediment. *I'm* disinterested in the matter—I shall marry, as I've had the honour to inform you, without having to think at all of impediments or failures. That's the difference between us, and it seems to me that it alters everything. I had a delicacy—but now I've nothing in the world but a fear."

Jean had got up before these remarks had gone far, but even though she fell back a few steps her dismay was a force that condemned her to take them in. "God forbid I should understand you," she panted; "I only make out that you say and mean horrible things and that you're doing your best to seek a quarrel with me from which you shall derive some advantage that, I'm happy to feel, is beyond my conception." Both the women were now as pale as death, and Rose was brought to her feet by the pure passion of this retort. The manner of it was such as to leave Jean nothing but to walk away, which she instantly proceeded to do. At the end of ten paces, however, she turned to look at their companion, who stood beside Rose, held by the hand, and whom, as if from a certain consideration for infant innocence and a certain instinct of fair play, she had not attempted to put on her side by a single direct appeal from intimate eyes. This appeal she now risked, and the way the little girl's face mutely met it suddenly precipitated her to blind supplication. She became weak—she broke down. "I beseech you to let me have her."

Rose Armiger's countenance made no secret of her appreciation of this collapse. "I'll let you have her on one condition," she presently replied.

"What condition?"

"That you deny to me on the spot that you've but one feeling in your soul. Oh, don't look vacant and dazed," Rose derisively pursued; "don't look as if you didn't know what feeling I mean! Renounce it—repudiate it, and I'll never touch her again!"

Jean gazed in sombre stupefaction. "I know what feeling you mean," she said at last, "and I'm incapable of meeting your condition. I 'deny,' I 'renounce,' I 'repudiate' as little as I hope, as I dream, or as I feel that I'm likely ever again even to utter——!" Then she brought out in her baffled sadness, but with so little vulgarity of pride that she sounded, rather, a note of compassion for a perversity so deep: "It's because of *that* that I want her!"

"Because you adore him—and she's his?"

Jean faltered, but she was launched. "Because I adore him—and she's his."

"*I* want her for another reason," Rose declared. "I adored her poor mother—and she's hers. That's *my* ground, that's *my* love, that's *my* faith." She caught Effie up again; she held her in two strong arms and dealt her a kiss that was a long consecration. "It's as your dear dead mother's, my own, my sweet, that—if it's time—I shall carry you to bed!" She passed swiftly down the slope with her burden and took the turn which led her out of sight. Jean stood watching her till she disappeared and then waited till she had emerged for the usual minute on the rise in the middle of the bridge. She saw her stop again there, she saw her again, as if in the triumph—a great open-air insolence—of possession, press her face to the little girl's. Then they dipped together to the further end and were lost, and Jean, after taking a few vague steps on the lawn, paused, as if sick with the aftertaste of her encounter, and turned to the nearest seat. It was close to Mrs. Beever's blighted tea-table, and when she had sunk into the chair she threw her arms upon this support and wearily dropped her head.

XXVI

A T THE END of some minutes, with the sense of being approached, she looked up and saw Paul Beever. Returning to the garden, he had stopped short at sight of her, and
his arrival made her spring to her feet with the fear of having,
in the belief that she was unobserved, shown him something
she had never shown. But as he bent upon her his kind, ugly
face there came into her own the comfort of a general admission, the drop of all attempt at a superfine surface: they stood
together without saying a word, and there passed between
them something sad and clear, something that was in its
essence a recognition of the great, pleasant oddity of their being drawn closer by their rupture. They knew everything
about each other now and, young and clean and good as they
were, could meet not only without attenuations, but with a
positive friendliness that was for each, from the other, a moral
help. Paul had no need of speech to show Jean how he
thanked her for understanding why he had not besieged her
with a pressure more heroic, and she, on her side, could enter with the tread of a nurse in a sick-room into the spirit of
that accommodation. They both, moreover, had been closeted with his mother—an experience on which they could,
with some dumb humour, compare notes. The girl, finally,
had now, to this dear boy she didn't love, something more to
give than she had ever given; and after a little she could see
the dawn of suspicion of it in the eyes with which he searched
her grave face.

"I knew Miss Armiger had come back here, and I thought
I should find her," he presently explained.

"She was here a few minutes ago—she has just left me,"
Jean said.

"To go in again?" Paul appeared to wonder he had not met
her on his way out.

"To go over to Bounds."

He continued to wonder. "With Mr. Bream?"

"No—with his little girl."

Paul's surprise increased. "She has taken *her* up?"

Jean hesitated; she uneasily laughed. "Up—up—up: away up in her arms!"

Her companion was more literal. "A young woman of Effie's age must be a weight!"

"I know what weight—I've carried her. Miss Armiger did it precisely to prevent that."

"To prevent your carrying her?"

"To prevent my touching or, if possible, looking at her. She snatched her up and fled with her—to get her away from me."

"Why should she wish to do that?" Paul inquired.

"I think you had better ask her directly." Then Jean added: "As you say, she has taken her up. She's *her* occupation, from this time."

"Why, suddenly, from this time?"

"Because of what has happened."

"Between you and me?"

"Yes—that's one of her reasons."

"One of them?" laughed Paul. "She has so many?"

"She tells me she has two."

"Two? She speaks of it?"

Jean saw, visibly, that she mystified him; but she as visibly tried to let him see that this was partly because she spared him. "She speaks of it with perfect frankness."

"Then what's her second reason?"

"That if I'm not engaged"—Jean hung fire, but she brought it out—"at least she herself is."

"She herself?—instead of you?"

Paul's blandness was so utter that his companion's sense of the comic was this time, and in spite of the cruelty involved in a correction, really touched. "To you? No, not to you, my dear Paul. To a gentleman I found with her here. To that Mr. Vidal," said Jean.

Paul gasped. "You found that Mr. Vidal with her?" He looked bewilderedly about. "Where then *is* he?"

"He went over to Bounds."

"And she went with him?"

"No, she went after."

Still Paul stood staring. "Where the dickens did he drop from?"

"I haven't the least idea."

The young man had a sudden light. "Why, I saw him with mamma! He was here when I came off the river—he borrowed the boat."

"But you didn't know it was he?"

"I never dreamed—and mamma never told me."

Jean thought a moment. "She was afraid. You see I'm not."

Paul Beever more pitifully wondered; he repeated again the word she had left ringing in his ears. "She's 'engaged'?"

"So she informed me."

His little eyes rested on her with a stupefaction so candid as almost to amount to a challenge; then they moved away, far away, and he stood lost in what he felt. She came, tenderly, nearer to him, and they turned back to her: on which he saw they were filled with the tears that another failure she knew of had no power to draw to them. "It's awfully odd!" he said.

"I've had to hurt you," she replied. "I'm very sorry for you."

"Oh, don't mind it!" Paul smiled.

"These are things for you to hear of—straight."

"From *her*? Ah, I don't want to do that! You see, of course, I shan't say anything." And he covered, for an instant, working it clumsily, one of his little eyes with the base of one of his big thumbs.

Jean held out her hand to him. "Do you love her?"

He took it, embarrassed, without meeting her look; then, suddenly, something of importance seemed to occur to him and he replied with simple alertness: "I never mentioned it!"

Dimly, but ever so kindly, Jean smiled. "Because you hadn't had your talk with *me*?" She kept hold of his hand. "Dear Paul, I must say it again—you're beautiful!"

He stared, not as yet taking this approval home; then with the same prompt veracity, "But she knows it, you know, all the same!" he exclaimed.

Jean laughed as she released him; but it kept no gravity out of the tone in which she presently repeated: "I'm sorry for you."

"Oh, it's all right! May I light a cigarette?" he asked.

"As many as you like. But I must leave you."

He had struck a match, and at this he paused. "Because I'm smoking?"

"Dear, no. Because I must go over to see Effie." Facing wistfully to her little friend's quarter, Jean thought aloud. "I always bid her 'Good-night.' I don't see why—on her birthday, of all evenings—I should omit it."

"Well, then, bid her 'Good-night' for me too." She was halfway down the slope; Paul went in the same direction, puffing his cigarette hard. Then, stopping short, "Tony puts him up?" he abruptly asked.

"Mr. Vidal? So it appears."

He gazed a little, blowing his smoke, at this appearance. "And she has gone over to see him?"

"That may be a part of her errand."

He hesitated again. "They can't have lost much time!"

"Very little indeed."

Jean went on again; but again he checked her with a question. "What has he, what has the matter you speak of, to do with her cutting in——?" He paused as if in the presence of things painfully obscure.

"To the interest others take in the child? Ah," said Jean, "if you feel as you do"—she hesitated—"don't ask me. Ask her!"

She went her way, and, standing there in thought, he waited for her to come, after an interval, into sight on the curve of the bridge. Then as the minutes elapsed without her doing so, he lounged, heavy and blank, up again to where he had found her. Manning, while his back was turned, had arrived with one of her aids to carry off the tea-things; and from a distance, planted on the lawn, he bent on these evolutions an attention unnaturally fixed. The women marched and countermarched, dismantling the table; he broodingly and vacantly watched them; then, as he lighted a fresh cigarette, he saw his mother come out of the house to give an eye to their work. She reached the spot and dropped a command or two; after which, joining him, she took in that her little company had dispersed.

"What has become of every one?"

Paul's replies were slow; but he gave her one now that was distinct. "After the talk on which I lately left you I should think you would know pretty well what had become of *me*."

She gave him a keen look; her face softened. "What on earth's the matter with you?"

He placidly smoked. "I've had my head punched."

"Nonsense—for all you mind me!" She scanned him again. "Are you ill, Paul?"

"I'm all right," he answered philosophically.

"Then kiss your old mammy." Solemnly, silently he obeyed her; but after he had done so she still held him before her eyes. She gave him a sharp pat. "You're worth them all!"

Paul made no acknowledgment of this tribute save to remark after an instant rather awkwardly: "I don't know where Tony is."

"I can do without Tony," said his mother. "But where's Tony's child?"

"Miss Armiger has taken her home."

"The clever thing!"—Mrs. Beever fairly applauded the feat. "She was here when you came out?"

"No, but Jean told me."

"Jean was here?"

"Yes; but she went over."

"Over to Bounds—after what has happened?" Mrs. Beever looked at first incredulous; then she looked stern again. "What in the name of goodness possesses her?"

"The wish to bid Effie good-night."

Mrs. Beever was silent a moment. "I wish to heaven she'd leave Effie alone!"

"Aren't there different ways of looking at that?"

"Plenty, no doubt—and only one decent one." The grossness of the girl's error seemed to loom larger. "I'm ashamed of her!" she declared.

"Well, I'm not!" Paul quietly returned.

"Oh, you—of course you excuse her!" In the agitation that he had produced Mrs. Beever bounced across an interval that brought her into view of an object from which, as she stopped short at the sight of it, her emotion drew fresh sustenance. "Why, there's the boat!"

"Mr. Vidal has brought it back," said Paul.

She faced round in surprise. "You've seen him?"

"No, but Jean told me."

The lady of Eastmead stared. "*She* has seen him? Then where on earth is he?"

"He's staying at Bounds," said Paul.

His mother's wonderment deepened. "He has got there already?"

Paul smoked a little: then he explained. "It's not very soon for Mr. Vidal—he puts things through. He's already engaged to her."

Mystified, at sea, Mrs. Beever dropped upon a bench. "Engaged to Jean?"

"Engaged to Miss Armiger."

She tossed her head with impatience. "What news is that? He was engaged to her five years ago!"

"Well, then he is still. They've patched it up."

Mrs. Beever was on her feet. "She has seen him?"

Tony Bream at this moment came rapidly down the lawn and had the effect of staying Paul's answer. The young man gave a jerk to the stump of his cigarette and turned away with marked nervousness.

XXVII

THE LADY of Eastmead fronted her neighbour with a certain grimness. "She has seen him—they've patched it up."

Breathless with curiosity, Tony yet made but a bite of her news. "It's on again—it's all right?"

"It's whatever you like to call it. I only know what Paul tells me."

Paul, at this, stopped in his slow retreat, wheeling about. "I only know what I had just now from Jean."

Tony's expression, in the presence of his young friend's, dropped almost comically into the considerate. "Oh, but I daresay it's so, old man. I was there when they met," he explained to Mrs. Beever, "and I saw for myself pretty well how it would go."

"I confess I didn't," she replied. Then she added: "It must have gone with a jump!"

"With a jump, precisely—and the jump was hers!" laughed Tony. "All's well that ends well!" He was heated—he wiped his excited brow, and Mrs. Beever looked at him as if it struck her that she had helped him to more emotion than she wished him. "She's a most extraordinary girl," he went on, "and the effort she made there, all unprepared for it"—he nodded at the very spot of the exploit—"was magnificent in its way, one of the finest things I've ever seen." His appreciation of the results of this effort seemed almost feverish, and his elation deepened so that he turned, rather blindly, to poor Paul. "Upon my honour she's cleverer, she has more domestic resources, as one may say, than—I don't care whom!"

"Oh, we all know how clever she is!" Mrs. Beever impatiently grunted.

Tony's enthusiasm, none the less, overflowed; he was nervous for joy. "I thought I did myself, but she had a lot more to show me!" He addressed himself again to Paul. "She told you—with her coolness?"

Paul was occupied with another cigarette; he emitted no

sound, and his mother, with a glance at him, spoke for him. "Didn't you hear him say it was Jean who told him?"

"Oh, Jean!"—Tony looked graver. "She told Jean?" But his gaiety, at this image, quickly came back. "That was charming of her!"

Mrs. Beever remained cold. "Why on earth was it charming?"

Tony, though he reddened, was pulled up but an instant—his spirits carried him on. "Oh, because there hasn't been much between them, and it was a pretty mark of confidence." He glanced at his watch. "They're in the house?"

"Not in mine—in yours."

Tony looked surprised. "Rose and Vidal?"

Paul spoke at last. "Jean also went over—went after them."

Tony thought a moment. "'After them'—Jean? How long ago?"

"About a quarter of an hour," said Paul.

Tony continued to wonder. "Aren't you mistaken? They're not there now."

"How do you know," asked Mrs. Beever, "if you've not been home?"

"I *have* been home—I was there five minutes ago."

"Then how did you get here——?"

"By the long way? I took a fly. I went back to get a paper I had stupidly forgotten and that I needed for a fellow with whom I had to talk. Our talk was a bore for the want of it, so I drove over there and got it, and, as he had his train to catch, I then overtook him at the station. I ran it close, but I saw him off; and here I am." Tony shook his head. "There's no one at Bounds."

Mrs. Beever looked at Paul. "Then where's Effie?"

"Effie's not here?" Tony asked.

"Miss Armiger took her home," said Paul.

"You saw them go?"

"No, but Jean told me."

"Then where's Miss Armiger?" Tony continued. "And where's Jean herself?"

"Where's Effie herself—that's the question," said Mrs. Beever.

"No," Tony laughed, "the question's Where's Vidal? *He's*

the fellow I want to catch. I asked him to stay with me, and he said he'd go over, and it was my finding just now he hadn't come over that made me drive on here from the station to pick him up."

Mrs. Beever gave ear to this statement, but she gave nothing else. "Mr. Vidal can take care of himself; but if Effie's not at home, where is she?" She pressed her son. "Are you sure of what Jean said to you?"

Paul bethought himself. "Perfectly, mamma. She said Miss Armiger carried off the little girl."

Tony appeared struck with this. "That's exactly what Rose told me she meant to do. Then they're simply in the garden—they simply hadn't come in."

"They've been in gardens enough!" Mrs. Beever declared. "I should like to know the child's simply in bed."

"So should I," said Tony with an irritation that was just perceptible; "but I none the less deprecate the time-honoured custom of a flurry—I may say indeed of a panic—whenever she's for a moment out of sight." He spoke almost as if Mrs. Beever were trying to spoil for him by the note of anxiety the pleasantness of the news about Rose. The next moment, however, he questioned Paul with an evident return of the sense that toward a young man to whom such a hope was lost it was a time for special tact. "You, at any rate, dear boy, saw Jean go?"

"Oh, yes—I saw Jean go."

"And you understood from her that Rose and Effie went with Vidal?"

Paul consulted his memory. "I think Mr. Vidal went first."

Tony thought a moment. "Thanks so much, old chap." Then with an exaggerated gaiety that might have struck his companions had it not been the sign of so much of his conversation: "They're all a jolly party in the garden together. I'll go over."

Mrs. Beever had been watching the bridge. "Here comes Rose—she'll tell us."

Tony looked, but their friend had already dropped on the hither side, and he turned to Paul. "You wouldn't object—a—to dining——?"

"To meet Mr. Vidal?" Mrs. Beever interposed. "Poor

Paul," she laughed, "you're between two fires! You and your guest," she said to her neighbour, "had better dine here."

"Both fires at once?"—Tony smiled at her son. "Should you like that better?"

Paul, where he stood, was lost in the act of watching for Rose. He shook his head absently. "I don't care a rap!" Then he turned away again, and his mother, addressing Tony, dropped her voice.

"He won't show."

"Do you mean his feelings?"

"I mean for either of us."

Tony observed him a moment. "Poor lad, I'll bring him round!" After which, "Do you mind if I speak to her of it?" he abruptly inquired.

"To Rose—of this news?" Mrs. Beever looked at him hard, and it led her to reply with severity: "Tony Bream, I don't know what to make of you!" She was apparently on the point of making something rather bad, but she now saw Rose at the bottom of the slope and straightway hailed her. "You took Effie home?"

Rose came quickly up. "Not I! She isn't here?"

"She's gone," said Mrs. Beever. "Where is she?"

"I'm afraid I don't know. I gave her up." Paul had wheeled round at her first negation; Tony had not moved. Bright and handsome, but a little out of breath, she looked from one of her friends to the other. "You're sure she's not here?" Her surprise was fine.

Mrs. Beever's, however, had greater freedom. "How can she be, when Jean says you took her away?"

Rose Armiger stared; she threw back her head. "'Jean says?'" She looked round her. "Where *is* 'Jean'?"

"She's nowhere about—she's not in the house." Mrs. Beever challenged the two men, echoing the question as if it were indeed pertinent. "Where *is* the girl?"

"She has gone to Bounds," said Tony. "She's not in my garden?"

"She wasn't five minutes ago—I've just come out of it."

"Then what took you there?" asked Mrs. Beever.

"Mr. Vidal." Rose smiled at Tony: "*You* know what!" She turned again to Mrs. Beever, looking her full in the face. "I've seen him. I went over with him."

"Leaving Effie with Jean—precisely," said Tony, in his arranging way.

"She came out—she begged so hard," Rose explained to Mrs. Beever. "So I gave in."

"And yet Jean says the contrary?" this lady demanded in stupefaction of her son.

Rose turned, incredulous, to Paul. "She said to *you*—anything so false?"

"My dear boy, you simply didn't understand!" Tony laughed. "Give me a cigarette."

Paul's eyes, contracted to the pin-points we have already seen them become in his moments of emotion, had been attached, while he smoked still harder, to Rose's face. He turned very red and, before answering her, held out his cigarette-case. "That was what I remember she said—that you had gone with Effie to Bounds."

Rose stood wonderstruck. "When she had taken her from me herself——?"

Mrs. Beever referred her to Paul. "But she wasn't with Jean when he saw her!"

Rose appealed to him. "You saw Miss Martle alone?"

"Oh yes, quite alone." Paul now was crimson and without visible sight.

"My dear boy," cried Tony, impatient, "you simply *don't* remember."

"Yes, Tony. I remember."

Rose had turned grave—she gave Paul a sombre stare. "Then what on earth had she done with her?"

"What she had done was evident: she had taken her home!" Tony declared with an air of incipient disgust. They made a silly mystery of nothing.

Rose gave him a quick, strained smile. "But if the child's not there——?"

"You just told us yourself she isn't!" Mrs. Beever reminded him.

He hunched his shoulders as if there might be many explanations. "Then she's somewhere else. She's wherever Jean took her."

"But if Jean was here without her?"

"Then Jean, my dear lady, had come back."

"Come back to lie?" asked Mrs. Beever.

Tony coloured at this, but he controlled himself. "Dearest Mrs. Beever, Jean doesn't lie."

"Then somebody does!" Mrs. Beever roundly brought out.

"It's not you, Mr. Paul, I know!" Rose declared, discomposed but still smiling. "Was it you who saw her go over?"

"Yes; she left me here."

"How long ago?"

Paul looked as if fifty persons had been watching him. "Oh, not long!"

Rose addressed herself to the trio. "Then why on earth haven't I met her? She must explain her astounding statement!"

"You'll see that she'll explain it easily," said Tony.

"Ah, but, meanwhile, where's your daughter, don't you know?" Rose demanded with resentment.

"I'm just going over to see."

"Then please go!" she replied with a nervous laugh. She presented to the others, as a criticism of his inaction, a white, uneasy face.

"I want first," said Tony, "to express to you my real joy. Please believe in it."

She thought—she seemed to come back from a distance. "Oh, you know?" Then to Paul: "She told you? It's a detail," she added impatiently. "*The* question"—she thought again—"is the poor child." Once more she appealed to Paul. "Will you go and see?"

"Yes, go, boy." Tony patted his back.

"Go this moment," his mother put in.

He none the less lingered long enough to offer Rose his blind face. "I want also to express——"

She took him up with a wonderful laugh. "*Your* real joy, deal Mr. Paul?"

"Please believe in that too." And Paul, at an unwonted pace, took his way.

"I believe in everything—I believe in every one," Rose went on. "But I don't believe——" She hesitated, then checked herself. "No matter. Can you forgive me?" she asked of Mrs. Beever.

"For giving up the child?" The lady of Eastmead looked at

her hard. "No!" she said curtly, and, turning straight away, went and dropped into a seat from which she watched the retreating figures of her two parlourmaids, who carried off between them a basket containing the paraphernalia of tea. Rose, with a queer expression, but with her straight back to the painful past, quietly transferred her plea to Tony. "It was his coming—it made the difference. It upset me."

"Upset you? You were splendid!"

The light of what had happened was in her face as she considered him. "*You* are!" she replied. Then she added: "But he's finer than either of us!"

"I told you four years ago what he is. He's all right."

"Yes," said Rose—"he's all right. And *I* am—now," she went on. "You've been good to me." She put out her hand. "Good-bye."

"Good-bye? You're going?"

"He takes me away."

"But not to-night!"—Tony's native kindness, expressed in his inflection, felt that it could now risk almost all the forms he essentially liked.

From the depth of Rose's eyes peeped a distracted, ironic sense of this. But she said with all quietude: "To-morrow early. I may not see you."

"Don't be absurd!" laughed Tony.

"Ah, well—if you will!" She stood a moment looking down; then raising her eyes, "Don't hold my hand so long," she abruptly said. "Mrs. Beever, who has dismissed the servants, is watching us."

Tony had the appearance of having felt as if he had let it go; but at this, after a glance at the person indicated, staring and smiling with a clear face, he retained his grasp of it. "How in the world, with your back turned, can you see that?"

"It's with my back turned that I see most. She's looking at us hard."

"I don't care a hang!" said Tony gaily.

"Oh, I don't say it for myself!" But Rose withdrew her hand.

Tony put both his own into his pockets. "I hope you'll let me say to you—very simply—that I believe you'll be very happy."

"I shall be as happy as a woman can be who has abandoned her post."

"Oh, your post!"—Tony made a joke of that now. But he instantly added: "Your post will be to honour us with your company at Bounds again; which, as a married woman, you see, you'll be perfectly able to do."

She smiled at him. "How you arrange things!" Then with a musing headshake: "We leave England."

"How *you* arrange them!" Tony exclaimed. "He goes back to China?"

"Very soon—he's doing so well."

Tony hesitated. "I hope he has made money."

"A great deal. I should look better—shouldn't I?—if he hadn't. But I show you enough how little I care how I look. I blow hot and cold; I'm all there—then I'm off. No matter," she repeated. In a moment she added: "I accept your hopes for my happiness. It will do, no doubt, soon as I learn——!" Her voice dropped for impatience; she turned to the quarter of the approach from the other house.

"That Effie's all right?" Tony saw their messenger already in the shrubbery. "Here comes Paul to tell us."

Mrs. Beever rejoined them as he spoke. "It wasn't Paul on the bridge. It was the Doctor—without his hat."

"Without his hat?" Rose murmured.

"He has it in his hand," Tony cheerfully asserted as their good friend emerged from cover.

But he hadn't it in his hand, and at sight of them on the top of the slope he stopped short, stopped long enough to give Rose time to call eagerly: "Is Effie there?"

It was long enough also to give them all time to see, across the space, that his hair was disordered and his look at them strange; but they had no sooner done so than he made a violent gesture—a motion to check the downward rush that he evidently felt his aspect would provoke. It was so imperative that, coming up, he was with them before they had moved, showing them splashed, wet clothes and a little hard white face that Wilverley had never seen. "There has been an accident." Neither had Wilverley, gathered into three pair of ears, heard that voice.

The first effect of these things was to hold it an instant while Tony cried: "She's hurt?"

"She's killed?" cried Mrs. Beever.

"Stay where you are!" was the Doctor's stern response. Tony had given a bound, but, caught by the arm, found himself jerked, flaming red, face to face with Rose, who had been caught as tightly by the wrist. The Doctor closed his eyes for a second with this effort of restraint, but in the force he had put into it, which was not all of the hands, his captives submissively quivered. "You're not to go!" he declared—quite as if it were for their own good.

"She's dead?" Tony panted.

"Who's *with* her—who *was?*" cried Rose.

"Paul's with her—by the water."

"By the water?" Rose shrieked.

"My child's *drowned?*"—Tony's cry was strange.

The Doctor had been looking from one of them to the other; then he looked at Mrs. Beever, who, instantly, admirably, with a strength quickly acknowledged by the mute motion of his expressive little chin toward her, had stilled herself into the appeal of a blanched, breathless wait. "May *I* go?" sovereignly came from her.

"Go. There's no one else," he said as she bounced down the bank.

"No one else? Then where's that girl?"—Rose's question was fierce. She gave, as fiercely, to free herself, a great wrench of her arm, but the Doctor held her as if still to spare her what he himself had too dreadfully seen. He looked at Tony, who said with quick quietness—

"Ramage, have I lost my child?"

"You'll see—be brave. Not *yet*—I've told Paul. Be quiet!" the Doctor repeated; then his hand dropped on feeling that the movement he had meant to check in his friend was the vibration of a man stricken to weakness and sickened on the spot. Tony's face had turned black; he was rooted to the ground; he stared at Rose, to whom the Doctor said: "Who, Miss Armiger, was with her?"

All her lividness wondered. "When *was* it——?"

"God knows! She was there—against the bridge."

"Against the bridge—where I passed just now? *I* saw nothing!" Rose jerked, while Tony dumbly closed his eyes.

"I came over because she wasn't at the house, and—from the bank—*there* she was. I reached her—with the boat, with a push. She might have been half an hour——"

"It was half an hour ago she took her!" Rose broke in. "She's not there?"

The Doctor looked at her hard. "Of whom do you speak?"

"Why, of Miss Martle—whose hands are never off her." Rose's mask was the mask of Medusa. "What has become of Miss Martle?"

Dr. Ramage turned with the question to Tony, whose eyes, open now, were half out of his head. "What has become of her?"

"She's not there?" Tony articulated.

"There's no one there."

"Not Dennis?" sprang bewilderedly from Rose.

The Doctor stared. "Mr. Vidal? No, thank God—only Paul." Then pressing Tony: "Miss Martle was with her?"

Tony's eyes rolled over all space. "No—not Miss Martle."

"But *somebody* was!" Rose clamoured. "She wasn't alone!"

Tony fixed her an instant. "Not Miss Martle," he repeated.

"But who then? And where is she now?"

"It's positive she's not here?" the Doctor asked of Rose.

"Positive—Mrs. Beever knew. Where *is* she?" Rose rang out.

"Where in the name——?" passed, as with the dawn of a deeper horror, from their companion to Tony.

Tony's eyes sounded Rose's, and hers blazed back. His silence was an anguish, his face a convulsion. "It isn't half an hour," he at last brought out.

"Since it happened?" The Doctor blinked at his sudden knowledge. "Then when——?"

Tony looked at him straight. "When I was there."

"And when was that?"

"After I called for you."

"To leave word for me to go?" The Doctor set his face. "But you were not going home then."

"I did go—I had a reason. You know it," Tony said to Rose.

"When you went for your paper?" She thought. "But Effie wasn't there then."

"Why not? She was there, but Miss Martle wasn't with her."

"Then, in God's name, who was?" cried the Doctor.

"*I* was," said Tony.

Rose gave the inarticulate cry of a person who has been holding her breath, and the Doctor an equally loud, but more stupefied "You?"

Tony fixed upon Rose a gaze that seemed to count her respirations. "I was with her," he repeated; "and I was with her alone. And what was done—*I* did." He paused while they both gasped: then he looked at the Doctor. "Now you know." They continued to gasp; his confession was a blinding glare, in the shock of which the Doctor staggered back from Rose and she fell away with a liberated spring. "God forgive me!" howled Tony—he broke now into a storm of sobs. He dropped upon a bench with his wretched face in his hands, while Rose, with a passionate wail, threw herself, appalled, on the grass, and their companion, in a colder dismay, looked from one prostrate figure to the other.

BOOK THIRD

XXVIII

T HE GREATEST of the parlourmaids came from the hall into the drawing-room at Eastmead—the high, square temple of mahogany and tapestry in which, the last few years, Mrs. Beever had spent much time in rejoicing that she had never set up new gods. She had left it, from the first, as it was—full of the old things that, on succeeding to her husband's mother, she had been obliged, as a young woman of that period, to accept as dolefully different from the things thought beautiful by other young women whose views of drawing-rooms, all about her, had also been intensified by marriage. She had not unassistedly discovered the beauty of her heritage, and she had not from any such subtle suspicion kept her hands off it. She had never in her life taken any course with regard to any object for reasons that had so little to do with her duty. Everything in her house stood, at an angle of its own, on the solid rock of the discipline it had cost her. She had therefore lived with mere dry wistfulness through the age of rosewood, and had been rewarded by finding that, like those who sit still in runaway vehicles, she was the only person not thrown out. Her mahogany had never moved, but the way people talked about it had, and the people who talked were now eager to sit down with her on everything that both she and they had anciently thought plainest and poorest. It was Jean, above all, who had opened her eyes—opened them in particular to the great wine-dark doors, polished and silver-hinged, with which the lady of Eastmead, arriving at the depressed formula that they were "gloomy," had for thirty years, prudently on the whole, as she considered, shut out the question of taste. One of these doors Manning now softly closed, standing, however, with her hand on the knob and looking across, as if, in the stillness, to listen at another which exactly balanced with it on the opposite side of the room. The light of the long day had not wholly faded, but what remained of it was the glow of the western sky, which showed through the wide, high window that was still open to the garden. The sensible hush in which Manning waited was broken after a moment by a movement, ever so gentle, of the other door. Mrs. Beever put her head out of the next room; then, seeing her servant, closed the door with precautions and came forward. Her face, hard but overcharged, had pressingly asked a question.

"Yes, ma'am—Mr. Vidal. I showed him, as you told me, into the library."

Mrs. Beever thought. "It may be wanted. I'll see him here." But she checked the woman's retreat. "Mr. Beever's in his room?"

"No, ma'am—he went out."

"But a minute ago?"

"Longer, ma'am. After he carried in——"

Mrs. Beever stayed the phrase on Manning's lips and quickly supplied her own. "The dear little girl—yes. He went to Mr. Bream?"

"No, ma'am—the other way."

Mrs. Beever thought afresh. "But Miss Armiger's in?"

"Oh, yes—in her room."

"She went straight?"

Manning, on her side, reflected. "Yes, ma'am. She always goes straight."

"Not always," said Mrs. Beever. "But she's quiet there?"

"Very quiet."

"Then call Mr. Vidal." While Manning obeyed she turned to the window and stared at the gathering dusk. Then the door that had been left open closed again, and she faced about to Dennis Vidal.

"Something dreadful has happened?" he instantly asked.

"Something dreadful has happened. You've come from Bounds?"

"As fast as I could run. I saw Doctor Ramage there."

"And what did he tell you?"

"That I must come straight here."

"Nothing else?"

"That you would tell me," Dennis said. "I saw the shock in his face."

"But you didn't ask?"

"Nothing. Here I am."

"Here you are, thank God!" Mrs. Beever gave a muffled moan.

She was going on, but, eagerly, he went before her. "Can I help you?"

"Yes—if there *is* help. You can do so first by not asking me a question till I have put those I wish to yourself."

"Put them—put them!" he said impatiently.

At his peremptory note she quivered, showing him she was in the state in which every sound startles. She locked her lips and closed her eyes an instant; she held herself together with an effort. "I'm in great trouble, and I venture to believe that if you came back to me to-day it was because——"

He took her up shorter than before. "Because I thought of you as a friend? For God's sake, think of *me* as one!"

She pressed to her lips while she looked at him the small tight knot into which her nerves had crumpled her pocket-handkerchief. She had no tears—only a visible terror. "I've never appealed to one," she replied, "as I shall appeal to you now. Effie Bream is dead." Then as instant horror was in his eyes: "She was found in the water."

"The water?" Dennis gasped.

"Under the bridge—at the other side. She had been caught, she was held, in the slow current by some obstruction, and by the pier. Don't ask me *how*—when I arrived, by the mercy of heaven, she had been brought to the bank. But she was gone." With a movement of the head toward the room she had quitted, "We carried her back here," she went on. Vidal's face, which was terrible in the intensity of its sudden vision, struck her apparently as for the instant an echo, wild but interrogative, of what she had last said; so she explained quickly: "To think—to get more time." He turned straight away from her; he went, as she had done, to the window and, with his back presented, stood looking out in the mere rigour of dismay.

She was silent long enough to show a respect for the particular consternation that her manner of watching him betrayed her impression of having stirred; then she went on: "How long were you at Bounds with Rose?"

Dennis turned round without meeting her eyes or, at first, understanding her question. "At Bounds?"

"When, on your joining her, she went over with you."

He thought a moment. "She didn't go over with me. I went alone—after the child came out."

"You were there when Manning brought her?"—Mrs. Beever wondered. "Manning didn't tell me that."

"I found Rose on the lawn—with Mr. Bream—when I brought back your boat. He left us together—after inviting me to Bounds—and then the little girl arrived. Rose let me hold her, and I was with them till Miss Martle appeared. Then I—rather uncivilly—went off."

"You went without Rose?" Mrs. Beever asked.

"Yes—I left her with the little girl and Miss Martle." The marked effect of this statement made him add: "Was it your impression I didn't?"

His companion, before answering him, dropped into a seat and stared up at him; after which she articulated: "I'll tell you later. You left them," she demanded, "in the garden with the child?"

"In the garden with the child."

"Then you hadn't taken her?"

Dennis had for some seconds a failure either of memory or of courage; but whichever it was he completely overcame it. "By no means. She was in Rose's arms."

Mrs. Beever, at this image, lowered her eyes to the floor; after which, raising them again, she continued: "You went to Bounds?"

"No—I turned off short. I *was* going, but if I had a great deal to think of," Dennis pursued, "after I had learned from you she was here, the quantity wasn't of course diminished by our personal encounter." He hesitated. "I had seen her with *him*."

"Well?" said Mrs. Beever as he paused again.

"I asked you if she was in love with him."

"And I bade you find out for yourself."

"I've found out," Dennis said.

"Well?" Mrs. Beever repeated.

It was evidently, even in this tighter tension, something of an ease to all his soreness to tell her. "I've never seen anything like it—and there's not much I've not seen."

"That's exactly what the Doctor says!"

Dennis stared, but after a moment, "And does the Doctor say Mr. Bream cares?" he somewhat artlessly inquired.

"Not a farthing."

"Not a farthing. I'm bound to say—I could see it for myself," he declared, "that he has behaved very well." Mrs. Beever, at this, turning in torment on her seat, gave a smothered wail which pulled him up so that he went on in surprise: "Don't you think that?"

"I'll tell you later," she answered. "In the presence of this misery I don't judge him.

"No more do I. But what I was going to say was that, all the same, the way he has with a woman, the way he had with *her* there, and his damned good looks and his great happiness——"

"His great happiness? God help him!" Mrs. Beever broke out, springing up again in her emotion. She stood before him with pleading hands. "Where *were* you then?"

"After I left the garden? I was upset, I was dissatisfied—I didn't go over. I lighted a cigar; I passed out of the gate by your little closed pavilion and kept on by the river."

"By the river?"—Mrs. Beever was blank. "Then why didn't you see——?"

"What happened to the child? Because if it happened near the bridge I had left the bridge behind."

"But you were in sight——"

"For five minutes," Dennis said. "I was in sight perhaps even for ten. I strolled there, I turned things over, I watched the stream and, finally—just at the sharp bend—I sat a little on the stile beyond that smart new boat-house."

"It's a horrid thing." Mrs. Beever considered. "But you see the bridge from the boat-house."

Dennis hesitated. "Yes—it's a good way, but you've a glimpse."

"Which showed you nothing at all?"

"Nothing at all?"—his echo of the question was interrogative, and it carried him uneasily to the window, where he again, for a little, stared out. The pink of the sky had faded and dusk had begun in the room. At last he faced about. "No—I saw something. But I'll not tell you what it was, please, till I've myself asked you a thing or two."

Mrs. Beever was silent at this: they stood face to face in the twilight. Then she slowly exhaled a throb of her anguish. "I think you'll be a help."

"How much of one," he bitterly demanded, "shall I be to myself?" But he continued before she could meet the question: "I went back to the bridge, and as I approached it Miss Martle came down to it from your garden."

Mrs. Beever grabbed his arm. "Without the child?" He was silent so long that she repeated it: "Without the child?"

He finally spoke. "Without the child."

She looked at him as she showed that she felt she had never looked at any man. "On your sacred honour?"

"On my sacred honour."

She closed her eyes as she had closed them at the beginning of their talk, and the same defeated spasm passed over her face. "You *are* a help," she said.

"Well," Dennis replied straightforwardly, "if it's being one to let you know that she was with me from that moment——"

Breathless she caught him up. "With *you?*—till when?"

"Till just now, when we again separated at the gate-house: I to go over to Bounds, as I had promised Mr. Bream, and Miss Martle——"

Again she snatched the words from him. "To come straight in? Oh, glory be to God!"

Dennis showed some bewilderment. "She *did* come——?"

"Mercy, yes—to meet this horror. She's with Effie." She returned to it, to have it again. "She was *with* you?"

"A quarter of an hour—perhaps more." At this Mrs. Beever dropped upon her sofa again and gave herself to the tears that had not sooner come. She sobbed softly, controlling them, and Dennis watched her with hard, haggard pity; after which he said: "As soon as I saw her I spoke to her—I felt that I wanted her."

"You wanted her?"—in the clearer medium through which Mrs. Beever now could look up there were still obscurities.

He hesitated. "For what she might say to me. I told you, when we spoke of Rose after my arrival, that I had not come to watch her. But while I was with them"—he jerked his head at the garden—"something remarkable took place."

Mrs. Beever rose again. "I know what took place."

He seemed struck. "You know it?"

"She told Jean."

Dennis stared. "I think not."

"Jean didn't speak of it to you?"

"Not a word."

"She spoke of it to Paul," said Mrs. Beever. Then, to be more specific: "Something highly remarkable. I mean your engagement."

Dennis was mute; but at last, in the gathered gloom, his voice was stranger than his silence. "My engagement?"

"Didn't you, on the spot, induce her to renew it?"

Again, for some time, he was dumb. "Has she said so?" he then asked.

"To every one."

Once more he waited. "I should like to see her."

"Here she is."

The door from the hall had opened as he spoke: Rose Armiger stood there. She addressed him straight and as if she had not seen Mrs. Beever. "I knew you'd be here—I must see you."

Mrs. Beever passed quickly to the side of the room at which she had entered, where her fifty years of order abruptly came out to Dennis. "Will you have lights?"

It was Rose who replied. "No lights, thanks." But she stayed her hostess. "May I see her?"

Mrs. Beever fixed a look through the dusk. "No!" And she slipped soundlessly away.

XXIX

Rose had come for a purpose, Vidal saw, to which she would make but a bound, and she seemed in fact to take the spring as she instantly broke out: "For what did you come back to me?—for what did you come back?" She approached him quickly, but he made, more quickly, a move that gained him space and that might well have been the result of two sharp impressions: one of these the sense that in a single hour she had so altered as to be ugly, without a trace of the charm that had haunted him; and the other the sense that, thus ravaged and disfigured, wrecked in the gust that had come and gone, she required of him something that she had never required. A monstrous reality flared up in their relation, the perception of which was a shock that he was conscious for the moment of betraying that he feared, finding no words to answer her and showing her, across the room, while she repeated her question, a face blanched by the change in her own. "For what did you come back to me?—for what did you come back?"

He gaped at her; then as if there were help for him in the simple fact that on his own side he could immediately recall, he stammered out: "To you—to you? I hadn't the slightest notion you were here!"

"Didn't you come to see where I was? Didn't you come absolutely and publicly *for* me?" He jerked round again to the window with the vague, wild gesture of a man in horrible pain, and she went on without vehemence, but with clear, deep intensity: "It was exactly when you found I was here that you did come back. You had a perfect chance, on learning it, not to show; but you didn't take the chance, you quickly put it aside. You reflected, you decided, you insisted we should meet." Her voice, as if in harmony with the power of her plea, dropped to a vibration more muffled, a soft but inexorable pressure. "I hadn't called you, I hadn't troubled you, I left you as perfectly alone as I've *been* alone. It was your own passion and your own act—you've dropped upon me, you've overwhelmed me. You've overwhelmed me, I say, because I speak from the depths of *my* surrender. But you didn't do it, I imagine, to be cruel, and if you didn't do it to be cruel you did it to take what it would give you." Gradually, as she talked, he faced round again; she stood there supported by the high back of a chair, either side of which she held tight. "You know what I am, if any man has known, and it's to the thing I am—whatever that is—you've come back at last from so far. It's the thing I am—whatever that is—I now count on you to stand by."

"Whatever that is?"—Dennis mournfully marvelled. "I feel, on the contrary, that I've never, never known!"

"Well, it's before anything a woman who has such a need as no woman has ever had." Then she eagerly added: "Why on earth did you descend on me if you hadn't need of *me*?"

Dennis took for an instant, quite as if she were not there, several turns in the wide place; moving in the dumb distress of a man confronted with the greatest danger of his life and obliged, while precious minutes lapse, to snatch at a way of safety. His whole air was an instinctive retreat from being carried by assault, and he had the effect both of keeping far from her and of revolving blindly round her. At last, in his hesitation, he pulled up before her. "What makes, all of a sudden, the tremendous need you speak of? Didn't you remind me but an hour ago of how remarkably low, at our last meeting, it had dropped?"

Rose's eyes, in the dimness, widened with their wonder. "You can speak to me in harshness of what I did an hour ago? You can taunt me with an act of penance that might have moved you—that did move you? Does it mean," she continued, "that you've none the less embraced the alternative that seems to you most worthy of your courage? Did I only stoop, in my deep contrition, to make it easier for you to knock me down? I gave you your chance to refuse me, and what you've come back for then will have been only, most handsomely, to take it. In that case you did injustice there to the question of your revenge. What fault have you to find with anything so splendid?"

Dennis had listened with his eyes averted, and he met her own again as if he had not heard, only bringing out his previous words with a harder iteration: "What makes your tremendous need? what makes your tremendous need?"—he spoke as

if that tone were the way of safety. "I don't in the least see
why it should have taken such a jump. You must do justice,
even after your act of this afternoon—a demonstration far
greater than any I dreamed of asking of you—you must do
justice to my absolute necessity for seeing everything clear. I
didn't there in the garden see anything clear at all—I was only
startled and wonder-struck and puzzled. Certainly I was
touched, as you say—I was so touched that I particularly suffered. But I couldn't pretend I was satisfied or gratified, or
even that I was particularly convinced. You often failed of old,
I know, to give me what I really wanted from you, and yet it
never prevented the success of your effect on—what shall I call
it?" He stopped short. "On God knows what baser, obscurer
part of me! I'm not such a brute as to say," he quickly went
on, "that that effect was not produced this afternoon——"

"You confine yourself to saying," Rose interrupted, "that
it's not produced in our actual situation."

He stared through the thicker dusk; after which, "I don't
understand you!" he dropped. "I do say," he declared, "that,
whatever your success to-day may be admitted to consist of, I
didn't at least then make the admission. I didn't at that moment understand you any more than I do now; and I don't
think I said anything to lead you to suppose I did. I showed
you simply that I was bewildered, and I couldn't have shown
it more than by the abrupt way I left you. I don't recognise
that I'm committed to anything that deprives me of the right
of asking you for a little more light."

"Do you recognise by chance," Rose returned, "the horrible blow——?"

"That has fallen on all this wretched place? I'm unutterably
shocked by it. But where does it come into our relations?"

Rose smiled in exquisite pity, which had the air, however, of
being more especially for herself. "You say you were painfully
affected; but you really invite me to go further still. Haven't
I put the dots on all the horrid i's and dragged myself
through the dust of enough confessions?"

Dennis slowly and grimly shook his head; he doggedly
clung to his only refuge. "I don't understand you—I don't
understand you."

Rose, at this, surmounted her scruples. "It would be inexpressibly horrible to me to appear to be free to profit by Mr. Bream's misfortune."

Dennis thought a moment. "To appear, you mean, to have an interest in the fact that the death of his daughter leaves him at liberty to invite you to become his wife?"

"You express it to admiration."

He discernibly wondered. "But why should you be in danger of that torment to your delicacy if Mr. Bream has the best of reasons for doing nothing to contribute to it?"

"The best of Mr. Bream's reasons," Rose rejoined, "won't be nearly so good as the worst of mine."

"That of your making a match with some one else? I see," her companion said. "That's the precaution I'm to have the privilege of putting in your power."

She gave the strangest of smiles; the whites of her excited eyes shimmered in the gloom. "Your loyalty makes my position perfect."

Dennis hesitated. "And what does it make my own?"

"Exactly the one you came to take. You *have* taken it by your startling presence; you're up to your eyes in it, and there's nothing that will become you so as to wear it bravely and gallantly. If you don't like it," Rose added, "you should have thought of that before!"

"You like it so much on your side," Dennis retorted, "that you appear to have engaged in measures to create it even before the argument for it had acquired the force that you give such a fine account of."

"Do you mean by giving it out as an accomplished fact? It was never too soon to give it out; the right moment was the moment you were there. Your arrival changed everything; it gave me on the spot my advantage; it precipitated my grasp of it."

Vidal's expression was like a thing battered dead, and his voice was a sound that matched it. "You call your grasp your announcement——?"

She threw back her head. "My announcement *has* reached you? Then you know I've cut off your retreat." Again he turned away from her; he flung himself on the sofa on which, shortly before, Mrs. Beever had sunk down to sob, and, as if with the need to hold on to something, buried his face in one of the hard, square cushions. She came a little nearer to him; she went on with her low lucidity: "So you can't abandon me—you can't. You came to me through doubts—you spoke to me through fears. You're mine!"

She left him to turn this over; she moved off and approached the door at which Mrs. Beever had gone out, standing there in strained attention till, in the silence, Dennis at last raised his head. "What is it you look to me to do?" he asked.

She came away from the door. "Simply to see me through."

He was on his feet again. "Through what, in the name of horror?"

"Through everything. If I count on you, it's to support me. If I say things, it's for you to say them."

"Even when they're black lies?" Dennis brought out.

Her answer was immediate. "What need should I have of you if they were white ones?" He was unable to tell her, only meeting her mettle with his stupor, and she continued, with the lightest hint of reproach in her quiet pain: "I thank you for giving that graceful name to my weak boast that you admire me."

He had a sense of comparative idiotcy. "Do you expect me—on that admiration—to marry you?"

"Bless your innocent heart, no!—for what do you take me? I expect you simply to make people believe that you mean to."

"And how long will they believe it if I don't?"

"Oh, if it should come to that," said Rose, "you can easily make them believe that you *have*!" She took a step so rapid that it was almost a spring; she had him now and, with her hands on his shoulders, she held him fast. "So you see, after all, dearest, how little I ask!"

He submitted, with no movement but to close his eyes before the new-born dread of her caress. Yet he took the caress when it came—the dire confession of her hard embrace, the long entreaty of her stony kiss. He might still have been a creature trapped in steel; after she had let him go he still stood at a loss how to turn. There was something, however, that he presently opened his eyes to try. "That you went over with *me*—that's what you wish me to say?"

"Over to Bounds? Is that what *I* said? I can't think." But she thought all the same. "Thank you for fixing it. If it's that, stick to it!"

"And to our having left the child with Miss Martle?"

This brought her up a moment. "Don't ask me—simply meet the case as it comes. I give you," she added in a marvellous manner, "a perfectly free hand!"

"You're very liberal," said Dennis, "but I think you simplify too much."

"I can hardly do that if to simplify is to leave it to your honour. It's the beauty of my position that *you're* believed."

"That, then, gives me a certain confidence in telling you that Miss Martle was the whole time with me."

Rose stared. "Of what time do you speak?"

"The time after you had gone over to Bounds with Effie."

Rose thought again. "Where was she with you?"

"By the river, on this side."

"On this side? You didn't go to Bounds?"

"Not when I left you for the purpose. I obeyed an impulse that made me do just the opposite. You see," said Dennis, "that there's a flaw in my honour! You had filled my cup too full—I couldn't carry it straight. I kept by the stream—I took a walk."

Rose gave a low, vague sound. "But Miss Martle and I were there together."

"You were together till you separated. On my return to the bridge I met her."

Rose hesitated. "Where was she going?"

"Over to Bounds—but I prevented her."

"You mean she joined you?"

"In the kindest manner—for another turn. I took her the same way again."

Once more Rose thought. "But if she was going over, why in the world should she have let you?"

Dennis considered. "I think she pitied me."

"Because she spoke to you of me?"

"No; because she didn't. But I spoke to her of you," said Dennis.

"And what did you say?"

He hung fire a moment. "That—a short time before—I saw you cross to Bounds."

Rose slowly sat down. "You saw me?"

"On the bridge, distinctly. With the child in your arms."

"Where were you then?"

"Far up the stream—beyond your observation."

She looked at him fixedly, her hands locked together between her knees. "You were watching me?" Portentous and ghostly, in the darker room, had become their confronted estrangement.

Dennis waited as if he had a choice of answers; but at last he simply said: "I saw no more."

His companion as slowly rose again and moved to the window, beyond which the garden had now grown vague. She stood before it a while; then, without coming away, turned her back to it, so that he saw her handsome head, with the face obscure, against the evening sky. "Shall I tell you who did it?" she asked.

Dennis Vidal faltered. "If you feel that you're prepared."

"I've been preparing. I see it's best." Again, however, she was silent.

This lasted so long that Dennis finally spoke. "Who did it?"

"Tony Bream—to marry Jean."

A loud sound leaped from him, which was thrown back by the sudden opening of the door and a consequent gush of light. Manning marched in with a high lamp, and Doctor Ramage stood on the threshold.

XXX

THE DOCTOR remained at the door while the maid put down her lamp, and he checked her as she proceeded to the blinds and the other duties of the moment.

"Leave the windows, please; it's warm. That will do—thanks." He closed the door on her extinguished presence and he held it a little, mutely, with observing eyes, in that of Dennis and Rose.

"Do you want *me?*" the latter promptly asked, in the tone, as he liked, of readiness either to meet him or to withdraw. She seemed to imply that at such an hour there was no knowing what any one might want. Dennis's eyes were on her as well as the Doctor's, and if the lamp now lighted her consciousness of looking horrible she could at least support herself with the sight of the crude embarrassment of others.

The Doctor, resorting to his inveterate practice when confronted with a question, consulted his watch. "I came in for Mr. Vidal, but I shall be glad of a word with you after I've seen him. I must ask you, therefore"—and he nodded at the third door of the room—"kindly to pass into the library."

Rose, without haste or delay, reached the point he indicated. "You wish me to wait there?"

"If you'll be so good."

"While you talk with *him?*"

"While I talk with 'him.'"

Her eyes held Vidal's a minute. "I'll wait." And she passed out.

The Doctor immediately attacked him. "I must appeal to you for a fraction of your time. I've seen Mrs. Beever."

Dennis hesitated. "I've done the same."

"It's because she has told me of your talk that I mention it. She sends you a message."

"A message?" Dennis looked as if it were open to him to question indirectness. "Where then is she?"

"With that distracted girl."

"Miss Martle?" Dennis hesitated. "Miss Martle so greatly feels the shock?"

"'Feels' it, my dear sir?" the Doctor cried. "She has been made so pitifully ill by it that there's no saying just what turn her condition may take, and she now calls for so much of my attention as to force me to plead, with you, that excuse for my brevity. Mrs. Beever," he rapidly pursued, "requests you to regard this hurried inquiry as the sequel to what you were so good as to say to her."

Dennis thought a moment; his face had changed as if by the action of Rose's disappearance and the instinctive revival, in a different relation, of the long, stiff habit of business, the art of treating affairs and meeting men. This was the art of not being surprised, and, with his emotion now controlled, he was discernibly on his guard. "I'm afraid," he replied, "that what I said to Mrs. Beever was a very small matter."

"She doesn't think it at all a small matter to have said you'd help her. You can do so—in the cruel demands our catastrophe makes of her—by considering that I represent her. It's in her name, therefore, that I ask you if you're engaged to be married to Miss Armiger."

Dennis had an irrepressible start; but it might have been quite as much at the freedom of the question as at the difficulty of the answer. "Please say to her that—I *am*." He spoke with a clearness that proved the steel surface he had in a few minutes forged for his despair.

The Doctor took the thing as he gave it, only drawing from his pocket a key, which he held straight up. "Then I feel it to be only right to say to you that this locks"—and he indicated the quarter to which Rose had retired—"the other door."

Dennis, with a diffident hand out, looked at him hard; but the good man showed with effect that he was professionally used to that. "You mean she's a prisoner?"

"On Mr. Vidal's honour."

"But whose prisoner?"

"Mrs. Beever's."

Dennis took the key, which passed into his pocket. "Don't you forget," he then asked with inscrutable gravity, "that we're here, all round, on a level——"

"With the garden?" the Doctor broke in. "I forget nothing. We've a friend on the terrace."

"A friend?"

"Mr. Beever. A friend of Miss Armiger's," he promptly added.

Still showing nothing in his face, Dennis perhaps showed something in the way that, with his eyes bent on the carpet and his hands interclenched behind him, he slowly walked across the room. At the end of it he turned round. "If I have this key, who has the other?"

"The other?"

"The key that confines Mr. Bream."

The Doctor winced, but he stood his ground. "I have it." Then he said as if with a due recognition of the weight of the circumstance: "She has told you?"

Dennis turned it over. "Mrs. Beever?"

"Miss Armiger." There was a faint sharpness in the Doctor's tone.

It had something evidently to do with the tone in which Dennis replied. "She has told me. But if you've left him——"

"I've not left him. I've brought him over."

Dennis showed himself at a loss. "To see *me?*"

The Doctor raised a solemn, reassuring hand; then, after an instant, "To see his child," he colourlessly said.

"He desires that?" Dennis asked with an accent that emulated this detachment.

"He desires that." Dennis turned away, and in the pause that followed the air seemed charged with a consciousness of all that between them was represented by the unspoken. It lasted indeed long enough to give to an auditor, had there been one, a sense of the dominant unspeakable. It was as if each were waiting to have something from the other first, and it was eventually clear that Dennis, who had not looked at his watch, was prepared to wait longest. The Doctor had moreover to recognise that he himself had sought the interview. He impatiently summed up his sense of their common attitude. "I do full justice to the difficulty created for you by your engagement. That's why it was important to have it from your own lips." His companion said nothing, and he went on: "Mrs. Beever, all the same, feels that it mustn't prevent us from putting you another question, or rather from reminding you that there's one that you led her just now to expect that you'll answer." The Doctor paused again, but he perceived he must go all the way. "From the bank of the river you saw something that bears upon this"—he hesitated; then daintily selected his words—"remarkable performance. We appeal to your sense of propriety to tell us what you saw."

Dennis considered. "My sense of propriety is strong; but so—just now—is my sense of some other things. My word to Mrs. Beever was contingent. There are points *I* want made clear."

"I'm here," said the Doctor, "to do what I can to satisfy you. Only be go good as to remember that time is everything." He added, to drive this home, in his neat, brisk way: "Some action has to be taken."

"You mean a declaration made?"

"Under penalty," the Doctor assented, "of consequences sufficiently tremendous. There has been an accident of a gravity——"

Dennis, with averted eyes, took him up. "That can't be explained away?"

The Doctor looked at his watch; then, still holding it, he quickly looked up at Dennis. "You wish her presented as dying of a natural cause?"

Vidal's haggard face turned red, but he instantly recovered himself. "Why do you ask, if you've a supreme duty?"

"I haven't *one*—worse luck. I've fifty."

Dennis fixed his eyes on the watch. "Does that mean you can keep the thing quiet?"

The Doctor put his talisman away. "Before I say I must know what you'll do for me."

Dennis stared at the lamp. "Hasn't it gone too far?"

"I know *how* far: not so far, by a peculiar mercy, as it might have gone. There has been an extraordinary coincidence of chances—a miracle of conditions. Everything appears to serve." He hesitated; then with great gravity: "We'll call it a providence and have done with it."

Dennis turned this over. "Do you allude to the absence of witnesses——?"

"At the moment the child was found. Only the blessed three of us. And she had been there——" Stupefaction left him counting.

Dennis jerked out a sick protest. "Don't tell me how long!

What do *I* want——?" What he wanted proved, the next moment, to be more knowledge. "How do you meet the servants?"

"Here? By giving a big name to her complaint. None of them have seen her. She was carried in with a success——!" The Doctor threw up triumphant little hands.

"But the people at the other house?"

"They know nothing but that over here she has had an attack which it will be one of the fifty duties of mine I mentioned to you to make sufficiently remarkable. She was out of sorts this morning—this afternoon I was summoned. That call of Tony's at my house is the providence!"

But still Dennis questioned. "Hadn't she some fond nurse—some devoted dragon?"

"The great Gorham? Yes: she didn't want her to come; she was cruelly overborne. Well," the Doctor lucidly pursued, "I must face the great Gorham. I'm already keeping her at bay—doctors, you see, are so luckily despots! They're blessedly bullies. She'll be tough—but it's all tough!"

Dennis, pressing his hand to his head, began wearily to pace again: it was far too tough for *him*. But he suddenly dropped upon the sofa, all but audibly moaning, falling back in the despair that broke through his false pluck. His interlocutor watched his pain as if he had something to hope from it; then abruptly the young man began: "I don't in the least conceive how——" He stopped short: even this he couldn't bring out.

"How was it done? Small blame to you! It was done in one minute—with the aid of a boat and the temptation (we'll call it!) of solitude. The boat's an old one of Tony's own—padlocked, but with a long chain. To see the place," said the Doctor after an instant, "is to see the deed."

Dennis threw back his head; he covered his distorted face with his two hands. "Why in thunder should I see it?"

The Doctor had moved towards him; at this he seated himself beside him and, going on with quiet clearness, applied a controlling, soothing grasp to his knee. "The child was taken into the boat and it was tilted: that was enough—the trick was played." Dennis remained motionless and dumb, and his companion completed the picture. "She was immersed—she

was held under water—she was made sure of. Oh, I grant you
it took a hand—and it took a spirit! But they were there.
Then she was left. A pull of the chain brought back the boat;
and the author of the crime walked away."

Dennis slowly shifted his position, dropped his head,
dropped his hands, sat staring lividly at the floor. "But how
could she be *caught*?"

The Doctor hesitated, as if in the presence of an ambiguity.
"The poor little girl? You'd see if you saw the place."

"I passed it to come back here," Dennis said. "But I didn't
look, for I didn't know."

The Doctor patted his knee. "If you had known you would
have looked still less. She rose; she drifted some yards; then
she was washed against the base of the bridge, and one of the
openings of her little dress hooked itself to an old loose
clamp. There she was kept."

"And no one came by?"

"No one came till, by the mercy of God, *I* came!"

Dennis took it in as if with a long, dry gulp, and the two
men sat for a minute looking at each other. At last the
younger one got up. "And yet the risk of anything but a
straight course is hideous."

The Doctor kept his place. "Everything's hideous. I appreciate greatly," he added, "the gallantry of your reminding me
of my danger. Don't think I don't know exactly what it is.
But I have to think of the danger of others. I can measure
mine; I can't measure theirs."

"I can return your compliment," Dennis replied. "'Theirs,'
as you call it, seems to me such a fine thing for you to care
for."

The Doctor, with his plump hands folded on his stomach,
gave a small stony smile. "My dear man, I care for my
friends!"

Dennis stood before him; he was visibly mystified. "There's
a person whom it's very good of you to take this occasion of
calling by that name!"

Doctor Ramage stared; with his vision of his interlocutor's
mistake all his tight curves grew tense. Then, as he sprang to
his feet, he seemed to crack in a grim little laugh. "The person you allude to is, I confess, not, my dear sir——"

"One of the persons," said Dennis, "whom you wish to protect? It certainly would have surprised me to hear it! But you spoke of your 'friends.' Who then is your second one?"

The Doctor looked astonished at the question. "Why, sweet Jean Martle."

Dennis equally wondered. "I should have supposed her the first! Who then is the other?"

The Doctor lifted his shoulders. "Who but poor Tony Bream?"

Dennis thought a moment. "What's *his* danger?"

The Doctor grew more amazed. "The danger we've been talking of!"

"Have we been talking of *that*?"

"You ask me, when you told me you knew——?"

Dennis, hesitating, recalled. "Knew that he's accused——?"

His companion fairly sprang at him. "Accused by *her* too?"

Dennis fell back at his onset. "Is he by anybody else?"

The Doctor, turning crimson, had grabbed his arm; he blazed up at him. "You don't know it all?"

Dennis faltered. "Is there any more?"

"Tony cries on the housetops that *he* did it!"

Dennis, blank and bewildered, sank once more on his sofa. "*He* cries——?"

"To cover Jean."

Dennis took it in. "But if she *is* covered?"

"Then to shield Miss Armiger."

Poor Dennis gazed aghast. "Who meanwhile denounces him?" He was on his feet again; again he moved to the open window and stood there while the Doctor in silence waited. Presently he turned round. "May I see him?"

The Doctor, as if he had expected this, was already at the door. "God bless you!" And he flashed out.

Dennis, left alone, remained rigid in the middle of the room, immersed apparently in a stupor of emotion; then, as if shaken out of it by a return of conscious suffering, he passed in a couple of strides to the door of the library. Here, however, with his hand on the knob, he yielded to another impulse, which kept him irresolute, listening, drawing his breath in pain. Suddenly he turned away—Tony Bream had come in.

XXXI

"I F IN this miserable hour I've asked you for a moment of your time," Dennis immediately said, "I beg you to believe it's only to let you know that anything in this world I can do for you——" Tony raised a hand that mutely discouraged as well as thanked him, but he completely delivered himself: "I'm ready, whatever it is, to do on the spot."

With his handsome face smitten, his red eyes contracted, his thick hair disordered and his black garments awry, Tony had the handled, hustled look of a man just dragged through some riot or some rescue and only released to take breath. Like Rose, for Dennis, he was deeply disfigured, but with a change more passive and tragic. His bloodshot eyes fixed his interlocutor's. "I'm afraid there's nothing any one can do for me. My disaster's overwhelming; but I must meet it myself."

There was courtesy in his voice; but there was something hard and dry in the way he stood there, something so opposed to his usual fine overflow that for a minute Dennis could only show by pitying silence the full sense of his wretchedness. He was in the presence of a passionate perversity—an attitude in which the whole man had already petrified. "Will it perhaps help you to think of something," he presently said, "if I tell you that your disaster is almost as much mine as yours, and that what's of aid to one of us may perhaps therefore be of aid to the other?"

"It's very good of you," Tony replied, "to be willing to take upon you the smallest corner of so big a burden. Don't do that—don't do that, Mr. Vidal," he repeated, with a heavy head-shake. "Don't come near such a thing; don't touch it; don't know it!" He straightened himself as if with a long, suppressed shudder; and then with a sharper and more sombre vehemence, "Stand from under it!" he exclaimed. Dennis, in deeper compassion, looked at him with an intensity that might have suggested submission, and Tony followed up what he apparently took for an advantage. "You came here for an hour, for your own reasons, for your relief: you came in all kindness and trust. You've encountered an unutterable horror, and you've only one thing to do."

"Be so good as to name it," said Dennis.

"Turn your back on it for ever—go your way this minute. I've come to you simply to say that."

"Leave you, in other words——?"

"By the very first train that will take you."

Dennis appeared to turn this over; then he spoke with a face that showed what he thought of it. "It has been my unfortunate fate in coming to this place—so wrapped, as one might suppose, in comfort and peace—to intrude a second time on obscure, unhappy things, on suffering and danger and death. I should have been glad, God knows, not to renew the adventure, but one's destiny kicks one before it, and I seem myself not the least part of the misery I speak of. You must accept that as my excuse for not taking your advice. I must stay at least till you understand me." On this he waited a moment; after which, abruptly, impatiently, "For God's sake, Mr. Bream, believe in me and meet me!" he broke out.

"Meet you?"

"Make use of the hand I hold out to you!"

Tony had remained just within the closed door, as if to guard against its moving from the other side. At this, with a faint flush in his dead vacancy, he came a few steps further. But there was something still locked in his conscious, altered eyes, and coldly absent from the tone in which he said: "You've come, I think, from China?"

"I've come, Mr. Bream, from China."

"And it's open to you to go back?"

Dennis frowned. "I can do as I wish."

"And yet you're not off like a shot?"

"My movements and my inclinations are my own affair. You won't accept my aid?"

Tony gave his sombre stare. "You ask me, as you call it, to meet you. I beg you to excuse me if on my side I first inquire on what definite ground——?"

Dennis took him straight up. "On the definite ground on which Doctor Ramage is good enough to do so. I'm afraid there's no better ground than my honour."

Tony's stare was long and deep; then he put out his hand, and while Dennis held it, "I understand you," he said. "Good-bye."

Dennis kept hold of him. "Good-bye?"

Tony had a supreme hesitation. "She's safe."

Dennis had a shorter one. "Do you speak of Miss Martle?"

"Not of Miss Martle."

"Then I can. *She's* safe."

"Thank you," said Tony. He drew away his hand.

"As for the person you do speak of, if *you* say it——" and Dennis paused.

"She's safe," Tony repeated.

"That's all I ask of you. The Doctor will do the rest."

"I know what the Doctor will do." Tony was silent a moment. "What will you do?"

Dennis waited, but at last he spoke. "Everything but marry her."

A flare of admiration rose and fell in Tony's eyes. "You're beyond me!"

"I don't in the least know where I am, save that I'm in a black, bloody nightmare and that it's not I, it's not she, it's not you, it's not any one. I shall wake up at last, I suppose, but meanwhile——"

"There's plenty more to come? Oh, as much as you like!" Tony excitedly declared.

"For me, but not for you. For you the worst's over," his companion boldly observed.

"Over? with all my life made hideous?"

There was a certain sturdiness in Vidal's momentary silence. "You think so now——!" Then he added more gently: "I grant you it's hideous enough."

Tony stood there in the agony of the actual; the tears welled into his hot eyes. "She murdered—she tortured my child. And she did it to incriminate Jean."

He brought it all back to Dennis, who exclaimed with simple solemnity: "The dear little girl—the sweet, kind little girl!" With a sudden impulse that, in the midst of this tenderness, seemed almost savage, he laid on Tony's shoulder a hard, conscientious hand. "She forced her in. She held her down. She left her."

The men turned paler as they looked at each other. "I'm infamous—I'm infamous," said Tony.

There was a long pause that was like a strange assent from Dennis, who at last, however, brought out in a different tone: "It was her passion."

"It was her passion."

"She loves you——!" Dennis went on with a drop, before the red real, of all vain terms.

"She loves me!"—Tony's face reflected the mere monstrous fact. "It has made what it has made—her awful act and my silence. My silence is a part of the crime and the cruelty—I shall live to be a horror to myself. But I see it, none the less, as I see it, and I shall keep the word I gave her in the first madness of my fear. It came to me—there it is."

"I know what came to you," Dennis said.

Tony wondered. "Then you've seen her?"

Dennis hesitated. "I know it from the Doctor."

"I see——" Tony thought a moment. "She, I imagine——"

"Will keep it to herself? Leave that to me!" Dennis put out his hand again. "Good-bye."

"You take her away?"

"To-night."

Tony kept his hand. "Will her flight help Ramage?"

"Everything falls in. Three hours ago I came for her."

"So it will seem pre-arranged?"

"For the event she announced to you. Our happy union!" said Dennis Vidal.

He reached the door to the hall, where Tony checked him. "There's nothing, then, I shall do for *you?*"

"It's done. We've helped each other."

What was deepest in Tony stirred again. "I mean when your trouble has passed."

"It will never pass. Think of that when you're happy yourself."

Tony's grey face stared. "How shall I ever be——?"

The door, as he spoke, opened from the room to which Mrs. Beever had returned, and Jean Martle appeared to them. Dennis retreated. "Ask *her!*" he said from the threshold.

XXXII

RUSHING to Tony, she wailed under her breath: "I must speak to you—I must speak to you! But how can you ever look at me?—how can you ever forgive me?" In an instant he had met her; in a flash the gulf was bridged: his arms had opened wide to her and she had thrown herself into them. They had only to be face to face to let themselves go; he making no answer but to press her close against him, she pouring out her tears upon him as if the contact quickened the source. He held her and she yielded with a passion no bliss could have given; they stood locked together in their misery with no sound and no motion but her sobs. Breast to breast and cheek to cheek, they felt simply that they had ceased to be apart. This long embrace was the extinction of all limits and questions—swept away in a flood which tossed them over the years and in which nothing remained erect but the sense and the need of each other. These things had now the beauty of all the tenderness that they had never spoken and that, for some time, even as they clung there, was too strange and too deep for speech. But what was extraordinary was that as Jean disengaged herself there was neither wonder nor fear between them; nothing but a recognition in which everything swam and, on the girl's part, the still higher tide of the remorse that harried her and that, to see him, had made her break away from the others. "They tell me I'm ill, I'm insane," she went on—"they want to shut me up, to give me things—they tell me to lie down, to try to sleep. But it's all to me, so dreadfully, as if it were *I* who had done it, that when they admitted to me that you were here I felt that if I didn't see you it would make me as crazy as they say. It's to have seen her go—to have seen her go: that's what I can't bear— it's too horrible!" She continued to sob; she stood there before him swayed to and fro in her grief. She stirred up his own, and that added to her pain; for a minute, in their separate sorrow, they moved asunder like creatures too stricken to communicate. But they were quickly face to face again, more intimate, with more understood, though with the air, on

either side and in the very freedom of their action, of a clear
vision of the effect of their precipitated union—the instinct of
not again touching it with unconsecrated hands. Tony had no
idle words, no easy consolation; she only made him see more
vividly what had happened, and they hung over it together
while she accused and reviled herself. "I let her go—I let her
go; that's what's so terrible, so hideous. I might have got
her—have kept her; I might have screamed, I might have
rushed for help. But how could I know or dream? How could
the worst of my fears——?" She broke off, she shuddered and
dropped; she sat and sobbed while he came and went. "I see
her little face as she left me—she looked at me as if she knew.
She wondered and dreaded: she knew—she knew! It was the
last little look I was to have from her, and I didn't even answer it with a kiss. She sat there where I could seize her, but
I never raised a hand. I was close, I was *there*—she must have
called for me in her terror! I didn't listen—I didn't come—I
only gave her up to be murdered! And now I shall be punished for ever: I shall see her in those arms—in those arms!"
Jean flung herself down and hid her face; her smothered wild
lament filled the room.

Tony stopped before her, seeing everything she brought
up, but only the more helpless in his pity. "It was the only
little minute in all the years that you had been forced to fail
her. She was always more yours than mine."

Jean could only look out through her storm-beaten window. "It was just because she was yours that she was mine. It
was because she was yours from the first hour that I——!"
She broke down again; she tried to hold herself; she got up.
"What could I do, you see? To you I couldn't be kind." She
was as exposed in her young, pure woe as a bride might have
been in her joy.

Tony looked as if he were retracing the saddest story on
earth. "I don't see how you could have been kinder."

She wondered with her blinded eyes. "That wasn't what
thought I was—it *couldn't* be, ever, ever. Didn't I try not to
think of you? But the child was a beautiful part of you—the
child I could take and keep. I could take her altogether, without thinking or remembering. It was the only thing I could
do for you, and you let me, always, and *she* did. So I thought

it would go on, for wasn't it happiness enough? But all the horrible things—I didn't know them till to-day! There they were—so near to us; and there they closed over her, and—oh!" She turned away in a fresh wild spasm, inarticulate and distracted.

They wandered in silence, as if it made them more companions; but at last Tony said: "She was a little radiant, perfect thing. Even if she had not been mine you would have loved her." Then he went on, as if feeling his way through his thickest darkness: "If she had not been mine she wouldn't be lying there as I've seen her. Yet I'm glad she was mine!" he said.

"She lies there because I loved her and because I so insanely showed it. That's why it's I who killed her!" broke passionately from Jean.

He answered nothing till he quietly and gently answered: "It was *I* who killed her."

She roamed to and fro, slowly controlling herself, taking this at first as a mere torment like her own. "We seem beautifully eager for the guilt!"

"It doesn't matter what any one else seems. I must tell you all—now. I've taken the act on myself."

She had stopped short, bewildered. "How have you taken it——?"

"To meet whatever may come."

She turned as white as ashes. "You mean you've accused yourself?"

"Any one may accuse me. Whom is it more natural to accuse? What had she to gain? My own motive is flagrant. There it is," said Tony.

Jean withered beneath this new stroke. "You'll say you did it?"

"I'll say I did it."

Her face grew old with terror. "You'll lie? You'll perjure yourself?"

"I'll say I did it for you."

She suddenly turned crimson. "Then what do you think *I'll* say?"

Tony coldly considered. "Whatever you say will tell against me."

"Against you?"

"If the crime was committed for you."

"'For' me?" she echoed again.

"To enable us to marry."

"Marry?—*we?*" Jean looked at it in blighted horror.

"It won't be of any consequence that we shan't, that we can't: it will only stand out clear that we *can.*" His sombre ingenuity halted, but he achieved his demonstration. "So I shall save—whom I wish to save."

Jean gave a fiercer wail. "You wish to save *her?*"

"I don't wish to hand her over. You can't conceive it?"

"I?" The girl looked about her for a negation not too vile. "I wish to hunt her to death! I wish to burn her alive!" All her emotion had changed to stupefaction; the flame in her eyes had dried them. "You mean she's not to suffer?"

"You want her to suffer—all?"

She was ablaze with the light of justice. "How can anything be enough? I could tear her limb from limb. That's what she tried to do to me!"

Tony lucidly concurred. "Yes—what she tried to do to you."

But she had already flashed round. "And yet you condone the atrocity——?"

Tony thought a moment. "Her doom will be to live."

"But how will such a fiend be suffered to live—when she went to it before my eyes?" Jean stared at the mountain of evidence; then eagerly: "And Mr. Vidal—her very lover, who'll swear what he knows—what he saw!"

Tony stubbornly shook his head. "Oh, Mr. Vidal!"

"To make me," Jean cried, "seem the monster——!"

Tony looked at her so strangely that she stopped. "She made it for the moment possible——"

She caught him up. "To suspect me——?"

"I was mad—and you're weren't there." With a muffled moan she sank down again; she covered her face with her hands. "I tell you all—I tell you all," he said. "He knows nothing—he saw nothing—he'll swear nothing. He's taking her away."

Jean started as if he had struck her. "She's here?"

Tony wondered. "You didn't know it?"

"She came back?" the girl panted.

"You thought she had fled?"

Jean hung there like a poised hawk. "Where *is* she?"

Tony gave her, with a grave gesture, a long, absolute look before which, gradually, her passion fell. "She has gone. Let her go."

She was silent a little. "But others: how will they——?"

"There are no others." After a moment he added: "She would have died for me."

The girl's pale wrath gave a flare. "So you want to die for *her*?"

"I shan't die. But I shall remember." Then, as she watched him, "I must tell you all," he said once more. "I knew it—I always knew it. And I made her come."

"You were kind to her—as you're always kind."

"No; I was more than that. And I should have been less." His face showed a rift in the blackness. "I remember."

She followed him in pain and at a distance. "You mean you liked it?"

"I liked it—while I was safe. Then I grew afraid."

"Afraid of what?"

"Afraid of everything. You don't know—but we're abysses. At least *I'm* one!" he groaned. He seemed to sound this depth. "There are other things. They go back far."

"Don't tell me all," said Jean. She had evidently enough to turn over. "What will become of her?" she asked.

"God knows. She goes forth."

"And Mr. Vidal with her?"

"Mr. Vidal with her."

Jean gazed at the tragic picture. "Because he still loves her?"

"Yes," said Tony Bream.

"Then what will he do?"

"Put the globe between them. Think of her torture," Tony added.

Jean looked as if she tried. "Do you mean *that*?"

He meant another matter. "To have only made us free."

Jean protested with all her woe. "It's her triumph—that our freedom is horrible!"

Tony hesitated; then his eyes distinguished in the outer

dusk Paul Beever, who had appeared at the long window which in the mild air stood open to the terrace. "It's horrible," he gravely replied.

Jean had not seen Paul; she only heard Tony's answer. It touched again the source of tears; she broke again into stifled sobs. So, blindly, slowly, while the two men watched her, she passed from the room by the door at which she had entered.

Y OU'RE looking for me?" Tony quickly asked.
Paul, blinking in the lamplight, showed the dismal
desert of his face. "I saw you through the open window, and
I thought I would let you know——"

"That some one wants me?" Tony was all ready.

"She hasn't asked for you; but I think that if you could do
it——"

"I can do anything," said Tony. "But of whom do you
speak?"

"Of one of your servants—poor Mrs. Gorham."

"Effie's nurse?—she has come over?"

"She's in the garden," Paul explained. "I've been flounder-
ing about—I came upon her."

Tony wondered. "But what's she doing?"

"Crying very hard—without a sound."

"And without coming in?"

"Out of discretion."

Tony thought a moment. "You mean because Jean and the
Doctor——?"

"Have taken complete charge. She bows to that, but she
sits there on a bench——"

"Weeping and wailing?" Tony asked. "Dear thing, I'll speak
to her."

He was about to leave the room in the summary manner
permitted by the long widow when Paul checked him with a
quiet reminder. "Hadn't you better have your hat?"

Tony looked about him—he had not brought it in.
"Why?—if it's a warm night?"

Paul approached him, laying on him as if to stay him a
heavy but friendly hand. "You never go out without it—don't
be too unusual."

"I see what you mean—I'll get it." And he made for the
door to the hall.

But Paul had not done with him. "It's much better you
should see her—it's unnatural you shouldn't. But do you

mind my just thinking for you the least bit—asking you for instance what it's your idea to say to her?"

Tony had the air of accepting this solicitude; but he met the inquiry with characteristic candour. "I think I've no idea but to talk with her of Effie."

Paul visibly wondered. "As dangerously ill? That's all she knows."

Tony considered an instant. "Yes, then—as dangerously ill. Whatever she's prepared for."

"But what are *you* prepared for? You're not afraid——?" Paul hesitated.

"Afraid of what?"

"Of suspicions—importunities; her making some noise."

Tony slowly shook his head. "I don't think," he said very gravely, "that I'm afraid of poor Gorham."

Paul looked as if he felt that his warning half failed. "Every one else is. She's tremendously devoted."

"Yes—that's what I mean."

Paul sounded him a moment. "You mean to *you?*"

The irony was so indulgent—and all irony on this young man's part was so rare—that Tony was to be excused for not perceiving it. "She'll do anything. We're the best of friends."

"Then get your hat," said Paul.

"It's much the best thing. Thank you for telling me." Even in a tragic hour there was so much in Tony of the ingenuous that, with his habit of good-nature and his hand on the door, he lingered for the comfort of his friend. "She'll be a re-source—a fund of memory. She'll know what I mean—I shall want some one. So we can always talk."

"Oh, *you're* safe!" Paul went on.

It had now all come to Tony. "I see my way with her."

"So do I!" said Paul.

Tony fairly brightened through his gloom. "I'll keep her on!" And he took his course by the front.

Left alone Paul closed the door on him, holding it a minute and lost evidently in reflections of which he was the subject. He exhaled a long sigh that was burdened with many things; then as he moved away his eyes attached themselves as if in sympathy with a vague impulse to the door of the library. He stood a moment irresolute; after which, deeply restless, he went to take up the hat that, on coming in, he had laid on one of the tables. He was in the act of doing this when the door of the library opened and Rose Armiger stood before him. She had since their last meeting changed her dress and, arrayed for a journey, wore a bonnet and a long, dark mantle. For some time after she appeared no word came from either; but at last she said: "Can you endure for a minute the sight of me?"

"I was hesitating—I thought of going to you," Paul replied. "I knew you were there."

At this she came into the room. "I knew you were here. You passed the window."

"I've passed and repassed—this hour."

"I've known that too, but this time I heard you stop. I've no light there," she went on, "but the window, on this side, is open. I could tell that you had come in."

Paul hesitated. "You ran a danger of not finding me alone."

"I took my chance—of course I knew. I've been in dread, but in spite of it I've seen nobody. I've been up to my room and come down. The coast was clear."

"You've not then seen Mr. Vidal?"

"Oh yes—*him*. But he's nobody." Then as if conscious of the strange sound of this: "Nobody, I mean, to fear."

Paul was silent a moment. "What in the world is it *you* fear?"

"In the sense of the awful things—you know? Here on the spot nothing. About those things I'm quite quiet. There may be plenty to come; but what I'm afraid of now is my safety. There's something in that——!" She broke down; there was more in it than she could say.

"Are you so sure of your safety?"

"You see how sure. It's in your face," said Rose. "And your face—for what it says—is terrible."

Whatever it said remained there as Paul looked at her. "Is it as terrible as yours?" he asked.

"Oh, mine—mine must be hideous; unutterably hideous forever! Yours is beautiful. Everything, every one here is beautiful."

"I don't understand you," said Paul.

"How should you? It isn't to ask you to do that that I've come to you."

He waited in his woful wonder. "For what have you come?"

"You *can* endure it, then, the sight of me?"

"Haven't I told you that I thought of going to you?"

"Yes—but you didn't go," said Rose. "You came and went like a sentinel, and if it was to watch me——"

Paul interrupted her. "It wasn't to watch you."

"Then what was it for?"

"It was to keep myself quiet," said Paul.

"But you're anything but quiet."

"Yes," he dismally allowed; "I'm anything but quiet."

"There's something then that may help you: it's one of two things for which I've come to you. And there's no one but you to care. You may care a very little; it may give you a grain of comfort. Let your comfort be that I've failed."

Paul, after a long look at her, turned away with a vague, dumb gesture, and it was a part of his sore trouble that, in his wasted strength, he had no outlet for emotion, no channel even for pain. She took in for a moment his clumsy, massive misery. "No—you loathe my presence," she said.

He stood awhile in silence with his back to her, as if within him some violence were struggling up; then with an effort, almost with a gasp, he turned round, his open watch in his hand. "I saw Mr. Vidal," was all he produced.

"And he told you too he would come back for me?"

"He said there was something he had to do, but that he would meanwhile get ready. He would return immediately with a carriage."

"That's why I've waited," Rose replied. "I'm ready enough. But he won't come."

"He'll come," said Paul. "But it's more than time."

She drearily shook her head. "Not after getting off—not back to the horror and the shame. He thought so; no doubt he has tried. But it's beyond him."

"Then what are you waiting for?"

She hesitated. "Nothing—now. Thank you." She looked about her. "How shall I go?"

Paul went to the window; for a moment he listened. "I thought I heard wheels."

She gave ear; but once more she shook her head. "There are no wheels, but I can go that way."

He turned back again, heavy and uncertain; he stood

wavering and wondering in her path. "What will become of you?" he asked.

"How do I know and what do I care?"

"What will become of you? what will become of you?" he went on as if he had not heard her.

"You pity me too much," she answered after an instant. "I've failed, but I did what I could. It was all that I saw—it was all that was left me. It took hold of me, it possessed me: it was the last gleam of a chance."

Paul flushed like a sick man under a new wave of weakness. "Of a chance for what?"

"To make him take her. You'll say my calculation was grotesque—my stupidity as ignoble as my crime. All I can answer is that I might none the less have succeeded. People *have*—in worse conditions. But I don't defend myself—I'm face to face with my mistake. I'm face to face with it forever—and that's how I wish you to see me. Look at me well!"

"I would have done anything for you!" Paul as if all talk with her were vain, wailed under his breath.

She considered this; her dreadful face was lighted by the response it kindled. "Would you do anything now?" He answered nothing; he seemed lost in the vision of what was carrying her through. "I saw it as I saw it," she continued: "there it was and there it is. There it is—there it is," she repeated in a tone sharp, for a flash, with all the excitement she contrived to keep under. "It has nothing to do now with any part or any other possibility even of what may be worst in me. It's a storm that's past, it's a debt that's paid. I may literally be better." At the expression this brought out in him she interrupted herself. "You don't understand a word I utter!"

He was following her—as she showed she could see—only in the light of his own emotion; not in that of any feeling that she herself could present. "Why didn't you speak to me—why didn't you tell me what you were thinking? There was nothing you couldn't have told me, nothing that wouldn't have brought me nearer. If I had known your abasement——"

"What would you have done?" Rose demanded.

"I would have saved you."

"What would you have done?" she pressed.

"Everything."

She was silent while he went to the window. "Yes, I've lost you—I've lost you," she said at last. "And you were the thing I might have had. *He* told me that, and I knew it."

"'He' told you?" Paul had faced round.

"He tried to put me off on you. That was what finished me. Of course they'll marry," she abruptly continued.

"Oh yes, they'll marry."

"But not soon, do you suppose?"

"Not soon. But sooner than they think."

Rose looked surprised. "Do you already know what they think?"

"Yes—that it will never be."

"Never?"

"Coming about so horribly. But some day—it will be."

"It will be," said Rose. "And I shall have done it for him. That's more," she said, "than even you would have done for *me*."

Strange tears had found their way between Paul's closed lids. "You're too horrible," he breathed; "you're too horrible."

"Oh, I talk only to you: it's *all* for you. Remember, please, that I shall never speak again. You see," she went on, "that he daren't come."

Paul looked afresh at his watch. "I'll go with you."

Rose hesitated. "How far?"

"I'll go with you," he simply repeated.

She looked at him hard; in her eyes too there were tears. "My safety—my safety!" she murmured as if awestruck.

Paul went round for his hat, which on his entrance he had put down. "I'll go with you," he said once more.

Still, however, she hesitated. "Won't *he* need you?"

"Tony?—for what?"

"For help."

It took Paul a moment to understand. "He wants none."

"You mean he has nothing to fear?"

"From any suspicion? Nothing."

"That's his advantage," said Rose. "People like him too much."

"People like him too much," Paul replied. Then he exclaimed: "Mr. Vidal!"—to which, as she looked, Rose responded with a low, deep moan.

Dennis had appeared at the window; he gave signal in a short, sharp gesture and remained standing in the dusk of the terrace. Paul put down his hat; he turned away to leave his companion free. She approached him while Dennis waited; she lingered desperately, she wavered, as if with a last word to speak. As he only stood rigid, however, she faltered, choking her impulse and giving her word the form of a look. The look held her a moment, held her so long that Dennis spoke sternly from the darkness: "Come!" At this, for a space as great, she fixed her eyes on him; then while the two men stood motionless she decided and reached the window. He put out a hand and seized her, and they passed quickly into the night. Paul, left alone, again sounded a long sigh; this time it was the deep breath of a man who has seen a great danger averted. It had scarcely died away before Tony Bream returned. He came in from the hall as eagerly as he had gone out, and, finding Paul, gave him his news: "Well—I took her home."

Paul required a minute to carry his thoughts back to Gorham. "Oh, she went quietly?"

"Like a bleating lamb. She's too glad to stay on."

Paul turned this over; but as if his confidence now had solid ground he asked no question. "Ah, you're all right!" he simply said.

Tony reached the door through which Jean had left the room; he paused there in surprise at this incongruous expression. Yet there was something absent in the way he echoed "All right?"

"I mean you have such a pull. You'll meet nothing but sympathy."

Tony looked indifferent and uncertain; but his optimism finally assented. "I daresay I shall get on. People perhaps won't challenge me."

"They like you too much."

Tony, with his hand on the door, appeared struck with this; but it embittered again the taste of his tragedy. He remembered with all his vividness to what tune he had been "liked," and he wearily bowed his head. "Oh, too much, Paul!" he sighed as he went out.

THE SPOILS OF POYNTON

I

MRS. GERETH had said she would go with the rest to
church, but suddenly it seemed to her that she should
not be able to wait even till church-time for relief: breakfast,
at Waterbath, was a punctual meal, and she had still nearly an
hour on her hands. Knowing the church to be near, she prepared in her room for the little rural walk, and on her way
down again, passing through corridors and observing imbe-
cilities of decoration, the æsthetic misery of the big com-
modious house, she felt a return of the tide of last night's
irritation, a renewal of everything she could secretly suffer
from ugliness and stupidity. Why did she consent to such contacts? why did she so rashly expose herself? She had had,
heaven knew, her reasons, but the whole experience was to be
sharper than she had feared. To get away from it and out into
the air, into the presence of sky and trees, flowers and birds,
was a necessity of every nerve. The flowers at Waterbath
would probably go wrong in colour and the nightingales sing
out of tune; but she remembered to have heard the place described as possessing those advantages that are usually spoken
of as natural. There were advantages enough it clearly didn't
possess. It was hard for her to believe that a woman could
look presentable who had been kept awake for hours by the
wall-paper in her room; yet none the less, as in her fresh
widow's weeds she rustled across the hall, she was sustained
by the consciousness, which always added to the unction of
her social Sundays, that she was, as usual, the only person in
the house incapable of wearing in her preparation the horrible
stamp of the same exceptional smartness that would be conspicuous in a grocer's wife. She would rather have perished
than have looked *endimanchée*.

She was fortunately not challenged, the hall being empty of
the other women, who were engaged precisely in arraying
themselves to that dire end. Once in the grounds, she recognised that, with a site, a view that struck the note, set an
example to its inmates, Waterbath ought to have been charming. How she herself, with such elements to handle, would

have taken the fine hint of nature! Suddenly, at the turn of a walk, she came on a member of the party, a young lady seated on a bench in deep and lonely meditation. She had observed the girl at dinner and afterwards: she was always looking at girls with an apprehensive or speculative reference to her son. Deep in her heart was a conviction that Owen would, in spite of all her spells, marry at last a frump; and this from no evidence that she could have represented as adequate, but simply from her deep uneasiness, her belief that such a special sensibility as her own could have been inflicted on a woman only as a source of anguish. It would be her fate, her discipline, her cross, to have a frump brought hideously home to her. This girl, one of the two Vetches, had no beauty, but Mrs. Gereth, scanning the dulness for a sign of life, had been straightway able to classify such a figure as the least, for the moment, of her afflictions. Fleda Vetch was dressed with an idea, though perhaps not with much else; and that made a bond when there was none other, especially as in this case the idea was real, not imitation. Mrs. Gereth had long ago generalised the truth that the temperament of the frump is amply consistent with a certain usual prettiness. There were five girls in the party, and the prettiness of this one, slim, pale and black-haired, was less likely than that of the others ever to occasion an exchange of platitudes. The two less developed Brigstocks, daughters of the house, were in particular tiresomely "lovely." A second glance, a sharp one, at the young lady before her conveyed to Mrs. Gereth the soothing assurance that she also was guiltless of looking hot and fine. They had had no talk as yet, but here was a note that would effectually introduce them if the girl should show herself in the least conscious of their community. She got up from her seat with a smile that but partly dissipated the prostration Mrs. Gereth had recognised in her attitude. The elder woman drew her down again, and for a minute, as they sat together, their eyes met and sent out mutual soundings. "Are you safe? Can I utter it?" each of them said to the other, quickly recognising, almost proclaiming, their common need to escape. The tremendous fancy, as it came to be called, that Mrs. Gereth was destined to take to Fleda Vetch virtually began with this discovery that the poor child had been moved to flight even more promptly than herself. That the poor child no less quickly perceived how far she could now go was proved by the immense friendliness with which she instantly broke out: "Isn't it too dreadful?"

"Horrible—horrible!" cried Mrs. Gereth with a laugh; "and it's really a comfort to be able to say it." She had an idea, for it was her ambition, that she successfully made a secret of that awkward oddity her proneness to be rendered unhappy by the presence of the dreadful. Her passion for the exquisite was the cause of this, but it was a passion she considered that she never advertised nor gloried in, contenting herself with letting it regulate her steps and show quietly in her life, remembering at all times that there are few things more soundless than a deep devotion. She was therefore struck with the acuteness of the little girl who had already put a finger on her hidden spring. What was dreadful now, what was horrible, was the intimate ugliness of Waterbath, and it was of that phenomenon these ladies talked while they sat in the shade and drew refreshment from the great tranquil sky, from which no blue saucers were suspended. It was an ugliness fundamental and systematic, the result of the abnormal nature of the Brigstocks, from whose composition the principle of taste had been extravagantly omitted. In the arrangement of their home some other principle, remarkably active, but uncanny and obscure, had operated instead, with consequences depressing to behold, consequences that took the form of a universal futility. The house was bad in all conscience, but it might have passed if they had only let it alone. This saving mercy was beyond them; they had smothered it with trumpery ornament and scrapbook art, with strange excrescences and bunchy draperies, with gimcracks that might have been keepsakes for maid-servants and nondescript conveniences that might have been prizes for the blind. They had gone wildly astray over carpets and curtains; they had an infallible instinct for disaster, and were so cruelly doom-ridden that it rendered them almost tragic. Their drawing-room, Mrs. Gereth lowered her voice to mention, caused her face to burn, and each of the new friends confided to the other that in her own apartment she had given way to tears. There was in the elder lady's a set of comic water-colours, a family joke by a family genius, and in the younger's a souvenir from some centennial or other Exhibition, that they shudderingly alluded to. The house was perversely full of souvenirs of places even more ugly than itself and of things it would have been a pious duty to forget. The worst horror was the acres of varnish, something advertised and smelly, with which everything was smeared: it was Fleda Vetch's conviction that the application of it, by their own hands and hilariously shoving each other, was the amusement of the Brigstocks on rainy days.

When, as criticism deepened, Fleda dropped the suggestion that some people would perhaps see something in Mona, Mrs. Gereth caught her up with a groan of protest, a smothered familiar cry of "Oh, my dear!" Mona was the eldest of the three, the one Mrs. Gereth most suspected. She confided to her young friend that it was her suspicion that had brought her to Waterbath; and this was going very far, for on the spot, as a refuge, a remedy, she had clutched at the idea that something might be done with the girl before her. It was her fancied exposure at any rate that had sharpened the shock; made her ask herself with a terrible chill if fate could really be plotting to saddle her with a daughter-in-law brought up in such a place. She had seen Mona in her appropriate setting and she had seen Owen, handsome and heavy, dangle beside her; but the effect of these first hours had happily not been to darken the prospect. It was clearer to her that she could never accept Mona, but it was after all by no means certain that Owen would ask her to. He had sat by somebody else at dinner, and afterwards he had talked to Mrs. Firmin, who was as dreadful as all the rest, but redeemingly married. His heaviness, which in her need of expansion she freely named, had two aspects: one of them his monstrous lack of taste, the other his exaggerated prudence. If it should come to a question of carrying Mona with a high hand there would be no need to worry, for that was rarely his manner of proceeding.

Invited by her companion, who had asked if it weren't wonderful, Mrs. Gereth had begun to say a word about Poynton; but she heard a sound of voices that made her stop short. The next moment she rose to her feet, and Fleda could see that her alarm was by no means quenched. Behind the place where they had been sitting the ground dropped with a certain steepness, forming a long grassy bank, up which Owen Gereth and Mona Brigstock, dressed for church but making a familiar joke of it, were in the act of scrambling and helping each other. When they had reached the even ground Fleda was able to read the meaning of the exclamation in which Mrs. Gereth had expressed her reserves on the subject of Miss Brigstock's personality. Miss Brigstock had been laughing and even romping, but the circumstance hadn't contributed the ghost of an expression to her countenance. Tall, straight and fair, long-limbed and strangely festooned, she stood there without a look in her eye or any perceptible intention of any sort in any other feature. She belonged to the type in which speech is an unaided emission of sound and the secret of being is impenetrably and incorruptibly kept. Her expression would probably have been beautiful if she had had one, but whatever she communicated she communicated, in a manner best known to herself, without signs. This was not the case with Owen Gereth, who had plenty of them, and all very simple and immediate. Robust and artless, eminently natural yet perfectly correct, he looked pointlessly active and pleasantly dull. Like his mother and like Fleda Vetch, but not for the same reason, this young pair had come out to take a turn before church.

The meeting of the two couples was sensibly awkward, and Fleda, who was sagacious, took the measure of the shock inflicted on Mrs. Gereth. There had been intimacy—oh yes, intimacy as well as puerility—in the horse-play of which they had just had a glimpse. The party began to stroll together to the house, and Fleda had again a sense of Mrs. Gereth's quick management in the way the lovers, or whatever they were, found themselves separated. She strolled behind with Mona, the mother possessing herself of her son, her exchange of remarks with whom, however, remained, as they went, suggestively inaudible. That member of the party in whose intenser consciousness we shall most profitably seek a reflection of the little drama with which we are concerned received an even livelier impression of Mrs. Gereth's intervention from the fact that ten minutes later, on the way to church, still another pairing had been effected. Owen walked with Fleda, and it was an amusement to the girl to feel sure that this was by his mother's direction. Fleda had other amusements as well: such as noting that Mrs. Gereth was now with Mona Brigstock; such as observing that she was all affability to that young woman; such as reflecting that, masterful and clever, with a great bright spirit, she was one of those who impose themselves as an influence; such as feeling finally that Owen Gereth was absolutely beautiful and delightfully dense. This young person had even from herself wonderful secrets of delicacy and pride; but she came as near distinctness as in the consideration of such matters she had ever come at all in now surrendering herself to the idea that it was of a pleasant effect and rather remarkable to be stupid without offence—of a pleasanter effect and more remarkable indeed than to be clever and horrid. Owen Gereth, at any rate, with his inches, his features and his lapses, was neither of these latter things. She herself was prepared, if she should ever marry, to contribute all the cleverness, and she liked to think that her husband would be a force grateful for direction. She was in her small way a spirit of the same family as Mrs. Gereth. On that flushed and huddled Sunday a great matter occurred; her little life became aware of a singular quickening. Her meagre past fell away from her like a garment of the wrong fashion, and as she came up to town on the Monday what she stared at from the train in the suburban fields was a future full of the things she particularly loved.

II

THESE WERE neither more nor less than the things with which she had had time to learn from Mrs. Gereth that Poynton overflowed. Poynton, in the south of England, was this lady's established, or rather her disestablished, home: it had recently passed into the possession of her son. The father of the boy, an only child, had died two years before, and in London, with his mother, Owen was occupying for May and June a house good-naturedly lent them by Colonel Gereth, their uncle and brother-in-law. His mother had laid her hand so engagingly on Fleda Vetch that in a very few days the girl knew it was possible they should suffer together in Cadogan Place almost as much as they had suffered together at Waterbath. The kind soldier's house was also an ordeal, but the two women, for the ensuing month, had at least the relief of their confessions. The great drawback of Mrs. Gereth's situation was that, thanks to the rare perfection of Poynton, she was condemned to wince wherever she turned. She had lived for a quarter of a century in such warm closeness with the beautiful that, as she frankly admitted, life had become for her a kind of fool's paradise. She couldn't leave her own house without peril of exposure. She didn't say it in so many words, but Fleda could see she held that there was nothing in England really to compare to Poynton. There were places much grander and richer, but there was no such complete work of art, nothing that would appeal so to those who were really informed. In putting such elements into her hand destiny had given her an inestimable chance; she knew how rarely well things had gone with her and that she had enjoyed an extraordinary fortune.

There had been in the first place the exquisite old house itself, early Jacobean, supreme in every part: it was a provocation, an inspiration, a matchless canvas for the picture. Then there had been her husband's sympathy and generosity, his knowledge and love, their perfect accord and beautiful life together, twenty-six years of planning and seeking, a long, sunny harvest of taste and curiosity. Lastly, she never denied, there had been her personal gift, the genius, the passion, the patience of the collector—a patience, an almost infernal cunning, that had enabled her to do it all with a limited command of money. There wouldn't have been money enough for any one else, she said with pride, but there have been money enough for her. They had saved on lots of things in life, and there were lots of things they hadn't had, but they had had in every corner of Europe their swing among the Jews. It was fascinating to poor Fleda, who hadn't a penny in the world nor anything nice at home, and whose only treasure was her subtle mind, to hear this genuine English lady, fresh and fair, young in the fifties, declare with gaiety and conviction that she was herself the greatest Jew who had ever tracked a victim. Fleda, with her mother dead, hadn't so much even as a home, and her nearest chance of one was that there was some appearance her sister would become engaged to a curate whose eldest brother was supposed to have property and would perhaps allow him something. Her father paid some of her bills, but he didn't like her to live with him; and she had lately, in Paris, with several hundred other young women, spent a year in a studio, arming herself for the battle of life by a course with an impressionist painter. She was determined to work, but her impressions, or somebody's else, were as yet her only material. Mrs. Gereth had told her she liked her because she had an extraordinary *flair*; but under the circumstances a *flair* was a questionable boon: in the dry spaces in which she had mainly moved she could have borne a chronic catarrh. She was constantly summoned to Cadogan Place and before the month was out was kept to stay, to pay a visit of which the end, it was agreed, should have nothing to do with the beginning. She had a sense, partly exultant and partly alarmed, of having quickly become necessary to her imperious friend, who indeed gave a reason quite sufficient for it in telling her there was nobody else who understood. From Mrs. Gereth there was in these days an immense deal to understand, though it might be freely summed up in the circumstance that she was wretched. She told Fleda that she couldn't completely know why till she should have seen the things at Poynton. Fleda could perfectly grasp this connection, which was exactly one of the matters that, in their inner mystery, were a blank to everybody else.

The girl had a promise that the wonderful house should be shown her early in July, when Mrs. Gereth would return to it as to her home; but even before this initiation she put her finger on the spot that in the poor lady's troubled soul ached hardest. This was the misery that haunted her, the dread of the inevitable surrender. What Fleda had to sit up to was the confirmed appearance that Owen Gereth would marry Mona Brigstock, marry her in his mother's teeth, and that such an act would have incalculable bearings. They were present to Mrs. Gereth, her companion could see, with a vividness that at moments almost ceased to be that of sanity. She would have to give up Poynton, and give it up to a product of Waterbath—that was the wrong that rankled, the humiliation at which Fleda would be able adequately to shudder only when she should know the place. She did know Waterbath and she despised it—she had that qualification for sympathy. Her sympathy was intelligent, for she read deep into the matter: she stared, aghast, as it came home to her for the first time, at the cruel English custom of the expropriation of the lonely mother. Mr. Gereth had apparently been a very amiable man, but Mr. Gereth had left things in a way that made the girl marvel. The house and its contents had been treated as a single splendid object; everything was to go straight to his son, and his widow was to have a maintenance and a cottage in another county. No account whatever had been taken of her relation to her treasures, of the passion with which she had waited for them, worked for them, picked them over, made them worthy of each other and the house, watched them, loved them, lived with them. He appeared to have assumed that she would settle questions with her son, that he could depend upon Owen's affection. And in truth, as poor Mrs. Gereth inquired, how could he possibly have had a prevision—he who turned his eyes instinctively from everything repulsive—of anything so abnormal as a Waterbath Brigstock? He had been in ugly houses enough, but had escaped that particular nightmare. Nothing so perverse could have been expected to happen as that the heir to the loveliest thing in England should be inspired to hand it over to a girl so exceptionally tainted. Mrs. Gereth spoke of poor Mona's taint as if to mention it were almost a violation of decency, and a person who had listened without enlightenment would have wondered of what fault the girl had been or had indeed not been guilty. But Owen had from a boy never cared, had never had the least pride or pleasure in his home.

"Well, then, if he doesn't care—!" Fleda exclaimed with some impetuosity; stopping short, however, before she completed her sentence.

Mrs. Gereth looked at her rather hard. "If he doesn't care?"

Fleda hesitated; she had not quite had a definite idea. "Well—he'll give them up."

"Give what up?"

"Why, those beautiful things."

"Give them up to whom?" Mrs. Gereth more boldly stared.

"To you, of course—to enjoy, to keep for yourself."

"And leave his house as bare as your hand? There's nothing in it that isn't precious."

Fleda considered; her friend had taken her up with a smothered ferocity by which she was slightly disconcerted. "I don't mean of course that he should surrender everything; but he might let you pick out the things to which you're most attached."

"I think he would if he were free," said Mrs. Gereth.

"And do you mean, as it is, that she'll prevent him?" Mona Brigstock, between these ladies, was now nothing but "she."

"By every means in her power."

"But surely not because she understands and appreciates them?"

"No," Mrs. Gereth replied, "but because they belong to the house and the house belongs to Owen. If I should wish to take anything she would simply say, with that motionless mask: 'It goes with the house.' And day after day, in the face of every argument, of every consideration of generosity, she would repeat, without winking, in that voice like the squeeze of a doll's stomach: 'It goes with the house—it goes with the house.' In that attitude they'll shut themselves up."

Fleda was struck, was even a little startled with the way Mrs. Gereth had turned this over—had faced, if indeed only to recognise its futility, the notion of a battle with her only son. These words led her to make an inquiry which she had not thought it discreet to make before: she brought out the idea of the possibility, after all, of her friend's continuing to live at Poynton. Would they really wish to proceed to extremities? Was no good-humoured, graceful compromise to be imagined or brought about? Couldn't the same roof cover them? Was it so very inconceivable that a married son should, for the rest of her days, share with so charming a mother the home she had devoted more than a score of years to making beautiful for him? Mrs. Gereth hailed this question with a wan, compassionate smile: she replied that a common household, in such a case, was exactly so inconceivable that Fleda had only to glance over the fair face of the English land to see how few people had ever conceived it. It was always thought a wonder, a "mistake," a piece of overstrained sentiment; and she confessed that she was as little capable of a flight of that sort as Owen himself. Even if they both had been capable they would still have Mona's hatred to reckon with. Fleda's breath was sometimes taken away by the great bounds and elisions which, on Mrs. Gereth's lips, the course of discussion could take.

This was the first she had heard of Mona's hatred, though she certainly had not needed Mrs. Gereth to tell her that in close quarters that young lady would prove secretly mulish. Later Fleda perceived indeed that perhaps almost any girl would hate a person who should be so markedly averse to having anything to do with her. Before this, however, in conversation with her young friend, Mrs. Gereth furnished a more vivid motive for her despair by asking how she could possibly be expected to sit there with the new proprietors and accept—or call it, for a day, endure—the horrors they would perpetrate in the house. Fleda reasoned that they wouldn't after all smash things nor burn them up; and Mrs. Gereth admitted when pushed that she didn't quite suppose they would. What she meant was that they would neglect them, ignore them, leave them to clumsy servants (there wasn't an object of them all but should be handled with perfect love), and in many cases probably wish to replace them by pieces answerable to some vulgar modern notion of the convenient. Above all she saw in advance with dilated eyes the abominations they would inevitably mix up with them—the maddening relics of Waterbath, the little brackets and pink vases, the sweepings of bazaars, the family photographs and illuminated texts, the "household art" and household piety of Mona's hideous home. Wasn't it enough simply to contend that Mona would approach Poynton in the spirit of a Brigstock and that in the spirit of a Brigstock she would deal with her acquisition? Did Fleda really see *her*, Mrs. Gereth demanded, spending the remainder of her days with such a creature's elbow in her eye?

Fleda had to declare that she certainly didn't and that Waterbath had been a warning it would be frivolous to overlook. At the same time she privately reflected that they were taking a great deal for granted and that, inasmuch as to her knowledge Owen Gereth had positively denied his betrothal, the ground of their speculations was by no means firm. It seemed to our young lady that in a difficult position Owen conducted himself with some natural art; treating this domesticated confidant of his mother's wrongs with a simple civility that almost troubled her conscience, so deeply she felt that she might have had for him the air of siding with that lady against him. She wondered if he would ever know how little really she did this and that she was there, since Mrs. Gereth had insisted, not to betray but essentially to confirm and protect. The fact that his mother disliked Mona Brigstock might have made him dislike the object of her preference, and it was detestable to Fleda to remember that she might have appeared to him to offer herself as an exemplary contrast. It was clear enough, however, that the happy youth had no more sense for a motive than a deaf man for a tune; a limitation by which, after all, she could gain as well as lose. He came and went very freely on the business with which London abundantly furnished him, but he found time more than once to say to her, "It's awfully nice of you to look after poor Mummy." As well as his quick speech, which shyness made obscure—it was usually as desperate as a "rush" at some violent game—his child's eyes in his man's face put it to her that, you know, this really meant a good deal for him and that he hoped she would stay on. With a person in the house who, like herself, was clever, poor Mummy was conveniently occupied; and Fleda found a beauty in the candour and even in the modesty which apparently kept him from suspecting that two such wiseheads could possibly be occupied with Owen Gereth.

III

THEY WENT at last, the wiseheads, down to Poynton, where the palpitating girl had the full revelation. "*Now* do you know how I feel?" Mrs. Gereth asked when in the wonderful hall, three minutes after their arrival, her pretty associate dropped on a seat with a soft gasp and a roll of dilated eyes. The answer came clearly enough, and in the rapture of that first walk through the house Fleda took a prodigious span. She perfectly understood how Mrs. Gereth felt—she had understood but meagrely before; and the two women embraced with tears over the tightening of their bond—tears which on the younger one's part were the natural and usual sign of her submission to perfect beauty. It was not the first time she had cried for the joy of admiration, but it was the first time the mistress of Poynton, often as she had shown her house, had been present at such an exhibition. She exulted in it; it quickened her own tears; she assured her companion that such an occasion made the poor old place fresh to her again and more precious than ever. Yes, nobody had ever, that way, felt what she had achieved: people were so grossly ignorant, and everybody, even the knowing ones, as they thought themselves, more or less dense. What Mrs. Gereth had achieved was indeed an exquisite work; and in such an art of the treasure-hunter, in selection and comparison refined to that point, there was an element of creation, of personality. She had commended Fleda's *flair*, and Fleda now gave herself up to satiety. Preoccupations and scruples fell away from her; she had never known a greater happiness than the week she passed in this initiation.

Wandering through clear chambers where the general effect made preferences almost as impossible as if they had been shocks, pausing at open doors where vistas were long and bland, she would, even if she had not already known, have discovered for herself that Poynton was the record of a life. It was written in great syllables of colour and form, the tongues of other countries and the hands of rare artists. It was all France and Italy, with their ages composed to rest. For England you looked out of old windows—it was England that was the wide embrace. While outside, on the low terraces, she contradicted gardeners and refined on nature, Mrs. Gereth left her guest to finger fondly the brasses that Louis Quinze might have thumbed, to sit with Venetian velvets just held in a loving palm, to hang over cases of enamels and pass and repass before cabinets. There were not many pictures—the panels and the stuffs were themselves the picture; and in all the great wainscoted house there was not an inch of pasted paper. What struck Fleda most in it was the high pride of her friend's taste, a fine arrogance, a sense of style which, however amused and amusing, never compromised nor stooped. She felt indeed, as this lady had intimated to her that she would, both a respect and a compassion that she had not known before; the vision of the coming surrender filled her with an equal pain. To give it all up, to die to it—that thought ached in her breast. She herself could imagine clinging there with a closeness separate from dignity. To have created such a place was to have had dignity enough; when there was a question of defending it the fiercest attitude was the right one. After so intense a taking of possession she too was to give it up; for she reflected that if Mrs. Gereth's remaining there would have offered her a sort of future—stretching away in safe years on the other side of a gulf—the advent of the others could only be, by the same law, a great vague menace, the ruffling of a still water. Such were the emotions of a hungry girl whose sensibility was almost as great as her opportunities for comparison had been small. The museums had done something for her, but nature had done more.

If Owen had not come down with them nor joined them later, it was because he still found London jolly; yet the question remained of whether the jollity of London was not merely the only name his small vocabulary yielded for the jollity of Mona Brigstock. There was indeed in his conduct another ambiguity—something that required explaining so long as his motive didn't come to the surface. If he was in love what was the matter? And what was the matter still more if he wasn't? The mystery was at last cleared up: this Fleda gathered from the tone in which, one morning at breakfast, a letter just opened made Mrs. Gereth cry out. Her dismay was almost a shriek: "Why, he's bringing her down—he wants her to see the house!" They flew, the two women, into each other's arms and, with their heads together, soon made out that the reason, the baffling reason why nothing had yet happened, was that Mona didn't know, or Owen didn't, whether Poynton would really please her. She was coming down to judge; and could anything in the world be more like poor Owen than the ponderous probity which had kept him from pressing her for a reply till she should have learned whether she approved what he had to offer her? That was a scruple it had naturally been impossible to impute. If only they might fondly hope, Mrs. Gereth wailed, that the girl's expectations would be dashed! There was a fine consistency, a sincerity quite affecting, in her arguing that the better the place should happen to look and to express the conceptions to which it owed its origin, the less it would speak to an intelligence so primitive. How could a Brigstock possibly understand what it was all about? How, really, could a Brigstock logically do anything but hate it? Mrs. Gereth, even as she whisked away linen shrouds, persuaded herself of the possibility on Mona's part of some bewildered blankness, some collapse of admiration that would prove disconcerting to her swain—a hope of which Fleda at least could see the absurdity and which gave the measure of the poor lady's strange, almost maniacal disposition to thrust in everywhere the question of "things," to read all behaviour in the light of some fancied relation to them. "Things" were of course the sum of the world; only, for Mrs. Gereth, the sum of the world was rare French furniture and oriental china. She could at a stretch imagine people's not having, but she couldn't imagine their not wanting and not missing.

The young couple were to be accompanied by Mrs. Brigstock, and with a prevision of how fiercely they would be watched Fleda became conscious, before the party arrived, of an amused, diplomatic pity for them. Almost as much as Mrs. Gereth's her taste was her life, but her life was somehow the larger for it. Besides, she had another care now: there was some one she wouldn't have liked to see humiliated even in the form of a young lady who would contribute to his never suspecting so much delicacy. When this young lady appeared Fleda tried, so far as the wish to efface herself allowed, to be mainly the person to take her about, show her the house and cover up her ignorance. Owen's announcement had been that, as trains made it convenient, they would present themselves for luncheon and depart before dinner; but Mrs. Gereth, true to her system of glaring civility, proposed and obtained an extension, a dining and spending of the night. She made her young friend wonder against what rebellion of fact she was sacrificing in advance so profusely to form. Fleda was appalled after the first hour by the rash innocence with which Mona had accepted the responsibility of observation, and indeed by the large levity with which, sitting there like a bored tourist in fine scenery, she exercised it. She felt in her nerves the effect of such a manner on her companion's, and it was this that made her want to entice the girl away, give her some merciful warning or some jocular cue. Mona met intense looks, however, with eyes that might have been blue beads, the only ones she had—eyes into which Fleda thought it strange Owen Gereth should have to plunge for his fate and his mother for a confession of whether Poynton was a success. She made no remark that helped to supply this light; her impression at any rate had nothing in common with the feeling that, as the beauty of the place throbbed out like music, had caused Fleda Vetch to burst into tears. She was as content to say nothing as if, Mrs. Gereth afterwards exclaimed, she had been keeping her mouth shut in a railway-tunnel. Mrs. Gereth contrived at the end of an hour to convey to Fleda that it was plain she was brutally ignorant; but Fleda more finely discovered that her ignorance was obscurely active.

She was not so stupid as not to see that something, though she scarcely knew what, was expected of her that she couldn't give; and the only mode her intelligence suggested of meeting the expectation was to plant her big feet and pull another way. Mrs. Gereth wanted her to rise, somehow or somewhere, and was prepared to hate her if she didn't: very well, she couldn't, she wouldn't rise; she already moved at the altitude that suited her, and was able to see that since she was exposed to the hatred she might at least enjoy the calm. The smallest trouble, for a girl with no nonsense about her, was to earn what she incurred; so that, a dim instinct teaching her she would earn it best by not being effusive, and combining with the conviction that she now held Owen, and therefore the place, she had the pleasure of her honesty as well as of her security. Didn't her very honesty lead her to be belligerently blank about Poynton, inasmuch as it was just Poynton that was forced upon her as a subject for effusiveness? Such subjects, to Mona Brigstock, had an air almost of indecency, and the house became uncanny to her through such an appeal— an appeal that, somewhere in the twilight of her being, as Fleda was sure, she thanked heaven she *was* the girl stiffly to draw back from. She was a person whom pressure at a given point infallibly caused to expand in the wrong place instead of, as it is usually administered in the hope of doing, the right one. Her mother, to make up for this, broke out universally, pronounced everything "most striking," and was visibly happy that Owen's captor should be so far on the way to strike: but she jarred upon Mrs. Gereth by her formula of admiration, which was that anything she looked at was "in the style" of something else. This was to show how much she had seen, but it only showed she had seen nothing; everything at Poynton was in the style of Poynton, and poor Mrs. Brigstock, who at least was determined to rise and had brought with her a trophy of her journey, a "lady's magazine" purchased at the station, a horrible thing with patterns for antimacassars, which, as it was quite new, the first number, and seemed so clever, she kindly offered to leave for the house, was in the style of a vulgar old woman who wore silver jewelry and tried to pass off a gross avidity as a sense of the beautiful.

By the day's end it was clear to Fleda Vetch that, however Mona judged, the day had been determinant. Whether or no she felt the charm she felt the challenge: at an early moment Owen Gereth would be able to tell his mother the worst. Nevertheless when the elder lady, at bedtime, coming in a dressing-gown and a high fever to the younger one's room, cried out, "She hates it; but what will she do?" Fleda pretended vagueness, played at obscurity and assented disingenuously to the proposition that they at least had a respite. The future was dark to her, but there was a silken thread she could clutch in the gloom—she would never give Owen away. He might give himself—he even certainly would; but that was his own affair, and his blunders, his innocence only added to the

appeal he made to her. She would cover him, she would protect him, and beyond thinking her a cheerful inmate he would
never guess her intention, any more than, beyond thinking
her clever enough for anything, his acute mother would discover it. From this hour, with Mrs. Gereth, there was a flaw
in her frankness. Her admirable friend continued to know
everything she did; what was to remain unknown was the
general motive.

From the window of her room, the next morning before
breakfast, the girl saw Owen in the garden with Mona, who
strolled beside him with a listening parasol but without a visible look for the great florid picture that had been hung there
by Mrs. Gereth's hand. Mona kept dropping her eyes, as she
walked, to catch the sheen of her patent-leather shoes, which
resembled a man's and which she kicked forward a little—it
gave her an odd movement—to help her see what she
thought of them. When Fleda came down Mrs. Gereth was in
the breakfast-room; and at that moment Owen, through a
long window, passed in alone from the terrace and very endearingly kissed his mother. It immediately struck the girl that
she was in their way, for hadn't he been borne on a wave of
joy exactly to announce, before the Brigstocks departed, that
Mona had at last faltered out the sweet word he had been
waiting for? He shook hands with his friendly violence, but
Fleda contrived not to look into his face: what she liked most
to see in it was not the reflection of Mona's big boot-toes.
She could bear well enough that young lady herself, but she
couldn't bear Owen's opinion of her. She was on the point of
slipping into the garden when the movement was checked by
Mrs. Gereth's suddenly drawing her close, as if for the morning embrace, and then, while she kept her there with the
bravery of the night's repose, breaking out: "Well, my dear
boy, what *does* your young friend there make of our odds and
ends?"

"Oh, she thinks they're all right!"

Fleda immediately guessed from his tone that he had not
come in to say what she supposed; there was even something
in it to confirm Mrs. Gereth's belief that their danger had
dropped. She was sure, moreover, that his tribute to Mona's
taste was a repetition of the eloquent words in which the girl

had herself recorded it; she could indeed hear, with all vividness, the pretty passage between the pair. "Don't you think it's rather jolly, the old shop?" "Oh, it's all right!" Mona had graciously remarked: and then they had probably, with a slap on a back, run another race up or down a green bank. Fleda knew Mrs. Gereth had not yet uttered a word to her son that would have shown him how much she feared; but it was impossible to feel her friend's arm round her and not become aware that this friend was now throbbing with a strange intention. Owen's reply had scarcely been of a nature to usher in a discussion of Mona's sensibilities; but Mrs. Gereth went on, in a moment, with an innocence of which Fleda could measure the cold hypocrisy: "Has she any sort of feeling for nice old things?" The question was as fresh as the morning light.

"Oh, of course she likes everything that's nice." And Owen, who constitutionally disliked questions—an answer was almost as hateful to him as a "trick" to a big dog—smiled kindly at Fleda and conveyed that she would understand what he meant even if his mother didn't. Fleda, however, mainly understood that Mrs. Gereth, with an odd, wild laugh, held her so hard that she hurt her.

"I could give up everything without a pang, I think, to a person I could trust, I could respect." The girl heard her voice tremble under the effort to show nothing but what she wanted to show, and felt the sincerity of her implication that the piety most real to her was to be on one's knees before one's high standard. "The best things here, as you know, are the things your father and I collected, things all that we worked for and waited for and suffered for. Yes," cried Mrs. Gereth, with a fine freedom of fancy, "there are things in the house that we almost starved for! They were our religion, they were our life, they were *us*! And now they're only *me*— except that they're also *you*, thank God, a little, you dear!" she continued, suddenly inflicting on Fleda a kiss apparently intended to knock her into position. "There isn't one of them I don't know and love—yes, as one remembers and cherishes the happiest moments of one's life. Blindfold, in the dark, with the brush of a finger, I could tell one from another. They're living things to me; they know me, they return the touch of my hand. But I could let them all go, since I have to, so strangely, to another affection, another conscience. There's a care they want, there's a sympathy that draws out their beauty. Rather than make them over to a woman ignorant and vulgar, I think I'd deface them with my own hands. Can't you see me, Fleda, and wouldn't you do it yourself?"— she appealed to her companion with glittering eyes. "I couldn't bear the thought of such a woman here—I *couldn't*. I don't know what she'd do; she'd be sure to invent some devilry, if it should be only to bring in her own little belongings and horrors. The world is full of cheap gimcracks, in this awful age, and they're thrust in at one at every turn. They'd be thrust in here, on top of my treasures, my own. Who would save *them* for me—I ask you who *would*?" and she turned again to Fleda with a dry, strained smile. Her handsome, high-nosed, excited face might have been that of Don Quixote tilting at a windmill. Drawn into the eddy of this outpouring, the girl, scared and embarrassed, laughed off her exposure; but only to feel herself more passionately caught up and, as it seemed to her, thrust down the fine open mouth (it showed such perfect teeth) with which poor Owen's slow cerebration gaped. "*You* would, of course—only you, in all the world, because you know, you feel, as I do myself, what's good and true and pure." No severity of the moral law could have taken a higher tone in this implication of the young lady who had not the only virtue Mrs. Gereth actively esteemed. "*You* would replace me, *you* would watch over them, *you* would keep the place right," she austerely pursued, "and with you here—yes, with you, I believe I might rest, at last, in my grave!" She threw herself on Fleda's neck, and before Fleda, horribly shamed, could shake her off, had burst into tears which couldn't have been explained, but which might perhaps have been understood.

IV

A WEEK LATER Owen Gereth came down to inform his mother that he had settled with Mona Brigstock; but it was not at all a joy to Fleda, aware of how much to himself it would be a surprise, that he should find her still in the house. That dreadful scene before breakfast had made her position false and odious; it had been followed, after they were left alone, by a scene of her own making with her extravagant friend. She notified Mrs. Gereth of her instant departure: she couldn't possibly remain after being offered to Owen that way, before his very face, as his mother's candidate for the honour of his hand. That was all he could have seen in such an outbreak and in the indecency of her standing there to enjoy it. Fleda had on the prior occasion dashed out of the room by the shortest course and in her confusion had fallen upon Mona in the garden. She had taken an aimless turn with her, and they had had some talk, rendered at first difficult and almost disagreeable by Mona's apparent suspicion that she had been sent out to spy, as Mrs. Gereth had tried to spy, into her opinions. Fleda was sagacious enough to treat these opinions as a mystery almost awful; which had an effect so much more than reassuring that at the end of five minutes the young lady from Waterbath suddenly and perversely said: "Why has she never had a winter garden thrown out? If ever I have a place of my own I mean to have one." Fleda, dismayed, could see the thing—something glazed and piped, on iron pillars, with untidy plants and cane sofas; a shiny excrescence on the noble face of Poynton. She remembered at Waterbath a conservatory where she had caught a bad cold in the company of a stuffed cockatoo fastened to a tropical bough and a waterless fountain composed of shells stuck into some hardened paste. She asked Mona if her idea would be to make something like this conservatory; to which Mona replied: "Oh no, much finer; we haven't got a winter garden at Waterbath." Fleda wondered if she meant to convey that it was the only grandeur they lacked, and in a moment Mona went on: "But we have got a billiard-room—that I will say for

233

us!" There was no billiard-room at Poynton, but there would evidently be one, and it would have, hung on its walls, framed at the "Stores," caricature-portraits of celebrities taken from a "society paper."

When the two girls had gone in to breakfast it was for Fleda to see at a glance that there had been a further passage, of some high colour, between Owen and his mother; and she had turned pale in guessing to what extremity, at her expense, Mrs. Gereth had found occasion to proceed. Hadn't she, after her clumsy flight, been pressed upon Owen in still clearer terms? Mrs. Gereth would practically have said to him: "If you'll take *her*, I'll move away without a sound. But if you take any one else, any one I'm not sure of as I am of her—heaven help me, I'll fight to the death!" Breakfast, this morning, at Poynton, had been a meal singularly silent, in spite of the vague little cries with which Mrs. Brigstock turned up the underside of plates and the knowing but alarming raps administered by her big knuckles to porcelain cups. Some one had to respond to her, and the duty assigned itself to Fleda, who, while pretending to meet her on the ground of explanation, wondered what Owen thought of a girl still indelicately anxious, after she had been grossly hurled at him, to prove by exhibitions of her fine taste that she was really what his mother pretended. This time, at any rate, their fate was sealed: Owen, as soon as he should get out of the house, would describe to Mona that lady's extraordinary conduct, and if anything more had been wanted to "fetch" Mona, as he would call it, the deficiency was now made up. Mrs. Gereth in fact took care of that—took care of it by the way, at the last, on the threshold, she said to the younger of her departing guests, with an irony of which the sting was wholly in the sense, not at all in the sound: "We haven't had the talk we might have had, have we? You'll feel that I've neglected you, and you'll treasure it up against me. *Don't*, because really, you know, it has been quite an accident, and I've all sorts of information at your disposal. If you should come down again (only you won't, ever—I feel that!) I should give you plenty of time to worry it out of me. Indeed there are some things I should quite insist on your learning; not permit you at all, in any settled way, *not* to learn. Yes indeed, you'd put me through, and I should put you, my dear! We should have each other to reckon with, and you would see me as I really am. I'm not a bit the vague, mooning, easy creature I dare say you think. However, if you won't come, you won't; *n'en parlons plus.* It *is* stupid here after what you're accustomed to. We can only, all round, do what we can, eh? For heaven's sake, don't let your mother forget her precious publication, the female magazine, with the what-do-you-call-'em?—the grease-catchers. There!"

Mrs. Gereth, delivering herself from the doorstep, had tossed the periodical higher in air than was absolutely needful—tossed it toward the carriage the retreating party was about to enter. Mona, from the force of habit, the reflex action of the custom of sport, had popped out, with a little spring, a long arm and intercepted the missile as easily as she would have caused a tennis-ball to rebound from a racket. "Good catch!" Owen had cried, so genuinely pleased that practically no notice was taken of his mother's impressive remarks. It was to the accompaniment of romping laughter, as Mrs. Gereth afterwards said, that the carriage had rolled away; but it was while that laughter was still in the air that Fleda Vetch, white and terrible, had turned upon her hostess with her scorching "How *could* you? Great God, how *could* you?" This lady's perfect blankness was from the first a sign of her serene conscience; and the fact that till indoctrinated she didn't even know what Fleda meant by resenting her late offence to every susceptibility, gave our young woman a sore, scared perception that her own value in the house was the mere value, as one might say, of a good agent. Mrs. Gereth was generously sorry, but she was still more surprised—surprised at Fleda's not having liked to be shown off to Owen as the right sort of wife for him. Why not, in the name of wonder, if she absolutely *was* the right sort? She had admitted on explanation that she could see what her young friend meant by having been laid, as Fleda called it, at his feet; but it struck the girl that the admission was only made to please her and that Mrs. Gereth was secretly surprised at her not being as happy to be sacrificed to the supremacy of a high standard as she was happy to sacrifice her. She had taken a tremendous fancy to her, but that was on account of the fancy—to

Poynton of course—Fleda herself had taken. Wasn't this latter fancy then so great after all? Fleda felt that she could declare it to be great indeed when really for the sake of it she could forgive what she had suffered and, after reproaches and ears, asseverations and kisses, after learning that she was cared for only as a priestess of the altar and a view of her bruised dignity which left no alternative to flight, could accept the shame with the balm, consent not to depart, take refuge in the thin comfort of at least knowing the truth. The truth was simply that all Mrs. Gereth's scruples were on one side and that her ruling passion had in a manner despoiled her of her humanity. On the second day, after the tide of emotion had somewhat ebbed, she said soothingly to her companion: "But you *would*, after all, marry him, you know, darling, wouldn't you, if that girl were not there? I mean of course if he were to ask you," Mrs. Gereth had thoughtfully added.

"Marry him if he were to ask me? Most distinctly not!"

The question had not come up with this definiteness before, and Mrs. Gereth was clearly more surprised than ever. She marvelled a moment. "Not even to have Poynton?"

"Not even to have Poynton."

"But why on earth?" Mrs. Gereth's sad eyes were fixed on her.

Fleda coloured; she hesitated. "Because he's too stupid!" Save on one other occasion, at which we shall in time arrive, little as the reader may believe it, she never came nearer to betraying to Mrs. Gereth that she was in love with Owen. She found a dim amusement in reflecting that if Mona had not been there and he had not been too stupid and he verily had asked her, she might, should she have wished to keep her secret, have found it possible to pass off the motive of her action as a mere passion for Poynton.

Mrs. Gereth evidently thought in these days of little but things hymeneal; for she broke out with sudden rapture in the middle of the week: "I know what they'll do: they *will* marry, but they'll go and live at Waterbath!" There was positive joy in that form of the idea, which she embroidered and developed: it seemed so much the safest thing that could happen. "Yes, I'll have you, but I won't go *there*!" Mona would have said with a vicious nod at the southern horizon: "we'll leave

your horrid mother alone there for life." It would be an ideal
solution, this ingress the lively pair, with their spiritual need
of a warmer medium, would playfully punch in the ribs of her
ancestral home; for it would not only prevent recurring panic
at Poynton—it would offer them, as in one of their gimcrack
baskets or other vessels of ugliness, a definite daily felicity that
Poynton could never give. Owen might manage his estate just
as he managed it now, and Mrs. Gereth would manage everything else. When in the hall, on the unforgettable day of his
return, she had heard his voice ring out like a call to a terrier,
she had still, as Fleda afterwards learned, clutched frantically
at the conceit that he had come, at the worst, to announce
some compromise; to tell her she would have to put up with
the girl, yes, but that some way would be arrived at of leaving
her in personal possession. Fleda Vetch, whom from the earliest hour no illusion had brushed with its wing, now held her
breath, went on tiptoe, wandered in outlying parts of the
house and through delicate, muffled rooms while the mother
and son faced each other below. From time to time she
stopped to listen; but all was so quiet she was almost frightened: she had vaguely expected a sound of contention. It
lasted longer than she would have supposed, whatever it was
they were doing; and when finally, from a window, she saw
Owen stroll out of the house, stop and light a cigarette and
then pensively lose himself in the plantations, she found other
matter for trepidation in the fact that Mrs. Gereth didn't immediately come rushing up into her arms. She wondered
whether she oughtn't to go down to her, and measured the
gravity of what had occurred by the circumstance, which she
presently ascertained, that the poor lady had retired to her
room and wished not to be disturbed. This admonition had
been for her maid, with whom Fleda conferred as at the door
of a death-chamber; but the girl, without either fatuity or resentment, judged that, since it could render Mrs. Gereth
indifferent even to the ministrations of disinterested attachment, the scene had been tremendous.

She was absent from luncheon, where indeed Fleda had
enough to do to look Owen in the face: there would be so
much to make that hateful in their common memory of the
passage in which his last visit had terminated. This had been

her apprehension at least; but as soon as he stood there she was constrained to wonder at the practical simplicity of the ordeal—a simplicity which was really just his own simplicity, the particular thing that, for Fleda Vetch, some other things of course aiding, made almost any direct relation with him pleasant. He had neither wit, nor tact, nor inspiration: all she could say was that when they were together the alienation these charms were usually depended on to allay didn't occur. On this occasion, for instance, he did so much better than "carry off" an awkward remembrance: he simply didn't have it. He had clean forgotten that she was the girl his mother would have fobbed off on him; he was conscious only that she was there in a manner for service—conscious of the dumb instinct that from the first had made him regard her not as complicating his intercourse with that personage, but as simplifying it. Fleda found beautiful that this theory should have survived the incident of the other day; found exquisite that whereas she was conscious, through faint reverberations, that for her kind little circle at large, whom it didn't concern, her tendency had begun to define itself as parasitical, this strong young man, who had a right to judge and even a reason to loathe her, didn't judge and didn't loathe, let her down gently, treated her as if she pleased him, and in fact evidently liked her to be just where she was. She asked herself what he did when Mona denounced her, and the only answer to the question was that perhaps Mona didn't denounce her. If Mona was inarticulate he wasn't such a fool, then, to marry her. That he was glad Fleda was there was at any rate sufficiently shown by the domestic familiarity with which he said to her: "I must tell you I've been having an awful row with my mother. I'm engaged to be married to Miss Brigstock."

"Ah, really?" cried Fleda, achieving a radiance of which she was secretly proud. "How very exciting!"

"Too exciting for poor Mummy. She won't hear of it. She has been slating her fearfully. She says she's a 'barbarian.'"

"Why, she's lovely!" Fleda exclaimed.

"Oh, she's all right. Mother must come round."

"Only give her time," said Fleda. She had advanced to the threshold of the door thus thrown open to her and, without exactly crossing it, she threw in an appreciative glance. She asked Owen when his marriage would take place, and in the light of his reply read that Mrs. Gereth's wretched attitude would have no influence at all on the event, absolutely fixed when he came down and distant by only three months. He liked Fleda's seeming to be on his side, though that was a secondary matter; for what really most concerned him now was the line his mother took about Poynton, her declared unwillingness to give it up.

"Naturally I want my own house, you know," he said, "and my father made every arrangement for me to have it. But she may make it devilish awkward. What in the world's a fellow to do?" This it was that Owen wanted to know, and there could be no better proof of his friendliness than his air of depending on Fleda Vetch to tell him. She questioned him, they spent an hour together, and, as he gave her the scale of the concussion from which he had rebounded, she found herself saddened and frightened by the material he seemed to offer her to deal with. It *was* devilish awkward, and it was so in part because Owen had no imagination. It had lodged itself in that empty chamber that his mother hated the surrender because she hated Mona. He didn't of course understand why she hated Mona, but this belonged to an order of mysteries that never troubled him: there were lots of things, especially in people's minds, that a fellow didn't understand. Poor Owen went through life with a frank dread of people's minds: there were explanations he would have been almost as shy of receiving as of giving. There was therefore nothing that accounted for anything, though in its way it was vivid enough, in his picture to Fleda of his mother's virtual refusal to move. That was simply what it was; for didn't she refuse to move when she as good as declared that she would move only with the furniture? It was the furniture he wouldn't give up; and what was the good of Poynton without the furniture? Besides, the furniture happened to be his, just as everything else happened to be. The furniture—the word, on his lips, had somehow, for Fleda, the sound of washing-stands and copious bedding, and she could well imagine the note it might have struck for Mrs. Gereth. The girl, in this interview with him, spoke of the contents of the house only as "the works of art." It didn't, however, in the least matter to Owen what they were called; what did matter, she easily guessed, was that it had been laid upon him by Mona, been made in effect a condition of her consent, that he should hold his mother to the strictest accountability for them. Mona had already entered upon the enjoyment of her rights. She had made him feel that Mrs. Gereth had been liberally provided for, and had asked him cogently what room there would be at Ricks for the innumerable treasures of the big house. Ricks, the sweet little place offered to the mistress of Poynton as the refuge of her declining years, had been left to the late Mr. Gereth a considerable time before his death by an old maternal aunt, a good lady who had spent most of her life there. The house had in recent times been let, but it was amply furnished, it contained all the defunct aunt's possessions. Owen had lately inspected it, and he communicated to Fleda that he had quietly taken Mona to see it. It wasn't a place like Poynton—what dowerhouse ever was?—but it was an awfully jolly little place, and Mona had taken a tremendous fancy to it. If there were a few things at Poynton that were Mrs. Gereth's peculiar property, of course she must take them away with her; but one of the matters that became clear to Fleda was that this transfer would be immediately subject to Miss Brigstock's approval. The special business that she herself now became aware of being charged with was that of seeing Mrs. Gereth safely and singly off the premises.

Her heart failed her, after Owen had returned to London, with the ugliness of this duty—with the ugliness indeed of the whole close conflict. She saw nothing of Mrs. Gereth that day; she spent it in roaming with sick sighs, in feeling, as she passed from room to room, that what was expected of her companion was really dreadful. It would have been better never to have had such a place than to have had it and lose it. It was odious to *her* to have to look for solutions: what a strange relation between mother and son when there was no fundamental tenderness out of which a solution would irrepressibly spring! Was it Owen who was mainly responsible for that poverty? Fleda couldn't think so when she remembered that, so far as he was concerned, Mrs. Gereth would still have been welcome to keep her seat by the Poynton fire. The fact that from the moment one accepted his marrying one saw no

very different course for Owen to take—this fact made her all
the rest of that aching day find her best relief in the mercy of
not having yet to face her hostess. She dodged and dreamed
and romanced away the time. Instead of inventing a remedy
or a compromise, instead of preparing a plan by which a scandal might be averted, she gave herself, in her sentient solitude, up to a mere fairy-tale, up to the very taste of the
beautiful peace with which she would have filled the air if only
something might have been that could never have been.

V

I'LL GIVE UP the house if they'll let me take what I require!"—that, on the morrow, was what Mrs. Gereth's stifled night had qualified her to say with a tragic face at
breakfast. Fleda reflected that what she "required" was simply
every object that surrounded them. The poor woman would
have admitted this truth and accepted the conclusion to be
drawn from it, the reduction to the absurd of her attitude, the
exaltation of her revolt. The girl's dread of a scandal, of spectators and critics, diminished the more she saw how little vulgar avidity had to do with this rigour. It was not the crude
love of possession; it was the need to be faithful to a trust and
loyal to an idea. The idea was surely noble; it was that of the
beauty Mrs. Gereth had so patiently and consummately
wrought. Pale but radiant, her back to the wall, she rose there
like a heroine guarding a treasure. To give up the ship was to
flinch from her duty; there was something in her eyes that declared she would die at her post. If their difference should
become public the shame would be all for the others. If
Waterbath thought it could afford to expose itself, then
Waterbath was welcome to the folly. Her fanaticism gave her
a new distinction, and Fleda perceived almost with awe that
she had never carried herself so well. She trod the place like a
reigning queen or a proud usurper; full as it was of splendid
pieces it could show in these days no ornament so effective as
its menaced mistress.

Our young lady's spirit was strangely divided; she had a
tenderness for Owen which she deeply concealed, yet it left
her occasion to marvel at the way a man was made who could
care in any relation for a creature like Mona Brigstock when
he had known in any relation a creature like Adela Gereth.
With such a mother to give him the pitch how could he take
it so low? She wondered that she didn't despise him for this,
but there was something that kept her from it. If there had
been nothing else it would have sufficed that she really found
herself from this moment the medium of communication
with him.

"He'll come back to assert himself," Mrs. Gereth had said; and the following week Owen in fact re-appeared. He might merely have written, Fleda could see, but he had come in person because it was at once "nicer" for his mother and stronger for his cause. He didn't like the row, though Mona probably did; if he hadn't a sense of beauty he had after all a sense of justice; but it was inevitable he should clearly announce at Poynton the date at which he must look to find the house vacant. "You don't think I'm rough or hard, do you?" he asked of Fleda, his impatience shining in his idle eyes as the dining-hour shines in club-windows. "The place at Ricks stands there with open arms. And then I give her lots of time. Tell her she can remove everything that belongs to her." Fleda recognised the elements of what the newspapers call a deadlock in the circumstance that nothing at Poynton belonged to Mrs. Gereth either more or less than anything else. She must either take everything or nothing, and the girl's suggestion was that it might perhaps be an inspiration to do the latter and begin again on a clean page. What, however, was the poor woman in that case to begin with? What was she to do at all on her meagre income but make the best of the *objets d'art* of Ricks, the treasures collected by Mr. Gereth's maiden-aunt? She had never been near the place: for long years it had been let to strangers, and after that the foreboding that it would be her doom had kept her from the abasement of it. She had felt that she should see it soon enough, but Fleda (who was careful not to betray to her that Mona had seen it and had been gratified) knew her reasons for believing that the maiden-aunt's principles had had much in common with the principles of Waterbath. The only thing, in short, that she would ever have to do with the *objets d'art* of Ricks would be to turn them out into the road. What belonged to her at Poynton, as Owen said, would conveniently mitigate the void resulting from that demonstration.

The exchange of observations between the friends had grown very direct by the time Fleda asked Mrs. Gereth whether she literally meant to shut herself up and stand a siege, or whether it was her idea to expose herself, more informally, to be dragged out of the house by constables. "Oh, I prefer the constables and the dragging!" the heroine of

Poynton had answered. "I want to make Owen and Mona do everything that will be most publicly odious." She gave it out that it was her one thought now to force them to a line that would dishonour them and dishonour the tradition they embodied, though Fleda was privately sure that she had visions of an alternative policy. The strange thing was that, proud and fastidious all her life, she now showed so little distaste for the world's hearing of the squabble. What had taken place in her above all was that a long resentment had ripened. She hated the effacement to which English usage reduced the widowed mother; she had discoursed of it passionately to Fleda; contrasted it with the beautiful homage paid in other countries to women in that position, women no better than herself, whom she had seen acclaimed and enthroned, whom she had known and envied; made in short as little as possible a secret of the injury, the bitterness she found in it. The great wrong Owen had done her was not his "taking up" with Mona—that was disgusting, but it was a detail, an accidental form; it was his failure from the first to understand what it was to have a mother at all, to appreciate the beauty and sanctity of the character. She was just his mother as his nose was just his nose, and he had never had the least imagination or tenderness or gallantry about her. One's mother, gracious heaven, if one were the kind of fine young man one ought to be, the only kind Mrs. Gereth cared for, was a subject for poetry, for idolatry. Hadn't she often told Fleda of her friend Madame de Jaume, the wittiest of women, but a small, black crooked person, each of whose three boys, when absent, wrote to her every day of their lives? She had the house in Paris, she had the house in Poitou, she had more than in the lifetime of her husband (to whom, in spite of her appearance, she had afforded repeated cause for jealousy), because she had to the end of her days the supreme word about everything. It was easy to see that Mrs. Gereth would have given again and again her complexion, her figure, and even perhaps the spotless virtue she had still more successfully retained, to have been the consecrated Madame de Jaume. She wasn't, alas, and this was what she had at present a magnificent occasion to protest against. She was of course fully aware of Owen's concession, his willingness to let her take away with her the few things she liked best; but as yet she only declared that to meet him on this ground would be to give him a triumph, to put him impossibly in the right. "Liked best?" There wasn't a thing in the house that she didn't like best, and what she liked better still was to be left where she was. How could Owen use such an expression without being conscious of his hypocrisy? Mrs. Gereth, whose criticism was often gay, dilated with sardonic humour on the happy look a dozen objects from Poynton would wear and the charming effect they would conduce to when interspersed with the peculiar features of Ricks. What had her whole life been but an effort toward completeness and perfection? Better Waterbath at once, in its cynical unity, than the ignominy of such a mixture!

All this was of no great help to Fleda, in so far as Fleda tried to rise to her mission of finding a way out. When at the end of a fortnight Owen came down once more, it was ostensibly to tackle a farmer whose proceedings had been irregular; the girl was sure, however, that he had really come, on the instance of Mona, to see what his mother was doing. He wished to satisfy himself that she was preparing her departure, and he wished to perform a duty, distinct but not less imperative, in regard to the question of the perquisites with which she would retreat. The tension between them was now such that he had to perpetrate these offences without meeting his adversary. Mrs. Gereth was as willing as himself that he should address to Fleda Vetch whatever cruel remarks he might have to make; she only pitied her poor young friend for repeated encounters with a person as to whom she perfectly understood the girl's repulsion. Fleda thought it nice of Owen not to have expected her to write to him; he wouldn't have wished any more than herself that she should have the air of spying on his mother in his interest. What made it comfortable to deal with him in this more familiar way was the sense that she understood so perfectly how poor Mrs. Gereth suffered, and that she measured so adequately the sacrifice the other side did take rather monstrously for granted. She understood equally how Owen himself suffered, now that Mona had already begun to make him do things he didn't like. Vividly Fleda apprehended how *she* would have first made him like anything she would have made him do; anything even as disagreeable as this appearing there to state, virtually on Mona's behalf, that of course there must be a definite limit to the number of articles appropriated. She took a longish stroll with him in order to talk the matter over; to say if she didn't think a dozen pieces, chosen absolutely at will, would be a handsome allowance; and above all to consider the very delicate question of whether the advantage enjoyed by Mrs. Gereth mightn't be left to her honour. To leave it so was what Owen wished; but there was plainly a young lady at Waterbath to whom, on his side, he already had to render an account. He was as touching in his off-hand annoyance as his mother was tragic in her intensity; for if he couldn't help having a sense of propriety about the whole matter, so he could as little help hating it. It was for his hating it, Fleda reasoned, that she liked him so, and her insistence to his mother on the hatred perilously resembled on one or two occasions a revelation of the liking. There were moments when, in conscience, that revelation pressed her; inasmuch as it was just on the ground of her not liking him that Mrs. Gereth trusted her so much. Mrs. Gereth herself didn't in these days like him at all, and she was of course and always on Mrs. Gereth's side. He ended really, while the preparations for his marriage went on, by quite a little custom of coming and going; but at no one of these junctures would his mother receive him. He talked only with Fleda and strolled with Fleda; and when he asked her, in regard to the great matter, if Mrs. Gereth were really doing nothing, the girl usually replied: "She pretends not to be, if I may say so; but I think she's really thinking over what she'll take." When her friend asked her what Owen was doing she could have but one answer: "He's waiting, dear lady, to see what *you* do!"

Mrs. Gereth, a month after she had received her great shock, did something abrupt and extraordinary: she caught up her companion and went to have a look at Ricks. They had come to London first and taken a train from Liverpool Street, and the least of the sufferings they were armed against was that of passing the night. Fleda's admirable dressing-bag had been given her by her friend. "Why, it's charming!" she exclaimed a few hours later, turning back again into the small prim parlour from a friendly advance to the single plate of the window. Mrs. Gereth hated such windows, the one flat glass, sliding up and down, especially when they enjoyed a view of four iron pots on pedestals, painted white and containing ugly geraniums, ranged on the edge of a gravel-path and doing their best to give it the air of a terrace. Fleda had instantly averted her eyes from these ornaments, but Mrs. Gereth grimly gazed, wondering of course how a place in the deepest depths of Essex and three miles from a small station could contrive to look so suburban. The room was practically a shallow box, with the junction of the walls and ceiling guiltless of curve or cornice and marked merely by the little band of crimson paper glued round the top of the other paper, a turbid grey sprigged with silver flowers. This decoration was rather new and quite fresh; and there was in the centre of the ceiling a big square beam papered over in white, as to which Fleda hesitated about venturing to remark that it was rather picturesque. She recognised in time that this remark would be weak and that, throughout, she should be able to say nothing either for the mantelpieces or for the doors, of which she saw her companion become sensible with a soundless moan. On the subject of doors especially Mrs. Gereth had the finest views: the thing in the world she most despised was the meanness of the single flap. From end to end, at Poynton, there were high double leaves. At Ricks the entrances to the rooms were like the holes of rabbit-hutches.

It was all, none the less, not so bad as Fleda had feared; it was faded and melancholy, whereas there had been a danger that it would be contradictious and positive, cheerful and loud. The house was crowded with objects of which the aggregation somehow made a thinness and the futility a grace; things that told her they had been gathered as slowly and as lovingly as the golden flowers of Poynton. She too, for a home, could have lived with them: they made her fond of the old maiden-aunt; they made her even wonder if it didn't work more for happiness not to have tasted, as she herself had done, of knowledge. Without resources, without a stick, as she said, of her own, Fleda was moved, after all, to some secret surprise at the pretensions of a shipwrecked woman who could hold such an asylum cheap. The more she looked about the surer she felt of the character of the maiden-aunt, the

sense of whose dim presence urged her to pacification: the
maiden-aunt had been a dear; she would have adored the
maiden-aunt. The poor lady had had some tender little story;
she had been sensitive and ignorant and exquisite: that too
was a sort of origin, a sort of atmosphere for relics and rarities, though different from the sorts most prized at Poynton.
Mrs. Gereth had of course more than once said that one of
the deepest mysteries of life was the way that, by certain natures, hideous objects could be loved. But it wasn't a question
of love, now, for these; it was only a question of a certain
practical patience. Perhaps some thought of that kind had
stolen over Mrs. Gereth when, at the end of a brooding hour,
she exclaimed, taking in the house with a strenuous sigh:
"Well, something can be done with it!" Fleda had repeated to
her more than once the indulgent fancy about the maiden-
aunt—she was so sure she had deeply suffered. "I'm sure I
hope she did!" was, however, all that Mrs. Gereth had replied.

VI

IT WAS a great relief to the girl at last to perceive that the dreadful move would really be made. What might happen if it shouldn't had been from the first indefinite. It was absurd to pretend that any violence was probable—a tussle, dishevelment, shrieks; yet Fleda had an imagination of a drama, a "great scene," a thing, somehow, of indignity and misery, of wounds inflicted and received, in which indeed, though Mrs. Gereth's presence, with movements and sounds, loomed large to her, Owen remained indistinct and on the whole unaggressive. He wouldn't be there with a cigarette in his teeth, very handsome and insolently quiet: that was only the way he would be in a novel, across whose interesting page some such figure, as she half closed her eyes, seemed to her to walk. Fleda had rather, and indeed with shame, a confused, pitying vision of Mrs. Gereth with her great scene left in a manner on her hands, Mrs. Gereth missing her effect and having to appear merely hot and injured and in the wrong. The symptoms that she would be spared even that spectacle resided not so much, through the chambers of Poynton, in an air of concentration as in the hum of buzzing alternatives. There was no common preparation, but one day, at the turn of a corridor, she found her hostess standing very still, with the hanging hands of an invalid and the active eyes of an adventurer. These eyes appeared to Fleda to meet her own with a strange, dim bravado, and there was a silence, almost awkward, before either of the friends spoke. The girl afterwards thought of the moment as one in which her hostess mutely accused her of an accusation, meeting it, however, at the same time, by a kind of defiant acceptance. Yet it was with mere melancholy candour that Mrs. Gereth at last sighingly exclaimed: "I'm thinking over what I had better take!" Fleda could have embraced her for this virtual promise of a concession, the announcement that she had finally accepted the problem of knocking together a shelter with the small salvage of the wreck.

It was true that when after their return from Ricks they
tried to lighten the ship the great embarrassment was still im-
mutably there, the odiousness of sacrificing the exquisite
things one wouldn't take to the exquisite things one would.
This immediately made the things one wouldn't take the very
things one ought to, and, as Mrs. Gereth said, condemned
one, in the whole business, to an eternal vicious circle. In
such a circle, for days, she had been tormentedly moving,
prowling up and down, comparing incomparables. It was for
that one had to cling to them and their faces of supplication.
Fleda herself could judge of these faces, so conscious of their
race and their danger, and she had little enough to say when
her companion asked her if the whole place, perversely fair on
October afternoons, looked like a place to give up. It looked,
to begin with, through some effect of season and light, larger
than ever, immense, and it was filled with the hush of sorrow,
which in turn was all charged with memories. Everything was
in the air—every history of every find, every circumstance of
every struggle. Mrs. Gereth had drawn back every curtain and
removed every cover; she prolonged the vistas, opened wide
the whole house, gave it an appearance of awaiting a royal
visit. The shimmer of wrought substances spent itself in the
brightness; the old golds and brasses, old ivories and bronzes,
the fresh old tapestries and deep old damasks threw out a radiance in which the poor woman saw in solution all her old
loves and patiences, all her old tricks and triumphs.

Fleda had a depressed sense of not, after all, helping her
much: this was lightened indeed by the fact that Mrs. Gereth,
letting her off easily, didn't now seem to expect it. Her sympathy, her interest, her feeling for everything for which Mrs.
Gereth felt, were a force that really worked to prolong the
deadlock. "I only wish I bored you and my possessions bored
you," that lady, with some humour, declared; "then you'd
make short work with me, bundle me off, tell me just to pile
certain things into a cart and have done." Fleda's sharpest
difficulty was in having to act up to the character of thinking Owen a brute, or at least to carry off the inconsistency of
seeing him when he came down. By good fortune it was her
duty, her function, as well as a protection to Mrs. Gereth. She
thought of him perpetually, and her eyes had come to rejoice

in his manly magnificence more even than they rejoiced in the royal cabinets of the red saloon. She wondered, very faintly at first, why he came so often; but of course she knew nothing about the business he had in hand, over which, with men red-faced and leather-legged, he was sometimes closeted for an hour in a room of his own that was the one monstrosity of Poynton: all tobacco-pots and bootjacks, his mother had said—such an array of arms of aggression and castigation that he himself had confessed to eighteen rifles and forty whips. He was arranging for settlements on his wife, he was doing things that would meet the views of the Brigstocks. Considering the house was his own, Fleda thought it nice of him to keep himself in the background while his mother remained; making his visits, at some cost of ingenuity about trains from town, only between meals, doing everything to let it press lightly upon her that he was there. This was rather a stoppage to her meeting Mrs. Gereth on the ground of his being a brute; the most she really at last could do was not to contradict her when she repeated that he was watching—just insultingly watching. He *was* watching, no doubt; but he watched somehow with his head turned away. He knew that Fleda knew at present what he wanted of her, so that it would be gross of him to say it over and over. It existed as a confidence between them and made him sometimes, with his wandering stare, meet her eyes as if a silence so pleasant could only unite them the more. He had no great flow of speech, certainly, and at first the girl took for granted that this was all there was to be said about the matter. Little by little she speculated as to whether, with a person who, like herself, could put him, after all, at a sort of domestic ease, it was not supposable that he would have more conversation if he were not keeping some of it back for Mona.

From the moment she suspected he might be thinking what Mona would say to his chattering so to an underhand "companion," an inmate all but paid, this young lady's repressed emotion began to require still more repression. She grew impatient of her situation at Poynton; she privately pronounced it false and horrid. She said to herself that she had let Owen know that she had, to the best of her power, directed his mother in the general sense he desired; that he quite understood it and that he also understood how unworthy it was of either of them to stand over the good lady with a notebook and a lash. Wasn't this practical unanimity just practical success? Fleda became aware of a sudden desire, as well as of pressing reasons, to bring her stay at Poynton to a close. She had not, on the one hand, like a minion of the law, undertaken to see Mrs. Gereth down to the train and locked, in sign of her abdication, into a compartment; neither had she on the other committed herself to hold Owen indefinitely in dalliance while his mother gained time or dug a countermine. Besides, people *were* saying that she fastened like a leech on other people—people who had houses where something was to be picked up: this revelation was frankly made her by her sister, now distinctly doomed to the curate and in view of whose nuptials she had almost finished, as a present, a wonderful piece of embroidery, suggested, at Poynton, by an old Spanish altar-cloth. She would have to exert herself still further for the intended recipient of this offering, turn her out for her marriage with more than that drapery. She would go up to town, in short, to dress Maggie; and their father, in lodgings at West Kensington, would stretch a point and take them in. He, to do him justice, never reproached her with profitable devotions; so far as they existed he consciously profited by them. Mrs. Gereth gave her up as heroically as if she had been a great bargain, and Fleda knew that she wouldn't at present miss any visit of Owen's, for Owen was shooting at Waterbath. Owen shooting was Owen lost, and there was scant sport at Poynton.

The first news she had from Mrs. Gereth was news of that lady's having accomplished, in form at least, her migration. The letter was dated from Ricks, to which place she had been transported by an impulse apparently as sudden as the inspiration she had obeyed before. "Yes, I've literally come," she wrote, "with a bandbox and a kitchen-maid; I've crossed the Rubicon, I've taken possession. It has been like plumping into cold water. I saw the only thing was to do it, not to stand shivering. I shall have warmed the place a little by simply being here for a week; when I come back the ice will have been broken. I didn't write to you to meet me on my way through town, because I know how busy you are and because, besides,

I'm too savage and odious to be fit company even for you. You'd say I really go too far, and there's no doubt whatever I do. I'm here, at any rate, just to look round once more, to see that certain things are done before I enter in force. I shall probably be at Poynton all next week. There's more room than I quite measured the other day, and a rather good set of old Worcester. But what are space and time, what's even old Worcester, to your wretched and affectionate A. G.?"

The day after Fleda received this letter she had occasion to go into a big shop in Oxford Street—a journey that she achieved circuitously, first on foot and then by the aid of two omnibuses. The second of these vehicles put her down on the side of the street opposite her shop, and while, on the curbstone, she humbly waited, with a parcel, an umbrella and a tucked-up frock, to cross in security, she became aware that, close beside her, a hansom had pulled up short, in obedience to the brandished stick of a demonstrative occupant. This occupant was Owen Gereth, who had caught sight of her as he rattled along and who, with an exhibition of white teeth that, from under the hood of the cab, had almost flashed through the fog, now alighted to ask her if he couldn't give her a lift. On finding that her destination was just over the way he dismissed his vehicle and joined her, not only piloting her to the shop, but taking her in; with the assurance that his errands didn't matter, that it amused him to be concerned with hers. She told him she had come to buy a trimming for her sister's frock, and he expressed an hilarious interest in the purchase. His hilarity was almost always out of proportion to the case, but it struck her at present as more so than ever; especially when she had suggested that he might find it a good time to buy a garnishment of some sort for Mona. After wondering an instant whether he gave the full satiric meaning, such as it was, to this remark, Fleda dismissed the possibility as inconceivable. He stammered out that it was for *her* he would like to buy something, something "ripping," and that she must give him the pleasure of telling him what would best please her. He couldn't have a better opportunity for making her a present—the present, in recognition of all she had done for Mummy that he had had in his head for weeks.

Fleda had more than one small errand in the big bazaar,

and he went up and down with her, pointedly patient, pretending to be interested in questions of tape and of change.
She had now not the least hesitation in wondering what
Mona would think of such proceedings. But they were not
her doing—they were Owen's; and Owen, inconsequent and
even extravagant, was unlike anything she had ever seen him
before. He broke off, he came back, he repeated questions
without heeding answers, he made vague abrupt remarks
about the resemblances of shopgirls and the uses of chiffon.
He unduly prolonged their business together, giving Fleda a
sense that he was putting off something particular that he had
to face. If she had ever dreamed of Owen Gereth as nervous
she would have seen him with some such manner as this. But
why should he be nervous? Even at the height of the crisis his
mother hadn't made him so, and at present he was satisfied
about his mother. The one idea he stuck to was that Fleda
should mention something she would let him give her: there
was everything in the world in the wonderful place, and he
made her incongruous offers—a travelling-rug, a massive
clock, a table for breakfast in bed, and above all, in a resplen-
dent binding, a set of somebody's "works." His notion was a
testimonial, a tribute, and the "works" would be a graceful
intimation that it was her cleverness he wished above all to
commemorate. He was immensely in earnest, but the articles
he pressed upon her betrayed a delicacy that went to her
heart: what he would really have liked, as he saw them tumbled about, was one of the splendid stuffs for a gown—a
choice proscribed by his fear of seeming to patronize her, to
refer to her small means and her deficiencies. Fleda found it
easy to chaff him about his exaggeration of her deserts; she
gave the just measure of them in consenting to accept a small
pin-cushion, costing sixpence, in which the letter F was
marked out with pins. A sense of loyalty to Mona was not
needed to enforce this discretion, and after that first allusion
to her she never sounded her name. She noticed on this occasion more things in Owen Gereth than she had ever noticed
before, but what she noticed most was that he said no word
of his intended. She asked herself what he had done, in so
long a parenthesis, with his loyalty or at least his "form"; and
then reflected that even if he had done something very good

with them the situation in which such a question could come up was already a little strange. Of course he wasn't doing anything so vulgar as to make love to her; but there was a kind of punctilio for a man who was engaged.

That punctilio didn't prevent Owen from remaining with her after they had left the shop, from hoping she had a lot more to do, and from pressing her to look with him, for a possible glimpse of something she might really let him give her, into the windows of other establishments. There was a moment when, under this pressure, she made up her mind that his tribute would be, if analysed, a tribute to her insignificance. But all the same he wanted her to come somewhere and have luncheon with him: what was that a tribute to? She must have counted very little if she didn't count too much for a romp in a restaurant. She had to get home with her trimming, and the most, in his company, she was amenable to was a retracing of her steps to the Marble Arch and then, after a discussion when they had reached it, a walk with him across the Park. She knew Mona would have considered that she ought to take the omnibus again; but she had now to think for Owen as well as for herself—she couldn't think for Mona. Even in the Park the autumn air was thick, and as they moved westward over the grass, which was what Owen preferred, the cool greyness made their words soft, made them at last rare and everything else dim. He wanted to stay with her—he wanted not to leave her: he had dropped into complete silence, but that was what his silence said. What was it he had postponed? What was it he wanted still to postpone? She grew a little scared as they strolled together and she thought. It was too confused to be believed, but it was as if somehow he felt differently. Fleda Vetch didn't suspect him at first of feeling differently to *her*, but only of feeling differently to Mona; yet she was not unconscious that this latter difference would have had something to do with his being on the grass beside her. She had read in novels about gentlemen who on the eve of marriage, winding up the past, had surrendered themselves for the occasion to the influence of a former tie; and there was something in Owen's behaviour now, something in his very face, that suggested a resemblance to one of those gentlemen. But whom and what, in that case,

would Fleda herself resemble? She wasn't a former tie, she
wasn't any tie at all; she was only a deep little person for
whom happiness was a kind of pearl-diving plunge. It was
down at the very bottom of all that had lately occurred; for all
that had lately occurred was that Owen Gereth had come and
gone at Poynton. That was the small sum of her experience,
and what it had made for her was her own affair, quite consistent with her not having dreamed it had made a tie—at
least what *she* called one—for Owen. The old one, at any rate,
was Mona—Mona whom he had known so very much longer.

They walked far, to the south-west corner of the great
Gardens, where, by the old round pond and the old red
palace, when she had put out her hand to him in farewell,
declaring that from the gate she must positively take a conveyance, it seemed suddenly to rise between them that this
was a real separation. She was on his mother's side, she belonged to his mother's life, and his mother, in the future,
would never come to Poynton. After what had passed she
wouldn't even be at his wedding, and it was not possible
now that Mr. Gereth should mention that ceremony to the
girl, much less express a wish that the girl should be present
at it. Mona, from decorum and with reference less to the
bridegroom than to the bridegroom's mother, would of
course not invite any such girl as Fleda. Everything therefore
was ended; they would go their different ways; this was the
last time they would stand face to face. They looked at each
other with the fuller sense of it and, on Owen's part, with
an expression of dumb trouble, the intensification of his
usual appeal to any interlocutor to add the right thing to
what he said. To Fleda at this moment it appeared that the
right thing might easily be the wrong. At any rate he only
said: "I want you to understand, you know—I want you to
understand."

What did he want her to understand? He seemed unable to
bring it out, and this understanding was moreover exactly
what she wished not to arrive at. Bewildered as she was, she
had already taken in as much as she should know what to do
with; the blood also was rushing into her face. He liked her—
it was stupefying—more than he really ought: that was what
was the matter with him and what he desired her to swallow;

so that she was suddenly as frightened as some thoughtless girl who finds herself the object of an overture from a married man.

"Good-bye, Mr. Gereth—I *must* get on!" she declared with a cheerfulness that she felt to be an unnatural grimace. She broke away from him sharply, smiling, backing across the grass and then turning altogether and moving as fast as she could. "Good-bye, good-bye!" she threw off again as she went, wondering if he would overtake her before she reached the gate; conscious with a red disgust that her movement was almost a run; conscious too of just the confused handsome face with which he would look after her. She felt as if she had answered a kindness with a great flouncing snub but in any case she had got away, though the distance to the gate, her ugly gallop down the Broad Walk, every graceless jerk of which hurt her, seemed endless. She signed from afar to a cab on the stand in the Kensington Road and scrambled into it, glad of the encompassment of the four-wheeler that had officiously obeyed her summons and that, at the end of twenty yards, when she had violently pulled up a glass, permitted her to recognise the fact that she was on the point of bursting into tears.

VII

As soon as her sister was married she went down to Mrs. Gereth at Ricks—a promise to this effect having been promptly exacted and given; and her inner vision was much more fixed on the alterations there, complete now as she understood, than on the success of her plotting and pinching for Maggie's happiness. Her imagination, in the interval, had indeed had plenty to do and numerous scenes to visit; for when on the summons just mentioned it had taken a flight from West Kensington to Ricks, it had hung but an hour over the terrace of painted pots and then yielded to a current of the upper air that swept it straight off to Poynton and to Waterbath. Not a sound had reached her of any supreme clash, and Mrs. Gereth had communicated next to nothing; giving out that, as was easily conceivable, she was too busy, too bitter and too tired for vain civilities. All she had written was that she had got the new place well in hand and that Fleda would be surprised at the way it was turning out. Everything was even yet upside down; nevertheless, in the sense of having passed the threshold of Poynton for the last time, the amputation, as she called it, had been performed. Her leg had come off—she had now begun to stump along with the lovely wooden substitute; she would stump for life, and what her young friend was to come and admire was the beauty of her movement and the noise she made about the house. The reserve of Poynton and Waterbath had been matched by the austerity of Fleda's own secret, under the discipline of which she had repeated to herself a hundred times a day that she rejoiced at having cares that excluded all thought of it. She had lavished herself, in act, on Maggie and the curate, and had opposed to her father's selfishness a sweetness quite ecstatic. The young couple wondered why they had waited so long, since everything was after all so easy. She had thought of everything, even to how the "quietness" of the wedding should be relieved by champagne and her father kept brilliant on a single bottle. Fleda knew, in short, and liked the knowledge, that for several weeks she had appeared exemplary in every relation of life.

She had been perfectly prepared to be surprised at Ricks, for Mrs. Gereth was a wonder-working wizard, with a command, when all was said, of good material; but the impression in wait for her on the threshold made her catch her breath and falter. Dusk had fallen when she arrived, and in the plain square hall, one of the few good features, the glow of a Venetian lamp just showed, on either wall, the richness of an admirable tapestry. This instant perception that the place had been dressed at the expense of Poynton was a shock: it was as if she had abruptly seen herself in the light of an accomplice. The next moment, folded in Mrs. Gereth's arms, her eyes were diverted; but she had already had, in a flash, the vision of the great gaps in the other house. The two tapestries, not the largest, but those most splendidly toned by time, had been on the whole its most uplifted pride. When she could really see again she was on a sofa in the drawing-room, staring with intensity at an object soon distinct as the great Italian cabinet that, at Poynton, had been in the red saloon. Without looking, she was sure the room was occupied with other objects like it, stuffed with as many as it could hold of the trophies of her friend's struggle. By this time the very fingers of her glove, resting on the seat of the sofa, had thrilled at the touch of an old velvet brocade, a wondrous texture that she could recognise, would have recognised among a thousand, without dropping her eyes on it. They stuck to the cabinet with a kind of dissimulated dread, while she painfully asked herself whether she should notice it, notice everything, or just pretend not to be affected. How could she pretend not to be affected, with the very pendants of the lustres tinkling at her, and with Mrs. Gereth beside her and staring at her even as she herself stared at the cabinet, hunching up a back like Atlas under his globe? She was appalled at this image of what Mrs. Gereth had on her shoulders. That lady was waiting and watching her, bracing herself and preparing the same face of confession and defiance she had shown the day, at Poynton, she had been surprised in the corridor. It was farcical not to speak; and yet to exclaim, to participate, would give one a bad sense of being mixed up with a theft. This ugly

word sounded, for herself, in Fleda's silence, and the very violence of it jarred her into a scared glance, as of a creature detected, to the right and left. But what again the full picture
most showed her was the far-away empty sockets, a scandal of
nakedness in high, bare walls. She at last uttered something
formal and incoherent—she didn't know what: it had no relation to either house. Then she felt Mrs. Gereth's hand once
more on her arm. "I've arranged a charming room for you—
it's really lovely. You'll be very happy there." This was spoken
with extraordinary sweetness and with a smile that meant:
"Oh, I know what you're thinking; but what does it matter
when you're so loyally on my side?" It had come indeed to a
question of "sides," Fleda thought, for the whole place was in
battle array. In the soft lamplight, with one fine feature after
another looming up into sombre richness, it defied her not to
pronounce it a triumph of taste. Her passion for beauty
leaped back into life; and was not what now most appealed to
it a certain gorgeous audacity? Mrs. Gereth's high hand was,
as mere great effect, the climax of the impression.

"It's too wonderful, what you've done with the house!"
—the visitor met her friend's eyes. They lighted up with
joy—that friend herself so pleased with what she had done.
This was not at all, in its accidental air of enthusiasm, what
Fleda wanted to have said: it offered her as stupidly announcing from the first minute on whose side she was. Such
was clearly the way Mrs. Gereth took it; she threw herself
upon the delightful girl and tenderly embraced her again; so
that Fleda soon went on, with a studied difference and a
cooler inspection: "Why, you brought away absolutely everything!"

"Oh, no, not everything. I saw how little I could get into
this scrap of a house. I only brought away what I required."

Fleda had got up; she took a turn round the room. "You
'required' the very best pieces—the *morceaux de musée*, the
individual gems!"

"I certainly didn't want the rubbish, if that's what you
mean." Mrs. Gereth, on the sofa, followed the direction of
her companion's eyes; with the light of her satisfaction still in
her face she slowly rubbed her large handsome hands. Wherever she was, she was herself the great piece in the gallery. It

was the first Fleda had heard of there being "rubbish" at Poynton, but she didn't for the moment take up this insincerity; she only, from where she stood in the room, called out, one after the other, as if she had had a list before her, the items that in the great house had been scattered and that now, if they had a fault, were too much like a minuet danced on a hearth-rug. She knew them each, in every chink and charm—knew them by the personal name their distinctive sign or story had given them; and a second time she felt how, against her intention, this uttered knowledge struck her hostess as so much free approval. Mrs. Gereth was never indifferent to approval, and there was nothing she could so love you for as for doing justice to her deep morality. There was a particular gleam in her eyes when Fleda exclaimed at last, dazzled by the display: "And even the Maltese cross!" That description, though technically incorrect, had always been applied at Poynton to a small but marvelous crucifix of ivory, a masterpiece of delicacy, of expression and of the great Spanish period, the existence and precarious accessibility of which she had heard of at Malta, years before, by an odd and romantic chance—a clue followed through mazes of secrecy till the treasure was at last unearthed.

"'Even' the Maltese cross?" Mrs. Gereth rose as she sharply echoed the words. "My dear child, you don't suppose I'd have sacrificed *that*! For what in the world would you have taken me?"

"A *bibelot* the more or less," Fleda said, "could have made little difference in this grand general view of you. I take you simply for the greatest of all conjurers. You've operated with a quickness—and with a quietness!" Her voice trembled a little as she spoke, for the plain meaning of her words was that what her friend had achieved belonged to the class of operation, essentially involving the protection of darkness. Fleda felt she really could say nothing at all if she couldn't say that she knew what the danger had been. She completed her thought by a resolute and perfectly candid question. "How in the world did you get off with them?"

Mrs. Gereth confessed to the fact of danger with a cynicism that surprised the girl. "By calculating, by choosing my time. I *was* quiet and I *was* quick. I manœuvred; then at the last rushed!" Fleda drew a long breath: she saw in the poor woman something much better than sophistical ease, a crude elation that was a comparatively simple state to deal with. Her elation, it was true, was not so much from what she had done as from the way she had done it—by as brilliant a stroke as any commemorated in the annals of crime. "I succeeded because I had thought it all out and left nothing to chance. The whole process was organised in advance, so that the mere carrying it into effect took but a few hours. It was largely a matter of money: oh, I was horribly extravagant—I had to turn on so many people. But they were all to be had—a little army of workers, the packers, the porters, the helpers of every sort, the men with the mighty vans. It was a question of arranging in Tottenham Court Road and of paying the price. I haven't paid it yet; there'll be a horrid bill; but at least the thing's done! Expedition pure and simple was the essence of the bargain. 'I can give you two days,' I said; 'I can't give you another second.' They undertook the job, and the two days saw them through. The people came down on a Tuesday morning; they were off on the Thursday. I admit that some of them worked all Wednesday night. I had thought it all out; I stood over them; I showed them how. Yes, I coaxed them, I made love to them. Oh, I was inspired—they found me wonderful. I neither ate nor slept, but I was as calm as I am now. I didn't know what was in me; it was worth finding out. I'm very remarkable, my dear: I lifted tons with my own arms. I'm tired, very, very tired; but there's neither a scratch nor a nick, there isn't a teacup missing." Magnificent both in her exhaustion and in her triumph, Mrs. Gereth sank on the sofa again, the sweep of her eyes a rich synthesis and the restless friction of her hands a clear betrayal. "Upon my word," she laughed, "they really look better here!"

Fleda had listened in awe. "And no one at Poynton said anything? There was no alarm?"

"What alarm should there have been? Owen left me almost defiantly alone. I had taken a time that I had reason to believe was safe from a descent." Fleda had another wonder, which she hesitated to express: it would scarcely do to ask Mrs. Gereth if she hadn't stood in fear of her servants. She knew moreover some of the secrets of her humorous household

rule, all made up of shocks to shyness and provocations to curiosity—a diplomacy so artful that several of the maids quite
yearned to accompany her to Ricks. Mrs. Gereth, reading
sharply the whole of her visitor's thought, caught it up with
fine frankness. "You mean that I was watched—that he had
his myrmidons, pledged to wire him if they should see what I
was 'up to'? Precisely. I know the three persons you have in
mind: I had them in mind myself. Well, I took a line with
them—I settled them."

Fleda had had no one in particular in mind; she had never
believed in the myrmidons; but the tone in which Mrs.
Gereth spoke added to her suspense. "What did you do to
them?"

"I took hold of them hard—I put them in the forefront. I
made them work."

"To move the furniture?"

"To help, and to help so as to please me. That was the way
to take them: it was what they had least expected. I marched
up to them and looked each straight in the eye, giving him
the chance to choose if he'd gratify me or gratify my son. He
gratified *me*. They were too stupid!"

Mrs. Gereth massed herself more and more as an immoral
woman, but Fleda had to recognise that she too would have
been stupid and she too would have gratified her. "And when
did all this take place?"

"Only last week; it seems a hundred years. We've worked
here as fast as we worked there, but I'm not settled yet: you'll
see in the rest of the house. However, the worst is over."

"Do you really think so?" Fleda presently inquired. "I
mean, does he, after the fact, as it were, accept it?"

"Owen—what I've done? I haven't the least idea," said
Mrs. Gereth.

"Does Mona?"

"You mean that she'll be the soul of the row?"

"I hardly see Mona as the 'soul' of anything," the girl
replied. "But have they made no sound? Have you heard
nothing at all?"

"Not a whisper, not a step, in all the eight days. Perhaps
they don't know. Perhaps they're crouching for a leap."

"But wouldn't they have gone down as soon as you left?"

"They may not have known of my leaving." Fleda wondered afresh; it struck her as scarcely supposable that some sign shouldn't have flashed from Poynton to London. If the storm was taking this term of silence to gather, even in Mona's breast, it would probably discharge itself in some startling form. The great hush of every one concerned was strange; but when she pressed Mrs. Gereth for some explanation of it that lady only replied with her brave irony: "Oh, I took their breath away!" She had no illusions, however; she was still prepared to fight. What indeed was her spoliation of Poynton but the first engagement of a campaign?

All this was exciting, but Fleda's spirit dropped, at bedtime, in the chamber embellished for her pleasure, where she found several of the objects that in her earlier room she had most admired. These had been reinforced by other pieces from other rooms, so that the quiet air of it was a harmony without a break, the finished picture of a maiden's bower. It was the sweetest Louis Seize, all assorted and combined—old chastened, figured, faded France. Fleda was impressed anew with her friend's genius for composition. She could say to herself that no girl in England, that night, went to rest with so picked a guard; but there was no joy for her in her privilege, no sleep even for the tired hours that made the place, in the embers of the fire and the winter dawn, look grey, somehow, and loveless. She couldn't care for such things when they came to her in such ways; there was a wrong about them all that turned them to ugliness. In the watches of the night she saw Poynton dishonoured; she had cherished it as a happy whole, she reasoned, and the parts of it now around her seemed to suffer like chopped limbs. Before going to bed she had walked about with Mrs. Gereth and seen at whose expense the whole house had been furnished. At poor Owen's, from top to bottom—there wasn't a chair he hadn't sat upon. The maiden aunt had been exterminated—no trace of her to tell her tale. Fleda tried to think of some of the things at Poynton still unappropriated, but her memory was a blank about them, and in trying to focus the old combinations she saw again nothing but gaps and scars, a vacancy that gathered at moments into something worse. This concrete image was her greatest trouble, for it was Owen Gereth's face, his sad, strange eyes, fixed upon her now as they had never been. They stared at her out of the darkness, and their expression was more than she could bear: it seemed to say that he was in pain and that it was somehow her fault. He had looked to her to help him, and this was what her help had been. He had done her the honour to ask her to exert herself in his interest, confiding to her a task of difficulty, but of the highest delicacy. Hadn't that been exactly the sort of service she longed to render him? Well, her way of rendering it had been simply to betray him and hand him over to his enemy. Shame, pity, resentment oppressed her in turn; in the last of these feelings the others were quickly submerged. Mrs. Gereth had imprisoned her in that torment of taste; but it was clear to her for an hour at least that she might hate Mrs. Gereth.

Something else, however, when morning came, was even more intensely definite: the most odious thing in the world for her would be ever again to meet Owen. She took on the spot a resolve to neglect no precaution that could lead to her going through life without that calamity. After this, while she dressed, she took still another. Her position had become in a few hours intolerably false; in as few more hours as possible she would therefore put an end to it. The way to put an end to it would be to inform Mrs. Gereth that, to her great regret, she couldn't be with her now, couldn't cleave to her to the point that everything about her so plainly urged. She dressed with a sort of violence, a symbol of the manner in which this purpose was precipitated. The more they parted company the less likely she was to come across Owen; for Owen would be drawn closer to his mother now by the very necessity of bringing her down. Fleda, in the inconsequence of distress, wished to have nothing to do with her fall; she had had too much to do with everything. She was well aware of the importance, before breakfast and in view of any light they might shed on the question of motive, of not suffering her invidious expression of a difference to be accompanied by the traces of tears; but it none the less came to pass, down-stairs, that after she had subtly put her back to the window to make a mystery of the state of her eyes she stupidly let a rich sob escape her before she could properly meet the consequences of being asked if she wasn't delighted with her room. This accident struck her on the spot as so grave that she felt the only refuge to be instant hypocrisy, some graceful impulse that would charge her emotion to the quickened sense of her friend's generosity—a demonstration entailing a flutter round the table and a renewed embrace, and not so successfully improvised but that Fleda fancied Mrs. Gereth to have been only half reassured. She had been startled at any rate and she might remain suspicious: this reflection interposed by the time, after breakfast, the girl had recovered sufficiently to say what was in her heart. She accordingly didn't say it that morning at all. She had absurdly veered about; she had encountered the shock of the fear that Mrs. Gereth, with sharpened eyes, might wonder why the deuce (she often wondered in that phrase) she had grown so warm about Owen's rights. She would doubtless at a pinch be able to defend them on abstract grounds, but that would involve a discussion, and the idea of a discussion made her nervous for her secret. Until in some way Poynton should return the blow and give her a cue she must keep nervousness down; and she called herself a fool for having forgotten, however briefly, that her one safety was in silence.

Directly after luncheon Mrs. Gereth took her into the garden for a glimpse of the revolution—or at least, said the mistress of Ricks, of the great row—that had been decreed there; but the ladies had scarcely placed themselves for this view before the younger one found herself embracing a prospect that opened in quite another quarter. Her attention was called to it, oddly, by the streamers of the parlour-maid's cap, which, flying straight behind the neat young woman who unexpectedly burst from the house and showed a long red face as she ambled over the grass, seemed to articulate in their flutter the name that Fleda lived at present only to catch. "Poynton— Poynton!" said the morsels of muslin; so that the parlour-maid became on the instant an actress in the drama, and Fleda, assuming pusillanimously that she herself was only a spectator, looked across the footlights at the exponent of the principal part. The manner in which this artist returned her look showed that she was equally preoccupied. Both were haunted alike by possibilities, but the apprehension of neither, before the announcement was made, took the form of the arrival at Ricks, in the flesh, of Mrs. Gereth's victim. When the messenger informed them that Mr. Gereth was in the drawing-room the blank "Oh!" emitted by Fleda was quite as precipitate as the sound on her hostess's lips, besides being, as she felt, much less pertinent. "I thought it would be somebody," that lady afterwards said; "but I expected on the whole a solicitor's clerk." Fleda didn't mention that she herself had expected on the whole a pair of constables. She was surprised by Mrs. Gereth's question to the parlour-maid.

"For whom did he ask?"

"Why, for *you*, of course, dearest friend!" Fleda interjected, falling instinctively into the address that embodied the intensest pressure. She wanted to put Mrs. Gereth between her and her danger.

"He asked for Miss Vetch, mum," the girl replied with a face that brought startlingly to Fleda's ear the muffled chorus of the kitchen.

"Quite proper," said Mrs. Gereth austerely. Then to Fleda: "Please go to him."

"But what to do?"

"What you always do—to see what he wants." Mrs. Gereth dismissed the maid. "Tell him Miss Vetch will come." Fleda saw that nothing was in the mother's imagination at this moment but the desire not to meet her son. She had completely broken with him, and there was little in what had just happened to repair the rupture. It would now take more to do so than his presenting himself uninvited at her door. "He's right in asking for you—he's aware that you're still our communicator; nothing has occurred to alter that. To what he wishes to transmit through you I'm ready, as I've been ready before, to listen. As far as *I'm* concerned, if I couldn't meet him a month ago how am I to meet him to-day? If he has come to say, 'My dear mother, you're here, in the hovel into which I've flung you, with consolations that give me pleasure,' I'll listen to him; but on no other footing. That's what you're to ascertain, please. You'll oblige me as you've obliged me before. There!" Mrs. Gereth turned her back and, with a fine imitation of superiority, began to redress the miseries immediately before her. Fleda meanwhile hesitated, lingered for some minutes where she had been left, feeling secretly that her fate still had her in hand. It had put her face to face with Owen Gereth and it evidently meant to keep her so. She was reminded afresh of two things: one of which was that, though she judged her friend's rigour, she had never really had the story of the scene enacted in the great awe-stricken house between the mother and the son weeks before—the day the former took to her bed in her overthrow. The other was that at Ricks as at Poynton it was before all things her place to accept thankfully a usefulness not, she must remember, universally acknowledged. What determined her at the last, while Mrs. Gereth disappeared in the shrubbery, was that, though she was at a distance from the house and the drawing-room was turned the other way, she could absolutely see the young man alone there with the sources of his pain. She saw his simple stare at his tapestries, heard his heavy tread on his carpets and the hard breath of his sense of unfairness. At this she went to him fast.

VIII

I ASKED for you," he said when she stood there, "because I heard from the flyman who drove me from the station to the inn that he had brought you here yesterday. We had some talk—he mentioned it."

"You didn't know I was here?"

"No. I knew only that you had had, in London, all that you told me, that day, to do; and it was Mona's idea that after your sister's marriage you were staying on with your father. So I thought you were with him still."

"I am," Fleda replied, idealising a little the fact. "I'm here only for a moment. But do you mean," she went on, "that if you had known I was with your mother you wouldn't have come down?"

The way Owen hung fire at this question made it sound more playful than she had intended. She had in fact no consciousness of any intention but that of confining herself rigidly to her function. She could already see that in whatever he had now braced himself for she was an element he had not reckoned with. His preparation had been of a different sort—the sort congruous with his having been careful to go first and lunch solidly at the inn. He had not been forced to ask for her, but she became aware in his presence of a particular desire to make him feel that no harm could really come to him. She might upset him, as people called it, but she would take no advantage of having done so. She had never seen a person with whom she wished more to be light and easy, to be exceptionally human. The account he presently gave of the matter was that he indeed wouldn't have come if he had known she was on the spot; because then, didn't she see? he could have written to her. He would have had her there to let fly at his mother.

"That would have saved me—well, it would have saved me a lot. Of course I would rather see you than her," he somewhat awkwardly added. "When the fellow spoke of you I assure you I quite jumped at you. In fact I've no real desire to see Mummy at all. If she thinks I *like* it—!" He sighed disgustedly. "I only came down because it seemed better than any other way. I didn't want her to be able to say I hadn't been all right. I dare say you know she has taken everything; or if not quite everything, why a lot more than one ever dreamed. You can see for yourself—she has got half the place down. She has got them crammed—you can see for yourself!" He had his old trick of artless repetition, his helpless iteration of the obvious; but he was sensibly different, for Fleda, if only by the difference of his clear face, mottled over and almost disfigured by little points of pain. He might have been a fine young man with a bad toothache; with the first even of his life. What ailed him above all, she felt, was that trouble was new to him. He had never known a difficulty; he had taken all his fences, his world wholly the world of the personally possible, rounded indeed by a grey suburb into which he had never had occasion to stray. In this vulgar and ill-lighted region he had evidently now lost himself. "We left it quite to her honour, you know," he said ruefully.

"Perhaps you've a right to say that you left it a little to mine." Mixed up with the spoils there, rising before him as if she were in a manner their keeper, she felt that she must absolutely dissociate herself. Mrs. Gereth had made it impossible to do anything but give her away. "I can only tell you that on my side I left it to her. I never dreamed either that she would pick out so many things."

"And you don't really think it's fair, do you? You *don't*!" He spoke very quickly; he really seemed to plead.

Fleda faltered a moment. "I think she has gone too far." Then she added: "I shall immediately tell her that I've said that to you."

He appeared puzzled by this statement, but he presently rejoined: "You haven't then said to mamma what you think?"

"Not yet; remember that I only got here last night." She appeared to herself ignobly weak. "I had had no idea what she was doing. I was taken completely by surprise. She managed it wonderfully."

"It's the sharpest thing I ever saw in *my* life!" They looked at each other with intelligence, in appreciation of the sharpness, and Owen quickly broke into a loud laugh. The laugh was in itself natural, but the occasion of its strange; and stranger still to Fleda, so that she too almost laughed, the inconsequent charity with which he added: "Poor dear old Mummy! That's one of the reasons I asked for you," he went on—"to see if you'd back her up."

Whatever he said or did she somehow liked him the better for it. "How can I back her up, Mr. Gereth, when I think, as I tell you, that she has made a great mistake?"

"A great mistake! That's all right." He spoke—it wasn't clear to her why—as if this declaration were a great point gained.

"Of course there are many things she hasn't taken," Fleda continued.

"Oh yes, a lot of things. But you wouldn't know the place, all the same." He looked about the room with his dis-coloured, swindled face, which deepened Fleda's compassion for him, conjuring away any smile at so candid an image of the dupe. "You'd know this one soon enough, wouldn't you? These are just the things she ought to have left. Is the whole house full of them?"

"The whole house," said Fleda uncompromisingly. She thought of her lovely room.

"I never knew how much I cared for them. They're awfully valuable, aren't they?" Owen's manner mystified her; she was conscious of a return of the agitation he had produced in her on that last bewildering day, and she reminded herself that, now she was warned, it would be inexcusable of her to allow him to justify the fear that had dropped on her. "Mother thinks I never took any notice, but I assure you I was awfully proud of everything. Upon my honour I *was* proud, Miss Vetch."

There was an oddity in his helplessness; he appeared to wish to persuade her and to satisfy himself that she sincerely felt how worthy he really was to treat what had happened as an injury. She could only exclaim almost as helplessly as himself: "Of course you did justice! It's all most painful. I shall instantly let your mother know," she again declared, "the way I've spoken of her to you." She clung to that idea as to the sign of her straightness.

"You'll tell her what you think she ought to do?" he asked with some eagerness.

"What she ought to do?"

"*Don't* you think it—I mean that she ought to give them up?"

"To give them up?" Fleda hesitated again.

"To send them back—to keep it quiet." The girl had not felt the impulse to ask him to sit down among the monuments of his wrong, so that, nervously, awkwardly, he fidgeted about the room with his hands in his pockets and an effect of returning a little into possession through the formulation of his view. "To have them packed and despatched again, since she knows so well how. She does it beautifully"— he looked close at two or three precious pieces. "What's sauce for the goose is sauce for the gander!"

He had laughed at his way of putting it, but Fleda remained grave. "Is that what you came to say to her?"

"Not exactly those words. But I did come to say"—he stammered, then brought it out—"I did come to say we must have them right back."

"And did you think your mother would see you?"

"I wasn't sure, but I thought it right to try—to put it to her kindly, don't you see? If she won't see me, then she has herself to thank. The only other way would have been to set the lawyers at her."

"I'm glad you didn't do that."

"I'm dashed if I want to!" Owen honestly responded. "But what's a fellow to do if she won't meet a fellow?"

"What do you call meeting a fellow?" Fleda asked with a smile.

"Why, letting *me* tell her a dozen things she can have."

This was a transaction that Fleda, after a moment, had to give up trying to represent to herself. "If she won't do that——?" she went on.

"I'll leave it all to my solicitor. *He* won't let her off, by Jove. I know the fellow!"

"That's horrible!" said Fleda, looking at him in woe.

"It's utterly beastly."

His want of logic as well as his vehemence startled her; and with her eyes still on his she considered before asking him the question these things suggested. At last she asked it. "Is Mona very angry?"

"Oh dear, yes!" said Owen.

She had perceived that he wouldn't speak of Mona without her beginning. After waiting fruitlessly now for him to say more she continued: "She has been there again? She has seen the state of the house?"

"Oh dear, yes!" Owen repeated.

Fleda disliked to appear not to take account of his brevity, but it was just because she was struck by it that she felt the pressure of the desire to know more. What it suggested was simply what her intelligence supplied, for he was incapable of any art of insinuation. Wasn't it at all events the rule of communication with him to say for him what he couldn't say? This truth was present to the girl as she inquired if Mona greatly resented what Mrs. Gereth had done. He satisfied her promptly; he was standing before the fire, his back to it, his long legs apart, his hands, behind him, rather violently jiggling his gloves. "She hates it awfully. In fact she refuses to put up with it at all. Don't you see?—she saw the place with all the things."

"So that of course she misses them."

"Misses them—rather! She was awfully sweet on them." Fleda remembered how sweet Mona had been, and reflected that if that was the sort of plea he had prepared it was indeed as well he shouldn't see his mother. This was not all she wanted to know, but it came over her that it was all she needed. "You see it puts me in the position of not carrying out what I promised," Owen said. "As she says herself"—he hesitated an instant— "it's just as if I had obtained her under false pretences." Just before, when he spoke with more drollery than he knew, it had left Fleda serious; but now his own clear gravity had the effect of exciting her mirth. She laughed out, and he looked surprised, but went on: "She regards it as a regular sell."

Fleda was silent; but finally, as he added nothing, she exclaimed: "Of course it makes a great difference!" She knew all she needed, but none the less she risked after another pause an interrogative remark. "I forget when it is that your marriage takes place?"

Owen came away from the fire and, apparently at a loss where to turn, ended by directing himself to one of the windows. "It's a little uncertain. The date isn't quite fixed."

"Oh, I thought I remembered that at Poynton you had told me a day, and that it was near at hand."

"I dare say I did; it was for the 19th. But we've altered that—she wants to shift it." He looked out of the window; then he said: "In fact it won't come off till Mummy has come round."

"Come round?"

"Put the place as it was." In his off-hand way he added: "You know what I mean!"

He spoke not impatiently, but with a kind of intimate familiarity, the sweetness of which made her feel a pang for having forced him to tell her what was embarrassing to him, what was even humiliating. Yes indeed, she knew all she needed: all she needed was that Mona had proved apt at putting down that wonderful patent-leather foot. Her type was misleading only to the superficial, and no one in the world was less superficial than Fleda. She had guessed the truth at Waterbath and she had suffered from it at Poynton; at Ricks the only thing she could do was to accept it with the dumb exaltation that she felt rising. Mona had been prompt with her exercise of the member in question, for it might be called prompt to do that sort of thing before marriage. That she had indeed been premature who should say save those who should have read the matter in the full light of results? Neither at Waterbath nor Poynton had even Fleda's thoroughness discovered all that there was—or rather all that there was not—in Owen Gereth. "Of course it makes all the difference!" she said in answer to his last words. She pursued, after considering: "What you wish me to say from you then to your mother is that you demand immediate and practically complete restitution?"

"Yes, please. It's tremendously good of you."

"Very well, then. Will you wait?"

"For Mummy's answer?" Owen stared and looked perplexed; he was more and more fevered with so much vivid expression of his case. "Don't you think that if I'm here she may hate it worse—think I may want to make her reply bang off?"

Fleda thought. "You don't, then?"

"I want to take her in the right way, don't you know?— treat her as if I gave her more than just an hour or two."

"I see," said Fleda. "Then if you don't wait—good-bye."

This again seemed not what he wanted. "Must *you* do it bang off?"

"I'm only thinking she'll be impatient—I mean, you know, to learn what will have passed between us."

"I see," said Owen, looking at his gloves. "I can give her a day or two, you know. Of course I didn't come down to sleep," he went on. "The inn seems a horrible hole. I know all about the trains—having no idea you were here." Almost as soon as his interlocutress he was struck with the absence of the visible, in this, as between effect and cause. "I mean because in that case I should have felt I could stop over. I should have felt I could talk with you a blessed sight longer than with Mummy."

"We've already talked a long time," smiled Fleda.

"Awfully, haven't we?" He spoke with the stupidity she didn't object to. Inarticulate as he was he had more to say; he lingered perhaps because he was vaguely aware of the want of sincerity in her encouragement to him to go. "There's one thing, please," he mentioned, as if there might be a great many others too. "Please don't say anything about Mona."

She didn't understand. "About Mona?"

"About it being *her* that thinks she has gone too far." This was still slightly obscure, but now Fleda understood. "It mustn't seem to come from *her* at all, don't you know? That would only make Mummy worse."

Fleda knew exactly how much worse, but she felt a delicacy about explicitly assenting: she was already immersed moreover in the deep consideration of what might make "Mummy" better. She couldn't see as yet at all; she could only clutch at the hope of some inspiration after he should go. Oh, there was a remedy, to be sure, but it was out of the question; in spite of which, in the strong light of Owen's troubled presence, of his anxious face and restless step, it hung there before her for some minutes. She felt that, remarkably, beneath the decent rigour of his errand, the poor young man, for reasons, for weariness, for disgust, would have been ready not to insist. His fitness to fight his mother had left him—he wasn't in fighting trim. He had no natural avidity and even no special wrath; he had none that had not been taught him, and it was doing his best to learn the lesson that had made him so sick. He had his delicacies, but he hid them away like presents before Christmas. He was hollow, perfunctory, pathetic; he had been girded by another hand. That hand had naturally been Mona's, and it was heavy even now on his strong, broad back. Why then had he originally rejoiced so in its touch? Fleda dashed aside this question, for it had nothing to do with her problem. Her problem was to help him to live as a gentlemen and carry through what he had undertaken; her problem was to reinstate him in his rights. It was quite irrelevant that Mona had no intelligence of what she had lost—quite irrelevant that she was moved not by the privation but by the insult. She had every reason to be moved, though she was so much more movable, in the vindictive way at any rate, than one might have supposed—assuredly more than Owen himself had imagined.

"Certainly I shall not mention Mona," Fleda said, "and there won't be the slightest necessity for it. The wrong's quite sufficiently yours, and the demand you make is perfectly justified by it."

"I can't tell you what it is to me to feel you on my side!" Owen exclaimed.

"Up to this time," said Fleda after a pause, "your mother has had no doubt of my being on hers."

"Then of course she won't like your changing."

"I dare say she won't like it at all."

"Do you mean to say you'll have a regular kick-up with her?"

"I don't exactly know what you mean by a regular kick-up. We shall naturally have a great deal of discussion—if she consents to discuss the matter at all. That's why you must decidedly give her two or three days."

"I see you think she *may* refuse to discuss it at all," said Owen.

"I'm only trying to be prepared for the worst. You must remember that to have to withdraw from the ground she has taken, to make a public surrender of what she had publicly appropriated, will go uncommonly hard with her pride."

Owen considered; his face seemed to broaden, but not into a smile. "I suppose she's tremendously proud, isn't she?" This might have been the first time it had occurred to him.

"You know better than I," said Fleda, speaking with high extravagance.

"I don't know anything in the world half so well as you. If I were as clever as you I might hope to get round her." Owen hesitated; then he went on: "In fact I don't quite see what even you can say or do that will really fetch her."

"Neither do I, as yet. I must think—I must pray!" the girl pursued, smiling. "I can only say to you that I'll try. I *want* to try, you know—I want to help you." He stood looking at her so long on this that she added with much distinctness: "So you must leave me, please, quite alone with her. You must go straight back."

"Back to the inn?"

"Oh, no, back to town. I'll write to you to-morrow."

He turned about vaguely for his hat. "There's the chance, of course, that she may be afraid."

"Afraid, you mean, of the legal steps you may take?"

"I've got a perfect case—I could have her up. The Brigstocks say it's simply stealing."

"I can easily fancy what the Brigstocks say!" Fleda permitted herself to remark without solemnity.

"It's none of their business, is it?" was Owen's unexpected rejoinder. Fleda had already noted that no one so slow could ever have had such rapid transitions.

She showed her amusement. "They've a much better right to say it's none of mine."

"Well, at any rate you don't call her names."

Fleda wondered whether Mona did; and this made it all the finer of her to exclaim in a moment: "You don't know what I shall call her if she holds out!"

Owen gave her a gloomy glance; then he blew a speck off the crown of his hat. "But if you do have a set-to with her?"

He paused so long for a reply that Fleda said, "I don't think I know what you mean by a set-to.

"Well, if she calls *you* names."

"I don't think she'll do that."

"What I mean to say is, if she's angry at your backing me up—what will you do then? She can't possibly like it, you know."

"She may very well not like it; but everything depends. I must see what I shall do. You mustn't worry about me."

She spoke with decision, but Owen seemed still unsatisfied. "You won't go away, I hope?"

"Go away?"

"If she does take it ill of you."

Fleda moved to the door and opened it. "I'm not prepared to say. You must have patience and see."

"Of course I must," said Owen—"of course, of course." But he took no more advantage of the open door than to say: "You want me to be off, and I'm off in a minute. Only, before I go, please answer me a question. If you *should* leave my mother, where would you go?"

Fleda smiled again. "I haven't the least idea."

"I suppose you'd go back to London."

"I haven't the least idea," Fleda repeated.

"You don't—a—live anywhere in particular, do you?" the young man went on. He looked conscious as soon as he had spoken; she could see that he felt himself to have alluded more grossly than he meant to the circumstance of her having, if one were plain about it, no home of her own. He had meant it as an allusion of a tender sort to all that she would sacrifice in the case of a quarrel with his mother; but there was indeed no graceful way of touching on that. One just couldn't be plain about it.

Fleda, wound up as she was, shrank from any treatment at all of the matter, and she made no answer to his question. "I *won't* leave your mother," she said. "I'll produce an effect on her; I'll convince her absolutely."

"I believe you will, if you look at her like that!"

She was wound up to such a height that there might well be a light in her pale, fine little face—a light that, while for all return at first she simply shone back at him, was intensely reflected in his own. "I'll make her see it; I'll make her see it!"—she rang out like a silver bell. She had at that moment a perfect faith that she should succeed; but it passed into something else when, the next instant, she became aware that Owen, quickly getting between her and the door she had opened, was sharply closing it, as might be said, in her face. He had done this before she could stop him, and he stood there with his hand on the knob and smiled at her strangely. Clearer than he could have spoken it was the sense of those seconds of silence.

"When I got into this I didn't know you, and now that I know you how can I tell you the difference? And *she's* so different, so ugly and vulgar, in the light of this squabble. No, like *you* I've never known one. It's another thing, it's a new thing altogether. Listen to me a little: can't something be done?" It was what had been in the air in those moments at Kensington, and it only wanted words to be a committed act. The more reason, to the girl's excited mind, why it shouldn't have words; her one thought was not to hear, to keep the act uncommitted. She would do this if she had to be horrid.

"Please let me out, Mr. Gereth," she said; on which he opened the door with a hesitation so very brief that in thinking of these things afterwards—for she was to think of them for ever—she wondered in what tone she could have spoken. They went into the hall, where she encountered the parlour-maid, of whom she inquired whether Mrs. Gereth had come in.

"No, miss; and I think she has left the garden. She has gone up the back road." In other words they had the whole place to themselves. It would have been a pleasure, in a different mood, to converse with that parlour-maid.

"Please open the house-door," said Fleda.

Owen, as if in quest of his umbrella, looked vaguely about the hall—looked even wistfully up the staircase—while the neat young woman complied with Fleda's request. Owen's eyes then wandered out of the open door. "I think it's awfully nice here," he observed. "I assure you I could do with it myself."

"I should think you might, with half your things here! It's Poynton itself—almost. Good-bye, Mr. Gereth," Fleda added. Her intention had naturally been that the neat young woman, opening the front door, should remain to close it on the departing guest. That functionary, however, had acutely vanished behind a stiff flap of green baize which Mrs. Gereth had not yet had time to abolish. Fleda put out her hand, but Owen turned away—he couldn't find his umbrella. She passed into the open air—she was determined to get him out; and in a moment he joined her in the little plastered portico which had small resemblance to any feature of Poynton. It was, as Mrs. Gereth had said, like the portico of a house in Brompton.

"Oh, I don't mean with all the things here," he explained in regard to the opinion he had just expressed. "I mean I could put up with it just as it was; it had a lot of good things, don't you think? I mean if everything was back at Poynton, if everything was all right." He brought out these last words with a sort of smothered sigh. Fleda, didn't understand his explanation unless it had reference to another and more wonderful exchange—the restoration to the great house not only of its tables and chairs but of its alienated mistress. This would imply the installation of his own life at Ricks, and obviously that of another person. Such another person could scarcely be Mona Brigstock. He put out his hand now; and once more she heard his unsounded words. "With everything patched up at the other place, I could live here with *you.* Don't you see what I mean?"

Fleda saw perfectly and, with a face in which she flattered herself that nothing of this vision appeared, gave him her hand and said: "Good-bye, good-bye."

Owen held her hand very firmly and kept it even after an effort made by her to recover it—an effort not repeated, as she felt it best not to show she was flurried. That solution—of her living with him at Ricks—disposed of him beautifully and disposed not less so of herself; it disposed admirably too of Mrs. Gereth. Fleda could only vainly wonder how it provided for poor Mona. While he looked at her, grasping her hand, she felt that now indeed she was paying for his mother's extravagance at Poynton—the vividness of that lady's public plea that little Fleda Vetch was the person to insure the general peace. It was to that vividness poor Owen had come back, and if Mrs. Gereth had had more discretion little Fleda Vetch wouldn't have been in a predicament. She saw that Owen had at this moment his sharpest necessity of speech, and so long as he didn't release her hand she could only submit to him. Her defence would be perhaps to look blank and hard; so she looked as blank and as hard as she could, with the reward of an immediate sense that this was not a bit what he wanted. It even made him hang fire as if he were suddenly ashamed of himself, were recalled to some idea of duty and of honour. Yet he none the less brought it out. "There's one thing I dare say I ought to tell you, if you're going so kindly to act for me; though of course you'll see for yourself it's a thing it won't do to tell *her*." What was it? He made her wait for it again, and while she waited, under firm coercion, she had the extraordinary impression that Owen's simplicity was in eclipse. His natural honesty was like the scent of a flower, and she felt at this moment as if her nose had been brushed by the bloom without the odour. The allusion was undoubtedly to his mother; and was not what he meant about the matter in question the opposite of what he said—that it just *would* do to tell her? It would have been the first time he had said the opposite of what he meant, and there was certainly a fascination in the phenomenon as well as a challenge to suspense in the ambiguity. "It's just that I understand from Mona, you know," he stammered; "it's just that she has made no bones about bringing home to me—" He tried to laugh, and in the effort he faltered again.

"About bringing home to you?"—Fleda encouraged him.

He was sensible of it, he achieved his performance. "Why, that if I don't get the things back—every blessed one of them except a few *she'll* pick out—she won't have anything more to say to me."

Fleda after an instant encouraged him again. "To say to you?"

"Why, she simply won't marry me, don't you see?"

Owen's legs, not to mention his voice, had wavered while he spoke, and she felt his possession of her hand loosen so that she was free again. Her stare of perception broke into a lively laugh. "Oh, you're all right, for you *will* get them. You will; you're quite safe; don't worry!" She fell back into the house with her hand on the door. "Good-bye, good-bye." She repeated it several times, laughing bravely, quite waving him away and, as he didn't move and save that he was on the other side of it, closing the door in his face quite as he had closed that of the drawing-room in hers. Never had a face, never at least had such a handsome one, been so presented to that offence. She even held the door a minute, lest he should try to come in again. At last as she heard nothing she made a dash for the stairs and ran up.

IX

IN KNOWING a while before all she needed she had been far from knowing as much as that; so that once up-stairs, where, in her room, with her sense of danger and trouble, the age of Louis Seize suddenly struck her as wanting in taste and point, she felt that she now for the first time knew her temptation. Owen had put it before her with an art beyond his own dream. Mona would cast him off if he didn't proceed to extremities; if his negotiation with his mother should fail he would be completely free. That negotiation depended on a young lady to whom he had pressingly suggested the condition of his freedom; and as if to aggravate the young lady's predicament, designing fate had sent Mrs. Gereth, as the parlour-maid said, "up the back road." This would give the young lady more time to make up her mind that nothing should come of the negotiation. There would be different ways of putting the question to Mrs. Gereth, and Fleda might profitably devote the moments before her return to a selection of the way that would most surely be tantamount to failure. This selection indeed required no great adroitness; it was so conspicuous that failure would be the reward of an effective introduction of Mona. If that abhorred name should be properly invoked Mrs. Gereth would resist to the death, and before envenomed resistance Owen would certainly retire. His retirement would be into single life, and Fleda reflected that he had now gone away conscious of having practically told her so. She could only say as she waited for the back road to disgorge that she hoped it was a consciousness he enjoyed. There was something *she* enjoyed; but that was a very different matter. To know that she had become to him an object of desire gave her wings that she felt herself flutter in the air: it was like the rush of a flood into her own accumulations. These stored depths had been fathomless and still, but now, for half-an-hour, in the empty house, they spread till they overflowed. He seemed to have made it right for her to confess to herself her secret. Strange then there should be for him in return nothing that such a confession could make right! How could it make right that he should give up Mona for another woman? His attitude was a sorry appeal to Fleda to legitimate that. But he didn't believe it himself and he had none of the courage of his perversity. She could easily see how wrong everything must be when a man so made to be manly was wanting in courage. She had upset him, as people called it, and he had spoken out from the force of the jar of finding her there. He had upset her too, heaven knew, but she was one of those who could pick themselves up. She had the real advantage, she considered, of having kept him from seeing that she had been overthrown.

She had moreover at present completely recovered her feet, though there was in the intensity of the effort required to do so a vibration which throbbed away into an immense allowance for the young man. How could she after all know what, in the disturbance wrought by his mother, Mona's relations with him might have become? If he had been able to keep his wits, such as they were, more about him he would probably have felt—as sharply as she felt on his behalf—that so long as those relations were not ended he had no right to say even the little he had said. He had no right to appear to wish to draw in another girl to help him to run away. If he was in a plight he must get out of the plight himself, he must get out of it first, and anything he should have to say to any one else must be deferred and detached. She herself, at any rate—it was her own case that was in question—couldn't dream of assisting him save in the sense of their common honour. She could never be the girl to be drawn in; she could never lift her finger against Mona. There was something in her that would make it a shame to her forever to have owed her happiness to an interference. It would seem intolerably vulgar to her to have "ousted" the daughter of the Brigstocks; and merely to have abstained even wouldn't assure her that she had been straight. Nothing was really straight but to justify her little pensioned presence by her use; and now, won over as she was to heroism, she could see her use only as some high and delicate deed. She couldn't, in short, do anything at all unless she could do it with a kind of pride, and there would be nothing to be proud of in having arranged for poor Owen to get off easily. Nobody had a right to get off easily from pledges so deep and sacred. How could Fleda doubt they had been tremendous when she knew so well what any pledge of her own would be? If Mona was so formed that she could hold such vows light, that was Mona's peculiar business. To have loved Owen apparently, and yet to have loved him only so much, only to the extent of a few tables and chairs, was not a thing she could so much as try to grasp. Of a different manner of loving she was herself ready to give an instance, an instance of which the beauty indeed would not be generally known. It would not perhaps if revealed be generally understood, inasmuch as the effect of the particular pressure she proposed to exercise would be, should success attend it, to keep him tied to an affection that had died a sudden and violent death. Even in the ardour of her meditation Fleda remained in sight of the truth that it would be an odd result of her magnanimity to prevent her friend's shaking off a woman he disliked. If he didn't dislike Mona what was the matter with him? And if he did, Fleda asked, what was the matter with her own silly self?

Our young lady met this branch of the temptation it pleased her frankly to recognise by declaring that to encourage any such cruelty would be tortuous and base. She had nothing to do with his dislikes; she had only to do with his good-nature and his good name. She had joy of him just as he was, but it was of these things she had the greatest. The worst aversion and the liveliest reaction moreover wouldn't alter the fact—since one was facing facts—that but the other day his strong arms must have clasped a remarkably handsome girl as close as she had permitted. Fleda's emotion at this time was a wondrous mixture, in which Mona's permissions and Mona's beauty figured powerfully as aids to reflection. She herself had no beauty, and *her* permissions were the stony stares she had just practised in the drawing-room—a consciousness of a kind appreciably to add to the particular sense of triumph that made her generous. I may not perhaps too much diminish the merit of that generosity if I mention that it could take the flight we are considering just because really, with the telescope of her long thought, Fleda saw what might bring her out of the wood. Mona herself would bring her out; at the least Mona possibly might. Deep down plunged the

idea that even should she achieve what she had promised
Owen there was still the contingency of Mona's independent
action. She might by that time, under stress of temper or of
whatever it was that was now moving her, have said or done
the things there is no patching up. If the rupture should
come from Waterbath they might all be happy yet. This was a
calculation that Fleda wouldn't have committed to paper, but
it affected the total of her sentiments. She was meanwhile so
remarkably constituted that while she refused to profit by
Owen's mistake, even while she judged it and hastened to
cover it up, she could drink a sweetness from it that consorted
little with her wishing it mightn't have been made. There was
no harm done, because he had instinctively known, poor dear,
with whom to make it, and it was a compensation for seeing
him worried that he hadn't made it with some horrid mean
girl who would immediately have dished him by making a still
bigger one. Their protected error (for she indulged a fancy
that it was hers too) was like some dangerous, lovely, living
thing that she had caught and could keep—keep vivid and
helpless in the cage of her own passion and look at and talk
to all day long. She had got it well locked up there by the
time that from an upper window she saw Mrs. Gereth again
in the garden. At this she went down to meet her.

X

FLEDA'S LINE had been taken, her word was quite ready: on the terrace of the painted pots she broke out before her interlocutress could put a question. "His errand was perfectly simple: he came to demand that you shall pack everything straight up again and send it back as fast as the railway will carry it."

The back road had apparently been fatiguing to Mrs. Gereth; she rose there rather white and wan with her walk. A certain sharp thinness was in her ejaculation of "Oh!"—after which she glanced about her for a place to sit down. The movement was a criticism of the order of events that offered such a piece of news to a lady coming in tired; but Fleda could see that in turning over the possibilities this particular peril was the one that during the last hour her friend had turned up oftenest. At the end of the short, grey day, which had been moist and mild, the sun was out; the terrace looked to the south, and a bench, formed as to legs and arms of iron representing knotted boughs, stood against the warmest wall of the house. The mistress of Ricks sank upon it and presented to her companion the handsome face she had composed to hear everything. Strangely enough it was just this fine vessel of her attention that made the girl most nervous about what she must drop in. "Quite a 'demand,' dear, is it?" asked Mrs. Gereth, drawing in her cloak.

"Oh, that's what I should call it!"—Fleda laughed, to her own surprise.

"I mean with the threat of enforcement and that sort of thing."

"Distinctly with the threat of enforcement—what would be called, I suppose, coercion."

"What sort of coercion?" said Mrs. Gereth.

"Why, legal, don't you know?—what he calls setting the lawyers at you."

"Is that what he calls it?" She seemed to speak with disinterested curiosity.

"That's what he calls it," said Fleda.

Mrs. Gereth considered an instant. "Oh, the lawyers!" she exclaimed lightly. Seated there almost cosily in the reddening winter sunset, only with her shoulders raised a little and her mantle tightened as if from a slight chill, she had never yet looked to Fleda so much in possession nor so far from meeting unsuspectedness half-way. "Is he going to send them down here?"

"I dare say he thinks it may come to that."

"The lawyers can scarcely do the packing," Mrs. Gereth playfully remarked.

"I suppose he means them—in the first place at least—to try to talk you over."

"In the first place, eh? And what does he mean in the second?"

Fleda hesitated; she had not foreseen that so simple an inquiry could disconcert her. "I'm afraid I don't know."

"Didn't you ask?" Mrs. Gereth spoke as if she might have said: "What then were you doing all the while?"

"I didn't ask very much," said her companion. "He has been gone some time. The great thing seemed to be to understand clearly that he wouldn't be content with anything less than what he mentioned."

"My just giving everything back?"

"Your just giving everything back."

"Well, darling, what did you tell him?" Mrs. Gereth blandly inquired.

Fleda faltered again, wincing at the term of endearment, at what the words took for granted, charged with the confidence she had now committed herself to betray. "I told him I would tell you!" She smiled, but she felt that her smile was rather hollow and even that Mrs. Gereth had begun to look at her with some fixedness.

"Did he seem very angry?"

"He seemed very sad. He takes it very hard," Fleda added.

"And how does *she* take it?"

"Ah, that—that I felt a delicacy about asking."

"So you didn't ask?" The words had the note of surprise.

Fleda was embarrassed; she had not made up her mind definitely to lie. "I didn't think you'd care." That small untruth she would risk.

"Well—I don't!" Mrs. Gereth declared; and Fleda felt less guilty to hear her, for the statement was as inexact as her own. "Didn't you say anything in return?" Mrs. Gereth presently continued.

"Do you mean in the way of justifying you?"

"I didn't mean to trouble you to do that. My justification," said Mrs. Gereth, sitting there warmly and, in the lucidity of her thought, which nevertheless hung back a little, dropping her eyes on the gravel—"my justification was all the past. My justification was the cruelty—!" But at this, with a short, sharp gesture, she checked herself. "It's too good of me to talk—now." She produced these sentences with a cold patience, as if addressing Fleda in the girl's virtual and actual character of Owen's representative. Our young lady crept to and fro before the bench, combating the sense that it was occupied by a judge, looking at her boot-toes, reminding herself in doing so of Mona, and lightly crunching the pebbles as she walked. She moved about because she was afraid, putting off from moment to moment the exercise of the courage she had been sure she possessed. That courage would all come to her if she could only be equally sure that what she should be called upon to do for Owen would be to suffer. She had wondered, while Mrs. Gereth spoke, how that lady would describe her justification. She had described it as if to be irreproachably fair, give her adversary the benefit of every doubt and then dismiss the question for ever. "Of course," Mrs. Gereth went on, "if we didn't succeed in showing him at Poynton the ground we took, it's simply that he shuts his eyes. What I supposed was that you would have given him your opinion that if I was the woman so signally to assert myself I'm also the woman to rest upon it imperturbably enough."

Fleda stopped in front of her hostess. "I gave him my opinion that you're very logical, very obstinate and very proud."

"Quite right, my dear: I'm a rank bigot—about that sort of thing!" and Mrs. Gereth jerked her head at the contents of the house. "I've never denied it. I'd kidnap—to save them, to convert them—the children of heretics. When I know I'm right I go to the stake. Oh, he may burn me alive!" she cried with a happy face. "Did he abuse me?" she then demanded.

Fleda had remained there, gathering in her purpose. "How little you know him!"

Mrs. Gereth stared, then broke into a laugh that her companion had not expected. "Ah, my dear, certainly not so well as you!" The girl, at this, turned away again—she felt she looked too conscious; and she was aware that during a pause Mrs. Gereth's eyes watched her as she went. She faced about afresh to meet them, but what she met was a question that reinforced them. "Why had you a 'delicacy' as to speaking of Mona?"

She stopped again before the bench, and an inspiration came to her. "I should think *you* would know," she said with proper dignity.

Blankness was for a moment on Mrs. Gereth's brow; then light broke—she visibly remembered the scene in the breakfast-room after Mona's night at Poynton. "Because I contrasted you—told him *you* were the one?" Her eyes looked deep. "You were—you are still!"

Fleda gave a bold dramatic laugh. "Thank you, my love—with all the best things at Ricks!"

Mrs. Gereth considered, trying to penetrate, as it seemed; but at last she brought out roundly: "For you, you know, I'd send them back!"

The girl's heart gave a tremendous bound; the right way dawned upon her in a flash. Obscurity indeed the next moment engulfed this course, but for a few thrilled seconds she had understood. To send the things back "for her" meant of course to send them back if there were even a dim chance that she might become mistress of them. Fleda's palpitation was not allayed as she asked herself what portent Mrs. Gereth had suddenly perceived of such a chance: that perception could come only from a sudden suspicion of her secret. This suspicion in turn was a tolerably straight consequence of that implied view of the propriety of surrender from which, she was well aware, she could say nothing to dissociate herself. What she first felt was that if she wished to rescue the spoils she wished also to rescue her secret. So she looked as innocent as she could and said as quickly as possible: "For me? Why in the world for me?"

"Because you're so awfully keen."

"Am I? Do I strike you so? You know I hate him," Fleda went on.

She had the sense for a while of Mrs. Gereth's regarding her with the detachment of some stern, clever stranger. "Then what's the matter with you? Why do you want me to give in?"

Fleda hesitated; she felt herself reddening. "I've only said your son wants it. I haven't said *I* do."

"Then say it and have done with it!"

This was more peremptory than any word her friend, though often speaking in her presence with much point, had ever yet deliberately addressed her. It affected her like the crack of a whip, but she confined herself with an effort to taking it as a reminder that she must keep her head. "I know he has his engagement to carry out."

"His engagement to marry? Why, it's just that engagement we loathe!"

"Why should *I* loathe it?" Fleda asked with a strained smile. Then before Mrs. Gereth could reply she pursued: "I'm thinking of his general undertaking—to give her the house as she originally saw it."

"To give her the house!"—Mrs. Gereth brought up the words from the depth of the unspeakable. The effect was like the moan of an autumn wind; it was in the power of such an image to make her turn pale.

"I'm thinking," Fleda continued, "of the simple question of his keeping faith on an important clause of his contract: it doesn't matter whether it's with a stupid person or with a monster of cleverness. I'm thinking of his honour and his good name."

"The honour and good name of a man you hate?"

"Certainly," the girl resolutely answered. "I don't see why you should talk as if one had a petty mind. You don't think so. It's not on that assumption you've ever dealt with me. I can do your son justice, as he put his case to me."

"Ah, then he did put his case to you!" Mrs. Gereth exclaimed with an accent of triumph. "You seemed to speak just now as if really nothing of any consequence had passed between you."

"Something always passes when one has a little imagination," our young lady declared.

"I take it you don't mean that Owen has any!" Mrs. Gereth cried with her large laugh.

Fleda was silent a moment. "No, I don't mean that Owen has any," she returned at last.

"Why is it you hate him so?" her hostess abruptly put to her.

"Should I love him for all he has made you suffer?"

Mrs. Gereth slowly rose at this and, coming over the walk, took her young friend to her breast and kissed her. She then passed into one of Fleda's an arm perversely and imperiously sociable. "Let us move a little," she said, holding her close and giving a slight shiver. They strolled along the terrace and she brought out another question. "He *was* eloquent, then, poor dear—he poured forth the story of his wrongs?"

Fleda smiled down at her companion, who, cloaked and perceptibly bowed, leaned on her heavily and gave her an odd, unwonted sense of age and cunning. She took refuge in an evasion. "He couldn't tell me anything that I didn't know pretty well already."

"It's very true that you know everything. No, dear, you haven't a petty mind; you've a lovely imagination and you're the nicest creature in the world. If you were inane, like most girls—like every one in fact—I would have insulted you, I would have outraged you, and then you would have fled from me in terror. No, now that I think of it," Mrs. Gereth went on, "you wouldn't have fled from me: nothing, on the contrary, would have made you budge. You would have cuddled into your warm corner, but you would have been wounded and weeping and martyrised, and you would have taken every opportunity to tell people I'm a brute—as indeed I should have been!" They went to and fro, and she would not allow Fleda, who laughed and protested, to attenuate with any light civiltiy this spirited picture. She praised her cleverness and her patience; then she said it was getting cold and dark and they must go in to tea. She delayed quitting the place, however, and reverted instead to Owen's ultimatum, about which she asked another question or two; in particular whether it had struck Fleda that he really believed she would comply with such a summons.

"I think he really believes that if I try hard enough I can

make you:" after uttering which words our young lady
stopped short and emulated the embrace she had received a
few moments before.

"And you've promised to try: I see. You didn't tell me that
either," Mrs. Gereth added as they moved. "But you're rascal
enough for anything!" While Fleda was occupied in thinking
in what terms she could explain why she had indeed been rascal enough for the reticence thus denounced, her companion
broke out with an inquiry somewhat irrelevant and even in
form somewhat profane. "Why the devil, at any rate, doesn't
it come off?"

Fleda hesitated. "You mean their marriage?"

"Of course I mean their marriage!"

Fleda hesitated again. "I haven't the least idea."

"You didn't ask him?"

"Oh, how in the world can you fancy?" She spoke in a
shocked tone.

"Fancy your putting a question so indelicate? *I* should have
put it—I mean in your place; but I'm quite coarse, thank
God!" Fleda felt privately that she herself was coarse, or at any
rate would presently have to be; and Mrs. Gereth, with a purpose that struck her as increasing, continued: "What, then,
was the day to be? Wasn't it just one of these?"

"I'm sure I don't remember."

It was part of the great rupture and an effect of Mrs.
Gereth's character that up to this moment she had been completely and haughtily indifferent to that detail. Now, however,
she had a visible reason for being sure. She bethought herself
and she broke out: "Isn't the day past?" Then stopping short
she added: "Upon my word they must have put it off!" As
Fleda made no answer to this she sharply pursued: "*Have* they
put it off?"

"I haven't the least idea," said the girl.

Her hostess was again looking at her hard. "Didn't he tell
you—didn't he say anything about it?"

Fleda meanwhile had had time to make her reflections,
which were moreover the continued throb of those that had
occupied the interval between Owen's departure and his
mother's return. If she should now repeat his words this
wouldn't at all play the game of her definite vow; it would

only play the game of her little gagged and blinded desire. She could calculate well enough the result of telling Mrs. Gereth how she had had it from Owen's troubled lips that Mona was only waiting for the restitution and would do nothing without it. The thing was to obtain the restitution without imparting that knowledge. The only way also not to impart it was not to tell any truth at all about it; and the only way to meet this last condition was to reply to her companion, as she presently did: "He told me nothing whatever. He didn't touch on the subject."

"Not in any way?"

"Not in any way."

Mrs. Gereth watched Fleda and considered. "You haven't any idea if they are waiting for the things?"

"How should I have? I'm not in their counsels."

"I dare say they are—or that Mona is." Mrs. Gereth reflected again; she had a bright idea. "If I don't give in I'll be hanged if she'll not break off."

"She'll never, never break off," said Fleda.

"Are you sure?"

"I can't be sure, but it's my belief."

"Derived from *him?*"

The girl hung fire a few seconds. "Derived from him."

Mrs. Gereth gave her a long last look, then turned abruptly away. "It's an awful bore you didn't really get it out of him! Well, come to tea," she added rather dryly, passing straight into the house.

XI

THE SENSE of her dryness, which was ominous of a complication, made Fleda, before complying, linger a little on the
terrace: she felt the need moreover of taking breath after such
a flight into the cold air of denial. When at last she rejoined
Mrs. Gereth she found her erect before the drawing-room fire.
Their tea had been set out in the same quarter, and the mistress
of the house, for whom the preparation of it was in general a
high and undelegated function, was in an attitude to which the
hissing urn made no appeal. This omission, for Fleda, was such
a further sign of something to come that, to disguise her apprehension, she immediately and without apology took the
duty in hand; only however to be promptly reminded that she
was performing it confusedly and not counting the journeys of
the little silver shovel she emptied into the pot. "Not *five*, my
dear—the usual three," said her hostess with the same reserve;
watching her then in silence while she clumsily corrected her
mistake. The tea took some minutes to draw, and Mrs. Gereth
availed herself of them suddenly to exclaim: "You haven't yet
told me, you know, how it is you propose to 'make' me!"

"Give everything back?" Fleda looked into the pot again
and uttered her question with a briskness that she felt to be a
trifle overdone. "Why, by putting the question well before
you; by being so eloquent that I shall persuade you, shall act
upon you; by making you sorry for having gone so far," she
said boldly. "By simply and earnestly asking it of you, in
short; and by reminding you at the same time that it's the first
thing I ever have so asked. Oh, you've done things for me—
endless and beautiful things," she exclaimed; "but you've
done them all from your own generous impulse. I've never so
much as hinted to you to lend me a postage-stamp."

"Give me a cup of tea," said Mrs. Gereth. A moment later,
taking the cup, she replied: "No, you've never asked me for a
postage-stamp."

"That gives me a pull!" Fleda returned, with a smile.

"Puts you in the situation of expecting that I shall do this
thing just simply to oblige you?"

The girl hesitated. "You said a while ago that for me you *would* do it."

"For you, but not for your eloquence. Do you understand what I mean by the difference?" Mrs. Gereth asked as she stood stirring her tea.

Fleda, to postpone answering, looked round, while she drank it, at the beautiful room. "I don't in the least like, you know, your having taken so much. It was a great shock to me, on my arrival here, to find you had done so."

"Give me some more tea," said Mrs. Gereth; and there was a moment's silence as Fleda poured out another cup. "If you were shocked, my dear, I'm bound to say you concealed your shock."

"I know I did. I was afraid to show it."

Mrs. Gereth drank off her second cup. "And you're not afraid now?"

"No, I'm not afraid now."

"What has made the difference?"

"I've pulled myself together." Fleda paused; then she added: "And I've seen Mr. Owen."

"You've seen Mr. Owen"—Mrs. Gereth concurred. She put down her cup and sank into a chair, in which she leaned back, resting her head and gazing at her young friend. "Yes, I did tell you a while ago that for you I'd do it. But you haven't told me yet what you'll do in return."

Fleda thought an instant. "Anything in the wide world you may require."

"Oh, 'anything' is nothing at all! That's too easily said." Mrs. Gereth, reclining more completely, closed her eyes with an air of disgust, an air indeed of inviting slumber.

Fleda looked at her quiet face, which the appearance of slumber always made particularly handsome; she noted how much the ordeal of the last few weeks had added to its indications of age. "Well then, try me with something. What is it you demand?"

At this, opening her eyes, Mrs. Gereth sprang straight up. "Get him away from her!"

Fleda marvelled: her companion had in an instant become young again. "Away from Mona? How in the world—?"

"By not looking like a fool!" cried Mrs. Gereth very

sharply. She kissed her, however, on the spot, to make up for this roughness, and with an officious hand took off the hat which, on coming into the house, our young lady had not removed. She applied a friendly touch to the girl's hair and gave a business-like pull to her jacket. "I say don't look like an idiot, because you happen not to be one, not the least bit. *I'm* idiotic; I've been so, I've just discovered, ever since our first days together. I've been a precious donkey; but that's another affair."

Fleda, as if she humbly assented, went through no form of controverting this; she simply stood passive to her companion's sudden refreshment of the charms of her person. "How can I get him away from her?" she presently demanded.

"By letting yourself go."

"By letting myself go?" She spoke mechanically, still more like an idiot, and felt as if her face flamed out the insincerity of her question. It was vividly back again, the vision of the real way to act on Mrs. Gereth. This lady's movements were now rapid; she turned off from her as quickly as she had seized her, and Fleda sat down to steady herself for full responsibility.

Her hostess, without taking up her ejaculation, gave a violent poke at the fire and then faced her again. "You've done two things, then, to-day—haven't you?—that you've never done before. One has been asking me the service or favour or concession—whatever you call it—that you just mentioned; the other has been telling me—certainly too for the first time—an immense little fib."

"An immense little fib?" Fleda felt weak; she was glad of the support of her seat.

"An immense big one then!" said Mrs. Gereth irritatedly. "You don't in the least 'hate' Owen, my darling. You care for him very much. In fact, my own, you're in love with him—there! Don't tell me any more lies!" cried Mrs. Gereth with a voice and a face in the presence of which Fleda recognised that there was nothing for her but to hold herself and take them. When once the truth was out it was out, and she could see more and more every instant that it would be the only way. She accepted therefore what had to come; she leaned back her head and closed her eyes as her companion had done just before. She would have covered her face with her hands but for the still greater shame. "Oh, you're a wonder, a wonder," said Mrs. Gereth; "you're magnificent, and I was right, as soon as I saw you, to pick you out and trust you!" Fleda closed her eyes tighter at this last word, but her friend kept it up. "I never dreamed of it till a while ago, when, after he had come and gone, we were face to face. Then something stuck out of you; it strongly impressed me, and I didn't know at first quite what to make of it. It was that you had just been with him and that you were not natural. Not natural to *me*," she added with a smile. "I pricked up my ears, and all that this might mean dawned upon me when you said you had asked nothing about Mona. It put me on the scent, but I didn't show you, did I? I felt it was *in* you, deep down, and that I must draw it out. Well, I *have* drawn it, and it's a blessing. Yesterday, when you shed tears at breakfast, I was awfully puzzled. What has been the matter with you all the while? Why, Fleda, it isn't a crime, don't you know that?" cried the delighted woman. "When I was a girl I was always in love, and not always with such nice people as Owen. I didn't behave as well as you; compared with you I think I must have been odious. But if you're proud and reserved it's your own affair; I'm proud too, though I'm not reserved—that's what spoils it. I'm stupid, above all—that's what I am; so dense that I really blush for it. However, no one but you could have deceived me. If I trusted you moreover, it was exactly to be cleverer than myself. You must be so now more than ever!" Suddenly Fleda felt her hands grasped: Mrs. Gereth had plumped down at her feet and was leaning on her knees. "Save him—save him: you *can*!" she passionately pleaded. "How could you not like him when he's such a dear? He *is* a dear, darling; there's no harm in my own boy! You can do what you will with him—you know you can! What else does he give us all this time for? Get him away from her: it's as if he besought you to, poor wretch! Don't abandon him to such a fate, and I'll never abandon *you*. Think of him with that creature, that future! If you'll take him I'll give up everything. There, it's a solemn promise, the most sacred of my life. Get the better of her and he shall have every stick I removed. Give me your word and I'll accept it. I'll write for the packers to-night!"

Fleda, before this, had fallen forward on her companion's neck, and the two women, clinging together, had got up while the younger wailed on the other's bosom. "You smooth it down because you see more in it than there can ever be; but after my hideous double game how will you be able to believe in me again?"

"I see in it simply what *must* be, if you've a single spark of pity. Where on earth was the double game, when you've behaved like such a saint? You've been beautiful, you've been exquisite, and all our trouble is over."

Fleda, drying her eyes, shook her head ever so sadly. "No, Mrs. Gereth, it isn't over. I can't do what you ask—I can't meet your condition."

Mrs. Gereth stared; the cloud gathered in her face again. "Why, in the name of goodness, when you adore him? I know what you see in him," she declared in another tone. "You're quite right!"

Fleda gave a faint, stubborn smile. "He cares for her too much."

"Then why doesn't he marry her? He's giving you an extraordinary chance."

"He doesn't dream I've ever thought of him," said Fleda. "Why should he, if you didn't?"

"It wasn't with me you were in love, my duck." Then Mrs. Gereth added: "I'll go and tell him."

"If you do any such thing you shall never see me again—absolutely, literally never!"

Mrs. Gereth looked hard at her young friend, betraying that she saw she must believe her. "Then you're perverse, you're wicked. Will you swear he doesn't know?"

"Of course he doesn't know!" cried Fleda indignantly.

Her interlocutress was silent a little. "And that he has no feeling on *his* side?"

"For me?" Fleda stared. "Before he has even married her?"

Mrs. Gereth gave a sharp laugh at this. "He ought at least to appreciate your wit. Oh, my dear, you *are* a treasure! Doesn't he appreciate anything? Has he given you absolutely no symptom—not looked a look, not breathed a sigh?"

"The case," said Fleda coldly, "is as I've had the honour to state it."

"Then he's as big a donkey as his mother! But you know you must account for their delay," Mrs. Gereth remarked.

"Why must I?" Fleda asked after a moment.

"Because you were closeted with him here so long. You can't pretend at present, you know, not to have any art."

The girl hesitated an instant; she was conscious that she must choose between two risks. She had had a secret and the secret was gone. Owen had one, which was still unbruised, and the greater risk now was that his mother should lay her formidable hand upon it. All Fleda's tenderness for him moved her to protect it; so she faced the smaller peril. "Their delay," she brought herself to reply, "may perhaps be Mona's doing. I mean because he has lost her the things."

Mrs. Gereth jumped at this. "So that she'll break altogether if I keep them?"

Fleda winced. "I've told you what I believe about that. She'll make scenes and conditions; she'll worry him. But she'll hold him fast; she'll never give him up."

Mrs. Gereth turned it over. "Well, I'll keep them to try her," she finally pronounced; at which Fleda felt quite sick, as if to have given everything and got nothing.

XII

I MUST in common decency let him know that I've talked of the matter with you," she said to her hostess that evening. "What answer do you wish me to write to him?"

"Write to him that you must see him again," said Mrs. Gereth.

Fleda looked very blank. "What on earth am I to see him for?"

"For anything you like!"

The girl would have been struck with the levity of this had she not already, in an hour, felt the extent of the change suddenly wrought in her commerce with her friend—wrought above all, to that friend's view, in her relation to the great issue. The effect of what had followed Owen's visit was to make this relation the very key of the crisis. Pressed upon her, goodness knew, the crisis had been, but it now seemed to put forth big encircling arms—arms that squeezed till they hurt and she must cry out. It was as if everything at Ricks had been poured into a common receptacle, a public ferment of emotion and zeal, out of which it was ladled up to be tasted and talked about; everything at least but the one little treasure of knowledge that she kept back. She ought to have liked this, she reflected, because it meant sympathy, meant a closer union with the source of so much in her life that had been beautiful and renovating; but there were fine instincts in her that stood off. She had had—and it was not merely at this time—to recognise that there were things for which Mrs. Gereth's *flair* was not so happy as for bargains and "marks." It wouldn't be happy now as to the best action on the knowledge she had just gained; yet as from this moment they were still more intimately together, so a person deeply in her debt would simply have to stand and meet what was to come. There were ways in which she could sharply incommode such a person, and not only with the best conscience in the world, but with a sort of brutality of good intentions. One of the straightest of these strokes, Fleda saw, would be the dance of delight over the mystery Mrs. Gereth had laid bare—the loud,

300

lawful, tactless joy of the explorer leaping upon the strand. Like any other lucky discoverer she would take possession of the fortunate island. She was nothing if not practical: almost the only thing she took account of in her young friend's soft secret was the excellent use she could make of it—a use so much to her taste that she refused to feel a hindrance in the quality of the material. Fleda put into Mrs. Gereth's answer to her question a good deal more meaning than it would have occurred to her a few hours before that she was prepared to put, but she had on the spot a foreboding that even so broad a hint would live to be bettered.

"Do you suggest that I shall propose to him to come down here again?" she presently inquired.

"Dear, no; say that you'll go up to town and meet him." It *was* bettered, the broad hint; and Fleda felt this to be still more the case when, returning to the subject before they went to bed, her companion said: "I make him over to you wholly, you know—to do what you please with. Deal with him in your own clever way—I ask no questions. All I ask is that you succeed."

"That's charming," Fleda replied, "but it doesn't tell me a bit, you'll be so good as to consider, in what terms to write to him. It's not an answer from you to the message I was to give you."

"The answer to his message is perfectly distinct: he shall have everything in the place the minute he'll say he'll marry you."

"You really pretend," Fleda asked, "to think me capable of transmitting him that news?"

"What else can I really pretend, when you threaten so to cast me off if I speak the word myself?"

"Oh, if *you* speak the word—!" the girl murmured very gravely, but happy at least to know that in this direction Mrs. Gereth confessed herself warned and helpless. Then she added: "How can I go on living with you on a footing of which I so deeply disapprove? Thinking as I do that you've despoiled him far more than is just or merciful—for if I ex-pected you to take something I didn't in the least expect you to take everything—how can I stay here without a sense that I am backing you up in your cruelty and participating in your

ill-gotten gains?" Fleda was determined that if she had the
chill of her exposed and investigated state she would also have
the convenience of it, and that if Mrs. Gereth popped in and
out of the chamber of her soul she would at least return the
freedom. "I shall quite hate, you know, in a day or two, every
object that surrounds you—become blind to all the beauty
and rarity that I formerly delighted in. Don't think me harsh;
there's no use in my not being frank now. If I leave you,
everything's at an end."

Mrs. Gereth, however, was imperturbable: Fleda had to
recognise that her advantage had become too real. "It's too
beautiful, the way you care for him; it's music in my ears. Nothing else but such a passion could make you say such things;
that's the way I should have been too, my dear. Why didn't you
tell me sooner? I'd have gone right in for you; I never would
have moved a candlestick. Don't stay with me if it torments
you: don't, if you suffer, be where you see the old rubbish. Go
up to town—go back for a little to your father's. It need be only
for a little; two or three weeks will see us through. Your father
will take you and be glad, if you only will make him understand
what it's a question of—of your getting yourself off his hands
forever. *I'll* make him understand, you know, if you feel shy. I'd
take you up myself, I'd go with you, to spare your being bored:
we'd put up at an hotel and we might amuse ourselves a bit. We
haven't had much pleasure since we met, have we? But of
course that wouldn't suit our book. I should be a bugaboo to
Owen—I should be fatally in the way. Your chance is there—
your chance is to be alone. For God's sake use it to the right
end. If you're in want of money I've a little I can give you. But
I ask no questions—not a question as small as your shoe!"

She asked no questions, but she took the most extraordinary things for granted: Fleda felt this still more at the end of
a couple of days. On the second of these our young lady
wrote to Owen: her emotion had to a certain degree cleared
itself—there was something she could briefly say. If she had
given everything to Mrs. Gereth and as yet got nothing, so
she had on the other hand quickly reacted—it took but a
night—against the discouragement of her first check. Her desire to serve him was too passionate, the sense that he
counted upon her too sweet: these things caught her up again

and gave her a new patience and a new subtlety. It shouldn't really be for nothing that she had given so much; deep within her burned again the resolve to get something back. So what she wrote to Owen was simply that she had had a great scene with his mother, but that he must be patient and give her time. It was difficult, as they both had expected, but she was working her hardest for him. She had made an impression—she would do everything to follow it up. Meanwhile he must keep intensely quiet and take no other steps; he must only trust her and pray for her and believe in her perfect loyalty. She made no allusion whatever to Mona's attitude, nor to his not being, as regarded that young lady, master of the situation; but she said in a postscript, in reference to his mother, "Of course she wonders a good deal why your marriage doesn't take place." After the letter had gone she regretted having used the word "loyalty"; there were two or three milder terms which she might as well have employed. The answer she immediately received from Owen was a little note of which she met all the deficiencies by describing it to herself as pathetically simple, but which, to prove that Mrs. Gereth might ask as many questions as she liked, she at once made his mother read. He had no art with his pen, he had not even a good hand, and his letter, a short profession of friendly confidence, consisted of but a few familiar and colourless words of acknowledgment and assent. The gist of it was that he would certainly, since Miss Vetch recommended it, not hurry mamma too much. He would not for the present cause her to be approached by any one else, but he would nevertheless continue to hope that she would see she *must* come round. "Of course, you know," he added, "she can't keep me waiting indefinitely. Please give her my love and tell her that. If it can be done peaceably I know you're just the one to do it."

Fleda had awaited his rejoinder in deep suspense; such was her imagination of the possibility of his having, as she tacitly phrased it, let himself go on paper that when it arrived she was at first almost afraid to open it. There was indeed a distinct danger, for if he should take it into his head to write her love-letters the whole chance of aiding him would drop: she would have to return them, she would have to decline all further communication with him; it would be quite the end of the business. This imagination of Fleda's was a faculty that easily embraced all the heights and depths and extremities of things; that made a single mouthful in particular of any tragic or desperate necessity. She was perhaps at first just a trifle disappointed not to find in the note in question a syllable that strayed from the text; but the next moment she had risen to a point of view from which it presented itself as a production almost inspired in its simplicity. It was simple even for Owen, and she wondered what had given him the cue to be more so than usual. Then she saw how natures that are right just do the things that are right. He wasn't clever—his manner of writing showed it; but the cleverest man in England couldn't have had more the instinct that, under the circumstances, was the supremely happy one, the instinct of giving her something that would do beautifully to be shown to Mrs. Gereth. This was a kind of divination, for naturally he couldn't know the line Mrs. Gereth was taking. It was furthermore explained—and that was the most touching part of all—by his wish that she herself should notice how awfully well he was behaving. His very bareness called her attention to his virtue; and these were the exact fruits of her beautiful and terrible admonition. He was cleaving to Mona; he was doing his duty; he was making tremendously sure he should be without reproach.

If Fleda handed this communication to her friend as a triumphant gage of the innocence of the young man's heart, her elation lived but a moment after Mrs. Gereth had pounced upon the tell-tale spot in it. "Why in the world, then," that lady cried, "does he still not breathe a breath about the day, the *day*, the DAY?" She repeated the word with a crescendo of superior acuteness; she proclaimed that nothing could be more marked than its absence—an absence that simply spoke volumes. What did it prove in fine but that she was producing the effect she had toiled for—that she had settled or was rapidly settling Mona?

Such a challenge Fleda was obliged in some manner to take up. "You may be settling Mona," she returned with a smile, "but I can hardly regard it as sufficient evidence that you're settling Mona's lover."

"Why not, with such a studied omission on his part to gloss over in any manner the painful tension existing between them—the painful tension that, under Providence, I've been the means of bringing about? He gives you by his silence clear notice that his marriage is practically off."

"He speaks to me of the only thing that concerns me. He gives me clear notice that he abates not one jot of his demand."

"Well, then, let him take the only way to get it satisfied."

Fleda had no need to ask again what such a way might be, nor was her support removed by the fine assurance with which Mrs. Gereth could make her argument wait upon her wish. These days, which dragged their length into a strange, uncomfortable fortnight, had already borne more testimony to that element than all the other time the two women had passed together. Our young lady had been at first far from measuring the whole of a feature that Owen himself would probably have described as her companion's "cheek." She lived now in a kind of bath of boldness, felt as if a fierce light poured in upon her from windows opened wide; and the singular part of the ordeal was that she couldn't protest against it fully without incurring even to her own mind some reproach of ingratitude, some charge of smallness. If Mrs. Gereth's apparent determination to hustle her into Owen's arms was accompanied with an air of holding her dignity rather cheap, this was after all only as a consequence of her being held in respect to some other attributes rather dear. It was a new version of the old story of being kicked up-stairs. The wonderful woman was the same woman who, in the summer, at Poynton, had been so puzzled to conceive why a good-natured girl shouldn't have contributed more to the personal rout of the Brigstocks—shouldn't have been grateful even for the handsome puff of Fleda Vetch. Only her passion was keener now and her scruple more absent; the fight made a demand upon her, and her pugnacity had become one with her constant habit of using such weapons as she could pick up. She had no imagination about anybody's life save on the side she bumped against. Fleda was quite aware that she would have otherwise been a rare creature; but a rare creature was originally just what she had struck her as being. Mrs. Gereth had really no perception of anybody's nature—had only one question about persons: were they clever or stupid? To be clever meant to know the marks. Fleda knew them by direct inspiration, and a warm recognition of this had been her friend's

tribute to her character. The girl had hours now of sombre
wishing that she might never see anything good again: that
kind of experience was evidently not an infallible source of
peace. She would be more at peace in some vulgar little place
that should owe its *cachet* to a Universal Provider. There were
nice strong horrors in West Kensington; it was as if they beckoned her and wooed her back to them. She had a relaxed recollection of Waterbath; and of her reasons for staying on at
Ricks the force was rapidly ebbing. One of these was her
pledge to Owen—her vow to press his mother close; the other
was the fact that of the two discomforts, that of being prod-
ded by Mrs. Gereth and that of appearing to run after somebody else, the former remained for a while the more
endurable.

As the days passed, however, it became plainer to Fleda that
her only chance of success would be in lending herself to this
low appearance. Then moreover, at last, her nerves settling
the question, the choice was simply imposed by the violence
done to her taste—to whatever was left of that high principle,
at least, after the free and reckless meeting, for months, of
great drafts and appeals. It was all very well to try to evade
discussion: Owen Gereth was looking to her for a struggle,
and it wasn't a bit of a struggle to be disgusted and dumb.
She was on too strange a footing—that of having presented
an ultimatum and having had it torn up in her face. In such a
case as that the envoy always departed; he never sat gaping
and dawdling before the city. Mrs. Gereth every morning
looked publicly into *The Morning Post*, the only newspaper
she received; and every morning she treated the blankness of
that journal as fresh evidence that everything was "off." What
did the *Post* exist for but to tell you your children were
wretchedly married?—so that if such a source of misery was
dry what could you do but infer that for once you had miraculously escaped? She almost taunted Fleda with supineness in
not getting something out of somebody—in the same breath
indeed in which she drenched her with a kind of appreciation
more onerous to the girl than blame. Mrs. Gereth herself had
of course washed her hands of the matter; but Fleda knew
people who knew Mona and would be sure to be in her confidence—inconceivable people who admired her and had the

"entrée" of Waterbath. What was the use therefore of being the most natural and the easiest of letter-writers if no sort of side-light—in some pretext for correspondence—was, by a brilliant creature, to be got out of such barbarians? Fleda was not only a brilliant creature, but she heard herself commended in these days for attractions new and strange; she figured suddenly in the queer conversations of Ricks as a distinguished, almost as a dangerous beauty. That retouching of her hair and dress in which her friend had impulsively indulged on a first glimpse of her secret was by implication very frequently repeated. She had the sense not only of being advertised and offered, but of being counselled and enlightened in ways that she scarcely understood—arts obscure even to a poor girl who had had, in good society and motherless poverty, to look straight at realities and fill out blanks.

These arts, when Mrs. Gereth's spirits were high, were handled with a brave and cynical humour with which Fleda's fancy could keep no step: they left our young lady wondering what on earth her companion wanted her to do. "I want you to cut in!"—that was Mrs. Gereth's familiar and comprehensive phrase for the course she prescribed. She challenged again and again Fleda's picture, as she called it (though the sketch was too slight to deserve the name), of the indifference to which a prior attachment had committed the proprietor of Poynton. "Do you mean to say that, Mona or no Mona, he could see you that way, day after day, and not have the ordinary feelings of a man? Don't you know a little more, you absurd, affected thing, what men *are*, the brutes?" This was the sort of interrogation to which Fleda was fitfully and irrelevantly treated. She had grown almost used to the refrain. "Do you mean to say that when, the other day, one had quite made you over to him, the great gawk, and he was, on this very spot, utterly alone with you—?" The poor girl at this point never left any doubt of what she meant to say; but Mrs. Gereth could be trusted to break out in another place and at another time. At last Fleda wrote to her father that he must take her in for a while; and when, to her companion's delight, she returned to London, that lady went with her to the station and wafted her on her way. *The Morning Post* had been delivered as they left the house, and Mrs. Gereth had brought it with her for the traveller, who never spent a penny on a newspaper. On the platform, however, when this young person was ticketed, labelled and seated, she opened it at the window of the carriage, exclaiming as usual, after looking into it a moment, "Nothing—nothing—nothing: don't tell *me*!" Every day that there was nothing was a nail in the coffin of the marriage. An instant later the train was off, but, moving quickly beside it, while Fleda leaned inscrutably forth, Mrs. Gereth grasped her friend's hand and looked up with wonderful eyes. "Only let yourself go, darling—only let yourself go!"

XIII

THAT she desired to ask no prudish questions Mrs. Gereth conscientiously proved by closing her lips tight after Fleda had gone to London. No letter from Ricks arrived at West Kensington, and Fleda, with nothing to communicate that could be to the taste of either party, forbore to open a correspondence. If her heart had been less heavy she might have been amused to perceive how much free rope this reticence of Ricks seemed to signify to her that she could take. She had at all events no good news for her friend save in the sense that her silence was not bad news. She was not yet in a position to write that she had "cut in"; but neither, on the other hand, had she gathered material for announcing that Mona was undisseverable from her prey. She had made no use of the pen so glorified by Mrs. Gereth to wake up the echoes of Waterbath; she had sedulously abstained from inquiring what in any quarter, far or near, was said or suggested or supposed. She only spent a matutinal penny on *The Morning Post*; she only saw, on each occasion, that that inspired sheet had as little to say about the imminence as about the abandonment of certain nuptials. It was at the same time obvious that Mrs. Gereth triumphed on these occasions much more than she trembled, and that with a few such triumphs repeated she would cease to tremble at all. What was most manifest, however, was that she had had a rare preconception of the circumstances that would have ministered, had Fleda been disposed, to the girl's cutting in. It was brought home to Fleda that these circumstances would have particularly favoured intervention; she was quickly forced to do them a secret justice. One of the effects of her intimacy with Mrs. Gereth was that she had quite lost all sense of intimacy with any one else. The lady of Ricks had made a desert around her, possessing and absorbing her so utterly that other partakers had fallen away. Hadn't she been admonished, months before, that people considered they had lost her and were reconciled on the whole to the privation? Her present position in the great unconscious town defined itself as obscure: she regarded it at any rate with eyes suspicious of that lesson. She neither wrote notes nor received them; she indulged in no reminders nor knocked at any doors; she wandered vaguely in the western wilderness or cultivated shy forms of that "household art" for which she had had a respect before tasting the bitter tree of knowledge. Her only plan was to be as quiet as a mouse, and when she failed in the attempt to lose herself in the flat suburb she felt like a lonely fly crawling over a dusty chart.

How had Mrs. Gereth known in advance that if she had chosen to be "vile" (that was what Fleda called it) everything would happen to help her?—especially the way her poor father, after breakfast, doddered off to his club, showing seventy when he was really fifty-seven and leaving her richly alone for the day. He came back about midnight, looking at her very hard and not risking long words—only making her feel by inimitable touches that the presence of his family compelled him to alter all his hours. She had in their common sitting-room the company of the objects he was fond of saying that he had collected—objects, shabby and battered, of a sort that appealed little to his daughter: old brandy-flasks and match-boxes, old calendars and hand-books, intermixed with an assortment of pen-wipers and ash-trays, a harvest he had gathered in from penny bazaars. He was blandly unconscious of that side of Fleda's nature which had endeared her to Mrs. Gereth, and she had often heard him wish to goodness there was something striking she cared for. Why didn't she try collecting something?—it didn't matter what. She would find it gave an interest to life, and there was no end of little curiosities one could easily pick up. He was conscious of having a taste for fine things which his children had unfortunately not inherited. This indicated the limits of their acquaintance with him—limits which, as Fleda was now sharply aware, could only leave him to wonder what the mischief she was there for. As she herself echoed this question to the letter she was not in a position to clear up the mystery. She couldn't have given a name to her errand in town or explained it save by saying that she had had to get away from Ricks. It was intensely provisional, but what was to come next? Nothing could come next but a deeper anxiety. She had neither a home nor an outlook—nothing in all the wide world but a feeling of suspense.

Of course she had her duty—her duty to Owen—a definite undertaking, re-affirmed, after his visit to Ricks, under her hand and seal; but there was no sense of possession attached to that: there was only a horrible sense of privation. She had quite moved from under Mrs. Gereth's wide wing; and now that she was really among the pen-wipers and ash-trays she was swept, at the thought of all the beauty she had forsworn, by short, wild gusts of despair. If her friend should really keep the spoils she would never return to her. If that friend should on the other hand part with them what on earth would there be to return to? The chill struck deep as Fleda thought of the mistress of Ricks reduced, in vulgar parlance, to what she had on her back: there was nothing to which she could compare such an image but her idea of Marie Antoinette in the Conciergerie, or perhaps the vision of some tropical bird, the creature of hot, dense forests, dropped on a frozen moor to pick up a living. The mind's eye could indeed see Mrs. Gereth only in her thick, coloured air; it took all the light of her treasures to make her concrete and distinct. She loomed for a moment, in any mere house, gaunt and unnatural; then she vanished as if she had suddenly sunk into a quicksand. Fleda lost herself in the rich fancy of how, if *she* were mistress of Poynton, a whole province, as an abode, should be assigned there to the august queen-mother. She would have returned from her campaign with her baggage-train and her loot, and the palace would unbar its shutters and the morning flash back from its halls. In the event of a surrender the poor woman would never again be able to begin to collect: she was now too old and too moneyless, and times were altered and good things impossibly dear. A surrender, furthermore, to any daughter-in-law save an oddity like Mona needn't at all be an abdication in fact; any other fairly nice girl whom Owen should have taken it into his head to marry would have been positively glad to have, for the museum, a custodian who was a walking catalogue and who understood beyond any one in England the hygiene and temperament of rare pieces. A fairly nice girl would somehow be away a good deal and would at such times count it a blessing to feel Mrs. Gereth at her post.

Fleda had fully recognised, the first days, that, quite apart from any question of letting Owen know where she was, it would be a charity to give him some sign: it would be weak, it would be ugly to be diverted from that kindness by the fact that Mrs. Gereth had attached a tinkling bell to it. A frank relation with him was only superficially discredited: she ought for his own sake to send him a word of cheer. So she repeatedly reasoned, but she as repeatedly delayed performance: if her general plan had been to be as still as a mouse an interview like the interview at Ricks would be an odd contribution to that ideal. Therefore with a confused preference of practice to theory she let the days go by; she felt that nothing was so imperative as the gain of precious time. She shouldn't be able to stay with her father for ever, but she might now reap the benefit of having married her sister—Maggie's union had been built up round a small spare room. Concealed in this apartment she might try to paint again, and abetted by the grateful Maggie—for Maggie at least was grateful, she might try to dispose of her work. She had not indeed struggled with a brush since her visit to Waterbath, where the sight of the family splotches had put her immensely on her guard. Poynton, moreover, had been an impossible place for producing; no active art could flourish there but a Buddhistic contemplation. It had stripped its mistress clean of all feeble accomplishments; her hands were imbrued neither with ink nor with water-colour. Close to Fleda's present abode was the little shop of a man who mounted and framed pictures and desolately dealt in artists' materials. She sometimes paused before it to look at a couple of shy experiments for which its dull window constituted publicity, small studies placed there for sale and full of warning to a young lady without fortune and without talent. Some such young lady had brought them forth in sorrow; some such young lady, to see if they had been snapped up, had passed and repassed as helplessly as she herself was doing. They never had been, they never would be snapped up; yet they were quite above the actual attainment of some other young ladies. It was a matter of discipline with Fleda to take an occasional lesson from them; besides which when she now quitted the house she had to look for reasons after she was out. The only place to find them was in the shop-windows. They made her feel like a servant-girl taking her "afternoon," but that didn't signify: perhaps some day she would resemble such a person still more closely. This continued a fortnight, at the end of which the feeling was suddenly dissipated. She had stopped as usual in the presence of the little pictures; then, as she turned away, she had found herself face to face with Owen Gereth.

At the sight of him two fresh waves passed quickly across her heart, one at the heels of the other. The first was an instant perception that this encounter was not an accident; the second a consciousness as prompt that the best place for it was the street. She knew before he told her that he had been to see her, and the next thing she knew was that he had had information from his mother. Her mind grasped these things while he said with a smile: "I saw only your back, but I was sure. I was over the way. I've been at your house."

"How came you to know my house?" Fleda asked.

"I like that!" he laughed. "How came you not to let me know that you were there?"

Fleda, at this, thought it best also to laugh. "Since I didn't let you know, why did you come?"

"Oh, I say!" cried Owen. "Don't add insult to injury. Why in the world didn't you let me know? I came because I want awfully to see you." He hesitated, then he added: "I got the tip from mother. She has written to me—fancy!"

They still stood where they had met. Fleda's instinct was to keep him there; the more so that she could already see him take for granted that they would immediately proceed together to her door. He rose before her with a different air: he looked less ruffled and bruised than he had done at Ricks; he showed a recovered freshness. Perhaps, however, this was only because she had scarcely seen him at all as yet in London form, as he would have called it—"turned out" as he was turned out in town. In the country, heated with the chase and splashed with the mire, he had always rather reminded her of a picturesque peasant in national costume. This costume, as Owen wore it, varied from day to day; it was as copious as the wardrobe of an actor; but it never failed of suggestions of the earth and the weather, the hedges and the ditches, the beasts and the birds. There had been days when he struck her as all nature in one pair of boots. It didn't make him now another person that he was delicately dressed, shining and splendid—that he had a higher hat and light gloves with black seams and a spear-like umbrella; but it made him, she soon decided, really handsomer, and that in turn gave him—for she never could think of him, or indeed of some other things, without the aid of his vocabulary—a tremendous pull. Yes, this was for the moment, as he looked at her, the great fact of their situation—his pull was tremendous. She tried to keep the acknowledgment of it from trembling in her voice as she said to him with more surprise than she really felt: "You've then re-opened relations with her?"

"It's she who has re-opened them with me. I got her letter this morning. She told me you were here and that she wished me to know it. She didn't say much; she just gave me your address. I wrote her back, you know, 'Thanks no end. Shall go to-day.' So we *are* in correspondence again, aren't we? She means of course that you've something to tell me from her, hey? But if you have, why haven't you let a fellow know?" He waited for no answer to this, he had so much to say. "At your house, just now, they told me how long you've been here. Haven't you known all the while that I'm counting the hours? I left a word for you—that I would be back at six; but I'm awfully glad to have caught you so much sooner. You don't mean to say you're not going home!" he exclaimed in dismay. "The young woman there told me you went out early."

"I've been out a very short time," said Fleda, who had hung back with the general purpose of making things difficult for him. The street would make them difficult; she could trust the street. She reflected in time, however, that to betray to him she was afraid to admit him would give him more a feeling of facility than of anything else. She moved on with him after a moment, letting him direct their course to her door, which was only round a corner; she considered as they went that it might not prove such a stroke to have been in London so long and yet not to have called him. She desired he should feel she was perfectly simple with him, and there was no simplicity in that. None the less, on the steps of the house, though she had a key, she rang the bell; and while they waited together and she averted her face she looked straight into the depths of what Mrs. Gereth had meant by giving him the "tip." This had been perfidious, had been monstrous of Mrs. Gereth, and Fleda wondered if her letter had contained only what Owen repeated.

XIV

WHEN they had passed together into her father's little place and, among the brandy-flasks and pen-wipers, still more disconcerted and divided, the girl—to do something, though it would make him stay—had ordered tea, he put the letter before her quite as if he had guessed her thought. "She's still a bit nasty—fancy!" He handed her the scrap of a note which he had pulled out of his pocket and from its envelope. "Fleda Vetch," it ran, "is at West Kensington—10 Raphael Road. Go to see her and try, for God's sake, to cultivate a glimmer of intelligence." When in handing it back to him she took in his face she saw that its heightened colour was the effect of his watching her read such an allusion to his want of wit. Fleda knew what it was an allusion to, and his pathetic air of having received this buffet, tall and fine and kind as he stood there, made her conscious of not quite concealing her knowledge. For a minute she was kept silent by an angered sense of the trick that had been played her. It was a trick because Fleda considered there had been a covenant; and the trick consisted of Mrs. Gereth's having broken the spirit of their agreement while conforming in a fashion to the letter. Under the girl's menace of a complete rupture she had been afraid to make of her secret the use she itched to make; but in the course of these days of separation she had gathered pluck to hazard an indirect betrayal. Fleda measured her hesitations and the impulse which she had finally obeyed and which the continued procrastination of Waterbath had encouraged, had at last made irresistible. If in her high-handed manner of playing their game she had not named the thing hidden she had named the hiding-place. It was over the sense of this wrong that Fleda's lips closed tight: she was afraid of aggravating her case by some ejaculation that would make Owen prick up his ears. A great, quick effort, however, helped her to avoid the danger; with her constant idea of keeping cool and repressing a visible flutter she found herself able to choose her words. Meanwhile he had exclaimed with his uncomfortable laugh: "That's a good one for me, Miss Vetch, isn't it?"

"Of course you know by this time that your mother's very sharp," said Fleda.

"I think I can understand well enough when I know what's to be understood," the young man asserted. "But I hope you won't mind my saying that you've kept me pretty well in the dark about that. I've been waiting, waiting, waiting—so much has depended on your news. If you've been working for me I'm afraid it has been a thankless job. Can't she say what she'll do, one way or the other? I can't tell in the least where I am, you know. I haven't really learnt from you, since I saw you there, where *she* is. You wrote me to be patient, and upon my soul I have been. But I'm afraid you don't quite realise what I'm to be patient with. At Waterbath, don't you know? I've simply to account and answer for the damned things. Mona glowers at me and waits, and I, hang it, I glower at you and do the same." Fleda had gathered fuller confidence as he continued; so plain was it that she had succeeded in not dropping into his mind the spark that might produce the glimmer his mother had tried to rub up. But even her small safety gave a start when after an appealing pause he went on: "I hope, you know, that after all you're not keeping anything back from me."

In the full face of what she was keeping back such a hope could only make her wince; but she was prompt with her explanations in proportion as she felt they failed to meet him. The smutty maid came in with tea-things, and Fleda, moving several objects, eagerly accepted the diversion of arranging a place for them on one of the tables. "I've been trying to break your mother down because it has seemed there may be some chance of it. That's why I've let you go on expecting it. She's too proud to veer round all at once, but I think I speak correctly in saying that I've made an impression."

In spite of ordering tea she had not invited him to sit down; she herself made a point of standing. He hovered by the window that looked into Raphael Road; she kept at the other side of the room; the stunted slavey, gazing wide-eyed at the beautiful gentleman and either stupidly or cunningly bringing but one thing at a time, came and went between the tea-tray and the open door.

"You pegged at her so hard?" Owen asked.

"I explained to her fully your position and put before her

much more strongly than she liked what seemed to me her absolute duty."

Owen waited a little. "And having done that you departed?"

Fleda felt the full need of giving a reason for her departure; but at first she only said with cheerful frankness: "I departed."

Her companion again looked at her in silence. "I thought you had gone to her for several months."

"Well," Fleda replied, "I couldn't stay. I didn't like it. I didn't like it at all—I couldn't bear it," she went on. "In the midst of those trophies of Poynton, living with them, touching them, using them, I felt as if I were backing her up. As I was not a bit of an accomplice, as I hate what she has done, I didn't want to be, even to the extent of the mere look of it—what is it you call such people?—an accessory after the fact." There was something she kept back so rigidly that the joy of uttering the rest was double. She felt the sharpest need of giving him all the other truth. There was a matter as to which she had deceived him, and there was a matter as to which she had deceived Mrs. Gereth, but her lack of pleasure in deception as such came home to her now. She busied herself with the tea and, to extend the occupation, cleared the table still more, spreading out the coarse cups and saucers and the vulgar little plates. She was aware that she produced more confusion than symmetry, but she was also aware that she was violently nervous. Owen tried to help her with something: this made indeed for disorder. "My reason for not writing to you," she pursued, "was simply that I was hoping to hear more from Ricks. I've waited from day to day for that."

"But you've heard nothing?"

"Not a word."

"Then what I understand," said Owen, "is that practically you and Mummy have quarrelled. And you've done it—I mean you personally—for *me*."

"Oh no, we haven't quarrelled a bit!" Then with a smile: "We've only diverged."

"You've diverged uncommonly far!"—Owen laughed pleasantly back. Fleda, with her hideous crockery and her father's collections, could conceive that these objects, to her visitor's perception even more strongly than to her own, measured the length of the swing from Poynton and Ricks; she was aware

too that her high standards figured vividly enough even to
Owen's simplicity to make him reflect that West Kensington
was a tremendous fall. If she had fallen it was because she had
acted for him. She was all the more content he should thus
see she *had* acted, as the cost of it, in his eyes, was none of
her own showing. "What seems to have happened," he exclaimed, "is that you've had a row with her and yet not
moved her!"

Fleda considered a moment; she was full of the impression
that, notwithstanding her scant help, he saw his way clearer
than he had seen it at Ricks. He might mean many things;
and what if the many should mean in their turn only one?
"The difficulty is, you understand, that she doesn't really see
into your situation." She hesitated. "She doesn't comprehend
why your marriage hasn't yet taken place."

Owen stared. "Why, for the reason I told you: that Mona
won't take another step till mother has given full satisfaction.
Everything must be there. You see everything *was* there the
day of that fatal visit."

"Yes, that's what I understood from you at Ricks," said
Fleda; "but I haven't repeated it to your mother." She had
hated at Ricks to talk with him about Mona, but now that
scruple was swept away. If he could speak of Mona's visit as
fatal she need at least not pretend not to notice it. It made all
the difference that she had tried to assist him and had failed:
to give him any faith in her service she must give him all her
reasons but one. She must give him, in other words, with a
corresponding omission, all Mrs. Gereth's. "You can easily see
that, as she dislikes your marriage, anything that may seem to
make it less certain works in her favour. Without my telling
her, she has suspicions and views that are simply suggested by
your delay. Therefore it didn't seem to me right to make
them worse. By holding off long enough, she thinks she may
put an end to your engagement. If Mona's waiting she believes she may at last tire Mona out." That, in all conscience,
Fleda felt was lucid enough.

So the young man, following her attentively, appeared
equally to feel. "So far as that goes," he promptly declared,
"she *has* at last tired Mona out." He uttered the words with
a strange approach to hilarity.

Fleda's surprise at this aberration left her a moment looking at him. "Do you mean your marriage is off?"

Owen answered with a kind of gay despair. "God knows, Miss Vetch, where or when or what my marriage is! If it isn't 'off,' it certainly, at the point things have reached, isn't *on*. I haven't seen Mona for ten days, and for a week I haven't heard from her. She used to write me every week, don't you know? She won't budge from Waterbath and I haven't budged from town." Then he suddenly broke out: "If she *does* chuck me, will mother come round?"

Fleda, at this, felt that her heroism had come to its real test—felt that in telling him the truth she should effectively raise a hand to push his impediment out of the way. Was the knowledge that such a motion would probably dispose forever of Mona capable of yielding to the conception of still giving her every chance she was entitled to? That conception was heroic, but at the same moment it reminded Fleda of the place it had held in her plan she was also reminded of the not less urgent claim of the truth. Ah, the truth—there was a limit to the impunity with which one could juggle with it! Wasn't what she had most to remember the fact that Owen had a right to his property and that he had also her vow to stand by him in the effort to recover it? How did she stand by him if she hid from him the single way to recover it of which she was quite sure? For an instant that seemed to her the fullest of her life she debated. "Yes," she said at last, "if your marriage is really abandoned she will give up everything she has taken."

"That's just what makes Mona hesitate!" Owen honestly exclaimed. "I mean the idea that I shall get back the things only if she gives me up."

Fleda thought an instant. "You mean makes her hesitate to keep you—not hesitate to renounce you?"

Owen looked a trifle befogged. "She doesn't see the use of hanging on, as I haven't even yet put the matter into legal hands. She's awfully keen about that, and awfully disgusted that I don't. She says it's the only real way, and she thinks I'm afraid to take it. She has given me time and then has given me again more. She says I give Mummy too much. She says I'm a muff to go pottering on. That's why she's drawing off so hard, don't you see?"

"I don't see very clearly. Of course you must give her what you offered her; of course you must keep your word. There must be no mistake about *that*!" the girl declared.

Owen's bewilderment visibly increased. "You think, then, as she does, that I *must* send down the police?"

The mixture of reluctance and dependence in this made her feel how much she was failing him: she had the sense of "chucking" him too. "No, no, not yet!" she said, though she had really no other and no better course to prescribe. "Doesn't it occur to you," she asked in a moment, "that if Mona is, as you say, drawing away, she may have, in doing so, a very high motive? She knows the immense value of all the objects detained by your mother, and to restore the spoils of Poynton she is ready—is that it?—to make a sacrifice. The sacrifice is that of an engagement she had entered upon with joy."

Owen had been blank a moment before, but he followed this argument with success—a success so immediate that it enabled him to produce with decision: "Ah, she's not that sort! She wants them herself," he added; "she wants to feel they're hers; she doesn't care whether I have them or not! And if she can't get them she doesn't want *me*. If she can't get them she doesn't want anything at all."

This was categoric: Fleda drank it in. "She takes such an interest in them?"

"So it appears."

"So much that they're *all*, and that she can let everything else absolutely depend upon them?"

Owen weighed her question as if he felt the responsibility of his answer. But that answer came in a moment and, as Fleda could see, out of a wealth of memory. "She never wanted them particularly till they seemed to be in danger. Now she has an idea about them; and when she gets hold of an idea—oh dear me!" He broke off, pausing and looking away as with a sense of the futility of expression: it was the first time Fleda had ever heard him explain a matter so pointedly or embark at all on a generalisation. It was striking, it was touching to her, as he faltered, that he appeared but half capable of floating his generalisation to the end. The girl, however, was so far competent to fill up his blank as that she had divined on the occasion of Mona's visit to Poynton what would happen in the event of the accident at which he glanced. She had there with her own eyes seen Owen's betrothed get hold of an idea. "I say, you know, *do* give me some tea!" he went on irrelevantly and familiarly.

Her profuse preparations had all this time had no sequel, and with a laugh that she felt to be awkward she hastily complied with his request. "It's sure to be horrid," she said; "we don't have at all good things." She offered him also bread and butter, of which he partook, holding his cup and saucer in his other hand and moving slowly about the room. She poured herself a cup, but not to take it; after which, without wanting it, she began to eat a small stale biscuit. She was struck with the extinction of the unwillingness she had felt at Ricks to contribute to the bandying between them of poor Mona's name; and under this influence she presently resumed: "Am I to understand that she engaged herself to marry you without caring for you?"

Owen looked out into Raphael Road. "She *did* care for me awfully. But she can't stand the strain."

"The strain of what?"

"Why, of the whole wretched thing."

"The whole thing has indeed been wretched, and I can easily conceive its effect upon her," Fleda said.

Her visitor turned sharp round. "You *can*?" There was a light in his strong stare. "You can understand it's spoiling her temper and making her come down on *me*? She behaves as if I were of no use to her at all!"

Fleda hesitated. "She's rankling under the sense of her wrong."

"Well, was it I, pray, who perpetrated the wrong? Ain't I doing what I can to get the thing arranged?"

The ring of his question made his anger at Mona almost resemble for a minute an anger at Fleda; and this resemblance in turn caused our young lady to observe how handsome he looked when he spoke, for the first time in her hearing, with that degree of heat, and used, also for the first time, such a term as "perpetrated." In addition his challenge rendered still more vivid to her the mere flimsiness of her own aid. "Yes, you've been perfect," she said. "You've had a most difficult part. You've had to show tact and patience, as well as firmness, with your mother, and you've strikingly shown them. It's I who, quite unintentionally, have deceived you. I haven't helped you at all to your remedy."

"Well, you wouldn't at all events have ceased to like me, would you?" Owen demanded. It evidently mattered to him to know if she really justified Mona. "I mean of course if you *had* liked me—liked me as *she* liked me," he explained.

Fleda looked this inquiry in the face only long enough to recognise that in her embarrassment she must take instant refuge in a superior one. "I can answer that better if I know how kind to her you've been. *Have* you been kind to her?" she asked as simply as she could.

"Why, rather, Miss Vetch!" Owen declared. "I've done every blessed thing she wished. I rushed down to Ricks, as you saw, with fire and sword, and the day after that I went to see her at Waterbath." At this point he checked himself, though it was just the point at which her interest deepened. A different look had come into his face as he put down his empty teacup. "But why should I tell you such things, for any good it does me? I gather that you've no suggestion to make me now except that I shall request my solicitor to act. *Shall* I request him to act?"

Fleda scarce caught his words: something new had suddenly come into her mind. "When you went to Waterbath after seeing me," she asked, "did you tell her all about that?"

Owen looked conscious. "All about it?"

"That you had had a long talk with me without seeing your mother at all?"

"Oh yes, I told her exactly, and that you had been most awfully kind and that I had placed the whole thing in your hands."

Fleda was silent a moment. "Perhaps that displeased her," she at last suggested.

"It displeased her fearfully," said Owen, looking very queer.

"Fearfully?" broke from the girl. Somehow, at the word, she was startled.

"She wanted to know what right you had to meddle. She said you were not honest."

"Oh!" Fleda cried with a long wail. Then she controlled herself. "I see."

"She abused you, and I defended you. She denounced you——"

She checked him with a gesture. "Don't tell me what she did!" She had coloured up to her eyes, where, as with the effect of a blow in the face, she quickly felt the tears gathering. It was a sudden drop in her great flight, a shock to her attempt to watch over what Mona was entitled to. While she had been straining her very soul in this attempt the object of her magnanimity had been practically pronouncing her vile. She took it all in, however, and after an instant was able to speak with a smile. She would not have been surprised to learn indeed that her smile was strange. "You had said a while ago that your mother and I quarrelled about you. It's much more true that you and Mona have quarrelled about *me*."

Owen hesitated, but at last he brought it out. "What I mean to say is, don't you know, that Mona, if you don't mind my saying so, has taken it into her head to be jealous."

"I see," said Fleda. "Well, I dare say our conferences have looked very odd."

"They've looked very beautiful, and they've been very beautiful. Oh, I've told her the sort you are!" the young man pursued.

"That of course hasn't made her love me better."

"No, nor love me," said Owen. "Of course, you know, she *says*—as far as that goes—that she loves me."

"And do you say you love her?"

"I say nothing else—I say it all the while. I said it the other day a dozen times." Fleda made no immediate rejoinder to this, and before she could choose one he repeated his question of a moment before. "*Am* I to tell my solicitor to act?"

She had at that moment turned away from this solution, precisely because she saw in it the great chance of her secret. If she should determine him to adopt it she might put out her hand and take him. It would shut in Mrs. Gereth's face the open door of surrender: she would flare up and fight, flying the flag of a passionate, an heroic defence. The case would obviously go against her, but the proceedings would last longer than Mona's patience or Owen's propriety. With a formal rupture he would be at large; and she had only to tighten her fingers round the string that would raise the curtain on that scene. "You tell me you 'say' you love her, but is there nothing more in it than your saying so? You wouldn't say so, would you, if it's not true? What in the world has become in so short a time of the affection that led to your engagement?"

"The deuce knows what has become of it, Miss Vetch!" Owen cried. "It seemed all to go to pot as this horrid struggle came on." He was close to her now and, with his face lighted again by the relief of it, he looked all his helpless history into her eyes. "As I saw you and noticed you more, as I knew you better and better, I felt less and less—I couldn't help it—about anything or any one else. I wished I had known you sooner—I knew I should have liked you better than any one in the world. But it wasn't you who made the difference," he eagerly continued, "and I was awfully determined to stick to Mona to the death. It was she herself who made it, upon my soul, by the state she got into, the way she sulked, the way she took things and the way she let me have it! She destroyed our prospects and our happiness, upon my honour. She made just the same smash of them as if she had kicked over that tea-table. She wanted to know all the while what was passing between us, between you and me; and she wouldn't take my solemn assurance that nothing was passing but what might have directly passed between me and old Mummy. She said a pretty girl like you was a nice old Mummy for me, and, if you'll believe it, she never called you anything else but that. I'll be hanged if I haven't been good, haven't I? I haven't breathed a breath of any sort to you, have I? You'd have been down on me hard if I had, wouldn't you? You're down on me pretty hard as it is, I think, aren't you? But I don't care what you say now, or what Mona says either, or a single rap what any one says: she has given me at last by her confounded behaviour a right to speak out, to utter the way I feel about it. The way I feel about it, don't you know, is that it had all better come to an end. You ask me if I don't love her, and I suppose it's natural enough you should. But you ask it at the very moment I'm half mad to say to you that there's only one person on the whole earth I *really* love, and that that person——" Here Owen pulled up short, and Fleda wondered if it were from the effect of his perceiving, through the closed door, the sound of steps and voices on the landing of the stairs. She had caught this sound herself with surprise and a vague uneasiness: it was not an hour at which her father ever came in, and there was no present reason why she should have a visitor. She had a fear which after a few seconds deepened: a visitor was at hand; the visitor would be simply Mrs. Gereth. That lady wished for a near view of the consequence of her note to Owen. Fleda straightened herself with the instant thought that if this was what Mrs. Gereth desired Mrs. Gereth should have it in a form not to be mistaken. Owen's pause was the matter of a moment, but during that moment our young couple stood with their eyes holding each other's eyes and their ears catching the suggestion, still through the door, of a murmured conference in the hall. Fleda had begun to make the movement to cut it short when Owen stopped her with a grasp of her arm. "You're surely able to guess," he said with his voice dropped and her arm pressed as she had never known such a drop or such a pressure—"you're surely able to guess the one person on earth I love?"

The handle of the door turned, and Fleda had only time to jerk at him: "Your mother!"

The door opened, and the smutty maid, edging in, announced "Mrs. Brigstock!"

XV

M<small>RS.</small> B<small>RIGSTOCK</small>, in the doorway, stood looking from one of the occupants of the room to the other; then they saw her eyes attach themselves to a small object that had lain hitherto unnoticed on the carpet. This was the biscuit of which, on giving Owen his tea, Fleda had taken a perfunctory nibble: she had immediately laid it on the table, and that subsequently, in some precipitate movement, she should have brushed it off was doubtless a sign of the agitation that possessed her. For Mrs. Brigstock there was apparently more in it than met the eye. Owen at any rate picked it up, and Fleda felt as if he were removing the traces of some scene that the newspapers would have characterised as lively. Mrs. Brigstock clearly took in also the sprawling tea-things and the mark as of high water in the full faces of her young friends. These elements made the little place a vivid picture of intimacy. A minute was filled by Fleda's relief at finding her visitor not to be Mrs. Gereth, and a longer space by the ensuing sense of what was really more compromising in the actual apparition. It dimly occurred to her that the lady of Ricks had also written to Waterbath. Not only had Mrs. Brigstock never paid her a call, but Fleda would have been unable to figure her so employed. A year before the girl had spent a day under her roof, but never feeling that Mrs. Brigstock regarded this as constituting a bond. She had never stayed in any house but Poynton, where the imagination of a bond, on one side or the other, prevailed. After the first astonishment she dashed gaily at her guest, emphasising her welcome and wondering how her whereabouts had become known at Waterbath. Had not Mrs. Brigstock quitted that residence for the very purpose of laying her hand on the associate of Mrs. Gereth's misconduct? The spirit in which this hand was to be laid our young lady was yet to ascertain; but she was a person who could think ten thoughts at once—a circumstance which, even putting her present plight at its worst, gave her a great advantage over a person who required easy conditions for dealing even with one. The very vibration of the air, however, told her that whatever Mrs. Brigstock's spirit might originally have been it had been sharply affected by the sight of Owen. He was essentially a surprise: she had reckoned with everything that concerned him but his personal presence. With that, in awkward silence, she was reckoning now, as Fleda could see, while she effected with friendly aid an embarrassed transit to the sofa. Owen would be useless, would be deplorable: that aspect of the case Fleda had taken in as well. Another aspect was that he would admire her, adore her, exactly in proportion as she herself should rise gracefully superior. Fleda felt for the first time free to let herself "go," as Mrs. Gereth had said, and she was full of the sense that to "go" meant now to aim straight at the effect of moving Owen to rapture at her simplicity and tact. It was her impression that he had no positive dislike of Mona's mother; but she couldn't entertain that notion without a glimpse of the implication that he had a positive dislike of Mrs. Brigstock's daughter. Mona's mother declined tea, declined a better seat, declined a cushion, declined to remove her boa: Fleda guessed that she had not come on purpose to be dry, but that the voice of the invaded room had itself given her the hint.

"I just came on the mere chance," she said. "Mona found yesterday somewhere the card of invitation to your sister's marriage that you sent us, or your father sent us, some time ago. We couldn't be present—it was impossible; but as it had this address on it I said to myself that I might find you here."

"I'm very glad to be at home," Fleda responded.

"Yes, that doesn't happen very often, does it?" Mrs. Brigstock looked round afresh at Fleda's home.

"Oh, I came back from Ricks last week. I shall be here now till I don't know when."

"We thought it very likely you would have come back. We knew of course of your having been at Ricks. If I didn't find you I thought I might perhaps find Mr. Vetch," Mrs. Brigstock went on.

"I'm sorry he's out. He's always out—all day long."

Mrs. Brigstock's round eyes grew rounder. "All day long?"

"All day long," Fleda smiled.

"Leaving you quite to yourself?"

"A good deal to myself, but a little, to-day, as you see, to

Mr. Gereth—" and the girl looked at Owen to draw him into their sociability. For Mrs. Brigstock he had immediately sat down; but the movement had not corrected the sombre stiffness taking possession of him at the sight of her. Before he found a response to the appeal addressed to him Fleda turned again to her other visitor. "It there any purpose for which you would like my father to call on you?"

Mrs. Brigstock received this question as if it were not to be unguardedly answered; upon which Owen intervened with pale irrelevance: "I wrote to Mona this morning of Miss Vetch's being in town; but of course the letter hadn't arrived when you left home."

"No, it hadn't arrived. I came up for the night—I've several matters to attend to." Then looking with an intention of fixedness from one of her companions to the other, "I'm afraid I've interrupted your conversation," Mrs. Brigstock said. She spoke without effectual point, had the air of merely announcing the fact. Fleda had not yet been confronted with the question of the sort of person Mrs. Brigstock was; she had only been confronted with the question of the sort person Mrs. Gereth scorned her for being. She was really somehow no sort of person at all, and it came home to Fleda that if Mrs. Gereth could see her at this moment she would scorn her more than ever. She had a face of which it was impossible to say anything but that it was pink, and a mind that it would be possible to describe only if one had been able to mark it in a similar fashion. As nature had made this organ neither green nor blue nor yellow there was nothing to know it by: it strayed and bleated like an unbranded sheep. Fleda felt for it at this moment much of the kindness of compassion, since Mrs. Brigstock had brought it with her to do something for her that she regarded as delicate. Fleda was quite prepared to help it to perform if she should be able to gather what it wanted to do. What she gathered, however, more and more was that it wanted to do something different from what it had wanted to do in leaving Waterbath. There was still nothing to enlighten her more specifically in the way her visitor continued: "You must be very much taken up. I believe you quite espouse his dreadful quarrel."

Fleda vaguely demurred. "His dreadful quarrel?"

"About the contents of the house. Aren't you looking after them for him?"

"She knows how awfully kind you've been to me," Owen said. He showed such discomfiture that he really gave away their situation; and Fleda found herself divided between the hope that he would take leave and the wish that he should see the whole of what the occasion might enable her to bring to pass for him.

She explained to Mrs. Brigstock. "Mrs. Gereth, at Ricks the other day, asked me particularly to see him for her."

"And did she ask you also particularly to see him here in town?" Mrs. Brigstock's hideous bonnet seemed to argue for the unsophisticated truth; and it was on Fleda's lips to reply that such had indeed been Mrs. Gereth's request. But she checked herself, and before she could say anything else Owen had addressed their companion.

"I made a point of letting Mona know that I should be here, don't you see? That's exactly what I wrote her this morning."

"She would have had no doubt you would be here if you had a chance," Mrs. Brigstock returned. "If your letter had arrived it might have prepared me for finding you here at tea. In that case I certainly wouldn't have come."

"I'm glad then it didn't arrive. Shouldn't you like him to go?" Fleda asked.

Mrs. Brigstock looked at Owen and considered: nothing showed in her face but that it turned a deeper pink. "I should like him to go with *me*." There was no menace in her tone, but she evidently knew what she wanted. As Owen made no response to this Fleda glanced at him to invite him to assent; then for fear that he wouldn't, and would thereby make his case worse, she took upon herself to declare that she was sure he would be very glad to meet such a wish. She had no sooner spoken than she felt that the words had a bad effect of intimacy: she had answered for him as if she had been his wife. Mrs. Brigstock continued to regard him as if she had observed nothing and she continued to address Fleda. "I've not seen him for a long time—I've particular things to say to him."

"So have I things to say to you, Mrs. Brigstock!" Owen

interjected. With this he took up his hat as if for immediate departure.

The other visitor meanwhile turned to Fleda. "What is Mrs. Gereth going to do?"

"Is that what you came to ask me?" Fleda demanded.

"That and several other things."

"Then you had much better let Mr. Gereth go, and stay by yourself and make me a pleasant visit. You can talk with him when you like, but it's the first time you've been to see me."

This appeal had evidently a certain effect; Mrs. Brigstock visibly wavered. "I can't talk with him whenever I like," she returned; "he hasn't been near us since I don't know when. But there are things that have brought me here."

"They can't be things of any importance," Owen, to Fleda's surprise, suddenly asserted. He had not at first taken up Mrs. Brigstock's expression of a wish to carry him off: Fleda could see that the instinct at the bottom of this was that of standing by her, of seeming not to abandon her. But abruptly, all his soreness working within him, it had struck him that he should abandon her still more if he should leave her to be dealt with by her other visitor. "You must allow me to say, you know, Mrs. Brigstock, that I don't think you should come down on Miss Vetch about anything. It's very good of her to take the smallest interest in us and our horrid, vulgar little squabble. If you want to talk about it, talk about it with *me*." He was flushed with the idea of protecting Fleda, of exhibiting his consideration for her. "I don't like you cross-questioning her, don't you see? She's as straight as a die: *I'll* tell you all about her!" he declared with an excited laugh. "Please come off with me and let her alone."

Mrs. Brigstock, at this, became vivid at once; Fleda thought she looked most peculiar. She stood straight up, with a queer distention of her whole person and of everything in her face but her mouth, which she gathered into a small, tight orifice. Fleda was painfully divided; her joy was deep within, but it was more relevant to the situation that she should not appear to associate herself with the tone of familiarity in which Owen addressed a lady who had been, and was perhaps still, about to become his mother-in-law. She laid on Mrs. Brigstock's arm a repressive, persuasive hand. Mrs. Brigstock, however, had already exclaimed on her having so wonderful a defender. "He speaks, upon my word, as if I had come here to be rude to you!"

At this, grasping her hard, Fleda laughed; then she achieved the exploit of delicately kissing her. "I'm not in the least afraid to be alone with you, or of your tearing me to pieces. I'll answer any question that you can possibly dream of putting to me."

"I'm the proper person to answer Mrs. Brigstock's questions," Owen broke in again, "and I'm not a bit less ready to meet them than you are." He was firmer than she had ever seen him; it was as if she had not dreamed he could be so firm.

"But she'll only have been here a few minutes. What sort of a visit is that?" Fleda cried.

"It has lasted long enough for my purpose. There was something I wanted to know, but I think I know it now."

"Anything you don't know I dare say I can tell you!" Owen observed as he impatiently smoothed his hat with the cuff of his coat.

Fleda by this time desired immensely to keep his companion, but she saw she could do so only at the cost of provoking on his part a further exhibition of the sheltering attitude which he exaggerated precisely because it was the first thing, since he had begun to "like" her, that he had been able frankly to do for her. It was not in her interest that Mrs. Brigstock should be more struck than she already was with that benevolence. "There may be things you know that I don't," she presently said to her with a smile. "But I've a sort of sense that you are labouring under some great mistake."

Mrs. Brigstock, at this, looked into her eyes more deeply and yearningly than she had supposed Mrs. Brigstock could look: it was the flicker of a mild, muddled willingness to give her a chance. Owen, however, quickly spoiled everything. "Nothing is more probable than that Mrs. Brigstock is doing what you say; but there's no one in the world to whom you owe an explanation. I may owe somebody one—I dare say I do. But not you—no!"

"But what if there's one that it's no difficulty at all for me to give?" Fleda inquired. "I'm sure that's the only one Mrs. Brigstock came to ask, if she came to ask any at all."

Again the good lady looked hard at her young hostess. "I came, I believe, Fleda, just, you know, to plead with you."

Fleda, with a bright face, hesitated a moment. "As if I were one of those bad women in a play?"

The remark was disastrous: Mrs. Brigstock, on whom her brightness was lost, evidently thought it singularly free. She turned away as from a presence that had really defined itself as objectionable, and Fleda had a vain sense that her good humour, in which there was an idea, was taken for impertinence or at least for levity. Her allusion was improper even if she herself wasn't. Mrs. Brigstock's emotion simplified: it came to the same thing. "I'm quite ready," that lady said to Owen rather mildly and woundedly. "I do want to speak to you very much."

"I'm completely at your service." Owen held out his hand to Fleda. "Good-bye, Miss Vetch. I hope to see you again to-morrow." He opened the door for Mrs. Brigstock, who passed before the girl with an oblique, averted salutation. Owen and Fleda, while he stood at the door, then faced each other darkly and without speaking. Their eyes met once more for a long moment, and she was conscious there was something in hers that the darkness didn't quench, that he had never seen before and that he was perhaps never to see again. He stayed long enough to take it—to take it with a sombre stare that just showed the dawn of wonder; then he followed Mrs. Brigstock out of the house.

XVI

H E HAD uttered the hope that he should see her the next day, but Fleda could easily reflect that he wouldn't see her if she were not there to be seen. If there was a thing in the world she desired at that moment it was that the next day should have no point of resemblance with the day that had just elapsed. She accordingly aspired to an absence: she would go immediately down to Maggie. She ran out that evening and telegraphed to her sister, and in the morning she quitted London by an early train. She required for this step no reason but the sense of necessity. It was a strong personal need; she wished to interpose something, and there was nothing she could interpose but distance, but time. If Mrs. Brigstock had to deal with Owen she would allow Mrs. Brigstock the chance. To be there, to be in the midst of it, was the reverse of what she craved: she had already been more in the midst of it than had ever entered into her plan. At any rate she had renounced her plan; she had no plan now but the plan of separation. This was to abandon Owen, to give up the fine office of helping him back to his own; but when she had undertaken that office she had not foreseen that Mrs. Gereth would defeat it by a manœuvre so remarkably simple. The scene at her father's rooms had extinguished all offices, and the scene at her father's rooms was of Mrs. Gereth's producing. Owen, at all events, must now act for himself: he had obligations to meet, he had satisfactions to give, and Fleda fairly ached with the wish that he might be equal to them. She never knew the extent of her tenderness for him till she became conscious of the present force of her desire that he should be superior, be perhaps even sublime. She obscurely made out that superiority, that sublimity mightn't after all be fatal. She closed her eyes and lived for a day or two in the mere beauty of confidence. It was with her on the short journey; it was with her at Maggie's; it glorified the mean little house in the stupid little town. Owen had grown larger to her: he would do, like a man, whatever he should have to do. He wouldn't be weak—not as she was: she herself was weak exceedingly.

Arranging her few possessions in Maggie's fewer receptacles, she caught a glimpse of the bright side of the fact that her old things were not such a problem as Mrs. Gereth's. Picking her way with Maggie through the local puddles, diving with her into smelly cottages and supporting her, at smellier shops, in firmness over the weight of joints and the taste of cheese, it was still her own secret that was universally interwoven. In the puddles, the cottages, the shops she was comfortably alone with it; that comfort prevailed even while, at the evening meal, her brother-in-law invited her attention to a diagram, drawn with a fork on too soiled a tablecloth, of the scandalous drains of the Convalescent Home. To be alone with it she had come away from Ricks; and now she knew that to be alone with it she had come away from London. This advantage was of course menaced, though not immediately destroyed, by the arrival on the second day of the note she had been sure she should receive from Owen. He had gone to West Kensington and found her flown, but he had got her address from the little maid and then hurried to a club and written to her. "Why have you left me just when I want you most?" he demanded. The next words, it was true, were more reassuring on the question of his steadiness. "I don't know what your reason may be," they went on, "nor why you've not left a line for me; but I don't think you can feel that I did anything yesterday that it wasn't right for me to do. As regards Mrs. Brigstock certainly I just felt what was right and I did it. She had no business whatever to attack you that way, and I should have been ashamed if I had left her there to worry you. I won't have you worried by any one. No one shall be disagreeable to you but me. I didn't mean to be so yesterday, and I don't to-day; but I'm perfectly free now to want you, and I want you much more than you've allowed me to explain. You'll see if I'm not all right, if you'll let me come to you. Don't be afraid—I'll not hurt you nor trouble you. I give you my honour I'll not hurt any one. Only I *must* see you, on what I had to say to Mrs. B. She was nastier than I thought she could be, but I'm behaving like an angel. I assure you I'm all right—that's exactly what I want you to see. You owe me something, you know, for what you said you would do and haven't done; what your departure without a

word gives me to understand—doesn't it?—that you definitely can't do. Don't simply forsake me. See me if you only
see me once. I sha'n't wait for any leave—I shall come down
to-morrow. I've been looking into trains and find there's
something that will bring me down just after lunch and something very good for getting me back. I won't stop long. For
God's sake, be there."

This communication arrived in the morning, but Fleda
would still have had time to wire a protest. She debated on
that alternative; then she read the note over and found in
one phrase an exact statement of her duty. Owen's simplicity
had expressed it, and her subtlety had nothing to answer. She
owed him something for her obvious failure, and what she
owed him was to receive him. If indeed she had known he
would make this attempt she might have been held to have
gained nothing by her flight. Well, she had gained what she
had gained—she had gained the interval. She had no compunction for the greater trouble she should give the young
man; it was now doubtless right that he should have as much
trouble as possible. Maggie, who thought she was in her
confidence, yet was immensely not, had reproached her for
having quitted Mrs. Gereth, and Maggie was just in this proportion gratified to hear of the visitor with whom, early in
the afternoon, Fleda would have to ask to be left alone.
Maggie liked to see far, and now she could sit up-stairs and
rake the whole future. She had known that, as she familiarly
said, there was something the matter with Fleda, and the
value of that knowledge was augmented by the fact that
there was apparently also something the matter with Mr.
Gereth.

Fleda, down-stairs, learned soon enough what this was. It
was simply that, as he announced the moment he stood before her, he was now all right. When she asked him what he
meant by that state he replied that he meant he could practically regard himself henceforth as a free man: he had had at
West Kensington, as soon as they got into the street, such a
horrid scene with Mrs. Brigstock.

"I knew what she wanted to say to me: that's why I was determined to get her off. I knew I shouldn't like it, but I was
perfectly prepared," said Owen. "She brought it out as soon

as we got round the corner. She asked me point-blank if I was in love with you."

"And what did you say to that?"

"That it was none of her business."

"Ah," said Fleda, "I'm not so sure!"

"Well, *I* am, and I'm the person most concerned. Of course I didn't use just those words: I was perfectly civil, quite as civil as she. But I told her I didn't consider she had a right to put me any such question. I said I wasn't sure that even Mona had, with the extraordinary line, you know, that Mona has taken. At any rate the whole thing, the way *I* put it, was between Mona and me; and between Mona and me, if she didn't mind, it would just have to remain."

Fleda was silent a little. "All that didn't answer her question."

"Then you think I ought to have told her?"

Again our young lady reflected. "I think I'm rather glad you didn't."

"I knew what I was about," said Owen. "It didn't strike me that she had the least right to come down on us that way and ask for explanations."

Fleda looked very grave, weighing the whole matter. "I dare say that when she started, when she arrived, she didn't mean to 'come down.'"

"What then did she mean to do?"

"What she said to me just before she went: she meant to plead with me."

"Oh, I heard her!" said Owen. "But plead with you for what?"

"For you, of course—to entreat me to give you up. She thinks me awfully designing—that I've taken some sort of possession of you."

Owen stared. "You haven't lifted a finger! It's I who have taken possession."

"Very true, you've done it all yourself." Fleda spoke gravely and gently, without a breath of coquetry. "But those are shades between which she's probably not obliged to distinguish. It's enough for her that we're repulsively intimate."

"I am, but you're not!" Owen exclaimed.

Fleda gave a dim smile. "You make me at least feel that I'm learning to know you very well when I hear you say such a

thing as that. Mrs. Brigstock came to get round me, to supplicate me," she went on; "but to find you there looking so
much at home, paying me a friendly call and shoving the tea-
things about—that was too much for her patience. She
doesn't know, you see, that I'm after all a decent girl. She simply made up her mind on the spot that I'm a very bad case."

"I couldn't stand the way she treated you, and that was
what I had to say to her," Owen returned.

"She's simple and slow, but she's not a fool: I think she
treated me on the whole very well." Fleda remembered how
Mrs. Gereth had treated Mona when the Brigstocks came
down to Poynton.

Owen evidently thought her painfully perverse. "It was you
who carried it off; you behaved like a brick. And so did I, I
consider. If you only knew the difficulty I had! I told her you
were the noblest and straightest of women."

"That can hardly have removed her impression that there
are things I put you up to."

"It didn't," Owen replied with candour. "She said our relation, yours and mine, isn't innocent."

"What did she mean by that?"

"As you may suppose, I particularly inquired. Do you
know what she had the cheek to tell me?" Owen asked. "She
didn't better it much. She said she meant that it's excessively
unnatural."

Fleda considered afresh. "Well, it is!" she brought out at
last.

"Then, upon my honour, it's only you who make it so!"
Her perversity was distinctly too much for him. "I mean you
make it so by the way you keep me off."

"Have I kept you off to-day?" Fleda sadly shook her head,
raising her arms a little and dropping them.

Her gesture of resignation gave him a pretext for catching
at her hand, but before he could take it she had put it behind
her. They had been seated together on Maggie's single sofa,
and her movement brought her to her feet while Owen, looking at her reproachfully, leaned back in discouragement.
"What good does it do me to be here when I find you only a
stone?"

She met his eyes with all the tenderness she had not yet uttered, and she had not known till this moment how great was the accumulation. "Perhaps, after all," she risked, "there may be even in a stone still some little help for you."

Owen sat there a minute staring at her. "Ah, you're beautiful, more beautiful than any one," he broke out, "but I'll be hanged if I can ever understand you! On Tuesday, at your father's, you were beautiful—as beautiful, just before I left, as you are at this instant. But the next day, when I went back, I found it had apparently meant nothing; and now again that you let me come here and you shine at me like an angel, it doesn't bring you an inch nearer to saying what I want you to say." He remained a moment longer in the same position; then he jerked himself up. "What I want you to say is that you like me—what I want you to say is that you pity me." He sprang up and came to her. "What I want you to say is that you'll *save* me!"

Fleda hesitated. "Why do you need saving when you announced to me just now that you're a free man?"

He too hesitated, but he was not checked. "It's just for the reason that I'm free. Don't you know what I mean, Miss Vetch? I want you to marry me."

Fleda, at this, put out her hand in charity; she held his own, which quickly grasped it a moment, and if he had described her as shining at him it may be assumed that she shone all the more in her deep, still smile. "Let me hear a little more about your freedom first," she said. "I gather that Mrs. Brigstock was not wholly satisfied with the way you disposed of her question."

"I dare say she wasn't. But the less she's satisfied the more I'm free."

"What bearing have *her* feelings, pray?" Fleda asked.

"Why, Mona's much worse than her mother, you know. She wants much more to give me up."

"Then why doesn't she do it?"

"She will, as soon as her mother gets home and tells her."

"Tells her what?" Fleda inquired.

"Why, that I'm in love with *you*!"

Fleda debated. "Are you so very sure she will?"

"Certainly I'm sure, with all the evidence I already have. That will finish her!" Owen declared.

This made his companion thoughtful again. "Can you take such pleasure in her being 'finished'—a poor girl you've once loved?"

Owen waited long enough to take in the question; then with a serenity startling even to her knowledge of his nature, "I don't think I can have *really* loved her, you know," he replied.

Fleda broke into a laugh which gave him a surprise as visible as the emotion it represented. "Then how am I to know that you 'really' love—anybody else?"

"Oh, I'll show you that!" said Owen.

"I must take it on trust," the girl pursued. "And what if Mona doesn't give you up?" she added.

Owen was baffled but a few seconds; he had thought of everything. "Why, that's just where you come in."

"To save you? I see. You mean I must get rid of her for you." His blankness showed for a little that he felt the chill of her cold logic; but as she waited for his rejoinder she knew to which of them it cost most. He gasped a minute, and that gave her time to say: "You see, Mr. Owen, how impossible it is to talk of such things yet!"

Like lightning he had grasped her arm. "You mean you *will* talk of them?" Then as he began to take the flood of assent from her eyes: "You *will* listen to me? Oh, you dear, you dear—when, when?"

"Ah, when it isn't mere misery!" The words had broken from her in a sudden loud cry, and what next happened was that the very sound of her pain upset her. She heard her own true note; she turned short away from him; in a moment she had burst into sobs; in another his arms were round her; the next she had let herself go so far that even Mrs. Gereth might have seen it. He clasped her, and she gave herself—she poured out her tears on his breast. Something prisoned and pent throbbed and gushed; something deep and sweet surged up—something that came from far within and far off, that had begun with the sight of him in his indifference and had never had rest since then. The surrender was short, but the relief was long: she felt his warm lips on her face and his arms tighten with his full divination. What she did, what she *had* done, she scarcely knew: she only was aware, as she broke from him again, of what had taken place in his panting soul. What had taken place was that, with the click of a spring, he saw. He had cleared the high wall at a bound; they were together without a veil. She had not a shred of a secret left; it was as if a whirlwind had come and gone, laying low the great false front that she had built up stone by stone. The strangest thing of all was the momentary sense of desolation.

"Ah, all the while you *cared*?" Owen read the truth with a wonder so great that it was visibly almost a sadness, a terror caused by his sudden perception of where the impossibility was not. That made it all perhaps elsewhere.

"I cared, I cared, I cared!"——Fleda moaned it as defiantly as if she were confessing a misdeed. "How couldn't I care? But you mustn't, you must never, never ask! It isn't for us to talk about," she insisted. "Don't speak of it, don't speak!"

It was easy indeed not to speak when the difficulty was to find words. He clasped his hands before her as he might have clasped them at an altar; his pressed palms shook together while he held his breath and while she stilled herself in the effort to come round again to the real and the right. He assisted this effort, soothing her into a seat with a touch as light as if she had really been something sacred. She sank into a chair and he dropped before her on his knees; she fell back with closed eyes and he buried his face in her lap. There was no way to thank her but this act of prostration, which lasted, in silence, till she laid consenting hands on him, touched his head and stroked it, held it in her tenderness till he acknowledged his long density. He made the avowal seem only his— made her, when she rose again, raise him at last, softly, as if from the abasement of shame. If in each other's eyes now, however, they saw the truth, this truth, to Fleda, looked harder even than before—all the harder that when, at the very moment she recognised it, he murmured to her ecstatically, in fresh possession of her hands, which he drew up to his breast, holding them tight there with both his own: "I'm saved, I'm saved—I *am*! I'm ready for anything. I have your word. Come!" he cried, as if from the sight of a response slower than he needed, and in the tone he so often had of a great boy at a great game.

She had once more disengaged herself with the private vow

that he shouldn't yet touch her again. It was all too horribly soon—her sense of this was rapidly surging back. "We mustn't talk, we mustn't talk; we must wait!" she intensely insisted. "I don't know what you mean by your freedom; I don't see it, I don't feel it. Where is it yet, where, your freedom? If it's real there's plenty of time, and if it isn't there's more than enough. I hate myself," she protested, "for having anything to say about her: it's like waiting for dead men's shoes! What business is it of mine what she does? She has her own trouble and her own plan. It's too hideous to watch her and count on her!"

Owen's face, at this, showed a reviving dread, the fear of some darksome process of her mind. "If you speak for yourself I can understand. But why is it hideous for me?"

"Oh, I mean for myself!" Fleda said impatiently.

"*I* watch her, *I* count on her: how can I do anything else? If I count on her to let me definitely know how we stand I do nothing in life but what she herself has led straight up to. I never thought of asking you to 'get rid of her' for me, and I never would have spoken to you if I hadn't held that I *am* rid of her, that she has backed out of the whole thing. Didn't she do so from the moment she began to put it off? I had already applied for the licence; the very invitations were half addressed. Who but she, all of a sudden, demanded an unnatural wait? It was none of *my* doing; I had never dreamed of anything but coming up to the scratch." Owen grew more and more lucid and more confident of the effect of his lucidity. "She called it 'taking a stand,' to see what mother would do. I told her mother would do what I would make her do; and to that she replied that she would like to see me make her first. I said I would arrange that everything should be all right, and she said she really preferred to arrange it herself. It was a flat refusal to trust me in the smallest degree. Why then had she pretended so tremendously to care for me? And of course at present," said Owen, "she trusts me, if possible, still less."

Fleda paid this statement the homage of a minute's muteness. "As to that, naturally, she has reason."

"Why on earth has she reason?" Then, as his companion, moving away, simply threw up her hands, "I never looked at you—not to call looking—till she had regularly driven me to it," he went on. "I know what I'm about. I do assure you I'm all right!"

"You're not all right—you're all wrong!" Fleda cried in despair. "You mustn't stay here, you mustn't!" she repeated with clear decision. "You make me say dreadful things, and I feel as if I made you say them." But before he could reply she took it up in another tone. "Why in the world, if everything had changed, didn't you break off?"

"I—?" The inquiry seemed to have moved him to stupefaction. "Can you ask me that question when I only wanted to please you? Didn't you seem to show me, in your wonderful way, that that was exactly how? I didn't break off just on purpose to leave it to Mona. I didn't break off so that there shouldn't be a thing to be said against me."

The instant after her challenge Fleda had faced him again in self-reproof. "There *isn't* a thing to be said against you, and I don't know what nonsense you make me talk! You *have* pleased me, and you've been right and good, and it's the only comfort, and you must go. Everything must come from Mona, and if it doesn't come we've said entirely too much. You must leave me alone—forever."

"Forever?" Owen gasped.

"I mean unless everything is different."

"Everything *is* different, when I know you!"

Fleda winced at his knowledge; she made a wild gesture which seemed to whirl it out of the room. The mere allusion was like another embrace. "You don't know me—you don't—and you must go and wait! You mustn't break down at this point."

He looked about him and took up his hat: it was as if in spite of frustration he had got the essence of what he wanted and could afford to agree with her to the extent of keeping up the forms. He covered her with his fine, simple smile, but made no other approach. "Oh, I'm so awfully happy!" he exclaimed.

She hesitated: she would only be impeccable even though she should have to be sententious. "You'll be happy if you're perfect!" she risked.

He laughed out at this, and she wondered if, with a new-born acuteness, he saw the absurdity of her speech and that no one was happy just because no one could be what she so easily prescribed. "I don't pretend to be perfect, but I shall find a letter to-night!"

"So much the better, if it's the kind of one you desire." That was the most she could say, and having made it sound as dry as possible she lapsed into a silence so pointed as to deprive him of all pretext for not leaving her. Still, nevertheless, he stood there, playing with his hat and filling the long pause with a strained and anxious smile. He wished to obey her thoroughly, to appear not to presume on any advantage he had won from her; but there was clearly something he longed for beside. While he showed this by hanging on she thought of two other things. One of these was that his countenance, after all, failed to bear out his description of his bliss. As for the other, it had no sooner come into her head than she found it seated, in spite of her resolution, on her lips. It took the form of an inconsequent question. "When did you say Mrs. Brigstock was to have gone back?"

Owen stared. "To Waterbath? She was to have spent the night in town, don't you know? But when she left me after our talk I said to myself that she would take an evening train. I know I made her want to get home."

"Where did you separate?" Fleda asked.

"At the West Kensington station—she was going to Victoria. I had walked with her there, and our talk was all on the way."

Fleda pondered a moment. "If she did go back that night you would have heard from Waterbath by this time."

"I don't know," said Owen. "I thought I might hear this morning."

"She can't have gone back," Fleda declared. "Mona would have written on the spot."

"Oh yes, she *will* have written bang off!" Owen cheerfully conceded.

Fleda thought again. "So that, even in the event of her mother's not having got home till the morning you would have had your letter at the latest to-day. You see she has had plenty of time."

Owen hesitated; then "Oh, she's all right!" he laughed. "I go by Mrs. Brigstock's certain effect on her—the effect of the

temper the old lady showed when we parted. Do you know
what she asked me?" he sociably continued. "She asked me in
a kind of nasty manner if I supposed you 'really' cared anything about me. Of course I told her I supposed you didn't—
not a solitary rap. How could I ever suppose you do, with
your extraordinary ways? It doesn't matter; I could see she
thought I lied."

"You should have told her, you know, that I had seen you
in town only that one time," Fleda suggested.

"By Jove, I did—for *you*! It was only for you."

Something in this touched the girl so that for a moment
she could not trust herself to speak. "You're an honest man,"
she said at last. She had gone to the door and opened it.
"Good-bye."

Even yet, however, Owen hung back. "But even if there's
no letter—" he began. He began, but there he left it.

"You mean even if she doesn't let you off? Ah, you ask me
too much!" Fleda spoke from the tiny hall, where she had
taken refuge between the old barometer and the old mackin-
tosh. "There are things too utterly for yourselves alone. How
can I tell? What do I know? Good-bye, good-bye! If she
doesn't let you off it will be because she *is* attached to you."

"She's not, she's not: there's nothing in it! Doesn't a fellow
know?—except with *you*!" Owen ruefully added. With this he
came out of the room, lowering his voice to secret supplication, pleading with her really to meet him on the ground of
the negation of Mona. It was this betrayal of his need of support and sanction that made her retreat, harden herself in the
effort to save what might remain of all she had given, given
probably for nothing. The very vision of him as he thus
morally clung to her was the vision of a weakness somewhere
in the core of his bloom, a blessed manly weakness of which,
if she had only the valid right, it would be all a sweetness to
take care. She faintly sickened, however, with the sense that
there was as yet no valid right poor Owen could give. "You
can take it from my honour, you know," he painfully brought
out, "that she loathes me."

Fleda had stood clutching the knob of Maggie's little
painted stair-rail; she took, on the stairs, a step backward.
"Why then doesn't she prove it in the only clear way?"

"She *has* proved it. Will you believe it if you see the letter?"

"I don't want to see any letter," said Fleda. "You'll miss your train."

Facing him, waving him away, she had taken another upward step; but he sprang to the side of the stairs, and brought his hand, above the banister, down hard on her wrist. "Do you mean to tell me that I must marry a woman I hate?"

From her step she looked down into his raised face. "Ah, you see it's not true that you're free!" She seemed almost to exult. "It's not true, it's not true!"

He only, at this, like a buffeting swimmer, gave a shake of his head and repeated his question: "Do you mean to tell me I must marry such a woman?"

Fleda hesitated; he held her fast. "No. Anything is better than that."

"Then, in God's name, what must I do?"

"You must settle that with Mona. You mustn't break faith. Anything is better than that. You must at any rate be utterly sure. She must love you—how can she help it? *I* wouldn't give you up!" said Fleda. She spoke in broken bits, panting out her words. "The great thing is to keep faith. Where is a man if he doesn't? If he doesn't he may be so cruel. So cruel, so cruel, so cruel!" Fleda repeated. "I couldn't have a hand in that, you know: that's my position—that's mine. You offered her marriage. It's a tremendous thing for her." Then looking at him another moment, "*I* wouldn't give you up!" she said again. He still had hold of her arm; she took in his blank dread. With a quick dip of her face she reached his hand with her lips, pressing them to the back of it with a force that doubled the force of her words. "Never, never, never!" she cried; and before he could succeed in seizing her she had turned and, flashing up the stairs, got away from him even faster than she had got away at Ricks.

XVII

TEN DAYS after his visit she received a communication from Mrs. Gereth—a telegram of eight words, exclusive of signature and date. "Come up immediately and stay with me here"—it was characteristically sharp, as Maggie said; but, as Maggie added, it was also characteristically kind. "Here" was an hotel in London, and Maggie had embraced a condition of life which already began to produce in her some yearning for hotels in London. She would have responded in an instant, and she was surprised that her sister seemed to hesitate. Fleda's hesitation, which lasted but an hour, was expressed in that young lady's own mind by the reflection that in obeying her friend's summons she shouldn't know what she should be "in for." Her friend's summons, however, was but another name for her friend's appeal; and Mrs. Gereth's bounty had laid her under obligations more sensible than any reluctance. In the event—that is at the end of her hour—she testified to her gratitude by taking the train and to her mistrust by not taking her luggage. She went as if she had gone up for the day. In the train, however, she had another thoughtful hour, during which it was her mistrust that mainly deepened. She felt as if for ten days she had sat in darkness, looking to the east for a dawn that had not yet glimmered. Her mind had lately been less occupied with Mrs. Gereth; it had been so exceptionally occupied with Mona. If the sequel was to justify Owen's prevision of Mrs. Brigstock's action upon her daughter, this action was at the end of a week as much a mystery as ever. The stillness, all round, had been exactly what Fleda desired, but it gave her for the time a deep sense of failure, the sense of a sudden drop from a height at which she had had all things beneath her. She had nothing beneath her now; she herself was at the bottom of the heap. No sign had reached her from Owen—poor Owen who had clearly no news to give about his precious letter from Waterbath. If Mrs. Brigstock had hurried back to obtain that this letter should be written Mrs. Brigstock might then have spared herself so great an inconvenience. Owen had been

346

silent for the best of all reasons—the reason that he had had nothing in life to say. If the letter had not been written he would simply have had to introduce some large qualification into his account of his freedom. He had left his young friend under her refusal to listen to him until he should be able, on the contrary, to extend that picture; and his present submission was all in keeping with the rigid honesty that his young friend had prescribed.

It was this that formed the element through which Mona loomed large; Fleda had enough imagination, a fine enough feeling for life, to be impressed with such an image of successful immobility. The massive maiden at Waterbath *was* successful from the moment she could entertain her resentments as if they had been poor relations who needn't put her to expense. She was a magnificent dead weight; there was something positive and portentous in her quietude. "What game are they all playing?" poor Fleda could only ask; for she had an intimate conviction that Owen was now under the roof of his betrothed. That was stupefying if he really hated Mona; and if he didn't really hate her what had brought him to Raphael Road and to Maggie's? Fleda had no real light, but she felt that to account for the absence of any result of their last meeting would take a supposition of the full sacrifice to charity that she had held up before him. If he had gone to Waterbath it had been simply because he had to go. She had as good as told him that he would have to go; that this was an inevitable incident of his keeping perfect faith—faith so literal that the smallest subterfuge would always be a reproach to him. When she tried to remember that it was for herself he was taking his risk she felt how weak a way that was of expressing Mona's supremacy. There would be no need of keeping him up if there was nothing to keep him up to. Her eyes grew wan as she discerned in the impenetrable air that Mona's thick outline never wavered an inch. She wondered fitfully what Mrs. Gereth had by this time made of it, and reflected with a strange elation that the sand on which the mistress of Ricks had built a momentary triumph was quaking beneath the surface. As *The Morning Post* still held its peace she would be of course more confident; but the hour was at hand at which Owen would have absolutely to do either one thing or the other. To keep perfect faith was to inform against his mother, and to hear the police at her door would be Mrs. Gereth's awakening. How much she was beguiled Fleda could see from her having been for a whole month quite as deep and dark as Mona. She had left her young friend alone because of the certitude, cultivated at Ricks, that Owen had done the opposite. He had done the opposite indeed, but much good had that brought forth! To have sent for her now, Fleda felt, was from this point of view wholly natural: she had sent for her to show at last how much she had scored. If, however, Owen was really at Waterbath the refutation of that boast was easy.

Fleda found Mrs. Gereth in modest apartments and with an air of fatigue in her distinguished face, a sign, as she privately remarked, of the strain of that effort to be discreet of which she herself had been having the benefit. It was a constant feature of their relation that this lady could make Fleda blench a little, and that the effect proceeded from the intense pressure of her confidence. If the confidence had been heavy even when the girl, in the early flush of devotion, had been able to feel herself most responsive, it drew her heart into her mouth now that she had reserves and conditions, now that she couldn't simplify with the same bold hand as her protectress. In the very brightening of the tired look and at the moment of their embrace Fleda felt on her shoulders the return of the load; whereupon her spirit quailed as she asked herself what she had brought up from her trusted seclusion to support it. Mrs. Gereth's free manner always made a joke of weakness, and there was in such a welcome a richness, a kind of familiar nobleness that suggested shame to a harried conscience. Something had happened, she could see, and she could also see, in the bravery that seemed to announce it had changed everything, a formidable assumption that what had happened was what a healthy young woman must like. The absence of luggage had made this young woman feel meagre even before her companion, taking in the bareness at a second glance, exclaimed upon it and roundly rebuked her. Of course she had expected her to stay.

Fleda thought best to show bravery too and to show it from the first. "What you expected, dear Mrs. Gereth, is exactly what I came up to ascertain. It struck me as right to do that first. Right, I mean, to ascertain without making preparations."

"Then you'll be so good as to make them on the spot!" Mrs. Gereth was most emphatic. "You're going abroad with me."

Fleda wondered, but she also smiled. "To-night—to-morrow?"

"In as few days as possible. That's all that's left for me now." Fleda's heart, at this, gave a bound; she wondered to what particular difference in Mrs. Gereth's situation as last known to her it was an allusion. "I've made my plan," her friend continued: "I go for at least a year. We shall go straight to Florence; we can manage there. I of course don't look to you, however," she added, "to stay with me all that time. That will require to be settled. Owen will have to join us as soon as possible; he may not be quite ready to get off with us. But I'm convinced it's quite the right thing to go. It will make a good change; it will put in a decent interval."

Fleda listened; she was deeply mystified. "How kind you are to me!" she presently said. The picture suggested so many questions that she scarcely knew which to ask first. She took one at a venture. "You really have it from Mr. Gereth that he'll give us his company?"

If Mr. Gereth's mother smiled in response to this Fleda knew that her smile was a tacit criticism of such a form of reference to her son. Fleda habitually spoke of him as Mr. Owen, and it was a part of her present vigilance to appear to have relinquished that right. Mrs. Gereth's manner confirmed a certain impression of her pretending to more than she felt; her very first words had conveyed it, and it reminded Fleda of the conscious courage with which, weeks before, the lady had met her visitor's first startled stare at the clustered spoils of Poynton. It was her practice to take immensely for granted whatever she wished. "Oh, if you'll answer for him, it will do quite as well!" she said. Then she put her hands on the girl's shoulders and held them at arm's length, as if to shake them a little, while in the depths of her shining eyes Fleda discovered something obscure and unquiet. "You bad, false thing, why didn't you tell me?" Her tone softened her harshness, and her visitor had never had such a sense of her indulgence. Mrs.

Gereth could show patience; it was a part of the general bribe, but it was also like the handing in of a heavy bill before which Fleda could only fumble in a penniless pocket. "You must perfectly have known at Ricks, and yet you practically denied it. That's why I call you bad and false!" It was apparently also why she again almost roughly kissed her.

"I think that before I answer you I had better know what you're talking about," Fleda said.

Mrs. Gereth looked at her with a slight increase of hardness. "You've done everything you need for modesty, my dear! If he's sick with love of you, you haven't had to wait for me to inform you."

Fleda hesitated. "Has he informed *you*, dear Mrs. Gereth?"

Dear Mrs. Gereth smiled sweetly. "How could he when our situation is such that he communicates with me only through you and that you are so tortuous you conceal everything?"

"Didn't he answer the note in which you let him know that I was in town?" Fleda asked.

"He answered it sufficiently by rushing off on the spot to see you."

Mrs. Gereth met that allusion with a prompt firmness that made almost insolently light of any ground of complaint, and Fleda's own sense of responsibility was now so vivid that all resentments turned comparatively pale. She had no heart to produce a grievance; she could only, left as she was with the little mystery on her hands, produce after a moment a question. "How then do you come to know that your son has ever thought—"

"That he would give his ears to get you?" Mrs. Gereth broke in. "I had a visit from Mrs. Brigstock."

Fleda opened her eyes. "She went down to Ricks?"

"The day after she had found Owen at your feet. She knows everything."

Fleda shook her head sadly: she was more startled than she cared to show. This odd journey of Mrs. Brigstock's, which, with a simplicity equal for once to Owen's, she had not divined, now struck her as having produced the hush of the last ten days. "There are things she doesn't know!" she presently exclaimed.

"She knows he would do anything to marry you."

"He hasn't told her so," Fleda said.

"No, but he has told you. That's better still!" laughed Mrs. Gereth. "My dear child," she went on with an air that affected the girl as a sort of blind profanity, "don't try to make yourself out better than you are. *I* know what your are—I haven't lived with you so much for nothing. You're not quite a saint in heaven yet. Lord, what a creature you'd have thought me in my good time! But you do like it fortunately, you idiot. You're pale with your passion, you sweet thing. That's exactly what I wanted to see. I can't for the life of me think where the shame comes in." Then with a finer significance, a look that seemed to Fleda strange she added: "It's all right."

"I've seen him but twice," said Fleda.

"But twice?" Mrs. Gereth still smiled.

"On the occasion, at papa's, that Mrs. Brigstock told you of, and one day, since then, down at Maggie's."

"Well, those things are between yourselves, and you seem to me both poor creatures at best." Mrs. Gereth spoke with a rich humour which tipped with light for an instant the real conviction. "I don't know what you've got in your veins. You absurdly exaggerate the difficulties. But enough is as good as a feast, and when once I get you abroad together—!" She checked herself as if from excess of meaning; what might happen when she should get them abroad together was to be gathered only from the way she slowly rubbed her hands.

The gesture, however, made the promise so definite that for a moment her companion was almost beguiled. But there was nothing to account as yet for the wealth of Mrs. Gereth's certitude: the visit of the lady of Waterbath appeared but half to explain it. "Is it permitted to be surprised," Fleda deferentially asked, "at Mrs. Brigstock's thinking it would help her to see you?"

"It's never permitted to be surprised at the aberrations of born fools," said Mrs. Gereth. "If a cow should try to calculate, that's the kind of happy thought she'd have. Mrs. Brigstock came down to plead with me."

Fleda mused a moment. "That's what she came to do with *me*," she then honestly returned. "But what did she expect to get of you, with your opposition so marked from the first?"

"She didn't know I want *you*, my dear. It's a wonder, with all my violence—the gross publicity I've given my desires. But she's as stupid as an owl—she doesn't feel your charm."

Fleda felt herself flush slightly, but she tried to smile. "Did you tell her all about it? Did you make her understand you want me?"

"For what do you take me? I wasn't such a donkey."

"So as not to aggravate Mona?" Fleda suggested.

"So as not to aggravate Mona, naturally. We've had a narrow course to steer, but thank God we're at last in the open!"

"What do you call the open, Mrs. Gereth?" Fleda demanded. Then as that lady faltered: "Do you know where Mr. Owen is to-day?"

Mrs Gereth stared. "Do you mean he's at Waterbath? Well, that's your own affair. I can bear it if *you* can."

"Wherever he is I can bear it," Fleda said. "But I haven't the least idea where he is."

"Then you ought to be ashamed of yourself!" Mrs. Gereth broke out with a change of note that showed how deep a passion underlay everything she had said. The poor woman, catching her companion's hand, however, the next moment, as if to retract something of this harshness, spoke more patiently. "Don't you understand, Fleda, how immensely, how devotedly I've trusted you!" Her tone was indeed a supplication.

Fleda was infinitely shaken; she was silent a little. "Yes, I understand. Did she go to you to complain of me?"

"She came to see what she could do. She had been tremendously upset the day before by what had taken place at your father's, and she had posted down to Ricks on the inspiration of the moment. She hadn't meant it on leaving home; it was the sight of you closeted there with Owen that had suddenly determined her. The whole story, she said, was written in your two faces: she spoke as if she had never seen such an exhibition. Owen was on the brink, but there might still be time to save him, and it was with this idea she had bearded me in my den. 'What won't a mother do, you know?'—that was one of the things she said. What wouldn't a mother do indeed? I thought I had sufficiently shown her what! She tried to break me down by an appeal to my good-nature, as she called it, and from the moment she opened on *you*, from the moment she denounced Owen's falsity, I was as good-natured as she could wish. I understood that it was a plea for mere mercy, that you and he between you were killing her child. Of course I was delighted that Mona should be killed, but I was studiously kind to Mrs. Brigstock. At the same time I was honest, I didn't pretend to anything I couldn't feel. I asked her why the marriage hadn't taken place months ago, when Owen was perfectly ready; and I showed her how completely that fatuous mistake on Mona's part cleared his responsibility. It was she who had killed him—it was she who had destroyed his affection, his illusions. Did she want him now when he was estranged, when he was disgusted, when he had a sore grievance? She reminded me that Mona had a sore grievance too, but she admitted that she hadn't come to me to speak of that. What she had come to me for was not to get the old things back, but simply to get Owen. What she wanted was that I would, in simple pity, see fair play. Owen had been awfully bedevilled—she didn't call it that, she called it 'misled'; but it was simply you who had bedevilled him. He would be all right still if I would see that you were out of the way. She asked me point-blank if it was possible I could want him to marry you."

Fleda had listened in unbearable pain and growing terror, as if her interlocutress, stone by stone, were piling some fatal mass upon her breast. She had the sense of being buried alive, smothered in the mere expansion of another will; and now there was but one gap left to the air. A single word, she felt, might close it, and with the question that came to her lips as Mrs. Gereth paused she seemed to herself to ask, in cold dread, for her doom. "What did you say to that?" she inquired.

"I was embarrassed, for I saw my danger—the danger of her going home and saying to Mona that I was backing you up. It had been a bliss to learn that Owen had really turned to you, but my joy didn't put me off my guard. I reflected intensely for a few seconds; then I saw my issue."

"Your issue?" Fleda murmured.

"I remembered how you had tied my hands about saying a word to Owen."

Fleda wondered. "And did you remember the little letter

that, with your hands tied, you still succeeded in writing to him?"

"Perfectly; my little letter was a model of reticence. What I remembered was all that in those few words I forbade myself to say. I had been an angel of delicacy—I had effaced myself like a saint. It was not for me to have done all that and then figure to such a woman as having done the opposite. Besides, it was none of her business."

"Is that what you said to her?" Fleda asked.

"I said to her that her question revealed a total misconception of the nature of my present relations with my son. I said to her that I had no relations with him at all and that nothing had passed between us for months. I said to her that my hands were spotlessly clean of any attempt to make up to you. I said to her that I had taken from Poynton what I had a right to take, but had done nothing else in the world. I was determined that if I had bit my tongue off to oblige you I would at least have the righteousness that my sacrifice gave me."

"And was Mrs. Brigstock satisfied with your answer?"

"She was visibly relieved."

"It was fortunate for you," said Fleda, "that she's apparently not aware of the manner in which, almost under her nose, you advertised me to him at Poynton."

Mrs. Gereth appeared to recall that scene; she smiled with a serenity remarkably effective as showing how cheerfully used she had grown to invidious allusions to it. "How should she be aware of it?"

"She would if Owen had described your outbreak to Mona."

"Yes, but he didn't describe it. All his instinct was to conceal it from Mona. He wasn't conscious, but he was already in love with you!" Mrs. Gereth declared.

Fleda shook her head wearily. "No—I was only in love with him!"

Here was a faint illumination with which Mrs. Gereth instantly mingled her fire. "You dear old wretch!" she exclaimed; and she again, with ferocity, embraced her young friend.

Fleda submitted like a sick animal: she would submit to everything now. "Then what further passed?"

"Only that she left me thinking she had got something."

"And what had she got?"

"Nothing but her luncheon. But *I* got everything!"

"Everything?" Fleda quavered.

Mrs. Gereth, struck apparently by something in her tone, looked at her from a tremendous height. "Don't fail me now!"

It sounded so like a menace that, with a full divination at last, the poor girl fell weakly into a chair. "What on earth have you done?"

Mrs. Gereth stood there in all the glory of a great stroke. "I've settled you." She filled the room, to Fleda's scared vision, with the glare of her magnificence. "I've sent everything back."

"Everything?" Fleda gasped.

"To the smallest snuff-box. The last load went yesterday. The same people did it. Poor little Ricks is empty." Then as if, for a crowning splendour, to check all deprecation, "They're yours, you goose!" Mrs. Gereth concluded, holding up her handsome head and rubbing her white hands. Fleda saw that there were tears in her deep eyes.

XVIII

SHE WAS slow to take in the announcement, but when she
had done so she felt it to be more than her cup of bitterness would hold. Her bitterness was her anxiety, the taste of
which suddenly sickened her. What had she on the spot become but a traitress to her friend? The treachery increased
with the view of the friend's motive, a motive superb as a tribute to her value. Mrs. Gereth had wished to make sure of her
and had reasoned that there would be no such way as by a
large appeal to her honour. If it be true, as men have declared, that the sense of honour is weak in women, some of
the bearings of this stroke might have thrown a light on the
question. What was now at all events put before Fleda was
that she had been made sure of, for the greatness of the surrender imposed an obligation as great. There was an expression she had heard used by young men with whom she
danced: the only word to fit Mrs. Gereth's intention was that
Mrs. Gereth had designed to "fetch" her. It was a calculated,
it was a crushing bribe; it looked her in the eyes and said simply: "That's what I do for you!" What Fleda was to do in return required no pointing out. The sense at present of how
little she had done made her almost cry aloud with pain; but
her first endeavour in face of the fact was to keep such a cry
from reaching her companion. How little she had done Mrs.
Gereth didn't yet know, and possibly there would be still
some way of turning round before the discovery. On her own
side too Fleda had almost made one: she had known she was
wanted, but she had not after all conceived how magnificently
much. She had been treated by her friend's act as a conscious
prize, but what made her a conscious prize was only the
power the act itself imputed to her. As high, bold diplomacy
it dazzled and carried her off her feet. She admired the noble
risk of it, a risk Mrs. Gereth had faced for the utterly poor
creature that the girl now felt herself. The change it instantly
wrought in her was moreover extraordinary: it transformed at
a touch her emotion on the subject of concessions. A few
weeks earlier she had jumped at the duty of pleading for

them, practically quarrelling with the lady of Ricks for her refusal to restore what she had taken. She had been sore with the wrong to Owen, she had bled with the wounds of Poynton; now, however, as she heard of the replenishment of the void that had so haunted her, she came as near sounding an alarm as if from the deck of a ship she had seen a person she loved jump into the sea. Mrs. Gereth had become in a flash the victim; poor little Ricks had been laid bare in a night. If Fleda's feeling about the old things had taken precipitate form the form would have been a frantic command. It was indeed for mere want of breath that she didn't shout: "Oh, stop them—it's no use; bring them back—it's too late!" And what most kept her breathless was her companion's very grandeur. Fleda distinguished as never before the purity of such a passion; it made Mrs. Gereth august and almost sublime. It was absolutely unselfish—she cared nothing for mere possession. She thought solely and incorruptibly of what was best for the things; she had surrendered them to the presumptive care of the one person of her acquaintance who felt about them as she felt herself, and whose long lease of the future would be the nearest approach that could be compassed to committing them to a museum. Now it was indeed that Fleda knew what rested on her; now it was also that she measured as if for the first time Mrs. Gereth's view of the natural influence of a fine acquisition. She had adopted the idea of blowing away the last doubt of what her young friend would gain, of making good still more than she was obliged to make it the promise of weeks before. It was one thing for the girl to have heard that in a certain event restitution would be made; it was another for her to see the condition, with a noble trust, treated in advance as performed, and to be able to feel that she should have only to open a door to find every old piece in every old corner. To have played such a card was therefore, for Mrs. Gereth, practically to have won the game. Fleda had certainly to recognise that, so far as the theory of the matter went, the game had been won. Oh, she had been made sure of!

She couldn't, however, succeed for so very many minutes in deferring her exposure. "Why didn't you wait, dearest? Ah, why didn't you wait?"—if that inconsequent appeal kept rising to her lips to be cut short before it was spoken, this was only because at first the humility of gratitude helped her to gain time, enabled her to present herself very honestly as too overcome to be clear. She kissed her companion's hands, she did homage at her feet, she murmured soft snatches of praise, and yet in the midst of it all was conscious that what she really showed most was the wan despair at her heart. She saw Mrs. Gereth's glimpse of this despair suddenly widen, heard the quick chill of her voice pierce through the false courage of endearments. "Do you mean to tell me at such an hour as this that you've really lost him?"

The tone of the question made the idea a possibility for which Fleda had nothing from this moment but terror. "I don't know, Mrs. Gereth; how can I say?" she asked. "I've not seen him for so long; as I told you just now, I don't even know where he is. That's by no fault of his," she hurried on: "he would have been with me every day if I had consented. But I made him understand, the last time, that I'll receive him again only when he's able to show me that his release has been complete and definite. Oh, he can't yet, don't you see?—and that's why he hasn't been back. It's far better than his coming only that we should both be miserable. When he does come he'll be in a better position. He'll be tremendously moved by the splendid thing you've done. I know you wish me to feel that you've done it as much for me as for Owen, but your having done it for me is just what will delight him most! When he hears of it," said Fleda, in desperate optimism, "when he hears of it—" There indeed, regretting her advance, she quite broke down. She was wholly powerless to say what Owen would do when he heard of it. "I don't know what he won't make of you and how he won't hug you!" she had to content herself with lamely declaring. She had drawn Mrs. Gereth to a sofa with a vague instinct of pacifying her and still, after all, gaining time; but it was a position in which her great duped benefactress, portentously patient again during this demonstration, looked far from inviting a "hug." Fleda found herself tricking out the situation with artificial flowers, trying to talk even herself into the fancy that Owen, whose name she now made simple and sweet, might come in upon them at any moment. She felt an immense need to be understood and justified; she averted her face in dread from all that she might have to be forgiven. She pressed on her companion's arm as if to keep her quiet till she should really know, and then, after a minute, she poured out the clear essence of what in happier days had been her "secret." "You mustn't think I don't adore him when I've told him so to his face. I love him so that I'd die for him—I love him so that it's horrible. Don't look at me therefore as if I had not been kind, as if I had not been as tender as if he were dying and my tenderness were what would save him. Look at me as if you believe me, as if you feel what I've been through. Darling Mrs. Gereth, I could kiss the ground he walks on. I haven't a rag of pride; I used to have, but it's gone. I used to have a secret, but every one knows it now, and any one who looks at me can say, I think, what's the matter with me. It's not so very fine, my secret, and the less one really says about it the better; but I want you to have it from me because I was stiff before. I want you to see for yourself that I've been brought as low as a girl can very well be. It serves me right," Fleda laughed, "if I was ever proud and horrid to you! I don't know what you wanted me, in those days at Ricks, to do, but I don't think you can have wanted much more than what I've done. The other day at Maggie's I did things that made me afterwards think of you! I don't know what girls may do; but if he doesn't know that there isn't an inch of me that isn't his—!" Fleda sighed as if she couldn't express it; she piled it up, as she would have said; holding Mrs. Gereth with dilated eyes she seemed to sound her for the effect of these professions. "It's idiotic," she wearily smiled; "it's so strange that I'm almost angry for it, and the strangest part of all is that it isn't even happiness. It's anguish—it was from the first; from the first there was a bitterness and a kind of dread. But I owe you every word of the truth. You don't do him justice either: he's a dear, I assure you he's a dear. I'd trust him to the last breath; I don't think you really know him. He's ever so much cleverer than he makes a show of; he's remarkable in his own shy way. You told me at Ricks that you wanted me to let myself go, and I've 'gone' quite far enough to discover as much as that, as well as all sorts of other delightful things about him. You'll tell me I make myself out worse than I am," said the girl, feeling more and more in her companion's attitude a

quality that treated her speech as a desperate rigmarole and
even perhaps as a piece of cold immodesty. She wanted to
make herself out "bad"—it was a part of her justification; but
it suddenly occurred to her that such a picture of her extravagance imputed a want of gallantry to the young man. "I
don't care for anything you think," she declared, "because
Owen, don't you know? sees me as I am. He's so kind that it
makes up for everything!"

This attempt at gaiety was futile; the silence with which
for a minute her adversary greeted her troubled plea
brought home to her afresh that she was on the bare defensive. "Is it a part of his kindness never to come near you?"
Mrs. Gereth inquired at last. "Is it a part of his kindness to
leave you without an inkling of where he is?" She rose again
from where Fleda had kept her down; she seemed to tower
there in the majesty of her gathered wrong. "Is it a part of
his kindness that after I've toiled as I've done for six days,
and with my own weak hands, which I haven't spared, to
denude myself, in your interest, to that point that I've nothing left, as I may say, but what I have on my back—is it a
part of his kindness that you're not even able to produce
him for me?"

There was a high contempt in this which was for Owen
quite as much, and in the light of which Fleda felt that her effort at plausibility had been mere grovelling. She rose from
the sofa with a humiliated sense of rising from ineffectual
knees. That discomfort, however, lived but an instant: it was
swept away in a rush of loyalty to the absent. She herself
could bear his mother's scorn; but to avert it from his sweet
innocence she broke out with a quickness that was like the
raising of an arm. "Don't blame him—don't blame him: he'd
do anything on earth for me! It was I," said Fleda eagerly,
"who sent him back to her; I made him go; I pushed him out
of the house; I declined to have anything to say to him except
on another footing."

Mrs. Gereth stared as at some gross material ravage. "Another footing? What other footing?"

"The one I've already made so clear to you: my having it in
black and white, as you may say, from her that she freely gives
him up."

"Then you think he lies when he tells you that he has recovered his liberty?"

Fleda hesitated a moment; after which she exclaimed with a certain hard pride: "He's enough in love with me for anything!"

"For anything apparently except to act like a man and impose his reason and his will on your incredible folly. For anything except to put an end, as any man worthy of the name would have put it, to your systematic, to your idiotic perversity. What are you, after all, my dear, I should like to know, that a gentleman who offers you what Owen offers should have to meet such wonderful exactions, to take such extraordinary precautions about your sweet little scruples?" Her resentment rose to a strange insolence which Fleda took full in the face and which, for the moment at least, had the horrible force to present to her vengefully a showy side of the truth. It gave her a blinding glimpse of lost alternatives. "I don't know what to think of him," Mrs. Gereth went on; "I don't know what to call him: I'm so ashamed of him that I can scarcely speak of him even to *you*. But indeed I'm so ashamed of you both together that I scarcely know in common decency where to look." She paused to give Fleda the full benefit of this remarkable statement; then she exclaimed: "Any one but a jackass would have tucked you under his arm and marched you off to the Registrar!"

Fleda wondered; with her free imagination she could wonder even while her cheek stung from a slap. "To the Registrar?"

"That would have been the sane, sound, immediate course to adopt. With a grain of gumption you'd both instantly have felt it. *I* should have found a way to take you, you know, if I'd been what Owen is supposed to be. *I* should have got the business over first; the rest could come when you liked! Good God, girl, your place was to stand before me as a woman honestly married. One doesn't know what one has hold of in touching you, and you must excuse my saying that you're literally unpleasant to me to meet as you are. Then at least we could have talked, and Owen, if he had the ghost of a sense of humour, could have snapped his fingers at your refinements."

This stirring speech affected our young lady as if it had been the shake of a tambourine borne towards her from a gipsy dance: her head seemed to go round and she felt a sudden passion in her feet. The emotion, however, was but meagrely expressed in the flatness with which she heard herself presently say: "I'll go to the Registrar now."

"Now?" Magnificent was the sound Mrs. Gereth threw into this monosyllable. "And pray who's to take you?" Fleda gave a colourless smile, and her companion continued: "Do you literally mean that you can't put your hand upon him?" Fleda's wan grimace appeared to irritate her; she made a short, imperious gesture. "Find him for me, you fool—*find* him for me!"

"What do you want of him," Fleda sadly asked, "feeling as you do to both of us?"

"Never mind how I feel, and never mind what I say when I'm furious!" Mrs. Gereth still more incisively added. "Of course I cling to you, you wretches, or I shouldn't suffer as I do. What I want of him is to see that he takes you; what I want of him is to go with you myself to the place." She looked round the room as if, in feverish haste, for a mantle to catch up; she bustled to the window as if to spy out a cab: she would allow half-an-hour for the job. Already in her bonnet, she had snatched from the sofa a garment for the street: she jerked it on as she came back. "Find him, find him," she repeated; "come straight out with me, to try, at least, to get at him!"

"How can I get at him? He'll come when he's ready," Fleda replied.

Mrs. Gereth turned on her sharply. "Ready for what? Ready to see me ruined without a reason or a reward?"

Fleda was silent; the worst of it all was that there was something unspoken between them. Neither of them dared to utter it, but the influence of it was in the girl's tone when she returned at last, with great gentleness: "Don't be harsh to me—I'm very unhappy." The words produced a visible impression on Mrs. Gereth, who held her face averted and sent off through the window a gaze that kept pace with the long caravan of her treasures. Fleda knew she was watching it wind up the avenue of Poynton—Fleda participated indeed fully in the vision; so that after a little the most consoling thing seemed to her to add: "I don't see why in the world you take so for granted that he's, as you say, 'lost.'"

Mrs. Gereth continued to stare out of the window, and her stillness denoted some success in controlling herself. "If he's not lost, why are you unhappy?"

"I'm unhappy because I torment you and you don't understand me."

"No, Fleda, I don't understand you," said Mrs. Gereth, finally facing her again. "I don't understand you at all, and it's as if you and Owen were of quite another race and another flesh. You make me feel very old-fashioned and simple and bad. But you must take me as I am, since you take so much else *with* me!" She spoke now with the drop of her resentment, with a dry and weary calm. "It would have been better for me if I had never known you," she pursued, "and certainly better if I hadn't taken such an extraordinary fancy to you. But that too was inevitable: everything, I suppose, is inevitable. It was all my own doing—you didn't run after me: I pounced on you and caught you up. You're a stiff little beggar, in spite of your pretty manners: yes, you're hideously misleading. I hope you feel how handsome it is of me to recognise the independence of your character. It was your clever sympathy that did it—your extraordinary feeling for those accursed vanities. You were sharper about them than any one I had ever known, and that was a thing I simply couldn't resist. Well," the poor lady concluded after a pause, "you see where it has landed us!"

"If you'll go for him yourself I'll wait here," said Fleda.

Mrs. Gereth, holding her mantle together, appeared for a while to consider. "To his club, do you mean?"

"Isn't it there, when he's in town, that he has a room? He has at present no other London address," Fleda said. "It's there one writes to him."

"How do *I* know, with my wretched relations with him?" Mrs. Gereth asked.

"Mine have not been quite so bad as that," Fleda desperately smiled. Then she added: "His silence, *her* silence, our hearing nothing at all—what are these but the very things on which, at Poynton and at Ricks, you rested your assurance that everything is at an end between them?"

Mrs. Gereth looked dark and void. "Yes, but I hadn't heard from you then that you could invent nothing better than, as you call it, to send him back to her."

"Ah, but, on the other hand, you've learned from them what you didn't know—you've learned by Mrs. Brigstock's visit that he cares for me." Fleda found herself in the position of availing herself of optimistic arguments that she formerly had repudiated; her refutation of her companion had completely changed its ground. She was in a fever of ingenuity and painfully conscious, on behalf of her success, that her fever was visible. She could herself see the reflection of it glitter in Mrs. Gereth's sombre eyes.

"You plunge me in stupefaction," that lady answered, "and at the same time you terrify me. Your account of Owen is inconceivable, and yet I don't know what to hold on by. He cares for you, it does appear, and yet in the same breath you inform me that nothing is more possible than that he's spending these days at Waterbath. Excuse me if I'm so dull as not to see my way in such darkness. If he's at Waterbath he doesn't care for you. If he cares for you he's not at Waterbath."

"Then where is he?" poor Fleda helplessly wailed. She caught herself up, however; she did her best to be brave and clear. Before Mrs. Gereth could reply, with due obviousness, that this was a question for her not to ask but to answer, she found an air of assurance to say: "You simplify far too much. You always did and you always will. The tangle of life is much more intricate than you've ever, I think, felt it to be. You slash into it," cried Fleda finely, "with a great pair of shears; you nip at it as if you were one of the Fates! If Owen's at Waterbath he's there to wind everything up."

Mrs. Gereth shook her head with slow austerity. "You don't believe a word you're saying. I've frightened you, as you've frightened me: you're whistling in the dark to keep up our courage. I do simplify, doubtless, if to simplify is to fail to comprehend the insanity of a passion that bewilders a young blockhead with bugaboo barriers, with hideous and monstrous sacrifices. I can only repeat that you're beyond me. Your perversity's a thing to howl over. However," the poor woman continued with a break in her voice, a long hesitation and then the dry triumph of her will, "I'll never mention it to you again! Owen I can just make out; for Owen *is* a blockhead. Owen's a blockhead," she repeated with a quiet, tragic finality, looking straight into Fleda's eyes. "I don't know why you dress up so the fact that he's disgustingly weak."

Fleda hesitated; at last, before her companion's, she lowered her look. "Because I love him. It's because he's weak that he needs me," she added.

"That was why his father, whom he exactly resembles, needed *me*. And I didn't fail his father," said Mrs. Gereth. She gave Fleda a moment to appreciate the remark; after which she pursued: "Mona Brigstock isn't weak. She's stronger than you!"

"I never thought she was weak," Fleda answered. She looked vaguely round the room with a new purpose: she had lost sight of her umbrella.

"I did tell you to let yourself go, but it's clear enough that you really haven't," Mrs. Gereth declared. "If Mona has got him——"

Fleda had accomplished her search; her interlocutress paused. "If Mona has got him?" the girl inquired, tightening the umbrella.

"Well," said Mrs. Gereth profoundly, "it will be clear enough that Mona *has*."

"Has let herself go?"

"Has let herself go." Mrs. Gereth spoke as if she saw it in every detail.

Fleda felt the tone and finished her preparation; then she went and opened the door. "We'll look for him together," she said to her friend, who stood a moment taking in her face. "They may know something about him at the Colonel's."

"We'll go there." Mrs. Gereth had picked up her gloves and her purse. "But the first thing," she went on, "will be to wire to Poynton."

"Why not to Waterbath at once?" Fleda asked.

Her companion hesitated. "In *your* name?"

"In my name. I noticed a place at the corner."

While Fleda held the door open Mrs. Gereth drew on her gloves. "Forgive me," she presently said. "Kiss me," she added.

Fleda, on the threshold, kissed her. Then they both went out.

XIX

I N THE PLACE at the corner, on the chance of its saving time,
Fleda wrote her telegram—wrote it in silence under Mrs.
Gereth's eye and then in silence handed it to her. "I send this
to Waterbath, on the possibility of your being there, to ask
you to come to me." Mrs. Gereth held it a moment, read it
more than once; then keeping it, and with her eyes on her
companion, seemed to consider. There was the dawn of a
kindness in her look; Fleda perceived in it, as if as the reward
of complete submission, a slight relaxation of her rigour.

"Wouldn't it perhaps after all be better," she asked, "before
doing this, to see if we can make his whereabouts certain?"

"Why so? It will be always so much done," said Fleda.
"Though I'm poor," she added with a smile, "I don't mind
the shilling."

"The shilling's *my* shilling," said Mrs. Gereth.

Fleda stayed her hand. "No, no—I'm superstitious."

"Superstitious?"

"To succeed, it must be all me!"

"Well, if that will make it succeed!" Mrs. Gereth took back
her shilling, but she still kept the telegram. "As he's most
probably not there——"

"If he shouldn't be there," Fleda interrupted, "there will
be no harm done."

"If he 'shouldn't be' there!" Mrs. Gereth ejaculated.
"Heaven help us, how you assume it!"

"I'm only prepared for the worst. The Brigstocks will simply send any telegram on."

"Where will they send it?"

"Presumably to Poynton."

"They'll read it first," said Mrs. Gereth.

"Read it?"

"Yes, Mona will. She'll open it under the pretext of having
it repeated; and then she'll probably do nothing. She'll keep
it as a proof of your immodesty."

"What of that?" asked Fleda.

"You don't mind her seeing it?"

Rather musingly and absently Fleda shook her head. "I don't mind anything."

"Well then, that's all right," said Mrs. Gereth as if she had only wanted to feel that she had been irreproachably considerate. After this she was gentler still, but she had another point to clear up. "Why have you given, for a reply, your sister's address?"

"Because if he does come to me he must come to me there. If that telegram goes," said Fleda, "I return to Maggie's to-night."

Mrs. Gereth seemed to wonder at this. "You won't receive him here with me?"

"No, I won't receive him here with you. Only where I received him last—only there again." She showed her companion that as to that she was firm.

But Mrs. Gereth had obviously now had some practice in following queer movements prompted by queer feelings. She resigned herself, though she fingered the paper a moment longer. She appeared to hesitate; then she brought out: "You couldn't then, if I release you, make your message a little stronger?"

Fleda gave her a faint smile. "He'll come if he can."

Mrs. Gereth met fully what this conveyed; with decision she pushed in the telegram. But she laid her hand quickly upon another form and with still greater decision wrote another message. "From *me*, this," she said to Fleda when she had finished: "to catch him possibly at Poynton. Will you read it?"

Fleda turned away. "Thank you."

"It's stronger than yours."

"I don't care," said Fleda, moving to the door. Mrs. Gereth, having paid for the second missive, rejoined her, and they drove together to Owen's club, where the elder lady alone got out. Fleda, from the hansom, watched through the glass doors her brief conversation with the hall-porter and then met in silence her return with the news that he had not seen Owen for a fortnight and was keeping his letters till called for. These had been the last orders; there were a dozen letters lying there. He had no more information to give, but they would see what they could find at Colonel Gereth's. To any connection with this inquiry, however, Fleda now roused herself to object, and her friend had indeed to recognise that on second thoughts it couldn't be quite to the taste of either of them to advertise in the remoter reaches of the family that they had forfeited the confidence of the master of Poynton. The letters lying at the club proved effectively that he was not in London, and this was the question that immediately concerned them. Nothing could concern them further till the answers to their telegrams should have had time to arrive. Mrs. Gereth had got back into the cab, and, still at the door of the club, they sat staring at their need of patience. Fleda's eyes rested, in the great hard street, on passing figures that struck her as puppets pulled by strings. After a little the driver challenged them through the hole in the top. "Anywhere in particular, ladies?"

Fleda decided. "Drive to Euston, please."

"You won't wait for what we may hear?" Mrs. Gereth asked.

"Whatever we hear, I must go." As the cab went on she added: "But I needn't drag *you* to the station."

Mrs. Gereth was silent a moment; then "Nonsense!" she sharply replied.

In spite of this sharpness they were now almost equally and almost tremulously mild; though their mildness took mainly the form of an inevitable sense of nothing left to say. It was the unsaid that occupied them—the thing that for more than an hour they had been going round and round without naming it. Much too early for Fleda's train, they encountered at the station a long half-hour to wait. Fleda made no further allusion to Mrs. Gereth's leaving her; their dumbness, with the elapsing minutes, grew to be in itself a reconstituted bond. They slowly paced the great grey platform, and presently Mrs. Gereth took the girl's arm and leaned on it with a hard demand for support. It seemed to Fleda not difficult for each to know of what the other was thinking—to know indeed that they had in common two alternating visions, one of which at moments brought them as by a common impulse to a pause. This was the one that was fixed; the other filled at times the whole space and then was shouldered away. Owen and Mona glared together out of the gloom and disappeared, but the replenishment of Poynton made a shining, steady light. The old splendour was there again, the old things were in their places.

Our friends looked at them with an equal yearning; face to face, on the platform, they counted them in each other's eyes. Fleda had come back to them by a road as strange as the road they themselves had followed. The wonder of their great journeys, the prodigy of this second one, was the question that made her occasionally stop. Several times she uttered it, asked how this and that difficulty had been met. Mrs. Gereth replied with pale lucidity—was naturally the person most familiar with the truth that what she undertook was always somehow achieved. To do it was to do it—she had more than one kind of magnificence. She confessed there, audaciously enough, to a sort of arrogance of energy, and Fleda, going on again, her inquiry more than answered and her arm rendering service, flushed in her diminished identity with the sense that such a woman was great.

"You do mean literally everything, to the last little miniature on the last little screen?"

"I mean literally everything. Go over them with the catalogue!"

Fleda went over them while they walked again; she had no need of the catalogue. At last she spoke once more. "Even the Maltese cross?"

"Even the Maltese cross. Why not that as well as everything else?—especially as I remembered how you like it."

Finally, after an interval, the girl exclaimed: "But the mere fatigue of it, the exhaustion of such a feat! I drag you to and fro here while you must be ready to drop."

"I'm very, very tired." Mrs. Gereth's slow head-shake was tragic. "I couldn't do it again."

"I doubt if they'd bear it again!"

"That's another matter: they'd bear it if I could. There won't have been, this time either, a shake or a scratch. But I'm too tired—I very nearly don't care."

"You must sit down then till I go," said Fleda. "We must find a bench."

"No. I'm tired of *them*: I'm not tired of you. This is the way for you to feel most how much I rest on you." Fleda had a compunction, wondering as they continued to stroll whether it was right after all to leave her. She believed however that if the flame might for the moment burn low it was far from dying out; an impression presently confirmed by the way Mrs. Gereth went on: "But one's fatigue is nothing. The idea under which one worked kept one up. For you I *could*— I can still. Nothing will have mattered if *she's* not there."

There was a question that this imposed, but Fleda at first found no voice to utter it: it was the thing that between them, since her arrival, had been so consciously and vividly unsaid. Finally she was able to breathe: "And if she *is* there— if she's there already?"

Mrs. Gereth's rejoinder too hung back; then when it came—from sad eyes as well as from lips barely moved—it was unexpectedly merciful. "It will be very hard." That was all now; and it was poignantly simple. The train Fleda was to take had drawn up; the girl kissed her as if in farewell. Mrs. Gereth submitted, then after a little brought out: "If we *have* lost——"

"If we have lost?" Fleda repeated as she paused again.

"You'll all the same come abroad with me?"

"It will seem very strange to me if you want me. But whatever you ask, whatever you need, that I will always do."

"I shall need your company," said Mrs. Gereth. Fleda wondered an instant if this were not practically a demand for penal submission—for a surrender that, in its complete humility, would be a long expiation. But there was none of the latent chill of the vindictive in the way Mrs. Gereth pursued: "We can always, as time goes on, talk of them together."

"Of the old things?" Fleda had selected a third-class compartment: she stood a moment looking into it and at a fat woman with a basket who had already taken possession. "Always?" she said, turning again to her companion. "Never!" she exclaimed. She got into the carriage, and two men with bags and boxes immediately followed, blocking up door and window so long that when she was able to look out again Mrs. Gereth had gone.

XX

THERE CAME to her at her sister's no telegram in answer to her own: the rest of that day and the whole of the next elapsed without a word either from Owen or from his mother. She was free, however, to her infinite relief, from any direct dealing with suspense, and conscious, to her surprise, of nothing that could show her, or could show Maggie and her brother-in-law, that she was excited. Her excitement was composed of pulses as swift and fine as the revolutions of a spinning top: she supposed she was going round, but she went round so fast that she couldn't even feel herself move. Her emotion occupied some quarter of her soul that had closed its doors for the day and shut out even her own sense of it; she might perhaps have heard something if she had pressed her ear to a partition. Instead of that she sat with her patience in a cold, still chamber from which she could look out in quite another direction. This was to have achieved an equilibrium to which she couldn't have given a name: indifference, resignation, despair were the terms of a forgotten tongue. The time even seemed not long, for the stages of the journey were the items of Mrs. Gereth's surrender. The detail of that performance, which filled the scene, was what Fleda had now before her eyes. The part of her loss that she could think of was the reconstituted splendour of Poynton. It was the beauty she was most touched by that, in tons, she had lost—the beauty that, charged upon big wagons, had safely crept back to its home. But the loss was a gain to memory and love; it was to her too at last that, in condonation of her treachery, the old things had crept back. She greeted them with open arms; she thought of them hour after hour; they made a company with which solitude was warm and a picture that, at this crisis, overlaid poor Maggie's scant mahogany. It was really her obliterated passion that had revived, and with it an immense assent to Mrs. Gereth's early judgment of her. She equally, she felt, was of the religion, and like any other of the passionately pious she could worship now even in the desert. Yes, it was all for her; far round as she had gone she had been strong enough: her love had gathered in the spoils. She wanted indeed no catalogue to count them over; the array of them, miles away, was complete; each piece, in its turn, was perfect to her; she could have drawn up a catalogue from memory. Thus again she lived with them, and she thought of them without a question of any personal right. That they might have been, that they might still be hers, that they were perhaps already another's, were ideas that had too little to say to her. They were nobody's at all—too proud, unlike base animals and humans, to be reducible to anything so narrow. It was Poynton that was theirs; they had simply recovered their own. The joy of that for them was the source of the strange peace in which the girl found herself floating.

It was broken on the third day by a telegram from Mrs. Gereth. "Shall be with you at 11.30—don't meet me at station." Fleda turned this over; she was sufficiently expert not to disobey the injunction. She had only an hour to take in its meaning, but that hour was longer than all the previous time. If Maggie had studied her convenience the day Owen came, Maggie was also at the present juncture a miracle of refinement. Increasingly and resentfully mystified, in spite of all reassurance, by the impression that Fleda suffered more than she gained from the grandeur of the Gereths, she had it at heart to exemplify the perhaps truer distinction of nature that characterised the house of Vetch. She was not, like poor Fleda, at every one's beck, and the visitor was to see no more of her than what the arrangement of luncheon might tantalisingly show. Maggie described herself to her sister as intending for a just provocation even the understanding she had had with her husband that he also should remain invisible. Fleda accordingly awaited alone the subject of so many manœuvres—a period that was slightly prolonged even after the drawing-room door, at 11:30, was thrown open. Mrs. Gereth stood there with a face that spoke plain, but no sound fell from her till the withdrawal of the maid, whose attention had immediately attached itself to the rearrangement of a window-blind and who seemed, while she bustled at it, to contribute to the pregnant silence; before the duration of which, however, she retreated with a sudden stare.

"He has done it," said Mrs. Gereth, turning her eyes avoid-

ingly but not unperceivingly about her and in spite of herself
dropping an opinion upon the few objects in the room. Fleda,
on her side, in her silence, observed how characteristically she
looked at Maggie's possessions before looking at Maggie's sister. The girl understood and at first had nothing to say; she
was still dumb while Mrs. Gereth selected, with hesitation, a
seat less distasteful than the one that happened to be nearest.
On the sofa near the window the poor woman finally showed
what the two past days had done for the age of her face. Her
eyes at last met Fleda's. "It's the end."

"They're married?"

"They're married."

Fleda came to the sofa in obedience to the impulse to sit
down by her; then paused before her while Mrs. Gereth
turned up a dead grey mask. A tired old woman sat there with
empty hands in her lap. "I've heard nothing," said Fleda. "No
answer came."

"That's the only answer. It's the answer to everything." So
Fleda saw; for a minute she looked over her companion's head
and far away. "He wasn't at Waterbath. Mrs. Brigstock must
have read your telegram and kept it. But mine, the one to Poynton, brought something. 'We are here—what do you want?'"
Mrs. Gereth stopped as if with a failure of voice; on which Fleda
sank upon the sofa and made a movement to take her hand. It
met no response; there could be no attenuation. Fleda waited;
they sat facing each other like strangers. "I wanted to go
down," Mrs. Gereth presently continued. "Well, I went."

All the girl's effort tended for the time to a single aim—
that of taking the thing with outward detachment, speaking
of it as having happened to Owen and to his mother and not
in any degree to herself. Something at least of this was in the
encouraging way she said: "Yesterday morning?"

"Yesterday morning. I saw him."

Fleda hesitated. "Did you see *her*?"

"Thank God, no!"

Fleda laid on her arm a hand of vague comfort, of which
Mrs. Gereth took no notice. "You've been capable, just to tell
me, of this wretched journey, of this consideration that I
don't deserve?"

"We're together, we're together," said Mrs. Gereth. She

looked helpless as she sat there, her eyes, unseeingly enough, on a tall Dutch clock, old but rather poor, that Maggie had had as a wedding-gift and that eked out the bareness of the room.

To Fleda, in the face of the event, it appeared that this was exactly what they were not: the last inch of common ground, the ground of their past intercourse, had fallen from under them. Yet what was still there was the grand style of her companion's treatment of her. Mrs. Gereth couldn't stand upon small questions, couldn't in conduct make small differences. "You're magnificent!" her young friend exclaimed. "There's an extraordinary greatness in your generosity."

"We're together, we're together," Mrs. Gereth lifelessly repeated. "That's all we *are* now; it's all we have." The words brought to Fleda a sudden vision of the empty little house at Ricks; such a vision might also have been what her companion found in the face of the stopped Dutch clock. Yet with this it was clear that she would now show no bitterness: she had done with that, had given the last drop to those horrible hours in London. No passion even was left to her, and her forbearance only added to the force with which she represented the final vanity of everything.

Fleda was so far from a wish to triumph that she was absolutely ashamed of having anything to say for herself; but there was one thing, all the same, that not to say was impossible. "That he has done it, that he couldn't *not* do it, shows how right I was." It settled forever her attitude, and she spoke as if for her own mind; then after a little she added very gently, for Mrs. Gereth's: "That's to say, it shows that he was bound to her by an obligation that, however much he may have wanted to, he couldn't in any sort of honour break."

Blanched and bleak, Mrs. Gereth looked at her. "What sort of an obligation do you call that? No such obligation exists for an hour between any man and any woman who have hatred on one side. He had ended by hating her, and now he hates her more than ever."

"Did he tell you so?" Fleda asked.

"No. He told me nothing but the great gawk of a fact. I saw him but for three minutes." She was silent again, and Fleda, as before some lurid image of this interview, sat without speaking. "Do you wish to appear as if you don't care?" Mrs. Gereth presently demanded.

"I'm trying not to think of myself."

"Then if you're thinking of Owen, how can you *bear* to think?"

Sadly and submissively Fleda shook her head; the slow tears had come into her eyes. "I can't. I don't understand—I don't understand!" she broke out.

"*I* do, then." Mrs. Gereth looked hard at the floor. "There was no obligation at the time you saw him last—when you sent him, hating her as he did, back to her."

"If he went," Fleda asked, "doesn't that exactly prove that he recognised one?"

"He recognised rot! You know what *I* think of him." Fleda knew; she had no wish to provoke a fresh statement. Mrs. Gereth made one—it was her sole, faint flicker of passion—to the extent of declaring that he was too abjectly weak to deserve the name of a man. For all Fleda cared!—it was his weakness she loved in him. "He took strange ways of pleasing you!" her friend went on. "There was no obligation till suddenly, the other day, the situation changed."

Fleda wondered. "The other day?"

"It came to Mona's knowledge—I can't tell you how, but it came—that the things I was sending back had begun to arrive at Poynton. I had sent them for you, but it was *her* I touched." Mrs. Gereth paused; Fleda was too absorbed in her explanation to do anything but take blankly the full, cold breath of this. "They were there, and that determined her."

"Determined her to what?"

"To act, to take means."

"To take means?" Fleda repeated.

"I can't tell you what they were, but they were powerful. She knew how," said Mrs. Gereth.

Fleda received with the same stoicism the quiet immensity of this allusion to the person who had not known how. But it made her think a little, and the thought found utterance, with unconscious irony, in the simple interrogation: "Mona?"

"Why not? She's a brute."

"But if he knew that so well, what chance was there in it for her?"

"How can I tell you? How can I talk of such horrors? I can only give you, of the situation, what I see. He knew it, yes. But as she couldn't make him forget it, she tried to make him like it. She tried and she succeeded: that's what she did. She's after all so much less of a fool than he. And what *else* had he originally liked?" Mrs. Gereth shrugged her shoulders. "She did what you wouldn't!" Fleda's face had grown dark with her wonder, but her friend's empty hands offered no balm to the pain in it. "It was that if it was anything. Nothing else meets the misery of it. Then there was quick work. Before he could turn round he was married."

Fleda, as if she had been holding her breath, gave the sigh of a listening child. "At that place you spoke of in town?"

"At a Registry-office—like a pair of low atheists."

The girl hesitated. "What do people say of that? I mean the 'world.'"

"Nothing, because nobody knows. They're to be married on the 17th at Waterbath church. If anything else comes out, everybody is a little prepared. It will pass for some stroke of diplomacy, some move in the game, some outwitting of *me*. It's known there has been a row with me."

Fleda was mystified. "People surely know at Poynton," she objected, "if, as you say, she's there."

"She was there, day before yesterday, only for a few hours. She met him in London and went down to see the things."

Fleda remembered that she had seen them only once. "Did *you* see them?" she then ventured to ask.

"Everything."

"Are they right?"

"Quite right. There's nothing like them," said Mrs. Gereth. At this her companion took up one of her hands again and kissed it as she had done in London. "Mona went back that night; she was not there yesterday. Owen stayed on," she added.

Fleda stared. "Then she's not to live there?"

"Rather! But not till after the public marriage." Mrs. Gereth seemed to muse; then she brought out: "She'll live there alone."

"Alone?"

"She'll have it to herself."

"He won't live with her?"

"Never! But she's none the less his wife, and you're not," said Mrs. Gereth, getting up. "Our only chance is the chance she may die."

Fleda appeared to consider: she appreciated her visitor's magnanimous use of the plural. "Mona won't die," she replied.

"Well, *I* shall, thank God! Till then"—and with this, for the first time, Mrs. Gereth put out her hand—"don't desert me."

Fleda took her hand, and her clasp of it was a reiteration of a promise already given. She said nothing, but her silence was an acceptance as responsible as the vow of a nun. The next moment something occurred to her. "I mustn't put myself in your son's way."

Mrs. Gereth gave a dry, flat laugh. "You're prodigious! But how shall you possibly be more out of it? Owen and I—" She didn't finish her sentence.

"That's your great feeling about him," Fleda said; "but how, after what has happened, can it be his about you?"

Mrs. Gereth hesitated. "How do you know what has happened? You don't know what I said to him."

"Yesterday?"

"Yesterday."

They looked at each other with a long, deep gaze. Then, as Mrs. Gereth seemed again about to speak, the girl, closing her eyes, made a gesture of strong prohibition. "Don't tell me!"

"Merciful powers, how you worship him!" Mrs. Gereth wonderingly moaned. It was for Fleda the shake that made the cup overflow. She had a pause, that of the child who takes time to know that he responds to an accident with pain; then, dropping again on the sofa, she broke into tears. They were beyond control, they came in long sobs, which for a moment Mrs. Gereth, almost with an air of indifference, stood hearing and watching. At last Mrs. Gereth too sank down again. Mrs. Gereth soundlessly, wearily wept.

XXI

"IT LOOKS just like Waterbath; but, after all, we bore *that* together:" these words formed part of a letter in which, before the 17th, Mrs. Gereth, writing from disfigured Ricks, named to Fleda the day on which she would be expected to arrive there on a second visit. "I shan't, for a long time to come," the missive continued, "be able to receive any one who may *like* it, who would try to smooth it down, and me with it; but there are always things you and I can comfortably hate together, for you're the only person who comfortably understands. You don't understand quite everything, but of all my acquaintance you're far away the least stupid. For action you're no good at all; but action is over, for me, forever, and you will have the great merit of knowing, when I'm brutally silent, what I shall be thinking about. Without setting myself up for your equal I dare say I shall also know what are your own thoughts. Moreover, with nothing else but my four walls, you'll at any rate be a bit of furniture. For that, you know, a little, I've always taken you—quite one of my best finds. So come, if possible, on the 15th."

The position of a bit of furniture was one that Fleda could conscientiously accept, and she by no means insisted on so high a place in the list. This communication made her easier, if only by its acknowledgment that her friend had something left: it still implied recognition of the principle of property. Something to hate, and to hate "comfortably," was at least not the utter destitution to which, after their last interview, she had helplessly seemed to see Mrs. Gereth go forth. She remembered indeed that, in the state in which they first saw it, she herself had "liked" the blessed refuge of Ricks; and she now wondered if the tact for which she was commended had then operated to make her keep her kindness out of sight. She was at present ashamed of such obliquity and made up her mind that if this happy impression, quenched in the spoils of Poynton, should revive on the spot, she would utter it to her companion without reserve. Yes, she was capable of as much "action" as that: all the more that the spirit of her hostess seemed, for the time at least, wholly to have failed. Mrs. Gereth's three minutes with Owen had been a blow to all talk of travel, and after her woeful hour at Maggie's she had, like some great moaning, wounded bird, made her way with wings of anguish back to the nest she knew she should find empty. Fleda, on that dire day, could neither keep her nor give her up; she had pressingly offered to return with her, but Mrs. Gereth, in spite of the theory that their common grief was a bond, had even declined all escort to the station, conscious apparently of something abject in her collapse and almost fiercely eager, as with a personal shame, to be unwatched. All she had said to Fleda was that she would go back to Ricks that night, and the girl had lived for days after with a dreadful image of her position and her misery there. She had had a vision of her now lying prone on some unmade bed, now pacing a bare floor like a lioness deprived of her cubs. There had been moments when her mind's ear was strained to listen for some sound of grief wild enough to be wafted from afar. But the first sound, at the end of a week, had been a note announcing, without reflections, that the plan of going abroad had been abandoned. "It has come to me indirectly, but with much appearance of truth, that *they* are going—for an indefinite time. That quite settles it; I shall stay where I am, and as soon as I've turned round again I shall look for you." The second letter had come a week later, and on the 15th Fleda was on her way to Ricks.

Her arrival took the form of a surprise very nearly as violent as that of the other time. The elements were different, but the effect, like the other, arrested her on the threshold: she stood there stupefied and delighted at the magic of a passion of which such a picture represented the low-water mark. Wound up but sincere, and passing quickly from room to room, Fleda broke out before she even sat down. "If you turn me out of the house for it, my dear, there isn't a woman in England for whom it wouldn't be a privilege to live here." Mrs. Gereth was as honestly bewildered as she had of old been falsely calm. She looked about at the few sticks that, as she afterwards phrased it, she had gathered in, and then hard at her guest, as if to protect herself against a joke sufficiently cruel. The girl's heart gave a leap, for this stare was the sign of an opportunity.

Mrs. Gereth was all unwitting; she didn't in the least know what she had done, and as Fleda could tell her, Fleda suddenly became the one who knew most. That counted for the moment as a magnificent position; it almost made all the difference. Yet what contradicted it was the vivid presence of the artist's idea. "Where on earth did you put your hand on such beautiful things?"

"Beautiful things?" Mrs. Gereth turned again to the little worn, bleached stuffs and the sweet spindle-legs. "They're the wretched things that were here—that stupid, starved old woman's."

"The maiden-aunt's, the nicest, the dearest old woman that ever lived? I thought you had got rid of the maiden-aunt."

"She was stored in an empty barn—stuck away for a sale; a matter that, fortunately, I've had neither time nor freedom of mind to arrange. I've simply, in my extremity, fished her out again."

"You've simply, in your extremity, made a delight of her." Fleda took the highest line and the upper hand, and as Mrs. Gereth, challenging her cheerfulness, turned again a lustreless eye over the contents of the place, she broke into a rapture that was unforced, but that she was conscious of an advantage in being able to feel. She moved, as she had done on the previous occasion, from one piece to another, with looks of recognition and hands that lightly lingered, but she was as feverishly jubilant now as she had formerly been anxious and mute. "Ah, the little melancholy, tender, tell-tale things: how can they *not* speak to you and find a way to your heart? It's not the great chorus of Poynton; but you're not, I'm sure, either so proud or so broken as to be reached by nothing but that. This is a voice so gentle, so human, so feminine—a faint, far-away voice with the little quaver of a heart-break. You've listened to it unawares; for the arrangement and effect of everything—when I compare them with what we found the first day we came down—shows, even if mechanically and disdainfully exercised, your admirable, infallible hand. It's your extraordinary genius; you make things 'compose' in spite of yourself. You've only to be a day or two in a place with four sticks for something to come of it!"

"Then if anything has come of it here, it has come precisely of just four. That's literally, by the inventory, all there are!" said Mrs. Gereth.

"If there were more there would be too many to convey the impression in which half the beauty resides—the impression, somehow, of something dreamed and missed, something reduced, relinquished, resigned: the poetry, as it were, of something sensibly *gone*." Fleda ingeniously and triumphantly worked it out. "Ah, there's something here that will never be in the inventory!"

"Does it happen to be in your power to give it a name?" Mrs. Gereth's face showed the dim dawn of an amusement at finding herself seated at the feet of her pupil.

"I can give it a dozen. It's a kind of fourth dimension. It's a presence, a perfume, a touch. It's a soul, a story, a life. There's ever so much more here than you and I. We're in fact just three!"

"Oh, if you count the ghosts!"

"Of course I count the ghosts. It seems to me ghosts count double—for what they were and for what they are. Somehow there were no ghosts at Poynton," Fleda went on. "That was the only fault."

Mrs. Gereth, considering, appeared to fall in with the girl's fine humour. "Poynton was too splendidly happy."

"Poynton was too splendidly happy," Fleda promptly echoed.

"But it's cured of that now," her companion added.

"Yes, henceforth there'll be a ghost or two."

Mrs. Gereth thought again: she found her young friend suggestive. "Only *she* won't see them."

"No, 'she' won't see them." Then Fleda said: "What I mean is, for this dear one of ours, that if she had (as I *know* she did; it's in the very taste of the air!) a great accepted pain——"

She had paused an instant, and Mrs. Gereth took her up. "Well, if she had?"

Fleda still hesitated. "Why, it was worse than yours."

Mrs. Gereth reflected. "Very likely." Then she too hesitated. "The question is if it was worse than yours."

"Mine?" Fleda looked vague.

"Precisely. Yours."

At this our young lady smiled. "Yes, because it was a disappointment. She had been so sure."

"I see. And you were never sure."

"Never. Besides, I'm happy," said Fleda.

Mrs. Gereth met her eyes awhile. "Goose!" she quietly remarked as she turned away. There was a curtness in it; nevertheless it represented a considerable part of the basis of their new life.

On the 18th *The Morning Post* had at last its clear message, a brief account of the marriage, from the residence of the bride's mother, of Mr. Owen Gereth of Poynton Park to Miss Mona Brigstock of Waterbath. There were two ecclesiastics and six bridesmaids and, as Mrs. Gereth subsequently said, a hundred frumps, as well as a special train from town: the scale of the affair sufficiently showed that the preparations had been complete for weeks. The happy pair were described as having taken their departure for Mr. Gereth's own seat, famous for its unique collection of artistic curiosities. The newspapers and letters, the fruits of the first London post, had been brought to the mistress of Ricks in the garden; and she lingered there alone a long time after receiving them. Fleda kept at a distance; she knew what must have happened, for from one of the windows she saw her rigid in a chair, her eyes strange and fixed, the newspaper open on the ground and the letters untouched in her lap. Before the morning's end she had disappeared, and the rest of that day she remained in her room: it recalled to Fleda, who had picked up the newspaper, the day, months before, on which Owen had come down to Poynton to make his engagement known. The hush of the house at least was the same, and the girl's own waiting, her soft wandering, through the hours: there was a difference indeed sufficiently great, of which her companion's absence might in some degree have represented a considerate recognition. That was at any rate the meaning Fleda, devoutly glad to be alone, attached to her opportunity. Mrs. Gereth's sole allusion the next day to the subject of their thoughts has already been mentioned: it was a dazzled glance at the fact that Mona's quiet pace had really never slackened.

Fleda fully assented. "I said of our disembodied friend here that she had suffered in proportion as she had been sure. But that's not always a source of suffering. It's Mona who must have been sure!"

"She was sure of *you*!" Mrs. Gereth returned. But this didn't diminish the satisfaction taken by Fleda in showing how serenely and lucidly she could talk.

XXII

HER RELATION with her wonderful friend had, however, in becoming a new one begun to shape itself almost wholly on breaches and omissions. Something had dropped out altogether, and the question between them, which time would answer, was whether the change had made them strangers or yokefellows. It was as if at last, for better or worse, they were, in a clearer, cruder air, really to know each other. Fleda wondered how Mrs. Gereth had escaped hating her: there were hours when it seemed that such a feat might leave after all a scant margin for future accidents. The thing indeed that now came out in its simplicity was that even in her shrunken state the lady of Ricks was larger than her wrongs. As for the girl herself, she had made up her mind that her feelings had no connection with the case. It was her pretension that they had never yet emerged from the seclusion into which, after her friend's visit to her at her sister's, we saw them precipitately retire: if she should suddenly meet them in straggling procession on the road it would be time enough to deal with them. They were all bundled there together, likes with dislikes and memories with fears; and she had for not thinking of them the excellent reason that she was too occupied with the actual. The actual was not that Owen Gereth had seen his necessity where she had pointed it out; it was that his mother's bare spaces demanded all the tapestry that the recipient of her bounty could furnish. There were moments during the month that followed when Mrs. Gereth struck her as still older and feebler and as likely to become quite easily amused.

At the end of it, one day, the London paper had another piece of news: "Mr. and Mrs. Owen Gereth, who arrived in town last week, proceed this morning to Paris." They exchanged no word about it till the evening, and none indeed would then have been uttered had not Mrs. Gereth irrelevantly broken out: "I dare say you wonder why I declared the other day with such assurance that he wouldn't live with her. He apparently *is* living with her."

"Surely it's the only proper thing for him to do."

384

"They're beyond me—I give it up," said Mrs. Gereth.

"I don't give it up—I never did," Fleda returned.

"Then what do you make of his aversion to her?"

"Oh, she has dispelled it."

Mrs. Gereth said nothing for a minute. "You're prodigious in your choice of terms!" she then simply ejaculated.

But Fleda went luminously on; she once more enjoyed her great command of her subject. "I think that when you came to see me at Maggie's you saw too many things, you had too many ideas."

"You had none," said Mrs. Gereth. "You were completely bewildered."

"Yes, I didn't quite understand—but I think I understand now. The case is simple and logical enough. She's a person who's upset by failure and who blooms and expands with success. There was something she had set her heart upon, set her teeth about—the house exactly as she had seen it."

"She never saw it at all, she never looked at it!" cried Mrs. Gereth.

"She doesn't look with her eyes; she looks with her ears. In her own way she had taken it in; she knew, she felt when it had been touched. That probably made her take an attitude that was extremely disagreeable. But the attitude lasted only while the reason for it lasted."

"Go on—I can bear it now," said Mrs. Gereth. Her companion had just perceptibly paused.

"I know you can, or I shouldn't dream of speaking. When the pressure was removed she came up again. From the moment the house was once more what it had to be, her natural charm reasserted itself."

"Her natural charm!" Mrs. Gereth could barely articulate.

"It's very great; everybody thinks so; there must be something in it. It operated as it had operated before. There's no need of imagining anything very monstrous. Her restored good humour, her splendid beauty and Mr. Owen's impressibility and generosity sufficiently cover the ground. His great bright sun came out!"

"And his great bright passion for another person went in. Your explanation would doubtless be perfection if he didn't love you."

Fleda was silent a little. "What do you know about his 'loving' me?"

"I know what Mrs. Brigstock herself told me."

"You never in your life took her word for any other matter."

"Then won't yours do?" Mrs. Gereth demanded. "Haven't I had it from your own mouth that he cares for you?"

Fleda turned pale, but she faced her companion and smiled. "You confound, Mrs. Gereth. You mix things up. You've only had it from my own mouth that I care for *him*!"

It was doubtless in contradictious allusion to this (which at the time had made her simply drop her head as in a strange, vain reverie) that Mrs. Gereth, a day or two later, said to Fleda: "Don't think I shall be a bit affected if I'm here to see it when he comes again to make up to you."

"He won't do that," the girl replied. Then she added, smiling: "But if he should be guilty of such bad taste it wouldn't be nice of you not to be disgusted."

"I'm not talking of disgust; I'm talking of its opposite," said Mrs. Gereth.

"Of its opposite?"

"Why, of any reviving pleasure that one might feel in such an exhibition. I shall feel none at all. You may personally take it as you like; but what conceivable good will it do?"

Fleda wondered. "To me, do you mean?"

"Deuce take you, no! To what we don't, you know, by your wish, ever talk about."

"The old things?" Fleda considered again. "It will do no good of any sort to anything or any one. That's another question I would rather we shouldn't discuss, please," she gently added.

Mrs. Gereth shrugged her shoulders. "It certainly isn't worth it!"

Something in her manner prompted her companion, with a certain inconsequence, to speak again. "That was partly why I came back to you, you know—that there should be the less possibility of anything painful."

"Painful?" Mrs. Gereth stared. "What pain can I ever feel again?"

"I meant painful to myself," Fleda, with a slight impatience, explained.

"Oh, I see." Her friend was silent a minute. "You use sometimes such odd expressions. Well, I shall last a little, but I sha'n't last forever."

"You'll last quite as long——" Here Fleda suddenly hesitated.

Mrs. Gereth took her up with a cold smile that seemed the warning of experience against hyperbole. "As long as what, please?"

The girl thought an instant; then met the difficulty by adopting, as an amendment, the same tone. "As any danger of the ridiculous."

That did for the time, and she had moreover, as the months went on, the protection of suspended allusions. This protection was marked when, in the following November, she received a letter directed in a hand at which a quick glance sufficed to make her hesitate to open it. She said nothing, then or afterwards; but she opened it, for reasons that had come to her, on the morrow. It consisted of a page and a half from Owen Gereth, dated from Florence, but with no other preliminary. She knew that during the summer he had returned to England with his wife, and that after a couple of months they had again gone abroad. She also knew, without communication, that Mrs. Gereth, round whom Ricks had grown submissively and indescribably sweet, had her own interpretation of her daughter-in-law's share in this second migration. It was a piece of calculated insolence—a stroke odiously directed at showing whom it might concern that now she had Poynton fast she was perfectly indifferent to living there. *The Morning Post*, at Ricks, had again been a resource: it was stated in that journal that Mr. and Mrs. Owen Gereth proposed to spend the winter in India. There was a person to whom it was clear that she led her wretched husband by the nose. Such was the light in which contemporary history was offered to Fleda until, in her own room, late at night, she broke the seal of her letter.

"I want you, inexpressibly, to have, as a remembrance, something of mine—something of real value. Something from Poynton is what I mean and what I should prefer. You know everything there, and far better than I what's best and what isn't. There are a lot of differences, but aren't some of the smaller things the most remarkable? I mean for judges, and for what they'd bring. What I want you to take from me, and to choose for yourself, is the thing in the whole house that's most beautiful and precious. I mean the 'gem of the collection,' don't you know? If it happens to be of such a sort that you can take immediate possession of it—carry it right away with you—so much the better. You're to have it on the spot, whatever it is. I humbly beg of you to go down there and see. The people have complete instructions: they'll act for you in every possible way and put the whole place at your service. There's a thing mamma used to call the Maltese cross and that I think I've heard her say is very wonderful. Is *that* the gem of the collection? Perhaps you would take it or anything equally convenient. Only I do want you awfully to let it be the very pick of the place. Let me feel that I can trust you for this. You won't refuse if you will think a little what it must be that makes me ask."

Fleda read that last sentence over more times even than the rest: she was baffled—she couldn't think at all of what it might be. This was indeed because it might be one of so many things. She made for the present no answer; she merely, little by little, fashioned for herself the form that her answer should eventually wear. There was only one form that was possible—the form of doing, at her time, what he wished. She would go down to Poynton as a pilgrim might go to a shrine, and as to this she must look out for her chance. She lived with her letter, before any chance came, a month, and even after a month it had mysteries for her that she couldn't meet. What did it mean, what did it represent, to what did it correspond in his imagination or his soul? What was behind it, what was before it, what was, in the deepest depth, within it? She said to herself that with these questions she was under no obligation to deal. There was an explanation of them that, for practical purposes, would do as well as another: he had found in his marriage a happiness so much greater than, in the distress of his dilemma, he had been able to take heart to believe, that he now felt he owed her a token of gratitude for having kept him in the straight path. That explanation, I say, she could throw off; but no explanation in the least mattered: what determined her was the simple strength of her impulse to respond. The passion for which what had happened had made

no difference, the passion that had taken this into account before as well as after, found here an issue that there was nothing whatever to choke. It found even a relief to which her
imagination immensely contributed. Would she act upon his
offer? She would act with secret rapture. To have as her own
something splendid that he had given her, of which the gift
had been his signed desire, would be a greater joy than the
greatest she had supposed to be left to her, and she felt that
till the sense of this came home she had even herself not
known what burned in her successful stillness. It was an hour
to dream of and watch for; to be patient was to draw out the
sweetness. She was capable of feeling it as an hour of triumph,
the triumph of everything in her recent life that had not held
up its head. She moved there in thought—in the great rooms
she knew; she should be able to say to herself that, for once
at least, her possession was as complete as that of either of the
others whom it had filled only with bitterness. And a thousand times yes—her choice should know no scruple: the thing
she should go down to take would be up to the height of her
privilege. The whole place was in her eyes, and she spent for
weeks her private hours in a luxury of comparison and debate.
It should be one of the smallest things because it should be
one she could have close to her; and it should be one of the
finest because it was in the finest he saw his symbol. She said
to herself that of what it would symbolise she was content to
know nothing more than just what her having it would tell
her. At bottom she inclined to the Maltese cross—with the
added reason that he had named it. But she would look again
and judge afresh; she would on the spot so handle and ponder that there shouldn't be the shade of a mistake.

Before Christmas she had a natural opportunity to go to
London: there was her periodical call upon her father to pay
as well as a promise to Maggie to redeem. She spent her first
night in West Kensington, with the idea of carrying out on
the morrow the purpose that had most of a motive. Her father's affection was not inquisitive, but when she mentioned
to him that she had business in the country that would oblige
her to catch an early train he deprecated her excursion in view
of the menace of the weather. It was spoiling for a storm: all
the signs of a winter gale were in the air. She replied that she

would see what the morning might bring; and it brought in fact what seemed in London an amendment. She was to go to Maggie the next day, and now that she started her eagerness had become suddenly a pain. She pictured her return that evening with her trophy under her cloak; so that after looking, from the doorstep, up and down the dark street, she decided with a new nervousness and sallied forth to the nearest place of access to the "Underground." The December dawn was dolorous, but there was neither rain nor snow; it was not even cold, and the atmosphere of West Kensington, purified by the wind, was like a dirty old coat that had been bettered by a dirty brush. At the end of almost an hour, in the larger station, she had taken her place in a third-class compartment; the prospect before her was the run of eighty minutes to Poynton. The train was a fast one, and she was familiar with the moderate measure of the walk to the park from the spot at which it would drop her.

Once in the country indeed she saw that her father was right: the breath of December was abroad with a force from which the London labyrinth had protected her. The green fields were black, the sky was all alive with the wind; she had, in her anxious sense of the elements, her wonder at what might happen, a reminder of the surmises, in the old days of going to the Continent, that used to worry her on the way, at night, to the horrid cheap crossings by long sea. Something, in a dire degree, at this last hour, had begun to press on her heart: it was the sudden imagination of a disaster, or at least of a check, before her errand was achieved. When she said to herself that something might happen she wanted to go faster than the train. But nothing could happen save a dismayed discovery that, by some altogether unlikely chance, the master and mistress of the house had already come back. In that case she must have had a warning, and the fear was but the excess of her hope. It was every one's being exactly where every one was that lent the quality to her visit. Beyond lands and seas and alienated forever, they in their different ways gave her the impression to take as she had never taken it. At last it was already there, though the darkness of the day had deepened; they had whizzed past Chater—Chater which was the station before the right one. Off in that quarter was an air of wild rain, but there shimmered straight across it a brightness that was the colour of the great interior she had been haunting. That vision settled before her—in the house the house was all; and as the train drew up she rose, in her mean compartment, quite proudly erect with the thought that all for Fleda Vetch then the house was standing there.

But with the opening of the door she encountered a shock, though for an instant she couldn't have named it: the next moment she saw it was given her by the face of the man advancing to let her out, an old lame porter of the station who had been there in Mrs. Gereth's time and who now recognised her. He looked up at her so hard that she took an alarm and before alighting broke out to him: "They've come back?" She had a confused, absurd sense that even he would know that in this case she mustn't be there. He hesitated, and in a few seconds her alarm had completely changed its ground: it seemed to leap, with her quick jump from the carriage, to the ground that was that of his stare at her. "Smoke?" She was on the platform with her frightened sniff; it had taken her a minute to become aware of an extraordinary smell. The air was full of it, and there were already heads at the windows of the train, looking out at something she couldn't see. Some one, the only other passenger, had got out of another carriage, and the old porter hobbled off to close his door. The smoke was in her eyes, but she saw the station-master, from the end of the platform, identify her too and come straight at her. He brought her a finer shade of surprise than the porter, and while he was coming she heard a voice at a window of the train say that something was "a good bit off—a mile from the town." That was just what Poynton was. Then her heart stood still at the white wonder in the station-master's face.

"You've come down to it, miss, already?"

At this she knew. "Poynton's on fire?"

"Gone, miss—with this awful gale. You weren't wired? Look out!" he cried in the next breath, seizing her; the train was going on, and she had given a lurch that almost made it catch her as it passed. When it had drawn away she became more conscious of the pervading smoke, which the wind seemed to hurl in her face.

"*Gone?*" She was in the man's hands; she clung to him.

"Burning still, miss. Ain't it quite too dreadful? Took early this morning—the whole place is up there."

In her bewildered horror she tried to think. "Have they come back?"

"Back? They'll be there all day!"

"Not Mr. Gereth, I mean—nor his wife?"

"Nor his mother, miss—not a soul of *them* back. A pack o' servants in charge—not the old lady's lot, eh? A nice job for care-takers! Some rotten chimley or one of them portable lamps set down in the wrong place. What has done it is this cruel, cruel night." Then as a great wave of smoke half-choked them, he drew her with force to the little waiting-room. "Awkward for you, miss—I see!"

She felt sick; she sank upon a seat, staring up at him. "Do you mean that great house is *lost?*"

"It was near it, I was told, an hour ago—the fury of the flames had got such a start. I was there myself at six, the very first I heard of it. They were fighting it then, but you couldn't quite say they had got it down."

Fleda jerked herself up. "Were they saving the things?"

"That's just where it was, miss—to get *at* the blessed things. And the want of right help—it maddened me to stand and see 'em muff it. This ain't a place, like, for anything or-ganised. They don't come up to a *reel* emergency."

She passed out of the door that opened toward the village, and met a great acrid gust. She heard a far-off windy roar which, in her dismay, she took for that of flames a mile away, and which, the first instant, acted upon her as a wild solicita-tion. "I must go there." She had scarcely spoken before the same omen had changed into an appalling check.

Her vivid friend moreover had got before her; he clearly suffered from the nature of the control he had to exercise. "Don't do that, miss—you won't care for it at all." Then as she waveringly stood her ground: "It's not a place for a young lady, nor, if you'll believe me, a sight for them as are in any way affected."

Fleda by this time knew in what way she was affected: she became limp and weak again; she felt herself give everything up. Mixed with the horror, with the kindness of the station-master, with the smell of cinders and the riot of sound was the raw bitterness of a hope that she might never again in life have to give up so much at such short notice. She heard herself repeat mechanically, yet as if asking it for the first time: "Poynton's *gone*?"

The man hesitated. "What can you call it, miss, if it ain't really saved?"

A minute later she had returned with him to the waiting-room, where, in the thick swim of things, she saw something like the disc of a clock. "Is there an up-train?" she asked.

"In seven minutes."

She came out on the platform: everywhere she met the smoke. She covered her face with her hands. "I'll go back."

WHAT MAISIE KNEW

WHAT MAISIE KNEW

T HE LITIGATION had seemed interminable and had in fact
been complicated; but by the decision on the appeal the
judgment of the divorce-court was confirmed as to the assign-
ment of the child. The father, who, though bespattered from
head to foot, had made good his case, was, in pursuance of this
triumph, appointed to keep her: it was not so much that the
mother's character had been more absolutely damaged as that
the brilliancy of a lady's complexion (and this lady's, in court,
was immensely remarked) might be more regarded as showing
the spots. Attached, however, to the second pronouncement
was a condition that detracted, for Beale Farange, from its
sweetness—an order that he should refund to his late wife the
twenty-six hundred pounds put down by her, as it was called,
some three years before, in the interest of the child's maintenance and precisely on a proved understanding that he would
take no proceedings: a sum of which he had had the adminis-
tration and of which he could render not the least account.
The obligation thus attributed to her adversary was no small
balm to Ida's resentment; it drew a part of the sting from her
defeat and compelled Mr. Farange perceptibly to lower his
crest. He was unable to produce the money or to raise it in any
way; so that after a squabble scarcely less public and scarcely
more decent than the original shock of battle his only issue
from his predicament was a compromise proposed by his legal
advisers and finally accepted by hers.

His debt was by this arrangement remitted to him and the
little girl disposed of in a manner worthy of the judgment-
seat of Solomon. She was divided in two and the portions
tossed impartially to the disputants. They would take her, in
rotation, for six months at a time; she would spend half the
year with each. This was odd justice in the eyes of those who
still blinked in the fierce light projected from the tribunal—a
light in which neither parent figured in the least as a happy
example to youth and innocence. What was to have been expected on the evidence was the nomination, *in loco parentis*,
of some proper third person, some respectable or at least
some presentable friend. Apparently, however, the circle of

the Faranges had been scanned in vain for any such ornament; so that the only solution finally meeting all the difficulties was, save that of sending Maisie to a Home, the partition of the tutelary office in the manner I have mentioned. There were more reasons for her parents to agree to it than there had ever been for them to agree to anything; and they now prepared with her help to enjoy the distinction that waits upon vulgarity sufficiently attested. Their rupture had resounded, and after being perfectly insignificant together they would be decidedly striking apart. Had they not produced an impression that warranted people in looking for appeals in the newspapers for the rescue of the little one—reverberation, amid a vociferous public, of the idea that some movement should be started or some benevolent person should come forward? A good lady came indeed a step or two: she was distantly related to Mrs. Farange, to whom she proposed that, having children and nurseries wound up and going, she should be allowed to take home the bone of contention and, by working it into her system, relieve at least one of the parents. This would make every time, for Maisie, after her inevitable six months with Beale, much more of a change.

"More of a change?" Ida cried. "Won't it be enough of a change for her to come from that low brute to the person in the world who detests him most?"

"No, because you detest him so much that you'll always talk to her about him. You'll keep him before her by perpetually abusing him."

Mrs. Farange stared. "Pray, then, am I to do nothing to counteract his villainous abuse of *me*?"

The good lady, for a moment, made no reply: her silence was a grim judgment of the whole point of view. "Poor little monkey!" she at last exclaimed; and the words were an epitaph for the tomb of Maisie's childhood. She was abandoned to her fate. What was clear to any spectator was that the only link binding her to either parent was this lamentable fact of her being a ready vessel for bitterness, a deep little porcelain cup in which biting acids could be mixed. They had wanted her not for any good they could do her, but for the harm they could, with her unconscious aid, do each other. She should serve their anger and seal their revenge, for husband and wife had been alike crippled by the heavy hand of justice, which, in the last resort, met on neither side their indignant claim to get, as they called it, everything. If each was only to get half, this seemed to concede that neither was so base as the other pretended, or, to put it differently, offered them as both bad indeed, since they were only as good as each other. The mother had wished to prevent the father from, as she said, "so much as looking" at the child; the father's plea was that the mother's lightest touch was "simply contamination." These were the opposed principles in which Maisie was to be educated—she was to fit them together as she might. Nothing could have been more touching at first than her failure to suspect the ordeal that awaited her little unspotted soul. There were persons horrified to think what those who had charge of it would combine to try to make of it: no one could conceive in advance that they would be able to make nothing ill.

This was a society in which, for the most part, people were occupied only with chatter, but the disunited couple had at last grounds for expecting a period of high activity. They girded their loins; they felt as if the quarrel had only begun. They felt indeed more married than ever, inasmuch as what marriage had mainly suggested to them was the high opportunity to quarrel. There had been "sides" before, and there were sides as much as ever; for the sider too the prospect opened out, taking the pleasant form of a superabundance of matter for desultory conversation. The many friends of the Faranges drew together to differ about them; contradiction grew young again over teacups and cigars. Everybody was always assuring everybody of something very shocking, and nobody would have been jolly if nobody had been outrageous. The pair appeared to have a social attraction which failed merely as regards each other: it was indeed a great deal to be able to say for Ida that no one but Beale desired her blood, and for Beale that if he should ever have his eyes scratched out it would be only by his wife. It was generally felt, to begin with, that they were awfully good-looking—they had really not been analysed to a deeper residuum. They made up together, for instance, some twelve feet of stature, and nothing was more discussed than the apportionment of this quantity. The sole flaw in Ida's beauty was a length and reach of arm conducive perhaps to her having so often beaten her ex-husband at billiards, a game in which she showed a superiority largely accountable, as she maintained, for the resentment finding expression in his physical violence. Billiards were her great accomplishment and the distinction her name always first produced the mention of. Notwithstanding some very long lines everything about her that might have been large and that in many women profited by the licence was, with a single exception, admired and cited for its smallness. The exception was her eyes, which might have been of mere regulation size, but which overstepped the modesty of nature; her mouth, on the other hand, was barely perceptible, and odds were freely taken as to the measurement of her waist. She was a person who, when she was out—and she was always out—produced everywhere a sense of having been seen often, the sense indeed of a kind of abuse of visibility, so that it would have been, in the usual places, rather vulgar to wonder at her. Strangers only did that; but they, to the amusement of the familiar, did it very much: it was an inevitable way of betraying an alien habit. Like her husband, she carried clothes, carried them as a train carries passengers: people had been known to compare their taste and dispute about the accommodation they gave these articles, though inclining on the whole to the commendation of Ida as less overcrowded, especially with jewellery and flowers. Beale Farange had natural decorations, a kind of costume in his vast fair beard, burnished like a gold breastplate, and in the eternal glitter of the teeth that his long moustache had been trained not to hide and that gave him, in every possible situation, the look of the joy of life. He had been destined in his youth for diplomacy and momentarily attached, without a salary, to a legation which enabled him often to say "In *my* time, in the East": but contemporary history had somehow had no use for him, had hurried past him and left him in perpetual Piccadilly. Every one knew what he had—only twenty-five hundred. Poor Ida, who had run through everything, had now nothing but her carriage and her paralysed uncle. This old brute, as he was called, was supposed to have a lot put away. The child was provided for, thanks to a crafty godmother, a defunct aunt of Beale's, who had left her something in such a manner that the parents could appropriate only the income.

I

THE CHILD was provided for, but the new arrangement was inevitably confounding to a young intelligence, intensely aware that something had happened which must matter a good deal and looking anxiously out for the effects of so great a cause. It was to be the fate of this patient little girl to see much more than, at first, she understood, but also, even at first, to understand much more than any little girl, however patient, had perhaps ever understood before. Only a drummer-boy in a ballad or a story could have been so in the thick of the fight. She was taken into the confidence of passions on which she fixed just the stare she might have had for images bounding across the wall in the slide of a magic-lantern. Her little world was phantasmagoric—strange shadows dancing on a sheet. It was as if the whole performance had been given for her—a mite of a half-scared infant in a great dim theatre. She was in short introduced to life with a liberality in which the selfishness of others found its account, and there was nothing to avert the sacrifice but the modesty of her youth.

Her first term was with her father, who spared her only in not letting her have the wild letters addressed to her by her mother: he confined himself to holding them up at her and shaking them, while he showed his teeth, and then amusing her by the way he chucked them, across the room, bang into the fire. Even at that moment, however, she had a scared anticipation of fatigue, a guilty sense of not rising to the occasion, feeling the charm of the violence with which the stiff unopened envelopes, whose big monograms—Ida bristled with monograms—she would have liked to see, were made to whizz, like dangerous missiles, through the air. The greatest effect of the great cause was her own greater importance, chiefly revealed to her in the larger freedom with which she was handled, pulled hither and thither and kissed, and the proportionately greater niceness she was obliged to show. Her features had somehow become prominent; they were so perpetually nipped by the gentlemen who came to see her father and the smoke of whose cigarettes went into her face. Some

of these gentlemen made her strike matches and light their
cigarettes; others, holding her on knees violently jolted,
pinched the calves of her legs until she shrieked—her shriek
was much admired—and reproached them with being toothpicks. The word stuck in her mind and contributed to her
feeling from this time that she was deficient in something that
would meet the general desire. She found out what it was: it
was a congenital tendency to the production of a substance to
which Moddle, her nurse, gave a short, ugly name, a name
painfully associated with the part of the joint, at dinner, that
she didn't like. She had left behind her the time when she had
no desires to meet, none at least save Moddle's, who, in
Kensington Gardens, was always on the bench when she came
back to see if she had been playing too far. Moddle's desire
was merely that she shouldn't do that, and she met it so easily that the only spots in that long brightness were the moments of her wondering what would become of her if, on her
rushing back, there should be no Moddle on the bench. They
still went to the Gardens, but there was a difference even
there; she was impelled perpetually to look at the legs of other
children and ask her nurse if *they* were toothpicks. Moddle
was terribly truthful; she always said: "Oh, my dear, you'll not
find such another pair as your own." It seemed to have to do
with something else that Moddle often said: "You feel the
strain—that's where it is; and you'll feel it still worse, you
know."

Thus, from the first, Maisie not only felt it, but knew that
she felt it. A part of it was the consequence of her father's
telling her that he felt it too, and telling Moddle, in her presence, that she must make a point of driving that home. She
was familiar, at the age of six, with the fact that everything
had been changed on her account, everything ordered to enable him to give himself up to her. She was to remember always the words in which Moddle impressed upon her that he
did so give himself: "Your papa wishes you never to forget,
you know, that he has been dreadfully put about." If the skin
on Moddle's face had to Maisie the air of being unduly, almost painfully, stretched, it never presented that appearance
so much as when she uttered, as she often had occasion to utter, such words. The child wondered if they didn't make it

hurt more than usual; but it was only after some time that she was able to attach to the picture of her father's sufferings, and more particularly to her nurse's manner about them, the meaning for which these things had waited. By the time she had grown sharper, as the gentlemen who had criticised her calves used to say, she found in her mind a collection of images and echoes to which meanings were attachable—images and echoes kept for her in the childish dusk, the dim closet, the high drawers, like games she wasn't yet big enough to play. The great strain meanwhile was that of carrying by the right end the things her father said about her mother—things mostly indeed that Moddle, on a glimpse of them, as if they had been complicated toys or difficult books, took out of her hands and put away in the closet. It was a wonderful assortment of objects of this kind that she discovered there later, all tumbled up too with the things, shuffled into the same receptacle, that her mother had said about her father.

She had the knowledge that, on a certain occasion which every day brought nearer, her mother would be at the door to take her away, and this would have darkened all the days if the ingenious Moddle had not written on a paper, in very big, easy words, ever so many pleasures that she would enjoy at the other house. These promises ranged from "a mother's fond love" to "a nice poached egg to your tea," and took by the way the prospect of sitting up ever so late to see the lady in question dressed, in silks and velvets and diamonds and pearls, to go out: so that it was a real support to Maisie, at the supreme hour, to feel that, by Moddle's direction, the paper was thrust away in her pocket and there clenched in her fist. The supreme hour was to furnish her with a vivid reminiscence, that of a strange outbreak in the drawing-room on the part of Moddle, who, in reply to something her father had just said, cried aloud: "You ought to be perfectly ashamed of yourself—you ought to blush, sir, for the way you go on!" The carriage, with her mother in it, was at the door; a gentleman who was there, who was always there, laughed out very loud; her father, who had her in his arms, said to Moddle: "My dear woman, I'll settle *you* presently!"—after which he repeated, showing his teeth more than ever at Maisie while he hugged her, the words for which her nurse had taken him up. Maisie was not at the moment so fully conscious of them as of the wonder of Moddle's sudden disrespect and crimson face; but she was able to produce them in the course of five minutes when, in the carriage, her mother, all kisses, ribbons, eyes, arms, strange sounds and sweet smells, said to her: "And did your beastly papa, my precious angel, send any message to your own loving mamma?" Then it was that she found the words spoken by her beastly papa to be, after all, in her little bewildered ears, from which, at her mother's appeal, they passed, in her clear, shrill voice, straight to her little innocent lips. "He said I was to tell you, from him," she faithfully reported, "that you're a nasty, horrid pig!"

II

I N THAT lively sense of the immediate which is the very air of a child's mind the past, on each occasion, became for her as indistinct as the future: she surrendered herself to the actual with a good faith that might have been touching to either parent. Crudely as they had calculated, they were at first justified by the event: she was the little feathered shuttlecock that they fiercely kept flying between them. The evil they had the gift of thinking, or pretending to think, of each other, they poured into her little gravely gazing soul as into a boundless receptacle; and each of them had, doubtless, the best conscience in the world as to the duty of teaching her the stern truth that should be her safeguard against the other. She was at the age for which all stories are true and all conceptions are stories. The actual was the absolute; the present alone was vivid. The objurgation, for instance, launched in the carriage by her mother after she had, at her father's bidding, punctually performed, was a missive that dropped into her memory with the dry rattle of a letter falling into a pillar-box. Like the letter it was, as part of the contents of a well-stuffed post-bag, delivered in due course at the right address. In the presence of these overflowings, after they had continued for a couple of years, the associates of either party sometimes felt that something should be done for what they called "the real good, don't you know?" of the child. The only thing done, however, in general, took place when it was sighingly remarked that she fortunately wasn't all the year round where she happened to be at the awkward moment, and that, furthermore, either from extreme cunning or from extreme stupidity, she appeared not to take things in.

The theory of her stupidity, eventually embraced by her parents, corresponded with a great date in her small, still life: the complete vision, private but final, of the strange office she filled. It was literally a moral revolution, and it was accomplished in the depths of her nature. The stiff dolls on the dusky shelves began to move their arms and legs: old forms and phrases began to have a sense that frightened her. She had a new feeling, the feeling of danger; on which a new remedy rose to meet it, the idea of an inner self, or, in other words, of concealment. She puzzled out with imperfect signs, but with a prodigious spirit, that she had been a centre of hatred and a messenger of insult, and that everything was bad because she had been employed to make it so. Her parted lips locked themselves with the determination to be employed no longer. She would forget everything, she would repeat nothing, and when, as a tribute to the successful application of her system, she began to be called a little idiot, she tasted a pleasure altogether new. When therefore, as she grew older, her parents in turn, in her presence, announced that she had grown shockingly dull, it was not from any real contraction of her little stream of life. She spoiled their fun, but she practically added to her own. She saw more and more; she saw too much. It was Miss Overmore, her first governess, who, on a momentous occasion, had sown the seeds of secrecy; sown them not by anything she said, but by a mere roll of those fine eyes which Maisie already admired. Moddle had become at this time, after alterations of residence of which the child had no clear record, an image faintly embalmed in the remembrance of hungry disappearances from the nursery and distressful lapses in the alphabet, sad embarrassments, in particular, when invited to recognise something that her nurse called "the important letter haitch." Miss Overmore, however hungry, never disappeared: this marked her somehow as a being more exalted, and the character was confirmed by a prettiness that Maisie supposed to be extraordinary. Mrs. Farange had said that she was almost too pretty, and some one had asked what that mattered so long as Beale wasn't there. "Beale or no Beale," Maisie had heard her mother reply, "I take her because she's a lady and yet awfully poor. Rather nice people, but there are seven sisters at home. What do people mean?"

Maisie didn't know what people meant, but she knew very soon all the names of all the sisters; she could say them off better than she could say the multiplication-table. She privately wondered moreover, though she never asked, about the awful poverty, of which her companion also never spoke. Food, at any rate, came up by mysterious laws; Miss Overmore never, like Moddle, had on an apron, and when she ate she held her fork with her little finger curled out. The child, who watched her at many moments, watched her particularly at that one. "I think you're lovely," she often said to her; even mamma, who was lovely too, had not such a pretty way with the fork. Maisie associated this showier presence with her now being "big," knowing of course that nursery-governesses were only for little girls who were not, as she said, "really" little. She vaguely knew, further, somehow, that the future was still bigger than she, and that a part of what made it so was the number of governesses lurking in it and ready to dart out. Everything that had happened when she was really little was dormant, everything but the positive certitude, bequeathed from afar by Moddle, that the natural way for a child to have her parents was separate and successive, like her mutton and her pudding or her bath and her nap.

"*Does* he know that he lies?"—that was what she had vivaciously asked Miss Overmore on the occasion which was so suddenly to lead to a change in her life.

"Does he know——?" Miss Overmore stared; she had a stocking pulled over her hand and was pricking at it with a needle which she poised in the act. Her task was homely, but her movement, like all her movements, graceful.

"Why, papa."

"That he 'lies'?"

"That's what mamma says I'm to tell him—'that he lies and he knows he lies.'" Miss Overmore turned very red, though she laughed out till her head fell back; then she pricked again at her muffled hand so hard that Maisie wondered how she could bear it. "*Am* I to tell him?" the child went on. It was then that her companion addressed her in the unmistakable language of a pair of eyes of deep dark-grey. "I can't say No," they replied as distinctly as possible; "I can't say No, because I'm afraid of your mamma, don't you see? Yet how can I say Yes after your papa has been so kind to me, talking to me so long the other day, smiling and flashing his beautiful teeth at me the time we met him in the Park, the time when, rejoicing at the sight of us, he left the gentleman he was with and turned and walked with us, stayed with us for half an hour?" Somehow, in the light of Miss Overmore's lovely eyes, that

incident came back to Maisie with a charm it hadn't had at
the time, and this in spite of the fact that after it was over her
governess had never but once alluded to it. On their way
home, when papa had quitted them, she had expressed the
hope that the child wouldn't mention it to mamma. Maisie
liked her so, and had so the charmed sense of being liked by
her, that she accepted this remark as settling the matter and
wonderingly conformed to it. The wonder now lived again,
lived in the recollection of what papa had said to Miss Overmore: "I've only to look at you to see that you're a person to
whom I can appeal to help me to save my daughter." Maisie's
ignorance of what she was to be saved from didn't diminish
the pleasure of the thought that Miss Overmore was saving
her. It seemed to make them cling together.

III

S HE WAS therefore all the more startled when her mother
said to her in connection with something to be done before her next migration: "You understand, of course, that
she's not going with you."

Maisie turned quite faint. "Oh, I thought she was."

"It doesn't in the least matter, you know, what you think,"
Mrs. Farange loudly replied; "and you had better indeed for
the future, miss, learn to keep your thoughts to yourself."
This was exactly what Maisie had already learned, and the accomplishment was just the source of her mother's irritation.
It was of a horrid little critical system, a tendency, in her silence, to judge her elders, that this lady suspected her, liking
as she did, for her own part, a child to be simple and confiding. She liked also to hear the report of the whacks she administered to Mr. Farange's character, to his pretensions to
peace of mind: the satisfaction of dealing them diminished
when nothing came back. The day was at hand, and she felt
it, when she should feel more delight in hurling Maisie at him
than in snatching her away; so much so that her conscience
winced under the acuteness of a candid friend who had
remarked that the real end of all their tugging would be
that each parent would try to make the little girl a burden to
the other—a sort of game in which a fond mother clearly
wouldn't show to advantage. The prospect of not showing to
advantage, a distinction in which she held that she had never
failed, begot in Ida Farange an ill-humour of which several
persons felt the effect. She determined that Beale, at any rate,
should feel it; she reflected afresh that in the study of how to
be odious to him she must never give way. Nothing could incommode him more than not to get the good, for the child,
of a nice female appendage who had clearly taken a fancy to
her. One of the things Ida said to the appendage was that
Beale's was a house in which no decent woman could consent
to be seen. It was Miss Overmore herself who explained to
Maisie that she had had a hope of being allowed to accompany her to her father's, and that this hope had been dashed

by the way her mother took it. "She says that if I ever do such
a thing as enter his service, I must never, in this house, expect
to show my face again. So I've promised not to attempt to go
with you. If I wait patiently till you come back here we shall
certainly be together once more."

Waiting patiently, and above all waiting till she should come
back there, seemed to Maisie a long way round—it reminded
her of all the things she had been told, first and last, that she
should have if she would be good, and that, in spite of her
goodness, she had never had at all. "Then who will take care
of me at papa's?"

"Heaven only knows, my own precious!" Miss Overmore
replied, tenderly embracing her. There was indeed no doubt
that she was dear to this beautiful friend. What could have
proved it better than the fact that before a week was out, in
spite of their distressing separation, and her mother's prohibition, and Miss Overmore's scruples and Miss Overmore's
promise, the beautiful friend had turned up at her father's?
The little lady already engaged there to come by the hour, a
fat, dark little lady, with a foreign name and dirty fingers, who
wore, throughout, a bonnet that had at first given her a de-
ceptive air of not staying long, besides asking her pupil questions that had nothing to do with lessons, questions that
Beale Farange himself, when two or three were repeated to
him, admitted to be awfully vulgar—this strange apparition
faded before the bright creature who had braved everything
for Maisie's sake. The bright creature told her little charge
frankly what had happened—that she had really been unable
to hold out. She had broken her vow to Mrs. Farange; she
had struggled for three days, then she had come straight to
Maisie's papa and told him the simple truth. She adored his
daughter; she couldn't give her up; she would make any sacrifice for her. On this basis it had been arranged that she
should stay; her courage had been rewarded; she left Maisie in
no doubt as to the amount of courage she had required.
Some of the things she said made a particular impression on
the child—her declaration, for instance, that when her pupil
should get older she would understand better just how
"dreadfully bold" a young lady, to do exactly what she had
done, had to be.

"Fortunately your papa appreciates it; he appreciates it *immensely*"—that was one of the things Miss Overmore also said, with a striking insistence on the adverb. Maisie herself was no less impressed with what her friend had gone through, especially after hearing of the terrible letter that had come from Mrs. Farange. Mamma had been so angry that, in Miss Overmore's own words, she had loaded her with insult—proof enough indeed that they must never look forward to being together again under mamma's roof. Mamma's roof, however, had its turn, this time, for the child, of appearing but remotely contingent, so that, to reassure her, there was scarce a need of her companion's secret, solemnly confided—the idea that there should be no going back to mamma at all. It was Miss Overmore's private conviction, and a part of the same communication, that if Mr. Farange's daughter would only show a really marked preference she would be backed up by "public opinion" in holding on to him. Poor Maisie could scarcely grasp that incentive, but she could surrender herself to the day. She had conceived her first passion, and the object of it was her governess. It had not been put to her, and she couldn't, or at any rate she didn't, put it to herself, that she liked Miss Overmore better than she liked papa; but it would have sustained her under such an imputation to feel herself able to reply that papa too liked Miss Overmore exactly as much. He had particularly told her so. Besides, she could easily see it.

IV

A LL THIS led her on, but it brought on her fate as well, the day when her mother would be at the door in the carriage in which Maisie now rode on no occasions but these. There was no question, at present, of Miss Overmore's going back with her: it was universally recognised that her quarrel with Mrs. Farange was much too acute. The child felt it from the first; there was no hugging nor exclaiming as that lady drove her away—there was only a frightening silence, unenlivened even by the invidious inquiries of former years, which culminated, according to its stern nature, in a still more frightening old woman, a figure awaiting her on the very doorstep. "You're to be under this lady's care," said her mother. "Take her, Mrs. Wix," she added, addressing the figure impatiently and giving the child a push in which Maisie felt that she wished to set Mrs. Wix an example of energy. Mrs. Wix took her, and Maisie felt, the next day, that she would never let her go. She had struck her at first, just after Miss Overmore, as terrible; but something in her voice at the end of an hour touched the little girl in a spot that had never even yet been reached. Maisie knew later what it was, though doubtless she couldn't have made a statement of it: these were things that a few days' conversation with Mrs. Wix lighted up. The principal one was a matter that Mrs. Wix herself always immediately mentioned: she had had a little girl quite of her own, and the little girl had been killed on the spot. She had had absolutely nothing else in all the world, and her affliction had broken her heart. It was comfortably established between them that Mrs. Wix's heart was broken. What Maisie felt was that she had been, with passion and anguish, a mother, and that this was something Miss Overmore was not, something, strangely, confusingly, that mamma was even less.

So it was that in the course of an extraordinarily short time she found herself as deeply absorbed in the image of the little dead Clara Matilda, who, on a crossing in the Harrow Road, had been knocked down and crushed by the cruellest of hansoms, than she had ever found herself in the family group made vivid by one of seven. "She's your little dead sister," Mrs. Wix ended by saying, and Maisie, all in a tremor of curiosity and compassion, addressed from that moment a particular piety to the small infectious sentiment. Somehow she wasn't a real sister, but that only made her the more romantic. It contributed to this view of her that she was never to be spoken of in that character to any one else—least of all to Mrs. Farange, who wouldn't care for her nor recognise the relationship: it was to be just an unutterable and inexhaustible little secret with Mrs. Wix. Maisie knew everything about her that could be known, everything she had said or done in her little mutilated life, exactly how lovely she was, exactly how her hair was curled and her frocks were trimmed. Her hair came down far below her waist—it was of the most wonderful golden brightness, just as Mrs. Wix's own had been a long time before. Mrs. Wix's own was indeed very remarkable still, and Maisie had felt at first that she should never get on with it. It played a large part in the sad and strange appearance, the appearance as of a kind of greasy greyness, which Mrs. Wix had presented on the child's arrival. It had originally been yellow, but time had turned its glow to ashes, to a turbid, sallow, unvenerable white. Still excessively abundant, it was dressed in a manner of which the poor lady appeared not yet to have recognised the supersession, with a glossy braid, like a large diadem, on the top of the head, and behind, at the nape of the neck, a dingy rosette like a large button. She wore glasses which, in humble reference to a divergent obliquity of vision, she called her straighteners, and a little ugly snuff-coloured dress trimmed with satin bands in the form of scallops and glazed with antiquity. The straighteners, she explained to Maisie, were put on for the sake of others, whom, as she believed, they helped to recognise the direction, otherwise misleading, of her glance; the rest of the melancholy attire could only have been put on for herself. With the added suggestion of her goggles it reminded her pupil of the polished shell or corslet of a horrid beetle. At first she had looked cross and almost cruel; but this impression passed away with the child's increased perception of her being in the eyes of the world a figure mainly for laughter. She was passively comical—a person whom people, to make talk lively, described to each other

V

THE SECOND parting from Miss Overmore had been bad enough, but this first parting from Mrs. Wix was much worse. The child had lately been to the dentist's and had a term of comparison for the screwed-up intensity of the scene. It was dreadfully silent, as it had been when her tooth was taken out; Mrs. Wix had on that occasion grabbed her hand and they had clung to each other with the frenzy of their determination not to scream. Maisie, at the dentist's, had been heroically still, but just when she felt most anguish had become aware, on the part of her companion, of an audible shriek, a spasm of stifled sympathy. This was reproduced by the only sound that broke their supreme embrace when, a month later, the "arrangement," as her periodical uprootings were called, played the part of the horrible forceps. Embedded in Mrs. Wix's nature as her tooth had been socketed in her gum, the operation of extracting her would really have been a case for chloroform. It was a hug that fortunately left nothing to say, for the poor woman's want of words at such an hour seemed to fall in with her want of everything. Maisie's alternate parent, in the outermost vestibule—he liked the impertinence of crossing as much as that of his late wife's threshold—stood over them with his open watch and his still more open grin, while from the only corner of an eye on which something of Mrs. Wix's didn't impinge the child saw at the door a brougham in which Miss Overmore also waited. She remembered the difference when, six months before, she had been torn from the breast of that more spirited protectress. Miss Overmore, then also in the vestibule, but of course in the other one, had been thoroughly audible and voluble; her protest had rung out bravely and she had declared that something—her pupil didn't know exactly what—was a regular wicked shame. That had at the time dimly recalled to Maisie the far-away moment of Moddle's great outbreak: there seemed always to be "shames" connected in one way or another with her migrations. At present, while Mrs. Wix's arms tightened and the smell of her hair was strong, she fur-

ther remembered how, in pacifying Miss Overmore, papa had
made use of the words "you dear old duck!"—an expression
which, by its oddity, had stuck fast in her young mind, having
moreover a place well prepared for it there by what she knew
of the governess whom she now always mentally characterised
as the pretty one. She wondered whether this affection would
be as great as before: that would at all events be the case with
the prettiness Maisie could see in the face which showed
brightly at the window of the brougham.

The brougham was a token of harmony, of the fine conditions papa, this time, would offer: he had usually come for her
in a hansom with a four-wheeler behind for the boxes. The
four-wheeler with the boxes on it was actually there: but
mamma was the only lady with whom she had ever been in a
conveyance of the kind always of old spoken of by Moddle as
a private carriage. Papa's carriage was, now that he had one,
still more private, somehow, than mamma's; and when at last
she found herself quite on top, as she felt, of its inmates and
gloriously rolling away she put to Miss Overmore, after another immense and talkative squeeze, a question of which the
motive was a desire for information as to the continuity of a
certain sentiment. "Did papa like you just the same while I
was gone?" she inquired—full of the sense of how markedly
his favour had been established in her presence. She had
bethought herself that this favour might, like her presence,
and as if depending on it, be only intermittent and for the
season. Papa, on whose knee she sat, burst into one of those
loud laughs of his that, however prepared she was, seemed always, like some trick in a frightening game, to leap forth to
make her jump; and before Miss Overmore could speak he
replied: "Why, you little donkey, when you're away what have
I left to do but just to love her?" Miss Overmore hereupon
immediately took her from him, and they had, over her, an
hilarious little scrimmage of which Maisie caught the surprised observation in the white stare of an old lady who
passed in a victoria. Then her beautiful friend remarked to her
very gravely: "I shall make him understand that if he ever
again says anything as horrid as that to you I shall carry you
straight off and we'll go and live somewhere together and be
good, quiet little girls." The child couldn't quite make out

why her father's speech had been horrid, since it only expressed that appreciation which their companion herself, of
old, described as "immense." To enter more into the truth of
the matter she appealed to him again directly, asked if in all
those months Miss Overmore hadn't been with him just as
she had been before and just as she would be now. "Of course
she has, old girl—where else could the poor dear be?" cried
Beale Farange, to the still greater scandal of their companion,
who protested that unless he straightway "took back" his
nasty wicked fib it would be, this time, not only him she
would leave, but his child too and his house and his tiresome
troubles—all the impossible things he had succeeded in
putting on her. Beale, under this frolic menace, took nothing
back at all: he was indeed apparently on the point of repeating his assertion, but Miss Overmore instructed her little
charge that she was not to listen to his bad jokes: she was to
understand that a lady couldn't stay with a gentleman that
way without some awfully proper reason.

Maisie looked from one of her companions to the other;
this was the freshest, merriest start she had yet enjoyed, but
she had a shy fear of not exactly believing them. "Well, what
reason *is* proper?" she thoughtfully demanded.

"Oh, a long-legged stick of a tomboy: there's none so
good as that." Her father enjoyed both her drollery and his
own and tried again to get possession of her—an effort deprecated by their comrade and leading again to something of a
public scuffle. Miss Overmore declared to the child that she
had been all the while with good friends; on which Beale
Farange went on: "She means good friends of mine, you
know—tremendous friends of mine. There has been no end
of *them* about—that I *will* say for her!" The child felt bewildered and was afterwards for some time conscious of a vagueness, just slightly embarrassing, as to the subject of so much
amusement and as to where her governess had really been.
She didn't feel at all as if she had been seriously told, and no
such feeling was supplied by anything that occurred later. Her
embarrassment, of a precocious, instinctive order, attached itself to the idea that this was another of the matters that it was
not for her, as her mother used to say, to go into. Therefore,
under her father's roof, during the time that followed, she

made no attempt to clear up her ambiguity by a sociable interrogation of housemaids; and it was an odd truth that the ambiguity itself took nothing from the fresh pleasure promised her by renewed contact with Miss Overmore. The confidence looked for by that young lady was of the fine sort that explanation cannot improve, and she herself at any rate was a person superior to any confusion. For Maisie moreover concealment had never necessarily seemed deception, and she had grown up among things as to which her foremost knowledge was that she was not to ask about them. It was far from new to her that the questions of the small are the peculiar diversion of the great: except the affairs of her doll Lisette there had scarcely ever been anything at her mother's that was explicable with a grave face. Nothing was so easy to her as to send the ladies who gathered there off into shrieks, and she might have practised upon them largely if she had been of a more calculating turn. Everything had something behind it: life was like a long, long corridor with rows of closed doors. She had learned that at these doors it was wise not to knock—this seemed to produce, from within, such sounds of derision. Little by little, however, she understood more, for it befell that she was enlightened by Lisette's questions, which reproduced the effect of her own upon those for whom she sat in the very darkness of Lisette. Was she not herself convulsed by such innocence? In the presence of it she often imitated the shrieking ladies. There were at any rate things she really couldn't tell even a French doll. She could only pass on her lessons and study to produce on Lisette the impression of having mysteries in her life, wondering the while whether she succeeded in the air of shading off, like her mother, into the unknowable. When the reign of Miss Overmore followed that of Mrs. Wix she took a fresh cue, emulating her governess and bridging over the interval with the simple expectation of trust. Yes, there were matters one couldn't "go into" with a pupil. There were for instance days when, after prolonged absence, Lisette, while she took off her things, tried hard to discover where she had been. Well, she discovered a little, but she never discovered all. There was an occasion when, on her being particularly indiscreet, Maisie replied to her—and precisely about the motive of a disappearance—as she, Maisie, had once been replied to by Mrs. Farange: "Find out for yourself!" She mimicked her mother's sharpness, but she was rather ashamed afterwards, though as to whether of the sharpness or the mimicry was not quite clear.

VI

S HE BECAME aware in time that this would be a period not remarkable for lessons, the care of her education being now only one of the many duties devolving on Miss Overmore; a circumstance as to which she was present at various passages between that lady and her father—passages significant, on either side, of dissent and even of displeasure. It was gathered by the child on these occasions that there was something in the situation for which her mother might "come down" on them all, though indeed the suggestion, always thrown out by her father, was greeted on his companion's part with particular derision. Such scenes were usually brought to a climax by Miss Overmore's demanding, in a harsher manner than she applied to any other subject, in what position under the sun such a person as Mrs. Farange would find herself for coming down. As the months went on the little girl's interpretations thickened, and the more effectually that this period was the longest she had yet known without a break. She became familiar with the idea that her mother, for some reason, was in no hurry to reinstate her: that idea was forcibly expressed by her father whenever Miss Overmore, differing and decided, took him up on the question, which he was always putting forward, of the urgency of sending her to school. For a governess Miss Overmore differed surprisingly; far more, for instance, than would ever have entered into the head of poor Mrs. Wix. She remarked to Maisie many times that she was quite conscious of not doing her justice, and that Mr. Farange equally measured and equally lamented this deficiency. The reason of it was that she had mysterious responsibilities that interfered—responsibilities, Miss Overmore intimated, to Mr. Farange himself and to the friendly, noisy little house and those who came there. Mr. Farange's remedy for every inconvenience was that the child should be put at school—there were such lots of splendid schools, as everybody knew, at Brighton and all over the place. That, however, Maisie learned, was just what would bring her mother down: from the moment he should delegate to others the housing of his little charge he hadn't a leg to stand on before the law. Didn't he keep her away from her mother precisely because Mrs. Farange was one of these others?

There was also the solution of a second governess, a young person to come in by the day and really do the work; but to this Miss Overmore wouldn't for a moment listen, arguing against it with great public relish and wanting to know from all comers (she put it even to Maisie herself) if they didn't see how frightfully it would give her away. "What am I supposed to be at all, don't you see, if I'm not here to look after her?" She was in a false position and so freely and loudly called attention to it that it seemed to become almost a source of glory. The way out of it of course was just to do her plain duty; but that was unfortunately what, with his excessive, his exorbitant demands on her, which every one indeed appeared quite to understand, he practically, he selfishly prevented. Beale Farange, for Miss Overmore, was now never anything but "he," and the house was as full as ever of lively gentlemen with whom, under that designation, she chaffingly talked about him. Maisie meanwhile, as a subject of familiar gossip on what was to be done with her, was left so much to herself that she had hours of wistful thought of the large loose discipline of Mrs. Wix: yet she none the less held it under her father's roof a point of superiority that none of his visitors were ladies. It added to this odd security that she had once heard a gentleman say to him as if it were a great joke and in obvious reference to Miss Overmore: "Hanged if she'll let another woman come near you—hanged if she ever will. She'd let fly a stick at her as they do at a strange cat!" Maisie greatly preferred gentlemen as inmates in spite of their also having their way—louder but sooner over—of laughing out at her. They pulled and pinched, they teased and tickled her; some of them even, as they termed it, shied things at her, and all of them thought it funny to call her by names having no resemblance to her own. The ladies, on the other hand, addressed her as "You poor pet" and scarcely touched her even to kiss her. But it was of the ladies she was most afraid.

She was old enough now to understand how disproportionate a stay she had already made with her father; and also

old enough to enter a little into the ambiguity that surrounded this circumstance and that oppressed her particularly
whenever the question had been touched upon in talk with
her governess. "Oh, you needn't worry: she doesn't care!"
Miss Overmore had often said to her in reference to any fear
that her mother might resent her prolonged detention. "She
has other people than poor little *you* to think about, and she
has gone abroad with them, and you needn't be in the least
afraid that she'll stickle this time for her rights." Maisie knew
Mrs. Farange had gone abroad, for she had had, weeks and
weeks before, a letter from her, beginning "My precious pet"
and taking leave of her for an indeterminate time; but she had
not seen in it a renunciation of hatred or of the writer's policy of asserting herself, for the sharpest of all her impressions
had been that there was nothing her mother would ever care
so much about as to torment Mr. Farange. What at last, however, in this connection was bewildering and a little frightening was the dawn of a suspicion that a better way had been
found to torment Mr. Farange than to deprive him of his periodical burden. This was the question that worried our
young lady and that Miss Overmore's confidences and the
frequent observations of her employer only rendered more
mystifying. It was a contradiction that if Ida had now a fancy
for shirking the devotion she had originally been so hot
about, her late husband shouldn't jump at the monopoly for
which he had also in the first instance so fiercely fought; but
when Maisie, with a subtlety beyond her years, sounded this
new ground her main success was in hearing her mother more
freshly abused. Miss Overmore, up to now, had rarely devi-
ated from a decent reserve, but the day came when she expressed herself with a vividness not inferior to Beale's own on
the subject of the lady who had fled to the Continent to
wriggle out of her job. It would serve this lady right, Maisie
gathered, if that contract, in the shape of an overgrown and
underdressed daughter, should be shipped straight out to her
and landed at her feet in the midst of scandalous pastimes.

The picture of these pursuits was what Miss Overmore took
refuge in when the child tried timidly to ascertain if her father
were in danger of feeling that he had too much of her. She
evaded the point and only kicked up all round it the dust of

Ida's heartlessness and folly, of which the supreme proof, it appeared, was the fact that she was accompanied on her journey by a gentleman whom, to be painfully plain about it, she had—well, "picked up." The only terms on which, unless they were married, ladies and gentlemen might, as Miss Overmore expressed it, knock about together, were the terms on which she and Mr. Farange had exposed themselves to possible misconception. She had indeed, as I have intimated, often explained this before, often said to Maisie: "I don't know what in the world, darling, your father and I should do without you, for you just make the difference, as I've told you, of keeping us perfectly proper." The child took in the office it was so endearingly presented to her that she performed a comfort that helped her to a sense of security even in the event of being abandoned by her mother. Familiar as she had become with the idea of the great alternative to the proper, she felt that her governess and her father would have a substantial reason for not emulating that detachment. At the same time she had heard somehow of little girls—of exalted rank, it was true—whose education was carried on by instructors of the other sex, and she knew that if she were at school at Brighton it would be thought an advantage to her to be more or less in the hands of masters. She meditated on these mysteries and she at last remarked to Miss Overmore that if she should go to her mother perhaps the gentleman might become her tutor.

"The gentleman?" The proposition was complicated enough to make Miss Overmore stare.

"The one who's with mamma. Mightn't that make it right—as right as your being my governess makes it for you to be with papa?"

Miss Overmore considered; she coloured a little; then she embraced her ingenious disciple. "You're too sweet! I'm a *real* governess."

"And couldn't he be a real tutor?"

"Of course not. He's ignorant and bad."

"Bad——?" Maisie echoed, with wonder.

Her companion gave a queer little laugh at her tone. "He's ever so much younger——" The speaker paused.

"Younger than you?"

Miss Overmore laughed again; it was the first time Maisie had seen her approach so nearly to a giggle. "Younger than— no matter whom. I don't know anything about him, and I don't want to," she rather inconsequently added. "He's not my sort, and I'm sure, my own darling, he's not yours." And she repeated the embrace with which her colloquies with Maisie almost always terminated and which made the child feel that *her* affection, at least, was a gage of safety. Parents had come to seem precarious, but governesses were evidently to be trusted. Maisie's faith in Mrs. Wix, for instance, had suffered no lapse from the fact that all communication with her was temporarily at an end. During the first weeks of their separation Clara Matilda's mamma had repeatedly and dolefully written to her, and Maisie had answered with an excitement qualified only by orthographical delays; but the correspondence had been duly submitted to Miss Overmore, with the final consequence of incurring a lively disapproval. It was this lady's view that Mr. Farange wouldn't care for it at all; and she ended by confessing—since her pupil pushed her—that she didn't care for it herself. She was furiously jealous, she said; and that circumstance was only a new proof of her disinterested affection. She pronounced Mrs. Wix's effusions moreover illiterate and unprofitable and made no scruple of declaring it extraordinary that a woman in her senses should have placed the formation of her daughter's mind in such ridiculous hands. Maisie was well aware that the proprietress of the old brown dress and the old, odd headgear was a very different class of person from Miss Overmore; but it was now brought home to her with pain that she was educationally quite out of the question. She was buried for the time beneath a conclusive remark of Miss Overmore's: "She's really beyond a joke!" This remark was made as that charming woman held in her hand the last letter that Maisie was to receive from Mrs. Wix; it was fortified by a decree abolishing the preposterous tie. "Must I then write and tell her?" the child bewilderingly inquired: she grew pale at the image of the dreadful things it appeared to be prescribed for her to say. "Don't dream of it, my dear—*I'll* write: you may trust me!" cried Miss Overmore; who indeed wrote to such purpose that a hush in which you could have heard a pin drop descended upon poor Mrs. Wix. She gave for weeks and weeks no sign whatever of life: it was as if she had been as effectually disposed of by Miss Overmore's communication as her little girl, in the Harrow Road, had been disposed of by the terrible hansom. Her very silence became, after this, one of the largest elements of Maisie's consciousness; it proved a warm and habitable air, into which the child penetrated further than she dared ever to mention to her companions. Somewhere in the depths of it the dim straighteners were fixed upon her; somewhere out of the troubled little current Mrs. Wix intensely waited.

VII

I T QUITE fell in with this intensity that one day, on returning from a walk with the housemaid, Maisie should have
found her in the hall, seated on the stool usually occupied by
the telegraph-boys who haunted Beale Farange's door and
kicked their heels while, in his room, answers were concocted
with the aid of smoke-puffs and growls. It had seemed to her
on their parting that Mrs. Wix had reached the last limits of
the squeeze, but she now felt those limits to be transcended
and that the duration of her visitor's hug was a direct reply to
Miss Overmore's act of abolition. She understood in a flash
how the visit had come to be possible—that Mrs. Wix, watching her chance, must have slipped in under protection of the
fact that papa, always tormented in spite of arguments with
the idea of a school, had, for a three days' excursion to
Brighton, absolutely insisted on the attendance of her adversary. It was true that when Maisie explained their absence and
their important motive Mrs. Wix wore an expression so peculiar that it could only have had its origin in surprise. This contradiction, however, peeped out only to vanish, for at the very
moment that, in the spirit of it, she threw herself afresh upon
her young friend a hansom crested with neat luggage rattled
up to the door and Miss Overmore bounded out. The shock
of her encounter with Mrs. Wix was less violent than Maisie
had feared on seeing her and didn't at all interfere with the
sociable tone in which, in the presence of her rival, she explained to her little charge that she had returned, for a particular reason, a day sooner than she first intended. She had
left papa—in such nice lodgings—at Brighton; but he would
come back to his dear little home on the morrow. As for Mrs.
Wix, papa's companion supplied Maisie in later converse with
the right word for the attitude of this personage: Mrs. Wix
"stood up" to her in a manner that the child herself felt at the
time to be astonishing. This occurred indeed after Miss Overmore had so far waived her interdict as to make a move to the
dining-room, where, in the absence of any suggestion of sitting down, it was scarcely more than natural that even poor

Mrs. Wix should stand up. Maisie immediately inquired if at Brighton, this time, anything had come of the possibility of a school; to which, much to her surprise, Miss Overmore, who had always grandly repudiated it, replied, after an instant, but quite as if Mrs. Wix were not there:

"It may be, darling, that something *will* come. The objection, I must tell you, has been quite removed."

At this it was still more startling to hear Mrs. Wix speak out with great firmness. "I don't think, if you'll allow me to say so, that there's any arrangement by which the objection *can* be 'removed.' What has brought me here to-day is that I've a message for Maisie from dear Mrs. Farange."

The child's heart gave a great thump. "Oh, mamma's come back?"

"Not yet, sweet love, but she's coming," said Mrs. Wix, "and she has—most thoughtfully, you know—sent me on to prepare you."

"To prepare her for what, pray?" asked Miss Overmore, whose original serenity began, with this news, to turn to sharpness.

Mrs. Wix quietly applied her straighteners to Miss Overmore's florid loveliness. "Well, miss, for a very important communication."

"Can't dear Mrs. Farange, as you so oddly call her, make her communications directly? Can't she take the trouble to write to her only daughter?" the younger lady demanded. "Maisie herself will tell you that it's months and months since she has had so much as a word from her."

"Oh, but I've written to mamma!" cried the child as if this would do quite as well.

"That makes her treatment of you all the greater scandal," the governess in possession promptly declared.

"Mrs. Farange is too well aware," said Mrs. Wix with sustained spirit, "of what becomes of her letters in this house."

Maisie's sense of fairness hereupon interposed for her visitor. "You know, Miss Overmore, that papa doesn't like everything of mamma's."

"No one likes, my dear, to be made the subject of such language as your mother's letters contain. They were not fit for the innocent child to see," Miss Overmore observed to Mrs. Wix.

"Then I don't know what you complain of, and she's better without them. It serves every purpose that I'm in Mrs. Farange's confidence."

Miss Overmore gave a scornful laugh. "Then you must be mixed up with some extraordinary proceedings!"

"None so extraordinary," cried Mrs. Wix, turning very pale, "as to say horrible things about the mother to the face of the helpless daughter!"

"Things not a bit more horrible, I think," Miss Overmore rejoined, "than those you, madam, appear to have come here to say about the father!"

Mrs. Wix looked for a moment hard at Maisie; then turning again to her other interlocutress she spoke with a trembling voice. "I came to say nothing about him, and you must excuse Mrs. Farange and me if we are not so irreproachable as the companion of his travels."

The young woman thus described stared an instant at the audacity of the description—she apparently needed time to take it in. Maisie, however, gazing solemnly from one of the disputants to the other, observed that her answer, when it came, perched upon smiling lips. "It will do quite as well, no doubt, if you come up to the requirements of the companion of Mrs. Farange's!"

Mrs. Wix broke into a queer laugh: it sounded to Maisie like an unsuccessful imitation of a neigh. "That's just what I'm here to make known—how perfectly the poor lady comes up to them herself." She straightened herself before the child. "You must take your mamma's message, Maisie, and you must feel that her wishing me to come to you with it this way is a great proof of interest and affection. She sends you her particular love and announces to you that she's engaged to be married to Sir Claude."

"Sir Claude?" Maisie wonderingly echoed. But while Mrs. Wix explained that this gentleman was a dear friend of Mrs. Farange's, who had been of great assistance to her in getting to Florence and in making herself comfortable there for the winter, she was not too violently shaken to perceive her old friend's enjoyment of the effect of this news on Miss Overmore. That young lady opened her eyes and flushed; she immediately remarked that Mrs. Farange's marriage would of

course put an end to any further pretension to take her
daughter back. Mrs. Wix inquired with astonishment why it
should do anything of the sort, and Miss Overmore promptly
gave as a reason that it was clearly but another dodge in a system of dodging. She wanted to get out of the bargain: why
else had she now left Maisie on her father's hands weeks and
weeks beyond the time about which she had originally made
such a fuss? It was vain for Mrs. Wix to represent—as she spe-
ciously proceeded to do—that all this time would be made up
as soon as Mrs. Farange returned: she, Miss Overmore, knew
nothing, thank heaven, about her confederate, but she was
very sure that any person capable of forming that sort of relation with the lady in Florence was a person who could easily
be put forward as objecting to the presence in his house of
the fruit of a union that his dignity must ignore. It was a
game like another, and Mrs. Wix's visit was clearly the first
move in it. Maisie found in this exchange of asperities a fresh
incitement to the unformulated fatalism in which her observation of her own career had long since taken refuge; and it
was the beginning for her of a deeper prevision that, in spite
of Miss Overmore's brilliancy and Mrs. Wix's passion, she
should live to see a change in the nature of the struggle she
appeared to have come into the world to produce. It would
still be essentially a struggle, but its object would now be *not*
to receive her.

Mrs. Wix, after Miss Overmore's last demonstration, addressed herself wholly to the little girl, and, drawing from the
pocket of her dingy old pelisse a small flat parcel, removed its
envelope and wished to know if *that* looked like a gentleman
who wouldn't be nice to everybody—let alone to a person he
would be so sure to find so nice. Mrs. Farange, in the geniality of new-found happiness, had enclosed a "cabinet" photograph of Sir Claude, and Maisie lost herself in admiration of
the fair, smooth face, the regular features, the kind eyes, the
amiable air, the general glossiness and smartness of her
prospective stepfather—only vaguely puzzled to think that
she should now have two fathers at once. Her researches had
hitherto indicated that to incur a second parent of the same
sex you had usually to lose the first. "*Isn't* he sympathetic?"
asked Mrs. Wix, who had clearly, on the strength of his

charming portrait, made up her mind that Sir Claude promised her a future. "You can see, I hope," she added, with much expression, "that *he's* a perfect gentleman!" Maisie had never before heard the word "sympathetic" applied to anybody's face; it struck her very much and from that moment it agreeably remained with her. She testified moreover to the force of her own perception in a long, soft little sigh of response to the pleasant eyes that seemed to seek her acquaintance, to speak to her directly. "He's quite lovely!" she declared to Mrs. Wix. Then eagerly, irrepressibly, as she still held the photograph and Sir Claude continued to fraternise, "Oh, can't I keep it?" she broke out. No sooner had she done so than she looked up from it at Miss Overmore: this was with the sudden instinct of appealing to the authority that had long ago impressed on her that she mustn't ask for things. Miss Overmore, to her surprise, looked distant and rather odd, hesitating and giving her time to turn again to Mrs. Wix. Then Maisie saw that lady's long face lengthen; it was stricken and almost scared, as if her young friend really expected more of her than she had to give. The photograph was a possession that, direly denuded, she clung to, and there was a momentary struggle between her fond clutch of it and her capability of every sacrifice for her precarious pupil. With the acuteness of her years, however, Maisie saw that her own avidity would triumph, and she held out the picture to Miss Overmore as if she were quite proud of her mother. "Isn't he just lovely?" she demanded while poor Mrs. Wix hungrily wavered, her straighteners largely covering it and her pelisse gathered about her with an intensity that strained its ancient seams.

"It was to *me*, darling," the visitor said, "that your mamma so generously sent it; but of course if it would give you particular pleasure——" She faltered, only gasping her surrender.

Miss Overmore continued extremely remote. "If the photograph's your property, my dear, I shall be happy to oblige you by looking at it on some future occasion. But you must excuse me if I decline to touch an object belonging to Mrs. Wix."

Mrs. Wix by this time had grown very red. "You might as well see him this way, miss," she retorted, "as you certainly never will, I believe, in any other! Keep the pretty picture, by all means, my precious," she went on: "Sir Claude will be happy himself, I daresay, to give me one with a kind inscription." The pathetic quaver of this brave little boast was not lost upon Maisie, who threw herself so gratefully upon Mrs. Wix's neck that on the termination of their embrace, the public tenderness of which, she felt, made up for the sacrifice she imposed, their companion had had time to lay a quick hand on Sir Claude and, with a glance at him or not, whisk him effectually out of sight. Released from the child's arms Mrs. Wix looked about for the picture; then she fixed Miss Overmore with a hard, dumb stare; and finally, with her eyes on the little girl again, achieved the grimmest of smiles. "Well, nothing matters, Maisie, because there's another thing your mamma wrote about. She has made sure of me." Even after her loyal hug Maisie felt a bit of a sneak as she glanced at Miss Overmore for permission to understand this. But Mrs. Wix left them in no doubt of what it meant. "She has definitely engaged me—for her return and for yours. Then you'll see for yourself." Maisie, on the spot, quite believed she should; but the prospect was suddenly thrown into confusion by an extraordinary demonstration from Miss Overmore.

"Mrs. Wix," said that young lady, "has some undiscoverable reason for regarding your mother's hold on you as strengthened by the fact that she's about to marry. I wonder then—on that system—what Mrs. Wix will say to your father's."

Miss Overmore's words were directed to her pupil, but her face, lighted with an irony that made it prettier even than ever before, was presented to the dingy figure that had stiffened itself for departure. The child's discipline had been bewildering—it had ranged freely between the prescription that she was to answer when spoken to and the experience of lively penalties on obeying that prescription. This time, nevertheless, she felt emboldened for risks; above all as something still more bewildering seemed to have leaped into her sense of the relations of things. She raised to Miss Overmore's face all the timidity of her eyes. "Do you mean papa's hold on me—do you mean *he's* about to marry?"

"Papa is not about to marry—papa *is* married, my dear. Papa was married the day before yesterday at Brighton." Miss

Overmore glittered more gaily; meanwhile it came over Maisie, and quite dazzlingly, that her pretty governess was a bride. "He's my husband, if you please, and I'm his little wife. So *now* we'll see who's your little mother!" She caught her pupil to her bosom in a manner that was not to be outdone by the emissary of her predecessor, and a few moments later, when things had lurched back into their places, that poor lady, quite defeated of the last word, had soundlessly taken flight.

VIII

AFTER Mrs. Wix's retreat Miss Overmore appeared to recognise that she was not exactly in a position to denounce Ida Farange's second union; but she drew from a table-drawer the photograph of Sir Claude and, standing there before Maisie, bent her eyes on it for some moments.

"Isn't he beautiful?" the child ingenuously asked.

Her companion hesitated. "No—he's horrid," she, to Maisie's surprise, sharply returned. But she considered another minute; after which she handed back the picture. It appeared to Maisie herself to exhibit a fresh attraction, and she was embarrassed, for she had never before had occasion to differ from her lovely friend. So she only could ask what, such being the case, she should do with it: should she put it quite away—where it wouldn't be there to offend? On this Miss Overmore again deliberated; then she said unexpectedly: "Put it on the schoolroom mantelpiece."

Maisie had apprehensions. "Won't papa dislike to see it there?"

"Very much indeed; but that won't matter *now*." Miss Overmore spoke with peculiar significance and to her pupil's mystification.

"On account of the marriage?" Maisie inquired.

Miss Overmore laughed, and Maisie could see that in spite of the irritation produced by Mrs. Wix she was in high spirits. "Which marriage do you mean?"

With the question put to her it suddenly seemed to the child that she didn't know, and she felt that she looked foolish. So she took refuge in saying: "Shall *you* be different——?" This was a full implication that the bride of Sir Claude would be.

"As your father's wedded wife? Utterly!" Miss Overmore replied. And the difference began of course in her being addressed, even by Maisie, from that day and by her particular request, as Mrs. Beale. It was there indeed principally that it ended, for except that the child could reflect that she should presently have four parents in all, and also that at the end of three months the staircase, for a little girl hanging over banisters, sent up the deepening rustle of more delicate advances, everything made the same impression as before. Mrs. Beale had very pretty frocks, but Miss Overmore's had been quite as good, and if papa was much fonder of his second wife than he had been of his first Maisie had foreseen that fondness and followed its development almost as closely as the victim of it. There was little indeed in the relations of her companions that her precocious experience couldn't explain, for if they struck her as after all rather deficient in that air of the honeymoon of which she had so often heard—in much detail, for instance, from Mrs. Wix—it was natural to judge this circumstance in the light of papa's proved disposition to contest the empire of the matrimonial tie. His honeymoon, when he came back from Brighton—not on the morrow of Mrs. Wix's visit, and not, oddly, till several days later—his honeymoon was perhaps perceptibly tinged with the dawn of a later stage of wedlock. There were things as to which, for Mrs. Beale, as the child had learnt, his dislike wouldn't matter now, and their number increased so that such a trifle as his hostility to the photograph of Sir Claude quite dropped out of view. This pleasing object found a conspicuous place in the schoolroom, which, in truth, Mr. Farange seldom entered and in which silent admiration formed, during the time I speak of, almost the sole scholastic exercise of Mrs. Beale's pupil.

Maisie was not long in seeing just what her stepmother had meant by the difference she should show as Mrs. Beale. If she was her father's wife she was not her own governess, and if her presence had had formerly to be made regular by the theory of a humble function she was now on a footing that dispensed with all theories and was inconsistent with all servitude. That was what she had meant by the removal of the obstacle to a school; her small companion was no longer required at home as—it was Mrs. Beale's own amusing word—a little duenna. The objection to a successor to Miss Overmore remained: it was composed frankly of the fact, of which Mrs. Beale granted the full absurdity, that she was too awfully fond of her stepdaughter to bring herself to see her in vulgar and mercenary hands. The note of this particular danger emboldened Maisie to put in a word for Mrs. Wix, the modest measure of whose avidity she had taken from the first; but Mrs. Beale disposed afresh and effectually of a candidate who would be sure to act in some horrible and insidious way for Ida's interest and who moreover was personally loathsome and as ignorant as a fish. She made also no less of a secret of the awkward fact that a good school would be hideously expensive, and of the further circumstance, which seemed to put an end to everything, that when it came to the point papa, in spite of his previous clamour, was really most nasty about paying. "Would you believe," Mrs. Beale confidentially asked of her little charge, "that he says I'm a worse expense than ever, and that a daughter and a wife together are really more than he can afford?" It was thus that the splendid school at Brighton lost itself in the haze of larger questions, though the fear that it would provoke Ida to leap into the breach subsided with her prolonged, her quite shameless non-appearance. Her daughter and her successor were therefore left to gaze in united but helpless blankness at all that Maisie was not learning.

This quantity was so great as to fill the child's days with a sense of intermission to which even French Lisette gave no accent—with finished games and unanswered questions and dreaded tests; with the habit, above all, in her watch for a change, of hanging over banisters when the door-bell sounded. This was the great refuge of her impatience, but what she heard at such times was a clatter of gaiety downstairs; the impression of which, from her earliest childhood, had built up in her the belief that the grown-up time was the time of real amusement and above all of real intimacy. Even Lisette, even Mrs. Wix had never, she felt, in spite of hugs and tears, been so intimate with her as so many persons at present were with Mrs. Beale and as so many others of old had been with Mrs. Farange. The note of hilarity brought people together still more than the note of melancholy, which was the one exclusively sounded, for instance, by poor Mrs. Wix. Maisie, in these days, preferred none the less that domestic revels should be wafted to her from a distance: she felt sadly unsupported for facing the interrogatory of the drawing-room. That was a reason the more for making the most of Susan Ash, who in her quality of under-housemaid moved at a very different level and who, none the less, was much depended upon out of doors. She was a guide to peregrinations that had little in common with those intensely definite airings that had left with the child a vivid memory of the regulated mind of Moddle. There were under Moddle's system no dawdles at shop-windows and no nudges, in Oxford Street, of "I *say*, look at *'er*!" There was an inexorable treatment of crossings and a serene exemption from the fear that—especially at corners, of which she was yet weakly fond—haunted the housemaid, the fear of being, as she ominously said, "spoken to." The dangers of the town equally with its diversions added to Maisie's sense of being untutored and unclaimed.

The situation, however, had taken a twist when, on another of her returns, at Susan's side, extremely tired, from the pursuit of exercise qualified by much hovering, she encountered another emotion. She on this occasion learnt at the door that her instant attendance was requested in the drawing-room. Crossing the threshold in a cloud of shame she discerned through the blur Mrs. Beale seated there with a gentleman who immediately drew the pain from her predicament by rising before her as the original of the photograph of Sir Claude. She felt the moment she looked at him that he was by far the most radiant person with whom she had yet been concerned, and her pleasure in seeing him, in knowing that he took hold of her and kissed her, as quickly throbbed into a strange, shy pride in him, a perception of his making up for her fallen state, for Susan's public nudges, which quite bruised her, and for all the lessons that, in the dead schoolroom, where at times she was almost afraid to stay alone, she was bored with not having. It was as if he had told her on the spot that he belonged to her, so that she could already show him off and see the effect he produced. No, nothing else that was most beautiful that had ever belonged to her could kindle that particular joy—not Mrs. Beale at that very moment, not papa when he was gay, nor mamma when she was dressed, nor Lisette when she was new. The joy almost overflowed in tears when he laid his hand on her and drew her to him, telling her, with a smile of which the promise was as bright as that of a Christmas-tree, that he knew her ever so well by her mother, but had come to see her now so that he might know her really.

She could see that his view of the way "really" to know her was to make her come away with him, and, further, that this was what he was there for and had already been some time: arranging it with Mrs. Beale and getting on with that lady in a manner evidently not at all affected by her having, on the arrival of his portrait, thought of him so ill. They had grown almost intimate—or had the air of it—over their discussion; and it was still further conveyed to Maisie that Mrs. Beale had made no secret, and would make yet less of one, of all that it cost to let her go. "You seem so tremendously eager," she said to the child, "that I hope you're at least clear about Sir Claude's relation to you. It doesn't appear to occur to him to give you the necessary reassurance."

Maisie, a trifle mystified, turned quickly to her new friend. "Why, it's of course that you're *married* to her, isn't it?"

Her anxious emphasis started them off, as she had learned to call it; this was the echo she infallibly and now quite resignedly produced; moreover, Sir Claude's laughter was an indistinguishable part of the sweetness of his being there. "We've been married, my dear child, three months, and my interest in you is a consequence, don't you know? of my great affection for your mother. In coming here it's of course for your mother I'm acting."

"Oh, I know," Maisie said with all the candour of her competence. "She can't come herself—except just to the door." Then as she thought afresh: "Can't she come even to the door now?"

"There you are!" Mrs. Beale exclaimed to Sir Claude. She spoke as if his dilemma were ludicrous.

His kind face, in an hesitation, seemed to recognise it; but he answered the child with a frank smile. "No—not very well."

"Because she has married you?"

He promptly accepted this reason. "Well, that has a good deal to do with it."

He was so delightful to talk to that Maisie pursued the subject. "But, papa—*he* has married Miss Overmore."

"Yes, and you'll see that he won't come for you at your mother's," that lady interposed.

"Yes, but that won't be for a long time," Maisie hastened to respond.

"We won't talk about it now—you've months and months to put in first." And Sir Claude drew her closer.

"Ah, that's what makes it so hard to give her up!" Mrs. Beale sighed, holding out her arms to her stepdaughter. Maisie, quitting Sir Claude, went over to them and, clasped in a still tenderer embrace, felt entrancingly the expansion of the field of happiness. "*I'll* come for you," said her stepmother, "if Sir Claude keeps you too long: we must make him quite understand that! Don't talk to me about her ladyship!" she went on, to their visitor, so familiarly that it was almost as if they must have met before. "I know her ladyship as if I had made her. They're a pretty pair of parents!" Mrs. Beale exclaimed.

Maisie had so often heard them called so that the remark diverted her but an instant from the agreeable wonder of this grand new form of allusion to her mother; and that, in its turn, presently left her free to catch at the pleasant possibility, in connection with herself, of a relation much happier as between Mrs. Beale and Sir Claude than as between mamma and papa. Still the next thing that happened was that her interest in such a relation brought to her lips a fresh question. "Have you seen papa?" she asked of Sir Claude.

It was the signal for their going off again, as her small stoicism had perfectly taken for granted that it would be. All that Mrs. Beale had nevertheless to add was the vague apparent sarcasm: "Oh, papa!"

"I'm assured he's not at home," Sir Claude replied to the child; "but if he had been I should have hoped for the pleasure of seeing him."

"Won't he mind your coming?" Maisie went on.

"Oh, you bad little girl!" Mrs. Beale humorously protested.

The child could see that at this Sir Claude, though still moved to mirth, coloured a little; but he spoke to her very kindly. "That's just what I came to see, you know—whether your father *would* mind. But Mrs. Beale appears strongly of the opinion that he won't."

This lady promptly justified her opinion to her stepdaughter. "It will be very interesting, my dear, you know, to find out what it is, to-day, that your father does mind. I'm sure *I* don't know!"—and she repeated, though with perceptible resignation, her sigh of a moment before. "Your father, darling, is a very odd person indeed." She turned with this, smiling, to Sir Claude. "But, perhaps, it's hardly civil for me to say that of his not objecting to have *you* in the house. If you knew some of the people he does have!"

Maisie knew them all, and none indeed were to be compared to Sir Claude. He laughed back at Mrs. Beale; he looked at such moments quite as Mrs. Wix, in the long stories she told her pupil, always described the lovers of her distressed beauties—"the perfect gentleman and strikingly handsome." He got up, to the child's regret, as if he were going. "Oh, I daresay we should be all right!"

Mrs. Beale once more gathered in her little charge, holding her close and looking thoughtfully over her head at their visitor. "It's so charming—for a man of your type—to have wanted her so much!"

"What do you know about my type?" Sir Claude inquired. "Whatever it may be, I daresay it deceives you. The truth about me is simply that I'm the most unappreciated of—what do you call the fellows?—'family-men.' Yes, I'm a family-man; upon my honour I am!"

"Then why on earth," cried Mrs. Beale, "didn't you marry a family-woman?"

Sir Claude looked at her hard. "*You* know who one marries, I think. Besides, there *are* no family-women—hanged if there are! None of them want any children—hanged if they do!"

His account of the matter was most interesting, and Maisie, as if it were of bad omen for her, stared at the picture in some dismay. At the same time she felt, through encircling arms, her protectress hesitate. "You do come out with things! But you mean her ladyship doesn't want any—really?"

"Won't hear of them—simply. But she can't help the one she *has* got." And with this Sir Claude's eyes rested on the little girl in a way that seemed to her to mask her mother's attitude with the conscientiousness of his own. "She must make the best of her, don't you see? If only for the look of the thing, don't you know? one wants one's wife to take the proper line about her child."

"Oh, I know what one wants!" Mrs. Beale asserted with a competence that evidently impressed her interlocutor.

"Well, if you keep *him* up—and I daresay you've had worry enough—why shouldn't I keep Ida? What's sauce for the goose is sauce for the gander—or the other way round, don't you know? I mean to see the thing through."

Mrs. Beale, for a minute, still with her eyes on him as he leaned upon the chimneypiece, appeared to turn this over. "You're just a wonder of kindness—that's what you are!" she said at last. "A lady's expected to have natural feelings. But *your* horrible sex——! Isn't it a horrible sex, little love?" she demanded with her cheek upon her stepdaughter's.

"Oh, I like gentlemen best," Maisie lucidly replied.

The words were taken up merrily. "That's a good one for *you*!" Sir Claude exclaimed to Mrs. Beale.

"No," said that lady: "I've only to remember the women she sees at her mother's."

"Ah, they're very nice now," Sir Claude returned.

"What do you call 'nice'?"

"Well, they're all right."

"That doesn't answer me," said Mrs. Beale; "but I daresay you do take care of them. That makes you more of an angel to want this job too." She playfully whacked her smaller companion.

"I'm not an angel—I'm an old grandmother," Sir Claude declared. "I like babies—I always did. If we go to smash I shall look for a place as responsible nurse."

Maisie, in her charmed mood, drank in an imputation on her years which at another moment might have been bitter; but the charm was sensibly interrupted by Mrs. Beale's screwing her round and gazing fondly into her eyes. "You're willing to leave me, you wretch?"

The little girl deliberated; even her attachment to this bright presence had become as a cord she must suddenly snap. But she snapped it very gently. "Isn't it my turn for mamma?"

"You're a horrible little hypocrite! The less, I think, now said about 'turns' the better," Mrs. Beale made answer. "*I* know whose turn it is. You've not such a passion for your mother!"

"I say, I say: *do* look out!" Sir Claude quite amiably protested.

"There's nothing she hasn't heard. But it doesn't matter—it hasn't spoiled her. If you know what it costs me to part with you!" she pursued to Maisie.

Sir Claude watched her as she charmingly clung to the child. "I'm so glad you really care for her. That's so much to the good."

Mrs. Beale slowly got up, still with her hands on Maisie, but emitting a little soft exhalation. "Well, if you're glad, that may help us; for I assure you that I shall never give up any rights in her that I may consider that, by my own sacrifices, I've acquired. I shall hold very fast to my interest in her. What seems to have happened is that she has brought you and me together."

"She has brought you and me together," said Sir Claude.

The cheerfulness of his assent to this proposition was contagious, and Maisie broke out almost with enthusiasm: "I've brought you and her together!"

Her companions of course laughed anew and Mrs. Beale gave her an affectionate shake. "You little monster—take care what you do! But that's what she does do," she continued to Sir Claude. "She did it to me and Beale."

"Well, then," he said to Maisie, "you must try the trick at *our* place." He held out his hand to her again. "Will you come now?"

"Now—just as I am?" She turned with an immense appeal to her stepmother, taking a leap over the mountain of "mending," the abyss of packing that had loomed and yawned before her. "Oh, *may* I?"

Mrs. Beale addressed her assent to Sir Claude. "As well so as any other way. I'll send on her things to-morrow." Then she gave a tug to the child's coat, glancing at her up and down with some ruefulness. "She's not turned out as I should like—her mother will pull her to pieces. But what's one to do—with nothing to do it on? And she's better than when she came—you can tell her mother that. I'm sorry to have to say it to you—but the poor child was a sight!"

"Oh, I'll turn her out myself!" the visitor cordially announced.

"I shall like to see how!"——Mrs. Beale appeared much amused. "You must bring her to show me—we can manage that. Good-bye, little fright!" And her last word to Sir Claude was that she would keep him up to the mark.

IX

THE IDEA of what she was to make up and the prodigious total it came to were kept well before Maisie at her mother's. These things were the constant occupation of Mrs. Wix, who arrived there by the back-stairs, but in tears of joy, the day after her own arrival. The process of making up, as to which the good lady had an immense deal to say, took, through its successive phases, so long that it promised to be a period at least equal to the child's last period with her father. But this was a fuller and richer time: it bounded along to the tune of Mrs. Wix's constant insistence on the energy they must both put forth. There was a fine intensity in the way the child agreed with her that under Mrs. Beale and Susan Ash she had learned nothing whatever; the wildness of the rescued castaway was one of the forces that would henceforth make for a career of conquest. The year therefore rounded itself as a receptacle of retarded knowledge—a cup brimming over with the sense that now at least she was learning. Mrs. Wix fed this sense from the stores of her conversation and with the immense bustle of her reminder that they must cull the fleeting hour. They were surrounded with subjects they must take at a rush and perpetually getting into the attitude of triumphant attack. They had certainly no idle hours, and the child went to bed each night as tired as from a long day's play. This had begun from the moment of their reunion, begun with all Mrs. Wix had to tell her young friend of the reasons of her ladyship's extraordinary behaviour at the very first.

It took the form of her ladyship's refusal for three days to see her child—three days during which Sir Claude made hasty, merry dashes into the schoolroom to smooth down the odd situation, to say "She'll come round, you know; I assure you she'll come round," and a little even to compensate Maisie for the indignity he had caused her to suffer. There had never in the child's life been, in all ways, such a delightful amount of reparation. It came out by his sociable admission that her ladyship had not known of his visit to her late husband's house and of his having made that person's daughter a pretext for striking up an acquaintance with the dreadful creature installed there. Heaven knew she wanted her child back and had made every plan of her own for removing her; what she couldn't for the present at least forgive any one concerned was the meddling, underhand way in which Sir Claude had brought about the transfer. Maisie carried more of the weight of this resentment than even Mrs. Wix's confidential ingenuity could lighten for her, especially as Sir Claude himself was not at all ingenuous, though indeed on the other hand he was not at all crushed. He was amused and intermittent and at moments most startling; he brought out to his young companion, with a frankness that agitated her much more than he seemed to guess, that he depended on her not letting her mother, when she should see her, get anything out of her about anything Mrs. Beale might have said to him. He came in and out; he professed, in joke, to take tremendous precautions; he showed a positive disposition to romp. He chaffed Mrs. Wix till she was purple with the pleasure of it, and reminded Maisie of the reticence he expected of her till she set her teeth like an Indian captive. Her lessons these first days and indeed for long after seemed to be all about Sir Claude, and yet she never really mentioned to Mrs. Wix that she was prepared, under his inspiring injunction, to be vainly tortured. This lady, however, had formulated the position of things with an acuteness that showed how little she needed to be coached. Her explanation of everything that seemed not quite pleasant—and if her own footing was perilous it met that danger as well—was that her ladyship was passionately in love. Maisie accepted this hint with infinite awe and pressed upon it much when she was at last summoned into the presence of her mother.

There she encountered matters in which it seemed really to help to give her a clue—an almost terrifying strangeness, full, none the less, after a little, of reverberations of Ida's old fierce, demonstrative recoveries of possession. They had been some time in the house together, and this demonstration came late. Preoccupied, however, as Maisie was with the idea of the sentiment Sir Claude had inspired, and familiar, in addition, by Mrs. Wix's anecdotes, with the ravages that in general such a sentiment could produce, she was able to make allowances for her ladyship's remarkable appearance, her violent splendour, the wonderful colour of her lips and even the hard stare, like that of some gorgeous idol described in a story-book, that had come into her eyes in consequence of a curious thickening of their already rich circumference. Her professions and explanations were mixed with eager challenges and sudden drops, in the midst of which Maisie recognised as a memory of other years the rattle of her trinkets and the scratch of her endearments, the odour of her clothes and the jumps of her conversation. She had all her old clever way—Mrs. Wix said it was "aristocratic"—of changing the subject as she might have slammed the door in your face. The principal thing that was different was the tint of her golden hair, which had changed to a coppery red and, with the head it profusely covered, struck the child as now lifted still further aloft. This picturesque parent showed literally a grander stature and a nobler presence, things which, with some others that might have been bewildering, were handsomely accounted for by the romantic state of her affections. It was her affections, Maisie could easily see, that led Ida to break out into questions as to what had passed at the other house between that horrible woman and Sir Claude; but it was also just here that the little girl was able to recall the effect with which in earlier days she had practised the pacific art of stupidity. This art again came to her aid: her mother, in getting rid of her after an interview in which she had achieved a hollowness beyond her years, allowed her fully to understand that she had not grown a bit more amusing.

She could bear that; she could bear anything that helped her to feel she had done something for Sir Claude. If she hadn't told Mrs. Wix how Mrs. Beale seemed to like him she certainly couldn't tell her ladyship. In the way the past revived for her there was a queer confusion. It was because mamma hated papa that she used to want to know bad things of him; but if at present she wanted to know the same of Sir Claude it was quite from the opposite motive. She was awe-struck at the manner in which a lady might be affected through the passion mentioned by Mrs. Wix; she held her breath with the sense of picking her steps among the tremendous things of life. What she did, however, now, after the interview with her mother, impart to Mrs. Wix was that, in spite of her having had her "good" effect, as she called it—the effect she studied, the effect of harmless vacancy—her ladyship's last words had been that her ladyship's duty by her would be thoroughly done. Over this announcement governess and pupil looked at each other in silent profundity; but as the weeks went by it had no consequences that interfered gravely with the breezy gallop of making up. Her ladyship's duty took at times the form of not seeing her child for days together, and Maisie led her life in great prosperity between Mrs. Wix and kind Sir Claude. Mrs. Wix had a new dress and, as she was the first to proclaim, a better position; so it all struck Maisie as a crowded, brilliant life, with, for the time, Mrs. Beale and Susan Ash simply "left out" like children not invited to a Christmas party. Mrs. Wix had a secret terror which, like most of her secret feelings, she discussed with her little companion, in great solemnity, by the hour: the possibility of her ladyship's coming down on them, in her sudden high-bred way, with a school. But she had also a balm to this fear in a conviction of the strength of Sir Claude's grasp of the situation. He was too pleased—didn't he constantly say as much?—with the good impression made, in a wide circle, by Ida's sacrifices; and he came into the schoolroom repeatedly to let them know how beautifully he felt everything had gone off and everything would go on.

He disappeared at times for days, when his patient friends understood that her ladyship would naturally absorb him; but he always came back with the drollest stories of where he had been, a wonderful picture of society, and even with pretty presents that showed how in absence he thought of his home. Besides giving Mrs. Wix by his conversation a sense that they almost themselves "went out," he gave her a five-pound note and the history of France and an umbrella with a malachite knob, and to Maisie both chocolate-creams and story-books, and a lovely great-coat (which he took her out all alone to buy), besides ever so many games in boxes, with printed directions, and a bright red frame for the protection of his famous photograph. The games were, as he said, to while away the evening hour; and the evening hour indeed often passed in futile attempts on Mrs. Wix's part to master what "it said" on the papers. When he asked the pair how they liked the games they always replied "Oh, immensely!" but they had earnest discussions as to whether they hadn't better appeal to him frankly for aid to understand them. This was a course their delicacy shrank from; they couldn't have told exactly why, but it was a part of their tenderness for him not to let him think they had trouble. What dazzled most was his kindness to Mrs. Wix, not only the five-pound note and the "not forgetting" her, but the perfect consideration, as she called it with an air to which her sounding of the words gave the only grandeur Maisie was to have seen her wear save on a certain occasion hereafter to be described, an occasion when the poor lady was grander than all of them put together. He shook hands with her, he recognised her, as she said, and above all, more than once, he took her, with his stepdaughter, to the pantomime and, in the crowd, coming out, publicly gave her his arm. When he met them in sunny Piccadilly he made merry and turned and walked with them, heroically suppressing his consciousness of the stamp of his company, a heroism that—needless for Mrs. Wix to sound *those* words—her ladyship, though a blood-relation, was little enough the woman to be capable of. Even to the hard heart of childhood there was something tragic in such elation at such humanities: it brought home to Maisie the way her humble companion had sidled and ducked through life. But it settled the question of the degree to which Sir Claude was a gentleman: he was more of one than anybody else in the world—"I don't care," Mrs. Wix repeatedly remarked, "whom you may meet in grand society, nor even to whom you may be contracted in marriage." There were questions that Maisie never asked; so her governess was spared the embarrassment of telling her if he were more of a gentleman than papa. This was not moreover from the want of opportunity, for there were no moments between them at which the topic could be irrelevant, no subject they were going into, not even the principal dates or the auxiliary verbs, in which it was further off than the turn of the page. The answer on the winter nights to the puzzle of cards and counters and little bewildering pamphlets was just to draw up to the fire and talk about him; and if the truth must be told this edifying interchange constituted for the time the little girl's chief education.

It must also be admitted that he took them far, farther perhaps than was always warranted by the old-fashioned conscience, the dingy decencies, of Maisie's simple instructress. There were hours when Mrs. Wix sighingly testified to the scruples she surmounted, seemed to ask what other line one *could* take with a young person whose experience had been, as it were, so peculiar. "It isn't as if you didn't already know everything, is it, love?" and "I can't make you any worse than you *are*, can I darling?"—these were the terms in which the good lady justified to herself and her pupil her pleasant conversational ease. What the pupil already knew was indeed rather taken for granted than expressed, but it performed the useful function of transcending all text-books and supplanting all studies. If the child couldn't be worse it was a comfort even to herself that she was bad—a comfort offering a broad, firm support to the fundamental fact of the present crisis: the fact that mamma was fearfully jealous. This was another side of the circumstance of mamma's passion, and the deep couple in the schoolroom were not long in working round to it. It brought them face to face with the idea of the inconvenience suffered by any lady who marries a gentleman producing on other ladies the charming effect of Sir Claude. That such ladies would freely fall in love with him was a reflection naturally irritating to his wife. One day when some accident, some crash of a banged door or some scurry of a scared maid, had rendered this truth particularly vivid, Maisie, receptive and profound, suddenly said to her companion: "And you, my dear, are you in love with him too?"

Even her profundity had left a margin for a laugh; so she was a trifle startled by the solemn promptitude with which Mrs. Wix plumped out: "Over head and ears. I've *never*, since you ask me, been so far gone."

This boldness had none the less no effect of deterrence for her when, a few days later—it was because several had elapsed without a visit from Sir Claude—her governess turned the tables. "May I ask you, miss, if *you* are?" Mrs. Wix brought it out, she could see, with hesitation, but clearly intending a joke. "Why, *yes*!" the child made answer, as if in surprise at

not having long ago seemed sufficiently to commit herself; on
which her friend gave a sigh of apparent satisfaction. It might
in fact have expressed positive relief. Everything was as it
should be.

Yet it was not with them, they were very sure, that her ladyship was furious, nor because she had forbidden it that
there befell at last a period—six months brought it round—
when for days together he scarcely came near them. He was
"off," and Ida was "off," and they were sometimes off together and sometimes apart; there were seasons when the
simple students had the house to themselves, when the very
servants seemed also to be "off" and dinner became a reckless
forage in pantries and sideboards. Mrs. Wix reminded her disciple on such occasions—hungry moments often, when all the
support of the reminder was required—that the "real life" of
their companions, the brilliant society in which it was inevitable they should move and the complicated pleasures in
which it was almost presumptuous of the mind to follow
them, must offer features literally not to be imagined without
being seen. At one of these times Maisie found her opening it
out that, though the difficulties were many, it was Mrs. Beale
who had now become the chief. Then somehow it was
brought fully to the child's knowledge that her stepmother
had been making attempts to see her, that her mother had
deeply resented it, that her stepfather had backed her stepmother up, that the latter had pretended to be acting as the
representative of her father, and that her mother took the
whole thing, in plain terms, very hard. The situation was, as
Mrs. Wix declared, an extraordinary muddle to be sure. Her
account of it brought back to Maisie the happy vision of the
way Sir Claude and Mrs. Beale had made acquaintance—an
incident to which, with her stepfather, though she had had
little to say about it to Mrs. Wix, she had during the first
weeks of her stay at her mother's found more than one opportunity to revert. As to what had taken place the day Sir
Claude came for her, she had been vaguely grateful to Mrs.
Wix for not attempting, as her mother had attempted, to put
her through. That was what Sir Claude had called the process
when he warned her of it, and again afterwards when he told
her she was an awfully good "chap" for having foiled it. Then

it was that, well aware Mrs. Beale hadn't in the least really given her up, she had asked him if he remained in communication with her and if for the time everything must really be held to be at an end between her stepmother and herself. This conversation had occurred in consequence of his one day popping into the schoolroom and finding Maisie alone.

X

H E WAS smoking a cigarette and he stood before the fire
and looked at the meagre appointments of the room in
a way that made her rather ashamed of them. Then before, on
the subject of Mrs. Beale, he let her "draw" him—that was
another of his words; it was astonishing how many she gathered in—he remarked that really mamma kept them rather
low on the question of decorations. Mrs. Wix had put up a
Japanese fan and two rather grim texts; she had wished they
were gayer, but they were all she happened to have. Without
Sir Claude's photograph, however, the place would have
been, as he said, as dull as a cold dinner. He had said as well
that there were all sorts of things they ought to have; yet governess and pupil, it had to be admitted, were still divided between discussing the places where any sort of thing would
look best if any sort of thing should ever come and acknowledging that mutability in the little girl's career which was naturally unfavourable to accumulation. She stayed long enough
only to miss things, not half long enough to deserve them.
The way Sir Claude looked about the schoolroom had made
her feel with humility as if it were not very different from the
shabby attic in which she had visited Susan Ash. Then he had
said, in abrupt reference to Mrs. Beale: "Do you think she
really cares for you?"

"Oh, awfully!" Maisie had replied.

"But, I mean, does she love you for yourself, as they call it,
don't you know? Is she as fond of you, now, as Mrs. Wix?"

The child turned it over. "Oh, I'm not every bit Mrs. Beale
has!"

Sir Claude seemed much amused at this. "No; you're not
every bit she has!"

He laughed for some moments; but that was an old story
to Maisie, and she was not too much disconcerted to go on:
"But she'll never give me up."

"Well, I won't either, old boy: so that's not so wonderful,
and she's not the only one. But if she's so fond of you, why
doesn't she write to you?"

"Oh, on account of mamma." This was rudimentary, and she was almost surprised at the simplicity of Sir Claude's question.

"I see—that's quite right," he answered. "She might get at you—there are all sorts of ways. But of course there's Mrs. Wix."

"There's Mrs. Wix," Maisie lucidly concurred. "Mrs. Wix can't endure her."

Sir Claude seemed interested. "Oh, she can't endure her? Then what does she say about her?"

"Nothing at all—because she knows I shouldn't like it. Isn't it sweet of her?" the child asked.

"Certainly; rather nice. Mrs. Beale wouldn't hold her tongue for any such thing as that, would she?"

Maisie remembered how little she had done so; but she desired to protect Mrs. Beale too. The only protection she could think of, however, was the plea: "Oh, at papa's, you know, they don't mind!"

At this Sir Claude only smiled. "No, I dare say not. But here we mind, don't we?—we take care what we say. I don't suppose it's the sort of thing I ought to say," he went on; "but I think we must on the whole be rather nicer here than at your father's. However, I don't press that; for it's a sort of question on which it's awfully awkward for you to speak. Don't worry, at any rate: I assure you I'll back you up." Then, after a moment, while he smoked, he reverted to Mrs. Beale and the child's first inquiry. "I'm afraid we can't do much for her just now. I haven't seen her since that day— upon my word I haven't seen her." The next instant, with a laugh the least bit foolish, the young man slightly coloured: he felt this profession of innocence to be excessive as addressed to Maisie. It was inevitable to say to her, however, that of course her mother loathed the lady of the other house. He couldn't go there again with his wife's consent, and he wasn't the man—he begged her to believe, falling once more, in spite of himself, into the scruple of showing the child he didn't trip—to go there without it. He was liable in talking with her to take the tone of her being also a man of the world. He had gone to Mrs. Beale's to fetch away Maisie; but that was altogether different. Now that she was in her mother's house what pretext had he to give her mother for

paying calls on her father's wife? And of course Mrs. Beale
couldn't come to Ida's—Ida would tear her limb from limb.
Maisie, with this talk of pretexts, remembered how much
Mrs. Beale had made of her being a good one, and how, for
such a function, it was her fate to be either much depended
on or much missed. Sir Claude moreover recognised on this
occasion that perhaps things would take a turn later on; and
he wound up by saying: "I'm sure she does sincerely care for
you—how can she possibly help it? She's very young and very
pretty and very clever: I think she's charming. But we must
walk very straight. If you'll help me, you know, I'll help *you*,"
he concluded in the pleasant fraternising, equalising, not a bit
patronising way which made the child ready to go through
anything for him and the beauty of which, as she dimly felt,
was that it was not a deceitful descent to her years, but a real
indifference to them.

It gave her moments of secret rapture—moments of believing she might help him indeed. The only mystification in this
was the imposing time of life that her elders spoke of as
youth. For Sir Claude then Mrs. Beale was "young," just as
for Mrs. Wix Sir Claude was: that was one of the merits for
which Mrs. Wix most commended him. What therefore was
Maisie herself, and, in another relation to the matter, what
therefore was mamma? It took her some time to puzzle out
with the aid of an experiment or two that it wouldn't do to
talk about mamma's youth. She even went so far one day, in
the presence of that lady's thick colour and marked lines, as
to wonder if it would occur to any one but herself to do so.
Yet if she wasn't young then she was old; and this threw an
odd light on her having a husband of a different generation.
Mr. Farange was still older—that Maisie perfectly knew; and it
brought her in due course to the perception of how much
more, since Mrs. Beale was younger than Sir Claude, papa
must be older than Mrs. Beale. Such discoveries were disconcerting and even a trifle confounding: these persons, it appeared, were not of the age they ought to be. This was
somehow particularly the case with mamma, and the fact
made her reflect with some relief on her not having gone with
Mrs. Wix into the question of Sir Claude's attachment to his
wife. She was conscious that in confining their attention to

the state of her ladyship's own affections they had been controlled—Mrs. Wix perhaps in especial—by delicacy and even by embarrassment. The end of her colloquy with her stepfather in the schoolroom was her saying: "Then if we're not to see Mrs. Beale at all it isn't what she seemed to think when you came for me."

He looked rather blank. "What did she seem to think?"

"Why, that I've brought you together."

"She thought that?" Sir Claude inquired.

Maisie was surprised at his already forgetting it. "Just as I had brought papa and her. Don't you remember she said so?"

It came back to Sir Claude in a peal of laughter. "Oh yes—she said so!"

"And *you* said so," Maisie lucidly pursued.

He recovered, with increasing mirth, the whole occasion. "And *you* said so!" he retorted as if they were playing a game.

"Then were we all mistaken?" the child asked.

He considered a little. "No; on the whole not. I dare say it's just what you *have* done. We *are* together—in an extraordinary sort of way. She's thinking of us—of you and me—though we don't meet. And I've no doubt you'll find it will be all right when you go back to her."

"Am I going back to her?" Maisie brought out with a little gasp which was like a sudden clutch of the happy present.

It appeared to make Sir Claude grave a moment; it might have made him feel the weight of the pledge his action had given. "Oh, some day, I suppose! We've lots of time."

"I've such a tremendous lot to make up," Maisie said with a sense of great boldness.

"Certainly; and you must make up every hour of it. Oh, I'll *see* that you do!"

This was encouraging; and to show, cheerfully, that she was reassured she replied: "That's what Mrs. Wix sees too."

"Oh yes," said Sir Claude; "Mrs. Wix and I are shoulder to shoulder."

Maisie took in a little this strong image; after which she exclaimed: "Then I've done it also to you and her—I've brought *you* together!"

"Blest if you haven't!" Sir Claude laughed. "And more, upon my word, than any of the lot. Oh, you've done for *us*!

Now, if you could—as I suggested, you know, that day—only manage me and your mother!"

The child wondered. "Bring you and *her* together?"

"You see we're not together—not a bit. But I oughtn't to tell you such things; all the more that you won't really do it—not you. No, old chap," the young man continued; "there you'll break down. But it won't matter—we'll rub along. The great thing is that you and I are all right."

"*We're* all right!" Maisie echoed devoutly. But the next moment, in the light of what he had just said, she asked: "How shall I ever leave you?" It was as if she must somehow take care of him.

His smile did justice to her anxiety. "Oh, well, you needn't! It won't come to that."

"Do you mean that when I do go you'll go with me?"

Sir Claude hesitated. "Not exactly 'with' you perhaps; but I shall never be far off."

"But how do you know where mamma may take you?"

He laughed again. "I don't, I confess!" Then he had an idea, but it seemed a little too jocose. "That will be for you to see—that she sha'n't take me too far."

"How can I help it?" Maisie inquired in surprise. "Mamma doesn't care for me," she said very simply. "Not really." Child as she was, her little long history was in the words; and it was as impossible to contradict her as if she had been venerable.

Sir Claude's silence was an admission of this, and still more the tone in which he presently replied: "That won't prevent her from—some time or other—leaving me with you."

"Then we'll live together?" she eagerly demanded.

"I'm afraid," said Sir Claude, smiling, "that that will be Mrs. Beale's real chance."

Her eagerness just slightly dropped at this; she remembered Mrs. Wix's pronouncement that it was all an extraordinary muddle. "To take me again? Well, can't you come to see me there?"

"Oh, I dare say!"

Though there were parts of childhood Maisie had lost she had all childhood's preference for the particular promise. "Then you *will* come—you'll come often, won't you?" she insisted, while at the moment she spoke the door opened for

the return of Mrs. Wix. Sir Claude hereupon, instead of replying, gave her a look which left her silent and embarrassed.

When he again found privacy convenient, however—which
happened to be long in coming—he took up their conversation very much where it had dropped. "You see, my dear, if I
shall be able to go to you at your father's it isn't at all the
same thing for Mrs. Beale to come to you here." Maisie gave
a thoughtful assent to this proposition, though conscious that
she could scarcely herself say just where the difference would
lie. She felt how much her stepfather saved her, as he said
with his habitual amusement, the trouble of that. "I shall
probably be able to go to Mrs. Beale's without your mother's
knowing it."

Maisie stared with a certain thrill at the dramatic element in
this. "And she couldn't come here without mamma's——?"
She was unable to articulate the word for what mamma
would do.

"My dear child, Mrs. Wix would tell of it."

"But I thought," Maisie objected, "that Mrs. Wix and
you——"

"Are such brothers-in-arms?"—Sir Claude caught her up.
"Oh yes, about everything but Mrs. Beale. And if you should
suggest," he went on, "that we might somehow or other hide
her peeping in from Mrs. Wix——"

"Oh, I don't suggest *that*!" Maisie in turn cut him short.

Sir Claude looked as if he could indeed quite see why. "No;
it would really be impossible." There came to her from this
glance at what they might hide the first small glimpse of
something in him that she wouldn't have expected. There had
been times when she had had to make the best of the impression that she was herself deceitful; yet she had never concealed anything bigger than a thought. Of course she now
concealed this thought of how strange it would be to see *him*
hide; and while she was so actively engaged he continued:
"Besides, you know, I'm not afraid of your father."

"And you are of my mother?"

"Rather, old man!" Sir Claude replied.

XI

IT MUST not be supposed that her ladyship's intermissions were not qualified by demonstrations of another order—triumphal entries and breathless pauses during which she seemed to take of everything in the room, from the state of the ceiling to that of her daughter's boot-toes, a survey that was rich in intentions. Sometimes she sat down and sometimes she surged about, but her attitude wore equally in either case the grand air of the practical. She found so much to deplore that she left a great deal to expect, and bristled so with calculations that she seemed to scatter remedies and pledges. Her visits were as good as an outfit; her manner, as Mrs. Wix once said, as good as a pair of curtains; but she was a person addicted to extremes—sometimes barely speaking to her child and sometimes pressing this tender shoot to a bosom cut, as Mrs. Wix had also observed, remarkably low. She was always in a fearful hurry, and the lower the bosom was cut the more it was to be gathered she was wanted elsewhere. She usually broke in alone, but sometimes Sir Claude was with her, and during all the earlier period there was nothing on which these appearances had had so delightful a bearing as on the way her ladyship was, as Mrs. Wix expressed it, under the spell. "But *isn't* she under it!" Maisie used in thoughtful but familiar reference to exclaim after Sir Claude had swept mamma away in peals of natural laughter. Not even in the old days of the convulsed ladies had she heard mamma laugh so freely as in these moments of conjugal surrender, to the gaiety of which even a little girl could see she had at last a right—a little girl whose thoughtfulness was now all happy selfish meditation on good omens and future fun.

Unaccompanied, in subsequent hours, and with an effect of changing to meet a change, Ida took a tone superficially disconcerting and abrupt—the tone of having, at an immense cost, made over everything to Sir Claude and wishing others to know that if everything wasn't right it was because Sir Claude was so dreadfully vague. "He has made from the first such a row about you," she said on one occasion to Maisie, "that I've told him to do for you himself and try how he likes it—see? I've washed my hands of you; I've made you over to him; and if you're discontented it's on him, please, you'll come down. So don't haul poor *me* up—I assure you I've worries enough." One of these, visibly, was that the spell rejoiced in by the schoolroom fire was already in danger of breaking; another was that she was finally forced to make no secret of her husband's unfitness for real responsibilities. The day came indeed when her breathless auditors learnt from her in bewilderment that what ailed him was that he was, alas, simply not serious. Maisie wept on Mrs. Wix's bosom after hearing that Sir Claude was a butterfly; considering moreover that her governess patched it up but ill in coming out at various moments the next few days with the opinion that it was proper to his "station" to be light and gay. That had been proper to every one's station that she had yet encountered save poor Mrs. Wix's own, and the particular merit of Sir Claude had seemed precisely that he was different from every one. She talked with him, however, as time went on, very freely about her mother; being with him, in this relation, wholly without the fear that had kept her silent before her father—the fear of bearing tales and making bad things worse. He appeared to accept the idea that he had taken her over and made her, as he said, his particular lark; he quite agreed also that he was an awful humbug and an idle beast and a sorry dunce. And he never said a word to her against her mother—he only remained dumb and discouraged in the face of her ladyship's own overtopping earnestness. There were occasions when he even spoke as if he had wrenched his little charge from the arms of a parent who had fought for her tooth and nail.

This was the very moral of a scene that flashed into vividness one day when the four happened to meet without company in the drawing-room and Maisie found herself clutched to her mother's breast and passionately sobbed and shrieked over, made the subject of a demonstration that evidently formed the sequel to a sharp passage enacted just before. The connection required that while she almost cradled the child in her arms Ida should speak of her as hideously, as fatally estranged, and should rail at Sir Claude as the cruel author of the outrage. "He has taken you *from* me," she cried; "he has set you *against* me, and you've been won away and your horrid little mind has been poisoned! You've gone over to him, you've given yourself up to side against me and hate me. You never open your mouth to me—you know you don't; and you chatter to him like a dozen magpies. Don't lie about it—I hear you all over the place. You hang about him in a way that's barely decent, and he can do what he likes with you. Well then, let him, to his heart's content: he has been in such a hurry to take you that we'll see if it suits him to keep you. I'm very good to break my heart about it when you've no more feeling for me than a clammy little fish!" She suddenly thrust the child away and, as a disgusted admission of failure, sent her flying across the room into the arms of Mrs. Wix, whom at this moment and even in the whirl of her transit Maisie saw, very red, exchange a quick, queer look with Sir Claude.

The impression of the look remained with her, confronting her with such a critical little view of her mother's explosion that she felt the less ashamed of herself for incurring the reproach with which she had been cast off. Her father had once called her a heartless little beast, and now, though decidedly scared, she was as stiff and cold as if the description had been just. She was not even frightened enough to cry, which would have been a tribute to her mother's wrongs: she was only, more than anything else, curious about the opinion mutely expressed by their companions. Taking the earliest opportunity to question Mrs. Wix on this subject she elicited the remarkable reply: "Well, my dear, it's her ladyship's game, and we must just hold on like grim death." Maisie could interpret at her leisure these ominous words. Her reflections indeed at this moment thickened apace, and one of them made her sure that her governess had conversations, private, earnest and not infrequent, with her frivolous stepfather. She perceived in the light of a second episode that something beyond her knowledge had taken place in the house. The things beyond her knowledge—numerous enough in truth—had not hitherto, she believed, been the things that had been nearest to her: she had even had in the past a small smug conviction that in the domestic labyrinth she always kept the clue. This time too, however, she at last found out, with the discreet aid, it had to be confessed, of Mrs. Wix. Sir Claude's own assistance was abruptly taken from her, for his comment on her ladyship's game was to start on the spot, quite alone, for Paris, evidently because he wished to show a spirit when accused of positive wickedness. He might be fond of his stepdaughter, Maisie felt, without wishing her to be after all thrust on him in such a way; his absence therefore, it was clear, was a protest against the thrusting. It was while this absence lasted that our young lady finally discovered what had happened in the house to be that her mother was no longer in love.

The limit of a passion for Sir Claude had certainly been reached, she judged, some time before the day on which her ladyship burst suddenly into the schoolroom to introduce Mr. Perriam, who, as she announced from the doorway to Maisie, wouldn't believe his ears that one had a great hoyden of a daughter. Mr. Perriam was short and massive—Mrs. Wix remarked afterwards that he was distinctly fat; and it would have been difficult to say of him whether his head were more bald or his black moustache more bushy. He seemed also to have moustaches over his eyes, which, however, by no means prevented these polished little globes from rolling round the room as if they had been billiard-balls impelled by Ida's celebrated stroke. Mr. Perriam wore on the hand that pulled his moustache a diamond of dazzling lustre, in consequence of which and of his general weight and mystery our young lady observed on his departure that if he had only had a turban he would have been quite her idea of a heathen Turk.

"He's quite my idea," Mrs. Wix replied, "of a heathen Jew."

"Well, I mean," said Maisie, "of a person who comes from the East."

"That's where he *must* come from," her governess opined—"he comes from the City." In a moment she added as if she knew all about him: "He's one of those people who have lately broken out. He'll be immensely rich."

"On the death of his papa?" the child interestedly inquired.

"Dear no—nothing hereditary. I mean he has made a lot of money."

"How much, do you think?" Maisie demanded.

Mrs. Wix reflected and sketched it. "Oh, many millions."

"A hundred?" said her questioner.

Mrs. Wix was not sure of the number, but there were enough of them to have seemed to warm up for the time the penury of the schoolroom—to linger there as an afterglow of the hot, heavy light Mr. Perriam sensibly shed. This was also, no doubt, on his part, an effect of that enjoyment of life with which, among her elders, Maisie had been in contact from her earliest years—the sign of happy maturity, the old familiar note of overflowing cheer. "How d'ye do, ma'am? How d'ye do, little miss?"—he laughed and nodded at the gaping figures. "She has brought me up for a peep—it's true I wouldn't take you on trust. She's always talking about you, but she would never produce you; so to-day I challenged her on the spot. Well, you ain't a myth, my dear—I back down on that," the visitor went on to Maisie; "nor you either, miss, though you might be, to be sure!"

"I bored him with you, darling—I bore every one," Ida said, "and to prove that you *are* a sweet thing, as well as a fearfully old one, I told him he could judge for himself. So now he sees that you're a dreadful bouncing business and that your poor old Mummy's at least sixty!"—and her ladyship smiled at Mr. Perriam with the charm that her daughter had heard imputed to her at papa's by the merry gentlemen who had so often wished to get from him what they called a "rise." Her manner at that instant gave the child a glimpse more vivid than any yet enjoyed of the attraction that papa, in remarkable language, always denied she could put forth.

Mr. Perriam, however, clearly recognised it in the grace with which he met her. "I never said you ain't wonderful— did I ever say it, hey?" and he appealed with pleasant confidence to the testimony of the schoolroom, about which itself also he evidently felt that he ought to have something to say. "So this is their little place, hey? Charming, charming, charming!" he repeated as he vaguely looked round. The interrupted students clung together as if they had been personally exposed; but Ida relieved their embarrassment by a hunch of her high shoulders. This time the smile she addressed to Mr. Perriam had a beauty of sudden sadness. "What on earth is a poor woman to do?"

The visitor's grimace grew more marked as he continued to look, and the conscious little schoolroom felt still more like a cage at a menagerie. "Charming, charming, charming!" Mr. Perriam insisted; but the parenthesis closed with a prompt click. "There you are!" said her ladyship. "By-bye!" she sharply added. The next minute they were on the stairs, and Mrs. Wix and her companion, at the open door and looking mutely at each other, were reached by the sound of the ample current that carried them back to their life.

It was singular perhaps after this that Maisie never put a question about Mr. Perriam, and it was still more singular that by the end of a week she knew all she didn't ask. What she most particularly knew—and the information came to her, unsought, straight from Mrs. Wix—was that Sir Claude wouldn't at all care for the visits of a millionaire who was in and out of the upper rooms. How little he would care was proved by the fact that under the sense of them Mrs. Wix's discretion broke down altogether: she was capable of a transfer of allegiance, capable, at the altar of propriety, of a desperate sacrifice of her ladyship. As against Mrs. Beale, she more than once intimated, she had been willing to do the best for her, but as against Sir Claude she could do nothing for her at all. It was extraordinary the number of things that, still without a question, Maisie knew by the time her stepfather came back from Paris—came bringing her a splendid apparatus for painting in water-colours and bringing Mrs. Wix, by a lapse of memory that would have been droll if it had not been a trifle disconcerting, a second and even a more elegant umbrella. He had forgotten all about the first, with which, buried in as many wrappers as a mummy of the Pharaohs, she wouldn't for the world have done anything so profane as use it. Maisie knew above all that though she was now, by what she called an informal understanding, on Sir Claude's "side," she had yet not uttered a word to him about Mr. Perriam. That gentleman became therefore a kind of flourishing public secret, out of the depths of which governess and pupil looked at each other portentously from the time their friend was restored to them. He was restored in great abundance, and it was marked that, though he appeared to have felt the need to take a stand against the risk of being too roughly saddled with the offspring of others, he at this period exposed himself more than ever before to the presumption of having created expectations.

If it had become now, for that matter, a question of sides, there was at least a certain amount of evidence as to where they all were. Maisie, of course, in such a delicate position, was on nobody's; but Sir Claude had all the air of being on hers. If therefore Mrs. Wix was on Sir Claude's, her ladyship on Mr. Perriam's, and Mr. Perriam presumably on her ladyship's, this left only Mrs. Beale and Mr. Farange to account for. Mrs. Beale clearly was, like Sir Claude, on Maisie's, and papa, it was to be supposed, on Mrs. Beale's. Here indeed was a slight ambiguity, as papa's being on Mrs. Beale's didn't somehow seem to place him quite on his daughter's. It sounded, as this young lady thought it over, very much like puss-in-the-corner, and she could only wonder if the distribution of parties would lead to a rushing to and fro and changing of places. She was in the presence, she felt, of restless change: wasn't it restless enough that her mother and her stepfather should already be on different sides? That was the great thing that had domestically happened. Mrs. Wix besides had turned another face: she had never been exactly gay, but her gravity was now an attitude as conspicuous as a poster. She seemed to sit in her new dress and brood over her lost delicacy, which had become almost as doleful a memory as that of poor Clara Matilda. "It *is* hard for him," she often said to her companion; and it was surprising how competent on this point Maisie was conscious of being to agree with her. Hard as it was, however, Sir Claude had never shown to greater advantage than in the gallant, generous, sociable way he carried it off: a way that drew from Mrs. Wix a hundred expressions of relief at his not having suffered it to embitter him. It threw him more and more at last into the schoolroom, where he had plainly begun to recognise that if he was to have the credit of perverting the innocent child he might also at least have the amusement. He never came into the place without telling its occupants that they were the nicest people in the house—a remark which always led them to say to each other "Mr. Perriam!" as loud as ever compressed lips and enlarged eyes could make them articulate. He caused

Maisie to remember what she had said to Mrs. Beale about his having the nature of a good nurse and, rather more than she intended before Mrs. Wix, to bring the whole thing out by once remarking to him that none of her good nurses had smoked quite so much in the nursery. This had no more effect than it was meant to on his cigarettes: he was always smoking, but always declaring that it was death to him not to lead a domestic life.

He led one after all in the schoolroom, and there were hours of late evening, when she had gone to bed, that Maisie knew he sat there talking with Mrs. Wix of how to meet his difficulties. His consideration for this unfortunate woman even in the midst of them continued to show him as the perfect gentleman and lifted the object of his courtesy into an upper air of beatitude in which her very pride had the hush of anxiety. "He leans on me—he leans on me!" she only announced from time to time; and she was more surprised than amused when, later on, she accidentally found she had given her pupil the impression of a support literally supplied by her person. This glimpse of a misconception led her to be explicit—to put before the child, with an air of mourning indeed for such a stoop to the common, that what they talked about in the small hours, as they said, was the question of his taking right hold of life. The life she wanted him to take right hold of was the public: "she," I hasten to add, was, in this connection, not the mistress of his fate, but only Mrs. Wix herself. She had phrases about him that were full of tenderness, yet full of morality. "He's a wonderful nature, but he can't live like the lilies. He's all right, you know, but he must have a high interest." She had more than once remarked that his affairs were sadly involved, but that they must get him—Maisie and she together apparently—into Parliament. The child took it from her with a flutter of importance that Parliament was his natural sphere, and she was the less prepared to recognise a hindrance as she had never heard of any affairs whatever that were not involved. She had in the old days once been told by Mrs. Beale that her very own were, and with the refreshment of knowing that she *had* affairs the information hadn't in the least overwhelmed her. It was true and perhaps a little alarming that she had never heard of any such matters since then. Full of charm at any rate was the prospect of some day getting Sir Claude in; especially after Mrs. Wix, as the fruit of more midnight colloquies, once went so far as to observe that she really believed it was all that was wanted to save him. Mrs. Wix, with these words, struck her pupil as cropping up, after the manner of mamma when mamma talked, quite in a new place. The child stared as at the jump of a kangaroo.

"Save him from what?"

Mrs. Wix hesitated; then she covered a still greater distance. "Why, just from awful misery."

XII

S HE HAD not at the moment explained her ominous speech, but the light of remarkable events soon enabled her companion to read it. It may indeed be said that these days brought on a high quickening of Maisie's direct perceptions, of her gratified sense of arriving by herself at conclusions. This was helped by an emotion intrinsically far from sweet—the increase of the alarm that had most haunted her meditations. She had no need to be told, as on the morrow of the revelation of Sir Claude's danger she was told by Mrs. Wix, that her mother wanted more and more to know why the devil her father didn't send for her: she had too long expected that mamma's curiosity on this point would break out with violence. Maisie could meet such pressure so far as meeting it was to be in a position to reply, in words directly inspired, that papa would be hanged before he'd again be saddled with her. She therefore recognised the hour that in troubled glimpses she had long foreseen, the hour when—the phrase for it came back to her from Mrs. Beale—with two fathers, two mothers and two homes, six protections in all, she shouldn't know "wherever" to go. Such apprehension as she felt on this score was not diminished by the fact that Mrs. Wix herself was suddenly white with terror: a circumstance leading Maisie to the further knowledge that this lady was still more scared on her own behalf than on that of her pupil. A governess who had only one frock was not likely to have either two fathers or two mothers: accordingly if even with these resources Maisie was to be in the streets, where in the name of all that was dreadful was poor Mrs. Wix to be? She had had, it appeared, a tremendous brush with Ida, which had begun and ended with the request that she would be pleased on the spot to "bundle." It had come suddenly but completely, this signal of which she had gone in fear. The companions confessed to each other their long foreboding, but Mrs. Wix was better off than Maisie in having a plan of defence. She declined indeed to communicate it till it was quite mature; but meanwhile, she hastened to declare, her feet were firm in the schoolroom. They could only be loosened by force: she would "leave" for the police perhaps, but she wouldn't leave for mere outrage. That would be to play her ladyship's game, and it would take another turn of the screw to make her desert her darling. Her ladyship had come down with extraordinary ferocity: it had been one of many symptoms of a situation strained—"between them all," as Mrs. Wix said, "but especially between the two"—to the point of God only knew what.

Her description of the crisis made the child reflect. "Between which two?—papa and mamma?"

"Dear, no. I mean between your mother and *him*."

Maisie, in this, recognised an opportunity to be really deep. "'Him'?—Mr. Perriam?"

She fairly brought a blush to the scared face. "Well, my dear, I must say what you *don't* know ain't worth mentioning. That it won't go on for ever with Mr. Perriam—since I *must* meet you—who can suppose? But I meant dear Sir Claude."

Maisie stood corrected rather than abashed. "I see. But it's about Mr. Perriam he's angry?"

Mrs. Wix hesitated. "He says he's not."

"Not angry? He has told you so?"

Mrs. Wix looked at her hard. "Not about *him*."

"Then about some one else?"

Mrs. Wix looked at her harder. "About some one else."

"Lord Eric?" the child promptly brought forth.

At this, of a sudden, her governess was more agitated. "Oh, why, little unfortunate, should we discuss their dreadful names?"—and she threw herself for the millionth time on Maisie's neck. It took her pupil but a moment to feel that she quivered with insecurity, and, the contact of her terror aiding, the pair in another instant were sobbing in each other's arms. Then it was that, completely relaxed, demoralised as she had never been, Mrs. Wix suffered her wound to bleed and her resentment to gush. Her great bitterness was that Ida had called her false, denounced her hypocrisy and duplicity, reviled her spying and tattling, her lying and grovelling to Sir Claude. "Me, *me*," the poor woman wailed, "who've seen what I've seen and gone through everything only to cover her up and ease her off and smooth her down? If I've been an 'ipocrite it's the other way round: I've pretended, to him and to her, to myself and to you and to every one, *not* to see! It serves me right to have held my tongue before such horrors!" What horrors they were her companion forbore too closely to inquire, showing even signs not a few of an ability to take them for granted. That put the couple more than ever, in this troubled sea, in the same boat, so that with the consciousness of ideas on the part of her fellow-mariner Maisie could sit close and wait. Sir Claude on the morrow came in to tea, and then the ideas were produced. It was extraordinary how the child's presence drew out their full richness. The principal one was startling, but Maisie appreciated the courage with which her governess handled it. It simply consisted of the proposal that whenever and wherever they should take refuge Sir Claude should consent to share their asylum. On his protesting with all the warmth in nature against this note of secession she asked what else in the world was left to them if her ladyship should stop supplies.

"Supplies be hanged, my dear woman!" said their delightful friend. "Leave supplies to me—I'll take care of supplies."

Mrs. Wix hesitated. "Well, it's exactly because I knew you'd be so glad to do so that I put the question before you. There's a way to look after us better than any other. That way is just to come *with* us."

It hung before Maisie, Mrs. Wix's way, like a glittering picture, and she clasped her hands in ecstasy. "Come with us, come with us!" she echoed.

Sir Claude looked from his stepdaughter back to her governess. "Do you mean leave this house and take up my abode with you?"

"It will be the right thing—if you feel as you've told me you feel." Mrs. Wix, sustained and uplifted, was now as clear as a bell.

Sir Claude had the air of trying to recall what he had told her; then the light broke that was always breaking to make his face more pleasant. "It's your suggestion that I shall take a house for you?"

"For the wretched homeless child. Any roof—over *our* heads—will do for us; but of course for you it will have to be something really nice."

Sir Claude's eyes reverted to Maisie, rather hard, as she thought; and there was a shade in his very smile that seemed to show her—though she also felt it didn't show Mrs. Wix—that the accommodation prescribed must loom to him pretty large. The next moment, however, he laughed gaily enough. "My dear lady, you exaggerate tremendously *my* poor little needs." Mrs. Wix had once mentioned to her young friend that when Sir Claude called her his dear lady he could do anything with her; and Maisie felt a certain anxiety to see what he would do now. Well, he only addressed her a remark of which the child herself was aware of feeling the force. "Your plan appeals to me immensely; but of course—don't you see?—I shall have to consider the position I put myself in by leaving my wife."

"You'll also have to remember," Mrs. Wix replied, "that if you don't look out your wife won't give you time to consider. Her ladyship will leave *you*."

"Ah, my good friend, I do look out!" the young man returned while Maisie helped herself afresh to bread and butter. "Of course if that happens I shall have somehow to turn round; but I hope with all my heart it won't. I beg your pardon," he continued to his stepdaughter, "for appearing to discuss that sort of possibility under your sharp little nose. But the fact is that I forget half the time that Ida is your sainted mother."

"So do I!" said Maisie, to put him the more in the right.

Her protectress, at this, was upon her again. "The little desolate, precious pet!" For the rest of the conversation she was enclosed in Mrs. Wix's arms, and as they sat there interlocked Sir Claude, before them with his tea-cup, looked down at them in deepening thought. Shrink together as they might they couldn't help, Maisie felt, being a very massive image, a large loose, ponderous presentment, of what Mrs. Wix required of him. She knew moreover that this lady didn't make it better by adding in a moment: "Of course *we* shouldn't dream of a whole house. Any sort of little lodging, however humble, would be only too blessed."

"But it would have to be something that would hold us all," said Sir Claude.

"Oh yes," Mrs. Wix concurred; "the whole point is our being together. While you're waiting, before you act, for her ladyship to take some step, our position here will come to an impossible pass. You don't know what I went through with her for you yesterday—and for our poor darling; but it's not a thing I can promise you often to face again. She has dismissed me in horrible language—she has instructed the servants not to wait on me."

"Oh, the poor servants are all right!" Sir Claude eagerly cried.

"They're certainly better than their mistress. It's too dreadful that I should sit here and say of your wife, Sir Claude, and of Maisie's own mother, that she's lower than a domestic; but my being betrayed into such remarks is just a reason the more for our getting away. I shall stay till I'm taken by the shoulders, but that may happen any day. What also may perfectly happen, you must permit me to repeat, is that she'll go off to get rid of us."

"Oh, if she'll only do that!" Sir Claude laughed. "That would be the very making of us!"

"Don't say it—don't say it!" Mrs. Wix pleaded. "Don't speak of anything so fatal. You know what I mean. We must all cling to the right. You mustn't be bad."

Sir Claude set down his tea-cup; he had become more grave and he pensively wiped his moustache. "Won't all the world say I'm awful if I leave the house before—before she has bolted? They'll say it was my doing it that made her bolt."

Maisie could grasp the force of this reasoning, but it offered no check to Mrs. Wix. "Why need you mind that—if you've done it for so high a motive? Think of the beauty of it," the good lady pressed.

"Of bolting with *you*?" Sir Claude ejaculated.

She faintly smiled—she even faintly coloured. "So far from doing you harm, it will do you the highest good. Sir Claude, if you'll listen to me, it will save you."

"Save me from what?"

Maisie, at this question, waited with renewed suspense for an answer that would bring the thing to a finer point than their companion had brought it to before. But there was on the contrary only more mystification in Mrs. Wix's reply. "Ah, from you know what!"

"Do you mean from some other woman?"

"Yes—from a real bad one."

Sir Claude at least, the child could see, was not mystified; so little indeed that a smile of intelligence broke afresh in his eyes. He turned them in vague discomfort to Maisie, and then something in the way she met them caused him to chuck her playfully under the chin. It was not till after this that he good-naturedly met Mrs. Wix. "You think me much worse than I am."

"If that were true," she returned, "I wouldn't appeal to you. I do, Sir Claude, in the name of all that's good in you—and, oh, so earnestly! We can help each other. What you'll do for our young friend here I needn't say. That isn't even what I want to speak of now. What I want to speak of is what you'll *get*—don't you see?—from such an opportunity to take hold. Take hold of *us*—take hold of *her*. Make her your duty—make her your life: she'll repay you a thousand-fold!"

It was to Mrs. Wix, during this appeal, that Maisie's contemplation transferred itself: partly because, though her heart was in her throat for trepidation, she felt a certain delicacy about appearing herself to press the question; partly from the coercion of seeing Mrs. Wix come out as Mrs. Wix had never come before—not even on the day of her call at Mrs. Beale's with the news of mamma's marriage. On that day Mrs. Beale had surpassed her in dignity; but nobody could have surpassed her now. There was in fact at this moment a fascination for her pupil in the hint she seemed to give that she had still more of that surprise behind. So the sharpened sense of spectatorship was the child's main support, the long habit, from the first, of seeing herself in discussion and finding in the fury of it—she had had a glimpse of the game of football—a sort of compensation for the doom of a peculiar passivity. It gave her often an odd air of being present at her history in as separate a manner as if she could only get at experience by flattening her nose against a pane of glass. Such she felt to be the application of her nose while she waited for the effect of Mrs. Wix's eloquence. Sir Claude, however, didn't keep her long in a position so ungraceful: he sat down and opened his arms to her as he had done the day he came for her at her father's, and while he held her there, looking at her kindly, but as if their companion had brought the blood a good deal to his face, he said:

"Dear Mrs. Wix is magnificent, but she's rather too grand about it. I mean the situation isn't after all quite so desperate or quite so simple. But I give you my word before her, and I give it to her before you, that I'll never, never, forsake you. Do you hear that, old fellow, and do you take it in? I'll stick to you through everything."

Maisie did take it in—took it with a long tremor of all her little being; and then as, to emphasise it, he drew her closer she buried her head on his shoulder and cried without sound and without pain. While she was so engaged she became aware that his own breast was agitated, and gathered from it with rapture that his tears were as silently flowing. Presently she heard a loud sob from Mrs. Wix—Mrs. Wix was the only one who made a noise.

She was to have made, for some time, none other but this, though within a few days, in conversation with her pupil, she described her relations with Ida as positively excruciating. There was as yet nevertheless no attempt to eject her by force, and she recognised that Sir Claude, taking such a stand as never before, had intervened with passion and with success. As Maisie remembered—and remembered wholly without disdain—that he had told her he was afraid of her ladyship, the little girl took this act of resolution as a proof of what, in the spirit of the engagement sealed by all their tears, he was really prepared to do. Mrs. Wix spoke to her of the pecuniary sacrifice by which she herself purchased the scant security she enjoyed and which, if it was a defence against the hand of violence, was far from making her safe from private aggression. Didn't her ladyship find every hour of the day some insidious means to humiliate and trample upon her? There was a quarter's salary owing her—a great name, even Maisie could suspect, for a small matter; she should never see it as long as she lived, but keeping quiet about it put her ladyship, thank heaven, a little in one's power. Now that he was doing so much else she could never have the grossness to apply for it to Sir Claude. He had sent home for schoolroom consumption a huge frosted cake, a wonderful delectable mountain with geological strata of jam, which might, with economy, see them through many days of their siege; but it was none the less known to Mrs. Wix that his affairs were more and more involved, and her fellow-partaker looked back tenderly, in the light of these involutions, at the expression of face with which he had greeted the proposal that he should set up another establishment. Maisie felt that if their maintenance should hang but by a thread they must still demean themselves with the highest delicacy. What he was doing was simply acting without delay, so far as his embarrassments permitted, on the inspiration of his elder friend. There was at this season a wonderful month of May—as soft as a drop of the wind in a gale that had kept one awake—when he took out his step-daughter with a fresh alacrity and they rambled the great town in search, as Mrs. Wix called it, of combined amusement and instruction.

They rode on the top of 'buses; they visited outlying parks; they went to cricket-matches where Maisie fell asleep; they tried a hundred places for the best one to have tea. This was his direct way of rising to Mrs. Wix's admirable lesson—of making his little accepted charge his duty and his life. They dropped, under incontrollable impulses, into shops that they agreed were too big, to look at things that they agreed were too small, and it was during these hours that Mrs. Wix, alone at home, but a subject of regretful reference as they pulled off their gloves for refreshment, subsequently described herself as most exposed to the blows that her ladyship had achieved such ingenuity in dealing. She again and again repeated that she would not so much have minded having her "attainments" held up to scorn and her knowledge of every subject denied if she were not habitually denounced to her face as the basest of her sex. There was by this time no pretence on the part of any one of denying it to be fortunate that her ladyship habitually left London every Saturday and was more and more disposed to a return late in the week. It was almost equally public that she regarded as a preposterous "pose," and indeed as a direct insult to herself, her husband's attitude of staying behind to look after a child for whom the most elaborate provision had been made. If there was a type Ida despised, Sir Claude communicated to Maisie, it was the man who pottered about town of a Sunday; and he also mentioned how often she had declared to him that if he had a grain of spirit he would be ashamed to accept a menial position about

Mr. Farange's daughter. It was her ladyship's contention that he was in craven fear of his predecessor—otherwise he would recognise it as an obligation of plain decency to protect his wife against the outrage of that person's barefaced attempt to swindle her. The swindle was that Mr. Farange put upon her the whole intolerable burden; "and even when I pay for you myself," Sir Claude averred to his young friend, "she accuses me the more of truckling and grovelling." It was Mrs. Wix's conviction, they both knew, arrived at on independent grounds, that Ida's weekly excursions were feelers for a more considerable absence. If she came back later each week the week would be sure to arrive when she wouldn't come back at all. This appearance had of course much to do with Mrs. Wix's actual valour. Could they but hold out long enough the snug little home with Sir Claude would find itself informally constituted.

XIII

THIS MIGHT moreover have been taken to be the sense of a remark made by her stepfather as—one rainy day when the streets were all splash and two umbrellas unsociable and the wanderers had sought shelter in the National Gallery—Maisie sat beside him staring rather sightlessly at a roomful of pictures which he had mystified her much by speaking of with a bored sigh as a "silly superstition." They represented, with patches of gold and cataracts of purple, with stiff saints and angular angels, with ugly Madonnas and uglier babies, strange prayers and prostrations; so that she at first took his words for a protest against devotional idolatry—all the more that he had of late often come with her and with Mrs. Wix to morning church, a place of worship of Mrs. Wix's own choosing, where there was nothing of that sort; no haloes on heads, but only, during long sermons, beguiling backs of bonnets, and where, as her governess always afterwards observed, he gave the most earnest attention. It presently appeared, however, that his reference was merely to the affectation of admiring such ridiculous works—an admonition that she received from him as submissively as she received everything. What turn it gave to their talk need not here be recorded: the transition to the colourless schoolroom and lonely Mrs. Wix was doubtless an effect of relaxed interest in what was before them. Maisie expressed in her own way the truth that she never went home nowadays without expecting to find the temple of her studies empty and the poor priestess cast out. This conveyed a full appreciation of her peril, and it was in rejoinder that Sir Claude uttered, acknowledging the source of that peril, the reassurance at which I have glanced. "Don't be afraid, my dear: I've squared her." It required indeed a supplement when he saw that it left the child momentarily blank. "I mean that your mother lets me do what I want so long as I let her do what she wants."

"So you *are* doing what you want?" Maisie asked.

"Rather, Miss Farange!"

Miss Farange turned it over. "And she's doing the same?"

"Up to the hilt!"

Again she considered. "Then, please, what may it be?"

"I wouldn't tell you for the whole world."

She gazed at a gaunt Madonna; after which she broke into a slow smile. "Well, I don't care, so long as you do let her."

"Oh, you monster!" laughed Sir Claude, getting up.

Another day, in another place—a place in Baker Street where at a hungry hour she had sat down with him to tea and buns—he brought out a question disconnected from previous talk. "I say, you know, what do you suppose your father *would* do?"

Maisie had not long to cast about nor to question his pleasant eyes. "If you were really to go with us? He would make a great complaint."

He seemed amused at the term she employed. "Oh, I shouldn't mind a 'complaint'!"

"He would talk to every one about it," said Maisie.

"Well, I shouldn't mind that either."

"Of course not," the child hastened to respond. "You've told me you're not afraid of him."

"The question is are you?" said Sir Claude.

Maisie candidly considered; then she spoke resolutely. "No, not of papa."

"But of somebody else?"

"Certainly, of lots of people."

"Of your mother first and foremost of course."

"Dear, yes; more of mamma than of——than of——"

"Than of what?" Sir Claude asked as she hesitated for a comparison.

She thought over all objects of dread. "Than of a wild elephant!" she at last declared. "And you are too," she reminded him as he laughed.

"Oh yes, I am too."

Again she meditated. "Why then did you marry her?"

"Just because I *was* afraid."

"Even when she loved you?"

"That made her the more alarming."

For Maisie herself, though her companion seemed to find it droll, this opened up depths of gravity. "More alarming than she is now?"

"Well, in a different way. Fear, unfortunately, is a very big thing, and there's a great variety of kinds."

She took this in with complete intelligence. "Then I think I've got them all."

"You?" her friend cried. "Nonsense! You're thoroughly 'game.'"

"I'm awfully afraid of Mrs. Beale," Maisie announced.

He raised his smooth brows. "That charming woman?"

"Well," she answered, "you can't understand it because you're not in the same state."

She had been going on with a luminous "But" when, across the table, he laid his hand on her arm. "I *can* understand it," he confessed. "I *am* in the same state."

"Oh, but she likes you so!" Maisie eagerly suggested.

Sir Claude literally coloured. "That has something to do with it."

Maisie wondered again. "Being liked with being afraid?"

"Yes, when it amounts to adoration."

"Then why aren't you afraid of *me*?"

"Because with you it amounts to that." He had kept his hand on her arm. "Well, what prevents is simply that you're the gentlest spirit on earth. Besides——" he pursued; but he came to a pause.

"Besides——?"

"I should be in fear if you were older—there! See—you already make me talk nonsense," the young man added. "The question's about your father. Is he likewise afraid of Mrs. Beale?"

"I think not. And yet he loves her," Maisie mused.

"Oh no—he doesn't; not a bit!" After which, as his companion stared, Sir Claude apparently felt that he must make his announcement fit with her recollections. "There's nothing of that sort *now*."

But Maisie only stared the more. "They've changed?"

"Like your mother and me."

She wondered how he knew. "Then you've seen Mrs. Beale again?"

He demurred. "Oh no. She has written to me," he presently subjoined. "*She's* not afraid of your father either. No one at all is—really." Then he went on while Maisie's little mind, with its filial spring too relaxed, from of old, for a pang at this want of parental majesty, speculated on the vague relation between Mrs. Beale's courage and the question, for Mrs. Wix and herself, of a neat lodging with their friend. "She wouldn't care a bit if Mr. Farange should make a row."

"Do you mean about you and me and Mrs. Wix? Why should she care? It wouldn't hurt *her*."

Sir Claude, with his legs out and his hand diving into his trousers-pocket, threw back his head with a laugh just perceptibly tempered, as she thought, by a sigh. "My dear stepchild, you're delightful! Look here, we must pay. You've had five buns?"

"How *can* you?" Maisie demanded, crimson under the eye of the young woman who had stepped to their board. "I've had three."

Shortly after this Mrs. Wix looked so ill that it was to be feared her ladyship had treated her to some unexampled passage. Maisie asked if anything worse than usual had occurred; whereupon the poor woman brought out with infinite gloom: "He has been seeing Mrs. Beale."

"Sir Claude?" The child remembered what he had said. "Oh no—not *seeing* her!"

"I beg your pardon. I absolutely know it." Mrs. Wix was as positive as she was dismal.

Maisie nevertheless ventured to challenge her. "And how, please, do you know it?"

She faltered a moment. "From herself. I've been to see her." Then on Maisie's visible surprise: "I went yesterday while you were out with him. He has seen her repeatedly."

It was not wholly clear to Maisie why Mrs. Wix should be prostrate at this discovery; but her general consciousness of the way things could be both perpetrated and resented always eased off for her the strain of the particular mystery. "There may be some mistake. He says he hasn't."

Mrs. Wix turned paler, as if this were a still deeper ground for alarm. "He says so?—he denies that he has seen her?"

"He told me so three days ago. Perhaps she's mistaken," Maisie suggested.

"Do you mean perhaps she lies? She lies whenever it suits her, I'm very sure. But I know when people lie—and that's what I've loved in you, that you never do. Mrs. Beale didn't yesterday at any rate. He *has* seen her."

Maisie was silent a little. "He says not," she then repeated. "Perhaps—perhaps——" Once more she paused.

"Do you mean perhaps *he* lies?"

"Gracious goodness, no!" Maisie shouted.

Mrs. Wix's bitterness, however, again overflowed. "He does, he does," she cried, "and it's that that's just the worst of it! They'll take you, they'll take you, and what in the world will then become of me?" She threw herself afresh upon her pupil and wept over her with the inevitable effect of causing the child's own tears to flow. But Maisie could not have told you if she had been crying at the image of their separation or at that of Sir Claude's untruth. As regards this deviation it was agreed between them that they were not in a position to bring it home to him. Mrs. Wix was in dread of doing anything to make him, as she said, "worse"; and Maisie was sufficiently initiated to be able to reflect that in speaking to her as he had done he had only wished to be tender of Mrs. Beale. It fell in with all her inclinations to think of him as tender, and she forbore to let him know that the two ladies had, as *she* would never do, betrayed him.

She had not long to keep her secret, for the next day, when she went out with him, he suddenly said in reference to some errand he had first proposed: "No, we won't do that—we'll do something else." On this, a few steps from the door, he stopped a hansom and helped her in; then following her he gave the driver over the top an address that she lost. When he was seated beside her she asked him where they were going; to which he replied: "My dear child, you'll see." She saw while she watched and wondered that they took the direction of the Regent's Park; but she didn't know why he should make a mystery of that, and it was not till they passed under a pretty arch and drew up at a white house in a terrace from which the view, she thought, must be lovely that, mystified, she clutched him and broke out: "I shall see papa?"

He looked down at her with a kind smile. "No, probably not. I haven't brought you for that."

"Then whose house is it?"

"It's your father's. They've moved here."

She looked about: she had known Mr. Farange in four or five houses, and there was nothing astonishing in this except that it was the nicest place yet. "But I shall see Mrs. Beale?"

"It's to see her that I brought you."

She stared, very white, and, with her hand on his arm, though they had stopped, kept him sitting in the cab. "To leave me, do you mean?"

He hesitated. "It's not for me to say if you *can* stay. We must look into it."

"But if I do I shall see papa?"

"Oh, some time or other, no doubt." Then Sir Claude went on: "Have you really so very great a dread of that?"

Maisie glanced away over the apron of the cab—gazed a minute at the green expanse of the Regent's Park and, at this moment colouring to the roots of her hair, felt the full, hot rush of an emotion more mature than any she had yet known. It consisted of an odd, unexpected shame at placing in an inferior light, to so perfect a gentleman and so charming a person as Sir Claude, so very near a relative as Mr. Farange. She remembered, however, her friend's telling her that no one was seriously afraid of her father, and she turned round with a small toss of her head. "Oh, I daresay I can manage him!"

Sir Claude smiled, but she noticed that the violence with which she had just changed colour had brought into his own face a slight compunctious and embarrassed flush. It was as if he had caught his first glimpse of her sense of responsibility. Neither of them made a movement to get out, and after an instant he said to her: "Look here, if you say so we won't after all go in."

"Ah, but I want to see Mrs. Beale!" the child murmured.

"But what if she does decide to take you? Then, you know, you'll have to remain."

Maisie turned it over. "Straight on—and give you up?"

"Well—I don't quite know about giving me up."

"I mean as I gave up Mrs. Beale when I last went to mamma's. I couldn't do without you here for anything like so long a time as that." It struck her as a hundred years since she had seen Mrs. Beale, who was on the other side of the door they were so near and whom she yet had not taken the jump to clasp in her arms.

"Oh, I daresay you'll see more of me than you've seen of Mrs. Beale. It isn't in *me* to be so beautifully discreet," Sir Claude said. "But all the same," he continued, "I leave the thing, now that we're here, absolutely with you. You must settle it. We'll only go in if you say so. If you don't say so we'll turn right round and drive away."

"So in that case Mrs. Beale won't take me?"

"Well—not by any act of ours."

"And I shall be able to go on with mamma?" Maisie asked.

"Oh, I don't say that!"

She considered. "But I thought you said you had squared her?"

Sir Claude poked his stick at the splashboard of the cab. "Not, my dear child, to the point she now requires."

"Then if she turns me out and I don't come here——?"

Sir Claude promptly took her up. "What do I offer you, you naturally inquire? My poor chick, that's just what I ask myself. I don't see it, I confess, quite as straight as Mrs. Wix."

His companion gazed a moment at what Mrs. Wix saw. "You mean *we* can't make a little family?"

"It's very base of me, no doubt, but I can't wholly chuck your mother."

Maisie, at this, emitted a low but lengthened sigh, a slight sound of reluctant assent which would certainly have been amusing to an auditor. "Then there isn't anything else?"

"I vow I don't quite see what there is."

Maisie waited a moment; her silence seemed to signify that she too had no alternative to suggest. But she made another appeal. "If I come here you'll come to see me?"

"I won't lose sight of you."

"But how often will you come?" As he hung fire she pressed him. "Often and often?"

Still he faltered. "My dear old woman——" he began. Then he paused again, going on at the next moment with a change of tone: "You're too funny! Yes, then," he said; "often and often."

"All right!" Maisie jumped out. Mrs. Beale was at home, but not in the drawing-room, and when the butler had gone for her the child suddenly broke out: "But when I'm here what will Mrs. Wix do?"

"Ah, you should have thought of that sooner!" said her companion with the first faint note of asperity she had ever heard him sound.

XIV

MRS. BEALE fairly swooped upon her, and the effect of the whole hour was to show the child how much, how quite formidably indeed, after all, she was loved. This was the more the case as her stepmother, so changed—in the very manner of her mother—that she really struck her as a new acquaintance, somehow recalled more familiarity than Maisie could feel. A rich, strong, expressive affection in short pounced upon her in the shape of a handsomer, ampler, older Mrs. Beale. It was like making a fine friend, and they hadn't been a minute together before she felt elated at the way she had met the choice imposed upon her in the cab. There was a whole future in the combination of Mrs. Beale's beauty and Mrs. Beale's hug. She seemed to Maisie charming to behold, and also to have no connection at all with anybody who had once mended underclothing and had meals in the nursery. The child knew one of her father's wives was a woman of fashion, but she had always dimly made a distinction, not applying that epithet without reserve to the other. Mrs. Beale since their separation had acquired a conspicuous right to it, and Maisie's first flush of response to her present delight coloured all her splendour with meanings that, this time, were sweet. She had told Sir Claude that she was afraid of the lady in the Regent's Park; but she was not too much afraid to rejoice, aloud, on the very spot. "Why, aren't you beautiful? Isn't she beautiful, Sir Claude, *isn't* she?"

"The handsomest woman in London, simply," Sir Claude gallantly replied. "Just as sure as you're the best little girl!"

Well, the handsomest woman in London gave herself up, with tender, lustrous looks and every demonstration of fondness, to a happiness at last recovered. There was almost as vivid a bloom in her maturity as in mamma's, and it took her but a short time to give her little friend an impression of positive power—an impression that opened up there like a new source of confidence. This was a perception, on Maisie's part, that neither mamma, nor Sir Claude, nor Mrs. Wix, with their immense and so varied respective attractions, had exactly kindled, and that made an immediate difference when the talk, as it promptly did, began to turn to her father. Oh yes, Mr. Farange was a complication, but she saw now that he would not be one for his daughter. For Mrs. Beale certainly he was an immense one; she speedily made known as much: but Mrs. Beale from this moment presented herself to Maisie as a person to whom a great gift had come. The great gift was just for handling complications. Maisie observed how little she made of them when, after she had dropped to Sir Claude some reference to a previous meeting, he exclaimed with an air of consternation and yet with something of a laugh that he had denied to their companion their having, since the day he came for her, seen each other till that moment.

Mrs. Beale diffused surprise. "Why did you do anything so silly?"

"To protect your reputation."

"From Maisie?" Mrs. Beale was much amused. "My reputation with Maisie is too good to suffer."

"But you believed me, you rascal, didn't you?" Sir Claude asked of the child.

She looked at him; she smiled. "Her reputation did suffer. I discovered you had been here."

He was not too chagrined to laugh. "The way, my dear, you talk of that sort of thing!"

"How should she talk," Mrs. Beale inquired, "after all this wretched time with her mother?"

"It was not mamma who told me," Maisie exclaimed. "It was only Mrs. Wix." She was hesitating whether to bring out before Sir Claude the source of Mrs. Wix's information; but Mrs. Beale, addressing the young man, showed her the vanity of her scruples.

"Do you know that preposterous person came to see me a day or two ago?—when I told her I had seen you repeatedly."

Sir Claude, for once in a way, was disconcerted. "The old cat! She never told me. Then you thought I had lied?" he demanded of Maisie.

She was flurried by the term with which he had qualified her gentle friend, but she felt the occasion to be one which she must in every manner lend herself. "Oh, I didn't mind! But Mrs. Wix did," she added with an intention benevolent to her governess.

Her intention was not very effective as regards Mrs. Beale. "Mrs. Wix is too idiotic!" that lady declared.

"But to you, of all people," Sir Claude asked, "what had she to say?"

"Why, that, like Mrs. Micawber—whom she must, I think, rather resemble—she will never, never, never desert Miss Farange."

"Oh, I'll make that all right!" Sir Claude cheerfully returned.

"I'm sure I hope so, my dear man," said Mrs. Beale, while Maisie wondered just how he would proceed. Before she had time to ask Mrs. Beale continued: "That's not all she came to do, if you please. But you'll never guess the rest."

"Shall *I* guess it?" Maisie demanded.

Mrs. Beale was again amused. "Why, you're just the person! It must be quite the sort of thing you've heard at your awful mother's. Have you never seen women there crying to her to 'spare' the men they love?"

Maisie, wondering, tried to remember; but Sir Claude was freshly diverted. "Oh, they don't trouble about Ida! Mrs. Wix cried to you to spare *me*?"

"She regularly went down on her knees to me."

"The darling old dear!" the young man exclaimed.

These words were a joy to Maisie—they made up for his previous description of Mrs. Wix. "And *will* you spare him?" she asked of Mrs. Beale.

Her stepmother, seizing her and kissing her again, seemed charmed with the tone of her question. "Not an inch of him! I'll pick him to the bone!"

"You mean that he'll really come often?" Maisie pressed.

Mrs. Beale turned lovely eyes to Sir Claude. "That's not for me to say—it's for him."

He said nothing for the time, however; with his hands in his pockets and vaguely humming a tune—even Maisie could see he was a little nervous—he only walked to the window and looked out at the Regent's Park. "Well, he has promised," Maisie said. "But how will papa like it?"

"His being in and out? Ah, that's a question that, to be frank with you, my dear, hardly matters. In point of fact, however, Beale greatly enjoys the idea that Sir Claude too, poor man, has been forced to quarrel with your mother."

Sir Claude turned round and spoke gravely and kindly. "Don't be afraid, Maisie; you won't lose sight of me."

"Thank you so much!" Maisie was radiant. "But what I meant—don't you know?—was what papa would say to *me*."

"Oh, I've been having that out with him," said Mrs. Beale. "He'll behave well enough. You see the great difficulty is that, though he changes every three days about everything else in the world, he has never changed about your mother. It's a caution, the way he hates her."

Sir Claude gave a short laugh. "It certainly can't beat the way she still hates *him*!"

"Well," Mrs. Beale went on obligingly, "nothing can take the place of that feeling with either of them, and the best way they can think of to show it is for each to leave you as long as possible on the hands of the other. There's nothing, as you've seen for yourself, that makes either so furious. It isn't, asking so little as you do, that you're much of an expense or a trouble; it's only that you make each feel so well how nasty the other wants to be. Therefore Beale goes on loathing your mother too much to have any great fury left for any one else. Besides, you know, I've squared him."

"Oh Lord!" Sir Claude cried with a louder laugh and turning again to the window.

"*I* know how!" Maisie was prompt to proclaim. "By letting him do what he wants on condition that he let's you also do it."

"You're too delicious, my own pet!"—she was involved in another hug. "How in the world have I got on so long without you? I've not been happy, love," said Mrs. Beale with her cheek to the child's.

"Be happy now!"—Maisie throbbed with shy tenderness.

"I think I shall be. You'll save me."

"As I'm saving Sir Claude?" the little girl asked eagerly.

Mrs. Beale, a trifle at a loss, appealed to her visitor. "Is she really?"

He showed high amusement at Maisie's question. "It's dear Mrs. Wix's idea. There may be something in it."

"He makes me his duty—he makes me his life," Maisie set forth to her stepmother.

"Why, that's what *I* want to do!"—Mrs. Beale, so anticipated, turned pink with astonishment.

"Well, you can do it together. Then he'll *have* to come!"

Mrs. Beale by this time had her young friend fairly in her lap and she smiled up at Sir Claude. "Shall we do it together?"

His laughter had dropped, and for a moment he turned his handsome, serious face not to his hostess, but to his step-daughter. "Well, it's rather more decent than some things. Upon my soul, the way things are going, it seems to me the only decency!" He had the air of arguing it out to Maisie, of presenting it, through an impulse of conscience, as a connection in which they could honourably see her participate; though his plea of mere "decency" might well have appeared to fall below her rosy little vision. "If we're not good for you," he exclaimed, "I'll be hanged if I know who we shall be good for!"

Mrs. Beale showed the child an intenser light. "I daresay you *will* save us—from one thing and another."

"Oh, I know what she'll save *me* from!" Sir Claude roundly asserted. "There'll be rows, of course," he went on.

Mrs. Beale quickly took him up. "Yes, but they'll be nothing—for you at least—to the rows your wife makes as it is. I can bear what *I* suffer—I can't bear what you do."

"We're doing a good deal for you, you know, young woman," Sir Claude went on to Maisie with the same gravity.

His little charge coloured with a sense of obligation and the eagerness of her desire it should be remarked how little was lost on her. "Oh, I know!"

"Then you must keep us all right!" This time he laughed.

"How you talk to her!" cried Mrs. Beale.

"No worse than you!" he gaily rejoined.

"Handsome is that handsome does!" she exclaimed in the same spirit. "You can take off your things," she went on, re-leasing Maisie.

The child, on her feet, was all emotion. "Then I'm just to stop—this way?"

"It will do as well as any other. Sir Claude, to-morrow, will have your things brought."

"I'll bring them myself. Upon my word I'll see them packed!" Sir Claude promised. "Come here and unbutton."

He had beckoned his young companion to where he sat, and he helped to disengage her from her coverings while Mrs.

Beale, from a little distance, smiled at the hand he displayed. "There's a stepfather for you! I'm bound to say, you know, that he makes up for the want of other people."

"He makes up for the want of a nurse!" Sir Claude laughed. "Don't you remember I told you so the very first time?"

"Remember? It was exactly what made me think so well of you!"

"Nothing would induce me," the young man said to Maisie, "to tell you what made me think so well of *her*." Having divested the child he kissed her gently and gave her a little pat to make her stand off. The pat was accompanied with a vague sigh in which his gravity of a moment before came back. "All the same, if you hadn't had the fatal gift of beauty——"

"Well, what?" Maisie asked, wondering why he paused. It was the first time she had heard of her beauty.

"Why, we shouldn't all be thinking so well of each other!"

"He isn't speaking of personal loveliness—you're not lovely in person, my dear, at all," Mrs. Beale explained. "He's just talking of plain, dull charm of character."

"Her character's the most extraordinary thing in all the world," Sir Claude communicated to Mrs. Beale.

"Oh, I know all about that sort of thing!"—she fairly bridled with the knowledge.

It gave Maisie somehow a sudden sense of responsibility from which she sought refuge. "Well, you've got it too, 'that sort of thing'—you've got the fatal gift; you both really have!" she broke out.

"Beauty of character? My dear boy, we haven't a pennyworth!" Sir Claude protested.

"Speak for yourself, sir!" leaped lightly from Mrs. Beale. "I'm good and I'm clever. What more do you want? For you, I'll spare your blushes and not be personal—I'll simply say that you're as handsome as you can stick together."

"You're both very lovely; you can't get out of it!"—Maisie felt the need of carrying her point. "And it's beautiful to see you together."

Sir Claude had taken his hat and stick; he stood looking at her a moment. "You're a comfort in trouble! But I must go home and pack you."

"And when will you come back?—to-morrow, to-morrow?"

"You see what we're in for!" he said to Mrs. Beale.

"Well, I can bear it," she replied, "if you can."

Their companion gazed from one of them to the other, thinking that though she had been happy indeed between Sir Claude and Mrs. Wix she should evidently be happier still between Sir Claude and Mrs. Beale. But it was like being perched on a prancing horse, and she made a movement to hold on to something. "Then, you know, sha'n't I bid good-bye to Mrs. Wix?"

"Oh, I'll make it all right with her," said Sir Claude.

Maisie considered. "And with mamma?"

"Ah, mamma!" he sadly laughed.

Even for the child this was scarcely ambiguous; but Mrs. Beale endeavoured to contribute to its clearness. "Your mother will crow, she'll crow——"

"Like the early bird!" said Sir Claude as she looked about for a comparison.

"She'll need no consolation," Mrs. Beale went on, "for having made your father grandly blaspheme."

Maisie stared. "Will he grandly blaspheme?" It sounded picturesque, almost scriptural, and her question produced a fresh play of caresses, in which Sir Claude also engaged. She wondered meanwhile who, if Mrs. Wix was disposed of, would represent in her life the element of geography and anecdote; and she presently surmounted the delicacy she felt about asking. "Won't there be any one to give me lessons?"

Mrs. Beale was prepared with a reply that struck her as absolutely magnificent. "You shall have such lessons as you've never had in all your life. You shall go to courses."

"Courses?" Maisie had never heard of such things.

"At institutions—on subjects."

Maisie continued to stare. "Subjects?"

Mrs. Beale was really splendid. "All the most important ones. French literature—and sacred history. You'll take part in classes—with awfully smart children."

"I'm going to look thoroughly into the whole thing, you know." And Sir Claude, with characteristic kindness, gave her a nod of assurance accompanied by a friendly wink.

But Mrs. Beale went much further. "My dear child, you shall attend lectures."

The horizon was suddenly vast and Maisie felt herself the smaller for it. "All alone?"

"Oh no; I'll attend them with you," said Sir Claude. "They'll teach me a lot I don't know."

"So they will me," Mrs. Beale gravely admitted. "We'll go with her together—it will be charming. It's ages," she confessed to Maisie, "since I've had any time for study. That's another sweet way in which you'll be a motive to us. Oh, won't the good she'll do us be immense?" she broke out uncontrollably to Sir Claude.

He weighed it; then he replied: "That's certainly our idea." Of this idea Maisie naturally had less of a grasp, but it inspired her with almost equal enthusiasm. If in so bright a prospect there would be nothing to long for it followed that she wouldn't long for Mrs. Wix; but her consciousness of her assent to the absence of that fond figure caused a pair of words that had often sounded in her ears to ring in them again. It showed her in short what her father had always meant by calling her mother a "low sneak" and her mother by calling her father one. She wondered if she herself shouldn't be a low sneak in learning to be so happy without Mrs. Wix. What would Mrs. Wix do? where would Mrs. Wix go? Before Maisie knew it, and at the door, as Sir Claude was off, these anxieties, on her lips, grew articulate and her stepfather had stopped long enough to answer them. "Oh, I'll square her!" he cried; and with this he departed.

Face to face with Mrs. Beale Maisie, giving a sigh of relief, looked round at what seemed to her the dawn of a higher order. "Then *every one* will be squared!" she peacefully said. On which her stepmother affectionately bent over her again.

XV

IT WAS Susan Ash who came to her with the news: "He's downstairs, miss, and he do look beautiful."

In the schoolroom at her father's, which had pretty blue curtains, she had been making out at the piano a lovely little thing, as Mrs. Beale called it, a "Moonlight Berceuse" sent her through the post by Sir Claude, who considered that her musical education had been deplorably neglected and who, the last months at her mother's, had been on the point of making arrangements for regular lessons. She knew from him familiarly that the real thing, as he said, was shockingly dear and that anything else was a waste of money, and she therefore rejoiced the more at the sacrifice represented by this composition, of which the price, five shillings, was marked on the cover and which was evidently the real thing. She was already on her feet. "Mrs. Beale has sent up for me?"

"Oh no—it's not that," said Susan Ash. "Mrs. Beale has been out this hour."

"Then papa!"

"Dear no—not papa. You'll do, miss, all but them wandering 'airs," Susan went on. "Your papa never came 'ome at all," she added.

"From where?" Maisie responded a little absently and very excitedly. She gave a wild manual brush of her locks.

"Oh, that, miss, I should be very sorry to tell you! I'd rather tuck away that white thing behind—though I'm blessed if it's my work."

"Do then, please. I know where papa was," Maisie impatiently continued.

"Well, in your place I wouldn't tell."

"He was at the club—the Chrysanthemum. So!"

"All night long? Why, the flowers shut up at night, you know!" cried Susan Ash.

"Well, I don't care"—the child was at the door. "Sir Claude asked for me *alone*?"

"The same as if you was a duchess."

Maisie was aware on her way downstairs that she was now

quite as happy as one, and also, a moment later, as she hung round his neck, that even such a personage would scarce commit herself more grandly. There was moreover a hint of the duchess in the infinite point with which, as she felt, she exclaimed: "And this is what you call coming *often*?"

Sir Claude met her, delightfully, in the same fine spirit. "My dear old man, don't make me a scene—I assure you it's what every woman does that I look at. Let us have some fun—it's a lovely day: clap on something smart and come out with me; then we'll talk it over quietly." They were on their way five minutes later to Hyde Park, and nothing that even in the good days at her mother's they had ever talked over had more of the sweetness of tranquillity than his present prompt explanations. He was at his best in such an office and with the exception of Mrs. Wix the only person she had met in her life who ever explained. With him, however, the act had an authority transcending the wisdom of woman. It all came back, all the plans that always failed, all the rewards and bribes that she was perpetually paying for in advance and perpetually out of pocket by afterwards—the whole great stress to be dealt with introduced her on each occasion afresh to the question of money. Even she herself almost knew how it would have expressed the strength of his empire to say that to shuffle away her sense of being duped he had only, from under his lovely moustache, to breathe upon it. It was somehow in the nature of plans to be expensive and in the nature of the expensive to be impossible. To be "involved" was of the essence of everybody's affairs, and also at every particular moment to be more involved than usual. This had been the case with Sir Claude's, with papa's, with mamma's, with Mrs. Beale's and with Maisie's own at the particular moment, a moment of several weeks, that had elapsed since our young lady had been re-established at her father's. There wasn't "two-and-tuppence" for anything or for any one, and that was why there had been no sequel to the classes in French literature with all the smart little girls. It was devilish awkward, didn't she see? to try, without even the modest sum mentioned, to mix her up with a remote array that glittered before her after this as the children of the rich. She was to feel henceforth as if she were flattening her nose upon the hard window-pane of the sweet-shop of knowledge. If the classes, however, that were select, and accordingly the only ones, were impossibly dear, the lectures at the institutions—at least at some of them—were directly addressed to the intelligent poor, and it therefore had to be easier still to produce on the spot the reason why she had been taken to none. This reason, Sir Claude said, was that she happened to be just going to be, though they had nothing to do with that in now directing their steps to the banks of the Serpentine. Maisie's own park, in the north, had been nearer at hand, but they rolled westward in a hansom because at the end of the sweet June days that was the direction taken by every one that any one looked at. They cultivated for an hour, on the Row and by the Drive, this opportunity for each observer to amuse and for one of them indeed, not a little hilariously, to mystify the other, and before the hour was over Maisie had elicited, in reply to her sharpest challenge, a further account of her friend's long absence.

"Why I've broken my word to you so dreadfully—promising so solemnly and then never coming? Well, my dear, that's a question that, not seeing me day after day, you must very often have put to Mrs. Beale."

"Oh yes," the child replied; "again and again."

"And what has she told you?"

"That you're as bad as you're beautiful."

"Is that what she says?"

"Those very words."

"Ah, the dear old soul!" Sir Claude was much diverted, and his loud, clear laugh was all his explanation. Those were just the words Maisie had last heard him use about Mrs. Wix. She clung to his hand, which was encased in a pearl-grey glove ornamented with the thick black lines that, at her mother's, always used to strike her as connected with the way the bestitched fists of the long ladies carried, with the elbows well out, their umbrellas upside down. The mere sense of it in her own covered the ground of loss just as much as the ground of gain. His presence was like an object brought so close to her face that she couldn't see round its edges. He himself, however, remained showman of the spectacle even after they had passed out of the Park and begun, under the charm of the spot and the season, to stroll in Kensington Gardens. What they had left behind them was, as he said, only a pretty bad circus, and, through engaging gates and over a bridge, they had come in a quarter of an hour, as he also remarked, a hundred miles from London. A great green glade was before them, and high old trees, and under the shade of these, in the fresh turf, the crooked course of a rural footpath: "It's the Forest of Arden," Sir Claude had just delightfully observed, "and I'm the banished duke, and you're—what was the young woman called?—the artless country wench. And there," he went on, "is the other girl—what's her name, Rosalind?—and (don't you know?) the fellow who was making up to her. Upon my word he *is* making up to her!"

His allusion was to a couple who, side by side, at the end of the glade, were moving in the same direction as themselves. These distant figures, in their slow stroll (which kept them so close together that their heads, drooping a little forward, almost touched), presented the back of a lady who looked tall, who was evidently a very fine woman, and that of a gentleman whose left hand appeared to be passed well into her arm, while his right, behind him, made jerky motions with the stick that it grasped. Maisie's fancy responded for an instant to her friend's idea that the sight was idyllic; then, stopping short, she brought out with all her clearness: "Why, mercy—if it isn't mamma!"

Sir Claude paused with a stare. "Mamma? Why, mamma's at Brussels."

Maisie, with her eyes on the lady, wondered. "At Brussels?"

"She's gone to play a match."

"At billiards? You didn't tell me."

"Of course I didn't!" Sir Claude ejaculated. "There's plenty I don't tell you. She went on Wednesday."

The couple had added to their distance, but Maisie's eyes more than kept pace with them. "Then she has come back."

Sir Claude watched the lady. "It's much more likely she never went!"

"It's mamma!" the child said with decision.

They had stood still, but Sir Claude had made the most of his opportunity, and it happened that just at this moment, at the end of the vista, the others halted and, still showing only their backs, seemed to stay talking. "Right you are, my duck!" he exclaimed at last. "It's my own sweet wife!"

He had spoken with a laugh, but he had changed colour, and Maisie quickly looked away from him. "Then who is it with her?"

"Blest if I know!" said Sir Claude.

"Is it Mr. Perriam?"

"Oh dear no—Perriam's smashed."

"Smashed?"

"Exposed, in the City. But there are quantities of others!" Sir Claude smiled.

Maisie appeared to count them; she studied the gentleman's back. "Then is this Lord Eric?"

For a moment her companion made no answer, and when she turned her eyes again to him he was looking at her, she thought, rather queerly. "What do you know about Lord Eric?"

She tried innocently to be odd in return. "Oh, I know more than you think! Is it Lord Eric?" she repeated.

"It may be. Blest if I care!"

Their friends had slightly separated and now, as Sir Claude spoke, suddenly faced round, showing all the splendour of her ladyship and all the mystery of her comrade. Maisie held her breath. "They're coming!"

"Let them come." And Sir Claude, pulling out his cigarettes, began to strike a light.

"We shall meet them!"

"No; they'll meet *us*."

Maisie stood her ground. "They see us. Just look."

Sir Claude threw away his match. "Come straight on." The others, in the return, evidently startled, had half paused again, keeping well apart. "She's horribly surprised and she wants to slope," he continued. "But it's too late."

Maisie advanced beside him, making out even across the interval that her ladyship was ill at ease. "Then what will she do?"

Sir Claude puffed his cigarette. "She's quickly thinking." He appeared to enjoy it.

Ida had faltered but an instant; her companion clearly gave her moral support. Maisie thought he somehow looked brave, and he had no likeness whatever to Mr. Perriam. His face, thin and rather sharp, was smooth, and it was not till they came nearer that she saw he had a remarkably fair little moustache. She could already see that his eyes were of the lightest blue. He was far nicer than Mr. Perriam. Mamma looked terrible from afar, but even under her guns the child's curiosity flickered and she appealed again to Sir Claude. "Is it—*is* it Lord Eric?"

Sir Claude smoked composedly enough. "I think it's the Count."

This was a happy solution—it fitted her idea of a count. But what idea, as she now came grandly on, did mamma fit?—unless that of an actress, in some tremendous situation, sweeping down to the footlights as if she would jump them. Maisie felt really frightened and before she knew it had passed her hand into Sir Claude's arm. Her pressure caused him to stop, and at the sight of this the other couple came equally to a stand and, beyond the diminished space, remained a moment more in talk. This, however, was the matter of an instant; leaving the Count apparently to come round more circuitously—an outflanking movement, if Maisie had but known—her ladyship resumed the onset. "What *will* she do now?" her daughter asked.

Sir Claude was at present in a position to say: "Try to pretend it's me."

"You?"

"Why, that I'm up to something."

In another minute poor Ida had justified this prediction, erect there before them like a figure of justice in full dress. There were parts of her face that grew whiter while Maisie looked, and other parts in which this change seemed to make other colours reign with more intensity. "What are you doing with my daughter?" she demanded of her husband; in spite of the indignant tone of which Maisie had a greater sense than ever in her life before of not being personally noticed. It seemed to her that Sir Claude also grew pale as an effect of the loud defiance with which Ida twice repeated this question. He put her, instead of answering it, an inquiry of his own: "Who the devil have you got hold of *now*?" and at this her ladyship turned tremendously to the child, glaring at her as if she were an equal plotter of sin. Maisie received in petrifaction the full force of her mother's huge painted eyes—they were like Japanese lanterns swung under festive arches. But life came back to her from a tone suddenly and strangely softened. "Go straight to that gentleman, my dear; I have asked him to take you a few minutes. He's charming—go. I've something to say to *this* creature."

Maisie felt Sir Claude immediately clutch her. "No, no— thank you; that won't do. She's mine."

"Yours?" It was confounding to Maisie to hear her speak quite as if she had never heard of Sir Claude before.

"Mine. You've given her up. You've not another word to say about her. I have her from her father," said Sir Claude—a statement that astonished his companion, who could also measure its lively action on her mother.

There was visibly, however, an influence that made Ida consider; she glanced at the gentleman she had left, who, having strolled with his hands in his pockets to some distance, stood there with unembarrassed vagueness. With her great hard eyes on him for a moment she smiled; then she looked again at Sir Claude. "I've given her up to her father to *keep*—not to get rid of by sending about the town either with you or any one else. If she's not to mind me, let *him* come and tell me so. I decline to take it from another person, and you're a fool to pretend that with your hypocritical meddling you've a leg to stand on. I know your game, and I've something now to say to you about it."

Sir Claude gave a squeeze of the child's arm. "Didn't I tell you she would have, Miss Farange?"

"You're uncommonly afraid to hear it," Ida went on; "but if you think she'll protect you from it you're mightily mistaken." She gave him a moment. "I'll give her the benefit as soon as look at you. Should you like her to know, my dear?" Maisie had a sense of her launching this inquiry at him with effect; yet our young lady was also conscious of hoping that Sir Claude would reply in the affirmative. We have already learned that she had come to like people's liking her to "know." Before he could reply at all, none the less, her mother opened a pair of arms of extraordinary elegance, and then she felt the loosening of his grasp. "My own child," Ida murmured in a voice—a voice of sudden confused tenderness—that it seemed to her she heard for the first time. She wavered but an instant, thrilled with the first direct appeal, as distinguished from the mere maternal pull, she had ever had from lips that, even in the old vociferous years, had always been sharp. The next moment she was on her mother's breast, where, amid a wilderness of trinkets, she felt as if she had suddenly been thrust into a jeweller's shop-front, but only to be as suddenly ejected with a push and the brisk injunction: "Now go to the Captain!"

Maisie glanced at the gentleman submissively, but felt the want of more introduction. "The Captain?"

Sir Claude broke into a laugh. "I told her he was the Count."

Ida stared; she rose so superior that she was colossal. "You're too utterly loathsome," she then declared. "Be off!" she repeated to her daughter.

Maisie started, moved backward and, looking at Sir Claude, "Only for a moment," pleaded to him in her bewilderment.

But he was too angry to heed her—too angry with his wife; as she turned away she heard his anger break out. "You damned old b——!"—she couldn't quite hear all. It was enough, it was too much: she fled before it, rushing even to a stranger in the terror of such a change of tone.

XVI

A s she met the Captain's light blue eyes the greatest marvel occurred; she felt a sudden relief at finding them reply with anxiety to the horror in her face. "What in the world
has he done?" He put it all on Sir Claude.

"He has called her a damned old brute." She couldn't help
bringing that out.

The Captain, at the same elevation as her ladyship, gaped
wide; then of course, like every one else, he was convulsed.
But he instantly caught himself up, echoing her bad words.
"A damned old brute—your mother?"

Maisie had already her second movement. "I think she tried
to make him angry."

The Captain's stupefaction was fine. "Angry—*she?* Why,
she's an angel!"

On the spot, as he said this, his face won her over; it was
so bright and kind, and his blue eyes had such a reflection of
some mysterious grace that, for him at least, her mother had
put forth. Her fund of observation enabled her as she gazed
up at him to place him: he was a candid, simple soldier; very
brave—she came back to that—but at the same time very
soft. At any rate he struck a note that was new to her and
that after a moment made her say: "Do you like her very
much?"

He smiled down at her, hesitating, looking pleasanter and
pleasanter. "Let me tell you about your mother."

He put out a big military hand which she immediately
took, and they turned off together to where a couple of chairs
had been placed under one of the trees. "She told me to
come to you," Maisie explained as they went; and presently
she was close to him in one of the chairs, with the prettiest of
pictures—the sheen of the lake through other trees—before
them, and the sound of birds, the plash of boats, the play of
children in the air. The Captain, inclining his military person,
sat sideways to be closer and kinder, and as her hand was on
the arm of her seat he put his own down on it again to emphasise something he had to say that would be good for her

to hear. He had already told her how her mother, from the moment of seeing her so unexpectedly with a person who was—well, not at all the right person, had promptly asked him to take charge of her while she herself tackled, as she said, the real culprit. He gave the child the sense of doing for the time what he liked with her; ten minutes before she had never seen him, but she could now sit there touching him, impressed by him and thinking it nice when a gentleman was thin and brown—brown with a kind of clear depth that made his straw-coloured moustache almost white and his eyes resemble little pale flowers. The most extraordinary thing was the way she didn't appear just then to mind Sir Claude's being "tackled." The Captain wasn't a bit like him, for it was an odd part of the pleasantness of mamma's friend that it resided in a manner in this friend's being ugly. An odder part still was that it finally made our young lady, to classify him further, say to herself that, of all people in the world, he reminded her most insidiously of Mrs. Wix. He had neither straighteners nor a diadem, nor, at least in the same place as the other, a button; he was sun-burnt and deep-voiced and smelt of cigars, yet he marvellously had more in common with her old governess than with her young stepfather. What he had to say to her that was good for her to hear was that her poor mother (didn't she know?) was the best friend he had ever had in his life. And he added: "She has told me ever so much about you. I'm awfully glad to know you."

She had never, she thought, been so addressed as a young lady, not even by Sir Claude the day, so long ago, that she found him with Mrs. Beale. It struck her as the way that at balls, by delightful partners, young ladies must be spoken to in the intervals of dances; and she tried to think of something that would meet it at the same high point. But this effort flurried her, and all she could produce was: "At first, you know, I thought you were Lord Eric."

The Captain looked vague. "Lord Eric?"

"And then Sir Claude thought you were the Count."

At this he laughed out. "Why he's only five foot high and as red as a lobster!" Maisie laughed in return—the young lady at the ball certainly would—and was on the point, as conscientiously, of pursuing the subject with an agreeable question.

But before she could speak her companion challenged her. "Who in the world is Lord Eric?"

"Don't you know him?" She judged her young lady would say that with light surprise.

"Do you mean a fat man with his mouth always open?" She had to confess that their acquaintance was so limited that she could only describe the bearer of the name as a friend of mamma's; but a light suddenly came to the Captain, who quickly declared that he knew her man. "What-do-you-call-him's brother, the fellow that owned Bobolink?" Then, with all his kindness, he contradicted her flat. "Oh dear no; your mother never knew *him*."

"But Mrs. Wix said so," the child risked.

"Mrs. Wix?"

"My old governess."

This again seemed amusing to the Captain. "She mixed him up, your old governess. He's an awful beast. Your mother never looked at him."

He was as positive as he was friendly, but he dropped for a minute after this into a silence that gave Maisie, confused but ingenious, a chance to redeem the mistake of pretending to know too much by the humility of inviting further correction. "And doesn't she know the Count?"

"Oh, I daresay! But he's another ass." After which abruptly, with a different look, he put down again on the back of her own the hand he had momentarily removed. Maisie even thought he coloured a little. "I want tremendously to speak to you. You must never believe any harm of your mother."

"Oh, I assure you I *don't*!" cried the child, blushing, herself, up to her eyes in a sudden surge of deprecation of such a thought.

The Captain, bending his head, raised her hand to his lips with a benevolence that made her wish her glove had been nicer. "Of course you don't when you know how fond she is of *you*."

"She's fond of me?" Maisie panted.

"Tremendously. But she thinks you don't like her. You *must* like her. She has had too much to bear."

"Oh yes—I know!" She rejoiced that she had never denied it.

"Of course I've no right to speak of her except as a partic-ular friend," the Captain went on. "But she's a splendid woman. She has never had any sort of justice."

"Hasn't she?"—his companion, to hear the words, felt a thrill altogether new.

"Perhaps I oughtn't to say it to you; but she has had every-thing to suffer."

"Oh yes—you can *say* it to me!" Maisie hastened to profess.

The Captain rejoiced. "Well, you needn't tell. It's all for *you*—do you see?"

Serious and smiling, she only wanted to take it from him. "It's between you and me! Oh, there are lots of things I've never told!"

"Well, keep this with the rest. I assure you she has had the most infernal time, no matter what any one says to the con-trary. She's the cleverest woman I ever saw in all my life. She's too charming." She had been touched already by his tone, and now she leaned back in her chair and felt something tremble within her. "She's tremendous fun—she can do all sorts of things better than I've ever seen any one. She has the pluck of fifty—and I know; I assure you I do. She has the nerve for a tiger-shoot—by Jove I'd *take* her! And she's awfully open and generous, don't you know? there are women that are such hor-rid sneaks. She'll go through anything for any one she likes." He appeared to watch for a moment the effect on his compan-ion of this emphasis; then he gave a small sigh that mourned the limits of the speakable. But it was almost with the note of a fresh challenge that he wound up: "Look here, she's *true*!"

Maisie had so little desire to assert the contrary that she found herself, in the intensity of her response, throbbing with a joy still less utterable than the essence of the Captain's ad-miration. She was fairly hushed with the sense that he spoke of her mother as she had never heard any one speak. It came over her as she sat silent that, after all, this admiration and this respect were quite new words, which took a distinction from the fact that nothing in the least resembling them in quality had on any occasion dropped from the lips of her father, of Mrs. Beale, of Sir Claude, or even of Mrs. Wix. What it ap-peared to her to come to was that, on the subject of her lady-ship, it was the first real kindness she had heard, so that, at the touch of it, something strange and deep and pitying surged up within her—a revelation that, practically and so far as she knew, her mother, apart from this, had only been disliked. Mrs. Wix's original account of Sir Claude's affection seemed as empty now as the chorus in a children's game, and the husband and wife, but a little way off at that moment, were face to face in hatred and with the dreadful name he had called her still in the air. What was it the Captain, on the other hand, had called her? Maisie wanted to hear that again. The tears filled her eyes and rolled down her cheeks, which burned, under them, with the rush of a consciousness that for her too, five minutes before, the vivid, towering beauty whose assault she awaited had been for the moment an object of pure dread. She became on the spot indifferent to her usual fear of showing what in children was notoriously most offensive—presented to her companion, soundlessly but hideously, her wet, distorted face. She cried, with a pang, straight *at* him, cried as she had never cried at any one in all her life. "Oh, do you love her?" she brought out with a gulp that was the effect of her trying not to make a noise.

It was, doubtless, another consequence of the thick mist through which she saw him that in reply to her question the Captain gave her such a queer blurred look. He stammered; yet in his voice there was also the ring of a great awkward insistence. "Of course I'm tremendously fond of her—I like her better than any woman I ever saw. I don't mind in the least telling you that," he went on, "and I should think myself a great beast if I did." Then to show that his position was superlatively clear he made her, with a kindness that even Sir Claude had never surpassed, tremble again as she had trembled at his first outbreak. He called her by her name, and her name drove it home. "My dear Maisie, your mother's an angel!"

It was an almost incredible balm—it soothed so her impression of danger and pain. She sank back in her chair; she covered her face with her hands. "Oh, mother, mother, mother!" she sobbed. She had an impression that the Captain, beside her, if more and more friendly, was by no means unembarrassed; in a minute, however, when her eyes were clearer, he was erect in front of her, very red and nervously looking about him and whacking his leg with his stick. "Say you love her, Mr. Captain; say it, say it!" she implored.

Mr. Captain's blue eyes fixed themselves very hard. "Of *course* I love her, damn it, you know!"

At this she also jumped up; she had fished out somehow her pocket-handkerchief. "So do *I* then. I do, I do, I do!" she passionately asseverated.

"Then will you come back to her?"

Maisie, staring, stopped the tight little plug of her handkerchief on the way to her eyes. "She won't have me."

"Yes, she will. She wants you."

"Back at the house—with Sir Claude?"

Again he hung fire. "No, not with him. In another place."

They stood looking at each other with an intensity unusual as between a Captain and a little girl. "She won't have me in any place."

"Oh, yes she will, if *I* ask her!"

Maisie's intensity continued. "Shall you be there?"

The Captain's, on the whole, did the same. "Oh yes—some day."

"Then you don't mean now?"

He broke into a quick smile. "Will you come now?—go with us for an hour?"

Maisie considered. "She wouldn't have me even now." She could see that he had his idea, but that her tone impressed him. That disappointed her a little, though in an instant he rang out again.

"She will if I ask her," he repeated. "I'll ask her this minute."

Maisie, turning at this, looked away to where her mother and her stepfather had stopped. At first, among the trees, nobody was visible; but the next moment she exclaimed with expression: "It's over—here he comes!"

The Captain watched the approach of her ladyship's husband, who lounged composedly over the grass, making to Maisie with his closed fingers a little movement in the air. "I've no desire to avoid him."

"Well, you mustn't see him," said Maisie.

"Oh, he's in no hurry himself!" Sir Claude had stopped to light another cigarette.

She was vague as to the way it was proper he should feel; but she had a sense that the Captain's remark was rather a free reflection on it. "Oh, he doesn't care!" she replied.

"Doesn't care for what?"

"Doesn't care who you are. He told me so. Go and ask mamma," she added.

"If you can come with us? Very good. You really want me not to wait for him?"

"*Please* don't." But Sir Claude was not yet near, and the Captain had with his left hand taken hold of her right, which he familiarly, sociably swung a little. "Only first," she continued, "tell me this. Are you going to *live* with mamma?"

The immemorial note of mirth broke out at her seriousness. "One of these days."

She wondered, wholly unperturbed by his laughter. "Then where will Sir Claude be?"

"He'll have left her of course."

"Does he really intend to do that?"

"You have every opportunity to ask him."

Maisie shook her head with decision. "He won't do it. Not first."

Her "first" made the Captain laugh out again. "Oh, he'll be sure to be nasty! But I've said too much to you."

"Well, you know, I'll never tell," said Maisie.

"No, it's all for yourself. Good-bye."

"Good-bye." Maisie kept his hand long enough to add: "I like you too." And then supremely: "You *do* love her?"

"My dear child——!" The Captain wanted words.

"Then don't do it only for just a little."

"A little?"

"Like all the others."

"All the others?"—he stood staring.

She pulled away her hand. "Do it always!" She bounded to meet Sir Claude, and as she left the Captain she heard him ring out with apparent gaiety:

"Oh, I'll keep it up!"

As she joined Sir Claude she perceived her mother, in the distance, move slowly off; and, glancing again at the Captain, saw him, swinging his stick, retreat in the same direction.

She had never seen Sir Claude look as he looked just then;

flushed yet not excited—settled rather in an immovable disgust and at once very sick and very hard. His conversation
with her mother had clearly drawn blood, and the child's old
horror came back to her, begetting the instant moral contraction of the days when her parents had looked to her to feed
their love of battle. Her greatest fear for the moment, however, was that her friend would see she had been crying. The
next she became aware that he glanced at her, and it presently
occurred to her that he didn't even wish to be looked at. At
this she quickly removed her gaze, while he said rather curtly:
"Well, who in the world *is* the fellow?"

She felt herself flooded with prudence. "Oh, *I* haven't
found out!" This sounded as if she meant he ought to have
done so himself; but she could only face doggedly the ugliness of seeming disagreeable, as she used to face it in the
hours when her father, for her blankness, called her a dirty
little donkey, and her mother, for her falsity, pushed her out
of the room.

"Then what have you been doing all this time?"

"Oh, I don't know!" It was of the essence of her method
not to be silly by halves.

"Then didn't the beast say anything?" They had got down
by the lake and were walking fast.

"Well, not very much."

"He didn't speak of your mother?"

"Oh yes, a little!"

"Then, what I ask you, please, is *how*?" She was silent a
minute—so long that he presently went on: "I say, you
know—don't you hear me?"

At this she produced: "Well, I'm afraid I didn't attend to
him very much."

Sir Claude, smoking rather hard, made no immediate rejoinder; but finally he exclaimed: "Then, my dear, you were
the perfection of an idiot!" He was so irritated—or she took
him to be—that for the rest of the time they were in the Gardens he spoke no other word; and she meanwhile subtly abstained from any attempt to pacify him. That would only lead
to more questions. At the gate of the Gardens he hailed a four-
wheeled cab and, in silence, without meeting her eyes, put her
into it, only saying "Give him *that*" as he tossed half a crown

upon the seat. Even when from outside he had closed the door and told the man where to go he never took her departing look. Nothing of this kind had ever yet happened to them, but it had no power to make her love him less, and she could not only bear it, she felt as she drove away that she could rejoice in it. It brought again the sweet sense of success that, ages before, she had had on an occasion when, on the stairs, returning from her father's, she had met a fierce question of her mother's with an imbecility as deep and had in consequence been dashed by Mrs. Farange almost to the bottom.

XVII

I F FOR reasons of her own she could bear the sense of Sir Claude's displeasure her young endurance might have been put to a serious test. The days went by without his knocking at her father's door, and the time would have turned to dreariness if something had not conspicuously happened to give it a new difference. What took place was a marked change in the attitude of Mrs. Beale—a change that somehow, even in his absence, seemed to bring Sir Claude again into the house. It began practically with a conversation that occurred between them the day Maisie came home alone in the cab. Mrs. Beale had by that time returned, and she was more successful than their friend in extracting from our young lady an account of the extraordinary passage with the Captain. She came back to it repeatedly, and on the very next day it grew distinct to Maisie that she was already in full possession of what at the same moment had been enacted between her ladyship and Sir Claude. This was the real origin of her final perception that though he didn't come to the house her stepmother had some rare secret for not being deprived of him. That produced eventually a strange, a deeper communion with Mrs. Beale, the first sign of which had been— not on Maisie's part—a wonderful outbreak of tears. Mrs. Beale was not, as she herself said, a crying creature: she had not cried, to Maisie's knowledge, since the lowly governess days, the grey dawn of their connection. But she wept now with passion, professing loudly that it did her good and saying remarkable things to the child, for whom the occasion was an equal benefit, an addition to all the fine reasons stored up for not making anything worse. It hadn't somehow made anything worse, Maisie felt, for her to have told Mrs. Beale what she had not told Sir Claude, inasmuch as the greatest strain, to her sense, was between Sir Claude and Sir Claude's wife, and his wife was just what Mrs. Beale was unfortunately not. He sent his stepdaughter three days after the incident in Kensington Gardens a message as frank as it was tender, and that was how Mrs. Beale had had to bring out in a manner

that seemed half an appeal, half a defiance: "Well, yes, hang
it—I *do* see him!"

How and when and where, however, were just what Maisie
was not to know—an exclusion moreover that she never questioned in the light of a participation large enough to make
him, in hours of solitude with Mrs. Beale, present like a picture on the wall. As far as her father was concerned such
hours had no interruption; and then it was clear between
them that they were each thinking of the absent and each
thinking that the other thought, so that he was an object of
conscious reference in everything they said or did. The
wretched truth, Mrs. Beale had to confess, was that she had
hoped against hope and that in the Regent's Park it was impossible Sir Claude should really be in and out. Hadn't they
at last to look the fact in the face?—it was too disgustingly evident that no one after all had been squared. Well, if no one
had been squared it was because every one had been vile. No
one and every one were of course Beale and Ida, the extent of
whose power to be nasty was a thing that, to a little girl, Mrs.
Beale simply couldn't communicate. Therefore it was that to
keep going at all, as she said, that lady had to make, as she
also said, another arrangement—the arrangement in which
Maisie was included only to the point of knowing that it existed and wondering wistfully what it was. Conspicuously at
any rate it had a side that was responsible for Mrs. Beale's
sudden emotion and sudden confidence—a demonstration,
however, of which the tearfulness was far from deterrent to
our heroine's thought of how happy she should be if she
could only make an arrangement for herself. Mrs. Beale's own
operated, it appeared, with regularity and frequency; for it
was almost every day or two that she was able to bring Maisie
a message and to take one back. It had been over the vision
of what, as she called it, he did for her that she broke down;
and this vision was kept in a manner before Maisie by a subsequent increase not only of the gaiety, but literally—it
seemed not presumptuous to perceive—of the actual virtue of
her friend. The friend was herself the first to proclaim it: he
had pulled her up immensely—he had quite pulled her round.
She had charming, tormenting words about him: he was her
good fairy, her hidden spring—above all he was just her con-

science. That was what had particularly come out with her startling tears: he had made her, dear man, think ever so much better of herself. It had been thus rather surprisingly revealed that she had been in a way to think ill, and Maisie was glad to hear of the corrective at the same time that she heard of the ailment.

She presently found herself supposing and in spite of her envy even hoping that whenever Mrs. Beale was out of the house Sir Claude had in some manner the satisfaction of it. This was now of more frequent occurrence than ever before—so much so that she would have thought of her stepmother as almost extravagantly absent had it not been that, in the first place, her father was a superior specimen of that habit: it was the frequent remark of his present wife, as it had been, before the tribunals of their country, a prominent plea of her predecessor, that he scarce came home even to sleep. In the second place Mrs. Beale, when she *was* on the spot, had now a beautiful air of longing to make up for everything. The only shadow in such bright intervals was that, as Maisie put it to herself, she could get nothing by questions. It was in the nature of things to be none of a small child's business, even when a small child had from the first been deluded into a fear that she might be only too much initiated. Things then were in Maisie's experience so true to their nature that questions were almost always improper; but she learned on the other hand soon to recognise that patient little silences and intelligent little looks could be rewarded from time to time by delightful little glimpses. There had been years at Beale Farange's when the monosyllable "he" meant always, meant almost violently the master; but all that was changed at a period at which Sir Claude's merits were of themselves so much in the air that it scarce took even two letters to name him. "He keeps me up splendidly—he does, my own precious," Mrs. Beale would observe to her comrade; or else she would say that the situation at the other establishment had reached a point that could scarcely be believed—the point, monstrous as it sounded, of his not having laid eyes upon her for twelve days. "She" of course at Beale Farange's had never meant any one but Ida, and there was the difference in this case that it now meant Ida with renewed intensity. Mrs. Beale was in a position strikingly to animadvert more and more upon her dreadfulness, the moral of all which appeared to be how abominably yet blessedly little she had to do with her husband. This flow of information came home to our two friends because, truly, Mrs. Beale had not much more to do with her own; but that was one of the reflections that Maisie could make without allowing it to break the spell of her present sympathy. How could such a spell be anything but deep when Sir Claude's influence, though operating from afar, at last really determined the resumption of his stepdaughter's studies? Mrs. Beale again took fire about them and was quite vivid, for Maisie, as to their being the great matter to which the dear absent one kept her up.

This was the second source—I have just alluded to the first—of the child's consciousness of something that, very hopefully, she described to herself as a new phase; and it also presented in the brightest light the fresh enthusiasm with which Mrs. Beale always reappeared and which really gave Maisie a happier sense than she had yet had of being very dear at least to two persons. That she had small remembrance at present of a third illustrates, I am afraid, a temporary oblivion of Mrs. Wix, an accident to be explained only by a state of unnatural excitement. For what was the form taken by Mrs. Beale's enthusiasm and acquiring relief in the domestic conditions still left to her but the delightful form of "reading" with her little charge on lines directly prescribed and in works profusely supplied by Sir Claude? He had got hold of an awfully good list—"mostly essays, don't you know?" Mrs. Beale had said; a word always august to Maisie, but henceforth to be softened by hazy, in fact by quite languorous edges. There was at any rate a week in which no less than nine volumes arrived, and the impression was to be gathered from Mrs. Beale that the obscure intercourse she enjoyed with Sir Claude not only involved an account and a criticism of studies, but was organised almost for the very purpose of report and consultation. It was for Maisie's education in short that, as she often repeated, she closed her door—closed it to the gentlemen who used to flock there in such numbers and whom her husband's practical desertion of her would have made it a course of the highest indelicacy to receive. Maisie was familiar from of old with the principle at least of the care that a woman, as Mrs. Beale phrased it, attractive and exposed must take of her "character," and was duly impressed with the rigour of her stepmother's scruples. There was literally no one of the other sex whom she seemed to feel at liberty to see at home, and when the child risked an inquiry about the ladies who, one by one, during her own previous period, had been made quite loudly welcome, Mrs. Beale hastened to inform her that, one by one, they had, the fiends, been found out, after all, to be awful. If she wished to know more about them she was recommended to approach her father.

Maisie had, however, at the very moment of this injunction much livelier curiosities, for the dream of lectures at an institution had at last become a reality, thanks to Sir Claude's now unbounded energy in discovering what could be done. It stood out in this connection that when you came to look into things in a spirit of earnestness an immense deal could be done for very little more than your fare in the Underground. The institution—there was a splendid one in a part of the town but little known to the child—became, in the glow of such a spirit, a thrilling place, and the walk to it from the station through Glower Street—a pronunciation for which Mrs. Beale once laughed at her little friend—a pathway literally strewn with "subjects." Maisie seemed to herself to pluck them as she passed, though they thickened in the great grey rooms where the fountain of knowledge, in the form usually of a high voice that she took at first to be angry, plashed in the stillness of rows of faces thrust out like empty jugs. "It *must* do us good—it's all so hideous," Mrs. Beale had immediately declared, manifesting a purity of resolution that made these occasions quite the most harmonious of all the many on which the pair had pulled together. Maisie certainly had never, in such an association, felt so uplifted and never above all been so carried off her feet as at the moments of Mrs. Beale's breathlessly re-entering the house and fairly shrieking upstairs to know if they would still be in time for a lecture. Her stepdaughter, all ready from the earliest hours, almost leaped over the banister to respond, and they dashed out together in quest of learning as hard as they often dashed back to release Mrs. Beale for other preoccupations. There had been in short no bustle like it since that last brief flurry when Mrs. Wix, blowing as if she were grooming her, "made up" for everything previously lost at her father's.

These weeks as well were too few, but they were flooded with a new emotion, a part of which indeed came from the possibility that, through the long telescope of Glower Street, or perhaps between the pillars of the institution—which were what Maisie thought most made it one—they should some day spy Sir Claude. That was what Mrs. Beale, under pressure, had said—doubtless a little impatiently: "Oh yes, oh yes— some day!" His joining them was clearly far less of a matter of course than was to have been gathered from his original profession of desire to improve, in their company, his own mind; and this sharpened our young lady's guess that since that occasion either something destructive had happened or something desirable hadn't. Mrs. Beale had thrown but a partial light in telling her how it had turned out that nobody had been squared. Maisie wished at any rate that somebody *would* be squared. However, though in every approach to the temple of knowledge she watched in vain for Sir Claude, there was no doubt about the action of his loved image as an incentive and a recompense. When the institution was most on pillars—or, as Mrs. Beale put it, on stilts—when the subject was deepest and the lecture longest and the listeners ugliest, then it was they both felt their patron in the background would be most pleased with them.

One day, abruptly, with a glance at this background, Mrs. Beale said to her companion: "We'll go to-night to the thingumbob at Earl's Court;" an announcement putting forth its full lustre when she had made known that she referred to the great Exhibition just opened in that quarter, a collection of extraordinary foreign things, in tremendous gardens, with illuminations, bands, elephants, switchbacks and side-shows, as well as crowds of people among whom they might possibly see some one they knew. Maisie flew in the same bound at the neck of her friend and at the name of Sir Claude, on which Mrs. Beale confessed that—well, yes, there was just a chance that he would be able to meet them. He never of course, in his terrible position, knew what might happen from hour to hour; but he hoped to be free and he had given Mrs. Beale the tip. "Bring her there on the quiet and I'll try to turn up"—this was clear enough on what so many weeks of privation had made of his desire to see the child: it even appeared to represent on his part a yearning as constant as her own. That in turn was just puzzling enough to make Maisie express a bewilderment. She couldn't see, if they were so intensely of the same mind, why the theory on which she had come back to Mrs. Beale—the general reunion, the delightful trio, should have broken down so in fact. Mrs. Beale, furthermore, only gave her more to think about in saying that their disappointment was the result of his having got into his head a kind of idea.

"What kind of idea?"

"Oh, goodness knows!" She spoke with an approach to asperity. "He's so awfully delicate."

"Delicate?"—that was ambiguous.

"About what he does, don't you know?" said Mrs. Beale. She fumbled. "Well, about what *we* do."

Maisie wondered. "You and me?"

"Me and *him*, silly!" cried Mrs. Beale with, this time, a real giggle.

"But you don't do any harm—*you* don't," said Maisie, wondering afresh and intending her emphasis as a decorous allusion to her parents.

"Of course we don't, you angel—that's just the ground *I* take!" her companion exultantly responded. "He says he doesn't want you mixed up."

"Mixed up with what?"

"That's exactly what *I* want to know: mixed up with what, and how you are any more mixed——?" But Mrs. Beale paused without ending her question. She ended after an instant in a different way. "All you can say is that it's his fancy."

The tone of this, in spite of its expressing a resignation, the fruit of weariness, that dismissed the subject, conveyed so vividly how much such a fancy was not Mrs. Beale's own that our young lady was led by the mere fact of contact to arrive at a dim apprehension of the unuttered and the unknown. The relation between her step-parents had then a kind of mysterious residuum: this was the first time she really had reflected that except as regards herself it was not a relationship.

To each other it was only what they might have happened to make it, and she gathered that this, in the event, had been something that led Sir Claude to keep away from her. Didn't he fear she would be compromised? The perception of such a scruple endeared him the more, and it flashed over her that she might simplify everything by showing him how little she made of such a danger. Hadn't she lived with her eyes on it from her third year? It was the condition most frequently discussed at the Faranges', where the word was always in the air and where at the age of five, amid rounds of applause, she could gabble it off. She knew as well in short that a person could be compromised as that a person could be slapped with a hair-brush or left alone in the dark, and it was equally familiar to her that each of these ordeals was in general held to have too little effect. But the first thing was to make absolutely sure of Mrs. Beale. This was done by saying to her thoughtfully: "Well, if you don't mind—and you really don't, do you?"

Mrs. Beale, with a dawn of amusement, considered. "Mixing you up? Not a bit. For what does it mean?"

"Whatever it means I don't in the least mind *being* mixed. Therefore if you don't and I don't," Maisie concluded, "don't you think that when I see him this evening I had better just tell him we don't and ask him why in the world *he* should?"

XVIII

T HE CHILD, however, was not destined to enjoy much of
Sir Claude at the "thingumbob," which took for them a
very different turn indeed. On the spot Mrs. Beale, with hilarity, had urged her to the course proposed; but later, at the
Exhibition, she withdrew this allowance, mentioning as a result of second thoughts that when a man was so sensitive such
a communication might only make him worse. It would have
been hard indeed for Sir Claude to be "worse," Maisie felt as,
in the gardens and the crowd, when the first dazzle had
dropped, she looked for him in vain up and down. They had
all their time, the couple, for frugal, wistful wandering: they
had partaken together at home of the light, vague meal—
Maisie's name for it was a "jam-supper"—to which they were
reduced when Mr. Farange sought his pleasure abroad. It was
abroad now entirely that Mr. Farange cultivated this philosophy, and it was the actual impression of his daughter, derived
from his wife, that he had three days before joined a friend's
yacht at Cowes.

The place was full of side-shows, to which Mrs. Beale could
introduce the little girl only, alas, by revealing to her so attractive, so enthralling a name: the side-shows, each time,
were sixpence apiece, and the fond allegiance enjoyed by the
elder of our pair had been established from the earliest time in
spite of a paucity of sixpences. Small coin dropped from her as
half-heartedly as answers from bad children to lessons that had
not been looked at. Maisie passed more slowly the great
painted posters, pressing with a linked arm closer to her
friend's pocket, where she hoped for the audible chink of a
shilling. But the upshot of this was but to deepen her yearning: if Sir Claude would only at last come the shillings would
begin to ring. The companions paused, for want of one, before the Flowers of the Forest, a large presentment of bright
brown ladies—they were brown all over—in a medium suggestive of tropical luxuriance, and there Maisie dolorously expressed her belief that he would never come at all. Mrs. Beale
hereupon, though discernibly disappointed, reminded her that

he had not been promised as a certainty—a remark that caused the child to gaze at the Flowers of the Forest through a blur in which they became more magnificent, yet oddly more confused, and by which moreover confusion was imparted to the aspect of a gentleman who at that moment, in the company of a lady, came out of the brilliant booth. The lady was so brown that Maisie at first took her for one of the Flowers; but during the few seconds that this required—a few seconds in which she had also desolately given up Sir Claude—she heard Mrs. Beale's voice, behind her, gather both wonder and pain into a single sharp little cry.

"Of all the wickedness—*Beale*!"

He had already, without distinguishing them in the mass of strollers, turned another way—it seemed at the brown lady's suggestion. Her course was marked, over heads and shoulders, by an upright scarlet plume, as to the ownership of which Maisie was instantly eager. "Who is she?—who is she?"

But Mrs. Beale for a moment only looked after them. "The liar—the liar!"

Maisie considered. "Because he's not—where one thought?" That was also, a month ago in Kensington Gardens, where her mother had not been. "Perhaps he has come back," she insinuated.

"He never went—the hound!"

That, according to Sir Claude, had been also what her mother had not done, and Maisie could only have a sense of something that in a maturer mind would be called the way history repeats itself. "Who *is* she?" she asked again.

Mrs. Beale, fixed to the spot, seemed lost in the vision of an opportunity missed. "If he had only seen me!"—it came from between her teeth. "She's a brand-new one. But he must have been with her since Tuesday."

Maisie took it in. "She's almost black," she then observed.

"They're always hideous," said Mrs. Beale.

This was a remark on which the child had again to reflect. "Oh, not his *wives*!" she remonstrantly exclaimed. The words at another moment would probably have set her friend off, but Mrs. Beale was now too intent in seeing what became of the others. "Did you ever in your life see such a feather?" Maisie presently continued.

This decoration appeared to have paused at some distance, and in spite of intervening groups they could both look at it. "Oh, that's the way they dress—the vulgarest of the vulgar!"

"They're coming back—they'll see us!" Maisie the next moment asserted; and while her companion answered that this was exactly what she wanted and the child returned "Here they are—here they are!" the unconscious objects of so much attention, with a change of mind about their direction, quickly retraced their steps and precipitated themselves upon their critics. Their unconsciousness gave Mrs. Beale time to leap, under her breath, to a recognition which Maisie caught.

"It must be Mrs. Cuddon!"

Maisie looked at Mrs. Cuddon hard—her lips even echoed the name. What followed was extraordinarily rapid—a minute of livelier battle than had ever yet, in so short a span at least, been waged round our heroine. The muffled shock—lest people should notice—was so violent that it was only for her later thought the steps fell into their order, the steps through which, in a bewilderment not so much of sound as of silence, she had come to find herself, too soon for comprehension and too strangely for fear, at the door of the Exhibition with her father. He thrust her into a hansom and got in after her, and then it was—as she drove along with him—that she recovered a little what had happened. Face to face with them in the gardens he had seen them, and there had been a moment of checked concussion during which, in a glare of black eyes and a toss of red plumage, Mrs. Cuddon had recognised them, ejaculated and vanished. There had been another moment at which she became aware of Sir Claude, also poised there in surprise, but out of her father's view, as if he had been warned off at the very moment of reaching them. It fell into its place with all the rest that she had heard Mrs. Beale say to her father, but whether low or loud was now lost to her, something about his having this time a new one; on which he had growled something indistinct, but apparently in the tone and of the sort that the child, from her earliest years, had associated with hearing somebody retort to somebody that somebody was "another." "Oh, I stick to the old!" Mrs. Beale had exclaimed at this; and her accent, even as the cab got away, was still in the air, for Maisie's companion had spoken no other word from the moment of whisking her off—none at least save the indistinguishable address which, over the top of the hansom and poised on the step, he had given the driver. Reconstructing these things later, Maisie believed that she at this point would have put a question to him had not the silence into which he charmed her or scared her—she could scarcely tell which—come from his suddenly making her feel his arm about her, feel, as he drew her close, that he was agitated in a way he had never yet shown her. It seemed to her that he trembled, trembled too much to speak, and this had the effect of making her, with an emotion which, though it had begun to throb in an instant, was by no means all dread, conform to his portentous hush. The act of possession that his pressure in a manner advertised came back to her after the longest of the long intermissions that had ever let anything come back. They drove and drove, and he kept her close; she stared straight before her, holding her breath, watching one dark street succeed another and strangely conscious that what it all meant was somehow that papa was less to be left out of everything than she had supposed. It took her but a minute to surrender to this discovery, which, in the form of his present embrace, suggested a fresh kind of importance in him and with that a confused confidence. She neither knew exactly what he had done nor what he was doing; she could only be rather impressed and a little proud, vibrate with the sense that he had jumped up to do something and that she had as quickly become a part of it. It was a part of it too that here they were at a house that seemed not large, but in the fresh white front of which the street-lamp showed a smartness of flower-boxes. The child had been in thousands of stories—all Mrs. Wix's and her own, to say nothing of the richest romances of French Elise—but she had never been in such a story as this. By the time he had helped her out of the cab, which drove away, and she heard in the door of the house the prompt little click of his key, the Arabian Nights had quite closed round her.

From this minute they were in everything, particularly in such an instant "Open Sesame" and in the departure of the cab, a rattling void filled with relinquished step-parents; they were, with the vividness, the almost blinding whiteness of the

light that sprang responsive to papa's quick touch of a little
brass knob on the wall, in a place that, at the top of a short,
soft staircase, struck her as the most beautiful she had ever
seen in her life. The next thing she perceived it to be was the
drawing-room of a lady—oh, of a lady, she could see in a moment, and not of a gentleman, not even of one like papa himself or even like Sir Claude—whose things were as much
prettier than mamma's as it had always had to be confessed
that mamma's were prettier than Mrs. Beale's. In the middle
of the small bright room and the presence of more curtains
and cushions, more pictures and mirrors, more palm-trees
drooping over brocaded and gilded nooks, more little silver
boxes scattered over little crooked tables and little oval miniatures hooked upon velvet screens than Mrs. Beale and her
ladyship together could, in an unnatural alliance, have dreamed
of mustering, the child became aware, with a swift possibility
of compassion, of something that was strangely like a relega-
tion to obscurity of each of those women of taste. It was a
stranger operation still that her father should on the spot be
presented to her as quite advantageously and even grandly at
home in the dazzling scene and himself by so much the more
separated from scenes inferior to it. She spent with him in it,
while explanations continued to hang back, twenty minutes
that, in their sudden drop of danger, affected her, though
there were neither buns nor ginger-beer, like an extemporised
expensive treat.

"Is she very rich?" He had begun to strike her as almost
embarrassed, so shy that he might have found himself with a
young lady with whom he had little in common. She was literally moved by this apprehension to offer him some tactful
relief.

Beale Farange stood and smiled at his young lady, his back
to the fanciful fireplace, his light overcoat—the very lightest
in London—wide open, and his wonderful lustrous beard
completely concealing the expanse of his shirt-front. It
pleased her more than ever to think that papa was handsome
and, though as high aloft as mamma and almost, in his spe-
cially florid evening-dress, as splendid, of a beauty somehow
less belligerent, less terrible. "The Countess? Why do you ask
me that?"

Maisie's eyes opened wider. "Is she a Countess?"

There was an unaccustomed geniality in his enjoyment of her wonder. "Oh yes, my dear, but it isn't an English title."

Maisie's manner appreciated this. "Is it a French one?"

"No, nor French either. It's American."

Maisie conversed agreeably. "Ah then of course she must be rich." She took in such a combination of nationality and rank. "I never saw anything so lovely."

"Did you have a sight of her?" Beale asked.

"At the Exhibition?" Maisie smiled. "She was gone too quick."

Her father laughed. "She did slope!" She was for a moment afraid he would say something about Mrs. Beale and Sir Claude: his unexpected gentleness was too mystifying. All he risked was, the next minute: "She has a horror of vulgar scenes."

This was something Maisie needn't take up; she could still continue bland. "But where do you suppose she went?"

"Oh, I thought she'd have taken a cab and have been here by this time. But she'll turn up all right."

"I'm sure I *hope* she will," Maisie said; she spoke with an earnestness begotten of the impression of all the beauty around her, to which, in person, the Countess might make further contribution. "We came awfully fast," she added.

Her father again laughed loud. "Yes, my dear, I made you step out!" Beale hesitated; then he pursued: "I want her to see you."

Maisie, at this, rejoiced in the attention that, for their evening out, Mrs. Beale, even to the extent of personally "doing up" her old hat, had given her appearance. Meanwhile her father went on. "You'll like her awfully."

"Oh, I'm sure I shall!" After which, either from the effect of having said so much or from that of a sudden glimpse of the impossibility of saying more, she felt an embarrassment and sought refuge in a minor branch of the subject. "I thought she was Mrs. Cuddon."

Beale's gaiety rather increased than diminished. "You mean my wife did? My dear child, my wife's a damned fool!" He had the oddest air of speaking of his wife as of a person whom she might scarcely have known, so that the refuge of her scruple didn't prove particularly happy. Beale on the other hand appeared after an instant himself to feel a scruple. "What I mean is, to speak seriously, that she doesn't really know anything about anything." He paused, following the child's charmed eyes and tentative step or two as they brought her nearer to the pretty things on one of the tables. "She thinks she has good things, don't you know!" He quite jeered at Mrs. Beale's delusion.

Maisie felt she must confess that it was one; everything she had missed at the side-shows was made up to her by the Countess's luxuries. "Yes," she considered; "she does think that."

There was again a dryness in the way Beale replied that it didn't matter what she thought; but there was an increasing sweetness for his daughter in being with him so long without his doing anything worse. The whole hour of course was to remain with her for days and weeks, ineffaceably illumined and confirmed; by the end of which she was able to read into it a hundred things that were at the moment mere miraculous pleasantness. What they then and there came to was simply that her companion was still excited, yet wished not to show it, and that just in proportion as he succeeded in this attempt he was able to encourage her to regard him as kind. He moved about the room after a little, showed her things, spoke to her as a person of taste, told her the name, which she remembered, of the famous French lady represented in one of the miniatures, and remarked, as if he had caught her wistful over a trinket or a trailing stuff, that he made no doubt the Countess, on coming in, would give her something jolly. He spied a pink satin box with a looking-glass let into the cover, which he raised, with a quick, facetious flourish, to offer her the privilege of six rows of chocolate bonbons, cutting out thereby Sir Claude, who had never gone beyond four rows. "I can do what I like with these," he said, "for I don't mind telling you I gave 'em to her myself." The Countess had evidently appreciated the gift; there were numerous gaps, a ravage now quite unchecked, in the array. Even while they waited together Maisie had her sense, which was the mark of what their separation had become, of her having grown for him, since the last time he had, as it were, noticed her, and by

increase of years and of inches if by nothing else, much more
of a little person to reckon with. Yes, that was a part of the
positive awkwardness that he carried off by being almost foolishly tender. There was a passage during which, on a yellow
silk sofa under one of the palms, he had her on his knee,
stroking her hair, playfully holding her off while he showed
his shining fangs and let her, with a vague, affectionate, helpless, pointless "Dear old girl, dear little daughter," inhale the
fragrance of his cherished beard. She must have been sorry for
him, she afterwards knew, so well could she privately follow
his difficulty in being specific to her about anything. She had
such possibilities of vibration, of response, that it needed
nothing more than this to make up to her in fact for omissions. The tears came into her eyes again as they had done
when in the Park that day the Captain told her so excitingly
that her mother was good. What was this but exciting too—
this still directer goodness of her father and this unexampled
shining solitude with him, out of which everything had
dropped but that he was papa and that he was magnificent? It
didn't spoil it that she finally felt he must have, as he became
restless, some purpose he didn't quite see his way to bring
out, for in the freshness of their recovered fellowship she
would have lent herself gleefully to his suggesting, or even to
his pretending, that their relations were easy and graceful.
There was something in him that seemed, and quite touchingly, to ask her to help him to pretend—pretend he knew
enough about her life and her education, her means of sub-
sistence and her view of himself, to give the questions he
couldn't put her a natural domestic tone. She would have
pretended with ecstasy if he could only have given her the
cue. She waited for it while, between his big teeth, he
breathed the sighs she didn't know to be stupid. And as if he
had drawn—rather red with the confusion of it—the pledge
of her preparation from her tears, he floundered about, wondering what the devil he could lay hold of.

XIX

W HEN HE had lighted a cigarette and begun to smoke in her face it was as if he had struck with the match the note of some queer, clumsy ferment of old professions, old scandals, old duties, a dim perception of what he possessed in her and what, if everything had only—damn it!—been totally different, she might still be able to give him. What she was able to give him, however, as his blinking eyes seemed to make out through the smoke, would be simply what he should be able to get from her. To give something, to give here on the spot, was all her own desire. Among the old things that came back was her little instinct of keeping the peace; it made her wonder more sharply what particular thing she could do or not do, what particular word she could speak or not speak, what particular line she could take or not take, that might for every one, even for the Countess, give a better turn to the crisis. She was ready, in this interest, for an immense surrender, a surrender of everything but Sir Claude, of everything but Mrs. Beale. The immensity didn't include *them*; but if he had an idea at the back of his head she had also one in a recess as deep, and for a time, while they sat together, there was an extraordinary mute passage between her vision of this vision of his, his vision of her vision, and her vision of his vision of her vision. What there was no effective record of indeed was the small strange pathos on the child's part of an innocence so saturated with knowledge and so directed to diplomacy. What, further, Beale finally laid hold of while he masked again with his fine presence half the flounces of the fireplace was: "Do you know, my dear, I shall soon be off to America?" It struck his daughter both as a short cut and as the way he wouldn't have said it to his wife. But his wife figured with a bright superficial assurance in her response.

"Do you mean with Mrs. Beale?"

Her father looked at her hard. "Don't be a little ass!"

Her silence appeared to represent a concentrated effort not to be. "Then with the Countess?"

"With her or without her, my dear; that concerns only your

poor daddy. She has big interests over there, and she wants me to take a look at them."

Maisie threw herself into them. "Will that take very long?"

"Yes; they're in such a muddle—it may take months. Now what I want to hear, you know, is whether you would like to come along?"

Planted once more before him in the middle of the room she felt herself turning white. "I?" she gasped, yet feeling as soon as she had spoken that such a note of dismay was not altogether pretty. She felt it still more while her father replied, with a shake of his legs, a toss of his cigarette-ash and a fidgety look—he was for ever taking one—all the length of his waistcoat and trousers, that she needn't be quite so disgusted. It helped her in a few seconds to appear more as he would like her that she saw, in the lovely light of the Countess's splendour, exactly, however she appeared, the right answer to make. "Dear papa, I'll go with you anywhere."

He turned his back to her and stood with his nose at the glass of the chimneypiece while he brushed specks of ash out of his beard. Then he abruptly said: "Do you know anything about your brute of a mother?"

It was just of her brute of a mother that the manner of the question in a remarkable degree reminded her: it had the free flight of one of Ida's fine bridgings of space. With the sense of this was kindled for Maisie at the same time an inspiration. "Oh yes, I know everything!" and she became so radiant that her father, seeing it in the mirror, turned back to her and presently, on the sofa, had her on his knee again and was again particularly stirring. Maisie's inspiration was to the effect that the more she should be able to say about mamma the less she would be called upon to speak of her step-parents. She kept hoping the Countess would come in before her power to protect them was exhausted; and it was now, in closer quarters with her companion, that the idea at the back of her head shifted its place to her lips. She told him she had met her mother in the Park with a gentleman who, while Sir Claude had strolled with her ladyship, had been kind and had sat and talked to her; narrating the scene with a remembrance of her pledge of secrecy to the Captain quite brushed away by the joy of seeing Beale listen without profane interposition. It was almost an amazement, but it was indeed all a joy, thus to be able to guess that papa was at last quite tired of his anger —of his anger at any rate about mamma. He was only bored with her now. That made it, however, the more imperative that his spent displeasure shouldn't be blown out again. It charmed the child to see how much she could interest him; and the charm remained even when, after asking her a dozen questions, he observed musingly and a little obscurely: "Yes, damned if she won't!" For in this too there was a detachment, a wise weariness that made her feel safe. She had had to mention Sir Claude, though she mentioned him as little as possible and Beale only appeared to look quite over his head. It pieced itself together for her that this was the mildness of general indifference, a source of profit so great for herself personally that if the Countess was the author of it she was prepared literally to hug the Countess. She betrayed that eagerness by a restless question about her, to which her father replied:

"Oh, she has a head on her shoulders. I'll back her to get out of anything!" He looked at Maisie quite as if he would trace the connection between her inquiry and the impatience of her gratitude. "Do you mean to say," he presently went on, "that you'd really come with me?"

She felt as if he were now looking at her very hard indeed, and also as if she had grown ever so much older. "I'll do anything in the world you ask me, papa."

He gave again, with a laugh and with his legs apart, his proprietary glance at his waistcoat and trousers. "That's a way, my dear, of saying 'No, thank you!' You know you don't want to go the least little mite. You can't humbug *me*!" Beale Farange laid down. "I don't want to bully you—I never bullied you in my life; but I make you the offer, and it's to take or to leave. Your mother will never again have any more to do with you than if you were a kitchenmaid she had turned out for going wrong. Therefore of course I'm your natural protector, and you've a right to get everything out of me you can. Now's your chance, you know—you'll be a great fool if you don't. You can't say I don't put it before you—you can't say I ain't kind to you or that I don't play fair. Mind you never say that, you know—it *would* bring me down on you. I know what's proper. I'll take you again, just as I *have* taken you again and again. And I'm much obliged to you for making up such a face."

She was conscious enough that her face indeed couldn't please him if it showed any sign—just as she hoped it didn't —of her sharp impression of what he now really wanted to do. Wasn't he trying to turn the tables on her, embarrass her somehow into admitting that what would really suit her little book would be, after doing so much for good manners, to leave her wholly at liberty to arrange for herself? She began to be nervous again; it rolled over her that this was their parting, their parting for ever, and that he had brought her there for so many caresses only because it was important such an occasion should look better for him than any other. For her to spoil it by the note of discord would certainly give him ground for complaint; and the child was momentarily bewildered between her alternatives of agreeing with him about her wanting to get rid of him and displeasing him by pretending to stick to him. So she found for the moment no solution but to murmur very helplessly: "Oh papa—oh papa!"

"I know what you're up to—don't tell *me*!" After which he came straight over and, in the most inconsequent way in the world, clasped her in his arms a moment and rubbed his beard against her cheek. Then she understood as well as if he had spoken it that what he wanted, hang it, was that she should let him off with all the honours—with all the appearance of virtue and sacrifice on his side. It was exactly as if he had broken out to her: "I say, you little donkey, help me to be irreproachable, to be noble, and yet to have none of the beastly bore of it. There's only impropriety enough for one of us; so *you* must take it all. Repudiate your dear old daddy—in the face, mind you, of his tender supplications. He can't be rough with you—it isn't in his nature: therefore you will have successfully chucked him because he was too generous to be as firm with you, poor man, as was, after all, his duty." This was what he communicated in a series of tremendous pats on the back; that portion of her person had never been so thumped since Moddle thumped her when she choked. After a moment he gave her the further impression of having become sure enough of her to be able very gracefully to say out: "You know your mother loathes you, loathes you simply. And I've been thinking over your precious man—the fellow you told me about."

"Well," Maisie replied with competence, "I'm sure of *him*."

Her father was vague in an instant. "Do you mean sure of his liking you?"

"Oh no; of his liking *her*!"

Beale had a return of gaiety. "There's no accounting for tastes! It's what they all say, you know."

"I don't care—I'm sure of him!" Maisie repeated.

"Sure, you mean, that she'll bolt?"

Maisie knew all about bolting, but, decidedly, she *was* older, and there was something in her that could wince at the way her father made the word boom out. It prompted her to amend his allusion, which she did by returning: "I don't know what she'll do. But she'll be happy."

"Let us hope so," said Beale with bright, unusual mildness. "The more happy she is at any rate the less she'll want you about. That's why I press you," he agreeably pursued, "to consider this handsome offer—I mean seriously, you know— of your sole surviving parent." Their eyes, at this, met again in a long and extraordinary communion which terminated in his ejaculating: "Ah, you little scoundrel!" She took it from him in the manner that it seemed to her he would prefer and with a success that encouraged him to go on: "You *are* a deep little devil!" Her silence, ticking like a watch, acknowledged even this, in confirmation of which he finally brought out: "You've settled it with the other pair!"

"Well, what if I have?" She sounded to herself most bold.

Her father, quite as in the old days, broke into a peal. "Why, don't you know they're awful?"

She grew bolder still. "I don't care—not a bit!"

"But they're probably the worst people in the world and the very greatest criminals," Beale pleasantly urged. "I'm not the man, my dear, not to let you know it."

"Well, it doesn't prevent them from loving me. They love me tremendously." Maisie turned crimson to hear herself.

Her companion fumbled; almost any one—let alone a daughter—would have seen how conscientious he wanted to

be. "I daresay. But do you know why?" She braved his eyes
and he added: "You're a jolly good pretext."

"For what?" Maisie asked.

"Why, for their game. I needn't tell you what that is."

The child reflected. "Well, then, that's all the more reason."

"Reason for what, pray?"

"For their being kind to me."

"And for your keeping in with them?" Beale roared again;
it was as if his spirits rose and rose. "Do you realise, pray, that
in saying that you're a monster?"

Maisie turned it over. "A monster?"

"They've made one of you. Upon my honour it's quite awful. It shows the kind of people they are. Don't you understand," Beale pursued, "that when they've made you as horrid
as they can—as horrid as themselves—they'll just simply
chuck you?"

Maisie, at this, had a flicker of passion. "They *won't* chuck
me!"

"Excuse me," her father courteously insisted; "it's my duty
to put it before you. I shouldn't forgive myself if I didn't
point out to you that they'll cease to require you." He spoke
as if with an appeal to her intelligence that she must be
ashamed not adequately to meet, and this gave a real distinction to his superior delicacy.

It had after an instant the illumining effect he intended.
"Cease to require me because they won't care?" She paused
with that sketch of her idea.

"Of course Sir Claude won't care if his wife bolts. That's
his game. It will suit him down to the ground."

This was a proposition Maisie could perfectly embrace, but
it still left a loophole for triumph. She considered a little.
"You mean if mamma doesn't come back ever at all?" The
composure with which her face was presented to that
prospect would have shown a spectator the long road she had
travelled. "Well, but that won't put Mrs. Beale——"

"In the same comfortable position——?" Beale took her up
with relish; he had sprung to his feet again, shaking his legs
and looking at his shoes. "Right you are, darling! Something
more will be wanted for Mrs. Beale." He hesitated, then he
added: "But she may not have long to wait for it."

Maisie also for a minute looked at his shoes, though they were not the pair she most admired, the laced yellow "uppers" and patent-leather complement. At last, with a question, she raised her eyes. "Are you not coming back?"

Once more he hung fire; after which he gave a small laugh that in the oddest way in the world reminded her of the unique sounds she had heard emitted by Mrs. Wix. "It may strike you as extraordinary that I should make you such an admission; and in point of fact you're not to understand that I do. But we'll put it that way to help your decision. The point is that that's the way my wife will presently be sure to put it. You'll hear her shrieking that she's deserted, so that she may just pile up her wrongs. She'll be as free as she likes then—as free, you see, as your mother's ass of a husband. They won't have anything more to consider and they'll just put you into the street. Do I understand," Beale inquired, "that, in the face of what I press upon you, you still prefer to take the risk of that?" It was the most wonderful appeal any gentleman had ever addressed to his daughter, and it had placed Maisie in the middle of the room again while her father moved slowly about her with his hands in his pockets and something in his step that seemed, more than anything else he had done, to show the habit of the place. She turned her fevered little eyes over his friend's brightnesses, as if, on her own side, to press for some help in a quandary unexampled. As if also the pressure reached him he after an instant stopped short, completing the prodigy of his attitude and the pride of his loyalty by a supreme formulation of the general inducement. "You have an eye, love! Yes, there's money. No end of money."

This affected her for a moment like some great flashing dazzle in one of the pantomimes to which Sir Claude had taken her: she saw nothing in it but what it directly conveyed. "And shall I never, never see you again——?"

"If I do go to America?" Beale brought it out like a man. "Never, never, never!"

Hereupon, with the utmost absurdity, she broke down; everything gave way, everything but the horror of hearing herself definitely utter such an ugliness as the acceptance of that. So she only stiffened herself and said: "Then I can't give you up."

She held him some seconds looking at her, showing her a strained grimace, a perfect parade of all his teeth, in which it seemed to her she could read the disgust he didn't quite like to express at this departure from the pliability she had practically promised. But before she could attenuate in any way the crudity of her collapse he gave an impatient jerk which took him to the window. She heard a vehicle stop; Beale looked out; then he freshly faced her. He still said nothing, but she knew the Countess had come back. There was a silence again between them, but with a different shade of embarrassment from that of their united arrival; and it was still without speaking that, abruptly repeating one of the embraces of which he had already been so prodigal, he whisked her back to the lemon sofa just before the door of the room was thrown open. It was thus in renewed and intimate union with him that she was presented to a person whom she instantly recognised as the brown lady.

The brown lady looked almost as astonished, though not quite as alarmed, as when, at the Exhibition, she had gasped in the face of Mrs. Beale. Maisie in truth almost gasped in her own; this was with the fuller perception that she was brown indeed. She literally struck the child more as an animal than as a "real" lady; she might have been a clever, frizzled poodle in a frill or a dreadful human monkey in a spangled petticoat. She had a nose that was far too big and eyes that were far too small and a moustache that was, well, not so happy a feature as Sir Claude's. Beale jumped up to her; while, to the child's astonishment, though as if in a quick intensity of thought, the Countess advanced as gaily as if, for many a day, nothing awkward had happened for any one. Maisie, in spite of a large acquaintance with the phenomenon, had never seen it so promptly established that nothing awkward was to be mentioned. The next minute the Countess had kissed her and exclaimed to Beale with bright, tender reproach: "Why, you never told me *half*! My dear child," she cried, "it was awfully nice of you to come!"

"But she hasn't come—she won't come!" Beale answered. "I've put it to her how much you'd like it, but she declines to have anything to do with us."

The Countess stood smiling, and after an instant that was

mainly taken up with the shock of her weird aspect Maisie felt
herself reminded of another smile, which was not ugly,
though also interested—the kind light thrown, that day in the
Park, from the clean, fair face of the Captain. Papa's Captain
—yes—was the Countess; but she wasn't nearly so nice as the
other: it all came back, doubtless, to Maisie's minor appreciation of ladies. "Shouldn't you like me," said this one endearingly, "to take you to Spa?"

"To Spa?" The child repeated the name to gain time, not to
show how the Countess brought back to her a dim remembrance of a strange woman with a horrid face who once, years
before, in an omnibus, bending to her from an opposite seat,
had suddenly produced an orange and murmured "Little
dearie, won't you have it?" She felt then, for some reason,
a small, silly terror, though afterwards conscious that her interlocutress, unfortunately hideous, had particularly meant to
be kind. This was also what the Countess meant; yet the few
words she had uttered and the smile with which she had uttered them immediately cleared everything up. Oh no, she
wanted to go nowhere with *her*, for her presence had already,
in a few seconds, dissipated the happy impression of the room
and put an end to the pride momentarily suggested by Beale's
association with so much taste. There was no taste in his association with the short, fat, wheedling, whiskered person
who had approached her and in whom she had to recognise
the only figure wholly without attraction that had become a
party to an intimate connection formed in her immediate circle. She was abashed meanwhile, however, at having appeared
to weigh the place to which she had been invited; and she
added as quickly as possible: "It isn't to America then?" The
Countess, at this, looked sharply at Beale, and Beale, airily
enough, asked what the deuce it mattered when she had
already given him to understand that she wanted to have
nothing to do with them. There followed between her companions a passage of which the sense was drowned for her in
the deepening inward hum of her mere desire to get off;
though she was able to guess later on that her father must
have put it to his friend that it was no use talking, that she was
an obstinate little pig and that, besides, she was really old
enough to choose for herself. It glimmered back to her indeed

that she must have failed quite dreadfully to seem responsive and polite, inasmuch as before she knew it she had visibly given the impression that if they didn't allow her to go home she should cry. Oh! if there had ever been a thing to cry about it was being found in that punishable little attitude toward the handsomest offers one had ever received. The great pain of the thing was that she could see the Countess liked her enough to wish to be liked in return, and it was from the idea of a return she sought to flee. It was the idea of a return that after a confusion of loud words had arisen between the others brought to her lips with the tremor preceding disaster: "Can't I, please, be sent home in a cab?" Yes, the Countess wanted her and the Countess was wounded and chilled, and she couldn't help it, and it was all the more dreadful because it only made the Countess more seductive and more impossible. The only thing that sustained either of them perhaps till the cab came—Maisie presently saw it would come—was its being in the air somehow that Beale had done what he wanted. He went out to look for a conveyance; the servants, he said, had gone to bed, but she shouldn't be kept beyond her time. The Countess left the room with him, and, alone in the possession of it, Maisie hoped she wouldn't come back. It was all the effect of her face—the child simply couldn't look at it and meet its expression half-way. All in a moment too that queer expression had leaped into the lovely things—all in a moment she had had to accept her father as liking some one whom she was sure neither her mother, nor Mrs. Beale, nor Mrs. Wix, nor Sir Claude, nor the Captain, nor even Mr. Perriam and Lord Eric could possibly have liked. Three minutes later, downstairs, with the cab at the door, it was perhaps as a final confession of not having much to boast of that, on taking leave of her, he managed to press her to his bosom without her seeing his face. For herself she was so eager to go that their parting reminded her of nothing, not even of a single one of all the "nevers" that above, as the penalty of not cleaving to him, he had attached to the question of their meeting again. There was something in the Countess that falsified everything, even the great interests in America and yet more the first flush of that superiority to Mrs. Beale and to mamma which had been expressed in silver boxes. These were still there, but perhaps there were no great interests in America. Mamma had known an American who was not a bit like this one. She was not, however, of noble rank; her name was only Mrs. Tucker. Maisie's detachment would all the same have been more complete if she had not suddenly had to exclaim: "Oh dear, I haven't any money!"

Her father's teeth, at this, were such a picture of appetite without action as to be a match for any plea of poverty. "Make your stepmother pay."

"Stepmothers *don't* pay!" cried the Countess. "No stepmother ever paid in her life!" The next moment they were in the street together, and the next the child was in the cab, with the Countess, on the pavement, but close to her, quickly taking money from a purse whisked out of a pocket. Her father had vanished and there was even yet nothing in that to reawaken the pang of loss. "Here's money," said the brown lady: "go!" The sound was commanding: the cab rattled off. Maisie sat there with her hand full of coin. All that for a cab? As they passed a street lamp she bent to see how much. What she saw was a cluster of sovereigns. There *must* then have been great interests in America. It was still at any rate the Arabian Nights.

XX

THE MONEY was far too much even for a fee in a fairy-tale, and in the absence of Mrs. Beale, who, though the hour was now late, had not yet returned to the Regent's Park, Susan Ash, in the hall, as loud as Maisie was low and as bold as she was bland, produced, on the exhibition offered under the dim vigil of the lamp that made the place a contrast to the child's recent scene of light, the half-crown that an unsophisticated cabman could pronounce to be the least he would take. It was apparently long before Mrs. Beale would arrive, and in the interval Maisie had been induced by the prompt Susan not only to go to bed like a darling dear, but, in still richer expression of that character, to devote to the repayment of obligations general as well as particular one of the sovereigns in the fanciful figure that, on the dressing-table upstairs, was naturally not less dazzling to a lone orphan of a housemaid than to the subject of the manœuvres of a quartette. This subject went to sleep with her property under her pillow; but the explanations that on the morrow were inevitably more complete with Mrs. Beale than they had been with her humble friend found a climax in a surrender also more becomingly free. There were explanations indeed that Mrs. Beale had to give as well as to ask, and the most striking of these was to the effect that it was dreadful for a little girl to take money from a woman who was simply the vilest of their sex. The sovereigns were examined with some attention, the result of which, however, was to make Mrs. Beale desire to know what, if one really went into the matter, they could be called but the wages of sin. Her companion went into it merely to the point of inquiring what then they were to do with them; on which Mrs. Beale, who had by this time put them into her pocket, replied with dignity and with her hand on the place: "We're to send them back on the spot!" Susan, the child soon afterwards learnt, had been invited to contribute to this act of restitution her one appropriated coin; but a closer clutch of the treasure showed in her private assurance to Maisie that there was a limit to the way she could be "done." Maisie had been open with Mrs. Beale about the whole of last night's transaction; but she now found herself on the part of their indignant inferior a recipient of remarks that she must feel to be scaring secrets. One of these bore upon the extraordinary hour—it was three in the morning if she really wanted to know—at which Mrs. Beale had re-entered the house; another, in accents as to which Maisie's criticism was still intensely tacit, characterised that lady's appeal as such a "gime," such a "shime" as one had never had to put up with; a third treated with some vigour the question of the enormous sums due below stairs, in every department, for gratuitous labour and wasted zeal. Our young lady's consciousness was indeed mainly filled for several days with the apprehension created by the too slow subsidence of her attendant's sense of wrong. These days would be exciting indeed if an outbreak in the kitchen should crown them; and to promote that prospect she had more than one glimpse through Susan's eyes of forces making for an earthquake. To listen to Susan was to gather that the spark applied to the inflammables and already causing them to crackle was the circumstance of one's being called a horrid low thief for refusing to part with one's own.

The redeeming point of this tension was, on the fifth day, that it actually appeared to have had to do with a breathless perception in our heroine's breast that scarcely more as the centre of Sir Claude's than as that of Susan's energies she had soon after breakfast been conveyed from London to Folkestone and established at a lovely hotel. These agents, before her wondering eyes, had combined to carry through the adventure and to give it the air of having owed its success to the fact that Mrs. Beale had, as Susan said, but just stepped out. When Sir Claude, watch in hand, had met this fact with the exclamation "Then pack Miss Farange and come off with us!" there had ensued on the stairs a series of gymnastics of a nature to bring Miss Farange's heart into her mouth. She sat with Sir Claude in a four-wheeler while he still held his watch; held it longer than any doctor who had ever felt her pulse; long enough to give her a vision of something like the ecstasy of neglecting such an opportunity to show impatience. The ecstasy had begun in the schoolroom and over the Berceuse, quite in the manner of the same foretaste on the day, a little while back, when Susan had panted up and she herself, after the hint about the duchess, had sailed down; for what harm then had there been in drops and disappointments if she could still have, even only a moment, the sensation of such a name "brought up?" It had remained with her that her father had told her that she would some day be in the street, but it clearly wouldn't be this day, and she felt justified of her preference as soon as her visitor had set Susan in motion and laid his hand, while she waited with him, kindly on her own. That was what the Captain, in Kensington Gardens, had done; her present situation reminded her a little of that one and renewed the dim wonder of the way in which, from the first, such pats and pulls had struck her as the steps and signs of other people's business and even a little as the wriggle or the overflow of their difficulties. What had failed her and what had frightened her on the night of the Exhibition lost themselves at present alike in the impression that what would come from Sir Claude was too big to come all at once. Any awe that might have sprung from his air of leaving out her stepmother was corrected by the force of a general rule, the odd truth that if Mrs. Beale now never came nor went without making her think of him, it was not, to balance that, the main character of his own contact to appear to be a reference to Mrs. Beale. To be with Sir Claude was to think of Sir Claude, and that law governed Maisie's mind until, through a sudden lurch of the cab, which had at last taken in Susan and ever so many bundles and almost reached Charing Cross, it popped again somehow into her dizzy head the long-lost image of Mrs. Wix.

It was singular, but from this time she understood and she followed, followed with the sense of an ample filling-out of any void created by symptoms of avoidance and of flight. Her ecstasy was a thing that had yet more of a face than of a back to turn, a pair of eyes still directed to Mrs. Wix even after the slight surprise of their not finding her, as the journey expanded, either at the London station or at the Folkestone hotel. It took few hours to make the child feel that if she was in neither of these places she was at least everywhere else. Maisie had known all along a great deal, but never so much as she was to know from this moment on and as she learned in particular during the couple of days that she was to hang in the air, as it were, over the sea which represented in breezy blueness and with a summer charm a crossing of more spaces than the Channel. It was granted her at this time to arrive at divinations so ample that I shall have no room for the goal if I attempt to trace the stages; as to which therefore I must be content to say that the fullest expression we may give to Sir Claude's conduct is a poor and pale copy of the picture it presented to his young friend. Abruptly, that morning, he had yielded to the action of the idea pumped into him for weeks by Mrs. Wix on lines of approach that she had been capable of the extraordinary art of preserving from entanglement with the fine network of his relations with Mrs. Beale. The breath of her sincerity, blowing without a break, had puffed him up to the flight by which, in the degree I have indicated, Maisie too was carried off her feet. This consisted in neither more nor less than the brave stroke of his getting off from Mrs. Beale as well as from his wife—of making with the child straight for some such foreign land as would give a support to Mrs. Wix's dream that she might still see his errors renounced and his delinquencies redeemed. It would all be a sacrifice—under eyes that would miss no faintest shade—to what even the strange frequenters of her ladyship's earlier period used to call the real good of the little unfortunate. Maisie's head held a suspicion of much that, during the last long interval, had confusedly, but quite candidly, come and gone in his own; a glimpse, almost awe-stricken in its gratitude, of the miracle her old governess had wrought. That functionary could not in this connection have been more impressive, even at second-hand, if she had been a prophetess with an open scroll or some ardent abbess speaking with the lips of the Church. She had clung day by day to their plastic associate, plying him with her deep, narrow passion, doing her simple utmost to convert him, and so inspiring him that he had at last really embraced his fine chance. That the chance was not delusive was sufficiently guaranteed by the completeness with which he could finally figure it out that, in case of his taking action, neither Ida nor Beale, whose book, on each side, it would only too well suit, would make any sort of row.

It sounds, no doubt, too penetrating, but it was by no means all through Sir Claude's betrayals that Maisie was able to piece together the beauty of the special influence through which, for such stretches of time, he had refined upon propriety by keeping, so far as possible, his sentimental interests distinct. She had ever of course in her mind fewer names than conceptions, but it was only with this drawback that she now made out her companion's absences to have had for their ground that he was the lover of her stepmother and that the lover of her stepmother could scarce logically pretend to a superior right to look after her. Maisie had by this time embraced the implication of a kind of natural divergence between lovers and little girls. It was just this indeed that could throw light on the probable contents of the pencilled note deposited on the hall-table in the Regent's Park and which would greet Mrs. Beale on her return. Maisie freely figured it as provisionally jocular in tone, even though to herself on this occasion Sir Claude turned a graver face than he had shown in any crisis but that of putting her into the cab when she had been horrid to him after her parting with the Captain. He might really be embarrassed, but he would be sure, to her view, to have muffled in some bravado of pleasantry the disturbance produced at her father's by the removal of a valued servant. Not that there wasn't a great deal too that wouldn't be in the note—a great deal for which a more comfortable place was Maisie's light little brain, where it hummed away hour after hour and caused the first outlook at Folkestone to swim in a softness of colour and sound. It became clear in this medium that her stepfather had really now only to take into account his entanglement with Mrs. Beale. Wasn't he at last disentangled from every one and everything else? The obstacle to the rupture pressed upon him by Mrs. Wix in the interest of his virtue would be simply that he was in love, or rather, to put it more precisely, that Mrs. Beale had left him no doubt of the degree in which *she* was. She was so much so as to have succeeded in making him accept for a time her infatuated grasp of him and even to some extent the idea of what they yet might do together with a little diplomacy and a good deal of patience. I may not even answer for it that Maisie was not aware of how, in this, Mrs. Beale failed to

share his all but insurmountable distaste for their allowing
their little charge to breathe the air of their gross irregularity
—his contention, in a word, that they should either cease to
be irregular or cease to be parental. Their little charge, for
herself, had long ago adopted the view that even Mrs. Wix
had at one time not thought prohibitively coarse—the view
that she was after all, *as* a little charge, morally at home in at-
mospheres it would be appalling to analyse. If Mrs. Wix, however, ultimately appalled, had now set her heart on strong
measures, Maisie, as I have intimated, could also work round
both to the reasons for them and to the quite other reasons
for that lady's not, as yet at least, appearing in them at first
hand.

Oh, decidedly, I shall never get you to believe the number
of things she saw and the number of secrets she discovered!
Why in the world, for instance, couldn't Sir Claude have kept
it from her—except on the hypothesis of his not caring to—
that, when you came to look at it and so far as it was a question of vested interests, he had quite as much right in her as
her stepmother and a right that Mrs. Beale was in no position
to dispute? He failed at all events of any such successful ambiguity as could keep her, when once they began to look
across at France, from regarding even what was least explained as most in the spirit of their old happy times, their
rambles and expeditions in the easier, better days of their first
acquaintance. Never before had she had so the sense of giving
him a lead for the sort of treatment of what was between
them that would best carry it off, or of his being grateful to
her for meeting him so much in the right place. She met him
literally at the very point where Mrs. Beale was most to be
reckoned with, the point of the jealousy that was sharp in that
lady and of the need of their keeping it as long as possible obscure to her that poor Mrs. Wix had still a hand. Yes, she met
him too in the truth of the matter that, as her stepmother had
had no one else to be jealous of, she had made up for so gross
a privation by directing the sentiment to a moral influence. Sir
Claude appeared absolutely to convey in a wink that a moral
influence that could pull a string was after all a moral influence that could have its eyes scratched out; and that, this
being the case, there was somebody they couldn't afford to

expose before they should see a little better what Mrs. Beale
was likely to do. Maisie, true enough, had not to put it into
words to rejoin, in the coffee-room, at luncheon: "What *can*
she do but come to you if papa does take a step that will
amount to legal desertion?" Neither had he then, in answer,
to articulate anything but the jollity of their having found a
table at a window from which, as they partook of cold beef
and apollinaris—for he hinted they would have to save lots of
money, they could let their eyes hover tenderly on the far-off
white cliffs that so often had signalled to the embarrassed
English a promise of safety. Maisie stared at them as if she
might really make out after a little a queer, dear figure
perched on them—a figure as to which she had already the
subtle sense that, wherever perched, it would be the very
oddest yet seen in France. But it was at least as exciting to feel
where Mrs. Wix wasn't as it would have been to know where
she was, and if she wasn't yet at Boulogne this only thickened
the plot.

If she was not to be seen that day, however, the evening
was marked by an apparition before which, none the less, the
savour of suspense folded on the spot its wings. Adjusting her
respirations and attaching, under dropped lashes, all her
thoughts to a smartness of frock and frill for which she could
reflect that she had not appealed in vain to a loyalty in Susan
Ash triumphant over the nice things their feverish flight had
left behind, Maisie spent on a bench in the garden of the hotel the half-hour before dinner, that mysterious ceremony of
the *table d'hôte* for which she had prepared with a punctuality
of flutter. Sir Claude, beside her, was occupied with a cigarette and the afternoon papers; and though the hotel was full
the garden showed the particular void that ensues upon the
sound of the dressing-bell. She had almost had time to weary
of the human scene; her own humanity at any rate, in the
shape of a smutch on her scanty skirt, had held her so long
that as soon as she raised her eyes they rested on a high, fair
drapery by which smutches were put to shame and which had
glided towards her over the grass without her noting its
rustle. She followed up its stiff sheen—up and up from the
ground, where it had stopped—till at the end of a considerable journey her impression felt the shock of the fixed face

which, surmounting it, seemed to offer the climax of the dressed condition. "Why, mamma!" she cried the next instant —cried in a tone that, as she sprang to her feet, brought Sir Claude to his own beside her and gave her ladyship, a few yards off, the advantage of their momentary confusion. Poor Maisie's was immense; her mother's drop had the effect of one of the iron shutters that, in evening walks with Susan Ash, she had seen suddenly, at the touch of a spring, rattle down over shining shopfronts. The light of foreign travel was darkened at a stroke; she had a horrible sense that they were caught; and for the first time in her life in Ida's presence she so far translated an impulse into an invidious act as to clutch straight at the hand of her responsible confederate. It didn't help her that he appeared at first equally hushed with horror; a minute during which, in the empty garden, with its long shadows on the lawn, its blue sea over the hedge and its star- tled peace in the air, both her elders remained as stiff as tall tumblers filled to the brim and held straight for fear of a spill. At last, in a tone that in its unexpected softness enriched the whole surprise, her mother said to Sir Claude: "Do you mind at all my speaking to her?"

"Oh no; *do* you?" His reply was so long in coming that Maisie was the first to find the right note.

He laughed as he seemed to take it from her, and she felt a sufficient concession in his manner of addressing their visitor. "How in the world did you know we were here?"

His wife, at this, came the rest of the way and sat down on the bench with a hand laid on her daughter, whom she grace- fully drew to her and in whom, at her touch, the fear just kin- dled gave a second jump, but now in quite another direction. Sir Claude, on the further side, resumed his seat and his newspapers, and the three grouped themselves like a family party; his connection, in the oddest way in the world, almost cynically and in a flash acknowledged, and the mother patting the child into conformities unspeakable. Maisie could already feel that it was not Sir Claude and she who were caught. She had the positive sense of catching their relative, catching her in the act of getting rid of her burden with a finality that showed her as unprecedentedly relaxed. Oh yes, the fear had dropped, and she had never been so irrevocably parted with

as in the pressure of possession now supremely exerted by
Ida's long-gloved and much-bangled arm. "I went to the Re-
gent's Park"—this was presently her ladyship's answer to Sir
Claude.

"Do you mean to-day?"

"This morning; just after your own call there. That's how I
found you out; that's what has brought me."

Sir Claude considered and Maisie waited. "Whom then did
you see?"

Ida gave a sound of indulgent mockery. "I like your scare.
I know your game. I didn't see the person I risked seeing, but
I had been ready to take my chance of her." She addressed
herself to Maisie; she had encircled her more closely. "I asked
for *you*, my dear, but I saw no one but a dirty parlourmaid.
She was red in the face with the great things that, as she told
me, had just happened in the absence of her mistress; and she
luckily had the sense to have made out the place to which Sir
Claude had come to take you. If he hadn't given a false scent
I should find you here: that was the supposition on which I've
proceeded." Ida had never been so explicit about proceeding
or supposing, and Maisie, drinking this in, was aware that Sir
Claude shared her fine impression of it. "I wanted to see
you," his wife continued, "and now you can judge of the
trouble I've taken. I had everything to do in town to-day, but
I managed to get off."

Maisie and her companion, for a moment, did justice to
this achievement; but Maisie was the first to express it. "I'm
glad you wanted to see me, mamma." Then, after a concentration more deep and with a plunge more brave: "A little
more and you'd have been too late." It stuck in her throat,
but she brought it out: "We're going to France."

Ida was magnificent: Ida kissed her on the forehead.
"That's just what I thought likely; it made me decide to run
down. I fancied that in spite of your scramble you'd wait to
cross, and it added to the reason I have for seeing you."

Maisie wondered intensely what the reason could be, but
she knew ever so much better than to ask. She was slightly
surprised indeed to perceive that Sir Claude didn't, and to
hear him immediately inquire: "What in the name of goodness can you have to say to her?"

His tone was not exactly rude, but it was impatient enough to make his wife's response a fresh specimen of the new softness. "That, my dear man, is all my own business."

"Do you mean," Sir Claude asked, "that you wish me to leave you with her?"

"Yes, if you'll be so good; that's the extraordinary request I take the liberty of making." Her ladyship had dropped to a mildness of irony by which, for a moment, poor Maisie was mystified and charmed, puzzled with a glimpse of something that in all the years had at intervals peeped out. Ida smiled at Sir Claude with the strange air she had on such occasions of defying an interlocutor to keep it up as long; her huge eyes, her red lips, the intense marks in her face formed an illumination as distinct and public as a lamp set in a window. The child seemed quite to see in it the very lamp that had lighted her path; she suddenly found herself reflecting that it was no wonder the gentlemen were guided. This must have been the way mamma had first looked at Sir Claude; it brought back the lustre of the time they had outlived. It must have been the way she looked also at Mr. Perriam and Lord Eric; above all, it contributed in Maisie's mind to a completer view of the Captain. Our young lady grasped this idea with a quick lifting of the heart; there was a stillness during which her mother flooded her with a wealth of support to the Captain's striking tribute. This stillness remained long enough unbroken to represent that Sir Claude too might literally be struggling again with the element that had originally upset him; so that Maisie quite hoped he would at least say something to show a recognition that she could be charming.

What he presently said was: "Are you putting up for the night?"

His wife hesitated. "Not here—I've come from Dover."

Over Maisie's head, at this, they still faced each other. "You spend the night there?"

"Yes, I brought some things. I went to the hotel and hastily arranged; then I caught the train that whisked me on here. You see what a day I've had of it."

The statement may surprise, but these were really as obliging if not as lucid words as, into her daughter's ears at least, Ida's lips had ever dropped; and there was a quick desire in the daughter that for the hour at any rate they should duly be welcomed as a ground of intercourse. Certainly mamma had a charm which, when turned on, became a large explanation; and the only danger now in an impulse to applaud it would be that of appearing to signalise its rarity. Maisie, however, risked the peril in the geniality of an admission that Ida had indeed had a rush; and she invited Sir Claude to expose himself by agreeing with her that the rush had been even worse than theirs. He appeared to meet this appeal by saying with detachment enough: "You go back there to-night?"

"Oh yes—there are plenty of trains."

Again Sir Claude hesitated; it would have been hard to say if the child, between them, more connected or divided them. Then he brought out quietly: "It will be late for you to knock about. I'll see you over."

"You needn't trouble, thank you. I think you won't deny that I can help myself and that it isn't the first time in my dreadful life that I've somehow managed it." Save for this allusion to her dreadful life they talked there, Maisie noted, as if they were only rather superficial friends; a special effect that she had often wondered at before in the midst of what she supposed to be intimacies. This effect was augmented by the almost casual manner in which her ladyship went on: "I daresay I shall go abroad."

"From Dover do you mean, straight?"

"How straight I can't say. I'm excessively ill." This for a minute struck Maisie as but a part of the conversation; at the end of which time she became aware that it ought to strike her—as it apparently didn't strike Sir Claude—as a part of something graver. It helped her to twist nearer. "Ill, mamma —really ill?"

She regretted her "really" as soon as she had spoken it; but there couldn't be a better proof of her mother's present polish than that Ida showed no gleam of a temper to take it up. She had taken up at other times much tinier things. She only pressed Maisie's head against her bosom and said: "Shockingly, my dear. I must go to that new place."

"What new place?" Sir Claude inquired.

Ida thought, but couldn't recall it. "Oh, 'Chose,' don't you know?—where every one goes. I want some proper treatment. It's all I've ever asked for on earth. But that's not what I came to say."

Sir Claude, in silence, folded one by one his newspapers; then he rose and stood whacking the palm of his hand with the bundle. "You'll stop and dine with us?"

"Dear no—I can't dine at this sort of hour. I ordered dinner at Dover."

Her ladyship's tone in this one instance showed a certain superiority to those conditions in which her daughter had artlessly found Folkestone a paradise. It was yet not so crushing as to nip in the bud the eagerness with which the latter broke out: "But won't you at least have a cup of tea?"

Ida kissed her again on the brow. "Thanks, love. I had tea before coming." She raised her eyes to Sir Claude. "She *is* sweet!" He made no more answer than if he didn't agree; but Maisie was at ease about that and was still taken up with the joy of this happier pitch of their talk, which put more and more of a meaning into the Captain's version of her ladyship and literally kindled a conjecture that this admirer might, over there at the other place, be waiting for her to dine. Was the same conjecture in Sir Claude's mind? He partly puzzled her, if it had risen there, by the slight perversity with which he returned to a question that his wife evidently thought she had disposed of.

He whacked his hand again with his papers. "I had really much better take you."

"And leave Maisie here alone?"

Mamma so clearly didn't want it that Maisie leaped at the vision of a Captain who had seen her on from Dover and who, while he waited to take her back, would be hovering just at the same distance at which, in Kensington Gardens, the companion of his walk had herself hovered. Of course, however, instead of breathing any such guess she let Sir Claude reply; all the more that his reply could contribute so much to her own present grandeur. "She won't be alone when she has a maid in attendance."

Maisie had never before had so much of a retinue, and she waited also to enjoy the effect of it on her ladyship. "You mean the woman you brought from town?" Ida considered. "The person at the house spoke of her in a way that scarcely made her out company for my child." Her tone was that her child had never wanted, in her hands, for prodigious company. But she as distinctly continued to decline Sir Claude's. "Don't be an old goose," she said charmingly. "Let us alone."

In front of them on the grass he looked graver than Maisie at all now thought the occasion warranted. "I don't see why you can't say it before me."

His wife smoothed one of her daughter's curls. "Say what, dear?"

"Why, what you came to say."

At this Maisie at last interposed: she appealed to Sir Claude. "Do let her say it to me."

He looked hard for a moment at his little friend. "How do you know what she may say?"

"She must risk it," Ida remarked.

"I only want to protect you," he continued to the child.

"You want to protect yourself—that's what you mean," his wife replied. "Don't be afraid. I won't touch you."

"She won't touch you—she *won't*!" Maisie declared. She felt by this time that she could really answer for it, and something of the emotion with which she had listened to the Captain came back to her. It made her so happy and so secure that she could positively patronise mamma. She did so in the Captain's very language. "She's good, she's good!" she proclaimed.

"Oh Lord!"—Sir Claude, at this, let himself go. He appeared to have emitted some sound of derision that was smothered, to Maisie's ears, by her being again embraced by his wife. Ida released her and held her off a little, looking at her with a very queer face. Then the child became aware that their companion had left them and that from the face in question a confirmatory remark had proceeded.

"I *am* good, love," said her ladyship.

XXI

A GOOD DEAL of the rest of Ida's visit was devoted to explaining, as it were, so extraordinary a statement. This explanation was more copious than any she had yet indulged in, and as the summer twilight gathered and she kept her child in the garden she was conciliatory to a degree that let her need to arrange things a little perceptibly peep out. It was not merely that she explained; she almost conversed; all that was wanting to that was that she should have positively chattered a little less. It was really the occasion of Maisie's life on which her mother was to have most to say to her. That alone was an implication of generosity and virtue, and no great stretch was required to make our young lady feel that she should best meet her and soonest have it over by simply seeming struck with the propriety of her contention. They sat together while the parent's gloved hand sometimes rested sociably on the child's and sometimes gave a corrective pull to a ribbon too meagre or a tress too thick; and Maisie was conscious of the effort to keep out of her eyes the wonder with which they were occasionally moved to blink. Oh, there would have been things to blink at if one had let one's self go; and it was lucky they were alone together, without Sir Claude or Mrs. Wix or even Mrs. Beale to catch an imprudent glance. Though profuse and prolonged her ladyship was not exhaustively lucid, and her account of her situation, so far as it could be called descriptive, was a muddle of inconsequent things, bruised fruit of an occasion she had rather too lightly affronted. None of them were really thought out and some were even not wholly insincere. It was as if she had asked outright what better proof could have been wanted of her goodness and her greatness than just this marvellous consent to give up what she had so cherished. It was as if she had said in so many words: "There have been things between us—between Sir Claude and me—which I needn't go into, you little nuisance, because you wouldn't understand them." It suited her to convey that Maisie had been kept, so far as *she* was concerned or could imagine, in a holy ignorance and that she must take for granted a supreme simplicity. She turned this way and that in the predicament she had sought and from which she could neither retreat with grace nor emerge with credit: she draped herself in the tatters of her impudence, postured to her utmost before the last little triangle of cracked glass to which so many fractures had reduced the polished plate of filial superstition. If neither Sir Claude nor Mrs. Wix was there this was perhaps all the more a pity: the scene had a style of its own that would have qualified it for presentation, especially at such a moment as that of her letting it betray that she quite did think her wretched offspring better placed with Sir Claude than in her own soiled hands. There was at any rate nothing scant either in her admissions or her perversions, the mixture of her fear of what Maisie might undiscoverably think and of the support she at the same time gathered from a necessity of selfishness and a habit of brutality. This habit flushed through the merit she now made, in terms explicit, of not having come to Folkestone to kick up a vulgar row. She had not come to box any ears or to bang any doors or even to use any language: she had come at the worst to lose the thread of her argument in an occasional dumb, disgusted twitch of the toggery in which Mrs. Beale's low domestic had had the impudence to serve up Miss Farange. She checked all criticism, not committing herself even as much as about those missing comforts of the schoolroom on which Mrs. Wix had presumed.

"I *am* good—I'm crazily, I'm criminally good. But it won't do for *you* any more, and if I've ceased to contend with him, and with you too, who have made most of the trouble between us, it's for reasons that you'll understand one of these days but too well—one of these days when I hope you'll know what it is to have lost a mother. I'm awfully ill, but you mustn't ask me anything about it. If I don't get off somewhere my doctor won't answer for the consequences. He's stupefied at what I've borne—he says it has been put on me because I was formed to suffer. I'm thinking of South Africa, but that's none of your business. You must take your choice —you can't ask me questions if you're so ready to give me up. No, I won't tell you; you can find out for yourself. South Africa is wonderful, they say, and if I do go it must be to give it a fair trial. It must be either one thing or the other; if he

takes you, you know, he takes you. I've struck my last blow
for you; I can follow you no longer from pillar to post. I must
live for myself at last, while there's still a handful left of me.
I'm very, very ill; I'm very, very tired; I'm very, very determined. There you have it. Make the most of it. Your frock is
too filthy; but I came to sacrifice myself." Maisie looked at
the peccant places; there were moments when it was a relief
to her to drop her eyes even on anything so sordid. All her interviews, all her ordeals with her mother had, as she had
grown older, seemed to have, before any other, the hard quality of duration; but longer than any, strangely, were these
minutes offered to her as so pacific and so agreeably winding
up the connection. It was her anxiety that made them long,
her fear of some hitch, some check of the current, one of her
ladyship's famous quick jumps. She held her breath; she only
wanted, by playing into her visitor's hands, to see the thing
through. But her impatience itself made at instants the whole
situation swim; there were things Ida said which she perhaps
didn't hear, and there were things she heard that Ida perhaps
didn't say. "You're all I have, and yet I'm capable of this. Your
father wishes you were dead—that, my dear, is what your father wishes. You'll have to get used to it as I've done—I mean
to his wishing that *I'm* dead. At all events you see for yourself
how wonderful I am to Sir Claude. He wishes me dead quite
as much; and I'm sure that if making me scenes about *you*
could have killed me——!" It was the mark of Ida's eloquence that she started more hares than she followed, and she
gave but a glance in the direction of this one; going on to say
that the very proof of her treating her husband like an angel
was that he had just stolen off not to be fairly shamed. She
spoke as if he had retired on tiptoe, as he might have with-
drawn from a place of worship in which he was not fit to be
present. "You'll never know what I've been through about
you—never, never, never. I spare you everything, as I always
have; though I daresay you know things that, if I did (I mean
if you knew them) would make me—well, no matter! You're
old enough at any rate to know there are a lot of things I
don't say that I easily might; though it would do me good,
I assure you, to have spoken my mind for once in my life. I
don't speak of your father's infamous wife: that may give you

a notion of the way I'm letting you off. When I say 'you' I mean your precious friends and backers. If you don't do justice to my forbearing, out of delicacy, to mention, just as a last word, about your stepfather, a little fact or two of a kind that really I should only *have* to mention to shine myself in comparison and after every calumny like pure gold: if you don't do me *that* justice you'll never do me justice at all!"

Maisie's desire to show what justice she did her had by this time become so intense as to have brought with it an inspiration. The great effect of their encounter had been to confirm her sense of being launched with Sir Claude, to make it rich and full beyond anything she had dreamed, and everything now conspired to suggest that a single soft touch of her small hand would complete the good work and set her ladyship so promptly and majestically afloat as to leave the great seaway clear for the morrow. This was the more the case as her hand had for some moments been rendered free by a marked manœuvre of both of her mother's. One of these capricious members had fumbled with visible impatience in some backward depth of drapery and had presently reappeared with a small article in its grasp. The act had a significance for a little person trained, in that relation, from an early age, to keep an eye on manual motions, and its possible bearing was not darkened by the memory of the handful of gold that Susan Ash would never, never believe Mrs. Beale had sent back— "not she; she's too false and too greedy!"—to the munificent Countess. To have guessed, none the less, that her ladyship's purse might be the real figure of the object extracted from the rustling covert of her rear—this suspicion gave on the spot to the child's eyes a direction carefully distant. It added moreover to the optimism that for an hour could ruffle the surface of her deep diplomacy, ruffle it to the point of making her forget that she had never been safe unless she had also been stupid. She in short forgot her habitual caution in her impulse to adopt her ladyship's practical interests and show her ladyship how perfectly she understood them. She saw without looking that her mother pressed a little clasp; heard, without wanting to the sharp click that marked the closing portemonnaie from which something had been taken. What this was she just didn't see; it was not too substantial to be locked with ease in the fold of her ladyship's fingers. Nothing was less new to Maisie than the art of not thinking singly, so that at this instant she could both bring out what was on her tongue's end and weigh, as to the object in her mother's palm, the question of its being a sovereign against the question of its being a shilling. No sooner had she begun to speak than she saw that within a few seconds this question would have been settled: she had foolishly checked the rising words of the little speech of presentation to which, under the circumstances, even such a high pride as Ida's had had to give some thought. She had checked it completely—that was the next thing she felt: the note she sounded brought into her companion's eyes a look that quickly enough seemed at variance with presentations.

"That was what the Captain said to me that day, mamma. I think it would have given you pleasure to hear the way he spoke of you."

The pleasure, Maisie could now in consternation reflect, would have been a long time coming if it had come no faster than the response evoked by her allusion to it. Her mother gave her one of the looks that slammed the door in her face; never in a career of unsuccessful experiments had Maisie had to take such a stare. It reminded her of the way that once, at one of the lectures in Glower Street, something in a big jar that, amid an array of strange glasses and bad smells, had been promised as a beautiful yellow was produced as a beautiful black. She had been sorry on that occasion for the lecturer, but she was at this moment sorrier for herself. Oh, nothing had ever made for twinges like mamma's manner of saying: "The Captain? What Captain?"

"Why, when we met you in the Gardens—the one who took me to sit with him. That was exactly what *he* said."

Ida met her so far as to appear for an instant to pick up a lost thread. "What on earth did he say?"

Maisie faltered supremely, but supremely she brought it out. "What you say, mamma—that you're so good."

"What 'I' say?" Ida slowly rose, keeping her eyes on her child, and the hand that had busied itself in her purse conformed at her side and amid the folds of her dress to a certain stiffening of the arm. "I say you're a precious idiot, and I won't have you put words into my mouth!" This was much more peremptory than a mere contradiction. Maisie could only feel on the spot that everything had broken short off and that their communication had abruptly ceased. That came out as Ida went on. "What business have you to speak to me of him?"

Her daughter turned scarlet. "I thought you liked him."

"Him!—the biggest cad in London!" Her ladyship towered again, and in the gathering dusk the whites of her eyes were huge.

Maisie's own, however, could by this time pretty well match them; and she had at least now, with the first flare of anger that had ever yet lighted her face for a foe, the sense of looking up quite as hard as any one could look down. "Well, he was kind about you then; he *was*, and it made me like him. He said things—they were beautiful, they were, they were!" She was almost capable of the violence of forcing this home, for even in the midst of her surge of passion—of which in fact it was a part—there rose in her a fear, a pain, a vision ominous, precocious, of what it might mean for her mother's fate to have forfeited such a loyalty as that. There was literally an instant in which Maisie fully saw—saw madness and desolation, saw ruin and darkness and death. "I've thought of him often since, and I hoped it was with him—with him——" Here, in her emotion, it failed her, the breath of her filial hope.

But Ida got it out of her. "You hoped, you little horror——?"

"That it was he who's at Dover, that it was he who's to take you. I mean to South Africa," Maisie said with another drop.

Ida's stupefaction, on this, kept her silent unnaturally long, so long that her daughter could not only wonder what was coming, but perfectly measure the decline of every symptom of her liberality. She loomed there in her grandeur, merely dark and dumb; her wrath was clearly still, as it had always been, a thing of resource and variety. What Maisie least expected of it was by this law what now occurred. It melted, in the summer twilight, gradually into pity, and the pity after a little found a cadence, to which the renewed click of her purse gave an accent. She had put back what she had taken out. "You're a dreadful, dismal, deplorable little thing," she murmured. And with this she turned back and rustled away over the lawn.

After she had disappeared Maisie dropped upon the bench again and for some time, in the empty garden and the deeper dusk, sat and stared at the image her flight had still left standing. It had ceased to be her mother only, in the strangest way, that it might become her father, the father of whose wish that she were dead the announcement still lingered in the air. It was a presence with vague edges—it continued to front her, to cover her. But what reality that she need reckon with did it represent if Mr. Farange were, on his side, also going off—going off to America with the Countess, or even only to Spa? That question had from the house a sudden gay answer in the great roar of a gong, and at the same moment she saw Sir Claude look out for her from the wide, lighted doorway. At this she went to him, and he came forward and met her on the lawn. For a minute she was with him there in silence, as, just before, at the last, she had been with her mother.

"She's gone?"

"She's gone."

Nothing more, for the instant, passed between them but to move together to the house, where, in the hall, he indulged in one of those sudden pleasantries with which, to the delight of his stepdaughter, his native animation abounded. "Will Miss Farange do me the honour to accept my arm?"

There was nothing in all her days that Miss Farange had accepted with such bliss, a bright, rich element that floated them together to their feast; before they reached which, however, she uttered, in the spirit of a glad young lady taken in to her first dinner, a sociable word that made him stop short. "She goes to South Africa."

"To South Africa?" His face, for a moment, seemed to swing for a jump; the next it took its spring into the extreme of hilarity. "Is that what she said?"

"Oh yes, quite distinctly. For the climate."

Sir Claude was now looking at a young woman with black hair, a red frock and a tiny terrier tucked under her elbow. She swept past them on her way to the dining-room, leaving an impression of a strong scent which mingled, amid the clatter of the place, with the hot aroma of food. He had become

a little graver; he still stopped to talk. "I see—I see." Other
people brushed by; he was not too grave to notice them.
"Did she say anything else?"

"Oh yes, a lot more."

On this he met her eyes again with some intensity, but only
repeated: "I see—I see."

Maisie had still her own vision, which she brought out. "I
thought she was going to give me something."

"What kind of a thing?"

"Some money that she took out of her purse and then put
back."

Sir Claude's amusement reappeared. "She thought better
of it. Dear thrifty soul! How much did she make by that
manœuvre?"

Maisie considered. "I didn't see. It was very small."

Sir Claude threw back his head. "Do you mean very little?
Sixpence?"

Maisie resented this almost as if, at dinner, she were already
bandying jokes with an agreeable neighbour. "It may have
been a sovereign."

"Or even," Sir Claude suggested, "a ten-pound note." She
flushed at this sudden picture of what she perhaps had lost,
and he made it more vivid by adding: "Rolled up in a tight
little ball, you know—her way of treating bank-notes as if they
were curl-papers!" Maisie's flush deepened both with the immense plausibility of this and with a fresh wave of the consciousness that was always there to remind her of his
cleverness—the consciousness of how immeasurably more
after all he knew about mamma than she. She had lived with
her so many times without discovering the material of her
curl-papers or assisting at any other of her dealings with bank-
notes. The tight little ball had at any rate rolled away from her
for ever—quite like one of the other balls that Ida's cue used
to send flying. Sir Claude gave her his arm again and by the
time she was seated at table she had perfectly made up her
mind as to the amount of the sum she had forfeited. Everything about her, however—the crowded room, the bedizened
banquet, the savour of dishes, the drama of figures—ministered to the joy of life. After dinner she smoked with her
friend—for that was exactly what she felt she did—on a porch,

a kind of terrace, where the red tips of cigars and the light dresses of ladies made, under the happy stars, a poetry that was almost intoxicating. They talked but little, and she was slightly surprised at his asking for no more news of what her mother had said; but she had no need of talk, for it seemed to her that without it her sense of everything overflowed. They smoked and smoked, and there was a sweetness in her step-father's silence. At last he said: "Let us take another turn— but you must go to bed soon. Oh, you know, we're going to have a system!" Their turn was back into the garden, along the dusky paths from which they could see the black masts and the red lights of boats and hear the calls and cries that evidently had to do with happy foreign travel; and their system was once more to get on beautifully in this further lounge without a definite exchange. Yet he finally spoke—he broke out as he tossed away the match from which he had taken a fresh light: "I must go for a stroll. I'm in a fidget—I must walk it off." She fell in with this as she fell in with everything; on which he went on: "You go up to Miss Ash"—it was the name they had started; "you must see she's not in mischief. Can you find your way alone?"

"Oh yes; I've been up and down seven times." She positively enjoyed the prospect of an eighth.

Still they didn't separate; they stood smoking together under the stars. Then at last Sir Claude produced it. "I'm free— I'm free."

She looked up at him; it was the very spot on which a couple of hours before she had looked up at her mother. "You're free—you're free."

"To-morrow we go to France." He spoke as if he had not heard her; but it didn't prevent her again concurring.

"To-morrow we go to France."

Again he appeared not to have heard her; and after a moment—it was an effect evidently of the depth of his reflections and the agitation of his soul—he also spoke as if he had not spoken before. "I'm free—I'm free!"

She repeated her form of assent. "You're free—you're free."

This time he did hear her; he fixed her through the darkness with a grave face. But he said nothing more; he simply stooped a little and drew her to him—simply held her a little and kissed her good-night; after which, having given her a silent push upstairs to Miss Ash, he turned round again to the black masts and the red lights. Maisie mounted as if France were at the top.

XXII

THE NEXT DAY it seemed to her at the bottom—down too far, in shuddering plunges, even to leave her a sense, on the Channel boat, of the height at which Sir Claude remained and which had never in every way been so great as when, much in the wet, though in the angle of a screen of canvas, he sociably sat with his stepdaughter's head in his lap and that of Mrs. Beale's housemaid fairly pillowed on his breast. Maisie was surprised to learn as they drew into port that they had had a lovely passage; but this emotion, at Boulogne, was speedily quenched in others, above all in the great ecstasy of a larger impression of life. She was "abroad" and she gave herself up to it, responded to it, in the bright air, before the pink houses, among the bare-legged fish-wives and the red-legged soldiers, with the instant certitude of a vocation. Her vocation was to see the world and to thrill with enjoyment of the picture; she had grown older in five minutes and had by the time they reached the hotel recognised in the institutions and manners of France a multitude of affinities and messages. Literally in the course of an hour she found her initiation; a consciousness much quickened by the superior part that, as soon as they had gobbled down a French breakfast—which was indeed a high note in the concert—she observed herself to play to Susan Ash. Sir Claude, who had already bumped against people he knew and who, as he said, had business and letters, sent them out together for a walk, a walk in which the child was avenged, so far as poetic justice required, not only for the loud giggles that in their London trudges used to break from her attendant, but for all the years of her tendency to produce socially that impression of an excess of the queer something which had seemed to waver so widely between in-nocence and guilt. On the spot, at Boulogne, though there might have been excess there was at least no wavering; she recognised, she understood, she adored and took possession; feeling herself attuned to everything and laying her hand, right and left, on what had simply been waiting for her. She explained to Susan, she laughed at Susan, she towered over

Susan; and it was somehow Susan's stupidity, of which she
had never yet been so sure, and Susan's bewilderment and ignorance and antagonism, that gave the liveliest rebound to
her immediate perceptions and adoptions. The place and the
people were all a picture together, a picture that, when they
went down to the wide sands, shimmered, in a thousand tints,
with the pretty organisation of the *plage*, with the gaiety of
spectators and bathers, with that of the language and the
weather and above all with that of our young lady's unprecedented situation. For it appeared to her that no one since the
beginning of time could have had such an adventure or, in an
hour, so much experience; as a sequel to which she only
needed, in order to feel with conscious wonder how the past
was changed, to hear Susan, inscrutably aggravated, express a
preference for the Edgware Road. The past was so changed
and the circle it had formed already so overstepped that on
that very afternoon, in the course of another walk, she found
herself inquiring of Sir Claude—and without a single scruple
—if he were prepared as yet to name the moment at which
they should start for Paris. His answer, it must be said, gave
her the least little chill.

"Oh Paris, my dear child—I don't quite know about
Paris!"

This required to be met, but it was much less to challenge
him than for the rich joy of her first discussion of the details
of a tour that, after looking at him a minute, she replied:
"Well, isn't that the *real* thing, the thing that when one does
come abroad——?"

He had turned grave again, and she merely threw that out;
it was a way of doing justice to the seriousness of their life.
She couldn't moreover be so much older since yesterday without reflecting that if by this time she probed a little he would
recognise that she had done enough for mere patience. There
was in fact something in his eyes that suddenly, to her own,
made her discretion shabby. Before she could remedy this he
had answered her last question, answered it in a way that, of
all ways, she had least expected. "The thing it doesn't do not
to do? Certainly, Paris is charming. But, my dear fellow, Paris
eats your head off; I mean it's so beastly expensive."

That note gave her a pang—it suddenly let in a harder

light. Were they poor then, that is was *he* poor, really poor beyond the pleasantry of apollinaris and cold beef? They had walked to the end of the long jetty that enclosed the harbour and were looking out at the dangers they had escaped, the grey horizon that was England, the tumbled surface of the sea and the brown smacks that bobbed upon it. Why had he chosen an embarrassed time to make this foreign dash? unless indeed it was just the dash economic, of which she had often heard and on which, after another look at the grey horizon and the bobbing boats, she was ready to turn round with elation. She replied to him quite in his own manner: "I see, I see." She smiled up at him. "Our affairs are involved."

"That's it." He returned her smile. "Mine are not quite so bad as yours; for yours are really, my dear man, in a state I can't see through at all. But mine will do—for a mess."

She thought this over. "But isn't France cheaper than England?"

England, over there in the thickening gloom, looked just then remarkably dear.

"I daresay; some parts."

"Then can't we live in those parts?"

There was something that for an instant, in satisfaction of this, he had the air of being about to say and yet not saying. What he presently said was: "This very place is one of them."

"Then we shall live here?"

He didn't treat it quite as definitely as she liked. "Since we've come to save money!"

This made her press him more. "How long shall we stay?"

"Oh, three or four days."

It took her breath away. "You can save money in that time?"

He burst out laughing, starting to walk again and taking her under his arm. He confessed to her on the way that she too had put a finger on the weakest of all his weaknesses, the fact, of which he was perfectly aware, that he probably might have lived within his means if he had never done anything for thrift. "It's the happy thoughts that do it," he said; "there's nothing so ruinous as putting in a cheap week." Maisie heard afresh among the pleasant sounds of the closing day that steel click of Ida's change of mind. She thought of the ten-pound note it would have been delightful at this juncture to produce for her companion's encouragement. But the idea was dissipated by his saying irrelevantly, in the presence of the next thing they stopped to admire: "We shall stay till she arrives."

She turned upon him. "Mrs. Beale?"

"Mrs. Wix. I've had a wire," he went on. "She has seen your mother."

"Seen mamma?" Maisie stared. "Where in the world?"

"Apparently in London. They've been together."

For an instant this looked ominous—a fear came into her eyes. "Then she hasn't gone?"

"Your mother?—to South Africa? I give it up, dear boy," Sir Claude said; and she seemed literally to see him give it up as he stood there and with a kind of absent gaze—absent, that is, from *her* affairs—followed the fine stride and shining limbs of a young fishwife who had just waded out of the sea with her basketful of shrimps. His thought came back to her sooner than his eyes. "But I daresay it's all right. She wouldn't come if it wasn't, poor old thing: she knows rather well what she's about."

This was so reassuring that Maisie, after turning it over, could make it fit into her dream. "Well, what *is* she about?"

He stopped looking at last at the fishwife—he met his companion's inquiry. "Oh, you know!" There was something in the way he said it that made, between them, more of an equality than she had yet imagined; but it had also more the effect of raising her up than of letting him down, and what it did with her was shown by the sound of her assent.

"Yes—I know!" What she knew, what she *could* know is by this time no secret to us: it grew and grew at any rate, the rest of that day, in the air of what he took for granted. It was better he should do that than attempt to test her knowledge; but there at the worst was the gist of the matter: it was open between them at last that their great change, as, speaking as if it had already lasted weeks, Maisie called it, was somehow built up round Mrs. Wix. Before she went to bed that night she knew further that Sir Claude, since, as *he* called it, they had been on the rush, had received more telegrams than one. But they separated again without speaking of Mrs. Beale.

Oh what a crossing for the straighteners and the old brown

dress—which latter appurtenance the child saw thriftily revived for the possible disasters of travel! The wind got up in
the night and from her little room at the inn Maisie could
hear the noise of the sea. The next day it was raining and
everything different: this was the case even with Susan Ash,
who positively crowed over the bad weather, partly, it seemed,
for relish of the time their visitor would have in the boat, and
partly to point the moral of the folly of coming to such holes.
In the wet, with Sir Claude, Maisie went to the Folkestone
packet, on the arrival of which, with many signs of the fray, he
made her wait under an umbrella on the quay; whence, almost ere the vessel touched, he was to be descried, in quest
of their friend, wriggling—that had been his word—through
the invalids massed upon the deck. It was long till he reappeared—it was not indeed till every one had landed; when he
presented the object of his benevolence in a light that Maisie
scarce knew whether to deem the depth of prostration or the
climax of success. The lady on his arm, still bent beneath her
late ordeal, was muffled in such draperies as had never before
offered so much support to so much woe. At the hotel, an
hour later, this ambiguity dropped: assisting Mrs. Wix in private to refresh and reinvest herself, Maisie heard from her in
detail how little she could have achieved if Sir Claude hadn't
put it in her power. It was a phrase that in her room she repeated in connections indescribable: he had put it in her
power to have "changes," as she said, of the most intimate order, adapted to climates and occasions so various as to fore-
shadow in themselves the stages of a vast itinerary. Cheap
weeks would of course be in their place after so much money
spent on a governess; sums not grudged, however, by this
lady's pupil even on her feeling her own appearance give rise,
through the straighteners, to an attention perceptibly mystified. Sir Claude in truth had had less time to devote to it than
to Mrs. Wix's; and moreover she would rather be in her own
shoes than in her friend's creaking new ones in the event of
an encounter with Mrs. Beale. Maisie was too lost in the idea
of Mrs. Beale's judgment of so much newness to pass any
judgment herself. Besides, after much luncheon and many endearments, the question took quite another turn, to say nothing of the pleasure of the child's quick view that there were

other eyes than Susan Ash's to open to what she could show.
She couldn't show much, alas, till it stopped raining, which it
declined to do that day; but this had only the effect of leaving more time for Mrs. Wix's own demonstration. It came as
they sat in the little white and gold *salon* which Maisie
thought the loveliest place she had ever seen except perhaps
the apartment of the Countess; it came while the hard summer storm lashed the windows and blew in such a chill that
Sir Claude, with his hands in his pockets and cigarettes in his
teeth, fidgeting, frowning, looking out and turning back,
ended by causing a smoky little fire to be made in the dressy
little chimney. It came in spite of something that could only
be named his air of wishing to put it off; an air that had
served him—oh, as all his airs served him!—to the extent of
his having for a couple of hours confined the conversation to
gratuitous jokes and generalities, kept it on the level of the
little empty coffee-cups and *petits verres* (Mrs. Wix had two of
each!) that struck Maisie, through the fumes of the French
fire and the English tobacco, as a token more than ever that
they were launched. She felt now, in close quarters and as
clearly as if Mrs. Wix had told her, that what this lady had
come over for was not merely to be chaffed and to hear her
pupil chaffed; not even to hear Sir Claude, who knew French
in perfection, imitate the strange sounds emitted by the English folk at the hotel. It was perhaps half an effect of her present renovations, as if her clothes had been somebody's else:
she had at any rate never produced such an impression of
high colour, of a redness really so vivid as to be feverish. Her
heart was not at all in the gossip about Boulogne; and if her
complexion was partly the result of the *déjeuner* and the *petits
verres* it was also the brave signal of what she was there to say.
Maisie knew when this did come how anxiously it had been
awaited by the youngest member of the party. "Her ladyship
packed me off—she almost put me into the cab!" That was
what Mrs. Wix at last brought out.

XXIII

S IR CLAUDE was stationed at the window; he didn't so much as turn round, and it was left to Maisie to take up the remark. "Do you mean you went to see her yesterday?"

"She came to see *me*. She knocked at my shabby door. She mounted my squalid stair. She told me she had seen you at Folkestone."

Maisie wondered. "She went back that evening?"

"No; yesterday morning. She drove to me straight from the station. It was most remarkable. If I had a job to get off she did nothing to make it worse—she did a great deal to make it better." Mrs. Wix hung fire, though the flame in her face burned brighter; then she became capable of saying: "Her ladyship is kind! She did what I didn't expect."

Maisie, on this, looked straight at her stepfather's back; it might well have been for her at that hour a monument of her ladyship's kindness. It remained, as such at all events, monumentally still, and for a time that permitted the child to ask of their companion: "Did she really help you?"

"Most practically." Again Mrs. Wix paused; again she quite resounded. "She gave me a ten-pound note."

At that, still looking out, Sir Claude, at the window, laughed loud. "So you see, Maisie, we've not quite lost it."

"Oh no," Maisie responded. "Isn't that too charming?" She smiled at Mrs. Wix. "We know all about it." Then on her friend's showing such blankness as was compatible with such a flush she pursued: "She does want me to have you?"

Mrs. Wix showed a final hesitation, which, however, while Sir Claude drummed on the window-pane, she presently surmounted. It came to Maisie that in spite of his drumming and of his not turning round he was really so much interested as to leave himself in a manner in her hands; which somehow suddenly seemed to her a greater proof than he could have given by interfering. "She wants me to have *you*!" Mrs. Wix declared.

Maisie answered this bang at Sir Claude. "Then that's nice for all of us."

Of course it was, his continued silence sufficiently admitted, while Mrs. Wix rose from her chair and, as if to take more of a stand, placed herself, not without majesty, before the fire. The incongruity of her smartness, the circumference of her stiff frock presented her as really more ready for Paris than any of them. She also gazed hard at Sir Claude's back. "Your wife was different from anything she had ever shown me. She recognises certain proprieties."

"Which? Do you happen to remember?" Sir Claude asked.

Mrs. Wix's reply was prompt. "The importance for Maisie of a gentlewoman, of some one who is not—well, so bad! She objects to a mere maid, and I don't in the least mind telling you what she wants me to do." One thing was clear—Mrs. Wix was now bold enough for anything. "She wants me to persuade you to get rid of the person from Mrs. Beale's."

Maisie waited for Sir Claude to pronounce on this; then she could only understand that he on his side waited, and she felt particularly full of common sense as she met her responsibility. "Oh, I don't want Susan with *you*!" she said to Mrs. Wix.

Sir Claude, always from the window, approved. "That's quite simple. I'll take her back."

Mrs. Wix gave a positive jump; Maisie caught her look of alarm. "'Take' her? You don't mean to go over on purpose?"

Sir Claude said nothing for a moment; after which, "Why shouldn't I leave you here?" he inquired.

Maisie, at this, sprang up. "Oh do, oh do, oh do!" The next moment she was interlaced with Mrs. Wix, and the two, on the hearth-rug, their eyes in each other's eyes, considered the plan with intensity. Then Maisie perceived the difference of what they saw in it.

"She can surely go back alone: why should you put yourself out?" Mrs. Wix demanded.

"Oh, she's an idiot—she's incapable. If anything should happen to her it would be awkward: it was I who brought her —without her asking. If I turn her away I ought with my own hand to place her exactly where I found her."

Mrs. Wix's face appealed to Maisie on such folly, and her manner, as directed to their companion, had, to her pupil's surprise, an unprecedented sharpness. "Dear Sir Claude, I think you're perverse. Pay her fare and give her a sovereign.

She has had an experience that she never dreamed of and that will be an advantage to her through life. If she goes wrong on the way it will be simply because she wants to, and, with her expenses and her remuneration—make it even what you like! —you will have treated her as handsomely as you always treat every one."

This was a new tone—as new as Mrs. Wix's cap; and it could strike a perceptive person as the upshot of a relation that had taken on a new character. It brought out for Maisie how much more even than she guessed her friends were fighting side by side. At the same time it needed so definite a justification that as Sir Claude now at last did face them she at first supposed it in resentment of excessive familiarity. She was therefore yet more puzzled to see him show the whole of his serene beauty as well as an equal interest in a matter quite distinct from any freedom but her ladyship's. "Did my wife come alone?" He could ask even that good-humouredly.

"When she called on me?" Mrs. Wix *was* red now: his good-humour wouldn't keep down her colour, which for a minute glowed there like her ugly honestly. "No—there was some one in the cab." The only attenuation she could think of was after a minute to add: "But they didn't come up."

Sir Claude broke into a laugh—Maisie herself could guess what it was at: while he now walked about, still laughing, and at the fire-place gave a gay kick to a displaced log, she felt more vague about almost everything than about the drollery of such a "they." She in fact could scarce have told you if it was to deepen or to cover the joke that she bethought herself to observe: "Perhaps it was her maid."

Mrs. Wix gave her a look that at any rate deprecated the wrong tone. "It was not her maid."

"Do you mean there are this time two?" Sir Claude asked as if he had not heard.

"Two maids?" Maisie went on as if she might assume he had.

The reproach of the straighteners darkened; but Sir Claude cut across it with a sudden: "See here; what do you mean? And what do you suppose *she* meant?"

Mrs. Wix let him for a moment, in silence, understand that the answer to his question, if he didn't take care, might give him more than he wanted. It was as if, with this scruple, she measured and adjusted all that she gave him in at last saying: "What she meant was to make me know that you're definitely free. To have that straight from her was a joy I, of course, hadn't hoped for: it made the assurance, and my delight at it, a thing I could really proceed upon. You already know I would have started even if she hadn't pressed me; you already know what, so long, we have been looking for and what, as soon as she told me of her step taken at Folkestone, I recognised with rapture that we *have*. It's your freedom that makes me right"—she fairly bristled with her logic. "But I don't mind telling you that it's her action that makes me happy!"

"Her action?" Sir Claude echoed. "Why, my dear woman, her action is just a hideous crime. It happens to satisfy our sympathies in a way that's quite delicious; but that doesn't in the least alter the fact that it's the most abominable thing ever done. She has chucked our friend here overboard not a bit less than if she had shoved her, shrieking and pleading, out of that window and down two floors to the paving-stones."

Maisie surveyed serenely the parties to the discussion. "Oh, your friend here, dear Sir Claude, doesn't plead and shriek!"

He looked at her a moment. "Never. Never. That's one, only one, but charming so far as it goes, of about a hundred things we love her for." Then he pursued to Mrs. Wix: "What I can't for the life of me make out is what Ida is *really* up to, what game she was playing in turning to you with that cursed cheek after the beastly way she has used you. Where—to explain her at all—does she fancy she can presently, when we least expect it, take it out of us?"

"She doesn't fancy anything, nor want anything out of any one. Her cursed cheek, as you call it, is the best thing I've ever seen in her. I don't care a fig for the beastly way she used me—I forgive it all a thousand times over!" Mrs. Wix raised her voice as she had never raised it; she quite triumphed in her lucidity. "I understand her, I almost admire her!" she proclaimed. She spoke as if this might practically suffice; yet in charity to fainter lights she threw out an explanation. "As I've said, she was different; upon my word I wouldn't have known her. She had a glimmering, she had an instinct; they brought her. It was a kind of happy thought, and if you couldn't have supposed she would ever have had such a thing, why, of course, I quite agree with you. But she did have it! There!"

Maisie could see that, from what it with liveliness lacked, this demonstration gathered a certain something that might almost have exasperated. But as she had often watched Sir Claude in apprehension of displeasures that didn't come, so now, instead of his saying "Oh hell!" as her father used, she observed him only to take refuge in a question that at the worst was abrupt.

"Who *is* it this time, do you know?"

Mrs. Wix tried blind dignity. "Who is what, Sir Claude?"

"The man who stands the cabs. Who was in the one that waited at your door?"

At this challenge she faltered so long that it occurred to Maisie's conscience to give her a hand. "It wasn't the Captain."

Her good intention, however, only changed her old friend's scruple to a more ambiguous stare; besides of course making Sir Claude go off. Mrs. Wix fairly appealed to him. "Must I really tell you?"

His amusement continued. "Did she make you promise not to?"

Mrs. Wix looked at him still harder. "I mean before Maisie."

Sir Claude laughed again. "Why, *she* can't hurt him!"

Maisie felt herself, as it passed, brushed by the light humour of this. "Yes, I can't hurt him."

The straighteners again roofed her over; after which they seemed to crack with the explosion of their wearer's honesty. Amid the flying splinters Mrs. Wix produced a name. "Mr. Tischbein."

There was for an instant a silence that, under Sir Claude's influence and while he and Maisie looked at each other, suddenly pretended to be that of gravity. "We don't know Mr. Tischbein, do we, dear?"

Maisie gave the point all needful thought. "No, not Mr. Tischbein."

It was a passage that worked visibly on their friend. "You must excuse me, Sir Claude," she said, with an austerity of which the note was real, "if I thank God to your face that he has in his mercy—I mean his mercy to our charge—allowed me to achieve this act." She gave out a long puff of pain. "It was time!" Then as if still more to point the moral: "I said just now I understood your wife. I said just now I admired her. I stand to it: I did both of those things when I saw how even *she*, poor thing, saw. If you want the dots on the i's you shall have them. What she came to me for, in spite of everything was that I'm just"—she quavered it out—"well, just clean! What she saw for her daughter was that there must at last be a *decent* person!"

Maisie was quick enough to jump a little at the sound of this implication that such a person was what Sir Claude was not; the next instant, however, she more profoundly guessed against whom the discrimination was made. She was therefore left the more surprised at the complete candour with which he embraced the worst. "If she's bent on decent persons, why has she given her to *me*? You don't call me a decent person, and I'll do Ida the justice that *she* never did. I think I'm as indecent as any one and that there's nothing in my behaviour that makes my wife's surrender a bit less ignoble!"

"Don't speak of your behaviour!" Mrs. Wix cried. "Don't say such horrible things; they're false, and they're wicked, and I forbid you! It's to *keep* you decent that I'm here and that I've done everything I have done. It's to save you—I won't say from yourself, because in yourself you're beautiful and good! It's to save you from the worst person of all. I haven't, after all, come over to be afraid to speak of her! That's the person in whose place her ladyship wants such a person as even me; and if she thought herself, as she as good as told me, not fit for Maisie's company, it's not, as you may well suppose, that she may make room for Mrs. Beale!"

Maisie watched his face as it took this outbreak, and the most she saw in it was that it turned a little white. That indeed made him look, as Susan Ash would have said, queer; and it was, perhaps, a part of the queerness that he intensely smiled. "You're too hard on Mrs. Beale. She has great merits of her own."

Mrs. Wix, at this, instead of immediately replying, did what Sir Claude had been doing before: she moved across to the window and stared awhile into the storm. There was for a minute, to Maisie's sense, a hush that resounded with wind and rain. Sir Claude, in spite of these things, glanced about for his hat; on which Maisie spied it first and, making a dash for it, held it out to him. He took it with a gleam of a "thank-you" in his face, but as he did so something moved her still to hold the other side of the brim, so that, united by their grasp of this object, they stood some seconds looking many things at each other. By this time Mrs. Wix had turned round. "Do you mean to tell me," she demanded, "that you *are* going back?"

"To Mrs. Beale?" Maisie surrendered his hat, and there was something that touched her in the embarrassed, almost humiliated way their companion's challenge made him turn it round and round. She had seen people do that who, she was sure, did nothing else that Sir Claude did. "I can't just say, my dear thing. We'll see about it—we'll talk of it to-morrow. Meantime I must get some air."

Mrs. Wix, with her back to the window, threw up her head to a height that, still for a moment, had the effect of detaining him. "All the air in France, Sir Claude, won't, I think, give you the courage to deny that you're simply afraid of her!"

Oh, this time he did look queer; Maisie had no need of Susan's vocabulary to note it! It would have come to her of itself as, with his hand on the door, he turned his eyes from his stepdaughter to her governess and then back again. Resting on Maisie's, though for ever so short a time, there was something they gave up to her and tried to explain. His lips, however, explained nothing; they only surrendered to Mrs. Wix. "Yes. I'm simply afraid of her!" He opened the door and passed out.

It brought back to Maisie his confession of fear of her mother; it made her stepmother then the second lady about whom he failed of the particular virtue that was supposed most to mark a gentleman. In fact there were three of them, if she counted in Mrs. Wix, before whom he had undeniably quailed. Well, his want of valour was but a deeper appeal to her tenderness. To thrill with response to it she had only to remember all the ladies she herself had, as they called it, funked.

XXIV

IT CONTINUED to rain so hard that our young lady's private
dream of explaining the Continent to their visitor had to
contain a provision for some adequate treatment of the
weather. At the *table d'hôte* that evening she threw out a variety of lights: this was the second ceremony of the sort she had
sat through, and she would have neglected her privilege and
dishonoured her vocabulary—which indeed consisted mainly
of the names of dishes—if she had not been proportionately
ready to dazzle with interpretations. Preoccupied and overawed, Mrs. Wix was apparently dim: she accepted her pupil's
version of the mysteries of the *menu* in a manner that might
have struck the child as the depression of a credulity conscious not so much of its needs as of its dimensions. Maisie
was soon enough—though it scarce happened before bedtime
—confronted again with the different sort of programme for
which she reserved her criticism. They remounted together to
their sitting-room while Sir Claude, who said he would join
them later, remained below to smoke and to converse with
the old acquaintances that he met wherever he turned. He
had proposed his companions, for coffee, the enjoyment of
the *salon de lecture*, but Mrs. Wix had replied promptly and
with something of an air that it struck her their own apartments offered them every convenience. They offered the
good lady herself, Maisie could immediately observe, not only
that of this rather grand reference, which, already emulous, so
far as it went, of her pupil, she made as if she had spent her
life in *salons*; but that of a stiff French sofa where she could sit
and stare at the faint French lamp, in default of the French
clock that had stopped, as if for some account of the time Sir
Claude would so markedly interpose. Her demeanour accused
him so directly of hovering beyond her reach that Maisie
sought to divert her by a report of Susan's quaint attitude toward what they had talked of after lunch. Maisie had mentioned to the young woman for sympathy's sake the plan for
her relief, but her disapproval of alien ways appeared, strange
to say, only to prompt her to hug her gloom; so that between

Mrs. Wix's effect of displacing her and the visible stiffening of her back the child had the sense of a double office, an enlarged play for pacific powers.

These powers played to no great purpose, it was true, in keeping before Mrs. Wix the vision of Sir Claude's perversity, which hung there in the pauses of talk and which he himself, after unmistakable delays, finally made quite lurid by bursting in—it was near ten o'clock—with an object held up in his hand. She knew, before he spoke, what it was; she knew at least from the underlying sense of all that, since the hour spent after the Exhibition with her father, had not sprung up to reinstate Mr. Farange—she knew it meant a triumph for Mrs. Beale. The mere present sight of Sir Claude's face caused her on the spot to drop straight through her last impression of Mr. Farange a plummet that reached still deeper down than the security of these days of flight. She had wrapped that impression in silence—a silence that had parted with half its veil to cover also, from the hour of Sir Claude's advent, the image of Mr. Farange's wife. But as the object in Sir Claude's hand revealed itself as a letter which he held up very high, so there was something in his mere motion that laid Mrs. Beale again bare. "Here we are!" he cried almost from the door, shaking his trophy at them and looking from one to the other. Then he came straight to Mrs. Wix; he had pulled two papers out of the envelope and glanced at them again to see which was which. He thrust one out open to Mrs. Wix. "Read that." She looked at him hard, as if in fear: it was impossible not to see that he was excited. Then she took the letter, but it was not her face that Maisie watched while she read. Neither, for that matter, was it this countenance that Sir Claude scanned: he stood before the fire and, more calmly, now that he had acted, communed in silence with his stepdaughter.

This silence was in truth quickly broken; Mrs. Wix rose to her feet with the violence of the sound she emitted. The letter had dropped from her and lay upon the floor; it had made her turn ghastly white and she was speechless with the effect of it. "It's too abominable—it's too unspeakable!" she then cried.

"Isn't it a charming thing?" Sir Claude asked. "It has just arrived, enclosed in a word of her own. She sends it on to me with the remark that comment is superfluous. I really think it is. That's all you can say."

"She oughtn't to pass such a horror about," said Mrs. Wix. "She ought to put it straight in the fire."

"My dear woman, she's not such a fool! It's much too precious." He had picked the letter up and he gave it again a glance of complacency which produced a light in his face. "Such a document"—he considered, then concluded with a slight drop—"such a document is, in fine, a basis!"

"A basis for what?"

"Well——for proceedings."

"Hers?" Mrs. Wix's voice had become outright the voice of derision. "How can *she* proceed?"

Sir Claude turned it over. "How can she get rid of him? Well—she *is* rid of him."

"Not legally." Mrs. Wix had never looked to her pupil so much as if she knew what she was talking about.

"I daresay," Sir Claude laughed; "but she's not a bit less deprived than I am!"

"Of the power to get a divorce? It's just your want of the power that makes the scandal of your connection with her. Therefore it's just her want of it that makes that of hers with you. That's all I contend!" Mrs. Wix concluded with an unparalleled neigh of battle. Oh, she did know what she was talking about!

Maisie had meanwhile appealed mutely to Sir Claude, who judged it easier to meet what she didn't say than to meet what Mrs. Wix did.

"It's a letter to Mrs. Beale from your father, my dear, written from Spa and making the rupture between them perfectly irrevocable. It lets her know, and not in pretty language, that, as we technically say, he deserts her. It puts an end for ever to their relations." He ran his eyes over it again, then appeared to make up his mind. "In fact it concerns you, Maisie, so nearly and refers to you so particularly that I really think you ought to see the terms in which this new situation is created for you." And he held out the letter.

Mrs. Wix, at this, pounced upon it; she had grabbed it too soon even for Maisie to become aware of being rather afraid of it. Thrusting it instantly behind her she positively glared at

Sir Claude. "See it, wretched man?—the innocent child *see* such a thing? I think you must be mad, and she shall not have a glimpse of it while I'm here to prevent!"

The breadth of her action had made Sir Claude turn red— he even looked a little foolish. "You think it's too bad, eh? But it's precisely because it's bad that it seemed to me it would have a lesson and a virtue for her."

Maisie could do a quick enough justice to his motive to be able clearly to interpose. She fairly smiled at him. "I assure you I can quite believe how bad it is!" She hesitated an instant; then she added: "I know what's in it!"

He of course burst out laughing, and while Mrs. Wix groaned an "Oh heavens!" he replied: "You wouldn't say that, old boy, if you did! The point I make is," he continued to Mrs. Wix with a blandness now re-established—"the point I make is simply that it sets Mrs. Beale free."

She hung fire but an instant. "Free to live with *you?*"

"Free not to live, not to pretend to live, with her husband."

"Ah, they're mighty different things!"—a truth as to which her earnestness could now with a fine, inconsequent look invite the participation of the child.

Before Maisie could commit herself, however, the ground was occupied by Sir Claude, who, as he stood before their visitor with an expression half rueful, half persuasive, rubbed his hand sharply up and down the back of his head. "Then why the deuce do you grant so—do you, I may even say, rejoice so —that by the desertion of my own precious partner I'm free?"

Mrs. Wix met this challenge first with silence, then with a demonstration the most extraordinary, the most unexpected. Maisie could scarcely believe her eyes as she saw the good lady, with whom she had never associated the faintest form of coquetry, actually, after an upward grimace, give Sir Claude a great giggling, insinuating, naughty slap. "You wretch—you *know* why!" And she turned away. The face that with this movement she left him to present to Maisie was to abide with his stepdaughter as the very image of stupefaction; but the pair lacked time to communicate either amusement or alarm before their interlocutress was upon them again. She had begun in fact to show infinite variety and she flashed about with a still quicker change of tone. "Have you brought me that thing as a pretext for going over?"

Sir Claude braced himself. "I can't, after such news, in common decency not. I mean, don't you know, in common courtesy and humanity. My dear lady, you can't chuck a woman that way, especially taking the moment when she has been most insulted and wronged. A fellow must behave like a gentleman, damn it, dear good Mrs. Wix. We didn't come away, we two, to hang right on, you know: it was only to try our paces and just put in a few days that might prove to every one concerned that we're in earnest. It's exactly because we're in earnest that, hang it, we needn't be so awfully particular. I mean, don't you know, we needn't be so awfully afraid." He showed a vivacity, an intensity of argument, and if Maisie counted his words she was all the more ready to swallow after a single swift gasp those that, the next thing, she became conscious he paused for a reply to. "We didn't come, old girl, did we," he pleaded straight, "to stop right away for ever and put it all in *now*?"

Maisie had never doubted she could be heroic for him. "Oh no!" It was as if she had been shocked at the bare thought. "We're just taking it as we find it." She had a sudden inspiration, which she backed up with a smile. "We're just seeing what we can afford." She had never yet in her life made any claim for herself, but she hoped that this time, frankly, what she was doing would somehow be counted to her. Indeed she felt Sir Claude *was* counting it, though she was afraid to look at him—afraid she should show him tears. She looked at Mrs. Wix; she reached her maximum. "I don't think I should be bad to Mrs. Beale."

She heard, on this, a deep sound, something inarticulate and sweet, from Sir Claude; but tears were what Mrs. Wix didn't scruple to show. "Do you think you should be bad to *me*?" The question was the more disconcerting that Mrs. Wix's emotion didn't deprive her of the advantage of her effect. "If you see that woman again you're lost!" she declared to their companion.

Sir Claude looked at the moony globe of the lamp; he seemed to see for an instant what seeing Mrs. Beale would consist of. It was also apparently from this vision that he drew strength to return: "Her situation, by what has happened, is completely changed; and it's no use your trying to prove to me that I needn't take any account of that."

"If you see that woman you're lost!" Mrs. Wix with greater force repeated.

"Do you think she'll not let me come back to you? My dear lady, I leave you here, you and Maisie, as a hostage to fortune, and I promise you by all that's sacred that I shall be with you again at the very latest on Saturday. I provide you with funds; I install you in these lovely rooms; I arrange with the people here that you be treated with every attention and supplied with every luxury. The weather, after this, will mend; it will be sure to be exquisite. You'll both be as free as air and you can roam all over the place and have tremendous larks. You shall have a carriage to drive you; the whole house shall be at your call. You'll have in a word a magnificent position." He paused, he looked from one of his companions to the other as if to see the impression he had made. Whether or no he judged it adequate he subjoined after a moment: "And you'll oblige me above all by not making a fuss."

Maisie could only answer for the impression on herself, though indeed from the heart even of Mrs. Wix's rigour there floated to her sense a faint fragrance of depraved concession. Maisie had her dumb word for the show such a speech could make, for the exquisite charm it could take from his exquisite sincerity; and before she could do anything but blink at excess of light she heard this very word sound on Mrs. Wix's lips, just as if the poor lady had guessed it and wished, snatching it from her, to blight it like a crumpled flower. "You're dreadful, you're terrible, for you know but too well that it's not a small thing to me that you should address me in a fashion that's princely!" Princely was what he stood there and looked and sounded; that was what Maisie for the occasion found herself reduced to simple worship of him for being. Yet strange to say too, as Mrs. Wix went on, an echo rang within her that matched the echo she had herself just produced. "How much you must *want* to see her to say such things as that and to be ready to do so much for the poor little likes of Maisie and me! She has a hold of you, and you know it, and you want to feel it again and—God knows, or at least *I* do,

what's your motive and desire—enjoy it once more and give
yourself up to it! It doesn't matter if it's one day or three:
enough is as good as a feast and the lovely time you'll have
with her is something you're willing to pay for! I daresay
you'd like me to believe that your pay is to get her to give you
up; but that's a matter on which I adjure you not to put
down your money in advance. Give *her* up first. Then pay her
what you please!"

Sir Claude took this to the end, though there were things in
it that made him colour, called into his face more of the apprehension than Maisie had ever perceived there of a particular sort of shock. She had an odd sense that it was the first
time she had seen any one but Mrs. Wix really and truly scandalised, and this fed her inference, which grew and grew from
moment to moment, that Mrs. Wix was proving more of a
force to reckon with than either of them had allowed so much
room for. It was true that, long before, she had obtained a
"hold" of him, as she called it, different in kind from that obtained by Mrs. Beale and originally by her ladyship. But Maisie
could quite feel with him now that he had really not expected
this advantage to be driven so home. Oh, they hadn't at all
got to where Mrs. Wix would stop, for the next minute she
was driving harder than ever. It was the result of his saying
with a certain dryness, though so kindly that what most affected Maisie in it was his patience: "My dear friend, it's simply a matter in which I must judge for myself. You've judged
for me, I know, a good deal, of late, in a way that I appreciate,
I assure you, down to the ground. But you can't do it always;
no one can do that for another, don't you see, in every case.
There are exceptions, particular cases that turn up and that are
awfully delicate. It would be too easy if I could shift it all off
on you: it would be allowing you to incur an amount of responsibility that I should simply become quite ashamed of.
You'll find, I'm sure, that you'll have quite as much as you'll
enjoy if you'll be so good as to accept the situation as circumstances happen to make it for you and to stay here with our
friend, till I rejoin you, on the footing of as much pleasantness
and as much comfort—and I think I have a right to add, to
both of you, of as much faith in *me*—as possible."

Oh, he was princely indeed: that came out more and more

with every word he said and with the particular way he said it, and Maisie could feel his monitress stiffen almost with anguish against the increase of his spell and then hurl herself as a desperate defence from it into the quite confessed poorness of violence, of iteration. "You're afraid of her—afraid, afraid, afraid! Oh dear, oh dear, oh dear!" Mrs. Wix wailed it with a high quaver, then broke down into a long shudder of helplessness and woe. The next minute she had flung herself again on the lean sofa and had burst into a passion of tears.

Sir Claude stood and looked at her a moment; he shook his head slowly, altogether tenderly. "I've already admitted it—I'm in mortal terror; so we'll let that settle the question. I think you had best go to bed," he added; "you've had a tremendous day and you must both be tired to death. I shall not expect you to concern yourselves in the morning with my movements. There's an early boat on; I shall have cleared out before you're up; and I shall moreover have dealt directly and most effectively, I assure you, with the haughty, but not quite hopeless Miss Ash." He turned to his stepdaughter as if at once to take leave of her and give her a sign of how, through all tension and friction, they were still united in such a way that she at least needn't worry. "Maisie, boy!"—he opened his arms to her. With her culpable lightness she flew into them and, while he kissed her, chose the soft method of silence to promise him the silence that after battles of talk was the best balm she could offer his wounds. They held each other long enough to reaffirm intensely their vows; after which they were almost forced apart by Mrs. Wix's jumping to her feet.

Her jump, either with a quick return or with a final lapse of courage, was also to supplication almost abject. "I beseech you not to take a step so miserable and so fatal. I know her but too well, even if you jeer at me for saying it; little as I've seen her I know her, I know her. I know what she'll do—I see it as I stand here. Since you are afraid of her it's the mercy of heaven. Don't, for God's sake, be afraid to show it, to profit by it and to arrive at the very safety that it gives you. *I'm* not afraid of her, I assure you; you must already have seen for yourself that there's nothing I'm afraid of now. Let me go to her—*I'll* settle her and I'll take that woman back without a hair of her touched. Let me put in the two or three days—let me wind up the connection. You stay here with Maisie, with the carriage and the larks and the luxury; then I'll return to you and we'll go off together—we'll live together without a cloud. Take me, take me," she went on and on—the tide of her eloquence was high. "Here I am; I know what I am and what I ain't; but I say boldly to the face of you both that I'll do better for you, far, than ever she will even try to. I say it to yours, Sir Claude, even though I owe you the very dress on my back and the very shoes on my feet. I owe you everything —that's just the reason; and to pay it back, in profusion, what can that be but what I want? Here I am, here I am!"—she spread herself into an exhibition that, combined with her intensity and her decorations, appeared to suggest her for strange offices and devotions, for ridiculous replacements and substitutions. She manipulated her gown as she talked, she insisted on the items of her debt. "I have nothing of my own, I know—no money, no clothes, no appearance, no anything, nothing but my hold of this little one truth, which is all in the world I can bribe you with: that the pair of you are more to me than all besides, and that if you'll let me help you and save you, make what you both want possible in the one way it *can* be, why, I'll work myself to the bone in your service!"

Sir Claude wavered there without an answer to this magnificent appeal; he plainly cast about for one, and in no small agitation and pain. He addressed himself in his quest, however, only to vague quarters until he met once more, as he so frequently and actively met it, the more than filial gaze of his intelligent little charge. That gave him—poor plastic and dependent male—his issue. If she was still a child she was yet of the sex that could help him out. He signified as much by a renewed invitation to an embrace. She freshly sprang to him and again they inaudibly conversed. "Be nice to her, be nice to her," he at last distinctly articulated; "be nice to her as you've not even been to *me*!" On which, without another look at Mrs. Wix, he somehow got out of the room, leaving Maisie under the slight oppression of these words as well as of the idea that he had unmistakably once more dodged.

XXV

EVERY SINGLE thing he had prophesied came so true that it was after all no more than fair to expect quite as much for what he had as good as promised. His pledges they could verify to the letter, down to his very guarantee that a way would be found with Miss Ash. Roused in the summer dawn and vehemently squeezed by that interesting exile, Maisie fell back upon her couch with a renewed appreciation of his policy, a memento of which, when she rose later on to dress, glittered at her from the carpet in the shape of a sixpence that had overflowed from Susan's pride of possession. Sixpences really for the forty-eight hours that followed seemed to abound in her life; she fancifully computed the number of them represented by such a period of "larks." The number was not kept down, she presently noticed, by any scheme of revenge for Sir Claude's flight which should take on Mrs. Wix's part the form of a refusal to avail herself of the facilities he had so bravely ordered. It was in fact impossible to escape them; it was in the good lady's own phrase ridiculous to go on foot when you had a carriage prancing at the door. Everything about them pranced: the very waiters even as they presented the dishes to which, from a similar sense of the absurdity of perversity, Mrs. Wix helped herself with a freedom that spoke to Maisie quite as much of her depletion as of her logic. Her appetite was a sign to her companion of a great many things and testified no less on the whole to her general than to her particular condition. She had arrears of dinner to make up, and it was touching that in a dinnerless state her moral passion should have burned so clear. She partook largely as a refuge from depression, and yet the opportunity to partake was just a mark of the sinister symptoms that depressed her. The affair was in short a combat in which the baser element triumphed between her refusal to be bought off and her consent to be clothed and fed. It was not at any rate to be gainsaid that there was comfort for her in the developments of France; comfort so great as to leave Maisie free to take with her all the security for granted and brush all the

581

danger aside. That was the way to carry out in detail Sir
Claude's injunction to be "nice"; that was the way, as well, to
look, with her, in a survey of the pleasures of life abroad,
straight over the head of any doubt.

They shrank at last, all doubts, as the weather cleared up: it
had an immense effect on them and became quite as lovely as
Sir Claude had engaged. This seemed to have put him so into
the secret of things and the joy of the world so waylaid the
steps of his friends that little by little the spirit of hope filled
the air and finally took possession of the scene. To drive on
the long cliff was splendid, but it was perhaps better still to
creep in the shade—for the sun was strong—along the many-
coloured and many-odoured *port* and through the streets in
which, to English eyes, everything that was the same was a
mystery and everything that was different a joke. Best of all
was to continue the creep up the long Grand' Rue to the gate
of the *haute ville* and, passing beneath it, mount to the quaint
and crooked rampart, with its rows of trees, its quiet corners
and friendly benches where brown old women in such white
frilled caps and such long gold earrings sat and knitted or
snoozed; its little yellow-faced houses that looked like the
homes of misers or of priests and its dark château where small
soldiers lounged on the bridge that stretched across an empty
moat and military washing hung from the windows of towers.
This was a part of the place that could lead Maisie to inquire
if it didn't just meet one's idea of the middle ages; and since
it was rather a satisfaction than a shock to perceive, and not
for the first time, the limits in Mrs. Wix's mind of the historic
imagination, that only added one more to the variety of kinds
of insight that she felt it her own present mission to show.
They sat together on the old grey bastion; they looked down
on the little new town which seemed to them quite as old,
and across at the great dome and the high gilt Virgin of the
church that, as they gathered, was famous and that pleased
them by its unlikeness to any place in which they had wor-
shipped. They wandered in this temple afterwards and Mrs.
Wix confessed that for herself she had probably early in life
made, in not being a Catholic, a fatal mistake. Her confession
in its turn caused Maisie to wonder rather interestedly what
degree of maturity it was that shut the door against an escape

from such an error. They went back to the rampart on the second morning; the spot on which they appeared to have come furthest in the journey that was to separate them from everything that in the past had been objectionable: it gave them afresh the impression that had most to do with their having worked round to a confidence that on Maisie's part was determined and that she could see to be on her companion's desperate. She had had for many hours the sense of showing Mrs. Wix so much that she was comparatively slow to become conscious of being at the same time the subject of a similar process. The process went the faster, however, from the moment she got her glimpse of it; it then fell into its place in her general, her habitual view of the particular phenomenon that, had she felt the need of words for it, she might have called her personal relation to her knowledge. This relation had never been so lively as during the time she waited with her old governess for Sir Claude; and what made it so was exactly that Mrs. Wix struck her as having a new suspicion of it. Mrs. Wix had never yet had a suspicion—that was certain—so calculated to throw her pupil, in spite of the closer union of such adventurous hours, upon the deep defensive. Her pupil made out indeed as many marvels as she had made out on the rush to Folkestone; and if in Sir Claude's company on that occasion Mrs. Wix was the constant implication, so in Mrs. Wix's in the actual crisis Sir Claude was—and most of all through long pauses—the perpetual, the insurmountable theme. It all took them back to the first flush of his marriage and to the place he held in the schoolroom in those months of love and pain: only he had himself blown to a much bigger balloon the large consciousness he then filled out.

They went through it all again, and indeed while the interval lingered with the very weight of its charm they went, in spite of defences and suspicions, through everything. Their intensified clutch of the future throbbed like a clock ticking seconds; but this was a timepiece that inevitably, as well, at the best, rang occasionally a portentous hour. Oh, there were several of these, and two or three of the worst on the old city-wall where everything else so made for peace. There was nothing in the world Maisie more wanted than to be to Mrs. Wix as nice as Sir Claude had desired; but it was exactly because this fell in with her inveterate instinct of keeping the peace that the instinct itself was quickened. From the moment it was quickened, however, it found other work, and that was how, to begin with, she produced the very complication she most sought to avert. What she had essentially done, these days, had been to read the unspoken into the spoken; so that thus, with accumulations, it had become more definite to her that the unspoken was, unspeakably, the completeness of the sacrifice of Mrs. Beale. There were times when every minute that Sir Claude stayed away was like a nail in Mrs. Beale's coffin. That brought back to Maisie—it was a roundabout way—the beauty and antiquity of her connection with the flower of the Overmores as well as that lady's own grace and charm, her peculiar prettiness and cleverness and even her peculiar tribulations. A hundred things hummed at the back of her head, but two of these were simple enough. Mrs. Beale was by the way, after all, just her stepmother and her relative. She was just— and partly for that very reason—Sir Claude's greatest intimate ("lady-intimate" was Maisie's term), so that what together they were on Mrs. Wix's programme to give up and break short off with was for one of them his particular favourite and for the other her father's wife. Strangely, indescribably her perception of reasons kept pace with her sense of trouble; but there was something in her that, without a supreme effort not to be shabby, could not take the reasons for granted. What it comes to perhaps for ourselves is that, disinherited and denuded as we have seen her, there still lingered in her life an echo of parental influence—she was still reminiscent of one of the sacred lessons of home. It was the only one she retained, but luckily she retained it with force. She enjoyed in a word an ineffaceable view of the fact that there were things papa called mamma and mamma called papa a low sneak for doing or for not doing. Now this rich memory gave her a name that she dreaded to invite to the lips of Mrs. Beale: she would personally wince so just to hear it. The very sweetness of the foreign life she was steeped in added with each hour of Sir Claude's absence to the possibility of such pangs. She watched beside Mrs. Wix the great golden Madonna, and one of the earringed old women who had been sitting at the end of their bench got up and pottered away.

"Adieu, mesdames!" said the old woman in a little cracked, civil voice—a demonstration by which our friends were so affected that they bobbed up and almost curtesied to her. They subsided again, and it was shortly after, in a summer hum of French insects and a phase of almost somnolent reverie, that Maisie most had the vision of what it was to shut out from such a perspective so appealing a participant. It had not yet appeared so vast as at that moment, this prospect of statues shining in the blue and of courtesy in romantic forms.

"Why, after all, should we have to choose between you? Why shouldn't we be four?" she finally demanded.

Mrs. Wix gave the jerk of a sleeper awakened or the start even of one who hears a bullet whiz at the flag of truce. Her stupefaction at such a breach of the peace delayed for a moment her answer. "Four improprieties, do you mean? Because two of us happen to be decent people! Do I gather you to wish that I should stay on with you even if that woman *is* capable——?"

Maisie took her up before she could further phrase Mrs. Beale's capability. "Stay on as *my* companion—yes. Stay on as just what you were at mamma's. Mrs. Beale *would* let you!" the child proclaimed.

Mrs. Wix had by this time fairly sprung to her arms. "And who, I'd like to know, would let Mrs. Beale? Do you mean, little unfortunate, that *you* would?"

"Why not, if now she's free?"

"Free? Are you imitating *him*? Well, if Sir Claude's old enough to know better, upon my word I think it's right to treat you as if you also were. You'll have to, at any rate, to know better, if that's the line you're proposing to take." Mrs. Wix had never been so harsh; but on the other hand Maisie could guess that she herself had never appeared so wanton. What was underlying, however, rather overawed than angered her; she felt she could still insist, not for contradiction, but for ultimate calm. Her wantonness meanwhile continued to work upon her friend, who caught again, on the rebound, the sound of deepest provocation. "Free, free, free? If she's as free as *you* are, my dear, she's free enough, to be sure!"

"As I am?" Maisie, after reflection and in the face of what, of portentous, this seemed to convey, risked a critical echo.

"Well," said Mrs. Wix, "nobody, you know, is free to commit a crime."

"A crime!" The word had come out in a way that made the child echo it again.

"You'd commit as great a one as their own—and so should I—if we were to condone their immorality by our presence."

Maisie waited a little; this seemed so fiercely conclusive. "Why is it immorality?" she nevertheless presently inquired.

Her companion now turned upon her with a reproach softer because it was somehow deeper. "You're too unspeakable! Do you know what we're talking about?"

In the interest of ultimate calm Maisie felt that she must be above all clear. "Certainly; about their taking advantage of their freedom."

"Well, to do what?"

"Why, to live with us."

Mrs. Wix's laugh, at this, was literally wild. "'Us'? Thank you!"

"Then to live with *me*."

The words made her friend jump. "You give me up? You break with me for ever? You turn me into the street?"

Maisie was dazzled by the enumeration, but she bore bravely up. "Those, it seems to me, are the things you do to *me*."

Mrs. Wix made little for her valour. "I can promise you that, whatever I do, I shall never let you out of my sight! You ask me why it's immorality when you've seen with your own eyes that Sir Claude has felt it to be so to that dire extent that, rather than make you face the shame of it, he has for months kept away from you altogether? Is it any more difficult to see that the first time he tries to do his duty he washes his hands of *her*—takes you straight away from her?"

Maisie turned this over, but more for apparent consideration than from any impulse to yield too easily. "Yes, I see what you mean. But at that time they weren't free." She felt Mrs. Wix rear up again at the offensive word, but she succeeded in touching her with a remonstrant hand. "I don't think you know how free they've become."

"I know, I believe, at least as much as you do!"

Maisie hesitated. "About the Countess?"

"Your father's—temptress?" Mrs. Wix gave her a sidelong squint. "Perfectly. She pays him!"

"Oh, *does* she?" At this the child's countenance fell: it seemed to give a reason for papa's behaviour and place it in a more favourable light. She wished to be just. "I don't say she's not generous. She was so to me."

"How, to you?"

"She gave me a lot of money."

Mrs. Wix stared. "And, pray, what did you do with a lot of money?"

"I gave it to Mrs. Beale."

"And what did Mrs. Beale do with it?"

"She sent it back."

"To the Countess? Gammon!" said Mrs. Wix. She disposed of that plea as effectually as Susan Ash.

"Well, I don't care!" Maisie replied. "What I mean is that you don't know about the rest."

"The rest? What rest?"

Maisie wondered how she could best put it. "Papa kept me there an hour."

"I do know—Sir Claude told me. Mrs. Beale had told him."

Maisie looked incredulity. "How could she—when I didn't speak of it?"

Mrs. Wix was mystified. "Speak of what?"

"Why, of her being so frightful."

"The Countess? Of course she's frightful," Mrs. Wix declared. After a moment she added: "That's why she pays him."

Maisie pondered. "It's the best thing about her then—if she gives him as much as she gave *me*."

"Well, it's not the best thing about *him*! Or rather perhaps it is too!" Mrs. Wix subjoined.

"But she's awful—really and truly," Maisie went on.

Mrs. Wix arrested her. "You needn't go into details!" It was visibly at variance with this injunction that she yet inquired: "How does that make it any better?"

"Their living with me? Why, for the Countess—and for her whiskers!—he has put me off on them. I understood him," Maisie profoundly said.

"I hope then he understood you. It's more than I do!" Mrs. Wix admitted.

That was a real challenge to be plainer, and our young lady immediately became so. "I mean it isn't a crime."

"Why then did Sir Claude steal you away?"

"He didn't steal—he only borrowed me. I knew it wasn't for long," Maisie audaciously professed.

"You must allow me to reply to that," cried Mrs. Wix, "that you knew nothing of the sort, and that you rather basely failed to back me up last night when you pretended so plump that you did! You hoped, in fact, exactly as much as I did and as in my senseless passion I even hope now, that this may be the beginning of better things."

Oh yes, Mrs. Wix was indeed, for the first time, sharp; so that there at last stirred in our heroine the sense not so much of being proved disingenuous as of being precisely accused of the meanness that had brought everything down on her through her very desire to shake herself clear of it. She suddenly felt herself swell with a passion of protest. "I never, *never* hoped I wasn't going again to see Mrs. Beale! I didn't, I didn't, I didn't!" she repeated. Mrs. Wix bounced about with a force of rejoinder of which she also felt that she must anticipate the concussion and which, though the good lady was evidently charged to the brim, hung fire long enough to give time for an aggravation. "She's beautiful and I love her! I love her and she's beautiful!"

"And I'm hideous and you hate *me*?" Mrs. Wix fixed her a moment, then caught herself up. "I won't embitter you by absolutely accusing you of that; though, as for my being hideous, it's hardly the first time I've been told so! I know it so well that even if I haven't whiskers—have I?—I daresay there are other ways in which the Countess is a Venus to me! My pretensions must therefore seem to you monstrous— which comes to the same thing as your not liking me. But do you mean to go so far as to tell me that you *want* to live with them in their sin?"

"You know what I want, you know what I want!"—Maisie spoke with the shudder of rising tears.

"Yes, I do; you want me to be as bad as yourself! Well, I won't. There! Mrs. Beale's as bad as your father!" Mrs. Wix went on.

"She's not!—she's not!" her pupil almost shrieked in retort.

"You mean because Sir Claude at least has beauty and wit and grace? But he pays just as the Countess pays!" Mrs. Wix, who now rose as she spoke, fairly revealed a latent cynicism.

It raised Maisie also to her feet; her companion had walked off a few steps and paused. The two looked at each other as they had never looked, and Mrs. Wix seemed to flaunt there in her finery. "Then doesn't he pay *you* too?" her unhappy charge demanded.

At this she bounded in her place. "Oh, you incredible little waif!" She brought it out with a wail of violence; after which, with another convulsion, she marched straight away.

Maisie dropped back on the bench and burst into sobs.

XXVI

OTHING so dreadful of course could be final or even for
many minutes prolonged: they rushed together again
too soon for either to feel that either had kept it up, and
though they went home in silence it was with a vivid perception for Maisie that her companion's hand had closed upon
her. That hand had shown altogether, these twenty-four
hours, a new capacity for closing, and one of the truths the
child could least resist was that a certain greatness had now
come to Mrs. Wix. The case was indeed that the quality of her
motive surpassed the sharpness of her angles; both the combination and the singularity of which things, when in the
afternoon they used the carriage, Maisie could borrow from
the contemplative hush of their grandeur the freedom to feel
to the utmost. She still bore the mark of the tone in which her
friend had thrown out that threat of never losing sight of her.
This friend had been converted in short from feebleness to
force; and it was the light of her present power that showed
from how far she had come. The threat in question, sharply
exultant, might have produced defiance; but before anything
so ugly could happen another process had insidiously forestalled it. The moment at which this process had begun to
mature was that of Mrs. Wix's breaking out with a dignity attuned to their own apartments and with an advantage now
measurably gained. They had ordered coffee after luncheon,
in the spirit of Sir Claude's provision, and it was served to
them while they awaited their equipage in the white and gold
saloon. It was flanked moreover with a couple of liqueurs, and
Maisie felt that Sir Claude could scarce have been taken more
at his word had it been followed by anecdotes and cigarettes.
The influence of these luxuries was at any rate in the air. It
seemed to her while she tiptoed at the chimney-glass, pulling
on her gloves and with a motion of her head shaking a feather
into place, to have had something to do with Mrs. Wix's suddenly saying: "Haven't you really and truly *any* moral sense?"

Maisie was aware that her answer, though it brought her
down to her heels, was vague even to imbecility and that this

was the first time she had appeared to practise with Mrs. Wix
an intellectual inaptitude to meet her—the infirmity to which
she had owed so much success with papa and mamma. The
appearance did her injustice, for it was not less through her
candour than through her playfellow's pressure that after this
the idea of a moral sense mainly coloured their intercourse.
She began, the poor child, with scarcely knowing what it was;
but it proved something that, with scarce an outward sign
save her surrender to the swing of the carriage, she could, before they came back from their drive, strike up a sort of acquaintance with. The beauty of the day only deepened, and
the splendour of the afternoon sea, and the haze of the far
headlands, and the taste of the sweet air. It was the coachman
indeed who, smiling and cracking his whip, turning in his
place, pointing to invisible objects and uttering unintelligible
sounds—all, our tourists recognised, strict features of a social
order principally devoted to language: it was this polite person, I say, who made their excursion fall so much short that
their return left them still a stretch of the long daylight and
an hour that, at his obliging suggestion, they spent on foot
on the shining sands. Maisie had seen the *plage* the day before
with Sir Claude, but that was a reason the more for showing
on the spot to Mrs. Wix that it was, as she said, another of the
places on her list and of the things of which she knew the
French name. The bathers, so late, were absent and the tide
was low; the sea-pools twinkled in the sunset and there were
dry places as well, where they could sit again and admire and
expatiate: a circumstance that, while they listened to the lap of
the waves, gave Mrs. Wix a fresh fulcrum for her challenge.
"Have you absolutely none at all?"

She had no need now, as to the question itself at least, to
be specific; that on the other hand was the eventual result of
their quiet conjoined apprehension of the thing that—well,
yes, since they must face it—Maisie absolutely and appallingly
had so little of. This marked more particularly the moment of
the child's perceiving that her friend had risen to a level which
might—till superseded at all events—pass almost for sublime.
Nothing more remarkable had taken place in the first heat of
her own departure, no phenomenon of perception more in-
scrutable by our rough method, than her vision, the rest of

that Boulogne day, of the manner in which she figured. I so despair of tracing her steps that I must crudely give you my word for its being from this time on a picture literally present to her. Mrs. Wix saw her as a little person knowing so extraordinarily much that, for the account to be taken of it, what she still didn't know would be ridiculous if it hadn't been embarrassing. Mrs. Wix was in truth more than ever qualified to meet embarrassment; I am not sure that Maisie had not even a dim discernment of the queer law of her own life that made her educate to that sort of proficiency those elders with whom she was concerned. She promoted, as it were, their development; nothing could have been more marked for instance than her success in promoting Mrs. Beale's. She judged that if her whole history, for Mrs. Wix, had been the successive stages of her knowledge, so the very climax of the concatenation would, in the same view, be the stage at which the knowledge should overflow. As she was condemned to know more and more, how could it logically stop before she should know Most? It came to her in fact as they sat there on the sands that she was distinctly on the road to know Everything. She had not had governesses for nothing: what in the world had she ever done but learn and learn and learn? She looked at the pink sky with a placid foreboding that she soon should have learnt All. They lingered in the flushed air till at last it turned to grey and she seemed fairly to receive new information from every brush of the breeze. By the time they moved homeward it was as if for Mrs. Wix this inevitability had become a long, tense cord, twitched by a nervous hand, on which the counted pearls of intelligence were to be neatly strung.

In the evening upstairs they had another strange sensation, as to which Maisie could not afterwards have told you whether it was bang in the middle or quite at the beginning that her companion sounded with fresh emphasis the note of the moral sense. What mattered was merely that she did exclaim, and again, as at first appeared, most disconnectedly: "God help me, it does seem to peep out!" Oh, the queer confusions that had wooed it at last to such peeping! None so queer, however, as the words of woe, and it might verily be said of rage, in which the poor lady bewailed the tragic end of her own rich ignorance. There was a point at which she seized the child and hugged her as close as in the old days of partings and returns; at which she was visibly at a loss how to make up to such a victim for such contaminations; appealing, as to what she had done and was doing, in bewilderment, in explanation, in supplication, for reassurance, for pardon and even outright for pity.

"I don't know what I've said to you, my own: I don't know what I'm saying or what the turn you've given my life has rendered me, heaven forgive me, capable of saying. Have I lost all delicacy, all decency, all measure of how far and how bad? It seems to me mostly that I have, though I'm the last of whom you would ever have thought it. I've just done it for *you*, precious—not to lose you, which would have been worst of all: so that I've had to pay with my own innocence, if you do laugh! for clinging to you and keeping you. Don't let me pay for nothing; don't let me have been thrust for nothing into such horrors and such shames. I never knew anything about them and I never wanted to know! Now I know too much, too much!" the poor woman lamented and groaned. "I know so much that with hearing such talk I ask myself where I am; and with uttering it too, which is worse, say to myself that I'm far, too far, from where I started! I ask myself what I should have thought with my lost one if I had heard myself cross the line. There are lines I've crossed with *you* that I should have fancied I had come to a pretty pass!" She gasped at the mere supposition. "I've gone from one thing to another, and all for the real love of you; and now what would any one say—I mean any one but *them*—if they were to hear the way I go on? I've had to keep up with you, haven't I?—and therefore what could I do less than look to you to keep up with *me*? But it's not *them* that are the worst—by which I mean to say it's not *him*: it's your dreadfully base papa and the one person in the world whom he could have found, I do believe—and she's not the Countess, duck—wickeder than himself. While they were about it at any rate, since they *were* ruining you, they might have done it so as to spare an honest woman. Then I shouldn't have had to do whatever it is that's the worst: throw up at you the badness you haven't taken in, or find my advantage in the vileness you *have*! What I did lose patience at this morning was at how it was without your seeming to condemn—for you didn't, you remember!—you yet did seem to *know*. Thank God in his mercy, at last, *if* you do!"

The night, this time, was warm and one of the windows stood open to the small balcony over the rail of which, on coming up from dinner, Maisie had hung a long time in the enjoyment of the chatter, the lights, the life of the quay made brilliant by the season and the hour. Mrs. Wix's requirements had drawn her in from this posture and Mrs. Wix's embrace had detained her even though midway in the outpouring her confusion and sympathy had permitted, or rather had positively helped, her to disengage herself. But the casement was still wide, the spectacle, the pleasure were still there, and from her place in the room, which, with its polished floor and its panels of elegance, was lighted from without more than from within, the child could still take account of them. She appeared to watch and listen; after which she answered Mrs. Wix with a question: "If I do know——?"

"If you do condemn." The correction was made with some austerity.

It had the effect of causing Maisie to heave a vague sigh of oppression and then after an instant and as if under cover of this ambiguity pass out again upon the balcony. She hung again over the rail; she felt the summer night; she dropped down into the manners of France. There was a *café* below the hotel, before which, with little chairs and tables, people sat on a space enclosed by plants in tubs; and the impression was enriched by the flash of the white aprons of waiters and the music of a man and a woman who, from beyond the precinct, sent up the strum of a guitar and the drawl of a song about "amour." Maisie knew what "amour" meant too, and wondered if Mrs. Wix did: Mrs. Wix remained within, as still as a mouse and perhaps not reached by the performance. After a while, but not till the musicians had ceased and begun to circulate with a little plate, her pupil came back to her. "*Is* it a crime?" Maisie then asked.

Mrs. Wix was as prompt as if she had been crouching in a lair. "Branded by the Bible."

"Well, he won't commit a crime."

Mrs. Wix looked at her gloomily. "He's committing one now."

"Now?"

"In being with her."

Maisie had it on her tongue's end to return once more: "But now he's free." She remembered, however, in time that one of the things she had known for the last entire hour was that this made no difference. After that and as if to turn the right way she was on the point of a blind dash, a weak reversion to the reminder that it might make a difference, might diminish the crime for Mrs. Beale; till such a reflection was in its order also quashed by the visibility in Mrs. Wix's face of the collapse produced by her inference from her pupil's manner that after all her pains her pupil didn't even yet adequately understand. Never so much as when confronted had Maisie wanted to understand, and all her thought for a minute centred in the effort to come out with something which should be a disproof of her simplicity. "Just trust me, dear; that's all!"—she came out finally with that; and it was perhaps a good sign of her action that with a long, impartial moan Mrs. Wix floated her to bed.

There was no letter the next morning from Sir Claude—which Mrs. Wix let out that she deemed the worst of omens; yet it was just for the quieter communion they so got with him that, when after the coffee and rolls which made them more foreign than ever, it came to going forth for fresh drafts upon his credit they wandered again up the hill to the rampart instead of plunging into distraction with the crowd on the sands or into the sea with the semi-nude bathers. They gazed once more at their gilded Virgin; they sank once more upon their battered bench; they felt once more their distance from the Regent's Park. At last Mrs. Wix became definite about their friend's silence. "He *is* afraid of her! She has forbidden him to write." The fact of his fear Maisie already knew; but her companion's mention of it had at this moment two unexpected results. The first was her wondering in dumb remonstrance how Mrs. Wix, with a devotion not after all inferior to her own, could put into such an allusion such a grimness of derision; the second was that she found herself suddenly drop into a deeper view of it. She too had been afraid, as we have seen, of the people of whom Sir Claude was afraid, and by that law she had had her due measure of latest apprehension of Mrs. Beale. What occurred at present, however, was that, whereas this sympathy appeared vain as for him, the ground of it loomed dimly as a reason for selfish alarm. That uneasiness had not carried her far before Mrs. Wix spoke again and with an abruptness so great as almost to seem irrelevant. "Has it never occurred to you to be jealous of her?"

It never had in the least; yet the words were scarce in the air before Maisie had jumped at them. She held them well, she looked at them hard; at last she brought out with an assurance which there was no one, alas, but herself to admire: "Well, yes—since you ask me." She hesitated, then continued: "Lots of times!"

Mrs. Wix glared askance an instant; such approval as her look expressed was not wholly unqualified. It expressed at any rate something that presumably had to do with her saying once more: "Yes. He's afraid of her."

Maisie heard, and it had afresh its effect on her even through the blur of the attention now required by the possibility of that idea of jealousy—a possibility created only by her feeling that she had thus found the way to show she was not simple. It stuck out of Mrs. Wix that this lady still believed her moral sense to be interested and feigned; so what could be such a gage of her sincerity as a peep of the most restless of the passions? Such a revelation would baffle discouragement, and discouragement was in fact so baffled that, helped in some degree by the mere intensity of their need to hope, which also, according to its nature, sprang from the dark portent of the absent letter, the real pitch of their morning was reached by the note, not of mutual scrutiny, but of unprecedented frankness. There were broodings indeed and silences, and Maisie sank deeper into the vision that for her friend she was, at the most, superficial, and that also, positively, she was the more so the more she tried to appear complete. Was the sum of all knowledge only to know how little in this presence one would ever reach it? The answer to that question luckily lost itself in the brightness suffusing the scene as soon as Maisie had thrown out in regard to Mrs. Beale such a remark as she had never dreamed she should live to make. "If I thought she was unkind to him—I don't know *what* I should do!"

Mrs. Wix dropped one of her squints; she even confirmed it by a wild grunt. "I know what *I* should!"

Maisie at this felt that she lagged. "Well, I can think of *one* thing."

Mrs. Wix more directly challenged her. "What is it then?"

Maisie met her expression as if it were a game with forfeits for winking. "I'd *kill* her!" That at least, she hoped as she looked away, would guarantee her moral sense. She looked away, but her companion said nothing for so long that she at last turned her head again. Then she saw the straighteners all blurred with tears which after a little seemed to have sprung from her own eyes. There were tears in fact on both sides of the spectacles, and they were even so thick that it was presently all Maisie could do to make out through them that slowly, finally Mrs. Wix put forth a hand. It was the material pressure that settled that and even at the end of some minutes more things besides. It settled in its own way one thing in particular, which, though often, between them, heaven knew, hovered round and hung over, was yet to be established without the shadow of an attenuating smile. Oh, there was no gleam of levity, as little of humour as of deprecation in the long time they now sat together or in the way in which at some unmeasured point of it Mrs. Wix became distinct enough for her own dignity and yet not loud enough for the snoozing old women.

"I adore him. I adore him."

Maisie took it well in; so well that in a moment more she would have answered profoundly: "So do I." But before that moment passed something took place that brought other words to her lips; nothing more, very possibly, than the closer consciousness in her hand of the significance of Mrs. Wix's. Their hands remained linked in unutterable sign of their union, and what Maisie at last said was simply and serenely: "Oh, I know!"

Their hands were so linked and their union was so confirmed that it took the far, deep note of a bell, borne to them on the summer air, to call them back to a sense of hours and proprieties. They had touched bottom and melted together, but they gave a start at last: the bell was the voice of the inn and the inn was the image of luncheon. They should be late for it; they got up, and their quickened step on the return had something of the swing of confidence. When they reached the hotel the *table d'hôte* had begun; this was clear from the threshold, clear from the absence in the hall and on the stairs of the "personnel," as Mrs. Wix said—she had picked *that* up —all collected in the dining-room. They mounted to their apartments for a brush before the glass, and it was Maisie who, in passing and from a vain impulse, threw open the white and gold door. She was thus first to utter the sound that brought Mrs. Wix almost on top of her, as by the other accident it would have brought her on top of Mrs. Wix. It had at any rate the effect of leaving them bunched together in a strained stare at their new situation. This situation had put on in a flash the bright form of Mrs. Beale: she stood there in her hat and her jacket, amid bags and shawls, smiling and holding out her arms. If she had just arrived it was a different figure from either of the two that for *their* benefit, wan and tottering and none too soon to save life, the Channel had recently disgorged. She was as lovely as the day that had brought her over, as fresh as the luck and the health that attended her: it came to Maisie on the spot that she was more beautiful than she had ever been. All this was too quick to count, but there was still time in it to give the child the sense of what had kindled the light. That leaped out of the open arms, the open eyes, the open mouth; it leaped out with Mrs. Beale's loud cry at her: "I'm free, I'm free!"

XXVII

THE GREATEST wonder of all was the way Mrs. Beale addressed her announcement, so far as could be judged, equally to Mrs. Wix, who, as if from sudden failure of strength, sank into a chair while Maisie surrendered to the visitor's embrace. As soon as the child was liberated she met with profundity Mrs. Wix's stupefaction and actually was able to see that while in a manner sustaining the encounter her face yet seemed with intensity to say: "Now, for God's sake, don't crow 'I told you so!'" Maisie was somehow on the spot aware of an absence of disposition to crow; it had taken her but an extra minute to arrive at such a quick survey of the objects surrounding Mrs. Beale as showed that among them was no appurtenance of Sir Claude's. She knew his dressing-bag now—oh, with the fondest knowledge!—and there was an instant during which its not being there was a stroke of the worst news. She was yet to learn what it could be to recognise in some perception of a gap the sign of extinction, and therefore remained unaware that this momentary pang was a foretaste of the experience of death. It passed in a flash of course with Mrs. Beale's brightness and with her own instant appeal. "You've come alone?"

"Without Sir Claude?" Strangely, Mrs. Beale looked even brighter. "Yes; in the eagerness to get *at* you. You abominable little villain!"—and her stepmother, laughing clear, administered to her cheek a pat that was partly a pinch. "What were you up to and what did you take me for? But I'm glad to be abroad, and after all it's you who have shown me the way. I mightn't without you have been able to come; that is so soon. Well, here I am at any rate and in a moment more I should have begun to worry about you. This will do very well"—she was good-natured about the place and even presently added that it was charming. Then with a rosier glow she made again her great point: "I'm free, I'm free!" Maisie made on her side her own: she carried back her gaze to Mrs. Wix, whom amazement continued to hold; she drew afresh her old friend's attention to the superior way she didn't take that up.

What she did take up, the next minute, was the question of Sir Claude. "Where is he? Won't he come?"

Mrs. Beale's consideration of this oscillated with a smile between the two expectancies with which she was flanked: it was conspicuous, it was extraordinary, her unblinking acceptance of Mrs. Wix, a miracle of which Maisie had even now begun to read a reflection in that lady's long visage. "He'll come, but we must *make* him!" she gaily brought forth.

"Make him?" Maisie echoed.

"We must give him time. We must play our cards."

"But he promised us awfully," Maisie replied.

"My dear child, he has promised *me* awfully; I mean lots of things, and not in every case kept his promise to the letter." Mrs. Beale's good-humour insisted on taking for granted Mrs. Wix's, to whom her attention had suddenly grown prodigious. "I daresay he has done the same with you and not always come to time. But he makes it up in his own way; and it isn't as if we didn't know exactly what he is. There's one thing he is," she went on, "which makes everything else only a question, for us, of tact." They scarce had time to wonder what this was before it was, as they might have said, right there. "He's as free as I am!"

"Yes, I know," said Maisie; as if, however, independently weighing the value of that. She really weighed also the oddity of her stepmother's treating it as news to *her*, who had been the first person literally to whom Sir Claude had mentioned it. For a few seconds, as if with the sound of it in her ears, she stood with him again, in memory and in the twilight, in the hotel garden at Folkestone.

Anything Mrs. Beale overlooked was, she indeed divined, but the effect of an exaltation of high spirits, a tendency to soar that showed even when she dropped—still quite impartially—almost to the confidential. "Well, then—we've only to wait. He can't do without us long. I'm sure, Mrs. Wix, he can't do without *you*! He's devoted to you; he has told me so much about you. The extent I count on you, you know, count on you to help me!"—was an extent that even all her radiance couldn't express. What it couldn't express quite as much as what it could made at any rate every instant her presence and even her famous freedom loom larger; and it was this mighty mass that once more led her companions, bewildered and scattered, to exchange with each other as through a thickening veil confused and ineffectual signs. They clung together at least on the common ground of unpreparedness, and Maisie watched without relief the havoc of wonder in Mrs. Wix. It had reduced her to perfect impotence, and, but that gloom was black upon her, she sat as if fascinated by Mrs. Beale's high style. It had plunged her into a long deep hush; for what had happened was the thing she had least allowed for and before which the particular rigour she had worked up could only grow limp and sick. Sir Claude was to have reappeared with his accomplice or without her; never, never his accomplice without *him*. Mrs. Beale had gained apparently by this time an advantage she could pursue: she looked at the droll, dumb figure with jesting reproach. "You really won't shake hands with me? Never mind; you'll come round!" She put the matter to no test, going on immediately and, instead of offering her hand, raising it, with a pretty gesture that her bent head met, to a long black pin that played a part in her back hair. "Are hats worn at luncheon? If you're as hungry as I am we must go right down."

Mrs. Wix stuck fast, but she met the question in a voice her pupil scarce recognised. "I wear mine."

Mrs. Beale, swallowing at one glance her brand-new bravery, which she appeared at once to refer to its origin and to follow in its flights, accepted this as conclusive. "Oh, but I've not such a beauty!" Then she turned rejoicingly to Maisie. "I've got a beauty for *you*, my dear."

"A beauty?"

"A love of a hat—in my luggage. I remembered *that*"—she nodded at the object on her stepdaughter's head—"and I've brought you one with a peacock's breast. It's the most gorgeous blue!"

It was too strange, this talking with her there already not about Sir Claude, but about peacocks—too strange for the child to have the presence of mind to thank her. But the felicity in which she had arrived was so proof against everything that Maisie felt more and more the depth of the purpose that must underlie it. She had a vague sense of its being abysmal, the spirit with which Mrs. Beale carried off the awkwardness, in the white and gold *salon*, of such a want of breath and of welcome. Mrs. Wix was more breathless than ever; the embarrassment of Mrs. Beale's isolation was as nothing to the embarrassment of her grace. The perception of this dilemma was the germ on the child's part of a new question altogether. What if *with* this indulgence——? But the idea lost itself in something too frightened for hope and too conjectured for fear; and while everything went by leaps and bounds one of the waiters stood at the door to remind them that the *table d'hôte* was half over.

"Had you come up to wash hands?" Mrs. Beale hereupon asked them. "Go and do it quickly and I'll be with you: they've put my boxes in that nice room—it was Sir Claude's. Trust him," she laughed, "to have a nice one!" The door of a neighbouring room stood open, and now from the threshold, addressing herself again to Mrs. Wix, she launched a note that gave the very key of what, as she would have said, she was up to. "Dear lady, please attend to my daughter."

She was up to a change of deportment so complete that it represented—oh, for offices still honourably subordinate if not too explicitly menial—an absolute coercion, an interested clutch of the old woman's respectability. There was response, to Maisie's view, I may say at once, in the jump of that respectability to its feet: it was itself capable of one of the leaps, one of the bounds just mentioned, and it carried its charge, with this momentum and while Mrs. Beale popped into Sir Claude's chamber, straight away to where, at the end of the passage, pupil and governess were quartered. The greatest stride of all, for that matter, was that within a few seconds the pupil had, in another relation, been converted into a daughter. Maisie's eyes were still following it when, after the rush, with the door almost slammed and no thought of soap and towels, the pair stood face to face. Mrs. Wix, in this position, was the first to gasp a sound. "Can it ever be that *she* has one?"

Maisie felt still more bewildered. "One what?"

"Why, moral sense."

They spoke as if you might have two, but Mrs. Wix looked as if it were not altogether a happy thought, and Maisie didn't see how even an affirmative from her own lips would clear up what had become most of a mystery. It was to this she sprang pretty straight. "*Is* she my mother now?"

It was a point as to which an horrific glimpse of the responsibility of an opinion appeared to affect Mrs. Wix like a blow in the stomach. She had evidently never thought of it; but she could think and rebound. "If she is, he's equally your father."

Maisie, however, thought further. "Then my father and my mother——!"

But she had already faltered and Mrs. Wix had already glared back: "Ought to live together? Don't begin it again!" She turned away with a groan, to reach the washing-stand, and Maisie could by this time recognise with a certain ease that that way verily madness did lie. Mrs. Wix gave a great untidy splash, but the next instant had faced round. "She has taken a new line."

"She was nice to you," Maisie concurred.

"What *she* thinks so—'go and dress the young lady!' But it's something!" she panted. Then she thought out the rest. "If he won't have her, why she'll have *you*. She'll be the one."

"The one to keep me abroad?"

"The one to give you a home." Mrs. Wix saw further; she mastered all the portents. "Oh, she's cruelly clever! It's not a moral sense." She reached her climax: "It's a game!"

"A game?"

"Not to lose him. She has sacrificed him—to her duty."

"Then won't he come?" Maisie pleaded.

Mrs. Wix made no answer; her vision absorbed her. "He has fought. But she has won."

"Then won't he come?" the child repeated.

Mrs. Wix hesitated. "Yes, hang him!" She had never been so profane.

For all Maisie minded! "Soon—to-morrow?"

"Too soon—whenever. Indecently soon."

"But then we *shall* be together!" the child went on. It made Mrs. Wix look at her as if in exasperation; but nothing had time to come before she precipitated: "Together with *you*!" The air of criticism continued, but took voice only in her companion's bidding her wash herself and come down.

The silence of quick ablutions fell upon them, presently broken, however, by one of Maisie's sudden reversions. "Mercy, isn't she handsome?"

Mrs. Wix had finished; she waited. "She'll attract attention." They were rapid, and it would have been noticed that the shock the beauty had given them acted, incongruously, as a positive spur to their preparations for rejoining her. She had none the less when they returned to the sitting-room already descended; the open door of her room showed it empty and the chambermaid explained. Here again they were delayed by another sharp thought of Mrs. Wix's. "But what will she live on meanwhile?"

Maisie stopped short. "Till Sir Claude comes?"

It was nothing to the violence with which her friend had been arrested. "Who'll pay the bills?"

Maisie thought. "Can't *she?*"

"She? She hasn't a penny."

The child wondered. "But didn't papa——?"

"Leave her a fortune?" Mrs. Wix would have appeared to speak of papa as dead had she not immediately added: "Why, he lives on other women!"

Oh yes, Maisie remembered. "Then can't he send——?" She faltered again; even to herself it sounded queer.

"Some of their money to his wife?" Mrs. Wix gave a laugh still stranger than the weird suggestion. "I daresay she'd take it!"

They hurried on again; yet again, on the stairs, Maisie pulled up. "Well, if she had stopped in England——!" she threw out.

Mrs. Wix considered. "And he had come over instead?"

"Yes, as we expected." Maisie launched her speculation. "What then would she have lived on?"

Mrs. Wix hung fire but an instant. "On other men!" And she marched downstairs.

XXVIII

M RS. BEALE at table between the pair, plainly attracted the
attention Mrs. Wix had foretold. No other lady present was nearly so handsome, nor did the beauty of any other
accommodate itself with such art to the homage it produced.
She talked mainly to her other neighbour, and that left Maisie
leisure both to note the manner in which eyes were riveted
and nudges interchanged, and to lose herself in the meanings
that, dimly as yet and disconnectedly, but with a vividness that
fed apprehension, she could begin to read into her stepmother's independent move. Mrs. Wix had helped her by
talking of a game; it was a connection in which the move
could put on a strategic air. Her notions of diplomacy were
thin, but it was a kind of cold diplomatic shoulder and an elbow of more than usual point that, temporarily at least, were
presented to her by the averted inclination of Mrs. Beale's
head. There was a phrase familiar to Maisie, so often was it
used by this lady to express the idea of one's getting what one
wanted: one got it—Mrs. Beale always said *she* at all events
always got it or proposed to get it—by "making love." She
was at present making love, singular as it appeared, to Mrs.
Wix, and her young friend's mind had never moved in such
freedom as on thus finding itself face to face with the question
of what she wanted to get. This period of the *omelette aux
rognons* and the *poulet sauté*, while her sole surviving parent,
her fourth, fairly chattered to her governess, left Maisie rather
wondering if her governess would hold out. It was strange,
but she became on the spot quite as interested in Mrs. Wix's
moral sense as Mrs. Wix could possibly be in hers: it had risen
before her so pressingly that this was something new for Mrs.
Wix to resist. Resisting Mrs. Beale herself promised at such a
rate to become a very different business from resisting Sir
Claude's view of her. More might come of what had happened—whatever it was—than Maisie felt she could have
expected. She put it together with a suspicion that, had she
ever in her life had a sovereign changed, would have resembled an impression, baffled by the want of arithmetic, that her

change was wrong: she groped about in it that she had perhaps become the victim of a violent substitution. A victim was
what she should surely be if the issue between her step-
parents had been settled by Mrs. Beale's saying: "Well, if she
can live with but one of us alone, with which in the world
should it be but me?" That answer was far from what, for
days, she had nursed herself in, and the desolation of it was
deepened by the absence of anything from Sir Claude to show
he had not had to take it as triumphant. Had not Mrs. Beale,
upstairs, as good as given out that she had quitted him with
the snap of a tension, left him, dropped him in London, after
some struggle as a sequel to which her own advent represented that she had practically sacrificed him? Maisie assisted
in fancy at the probable episode in the Regent's Park, finding
elements almost of terror in the suggestion that Sir Claude
had not had fair play. They drew something, as she sat there,
even from the pride of an association with such beauty as Mrs.
Beale's; and the child quite forgot that, though the sacrifice of
Mrs. Beale herself was a solution she had not invented, she
would probably have seen Sir Claude embark upon it without
a direct remonstrance.

What her stepmother had clearly now promised herself to
wring from Mrs. Wix was an assent to the great modification,
the change, as smart as a juggler's trick, in the interest of
which nothing so much mattered as the new convenience of
Mrs. Beale. Maisie could positively seize the moral that her elbow seemed to point in ribs thinly defended—the moral of its
not mattering a straw which of the step-parents was the
guardian. The essence of the question was that a girl wasn't a
boy: if Maisie had been a mere trousered thing Sir Claude
would have been welcome. As the case stood he had simply
tumbled out, and Mrs. Wix would henceforth find herself in
the employ of the right person. These arguments had really
fallen, for our young lady, into their place at the very touch of
that tone in which she had heard her new title declared. She
was still, as result of so many parents, a daughter to somebody
even after papa and mamma were to all intents dead. If her father's wife and her mother's husband, by the operation of a
natural or, for all she knew, a legal rule, were in the shoes of
their defunct partners, then Mrs. Beale's was exactly as de-

funct as Sir Claude's and her shoes the very pair to which, in
"Farange *v.* Farange and Others," the divorce court had given
priority. The subject of that celebrated settlement saw the rest
of her day really filled out with the pomp of all that Mrs.
Beale assumed. The assumption rounded itself there between
this lady's entertainers, flourished in a way that left them, in
their bottomless element, scarce a free pair of eyes to exchange signals. It struck Maisie even a little that there was a
rope or two Mrs. Wix might have thrown out if she would, or
a rocket or two she might have sent up. They had at any rate
never been so long together without communion or telegra-
phy, and their companion kept them apart by simply keeping
them with her. From this situation they saw the grandeur of
their intenser relation to her pass and pass like an endless procession. It was a day of lively movement and of talk on Mrs.
Beale's part so brilliant and overflowing as to represent music
and banners. She took them out with her promptly to walk
and to drive, and even—towards night—sketched a plan for
carrying them to the Établissement, where, for only a franc
apiece, they should listen to a concert of celebrities. It reminded Maisie, the plan, of the sideshows at Earl's Court,
and the franc sounded brighter than the shillings which had
at that time failed; yet this too, like the other, was a frustrated
hope: the francs failed like the shillings and the sideshows had
set an example to the concert. The Établissement in short
melted away, and it was little wonder that a lady whom from
the moment of her arrival had been so gallantly in the breach
should confess herself at last done up. Maisie could appreciate
her fatigue; the day had not passed without such an observer's discovering that she was excited and even mentally
comparing her state to that of the breakers after a gale. It had
blown hard in London, and she would take time to subside.
It was of the condition known to the child by report as that
of talking against time that her decision, her spirit, her humour, which had never dropped, now gave the impression.

She too was delighted with foreign manners; but her
daughter's opportunities of explaining them to her were unexpectedly forestalled by her tone of large acquaintance with
them. One of the things that nipped in the bud all response to
her volubility was Maisie's surprised retreat before the fact

that Continental life was what she had been almost brought up on. It was Mrs. Beale, disconcertingly, who began to explain it to her friends; it was she who, wherever they turned, was the interpreter, the historian and the guide. She was full of reference to her early travels—at the age of eighteen: she had at that period made, with a distinguished Dutch family, a stay on the Lake of Geneva. Maisie had in the old days been regaled with anecdotes of these adventures, but they had with time become phantasmal, and the heroine's quite showy exemption from bewilderment at Boulogne, her acuteness on some of the very subjects on which Maisie had been acute to Mrs. Wix, were a high note of the majesty, of the variety of advantage, with which she had alighted. It was all a part of the wind in her sails and of the weight with which her daughter was now to feel her hand. The effect of it on Maisie was to add already the burden of time to her separation from Sir Claude. This might, to her sense, have lasted for days; it was as if, with their main agitation transferred thus to France and with neither mamma now nor Mrs. Beale nor Mrs. Wix nor herself at his side, he must be fearfully alone in England. Hour after hour she felt as if she were waiting; yet she couldn't have said exactly for what. There were moments when Mrs. Beale's flow of talk was a mere rattle to smother a knock. At no part of the crisis had the rattle so public a purpose as when, instead of letting Maisie go with Mrs. Wix to prepare for dinner, she pushed her—with a push at last incontestably maternal— straight into the room inherited from Sir Claude. She titivated her little charge with her own brisk hands; then she brought out: "I'm going to divorce your father."

This was so different from anything Maisie had expected that it took some time to reach her mind. She was aware meanwhile that she probably looked rather wan. "To marry Sir Claude?"

Mrs. Beale rewarded her with a kiss. "It's sweet to hear you put it so."

This was a tribute, but it left Maisie balancing for an objection. "How *can* you when he's married?"

"He isn't—practically. He's free, you know."

"Free to marry?"

"Free, first, to divorce his own fiend."

The benefit that these last days she had felt she owed a certain person left Maisie a moment so ill-prepared for recognising this lurid label that she hesitated long enough to risk: "Mamma?"

"She isn't your mamma any longer," Mrs. Beale replied. "Sir Claude has paid her money to cease to be." Then as if remembering how little, to the child, a pecuniary transaction must represent: "She lets him off supporting her if he'll let her off supporting you."

Mrs. Beale appeared, however, to have done injustice to her daughter's financial grasp. "And support me himself?" Maisie asked.

"Take the whole bother and burden of you and never let her hear of you again. It's a regular signed contract."

"Why, that's lovely of her!" Maisie cried.

"It's not so lovely, my dear, but that he'll get his divorce."

Maisie was briefly silent; after which, "No—he won't get it," she said. Then she added still more boldly: "And you won't get yours."

Mrs. Beale, who was at the dressing-glass, turned round with amusement and surprise. "How do you know that?"

"Oh, I know!" cried Maisie.

"From Mrs. Wix?"

Maisie debated, then, after an instant, was determined by Mrs. Beale's absence of anger, which struck her the more as she had felt she must take her courage in her hands. "From Mrs. Wix," she admitted.

Mrs. Beale, at the glass again, made play with a powder-puff. "My own sweet, she's mistaken!" was all she said.

There was a certain force in the very amenity of this, but our young lady reflected long enough to remember that it was not the answer Sir Claude himself had made. The recollection nevertheless failed to prevent her saying: "Do you mean then that he won't come till he has got it?"

Mrs. Beale gave a last touch; she was ready; she stood there in all her elegance. "I mean, my dear, that it's because he hasn't got it that I left him."

This opened out a view that stretched further than Maisie could reach. She turned away from it, but she spoke before they went out again. "Do you like Mrs. Wix now?"

"Why, my chick, I was just going to ask you if you think she has come at all to like poor bad me!"

Maisie thought, at this hint; but unsuccessfully. "I haven't the least idea. But I'll find out."

"Do!" said Mrs. Beale, rustling out with her in a scented air and as if it would be a very particular favour.

The child tried promptly at bed-time, relieved now of the fear that their visitor would wish to separate her for the night from her attendant. "Have you held out?" she began as soon as the two doors at the end of the passage were again closed on them.

Mrs. Wix looked hard at the flame of the candle. "Held out——?"

"Why, she has been making love to you. Has she won you over?"

Mrs. Wix transferred her intensity to her pupil's face. "Over to what?"

"To *her* keeping me instead."

"Instead of Sir Claude?" Mrs. Wix was distinctly gaining time.

"Yes; who else? since it's not instead of you."

Mrs. Wix coloured at this lucidity. "Yes, that *is* what she means."

"Well, do you like it?" Maisie asked.

She actually had to wait, for, oh, her friend was embarrassed! "My opposition to the connection—theirs—would then naturally to some extent fall. She has treated me to-day with peculiar consideration; not that I don't know very well where she got the pattern of it! But of course," Mrs. Wix hastened to add, "I shouldn't like her as *the* one nearly so well as him."

"'Nearly so well!'" Maisie echoed: "I should hope indeed not." She spoke with a firmness under which she was herself the first to quiver. "I thought you 'adored' him."

"I do," Mrs Wix sturdily allowed.

"Then have you suddenly begun to adore her too?"

Mrs. Wix, instead of directly answering, only blinked in support of her sturdiness. "My dear, in what a tone you ask that! You're coming out."

"Why shouldn't I? You've come out. Mrs. Beale has come

out. We each have our turn!" And Maisie threw off the most extraordinary little laugh that had ever passed her young lips.

There passed Mrs. Wix's indeed the next moment a sound that more than matched it. "You're most remarkable!" she neighed.

Her pupil faltered a few seconds. "I think you've done a great deal to make me so."

"Very true, I have." She dropped to humility, as if she recalled her so recent self-arraignment.

"Would you accept her then? That's what I ask," said Maisie.

"As a substitute?" Mrs. Wix turned it over; she met again the child's eyes. "She has literally almost fawned upon me."

"She hasn't fawned upon *him*. She hasn't even been kind to him."

Mrs. Wix looked as if she had now an advantage. "Then do you propose to 'kill' her?"

"You don't answer my question," Maisie persisted. "I want to know if you accept her."

Mrs. Wix continued to dodge. "I want to know if *you* do!"

Everything in the child's person, at this, announced that it was easy to know. "Not for a moment."

"Not the two now?" Mrs. Wix had caught on; she flushed with it. "Only him alone?"

"Him alone or nobody."

"Not even *me*?" cried Mrs. Wix.

Maisie looked at her a moment, then began to undress. "Oh, you're nobody!"

XXIX

H ER SLEEP was drawn out; she instantly recognised lateness in the way her eyes opened to Mrs. Wix, erect,
completely dressed, more dressed than ever, and gazing at her
from the centre of the room. The next thing she was sitting
straight up, wide awake with the fear of the hours of "abroad"
that she might have lost. Mrs. Wix looked as if the day had already made itself felt, and the process of catching up with it
began for Maisie with hearing her distinctly say: "My poor
dear, he has come!"

"Sir Claude?" Maisie, clearing the little bed-rug with the
width of her spring, felt the polished floor under her bare
feet.

"He crossed in the night; he got in early." Mrs. Wix's head
jerked stiffly backward. "He's there."

"And you've seen him?"

"No. He's there—he's there," Mrs. Wix repeated. Her
voice came out with a queer extinction that was not a volun-
tary drop, and she trembled so that it added to their common
emotion. Visibly pale, they gazed at each other.

"Isn't it too *beautiful?*" Maisie panted back at her; an appeal to which, however, she was not ready with a response.
The term Maisie had used was a flash of diplomacy—to prevent at any rate Mrs. Wix's using another. To that degree it
was successful; there was only an appeal, strange and mute, in
the white old face, which produced the effect of a want of decision greater than could by any stretch of optimism have
been associated with her attitude toward what had happened.
For Maisie herself indeed what had happened was oddly, as
she could feel, less of a simple rapture than any arrival or return of the same supreme friend had ever been before. What
had become overnight, what had become while she slept, of
the comfortable faculty of gladness? She tried to wake it up a
little wider by talking, by rejoicing, by plunging into water
and into clothes, and she made out that it was ten o'clock,
but also that Mrs. Wix had not yet breakfasted. The day before, at nine, they had had together a *café complet* in their sit-

ting-room. Mrs. Wix on her side had evidently also a refuge to seek. She sought it in checking the precipitation of some of her pupil's present steps, in recalling to her with an approach to sternness that of such preliminaries ablutions should be the through, and in throwing even a certain reprobation on the idea of hurrying into clothes for the sake of a mere stepfather. She took her in fact with a sort of silent insistence in hand; she reduced the process to sequences more definite than any it had known since the days of Moddle. Whatever it might be that was now, with a difference, attached to Sir Claude's presence was still after all compatible, for our young lady, with the instinct of dressing to see him with almost untidy haste. Mrs. Wix meanwhile luckily was not wholly directed to repression. "He's there—he's there!" she had said over several times. It was her answer to every invitation to mention how long she had been up and her motive for respecting so rigidly the slumber of her companion. It formed for some minutes her only account of the whereabouts of the others and her reason for not having yet seen them, as well as of the possibility of their presently being found in the *salon*.

"He's there—he's there!" she declared once more as she made, on the child, with an almost invidious tug, a strained undergarment "meet."

"Do you mean he's in the *salon*?" Maisie asked again.

"He's *with* her," Mrs. Wix desolately said. "He's with her," she reiterated.

"Do you mean in her room?" Maisie continued.

She waited an instant. "God knows!"

Maisie wondered a little why, or how, God should know; this, however, delayed but an instant her bringing out: "Well, won't she go back?"

"Go back? Never!"

"She'll stay all the same?"

"All the more."

"Then won't Sir Claude go?" Maisie asked.

"Go back—if *she* doesn't?" Mrs. Wix appeared to give this question the benefit of a minute's thought. "Why should he have come—only to go back?"

Maisie produced an ingenious solution. "To *make* her go. To take her."

Mrs. Wix met it without a concession. "If he can make her go so easily, why should he have let her come?"

Maisie considered. "Oh, just to see *me*. She has a right."

"Yes—she has a right."

"She's my mother!" Maisie tentatively tittered.

"Yes—she's your mother."

"Besides," Maisie went on, "he didn't let her come. He doesn't like her coming, and if he doesn't like it——"

Mrs. Wix took her up. "He must lump it—that's what he must do! Your mother was right about him—I mean your real one. He has no strength. No—none at all." She seemed more profoundly to muse. "He might have had some even with *her* —I mean with her ladyship. He's just a poor, sunk slave," she asserted with sudden energy.

Maisie wondered again. "A slave?"

"To his passions."

She continued to wonder and even to be impressed; after which she went on: "But how do you know he'll stay?"

"Because he likes us!"—and Mrs. Wix, with her emphasis of the word, whirled her charge round again to deal with posterior hooks. She had positively never shaken her so.

It was as if she quite shook something out of her. "But how will that help him if we—in spite of his liking!—don't stay?"

"Do you mean if we go off and leave him with her?"—Mrs. Wix put the question to the back of her pupil's head. "It *won't* help him. It will be his ruin. He'll have got nothing. He'll have lost everything. It will be his utter destruction, for he's certain after a while to loathe her."

"Then when he loathes her"—it was astonishing how she caught the idea—"he'll just come right after us!" Maisie announced.

"Never."

"Never?"

"She'll keep him. She'll hold him for ever."

Maisie doubted. "When he 'loathes' her?"

"That won't matter. She won't loathe *him*. People don't!" Mrs. Wix brought up.

"Some do. Mamma does," Maisie contended.

"Mamma does *not*!" It was startling—her friend contradicted her flat. "She loves him—she adores him. A woman knows." Mrs. Wix spoke not only as if Maisie were not a woman, but as if she would never be one. "*I* know!" she cried.

"The why on earth has she left him?"

Mrs. Wix hesitated. "He hates *her*. Don't stoop so—lift up your hair. You know how I'm affected toward him," she added with dignity; "but you must also know that I see clear."

Maisie all this time was trying hard to do likewise. "Then, if she has left him for that, why shouldn't Mrs. Beale leave him?"

"Because she's not such a fool!"

"Not such a fool as mamma?"

"Precisely—if you *will* have it. Does it look like her leaving him?" Mrs. Wix inquired. She hung fire again; then she went on with more intensity: "Do you want to know really and truly why? So that she may be his wretchedness and his punishment."

"His punishment?"—this was more than as yet Maisie could quite accept. "For what?"

"For everything. That's what will happen: he'll be tied to her for ever. She won't mind in the least his hating her, and she won't hate him back. She'll only hate *us*."

"Us?" the child faintly echoed.

"She'll hate *you*."

"Me? Why, I brought them together!" Maisie resentfully cried.

"You brought them together." There was a completeness in Mrs. Wix's assent. "Yes; it was a pretty job. Sit down." She began to brush her pupil's hair and, as she took up the mass of it with some force of hand, went on with a sharp recall: "Your mother adored him at first—it might have lasted. But he began too soon with Mrs. Beale. As you say," she pursued with a brisk application of the brush, "you brought them together."

"I brought them together"—Maisie was ready to reaffirm it. She left none the less for a moment at the bottom of a hole; then she seemed to see a way out. "But I didn't bring mamma together——" She just faltered.

"With all those gentlemen?"—Mrs. Wix pulled her up. "No; it isn't quite so bad as that."

"I only said to the Captain"—Maisie had the quick memory of it—"that I hoped he at least (he was awfully nice!) would love her and keep her."

"And even that wasn't much harm," threw in Mrs. Wix.

"It wasn't much good," Maisie was obliged to recognise. "She can't bear him—not even a mite. She told me at Folkestone."

Mrs. Wix suppressed a gasp; then after a bridling instant during which she might have appeared to deflect with difficulty from her odd consideration of Ida's wrongs: "He was a nice sort of person for her to talk to you about!"

"Oh, I *like* him!" Maisie promptly rejoined; and at this, with an inarticulate sound and an inconsequence still more marked, her companion bent over and dealt her on the cheek a rapid peck which had the apparent intention of a kiss.

"Well, if her ladyship doesn't agree with you, what does it only prove?" Mrs. Wix demanded in conclusion. "It proves that she's fond of Sir Claude!"

Maisie, in the light of some of the evidence, reflected on that till her hair was finished, but when she at last started up she gave a sign of no very close embrace of it. She grasped at this moment Mrs. Wix's arm. "He must have got his divorce!"

"Since day before yesterday? Don't talk trash."

This was spoken with an impatience which left the child nothing to reply; whereupon she sought her defence in a completely different relation to the fact. "Well, I knew he would come!"

"So did I; but not in twenty-four hours. I gave him a few days!" Mrs. Wix wailed.

Maisie, whom she had now released, looked at her with interest. "How many did *she* give him?"

Mrs. Wix faced her a moment; then as if with a bewildered sniff: "You had better ask her!" But she had no sooner uttered the words than she caught herself up. "Lord of mercy, how we talk!"

Maisie felt that however they talked she must see him, but she said nothing more for a time, a time during which she conscientiously finished dressing and Mrs. Wix also kept silence. It was as if they each had almost too much to think of and even as if the child had the sense that her friend was watching her and seeing if she herself were watched. At last Mrs. Wix turned to the window and stood—sightlessly, as Maisie could guess—looking away. Then our young lady, before the glass, gave the supreme shake. "Well, I'm ready. And now to *see* him!"

Mrs. Wix turned round, but as if without having heard her. "It's tremendously grave." There were slow, still tears behind the straighteners.

"It is—it is." Maisie spoke as if she were now dressed quite up to the occasion; as if indeed with the last touch she had put on the judgment-cap. "I must see him immediately."

"How can you see him if he doesn't send for you?"

"Why can't I go and find him?"

"Because you don't know where he is."

"Can't I just look in the *salon*?" That still seemed simple to Maisie.

Mrs. Wix, however, instantly cut it off. "I wouldn't have you look in the *salon* for all the world!" Then she explained a little: "The *salon* isn't ours now."

"Ours?"

"Yours and mine. It's theirs."

"Theirs?" Maisie, with her stare, continued to echo. "You mean they want to keep us out?"

Mrs. Wix faltered; she sank into a chair and, as Maisie had often enough seen her do before, covered her face with her hands. "They ought to, at least. The situation's too monstrous!"

Maisie stood there a moment—she looked about the room. "I'll go to him—I'll find him."

"*I* won't! I won't go *near* them!" cried Mrs. Wix.

"Then I'll see him alone." The child spied what she had been looking for—she possessed herself of her hat. "Perhaps I'll take him out!" And with decision she quitted the room.

When she entered the *salon* it was empty, but at the sound of the opened door some one stirred on the balcony, and Sir Claude, stepping straight in, stood before her. He was in light, fresh clothes and wore a straw hat with a bright ribbon; these things, besides striking her in themselves as the very promise of the grandest of grand tours, gave him a certain radiance and, as it were, a tropical ease; but such an effect only marked rather more his having stopped short and, for a longer minute than had ever at such a juncture elapsed, not opened his arms to her. His pause made her pause and enabled her to reflect that he must have been up some time, for there were no traces of breakfast; and that though it was so late he had rather markedly not caused her to be called to him. Had Mrs. Wix been right about their forfeiture of the *salon?* Was it all his now, all his and Mrs. Beale's? Such an idea, at the rate her small thoughts throbbed, could only remind her of the way in which what had been hers hitherto was what was exactly most Mrs. Beale's and his. It was strange to be standing there and greeting him across a gulf, for he had by this time spoken, smiled and said: "My dear child, my dear child!" but without coming any nearer. In a flash she saw that he was different—more so than he knew or designed. The next minute indeed it was as if he caught an impression from her face: this made him hold out his hand. Then they met, he kissed her, he laughed, she thought he even blushed: something of his affection rang out as usual. "Here I am, you see, again—as I promised you."

It was not as he had promised them—he had not promised them Mrs. Beale; but Maisie said nothing about that. What she said was simply: "I knew you had come. Mrs. Wix told me."

"Oh yes. And where is she?"

"In her room. She got me up—she dressed me."

Sir Claude looked at her up and down; a sweetness of mockery that she particularly loved came out in his face whenever he did that, and it was not wanting now. He raised his eyebrows and his arms to play at admiration; he was evidently after all disposed to be gay. "Got you up?—I should think so! She has dressed you most beautifully. Isn't she coming?"

Maisie wondered if she had better tell. "She said not."

"Doesn't she want to see a poor devil?"

She looked about under the vibration of the way he described himself, and her eyes rested on the door of the room he had previously occupied. "Is Mrs. Beale in there?"

Sir Claude looked blankly at the same object. "I haven't the least idea!"

"You haven't seen her?"

"Not the tip of her nose."

Maisie thought: there settled on her, in the light of his beautiful smiling eyes, the faintest, purest, coldest conviction that he was not telling the truth. "She hasn't welcomed you?"

"Not by a single sign."

"Then where is she?"

Sir Claude laughed; he seemed both amused and surprised at the point she made of it. "I give it up!"

"Doesn't she know you've come?"

He laughed again. "Perhaps she doesn't care!"

Maisie, with an inspiration, pounced on his arm. "Has she *gone?*"

He met her eyes and then she could see that his own were really much graver than his manner. "Gone?" She had flown to the door, but before she could raise her hand to knock he was beside her and had caught it. "Let her be. I don't care about her. I want to see *you.*"

Maisie fell back with him. "Then she *hasn't* gone?"

He still looked as if it were a joke, but the more she saw of him the more she could make out that he was troubled. "It wouldn't be like her!"

She stood wondering at him. "Did you want her to come?"

"How can you suppose——?" He put it to her candidly. "We had an immense row over it."

"Do you mean you've quarrelled?"

Sir Claude was at a loss. "What has she told you?"

"That I'm hers as much as yours. That she represents papa."

His gaze struck away through the open window and up to the sky; she could hear him rattle in his trousers-pocket his money or his keys. "Yes—that's what she keeps saying." It gave him for a moment an air that was almost helpless.

"You say you don't care about her," Maisie went on. "*Do* you mean you've quarrelled?"

"We do nothing in life but quarrel."

He rose before her, as he said this, so soft and fair, so rich, in spite of what might worry him, in restored familiarities, that it gave a bright blur to the meaning—to what would otherwise perhaps have been the tangible promise—of the words. "Oh, *your* quarrels!" she exclaimed with discouragement.

"I assure you hers are quite fearful!"

"I don't speak of hers. I speak of yours."

"Ah, don't do it till I've had my coffee! You're growing up clever," he added. Then he said: "I suppose you've breakfasted?"

"Oh no—I've had nothing."

"Nothing in your room?"—he was all compunction. "My dear old man!—we'll breakfast then together." He had one of his happy thoughts. "I say—we'll go out."

"That was just what I hoped. I've brought my hat."

"You *are* clever! We'll go to a *café*." Maisie was already at the door; he glanced round the room. "A moment—my stick." But there appeared to be no stick. "No matter; I left it —oh!" He remembered with an odd drop and came out.

"You left it in London?" she asked as they went downstairs.

"Yes—in London: fancy!"

"You were in such a hurry to come," Maisie explained.

He had his arm round her. "That must have been the reason." Half way down he stopped short again, slapping his leg. "And poor Mrs. Wix?"

Maisie's face just showed a shadow. "Do you want her to come?"

"Dear, no—I want to see you alone."

"That's the way I want to see *you*!" she replied. "Like before."

"Like before!" he gaily echoed. "But I mean has she had her coffee?"

"No, nothing."

"Then I'll send it up to her. Madame!" He had already, at the foot of the stair, called out to the stout *patronne*, a lady who turned to him from the bustling, breezy hall a countenance covered with fresh matutinal powder and a bosom as capacious as the velvet shelf of a chimneypiece, over which her round white face, framed in its golden frizzle, might have figured as a showy clock. He ordered, with particular recommendations, Mrs. Wix's repast, and it was a charm to hear his easy, brilliant French: even his companion's ignorance could measure the perfection of it. The *patronne*, rubbing her hands and breaking in with high, swift notes as into a florid duet, went with him to the street, and while they talked a moment longer Maisie remembered what Mrs. Wix had said about every one's liking him. It came out enough through the morning powder, it came out enough in the heaving bosom how the landlady liked him. He had evidently ordered something lovely for Mrs. Wix. "*Et bien soigné, n'est-ce-pas?*"

"*Soyez tranquille*"—the *patronne* beamed upon him. "*Et pour Madame?*"

"*Madame?*" he echoed—it just pulled him up a little.

"*Rien encore?*"

"*Rien encore.* Come, Maisie." She hurried along with him, but on the way to the *café* he said nothing.

XXX

A FTER they were seated there it was different: the place was
not below the hotel, but further along the quay; with
wide, clear windows and a floor sprinkled with bran in a manner that gave it for Maisie something of the added charm of a
circus. They had pretty much to themselves the painted spaces
and the red plush benches; these were shared by a few scattered gentlemen who picked teeth, with facial contortions,
behind little bare tables, and by an old personage in particular, a very old personage with a red ribbon in his buttonhole,
whose manner of soaking buttered rolls in coffee and then
disposing of them in the little that was left of the interval between his nose and chin might at a less anxious hour have cast
upon Maisie an almost envious spell. They too had their *café
au lait* and their buttered rolls, determined by Sir Claude's
asking her if she could with that light aid wait till the hour of
déjeuner. His allusion to this meal gave her, in the shaded,
sprinkled coolness, the scene, as she vaguely felt, of a sort of
ordered, mirrored licence, the haunt of those—the irregular,
like herself—who went to bed or who rose too late, something to think over while she watched the white-aproned
waiter perform as nimbly with plates and saucers as a certain
conjurer her friend had in London taken her to a music-hall
to see. Sir Claude had presently begun to talk again, to tell
her how London had looked and how long he had felt himself, on either side, to have been absent; all about Susan Ash
too and the amusement as well as the difficulty he had had
with her; then all about his return journey and the Channel in
the night and the crowd of people coming over and the way
there were always too many one knew. He spoke of other
matters beside, especially of what she must tell him of the oc-
cupations, while he was away, of Mrs. Wix and her pupil.
Hadn't they had the good time he had promised?—had he
exaggerated a bit the arrangements made for their pleasure?
Maisie had something—not all there was—to say of his success and of their gratitude: she had a complication of thought
that grew every minute, grew with the consciousness that she

had never seen him in this particular state in which he had been given back.

Mrs. Wix had once said—it was once or fifty times; once was enough for Maisie, but more was not too much—that he was wonderfully various. Well, he was certainly so, to the child's mind, on the present occasion: he was much more various than he was anything else. The fact that they were together in a shop, at a nice little intimate table as they had so often been in London, only, besides, made greater the difference of what they were together about. This difference was in his face, in his voice, in every look he gave her and every movement he made. They were not the looks and the movements he really wanted to show, and she could feel as well that they were not those she herself wanted. She had seen him nervous, she had seen every one she had come in contact with nervous, but she had never seen him so nervous as this. Little by little it gave her a settled terror, a terror that partook of the coldness she had felt just before, at the hotel, to find herself, on his answer about Mrs. Beale, disbelieve him. She seemed to see at present, to touch across the table, as if by laying her hand on it, what he had meant when he confessed on those several occasions to fear. Why was such a man so often afraid? It must have begun to come to her now that there was one thing just such a man above all could be afraid of. He could be afraid of himself. His fear at all events was there; his fear was sweet to her, beautiful and tender to her, was having coffee and buttered rolls and talk and laughter that were no talk and laughter at all with her; his fear was in his jesting, postponing, perverting voice; it was in just this make-believe way he had brought her out to imitate the old London playtimes, to imitate indeed a relation that had wholly changed, a relation that she had with her very eyes seen in the act of change when, the day before in the *salon*, Mrs. Beale rose suddenly before her. She rose before her, for that matter, now, and even while their refreshment delayed Maisie arrived at the straight question for which, on their entrance, his first word had given opportunity. "Are we going to have *déjeuner* with Mrs. Beale?"

His reply was anything but straight. "You and I?"

Maisie sat back in her chair. "Mrs. Wix and me."

Sir Claude also shifted. "That's an inquiry, my dear child, that Mrs. Beale herself must answer." Yes, he had shifted; but abruptly, after a moment during which something seemed to hang there between them and, as it heavily swayed, just fan them with the air of its motion, she felt that the whole thing was upon them. "Do you mind," he broke out, "my asking you what Mrs. Wix has said to you?"

"Said to me?"

"This day or two—while I was away."

"Do you mean about you and Mrs. Beale?"

Sir Claude, resting on his elbows, fixed his eyes a moment on the white marble beneath them. "No; I think we had a good deal of that—didn't we?—before I left you. It seems to me we had it pretty well all out. I mean about yourself, about your—don't you know?—associating with us, as I might say, and staying on with us. While you were alone with our friend what did she say?"

Maisie felt the weight of the question; it kept her silent for a space during which she looked at Sir Claude, whose eyes remained bent. "Nothing," she rejoined at last.

He showed incredulity. "Nothing?"

"Nothing," Maisie repeated; on which an interruption descended in the form of a tray bearing the preparations for their breakfast.

These preparations were as amusing as everything else; the waiter poured their coffee from a vessel like a watering-pot and then made it froth with the curved stream of hot milk that dropped from the height of his raised arm; but the two looked across at each other through the whole play of French pleasantness with a gravity that had now ceased to dissemble. Sir Claude sent the waiter off again for something and then took up her answer. "Hasn't she tried to affect you?"

Face to face with him thus it seemed to Maisie that she had tried so little as to be scarce worth mentioning; again therefore an instant she shut herself up. Presently she found her middle course. "Mrs. Beale likes her now; and there's one thing I've found out—a great thing. Mrs. Wix enjoys her being so kind. She was tremendously kind all day yesterday."

"I see. And what did she do?" Sir Claude asked.

Maisie was now busy with her breakfast, and her companion attacked his own; so that it was all, in form at least, even more than their old sociability. "Everything she could think of. She was as nice to her as you are," the child said. "She talked to her all day."

"And what did she say to her?"

"Oh, I don't know." Maisie was a little bewildered with his pressing her so for knowledge; it didn't fit into the degree of intimacy with Mrs. Beale that Mrs. Wix had so denounced and that, according to that lady, had now brought him back in bondage. Wasn't he more aware than his stepdaughter of what would be done by the person to whom he was bound? In a moment, however, she added: "She made love to her."

Sir Claude looked at her harder, and it was clearly something in her tone that made him quickly say: "You don't mind my asking you, do you?"

"Not at all; only I should think you'd know better than I."

"What Mrs. Beale did yesterday?"

She thought he coloured a trifle; but almost simultaneously with that impression she found herself answering: "Yes—if you *have* seen her."

He broke into the loudest of laughs. "Why, my dear boy, I told you just now I've absolutely not. I say, don't you believe me?"

There was something she was already so afraid of that it covered up other fears. "Didn't you come back to see her?" she inquired in a moment. "Didn't you come back because you always want to so much?"

He received her inquiry as he had received her doubt—with an extraordinary absence of resentment. "I can imagine of course why you think that. But it doesn't explain my doing what I have. It was, as I said to you just now at the inn, really and truly you I wanted to see."

She felt an instant as she used to feel when, in the backgarden at her mother's, she took from him the highest push of a swing—high, high, high—that he had had put there for her pleasure and that had finally broken down under the weight and the extravagant patronage of Susan Ash. "Well, that's beautiful. But to see me, you mean, and go away again?"

"My going away again is just the point. I can't tell yet—it all depends."

"On Mrs. Beale?" Maisie asked. "*She* won't go away." He finished emptying his coffee-cup and then, when he had put it down, leaned back in his chair, where she could see that he smiled at her. This only added to her idea that he was in trouble, that he was turning somehow in his pain and trying different things. He continued to smile and she went on: "Don't you know that?"

"Yes, I may as well confess to you that as much as that I do know. *She* won't go away. She'll stay."

"She'll stay. She'll stay," Maisie repeated.

"Just so. Won't you have some more coffee?"

"Yes, please."

"And another buttered roll?"

"Yes, please."

He signed to the hovering waiter, who arrived with the shining spout of plenty in either hand and with the friendliest interest in mademoiselle. "*Les tartines sont là.*" Their cups were replenished and, while he watched almost musingly the bubbles in the fragrant mixture, "Just so—just so," Sir Claude said again and again. "It's awfully awkward!" he exclaimed when the waiter had gone.

"That she won't go?"

"Well—everything! Well, well, well!" But he pulled himself together; he began again to eat. "I came back to ask you something. That's what I came back for."

"I know what you want to ask me," Maisie said.

"Are you very sure?"

"I'm *almost* very."

"Well then, risk it. You mustn't make *me* risk everything."

She was struck with the force of this. "You want to know if I should be happy with *them*."

"With those two ladies only? No, no, old man: *vous n'y êtes pas*. So now—there!" Sir Claude laughed.

"Well then, what is it?"

The next minute, instead of telling her what it was, he laid his hand across the table on her own and held her as if under the prompting of a thought. "Mrs. Wix would stay with *her*?"

"Without you? Oh yes—now."

"On account, as you just intimated, of Mrs. Beale's changed manner?"

Maisie, with her sense of responsibility, focused both Mrs. Beale's changed manner and Mrs. Wix's human weakness. "I think she talked her over."

Sir Claude thought a moment. "Ah, poor dear!"

"Do you mean Mrs. Beale?"

"Oh no—Mrs. Wix."

"She likes being talked over—treated like any one else. Oh, she likes great politeness," Maisie expatiated. "It affects her very much."

Sir Claude, to her surprise, demurred a little to this. "Very much—up to a certain point."

"Oh, up to any point!" Maisie returned with emphasis.

"Well, haven't I been polite to her?"

"Lovely—and she perfectly worships you."

"Then, my dear child, why can't she let me alone?"—this time Sir Claude unmistakably blushed. Before Maisie, however, could answer his question, which would indeed have taken her long, he went on in another tone: "Mrs. Beale thinks she has probably quite broken her down. But she hasn't."

Though he spoke as if he were sure, Maisie was strong in the impression she had just uttered and that she now again produced. "She has talked her over."

"Ah yes; over to herself, but not over to me."

Oh, she couldn't bear to hear him say that! "To you? Don't you really believe how she loves you?"

Sir Claude examined his belief. "Of course I know she's wonderful."

"She's just every bit as fond of you as *I* am," said Maisie. "She told me so yesterday."

"Ah then," he promptly exclaimed, "she *has* tried to affect you! I don't love *her*, don't you see? I do her perfect justice," he pursued, "but I mean I don't love her as I do you, and I'm sure you wouldn't seriously expect it. She's not my daughter —come, old chap! She's not even my mother, though I daresay it would have been better for me if she had been. I'll do for her what I'd do for my mother, but I won't do more." His real excitement broke out in a need to explain and justify himself, though he kept trying to correct and conceal it with laughs and mouthfuls and other vain familiarities. Suddenly he broke off, wiping his moustache with sharp pulls and coming back to Mrs. Beale. "Did she try to talk *you* over?"

"No—to me she said very little. Very little indeed," Maisie continued.

Sir Claude seemed struck with this. "She was only sweet to Mrs. Wix?"

"As sweet as sugar!" cried Maisie.

He looked amused at her comparison, but he didn't contest it; he uttered on the contrary, in an assenting way, a little inarticulate sound. "I know what she *can* be. But much good may it have done her! Mrs. Wix won't come round. That's what makes it so fearfully awkward."

Maisie knew it was fearfully awkward; she had known this now, she felt, for some time, and there was something else it more pressingly concerned her to learn. "What is it that you meant you came over to ask me?"

"Well," said Sir Claude, "I was just going to say. Let me tell you it will surprise you." She had finished breakfast now and she sat back in her chair again: she waited in silence to hear. He had pushed the things before him a little way and had his elbows on the table. This time, she was convinced, she knew what was coming, and once more, for the crash, as with Mrs. Wix lately in her room, she held her breath and drew together her eyes. He was going to say that she must give him up. He looked hard at her again; then he made his effort. "Should you see your way to let her go?"

She was bewildered. "To let who——?"

"Mrs. Wix, simply. I put it at the worst. Should you see your way to sacrifice her? Of course I know what I'm asking."

Maisie's eyes opened wide again; this was so different from what she had expected. "And stay with you alone?"

He gave another push to his coffee-cup. "With me and Mrs. Beale. Of course it would be rather rum; but everything in our whole story is rather rum, you know. What is more unusual than for any one to be given up, like you, by her parents?"

"Oh, nothing is more unusual than *that*!" Maisie concurred, relieved at the contact of a proposition as to which concurrence could have lucidity.

"Of course it would be quite unconventional," Sir Claude went on—"I mean the little household we three should make

together; but things have got beyond that, don't you see?
They got beyond that long ago. We shall stay abroad at any
rate—it's ever so much easier and it's our affair and nobody
else's: it's no one's business but ours on all the blessed earth.
I don't say that for Mrs. Wix, poor dear—I do her absolute
justice. I respect her; I see what she means; she has done me
a lot of good. But there are the facts. There they are, simply.
And here am I, and here are you. And she won't come round.
She's right from her point of view. I'm talking to you in the
most extraordinary way—I'm always talking to you in the
most extraordinary way, ain't I? One would think you were
about sixty and that I—I don't know what any one would
think *I* am. Unless a beastly cad!" he suggested. "I've been
awfully worried, and this is what it has come to. You've done
us the most tremendous good, and you'll do it still and always, don't you see? We can't let you go—you're everything.
There are the facts as I say. She *is* your mother now, Mrs.
Beale, by what has happened, and I, in the same way, I'm
your father. No one can contradict that, and we can't get out
of it. My idea would be a nice little place—somewhere in the
south—where she and you would be together and as good as
any one else. And I should be as good too, don't you see? for
I shouldn't live with you, but I should be close to you—just
round the corner, and it would be just the same. My idea
would be that it should all be perfectly open and frank. *Honi
soit qui mal y pense*, don't you know? You're the best thing—
you and what we can do for you—that either of us has ever
known:" he came back to that. "When I say to her 'Give her
up, come,' she lets me have it bang in the face: 'Give her up
yourself!' It's the same old vicious circle—and when I say vicious I don't mean a pun or a what-d'ye-call-'em. Mrs. Wix is
the obstacle; I mean, you know, if she has affected you. She
has affected *me*, and yet here I am. I never was in such a tight
place: please believe it's only that that makes me put it to you
as I do. My dear child, isn't that—to put it so—just the way
out of it? That came to me yesterday, in London, after Mrs.
Beale had gone: I had the most infernal, atrocious day. 'Go
straight over and put it to her: let her choose, freely, her own
self.' So I do, old girl—I put it to you. *Can* you choose
freely?"

This long address, slowly and brokenly uttered, with fidgets and falterings, with lapses and recoveries, with a mottled face and embarrassed but supplicating eyes, reached the child from a quarter so close that after the shock of the first sharpness she could see intensely its direction and follow it from point to point; all the more that it came back to the point at which it had started. There was a word that had hummed all through it. "Do you call it a 'sacrifice'?"

"Of Mrs. Wix? I'll call it whatever *you* call it. I won't funk it—I haven't, have I? I'll face it in all its baseness. Does it strike you it *is* base for me to get you well away from her, to smuggle you off here into a corner and bribe you with sophistries and buttered rolls to betray her?"

"To betray her?"

"Well—to part with her."

Maisie let the question wait; the concrete image it presented was the most vivid side of it. "If I part with her where will she go?"

"Back to London."

"But I mean what will she do?"

"Oh, as for that I won't pretend I know. I don't. We all have our difficulties."

That, to Maisie, was at this moment more striking than it had ever been. "Then who will teach me?"

Sir Claude laughed out. "What Mrs. Wix teaches?"

Maisie smiled dimly; she saw what he meant. "It isn't so very, very much."

"It's so very, very little," he rejoined, "that that's a thing we've positively to consider. We probably shouldn't give you another governess. To begin with, we shouldn't be able to get one—not of the only kind that would do. It wouldn't do—the kind that *would* do," he queerly enough explained. "I mean they wouldn't stay—heigh-ho! We'd do you ourselves. Particularly me. You see I *can* now; I haven't got to mind—what I used to. I won't fight shy as I did—she can show out *with* me. Our relation, all round, is more regular."

It seemed wonderfully regular, the way he put it; yet none the less, while she looked at it as judiciously as she could, the picture it made persisted somehow in being a combination quite distinct—an old woman and a little girl seated in deep silence on a battered old bench by the rampart of the *haute ville*. It was just at that hour yesterday; they were hand in hand; they had melted together. "I don't think you yet understand how she clings to you," Maisie said at last.

"I do—I do. But for all that——!" And he gave, turning in his conscious exposure, an oppressed, impatient sigh; the sigh, even his companion could recognise, of the man naturally accustomed to that argument, the man who wanted thoroughly to be reasonable, but who, if really he had to mind so many things, would be always impossibly hampered. What it came to indeed was that he understood quite perfectly. If Mrs. Wix clung it was all the more reason for shaking Mrs. Wix off.

This vision of what she had brought him to occupied our young lady while, to ask what he owed, he called the waiter and put down a gold piece that the man carried off for change. Sir Claude looked after him, then went on: "How could a woman have less to reproach a fellow with? I mean as regards herself."

Maisie entertained the question. "Yes. How *could* she have less? So why are you so sure she'll go?"

"Surely you heard why—you heard her come out three nights ago? How can she do anything but go—after what she then said? I've done what she warned me of—she was absolutely right. So here we are. Her liking Mrs. Beale, as you call it now, is a motive sufficient with other things to make her, for your sake, stay on without me; it's not a motive sufficient to make her, even for yours, stay on *with* me—swallow, in short, what she can't swallow. And when you say she's as fond of me as you are I think I can, if that's the case, challenge you a little on it. Would *you*, only with those two, stay on without me?" The waiter came back with the change, and that gave her, under this appeal, a moment's respite. But when he had retreated again with the "tip" gathered in with graceful thanks on a subtle hint from Sir Claude's forefinger, the latter, while he pocketed the money, followed the appeal up. "Would you let her make you live with Mrs. Beale?"

"Without you? Never," Maisie then answered. "Never," she said again.

It made him quite triumph, and she was indeed herself

shaken by the mere sound of it. "So you see you're not, like
her," he exclaimed, "so ready to give me away!" Then he
came back to his original question. "*Can* you choose? I mean
can you settle it, by a word, yourself? Will you stay on with us
without her?"

Now in truth she felt the coldness of her terror, and it
seemed to her that suddenly she knew, as she knew it about
Sir Claude, what she was afraid of. She was afraid of herself.
She looked at him in such a way that it brought, she could
see, wonder into his face, a wonder held in check, however,
by his frank pretension to play fair with her, not to use advantages, not to hurry nor hustle her—only to put her chance
clearly and kindly before her. "May I think?" she finally asked.

"Certainly, certainly. But how long?"

"Oh, only a little while," she said meekly.

He had for a moment the air of wishing to look at it as if it
were the most cheerful prospect in the world. "But what shall
we do while you're thinking?" He spoke as if thought were
compatible with almost any distraction.

There was but one thing Maisie wished to do, and after an
instant she expressed it. "Have we got to go back to the hotel?"

"Do you want to?"

"Oh no."

"There's not the least necessity for it." He bent his eyes on
his watch; his face was now very grave. "We can do anything
else in the world." He looked at her again almost as if he were
on the point of saying that they might for instance start off
for Paris. But even while she wondered if that were not coming he had a sudden drop. "We can take a walk."

She was all ready, but he sat there as if he had still something more to say. This too, however, didn't come; so she
herself spoke. "I think I should like to see Mrs. Wix first."

"Before you decide? All right—all right." He had put on
his hat, but he had still to light a cigarette. He smoked a
minute, with his head thrown back, looking at the ceiling;
then he said: "There's one thing to remember—I've a right to
impress it on you: we stand absolutely in the place of your
parents. It's their defection, their extraordinary baseness, that
has made our responsibility. Never was a young person more
directly committed and confided." He appeared to say this

over, at the ceiling, through his smoke, a little for his own illumination. It carried him after a pause somewhat further.
"Though, I admit, it was to each of us separately."

He gave her so, at that moment and in that attitude, the
sense of wanting, as it were, to be on her side—on the side of
what would be in every way most right and wise and charming for her—that she felt a sudden desire to show herself as
not less delicate and magnanimous, not less solicitous for his
own interests. What were these but that of the "regularity" he
had just before spoken of? "It *was* to each of you separately,"
she accordingly with much earnestness remarked. "But don't
you remember? I brought you together."

He jumped up with a delighted laugh. "Remember?
Rather! You brought us together, you brought us together.
Come!"

XXXI

S HE REMAINED out with him for a time of which she could take no measure save that it was too short for what she wished to make of it—an interval, a barrier indefinite, insurmountable. They walked about, they dawdled, they looked in shop-windows; they did all the old things exactly as if to try to get back all the old safety, to get something out of them that they had always got before. This had come before, whatever it was, without their trying, and nothing came now but the intenser consciousness of their quest and their subterfuge. The strangest thing of all was what had really happened to the old safety. What had really happened was that Sir Claude was "free" and that Mrs. Beale was "free," and yet that the new medium was somehow still more oppressive than the old. She could feel that Sir Claude concurred with her in the sense that the oppression would be worst at the inn, where, till something should be settled, they would feel the want of something—of what could they call it but a footing? The question of the settlement loomed larger to her now: it depended, she had learned, so completely on herself. Her choice, as her friend had called it, was there before her like an impossible sum on a slate, a sum that in spite of her plea for consideration she simply got off from doing while she walked about with him. She must see Mrs. Wix before she could do her sum; therefore the longer before she saw her the more distant would be the ordeal. She met at present no demand whatever of her obligation; she simply plunged, to avoid it, deeper into the company of Sir Claude. She saw nothing that she had seen hitherto—no touch in the foreign picture that had at first been always before her. The only touch was that of Sir Claude's hand, and to feel her own in it was her mute resistance to time. She went about as sightlessly as if he had been leading her blindfold. If they were afraid of themselves it was themselves they would find at the inn. She was certain now that what awaited them there would be to lunch with Mrs. Beale. All her instinct was to avoid that, to draw out their walk, to find pretexts, to take him down upon the beach, to

take him to the end of the pier. He said not another word to
her about what they had talked of at breakfast, and she had a
dim vision of how his way of not letting her see that he was
waiting for anything from her would make any one who
should know of it, would make Mrs. Wix for instance, think
him more than ever a gentleman. It was true that once or
twice, on the jetty, on the sands, he looked at her for a minute
with eyes that seemed to propose to her to come straight off
with him to Paris. That, however, was not to give her a nudge
about her responsibility. He evidently wanted to procrastinate
quite as much as she did; he was not a bit more in a hurry to
get back to the others. Maisie herself at this moment could be
secretly merciless to Mrs. Wix—to the extent at any rate of
not caring if her continued disappearance did make that lady
begin to worry about what had become of her, even begin to
wonder perhaps if the truants hadn't found their remedy. Her
want of mercy to Mrs. Beale indeed was at least as great; for
Mrs. Beale's worry and wonder would be as much greater as
the object at which they were directed. When at last Sir
Claude, at the far end of the *plage*, which they had already, in
the many-coloured crowd, once traversed, suddenly, with a
look at his watch, remarked that it was time, not to get back
to the *table d'hôte*, but to get over to the station and meet the
Paris papers—when he did this she found herself thinking
quite with intensity what Mrs. Beale and Mrs. Wix *would* say.
On the way over to the station she had even a mental picture
of the stepfather and the pupil established in a little place in
the south while the governess and the stepmother, in a little
place in the north, remained linked by a community of blankness and by the endless theme of intercourse it would afford.
The Paris papers had come in and her companion with a
strange extravagance bought no less of them than nine: it
took up time while they hovered at the bookstall on the restless platform, where the little volumes in a row were all yellow and pink and one of her favourite old women in one of
her favourite old caps absolutely wheedled him into the purchase of three. They had thus so much to carry home that it
would have seemed simpler, with such a provision for a nice
straight journey through France, just to "nip," as she phrased
it to herself, into the *coupé* of the train that, a little further

along, stood waiting to start. She asked Sir Claude where it was going.

"To Paris. Fancy!"

She could fancy well enough. They stood there and smiled, he with all the newspapers under his arm and she with the three books, one yellow and two pink. He had told her the pink were for herself and the yellow one for Mrs. Beale, implying in an interesting way that these were the vivid divisions in France of literature for the young and for the old. She knew that they looked exactly as if they were going to get into the train, and she presently brought out to her companion: "I wish we could go. Won't you take me?"

He continued to smile. "Would you really come?"

"Oh yes, oh yes. Try."

"Do you want me to take our tickets?"

"Yes, take them."

"Without any luggage?"

She showed their two armfuls, smiling at him as he smiled at her, but so conscious of being more frightened than she had ever been in her life that she seemed to see her whiteness as in a glass. Then she knew that what she saw was Sir Claude's whiteness: he was as frightened as herself. "Haven't we got plenty of luggage?" she asked. "Take the tickets—haven't you time? When does the train go?"

Sir Claude turned to a porter. "When does the train go?"

The man looked up at the station clock. "In two minutes. *Monsieur est placé?*"

"*Pas encore.*"

"*Et vos billets?—vous n'avez que le temps.*" Then, after a look at Maisie, "*Monsieur veut-il que je les prenne?*" the man inquired.

Sir Claude turned back to her. "*Veux-tu bien qu'il en prenne?*"

It was the most extraordinary thing in the world: in the intensity of her excitement she not only by illumination understood all their French, but fell into it with an active perfection. She addressed herself straight to the porter. "*Prenny, prenny. Oh prenny!*"

"*Ah, si mademoiselle le veut——!*" He waited there for the money.

But Sir Claude only stared—stared at her with his white face. "You *have* chosen then? You'll let her go?"

Maisie carried her eyes wistfully to the train, where, amid cries of "*En voiture, en voiture!*" heads were at windows and doors banging loud. The porter was pressing. "*Ah, vous n'avez plus le temps!*"

"It's going—it's going!" cried Maisie.

They watched it move, they watched it start; then the man went his way with a shrug. "It's gone!" Sir Claude said.

Maisie crept some distance up the platform; she stood there with her back to her companion, following it with her eyes, keeping down tears, nursing her pink and yellow books. She had had a real fright, but had fallen back to earth. The odd thing was that in her fall her fear too had been dashed down and broken. It was gone. She looked round at last from where she had paused at Sir Claude's, and then she saw that his was not. It sat there with him on the bench to which, against the wall of the station, he had retreated, and where, leaning back and, as she thought, rather queer, he still waited. She came down to him and he continued to offer his ineffectual intention of pleasantry. "Yes, I've chosen," she said to him. "I'll let her go if you—if you——"

She faltered; he quickly took her up. "If I, if I——?"

"If you'll give up Mrs. Beale."

"Oh!" he exclaimed; on which she saw how much, how hopelessly he was afraid. She had supposed at the *café* that it was of his rebellion, of his gathering motive; but how could that be when his temptations—that temptation for example of the train they had just lost—were after all so slight? Mrs. Wix was right. He was afraid of his weakness—of his weakness.

She could not have told you afterwards how they got back to the inn: she could only have told you that even from this point they had not gone straight, but once more had wandered and loitered and, in the course of it, had found themselves on the edge of the quay where—still apparently with half an hour to spare—the boat prepared for Folkestone was drawn up. Here they hovered as they had done at the station; here they exchanged silences again, but only exchanged silences. There were punctual people on the deck, choosing places, taking the best; some of them already contented, all

established and shawled, facing to England and attended by
the steward, who, confined on such a day to the lighter offices, tucked up the ladies' feet or opened bottles with a pop.
They looked down at these things without a word; they even
picked out a good place for two that was left in the lee of a
lifeboat; and if they lingered rather stupidly, neither deciding
to go aboard nor deciding to come away, it was quite as much
as she Sir Claude who wouldn't move. It was Sir Claude who
cultivated the supreme stillness by which she knew best what
he meant. He simply meant that he knew all she herself
meant. But there was no pretence of pleasantry now: their
faces were grave and tired. When at last they lounged off it
was as if his fear, his fear of his weakness, leaned upon her
heavily as they followed the harbour. In the hall of the hotel
as they passed in she saw a battered old box that she recognised, an ancient receptacle with dangling labels that she
knew and a big painted W, lately done over and intensely personal, that seemed to stare at her with a recognition and even
with some suspicion of its own. Sir Claude caught it too, and
there was agitation for both of them in the sight of this object on the move. Was Mrs. Wix going and was the responsibility of giving her up lifted, at a touch, from her pupil? Her
pupil and her pupil's companion, transfixed a moment, held,
in the presence of the omen, communication more intense
than in the presence either of the Paris train or of the Channel steamer; then, and still without a word, they went straight
upstairs. There, however, on the landing, out of sight of the
people below, they collapsed so that they had to sink down
together for support: they simply seated themselves on the
uppermost step while Sir Claude grasped the hand of his stepdaughter with a pressure that at another moment would
probably have made her squeal. Their books and papers were
all scattered. "She thinks you've given her up!"

"Then I must see her—I must see her," Maisie said.

"To bid her good-bye?"

"I must see her—I must see her," the child only repeated.

They sat a minute longer, Sir Claude with his tight grip of
her hand and looking away from her, looking straight down
the staircase to where, round the turn, electric bells rattled
and the pleasant sea-draught blew. At last, loosening his grasp,

he slowly got up while she did the same. They went together along the lobby, but before they reached the *salon* he stopped again. "If I give up Mrs. Beale——?"

"I'll go straight out with you again and not come back till she has gone."

He seemed to wonder. "Till Mrs. Beale——?"

He had made it sound like a bad joke. "I mean till Mrs. Wix leaves—in that boat."

Sir Claude looked almost foolish. "Is she going in that boat?"

"I suppose so. I won't even bid her good-bye," Maisie continued. "I'll stay out till the boat has gone. I'll go up to the old rampart."

"The old rampart?"

"I'll sit on that old bench where you see the gold Virgin."

"The gold Virgin?" he vaguely echoed. But it brought his eyes back to her as if after an instant he could see the place and the thing she named—could see her sitting there alone. "While I break with Mrs. Beale?"

"While you break with Mrs. Beale."

He gave a long, deep, smothered sigh. "I must see her first."

"You won't do as I do? Go out and wait?"

"Wait?"—once more he appeared at a loss.

"Till they both have gone," Maisie said.

"Giving *us* up?"

"Giving *us* up."

Oh, with what a face, for an instant, he wondered if that could be! But his wonder the next moment only made him go to the door and, with his hand on the knob, stand as if listening for voices. Maisie listened, but she heard none. All she heard presently was Sir Claude's saying with speculation quite averted, but so as not to be heard in the *salon*: "Mrs. Beale will never go." On this he pushed open the door and she went in with him. The *salon* was empty, but as an effect of their entrance the lady he had just mentioned appeared at the door of the bedroom. "Is she going?" he then demanded.

Mrs. Beale came forward, closing her door behind her. "I've had the most extraordinary scene with her. She told me yesterday she'd stay."

"And my arrival has altered it?"

"Oh, we took that into account!" Mrs. Beale was flushed, which was never quite becoming to her, and her face visibly testified to the encounter to which she alluded. Evidently, however, she had not been worsted, and she held up her head and smiled and rubbed her hands as if in sudden emulation of the *patronne*. "She promised she'd stay even if you should come."

"Then why has she changed?"

"Because she's a hound. The reason she herself gives is that you've been out too long."

Sir Claude stared. "What has that to do with it?"

"You've been out an age," Mrs. Beale continued; "I myself couldn't imagine what had become of you. The whole morning," she exclaimed, "and luncheon long since over!"

Sir Claude appeared indifferent to that. "Did Mrs. Wix go down with you?" he only asked.

"Not she; she never budged!"—and Mrs. Beale's flush, to Maisie's vision, deepened. "She moped there—she didn't so much as come out to me; and when I sent to invite her she simply declined to appear. She said she wanted nothing, and I went down alone. But when I came up, fortunately a little primed"—and Mrs. Beale smiled a fine smile of battle—"she *was* in the field!"

"And you had a big row?"

"We had a big row"—she assented with a frankness as large. "And while you left me to that sort of thing, I should like to know where you were!" She paused for a reply, but Sir Claude merely looked at Maisie; a movement that promptly quickened her challenge. "Where the mischief have you been?"

"You seem to take it as hard as Mrs. Wix," Sir Claude returned.

"I take it as I choose to take it, and you don't answer my question."

He looked again at Maisie, and as if for an aid to this effort; whereupon she smiled at her stepmother and offered: "We've been everywhere."

Mrs. Beale, however, made her no response, thereby adding to a surprise of which our young lady had already felt the light brush. She had received neither a greeting nor a glance, but perhaps this was not more remarkable than the omission, in respect to Sir Claude, parted with in London two days before, of any sign of a sense of their reunion. Most remarkable of all was Mrs. Beale's announcement of the pledge given by Mrs. Wix and not hitherto revealed to her pupil. Instead of heeding this witness she went on with acerbity: "It might surely have occurred to you that something would come up."

Sir Claude looked at his watch. "I had no idea it was so late, nor that we had been out so long. We weren't hungry. It passed like a flash. What *has* come up?"

"Oh, that she's disgusted," said Mrs. Beale.

"With whom then?"

"With Maisie." Even now she never looked at the child, who stood there equally associated and disconnected. "For having no moral sense."

"How *should* she have?" Sir Claude tried again to shine a little at the companion of his walk. "How at any rate is it proved by her going out with me?"

"Don't ask *me*; ask that woman. She drivels when she doesn't rage," Mrs. Beale declared.

"And she leaves the child?"

"She leaves the child," said Mrs. Beale with great emphasis and looking more than ever over Maisie's head.

In this position suddenly a change came into her face, caused, as the others could the next thing see, by the reappearance of Mrs. Wix in the doorway which, on coming in at Sir Claude's heels, Maisie had left gaping. "I *don't* leave the child—I don't, I don't!" she thundered from the threshold, advancing upon the opposed three, but addressing herself directly to Maisie. She was girded—positively harnessed—for departure, arrayed as she had been arrayed on her advent and armed with a small, fat, rusty reticule which, almost in the manner of a battle-axe, she brandished in support of her words. She had clearly come straight from her room, where Maisie in an instant guessed she had directed the removal of her minor effects. "I don't leave you till I've given you another chance: will you come *with* me?"

Maisie turned to Sir Claude, who struck her as having been

removed to a distance of about a mile. To Mrs. Beale she
turned no more than Mrs. Beale had turned: she felt as if already their difference had been disclosed. What had come out
about that in the scene between the two women? Enough
came out now, at all events, as she put it practically to her
stepfather. "Will *you* come? Won't you?" she inquired as if she
had not already seen that she should have to give him up. It
was the last flare of her dream. By this time she was afraid of
nothing.

"I should think you'd be too proud to ask!" Mrs. Wix interposed. Mrs. Wix was herself conspicuously too proud.

But at the child's words Mrs. Beale had fairly bounded.
"Come away from *me*, Maisie?" It was a wail of dismay and
reproach, in which her stepdaughter was astonished to read
that she had had no hostile consciousness and that if she had
been so actively grand it was not from suspicion, but from
strange entanglements of modesty.

Sir Claude presented to Mrs. Beale an expression positively
sick. "Don't put it to her *that* way!" There had indeed been
something in Mrs. Beale's tone, and for a moment our young
lady was reminded of the old days in which so many of her
friends had been "compromised."

This friend blushed—it was before Mrs. Wix, and though
she bridled she took the hint. "No—it isn't the way." Then
she showed she knew the way. "Don't be a still bigger fool,
dear, but go straight to your room and wait there till I can
come to you."

Maisie made no motion to obey, but Mrs. Wix raised a
hand that forestalled every evasion. "Don't move till you've
heard me. *I'm* going, but I must first understand. Have you
lost it again?"

Maisie surveyed for the idea of a describable loss the immensity of space. Then she replied lamely enough: "I feel as
if I had lost everything."

Mrs. Wix looked dark. "Do you mean to say you *have* lost
what we found together with so much difficulty two days ago?"
As her pupil failed of response she continued: "Do you mean
to say you've already forgotten what we found together?"

Maisie dimly remembered. "My moral sense?"

"You moral sense. *Haven't* I, after all, brought it out?" She spoke as she had never spoken even in the schoolroom and with the book in her hand.

It brought back to the child's recollection of how sometimes she couldn't repeat on Friday the sentence that had been glib on Wednesday, and she thought with conscious stupidity of the mystery on which she was now pulled up. Sir Claude and Mrs. Beale stood there like visitors at an "exam." She had indeed an instant a whiff of the faint flower that Mrs. Wix pretended to have plucked and now with such a peremptory hand passed under her nose. Then it left her, and, as if she were sinking with a slip from a foothold, her arms made a short jerk. What this jerk represented was the spasm within her of something still deeper than a moral sense. She looked at her examiner; she looked at the visitors; she felt the rising of the tears she had kept down at the station. The only thing was the old flat, shameful schoolroom plea. "I don't know— I don't know."

"Then you've lost it." Mrs. Wix seemed to close the book as she fixed the straighteners on Sir Claude. "You've nipped it in the bud. You've killed it when it had begun to live."

She was a newer Mrs. Wix than ever, a Mrs. Wix high and great; but Sir Claude was not after all to be treated as a little boy with a missed lesson. "I've not killed anything," he said; "on the contrary I think I've produced life. I don't know what to call it—I haven't even known how decently to deal with it, to approach it; but, whatever it is, it's the most beautiful thing I've ever met—it's exquisite, it's sacred." He had his hands in his pockets and, though a trace of the sickness he had just shown still perhaps lingered there, his face bent itself with extraordinary gentleness on both the friends he was about to lose. "Do you know what I came back for?" he asked of the elder.

"I think I do!" cried Mrs. Wix, surprisingly unmollified and with a crimson on her brow that was like a wave of colour reflected from the luridness lately enacted with Mrs. Beale. That lady, as if a little besprinkled by such turns of the tide, uttered a loud inarticulate protest and, averting herself, stood a moment at the window.

"I came back with a proposal," said Sir Claude.

"To me?" Mrs. Wix asked.

"To Maisie. That she should give you up."

"And does she?"

Sir Claude wavered. "Tell her!" he then exclaimed to the child, also turning away as if to give her the chance. But Mrs. Wix and her pupil stood confronted in silence, Maisie whiter than ever—more awkward, more rigid and yet more dumb. They looked at each other hard, and as nothing came from them Sir Claude faced about again. "You won't tell her?— you can't?" Still she said nothing: whereupon, addressing Mrs. Wix, he broke into a kind of ecstasy. "She refused—she refused!"

Maisie, at this, found her voice. "I didn't refuse. I didn't," she repeated.

It brought Mrs. Beale straight back to her. "You accepted, angel—you accepted!" She threw herself upon the child and, before Maisie could resist, had sunk with her upon the sofa, possessed of her, encircling her. "You've given her up already, you've given her up for ever, and you're ours and ours only now, and the sooner she's off the better!"

Maisie had shut her eyes, but at a word of Sir Claude's they opened. "Let her go!" he said to Mrs. Beale.

"Never, never, never!" cried Mrs. Beale. Maisie felt herself more compressed.

"Let her go!" Sir Claude more intensely repeated. He was looking at Mrs. Beale and there was something in his voice. Maisie knew from a loosening of arms that she had become conscious of what it was; she slowly rose from the sofa, and the child stood there again dropped and divided. "You're free —you're free," Sir Claude went on; at which Maisie's back became aware of a push that vented resentment and that placed her again in the centre of the room, the cynosure of every eye and not knowing which way to turn.

She turned with an effort to Mrs. Wix. "I didn't refuse to give you up. I said I would if *he'd* give up——!"

"Give up Mrs. Beale?" burst from Mrs. Wix.

"Give up Mrs. Beale. What do you call that but exquisite?" Sir Claude demanded of all of them, the lady mentioned included; speaking with a relish as intense now as if some lovely work of art or of nature had suddenly been set down among them. He was rapidly recovering himself on this basis of fine appreciation. "She made her condition—with such a sense of what it should be! She made the only right one."

"The only right one?"—Mrs. Beale returned to the charge. She had taken a moment before a snub from him, but she was not to be snubbed on this. "How can you talk such rubbish and how can you back her up in such impertinence? What in the world have you done to her to make her think of such stuff?" She stood there in righteous wrath; she flashed her eyes round the circle. Maisie took them full in her own, knowing that here at last was the moment she had had most to reckon with. But as regards her stepdaughter Mrs. Beale subdued herself to an inquiry deeply mild. "*Have* you made, my own love, any such condition as that?"

Somehow, now that it was there, the great moment was not so bad. What helped the child was that she knew what she wanted. All her learning and learning had made her at last learn that; so that if she waited an instant to reply it was only from the desire to be nice. Bewilderment had simply gone or at any rate was going fast. Finally she answered. "Will you give *him* up? Will you?"

"Ah, leave her alone—leave her, leave her!" Sir Claude in sudden supplication murmured to Mrs. Beale

Mrs. Wix at the same instant found another apostrophe. "Isn't it enough for you, madam, to have brought her to discussing your relations?"

Mrs. Beale left Sir Claude unheeded, but Mrs. Wix could make her flame. "My relations? What do you know, you hideous creature, about my relations, and what business on earth have you to speak of them? Leave the room this instant, you horrible old woman!"

"I think you had better go—you must really catch your boat," Sir Claude said distressfully to Mrs. Wix. He was out of it now, or wanted to be; he knew the worst and had accepted it: what now concerned him was to prevent, to dissipate vulgarities. "Won't you go—won't you just get off quickly?"

"With the child as quickly as you like. Not without her." Mrs. Wix was adamant.

"Then why did you lie to me, you fiend?" Mrs. Beale almost yelled. "Why did you tell me an hour ago that you had given her up?"

"Because I despaired of her—because I thought she had left me." Mrs. Wix turned to Maisie. "You were *with* them—in their connection. But now your eyes are open, and I take you!"

"No you don't!" and Mrs. Beale made, with a great fierce jump, a wild snatch at her stepdaughter. She caught her by the arm and, completing an instinctive movement, whirled her round in a further leap to the door, which had been closed by Sir Claude the instant their voices had risen. She fell back against it and, even while denouncing and waving off Mrs. Wix, kept it closed in an incoherence of passion. "You don't take her, but you bundle yourself: she stays with her own people and she's rid of you! I never heard anything so monstrous!" Sir Claude had rescued Maisie and kept hold of her; he held her in front of him, resting his hands very lightly on her shoulders and facing the loud adversaries. Mrs. Beale's flush had dropped; she had turned pale with a splendid wrath. She kept protesting and dismissing Mrs. Wix; she glued her back to the door to prevent Maisie's flight; she drove out Mrs. Wix by the window or the chimney. "You're a nice one—'discussing relations'—with your talk of our 'connection' and your insults! What in the world is our connection but the love of the child who is our duty and our life and who holds us together as closely as she originally brought us?"

"I know, I know!" Maisie said with a burst of eagerness. "I did bring you."

The strangest of laughs escaped from Sir Claude. "You did bring us—you did!" His hands went up and down gently on her shoulders.

Mrs. Wix so dominated the situation that she had something sharp for every one. "There you have it, you see!" she pregnantly remarked to her pupil.

"*Will* you give him up?" Maisie persisted to Mrs. Beale.

"To *you*, you abominable little horror?" that lady indignantly inquired, "and to this raving old demon who has filled your dreadful little mind with her wickedness? Have you been a hideous little hypocrite all these years that I've slaved to make you love me and deludedly believed that you did?"

"I love Sir Claude—I love *him*," Maisie replied with a sense slightly rueful and embarrassed that she appeared to offer it as something that would do as well. Sir Claude had continued to pat her, and it was really an answer to his pats.

"She hates you—she hates you," he observed with the oddest quietness to Mrs. Beale.

His quietness made her blaze. "And you back her up in it and give me up to outrage?"

"No; I only insist that she's free—she's free."

Mrs. Beale stared—Mrs. Beale glared. "Free to starve with this pauper lunatic?"

"I'll do more for her than *you* ever did!" Mrs. Wix retorted. "I'll work my fingers to the bone."

Maisie, with Sir Claude's hands still on her shoulders, felt, just as she felt the fine surrender in them, that over her head he looked in a certain way at Mrs. Wix. "You needn't do that," she heard him say. "She has means."

"Means?—Maisie?" Mrs. Beale shrieked. "Means that her vile father has stolen!"

"I'll get them back—I'll get them back. I'll look into it." He smiled and nodded at Mrs. Wix.

This had a fearful effect on his other friend. "Haven't *I* looked into it, I should like to know, and haven't I found an abyss? It's too inconceivable—your cruelty to me!" she wildly broke out. She had hot tears in her eyes.

He spoke to her very kindly, almost coaxingly. "We'll look into it again; we'll look into it together. It *is* an abyss, but he *can* be made—or Ida can. Think of the money they're getting now!" he laughed. "It's all right, it's all right," he continued. "It wouldn't do—it wouldn't do. We *can't* work her in. It's perfectly true—she's unique. We're not good enough—oh no!" and, quite exuberantly, he laughed again.

"Not good enough, and that beast *is*?" Mrs. Beale shouted.

At this for a moment there was a hush in the room, and in the midst of it Sir Claude replied to the question by moving with Maisie to Mrs. Wix. The next thing the child knew she was at that lady's side with an arm firmly grasped. Mrs. Beale still guarded the door. "Let them pass," said Sir Claude at last.

She remained there, however; Maisie saw the pair look at each other. Then she saw Mrs. Beale turn to her. "I'm your mother now, Maisie. And he's your father."

"That's just where it is!" sighed Mrs. Wix with an effect of irony positively detached and philosophic.

Mrs. Beale continued to address her young friend, and her effort to be reasonable and tender was in its way remarkable. "We're representative, you know, of Mr. Farange and his former wife. This person represents mere illiterate presumption. We take our stand on the law."

"Oh the law, the law!" Mrs. Wix superbly jeered. "You had better indeed let the law have a look at you!"

"Let them pass—let them pass!" Sir Claude pressed his friend—he pleaded.

But she fastened herself still to Maisie. "*Do* you hate me, dearest?"

Maisie looked at her with new eyes, but answered as she had answered before. "Will you give him up?"

Mrs. Beale's rejoinder hung fire, but when it came it was noble. "You shouldn't talk to me of such things!" She was shocked, she was scandalised to tears.

For Mrs. Wix, however, it was her discrimination that was indelicate. "You ought to be ashamed of yourself!" she roundly cried.

Sir Claude made a supreme appeal. "Will you be so good as to allow these horrors to terminate?"

Mrs. Beale fixed her eyes on him, and again Maisie watched them. "You should do him justice," Mrs. Wix went on to Mrs. Beale. "We've always been devoted to him, Maisie and I —and he has shown how much he likes us. He would like to please her; he would like even, I think, to please me. But he hasn't given you up."

They stood confronted, the step-parents, still under Maisie's observation. That observation had never sunk so deep as at this particular moment. "Yes, my dear, I haven't given you up," Sir Claude said to Mrs. Beale at last, "and if you'd like me to treat our friends here as solemn witnesses I don't mind giving you my word for it that I never, never will. There!" he dauntlessly exclaimed.

"He can't!" Mrs. Wix tragically commented.

Mrs. Beale, erect and alive in her defeat, jerked her handsome face about. "He can't!" she literally mocked.

"He can't, he can't, he can't!" Sir Claude's gay emphasis wonderfully carried it off.

Mrs. Beale took it all in, yet she held her ground; on which Maisie addressed Mrs. Wix. "Shan't we lose the boat?"

"Yes, we shall lose the boat," Mrs. Wix remarked to Sir Claude.

Mrs. Beale meanwhile faced full at Maisie. "I don't know what to make of you!" she launched.

"Good-bye," said Maisie to Sir Claude.

"Good-bye, Maisie," Sir Claude answered.

Mrs. Beale came away from the door. "Good-bye!" she hurled at Maisie; then passed straight across the room and disappeared in the adjoining one.

Sir Claude had reached the other door and opened it. Mrs. Wix was already out. On the threshold Maisie paused; she put out her hand to her stepfather. He took it and held it a moment, and their eyes met as the eyes of those who have done for each other what they can. "Good-bye," he repeated.

"Good-bye." And Maisie followed Mrs. Wix.

They caught the steamer, which was just putting off, and, hustled across the gulf, found themselves on the deck so breathless and so scared that they gave up half the voyage to letting their emotion sink. It sank slowly and imperfectly; but at last, in mid-channel, surrounded by the quiet sea, Mrs. Wix had courage to revert. "I didn't look back, did you?"

"Yes. He wasn't there," said Maisie.

"Not on the balcony?"

Maisie waited a moment; then, "He wasn't there," she simply said again.

Mrs. Wix also was silent awhile. "He went to *her*," she finally observed.

"Oh, I know!" the child replied.

Mrs. Wix gave a sidelong look. She still had room for wonder at what Maisie knew.

THE AWKWARD AGE

Contents

BOOK FIRST

Lady Julia

I

SAVE when it happened to rain Vanderbank always walked home, but he usually took a hansom when the rain was moderate and adopted the preference of the philosopher when it was heavy. On this occasion he therefore recognised, as the servant opened the door, a congruity between the weather and the "four-wheeler" that, in the empty street, under the glazed radiance, waited and trickled and blackly glittered. The butler mentioned it as, on such a wild night, the only thing they could get, and Vanderbank, having replied that it was exactly what would do best, prepared, in the doorway, to put up his umbrella and dash down to it. At this moment he heard his name pronounced from behind, and, on turning, found himself joined by the elderly fellow-guest with whom he had talked after dinner and about whom, later on, upstairs, he had sounded his hostess. It was at present a clear question of how this amiable, this apparently unassertive person should get home—of the possibility of the other cab for which even now one of the footmen, with a whistle to his lips, craned out his head and listened through the storm. Mr. Longdon wondered, to Vanderbank, if their course might by any chance be the same; which led our young friend immediately to express a readiness to see him safely in any direction that should accommodate him. As the footman's whistle spent itself in vain they got together into the four-wheeler, where, at the end of a few moments more, Vanderbank became conscious of having proposed his own rooms as a wind-up to their drive. Wouldn't that be a better finish of the evening than just separating in the wet? He liked his new acquaintance, who struck him as in a manner clinging to him, who was staying at an hotel presumably at that hour dismal, and who, confessing with easy humility to a connection positively timid with a club at which one couldn't have a visitor, accepted, under pressure, his invitation. Vanderbank, when they arrived, was amused at the air of added extravagance with which he said he would keep the cab: he so clearly enjoyed to that extent the sense of making a night of it.

"You young men, I believe, keep them for hours, eh? At least they did in my time," he laughed—"the wild ones! But I think of them as all wild then. I dare say that when one settles in town one learns how to manage; only I'm afraid, you know, that I've got completely out of it. I do feel really quite mouldy. It's a matter of thirty years——"

"Since you've been in London?"

"For more than a few days at a time, upon my honour. You won't understand that—any more, I dare say, than I myself quite understand how, at the end of all, I've accepted this queer view of the doom of coming back. But I don't doubt I shall ask you, if you'll be so good as to let me, for the help of a hint or two: as to how to do, don't you know? and not to —what do you fellows call it?—*be* done. Now about one of *these* things——"

One of these things was the lift in which, at no great pace and with much rumbling and creaking, the porter conveyed the two gentlemen to the alarming eminence, as Mr. Longdon measured their flight, at which Vanderbank perched. The impression made on him by this contrivance showed him as unsophisticated, yet when his companion, at the top, ushering him in, gave a touch to the quick light and, in the pleasant, ruddy room, all convenience and character, had before the fire another look at him, it was not to catch in him any protrusive angle. Mr. Longdon was slight and neat, delicate of body and both keen and kind of face, with black brows finely marked and thick, smooth hair in which the silver had deep shadows. He wore neither whisker nor moustache and seemed to carry in the flicker of his quick brown eyes and the positive sun-play of his smile even more than the equivalent of what might, superficially or stupidly, elsewhere be missed in him; which was mass, substance, presence—what is vulgarly called importance. He had indeed no presence, but he had somehow an effect. He might almost have been a priest, if priests, as it occurred to Vanderbank, were ever such dandies. He had at all events conclusively doubled the Cape of the years—he would never again see fifty-five: to the warning light of that bleak headland he presented a back sufficiently conscious. Yet, though, to Vanderbank, he could not look young, he came near—strikingly and amusingly—looking new: this, after a minute, appeared mainly perhaps indeed in the perfection of his evening dress and the special smartness of the sleeveless overcoat he had evidently had made to wear with it and might even actually be wearing for the first time. He had talked to Vanderbank at Mrs. Brookenham's about Beccles and Suffolk; but it was not at Beccles, nor anywhere in the county, that these ornaments had been designed. His action had already been, with however little purpose, to present the region to his interlocutor in a favourable light. Vanderbank, for that matter, had the kind of imagination that liked to place an object, even to the point of losing sight of it in the conditions; he already saw the nice old nook it must have taken to keep a man of intelligence so fresh while suffering him to remain so fine. The product of Beccles accepted at all events a cigarette—still much as a joke and an adventure—and looked about him as if even more pleased than he had expected. Then he broke, through his double eye-glass, into an exclamation that was like a passing pang of envy and regret. "You young men, you young men——!"

"Well, what about us?" Vanderbank's tone encouraged the courtesy of the reference. "I'm not so young, moreover, as that comes to."

"How old are you then, pray?"

"Why, I'm thirty-four."

"What do you call that? I'm a hundred and three!" Mr. Longdon took out his watch. "It's only a quarter past eleven." Then with a quick change of interest, "What did you say is your public office?" he inquired.

"The General Audit. I'm Deputy Chairman."

"Dear!" Mr. Longdon looked at him as if he had had fifty windows. "What a head you must have!"

"Oh yes—our head's Sir Digby Dence."

"And what do we do for you?"

"Well, you gild the pill—though not perhaps very thick. But it's a decent berth."

"A thing a good many fellows would give a pound of their flesh for?"

The old man appeared so to deprecate too faint a picture that his companion dropped all scruples. "I'm the most envied man I know—so that if I were a shade less amiable I should be one of the most hated."

Mr. Longdon laughed, yet not quite as if they were joking. "I see. Your pleasant way carries it off."

Vanderbank was, however, not serious. "Wouldn't it carry off anything?"

Again his visitor, through the *pince-nez*, appeared to crown him with a Whitehall cornice. "I think I ought to let you know I'm studying you. It's really fair to tell you," he continued, with an earnestness not discomposed by the indulgence in Vanderbank's face. "It's all right—all right!" he reassuringly added, having meanwhile stopped before a photograph suspended on the wall. "That's your mother!" he exclaimed with something of the elation of a child making a discovery or guessing a riddle. "I don't make you out in her yet—in my recollection of her, which, as I told you, is perfect; but I dare say I soon shall."

Vanderbank was more and more aware that the kind of hilarity he excited would never in the least be a bar to affection. "Please take all your time."

Mr. Longdon looked at his watch again. "Do you think I *had* better keep it?"

"The cab?" Vanderbank liked him so, found in him such a promise of pleasant things, that he was almost tempted to say: "Dear and delightful sir, don't weigh that question; I'll pay, myself, for the man's whole night!" His approval at all events was complete. "Most certainly. That's the only way not to think of it."

"Oh, you young men, you young men!" his guest again murmured. He had passed on to the photograph—Vanderbank had many, too many photographs—of some other relation, and stood wiping the gold-mounted glasses through which he had been darting admirations and catching sidelights of shocks. "Don't talk nonsense," he continued as his friend attempted once more to throw in a protest; "I belong to a different period of history. There have been things this evening that have made me feel as if I had been disinterred—

literally dug up from a long sleep. I assure you there have!"
—he really pressed the point.

Vanderbank wondered a moment what things in particular
these might be; he found himself wanting to get at everything
his visitor represented, to enter into his consciousness and be,
as it were, on his side. He glanced, with an intention freely
sarcastic, at an easy possibility. "The extraordinary vitality of
Brookenham?"

Mr. Longdon, with the nippers in place again, fixed on him
a gravity that failed to prevent his discovering in the eyes behind them a shy reflection of his irony. "Oh, Brookenham!
You must tell me all about Brookenham."

"I see that's not what you mean."

Mr. Longdon forbore to deny it. "I wonder if you'll understand what I mean." Vanderbank bristled with the wish to
be put to the test, but was checked before he could say so.
"And what's *his* place—Brookenham's?"

"Oh, Rivers and Lakes—an awfully good thing. He got it
last year."

Mr. Longdon—but not too grossly—wondered. "How did
he get it?"

Vanderbank laughed. "Well, *she* got it."

His friend remained grave. "And about how much now——?"

"Oh, twelve hundred—and lots of allowances and boats
and things. To do the work!" Vanderbank, still with a certain
levity, exclaimed.

"And what *is* the work?"

The young man hesitated. "Ask *him*. He'll like to tell you."

"Yet he seemed to have but little to say." Mr. Longdon exactly measured it again.

"Ah, not about that. Try him."

He looked more sharply at his host, as if vaguely suspicious
of a trap; then, not less vaguely, he sighed. "Well, it's what I
came up for—to try you all. But do they live on that?" he
continued.

Vanderbank once more just faltered. "One doesn't quite
know what they live on. But they've means—for it was just
that fact, I remember, that showed Brookenham's getting the
place wasn't a job. It was given, I mean, not to his mere

domestic need, but to his notorious efficiency. He has a property—an ugly little place in Gloucestershire—which they
sometimes let. His elder brother has the better one, but they
make up an income."

Mr. Longdon, for an instant, lost himself. "Yes, I remember—one heard of those things at the time. And *she* must have
had something."

"Yes indeed, she had something—and she always has her
intense cleverness. She knows thoroughly how. They do it
tremendously well."

"Tremendously well," Mr. Longdon intelligently echoed.
"But a house in Buckingham Crescent, with the way they
seem to have built through to all sorts of other places——"

"Oh, they're all right," Vanderbank soothingly dropped.

"One likes to feel that of people with whom one has dined.
There are four children?" his friend went on.

"The older boy, whom you saw and who, in his way, is a
wonder, the older girl, whom you must see, and two youngsters, male and female, whom you mustn't."

There might by this time, in the growing interest of their
talk, have been almost nothing too uncanny for Mr. Longdon
to fear it. "You mean the youngsters are—unfortunate?"

"No—they're only, like all the modern young, I think,
mysteries, terrible little baffling mysteries." Vanderbank had
broken into mirth again—it flickered so from his friend's face
that, really at moments to the point of alarm, his explanations deepened darkness. Then with more interest he harked
back. "I know the thing you just mentioned—the thing that
strikes you as odd." He produced his knowledge quite with
elation. "The talk." Mr. Longdon, on this, only looked at
him, in silence, harder, but he went on with assurance: "Yes,
the talk—for we do talk, I think." Still his guest left him
without relief, only fixing him, on his suggestion, with a sort
of suspended eloquence. Whatever the old man was on the
point of saying, however, he disposed of in a curtailed murmur; he had already turned afresh to the series of portraits,
and as he glanced at another Vanderbank spoke afresh. "It
was very interesting to me to hear from you there, when the
ladies had left us, how many old threads you were prepared
to pick up."

Mr. Longdon had paused. "I'm an old boy who remembers the mothers," he at last replied.

"Yes, you told me how well you remember Mrs. Brookenham's."

"Oh, oh!"—and he arrived at a new subject. "This must be your sister Mary."

"Yes; it's very bad, but as she's dead——"

"Dead? Dear, dear!"

"Oh, long ago"—Vanderbank eased him off. "It's delightful of you," he went on, "to have known also such a lot of *my* people."

Mr. Longdon turned from his contemplation with a visible effort. "I feel obliged to you for taking it so; it mightn't—one never knows—have amused you. As I told you there, the first thing I did was to ask Fernanda about the company; and when she mentioned your name I immediately said, 'Would he like me to speak to him?'"

"And what did Fernanda say?"

Mr. Longdon stared. "Do *you* call her Fernanda?"

Vanderbank felt positively more guilty than he would have expected. "You think it too much in the manner we just mentioned?"

His friend hesitated; then with a smile a trifle strange: "Excuse me; *I* didn't mention——"

"No, you didn't; and your scruple was magnificent. In point of fact," Vanderbank pursued, "I *don't* call Mrs. Brookenham by her Christian name."

Mr. Longdon's clear eyes were searching. "Unless in speaking of her to others?" He seemed really to wish to know.

Vanderbank was but too ready to satisfy him. "I dare say we seem to you a vulgar lot of people. That's not the way, I can see, you speak of ladies at Beccles."

"Oh, if you laugh at me!" And the old man turned off.

"Don't threaten me," said Vanderbank, "or I *will* send away the cab. Of course I know what you mean. It will be tremendously interesting to hear how the sort of thing we've fallen into—oh, we *have* fallen in!—strikes your fresh ear. Do have another cigarette. Sunk as I must appear to you, it sometimes strikes mine. But I'm not sure as regards Mrs. Brookenham, whom I've known a long time."

Mr. Longdon again took him up. "What do you people call a long time?"

Vanderbank considered. "Ah, there you are! And now we're 'we people'! That's right; give it to us. I'm sure that in one way or another it's all earned. Well, I've known her ten years. But awfully well."

"What do you call awfully well?"

"We people?" Vanderbank's inquirer, with his continued restless observation, moving nearer, the young man had laid on his shoulder the most considerate of hands. "Don't you perhaps ask too much? But no," he added, quickly and gaily, "of course you don't: if I don't look out I shall have, on you, exactly the effect I don't want. I dare say I don't know *how* well I know Mrs. Brookenham. Mustn't that sort of thing be put, in a manner, to the proof? What I meant to say just now was that I wouldn't—at least I hope I shouldn't—have named her as I did save to an old friend."

Mr. Longdon looked promptly satisfied and reassured. "You probably heard me address her myself."

"I did, but you have your rights, and that wouldn't excuse me. The only thing is that I go to see her every Sunday."

Mr. Longdon pondered; then, a little to Vanderbank's surprise, at any rate to his deeper amusement, candidly asked: "Only Fernanda? No other lady?"

"Oh yes, several other ladies."

Mr. Longdon appeared to hear this with pleasure. "You're quite right. We don't make enough of Sunday at Beccles."

"Oh, we make plenty of it in London!" Vanderbank said. "And I think it's rather in my interest I should mention that Mrs. Brookenham calls *me*——"

His visitor covered him now with an attention that just operated as a check. "By your Christian name?" Before Vanderbank could in any degree attenuate, "What *is* your Christian name?" Mr. Longdon asked.

Vanderbank felt of a sudden almost guilty—as if his answer could only impute extravagance to the lady. "My Christian name"—he blushed it out—"is Gustavus."

His friend took a droll, conscious leap. "And she calls you Gussy?"

"No, not even Gussy. But I scarcely think I ought to tell

you," he pursued, "if she herself gave you no glimpse of the fact. Any implication that she consciously avoided it might make you see deeper depths."

Vanderbank spoke with pointed levity, but his companion showed him after an instant a face just covered—and a little painfully—with the vision of the possibility brushed away by the joke. "Oh, I'm not so bad as that!" Mr. Longdon modestly ejaculated.

"Well, she doesn't do it always," Vanderbank laughed, "and it's nothing, moreover, to what some people are called. Why, there was a fellow there——" He pulled up, however, and, thinking better of it, selected another instance. "The Duchess —weren't you introduced to the Duchess?—never calls me anything but 'Vanderbank' unless she calls me '*caro mio.*' It wouldn't have taken much to make her appeal to *you* with an 'I say, Longdon!' I can quite hear her."

Mr. Longdon, focussing the effect of the sketch, pointed its moral with an indulgent: "Oh well, a *foreign* duchess!" He could make his distinctions.

"Yes, she's invidiously, cruelly foreign," Vanderbank concurred: "I've never indeed seen a woman avail herself so cleverly, to make up for the obloquy of that state, of the benefits and immunities it brings with it. She has bloomed in the hothouse of her widowhood—she's a Neapolitan hatched by an incubator."

"A Neapolitan?"—Mr. Longdon, civilly, seemed to wish he had only known it.

"Her husband was one; but I believe that dukes at Naples are as thick as princes at Petersburg. He's dead, at any rate, poor man, and she has come back here to live."

"Gloomily, I should think—after Naples?" Mr. Longdon threw out.

"Oh, it would take more than even a Neapolitan past——! However," the young man added, catching himself up, "she lives not in what is behind her, but in what is before—she lives in her precious little Aggie."

"Little Aggie?" Mr. Longdon took a cautious interest.

"I don't take a liberty there," Vanderbank smiled. "I speak only of the young Agnesina, a little girl, the Duchess's niece, or rather, I believe, her husband's, whom she has adopted—

in the place of a daughter early lost—and has brought to England to marry."

"Ah, to some great man, of course."

Vanderbank thought. "I don't know." He gave a vague but expressive sigh. "She's rather lovely, little Aggie."

Mr. Longdon looked conspicuously subtle. "Then perhaps *you're* the man——"

"Do I look like a great one?" Vanderbank broke in.

His visitor, turning away from him, again embraced the room. "Oh dear, yes!"

"Well then, to show how right you are, there's the young lady." He pointed to an object on one of the tables, a small photograph with a very wide border of something that looked like crimson fur.

Mr. Longdon took up the picture; he was serious now. "She's very beautiful—but she's not a little girl."

"At Naples they develop early. She's only seventeen or eighteen, I suppose; but I never know how old—or at least how young—girls are, and I'm not sure. An aunt, at any rate, has of course nothing to conceal. She *is* extremely pretty—with extraordinary red hair and a complexion to match; great rarities, I believe, in that race and latitude. She gave me the portrait—frame and all. The frame is Neapolitan enough, and little Aggie is charming." Then Vanderbank subjoined: "But not so charming as little Nanda."

"Little Nanda?—have you got *her?*" The old man was all eagerness.

"She's over there beside the lamp—also a present from the original."

II

Mr. Longdon had gone to the place—little Nanda was in glazed white wood. He took her up and held her out; for a moment he said nothing, but presently, over his glasses, rested on his host a look intenser even than his scrutiny of the faded image. "Do they give their portraits now?"

"Little girls—innocent lambs? Surely, to old friends. Didn't they in your time?"

Mr. Longdon studied the portrait again; after which, with

an exhalation of something between superiority and regret, "They never did to me," he replied.

"Well, you can have all you want now!" Vanderbank laughed.

His friend gave a slow, droll head-shake. "I don't want them 'now'!"

"You could do with them, my dear sir, still," Vanderbank continued in the same manner, "every bit *I* do!"

"I'm sure you do nothing you oughtn't." Mr. Longdon kept the photograph and continued to look at it. "Her mother told me about her—promised me I should see her next time."

"You must—she's a great friend of mine."

Mr. Longdon remained absorbed. "Is she clever?"

Vanderbank turned it over. "Well, you'll tell me if you think so."

"Ah, with a child of seventeen——!" Mr. Longdon murmured it as if in dread of having to pronounce. "This one, too, *is* seventeen?"

Vanderbank again considered. "Eighteen." He just hung fire once more, then brought out: "Well, call it nearly nineteen. I've kept her birthdays," he laughed.

His companion caught at the idea. "Upon my honour, *I* should like to! When is the next?"

"You've plenty of time—the fifteenth of June."

"I'm only too sorry to wait." Laying down the object he had been examining, Mr. Longdon took another turn about the room, and his manner was such an appeal to his host to accept his restlessness that, from the corner of a lounge, the latter watched him with encouragement. "I said to you just now that I knew the mothers, but it would have been more to the point to say the grandmothers." He stopped before the lounge, then nodded at the image of Nanda. "I knew *hers*. She put it at something less."

Vanderbank rather failed to understand. "The old lady? Put what?"

Mr. Longdon's face, for a moment, showed him as feeling his way. "I'm speaking of Mrs. Brookenham. She spoke of her daughter as only sixteen."

His companion's amusement at the tone of this broke out.

"She usually does! She has done so, I think, for the last year or two."

Mr. Longdon dropped upon the lounge as if with the weight of something sudden and fresh; then, from where he sat, with a sharp little movement, tossed into the fire the end of his cigarette. Vanderbank offered him another, a second, and as he accepted it and took a light he said: "I don't know what you're doing with me—I never, at home, smoke so much!" But he puffed away, and, seated so near him, laid his hand on Vanderbank's arm as if to help himself to utter something that was too delicate not to be guarded and yet too important not to be risked. "Now that's the sort of thing I did mean—as one of my impressions." Vanderbank continued at a loss, and he went on: "I refer—if you don't mind my saying so—to what you said just now."

Vanderbank was conscious of a deep desire to draw from him whatever might come; so sensible was it somehow that whatever in him was good was also thoroughly personal. But our young friend had to think a minute. "I see, I see. Nothing is more probable than that I've said something nasty; but which of my particular horrors?"

"Well, then, your conveying that she makes her daughter out younger——"

"To make herself out the same?" Vanderbank took him straight up. "It was nasty my doing that? I see, I see. Yes, yes: I rather gave her away, and you're struck by it—as is most delightful you *should* be—because you're, in every way, of a better tradition, and, knowing Mrs. Brookenham's my friend, can't conceive of one's playing on a friend a trick so vulgar and odious. It strikes you also probably as the kind of thing we must be constantly doing; it strikes you that right and left, probably, we keep giving each other away. Well, I dare say we do. Yes, 'come to think of it,' as they say in America, we do. But what shall I tell you? Practically we all know it and allow for it, and it's as broad as it's long. What's London life after all? It's tit for tat!"

"Ah, but what becomes of friendship?" Mr. Longdon earnestly and pleadingly asked, while he still held Vanderbank's arm as if under the spell of the vivid explanation with which he had been furnished.

The young man met his eyes only the more sociably. "Friendship?"

"Friendship." Mr. Longdon maintained the full value of the word.

"Well," his companion risked, "I daresay it isn't in London by any means what it is at Beccles. I quite literally mean that," Vanderbank reassuringly added; "I never really have believed in the existence of friendship in big societies—in great towns and great crowds. It's a plant that takes time and space and air; and London society is a huge 'squash,' as we elegantly call it—an elbowing, pushing, perspiring, chattering mob."

"Ah, I don't say *that* of you!" Mr. Longdon murmured with a withdrawal of his hand and a visible scruple for the sweeping concession he had evoked.

"Do say it, then—for God's sake; let some one say it, so that something or other, whatever it may be, may come of it! It's impossible to say too much—it's impossible to say enough. There isn't anything any one can say that I won't agree to."

"That shows you really don't care," the old man returned with acuteness.

"Oh, we're past saving, if that's what you mean!" Vanderbank laughed.

"You don't care, you don't care!" his visitor repeated, "and —if I may be frank with you—I shouldn't wonder if it were rather a pity."

"A pity I don't care?"

"You ought to, you ought to." Mr. Longdon paused. "May I say all I think?"

"I assure you *I* shall! You're awfully interesting."

"So are you, if you come to that. It's just what I've had in my head. There's something I seem to make out in you——!" He abruptly dropped this, however, going on in another way. "I remember the rest of you, but why did I never see *you?*"

"I must have been at school—at college. Perhaps you did know my brothers, elder and younger."

"There was a boy with your mother at Malvern. I was near her there for three months in—what *was* the year?"

"Yes, I know," Vanderbank replied while his guest tried to

fix the date. "It was my brother Miles. He was awfully clever, but he had no health, poor chap, and we lost him at seventeen. She used to take houses at such places with him—it was supposed to be for his benefit."

Mr. Longdon listened with a visible recovery. "He used to talk to me—I remember he asked me questions I couldn't answer and made me dreadfully ashamed. But I lent him books —partly, upon my honour, to make him think that, as I had them, I did know something. He read everything and had a lot to say about it. I used to tell your mother he had a great future."

Vanderbank shook his head sadly and kindly. "So he had. And you remember Nancy, who was handsome and who was usually with them?" he went on.

Mr. Longdon looked so uncertain that he explained he meant his other sister; on which his companion said: "Oh, her? Yes, she was charming—she evidently had a future too."

"Well, she's in the midst of it now. She's married."

"And whom did she marry?"

"A fellow called Toovey. A man in the City."

"Oh!" said Mr. Longdon a little blankly. Then as if to retrieve his blankness: "But why do you call her Nancy? Wasn't her name Blanche?"

"Exactly—Blanche Bertha Vanderbank."

Mr. Longdon looked half mystified and half distressed. "And now she's Nancy Toovey?"

Vanderbank broke into laughter at his dismay. "That's what every one calls her."

"But why?"

"Nobody knows. You see you were right about her future."

Mr. Longdon gave another of his soft, smothered sighs; he had turned back again to the first photograph, which he looked at for a longer time. "Well, it wasn't *her* way."

"My mother's? No, indeed. Oh, my mother's way!" Vanderbank waited, then added gravely: "She was taken in time."

Mr. Longdon turned half round and looked as if he were about to reply to this; but instead of so doing he proceeded afresh to an examination of the expressive oval in the red plush frame. He took up little Aggie, who appeared to interest him, and abruptly observed: "Nanda isn't so pretty."

"No, not nearly. There's a great question whether Nanda is pretty at all."

Mr. Longdon continued to inspect her more favoured friend; which led him after a moment to bring out: "She ought to be, you know. Her grandmother was."

"Oh, and her mother," Vanderbank threw in. "Don't you think Mrs. Brookenham lovely?"

Mr. Longdon kept him waiting a little. "Not so lovely as Lady Julia. Lady Julia had——" He faltered; then, as if there were too much to say, disposed of the question. "Lady Julia had everything."

Vanderbank gathered from the sound of the words an impression that determined him more and more to diplomacy. "But isn't that just what Mrs. Brookenham has?"

This time the old man was prompt. "Yes, she's very brilliant, but it's a totally different thing." He laid little Aggie down and moved away as if without a purpose; but Vanderbank presently perceived his purpose to be another glance at the other young lady. As if accidentally and absently, he bent again over the portrait of Nanda. "Lady Julia was exquisite, and this child's exactly like her."

Vanderbank, more and more conscious of something working in him, was more and more interested. "If Nanda's so like her, *was* she so exquisite?" he hazarded.

"Oh yes; every one was agreed about that." Mr. Longdon kept his eyes on the face, trying a little, Vanderbank even thought, to conceal his own. "She was one of the greatest beauties of her day."

"Then *is* Nanda so like her?" Vanderbank persisted, amused at his friend's transparency.

"Extraordinarily. Her mother told me all about her."

"Told you she's as beautiful as her grandmother?"

Mr. Longdon turned it over. "Well, that she has just Lady Julia's expression. She absolutely *has* it—I see it here." He was delightfully positive. "She's much more like the dead than like the living."

Vanderbank saw in this too many deep things not to follow them up. One of these was, to begin with, that his friend had not more than half succumbed to Mrs. Brookenham's attraction, if indeed, by a fine originality, he had not resisted it altogether. That in itself, for an observer deeply versed in this lady, was delightful and beguiling. Another indication was that he found himself, in spite of such a break in the chain, distinctly predisposed to Nanda. "If she reproduces then so vividly Lady Julia," the young man threw out, "why does she strike you as so much less pretty than her foreign friend there, who is after all by no means a prodigy?"

The subject of this address, with one of the photographs in his hand, glanced, while he reflected, at the other. Then with a subtlety that matched itself for the moment with Vanderbank's: "You just told me yourself that the little foreign person——"

"Is ever so much the lovelier of the two? So I did. But you've promptly recognised it. It's the first time," Vanderbank went on, to let him down more gently, "that I've heard Mrs. Brookenham admit the girl's looks."

"Her own girl's? 'Admit' them?"

"I mean grant them to be even as good as they are. I myself, I must tell you, extremely like them. I think Lady Julia's granddaughter has in her face, in spite of everything——"

"What do you mean by everything?" Mr. Longdon broke in with such an approach to resentment that his host's amusement overflowed.

"You'll see—when you do see. She has no features. No, not one," Vanderbank inexorably pursued; "unless indeed you put it that she has two or three too many. What I was going to say was that she has in her expression all that's charming in her nature. But beauty, in London"—and, feeling that he held his visitor's attention, he gave himself the pleasure of freely unfolding his idea—"staring, glaring, obvious, knock-down beauty, as plain as a poster on a wall, an advertisement of soap or whisky, something that speaks to the crowd and crosses the footlights, fetches such a price in the market that the absence of it, for a woman with a girl to marry, inspires endless terrors and constitutes for the wretched pair—to speak of mother and daughter alone—a sort of social bankruptcy. London doesn't love the latent or the lurking, has neither time, nor taste, nor sense for anything less discernible than the red flag in front of the steam-roller. It wants cash over the counter and letters ten feet high. Therefore, you see, it's all as yet rather a dark question for poor Nanda—a question that, in a way, quite occupies the foreground of her mother's earnest little life. How *will* she look, what will be thought of her and what will she be able to do for herself? She's at the age when the whole thing—speaking of her appearance, her possible share of good looks—is still, in a manner, in a fog. But everything depends on it."

Mr. Longdon, by this time, had come back to him. "Excuse my asking it again—for you take such jumps: what, once more, do you mean by everything?"

"Why, naturally, her marrying. Above all her marrying early."

Mr. Longdon stood before the sofa. "What do you mean by early?"

"Well, we do doubtless get up later than at Beccles; but that gives us, you see, shorter days. I mean in a couple of seasons. Soon enough," Vanderbank developed, "to limit the strain——" He broke down, in gaiety, at his friend's expression.

"What do you mean by the strain?"

"Well, the complication of her being there."

"Being where?"

"You do put one through!" Vanderbank laughed. But he showed himself perfectly prepared. "Out of the school-room, where she is now. In her mother's drawing-room. At her mother's fireside."

Mr. Longdon stared. "But where else should she be?"

"At her husband's, don't you see?"

Mr. Longdon looked as if he quite saw, yet he was nevertheless, as regards his original challenge, not to be put off. "Ah, certainly," he replied with a slight stiffness, "but not as if she had been pushed down the chimney. All in good time."

Vanderbank turned the tables on him. "What do you call good time?"

"Why, time to make herself loved."

Vanderbank wondered. "By the men who come to the house?"

Mr. Longdon slightly attenuated this way of putting it.

"Yes—and in the home circle. Where's the 'strain'—of her being suffered to be a member of it?"

III

Vanderbank, at this, left his corner of the sofa and, with his hands in his pockets and a manner so amused that it might have passed for excited, took several paces about the room while his interlocutor, watching him, waited for his response. The old man, as this response for a minute hung fire, took his turn at sitting down, and then Vanderbank stopped before him with a face in which something had been still more brightly kindled. "You ask me more things than I can tell you. You ask me more than I think you suspect. You must come and see me again—you must let me come and see you. You raise the most interesting questions, and we must sooner or later have them all out."

Mr. Longdon looked happy in such a prospect, but he once more took out his watch. "It wants five minutes to midnight. Which means that I must go now."

"Not in the least. There are satisfactions you too must give." Vanderbank, with an irresistible hand, confirmed him in his position and pressed upon him another cigarette. His resistance rang hollow—it was clearly, he judged, such an occasion for sacrifices. His companion's view of it meanwhile was quite as marked. "You see there's ever so much more you must in common kindness tell me."

Mr. Longdon sat there like a shy singer invited to strike up. "I told you everything at Mrs. Brookenham's. It comes over me now how I dropped on you."

"What you told me," Vanderbank returned, "was excellent so far as it went; but it was only after all that, having caught my name, you had asked of our friend if I belonged to people you had known years before, and then, from what she had said, had, with what you were so good as to call great pleasure, made out that I did. You came round to me, on this, after dinner, and gave me a pleasure still greater. But that only takes us part of the way." Mr. Longdon said nothing, but there was something appreciative in his conscious lapses; they were a tribute to his young friend's frequent felicity. This personage indeed appeared more and more to take them for that; which was not without its effect upon his spirits. At last, with a flight of some freedom, he brought their pause to a close. "You loved Lady Julia." Then as the attitude of his guest, who serenely met his eyes, was practically a contribution to the subject, he went on with a feeling that he had positively pleased. "You lost her, and you're unmarried."

Mr. Longdon's smile was beautiful—it supplied so many meanings that when presently he spoke he seemed already to have told half his story. "Well, my life took a form. It had to, or I don't know what would have become of me, and several things that all happened at once helped me out. My father died—I came into the little place in Suffolk. My sister, my only one, who had married and was older than I, lost within a year or two both her husband and her little boy. I offered her, in the country, a home, for her trouble was greater than any trouble of mine. She came, she stayed; it went on and on, and we lived there together. We were sorry for each other, and it somehow suited us. But she died two years ago."

Vanderbank took all this in, only wishing to show—wishing by this time quite tenderly—that he even read into it deeply enough all the unsaid. He filled out another of his friend's gaps. "And here you are." Then he invited Mr. Longdon himself to make the stride. "Well, you'll be a great success."

"What do you mean by that?"

"Why, that we shall be so infatuated with you that it will make your life a burden to you. You'll see soon enough what I mean by it."

"Possibly," the old man said; "to understand you I shall have to. You speak of something that, as yet—with my race practically run—I know nothing about. I was no success as a young man. I mean of the sort that would have made most difference. People wouldn't look at me."

"Well, *we* shall look at you," Vanderbank declared. Then he added: "What people do you mean?" And before his friend could reply: "Lady Julia?"

Mr. Longdon's assent was mute. "Ah, she was not the worst! I mean that what made it so bad," he continued, "was that they all really liked me. Your mother, I think—as to *that*, the dreadful, consolatory 'liking'—even more than the others."

"My mother?"—Vanderbank was surprised. "You mean there was a question——?"

"Oh, but for half a minute. It didn't take her long. It was five years after your father's death." This explanation was very delicately made. "She *could* marry again."

"And I suppose you know she did," Vanderbank replied.

"I knew it soon enough!" With this, abruptly, Mr. Longdon pulled himself forward. "Good-night, good-night."

"Good-night," said Vanderbank. "But wasn't that *after* Lady Julia?"

On the edge of the sofa, his hands supporting him, Mr. Longdon looked straight. "There was nothing after Lady Julia."

"I see." His companion smiled. "My mother was earlier."

"She was extremely good to me. I'm not speaking of that time at Malvern—that came later."

"Precisely—I understand. You're speaking of the first years of her widowhood."

Mr. Longdon just faltered. "I should call them rather the last. Six months later came her second marriage."

Vanderbank's interest visibly improved. "Ah, it was *then*? That was my seventh year." He called things back and pieced them together. "But she must have been older than you."

"Yes—a little. She was kindness itself to me, at all events, then and afterwards. That was the charm of the weeks at Malvern."

"I see," the young man laughed. "The charm was that you had recovered."

"Oh dear, no!" Mr. Longdon, rather to his mystification, exclaimed. "I'm afraid I hadn't recovered at all—hadn't, if that's what you mean, got over my misery and my melancholy. She knew I hadn't—and that was what was nice of her. She was a person with whom I could talk about her."

Vanderbank took a moment to clear up the ambiguity. "Oh, you mean you could talk about the *other*! You hadn't got over Lady Julia."

Mr. Longdon sadly smiled at him. "I haven't got over her yet!" Then, however, as if not to look too woeful, he took pains to be lucid. "The first wound was bad—but from that one always comes round. Your mother, dear woman, had known how to help me. Lady Julia was at that time her intimate friend—it was she who introduced me there. She couldn't help what happened—she did her best. What I meant just now was that, in the aftertime, when opportunity occurred, she was the one person with whom I could always talk and who always understood." Mr. Longdon appeared to lose himself an instant in the deep memories to which alone he now survived to testify; then he sighed out as if the taste of it all came back to him with a faint sweetness: "I think they must both have been good to me. At the period at Malvern—the particular time I just mentioned to you—Lady Julia was already married, and during those first years she was whirled out of my ken. Then her own life took a quieter turn; we met again; I went, for a long time, often to her house. I think she rather liked the state to which she had reduced me, though she didn't, you know, in the least presume upon it. The better a woman is—it has often struck me—the more she enjoys, in a quiet way, some fellow's having been rather bad, rather dark and desperate, about her—for her. I dare say, I mean, that, though Lady Julia insisted I ought to marry, she wouldn't really have liked it much if I had. At any rate it was in those years that I saw her daughter just cease to be a child —the little girl who was to be transformed by time into the so different person with whom we dined to-night. That comes back to me when I hear you speak of the growing up, in turn, of that person's own daughter."

"I follow you with a sympathy!" Vanderbank replied. "The situation's reproduced."

"Ah, partly—not altogether. The things that are unlike—well, are so *very* unlike." Mr. Longdon for a moment, on this, fixed his companion with eyes that betrayed one of the restless little jumps of his mind. "I told you just now that there's something I seem to make out in you."

"Yes, that was meant for better things?"—Vanderbank gaily took him up. "There *is* something, I really believe—meant for ever so much better ones. Those are just the sort I like to be supposed to have a real affinity with. Help me to them, Mr. Longdon; help me to them, and I don't know what I won't do for you!"

"Then, after all"—and the old man made his point with innocent sharpness—"you're *not* past saving!"

"Well, I individually—how shall I put it to you? If I tell you," Vanderbank went on, "that I've that sort of fulcrum for salvation which consists at least in a deep consciousness and the absence of a rag of illusion, I shall appear to say that I'm different from the world I live in and to that extent present myself as superior and fatuous. Try me at any rate. Let me try myself. Don't abandon me. See what can be done with me. Perhaps I'm after all a case. I shall certainly cling to you."

"You're too clever—you're too clever: that's what's the matter with you all!" Mr. Longdon sighed.

"With us *all?*" Vanderbank echoed. "Dear Mr. Longdon, it's the first time I've heard it. If you should say with *me* in particular, why there might be something in it. What you mean, at any rate—I see where you come out—is that we're cold and sarcastic and cynical, without the soft human spot. I think you flatter us even while you attempt to warn; but what's extremely interesting at all events is that, as I gather, we made on you this evening, in a particular way, a collective impression—something in which our trifling varieties are merged." His visitor's face, at this, appeared to say to him that he was putting the case in perfection, so that he was encouraged to go on. "There was something particular with which you were not altogether pleasantly struck."

Mr. Longdon, who, decidedly, changed colour easily, showed in his clear cheek the effect at once of feeling a finger on his fault and of admiration for his companion's insight. But he accepted the situation. "I couldn't help noticing your tone."

"Do you mean its being so low?"

Mr. Longdon, who had smiled at first, looked grave now. "Do you really want to know?"

"Just how you were affected? I assure you that there's nothing, at this moment, I desire nearly so much."

"I'm no judge," the old man went on; "I'm no critic; I'm no talker myself. I'm old-fashioned and narrow and dull. I've lived for years in a hole. I'm not a man of the world."

Vanderbank considered him with a benevolence, a geniality of approval, that he literally had to hold in check for fear of seeming to patronise. "There's not one of us who can touch you. You're delightful, you're wonderful, and I'm intensely curious to hear you," the young man pursued. "Were we absolutely odious?" Before his friend's puzzled, finally almost pained face, such an air of appreciating so much candour, yet looking askance at so much freedom, he could only endeavour to smooth the way and light the subject. "You see we don't in the least know where we are. We're lost—and you find us." Mr. Longdon, as he spoke, had prepared at last really to go, reaching the door with a manner that denoted, however, by no means so much satiety as an attention that felt itself positively too agitated. Vanderbank had helped him on with the Inverness cape and for an instant detained him by it. "Just tell me as a kindness. *Do* we talk—?"

"Too freely?" Mr. Longdon, with his clear eyes so untouched by time, speculatively murmured.

"Too outrageously. I want the truth."

The truth evidently for Mr. Longdon was difficult to tell. "Well—it was certainly different."

"From you and Lady Julia, I see. Well, of course with time *some* change is natural, isn't it? But so different," Vanderbank pressed, "that you were really shocked?"

His visitor, at this, smiled, but the smile somehow made the face graver. "I think I was rather frightened. Good-night."

BOOK SECOND

Little Aggie

IV

M RS. BROOKENHAM stopped on the threshold with the sharp surprise of the sight of her son, and there was disappointment, though rather of the afflicted than of the irritated sort, in the question that, slowly advancing, she launched at him. "If you're still lolling about, why did you tell me two hours ago that you were leaving immediately?"

Deep in a large brocaded chair, with his little legs stuck out to the fire, he was so much at his ease that he was almost flat on his back. She had evidently roused him from sleep, and it took him a couple of minutes, during which, without again looking at him, she directly approached a beautiful old French secretary, a fine piece of the period of Louis Seize, to justify his presence. "I changed my mind—I couldn't get off."

"Do you mean to say you're not going?"

"Well, I'm thinking it over. What's a fellow to do?" He sat up a little, staring with conscious solemnity at the fire, and if it had been—as it was not—one of the annoyances she in general expected from him, she might have received the impression that his flush was the heat of liquor.

"He's to keep out of the way," she replied—"when he has led one so deeply to hope it." There had been a bunch of keys suspended in the lock of the secretary, of which as she said these words Mrs. Brookenham took possession. Her air on observing them had promptly become that of having been in search of them, and a moment after she had passed across the room they were in her pocket. "If you don't go, what excuse will you give?"

"Do you mean to *you*, mummy?"

She stood before him, and now she dismally looked at him. "What's the matter with you? What an extraordinary time to take a nap!"

He had fallen back in the chair, from the depths of which

he met her eyes. "Why, it's just *the* time, mummy. I did it on purpose. I can always go to sleep when I like. I assure you it sees one through things!"

She turned away with impatience and, glancing about the room, perceived on a small table of the same type as the secretary a somewhat massive book with the label of a circulating library, which she proceeded to pick up as for refuge from the impression made on her by the boy. He watched her do this and watched her then slightly pause at the wide window that, in Buckingham Crescent, commanded the prospect they had ramified rearward to enjoy; a medley of smoky brick and spotty stucco, of other undressed backs, of glass invidiously opaque, of roofs and chimney-pots and stables unnaturally near—one of the private pictures that in London, in select situations, run up, as the phrase is, the rent. There was no indication of value now, however, in the character conferred on the scene by a cold spring rain. The place had moreover a confessed out-of-season vacancy. She appeared to have determined on silence for the present mark of her relation with Harold, yet she soon failed to resist a sufficiently poor reason for breaking it. "Be so good as to get out of my chair."

"What will you do for me," he asked, "if I oblige you?"

He never moved—but as if only the more directly and intimately to meet her—and she stood again before the fire and sounded his strange little face. "I don't know what it is, but you give me sometimes a kind of terror."

"A terror, mamma?"

She found another place, sinking sadly down and opening her book, and the next moment he got up and came over to kiss her, on which she drew her cheek wearily aside. "You bore me quite to death," she panted, "and I give you up to your fate."

"What do you call my fate?"

"Oh, something dreadful—if only by its being publicly ridiculous." She turned vaguely the pages of her book. "You're too selfish—too sickening."

"Oh, dear, dear!" he wonderingly whistled while he wandered back to the hearthrug on which, with his hands behind him, he lingered awhile. He was small and had a slight stoop, which somehow gave him character—a character somewhat of the insidious sort, carried out in the acuteness, difficult to trace to a source, of his smooth fair face, whose lines were all curves and its expression all needles. He had the voice of a man of forty and was dressed—as if markedly not for London —with an air of experience that seemed to match it. He pulled down his waistcoat, smoothing himself, feeling his neat hair and looking at his shoes; then he said to his mother: "I took your five pounds. Also two of the sovereigns," he went on. "I left you two pound ten." She jerked up her head at this, facing him in dismay, and, immediately on her feet, passed back to the secretary. "It's quite as I say," he insisted; "you should have locked it *before*, don't you know? It grinned at me there with all its charming brasses, and what was I to do? Darling mummy, I *couldn't* start—that was the truth. I thought I should find something—I had noticed; and I do hope you'll let me keep it, because if you don't it's all up with me. I stopped over on purpose—on purpose, I mean, to tell you what I've done. Don't you call that a sense of honour? And now you only stand and glower at me."

Mrs. Brookenham was, in her forty-first year, still charmingly pretty, and the nearest approach she made at this moment to meeting her son's description of her was by looking beautifully desperate. She had about her the pure light of youth—would always have it; her head, her figure, her flexibility, her flickering colour, her lovely, silly eyes, her natural, quavering tone all played together toward this effect by some trick that had never yet been exposed. It was at the same time remarkable that—at least in the bosom of her family—she rarely wore an appearance of gaiety less qualified than at the present juncture; she suggested, for the most part, the luxury, the novelty, of woe, the excitement of strange sorrows and the cultivation of fine indifferences. This was her special sign —an innocence dimly tragic. It gave immense effect to her other resources. She opened the secretary with the key she had quickly found, then with the aid of another rattled out a small drawer; after which she pushed the drawer back, closing the whole thing. "You terrify me—you terrify me," she again said.

"How can you say that when you showed me just now how well you know me? Wasn't it just on account of what you thought I might do that you took out the keys as soon as you

came in?" Harold's manner had a way of clearing up whenever he could talk of himself.

"You're too utterly disgusting, and I shall speak to your father:" with which, going to the chair he had given up, his
mother sank down again with her heavy book. There was no
anger, however, in her voice, and not even a harsh plaint; only
a detached, accepted disenchantment. Mrs. Brookenham's
supreme rebellion against fate was just to show with the last
frankness how much she was bored.

"No, darling mummy, you won't speak to my father—
you'll do anything in the world rather than that," Harold
replied, quite as if he were kindly explaining her to herself. "I
thank you immensely for the charming way you take what I
have done; it was because I had a conviction of that that
I waited for you to know it. It was all very well to tell you I
would start on my visit—but how the deuce was I to start
without a penny in the world? Don't you see that if you want
me to go about you must really enter into my needs?"

"I wish to heaven you would leave me—I wish to heaven
you would get out of the house," Mrs. Brookenham went on
without looking up.

Harold took out his watch. "Well, mamma, now I *am*
ready: I wasn't in the least before. But it will be going forth,
you know, quite to seek my fortune. For do you really think
—I must have from you what you do think—that it will be all
right for me?"

She fixed him at last with her pretty pathos. "You mean for
you to go to Brander?"

"You know," he answered with his manner as of letting her
see her own attitude, "you know you try to make me do
things that you wouldn't at all do yourself. At least I hope
you wouldn't. And don't you see that if I so far oblige you I
must at least be paid for it?"

His mother leaned back in her chair, gazed for a moment
at the ceiling and then closed her eyes. "You *are* frightful,"
she said; "you're appalling."

"You're always wanting to get me out of the house," he
continued; "I think you want to get us *all* out, for you manage to keep Nanda from showing even more than you do me.
Don't you think your children are good enough, mummy

dear? At any rate it's as plain as possible that if you don't keep us at home you must keep us in other places. One can't live anywhere for nothing—it's all bosh that a fellow saves by staying with people. I don't know how it is for a lady, but a man practically, is let in——"

"Do you know you kill me, Harold?" Mrs. Brookenham woefully interposed. But it was with the same remote melancholy that, in the next breath, she asked: "It wasn't an *invitation*—to Brander?"

"It's as I told you. She said she'd write, fixing a time; but she never did write."

"But if *you* wrote——"

"It comes to the same thing? *Does* it?—that's the question. If on my note she didn't write—that's what I mean. Should one simply take it that one is wanted? I like to have these things *from* you, mother. I do, I believe, everything you say; but to feel safe and right I must just *have* them. Any one *would* want me, eh?"

Mrs. Brookenham had opened her eyes, but she still attached them to the cornice. "If she hadn't wanted you she would have written. In a great house like that there's always room."

The young man watched her a moment. "How you *do* like to tuck us in and then sit up yourself! What do you want to do, anyway? What *are* you up to, mummy?"

She rose, at this, turning her eyes about the room as if from the extremity of martyrdom or the wistfulness of some deep thought. Yet when she spoke it was with a different expression, an expression that would have served for an observer as a marked illustration of that disconnectedness of her parts which frequently was laughable even to the degree of contributing to her social success. "You've spent then more than four pounds in five days. It was on Friday I gave them to you. What in the world do you suppose is going to become of me?"

Harold continued to look at her as if the question demanded some answer really helpful. "Do we live beyond our means?"

She now moved her gaze to the floor. "Will you *please* get away?"

"Anything to assist you. Only, if I *should* find I'm not wanted——?"

She met, after an instant, his look, and the wan loveliness and silliness of her own had never been greater. "*Be* wanted, and you won't find it. You're odious, but you're not a fool."

He put his arms about her now for farewell, and she submitted as if it were absolutely indifferent to her to whose bosom she was pressed. "You do, dearest," he laughed, "say such sweet things!" And with that he reached the door, on opening which he pulled up at a sound from below. "The Duchess! She's coming up."

Mrs. Brookenham looked quickly round the room, but she spoke with utter detachment. "Well, let her come."

"As I'd let her go. I take it as a happy sign *she* won't be at Brander." He stood with his hand on the knob; he had another quick appeal. "But after Tuesday?"

Mrs. Brookenham had passed half round the room with the glide that looked languid but that was really a remarkable form of activity, and had given a transforming touch, on sofa and chairs, to three or four crushed cushions. It was all with the sad, inclined head of a broken lily. "You're to stay till the twelfth."

"But if I *am* kicked out?"

It was as a broken lily that she considered it. "Then go to the Mangers."

"Happy thought! And shall I write?"

His mother raised a little more a window-blind. "No—I will."

"Delicious mummy!" And Harold blew her a kiss.

"Yes, rather"—she corrected herself. "Do write—from Brander. It's the sort of thing for the Mangers. Or even wire."

"Both?" the young man laughed. "Oh, you duck!" he cried. "And from where will *you* let them have it?"

"From Pewbury," she replied without wincing. "I'll write on Sunday."

"Good. How d'ye do, Duchess?"—and Harold, before he disappeared, greeted with a rapid concentration of all the shades of familiarity a large, high lady, the visitor he had announced, who rose in the doorway with the manner of a person used to arriving on thresholds very much as people arrive at stations—with the expectation of being "met."

V

"Good-bye. He's off," Mrs. Brookenham, who had remained quite on her own side of the room, explained to her friend.

"Where's he off to?" this friend inquired with a casual advance and a look not so much at her hostess as at the cushions just rearranged.

"Oh, to some places. To Brander to-day."

"How he does run about!" And the Duchess, still with a glance hither and yon, sank upon the sofa to which she had made her way unaided. Mrs. Brookenham knew perfectly the meaning of this glance: she had but three or four comparatively good pieces, whereas the Duchess, rich with the spoils of Italy, had but three or four comparatively bad. This was the relation, as between intimate friends, that the Duchess visibly preferred, and it was quite groundless, in Buckingham Crescent, ever to enter the drawing-room with an expression suspicious of disloyalty. The Duchess was a woman who so cultivated her passions that she would have regarded it as disloyal to introduce there a new piece of furniture in an underhand way—that is without a full appeal to herself, the highest authority, and the consequent bestowal of opportunity to nip the mistake in the bud. Mrs. Brookenham had repeatedly asked herself where in the world she might have found the money to be disloyal. The Duchess's standard was of a height—! It matched for that matter her other elements, which were as conspicuous as usual as she sat there suggestive of early tea. She always suggested tea before the hour, and her friend always, but with so different a wistfulness, rang for it. "Who's to be at Brander?" she asked.

"I haven't the least idea—he didn't tell me. But they've always a lot of people."

"Oh, I know—extraordinary mixtures. Has he been there before?"

Mrs. Brookenham thought. "Oh yes—if I remember—more than once. In fact her note—which he showed me, but which only mentioned 'some friends'—was a sort of appeal on the ground of something or other that had happened the last time."

The Duchess was silent a moment. "She writes the most extraordinary notes."

"Well, this was nice, I thought," Mrs. Brookenham said—"from a woman of her age and her immense position to so young a man."

Again the Duchess reflected. "My dear, she's not an American and she's not on the stage. Aren't those what you call positions in this country? And she's also not a hundred."

"Yes, but Harold's a mere baby."

"Then he doesn't seem to want for nurses!" the Duchess replied. She smiled at her friend. "Your children are like their mother—they're eternally young."

"Well, *I'm* not a hundred!" moaned Mrs. Brookenham as if she wished with dim perversity that she were. "Every one, at any rate, is awfully kind to Harold." She waited a moment to give her visitor the chance to pronounce it eminently natural, but no pronouncement came—nothing but the footman who had answered her ring and of whom she ordered tea. "And where did you say *you're* going?" she inquired after this.

"For Easter?" The Duchess achieved a direct encounter with her charming eyes—which was not, in general, an easy feat. "I didn't say I was going anywhere. I haven't, of a sudden, changed my habits. You know whether I leave my child —except in the sense of having left her an hour ago at Mr. Garlick's class in Modern Light Literature. I confess I'm a little nervous about the subjects and am going for her at five."

"And then where do you take her?"

"Home to her tea—where should you think?"

Mrs. Brookenham declined, in connection with the matter, any responsibility of thought; she did indeed much better by saying after a moment: "You *are* devoted!"

"Miss Merriman has her afternoon—I can't imagine what they do with their afternoons," the Duchess went on. "But she's to be back in the schoolroom at seven."

"And you have Aggie till then?"

"Till then," said the Duchess cheerfully. "You're off, for Easter, to—where is it?" she continued.

Mrs. Brookenham had received with no flush of betrayal the various discriminations thus conveyed by her visitor, and her only revenge for the moment was to look as sweetly resigned as if she really saw what was in them. Where were they going for Easter? She had to think an instant, but she brought it out. "Oh, to Pewbury—we've been engaged so long that I had forgotten. We go once a year—one does it for Edward."

"Ah, you spoil him!" smiled the Duchess. "Who's to be there?"

"Oh, the usual thing, I suppose. A lot of my lord's tiresome supporters."

"To pay his debt? Then why are you poor things asked?"

Mrs. Brookenham looked, on this, quite adorably—that is most wonderingly—grave. "How do I know, my dear Jane, why in the world we're ever asked anywhere? Fancy people wanting Edward!" she quavered with stupefaction. "Yet we can never get off Pewbury."

"You're better for getting on, *cara mia*, than for getting off!" the Duchess blandly returned. She was a person of no small presence, filling her place, however, without ponderosity, with a massiveness indeed rather artfully kept in bounds. Her head, her chin, her shoulders were well aloft, but she had not abandoned the cultivation of a "figure," or any of the distinctively finer reasons for passing as a handsome woman. She was secretly at war moreover, in this endeavour, with a lurking no less than with a public foe, and thoroughly aware that if she didn't look well she might at times only, and quite dreadfully, look good. There were definite ways of escape, none of which she neglected and from the total of which, as she flattered herself, the air of distinction almost mathematically resulted. This air corresponded superficially with her acquired Calabrian sonorities, from her voluminous title down, but the colourless hair, the passionless forehead, the mild cheek and long lip of the British matron, the type that had set its trap for her earlier than any other, were elements difficult to deal with and were all, at moments, that a sharp observer saw. The battle-ground then was the haunting danger of the *bourgeois*. She gave Mrs. Brookenham no time to resent her last note before inquiring if Nanda were to accompany the couple.

"Mercy, mercy no—she's not asked." Mrs. Brookenham, on Nanda's behalf, fairly radiated obscurity. "My children don't go where they're not asked."

"I never said they did, love," the Duchess returned. "But what then do you do with her?"

"If you mean socially"—Mrs. Brookenham looked as if there might be in some distant sphere, for which she almost yearned, a maternal opportunity very different from that—"if you mean socially, I don't do anything at all. I've never pretended to do anything. You know as well as I, dear Jane, that I haven't begun yet." Jane's hostess now spoke as simply as an earnest, anxious child. She gave a vague, patient sigh. "I suppose I must begin!"

The Duchess remained for a little rather grimly silent. "How old is she—twenty?"

"Thirty!" said Mrs. Brookenham with distilled sweetness. Then with no transition of tone: "She has gone for a few days to Tishy Grendon's."

"In the country?"

"She stays with her to-night in Hill Street. They go down together to-morrow. Why hasn't Aggie been?" Mrs. Brookenham went on.

The Duchess handsomely stared. "Been where?"

"Why, here to see Nanda."

"Here?" the Duchess echoed, fairly looking again about the room. "When is Nanda ever here?"

"Ah, you know I've given her a room of her own—the sweetest little room in the world." Mrs. Brookenham never looked so happy as when obliged to explain. "She has everything there that a girl can want."

"My dear woman," asked the Duchess, "has she sometimes her own mother?"

The men had now come in to place the tea-table, and it was the movements of the red-haired footman that Mrs. Brookenham followed. "You had better ask my child herself."

The Duchess was frank and jovial. "I would, I promise you, if I could get at her! But isn't that woman always with her?"

Mrs. Brookenham smoothed the little embroidered tea-cloth. "Do you call Tishy Grendon a woman?"

Again the Duchess had one of her pauses, which were indeed so frequent in her talks with this intimate that an auditor could sometimes wonder what particular form of relief they represented. They might have been a habit proceeding from the fear of undue impatience. If the Duchess had been as impatient with Mrs. Brookenham as she would possibly have seemed without them, her frequent visits, in the face of irritation, would have had to be accounted for. "What do *you* call her?" she demanded.

"Why, Nanda's best friend—if not her only one. That's the place I *should* have liked for Aggie," Mrs. Brookenham ever so graciously smiled.

The Duchess, hereupon, going beyond her, gave way to free mirth. "My dear thing, you're delightful, Aggie *or* Tishy is a sweet thought. Since you're so good as to ask why Aggie has fallen off, you'll excuse my telling you that you've just named the reason. You've known ever since we came to England what I feel about the proper persons—and the most improper—for her to meet. The Tishy Grendons are far from the proper."

Mrs. Brookenham continued to assist a little in the preparations for tea. "Why not say at once, Jane"—and her tone, in its appeal, was almost infantine—"that you've come at last to placing even poor Nanda, for Aggie's wonderful purpose, in the same impossible class?"

The Duchess took her time, but at last she accepted her duty. "Well, if you will have it. You know my ideas. If it isn't my notion of the way to bring up a girl to give her up, in extreme youth, to an intimacy with a young married woman who is both unhappy and silly, whose conversation has absolutely no limits, who says everything that comes into her head and talks to the poor child about God only knows what —if I should never dream of such an arrangement for my niece I can almost as little face the prospect of throwing her *much*, don't you see? with any young person exposed to such an association. It would be in the natural order certainly"—in spite of which natural order the Duchess made the point with but moderate emphasis—"that, since dear Edward is my cousin, Aggie should see at least as much of Nanda as of any other girl of their age. But what will you have? I must recognise the predicament I'm placed in by the more and more extraordinary development of English manners. Many things have altered, goodness knows, since I was Aggie's age, but nothing is so different as what you all do with your girls. It's all a muddle, a compromise, a monstrosity, like everything else you produce; there's nothing in it that goes on all-fours. *I* see but one consistent way, which is our fine old foreign way and which makes—in the upper classes, mind you, for it's with them only I'm concerned—*des femmes bien gracieuses*. I allude to the immemorial custom of my husband's race, which was good enough for his mother and his mother's mother, for Aggie's own, for his other sisters, for *toutes ces dames*. It would have been good enough for my child, as I call her—my dear husband called her *his*—if, not losing her parents, she had remained in her own country. She would have been brought up there under an anxious eye—that's the great point; privately, carefully, tenderly, and with what she was *not* to learn—till the proper time—looked after quite as much as the rest. I can only go on with her in that spirit and make of her, under Providence, what I consider any young person of her condition, of her name, of her particular traditions, should be. *Voilà, ma chère*. Should you put it to me if I think you're surrounding Nanda with any such security as that, I shouldn't be able to help it if I offended you by an honest answer. What it comes to, simply stated, is that really she must choose between Aggie and Tishy. I'm afraid I should shock you were I to tell you what I should think of myself for packing *my* child, all alone, off for a week with Mrs. Grendon."

Mrs. Brookenham, who had many talents, had none perhaps that she oftener found useful than that of listening with the appearance of being fairly hypnotised. It was the way she listened to her housekeeper at their regular morning conference, and if the rejoinder ensuing upon it frequently appeared to have nothing to do with her manner, that was a puzzle for her interlocutor alone. "Oh, of course I know your theory, dear Jane, and I daresay it's very charming and old-fashioned and, if you like, aristocratic, in a frowsy, foolish old way—though even upon that, at the same time, there would be something too to be said. But I can only congratulate you on finding it more workable than there can be any question of *my* finding it. If you're all armed for the sacrifices you speak of, I simply am not. I don't think I'm quite a monster, but I don't pretend to be a saint. I'm an English wife and an English mother, and I live in the mixed English world. My daughter, at any rate, is just my daughter—thank Heaven, and one of a good English bunch; she's not the unique niece of my

dead Italian husband, nor doubtless either, in spite of her excellent birth, of a lineage, like Aggie's, so very tremendous.
I've my life to lead, and she's a part of it. Sugar?" She wound
up on a still softer note as she handed the cup of tea.

"Never! Well, with *me*," said the Duchess with spirit, "she
would be all."

"'All' is soon said! Life is composed of many things." Mrs.
Brookenham gently rang out—"of such mingled, intertwisted
strands!" Then still with the silver bell, "Don't you really
think Tishy nice?" she asked.

"I think little girls should live with little girls, and young
femmes du monde so immensely initiated should—well," said
the Duchess with a toss of her head, "let them alone. What
do they want of them 'at all, at all'?"

"Well, my dear, if Tishy strikes you as 'initiated,' all one can
ask is 'Initiated into what'? I should as soon think of applying
such a term to a little shivering shorn lamb. Is it your theory,"
Mrs. Brookenham pursued, "that our unfortunate unmarried
daughters are to have no intelligent friends?"

"Unfortunate indeed," cried the Duchess, "precisely *because* they're unmarried, and unmarried, if you don't mind
my saying so, a good deal because they're unmarriageable.
Men, after all, the nice ones—by which I mean the possible
ones—are not on the look-out for little brides whose usual associates are so up to snuff. It's not their idea that the girls
they marry shall already have been pitchforked—by talk and
contacts and visits and newspapers, and the way the poor
creatures rush about and all the extraordinary things they do
—quite into *everything*. A girl's most intelligent friend is her
mother—or the relative acting as such. Perhaps you consider
that Tishy takes your place!"

Mrs. Brookenham waited so long to say what she considered that before she next spoke the question appeared to have
dropped. Then she only replied as if suddenly remembering
her manners: "Won't you eat something?" She indicated a
particular plate. "One of the nice little round ones?" The
Duchess appropriated a nice little round one, and her hostess
presently went on: "There's one thing I mustn't forget—
don't let us eat them *all*. I believe they're what Lord Petherton really comes for."

The Duchess finished her mouthful imperturbably before she took this up. "Does he come so often?"

Mrs. Brookenham hesitated. "I don't know what he calls it; but he said yesterday that he'd come to-day. I've had tea earlier for you," she went on with her most melancholy kindness —"and he's always late. But we mustn't, between us, lick the platter clean."

The Duchess entered very sufficiently into her companion's tone. "Oh, I don't feel at all obliged to consider him, for he has not of late particularly put himself out for me. He has not been to see me since I don't know when, and the last time he did come he brought Mr. Mitchett."

"Here it was the other way round. It was Mr. Mitchett, the other year, who first brought Lord Petherton."

"And who," asked the Duchess, "had first brought Mr. Mitchett?"

Mrs. Brookenham, meeting her friend's eyes, looked for an instant as if trying to remember. "I give it up. I muddle beginnings."

"That doesn't matter, if you only *make* them," the Duchess smiled.

"No, does it?" To which Mrs. Brookenham added: "Did he bring Mr. Mitchett for Aggie?"

"If he did they will have been disappointed. Neither of them has seen, in my house, the tip of her nose." The Duchess announced this circumstance with a pomp of pride.

"Ah, but with your ideas that doesn't prevent."

"Prevent what?"

"Why, what you call, I suppose, the *pourparlers.*"

"For Aggie's hand? My dear," said the Duchess, "I'm glad you do me the justice of feeling that I'm a person to take time by the forelock. It was not, as you seem to remember, with the sight of Mr. Mitchett that the question of Aggie's hand began to occupy me. I should be ashamed of myself if it were not constantly before me and if I had not my feelers out in more quarters than one. But I've not so much as thought of Mr. Mitchett—who, rich as he may be, is the son of a shoemaker and superlatively hideous—for a reason I don't at all mind telling you. Don't be outraged if I say that I've for a long time hoped you yourself would find the right use for

him." She paused—at present with a momentary failure of assurance, from which she rallied, however, to proceed with a
burst of earnestness that was fairly noble. "Forgive me if I just
tell you once for all how it strikes me. I'm stupefied at your
not seeming to recognise either your interest or your duty.
Oh, I know you want to, but you appear to me—in your perfect good faith, of course—utterly at sea. They're one and the
same thing, don't you make out? your interest and your duty.
Why isn't it as plain as a pikestaff that the thing to do with
Nanda is simply to marry her—and to marry her soon? That's
the great thing—do it while you *can*. If you don't want her
downstairs—at which, let me say, I don't in the least wonder
—your remedy is to take the right alternative. Don't send her
to Tishy——"

"Send her to Mr. Mitchett?" Mrs. Brookenham unresent-
fully quavered. Her colour, during her visitor's allocution,
had distinctly risen, but there was no irritation in her voice.
"How do you know, Jane, that I don't want her downstairs?"

The Duchess looked at her with an audacity confirmed by
the absence from her face of everything but the plaintive.
"There you are, with your eternal English false positions!
J'aime, moi, les situations nettes—je n'en comprends pas d'autres.
It wouldn't be to your honour—to that of your delicacy—that,
with your impossible house, you *should* wish to plant your girl
in your drawing-room. But such a way of keeping her out of it
as throwing her into a worse——"

"Well, Jane, you do say things to me!" Mrs. Brookenham
blandly broke in. She had sunk back into her chair; her hands,
in her lap, pressed themselves together, and her wan smile
brought a tear into each of her eyes by the very effort to be
brighter. It might have been guessed of her that she hated to
seem to care, but that she had other dislikes too. "If one were
to take up, you know, some of the things you say—!" And she
positively sighed for the fulness of amusement at them of
which her tears were the sign.

Her friend could quite match her indifference. "Well, my
child, *take* them up; if you were to do that with them candidly, one by one, you would do really very much what I
should like to bring you to. Do you see?" Mrs. Brookenham's
failure to repudiate the vision appeared to suffice, and her

visitor cheerfully took a further jump. "As much of Tishy as she wants—*after*. But not before."

"After what?"

"Well—say after Mr. Mitchett. Mr. Mitchett won't take her after Mrs. Grendon."

"And what are your grounds for assuming that he'll take her at all?" Then as the Duchess hung fire a moment: "Have you got it by chance from Lord Petherton?"

The eyes of the two women met for a little on this, and there might have been a consequence of it in the manner of the rejoinder. "I've got it from not being a fool. Men, I repeat, like the girls they marry——"

"Oh, I already know your old song! The way they like the girls they *don't* marry seems to be," Mrs. Brookenham mused, "what more immediately concerns us. You had better wait till you *have* made Aggie's fortune, perhaps, to be so sure of the working of your system. Excuse me, darling, if I don't take you for an example until you've a little more successfully become one. The sort of men *I* know anything about, at any rate, are not looking for mechanical dolls. They're looking for smart, safe, sensible English girls."

The Duchess glanced at the clock. "What is Mr. Vanderbank looking for?"

Her hostess appeared to oblige her by anxiously thinking. "Oh, *he*, I'm afraid, poor dear—for nothing at all!"

The Duchess had taken off a glove to appease her appetite, and now, drawing it on, she smoothed it down. "I think he has his ideas."

"The same as yours?"

"Well, more like them than like yours."

"Ah, perhaps then—for he and I," said Mrs. Brookenham, "don't agree, I think, on two things in the world. You think poor Mitchy then," she went on, "who's the son of a shoemaker and who might be the grandson of a grasshopper, good enough for my child."

The Duchess appreciated for a moment the superior fit of her glove. "I look facts in the face. It's exactly what I'm doing for Aggie." Then she broke into a certain conscious airiness. "What are you giving her?"

But Mrs. Brookenham took without wincing whatever, as

between a masterful relative and an exposed frivolity, might have been the sting of it. "That you must ask Edward. I haven't the least idea."

"There you are again—the virtuous English mother! I've got Aggie's little fortune in an old stocking, and I count it over every night. If you've no old stocking for Nanda, there are worse fates than shoemakers and grasshoppers. Even *with* one, you know, I don't at all say that I should sniff at poor Mitchy. We must take what we can get, and I shall be the first to take it. You can't have everything for nine-pence." And the Duchess got up, shining, however, with a confessed light of fantasy. "Speak to him, my dear—speak to him!"

"Do you mean offer him my child?"

The Duchess laughed at the intonation. "There you are once more—*vous autres!* If you're shocked at the idea, you place *drôlement* your delicacy. I'd offer mine to the son of a chimney-sweep if the principal guarantees were there. Nanda's charming—you don't do her justice. I don't say Mr. Mitchett is either beautiful or noble, and he hasn't as much distinction as would cover the point of a pin. He takes moreover his ease in talk—but that," added the Duchess with decision, "is much a matter of whom he talks with. And after marriage, what does it signify? He has forty thousand a year, an excellent idea of how to take care of it, and a good disposition."

Mrs. Brookenham sat still; she only looked up at her friend. "Is it by Lord Petherton that you know of his excellent idea?"

The Duchess showed she was challenged, but also that she was indulgent. "I go by my impression. But Lord Petherton *has* spoken for him."

"He ought to do that," said Mrs. Brookenham—"since he wholly lives on him."

"Lord Petherton—on Mr. Mitchett?" The Duchess stared, but rather in amusement than in horror. "Why, hasn't he a—property?"

"The loveliest. Mr. Mitchett's his property. Didn't you *know*?" There was an artless wail in Mrs. Brookenham's surprise.

"How should I know—still a stranger as I'm often rather

happy to feel myself here, and choosing my friends and picking my steps very much, I can assure you—how should I
know about all your social scandals and things?"

"Oh, we don't call *that* a social scandal!" Mrs. Brookenham
inimitably returned.

"Well, if you should wish to, you'd have the way that I told
you of to stop it. Divert the stream of Mr. Mitchett's
wealth."

"Oh, there's plenty for every one!"—Mrs. Brookenham
kept up her tone. "He's always giving us things—bonbons
and dinners and opera-boxes."

"He has never given *me* any," the Duchess contentedly
declared.

Mrs. Brookenham waited a little. "Lord Petherton has the
giving of some. He has never in his life before, I imagine,
made so many presents."

"Ah then it's a shame one has nothing!" On which, before
reaching the door, the Duchess changed the subject. "You say
I never bring Aggie. If you like I'll bring her back."

Mrs. Brookenham wondered. "Do you mean to-day?"

"Yes, when I've picked her up. It will be something to do
with her till Miss Merriman can take her."

"Delighted, dearest; do bring her. And I think she should
see Mr. Mitchett."

"Shall I find him too, then?"

"Oh, take the chance."

The two women, on this, exchanged, tacitly and across the
room—the Duchess at the door, which a servant had arrived
to open for her, and Mrs. Brookenham still at her tea-table—
a further stroke of intercourse, over which the latter was not
on this occasion the first to lower her lids. "I think I've shown
high scruples," the Duchess said, "but I understand then that
I'm free."

"Free as air, dear Jane."

"Good." Then just as she was off, "Ah, dear old Edward!"
the guest exclaimed. Her kinsman, as she was fond of calling
him, had reached the top of the staircase, and Mrs. Brookenham, by the fire, heard them meet on the landing—heard also
the Duchess protest against his turning to see her down. Mrs.
Brookenham, listening to them, hoped that Edward would

accept the protest and think it sufficient to leave her with the footman. Their common consciousness, not devoid of satisfaction, that she was a kind of cousin was quite consistent with a view, early arrived at, of the absurdity of any fuss about her.

VI

When Mr. Brookenham appeared his wife was prompt. "She's coming back for Lord Petherton."

"Oh!" he simply said.

"There's something between them."

"Oh!" he merely repeated. And it would have taken many such sounds on his part to represent a spirit of response discernible to any one but his wife.

"There have been things before," she went on, "but I haven't felt sure. Don't you know how one has sometimes a flash?"

It could not be said of Edward Brookenham, who seemed to bend for sitting down more hinges than most men, that he looked as if he knew either this or anything else. He had a pale, cold face, marked and made regular, made even in a manner handsome, by a hardness of line in which, oddly, there was no significance, no accent. Clean-shaven, slightly bald, with unlighted grey eyes and a mouth that gave the impression of not working easily, he suggested a stippled drawing by an inferior master. Lean moreover and stiff, and with the air of having here and there in his person a bone or two more than his share, he had once or twice, at fancy-balls, been thought striking in a dress copied from one of Holbein's English portraits. But when once some such meaning as that had been put into him it took a long time to put another, a longer time than even his extreme exposure, or anybody's study of the problem, had yet made possible. If anything particular had finally been expected from him it might have been a summary or an explanation of the things he had always not said, but there was something in him that had long since pacified impatience and drugged curiosity. He had never in his life answered such a question as his wife had just put him and which she would not have put had she feared a reply. So dry and decent and even distinguished did he look, as if he had positively been created to meet a propriety and match some other piece, his wife, with her notorious perceptions, would no more have appealed to him seriously on a general proposition than she would, for such a response, have rung the drawing-room bell. He was none the less held to have a great general adequacy. "What is it that's between them?" he demanded.

"What's between any woman and the man she's making up to?"

"Why, there may often be nothing. I didn't know she even particularly knew him," Brookenham added.

"It's exactly what she would like to prevent any one's knowing, and her coming here to be with him when she knows I know *she* knows—don't you see?—that he's to be here, is just one of those calculations that *are* subtle enough to put off the scent a woman who has but half a nose." Mrs. Brookenham, as she spoke, appeared to testify, by the pretty star-gazing way she thrust it into the air, to her own possession of the totality of such a feature. "I don't know yet quite what I think, but one wakes up to such things soon enough."

"Do you suppose it's her idea that he'll marry her?" Brookenham asked in his colourless way.

"My dear Edward!" his wife murmured for all answer.

"But if she can see him in other places why should she want to see him here?" Edward persisted in a voice destitute of intonation.

Mrs. Brookenham now had plenty of that. "Do you mean if she can see him in his own house?"

"No cream, please," her husband said. "Hasn't she a house too?"

"Yes, but so pervaded all over by Aggie and Miss Merriman."

"Oh!" Brookenham observed.

"There has always been some man—I've always known there has. And now it's Petherton," said his companion.

"But where's the attraction?"

"In *him*? Why, lots of women could tell you. Petherton has had a career."

"But I mean in old Jane."

"Well, I daresay lots of men could tell you. She's no older than any one else. She has also such great elements."

"Oh, I daresay she's all right," Brookenham returned as if

his interest in the case had dropped. You might have felt you got a little nearer to him on guessing that in so peopled a circle satiety was never far from him.

"I mean for instance she has such a grand idea of duty. She thinks we're nowhere!"

"Nowhere?"

"With our children—with our home life. She's awfully down on Tishy."

"Tishy?"—Brookenham appeared for a moment at a loss.

"Tishy Grendon—and her craze for Nanda."

"Has she a craze for Nanda?"

"Surely I told you Nanda's to be with her for Easter."

"I believe you did," Brookenham bethought himself, "but you didn't say anything about a craze. And where's Harold?" he went on.

"He's at Brander. That is, he will be by dinner. He has just gone."

"And how does he get there?"

"Why, by the South-Western. They'll send to meet him."

Brookenham appeared for a moment to view this statement in the dry light of experience. "They'll only send if there are others too."

"Of course then there'll be others—lots. The more the better for Harold."

This young man's father was silent a little. "Perhaps—if they don't play high."

"Ah," said his mother, "however Harold plays he has a way of winning."

"He has a way too of being a hopeless ass. What I meant was how he comes there at all," Brookenham explained.

"Why, as any one comes—by being invited. She wrote to him—weeks ago."

Brookenham was discoverably affected by this fact, but it would not have been possible to say if his satisfaction exceeded his surprise. "To Harold? Very good-natured." He had another short reflection, after which he continued: "If they don't send he'll be in for five miles in a fly—and the man will see that he gets his money."

"They *will* send—after her note."

"Did it say so?"

Mrs. Brookenham's melancholy eyes seemed, from afar, to run over the page. "I don't remember—but it was so cordial."

Again Brookenham meditated. "That often doesn't prevent one's being let in for ten shillings."

There was more gloom in this forecast than his wife had desired to produce. "Well, my dear Edward, what do you want me to do? Whatever a young man does, it seems to me, he's let in for ten shillings."

"Ah, but he needn't be—that's my point. *I* wasn't at his age."

Harold's mother took up her book again. "Perhaps you weren't the same success! I mean at such places."

"Well, I didn't borrow money to make me one—as I have a sharp idea our young scamp does."

Mrs. Brookenham hesitated. "From whom do you mean—the Jews?"

He looked at her as if her vagueness might be assumed. "No. They, I take it, are not quite so 'cordial' to him, as you call it, as the old ladies. He gets it from Mitchy."

"Oh!" said Mrs. Brookenham. "Are you very sure?" she then demanded.

He had got up and put his empty cup back upon the tea-table, wandering afterwards a little about the room and looking out, as his wife had done half-an-hour before, at the dreary rain and the now duskier ugliness. He reverted in this attitude, with a complete unconsciousness of making for irritation, to a question they might be supposed to have dropped. "He'll have a lovely drive for his money!" His companion, however, said nothing, and he presently came round again. "No, I'm not absolutely sure—of his having had it from Mitchy. If I were I should do something."

"What would you do?" She put it as if she couldn't possibly imagine.

"I would speak to him."

"To Harold?"

"No—that might just put it into his head." Brookenham walked up and down a little with his hands in his pockets; then, with a complete concealment of the steps of the transition, "Where are we dining to-night?" he brought out.

"Nowhere, thank heaven. We grace our own board."

"Oh—with those fellows, as you said, and Jane?"

"That's not for dinner. The Baggers and Mary Pinthorpe and—upon my word, I forget."

"You'll see when she comes," suggested Brookenham, who was again at the window.

"It isn't a she—it's two or three he's, I think," his wife replied with her indifferent anxiety. "But I don't know what dinner it is," she bethought herself; "it may be the one that's after Easter. Then that ones this one," she added with her eyes once more on her book.

"Well, it's a relief to dine at home"—and Brookenham faced about. "Would you mind finding out?" he asked with some abruptness.

"Do you mean who's to dine?"

"No, that doesn't matter. But whether Mitchy *has* come down."

"I can only find out by asking him."

"Oh, *I* could ask him." He seemed disappointed at his wife's want of resource.

"And you don't want to?"

He looked coldly, from before the fire, over the prettiness of her brown, bent head. "It will be such a beastly bore if he admits it."

"And you think poor I can make him not admit it?" She put the question as if it were really her own thought too, but they were a couple who could, even face to face and unlike the augurs behind the altar, think these things without laughing. "If he *should* admit it," Mrs. Brookenham threw in, "will you give me the money?"

"The money?"

"To pay Mitchy back."

She had now raised her eyes to her husband, but, turning away, he failed to meet them. "He'll deny it."

"Well, if they all deny it," she presently remarked, "it's a simple enough matter. I'm sure *I* don't want them to come down on us! But that's the advantage," she almost prattled on, "of having so many such charming friends—they *don't* come down."

This again was a remark of a sweep that there appeared to be nothing in Brookenham's mind to match; so that, scarcely pausing in the walk into which he had again fallen, he only said: "Who do you mean by 'all'?"

"Why, if he has had anything from Mitchy I dare say he has had something from Van."

"Oh!" Brookenham returned as if with a still greater drop of interest.

"They oughtn't to do it," she declared; "they ought to tell us, and when they don't it serves them right." Even this observation, however, failed to rouse in her husband a response, and, as she had quite formed the habit of doing, she philosophically answered herself. "But I don't suppose they do it on spec."

It was less apparent than ever what Edward supposed. "Oh, Van hasn't money to chuck about."

"Ah, I only mean a sovereign here and there."

"Well," Brookenham threw out after another turn, "I think Van, you know, is your affair."

"It *all* seems to be my affair!" she exclaimed with too dolorous a little wail to have other than a comic effect. "And of course then it will be still more so if he should begin to apply to Mr. Longdon."

"We must stop that in time."

"Do you mean by warning Mr. Longdon and requesting him immediately to tell us? That won't be very pleasant," Mrs. Brookenham sighed.

"Well, then, wait and see."

She waited only a minute—it might have seemed that she already saw. "I want him to be kind to Harold, and I can't help thinking he will."

"Yes, but I fancy that that will be his notion of it—keeping him from making debts. I dare say one needn't trouble about him," Brookenham added. "He can take care of himself."

"He appears to have done so pretty well all these years," his wife mused. "As I saw him in my childhood I see him now, and I see now that I saw then even how awfully in love he was with mamma. He's too lovely about mamma," Mrs. Brookenham pursued.

"Oh!" her husband replied.

This delicate past held her a moment. "I see now I must have known a lot as a child."

"Oh!" her companion repeated.

"I want him to take an interest in us. Above all in the children. He ought to like us"—she followed it up. "It will be a sort of 'poetic justice.' He sees, himself, the reasons, and we mustn't prevent it." She turned the possibilities over a moment, but they produced another soft wail. "The thing is that I don't see how he *can* like Harold."

"Then he won't lend him money," said Brookenham.

This contingency too she considered. "You make me feel as if I wished he would—which is too dreadful. And I don't think he really likes *me*," she went on.

"Oh!" her husband again ejaculated.

"I mean not utterly *really*. He has to try to. But it won't make any difference," she next remarked.

"Do you mean his trying?" Brookenham inquired.

"No, I mean his not succeeding. He'll be just the same." She saw it steadily and saw it whole. "On account of mamma."

Her husband also, with his perfect propriety, put it before himself. "And will he—on account of your mother—also like *me*?"

Mrs. Brookenham weighed it. "No, Edward." She covered him with her loveliest expression. "No, not really either. But it won't make any difference." This time she had pulled him up.

"Not if he doesn't like Harold, or like you, or like me?" Brookenham clearly found himself able to accept only the premise.

"He'll be perfectly loyal. It will be the advantage of mamma!" Mrs. Brookenham exclaimed. "Mamma, Edward," she brought out with a flash of solemnity—"mamma *was* wonderful. There have been times when I've felt that she's still with us, but Mr. Longdon makes it vivid. Whether she's with me or not, at any rate, she's with *him*; so that when *he's* with me, don't you see——"

"It comes to the same thing?" her husband intelligently asked. "I see. And when was he with you last?"

"Not since the day he dined—but that was only last week. He'll come soon—I know from Van."

"And what does Van know?"

"Oh, all sorts of things. He has taken the greatest fancy to him."

"The old man—to Van?"

"Van to Mr. Longdon. And the other way too. Mr. Longdon has been most kind to him."

Brookenham still moved about. "Well, if he likes Van and doesn't like *us*, what good will that do us?"

"You would understand soon enough if you felt Van's loyalty."

"Oh, the things you expect me to feel, my dear!" Edward Brookenham lightly moaned.

"Well, it doesn't matter. But he *is* as loyal to me as Mr. Longdon to mamma."

The statement produced on Brookenham's part an unusual vision of the comedy of things. "Every Jenny has her Jockey!" Yet perhaps—remarkably enough—there was even more imagination in his next words. "And what sort of means?"

"Mr. Longdon? Oh, very good. Mamma wouldn't have been the loser. Not that she cared. He *must* like Nanda," Mrs. Brookenham wound up.

Her companion appeared to look at the idea and then meet it. "He'll have to see her first."

"Oh, he shall see her!" Mrs. Brookenham affirmed. "It's time for her at any rate to sit downstairs."

"It was time, you know, *I* thought, a year ago."

"Yes, I know what you thought. But it wasn't."

She had spoken with decision, but he seemed unwilling to concede the point. "You admitted yourself that she was ready."

"*She* was ready—yes. But I wasn't. I am now," Mrs. Brookenham, with a fine emphasis on her adverb, proclaimed as she turned to meet the opening of the door and the appearance of the butler, whose announcement—"Lord Petherton and Mr. Mitchett"—might for an observer have seemed immediately to offer support to her changed state.

VII

Lord Petherton, a man of five-and-thirty, whose robust but symmetrical proportions gave to his dark blue double-breasted coat an air of tightness that just failed of compromising his tailor, had for his main facial sign a certain pleasant brutality, the effect partly of a bold, handsome parade of carnivorous teeth, partly of an expression of nose suggesting that this feature had paid a little, in the heat of youth, for some aggression at the time admired and even publicly commemorated. He would have been ugly, he substantively granted, had he not been happy; he would have been dangerous had he not been warranted. Many things doubtless performed for him this last service, but none so much as the delightful sound of his voice, the voice, as it were, of another man, a nature reclaimed, supercivilised, adjusted to the perpetual "chaff" that kept him smiling in a way that would have been a mistake, and indeed an impossibility, if he had really been witty. His bright familiarity was that of a young prince whose confidence had never had to falter, and the only thing that at all qualified the resemblance was the equal familiarity excited in his subjects.

Mr. Mitchett had so little intrinsic appearance that an observer would have felt indebted, as an aid to memory, to the rare prominence of his colourless eyes and the positive attention drawn to his chin by the precipitation of its retreat from detection. Dressed, on the other hand, not as gentlemen dress in London to pay their respects to the fair, he excited, by the exhibition of garments that had nothing in common save the violence and the independence of their pattern, a suspicion that in the desperation of humility he wished to make it public that he had thrown to the winds the effort to please. It was written all over him that he had judged once for all his personal case and that as his character, superficially disposed to gaiety, deprived him of the resource of shyness and shade, the effect of comedy might not escape him if secured by a real plunge. There was comedy therefore in the form of his pothat and the colour of his spotted shirt, in the systematic disagreement, above all, of his coat, waistcoat and trousers. It was only on long acquaintance that his so many ingenious ways of showing that he recognised his commonness could present him as secretly rare.

"And where's the child this time?" he asked of his hostess as soon as he was seated near her.

"Why do you say 'this time,' as if it were different from any other time?" she replied, as she gave him his tea.

"Only because, as the months and the years elapse, it's more and more of a wonder, whenever I don't see her, to think what she does with herself—of what you do with her. What it does show, I suppose," Mr. Mitchett went on, "is that she takes no trouble to meet me."

"My dear Mitchy," said Mrs. Brookenham, "what do *you* know about 'trouble'—either poor Nanda's or mine or any-body's else? You've never had to take any in your life, you're the spoiled child of fortune, and you skim over the surface of things in a way that seems often to represent you as suppos-ing that everybody else has wings. Most other people are sticking fast in their native mud."

"Mud, Mrs. Brook—mud, mud!" he protestingly cried as, while he watched his fellow-visitor move to a distance with their host, he glanced about the room, taking in afresh the Louis Seize secretary, which looked better closed than open and for which he always had a knowing eye. "Remarkably charming mud!"

"Well, that's what a great deal of the element really appears, to-day, to be thought; and precisely, as a specimen, Mitchy dear, those two French books you were so good as to send me and which—really, this time, you extraordinary man!" She fell back, intimately reproachful, from the effect produced on her, renouncing all expression save that of the rolled eye.

"Why, were they particularly dreadful?"—Mitchy was hon-estly surprised. "I rather liked the one in the pink cover—what's the confounded thing called?—I thought it had a sort of a something-or-other." He had cast his eye about as if for a glimpse of the forgotten title, and she caught the question as he vaguely and good-humouredly dropped it.

"A kind of a morbid modernity? There *is* that," she dimly conceded.

"Is that what they call it? Awfully good name. You must have got it from old Van!" he gaily declared.

"I dare say I did. I get the good things from him and the bad ones from you. But you're not to suppose," Mrs. Brookenham went on, "that I've discussed your horrible book with him."

"Come, I say!" Mr. Mitchett protested; "I've seen you with books from Vanderbank which, if you *have* discussed them with him—well," he laughed, "I should like to have been there!"

"You haven't seen me with anything like yours—no, no, never, never!" She was particularly positive. "He, on the contrary, gives tremendous warnings, makes apologies, in advance, for things that—well, after all, haven't killed one."

"That have even perhaps a little, after the warnings, let one down?"

Mrs. Brookenham took no notice of this pleasantry; she simply adhered to her thesis. "One has taken one's dose and one isn't such a fool as to be deaf to some fresh, true note, if it happens to turn up. But for abject, horrid, unredeemed vileness from beginning to end——"

"So you read to the end?" Mr. Mitchett interposed.

"I read to see what you could possibly have sent such things to me for, and because so long as they were in my hands they were not in the hands of others. Please to remember in future that the children are all over the place, and that Harold and Nanda have their nose in everything."

"I promise to remember," Mr. Mitchett returned, "as soon as you make old Van do the same."

"I do make old Van—I pull old Van up much oftener than I succeed in pulling you. I must say," Mrs. Brookenham went on, "you're all getting to require among you in general an amount of what one may call editing!" She gave one of her droll universal sighs. "I've got your books at any rate locked up, and I wish you'd send for them quickly again; one's too nervous about anything happening and their being perhaps found among one's relics. Charming literary remains!" she laughed.

The friendly Mitchy was also much amused. "By Jove, the most awful things *are* found! Have you heard about old Randage and what his executors have just come across? The most abominable——"

"I haven't heard," she broke in, "and I don't want to; but you give me a shudder, and I beg you'll have your offerings removed, for I can't think of confiding them, for the purpose, to any one in this house. I might burn them up in the dead of night, but even then I should be fearfully nervous."

"I'll send then my usual messenger," said Mitchy, "a person

I keep for such jobs, thoroughly seasoned, as you may imagine, and of a discretion—what do you call it?—*à toute épreuve.* Only you must let me say that I like your terror about Harold! Do you suppose he spends his time over Dr. Watts's hymns?"

Mrs. Brookenham just hesitated, and nothing, in general, was so becoming to her as the act of hesitation. "Dear Mitchy, do you know I want awfully to talk to you about Harold?"

"About his reading, Mrs. Brook?" Mitchy responded with interest. "The worse things are, let me just mention to you about that, the better they seem positively to be for one's feeling up in the language. They're more difficult, the bad ones—and there's a lot in that. All the young men know it —those who are going up for exams."

She had her eyes for a little on Lord Petherton and her husband; then, as if she had not heard what her interlocutor had just said, she overcame her last scruple. "Dear Mitchy, has he had money from you?"

He stared with his good goggle eyes—he laughed out. "Why on earth——? But do you suppose I'd tell you if he had?"

"He hasn't really borrowed the most dreadful sums?"

Mitchy was highly diverted. "Why should he? For what, please?"

"That's just it—for what? What does he do with it all? What in the world becomes of it?"

"Well," MItchy suggested, "he's saving up to start a business. Harold's irreproachable—hasn't a vice. Who knows, in these days, what may happen? He sees further than any young man I know. Do let him save."

She looked far away with her sweet world-weariness. "If you weren't an angel it would be a horror to be talking to you. But I insist on knowing." She insisted now with her absurdly pathetic eyes on him. "What kind of sums?"

"You shall never, never find out," Mr. Mitchett replied with extravagant firmness. "Harold is one of my great amusements —I really have awfully few; and if you deprive me of him you'll be a fiend. There are only one or two things I want to live for, but one of them is to see how far Harold will go. Please give me some more tea."

"Do you positively swear?" she asked with intensity as she helped him. Then without waiting for his answer: "You have the common charity to *us*, I suppose, to see the position you would put us in. Fancy Edward!" she quite austerely threw off.

Mr. Mitchett, at this, had, on his side, a hesitation. "Does Edward imagine——?"

"My dear man, Edward never 'imagined' anything in life." She still had her eyes on her interlocutor. "Therefore if he *sees* a thing, don't you know? it must exist."

Mitchy for a little fixed the person mentioned as he sat with his other guest, but, whatever this person saw, he failed just then to see his wife's companion, whose eyes he never met. His face only offered itself, like a clean domestic vessel, a receptacle with the peculiar property of constantly serving yet never filling, to Lord Petherton's talkative splash. "Well, only don't let him take it up. Let it be only between you and me," Mr. Mitchett pleaded; "keep him quiet—don't let him speak to me." He appeared to convey, with his pleasant extravagance, that Edward looked dangerous, and he went on with a rigour of levity: "It must be *our* little quarrel."

There were different ways of meeting such a tone, but Mrs. Brookenham's choice was remarkably prompt. "I don't think I quite understand what dreadful joke you may be making, but I dare say if you *had* let Harold borrow you would have another manner, and I was at any rate determined to have the question out with you."

"Let us always have everything out—that's quite my own idea. It's you," said Mr. Mitchett, "who are by no means always so frank with me as I recognise—oh, I do *that*!—what it must have cost you to be over this little question of Harold. There's one thing, Mrs. Brook, you do dodge."

"What do I ever dodge, dear Mitchy?" Mrs. Brook quite tenderly asked.

"Why, when I ask you about your other child you're off like a frightened fawn. When have you ever, on my doing so, said 'My darling Mitchy, I'll ring for her to be asked to come down, and you can see her for yourself'—when have you ever said anything like that?"

"I see," Mrs. Brookenham mused; "you think I sacrifice

her. You're very interesting among you all, and I've certainly
a delightful circle. The Duchess has just been letting me have
it most remarkably hot, and as she's presently coming back
you'll be able to join forces with her."

Mitchy looked a little of a loss. "On the subject of your
sacrifice——"

"Of my innocent and helpless, yet somehow at the same
time, as a consequence of my cynicism, dreadfully damaged
and depraved daughter." She took in for an instant the slight
bewilderment against which, as a result of her speech, even so
expert an intelligence as Mr. Mitchett's had not been proof;
then, with a small jerk of her head at the other side of the
room, she made the quickest of transitions. "What *is* there between her and him?"

Mitchy wondered at the other two. "Between Edward and
the girl?"

"Don't talk nonsense. Between Petherton and Jane."

Mitchy could only stare, and the wide noonday light of his
regard was at such moments really the redemption of his ugliness. "What 'is' there? Is there anything?"

"It's too beautiful," Mrs. Brookenham appreciatively
sighed, "your relation with him! You won't compromise him."

"It would be nicer of me," Mitchy laughed, "not to want
to compromise *her.*"

"Oh Jane!" Mrs. Brookenham dropped. "*Does* he like her?"
she continued. "You must know."

"Ah, it's just my knowing that constitutes the beauty of my
loyalty—of my delicacy." He had his quick jumps too. "Am I
never, never to see the child?"

This inquiry appeared only to confirm his companion in the
contemplation of what was touching in him. "You're the
most delicate thing I know, and it crops up, in the oddest
way, in the intervals of your depravity. Your talk's half the
time impossible; you respect neither age nor sex nor condition; one doesn't know what you'll say or do next; and one
has to return your books—*c'est tout dire*—under cover of
darkness. Yet there's in the midst of all this, and in the depths
of you, a little deep-down delicious niceness, a sweet sensibility, that one has actually one's self, shocked as one perpetually
is at you, quite to hold one's breath and stay one's hand for

fear of ruffling or bruising. There's no one with whom, in talking," she balmily continued, "I find myself half so often suddenly moved to pull up short. You've more little toes to tread on—though you pretend you haven't: I mean morally speaking, don't you know?—than even I have myself, and I've so many that I could wish most of them cut off. You never spare me a shock—no, you don't do that: it isn't the form your delicacy takes. But you'll know what I mean, all the same, I think, when I tell you that there are lots I spare *you*!"

Mr. Mitchett fairly glowed with the candour of his attention. "Know what you mean, dearest lady? How can a man handicapped to death, a man of my origin, my appearance, my general weaknesses, drawbacks, immense indebtedness, all round, for the start, as it were, that I feel my friends have been so good as to allow me: how can such a man not be conscious every moment that every one about him goes on tiptoe and winks at every one else? What *can* you all mention in my presence, poor things, that isn't personal?"

Mrs. Brookenham's face covered him for an instant as no painted Madonna's had ever covered the little charge at the breast beneath it. "And the finest thing of all in you is your beautiful, beautiful pride! You're prouder than all of us put together." She checked a motion that he had apparently meant as a protest—she went on with her muffled wisdom. "There isn't a man but *you* whom Petherton wouldn't have made vulgar. He isn't vulgar himself—at least not exceptionally; but he's just one of those people, a class one knows well, who are so fearfully, in this country, the cause of it in others. For all I know he's the cause of it in me—the cause of it even in poor Edward. For *I'm* vulgar, Mitchy, dear—very often; and the marvel of you is that you never are."

"Thank you for everything. Thank you, above all, for 'marvel'!" Mitchy grinned.

"Oh, I know what I say!"—she didn't in the least blush. "I'll tell you something," she pursued with the same gravity, "if you'll promise to tell no one on earth. If you're proud, I'm not. There! It's most extraordinary, and I try to conceal it, even to myself; but there's no doubt whatever about it— I'm not proud *pour deux sous*. And some day, on some awful occasion, I shall show it. So—I notify you. Shall you love me still?"

"To the bitter end," Mitchy loyally responded. "For how *can*, how need, a woman be 'proud' who's so preternaturally clever? Pride's only for use when wit breaks down—it's the train the cyclist takes when his tire's deflated. When that happens to *your* tire, Mrs. Brook, you'll let me know. And you do make me wonder just now," he confessed, "why you're taking such particular precautions and throwing out such a cloud of skirmishes. If you want to shoot me dead a single bullet will do." He faltered but an instant before completing his sense. "Where you really want to come out is at the fact that Nanda loathes me and that I might as well give up asking for her."

"Are you quite serious?" his companion after a moment asked. "Do you really and truly like her, Mitchy?"

"I like her as much as I dare to—as much as a man can like a girl when, from the very first of his seeing her and judging her, he has also seen, and seen with all the reasons, that there's no chance for him whatever. Of course, with all that, he has done his best not to let himself go. But there are moments," Mr. Mitchett ruefully added, "when it would relieve him awfully to feel free for a good spin."

"I think you exaggerate," his hostess replied, "the difficulties in your way. What do you mean by 'all the reasons'?"

"Why, one of them I've already mentioned. I make her flesh creep."

"My own Mitchy!" Mrs. Brookenham protestingly moaned.

"The other is that—very naturally—she's in love."

"With whom, under the sun?"

Mrs. Brookenham had, with her startled stare, met his eyes long enough to have taken something from him before he next spoke. "You really have never suspected? With whom conceivably but old Van?"

"Nanda's in love with old Van?"—the degree to which she had never suspected was scarce to be expressed. "Why, he's twice her age—he has seen her in a pinafore with a dirty face, and well slapped for it: he has never thought of her in the world."

"How can a person of your acuteness, my dear woman,"

Mitchy asked, "mention such trifles as having the least to do with the case? How can you possibly have such a fellow about, so beastly good-looking, so infernally well turned out in the way of 'culture,' and so bringing them down in short on every side, and expect in the bosom of your family the absence of history of the reigns of the good kings? If *you* were a girl, wouldn't *you* turn purple? If I were a girl shouldn't I—unless, as is more likely, I turned green?"

Mrs. Brookenham was deeply affected. "Nanda does turn purple—?"

"The loveliest shade you ever saw. It's too absurd that you haven't noticed."

It was characteristic of Mrs. Brookenham's amiability that, with her sudden sense of the importance of this new light, she should be quite ready to abase herself. "There are so many things in one's life; one follows false scents; one doesn't make out everything at once. If you're right you must help me. We must see more of her."

"But what good will that do me?" Mitchy inquired.

"Don't you care enough for her to want to help *her*?" Then before he could speak, "Poor little darling dear!" his hostess tenderly ejaculated. "What does she think or dream? Truly she's laying up treasure!"

"Oh, he likes her," said Mitchy. "He likes her in fact extremely."

"Do you mean he has told you so?"

"Oh no—we never mention it! But he likes her," Mr. Mitchett stubbornly repeated. "And he's thoroughly straight."

Mrs. Brookenham for a moment turned these things over; after which she came out in a manner that visibly surprised him. "It isn't as if you wished to be nasty about him, is it?—because I know you like him yourself. You're so wonderful to your friends"—oh, she could let him see that she knew!—"and in such different and exquisite ways. There are those, like *him*"—she signified her other visitor—"who get everything out of you and whom you really appear to like, or at least to put up with, just *for* that. Then there are those who ask nothing—and whom you like in spite of it."

Mitchy leaned back, at this, fist within fist, watching her

with a certain disguised emotion. He grinned almost too much for mere amusement. "That's the class to which *you* belong."

"It's the best one," she returned, "and I'm careful to remain in it. You try to get us, by bribery, into the inferior place, because, proud as you are, it bores you a little that you like us so much. But we won't go—at least *I* won't. You may make Van," she wonderfully continued. "There's nothing you wouldn't do for him or give him." Mitchy admired her from his position, slowly shaking his head with it. "He's the man—with no fortune and just as he is, to the smallest particular —whom you would have liked to be, whom you intensely envy, and yet to whom you're magnanimous enough to be ready for almost any sacrifice."

Mitchy's appreciation had fairly deepened to a flush. "Magnificent—magnificent Mrs. Brook! What *are* you, in thunder, up to?"

"Therefore, as I say," she imperturbably went on, "it's not to do him an ill turn that you maintain what you've just told me."

Mr. Mitchett for a minute gave no sign but his high colour and his queer glare. "How could it do him an ill turn?"

"Oh, it *would* be a way, don't you see? to put before me the need of getting rid of him. For he may 'like' Nanda as much as you please: he'll never, never," Mrs. Brookenham resolutely quavered—"he'll never come to the scratch. And to feel that as *I* do," she explained, "can only be, don't you also see? to want to save her."

It would have appeared at last that poor Mitchy did see. "By taking it in time? By forbidding him the house?"

She seemed to stand with little nipping scissors in a garden of alternatives. "Or by shipping *her* off. Will you help me to save her?" she broke out again after a moment. "It isn't true," she continued, "that she has any aversion to you."

"Have you charged her with it?" Mitchy demanded with a courage that amounted to high gallantry.

It inspired, on the spot, his interlocutress; and her own, of as fine a quality now as her diplomacy, which was saying much, fell but little below. "Yes, my dear friend—frankly."

"Good. Then I know what she said."

"She absolutely denied it."

"Oh yes—they always do, because they pity me," Mitchy smiled. "She said what they always say—that the effect I produce is, though at first upsetting, one that little by little they find it possible to get used to. The world's full of people who are getting used to me," Mr. Mitchett concluded.

"It's what *I* shall never do, for you're quite too delicious!" Mrs. Brookenham declared. "If I haven't threshed you out really *more* with Nanda," she continued, "it has been from a scruple of a sort you people never do a woman the justice to impute. You're the object of views that have so much more to set them off."

Mr. Mitchett, on this, jumped up; he was clearly conscious of his nerves; he fidgeted away a few steps, then, with his hands in his pockets, fixed on his hostess a countenance more controlled. "What does the Duchess mean by your daughter's being—as I understood you to quote her just now—'damaged and depraved'?"

Mrs. Brookenham came up—she literally rose—smiling. "You fit the cap. You know how she would like you for little Aggie!"

"What does she mean, what does she mean?" Mitchy repeated.

The door, as he spoke, was thrown open; Mrs. Brookenham glanced round. "You've the chance to find out from herself!" The Duchess had come back and little Aggie was in her wake.

VIII

That young lady, in this relation, was certainly a figure to have offered a foundation for the highest hopes. As slight and white, as delicately lovely, as a gathered garden lily, her admirable training appeared to hold her out to them all as with precautionary finger-tips. She presumed, however, so little on any introduction that, shyly and submissively, waiting for the word of direction, she stopped short in the centre of the general friendliness till Mrs. Brookenham fairly became, to meet her, also a shy little girl—put out a timid hand with wonder-struck, innocent eyes that hesitated whether a kiss of greeting might be dared. "Why, you dear, good, strange 'ickle' thing, you haven't been here for ages, but it *is* a joy to see you, and I do hope you've brought your doll!"—such might have been the sense of our friend's fond murmur while, looking at her up and down with pure pleasure, she drew the rare creature to a sofa. Little Aggie presented, up and down, an arrangement of dress exactly in the key of her age, her complexion, her emphasised virginity. She might have been prepared for her visit by a cluster of doting nuns, cloistered daughters of ancient houses and educators of similar products, whose taste, hereditarily good, had grown, out of the world and most delightfully, so queer as to leave on everything they touched a particular shade of distinction. The Duchess had brought in with the child an air of added confidence for which, in a moment, an observer would have seen the grounds, the association of the pair being so markedly favourable to each. Its younger member carried out the style of her aunt's presence quite as one of the accessory figures effectively thrown into old portraits. The Duchess, on the other hand, seemed, with becoming blandness, to draw from her niece the dignity of a kind of office of state—hereditary governess of the children of the blood. Little Aggie had a smile as softly bright as a southern dawn, and the friends of her relative looked at each other, according to a fashion frequent in Mrs. Brookenhams drawing-room, in free communication of their happy impression. Mr. Mitchett was, none the less, scantly diverted from his recognition of the occasion Mrs. Brookenham had just named to him.

"My dear Duchess," he promptly asked, "do you mind explaining to me an opinion that I have just heard of your—with marked originality—holding?"

The Duchess, with her head in the air, considered an instant her little ivory princess. "I'm always ready, Mr. Mitchett, to defend my opinions; but if it's a question of going much into the things that are the subjects of some of them, perhaps we had better, if you don't mind, choose our time and our place."

"No 'time,' gracious lady, for my impatience," Mr. Mitchett replied, "could be better than the present—but if you've reasons for wanting a better place, why shouldn't we go, on the spot, into another room?"

Lord Petherton, at this inquiry, broke into instant mirth. "Well, of all the coolness, Mitchy!—he does go at it, doesn't he, Mrs. Brook? What do you want to do in another room?" he demanded of his friend. "Upon my word, Duchess, under the nose of those ——"

The Duchess, on the first blush, lent herself to the humour of the case. "Well, Petherton, of 'those'?—I defy him to finish his sentence!" she smiled to the others.

"Of those," said his lordship, "who flatter themselves that when you do happen to find them somewhere your first idea is not quite to jump at a pretext for getting off somewhere else. Especially," he continued to jest, "with a man of Mitchy's vile reputation."

"Oh!" Edward Brookenham exclaimed at this, but only as if with quiet relief.

"Mitchy's offer is perfectly safe, I may let him know," his wife remarked, "for I happen to be sure that nothing would really induce Jane to leave Aggie five minutes among us here without remaining herself to see that we don't become improper."

"Well then, if we're already pretty far on the way to it," Lord Petherton resumed, "what on earth *might* we arrive at in the absence of your control? I warn you, Duchess," he joyously pursued, "that if you go out of the room with Mitchy I shall rapidly become quite awful."

The Duchess, during this brief passage, never took her eyes from her niece, who rewarded her attention with the sweetness of consenting dependence. The child's foreign origin was so delicately but unmistakably written in all her exquisite lines that her look might have expressed the modest detachment of a person to whom the language of her companions was unknown. The Duchess then glanced round the circle. "You're very odd people, all of you, and I don't think you quite know how ridiculous you are. Aggie and I are simple stranger-folk; there's a great deal we don't understand; yet we're none the less not easily frightened. In what is it, Mr. Mitchett," she asked, "that I've wounded your susceptibilities?"

Mr. Mitchett hesitated; he had apparently found time to reflect on his precipitation. "I see what Petherton's up to, and I won't, by drawing you aside just now, expose your niece to anything that might immediately oblige Mrs. Brook to catch her up and flee with her. But the first time I find you more isolated—well," he laughed, though not with the clearest ring, "all I can say is, Mind your eyes, dear Duchess!"

"It's about your thinking, Jane," Mrs. Brookenham placidly explained, "that Nanda suffers—in her morals, don't you know?—by my neglect. I wouldn't say anything about you that I can't bravely say *to* you; therefore, since he has plumped out with it, I do confess that I've appealed to him on what, as so good an old friend, *he* thinks of your contention."

"What in the world *is* Jane's contention?" Edward Brookenham put the question as if they were "stuck" at cards.

"You really, all of you," the Duchess replied with excellent coolness, "choose extraordinary conditions for the discussion of delicate matters. There are decidedly too many things on which we don't feel alike. You're all inconceivable just now. *Je ne peux pourtant pas la mettre à la porte, cette chérie*"—whom she covered again with the gay solicitude that seemed to have in it a vibration of private entreaty: "Don't understand, my own darling—don't understand!"

Little Aggie looked around with an impartial politeness that, as an expression of the general blind sense of her being, in every particular, in hands at full liberty either to spot or to spare her, was touching enough to bring tears to all eyes. It perhaps had to do with the sudden emotion with which—using now quite a different manner—Mrs. Brookenham again embraced her, and even with this lady's equally abrupt and altogether wonderful address to her: "Between you and me straight, my dear, and as from friend to friend, I know that you'll never doubt that everything must be all right!—What I spoke of to poor Mitchy," she went on to the Duchess, "is the dreadful view you take of my letting Nanda go to Tishy—and indeed of the general question of any acquaintance between young unmarried and young married females. Mr. Mitchett is sufficiently interested in us, Jane, to make it natural of me to take him into our confidence in one of our difficulties. On the other hand we feel your solicitude, and I needn't tell you at this time of day what weight in every respect we attach to your judgment. Therefore it *will* be a difficulty for us, *cara mia*, don't you see? if we decide suddenly, under the spell of your influence, that our daughter must break off a friendship—it *will* be a difficulty for us to put the thing to Nanda herself in such a way as that she shall have some sort of notion of what suddenly possesses us. Then there'll be the much stiffer job of putting it to poor Tishy. Yet if her house *is* an impossible place, what else is one to do? Carrie Donner's to be there, and Carrie Donner's a nature apart; but how can we ask even a little lamb like Tishy to give up her own sister?"

The question had been launched with an argumentative sharpness that made it for a moment keep possession of the air, and during this moment, before a single member of the circle could rally, Mrs. Brookenham's effect was superseded by that of the reappearance of the butler. "I say, my dear, don't shriek!"—Edward Brookenham had only time to sound this warning before a lady, presenting herself in the open doorway, followed close on the announcement of her name. "Mrs. Beach Donner!"—the impression was naturally marked. Every one betrayed it a little but Mrs. Brookenham, who, more than the others, appeared to have the help of seeing that, by a merciful stroke, her visitor has just failed to hear. This visitor, a young woman of striking, of startling appearance, who, in the manner of certain shiny housedoors and railings, instantly created a presumption of the lurking label "Fresh paint," found herself, with an embarrassment oddly opposed to the positive pitch of her complexion, in the presence of a group in which it was yet immediately evident that every one was a friend. Every one, to show no one had been caught, said something extremely easy; so that it was after a moment only poor Mrs. Donner who, seated close to her hostess, seemed to be in any degree in the wrong. This moreover was essentially her fault, so extreme was the anomaly of her having, without the means to back it up, committed herself to a "scheme of colour" that was practically an advertisement of courage. Irregularly pretty and painfully shy, she was retouched, from brow to chin, like a suburban photograph—the moral of which was simply that she should either have left more to nature or taken more from art. The Duchess had quickly reached her kinsman with a smothered hiss, an "Edward dear, for God's sake take Aggie!" and at the end of a few minutes had formed for herself in one of Mrs. Brookenham's admirable "corners" a society consisting of Lord Petherton and Mr. Mitchett, the latter of whom regarded Mrs. Donner, across the room, with articulate wonder and compassion.

"It's all right, it's all right—she's frightened only at herself!"

The Duchess watched her as from a box at the play, comfortably shut in, as in the old operatic days at Naples, with a pair of entertainers. "You're the most interesting nation in the world. One never gets to the end of your hatred of the *nuance*. The sense of the suitable, the harmony of parts—what on earth were you doomed to do that, to be punished sufficiently in advance, you had to be deprived of it in your very cradles? Look at her little black dress—rather good, but not so good as it ought to be, and, mixed up with all the rest, see her type, her beauty, her timidity, her wickedness, her notoriety and her *impudeur*. It's only in this country that a woman is both so shocking and so shaky." The Duchess's displeasure overflowed. "If she doesn't know how to be good——"

"Let her at least know how to be bad? Ah," Mitchy replied, "your irritation testifies more than anything else could do to our peculiar genius or our peculiar want of it. Our vice is intolerably clumsy—if it can possibly be a question of vice in regard to that charming child, who looks like one of the new-fashioned bill-posters, only, in the way of 'morbid modernity' as Mrs. Brook would say, more extravagant and funny than any that have yet been risked. I remember," he continued, "Mrs. Brook's having spoken of her to me lately as 'wild.' Wild?—why, she's simply tameness run to seed. Such an expression shows the state of training to which Mrs. Brook has reduced the rest of us."

"It doesn't prevent, at any rate, Mrs. Brook's training, some of the rest of you being horrible," the Duchess declared. "What did you mean just now, really, by asking me to explain before Aggie this so serious matter of Nanda's exposure?" Then instantly, taking herself up before Mr. Mitchett could answer: "What on earth do you suppose Edward's saying to my darling?"

Brookenham had placed himself, side by side with the child, on a distant little settee, but it was impossible to make out from the countenance of either whether a sound had passed between them. Aggie's little manner was too developed to show, and her host's not developed enough. "Oh, he's awfully careful," Lord Petherton reassuringly observed. "If you or I or Mitchy say anything bad, it's sure to be before we know it and without particularly meaning it. But old Edward means it——"

"So much that, as a general thing, he doesn't dare to say it?" the Duchess asked. "That's a pretty picture of him, inasmuch as, for the most part, he never speaks. What therefore must he mean?"

"He's an abyss—he's magnificent!" Mr. Mitchett laughed. "I don't know a man of an understanding more profound, and he's equally incapable of uttering and of wincing. If, by the same token, I'm 'horrible,' as you call me," he pursued, "it's only because, in every way, I'm so beastly superficial. All the same, I do sometimes go into things, and I insist upon knowing," he again broke out, "what it exactly was you had in mind in saying to Mrs. Brook, about Nanda, what she repeated to me."

"You 'insist,' you silly man?"—the Duchess had veered a little to indulgence. "Pray, on what ground of right, in such a connection, do you do anything of the sort?"

Poor Mitchy showed but for a moment that he felt pulled up. "Do you mean that when a girl liked by a fellow likes him so little in return——?"

"I don't mean anything," said the Duchess, "that may provoke you to suppose me vulgar and odious enough to try to put you out of conceit of a most interesting and unfortunate creature; and I don't quite, as yet, see—though I dare say I shall soon make it out!—what our friend has in her head in tattling to you on these matters as soon as my back is turned. Petherton will tell you—I wonder he hasn't told you before— why Mrs. Grendon, though not perhaps herself quite the rose, is decidedly, in these days, too near it."

"Oh, Petherton never tells me anything!" Mitchy's answer was brisk and impatient, but evidently quite as sincere as if the person alluded to had not been there.

The person alluded to, meanwhile, fidgeting frankly in his chair, alternately stretching his legs and resting his elbows on his knees, had reckoned as small the profit he might derive from this colloquy. His bored state indeed—if he was bored—prompted in him the honest impulse to clear, as he would have perhaps considered it, the atmosphere. He indicated Mrs. Donner with a remarkable absence of precautions. "Why, what the Duchess alludes to is my poor sister Fanny's stupid grievance—surely you know about that." He made oddly vivid for a moment the nature of his relative's allegation, his somewhat cynical treatment of which became peculiarly derisive in the light of the attitude and expression, at that minute, of the figure incriminated. "My brother-in-law's too thick with her. But Cashmore's such a fine old ass. It's excessively unpleasant," he added, "for affairs are just in that position in which, from one day to another, there may be something that people will get hold of. Fancy a man," he robustly reflected while the three took in more completely the subject of Mrs. Brookenham's attention—"fancy a man with that apparition on his hands! The beauty of it is that the two women seem never to have broken off. Blest if they don't still keep seeing each other!"

The Duchess, as on everything else, passed succinctly on this. "Ah, how can hatreds comfortably flourish without the nourishment of such regular 'seeing' as what you call here bosom friendship alone supplies? What are parties given for in London but that enemies may meet? I grant you it's inconceivable that the husband of a superb creature like your sister should find his requirements better met by an object *comme cette petite*, who looks like a pen-wiper—an actress's idea of one—made up for a theatrical bazaar. At the same time, if you'll allow me to say so, it scarcely strikes one that your sister's prudence is such as to have placed all the cards in her hands. She's the most beautiful woman in England, but her *esprit de conduite* isn't quite on a level. One can't have everything!" she philosophically sighed.

Lord Petherton met her comfortably enough on this assumption of his detachments. "If you mean by that her being the biggest fool alive I'm quite ready to agree with you. It's exactly what makes me afraid. Yet how can I decently say in particular," he asked, "of what?"

The Duchess still perched on her critical height. "Of what but one of your amazing English periodical public washings of dirty linen? There's not the least necessity to 'say'!" she laughed. "If there's anything more remarkable than these purifications, it's the domestic comfort with which, when all has come and gone, you sport the articles purified."

"It comes back, in all that sphere," Mr. Mitchett instructively suggested, "to our national, our fatal want of style. We can never, dear Duchess, take too many lessons, and there's probably at the present time no more useful function performed among us than that dissemination of neater methods to which you are so good as to contribute."

He had had another idea, but before he reached it his companion had gaily broken in. "Awfully good one for you, Duchess—and I'm bound to say that, for a clever woman, you exposed yourself! I've at any rate a sense of comfort," Lord Petherton pursued, "in the good relations now more and more established between poor Fanny and Mrs. Brook. Mrs. Brook's awfully kind to her and awfully sharp, and Fanny will take things from her that she won't take from me. I keep saying to Mrs. Brook—don't you know?—'Do keep hold of her, and let her have it strong.' She hasn't, upon my honour, any one in the world but me."

"And we know the extent of *that* resource!" the Duchess freely exclaimed.

"That's exactly what Fanny says—that *she* knows it," Petherton good-humouredly assented. "She says my beastly hypocrisy makes her sick. There are people," he pleasantly rambled on, "who are awfully free with their advice, but it's mostly fearful rot. Mrs. Brook's isn't, upon my word—I've tried some myself!"

"You talk as if it were something nasty and home-made—gooseberry wine!" the Duchess laughed; "but one can't know the dear soul, of course, without knowing that she has set up, for the convenience of her friends, a little office for consultations. She listens to the case, she strokes her chin and prescribes——"

"And the beauty of it is," cried Lord Petherton, "that she makes no charge whatever!"

"She doesn't take a guinea at the time, but you may still get your account," the Duchess returned. "Of course we know that the great business she does is in husbands and wives."

"This then seems the day of the wives!" Mr. Mitchett interposed as he became aware, the first, of the illustration that the Duchess's image was in the act of receiving. "Lady Fanny Cashmore!"—the butler was already in the field, and the company, with the exception of Mrs. Donner, who remained seated, was apparently conscious of a vibration that brought it afresh, but still more nimbly than on Aggie's advent, to its feet.

IX

"Go to her straight—be nice to her: you must have plenty to say. You stay with me—we have our affair." The latter of these commands the Duchess addressed to Mr. Mitchett, while their companion, in obedience to the former and affected, as it seemed, by an unrepressed familiar accent that stirred a fresh flicker of Mitchy's grin, met the new arrival in the middle of the room before Mrs. Brookenham had had time to reach her. The Duchess, quickly reseated, watched an instant the inexpressive concussion of the tall brother and sister; then while Mitchy again subsided in his place, "You're not, as a race, clever, you're not delicate, you're not sane, but you're capable of extraordinary good looks," she resumed. "*Vous avez parfois la grande beauté.*"

Mitchy was much amused. "Do you really think Petherton has?"

The Duchess withstood it. "They've got, both outside and in, the same great general things, only turned, in each, rather different ways, a way safer for him as a man, and more triumphant for her as—whatever you choose to call her! What *can* a woman do," she richly mused, "with such beauty as that——"

"Except come desperately to advise with Mrs. Brook"—Mitchy undertook to complete her question—"as to the highest use to make of it? But see," he immediately added, "how perfectly competent to instruct her our friend now looks." Their hostess had advanced to Lady Fanny with an outstretched hand but with an eagerness of greeting merged a little in the sweet predominance of wonder as well as in the habit, at such moments most perceptible, of the languid

lily-bend. Nothing in general could have been less poorly
conventional than the kind of reception given in Mrs.
Brookenham's drawing-room to the particular element—the
element of physical splendour void of those disparities that
make the question of others tiresome—comprised in Lady
Fanny's presence. It was a place in which, at all times, before
interesting objects, the unanimous occupants, almost more
concerned for each other's vibrations than for anything else,
were apt rather more to exchange sharp and silent searchings
than to fix their eyes on the object itself—and quite by the
same law that had worked, though less profoundly, on the entrance of little Aggie—superseded the usual rapt communion
very much in the manner of some beautiful tame tigress who
might really coerce attention. There was in Mrs. Brookenham's way of looking up at her a dim, despairing abandonment of the idea of any common personal ground. Lady Fanny,
magnificent, simple, stupid, had almost the stature of her
brother, a forehead unsurpassably low and an air of sombre
concentration just sufficiently corrected by something in her
movements that failed to give it a point. Her blue eyes were
heavy in spite of being perhaps a couple of shades too clear,
and the wealth of her black hair, the disposition of the massive coils of which was all her own, had possibly a satin sheen
depreciated by the current fashion. But the great thing in her
was that she was, with unconscious heroism, thoroughly herself; and what were Mrs. Brook and Mrs. Brook's intimates
after all, in their free surrender to the play of perception, but
a happy association for keeping her so? The Duchess was
moved to the liveliest admiration by the grand, simple sweetness of her encounter with Mrs. Donner, a combination indeed in which it was a question if she or Mrs. Brook appeared
to the higher advantage. It was poor Mrs. Donner—not, like
Mrs. Brook, subtle in sufficiency, nor, like Lady Fanny, almost
too simple—who made the poorest show. The Duchess immediately marked it to Mitchy as infinitely characteristic that
their hostess, instead of letting one of her visitors go, kept
them together by some sweet ingenuity and while Lord
Petherton, dropping his sister, joined Edward and Aggie in
the other angle, sat there between them as if, in pursuance of
some awfully clever line of her own, she were holding a hand

of each. Mr. Mitchett of course did justice all round, or at least, as would have seemed from an inquiry he presently made, wished not to fail of it. "Is it your real impression then that Lady Fanny has serious grounds——?"

"For jealousy of that preposterous little person? My dear Mitchett," the Duchess resumed after a moment's reflection, "if you're so rash as to ask me in any of these connections for my 'real' impression you deserve whatever you may get." The penalty Mitchy had incurred was apparently grave enough to make his companion just falter in the infliction of it; which gave him the opportunity of replying that the little person was perhaps not more preposterous than any one else, that there was something in her he rather liked, and that there were many different ways in which a woman could be interesting. This further levity it was therefore that laid him fully open. "Do you mean to say you've been living with Petherton so long without becoming aware that he's shockingly worried?"

"My dear Duchess," Mitchy smiled, "Petherton carries his worries with a bravery! They're so many that I've long since ceased to count them; and in general I've been disposed to let those pass that I can't help him to meet. *You've* made, I judge," he went on, "a better use of opportunities perhaps not so good—such as at any rate enables you to see further than I into the meaning of the impatience he just now expressed."

The Duchess was admirable, in conversation, for neglecting everything not essential to her present plausibility. "A woman like Lady Fanny can have no 'grounds' for anything—for any indignation, I mean, or for any revenge worth twopence. In this particular case at all events they've been sacrificed with such extravagance that, as an injured wife, she hasn't had the gumption to keep back an inch or two to stand on. She can do absolutely nothing."

"Then you take the view—?" Mitchy, who had, after all, his delicacies, pulled up as at sight of a name.

"I take the view," said the Duchess, "and I know exactly why. *Elle se les passe*—her little fancies!—She's a phenomenon, poor dear. And all with—what shall I call it?—the absence of haunting remorse of a good house-mother who makes the family accounts balance. She looks—and it's what they love her for here when they say 'Watch her now!'—like an angry saint; but she's neither a saint, nor, to be perfectly fair to her, really angry at all. She has only just enough reflection to make out that it may some day be a little better for her that her husband shall, on his side too, have committed himself; and she's only, in secret, too pleased to be sure whom it has been with. All the same I must tell you," the Duchess still more crisply added, "that our little friend Nanda is of the opinion—which I gather her to be quite ready to defend—that Lady Fanny is wrong."

Poor Mitchy found himself staring. "But what has our little friend Nanda to do with it?"

"What indeed, bless her heart? If you *will* ask questions, however, you must take, as I say, your risks. There are days when between you all you stupefy me. One of them was when I happened about a month ago to make some allusion to the charming example of Mr. Cashmore's fine taste that we have there before us: what was my surprise at the tone taken by Mrs. Brook to deny on this little lady's behalf the soft impeachment? It was quite a mistake that anything had happened—Mrs. Donner had pulled through unscathed. She had been but a day or two at the most in danger, for her family and friends—the best influences—had rallied to her support: the flurry was all over. She was now perfectly safe. Do you think she looks so?" the Duchess asked.

This was not a point that Mitchy was conscious of freedom of mind to examine. "Do I understand you that Nanda was her mother's authority—?"

"For the exact shade of the intimacy of the two friends and the state of Mrs. Brook's information? Precisely—it was 'the latest before going to press.' 'Our own correspondent!' Her mother quoted her."

Mr. Mitchett visibly wondered. "But how should Nanda know——"

"Anything about the matter? How should she *not* know everything? You've not, I suppose, lost sight of the fact that this lady and Mrs. Grendon are sisters. Carrie's situation and Carrie's perils are naturally very present to the extremely unoccupied Tishy, who is unhappily married into the bargain, who has no children, and whose house, as you may imagine, has a good thick air of partisanship. So, as with Nanda, on *her* side, there is no more absorbing interest than her dear friend Tishy, with whom she's at present staying and under whose roof she perpetually meets this victim of unjust aspersions——"

"I see the whole thing from here, you imply?" Mr. Mitchett, under the influence of this rapid evocation, had already taken his line. "Well," he said bravely, "Nanda's not a fool."

A momentary silence on the part of the Duchess might have been her tribute to his courage. "No. I don't agree with her, as it happens, here; but that there are matters as to which she's not in general at all befogged is exactly the worst I ever said of her. And I hold that in putting it so—on the basis of my little anecdote—you clearly give out that you're answered."

Mitchy turned it over. "Answered?"

"In the quarrel that, awhile back, you sought to pick with me. What I touched on to her mother was the peculiar range of aspects and interests she's compelled to cultivate by the special intimacies that Mrs. Brook permits her. There they are —and that's all I said. Judge them for yourself."

The Duchess had risen as she spoke, which was also what Mrs. Donner and Mrs. Brookenham had done; and Mr. Mitchett was on his feet as well, to act on this last admonition. Mrs. Donner was taking leave, and there occurred among the three ladies in connection with the circumstance a somewhat striking exchange of endearments. Mr. Mitchett, observing this, expressed himself suddenly as diverted. "By Jove, they're kissing—she's in Lady Fanny's arms!" But his hilarity was still to deepen. "And Lady Fanny, by Jove, is in Mrs. Brook's!"

"Oh, it's all beyond *me*!" the Duchess cried; and the little wail of her baffled imagination had almost the austerity of a complaint.

"Not a bit—they're all right. Mrs. Brook has acted!" Mitchy went on.

"Oh, it isn't that she doesn't 'act'!" his interlocutress ejaculated.

Mrs. Donner's face presented, as she now crossed the room, something that resembled the ravage of a death-struggle between its artificial and its natural elegance. "Well," Mitchy said with decision as he caught it—"I back Nanda." And while a whiff of derision reached him from the Duchess, "Nothing *has* happened!" he murmured.

As if to reward him for an indulgence that she must much more have divined than overheard, the visitor approached him with her bravery of awkwardness. "I go on Thursday to my sister's, where I shall find Nanda Brookenham. Can I take her any message from you?"

Mr. Mitchett showed a tint that might positively have been reflected. "Why should you dream of her expecting one?"

"Oh," said the Duchess with a gaiety that but half carried off her asperity, "Mrs. Brook must have told Mrs. Donner to ask you!"

The latter lady, at this, rested strange eyes on the speaker, and they had perhaps something to do with a quick flare of Mitchy's wit. "Tell her, please—if, as I suppose you came here to ask the same of her mother—that I adore her still more for keeping in such happy relations with you as enable me thus to meet you."

Mrs. Donner, overwhelmed, took flight with a nervous laugh, leaving Mr. Mitchett and the Duchess still confronted. Nothing had passed between the two ladies, yet it was as if there were a trace of something in the eyes of the elder, which, during a moment's silence, moved from the retreating visitor, now formally taken over at the door by Edward Brookenham, to Lady Fanny and her hostess, who, in spite of the embraces just performed, had again subsided together while Mrs. Brook gazed up in exalted intelligence. "It's a funny house," said the Duchess at last. "She makes me such a scene over my not bringing Aggie, and still more over my very faint hint of my reasons for it, that I fly off, in compunction, to do what I can, on the spot, to repair my excess of prudence. I reappear, panting, with my niece—and it's to *this* company I introduce her!"

Her companion looked at the charming child, to whom Lord Petherton was talking with evident kindness and gaiety —a conjunction that evidently excited Mitchy's interest. "May *we* then know her?" he asked with an effect of drollery. "May I—if *he* may?"

The Duchess's eyes, turned to him, had taken another light. He even gaped a little at their expression, which was, in

a manner, carried out by her tone. "Go and talk to her, you
perverse creature, and send him over to me." Lord Petherton,
a minute later, had joined her; Brookenham had left the room
with Mrs. Donner; his wife and Lady Fanny were still more
closely engaged; and the young Agnesina, though visibly a
little scared at Mitchy's queer countenance, had begun, after
the fashion he had touched on to Mrs. Brook, politely to in-
voke the aid of the idea of habit. "Look here—you must help
me," the Duchess said to Petherton. "You can, perfectly—and
it's the first thing I've yet asked of you.

"Oh, oh, oh!" her interlocutor laughed.

"I must have Mitchy," she went on without noticing his
particular shade of humour.

"Mitchy too?"—he appeared to wish to leave her in no
doubt of it.

"How low you are!" she simply said. "There are times
when I despair of you, He's in every way your superior, and I
like him so that—well, he must like *her*. Make him feel that he
does."

Lord Petherton turned it over as something put to him
practically. "I could wish for him that he would. I see in her
possibilities!" he continued to laugh.

"I daresay you do. *I* see them in Mitchett, and I trust you'll
understand me when I say that I appeal to you."

"Appeal to *him* straight. That's much better," Petherton
lucidly observed.

The Duchess wore for a moment her proudest air, which
made her, in the connection, exceptionally gentle. "He doesn't
like me."

Her interlocutor looked at her with all his bright brutality.
"Oh, my dear, I can speak for you—if *that's* what you want!"

The Duchess met his eyes, and so, for an instant, they
sounded each other. "You're so abysmally coarse that I often
wonder——" But as the door reopened she caught herself. It
was the effect of a face apparently directed at her. "Be quiet.
Here's Edward."

BOOK THIRD

Mr. Longdon

X

I F MITCHY arrived exactly at the hour it was quite by design and on a calculation—over and above the little pleasure it might give him—of ten minutes clear with his host, whom it rarely befell him to see alone. He had a theory of something special to go into, of a plummet to sink or a feeler to put forth; his state of mind in short was diplomatic and anxious. But his hopes had a drop as he crossed the threshold. His precaution had only assured him the company of a stranger, for the person in the room to whom the servant announced him was not old Van. On the other hand this gentleman would clearly be old—what was it? the fellow Vanderbank had made it a matter of such importance he should "really know." But were they then simply to have tea there together? No; the candidate for Mr. Mitchett's acquaintance, as if quickly guessing his apprehension, mentioned on the spot that their entertainer would be with them: he had just come home in a hurry, fearing he was late, and then had rushed off to make a change. "Fortunately," said the speaker, who offered his explanation as if he had had it on his mind—"fortunately the ladies haven't yet come."

"Oh, there *are* to be ladies?" Mr. Mitchett genially replied.

His fellow-guest, who was shy and apparently nervous, sidled about a little, swinging an eye-glass, yet glancing in a manner a trifle birdlike from object to object. "Mrs. Edward Brookenham, I think."

"Oh!" Mitchy himself felt, as soon as this comment had quitted his lips, that it might sound even to a stranger like a sign, such as the votaries of Mrs. Edward Brookenham had fallen into the way of constantly throwing off, that he recognised her hand in the matter. There was, however, something in his entertainer's face that somehow encouraged frankness; it had the sociability of surprise—it hadn't the chill. Mitchy saw at the same time that this friend of old Van's would never really understand him; though that was a thing he at times liked people as much for as he liked them little for it at others. It was in fact when he most liked that he was on the whole most tempted to mystify. "Only Mrs. Brook?—no others?"

"'Mrs. Brook'?" his friend echoed; staring an instant as if literally missing the connection; but quickly after, to show he was not stupid—and indeed it seemed to show he was delightful—smiling with extravagant intelligence. "Is that the right thing to say?"

Mitchy gave the kindest of laughs. "Well, I dare say I oughtn't to."

"Oh, I didn't mean to correct you," his interlocutor hastened to profess; "I meant, on the contrary, will it be right for me too?"

Mitchy's great goggle attentively fixed him. "Try it."

"To *her*?"

"To every one."

"To her husband?"

"Oh, to Edward," Mitchy laughed again, "perfectly!"

"And must I call him 'Edward'?"

"Whatever you do will be right," Mitchy returned—"even though it happen to be sometimes what I do."

His companion, as if to look at him with a due appreciation of this, stopped swinging the nippers and put them on. "You people here have a pleasant way——'

"Oh, we *have*!"—Mitchy, taking him up, was gaily emphatic. He began, however, already to perceive the mystification which in this case was to be his happy effect.

"Mr. Vanderbank," his victim remarked with perhaps a shade more of reserve, "has told me a good deal about you." Then as if, in a finer manner, to keep the talk off themselves: "He knows a great many ladies."

"Oh yes, poor chap, he can't help it. He finds a lady wherever he turns."

The stranger took this in, but seemed a little to challenge it. "Well, that's reassuring, if one sometimes fancies there are fewer."

"Fewer than there used to be?—I see what you mean," said Mitchy. "But if it has struck you so, that's awfully interesting." He glared and grinned and mused. "I wonder."

"Well, we shall see." His friend seemed to wish not to dogmatise.

"*Shall* we?" Mitchy considered it again in its high suggestive light. "You will—but how shall I?" Then he caught himself up with a blush. "What a beastly thing to say—as if it were mere years that make you see it!"

His companion this time gave way to the joke. "What else can it be—if I've thought so?"

"Why, it's the facts themselves, and the fine taste, and above all something *qui ne court pas les rues*, an approach to some experience of what a lady *is*." The young man's acute reflection appeared suddenly to flower into a vision of opportunity that swept everything else away. "Excuse my insisting on your time of life—but you *have* seen some?" The question was of such interest that he had already begun to follow it. "Oh, the charm of talk with some one who can meet one's conception of the really distinguished women of the past! If I could get you," he continued, "to be so awfully valuable as to meet mine!"

His fellow-visitor, on this, made, in a pause, a nearer approach to taking visibly his measure. "Are you sure you've got one?"

Mr. Mitchett brightly thought. "No. That must be just why I appeal to you. And it can't therefore be for confirmation, can it?" he went on. "It must therefore be for the beautiful primary hint altogether."

His interlocutor began, with a shake of the eye-glass, to shift and sidle again, as if distinctly excited by the subject. But it was as if his very excitement made him a trifle coy. "Are there no nice ones now?"

"Oh yes, there must be lots. In fact I know quantities."

This had the effect of pulling the stranger up. "Ah, 'quantities'! There it is."

"Yes," said Mitchy, "fancy the 'lady' in her millions. Have you come up to London, wondering, as you must, about what's happening—for Vanderbank mentioned, I think, that you *have* come up—in pursuit of her?"

"Ah," laughed the subject of Vanderbank's information, "I'm afraid 'pursuit,' with me, is over."

"Why, you're at the age," Mitchy returned, "of the most exquisite form of it. Observation."

"Yet it's a form, I seem to see, that you've not waited for my age to cultivate." This was followed by a decisive head-shake. "I'm not an observer. I'm a hater."

"That only means," Mitchy explained, "that you keep your observation for your likes—which is more admirable than prudent. But between my fear in the one direction and my desire in the other," he lightly added, "I scarcely know how to present myself. I must study the ground. Meanwhile *has* old Van told you much about me?"

Old Van's possible confidant, instead of immediately answering, again assumed the *pince-nez*. "Is that what you call him?"

"In general, I think—for shortness."

"And also"—the speaker hesitated—"for esteem?"

Mitchy laughed out. "For veneration! Our disrespects, I think, are all tender, and we wouldn't for the world do to a person we don't like anything so nice as to call him, or even to call her, don't you know——"

His questioner had quickly looked as if he knew. "Something pleasant and vulgar?"

Mitchy's gaiety deepened. "That discrimination is our only austerity. You must fall in."

"Then what will you call me?"

"What can we?" After which, sustainingly, "I'm 'Mitchy,'" our friend revealed.

His interlocutor looked slightly queer. "I don't think I can quite begin. I'm Mr. Longdon," he almost blushed to articulate.

"Absolutely and essentially—that's exactly what I recognise. I defy any one to see you," Mitchy declared, "as anything else, and on that footing you'll be, among us, unique."

Mr. Longdon appeared to accept his prospect of isolation with a certain gravity. "I gather from you—I've gathered indeed from Mr. Vanderbank—that you're a little sort of a set that hang very much together."

"Oh yes; not a formal association nor a secret society—still less a 'dangerous gang' or an organisation for any definite end. We're simply a collection of natural affinities," Mitchy explained; "meeting perhaps principally in Mrs. Brook's drawing-room—though sometimes also in old Van's, as you see,

sometimes even in mine—and governed at any rate everywhere by Mrs. Brook, in our mysterious ebbs and flows, very
much as the tides are governed by the moon. As I say,"
Mitchy pursued, "you must join. But if Van has got hold of
you," he added, "or you've got hold of him, you *have* joined.
We're not quite so numerous as I could wish, and we want
variety; we want just what I'm sure you'll bring us—a fresh
eye, an outside mind."

Mr. Longdon wore for a minute the air of a man knowing
but too well what it was to be asked to put down his name.
"My friend Vanderbank swaggers so little that it's rather from
you than from himself that I seem to catch the idea——"

"Of his being a great figure among us? I don't know what
he may have said to you, or have suppressed; but you may
take it from me—as between ourselves, you know—that he's
very much the best of us. Old Van, in fact—if you really want
a candid opinion," and Mitchy shone still brighter as he
talked, "is formed for a distinctly higher sphere. I should go
so far as to say that on our level he's positively wasted."

"And are you very sure you're not?" Mr. Longdon asked
with a smile.

"Dear no—I'm in my element. My element is to grovel before Van. You've only to look at me, as you must already have
made out, to see I'm everything dreadful that he isn't. But
you've seen him for yourself—I needn't tell you!" Mitchy
ejaculated.

Mr. Longdon, as if under the coercion of so much confidence, had stood in place longer than for any previous moment, and the spell continued for a minute after Mitchy had
paused. Then nervously, abruptly he turned away, and his
friend watched him rather aimlessly wander. "Our host has
spoken of you to me in high terms," he said as he came back.
"You would have no fault to find with them."

Mitchy took it with his highest light. "I know from your
taking the trouble to remember that, how much what I've
said of him pleases and touches you. We're a little sort of a set
then, you and I; we're an organisation of two, at any rate, and
we can't help ourselves. There—that's settled." He glanced at
the clock on the chimney. "But what's the matter with him?"

"You gentlemen dress so much," said Mr. Longdon.

Mitchy met the explanation quite half-way. "*I* try to look funny—but why should Apollo in person?"

Mr. Longdon weighed it. "Do you think him like Apollo?"

"The very image. Ask any of the women!"

"But do *they* know——"

"How Apollo must look?" Mitchy considered. "Why, the way it works is that it's just from Van's appearance they get the tip, and that then, don't you see? they've their term of comparison. Isn't it what you call a vicious circle? I borrow a little their vice."

Mr. Longdon, who had once more been arrested, once more sidled away. Then he spoke from the other side of the expanse of a table covered with books for which the shelves had no space—covered with portfolios, with well-worn leather-cased boxes, with documents in neat piles. The place was a miscellany, yet not a litter, the picture of an admirable order. "If we're an association of two, you and I, let me, accepting your idea, do what, this way, under a gentleman's roof and while enjoying his hospitality, I should in ordinary circumstances think perhaps something of a breach."

"Oh, strike out!" Mitchy laughed. It possibly chilled his interlocutor, who again hung fire so long that he himself at last adopted his image. "Why doesn't he marry, you mean?"

Mr. Longdon fairly flushed with recognition. "You're very deep, but with what we perceive—why doesn't he?"

Mitchy continued visibly to have his amusement, which might have been, this time and in spite of the amalgamation he had pictured, for what "they" perceived. But he threw off after an instant an answer clearly intended to meet the case. "He thinks he hasn't the means. He has great ideas of what a fellow must offer a woman."

Mr. Longdon's eyes travelled awhile over the amenities about him. "He hasn't such a view of himself alone——"

"As to make him think he's enough as he stands? No," said Mitchy, "I don't fancy he has a very awful view of himself alone. And since we *are* burning this incense under his nose," he added, "it's also my impression that he has no private means. Women in London cost so much."

Mr. Longdon was silent a little. "They come very high, I daresay."

"Oh, tremendously. They want so much—they want every-thing. I mean the sort of women he lives with. A modest man —who's also poor—isn't in it. I give you that, at any rate, as his view. There are lots of them that would—and only too glad—'love him for himself'; but things are much mixed, and these not necessarily the right ones, and at all events he doesn't see it. The result of which is that he's waiting."

"Waiting to feel himself in love?"

Mitchy just hesitated. "Well, we're talking of marriage. Of course you'll say there are women with money. There *are*"— he seemed for a moment to meditate—"dreadful ones!"

The two men, on this, exchanged a long regard. "He mustn't do that."

Mitchy again hesitated. "He won't."

Mr. Longdon had also a silence, which he presently termi-nated by one of his jerks into motion. "He shan't!"

Once more Mitchy watched him revolve a little, but now, familiarly yet with a sharp emphasis, he himself resumed their colloquy. "See here, Mr. Longdon. Are you seriously taking him up?"

Yet again, at the tone of this appeal, the old man percepti-bly coloured. It was as if his friend had brought to the surface an inward excitement, and he laughed for embarrassment. "You see things with a freedom——"

"Yes, and it's so I express them. I see them, I know, with a *raccourci*; but time after all rather presses, and at any rate we understand each other. What I want now is just to say—" and Mitchy spoke with a simplicity and a gravity he had not yet used—"that if your interest in him should at any time reach the point of your wishing to do something or other (no mat-ter what, don't you see?) *for* him——"

Mr. Longdon, as he faltered, appeared to wonder, but emitted a sound of gentleness. "Yes?"

"Why," said the stimulated Mitchy, "do, for God's sake, just let me have a finger in it."

Mr. Longdon's momentary mystification was perhaps partly but the natural effect of constitutional prudence. "A finger?"

"I mean—let me help."

"Oh!" breathed the old man thoughtfully and without meeting his eyes.

Mitchy, as if with more to say, watched him an instant; then before speaking caught himself up. "Look out—here he comes."

Hearing the stir of the door by which he had entered, he looked round; but it opened at first only to admit Vanderbank's servant. "Miss Brookenham!" the man announced; on which the two gentlemen in the room were—audibly, almost violently—precipitated into a union of surprise.

XI

However she might have been discussed, Nanda was not one to shrink, for, though she drew up an instant on failing to find in the room the person whose invitation she had obeyed, she advanced the next moment as if either of the gentlemen before her would answer as well. "How do you do, Mr. Mitchy? How do you do, Mr. Longdon?" She made no difference for them, speaking to the elder, whom she had not yet seen, as if they were already acquainted. There was moreover in the air of that personage at this juncture little to invite such a confidence: he appeared to have been startled, in the oddest manner, into stillness and, holding out no hand to meet her, only stared rather stiffly and without a smile. An observer disposed to interpret the scene might have fancied him a trifle put off by the girl's familiarity, or even, as by a singular effect of her self-possession, stricken into deeper diffidence. This self-possession, however, took on her own part no account of any awkwardness; it seemed the greater from the fact that she was almost unnaturally grave; and it overflowed in the immediate challenge: "Do you mean to say Van isn't here?—I've come without mother—she said I could, to see *him*," she went on, addressing herself more particularly to Mitchy. "But she didn't say I might do anything of that sort to see *you*."

If there was something serious in Nanda and something blank in their companion, there was, superficially at least, nothing in Mr. Mitchett but his usual flush of gaiety. "Did she really send you off this way alone?" Then while the girl's face met his own with the clear confession of it, "Isn't she too splendid for anything?" he asked with immense enjoyment. "What do you suppose is her idea?" Nanda's eyes had now turned to Mr. Longdon, whom she fixed with her mild straightness; which led to Mitchy's carrying on and repeating the appeal. "Isn't Mrs. Brook charming? What do you suppose is her idea?"

It was a bound into the mystery, a bound of which his fellow-visitor stood quite unconscious, only looking at Nanda still with the same coldness of wonder. All expression had for the minute been arrested in Mr. Longdon, but he at last began to show that it had merely been retarded. Yet it was almost with solemnity that he put forth his hand. "How do you do? How do you do? I'm so glad!"

Nanda shook hands with him as if she had done so already, though it might have been just her look of curiosity that detracted from her air of amusing herself. "Mother has wanted me awfully to see you. She told me to give you her love," she said. Then she added with odd irrelevance: "I didn't come in the carriage, nor in a cab or an omnibus."

"You came on a bicycle?" Mitchy inquired.

"No, I walked." She still spoke without a gleam. "Mother wants me to do everything."

"Even to walk!" Mitchy laughed. "Oh yes, we must, in these times, keep up our walking!" The ingenious observer just now suggested might even have detected in the still higher rise of this visitor's spirits a want of mere inward ease.

She had taken no notice of the effect upon him of her mention of her mother, and she took none, visibly, of Mr. Longdon's manner or of his words. What she did, while the two men, without offering her, either, a seat, practically lost themselves in their deepening vision, was to give her attention to all the place, looking at the books, pictures and other significant objects, and especially at the small table set out for tea, to which the servant who had admitted her now returned with a steaming kettle. "Isn't it charming here? Will there be any one else? Where *is* Mr. Van? Shall I make tea?" There was just a faint quaver, showing a command of the situation more desired perhaps than achieved, in the very rapid sequence of these ejaculations. The servant meanwhile had placed the hot water above the little silver lamp and left the room.

"Do you suppose there's anything the matter? Oughtn't

the man—or do you know our host's room?" Mr. Longdon, addressing Mitchy with solicitude, yet began to show, in a countenance less blank, a return of his sense of relations. It was as if something had happened to him and he were in haste to convert the signs of it into an appearance of care for the proprieties.

"Oh," said Mitchy, "Van's only making himself beautiful" —which account of their absent entertainer drew some point from his appearance at the moment in the doorway farthest removed from the place where the three were gathered.

Vanderbank came in with friendly haste and with something of the look indeed—refreshed, almost rosy, brightly brushed and quickly buttoned—of emerging, out of breath, from pleasant ablutions and renewals. "What a brute to have kept you waiting! I come back from work quite begrimed. How d'ye do, how d'ye do, how d'ye do? What's the matter with you, huddled there as if you were on a street-crossing? I want you to think this a refuge—but not of that kind!" he laughed. "Sit down, for heaven's sake; lie down—be happy! Of course you've made acquaintance all—except that Mitchy's so modest! Tea, tea!"—and he bustled to the table, where, the next minute, he appeared rather helpless. "Nanda, you blessed child, do *you* mind making it? How jolly of you! —are you all right?" He seemed, with this, for the first time, to be aware of somebody's absence. "Your mother isn't coming? She let you come alone? How jolly of her!" Pulling off her gloves, Nanda had come immediately to his assistance; on which, quitting the table and laying hands on Mr. Longdon's shoulder to push him toward a sofa, he continued to talk, to sound a note of which the humour was the exaggeration of his flurry. "How jolly of you to be willing to come—most awfully kind! I hope she isn't ill? Do, Mitchy, lie down. Down, Mitchy, down!—that's the only way to keep you." He had waited for no account of Mrs. Brookenham's health, and it might have been apparent—still to our sharp spectator—that he found nothing wonderful in her daughter's unsupported arrival.

"I can make tea beautifully," she said from behind her table. "Mother showed me how this morning."

"This morning?"—and Mitchy, who, before the fire and

still erect, had declined to be laid low, greeted the simple remark with uproarious mirth. "Dear young lady, you're the most delicious family!"

"She showed me at breakfast about the little things to do. She thought I might have to make it here and told me to offer," the girl went on. "I haven't yet done it this way at home —I usually have my tea upstairs. They bring it up in a cup, all made and very weak, with a piece of bread-and-butter in the saucer. That's because I'm so young. Tishy never lets me touch hers either; so we had to make up for lost time. That's what mother said"—she followed up her story, and her young distinctness had clearly something to do with a certain pale concentration in Mr. Longdon's face. "Mother isn't ill, but she told me already yesterday she wouldn't come. She said it's really all for *me*. I'm sure I hope it is!"—with which there flickered in her eyes, dimly but perhaps all the more prettily, the first intimation they had given of the light of laughter. "She told me you would understand, Mr. Van—from something you've said to her. It's for my seeing Mr. Longdon without—she thinks—her spoiling it."

"Oh, my dear child, 'spoiling it'!" Vanderbank protested as he took a cup of tea from her to carry to their friend. "When did your mother ever spoil anything? I told her Mr. Longdon wanted to see you, but I didn't say anything of his not yearning also for the rest of the family."

A sound of protest rather formless escaped from the gentleman named, but Nanda continued to carry out her duty. "She told me to ask why he hadn't been again to see her. Mr. Mitchy, sugar?—isn't that the way to say it? Three lumps? You're like me, only that I more often take five." Mitchy had dashed forward for his tea; she gave it to him; then she added with her eyes on Mr. Longdon's, which she had had no difficulty in catching: "She told me to ask you all sorts of things."

The old man had got up to take his cup from Vanderbank, whose hand, however, dealt with him on the question of sitting down again. Mr. Longdon, resisting, kept erect with a low gasp that his host only was near enough to catch. This suddenly appeared to confirm an impression gathered by Vanderbank in their contact, a strange sense that his visitor was so agitated as to be trembling in every limb. It brought to his lips a kind of ejaculation—"I *say!*" But even as he spoke Mr. Longdon's face, still white, but with a smile that was not all pain, seemed to supplicate him not to notice; and he was not a man to require more than this to achieve a divination as deep as it was rapid. "Why, we've all been scattered for Easter, haven't we?" he asked of Nanda. "Mr. Longdon has been at home, your mother and father have been paying visits, I myself have been out of London, Mitchy has been to Paris, and you—oh yes, I know where you've been."

"Ah, we all know that—there has been such a row made about it!" Mitchy said.

"Yes, I've heard of the feeling there is," Nanda replied. "It's supposed to be awful, my knowing Tishy—quite too awful."

Mr. Longdon, with Vanderbank's covert aid, had begun to appear to have pulled himself together, dropping back upon his sofa and giving some attention to his tea. It might have been with the notion of showing himself at ease that he turned, on this, a benevolent smile to the girl. "But what, my dear, is the objection——?"

She looked gravely from him to Vanderbank and to Mitchy, and then back again from one of these to the other. "Do you think I ought to say?"

They both laughed and they both just appeared uncertain, but Vanderbank spoke first. "I don't imagine, Nanda, that you really know."

"No—as a family, you're perfection!" Mitchy broke out. Before the fire again, with his cup, he addressed his hilarity to Mr. Longdon. "I told you a tremendous lot, didn't I? But I didn't tell you about that."

The old man maintained, yet with a certain vagueness, the attitude of amiable inquiry. "About the—a—family?"

"Well," Mitchy smiled, "about its ramifications. This young lady has a tremendous friendship—and in short it's all very complicated."

"My dear Nanda," said Vanderbank, "it's all very simple. Don't believe a word of anything of the sort."

He had spoken as with the intention of a large, light optimism; but there was clearly something in the girl that would always make for lucidity. "Do you mean about Carrie Donner? I *don't* believe it, and at any rate I don't think it's any one's business. I shouldn't have a very high opinion of a person who would give up a friend." She stopped short, with the sense apparently that she was saying more than she meant, though, strangely, as if it had been an effect of her type and of her voice, there was neither pertness nor passion in the profession she had just made. Curiously wanting as she seemed both in timidity and in levity, she was to a certainty not self-conscious—she was extraordinarily simple. Mr. Longdon looked at her now with an evident surrender to his extreme interest, and it might well have perplexed him to see her at once so downright and yet of so fresh and sweet a tenderness of youth.

"That's right, that's right, my dear young lady: never, never give up a friend for anything any one says!" It was Mitchy who rang out with this lively wisdom, the action of which on Mr. Longdon—unless indeed it was the action of something else—was to make that personage, in a manner that held the others watching him in slight suspense, suddenly spring to his feet again, put down his teacup carefully on a table near him and then without a word, as if no one had been present, quietly wander away and disappear through the door left open on Vanderbank's entrance. It opened into a second, a smaller sitting-room, into which the eyes of his companions followed him.

"What's the matter?" Nanda asked. "Has he been taken ill?"

"He *is* 'rum,' my dear Van," Mitchy said; "but you're right —of a charm, a distinction! In short just the sort of thing we want."

"The sort of thing we 'want'—I dare say!" Vanderbank laughed. "But it's not the sort of thing that's to be had for the asking—it's a sort we shall be mighty lucky if we can get!"

Mitchy turned with amusement to Nanda. "Van has invented him and, with the natural greed of the inventor, won't let us have him cheap. Well," he went on, "I'll pay my share of the expense."

"The difficulty is that he's so much too good for us," Vanderbank explained.

"Ungrateful wretch," his friend cried, "that's just what I've been telling him that *you* are! Let the return you make not be to deprive me——!"

"Mr. Van's not at all too good for *me*, if you mean that," Nanda broke in. She had finished her tea-making and leaned back in her chair with her hands folded on the edge of the tray.

Vanderbank only smiled at her in silence, but Mitchy took it up. "There's nobody too good for you, of course; only you're not quite, don't you know? *in* our set. You're in Mrs. Grendon's. I know what you're going to say—that she hasn't got any set, that she's just a loose little white flower dropped on the indifferent bosom of the world. But you're the small sprig of tender green that, added to her, makes her immediately 'compose.'"

Nanda looked at him with her cold kindness. "What nonsense you do talk!"

"Your tone's sweet to me," he returned, "as showing that you don't think *me*, either, too good for you. No one, remember, will take that for your excuse when the world some day sees me annihilated by your having put an end to our so harmless relations."

The girl appeared to lose herself a moment in the abysmal humanity over which his fairly fascinating ugliness played like the whirl of an eddy. "Martyr!" she gently exclaimed. But there was no smile with it. She turned to Vanderbank, who, during the previous minute, had moved toward the neighbouring room, then, hesitating, taking counsel of discretion, had come back a little nervous. "What *is* the matter?"

"What do you want to get out of him, you wretch?" Mitchy went on as their host for an instant produced no answer.

Vanderbank, whose handsome face had a fine thought in it, looked a trifle absently from one of them to the other; but it was to Nanda he spoke. "Do you like him, Nanda?"

She showed surprise at the question. "How can I know so soon?"

"*He* knows already."

Mitchy, with his eyes on her, became radiant to interpret. "He knows that he's pierced to the heart!"

"The matter with him, as you call it," Vanderbank brought out, "is one of the most beautiful things I've ever seen." He looked at her as with a hope that she would understand it. "Beautiful, beautiful, beautiful!"

"Precisely," Mitchy continued; "the victim done for by one glance of the goddess!"

Nanda, motionless in her chair, fixed her other friend with clear curiosity. "'Beautiful'? Why beautiful?"

Vanderbank, about to speak, checked himself. "I won't spoil it. Have it from *him*!"—and, returning to the old man, he this time went out.

Mitchy and Nanda looked at each other. "But isn't it rather awful?" Mitchy demanded.

She got up without answering; she slowly came away from the table. "I think I do know if I like him."

"Well you may," Mitchy exclaimed, "after his putting before you probably, on the whole, the greatest of your triumphs."

"And I also know, I think, Mr. Mitchy, that I like *you*." She spoke without attention to this hyperbole.

"In spite of my ineffectual attempts to be brilliant? That's a joy," he went on, "if it's not drawn out by the mere clumsiness of my flattery." She had turned away from him, kindly enough, as if time for his talk in the air were always to be allowed him; she took in vaguely Vanderbank's books and prints. "Why didn't your mother come?" Mitchy then inquired.

At this she again looked at him. "Do you mention her as a way of alluding to something you guess she must have told me?"

"That I've always supposed I make your flesh creep? Yes," Mitchy admitted; "I see that she must have said to you: 'Be nice to him, to show him it isn't quite so bad as that!' So you *are* nice—so you always *will* be nice. But I adore you, all the same, without illusions."

She had opened at one of the tables, unperceivingly, a big volume of which she turned the leaves. "Don't 'adore' a girl, Mr. Mitchy—just help her. That's more to the purpose."

"Help you?" he cried. "You bring tears to my eyes!"

"Can't a girl have friends?" she went on. "I never heard of anything so idiotic." Giving him, however, no chance to take her up on this, she made a quick transition. "Mother didn't come because she wants me now, as she says, more to share her own life."

Mitchy looked at it. "But is this the way for her to share yours?"

"Ah, that's another matter—about which you must talk to *her*. She wants me not, any more, to see only with her eyes. She's throwing me into the world."

Mitchy had listened with the liveliest interest, but he presently broke into a laugh. "What a good thing, then, that I'm there to catch you!"

Without—it might have been seen—having gathered the smallest impression of what they enclosed, she carefully drew together again the covers of her folio. There was deliberation in her movements. "I shall always be glad when you're there. But where do you suppose they've gone?" Her eyes were on what was visible of the other room, from which there arrived no sound of voices.

"They are there," said Mitchy, "but simply looking unutterable things about you. The impression's too deep. Let them look, and tell me meanwhile if Mrs. Donner gave you my message."

"Oh yes, she told me some humbug."

"The humbug then was in the tone my perfectly sincere speech took from herself. She gives things, I recognise, rather that sound. It's her weakness," he continued, "and perhaps even one may say her danger. All the more reason you should help her, as I believe you're supposed to be doing, aren't you? I hope you feel that you are," he earnestly added.

He had spoken this time gravely enough, and with magnificent gravity Nanda replied. "I *have* helped her. Tishy is sure I have. That's what Tishy wants me for. She says that to be with some nice girl is really the best thing for her."

Poor Mitchy's face hereupon would have been interesting, would have been distinctly touching to other eyes; but Nanda's were not heedful of it. "Oh," he returned after an instant and without profane mirth, "that seems to me the best thing for any one."

Vanderbank, however, might have caught his expression, for Vanderbank now reappeared, smiling on the pair as if struck by their intimacy. "How you *are* keeping it up!" Then to Nanda, persuasively: "Do you mind going to him in there? I want him so really to see you. It's quite, you know, what he came for."

Nanda seemed to wonder. "What will he do to me? Anything dreadful?"

"He'll tell you what I meant just now."

"Oh," said Nanda, "if he's a person who can tell me sometimes what you mean—!" With which she went quickly off.

"And can't *I* hear?" Mitchy asked of his host while they
looked after her.

"Yes, but only from me." Vanderbank had pushed him to a
seat again and was casting about for cigarettes. "Be quiet and
smoke, and I'll tell you."

Mitchy, on the sofa, received with meditation a light. "Will
she understand? She has everything in the world but one," he
added. "But that's half."

Vanderbank, before him, lighted for himself. "What is it?"

"A sense of humour."

"Oh yes, she's serious."

Mitchy smoked a little. "She's tragic."

His friend, at the fire, watched a moment the empty portion of the other room, then walked across to give the door a
light push that all but closed it. "It's rather odd," he remarked as he came back—"that's quite what I just said to
him. But he won't treat her to comedy."

XII

"Is it the shock of the resemblance to her grandmother?" Vanderbank had asked of Mr. Longdon on rejoining him in his retreat. The old man, with his back turned, was gazing out of the
window, and when in answer he showed his face there were
tears in his eyes. His answer in fact was just these tears, the significance of which Vanderbank immediately recognised. "It's
still greater then than you gathered from her photograph."

"It's the most extraordinary thing in the world. I'm too absurd to be so upset"—Mr. Longdon smiled through his tears
—"but if you had known Lady Julia you would understand.
It's *she* again, as I first knew her, to the life; and not only in
feature, in stature, in colour, in movement, but in every bodily mark and sign, in every look of the eyes, above all—oh, to
a degree!—in the sound, in the charm of the voice." He
spoke low and confidentially, but with an intensity that now
relieved him—he was restless in his emotion. He moved
about, in his excitement, gently, as if with a sacred awe—as if

but a few steps away he had been in the very presence. "She's *all* Lady Julia. There isn't a touch of her mother. It's unique —an absolute revival. I see nothing of her father, either—I see nothing of any one else. Isn't it thought wonderful by every one?" he went on. "Why didn't you tell me?"

"To have prepared you a little?"—Vanderbank felt almost guilty. "I see—I should have liked to make more of it; though," he added, smiling, "I might so, by putting you on your guard, have caused myself to lose what, if you'll allow me to say so, strikes me as one of the most touching tributes I've ever seen rendered to a woman. In fact, however, how could I know? I never saw Lady Julia, and you had in advance all the evidence that I could have: the portrait—pretty bad, in the taste of the time, I admit—and the three or four photographs that, with it, you must have noticed at Mrs. Brook's. These things must have compared themselves, for you, with my photograph in there of the granddaughter. The similarity of course we had all observed, but it has taken your wonderful memory and your admirable vision to put into it all the detail."

Mr. Longdon thought a moment, giving a dab with his pocket-handkerchief. "Very true—you're quite right. It's far beyond any identity in the pictures. But why did you tell me," he added more sharply, "that she isn't beautiful?"

"You've deprived me," Vanderbank laughed, "of the power of expressing civilly any surprise at your finding her so. But I said to you, please remember, nothing that qualified a jot my sense of the curious character of her face. I have always positively found in it a recall of the type of the period you must be thinking of. It isn't a bit modern. It's a face of Sir Thomas Lawrence——"

"It's a face of Gainsborough!" Mr. Longdon returned with spirit. "Lady Julia herself harked back."

Vanderbank, clearly, was equally touched and amused. "Let us say at once that it's a face of Raphael."

His old friend's hand was instantly on his arm. "That's exactly what I often said to myself of Lady Julia's."

"The forehead's a little too high," said Vanderbank.

"But it's just that excess that, with the exquisite eyes and the particular disposition round it of the fair hair, makes the individual grace, makes the beauty of the remainder."

Released by Lady Julia's lover, the young man in turn grasped him as an encouragement to confidence. "It's a face that should have the long side-ringlets of 1830. It should have the rest of the personal arrangement, the pelisse, the shape of bonnet, the sprigged muslin dress and the cross-laced sandals. It should have arrived in a pea-green 'tilbury' and it should be a reader of Mrs. Radcliffe. And all this to complete the Raphael!"

Mr. Longdon, who, relieved by expression, had begun to recover himself, looked hard a moment at his companion. "How you've observed her!"

Vanderbank met it without confusion. "Whom haven't I observed? Do you like her?" he then rather oddly and abruptly asked.

The old man broke away again. "How can I tell—with such disparities?"

"The manner must be different," Vanderbank suggested. "And the things she says."

His visitor was before him again. "I don't know what to make of them. They don't go with the rest of her. Lady Julia," said Mr. Longdon, "was rather shy."

On this too his host could meet him. "She must have been. And Nanda—yes, certainly—doesn't give that impression."

"On the contrary. But Lady Julia was gay!" he added with an eagerness that made Vanderbank smile.

"I can also see that. Nanda doesn't joke. And yet," Vanderbank continued with his exemplary candour, "we mustn't speak of her, must we? as if she were bold and grim."

Mr. Longdon fixed him. "Do you think she's sad?"

They had preserved their dropped tone and might, with their heads together, have been conferring as the party "out" in some game with the couple in the other room. "Yes. Sad." But Vanderbank broke off. "I'll send her to you." Thus it was he had come back to her.

Nanda, on joining Mr. Longdon, went straight to the point. "He says it's so beautiful—what you feel on seeing me: if that *is* what he meant." The old man said nothing again at first; he only smiled at her, but less strangely now, and then appeared to look about him for some place where she could sit near him. There was a sofa in this room too, on which, observing it, she quickly sank down, so that they were presently together, placed a little sideways and face to face. She had shown perhaps that she supposed him to have wished to take her hand, but he forbore to touch her, only letting her feel all the kindness of his eyes and their long, backward vision. These things she evidently felt soon enough; she went on before he had spoken. "I know how well you knew my grandmother. Mother has told me—and I'm so glad. She told me to say to you that she wants *you* to tell me." Just a shade, at this, might, over the old man's face, have appeared to drop; but who was there to detect whether the girl observed it? It didn't prevent at any rate her completing her statement. "That's why, to-day, she wished me to come alone. She wished you to have me, she said, all to yourself."

No, decidedly, she was not shy: that mute reflection was in the air an instant. "That, no doubt, is the best way. I thank her very much. I called, after having had the honour of dining—I called, I think, three times," he went on, with a sudden displacement of the question; "but I had the misfortune each time to miss her."

She kept looking at him with her crude young clearness. "I didn't know about that. Mother thinks she's more at home than almost any one. She does it on purpose: she knows what it is," Nanda pursued, with her perfect gravity, "for people to be disappointed of finding her."

"Oh, I shall find her yet," said Mr. Longdon. "And then I hope I shall also find *you*."

She appeared simply to consider the possibility and after an instant to think well of it. "I dare say you will now, for now I shall be down."

Her companion just blinked. "In the drawing-room, you mean—always?"

It was quite what she meant. "Always. I shall see all the people who come. It will be a great thing for me. I want to hear all the talk. Mr. Mitchett says I ought to—that it helps to form the young mind. I hoped, for that reason," she went on with the directness that made her honesty almost violent—"I hoped there would be more people here to day."

"I'm very glad there are not!"—the old man rang equally

clear. "Mr. Vanderbank kindly arranged the matter for me just this way. I met him at dinner, at your mother's, three weeks ago, and he brought me home here that night, when, as knowing you so differently, we took the liberty of talking you all over. It had the effect, naturally, of making me want to begin with you afresh—only that seemed difficult too without further help. This he good-naturedly offered me; he said"—and Mr. Longdon recovered his spirits to repeat it—"'Hang it, I'll have them here for you!'"

"I see—he knew we would come." Then she caught herself up. "But we haven't come, have we?"

"Oh, it's all right—it's all right. To me the occasion's brilliant and the affluence great. I've had such talk with those young men——"

"I see"—she was again prompt, but beyond any young person he had ever met she might have struck him as literal. "You're not used to such talk. Neither am I. It's rather wonderful, isn't it? They're thought awfully clever, Mr. Van and Mr. Mitchy. Do you like them?" she pushed on.

Mr. Longdon, who, as compared with her, might have struck a spectator as infernally subtle, took an instant to think. "I've never met Mr. Mitchett before."

"Well, he always thinks one doesn't like him," Nanda explained. "But one does. One ought to," she added.

Her companion had another pause. "He likes *you*."

Oh, Mr. Longdon needn't have hesitated! "I know he does. He has told mother. He has told lots of people."

"He has told even you," Mr. Longdon smiled.

"Yes—but that isn't the same. I don't think he's a bit dreadful," she pursued. Still, there was a greater interest. "Do you like Mr. Van?"

This time her interlocutor indeed hung fire. "How can I tell? He dazzles me."

"But don't you like that?" Then before he could really say: "You're afraid he may be false?"

At this he fairly laughed. "You go to the point!" She just coloured to have amused him so, but he quickly went on: "I think one has a little natural nervousness at being carried off one's feet. I'm afraid I've always liked too much to see where I'm going."

"And you don't with him?" She spoke with her curious hard interest. "I understand. But I think I like to be dazzled."

"Oh, you've got time—you can come round again; you've a margin for accidents, for disappointments and recoveries; you can take one thing with another. But I've only my last little scrap."

"And you want to make no mistakes—I see."

"Well, I'm too easily upset."

"Ah, so am I," said Nanda. "I assure you that in spite of what you say I want to make no mistakes either. I've seen a great many—though you mightn't think it," she persisted; "I really know what they may be. Do you like *me?*" she brought forth. But even on this she spared him too; a look appeared to have been enough for her. "How can you say, of course, already?—if you can't say for Mr. Van. I mean as you've seen him so much. When he asked me just now if I liked *you* I told him it was too soon. But it isn't now; you see it goes fast. I *do* like you." She gave him no time to acknowledge this tribute, but, as if it were a matter of course, tried him quickly with something else. "Can you say if you like mother?"

He could meet it pretty well now. "There are immense reasons why I should."

"Yes—I know about them, as I mentioned: mother has told me." But what she had to put to him kept up his surprise. "Have reasons anything to do with it? I don't believe you like her!" she exclaimed. "*She* doesn't think so," she added.

The old man's face at last, partly bewildered, partly reassured, showed even more something finer still in the effect she produced. "Into what mysteries you plunge!"

"Oh, we do; that's what every one says of us. We discuss everything and every one—we're always discussing each other. I think we must be rather celebrated for it, and it's a kind of trick—isn't it?—that's catching. But don't you think it's the most interesting sort of talk? Mother says we haven't any prejudices. *You* have, probably, quantities—and beautiful ones: so perhaps I oughtn't to tell you. But you'll find out for yourself."

"Yes—I'm rather slow; but I generally end by finding out. And I've got, thank heaven," said Mr. Longdon, "quite prejudices enough."

"Then I hope you'll tell me some of them," Nanda replied in a tone evidently marking how much he pleased her.

"Ah, you must do as *I* do—you must find out for yourself. Your resemblance to your grandmother is quite prodigious," he immediately added.

"That's what I wish you'd tell me about—your recollection of her and your wonderful feeling about her. Mother has told me things, but that I should have something straight from you is exactly what she also wants. My grandmother must have been awfully nice," the girl rambled on, "and I somehow don't see myself at all as the same sort of person."

"Oh, I don't say you're in the least the same sort: all I allude to," Mr. Longdon returned, "is the miracle of the physical heredity. Nothing could be less like her than your manner and your talk."

Nanda looked at him with all her honesty. "They're not so good, you must think."

He hung fire an instant, but was as honest as she. "You're separated from her by a gulf—and not only of time. Personally, you see, you breathe a different air."

She thought—she quite took it in. "Of course. And you breathe the same—the same old one, I mean, as my grandmother."

"The same old one," Mr. Longdon smiled, "as much as possible. Some day I'll tell you more of what you desire. I can't go into it now."

"Because I've upset you so?" Nanda frankly asked.

"That's one of the reasons."

"I think I can see another too," she observed after a moment. "You're not sure how much I shall understand. But I shall understand," she went on, "more, perhaps, than you think. In fact," she said earnestly, "I *promise* to understand. I've some imagination. Had my grandmother?" she asked. Her actual sequences were not rapid, but she had already anticipated him. "I've thought of that before, because I put the same question to mother."

"And what did your mother say?"

"'Imagination—dear mamma? Not a grain!'"

The old man showed a faint flush. "Your mother then has a supply that makes up for it."

The girl fixed him, on this, with a deeper attention. "You don't like her having said that."

His colour came stronger, though a slightly strained smile did what it could to diffuse coolness. "I don't care a single scrap, my dear, in respect to the friend I'm speaking of, for any judgment but my own."

"Not even for her daughter's?"

"Not even for her daughter's." Mr. Longdon had not spoken loud, but he rang as clear as a bell.

Nanda, for admiration of it, broke almost for the first time into the semblance of a smile. "You feel as if my grandmother were quite *your* property!"

"Oh, quite."

"I say—that's splendid!"

"I'm glad you like it," he answered kindly.

The very kindness pulled her up. "Excuse my speaking so, but I'm sure you know what I mean. You mustn't think," she eagerly continued, "that mother won't also want to hear you."

"On the subject of Lady Julia?" He gently, but very effectively, shook his head. "Your mother shall never hear me."

Nanda appeared to wonder at it an instant, and it made her completely grave again. "It will be all for *me*?"

"Whatever there may be of it, my dear."

"Oh, I shall get it all out of you," she returned without hesitation. Her mixture of free familiarity and of the vividness of evocation of something, whatever it was, sharply opposed —the little worry of this contradiction, not altogether unpleasant, continued to fill his consciousness more discernibly than anything else. It was really reflected in his quick brown eyes that she alternately drew him on and warned him off, but also that what they were beginning more and more to make out was an emotion of her own trembling there beneath her tension. His glimpse of it widened—his glimpse of it fairly triumphed when suddenly, after this last declaration, she threw off with quite the same accent but quite another effect: "I'm glad to be like any one the thought of whom makes you so good! You *are* good," she continued; "I see already how I shall feel it." She stared at him with tears, the sight of which brought his own straight back, so that thus for a moment they sat there together.

"My dear child!" he at last simply murmured. But he laid his hand on her now, and her own immediately met it.

"You'll get used to me," she said with the same gentleness that the response of her touch had tried to express; "and I shall be so careful with you that—well, you'll see!" She broke short off with a quaver and the next instant she turned—there was some one at the door. Vanderbank, still not quite at his ease, had come back to smile upon them. Detaching herself from Mr. Longdon, she got straight up to meet him. "You were right, Mr. Van. It's beautiful, beautiful, beautiful!"

BOOK FOURTH

Mr. Cashmore

XIII

HAROLD BROOKENHAM, whom Mr. Cashmore, ushered in and announced, had found in the act of helping himself to a cup of tea at the table apparently just prepared—Harold Brookenham arrived at the point with a dash so direct as to leave the visitor an option between but two suppositions: that of a desperate plunge, to have his shame soon over, or that of the acquired habit of such appeals, which had taught him the easiest way. There was no great sharpness in the face of Mr. Cashmore, who was somehow massive without majesty; yet he might not have been proof against the suspicion that his young friend's embarrassment was an easy precaution, a conscious corrective to the danger of audacity. It would not have been impossible to divine that if Harold shut his eyes and jumped it was mainly for the appearance of doing so. Experience was to be taken as showing that one might get a five-pound note as one got a light for a cigarette; but one had to check the friendly impulse to ask for it in the same way. Mr. Cashmore had in fact looked surprised, yet not on the whole so surprised as the young man seemed to have expected of him. There was almost a quiet grace in the combination of promptitude and diffidence with which Harold took over the responsibility of all proprietorship of the crisp morsel of paper that he slipped with slow firmness into the pocket of his waistcoat, rubbing it gently in its passage against the delicately buff-coloured duck of which that garment was composed. "So quite too awfully kind of you that I really don't know what to say"—there was a marked recall, in the manner of this speech, of the sweetness of his mother's droop and the tenderness of her wail. It was as if he had been moved for the moment to moralise, but the eyes he raised to his benefactor had the oddest effect of marking that personage himself as the source of the lesson.

Mr. Cashmore, who would have been very red-haired if he had not been very bald, showed a single eye-glass and a long

upper-lip; he was large and jaunty, with little petulant movements and intense ejaculations that were not in the line of his
type. "You may say anything you like if you don't say you'll
repay it. That's always nonsense—I hate it."

Harold remained sad, but showed himself really superior.
"Then I won't say it." Pensively, a minute, he appeared to figure the words, in their absurdity, on the lips of some young
man not, like himself, tactful. "I know just what you mean."

"But I think, you know, that you ought to tell your father,"
Mr. Cashmore said.

"Tell him I've borrowed of you?"

Mr. Cashmore good-humouredly demurred. "It would
serve me right—it's so shocking my having listened to you.
Tell him, certainly," he went on after an instant. "But what I
mean is that if you're in such straits you should speak to him
like a man."

Harold smiled at the innocence of a friend who could suppose him not to have exhausted that resource. "I'm *always*
speaking to him like a man, and that's just what puts him so
awfully out. He denies to my face that I *am* one. One would
suppose, to hear him, not only that I'm a small objectionable
child, but that I'm scarcely even human. He doesn't conceive
me as with any wants."

"Oh," Mr. Cashmore laughed, "you've all—you youngsters
—as many wants, I know, as an advertisement page of the
Times."

Harold showed an admiration. "That's awfully good. If you
think you ought to speak of it," he continued, "do it rather
to mamma." He noted the hour. "I'll go, if you'll excuse me,
to give you the chance."

The visitor referred to his own watch. "It's your mother
herself who gives the chances—the chances *you* take."

Harold looked kind and simple. "She *has* come in, I know.
She'll be with you in a moment."

He was half-way to the door, but Mr. Cashmore, though so
easy, had not done with him. "I suppose you mean that if it's
only your mother who's told, you may depend on her to
shield you."

Harold turned this over as if it were a questionable sovereign, but on second thoughts he wonderfully smiled. "Do

you think that after you've let me have it you can tell? You could, of course, if you hadn't." He appeared to work it out for Mr. Cashmore's benefit. "But I don't mind," he added, "your telling mamma."

"Don't mind, you mean really, it's annoying her so awfully?"

The invitation to repent thrown off in this could only strike the young man as absurd—it was so previous to any enjoyment. Harold liked things in their proper order; but at the same time his evolutions were quick. "I dare say I *am* selfish, but what I was thinking was that the terrific wigging, don't you know?—well, I'd take it from *her*. She knows about one's life—about our having to go on, by no fault of our own, as our parents start us. She knows all about wants—no one has more than mamma."

Mr. Cashmore stared, but there was amusement in it too. "So she'll say it's all right?"

"Oh no; she'll let me have it hot. But she'll recognise that at such a pass more must be done for a fellow, and that may lead to something—indirectly, don't you see? for she won't *tell* my father, she'll only, in her own way, work on him—that will put me on a better footing and for which therefore at bottom I shall have to thank *you*."

The eye assisted by Mr. Cashmore's glass had fixed, during this address, with a discernible growth of something like alarm, the subject of his beneficence. The thread of their relations somehow lost itself in this subtler twist, and he fell back on mere stature, position and property, things always convenient in the presence of crookedness. "I shall say nothing to your mother, but I think I shall be rather glad that you're not a son of mine."

Harold wondered at this new element in their talk. "Do your sons never——"

"Borrow money of their mother's visitors?" Mr. Cashmore had taken him up, eager, evidently, quite to satisfy him; but the question was caught on the wing by Mrs. Brookenham herself, who had opened the door as her friend spoke and who quickly advanced with an echo of it.

"Lady Fanny's visitors?"—and, though her eyes rather avoided than met his own, she seemed to cover her ladyship's husband with a vague but practised sympathy. "What on earth

are you saying to Harold about them?" Thus it was that at the
end of a few minutes Mr. Cashmore, on the sofa face to face
with her, found his consciousness quite purged of its actual
sense of his weakness and a new turn given to the idea of
what, in one's very drawing-room, might go on behind one's
back. Harold had quickly vanished—had been tacitly disposed
of, and Mrs. Brook's caller had moved even in the short space
of time so far in quite another direction as to have drawn
from her the little cold question: "'Presents'? You don't mean
money?"

He clearly felt the importance of expressing at least by his
silence and his eye-glass what he meant. "Her extravagance is
beyond everything, and though there are bills enough, God
knows, that do come in to me, I don't see how she pulls
through unless there are others that go elsewhere."

Mrs. Brookenham had given him his tea—her own she had
placed on a small table near her, and she could now respond
freely to the impulse felt, on this, of settling herself to something of real interest. Except to Harold she was incapable of
reproach, though there were shades, of course, in her resignation, and her daughter's report of her to Mr. Longdon as
conscious of an absence of prejudice would have been justified for a spectator by the particular feeling that Mr. Cashmore's speech caused her to disclose. What did this feeling
wonderfully appear unless strangely irrelevant? "I've no patience when I hear you talk as if you weren't horribly rich."

He looked at her an instant as if with the fancy that she
might have derived that impression from Harold. "What has
that to do with it? Does a rich man enjoy any more than a
poor his wife's making a fool of him?"

Her eyes opened wider: it was one of her very few ways of
betraying amusement. There was little indeed to be amused at
here except his choice of the particular invidious name. "You
know I don't believe a word you say."

Mr. Cashmore drank his tea, then rose to carry the cup
somewhere and put it down, declining with a motion any
assistance. When he was on the sofa again he resumed their
intimate talk. "I like tremendously to be with you, but you
mustn't think I've come here to let you say to me such dreadful things as that." He was an odd compound, Mr. Cashmore,

and the air of personal good health, the untarnished bloom which sometimes lent a monstrous serenity to his mention of the barely mentionable, was on occasion balanced or matched by his playful application of extravagant terms to matters of much less moment. "You know what I come to you for, Mrs. Brook: I won't come any more if you're going to be horrid and impossible."

"You come to me, I suppose, because—for my deep misfortune, I assure you—I've a kind of vision of things, of the wretched miseries in which you all knot yourselves up, which you yourselves are as little blessed with as if, tumbling about together in your heap, you were a litter of blind kittens."

"Awfully good, that—you do lift the burden of my trouble!" He had laughed out in the manner of the man who made notes for platform use of things that might serve; but the next moment he was grave again, as if his observation had reminded him of Harold's praise of his wit. It was in this spirit that he abruptly brought out: "Where, by-the-way, is your daughter?"

"I haven't the least idea. I do all I can to enter into her life, but you can't get into a railway train while it's on the rush."

Mr. Cashmore swung back to hilarity. "You give me lots of things. Do you mean she's so 'fast'?" He could keep the ball going.

Mrs. Brookenham hesitated. "No; she's a tremendous dear, and we're great friends. But she has her free young life, which, by that law of our time that I'm sure I only want, like all other laws, once I know what they *are*, to accept—she has her precious freshness of feeling which I say to myself that, so far as control is concerned, I ought to respect. I try to get her to sit with me, and she does so often, because she's kind. But before I know it she leaves me again: she feels that her presence makes a difference in one's liberty of talk."

Mr. Cashmore was struck by this picture. "That's awfully charming of her."

"Isn't it too dear?" The thought of it, for Mrs. Brook, seemed fairly to open out vistas. "The modern daughter!"

"But not the ancient mother!" Mr. Cashmore smiled.

She shook her head with a world of accepted woe. "'Give me back, give me back one hour of my youth'! Oh, I haven't a single thrill left to answer a compliment. I sit here now face to face with things as they are. They come in their turn, I assure you—and they find me," Mrs. Brook sighed, "ready. Nanda has stepped on the stage, and I give her up the house. Besides," she went on musingly, "it's awfully interesting. It *is* the modern daughter—we're really 'doing' her, the child and I; and as the modern has always been my own note—I've gone in, I mean, frankly for my very own Time—who is one, after all, that one should pretend to decline to go where it may lead?" Mr. Cashmore was unprepared with an answer to this question, and his hostess continued in a different tone: "It's sweet her sparing one!"

This, for the visitor, was firmer ground. "Do you mean about talking before her?"

Mrs. Brook's assent was positively tender. "She won't have a difference in my freedom. It's as if the dear thing *knew*, don't you see? what we must keep back. She wants us not to have to think. It's quite maternal!" she mused again. Then as if with the pleasure of presenting it to him afresh: "That's the modern daughter!"

"Well," said Mr. Cashmore, "I can't help wishing she were a trifle less considerate. In that case I might find her with you, and I may tell you frankly that I get more from her than I do from you. She has the great merit for me, in the first place, of not being such an admirer of my wife."

Mrs. Brookenham took this up with interest. "No—you're right; she doesn't, as I do, *see* Lady Fanny, and that's a kind of mercy."

"There you are then, you inconsistent creature," he cried with a laugh; "after all you *do* believe me! You recognise how benighted it would be for your daughter not to feel that Fanny's bad."

"You're too tiresome, my dear man," Mrs. Brook returned, "with your ridiculous simplifications. Fanny's *not* 'bad'; she's magnificently good—in the sense of being generous and simple and true, too adorably unaffected and without the least *mesquinerie*. She's a great calm silver statue."

Mr. Cashmore showed, on this, something of the strength that comes from the practice of public debate. "Then why are you glad that your daughter doesn't like her?"

Mrs. Brook smiled as with the sadness of having too much to triumph. "Because I'm not, like Fanny, without *mesquinerie*. I'm not generous and simple. I'm exaggeratedly anxious about Nanda. I care, in spite of myself, for what people may say. Your wife doesn't—she towers above them. I can be a shade less brave through the chance of my girl's not happening to feel her as the rest of us do."

Mr. Cashmore too heavily followed. "To 'feel' her?"

Mrs. Brook floated over. "There would be, in that case perhaps, something to hint to her not to shriek on the house-tops. When you say," she continued, "that one admits, as regards Fanny, anything wrong, you pervert dreadfully what one does freely grant—that she's a great glorious pagan. It's a real relief to know such a type—it's like a flash of insight into history. None the less, if you ask me why then it isn't all right for young things to 'shriek' as I say, I have my answer perfectly ready." After which, as her visitor seemed not only too reduced to doubt it, but too baffled to distinguish audibly, for his credit, between resignation and admiration, she produced: "Because she's purely instinctive. Her instincts are splendid—but it's terrific."

"That's all I ever maintained it to be!" Mr. Cashmore cried. "It *is* terrific."

"Well," his friend answered, "I'm watching her. We're all watching her. It's like some great natural poetic thing—an Alpine sunrise or a big high tide."

"You're amazing!" Mr. Cashmore laughed. "I'm watching her too."

"And I'm also watching *you*," Mrs. Brook lucidly continued. "What I don't for a moment believe is that her bills are paid by any one. It's *much* more probable," she sagaciously observed, "that they're not paid at all."

"Oh, well, if she can get on that way—!"

"There can't be a place in London," Mrs. Brook pursued, "where they're not delighted to dress such a woman. She shows things, don't you see? as some fine tourist region shows the placards in the fields and the posters on the rocks. And what proof can you adduce?" she asked.

Mr. Cashmore had grown restless; he picked a stray thread off the knee of his trousers. "Ah, when you talk about 'adducing'—!" He appeared to intimate, as if with the hint that if she didn't take care she might bore him, that it was the kind of word he used only in the House of Commons.

"When I talk about it you can't meet me," she placidly returned. But she fixed him with her weary penetration. "You try to believe what you *can't* believe, in order to give yourself excuses. And she does the same—only less, for she recognises less, in general, the need of them. She's so grand and simple."

Poor Mr. Cashmore stared. "Grander and simpler than I, you mean?"

Mrs. Brookenham thought. "Not simpler—no; but very much grander. She wouldn't, in the case you conceive, recognise really the need of *what* you conceive."

Mr. Cashmore wondered—it was almost mystic. "I don't understand you."

Mrs. Brook, seeing it all from dim depths, tracked it further and further. "We've talked her over so!"

Mr. Cashmore groaned as if too conscious of it. "Indeed we have!"

"I mean *we*"—and it was wonderful how her accent discriminated. "We've talked you too—but of course we talk every one." She had a pause through which there glimmered a ray from luminous hours, the inner intimacy which, privileged as he was, he couldn't pretend to share; then she broke out almost impatiently: "We're looking after her—leave her to *us!*"

He looked suddenly so curious as to seem really envious, but he tried to throw it off. "I doubt if after all you're good for her."

But Mrs. Brookenham knew. "She's just the sort of person we *are* good for, and the thing for her is to be with us as much as possible—just live with us naturally and easily, listen to our talk, feel our confidence in her, be kept up, don't you know? by the sense of what we expect of her splendid type, and so, little by little, let our influence act. What I meant to say just now is that I do perfectly see her taking what you call presents."

"Well, then," Mr. Cashmore inquired, "what do you want more?"

Mrs. Brook hung fire an instant—she seemed on the point of telling him. "I don't see her, as I said, recognising the obligation."

"The obligation——?"

"To give anything back. Anything at all." Mrs. Brook was positive. "The comprehension of petty calculations? Never!"

"I don't say the calculations are petty," Mr. Cashmore objected.

"Well, she's a great creature. If she does fall—!" His hostess lost herself in the view, which was at last all before her. "Be sure we shall all know it."

"That's exactly what I'm afraid of!"

"Then don't be afraid till we do. She would fall, as it were, on *us*, don't you see? and," said Mrs. Brook, with decision this time in her head-shake, "that couldn't be. We *must* keep her up—that's your guarantee. It's rather too much," she added with the same increase of briskness, "to have to keep *you* up too. Be very sure that if Carrie really wavers——"

"Carrie?"

His interruption was clearly too vague to be sincere, and it was as such that, going straight on, she treated it. "I shall never again give her three minutes' attention. To answer to you for Fanny without being able——"

"To answer to Fanny for me, do you mean?" He had flushed quickly as if he awaited her there. "It wouldn't suit you, you contend? Well then, I hope it will ease you off," he went on with spirit, "to know that I wholly *loathe* Mrs. Donner."

Mrs. Brook, staring, met the announcement with an absolute change of colour. "And since when, pray?" It was as if a fabric had crumbled. "She was here but the other day, and as full of you, poor thing, as an egg of meat."

Mr. Cashmore could only blush for her. "I don't say she wasn't. My life's a burden from her."

Nothing, for a spectator, could have been so odd as Mrs. Brook's disappointment unless it had been her determination. "Have you done with her already?"

"One has never done with a buzzing insect——!"

"Until one has literally killed it?" Mrs. Brookenham wailed. "I can't take that from you, my dear man: it was yourself who originally distilled the poison that courses through her veins." He jumped up at this as if he couldn't bear it, presenting as he walked across the room, however, a large, foolish, fugitive back on which her eyes rested as on a proof of her penetration. "If you spoil everything by trying to deceive me, how can I help you?"

He had looked, in his restlessness, at a picture or two, but he finally turned round. "With whom is it you talk us over? With Petherton and his friend Mitchy? With your adored Vanderbank? With your awful Duchess?"

"You know my little circle, and you've not always despised it." She met him on his return with a figure that had visibly flashed out for her. "Don't foul your own nest! Remember that after all we've more or less produced you." She had a smile that attenuated a little her image, for there were things that on a second thought he appeared ready to take from her. She patted the sofa as if to invite him again to be seated, and though he still stood before her it was with a face that seemed to show how her touch went home. "You know I've never quite thought you do us full honour, but it was because *she* took you for one of us that Carrie first——"

At this, to stop her, he dropped straight into the seat. "I assure you there has really been nothing." With a continuation of his fidget he pulled out his watch. "Won't she come in at all?"

"Do you mean Nanda?"

"Talk me over with *her*," he smiled, "if you like. If you don't believe Mrs. Donner is dust and ashes to me," he continued, "you do little justice to your daughter."

"Do you wish to break it to me that you're in love with Nanda?"

He hesitated, but only as if to give weight to his reply. "Awfully. I can't tell you how I like her."

She wondered. "And pray how will *that* help me? Help me, I mean, to help you. Is it what I'm to tell your wife?"

He sat looking away, but he evidently had his idea, which he at last produced. "Why wouldn't it be just the thing? It would exactly prove my purity."

There might have been in her momentary silence a hint of acceptance of it as a practical contribution to their problem, and there were indeed several lights in which it could be considered. Mrs. Brook, on a quick survey, selected the ironic. "I see, I see. I might by the same law arrange somehow that Lady Fanny should find herself in love with Edward. That would 'prove' *her* purity. And you could be quite at ease," she laughed—"he wouldn't make any presents!"

Mr. Cashmore regarded her with a candour that was almost a reproach to her mirth. "I like your daughter better than I like you."

But it only amused her more. "Is that perhaps because *I* don't prove your purity?"

What he might have replied remained in the air, for the door opened so exactly at the moment she spoke that he rose again with a start, and the butler, coming in, received her inquiry full in the face. This functionary's answer to it, however, had no more than the usual austerity. "Mr. Vanderbank and Mr. Longdon."

These visitors took a minute to appear, and Mrs. Brook, not stirring—still only looking from the sofa calmly up at Mr. Cashmore—used the time, it might have seemed, for correcting any impression of undue levity made by her recent question. "Where did you last meet Nanda?"

He glanced at the door to see if he were heard. "At the Grendons'."

"So you do go there?"

"I went over from Hicks the other day for an hour."

"And Carrie was there?"

"Yes. It was a dreadful horrid bore. But I talked only to your daughter."

She got up—the others were at hand—and offered Mr. Cashmore a face that might have struck him as strange. "It's serious."

"Serious?"—he had no eyes for the others.

"She didn't tell me."

He gave a sound, controlled by discretion, which sufficed none the less to make Mr. Longdon—beholding him for the first time—receive it with a little of the stiffness of a person greeted with a guffaw. Mr. Cashmore visibly liked this silence of Nanda's about their meeting.

XIV

Mrs. Brookenham, who had introduced him to the elder of her visitors, had also found, in serving these gentlemen with tea, a chance to edge at him with an intensity not to be resisted: "Talk to Mr. Longdon—take him off *there*." She had indicated the sofa at the opposite end of the room and had set him an example by possessing herself, in the place she already occupied, of her "adored" Vanderbank. This arrangement, however, when she had made it constituted for her, in her own corner, the ground of an instant appeal. "Will he hate me any worse for doing that?"

Vanderbank glanced at the others. "Will Cashmore, do you mean?"

"Dear no—I don't care whom *he* hates. But with Mr. Longdon I want to avoid mistakes."

"Then don't try quite so hard!" Vanderbank laughed. "Is that your reason for throwing him into Cashmore's arms?"

"Yes, precisely—so that I shall have these few moments to ask you for directions: you must know him, by this time, so well. I only want, heaven help me, to be as nice to him as I possibly can."

"That's quite the best thing for you and altogether why, this afternoon, I brought him: he might have better luck in finding you—it was he who suggested it—than he has had by himself. I'm in a general way," Vanderbank added, "watching over him."

"I see—and he's watching over you." Mrs. Brook's lovely vacancy had already taken in so much. "He wants to judge of what I may be doing to you—he wants to save you from me. He quite detests me."

Vanderbank, with the interest as well as the amusement, fairly threw himself back. "There's nobody like you—you're too magnificent!"

"I *am*; and that I can look the truth in the face and not be angry or silly about it is, as you know, the one thing in the world for which I think a bit well of myself."

"Oh yes, I know—I know; you're too wonderful!"

Mrs. Brookenham, in a brief pause, completed her consciousness. "They're doing beautifully—he's taking Cashmore with a seriousness!"

"And with what is Cashmore taking him?"

"With the hope that, from one moment to another, Nanda may come in."

"But how on earth does that concern him?"

"Through an extraordinary fancy he has suddenly taken to her." Mrs. Brook had been swift to master the facts. "He has been meeting her at Tishy's, and she has talked to him so effectually about his behaviour that she has quite made him cease to think about Carrie. He prefers *her* now—and of course she's much nicer."

Vanderbank's attention, it was clear, had now been fully seized. "She's much nicer. Rather! What you mean is," he asked the next moment, "that Nanda, this afternoon, has been the object of his call?"

"Yes—really; though he tried to keep it from me. She makes him feel," she went on, "so innocent and good."

Her companion for a moment said nothing; but then at last: "And *will* she come in?"

"I haven't the least idea."

"Don't you know where she is?"

"I suppose she's with Tishy, who has returned to town."

Vanderbank turned this over. "Is that your system now—to ask no questions?"

"Why *should* I ask any—when I want her life to be as much as possible like my own? It's simply that the hour has struck, as you know. From the moment she *is* down, the only thing for us is to live as friends. I think it's so vulgar," Mrs. Brook sighed, "not to have the same good manners with one's children as one has with other people. She asks *me* nothing."

"Nothing?" Vanderbank echoed.

"Nothing."

He paused again; after which, "It's very disgusting!" he exclaimed. Then as she took it up as he had taken her word of a moment before, "It's very preposterous," he continued.

Mrs. Brook appeared at a loss. "Do you mean her helping him?"

"It's not of Nanda I'm speaking—it's of him." Vanderbank spoke with a certain impatience. "His being with her in any sort of direct relation at all. His mixing her up with his other beastly affairs."

Mrs. Brook looked intelligent and wan about it, but also perfectly good-humoured. "My dear man, he and his affairs *are* such twaddle!"

Vanderbank laughed in spite of himself. "And does that make it any better?"

Mrs. Brook thought, but presently had a light—she almost smiled with it. "For *us.*" Then more woefully, "Don't you want Carrie to be saved?" she asked.

"Why should I? Not a jot. Carrie be hanged!"

"But it's for Fanny," Mrs. Brook protested. "If Carrie *is* rescued, it's a pretext the less for *her.*" As the young man looked for an instant rather gloomily vague she softly quavered: "I suppose you don't positively *want* her to bolt?"

"To bolt?"

"Surely I've not to remind you at this time of day how Captain Dent-Douglas is always round the corner with the post-chaise, and how tight, on our side, we're all clutching her."

"But why not let her go?"

Mrs. Brook, at this, showed a sentiment more sharp. "'Go'? Then what would become of us?" She recalled his wandering fancy. "She's the delight of our life."

"Oh!" Vanderbank sceptically murmured.

"She's the ornament of our circle," his companion insisted. "She will, she won't—she won't, she will! It's the excitement, every day, of plucking the daisy over." Vanderbank's attention, as she spoke, had attached itself, across the room, to Mr. Longdon; it gave her thus an image of the way his imagination had just seemed to her to stray, and she saw a reason in it moreover for her coming up in another place. "Isn't he rather rich?" She allowed the question all its effect of abruptness.

Vanderbank looked round at her. "Mr. Longdon? I haven't the least idea."

"Not after becoming so intimate? It's usually, with people, the very first thing I get my impression of." There came into her face, for another glance at their friend, no crudity of curiosity, but an expression more tenderly wistful. "He must have some mysterious box under his bed."

"Down in Suffolk?—a miser's hoard? Who knows? I dare say," Vanderbank went on. "He isn't a miser, but he strikes me as careful."

Mrs. Brook meanwhile had thought it out. "Then he has something to be careful of; it would take something really handsome to inspire in a man like him that sort of interest. With his small expenses all these years his savings must be immense. And how could he have proposed to mamma unless he had originally had money?"

If Vanderbank hesitated he also laughed. "You must remember your mother refused him."

"Ah, but not because there was not enough."

"No—I imagine the force of the blow, for him, was just in the other reason."

"Well, it would have been in that one just as much if that one had been the other." Mrs. Brook was sagacious, though a trifle obscure, and she pursued the next moment: "Mamma was so sincere. The fortune was nothing to her. That shows it was immense."

"It couldn't have been as great as your logic," Vanderbank smiled; "but of course if it has been growing ever since—!"

"I can see it grow while he sits there," Mrs. Brook declared. But her logic had in fact its own law, and her next transition was an equal jump. "It was too lovely, the frankness of your admission a minute ago that I affect him uncannily. Ah, don't spoil it by explanations!" she beautifully pleaded: "he's not the first and he won't be the last with whom I shall not have been what they call a combination. The only thing that matters is that I shouldn't if possible make the case worse. So you must guide me. What *is* one to do?"

Vanderbank, now amused again, looked at her kindly. "Be yourself, my dear woman. Obey your fine instincts."

"How can you be," she sweetly asked, "so hideously hypocritical? You know as well as you sit there that my fine instincts are the thing in the world you're most in terror of. 'Be myself'?" she echoed. "What you would *like* to say is: 'Be somebody else—that's your only chance.' Well, I'll try—I'll try."

He laughed again, shaking his head. "Don't—don't."

"You mean it's too hopeless? There's no way of effacing the bad impression or of starting a good one?" On this, with a drop of his mirth, he met her eyes, and for an instant through the superficial levity of their talk they might have appeared to sound each other. It lasted till Mrs. Brook went on: "I should really like not to lose him."

Vanderbank seemed to understand and at last said: "I think you won't lose him."

"Do you mean you'll help me, Van—you *will*?" Her voice had at moments the most touching tones of any in England, and humble, helpless, affectionate, she spoke with a familiarity of friendship. "It's for the sense of the link with mamma," she explained. "He's simply full of her."

"Oh, I know. He's prodigious."

"He has told you more—he comes back to it?" Mrs. Brook eagerly asked.

"Well," the young man replied a trifle evasively, "we've had a great deal of talk, and he's the jolliest old boy possible, and in short I like him."

"I see," said Mrs. Brook blandly, "and he likes you, in return, as much as he despises *me*. That makes it all right—makes me somehow so happy for you. There's something in him—what is it?—that suggests the *oncle d'Amérique*, the eccentric benefactor, the fairy godmother. He's a little of an old woman—but all the better for it." She hung fire but an instant before she pursued: "What can we make him do for you?"

Vanderbank at this was very blank. "Do for me?"

"How can any one love you," she asked, "without wanting to show it in some way? You know all the ways, dear Van," she breathed, "in which *I* want to show it."

He might have known them, something suddenly fixed in his face appeared to say, but they were not what was, on this speech of hers, most immediately present to him. "That, for instance, is the tone not to take with him."

"There you are!" she sighed with discouragement. "Well, only *tell* me." Then as he said nothing: "I must be more like mamma?"

His expression confessed to his feeling an awkwardness. "You're perhaps not quite enough like her."

"Oh, I know that if he deplores me as I am now she would have done so quite as much; in fact probably, as seeing it nearer, a good deal more. She would have despised me even more than he. But if it's a question," Mrs. Brook went on, "of not saying what mamma wouldn't, how can I know, don't you see, what she *would* have said?" Mrs. Brook became as

wonderful as if she saw in her friend's face some admiring reflection of the fine freedom of mind that—in such a connection quite as much as in any other—she could always show.
"Of course I revere mamma just as much as he does, and
there was everything in her to revere. But she was none the
less in every way a charming woman too, and I don't know,
after all, do I? what even she—in their peculiar relation—may
not have said to him."

Vanderbank's laugh came back. "Very good—very good. I
return to my first idea. Try with him whatever comes into
your head. You're a woman of genius after all, and genius
mostly justifies itself. To make you right," he went on pleasantly and inexorably, "might perhaps be to make you wrong.
Since you *have* so great a charm, trust it not at all or all in
all. That, I dare say, is all you can do. Therefore—yes—be
yourself."

These remarks were followed on either side by the repetition of a somewhat intenser mutual gaze, though indeed the
speaker's eyes had more the air of meeting his friend's than of
seeking them. "I can't be *you*, certainly, Van," Mrs. Brook
sadly brought forth.

"I know what you mean by that," he rejoined in a moment.
"You mean I'm hypocritical."

"Hypocritical?"

"I'm diplomatic and calculating—I don't show him how
bad I am; whereas with you he knows the worst."

Of this observation Mrs. Brook, whose eyes attached themselves again to Mr. Longdon, took at first no further notice
than might have been indicated by the way it set her musing.
"'Calculating'?"—she at last took him up. "On what is there
to calculate?"

"Why," said Vanderbank, "if, as you just hinted, he's a
blessing in disguise—! I perfectly admit," he resumed, "that
I'm capable of sacrifices to keep on good terms with him."

"You're not afraid he'll bore you?"

"Oh yes—distinctly."

"But it will be worth it? Then," Mrs. Brook said as he appeared to assent, "it will be worth a great deal." She continued to watch Mr. Longdon, who, without his glasses, stared

straight at the floor while Mr. Cashmore talked to him. She pursued, however, dispassionately enough: "He must be of a narrowness——!"

"Oh, beautiful!"

She was silent again. "I shall broaden him. *You* won't."

"Heaven forbid!" Vanderbank heartily concurred. "But none the less, as I've said, I'll help you."

Her attention was still fixed. "It will be him you'll help. If you're to make sacrifices to keep on good terms with him, the first sacrifice will be of me." Then on his leaving this remark so long unanswered that she had finally looked at him again: "I'm perfectly prepared for it."

It was as if, jocosely enough, he had had time to make up his mind how to meet her. "What will you have—when he loved my mother?"

Nothing could have been droller than the gloom of her surprise. "Yours too?"

"I didn't tell you the other day—out of delicacy."

Mrs. Brookenham darkly thought. "*He* didn't tell me either."

"The same consideration deterred him. But if I didn't speak of it," Vanderbank continued, "when I arranged with you, after meeting him here at dinner, that you should come to tea with him at my rooms—it I didn't mention it then it wasn't because I hadn't learnt it early."

Mrs. Brook more deeply sounded this affair, but she spoke with the exaggerated mildness which was the form mostly taken by her gaiety. "It was because of course it makes him out such a wretch! What becomes in that case of his loyalty?"

"To *your* mother's memory? Oh, it's all right—he has it quite straight. She came later. Mine, after my father's death, had refused him. But you see he might have been my stepfather."

Mrs. Brookenham took it in, but she had suddenly a brighter light. "He might have been my *own* father! Besides," she went on, "if his line is to love the mothers why on earth doesn't he love *me*? I'm in all conscience enough of one."

"Ah, but isn't there in your case the fact of a daughter?" Vanderbank asked with a slight embarrassment.

Mrs. Brookenham stared. "What good does that do me?"

"Why, didn't she tell you?"

"Nanda? She told me he doesn't like her any better than he likes me."

Vanderbank in his turn showed surprise. "That's really what she said?"

"She had on her return from your rooms a most unusual fit of frankness, for she generally tells me nothing."

"Well," said Vanderbank, "how did she put it?"

Mrs. Brook reflected—recovered it. "'I like him awfully, but I'm not in the least *his* idea.'"

"His idea of what?"

"That's just what I asked her. Of the proper grandchild for mamma."

Vanderbank hesitated. "Well, she isn't." Then after another pause: "But she'll do."

His companion gave him a deep look. "You'll make her?"

He got up, and on seeing him move Mr. Longdon also rose, so that, facing each other across the room, they exchanged a friendly signal or two. "I'll make her."

XV

Their hostess's account of Mr. Cashmore's motive for his staying on was so far justified as that Vanderbank, while Mr. Longdon came over to Mrs. Brook, appeared without difficulty further to engage him. The lady in question meanwhile had drawn her old friend down, and her present method of approach would have interested an observer aware of the unhappy conviction that she had just privately expressed. Some trace indeed of the glimpse of it enjoyed by Mr. Cashmore's present interlocutor might have been detected in the restlessness that Vanderbank's desire to keep the other pair uninterrupted was still not able to banish from his attitude. Not, however, that Mrs. Brook took the smallest account of it as she quickly broke out: "How can we thank you enough, my dear man, for your extraordinary kindness?" The reference was vivid, yet Mr. Longdon looked so blank about it that she had immediately to explain. "I mean to dear Van, who has told us of your giving him the great happiness—unless he's too dreadfully mistaken—of letting him really know you. He's such a tremendous friend of ours that nothing so delightful can befall him without its affecting us in the same way." She had proceeded with confidence, but suddenly she pulled up. "Don't tell me he *is* mistaken—I shouldn't be able to bear it." She challenged the pale old man with a loveliness that was for the moment absolutely juvenile. "Aren't you letting him —really?"

Mr. Longdon's smile was queer. "I can't prevent him. I'm not a great house—to give orders to go over me. The kindness is Mr. Vanderbank's own, and I've taken up, I'm afraid, a great deal of his precious time."

"You have indeed." Mrs. Brook was undiscouraged. "He has been talking with me just now of nothing else. You may say," she went on, "that it's I who have kept him at it. So I have, for his pleasure's a joy to us. If you can't prevent what he feels, you know, you can't prevent either what *we* feel."

Mr. Longdon's face reflected for a minute something he could scarcely have supposed her acute enough to make out, the struggle between his real mistrust of her, founded on the unconscious violence offered by her nature to his every memory of her mother, and his sense, on the other hand, of the high propriety of his liking her; to which latter force his interest in Vanderbank was a contribution, inasmuch as he was obliged to recognise on the part of the pair an alliance it would have been difficult to explain at Beccles. "Perhaps I don't quite see the value of what your husband and you and I are in a position to do for him."

"Do you mean because he's himself so clever?"

"Well," said Mr. Longdon, "I dare say that's at the bottom of my feeling so proud to be taken up by him. I think of the young men of *my* time, and I see that he takes in more. But that's what you all do," he rather helplessly sighed. "You're very, very wonderful!"

She met him with an almost extravagant eagerness that the meeting should be just where he wished. "I don't take in everything, but I take in all I can. That's a great affair in London to-day, and I often feel as if I were a circus-woman, in pink tights and no particular skirts, riding half-a-dozen horses at once. We're all in the troupe now, I suppose," she smiled, "and we must travel with the show. But when you say we're different," she added, "think, after all, of mamma."

Mr. Longdon stared. "It's from her you *are* different."

"Ah, but she had an awfully fine mind. We're not cleverer than she."

His conscious, honest eyes looked away an instant. "It's perhaps enough for the present that you're cleverer than I! I was very glad the other day," he continued, "to make the acquaintance of your daughter. I hoped I should find her with you."

If Mrs. Brook cast about it was but for a few seconds. "If she had known you were coming, she would certainly have been here. She wanted so to please you." Then as her visitor took no further notice of this speech than to ask if Nanda were out of the house, she had to admit it as an aggravation of failure; but she pursued in the next breath: "Of course you won't care, but she raves about you."

He appeared indeed at first not to care. "Isn't she eighteen?"—it was oddly abrupt.

"I have to think. Wouldn't it be nearer twenty?" Mrs. Brook audaciously returned. She tried again. "She told me all about your interview. I stayed away on purpose—I had my idea."

"And what *was* your idea?"

"I thought she would remind you more of mamma if I wasn't there. But she's a little person who sees. Perhaps you didn't think it, but she knew."

"And what did she know?" asked Mr. Longdon, who was unable, however, to keep from his tone a certain coldness which really deprived the question of its proper curiosity.

Mrs. Brook just showed the chill of it, but she had always her courage. "Why, that you don't like her." She had the courage of carrying off as well as of backing out. "She too has her little place with the circus—it's the way we earn our living."

Mr. Longdon said nothing for a moment and when he at last spoke it was almost with an air of contradiction. "She's your mother to the life."

His hostess, for three seconds, looked at him hard. "Ah, but with such differences! You'll lose it," she added with a head-shake of pity.

He had his eyes only on Vanderbank. "Well, my losses are my own affair." Then his eyes came back. "Did she tell you I didn't like her?"

The indulgence in Mrs. Brook's view of his simplicity was marked. "You thought you succeeded so in hiding it? No matter—she bears up. I think she really feels a great deal as I do—that it's no matter how many of us you hate if you'll only go on feeling as you do about mamma. To show us *that*— that's what we want."

Nothing could have expressed more the balm of reassurance, but the mild drops had fallen short of the spot to which they were directed. "'Show' you?"

Oh, how he had sounded the word! "I see—you *don't* show. That's just what Nanda saw you thought! But you can't keep us from knowing it—can't keep it in fact, I think, from affecting your own behaviour. You'd be much worse to us if it wasn't for the still warm ashes of your old passion." It was an immense pity that Vanderbank was at this moment too far off to fit, for his amusement, to the expression of his old friend's face so much of the cause of it as had sprung from the deeply informed tone of Mrs. Brook's allusion. To what degree the speaker herself made the connection will never be known to history, nor whether as she went on she thought she bettered her case or simply lost her head. "The great thing for us is that we can never be for you quite like other ordinary people."

"And what's the great thing for *me*?"

"Oh, for you, there's nothing, I'm afraid, but small things —so small that they can scarcely be worth the trouble of your making them out. Our being so happy that you've come back to us—if only just for a glimpse and to leave us again, in no matter what horror, for ever; our positive delight in your being exactly so different; the pleasure we have in talking about you, and shall still have—or indeed all the more—even if we've seen you only to lose you: whatever all this represents for ourselves, it's for none of us to pretend to say how much or how little *you* may pick out of it. And yet," Mrs. Brook wandered on, "however much we may disappoint you, some little spark of the past can't help being in us—for the past is the one thing beyond all spoiling: there it is, don't you think? —to speak for itself and, if need be, only *of* itself." She stopped a moment, but she appeared to have destroyed all power of speech in him, so that while she waited she had time for a fresh inspiration. It might perhaps frankly have been mentioned as on the whole her finest. "Don't you think it possible that if you once get the point of view of realising that I *know*——"

She held the note so long that he at last supplied a sound. "That you know what?"

"Why, that, compared with her, I'm a poor creeping thing. I mean"—she hastened to forestall any protest of mere decency that would spoil her idea—"that of course I ache in every limb with the certainty of my dreadful difference. It isn't as if I *didn't* know it, don't you see? There it is, as a matter of course: I've helplessly, but finally and completely, accepted it. Won't *that* help you?" she so ingeniously pleaded. "It isn't as if I tormented you with any recall of her whatever. I can quite see how awful it would be for you if, with the effect I produce on you, I did have her lovely eyes or her distinguished nose or the shape of her forehead or the colour of her hair. Strange as it is in a daughter, I'm disconnected altogether, and don't you think I *may* be a little saved for you by becoming thus simply out of the question? Of course," she continued, "your real trial is poor Nanda—she's likewise so fearfully out of it and yet she's so fearfully in it. And she," said Mrs. Brook wonderfully—"*she* doesn't know!"

A strange faint flush, while she talked, had come into Mr. Longdon's face, and, whatever effect, as she put it, she produced on him, it was clearly not that of causing his attention to wander. She held him at least, for weal or woe; his bright eyes grew brighter and opened into a stare that finally seemed to offer him as submerged in mere wonder. At last, however, he rose to the surface, and he appeared to have lighted, at the bottom of the sea, on the pearl of the particular wisdom he needed. "I daresay there may be something in what you so extraordinarily suggest."

She jumped at it as if in pleasant pain. "In just letting me go——"

But at this he dropped. "I shall never let you go."

It renewed her fear. "Not just for what I *am*?"

He rose from his place beside her, but looking away from her and with his colour marked. "I shall never let you go," he repeated.

"Oh, you angel!" She sprang up more quickly, and the others were by this time on their feet. "I've done it, I've done it!" she joyously cried to Vanderbank; "he likes me, or at least he can bear me—I've found him the way; and now I don't care even if he *says* I haven't." Then she turned again to her old friend. "We can manage about Nanda—you needn't ever see her. She's 'down' now, but she can go up again. We can arrange it at any rate—*c'est la moindre des choses.*"

"Upon my honour I protest," Mr. Cashmore exclaimed, "against anything of the sort! I defy you to 'arrange' that young lady in any such manner without also arranging *me*. I'm one of her greatest admirers," he gaily announced to Mr. Longdon.

Vanderbank said nothing, and Mr. Longdon seemed to show that he would have preferred to do the same: the old man's eyes might have represented an appeal to him somehow to intervene, to show the due acquaintance, springing from practice and wanting in himself, with the art of conversation developed to the point at which it could thus sustain a lady in the upper air. Vanderbank's silence might, without his mere kind, amused look, have seemed almost inhuman. Poor Mr. Longdon had finally to do his own simple best. "Will you bring your daughter to see me?" he asked of Mrs. Brookenham.

"Oh, oh—that's an idea: will you bring her to see *me*?" Mr. Cashmore again broke out.

Mrs. Brook had only fixed Mr. Longdon with the air of unutterable things. "You angel, you angel!"—they found expression but in that.

"*I* don't need to ask you to bring her, do I?" Vanderbank now said to his hostess. "I hope you don't mind my bragging all over the place of the great honour she did me the other day in appearing quite by herself."

"Quite by herself? I say, Mrs. Brook!" Mr. Cashmore flourished on.

It was only now that she noticed him; which she did indeed but by answering Vanderbank. "She didn't go for *you*, I'm afraid—though of course she might: she went because you had promised her Mr. Longdon. But I should have no more feeling about her going to you—and should expect her to have no more—than about her taking a pound of tea, as she sometimes does, to her old nurse, or her going to read to the old women at the workhouse. May you never have less to brag of!"

"I wish she'd bring *me* a pound of tea!" Mr. Cashmore resumed. "Or ain't I enough of an old woman for her to come and read to me at home?"

"Does she habitually visit the workhouse?" Mr. Longdon inquired of Mrs. Brook.

This lady kept him in a moment's suspense, which another pair of eyes might moreover have detected that Vanderbank in some degree shared. "Every Friday at three."

Vanderbank, with a sudden turn, moved slowly to one of the windows, and Mr. Cashmore had a happy remembrance. "Why, this is Friday—she must have gone to-day. But does she stay so late?"

"She was to go afterwards to little Aggie: I'm trying so, in spite of difficulties," Mrs. Brook explained, "to keep them on together." She addressed herself with a new thought to Mr. Longdon. "You must know little Aggie—the niece of the Duchess: I forget if you've met the Duchess, but you must know *her* too—there are so many things on which, I'm sure, she'll feel with you. Little Aggie's the one," she continued; "you'll delight in her; *she* ought to have been mamma's grandchild."

"Dearest lady, how can you pretend, or for a moment compare her—?" Mr. Cashmore broke in. "She says nothing to me at all."

"She says nothing to any one," Mrs. Brook serenely replied; "that's just her type and her charm—just, above all, her education." Then she appealed to Vanderbank. "Won't Mr. Longdon be struck with little Aggie, and won't he find it interesting to talk about all that sort of thing with the Duchess?"

Vanderbank came back laughing, but Mr. Longdon anticipated his reply. "What sort of thing do you mean?"

"Oh," said Mrs. Brook, "the whole question, don't you know? of bringing girls forward or not. The question of—well, what do you call it?—their exposure. It's *the* question, it appears—the question of the future; it's awfully interesting, and the Duchess at any rate is great on it. Nanda of course is exposed," Mrs. Brook pursued—"fearfully."

"And what on earth is she exposed to?" Mr. Cashmore gaily demanded.

"She's exposed to *you*, it would seem, my dear fellow!" Vanderbank spoke with a certain discernible impatience not so much of the fact he mentioned as of the turn of their talk.

It might have been in almost compassionate deprecation of this weak note that Mrs. Brookenham looked at him. Her reply to Mr. Cashmore's question, however, was uttered at Mr. Longdon. "She's exposed—it's much worse—to *me*. But Aggie isn't exposed to anything—never has been and never is to be; and we're watching to see if the Duchess can carry it through."

"Why not," asked Mr. Cashmore, "if there's nothing she *can* be exposed to but the Duchess herself?"

He had appealed to his companions impartially, but Mr. Longdon, whose attention was now all for his hostess, appeared unconscious. "If you're all watching, is it your idea that I should watch *with* you?"

The inquiry, on his lips, was a waft of cold air, the sense of which clearly led Mrs. Brook to put her invitation on the right ground. "Not of course on the chance of anything's happening to the dear child—to whom nothing obviously *can* happen but that her aunt will marry her off in the shortest possible time and in the best possible conditions. No, the interest is, much more, in the way the Duchess herself steers."

"Ah, she's in a boat," Mr. Cashmore fully concurred, "that will take a good bit of that."

It is not for Mr. Longdon's historian to overlook that if he was not unnaturally mystified, he was yet also visibly interested. "What boat is she in?"

He had addressed his curiosity, with politeness, to Mr. Cashmore, but they were all arrested by the wonderful way in which Mrs. Brook managed to smile at once very dimly, very darkly, and yet make it take them all in. "I think *you* must tell him, Van."

"Heaven forbid!"—and Vanderbank again retreated.

"*I'll* tell him like a shot—if you really give me leave," said Mr. Cashmore, for whom any scruple referred itself manifestly not to the subject of the information, but to the presence of a lady.

"I *don't* give you leave, and I beg you'll hold your tongue," Mrs. Brookenham replied. "You handle such matters with a minuteness—! In short," she broke off to Mr. Longdon, "he would tell you a good deal more than you'll care to know. She *is* in a boat—but she's an experienced mariner. *Basta*, as she would say. Do you know Mitchy?" Mrs. Brook suddenly asked.

"Oh yes, he knows Mitchy"—Vanderbank had approached again.

"Then make *him* tell him"—she put it before the young man as a charming turn for them all. "Mitchy *can* be refined when he tries."

"Oh dear—when Mitchy 'tries'!" Vanderbank laughed. "I think I should rather, for the job, offer him to Mr. Longdon as abandoned to his native wild impulse."

"I *like* Mr. Mitchett," the old man said, endeavouring to look his hostess straight in the eye and speaking as if somewhat to defy her to convict him, even from the point of view of Beccles, of a mistake.

Mrs. Brookenham took it with a wonderful bright emotion. "My dear friend, *vous me rendez la vie!* If you can stand Mitchy you can stand any of us!"

"Upon my honour, I should think so!" Mr. Cashmore was eager to remark. "What on earth do you mean," he demanded of Mrs. Brook, "by saying that I'm more 'minute' than he?"

She turned her beauty an instant on this visitor. "I don't say you're more minute—I say he's more brilliant. Besides, as I've told you before, you're not one of us." With which, as a check to further discussion, she went straight on to Mr. Longdon: "The point about Aggie's conservative education is the wonderful sincerity with which the Duchess feels that one's girl may so perfectly and consistently be hedged in without one's really ever (for it comes to that) depriving one's own self——"

"Well, of what?" Mr. Longdon boldly demanded while his hostess appeared thoughtfully to falter.

She addressed herself mutely to Vanderbank, in whom the movement produced a laugh. "I defy you," he exclaimed, "to say!"

"Well, you don't defy *me*!" Mr. Cashmore cried as Mrs. Brook failed to take up the challenge. "If you know Mitchy," he went on to Mr. Longdon, "you must know Petherton."

The old man remained vague and not imperceptibly cold. "Petherton?"

"My brother-in-law—whom, God knows why, Mitchy runs."

"Runs?" Mr. Longdon again echoed.

Mrs. Brook appealed afresh to Vanderbank. "I think we ought to spare him. I may not remind you of mamma," she continued to their companion, "but I hope you don't mind my saying how much you remind me. Explanations, after all, spoil things, and if you *can* make anything of us and will sometimes come back you'll find everything in its native freshness. You'll see, you'll feel for yourself."

Mr. Longdon stood before her and raised to Vanderbank, when she had ceased, the eyes he had attached to the carpet while she talked. "And must I go now?" Explanations, she had said, spoiled things, but he might have been a stranger at an Eastern court, comically helpless without his interpreter.

"If Mrs. Brook desires to 'spare' you," Vanderbank kindly replied, "the best way to make sure of it would perhaps indeed be to remove you. But hadn't we a hope of Nanda?"

"It might be of use for us to wait for her?"—it was still to his young friend that Mr. Longdon put it.

"Ah, when she's once on the loose—!" Mrs. Brookenham sighed. "Unless *la voilà*," she said as a hand was heard at the door-latch. It was only, however, a footman who entered with a little tray that, on his approaching his mistress, offered to sight the brown envelope of a telegram. She immediately took leave to open this missive, after the quick perusal of which she had another vision of them all. "It *is* she—the modern daughter. 'Tishy keeps me dinner and opera; clothes all right; return uncertain, but if before morning have latch-key.' She won't come home till morning!" said Mrs. Brook.

"But think of the comfort of the latch-key!" Vanderbank laughed. "You might go to the opera," he said to Mr. Longdon.

"Hanged if *I* don't!" Mr. Cashmore exclaimed.

Mr. Longdon appeared to have caught from Nanda's message an obscure agitation; he met his young friend's suggestion at all events with a visible intensity. "Will you go with me?"

Vanderbank had just hesitated, recalling engagements; which gave Mrs. Brook time to intervene. "Can't you live without him?" she asked of her elder friend.

Vanderbank had looked at her an instant. "I think I can get there late," he then replied to Mr. Longdon.

"I think *I* can get there early," Mr. Cashmore declared. "Mrs. Grendon must have a box; in fact I know which, and *they* don't," he jocosely continued to his hostess.

Mrs. Brook meanwhile had given Mr. Longdon her hand. "Well, at any rate, the child *shall* soon come to you. And oh, alone," she insisted: "you needn't make phrases—I know too well what I'm about."

"One hopes really you do," pursued the unquenched Mr. Cashmore. "If that's what one gets by having known your mother——!"

"It wouldn't have helped *you*," Mrs. Brook retorted. "And won't you have to say it's *all* you were to get?" she pityingly murmured to her other visitor.

He turned to Vanderbank with a strange gasp, and Vanderbank said "Come!"

BOOK FIFTH

The Duchess

XVI

THE LOWER windows of the great white house, which stood high and square, opened to a wide flagged terrace, the parapet of which, an old balustrade of stone, was broken in the middle of its course by a flight of stone steps that descended to a wonderful garden. The terrace had the afternoon shade and fairly hung over the prospect that dropped away and circled it—the prospect, beyond the series of gardens, of scattered, splendid trees and green glades, an horizon mainly of woods. Nanda Brookenham, one day at the end of July, coming out to find the place unoccupied as yet by other visitors, stood there awhile with an air of happy possession. She moved from end to end of the terrace, pausing, gazing about her, taking in with a face that showed the pleasure of a brief independence the combination of delightful things—of old rooms with old decorations that gleamed and gloomed through the high windows, of old gardens that squared themselves in the wide angles of old walls, of wood-walks rustling in the afternoon breeze and stretching away to further reaches of solitude and summer. The scene had an expectant stillness that she was too charmed to desire to break; she watched it, listened to it, followed with her eyes the white butterflies among the flowers below her, then gave a start as the cry of a peacock came to her from an unseen alley. It set her after a minute into less difficult motion; she passed slowly down the steps, wandering further, looking back at the big bright house but pleased again to see no one else appear. If the sun was still high enough she had a pink parasol. She went through the gardens one by one, skirting the high walls that were so like "collections" and thinking how, later on, the nectarines and plums would flush there. She exchanged a friendly greeting with a man at work, passed through an open door and, turning this way and that, finally found herself in the park, at some distance from the house. It was a point she had

784

had to take another rise to reach, a place marked by an old green bench for a larger sweep of the view, which, in the distance where the woods stopped, showed, in the most English way in the world, the colour-spot of an old red village and the tower of an old grey church. She had sunk down upon the bench almost with a sense of adventure, yet not too fluttered to wonder if it wouldn't have been happy to bring a book; the charm of which precisely would have been in feeling everything about her too beautiful to let her read.

The sense of adventure grew in her, presently becoming aware of a stir in the thicket below, followed by the coming into sight, on a path that, mounting, passed near her seat, of a wanderer whom, had his particular, his exceptional identity not quickly appeared, it might have disappointed her a trifle to have to recognise as a friend. He saw her immediately, stopped, laughed, waved his hat, then bounded up the slope and, brushing his forehead with his handkerchief, confessing to being hot, was rejoicingly there before her. Her own ejaculation on first seeing him—"Why, Mr. Van!"—had had an ambiguous sharpness that was rather for herself than for her visitor. She made room for him on the bench, and in a moment he was cooling off and they were both explaining. The great thing was that he had walked from the station to stretch his legs, coming far round, for the lovely hour and the pleasure of it, by a way he had learnt on some previous occasion of being at Mertle.

"You've already stayed here then?" Nanda, who had arrived but half-an-hour before, spoke as if she had lost the chance to give him a new impression.

"I've stayed here—yes, but not with Mitchy; with some people or other—who the deuce can they have been?—who had the place for a few months a year or two ago."

"Don't you even remember?"

Vanderbank wondered and laughed. "It will come to me. But it's a charming sign of London relations, isn't it?—that one *can* come down to people this way and be awfully well 'done for' and all that, and then go away and lose the whole thing, quite forget to whom one has been beholden. It's a queer life."

Nanda seemed for an instant to wish to say that one might deny the queerness, but she said something else instead. "I suppose a man like you doesn't quite feel that he *is* beholden.

It's awfully good of him—it's doing a great deal for anybody —that he should come down at all; so that it would add immensely to his burden if anybody had to be remembered for it."

"I don't know what you mean by a man 'like me,'" Vanderbank returned. "I'm not any particular kind of a man." She had been looking at him, but she looked away on this, and he continued good-humoured and explanatory. "If you mean that I go about such a lot, how do you know it but by the fact that you're everywhere now yourself?—so that, whatever I am, in short, you're just as bad."

"You admit then that you *are* everywhere. I may be just as bad," the girl went on, "but the point is that I'm not nearly so good. Girls are such hacks—they can't be anything else."

"And, pray, what are fellows who are in the beastly grind of fearfully busy offices? There isn't an old cab-horse in London that's kept at it, I assure you, as I am. Besides," the young man added, "if I'm out every night and off somewhere like this for Sunday, can't you understand, my dear child, the fundamental reason of it?"

Nanda, with her eyes on him again, studied an instant this mystery. "Am I to infer with delight that it's the sweet hope of meeting *me*? It isn't," she continued in a moment, "as if there were any necessity for your saying that. What's the use—?" But, impatiently, she stopped short.

He was eminently gay even if his companion was not. "Because we're such jolly old friends that we really needn't so much as speak at all? Yes, thank goodness—thank goodness." He had been looking around him, taking in the scene; he had dropped his hat on the ground and, completely at his ease, though still more wishing to show it, had crossed his legs and closely folded his arms. "What a tremendously jolly place! If I can't for the life of me recall who they were—the other people—I've the comfort of being sure their minds are an equal blank. Do they even remember the place they had? 'We had some fellows down at—where was it, the big white house last November?—and there was one of them, out of the What-do-you-call-it?—*you* know—who might have been a decent enough chap if he had not presumed so on his gifts.'" Vanderbank paused a minute, but his companion said nothing, and he pursued: "It does show, doesn't it?—the fact that we do meet this way—the tremendous change that has taken place in your life in the last three months. I mean, if I'm everywhere as you said just now, your being just the same."

"Yes—you see what you've done."

"How, what *I've* done?"

"You plunge into the woods for change, for solitude," the girl said, "and the first thing you do is to find me waylaying you in the depths of the forest. But I really couldn't—if you'll reflect upon it—know you were coming this way."

Vanderbank sat there with his position unchanged but with a constant little shake in the foot that hung down, as if every-thing—and what she now put before him not least—was much too pleasant to be reflected on. "May I smoke a cigarette?"

Nanda waited a little; her friend had taken out his silver case, which was of ample form, and as he extracted a cigarette she put forth her hand. "May *I*?" She turned the case over with admiration.

Vanderbank demurred. "Do you smoke with Mr. Longdon?"

"Immensely. But what has that to do with it?"

"Everything, everything." He spoke with a faint ring of im-patience. "I want you to do with me exactly as you do with him."

"Ah, that's soon said!" the girl replied in a peculiar tone. "How do you mean, to 'do'?"

"Well then, to *be*. What shall I say?" Vanderbank pleasantly wondered while his foot kept up its motion. "To feel."

She continued to handle the cigarette-case, without, how-ever, having profited by its contents. "I don't think that, as regards Mr. Longdon and me, you know quite so much as you suppose."

Vanderbank laughed and smoked. "I take for granted he tells me everything."

"Ah, but you scarcely take for granted *I* do!" She rubbed her cheek an instant with the polished silver, again, the next moment, turning over the case. "This is the kind of one I should like."

Her companion glanced down at it. "Why, it holds twenty."

"Well, I want one that holds twenty."

Vanderbank only threw out his smoke. "I want so to give you something," he said at last, "that in my relief at lighting on an object that will do, I will, if you don't look out, give you either that or a pipe."

"Do you mean this particular one?"

"I've had it for years—but even that one if you like it."

She kept it—continued to finger it. "And by whom was it given you?"

At this he turned to her smiling. "You think I've forgotten that too?"

"Certainly you must have forgotten, to be willing to give it away again."

"But how do you know it was a present?"

"Such things always are—people don't buy them for themselves."

She had now relinquished the object, laying it upon the bench, and Vanderbank took it up. "Its origin is lost in the night of time—it has no history except that I've used it. But I assure you that I do want to give you something. I've never given you anything."

She was silent a little. "The exhibition you're making," she seriously sighed at last, "of your inconstancy and superficiality! All the relics of you that I've treasured and that I supposed at the time to have meant something!"

"The 'relics'? Have you a lock of my hair?" Then as her meaning came to him: "Oh, little Christmas things? Have you really kept them?"

"Laid away in a drawer of their own—done up in pink paper."

"I know what you're coming to," Vanderbank said. "You've given *me* things, and you're trying to convict me of having lost the sweet sense of them. But you can't do it. Where my heart's concerned I'm a walking reliquary. Pink paper? *I* use gold paper—and the finest of all, the gold paper of the mind." He gave a flip with a fingernail to his cigarette and looked at its quickened fire; after which he pursued very familiarly, but with a kindness that of itself qualified the mere humour of the thing: "Don't talk, my dear child, as if you didn't really know me for the best friend you have in the world." As soon as he had spoken he pulled out his watch, so that if his words had led to something of a pause this movement offered a pretext for breaking it. Nanda asked the hour and, on his replying "Five-fifteen," remarked that there would now be tea on the terrace with every one gathered at it. "Then shall we go and join them?" her companion demanded.

He had made, however, no other motion, and when, after hesitating, she said "Yes, with pleasure," it was also without a change of position. "I like this," she inconsequently added.

"So do I, awfully. Tea on the terrace," Vanderbank went on, "isn't 'in' it. But who's here?"

"Oh, every one. All your set."

"Mine? Have I still a set—with the universal vagabondism you accuse me of?"

"Well then Mitchy's—whoever they are."

"And nobody of yours?"

"Oh yes," Nanda said, "all mine. He must at least have arrived by this time. My set's Mr. Longdon," she explained. "He's all of it now."

"Then where in the world am I?"

"Oh, you're an extra. There are always extras."

"A complete set and one over?" Vanderbank laughed. "Where then is Tishy?"

Charming and grave, the girl thought a moment. "She's in Paris with her mother—on their way to Aix-les-Bains." Then with impatience she continued: "Do you know that's a great deal to say—what you said just now? I mean about your being the best friend I have."

"Of course I do, and that's exactly why I said it. You see I am not in the least delicate or graceful or shy about it—I just come out with it and defy you to contradict me. Who, if I'm not the best, is a better one?"

"Well," Nanda replied, "I feel since I've known Mr. Longdon that I've almost the sort of friend who makes nobody else count."

"Then at the end of three months he has arrived at a value for you that I haven't reached in all these years?"

"Yes," she returned—"the value of my not being afraid of him."

Vanderbank, on the bench, shifted his position, turning

more to her with an arm over the back. "And you're afraid of *me?*"

"Horribly—hideously."

"Then our long, happy relations——?"

"They're just what make my terror," she broke in, "particularly abject. Happy relations don't matter. I always think of you with fear."

His elbow was on the back of the seat and his hand supported his head. "How awfully curious—if it be true!"

She had been looking away to the sweet English distance, but at this she made a movement. "Oh Mr. Van, I'm 'true!'"

As Mr. Van himself could not have expressed at any subsequent time to any interested friend the particular effect upon him of the tone of these words his chronicler takes advantage of the fact not to pretend to a greater intelligence—to limit himself on the contrary to the simple statement that they produced in Mr. Van's cheek a flush just discernible. "Fear of what?"

"I don't know. Fear is fear."

"Yes, yes—I see." He took out another cigarette and occupied a moment in lighting it. "Well, kindness is kindness too —that's all one can say."

He had smoked again awhile before she turned to him. "Have I wounded you by saying that?"

A certain effect of his flush was still in his smile. "It seems to me I should like you to wound me. I did what I wanted a moment ago," he continued with some precipitation: "I brought you out handsomely on the subject of Mr. Longdon. That was my idea—just to draw you."

"Well," said Nanda, looking away again, "he has come into my life."

"He couldn't have come into a place where it gives me more pleasure to see him."

"But he didn't like, the other day, when I used it to him, that expression," the girl returned. "He called it 'mannered modern slang' and came back again to the extraordinary difference between my speech and my grandmother's."

"Of course," the young man understandingly assented. "But I rather like your speech. Hasn't he by this time, with you," he pursued, "crossed the gulf? He has with me."

"Ah, with you there was no gulf. He liked you from the first."

Vanderbank wondered. "You mean I managed him so well?"

"I don't know how you managed him, but liking me has been for him a painful, gradual process. I think he does now," Nanda declared. "He accepts me at last as different—he's trying with me on that basis. He has ended by understanding that when he talks to me of Granny I can't even imagine her."

Vanderbank puffed away. "*I* can."

"That's what Mitchy says too. But you've both probably got her wrong."

"I don't know," said Vanderbank—"I've gone into it a good deal. But it's too late. We can't be Greeks if we would."

Even for this Nanda had no laugh, though she had a quick attention. "Do you call Granny a Greek?"

Her companion slowly rose. "Yes—to finish her off handsomely and have done with her." He looked again at his watch. "Shall we go?—I want to see if my man and my things have turned up."

She kept her seat; there was something to revert to. "My fear of you isn't superficial. I mean it isn't immediate—not of you just as you stand," she explained. "It's of some dreadfully possible future you."

"Well," said the young man, smiling down at her, "don't forget that if there's to be such a monster there'll also be a future you, proportionately developed, to deal with him."

Nanda in the shade had closed her parasol, and her eyes attached themselves to the small hole she had dug in the ground with its point. "We shall both have moved, you mean?"

"It's charming to think that we shall probably have moved together."

"Ah, if moving is changing," she returned, "there won't be much for me in that. I shall never change—I shall be always just the same. The same old mannered, modern, slangy hack," she continued quite gravely. "Mr. Longdon has made me feel that."

Vanderbank laughed aloud, and it was especially at her seriousness. "Well, upon my soul!"

"Yes," she pursued, "what I am I must remain. I haven't what's called a principle of growth." Making marks in the earth with her umbrella, she appeared to cipher it out. "I'm about as good as I can be—and about as bad. If Mr. Longdon can't make me different, nobody can."

Vanderbank could only speak in the tone of high amusement. "And he has given up the hope?"

"Yes—though not *me* quite, altogether. But the hope he originally had."

"He gives up quickly—in three months!"

"Oh, these three months," she answered, "have been a long time: the fullest, the most important, for what has happened in them, of my life." She still poked at the ground; then she added: "And all thanks to *you*."

"To me?"—Vanderbank couldn't fancy.

"Why, for what we were speaking of just now—my being now so in everything and squeezing up and down no matter whose staircase. Isn't it one crowded hour of glorious life?" she asked. "What preceded it was an age, no doubt—but an age without a name."

Vanderbank watched her a little in silence, then spoke quite beside the question. "It's astonishing how at moments you remind me of your mother!"

At this she got up. "Ah, there it is! It's what I shall never shake off. That, I imagine, is what Mr. Longdon feels."

Both on their feet now, as if ready for the others, they yet —and even a trifle awkwardly—lingered. It might in fact have appeared to a spectator that some climax had come, on the young man's part, to some state of irresolution as to the utterance of something. What were the words repeatedly on his lips, yet repeatedly not sounded? It would have struck our observer that they were probably not those his lips even now actually formed. "Doesn't he perhaps talk to you too much about yourself?"

Nanda gave him a dim smile, and he might indeed then have exclaimed on a certain resemblance, a resemblance of expression that had nothing to do with form. It would not have been diminished for him moreover by her successful suppression of every sign that she felt his inquiry a little of a snub. The recall he had previously mentioned could, however, as

she answered him, only have been brushed away by a super-
vening sense of his roughness. "It isn't so much that probably as my own way of going on." She spoke with a mildness
that could scarce have been so full without being an effort.
"Between his patience and my egotism anything is possible. It
isn't his talking—it's his listening." She gave up the point at
any rate as if from softness to her actual companion. "Wasn't
it you who spoke to mamma about my sitting with her?
That's what I mean by my debt to you. It's through you that
I'm always there—through you and perhaps a little through
Mitchy."

"Oh, through Mitchy—it *must* have been—more than
through me." Vanderbank spoke with the manner of humouring her about a trifle. "Mitchy, delightful man, felt on
the subject, I think, still more strongly."

They quitted their place together and at the end of a few
steps became aware of the approach of one of the others, a
figure but a few yards off, arriving from the quarter from
which Nanda had come. "Ah, Mr. Longdon!"—she spoke
with eagerness now.

Vanderbank instantly waved a hat. "Dear old boy!"

"Between you all, at any rate," she said more gaily, "you've
brought me down."

Vanderbank made no answer till they met their friend,
when, by way of greeting, he simply echoed her words. "Between us all, you'll be glad to know, we've brought her
down."

Mr. Longdon looked from one of them to the other.
"Where have you been together?"

Nanda was the first to respond. "Only talking—on a
bench."

"Well, *I* want to talk on a bench!" The old man showed a
spirit.

"With me, of course?"—Vanderbank met it with encouragement.

The girl said nothing, but Mr. Longdon sought her eyes.
"No—with Nanda. You must mingle in the crowd."

"Ah," their companion laughed, "you two are the crowd!"

"Well—have your tea first."

Vanderbank on this, giving it up with his laugh, offered to

Mr. Longdon, before withdrawing, the hand-shake of greeting he had omitted—a demonstration really the warmer for
the tone of the joke that went with it. "*Intrigant!*"

XVII

Nanda praised to Mr. Longdon the charming spot she had
quitted, with the effect that they presently took a fresh possession of it, finding the beauty of the view deepened as the
afternoon grew old and the shadows long. They were of a
comfortable agreement on these matters, by which moreover
they were not long delayed, one of the pair at least being too
conscious, for the hour, of still other phenomena than the
natural and peaceful process that filled the air. "Well, you
must tell me about these things," Mr. Longdon sociably said:
he had joined his young friend with a budget of impressions
rapidly gathered at the house; as to which his appeal to her
for a light or two may be taken as the measure of the confidence now ruling their relations. He had come to feel at last,
he mentioned, that he could allow for most differences; yet in
such a situation as the present bewilderment could only come
back. There were no differences in the world—so it had all
ended for him—but those that marked at every turn the manners he had for three months been observing in good society.
The general wide deviation of this body occupied his mind to
the exclusion of almost everything else, and he had finally
been brought to believe that even in his slow-paced prime he
must have hung behind his contemporaries. He had not supposed at the moment—in the fifties and the sixties—that he
passed for old-fashioned, but life couldn't have left him so far
in the rear had the start between them originally been fair.
This was the way that, more than once, he had put the matter to the girl; which gives a sufficient hint, it is hoped, of the
range of some of their talk. It had always wound up indeed,
their talk, with some assumption of the growth of his actual
understanding; but it was just these pauses in the fray that
seemed to lead from time to time to a sharper clash. It was
when he felt, in a word, as if he had exhausted surprises that
he received his greatest shocks. There were no such strange
tastes as some of those drawn from the bucket that had re-

peatedly, as he imagined, touched the bottom of the well. "Now this sudden invasion of somebody's—heaven knows whose—house, and our dropping down on it like a swarm of locusts: I dare say it isn't civil to criticise it when one's going too, so almost culpably, with the stream; but what are people made of that they consent, just for money, to the violation of their homes?"

Nanda wondered; she cultivated the sense that he made her intensely reflect. "But haven't people in England always let their places?"

"If we're a nation of shopkeepers, you mean, it can't date, on the scale on which we show it, only from last week? No doubt, no doubt, and the more one thinks of it the more one seems to see that society—for we're *in* society, aren't we, and that's our horizon?—can never have been anything but increasingly vulgar. The point is that in the twilight of time— and I belong, you see, to the twilight—it had made out much less how vulgar it *could* be. It did its best, very probably, but there were too many superstitions it had to get rid of. It has been throwing them overboard one by one, so that now the ship sails uncommonly light. That's the way"—and the old man, with his eyes on the golden distance, ingeniously followed it out—"I come to feel so the lurching and pitching. If I weren't a pretty fair sailor—well, as it is, my dear," he interrupted himself with a laugh, "I show you often enough what grabs I make for support." He gave a faint gasp, half amusement, half anguish, then abruptly relieved himself by a question. "To whom in point of fact does the place belong?"

"I'm awfully ashamed, but I'm afraid I don't know. That just came up here," the girl went on, "for Mr. Van."

Mr. Longdon seemed to think an instant. "Oh, it came up, did it? And Mr. Van couldn't tell?"

"He has quite forgotten—though he has been here before. Of course it may have been with other people," she added in extenuation. "I mean it mayn't have been theirs then any more than it's Mitchy's."

"I see. They too had just bundled in."

Nanda completed the simple history. "To-day it's Mitchy who bundles, and I believe that really he bundled only yesterday. He turned in his people, and here we are."

"Here we are, here we are!" her friend more gravely echoed. "Well, it's splendid!"

As if at a note in his voice her eyes, while his own still strayed away, just fixed him. "Don't you think it's really rather exciting? Everything's ready, the feast all spread, and with nothing to blunt our curiosity but the general knowledge that there will be people and things, we comfortably take our places." He answered nothing, though her picture apparently reached him. "There *are* people, there *are* things, and all in a plenty. Had every one, when you came away, turned up?" she asked as he was still silent.

"I dare say. There were some ladies and gentlemen on the terrace that I didn't know. But I looked only for you and came this way on an indication of your mother's."

"And did she ask that if you should find me with Mr. Van you would make him come to her?"

Mr. Longdon replied to this with some delay but without movement. "How could she have supposed he was here?"

"Since he had not yet been to the house? Oh, it has always been a wonder to me, the things that mamma supposes! I see she asked you," Nanda observed.

At this her old friend turned to her. "But it wasn't because of that I got rid of him."

Nanda hesitated. "No—you don't mind everything mamma says."

"I don't mind 'everything' anybody says: not even, my dear, when the person's you."

Again she waited an instant. "Not even when it's Mr. Van?"

Mr. Longdon candidly considered. "Oh, I take him up on all sorts of things."

"That shows then the importance they have for you. Is *he* like his grandmother?" the girl pursued. Then as her companion looked vague: "Wasn't it his grandmother too you knew?"

He had an extraordinary smile. "His mother." She exclaimed, colouring, on her mistake, and he added: "I'm not so bad as that. But you're none of you like them."

"Wasn't she pretty?" Nanda inquired.

"Very handsome. But it makes no difference. She herself, to-day, wouldn't know him."

She gave a small gasp. "His own mother wouldn't——?"

His head-shake just failed of sharpness. "No, nor he her. There's a link missing." Then as if after all she might take him too seriously, "Of course it's I," he more gently moralised, "who have lost the link in my sleep. I've slept half the century —I'm Rip Van Winkle." He went back after a moment to her question. "He's not, at any rate, like his mother."

Nanda turned it over. "Perhaps you wouldn't think so much of her now."

"Perhaps not. At all events my parting you from Mr. Vanderbank was my own idea."

"I wasn't thinking," Nanda said, "of your parting me. I was thinking of your parting yourself."

"I might have sent *you* to the house? Well," Mr. Longdon replied, "I find I take more and more the economical view of my pleasures. I run them less and less together—I get all I can out of each."

"So now you're getting all you can out of *me?*"

"All I can, my dear—all I can." He watched a little the flushed distance, then mildly broke out: "It *is*, as you said just now, exciting! But it makes me"—and he became abrupt again—"want you, as I've already told you, to come to *my* place. Not, however, that we may be still more mad together."

The girl from the bench shared his contemplation. "Do you call *this* madness?"

He hesitated. "You spoke of it yourself as excitement. You'll make of course one of your fine distinctions, but I take it, in my rough way, as a whirl. We're going round and round." In a minute he had folded his arms with the same closeness Vanderbank had used—in a minute he too was nervously shaking his foot. "Steady, steady; if we sit close we shall see it through. But come down to Suffolk for sanity."

"You do mean then that I may come alone?"

"I won't receive you, I assure you, on any other terms. I want to show you," he continued, "what life *can* give. Not of course," he subjoined, "of this sort of thing."

"No—you've told me. Of peace."

"Of peace," said Mr. Longdon. "Oh, you don't know— you haven't the least idea. That's just why I want to show you."

Nanda looked as if already she saw it in the distance. "But will it be peace if I'm there? I mean for *you*," she added.

"It isn't a question of 'me.' Everybody's omelette is made of somebody's eggs. Besides, I think that when we're alone together——"

He had dropped for so long that she wondered. "Well, when we are—?"

"Why, it will be all right," he simply concluded. "Temples of peace, the ancients used to call them. We'll set up one, and I shall be at least doorkeeper. You'll come down whenever you like."

She gave herself to him in her silence more than she could have done in words. "Have you arranged it with mamma?" she said, however, at last.

"I've arranged everything."

"*She* won't want to come?"

Her friend's laugh turned him to her. "Don't be nervous. There are things as to which your mother trusts me."

"But others as to which not."

Their eyes met for some time on this, and it ended in his saying: "Well, you must help me." Nanda, but without shrinking, looked away again, and Mr. Longdon, as if to consecrate their understanding by the air of ease, passed to another subject. "Mr. Mitchett's the most princely host."

"Isn't he too kind for anything? Do you know what he pretends?" Nanda went on. "He says, in the most extraordinary way, that he does it all for *me*."

"Takes this great place and fills it with servants and company—?"

"Yes, just so that I may come down for a Sunday or two. Of course he has only taken it for three or four weeks, but even for that time it's a handsome compliment. He doesn't care what he does. It's his way of amusing himself. He amuses himself at our expense," the girl continued.

"Well, I hope that makes up, my dear, for the rate at which we're doing so at his!"

"His amusement," said Nanda, "is to see us believe what he says."

Mr. Longdon thought a moment. "Really, my child, you're most acute."

"Oh, I haven't watched life for nothing! Mitchy doesn't care," she repeated.

Her companion seemed divided between a desire to draw and a certain fear to encourage her. "Doesn't care for what?"

She reflected an instant, in her seriousness, and it might have added to Mr. Longdon's impression of her depth. "Well, for himself. I mean for his money. For anything any one may think. For Lord Petherton, for instance, really at all. Lord Petherton thinks he has helped him—thinks, that is, that Mitchy thinks he has. But Mitchy's more amused at *him* than at anybody else. He takes every one in."

"Every one but you?"

"Oh, I like him."

"My poor child, you're of a profundity!" Mr. Longdon murmured.

He spoke almost uneasily, but she was not too much alarmed to continue lucid. "And he likes me, and I know just how much—and just how little. He's the most generous man in the world. It pleases him to feel that he's indifferent and splendid—there are so many things it makes up to him for." The old man listened with attention, and his young friend, conscious of it, proceeded as on ground of which she knew every inch. "He's the son, as you know, of a great bootmaker —'to all the Courts of Europe'—who left him a large fortune, which had been made, I believe, in the most extraordinary way, in building-speculations as well."

"Oh yes, I know. It's astonishing!" her companion sighed.

"That he should be of such extraction?"

"Well, everything. That you should be talking as you are— that you should have 'watched life,' as you say, to such purpose. That we should any of us be here—most of all that Mr. Mitchett himself should. That your grandmother's daughter should have brought *her* daughter——"

"To stay with a person"—Nanda took it up as, apparently out of delicacy, he fairly failed—"whose father used to take the measure, down on his knees on a little mat, as mamma says, of my grandfather's remarkably large foot? Yes, we none of us mind. Do you think we should?" Nanda asked.

Mr. Longdon turned it over. "I'll answer you by a question. Would you marry him?"

"Never." Then as if to show there was no weakness in her mildness, "Never, never, never," she repeated.

"And yet I dare say you know—?" But Mr. Longdon once more faltered; his scruple came uppermost. "You don't mind my speaking of it?"

"Of his thinking he wants to marry me? Not a bit. I positively enjoy telling you there's nothing in it."

"Not even for *him*?"

Nanda considered. "Not more than is made up to him by his having found out, through talk and things—which mightn't otherwise have occurred—that I do like him. I wouldn't have come down here if I hadn't."

"Not for any other reason?" Mr. Longdon gravely inquired.

"Not for *your* being here, do you mean?"

He hesitated. "Me and other persons."

She showed somehow that she wouldn't flinch. "You weren't asked till after he had made sure I'd come. We've become, you and I," she smiled, "one of the couples who are invited together."

These were couples, his speculative eye seemed to show, he didn't even yet know about, and if he mentally took them up a moment it was only promptly to drop them. "I don't think you put it quite strong enough, you know."

"That Mitchy *is* hard hit? He puts it so strong himself that it will surely do for both of us. I'm a part of what I just spoke of—his indifference and magnificence. It's as if he could only afford to do what's not vulgar. He might perfectly marry a duke's daughter, but that *would* be vulgar—would be the absolute necessity and ideal of nine out of ten of the sons of shoemakers made ambitious by riches. Mitchy says 'No; I take my own line; I go in for a beggar-maid.' And it's only because I'm a beggar-maid that he wants me."

"But there are plenty of others," Mr. Longdon objected.

"Oh, I admit I'm the one he least dislikes. But if I had any money," Nanda went on, "or if I were really good-looking—for that to-day, the real thing, will do as well as being a duke's daughter—he wouldn't come near me. And I think that ought to settle it. Besides, he must marry Aggie. She's a beggar-maid too—as well as an angel; so there's nothing against it."

Mr. Longdon stared, but even in his surprise seemed to take from the swiftness with which she made him move over the ground a certain agreeable glow. "Does 'Aggie' like him?"

"She likes every one. As I say, she's an angel—but a real, real, real one. The kindest man in the world is therefore the proper husband for her. If Mitchy wants to do something thoroughly nice," she declared with the same high competence, "he'll take her out of her situation, which is awful."

Mr. Longdon looked graver. "In what way awful?"

"Why, don't you know?" His eye was now cold enough to give her, in her chill, a flurried sense that she might displease him least by a graceful lightness. "The Duchess and Lord Petherton are like you and me."

"Is it a conundrum?" He was serious indeed.

"They're one of the couples who are invited together." But his face reflected so little success for her levity that it was in another tone she presently added: "Mitchy really oughtn't." Her friend, in silence, fixed his eyes on the ground; an attitude in which there was something to make her strike rather wild. "But of course, kind as he is, he can scarcely be called particular. He has his ideas—he thinks nothing matters. He says we've all come to a pass that's the end of everything."

Mr. Longdon remained mute a while, and when he at last raised his eyes it was without meeting Nanda's and with some dryness of manner. "The end of everything? One might easily receive that impression."

He again became mute, and there was a pause between them of some length, accepted by Nanda with an anxious stillness that it might have touched a spectator to observe. She sat there as if waiting for some further sign, only wanting not to displease her friend, yet unable to pretend to play any part and with something in her really that she couldn't take back now, something involved in her original assumption that there was to be a kind of intelligence in their relation. "I dare say," she said at last, "that I make allusions you don't like. But I keep forgetting."

He waited a moment longer, then turned to her with a look rendered a little strange by the way it happened to reach over his glasses. It was even austerer than before. "Keep forgetting what?"

She gave after an instant a faint, feeble smile which seemed to speak of helplessness and which, when at rare moments it played in her face, was expressive from her positive lack of personal, superficial diffidence. "Well—I don't know." It was as if appearances became at times so complicated that—so far as helping others to understand was concerned—she could only give up.

"I hope you don't think I want you to be with me as you wouldn't be—as it were—with yourself. I hope you don't think I don't want you to be frank. If you were to try to *appear* to me anything—!" He ended in simple sadness; that, for instance, would be so little what he should like.

"Anything different, you mean, from what I am? That's just what I've thought from the first. One's just what one *is*—isn't one? I don't mean so much," she went on, "in one's character or temper—for they have, haven't they? to be what's called 'properly controlled'—as in one's mind and what one sees and feels and the sort of thing one notices." Nanda paused an instant; then "There you are!" she simply but rather desperately brought out.

Mr. Longdon considered this with visible intensity. "What you suggest is that the things you speak of depend upon other people?"

"Well, every one isn't so beautiful as you." Nanda had met him with promptitude, yet no sooner had she spoken than she appeared again to encounter a difficulty. "But there it is—my just saying even that. Oh, how I always know—as I've told you before—whenever I'm different! I can't ask you to tell me the things Granny *would* have said, because that's simply arranging to keep myself back from you, and so being nasty and underhand, which you naturally don't want, nor I either. Nevertheless when I say the things she wouldn't, then I put before you too much—too much for your liking it—what I know and see and feel. If we're both partly the result of other people, *her* other people were so different." The girl's sensitive boldness kept it up, but there was something in her that pleaded for patience. "And yet if she had *you*, so I've got you too. It's the flattery of that, or the sound of it, I know, that must be so unlike her. Of course it's awfully like mother; yet it isn't as if you hadn't already let me see—is it?—that you don't really think me the same." Again she stopped a minute, as if to find her way with him; and again, for the time, he gave no sign. She struck out again with her strange, cool limpidity. "Granny wasn't the kind of girl she *couldn't* be—and so neither am I."

Mr. Longdon had fallen while she talked into something that might have been taken for a conscious temporary submission to her; he had uncrossed his fidgety legs and, thrusting them out with the feet together, sat looking very hard before him, his chin sunk on his breast and his hands, clasped as they met, rapidly twirling their thumbs. So he remained for a time that might have given his young friend the sense of having made herself right with him so far as she had been wrong. He still had all her attention, just as previously she had had his, but while he now simply gazed and thought she watched him with a discreet solicitude that would almost have represented him as a near relative whom she supposed unwell. At the end he looked round, and then, obeying some impulse that had gathered in her while they sat mute, she put out to him the tender hand she might have offered to a sick child. They had been talking about frankness, but she showed a frankness in this instance that made him perceptibly colour. For that in turn, however, he responded only the more completely, taking her hand and holding it, keeping it a long minute during which their eyes met and something seemed to clear up that had been too obscure to be dispelled by words. Finally he brought out as if, though it was what he had been thinking of, her gesture had most determined him: "I wish immensely you'd get married!"

His tone betrayed so special a meaning that the words had a sound of suddenness; yet there was always in Nanda's face that odd preparedness of the young person who has unlearned surprise through the habit, in company, of studiously not compromising her innocence by blinking at things said. "How *can* I?" she asked, but appearing rather to take up the proposal than to put it by.

"Can't you, *can't* you?" He spoke pressingly and kept her hand. She shook her head slowly, markedly; on which he continued: "You don't do justice to Mr. Mitchy." She said nothing, but her look was there, and it made him resume: "Impossible?"

"Impossible." At this, letting her go, Mr. Longdon got up; he pulled out his watch. "We must go back." She had risen with him, and they stood face to face in the faded light while he slipped the watch away. "Well, that doesn't make me wish it any less."

"It's lovely of you to wish it, but I shall be one of the people who don't. I shall be at the end," said Nanda, "one of those who haven't."

"No, my child," he returned gravely—"you shall never be anything so sad."

"Why not—if *you've* been?"

He looked at her a little, quietly; then, putting out his hand, passed her own into his arm. "Exactly because I have."

XVIII

"Would you," the Duchess said to him the next day, "be for five minutes awfully kind to my poor little niece?" The words were spoken in charming entreaty as he issued from the house late on the Sunday afternoon—the second evening of his stay, which the next morning was to bring to an end—and on his meeting the speaker at one of the extremities of the wide cool terrace. There was at this point a subsidiary flight of steps by which she had just mounted from the grounds, one of her purposes being apparently to testify afresh to that anxious supervision of little Aggie from which she had momentarily suffered herself to be diverted. This young lady, established in the pleasant shade on a sofa of light construction designed for the open air, offered the image of a patience of which it was a questionable kindness to break the spell. It was that beautiful hour when, toward the close of the happiest days of summer, such places as the great terrace at Mertle present to the fancy a recall of the banquet-hall deserted—deserted by the company lately gathered at tea and now dispersed, according to affinities and combinations promptly felt and perhaps quite as promptly criticised, either in quieter chambers where intimacy might deepen or in gardens and under trees where the stillness knew the click of balls and the good-humour of games. There had been chairs, on the terrace, pushed about; there were ungathered teacups on the level top of the parapet;

the servants in fact, in the manner of "hands" mustered by a whistle on the deck of a ship, had just arrived to restore things to an order soon again to be broken. There were scattered couples in sight below and an idle group on the lawn, out of the midst of which, in spite of its detachment, somebody was sharp enough sometimes to cry "Out!" The high daylight was still in the sky, but with just the foreknowledge already of the long golden glow in which the many-voiced caw of the rooks would sound at once sociable and sad. There was a great deal all about to be aware of and to look at, but little Aggie had her eyes on a book over which her pretty head was bent with a docility visible even from afar. "I've a friend —down there by the lake—to go back to," the Duchess went on, "and I'm on my way to my room to get a letter that I've promised to show him. I shall immediately bring it down and then in a few minutes be able to relieve you. I don't leave her alone too much—one doesn't, you know, in a house full of people, a child of that age. Besides"—and Mr. Longdon's interlocutress was even more confiding—"I do want you so very intensely to know her. You, *par exemple*, you're what I *should* like to give her." Mr. Longdon looked the Duchess, in acknowledgment of her appeal, straight in the face, and who can tell whether or no she acutely guessed from his expression that he recognised this particular juncture as written on the page of his doom?—whether she heard him inaudibly say "Ah, here it is: I knew it would have to come!" She would at any rate have been astute enough, had this miracle occurred, quite to complete his sense for her own understanding and suffer it to make no difference in the tone in which she still confronted him. "Oh, I take the bull by the horns—I know you haven't wanted to know me. If you had you would have called on me—I've given you plenty of hints and little coughs. Now, you see, I don't cough any more—I just rush at you and grab you. You don't call on me—so I call on *you*. There isn't any indecency moreover that I won't commit for my child."

Mr. Longdon's impenetrability crashed like glass at the elbow-touch of this large, handsome, practised woman, who walked for him, like some brazen pagan goddess, in a cloud of queer legend. He looked off at her child, who, at a distance and not hearing them, had not moved. "I know she's a great friend of Nanda's."

"Has Nanda told you that?"

"Often—taking such an interest in her."

"I'm glad she thinks so then—though really her interests are so various. But come to my baby. I don't make *her* come," she explained as she swept him along, "because I want you just to sit down by her there and keep the place, as one may say——!"

"Well, for whom?" he demanded as she stopped.

It was her step that had checked itself as well as her tongue, and again, suddenly, they stood quite consciously and vividly opposed. "Can I trust you?" the Duchess brought out. Again then she took herself up. "But as if I weren't already doing it! It's because I do trust you so utterly that I haven't been able any longer to keep my hands off you. The person I want the place for is none other than Mitchy himself, and half my occupation now is to get it properly kept for him. Lord Petherton's immensely kind, but Lord Petherton can't do everything. I know you really like our host——"

Mr. Longdon, at this, interrupted her with a certain coldness. "How, may I ask, do you know it?"

But with a brazen goddess to deal with—! This personage had to fix him but an instant. "Because, you dear honest man, you're here. You wouldn't be if you hated him, for you don't practically condone——!"

This time he broke in with his eyes on the child. "I feel on the contrary, I assure you, that I condone a great deal."

"Well, don't boast of your cynicism," she laughed, "till you're sure of all it covers. Let the right thing for you be," she went on, "that Nanda herself wants it."

"Nanda herself?" He continued to watch little Aggie, who had never yet turned her head. "I'm afraid I don't understand you."

She swept him on again. "I'll come to you presently and explain. I *must* get my letter for Petherton; after which I'll give up Mitchy, whom I was going to find, and since I've broken the ice—if it isn't too much to say to such a polar bear! —I'll show you *le fond de ma pensée*. Baby darling," she said to her niece, "keep Mr. Longdon. Show him," she benevolently suggested, "what you've been reading." Then again to her fellow-visitor, as arrested by this very question: "Caro signore, have *you* a possible book?"

Little Aggie had got straight up and was holding out her volume, which Mr. Longdon, all courtesy for her, glanced at. "*Stories from English History.* Oh!"

His ejaculation, though vague, was not such as to prevent the girl from venturing gently: "Have you read it?"

Mr. Longdon, receiving her pure little smile, showed he felt that he had never so taken her in as at this moment and also that she was a person with whom he should surely get on. "I think I must have."

Little Aggie was still more encouraged, but not to the point of keeping anything back. "It hasn't any author. It's anonymous."

The Duchess borrowed, for another question to Mr. Longdon, not a little of her gravity. "Is it all right?"

"I don't know"—his answer was to Aggie. "There have been some horrid things in English history."

"Oh, horrid—*haven't* there?" Aggie, whose speech had the prettiest, faintest foreignness, sweetly and eagerly quavered.

"Well, darling, Mr. Longdon will recommend to you some nice historical work—for we love history, don't we?—that leaves the horrors out. We like to know," the Duchess explained to the authority she invoked, "the cheerful, happy, *right* things. There are so many, after all, and this is the place to remember them. *A tantôt.*"

As she passed into the house by the nearest of the long windows that stood open Mr. Longdon placed himself beside her little charge, whom he treated, for the next ten minutes, with an exquisite courtesy. A person who knew him well would, if present at the scene, have found occasion in it to be freshly aware that he was in his quiet way master of two distinct kinds of urbanity, the kind that added to distance and the kind that diminished it. Such an analyst would furthermore have noted, in respect to the aunt and the niece, of which kind each had the benefit, and might even have gone so far as to detect in him some absolute betrayal of the impression produced on him by his actual companion, some irradiation of his certitude that, from the point of view under which she had been formed, she was a remarkable, a rare success. Since to create a particular little rounded and tinted innocence had been aimed at, the fruit had been grown to the perfection of a peach on a sheltered wall, and this quality of the object resulting from a process might well make him feel himself in contact with something wholly new. Little Aggie differed from any young person he had ever met in that she had been deliberately prepared for consumption and in that furthermore the gentleness of her spirit had immensely helped the preparation. Nanda, beside her, was a northern savage, and the reason was partly that the elements of that young lady's nature were already, were publicly, were almost indecorously active. They were practically there for good or for ill; experience was still to come and what they might work out to still a mystery; but the sum would get itself done with the figures now on the slate. On little Aggie's slate the figures were yet to be written; which sufficiently accounted for the difference of the two surfaces. Both the girls struck him as lambs with the great shambles of life in their future; but while one, with its neck in a pink ribbon, had no consciousness but that of being fed from the hand with the small sweet biscuit of unobjectionable knowledge, the other struggled with instincts and forebodings, with the suspicion of its doom and the far-borne scent, in the flowery fields, of blood.

"Oh, Nanda, she's my best friend after three or four others."

"After so many?" Mr. Longdon laughed. "Don't you think that's rather a back seat, as they say, for one's best?"

"A back seat?"—she wondered with a purity!

"If you don't understand," said her companion, "it serves me right, as your aunt didn't leave me with you to teach you the slang of the day."

"The 'slang'?"—she again spotlessly speculated.

"You've never even heard the expression? I should think that a great compliment to our time if it weren't that I fear it may have been only the name that has been kept from you."

The light of ignorance in the child's smile was positively golden. "The name?" she again echoed.

She understood too little—he gave it up. "And who are all the other best friends whom poor Nanda comes after?"

"Well, there's my aunt, and Miss Merriman, and Gelsomina, and Dr. Beltram."

"And who, please, is Miss Merriman?"

"She's my governess, don't you know?—but such a deliciously easy governess."

"That, I suppose, is because she has such a deliciously easy pupil. And who is Gelsomina?" Mr. Longdon inquired.

"She's my old nurse—my old maid."

"I see. Well, one must always be kind to old maids. But who is Dr. Beltram?"

"Oh, the most intimate friend of all. We tell him everything."

There was for Mr. Longdon in this, with a slight uncertainty, an effect of drollery. "Your little troubles?"

"Ah, they're not always so little! And he takes them all away."

"Always?—on the spot?"

"Sooner or later," said little Aggie with serenity. "But why not?"

"Why not indeed?" he laughed. "It must be very plain sailing." Decidedly she was, as Nanda had said, an angel, and there was a wonder in her possession on this footing of one of the most expressive little faces that even her expressive race had ever shown him. Formed to express everything, it scarce expressed as yet even a consciousness. All the elements of play were in it, but they had nothing to play with. It was a rest moreover, after so much that he had lately been through, to be with a person for whom questions were so simple. "But he sounds all the same like the kind of doctor whom, as soon as one hears of him, one wants to send for."

The young girl had at this a small light of confusion. "Oh, I don't mean he's a doctor for medicine. He's a clergyman—and my aunt says he's a saint. I don't think you've many in England," little Aggie continued to explain.

"Many saints? I'm afraid not. Your aunt's very happy to know one. We should call Dr. Beltram in England a priest."

"Oh, but he's English. And he knows everything we do—and everything we think."

"'We'—your aunt, your governess and your nurse? What a varied wealth of knowledge!"

"Ah, Miss Merriman and Gelsomina tell him only what they like."

"And do you and the Duchess tell him what you *don't* like?"

"Oh, often—but we always like *him*—no matter what we tell him. And we know that just the same he always likes us."

"I see then of course," said Mr. Longdon, very gravely now, "what a friend he must be. So it's after all this," he continued in a moment, "that Nanda comes in?"

His companion had to consider, but suddenly she caught assistance. "This one, I think, comes before." Lord Petherton, arriving apparently from the garden, had drawn near unobserved by Mr. Longdon and the next moment was within hail. "I see him very often," she continued—"oftener than Nanda. Oh, but *then* Nanda. And then," little Aggie wound up, "Mr. Mitchy."

"Oh, I'm glad *he* comes in," Mr. Longdon returned, "though rather far down in the list." Lord Petherton was now before them, there being no one else on the terrace to speak to, and with the odd look of an excess of physical power that almost blocked the way, he seemed to give them in the flare of his big teeth the benefit of a kind of brutal geniality. It was always to be remembered for him that he could scarce show without surprising you an adjustment to the smaller conveniences; so that when he took up a trifle it was not perforce in every case the sign of an uncanny calculation. When the elephant in the show plays the fiddle it must be mainly with the presumption of consequent apples; which was why, doubtless, this personage had half the time the air of assuring you that, really civilised as his type had now become, no apples were required. Mr. Longdon viewed him with a vague apprehension and as if quite unable to meet the question of what he would have called for such a personage the social responsibility. Did this specimen of his class pull the tradition down or did he just take it where he found it—in the very different place from that in which, on ceasing so long ago to "go out," Mr. Longdon had left it? Our friend doubtless averted himself from the possibility of a mental dilemma; if the man didn't lower the position was it the position then that let down the man? Somehow he wasn't positively up. More evidence would be needed to decide; yet it was just of more evidence that one remained rather in dread. Lord Petherton was kind to little Aggie, kind to her companion, kind to every one, after Mr. Longdon had explained that she was so good as to be giving him the list of her dear friends. "I'm only a little dismayed," the elder man said, "to find Mr. Mitchett at the bottom."

"Oh, but it's an awfully short list, isn't it? If it consists only of me and Mitchy he's not so very low down. We don't allow her very *many* friends; we look out too well for ourselves." He addressed the child as on an easy jocose understanding. "Is the question, Aggie, whether we shall allow you Mr. Longdon? Won't that rather 'do' for us—for Mitchy and me? I say, Duchess," he went on as this lady reappeared, "*are* we going to allow her Mr. Longdon and do we quite realise what we're about? We mount guard awfully, you know"—he carried the joke back to the person he had named. "We sift and we sort, we pick the candidates over, and I should like to hear any one say that in this case at least I don't keep a watch on my taste. Oh, we close in!"

The Duchess, with the object of her quest in her hand, had come back. "Well then Mr. Longdon will close *with* us—you'll consider henceforth that he's as safe as yourself. Here's the letter that I wanted you to read—with which you'll please take a turn, in strict charge of the child, and then restore her to us. If you don't come I shall know you have found Mitchy and shall be at peace. Go, little heart," she continued to the child, "but leave me your book to look over again. I don't know that I'm quite sure!" She sent them off together, but had a grave protest as her friend put out his hand for the volume. "No, Petherton—not for books; for her reading I can't say I do trust you. But for everything else—quite!" she declared to Mr. Longdon with a look of conscientious courage as their companion withdrew. "I do believe," she pursued in the same spirit, "in a certain amount of intelligent confidence. Really nice men are steadied by the sense of your having had it. But I wouldn't," she added gaily, "trust *him* all around!"

XIX

Many things at Mertle were strange for her interlocutor, but nothing perhaps as yet had been so strange as the sight of this arrangement for little Aggie's protection—an arrangement made in the interest of her remaining as a young person of her age and her *monde*, as her aunt would have said, should remain. The strangest part of this impression too was that the provision might really have its happy side and his lordship really understand better than any one else his noble friend's whole theory of perils and precautions. The child herself, the spectator of the incident was sure enough, understood nothing, but the understandings that surrounded her, filling all the air, made it a heavier compound to breathe than any Mr. Longdon had yet tasted. This heaviness had grown for him through the long, sweet summer day, and there was something in his at last finding himself ensconced with the Duchess that made it supremely oppressive. The contact was one that, none the less, he would not have availed himself of a decent pretext to avoid. With so many fine mysteries playing about him there was relief, at the point he had reached, rather than alarm, in the thought of knowing the worst; which it pressed upon him somehow that the Duchess must not only supremely know but must in any relation most naturally communicate. It fluttered him rather that a person who had an understanding with Lord Petherton should so single him out as to wish for one also with himself: such a person must either have great variety of mind or have a wonderful idea of *his* variety. It was true indeed that Mr. Mitchett must have the most extraordinary understanding, and yet with Mr. Mitchett he now found himself quite pleasantly at his ease. Their host, however, was a person *sui generis*, whom he had accepted, once for all, the inconsequence of liking in pursuance of the need he occasionally felt to put it on record that he was not narrow-minded. Perhaps at bottom he most liked Mitchy because Mitchy most liked Nanda; there hung about him still moreover the faded fragrance of the superstition that hospitality not declined is one of the things that "oblige." It obliged the thoughts for Mr. Longdon as well as the manners and in the especial form in which he was now committed to it would have made him, had he really thought any ill, ask himself what the deuce then he was doing in the man's house. All of which didn't prevent some of Mitchy's queer condonations—if condonations in fact they were—from not wholly, by themselves, soothing his vague unrest, an unrest which never had been so great as at the moment he heard the Duchess abruptly say to him: "Do you know my idea about Nanda? It's my particular desire that you should—the reason, really, why I've thus laid violent hands on you. Nanda, my dear man, should marry at the very first moment."

This was more interesting than he had expected, and the effect produced by his interlocutress, and doubtless not lost on her, was shown in his suppressed start. "There has been no reason why I should attribute to you any judgment of the matter; but I've had one myself, and I don't see why I shouldn't say frankly that it's very much the one you express. It would be a very good thing."

"A very good thing, but none of my business?"—the Duchess's briskness was not unamiable.

It was on this circumstance that her companion for an instant perhaps meditated. "It's probably not in my interest to say that—I should give you too easy a retort. It would strike any one as quite as much your business as mine."

"Well, it ought to be somebody's, you know. One would suppose it to be her mother's—her father's; but in this country the parents are even more emancipated than the children. Suppose, really, since it appears to be nobody's affair, that you and I *do* make it ours. We needn't either of us," she continued, "be concerned for the other's reasons, though I'm perfectly ready, I assure you, to put my cards on the table. You've your feelings—we know they're beautiful. I, on my side, have mine—for which I don't pretend anything but that they're strong. They can dispense with being beautiful when they're so perfectly settled. Besides, I may mention, they're rather nice than otherwise. Edward and I have a *cousinage*, though for all he does to keep it up—! If he leaves his children to play in the street I take it seriously enough to make an occasional dash for them before they're run over. And I want for Nanda simply the man she herself wants—it isn't as if I wanted for her a dwarf or a hunchback or a *coureur* or a drunkard. Vanderbank's a man whom any woman, don't you think? might be—whom more than one woman *is*—glad of for herself: *beau comme le jour*, awfully conceited and awfully patronising, but clever and successful and yet liked, and without, so far as

I know, any of the terrific appendages which in this country
so often diminish the value of even the pleasantest people. He
hasn't five horrible unmarried sisters for his wife to have always on a visit. The way your women don't marry is the ruin
here of society, and I've been assured in good quarters—
though I don't know so much about that—the ruin also of
conversation and of literature. Isn't it precisely just a little to
keep Nanda herself from becoming that kind of appendage—
say to poor Harold, say, one of these days, to her younger
brother and sister—that friends like you and me feel the importance of bestirring ourselves in time? Of course she's sup-
posedly young, but she's really any age you like: your London
world so fearfully batters and bruises them."

She had gone fast and far, but it had given Mr. Longdon
time to feel himself well afloat. There were so many things in
it all to take up that he laid his hand—of which, he was not
unconscious, the feebleness exposed him—on the nearest.
"Why, I'm sure her mother—after twenty years of it—is fresh
enough."

"Fresh? You find Mrs. Brook fresh?"

The Duchess had a manner that, in its all-knowingness,
rather humiliated than encouraged; but he was all the more
resolute for being conscious of his own reserves. "It seems to
me it's fresh to look about thirty."

"That indeed would be perfect. But she doesn't—she looks
about three. She simply looks a baby."

"Oh Duchess, you're really too particular!" he returned,
feeling that, as the trodden worm will turn, anxiety itself may
sometimes tend to wit.

She met him in her own way. "I know what I mean. My
niece is a person *I* call fresh. It's warranted, as they say in the
shops. Besides," she went on, "if a married woman has been
knocked about, that's only a part of her condition. *Elle l'a
bien voulu,* and if you're married you're married; it's the
smoke—or call it the soot!—of the fire. You know, yourself,"
she roundly pursued, "that Nanda's situation appals you."

"Oh, 'appals'!" he restrictively murmured.

It even tried a little his companion's patience. "There you
are, you English—you'll never face your own music. It's
amazing what you'd rather do with a thing—anything not to

shoot at or to make money with—than look at its meaning. If I wished to save the girl as *you* wish it I should know exactly from what. But why differ about reasons," she asked, "when we're at one about the fact? I don't mention the greatest of Vanderbank's merits," she added—"his having so delicious a friend. By whom, let me hasten to assure you," she laughed, "I don't in the least mean Mrs. Brook! She *is* delicious, if you like, but believe me when I tell you, *caro mio*—if you need to be told—that for effective action on him you're worth twenty of her."

What was most visible in Mr. Longdon was that, however it came to him, he had rarely before, all at once, had so much given him to think about. Again the only way to manage was to take what came uppermost. "By effective action you mean action on the matter of his proposing for Nanda?"

The Duchess's assent was noble. "You can make him propose—you can make, I mean, a sure thing of it. You can *doter* the bride." Then as with the impulse to meet benevolently and more than half-way her companion's imperfect apprehension: "You can settle on her something that will make her a *parti*." His apprehension was perhaps imperfect, but it could still lead somehow to his flushing all over, and this demonstration the Duchess as quickly took into account. "Poor Edward, you know, won't give her a penny."

Decidedly she went fast, but Mr. Longdon in a moment had caught up. "Mr. Vanderbank—your idea is—would require on the part of his wife something of that sort?"

"Pray, who wouldn't—in the world we all move in—require it quite as much? Mr. Vanderbank, I'm assured, has no means of his own at all, and if he doesn't believe in impecunious marriages it's not I who shall be shocked at him. For myself I simply despise them. He has nothing but a poor official salary. If it's enough for one it would be little for two, and would be still less for half-a-dozen. They're just the people to have, that blessed pair, a fine old English family."

Mr. Longdon was now fairly abreast of it. "What it comes to then, the idea you're so good as to put before me, is to bribe him to take her."

The Duchess remained bland, but she fixed him. "You say that as if you were scandalised, but if you try Mr. Van with it

I don't think he'll be. And you won't persuade me," she went on finely, "that you haven't, yourself, thought of it." She kept her eyes on him, and the effect of them, soon enough visible in his face, was such as presently to make her exult at her felicity. "You're of a limpidity, dear man!—you've only to be said 'bo!' to and you confess. Consciously or unconsciously— the former, really, I'm inclined to think—you've wanted him for her." She paused an instant to enjoy her triumph; after which she continued: "And you've wanted her for him. I make you out, you'll say—for I see you coming—one of those horrible benevolent busybodies who are the worst of the class, but you've only to think a little—if I may go so far—to see that no 'making' at all is required. You've only one link with the Brooks, but that link is golden. How can we, all of us, by this time, not have grasped and admired the beauty of your feeling for Lady Julia? There it is—I make you wince: to speak of it is to profane it. Let us by all means not speak of it then, but let us act on it." He had at last turned his face from her, and it now took in, from the vantage of his high position, only the loveliness of the place and the hour, which included a glimpse of Lord Petherton and little Aggie, who, down in the garden, slowly strolled in familiar union. Each had a hand in the other's, swinging easily as they went; their talk was evidently of flowers and fruits and birds; it was quite like father and daughter. And one could see half a mile off in short that *they* weren't flirting. Our friend's bewilderment came in odd, cold gusts: these were unreasoned and capricious; one of them, at all events, during his companion's pause, must have roared in his ears. Was it not therefore through some continuance of the sound that he heard her go on speaking? "Of course you know the poor child's own condition."

It took him a good while to answer. "Do *you* know it?" he asked with his eyes still away.

"If your question's ironical," she laughed, "your irony's perfectly wasted. I should be ashamed of myself if, with my relationship and my interest, I hadn't made sure. Nanda's fairly sick—as sick as a little cat—with her passion." It was with an intensity of silence that Mr. Longdon appeared to accept this; he was even so dumb for a minute that the oddity of the image could draw from him no natural sound. The

Duchess once more, accordingly, recognised an opportunity. "It has doubtless already occurred to you that, since your sentiment for the living is the charming fruit of your sentiment for the dead, there would be a sacrifice to Lady Julia's memory more exquisite than any other."

At this finally Mr. Longdon turned. "The effort—on the lines you speak of—for Nanda's happiness?"

She fairly glowed with hope. "And by the same token such a piece of poetic justice! Quite the loveliest it would be, I think, one had ever heard of."

So, for some time more, they sat confronted. "I don't quite see your difficulty," he said at last. "I do happen to know, I confess, that Nanda herself extremely desires the execution of your project."

His friend's smile betrayed no surprise at this effect of her eloquence. "You're bad at dodging. Nanda's desire is inevitably to stop off for herself every question of any one but Vanderbank. If she wants me to succeed in arranging with Mr. Mitchett can you ask for a plainer sign of her private predicament? But you've signs enough, I see"—she caught herself up: "we may take them all for granted. I've seen perfectly from the first that the only difficulty would come from her mother—but also that that would be stiff."

The movement with which Mr. Longdon removed his glasses might have denoted a certain fear to participate in too much of what the Duchess could see. "I've not been ignorant that Mrs. Brookenham favours Mr. Mitchett."

But he was not to be let off with that. "Then you've not been blind, I suppose, to her reason for doing so." He might not have been blind, but his vision, at this, scarce showed sharpness, and it determined in his interlocutress the shortest of short-cuts. "She favours Mr. Mitchett because she wants 'old Van' herself."

He was evidently conscious of looking at her hard. "In what sense—herself?"

"Ah, you must supply the sense; I can give you only the fact—and it's the fact that concerns us. *Voyons*," she almost impatiently broke out; "don't try to create unnecessary obscurities by being unnecessarily modest. Besides, I'm not touching your modesty. Supply any sense whatever that may miraculously satisfy your fond English imagination: I don't insist in the least on a bad one. She does want him herself—that's all I say. '*Pourquoi faire?*' you ask—or rather, being too shy, don't ask, but would like to if you dared or didn't fear I'd be shocked. I *can't* be shocked, but, frankly, I can't tell you either. The situation belongs, I think, to an order I don't understand. I understand either one thing or the other—I understand taking a man up or letting him alone. But I don't really get at Mrs. Brook. You must judge at any rate for yourself. Vanderbank could of course tell you if he would—but it wouldn't be right that he should. So the one thing we have to do with is that she's in fact against us. I can only work Mitchy through Petherton, but Mrs. Brook can work him straight. On the other hand that's the way you, my dear man, can work Vanderbank."

One thing evidently beyond the rest, as a result of this vivid demonstration, disengaged itself to Mr. Longdon's undismayed sense, but his consternation needed a minute or two to produce it. "I can absolutely assure you that Mr. Vanderbank entertains no sentiment for Mrs. Brookenham——"

"That he may not keep under by just setting his teeth and holding on? I never dreamed that he does, and have nothing so alarming in store for you—*rassurez-vous bien!*—as to propose that he shall be invited to sink a feeling for the mother in order to take one up for the child. Don't, please, flutter out of the whole question by a premature scare. I never supposed it's he who wants to keep *her*. He's not in love with her—be comforted! But she's amusing—highly amusing. I do her perfect justice. As your women go, she's rare. If she were French she'd be a *femme d'esprit*. She has invented a *nuance* of her own and she has done it all by herself, for Edward figures in her drawing-room only as one of those queer extinguishers of fire in the corridors of hotels. He's just a bucket on a peg. The men, the young and the clever ones, find it a house—and heaven knows they're right—with intellectual elbow-room, with freedom of talk. Most English talk is a quadrille in a sentry-box. You'll tell me we go further in Italy, and I won't deny it, but in Italy we have the common-sense not to have little girls in the room. The young men hang about Mrs. Brook and the clever ones ply her with the uproarious appreciation that keeps her up to the mark. She's in a prodigious fix—she must sacrifice either her daughter or what she once called to me her intellectual habits. Mr. Vanderbank, you've seen for yourself, is of these one of the most cherished, the most confirmed. Three months ago—it couldn't be any longer kept off —Nanda began definitely to 'sit'—to be there and look, by the tea-table, modestly and conveniently abstracted."

"I beg your pardon—I don't think she looks *that*, Duchess," Mr. Longdon lucidly broke in. How much she had carried him with her in spite of himself was betrayed by the very terms of his dissent. "I don't think it would strike any one that she looks 'convenient.'"

His companion, laughing, gave a shrug. "Try her and perhaps you'll find her so!" But his objection had none the less pulled her up a little. "I don't say she's a hypocrite, for it would certainly be less decent for her to giggle and wink. It's Mrs. Brook's theory moreover, isn't it? that she has, from five to seven at least, lowered the pitch. Doesn't she pretend that she bears in mind every moment the tiresome difference made by the presence of sweet virginal eighteen?"

"I haven't, I'm afraid, a notion of what she pretends!"

Mr. Longdon had spoken with a curtness to which his friend's particular manner of overlooking it only added significance. "They've become," she pursued, "superficial or insincere or frivolous, but at least they've become, with the way the drag's put on, quite as dull as other people."

He showed no sign of taking this up; instead of it he said abruptly: "But if it isn't Mr. Mitchett's own idea?"

His fellow-visitor barely hesitated. "It would be his own if he were free—and it would be Lord Petherton's *for* him. I mean by his being free Nanda's becoming definitely lost to him. Then it would be impossible for Mrs. Brook to continue to persuade him, as she does now, that by a waiting game he'll come to his chance. His chance will cease to exist, and he wants so, poor darling, to marry. You've really now seen my niece," she went on. "That's another reason why I hold you can help me."

"Yes—I've seen her."

"Well, there she is." It was as if in the pause that followed this they sat looking at little absent Aggie with a wonder that was almost equal. "The good God has given her to me," the Duchess said at last.

"It seems to me then that she herself is, in her remarkable loveliness, really your help."

"She will be doubly so if you give me proofs that you believe in her." And the Duchess, appearing to consider that with this she had made herself clear and her interlocutor plastic, rose in confident majesty. "I leave it to you."

Mr. Longdon did the same, but with more consideration now. "Is it your expectation that I will speak to Mr. Mitchett?"

"Don't flatter yourself he won't speak to *you*!"

Mr. Longdon made it out. "As supposing me, you mean, an interested party?"

She clapped her gloved hands with joy. "It's a delight to hear you practically admit that you *are* one! Mr. Mitchett will take anything from you—above all perfect candor. It isn't every day one meets *your* kind, and he's a connoisseur. I leave it to you—I leave it to you."

She spoke as if it were something she had thrust bodily into his hands and wished to hurry away from. He put his hands behind him—straightening himself a little, half kindled, still half confused. "You're all extraordinary people!"

She gave a toss of her head that showed a limited enthusiasm. "You're the best of us, *caro mio*—you and Aggie: for Aggie's as good as you. Mitchy's good too, however—Mitchy's beautiful. You see it's not only his money. He's a gentleman. So are you. There aren't so many. But we must move fast," she added more sharply.

"What do you mean by fast?"

"What should I mean but what I say? If Nanda doesn't get a husband early in the business——"

"Well?" said Mr. Longdon, as she appeared to pause with the weight of her idea.

"Why, she won't get one late—she won't get one at all. One, I mean, of the kind she'll take. She'll have been in it long for *their* taste."

She had moved, looking off and about her—little Aggie always on her mind—to the flight of steps, where she again hung fire; and had really succeeded in producing in him the manner of keeping up with her to challenge her. "Been in what?"

She went down a few steps while he stood with his face full
of perceptions strained and scattered. "Why, in the *mal' aria*
they themselves have made for her!"

XX

Late that night in the smoking-room at Mertle, as the smok-
ers—talkers and listeners alike—were about to disperse, Mr.
Longdon asked Vanderbank to stay, and then it was that the
young man, to whom all the evening he had not addressed a
word, could make out why, a little unnaturally, he had prolonged his vigil. "I've something particular to say to you and
I've been waiting. I hope you don't mind. It's rather important." Vanderbank expressed on the spot the liveliest desire to
oblige him and, quickly lighting another cigarette, mounted
again to the deep divan with which a part of the place was
furnished. The smoking-room at Mertle was not unworthy of
the general nobleness, and the fastidious spectator had clearly
been reckoned on in the great leather-covered lounge that,
raised by a step or two above the floor, applied its back to
two quarters of the wall and enjoyed, most immediately, a
view of the billiard-table. Mr. Longdon continued for a
minute to roam with the air of dissimulated absence that,
during the previous hour and among the other men, his companion's eye had not lost; he pushed a ball or two about, examined the form of an ash-stand, swung his glasses almost
with violence and declined either to smoke or to sit down.
Vanderbank, perched aloft on the bench and awaiting developments, had a little the look of some prepossessing criminal
who, in court, should have changed places with the judge.
He was unlike many a man of marked good looks in that the
effect of evening dress was not, with a perversity often observed in such cases, to over-emphasise his fineness. His type
was rather chastened than heightened, and he sat there moreover with a primary discretion quite in the note of the deference that, from the first with his friend of the elder fashion,
he had taken as imposed. He had a strong sense for shades of
respect and was now careful to loll scarcely more than with an
official superior. "If you ask me," Mr. Longdon presently
continued, "why at this hour of the night—after a day at best

too heterogeneous—I don't keep over till to-morrow whatever I may have to say, I can only tell you that I appeal to you
now because I've something on my mind that I shall sleep the
better for being rid of."

There was space to circulate in front of the daïs, where he
had still paced and still swung his glasses; but with these
words he had paused, leaning against the billiard-table, to
meet the interested urbanity of the reply they produced. "Are
you very sure that, having got rid of it, you *will* sleep? Is it a
pure confidence," Vanderbank said, "that you do me the
honour to make to me? Is it something terrific that requires a
reply, so that I shall have to take account, on my side, of the
rest I may deprive you of?"

"Don't take account of anything—I'm myself a man who
always takes too much. It isn't a matter about which I press
you for an immediate answer. You can give me no answer
probably without a good deal of thought. *I've* thought a
good deal—otherwise I wouldn't speak. I only want to put
something before you and leave it there."

"I never see you," said Vanderbank, "that you don't put
something before me."

"That sounds," his friend returned, "as if I rather over-
loaded—what's the sort of thing you fellows nowadays say?—
your intellectual board. If there's a congestion of dishes sweep
everything without scruple away. I've never put before you
anything like this."

He spoke with a weight that in the great space, where it resounded a little, made an impression—an impression marked
by the momentary pause that fell between them. He partly
broke the silence first by beginning to walk again, and then
Vanderbank broke it as through the apprehension of their becoming perhaps too solemn. "Well, you immensely interest
me and you really couldn't have chosen a better time. A secret—for we shall make it that of course, shan't we?—at this
witching hour, in this great old house, is all that my visit here
will have required to make the whole thing a rare remembrance. So, I assure you, the more you put before me the
better."

Mr. Longdon took up another ash-tray, but with the air of
doing so as a direct consequence of Vanderbank's tone. After

he had laid it down he put on his glasses; then fixing his companion he brought out: "Have you no idea at all——?"

"Of what you have in your head? Dear Mr. Longdon, how *should* I have?"

"Well, I'm wondering if I shouldn't perhaps have a little in your place. There's nothing that in the circumstances occurs to you as likely for me to want to say?"

Vanderbank gave a laugh that might have struck an auditor as slightly uneasy. "When you speak of 'the circumstances' you do a thing that—unless you mean the simple thrilling ones of this particular moment—always of course opens the door of the lurid for a man of any imagination. To such a man you've only to give a nudge for his conscience to jump. That's at any rate the case with mine. It's never quite on its feet—so it's now already on its back." He stopped a little—his smile was a trifle strained. "Is what you want to put before me something awful I've done?"

"Excuse me if I press this point." Mr. Longdon spoke kindly, but if his friend's want of ease grew his own thereby diminished. "Can you think of nothing at all?"

"Do you mean that I've done?"

"No, but that—whether you've done it or not—I may have become aware of."

There could have been no better proof than Vanderbank's expression, on this, of his having mastered the secret of humouring without appearing to patronise. "I think you ought to give me a little more of a clue."

Mr. Longdon took off his glasses. "Well—the clue's Nanda Brookenham."

"Oh, I see." Vanderbank had responded quickly, but for a minute he said nothing more, and the great marble clock that gave the place the air of a club ticked louder in the stillness. Mr. Longdon waited with a benevolent want of mercy, yet with a look in his face that spoke of what depended for him —though indeed very far within—on the upshot of his patience. The hush, for that matter, between them became a conscious public measure of the young man's honesty. He evidently at last felt it as such, and there would have been for an observer of his handsome, controlled face a study of some sharp things. "I judge that you ask me for an utterance," he finally said, "that very few persons at any time have the right to expect of a man. Think of the people—and very decent ones—to whom on many a question one can only reply at best that it's none of their business."

"I see you know what I mean," said Mr. Longdon.

"Then you know also the distinguished exception I make of you. There isn't another man with whom I'd talk of it."

"And even to me you don't! But I'm none the less obliged to you," Mr. Longdon added.

"It isn't only the gravity," his friend went on; "it's the ridicule that inevitably attaches——"

The manner in which Mr. Longdon indicated the empty room was in itself an interruption. "Don't I sufficiently spare you?"

"Thank you, thank you," said Vanderbank.

"Besides, it's not for nothing."

"Of course not!" the young man returned, but with a look of noting the next moment a certain awkwardness in his concurrence. "But don't spare me now."

"I don't mean to." Mr. Longdon had his back to the table again, on which he rested with each hand on the rim. "I don't mean to," he repeated.

His companion gave a laugh that betrayed at least the drop of a tension. "Yet I don't quite see what you can do to me."

"It's just what, for some time past, I've been trying to think."

"And at last you've discovered?"

"Well—it has finally glimmered out a little in this extraordinary place."

Vanderbank frankly wondered. "In consequence of anything particular that has happened?"

Mr. Longdon had a pause. "For an old idiot who notices as much as I, something particular is always happening. If you're a man of imagination——"

"Oh," Vanderbank broke in, "I know how much more in that case you're one! It only makes me regret," he continued, "that I've not attended more since yesterday to what you've been about."

"I've been about nothing but what among you people I'm always about. I've been seeing, feeling, thinking. That makes no show, of course I'm aware, for any one but myself, and it's wholly my own affair. Except indeed," he added, "so far as I've taken into my head to make, on it all, this special appeal. There are things that have come home to me."

"Oh, I see, I see." Vanderbank showed the friendliest alertness. "I'm to take it from you then, with all the avidity of my vanity, that I strike you as the person best able to understand what they are."

Mr. Longdon appeared to wonder an instant if his intelligence now had not almost too much of a glitter; he kept the same position, his back against the table, and while Vanderbank, on the settee, pressed upright against the wall, they recognised in silence that they were trying each other. "You're much the best of them. I've my ideas about you. You've great gifts."

"Well, then, we're worthy of each other. When Greek meets Greek—!" and the young man laughed as, a little with the air of bracing himself, he folded his arms. "Here we are."

His companion looked at him a moment longer, then, turning away, went slowly round the table. On the further side of it he stopped again and, after a minute, with a nervous movement, set a ball or two in motion. "It's beautiful—but it's terrible!" he finally murmured. He had not his eyes on Vanderbank, who for a minute said nothing, and he presently went on: "To see it and not to want to try to help—well, I can't do that." Vanderbank still neither spoke nor moved, remained as if he might interrupt something of high importance to him, and his friend, passing along the opposite edge of the table, continued to produce in the stillness, without the cue, the small click of the ivory. "How long—if you don't mind my asking—have you known it?"

Even for this at first Vanderbank had no answer—none but to rise from his place, come down to the floor and, standing there, look at Mr. Longdon across the table. He was serious now, but without being solemn. "How can one tell? One can never be sure. A man may fancy, may wonder, but with a girl, a person so much younger than himself and so much more helpless, he feels a—what shall I call it?"

"A delicacy?" Mr. Longdon suggested.

"It may be that; the name doesn't matter; at all events he's embarrassed. He wants not to be an ass on the one side and yet not some other kind of brute on the other."

Mr. Longdon listened with consideration—with a beautiful little air indeed of being, in his all but finally contracted state, earnestly open to information on such points from a magnificent young man. "He doesn't want, you mean, to be a coxcomb?—and he doesn't want to be cruel?"

Vanderbank, visibly preoccupied, produced a faint, kind smile. "Oh, *you* know!"

"I? I should know less than any one."

Mr. Longdon had turned away from the table on this, and the eyes of his companion, who after an instant had caught his meaning, watched him move along the room and approach another part of the divan. The consequence of the passage was that Vanderbank's only rejoinder was presently to say: "I can't tell you how long I've imagined—have asked myself. She's so charming—so interesting, and I feel as if I had known her always. I've thought of one thing and another to do—and then, on purpose, I haven't thought at all. That has mostly seemed to me best."

"Then I gather," said Mr. Longdon, "that your interest in her——"

"Hasn't the same character as her interest in *me?*" Vanderbank had taken him up responsively, but after speaking looked about for a match and lighted a new cigarette. "I'm sure you understand," he broke out, "what an extreme effort it is to me to talk of such things!"

"Yes, yes. But it's just effort only? It gives you no pleasure? I mean the fact of her condition," Mr. Longdon explained.

Vanderbank had really to think a little. "However much it might give me I should probably not be a fellow to gush. I'm a self-conscious stick of a Briton."

"But even a stick of a Briton—!" Mr. Longdon hesitated. "I've gushed in short to *you.*"

"About Lady Julia?" the young man frankly asked. "Is that what you call it?"

"Say then we're sticks of Britons. You're not in any degree at all in love?"

There fell between them, before Vanderbank replied, another pause, of which he took advantage to move once more round the table. Mr. Longdon meanwhile had mounted to the high bench and sat there as if the judge were now in his proper place. At last his companion spoke. "What you're coming to is of course that you've conceived a desire."

"That's it—strange as it may seem. But, believe me, it has not been precipitate. I've watched you both."

"Oh, I knew you were watching *her*," said Vanderbank.

"To such a tune that I've made up my mind. I want her so to marry—" But on the odd little quaver of longing with which he brought it out the old man fairly hung.

"Well?" said Vanderbank.

"Well, so that on the day she does she'll come into the interest of a considerable sum of money—already very decently invested—that I've determined to settle upon her."

Vanderbank's instant admiration flushed across the room. "How awfully jolly of you—how beautiful!"

"Oh, there's a way to show practically your appreciation of it."

But Vanderbank, for enthusiasm, scarcely heard him. "I can't tell you how admirable I think you." Then eagerly, "Does Nanda know it?" he demanded.

Mr. Longdon, after an hesitation, spoke with comparative dryness. "My idea has been that for the present you alone shall."

Vanderbank also hesitated. "No other man?"

His companion looked still graver. "I need scarcely say that I depend on you to keep the fact to yourself."

"Absolutely then and utterly. But that won't prevent what I think of it. Nothing for a long time has given me such joy."

Shining and sincere, he had held for a minute Mr. Longdon's eyes. "Why, you do care for her."

"Immensely. Never, I think, so much as now. That sounds of a grossness, doesn't it?" he laughed. "But your announcement really lights up the mind."

His friend for a moment almost glowed with his pleasure. "The sum I've fixed upon would be, I may mention, substantial, and I should of course be prepared with a clear statement—a very definite pledge—of my intentions."

"So much the better! Only"—Vanderbank suddenly pulled himself up—"to get it she *must* marry?"

"It's not in my interest to allow you to suppose she needn't, and it's only because of my intense wish for her marriage that I've spoken to you."

"And on the ground also, with it"—Vanderbank so far concurred—"of your quite taking for granted my only having to put myself forward?"

If his friend seemed to cast about, it proved but to be for the fullest expression. Nothing in fact could have been more charged than the quiet way in which he presently said: "My dear boy, I back you."

Vanderbank clearly was touched by it. "How extraordinarily kind you are to me!" Mr. Longdon's silence appeared to reply that he was willing to let it go for that, and the young man next went on: "What it comes to then—as you put it—is that it's a way for me to add something handsome to my income."

Mr. Longdon sat for a little with his eyes attached to the green field of the billiard-table, vivid in the spreading suspended lamp-light. "I think I ought to tell you the figure I have in mind."

Another person present might have felt rather taxed either to determine the degree of provocation represented by Vanderbank's considerate smile, or to say if there was an appreciable interval before he rang out: "I think, you know, you oughtn't to do anything of the sort. Let that alone, please. The great thing is the interest—the great thing is the wish you express. It represents a view of me, an attitude toward me—!" He pulled up, dropping his arms and turning away before the complete image.

"There's nothing in those things that need overwhelm you. It would be odd if you hadn't yourself, about your value and your future, a feeling quite as lively as any feeling of mine. There *is* mine at all events. I can't help it. Accept it. Then of the other feeling—how *she* moves me—I won't speak."

"You sufficiently show it!"

Mr. Longdon continued to watch the bright circle on the table, lost in which a moment he let his friend's answer pass. "I won't begin to you on Nanda."

"Don't," said Vanderbank. But in the pause that ensued each, in one way or another, might have been thinking of her for himself.

It was broken by Mr. Longdon's presently going on: "Of course what it superficially has the air of is my offering to pay you for taking a certain step. It's open to you to be grand and proud—to wrap yourself in your majesty and ask if I suppose you bribeable. I haven't spoken without having thought of that."

"Yes," said Vanderbank sympathetically, "but it isn't as if you proposed to me, is it, anything dreadful? If one cares for a girl one's deucedly glad she has money. The more of anything good she has the better. I may assure you," he added with the brightness of his friendly intelligence and quite as if to show his companion the way to be least concerned—"I may assure you that once I were disposed to act on your suggestion I would make short work of any vulgar interpretation of my motive. I should simply try to be as magnificent as yourself." He smoked, he moved about; then he came up in another place. "I dare say you know that dear old Mitchy, under whose blessed roof we're plotting this midnight treason, would marry her like a shot and without a penny."

"I think I know everything—I think I've thought of everything. Mr. Mitchett," Mr. Longdon added, "is impossible."

Vanderbank appeared for an instant to wonder. "Wholly then through *her* attitude?"

"Altogether."

Again he hesitated. "You've asked her?"

"I've asked her."

Once more Vanderbank faltered. "And that's how you know?"

"About *your* chance? That's how I know."

The young man, consuming his cigarette with concentration, took again several turns. "And your idea *is* to give one time?"

Mr. Longdon had for a minute to turn his idea over. "How much time do you want?"

Vanderbank gave a head-shake that was both restrictive and indulgent. "I must live into it a little. Your offer has been before me only these few minutes, and it's too soon for me to commit myself to anything whatever. Except," he added gallantly, "my gratitude."

Mr. Longdon, at this, on the divan, got up, as Vanderbank

had previously done, under the spring of emotion; only, un-like Vanderbank, he still stood there, his hands in his pockets and his face, a little paler, directed straight. There was disappointment in him even before he spoke. "You've no strong enough impulse——?"

His friend met him with admirable candour. "Wouldn't it seem that if I had I would by this time have taken the jump?"

"Without waiting, you mean, for anybody's money?" Mr. Longdon cultivated for a little a doubt. "Of course she has seemed—till now—tremendously young."

Vanderbank looked about once more for matches and occupied a time with relighting. "Till now—yes. But it's not," he pursued, "only because she's so young that—for each of us, and for dear old Mitchy too—she's so interesting." Mr. Longdon had now stepped down, and Vanderbank's eyes followed him till he stopped again. "I make out that, in spite of what you said to begin with, you're conscious of a certain pressure."

"In the matter of time? Oh yes, I do want it *done*. That," the old man simply explained, "is why I myself put on the screw." He spoke with the ring of impatience. "I want her got out."

"'Out'?"

"Out of her mother's house."

Vanderbank laughed, though, more immediately, he had coloured. "Why her mother's house is just where I see her!"

"Precisely; and if it only were not we might get on faster."

Vanderbank, for all his kindness, looked still more amused. "But if it only were not, as you say, I seem to see that you wouldn't have your particular vision of urgency."

Mr. Longdon, through adjusted glasses, took him in with a look that was sad as well as sharp, then jerked the glasses off. "Oh, you understand me."

"Ah," said Vanderbank, "I'm a mass of corruption!"

"You may perfectly be, but you shall not," Mr. Longdon returned with decision, "get off on any such plea. If you're good enough for me you're good enough, as you thoroughly know, on whatever head, for any one."

"Thank you." But Vanderbank, for all his happy appreciation, thought again. "We ought at any rate to remember, oughtn't we? that we should have Mrs. Brook against us."

His companion faltered but an instant. "Ah, that's another thing I know. But it's also exactly why. Why I want Nanda away."

"I see, I see."

The response had been prompt, yet Mr. Longdon seemed suddenly to show that he suspected the superficial. "Unless it's with Mrs. Brook you're in love." Then on his friend's taking the idea with a mere head-shake of negation, a repudiation that might even have astonished by its own lack of surprise, "Or unless Mrs. Brook's in love with you," he amended.

Vanderbank had for this any decent gaiety. "Ah, that of course may perfectly be!"

"But *is* it? That's the question."

He continued light. "If she had declared her passion shouldn't I rather compromise her——?"

"By letting me know?" Mr. Longdon reflected. "I'm sure I can't say—it's a sort of thing for which I haven't a measure or a precedent. In my time women didn't declare their passion. I'm thinking of what the meaning is of Mrs. Brookenham's wanting you—as I've heard it called—herself."

Vanderbank, still with his smile, smoked a minute. "That's what you've heard it called?"

"Yes, but you must excuse me from telling you by whom."

He was amused at his friend's discretion. "It's unimaginable. But it doesn't matter. We all call everything—anything. The meaning of it, if you and I put it so, is—well, a modern shade."

"You must deal then yourself," said Mr. Longdon, "with your modern shades." He spoke now as if the case simply awaited such dealing.

But at this his young friend was more grave. "*You* could do nothing?—to bring, I mean, Mrs. Brook round."

Mr. Longdon fairly started. "Propose, on your behalf, for her daughter? With your authority—to-morrow. Authorise me, and I instantly act."

Vanderbank's colour again rose—his flush was complete. "How awfully you want it!"

Mr. Longdon, after a look at him, turned away. "How awfully *you* don't!"

The young man continued to blush. "No—you must do me justice. You've not made a mistake about me—I see in your proposal all, I think, that you can desire I should. Only *you* see it much more simply—and yet I can't just now explain. If it *were* so simple I should say to you in a moment 'Do speak to them for me'—I should leave the matter with delight in your hands. But I require time, let me remind you, and you haven't yet told me how much I may take."

This appeal had brought them again face to face, and Mr. Longdon's first reply to it was a look at his watch. "It's one o'clock."

"Oh, I require"—Vanderbank had recovered his pleasant humour—"more than to-night!"

Mr. Longdon went off to the smaller table that still offered to view two bedroom candles. "You must take of course the time you need. I won't trouble you—I won't hurry you. I'm going to bed."

Vanderbank, overtaking him, lighted his candle for him; after which, handing it and smiling: "Shall we have conduced to your rest?"

Mr. Longdon looked at the other candle. "You're not coming to bed?"

"To *my* rest we shall not have conduced. I stay up a while longer."

"Good." Mr. Longdon was pleased. "You won't forget then, as we promised, to put out the lights?"

"If you trust me for the greater you can trust me for the less. Good-night."

Vanderbank had put out his hand. "Good-night." But Mr. Longdon kept him a moment. "You *don't* care for my figure?"

"Not yet—not yet. *Please.*" Vanderbank seemed really to fear it, but on Mr. Longdon's releasing him with a little drop of disappointment they went together to the door of the room, where they had another pause.

"She's to come down to me—alone—in September."

Vanderbank hesitated. "Then may *I* come?"

His friend, on this footing, had to consider. "Shall you know by that time?"

"I'm afraid I can't promise—if you must regard my coming as a pledge."

Mr. Longdon thought on; then raising his eyes: "I don't quite see why you won't suffer me to tell you——"

"The detail of your intention? *I* do then. You've said quite enough. If my visit positively must commit me," Vanderbank pursued, "I'm afraid I can't come"

Mr. Longdon, who had passed into the corridor, gave a dry sad little laugh. "Come then—as the ladies say—'as you are'!"

On which, rather softly closing the door, Vanderbank remained alone in the great empty, lighted billiard-room.

BOOK SIXTH

Mrs. Brook

XXI

PRESENTING himself in Buckingham Crescent three days after the Sunday spent at Mertle, Vanderbank found Lady Fanny Cashmore in the act of taking leave of Mrs. Brook and found Mrs. Brook herself in the state of muffled exaltation that was the mark of all her intercourse—and most of all perhaps of her farewells—with Lady Fanny. This splendid creature gave out, as it were, so little that Vanderbank was freshly struck with all Mrs. Brook could take in, though nothing, for that matter, in Buckingham Crescent, had been more fully formulated than the imperturbable grandeur of the almost total absence, on the part of the famous beauty, of articulation. Every aspect of the phenomenon had been freely discussed there and endless ingenuity lavished on the question of how exactly it was that so much of what the world would in another case have called complete stupidity could be kept by a mere wonderful face from boring one to death. It was Mrs. Brook who, in this relation as in many others, had arrived at the supreme expression of the law, had thrown off, happily enough, to whomever it might have concerned: "My dear thing, it all comes back, as everything always does, simply to personal pluck. It's only a question, no matter when or where, of having enough. Lady Fanny has the courage of all her silence—so much therefore that it sees her completely through and is what really makes her interesting. Not to be afraid of what may happen to you when you've no more to say for yourself than a steamer without a light—that truly is the highest heroism, and Lady Fanny's greatness is that she's never afraid. She takes the risk every time she goes out—takes, as you may say, her life in her hand. She just turns that glorious mask upon you and practically says: 'No, I won't open my lips—to call it really open—for the forty minutes I shall stay; but I calmly defy you, all the same, to kill me for it.' And we don't kill her—we delight in her; though when either of us watches her in a circle of others it's like seeing a very large blind person in the middle of Oxford Street. One fairly looks about for the police." Vanderbank, before his fellow-visitor withdrew it, had the benefit of the glorious mask and could scarce have failed to be amused at the manner in which Mrs. Brook alone showed the stress of thought. Lady Fanny, in the other scale, sat aloft and Olympian, so that though visibly much had happened between the two ladies it had all happened only to the hostess. The sense in the air in short was just of Lady Fanny herself, who came to an end like a banquet or a procession. Mrs. Brook left the room with her and, on coming back, was full of it. "She'll go, she'll go!"

"Go where?" Vanderbank appeared to have for the question less attention than usual.

"Well, to the place her companion will propose; probably—like Anna Karénine—to one of the smaller Italian towns."

"Anna Karénine? She isn't a bit like Anna."

"Of course she isn't so clever," said Mrs. Brook. "But that would spoil her. So it's all right."

"I'm glad it's all right," Vanderbank laughed. "But I dare say we shall still have her with us a while."

"We shall do that, I trust, whatever happens. She'll come up again—she'll remain, I feel, one of those enormous things that fate seems somehow to have given me as the occupation of my odd moments. I don't see," Mrs. Brook added, "what still keeps her on the edge, which isn't an inch wide."

Vanderbank looked this time as if he only tried to wonder. "Isn't it *you*?"

Mrs. Brook mused more deeply. "Sometimes I think so. But I don't know."

"Yes, how *can* you of course know, since she can't tell you?"

"Oh, if I depended on her telling—!" Mrs. Brook shook out, with this, a sofa-cushion or two and sank into the corner she had arranged. The August afternoon was hot and the London air heavy; the room moreover, though agreeably be-dimmed, gave out the staleness of the season's end. "If you hadn't come to-day," she went on, "you would have missed me till I don't know when, for we've let the Hovel again—wretchedly, but still we've let it—and I go down on Friday to see that it isn't too filthy. Edward, who's furious at what I've taken for it, had his idea that we should go there this year ourselves."

"And now"—Vanderbank took her up—"that fond fancy has become simply the ghost of a dead thought, a ghost that, in company with a thousand predecessors, haunts the house in the twilight and pops at you out of odd corners."

"Oh, Edward's dead thoughts are indeed a cheerful company and worthy of the perpetual mental mourning we seem to go about in. They're worse than the relations we're always losing without seeming to have any fewer, and I expect every day to hear that the *Morning Post* regrets to have to announce in that line too some new bereavement. The apparitions following the deaths of so many thoughts *are* particularly awful in the twilight, so that at this season, while the day drags and drags, I'm glad to have any one with me who may keep them at a distance."

Vanderbank had not sat down; slowly, familiarly he turned about. "And where's Nanda?"

"Oh, *she* doesn't help—she attracts rather the worst of the bogies. Edward and Nanda and Harold and I seated together are fairly a case for that—what do you call it?—investigating Society. Deprived of the sweet resource of the Hovel," Mrs. Brook continued, "we shall each, from about the tenth on, forage somehow or other for ourselves. Mitchy perhaps," she added, "will insist on taking us to Baireuth."

"That will be the form, you mean, of his own forage?"

Mrs. Brook just hesitated. "Unless you should prefer to take it as the form of yours."

Vanderbank appeared for a moment obligingly enough to turn this over, but with the effect of perceiving an objection. "Oh, I'm afraid I shall have to grind straight through the month and that by the time I'm free every Ring at Baireuth will certainly have been rung. Is it your idea to take Nanda?" he asked.

She reached out for another cushion. "If it's impossible for you to manage what I suggest why should that question interest you?"

"My dear woman"—and her visitor dropped into a chair—"do you suppose my interest depends on such poverties as what *I* can manage? You know well enough," he went on in another tone, "why I care for Nanda and inquire about her."

She was perfectly ready. "I know it, but only as a bad reason. Don't be too sure!"

For a moment they looked at each other. "Don't be so sure, you mean, that the elation of it may go to my head? Are you really warning me against vanity?"

"Your 'reallys,' my dear Van, are a little formidable, but it strikes me that, before I tell you, there's something I've a right to ask. Are you 'really' what they call thinking of my daughter?"

"Your asking," Vanderbank returned, "exactly shows the state of your knowledge of the matter. I don't quite see more-over why you speak as if I were paying an abrupt and unnat-ural attention. What have I done the last three months but talk to you about her? What have you done but talk to *me* about her? From the moment you first spoke to me—'mon-strously,' I remember you called it—of the difference made in your social life by her finally established, her perpetual, her in-exorable participation: from that moment what have we both done but put our heads together over the question of keep-ing the place tidy, as you called it—or as *I* called it, was it?—for the young female mind?"

Mrs. Brook faced serenely enough the directness of this challenge. "Well, what are you coming to? I spoke of the change in my life of course; I happen to be so constituted that my life has something to do with my mind and my mind some-thing to do with my talk. Good talk: you know—no one, dear Van, should know better—what part for me that plays. There-fore when one has deliberately to make one's talk bad——!"

"'Bad'?" Vanderbank, in his amusement, fell back in his chair. "Dear Mrs. Brook, you're too delightful!"

"You know what I mean—stupid, flat, fourth-rate. When one has to take in sail to that degree—and for a perfectly out-side reason—there's nothing strange in one's taking a friend sometimes into the confidence of one's irritation."

"Ah," Vanderbank protested, "you do yourself injustice. Ir-ritation hasn't been for you the only consequence of the affair."

Mrs. Brook gloomily thought. "No, no—I've had my calm-ness: the calmness of deep despair. I've seemed to see every-thing go."

"Oh, how can you say that," her visitor demanded, "when just what we've most been agreed upon so often is the practical impossibility of making any change? Hasn't it seemed as if we really can't overcome conversational habits so thoroughly formed?"

Again Mrs. Brook reflected. "As if our way of looking at things were too serious to be trifled with? I don't know—I think it's only you who have denied our sacrifices, our compromises and concessions. I myself have constantly felt smothered in them. But there it is," she impatiently went on. "What I don't admit is that you've given me ground to take for a proof of your 'intentions'—to use the odious term—your association with me on behalf of the preposterous fiction, as it after all is, of Nanda's blankness of mind."

Vanderbank's head, in his chair, was thrown back; his eyes ranged over the top of the room. "There never has been any mystery about my thinking her—all in her own way—the nicest girl in London. She *is*."

His companion was silent a little. "She is, by all means. Well," she then added, "so far as I may have been alive to the fact of any one's thinking her so, it's not out of place I should mention to you the difference made in my appreciation of it by our delightful little stay at Mertle. My views of Nanda," said Mrs. Brook, "have somehow gone up."

Vanderbank was prompt to show how he could understand it. "So that you wouldn't consider even Mitchy now?"

But his friend took no notice of the question. "The way Mr. Longdon distinguishes her is quite the sort of thing that gives a girl, as Harold says, a 'leg up.' It's awfully curious and has made me think: he isn't anything whatever, as London estimates go, in himself—so that what is it, pray, that makes him, when 'added on' to her, so double Nanda's value? I somehow or other see, through his being known to back her and through the pretty story of his loyalty to mamma and all the rest of it (oh, if one chose to *work* that!) ever so much more of a chance for her."

Vanderbank's eyes were on the ceiling. "It *is* curious, isn't it?—though I think he's rather more 'in himself,' even for the London estimate, than you quite understand." He appeared to give her time to take this up, but as she said nothing he pursued: "I daresay that if even I now *were* to enter myself it would strike you as too late."

Her attention to this was but indirect. "It's awfully vulgar to be talking about it, but I can't help feeling that something possibly rather big will come of Mr. Longdon."

"Ah, we've talked of that before," said Vanderbank, "and you know you did think something might come even for me."

She continued however, as if she scarce heard him, to work out her own vision. "It's very true that up to now——"

"Well, up to now?" he asked as she faltered.

She faltered still a little. "I do say the most hideous things. But we *have* said worse, haven't we? Up to now, I mean, he hasn't given her anything. Unless indeed," she mused, "she may have had something without telling me."

Vanderbank went much straighter. "What sort of thing have you in mind? Are you thinking of money?"

"Yes. Isn't it awful?"

"That you should think of it?"

"That I should talk this way." Her friend was apparently not prepared with an assent, and she quickly enough pursued: "If he *had* given her any it would come out somehow in her expenditure. She has tremendous liberty and is very secretive, but still it would come out."

"He wouldn't give her any without letting you know. Nor would she, without doing so," Vanderbank added, "take it."

"Ah," Mrs. Brook quietly said, "she hates me enough for anything."

"That's only your romantic theory."

Once more she appeared not to hear him; she came up suddenly in another place. "Has he given *you* anything?"

Her visitor smiled. "Not so much as a cigarette. I've always my pockets full of them, and *he* never; so he only takes mine. Oh, Mrs. Brook," he continued, "with me too—though I've also tremendous liberty!—it would come out."

"I think you'd let me know," she returned.

"Yes, I'd let you know."

Silence, upon this, fell between them a little; which Mrs. Brook was the first to break. "She has gone with him this afternoon—by solemn appointment—to the South Kensington Museum."

There was something in Mrs. Brook's dolorous drop that yet presented the news as a portent so great that he was moved again to mirth. "Ah, that's where she is? Then I confess she has scored. He has never taken *me* to the South Kensington Museum."

"You were asking what we're going to do," she went on. "What I meant was—about Baireuth—that the question for Nanda is simplified. He has pressed her so to pay him a visit."

Vanderbank's assent was marked. "I see: so that if you do go abroad she'll be provided for by that engagement."

"And by lots of other invitations."

These were such things as, for the most part, the young man could turn over. "Do you mean you'd let her go alone——?"

"To wherever she's asked?" said Mrs. Brook. "Why not? Don't talk like the Duchess."

Vanderbank seemed for a moment to try not to. "Couldn't Mr. Longdon take her? Why not?"

His friend looked really struck with it. "That *would* be working him. But to a beautiful end!" she meditated. "The only thing would be to get him also asked."

"Ah, but there you are, don't you see? Fancy 'getting' Mr. Longdon anything or anywhere whatever! Don't you feel," Vanderbank threw out, "how the impossibility of exerting that sort of patronage for him immediately places him?"

Mrs. Brook gave her companion one of those fitful glances of almost grateful appreciation with which their intercourse was even at its darkest hours frequently illumined. "As if he were the Primate or the French Ambassador? Yes, you're right —one couldn't do it; though it's very odd and one doesn't quite see why. It does place him. But he becomes thereby exactly the very sort of person with whom it would be most of an advantage for her to go about. What a pity," Mrs. Brook sighed, "he doesn't know more people!"

"Ah well, we *are*, in our way, bringing that to pass. Only we mustn't rush it. Leave it to Nanda herself," Vanderbank presently added; on which his companion so manifestly left it that she touched after a moment's silence on quite a different matter.

"I dare say he'd tell *you*—wouldn't he?—if he were to give her any considerable sum."

She had only obeyed his injunction, but he stared at the length of her jump. "He might attempt to do so, but I shouldn't at all like it." He was moved immediately to drop this branch of the subject and, apparently to help himself, take up another. "Do you mean she understands he has asked her down for a regular long stay?"

Mrs. Brook barely hesitated. "She understands, I think, that what I expect of her is to make it as long as possible."

Vanderbank laughed out—as it was even after ten years still possible to laugh—at the childlike innocence with which her voice could invest the hardest teachings of life; then with something a trifle nervous in the whole sound and manner he sprang up from his chair. "What a blessing he is to us all!"

"Yes, but think what we must be to *him*."

"An immense interest, no doubt." He took a few aimless steps and, stooping over a basket of flowers, inhaled it with violence, almost buried his face. "I dare say we *are* interesting."

He had spoken rather vaguely, but Mrs. Brook knew exactly why. "We render him no end of a service. We keep him in touch with old memories."

Vanderbank had reached one of the windows, shaded from without by a great striped sun-blind beneath which and between the flower-pots of the balcony he could see a stretch of hot, relaxed street. He looked a minute at these things. "I do so like your phrases!"

She had a pause that challenged his tone. "Do you call mamma a 'phrase'?"

He went off again, quite with extravagance, but quickly, leaving the window, pulled himself up. "I dare say we *must* put things for him—he does it, cares or is able to do it, so little himself."

"Precisely. He just quietly acts. That's his nature dear thing. We must *let* him act."

Vanderbank seemed to stifle again too vivid a sense of her particular emphasis. "Yes, yes—we must let him."

"Though it won't prevent Nanda, I imagine," his hostess pursued, "from finding the fun of a whole month at Beccles —or whatever she puts in—not exactly fast and furious."

Vanderbank had the look of measuring what the girl might

"put in." "The place will be quiet, of course, but when a person's so fond of a person——!"

"As she is of him, you mean?"

He hesitated. "Yes. Then it's all right."

"She *is* fond of him, thank God!" said Mrs. Brook.

He was before her now with the air of a man who had suddenly determined on a great blind leap. "Do you know what he has done? He wants me so to marry her that he has proposed a definite basis."

Mrs. Brook got straight up. "'Proposed'? To *her*?"

"No, I don't think he has said a word to Nanda—in fact I'm sure that, very properly, he doesn't mean to. But he spoke to me on Sunday night at Mertle—I had a big talk with him there alone, very late, in the smoking-room." Mrs. Brook's stare was serious, and Vanderbank now went on as if the sound of his voice helped him to meet it. "We had things out very much and his kindness was extraordinary—he's the most beautiful old boy that ever lived. I don't know, now that I come to think of it, if I'm within my rights in telling you— and of course I shall immediately let him know that I *have* told you; but I feel I can't arrive at any respectable sort of attitude in the matter without taking you into my confidence— which is really what I came here to-day to do, though till this moment I've funked it."

It was either, as her friends chose to think it, an advantage or a drawback of intercourse with Mrs. Brook that, her face being at any moment charged with the woe of the world, it was unavoidable to remain rather in the dark as to the effect of particular strokes. There was therefore something in Vanderbank's present study of the signs that showed he had had to learn to feel his way and had more or less mastered the trick. That she had turned a little pale was really the one fresh mark. "'Funked' it? Why in the world—?" His own colour deepened at her accent, which was a sufficient light on his having been stupid. "Do you mean you've declined the arrangement?"

He only, with a smile somewhat strained, continued for a moment to look at her; clearly, however, at last feeling, and not much caring, that he got in still deeper. "You're magnificent. You're magnificent."

Her lovely gaze widened out. "*Comment donc?* Where—why? You *have* declined her?" she went on. After which, as he replied only with a slow head-shake that seemed to say it was not for the moment all so simple as that, she had one of the inspirations to which she was constitutionally subject. "Do you imagine I want you myself?"

"Dear Mrs. Brook, you're so admirable," he answered, laughing, "that if by any chance you did, upon my honour I don't see how I should be able not to say 'All right.'" Then he spoke more gravely. "I was shy of really bringing out to you what has happened to me, for a reason that I have of course to look in the face. Whatever you want yourself, for Nanda you want Mitchy."

"I see, I see." She did full justice to his explanation. "And what did you say about a 'basis'? The blessed man offers to settle——?"

"You're a wonderful woman," her visitor returned, "and your imagination takes its fences in a way that, when I'm out with you, quite puts mine to shame. When he mentioned it to me I was quite surprised."

"And I," Mrs. Brook asked, "am not surprised a bit? Isn't it only," she modestly suggested, "because I've taken him in more than you? Didn't you know he *would*?" she quavered.

Vanderbank thought or at least pretended to. "Make *me* the condition? How could I be sure of it?"

But the point of his question was lost for her in the growing light. "Oh then, the condition's you only——?"

"That, at any rate, is all I have to do with. He's ready to settle it if I'm ready to do the rest."

"To propose to her straight, you mean?" She waited, but as he said nothing she went on: "And you're not ready. Is that it?"

"I'm taking my time."

"Of course you know," said Mrs. Brook, "that she'd jump at you."

He turned away from her now, but after some steps came back. "Then you do admit it."

She hesitated. "To *you*."

He had a strange faint smile. "Well, as I don't speak of it——!"

"No—only to me. What is it he settles?" Mrs. Brook demanded.

"I can't tell you."

"You didn't ask?"

"On the contrary I stopped him off."

"Oh then," Mrs. Brook exclaimed, "that's what I call declining."

The words appeared for an instant to strike her companion. "Is it? Is it?" he almost musingly repeated. But he shook himself the next moment free of his wonder, was more what would have been called in Buckingham Crescent on the spot. "Isn't there rather something in my having thus thought it my duty to warn you that I'm definitely his candidate?"

Mrs. Brook turned impatiently away. "You've certainly—with your talk about 'warning'—the happiest expressions!" She put her face into the flowers as he had done just before; then as she raised it: "What kind of a monster are you trying to make me out?"

"My dear lady"—Vanderbank was prompt—"I really don't think I say anything but what's fair. Isn't it just my loyalty to you in fact that has in this case positively strained my discretion?"

She shook her head in mere mild despair. "'Loyalty' again is exquisite. The tact of men has a charm quite its own. And you're rather good," she continued, "as men go."

His laugh was now a little awkward, as if she had already succeeded in making him uncomfortable. "I always become aware with you sooner or later that they don't go at all—in your sense; but how am I, after all, so far out if you *have* put your money on another man?"

"You keep coming back to that?" she wearily sighed.

He thought a little. "No, then. You've only to tell me not to, and I'll never speak of it again."

"You'll be in an odd position for speaking of it if you do really go in. You deny that you've declined," said Mrs. Brook; "which means then that you've allowed our friend to hope."

Vanderbank met it bravely. "Yes, I think he hopes."

"And imparts his hope to my child?"

This arrested the young man, but only for a moment. "I've the most perfect faith in his wisdom with her. I trust his particular delicacy. He cares more for her," he presently added, "even than we do."

Mrs. Brook gazed away at the infinite of space. "'We,' my dear Van," she at last returned, "is one of your own real, wonderful touches. But there's something in what you say: I *have*, as between ourselves—between me and him—been backing Mitchy. That is I've been saying to him 'Wait, wait: don't at any rate do anything else.' Only it's just from the depth of my thought for my daughter's happiness that I've clung to this resource. He would so absolutely, so unreservedly do anything for her." She had reached now, with her extraordinary self-control, the pitch of quiet, bland demonstration. "I want the poor thing, *que diable*, to have another string to her bow and another loaf, for her desolate old age, on the shelf. When everything else is gone, Mitchy will still be there. Then it will be at least her own fault—!" Mrs. Brook continued. "What can relieve me of the primary duty of taking precautions," she wound up, "when I know as well as that I stand here and look at you——"

"Yes, what?" he asked as she just paused.

"Why, that so far as they count on you, they count, my dear Van, on a blank." Holding him a minute as with the soft, low voice of his fate, she sadly but firmly shook her head. "You won't do it."

"Oh!" he almost too loudly protested.

"You won't do it," she went on.

"I *say*!"—he made a joke of it.

"You won't do it," she repeated.

It was as if he could not at last but show himself really struck; yet what he exclaimed on was what might in truth most have impressed him. "You *are* magnificent, really!"

"Mr. Mitchett!" the butler, appearing at the door, almost familiarly dropped; on which Vanderbank turned straight to the person announced.

Mr. Mitchett was there, and, anticipating Mrs. Brook in receiving him, her companion passed it straight on. "She's magnificent!"

Mitchy was already all interest. "Rather! But what's her last?"

It had been, though so great, so subtle, as they said in

Buckingham Crescent, that Vanderbank scarce knew how to put it. "Well, she's so thoroughly superior."

"Oh, to whom do you say it?" Mitchy cried as he greeted her.

XXII

The subject of this eulogy had meanwhile returned to her sofa, where she received the homage of her new visitor. "It's not I who am magnificent a bit—it's dear Mr. Longdon. I've just had from Van the most wonderful piece of news about him—his announcement of his wish to make it worth somebody's while to marry my child."

"'Make it'?"—Mitchy stared. "But *isn't* it?"

"My dear friend, you must ask Van. Of course you've always thought so. But I must tell you all the same," Mrs. Brook went on, "that I'm delighted."

Mitchy had seated himself, but Vanderbank remained erect and became perhaps even slightly stiff. He was not angry—none of the inner circle at Buckingham Crescent was ever angry—but he looked grave and rather troubled. "Even if it *is* decidedly fine"—he addressed his hostess straight—"I can't make out quite why you're doing *this*. I mean immediately making it known."

"Ah, but what do we keep from Mitchy?" Mrs. Brook asked.

"What *can* you keep? It comes to the same thing," Mitchy said. "Besides, here we are together, share and share alike—one beautiful intelligence. Mr. Longdon's 'somebody' is of course Van. Don't try to treat me as an outsider."

Vanderbank looked a little foolishly, though it was but the shade of a shade, from one of them to the other. "I think I've been rather an ass!"

"What then by the terms of our friendship—just as Mitchy says—can he and I have a better right to know and to feel with you about? You will want, Mitchy, won't you?" Mrs. Brook went on, "to hear all about *that*?"

"Oh, I only mean," Vanderbank explained, "in having just now blurted my tale out to you. However, I of course do know," he pursued to Mitchy, "that whatever is really between us will remain between us. Let me then tell you myself exactly what's the matter." The length of his pause after these words showed at last that he had stopped short; on which his companions, as they waited, exchanged a sympathetic look. They waited another minute, and then he dropped into a chair where, leaning forward, his elbows on the arms and his gaze attached to the carpet, he drew out the silence. Finally he looked at Mrs. Brook. "*You* make it clear."

The appeal called up for some reason her most infantine manner. "I don't think I *can*, dear Van—really *clear*. You know however yourself," she continued to Mitchy, "enough by this time about Mr. Longdon and mamma."

"Oh, rather!" Mitchy laughed.

"And about mamma and Nanda."

"Oh, perfectly: the way Nanda reminds him, and the 'beautiful loyalty' that has made him take such a fancy to her. But I've already embraced the facts—you needn't dot any i's." With another glance at his fellow-visitor Mitchy jumped up and stood there florid. "He has offered you money to marry her." He said this to Vanderbank as if it were the most natural thing in the world.

"Oh *no*," Mrs. Brook interposed with promptitude: "he has simply let him know before any one else that the money is there *for* Nanda, and that therefore——"

"First come, first served?" Mitchy had already taken her up. "I see, I see. Then, to make her sure of the money," he inquired of Vanderbank, "you *must* marry her?"

"If it depends upon that she'll never get it," Mrs. Brook returned. "Dear Van will think conscientiously a lot about it, but he won't do it."

"Won't you, Van, really?" Mitchy asked from the hearthrug.

"Never, never. We shall be very kind to him, we shall help him, hope and pray for him, but we shall be at the end," said Mrs. Brook, "just where we are now. Dear Van will have done his best, and we shall have done ours. Mr. Longdon will have done his—poor Nanda even will have done hers. But it will all have been in vain. However," Mrs. Brook continued to expound, "she'll probably have the money. Mr. Longdon will surely consider that she'll want it if she doesn't marry still

more than if she does. So we shall be *so* much at least," she
wound up—"I mean Edward and I and the child will be—to
the good."

Mitchy, for an equal certainty, required but an instant's
thought. "Oh, there can be no doubt about *that*. The things
about which your mind may now be at ease—!" he cheerfully
exclaimed.

"It does make a great difference!" Mrs. Brook comfortably
sighed. Then in a different tone: "What dear Van will find at
the end that he can't face will be, don't you see? just this fact
of appearing to have accepted a bribe. He won't want, on the
one hand—out of kindness for Nanda—to have the money
suppressed; and yet he won't want to have the pecuniary
question mixed up with the matter—to look in short as if he
had had to be paid. He's like you, you know—he's proud;
and it will be there we shall break down."

Mitchy had been watching his friend, who, a few minutes
before perceptibly embarrassed, had now recovered himself
and, at his ease, though still perhaps with a smile a trifle
strained, leaned back and let his eyes play everywhere but over
the faces of the others. Vanderbank evidently wished now to
show a good-humoured detachment.

"See here," Mitchy said to him: "I remember your once
submitting to me a case of some delicacy."

"Oh, he'll submit it to you—he'll submit it even to *me*,"
Mrs. Brook broke in. "He'll be charming, touching, confiding—above all he'll be awfully *interesting* about it. But he'll
make up his mind in his own way, and his own way won't be
to accommodate Mr. Longdon."

Mitchy continued to study their companion in the light of
these remarks, then turned upon his hostess his sociable glare.
"Splendid, isn't it, the old boy's infatuation with him?"

Mrs. Brook just hesitated. "From the point of view of the
immense interest it—just now, for instance—makes for you and
me? Oh yes, it's one of our best things yet. It places him a little
with Lady Fanny—'He will, he won't; he won't, he will!' Only,
to be perfect, it lacks, as I say, the element of real suspense."

Mitchy frankly wondered. "It does, you think? Not for me
—not wholly." He turned again quite pleadingly to their
friend. "I hope it doesn't for yourself totally either?"

Vanderbank, cultivating his detachment, made at first no more reply than if he had not heard, and the others meanwhile showed faces that testified perhaps less than their respective speeches had done to the absence of anxiety. The only token he immediately gave was to get up and approach Mitchy, before whom he stood a minute laughing kindly enough but not altogether gaily. As if then for a better proof of gaiety he presently seized him by the shoulders and, still without speaking, pushed him backward into the chair he himself had just quitted. Mrs. Brook's eyes, from the sofa, while this went on attached themselves to her visitors. It took Vanderbank, as he moved about and his companions waited, a minute longer to produce what he had in mind. "What *is* splendid, as we call it, is this extraordinary freedom and good-humour of our intercourse and the fact that we do care —so independently of our personal interests, with so little selfishness or other vulgarity—to get at the idea of things. The beautiful specimen Mrs. Brook had just given me of that," he continued to Mitchy, "was what made me break out to you about her when you came in." He spoke to one friend, but he looked at the other. "What's really 'superior' in her is that, though I suddenly show her an interference with a favourite plan, her personal resentment is nothing—all she wants is to see what may really happen, to take in the truth of the case and make the best of that. She offers me the truth, as she sees it, about myself, and with no nasty elation if it does chance to be the truth that suits her best. It was a charming, charming stroke."

Mitchy's appreciation was no bar to his amusement. "You're wonderfully right about us. But still it was a stroke."

If Mrs. Brook was less diverted she followed perhaps more closely. "If you do me so much justice then, why did you put to me such a cold, cruel question?—I mean when you so oddly challenged me on my handing on your news to Mitchy. If the principal beauty of our effort to live together is—and quite according to your own eloquence—in our sincerity, I simply obeyed the impulse to do the sincere thing. If we're not sincere, we're nothing."

"Nothing!"—it was Mitchy who first responded. "But we *are* sincere."

"Yes, we *are* sincere," Vanderbank presently said. "It's a great chance for us not to fall below ourselves; no doubt therefore we shall continue to soar and sing. We pay for it, people who don't like us say, in our self-consciousness——"

"But people who don't like us," Mitchy broke in "don't matter. Besides, how can we be properly conscious of each other——?"

"That's it!"—Vanderbank completed his idea: "without my finding myself, for instance, in you and Mrs. Brook? We see ourselves reflected—we're conscious of the charming whole. I thank you," he pursued after an instant to Mrs. Brook—"I thank you for your sincerity."

It was a business sometimes really to hold her eyes, but they had, it must be said for her, their steady moments. She exchanged with Vanderbank a somewhat remarkable look, then, with an art of her own, broke short off without appearing to drop him. "The thing is, don't you think?"—she appealed to Mitchy—"for us not to be so awfully clever as to make it believed that we can never be simple. We mustn't see *too* tremendous things—even in each other." She quite lost patience with the danger she glanced at. "We *can* be simple!"

"We *can*, by God!" Mitchy laughed.

"Well, we are now—and it's a great comfort to have it settled," said Vanderbank.

"Then you see," Mrs. Brook returned, "what a mistake you would make to see abysses of subtlety in my having been merely natural."

"We *can* be natural," Mitchy declared.

"We can, by God!" Vanderbank laughed.

Mrs. Brook had turned to Mitchy. "I just wanted you to know. So I spoke. It's not more complicated than that. As for *why* I wanted you to know——"

"What better reason could there be," Mitchy interrupted, "than your being filled to the finger-tips with the sense of how I would want it myself, and of the misery, the absolute pathos, of my being left out? Fancy, my dear chap"—he had only to put it to Van—"my *not* knowing!"

Vanderbank evidently couldn't fancy it, but he said quietly enough: "I should probably have told you myself."

"Well, what's the difference?"

"Oh, there *is* a difference," Mrs. Brook loyally said. Then she opened an inch or two, for Vanderbank, the door of her dim radiance. "Only I should have thought it a difference for the better. Of course," she added, "it remains absolutely with us three alone, and don't you already feel from it the fresh charm—with it here between us—of our being together?"

It was as if each of the men had waited for the other to assent better than he himself could and Mitchy then, as Vanderbank failed, had gracefully, to cover him, changed the subject. "But isn't Nanda, the person most interested, to know?"

Vanderbank gave on this a strange sound of hilarity. "Ah, that would finish it off!"

It produced for a few seconds something like a chill, a chill that had for consequence a momentary pause which in its turn added weight to the words next uttered. "It's not I who shall tell her," Mrs. Brook said gently and gravely. "There!—you may be sure. If you want a promise, it's a promise. So that if Mr. Longdon's silent," she went on, "and you are, Mitchy, and I am, how in the world shall she have a suspicion?"

"You mean of course except by Van's deciding to mention it himself."

Van might have been, from the way they looked at him, some beautiful unconscious object, but Mrs. Brook was quite ready to answer. "Oh, poor man, *he'll* never breathe."

"I see. So there we are."

To this discussion the subject of it had for the time nothing to contribute, even when Mitchy, rising with the words he had last uttered from the chair in which he had been placed, took sociably as well, on the hearthrug, a position before their hostess. This move ministered apparently to Vanderbank's mere silence, for it was still without speaking that, after a little, he turned away from his friend and dropped once more into the same seat. "I've shown you already, you of course remember," Vanderbank presently said to him, "that I'm perfectly aware of how much better Mrs. Brook would like *you* for the position."

"He thinks I want him myself," Mrs. Brook blandly explained.

She was indeed, as they always thought her, "wonderful,"

but she was perhaps not even now so much so as Mitchy found himself able to be. "But how would you lose old Van —even at the worst?" he earnestly asked of her.

She just hesitated. "What do you mean by the worst?"

"Then even at the best," Mitchy smiled. "In the event of his falsifying your prediction; which, by-the-way, has the danger, hasn't it?—I mean for your intellectual credit—of making him, as we all used to be called by our nurse-maids, 'contrairy.'"

"Oh, I've thought of that," Mrs. Brook returned. "But he won't do, on the whole, even for the sweetness of spiting me, what he won't want to do. *I* haven't said I should lose him," she went on; "that's only the view he himself takes—or, to do him perfect justice, the idea he candidly imputes to me; though without, I imagine—for I don't go so far as that—attributing to me anything so unutterably *bête* as a feeling of jealousy."

"You wouldn't dream of my supposing anything inept of you," Vanderbank said on this, "if you understood to the full how I keep on admiring you. Only what stupefies me a little," he continued, "is the extraordinary critical freedom—or we may call it if we like the high intellectual detachment—with which we discuss a question touching you, dear Mrs. Brook, so nearly and engaging so your most private and most sacred sentiments. What are we playing with, after all, but the idea of Nanda's happiness?"

"Oh, I'm not playing!" Mrs. Brook declared with a little rattle of emotion.

"She's not playing"—Mr. Mitchett gravely confirmed it. "Don't you feel in the very air the vibration of the passion that she's simply too charming to shake at the window as the housemaid shakes the tablecloth or the jingo the flag?" Then he took up what Vanderbank had previously said. "Of course, my dear man, I'm 'aware,' as you just now put it, of everything, and I'm not indiscreet, am I, Mrs. Brook? in admitting for you as well as for myself that there *was* an impossibility that you and I used sometimes to turn over together. Only— Lord bless us all!—it isn't as if I hadn't long ago seen that there's nothing at all *for* me."

"Ah, wait, wait!" Mrs. Brook put in.

"She has a theory"—Vanderbank, from his chair, lighted it

up for Mitchy, who hovered before them—"that your chance *will* come, later on, after I've given my measure."

"Oh, but that's exactly," Mitchy was quick to respond, "what you'll never do! You'll walk in magnificent mystery 'later on' not a bit less than you do to-day; you'll continue to have the benefit of everything that our imagination, perpetually engaged, often baffled and never fatigued, will continue to bedeck you with. Nanda, in the same way, to the end of all her time, will simply remain exquisite, or genuine, or generous—whatever we choose to call it. It may make a difference to us, who are comparatively vulgar, but what difference will it make to *her* whether you do or you don't decide for her? You can't belong to her more, for herself, than you do already—and that's precisely so much that there's no room for any one else. Where, therefore, without that room, do I come in?"

"Nowhere, I see"—Vanderbank seemed obligingly to muse.

Mrs. Brook had followed Mitchy with marked admiration, but she gave on this at Van a glance that was like the toss of a blossom from the same branch. "Oh then, shall I just go on with you *both*? That *will* be joy!" She had, however, the next thing, a sudden drop which shaded the picture. "You're so divine, Mitchy, that how can you not, in the long-run, break *any* woman down?"

It was not as if Mitchy was struck—it was only that he was courteous. "What do you call the long-run? Taking about till I'm eighty?"

"Ah, your genius is of a kind to which middle life will be particularly favourable. You'll reap then somehow, one feels, everything you've sown."

Mitchy still accepted the prophecy only to control it. "Do you call eighty middle life? Why, my moral beauty, my dear woman—if that's what you mean by my genius—is precisely my curse. What on earth is left for a man just rotten with goodness? It renders necessary the kind of liking that renders *un*necessary anything else."

"Now that *is* cheap paradox!" Vanderbank patiently sighed. "You're down for a fine."

It was with less of the patience perhaps that Mrs. Brook took this up. "Yes, on that we *are* stiff. Five pounds, please."

Mitchy drew out his pocket-book even though he explained. "What I mean is that I don't give out the great thing." With which he produced a crisp bank-note.

"*Don't* you?" asked Vanderbank, who, having taken it from him to hand to Mrs. Brook, held it a moment, delicately, to accentuate the doubt.

"The great thing's the sacred terror. It's you who give *that* out."

"Oh!"—and Vanderbank laid the money on the small stand at Mrs. Brook's elbow.

"Ain't I right, Mrs. Brook?—doesn't he, tremendously, and isn't that more than anything else what does it?"

The two again, as if they understood each other, gazed in a unity of interest at their companion, who sustained it with an air clearly intended as the happy mean between embarrassment and triumph. Then Mrs. Brook showed she liked the phrase. "The sacred terror! Yes, one feels it. It *is* that."

"The finest case of it," Mitchy pursued, "that I've ever met. So my moral's sufficiently pointed."

"Oh, I don't think it can be said to be that," Vanderbank returned, "till you've put the whole thing into a box by doing for Nanda what she does most want you to do."

Mitchy caught on without a shade of wonder. "Oh, by proposing to the Duchess for little Aggie?" He took but an instant to turn it over. "Well, I *would* propose, to please Nanda. Only I've never yet quite made out the reason of her wish."

"The reason is largely," his friend answered, "that, being very fond of Aggie, and in fact extremely admiring her, she wants to do something good for her and to keep her from anything bad. Don't you know—it's too charming—she regularly believes in her?"

Mitchy, with all his recognition, vibrated to the touch. "Isn't it too charming?"

"Well then," Vanderbank went on, "she secures for her friend a phœnix like you, and secures for you a phœnix like her friend. It's hard to say for which of you she desires most to do the handsome thing. She loves you both in short"—he followed it up—"though perhaps, when one thinks of it, the price she puts on you, Mitchy, in the arrangement, is a little the higher. Awfully fine at any rate—and yet awfully odd too —her feeling for Aggie's type, which is divided by such abysses from her own."

"Ah," laughed Mitchy, "but think then of her feeling for mine!"

Vanderbank, still more at his ease now and with his head back, had his eyes aloft and far. "Oh, there are things in Nanda—!" The others exchanged a glance at this, while their companion added: "Little Aggie's really the sort of creature she would have liked to be able to be."

"Well," Mitchy said, "I should have adored her even if she *had* been able."

Mrs. Brook, for some minutes, had played no audible part, but the acute observer we are constantly taking for granted would perhaps have detected in her, as one of the effects of the special complexion to-day of Vanderbank's presence, a certain smothered irritation. "She couldn't possibly have been able," she now interposed, "with so loose—or rather, to express it more properly, with so perverse—a mother."

"And yet, my dear lady," Mitchy promptly reflected, "how if, in little Aggie's case, the Duchess hasn't prevented——?"

Mrs. Brook was full of wisdom. "Well, it's a different thing. I'm not, as a mother—am I, Van?—bad *enough*. That's what's the matter with me. Aggie, don't you see? is the Duchess's morality, her virtue; which, by having it, that way, outside of you, as one may say, you can make a much better thing of. The child has been for Jane, I admit, a capital little subject, but Jane has kept her on hand and finished her like some wonderful piece of stitching. Oh, as work, it's of a *soigné*! There it is—to show. A woman like me has to be *herself*, poor thing, her virtue and her morality. What will you have? It's our lumbering English plan."

"So that her daughter," Mitchy sympathised, "can only, by the arrangement, hope to become at the best her immorality and her vice?"

But Mrs. Brook, without an answer for the question, appeared suddenly to have plunged into a sea of thought. "The only way for Nanda to have been *really* nice——"

"Would have been for you to be like Jane?"

Mitchy and his hostess seemed for a minute, on this, to gaze together at the tragic truth. Then she shook her head. "We see our mistakes too late." She repeated the movement, but as if to let it all go, and Vanderbank meanwhile, pulling out his watch, had got up with a laugh that showed some inattention and made to Mitchy a remark about their walking away together. Mitchy, engaged for the instant with Mrs. Brook, had assented only with a nod, but the attitude of the two men had become that of departure. Their friend looked at them as if she would like to keep one of them, and for a purpose connected somehow with the other, but was oddly, almost ludicrously embarrassed to choose. What was in her face indeed during this short passage might prove to have been, should we penetrate, the flicker of a sense that, in spite of all intimacy and amiability, they could, at bottom and as things commonly turned out, only be united against her. Yet she made at the end a sort of choice in going on to Mitchy: "He hasn't at all told you the real reason of Nanda's idea that you should go in for Aggie."

"Oh, I draw the line there," said Vanderbank. "Besides, he understands that too."

Mitchy did, on the spot, himself and every one justice. "Why, it just disposes of me, doesn't it?"

Vanderbank, restless now and turning about the room, stopped, on this, with a smile for Mrs. Brook. "We understand too well!"

"Not if he doesn't understand," she replied after a moment while she turned to Mitchy, "that his real 'combination' can in the nature of the case only be——"

"Oh yes"—Mitchy took her straight up—"with the young thing who is, as you say, positively and helplessly modern and the pious fraud of whose classic identity with a sheet of white paper has been—oh tacitly of course, but none the less practically—dropped. You've so often reminded me. I do understand. If I were to go in for Aggie it would only be to oblige. The modern girl, the product of our hard London facts and of her inevitable consciousness of them just as they are—she, wonderful being, *is*, I fully recognise, my real affair, and I'm not ashamed to say that when I like the individual I'm not afraid of the type. She knows too much—I don't say; but she doesn't know after all a millionth part of what *I* do."

"I'm not sure!" Mrs. Brook earnestly exclaimed.

He had rung out and he kept it up with a limpidity unusual. "And product for product, when you come to that, I'm a queerer one myself than any other. The traditions *I* smash!" Mitchy laughed.

Mrs. Brook had got up and Vanderbank had gone again to the window. "That's exactly why," she returned: "you're a pair of monsters and your monstrosity fits. She does know too much," she added.

"Well," said Mitchy with resolution, "it's all my fault."

"Not *all*—unless," Mrs. Brook returned, "that's only a sweet way of saying that it's mostly mine."

"Oh, yours too—immensely; in fact every one's. Even Edward's, I dare say; and certainly, unmistakably, Harold's. Ah, and Van's own—rather!" Mitchy continued; "for all he turns his back and will have nothing to say to it."

It was on the back Vanderbank turned that Mrs. Brook's eyes now rested. "That's precisely why he shouldn't be afraid of her."

He faced straight about. "Oh, I don't deny my part."

He shone at them brightly enough, and Mrs. Brook, thoughtful, wistful, candid, took in for a moment the radiance. "And yet to think that after all it has been mere *talk*!"

Something in her tone again made her hearers laugh out; so it was still with the air of good-humour that Vanderbank rejoined: "Mere, mere, mere. But perhaps it's exactly the 'mere' that has made us range so wide."

Mrs. Brook's intelligence abounded. "You mean that we haven't had the excuse of passion?"

Her companions once more gave way to merriment, but "There you are!" Vanderbank said after an instant less sociably. With it too he held out his hand.

"You *are* afraid," she answered as she gave him her own; on which, as he made no rejoiner, she held him before her. "Do you mean you *really* don't know if she gets it?"

"The money, if he *doesn't* go in?"—Mitchy broke almost with an air of responsibility into Vanderbank's silence. "Ah but, as we said, surely——!"

It was Mitchy's eyes that Vanderbank met. "Yes, I should suppose she gets it."

"Perhaps then, as a compensation, she'll even get *more*——!"

"If I don't go in? Oh!" said Vanderbank. And he changed colour.

He was by this time off, but Mrs. Brook kept Mitchy a moment. "Now—by that suggestion—he has something to show. He won't go in."

XXIII

Her visitors had been gone half-an-hour, but she was still in the drawing-room when Nanda came back. The girl found her, on the sofa, in a posture that might have represented restful oblivion but that, after a glance, our young lady appeared to interpret as mere intensity of thought. It was a condition from which at all events Mrs. Brook was quickly roused by her daughter's presence; she opened her eyes and put down her feet, so that the two were confronted as closely as persons may be when it is only one of them who looks at the other. Nanda, gazing vaguely about and not seeking a seat, slowly drew off her gloves while her mother's sad eyes considered her from top to toe. "Tea's gone," Mrs. Brook then said as if there were something in the loss peculiarly irretrievable. "But I suppose," she added, "he gave you all you want."

"Oh dear yes, thank you—I've had lots."

Nanda hovered there slim and charming, feathered and ribboned, dressed in thin, fresh fabrics and faint colours, with something in the effect of it all to which the sweeter, deeper melancholy in her mother's eyes seemed happily to testify. "Just turn round, dear." The girl immediately obeyed, and Mrs. Brook once more took everything in. "The back's best —only she didn't do what she said she would. How they do lie!" she gently quavered.

"Yes, but we lie so to *them*." Nanda had swung round again, producing evidently on her mother's part, by the admirable "hang" of her light skirts, a still deeper peace. "Do you mean the middle fold?—I knew she wouldn't. I don't want my back to be best—I don't walk backward."

"Yes," Mrs. Brook resignedly mused; "you dress for yourself."

"Oh, how can you say that," the girl asked, "when I never stick in a pin but what I think of *you*?"

"Well," Mrs. Brook moralised, "one must always, I consider, think, as a sort of *point de repère*, of some one good person. Only it's best if it's a person one's afraid of. You do very well, but I'm not enough. What one really requires is a kind of salutary terror. *I* never stick in a pin without thinking of your cousin Jane. What is it that some one quotes somewhere about some one's having said that 'Our antagonist is our helper—he prevents our being superficial'? The extent to which, with my poor clothes, the Duchess prevents *me*—!" It was a measure Mrs. Brook could give only by the general soft wail of her submission to fate.

"Yes, the Duchess isn't a woman, is she? She's a standard."

The speech had for Nanda's companion, however, no effect of pleasantry or irony, and it was a mark of the special intercourse of these good friends that though they had for each other, in manner and tone, such a fund of consideration as might almost have given it the stamp of diplomacy, there was yet in it also something of that economy of expression which is the result of a common experience. The recurrence of opportunity to observe them together would have taught a spectator that—on Mrs. Brook's side, doubtless, more particularly—their relation was governed by two or three remarkably established and, as might have been said, refined laws, the spirit of which was to guard against the vulgarity so often coming to the surface between parent and child. That they *were* as good friends as if Nanda had not been her daughter was a truth that no passage between them might fail in one way or another to illustrate. Nanda had gathered up, for that matter, early in life, a flower of maternal wisdom: "People talk about the conscience, but it seems to me one must just bring it up to a certain point and leave it there. You can let your conscience alone if you're nice to the second housemaid." Mrs. Brook was as "nice" to Nanda as she was to Sarah Curd —which involved, as may easily be imagined, the happiest conditions for Sarah. "Well," she resumed, reverting to the Duchess on a final appraisement of the girl's air, "I really think I do well by you and that Jane wouldn't have anything to say to-day. You look awfully like mamma," she then threw off as if for the first time of mentioning it.

"Oh, Cousin Jane doesn't care for that," Nanda returned. "What I don't look like is Aggie, for all I try."

"Ah, you shouldn't try—you can do nothing with it. One must be what one is."

Mrs. Brook was almost sententious, but Nanda, with civility, let it pass. "No one in London touches her. She's quite by herself. When one sees her one feels her to be the real thing."

Mrs. Brook, without harshness, wondered. "What do you mean by the real thing?"

Even Nanda, however, had to think a moment. "Well, the real young one. That's what Lord Petherton calls her," she mildly joked—"'the young 'un.'"

Her mother's echo was not for the joke, but for something else. "I know what you mean. What's the use of being good?"

"Oh, I didn't mean that," said Nanda. "Besides, isn't Aggie of a goodness——?"

"I wasn't talking of her. I was asking myself what's the use of *my* being."

"Well, you can't help it any more than the Duchess can help——"

"Ah, but she could if she would!" Mrs. Brook broke in with a sharper ring than she had yet given. "We can't help being good perhaps, if that burden is laid on us—but there are lengths in other directions we're not absolutely obliged to go. And what I think of when I stick in the pins," she went on, "is that Jane seems to me really never to have had to pay." She appeared for a minute to brood on this till she could no longer bear it; after which she jerked out: "Why, she has never had to pay for *any*thing!"

Nanda had by this time seated herself, taking her place, under the interest of their talk, on her mother's sofa, where, except for the removal of her long, soft gloves, which one of her hands again and again drew caressingly through the other, she remained very much as if she were some friendly yet circumspect young visitor to whom Mrs. Brook had on some occasion dropped "*Do* come." But there was something perhaps more expressly conciliatory in the way she had kept everything on: as if, in particular serenity and to confirm kindly Mrs. Brook's sense of what had been done for her, she had neither taken off her great feathered hat nor laid down her parasol of pale green silk, the "match" of hat and ribbons and which had an expensive, precious knob. Our spectator would possibly have found too much earnestness in her face to be sure if there was also candour "And do you mean that *you* have had to pay——?"

"Oh yes—all the while." With this Mrs. Brook was a little short, and also as she added as if to banish a slight awkwardness: "But don't let it discourage you."

Nanda seemed an instant to weigh the advice, and the whole thing would have been striking as another touch in the picture of the odd want, on the part of each, of any sense of levity in the other. Whatever escape when together mother or daughter might ever seek would never be the humorous one—a circumstance, notwithstanding, that would not in every case have failed to make their interviews droll for a third person. It would always indeed for such a person have produced an impression of tension beneath the surface. "I could have done much better at the start and have lost less time," the girl at last said, "if I hadn't had the drawback of not really remembering Granny."

"Oh well, *I* remember her!" Mrs. Brook moaned with an accent that evidently struck her the next moment as so much out of place that she slightly deflected. She took Nanda's parasol and held it as if—a more delicate thing much than any one of hers—she simply liked to have it. "Her clothes—at your age at least—must have been hideous. Was it at the place he took you to that he gave you tea?" she then went on.

"Yes, at the Museum. We had an orgy in the refreshment-room. But he took me afterwards to Tishy's, where we had another."

"He went *in* with you?" Mrs. Brook had suddenly flashed into eagerness.

"Oh yes—I made him."

"He didn't want to?"

"On the contrary—very much. But he doesn't do everything he wants," said Nanda.

Mrs. Brook seemed to wonder. "You mean you've also to want it?"

"Oh no—*that* isn't enough. What I suppose I mean," Nanda continued, "is that he doesn't do anything he doesn't want. But he does quite enough," she added.

"And who then was at Tishy's?"

"Oh, poor Tish herself, naturally, and Carrie Donner."

"And no one else?"

The girl just waited. "Yes, Mr. Cashmore came in."

Her mother gave a groan of impatience. "Ah, *again?*"

Nanda thought an instant. "How do you mean, 'again'? He just lives there as much as he ever did, and Tishy can't prevent him."

"I was thinking of Mr. Longdon—of *their* meeting. When he met him here that time he liked it so little. Did he like it any more to-day?" Mrs. Brook quavered.

"Oh no, he hated it."

"But hadn't he—if he should go in—known he *would?*"

"Yes, perfectly—but he wanted to see."

"To see—?" Mrs. Brook just threw out.

"Well, where I go so much. And he knew I wished it."

"I don't quite see why," Mrs. Brook mildly observed. And then as her daughter said nothing to help her: "At any rate he did loathe it?"

Nanda, for a reply, simply after an instant put a question. "Well, how can he understand?"

"You mean, like me, why you do go there so much? How can he indeed?"

"I don't mean that," the girl returned—"it's just that he understands perfectly, because he saw them all, in such an extraordinary way—well, what can I ever call it?—clutch me and cling to me."

Mrs. Brook with full gravity considered this picture. "And was Mr. Cashmore, to-day, so ridiculous?"

"Ah, he's not ridiculous, mamma—he's very unhappy. He thinks now Lady Fanny probably won't go, but he feels that may be, after all, only the worse for him."

"She *will* go," Mrs. Brook answered with one of her roundabout approaches to decision. "He *is* too great an idiot. She was here an hour ago, and if ever a woman was packed——!"

"Well," Nanda objected, "but doesn't she spend her time in packing and unpacking?"

This inquiry, however, scarce pulled up her mother. "No—though she *has*, no doubt, hitherto wasted plenty of labour. She has now a dozen boxes—I could see them there in her wonderful eyes—just waiting to be called for. So if you're counting on her not going, my dear—!" Mrs. Brook gave a head-shake that was the warning of wisdom.

"Oh, I don't care what she does!" Nanda replied. "What I meant just now was that Mr. Longdon couldn't understand why, with so much to make them so, they couldn't be decently happy."

"And did he wish you to explain?"

"I tried to, but I didn't make it any better. He doesn't like them. He doesn't even care for Tish."

"He told you so—right out?"

"Oh," Nanda said, "of course I asked him. I didn't press him, because I never do——!"

"You never do?" Mrs. Brook broke in as with the glimpse of a new light.

The girl showed an indulgence for this interest that was for a moment almost elderly. "I enjoy awfully, with him, seeing just how to take him."

Her tone and her face evidently put forth for her companion at this juncture something freshly, even quite supremely suggestive; and yet the effect of them on Mrs. Brook's part was only a question so off-hand that it might already often have been asked. The mother's eyes, to ask it, we may none the less add, attached themselves closely to the daughter's, and her own face just glowed. "You like him so very awfully?"

It was as if the next instant Nanda felt herself on her guard. Yet she spoke with a certain surrender. "Well, it's rather intoxicating to be one's self—!" She had only a drop over the choice of her term.

"So tremendously made up to, you mean—even by a little fussy, ancient man? But *doesn't* he, my dear," Mrs. Brook continued with encouragement, "make up to you?"

A supposititious spectator would certainly on this have imagined in the girl's face the delicate dawn of a sense that her mother had suddenly become vulgar, together with a general consciousness that the way to meet vulgarity was always to be frank and simple. "He makes one enjoy being liked so much—liked better, I do think, than I've ever been liked by any one."

If Mrs. Brook hesitated it was, however, clearly not because she had noticed. "Not better surely than by dear Mitchy? Or even if you come to that by Tishy herself."

Nanda's simplicity maintained itself. "Oh, Mr. Longdon's different from Tishy."

Her mother again hesitated. "You mean of course he knows more?"

The girl considered it. "He doesn't know *more*. But he knows other things—and he's pleasanter than Mitchy."

"You mean because he doesn't want to marry you?"

It was as if she had not heard that Nanda continued: "Well, he's more beautiful."

"O-oh!" cried Mrs. Brook, with a drawn-out extravagance of comment that amounted to an impugnment even by her-self of her taste.

It contributed to Nanda's quietness. "He's one of the most beautiful people in the world."

Her companion at this, with a quick wonder, fixed her. "*Does* he, my dear, want to marry you?"

"Yes—to all sorts of ridiculous people."

"But I mean—would you take *him*?"

Nanda, rising, met the question with a short ironic "Yes!" that showed her first impatience. "It's so charming being liked," she went on, "without being approved."

But Mrs. Brook only wanted to know. "He doesn't ap-prove——?"

"No, but it makes no difference. It's all exactly right, all the same."

Mrs. Brook seemed to wonder, however, exactly how it could be. "He doesn't want you to give up anything?" She looked as if she were rapidly thinking what Nanda *might* give up.

"Oh yes, everything."

It was as if for an instant she found her daughter in-scrutable; then she had a strange smile. "Me?"

The girl was perfectly prompt. "Everything. But he wouldn't like me nearly so much if I really did."

Her mother had a further pause. "Does he want to *adopt*

you?" Then more quickly and sadly, though also a little as if lacking courage to push the inquiry: "We couldn't give you up, Nanda."

"Thank you so much, mamma. But we shan't be very much tried," Nanda said, "because what it comes to seems to be that I'm really what you may call adopting *him*. I mean I'm little by little changing him—gradually showing him that, as I couldn't possibly have been different, and as also of course one can't keep giving up, the only way is for him not to mind and to take me just as I am. That, don't you see? is what he would never have expected to do."

Mrs. Brook recognised in a manner the explanation, but still had her wistfulness. "But—a—to take you, 'as you are,' *where?*"

"Well, to the South Kensington Museum."

"Oh!" said Mrs. Brook. Then, however, in a more exemplary tone: "Do you enjoy so very much your long hours with him?"

Nanda appeared for an instant to think how to express it. "Well, we're great friends."

"And always talking about Granny?"

"Oh no—really almost never now."

"He doesn't think so awfully much of her?" There was an oddity of eagerness in the question—a hope, a kind of dash, for something that might have been in Nanda's interest.

The girl met these things only with obliging gravity. "I think he's losing any sense of my likeness. He's too used to it, or too many things that are too different now cover it up."

"Well," said Mrs. Brook as she took this in, "I think it's awfully clever of you to get only the good of him and have none of the worry."

Nanda wondered. "The worry?"

"You leave that all to *me*," her mother went on, but quite forgivingly. "I hope at any rate that the good, for you, will be real."

"Real?" the girl, remaining vague, again echoed.

Mrs. Brook at this showed, though not an irritation, a flicker of austerity. "You must remember that we've a great many things to think about. There are things we must take for granted in each other—we must all help, in our way, to pull the coach. That's what I mean by worry, and if you don't have any, so much the better for you. For me it's in the day's work. Your father and I have most to think about always at this time, as you perfectly know—when we have to turn things round and manage somehow or other to get out of town, have to provide and pinch, to meet all the necessities, with money, money, money at every turn running away like water. The children this year seem to fit into nothing, into nowhere, and Harold's more dreadful than he has ever been, doing nothing at all for himself and requiring everything to be done for him. He talks about his American girl, with millions, who's so awfully taken with him, but I can't find out anything about her; the only one, just now, that people seem to have heard of is the one Booby Manger's engaged to. The Mangers literally snap up everything," Mrs. Brook quite wailingly now continued: "the Jew man, so gigantically rich— who is he? Baron Schack or Schmack—who has just taken Cumberland House and who has the awful stammer—or what is it? no roof to his mouth—is to give that horrid little Algie, to do his conversation for him, four hundred a year, which Harold pretended to me that, of all the rush of young men— dozens!—*he* was most in the running for. Your father's settled gloom is terrible, and I bear all the brunt of it; we get literally nothing this year for the Hovel, yet have to spend on it heaven knows what; and everybody, for the next three months, in Scotland and everywhere, has asked us for the wrong time and nobody for the right: so that I assure you I don't know where to turn—which doesn't, however, in the least prevent every one coming to me with their own selfish troubles." It was as if Mrs. Brook had found the cup of her secret sorrows suddenly jostled by some touch of which the perversity, though not completely noted at the moment, proved, as she a little let herself go, sufficient to make it flow over; but she drew, the next thing, from her daughter's stillness a reflection of the vanity of such heat and speedily recovered herself as if in order with more dignity to point the moral. "I can carry my burden and shall do so to the end; but we must each remember that we shall fall to pieces if we don't manage to keep hold of some little idea of responsibility. I positively can't arrange without knowing when it is you go to him."

"To Mr. Longdon? Oh, whenever I like," Nanda replied very gently and simply.

"And when shall you be so good as to like?"

"Well, he goes himself on Saturday, and if I want I can go a few days later."

"And what day can you go if *I* want?" Mrs. Brook spoke as with a small sharpness—just softened indeed in time—produced by the sight of a freedom on her daughter's part that suddenly loomed larger than any freedom of her own. It was still a part of the unsteadiness of the vessel of her anxieties; but she never after all remained publicly long subject to the influence that she often comprehensively designated to others as well as to herself as "nastiness." "What I mean is that you might go the same day, mightn't you?"

"With him—in the train? I should think so if you wish it."

"But would *he* wish it? I mean would he hate it?"

"I don't think so at all, but I can easily ask him."

Mrs. Brook's head inclined to the chimney and her eyes to the window. "Easily?"

Nanda looked for a moment mystified by her mother's insistence. "I can at any rate perfectly try it."

"Remembering even that mamma would never have pushed so?"

Nanda's face seemed to concede even that condition. "Well," she at all events serenely replied, "I really think we're good friends enough for anything."

It might have been, for the light it quickly produced, exactly what her mother had been working to make her say. "What do you call that then, I should like to know, but his adopting you?"

"Ah, I don't know that it matters much what it's called."

"So long as it brings with it, you mean," Mrs. Brook asked, "all the advantages?"

"Well yes," said Nanda, who had now begun dimly to smile —"call them advantages."

Mrs. Brook had a pause. "One would be quite ready to do that if one only knew a little more exactly what they're to consist of."

"Oh, the great advantage, I feel, is doing something for *him*."

Nanda's companion, at this, hesitated afresh. "But doesn't that, my dear, put the extravagance of your surrender to him on rather an odd footing? Charity, love, begins at home, and if it's a question of merely *giving*, you've objects enough for your bounty without going so far."

The girl, as her stare showed, was held a moment by her surprise, which presently broke out. "Why, I thought you wanted me so to be nice to him!"

"Well, I hope you won't think me very vulgar," said Mrs. Brook, "if I tell you that I want you still more to have some idea of what you'll get by it. I've no wish," she added, "to keep on boring you with Mitchy——"

"Don't, don't!" Nanda pleaded.

Her mother stopped short, as if there were something in her tone that set the limit all the more utterly for being un-studied. Yet poor Mrs. Brook couldn't leave it there. "Then what do you get instead?"

"Instead of Mitchy? Oh," said Nanda, "I shall never marry."

Mrs. Brook at this turned away, moving over to the win-dow with quickened weariness. Nanda, on her side, as if their talk had ended, went across to the sofa to take up her parasol before leaving the room, an impulse rather favoured than ar-rested by the arrival of her brother Harold, who came in at the moment both his relatives had turned a back to the door and who gave his sister, as she faced him, a greeting that made their mother look round. "Hallo, Nan—you *are* lovely! Ain't she lovely, mother?"

"No!" Mrs. Brook answered, not, however, otherwise noticing him. Her domestic despair centred at this instant all in her daughter. "Well then, we shall consider—your father and I—that he must take the consequence."

Nanda had now her hand on the door, while Harold had dropped on the sofa. "'He'?" she just sounded.

"I mean Mr. Longdon."

"And what do you mean by the consequence?"

"Well, it will do for the beginning of it that you'll please go down *with* him."

"On Saturday then? Thanks, mamma," the girl returned.

She was instantly gone, on which Mrs. Brook had more attention for her son. This, after an instant, as she approached the sofa and raised her eyes from the little table beside it, came straight out. "Where in the world is that five-pound note?"

Harold looked vacantly about him. "What five-pound note?"

Mitchy

XXIV

M<small>R.</small> L<small>ONGDON'S</small> garden took in three acres and, full of charming features, had for its greatest wonder the extent and colour of its old brick wall, in which the pink and purple surface was the fruit of the mild ages and the protective function, for a visitor strolling, sitting, talking, reading, that of a nurse of reverie. The air of the place, in the August time, thrilled all the while with the bliss of birds, the hum of little lives unseen and the flicker of white butterflies. It was on the large flat enclosed lawn that Nanda spoke to Vanderbank of the three weeks that she would have completed there on the morrow and that had been—she made no secret of it—the happiest she had yet spent anywhere. The greyish day was soft and still and the sky faintly marbled, while the more newly arrived of the visitors from London, who had come late on the Friday afternoon, lounged away the morning in an attitude of which every relaxed line referred to the holiday he had, as it were—at first merely looking about and victualling —sat down in front of as a captain before a city. There were sitting-places, just there, out of the full light, cushioned benches in the thick wide spread of old mulberry-boughs. A large book of facts lay in the young man's lap, and Nanda had come out to him, half-an-hour before luncheon, somewhat as Beatrice came out to Benedick: not to call him immediately indeed to the meal, but mentioning promptly that she had come at a bidding. Mr. Longdon had rebuked her, it appeared, for her want of attention to their guest, showing her in this way, to her pleasure, how far he had gone toward taking her, as he called it, into the house.

"You've been thinking of yourself," Vanderbank asked, "as a mere clerk at a salary, and you now find that you're a partner and have a share in the concern?"

"It seems to be something like that. But doesn't a partner put in something? What have I put in?"

"Well—*me*, for one thing. Isn't it your being here that has brought me down?"

"Do you mean you wouldn't have come for him alone? Then don't you make anything of his attraction? You ought to," said Nanda, "when he likes you so."

Vanderbank, longing for a river, was in white flannels, and he took her question with a happy laugh, a handsome face of good-humour, that completed the effect of his long, cool fairness. "Do you mind my just sitting still, and letting me smoke and staying with me awhile? Perhaps after a little we'll walk about—shan't we? But face to face with this dear old house, in this jolly old nook, one is too contented to move, lest raising a finger even should break the spell. What *will* be perfect will be your just sitting down—*do* sit down—and scolding me a little. That, my dear Nanda, will deepen the peace." Some minutes later, while, near him but in another chair, she fingered the impossible book, as she pronounced it, that she had taken from him, he came back to what she had last said. "Has he talked to you much about his 'liking' me?"

Nanda waited a minute, turning over the book. "No."

"Then how are you just now so struck with it?"

"I'm not struck only with what I'm talked to about. I don't only know," she went on, "what people tell me."

"Ah no—you're too much your mother's daughter for that!" Vanderbank leaned back and smoked, and though all his air seemed to say that when one was so at ease for gossip almost any subject would do, he kept jogging his foot with the same small nervous motion as during the half-hour at Mertle that this record has commemorated. "You're too much one of us all," he continued. "We've tremendous perceptions," he laughed. "Of course I *should* have come for him. But after all," he added as if all sorts of nonsense would equally serve, "he mightn't, except for you, you know, have asked me."

Nanda so far accepted this view as to reply: "That's awfully weak. He's so modest that he might have been afraid of your boring yourself."

"That's just what I mean."

"Well, if you do," Nanda returned, "the explanation's a little conceited."

"Oh, I only made it," Vanderbank said, "in reference to his

modesty." Beyond the lawn the house was before him, old, square, red-roofed, well assured of its right to the place it took up in the world. This was a considerable space—in the little world at least of Beccles—and the look of possession had everywhere mixed with it, in the form of old windows and doors, the tone of old red surfaces, the style of old white facings, the age of old high creepers, the long confirmation of time. Suggestive of panelled rooms, of precious mahogany, of portraits of women dead, of coloured china glimmering though glass doors and delicate silver reflected on bared tables, the thing was one of those impressions of a particular period that it takes two centuries to produce. "Fancy," the young man incoherently exclaimed, "his caring to leave anything so loveable as all this to come up and live with *us*!"

The girl, for a little, also lost herself. "Oh, you don't know what it is—the charm comes out so as one stays. Little by little it grows and grows. There are old things everywhere that are too delightful. He lets me explore so—he lets me rummage and rifle; and every day I make discoveries."

Vanderbank wondered as he smoked. "You mean he lets you take things——?"

"Oh yes—up to my room, to study or to copy. There are old patterns that are too dear for anything. It's when you live with them, you see, that you know. Everything in the place is such good company."

"Your mother ought to be here," Vanderbank presently suggested. "She's so fond of good company." Then as Nanda answered nothing he went on: "Was your grandmother ever?"

"Never," the girl promptly said. "Never," she repeated in a tone quite different. After which she added: "I'm the only one."

"Oh, and I. 'Me and you,' as they say," her companion amended.

"Yes, and Mr. Mitchy, who's to come down—please don't forget—this afternoon."

Vanderbank had another of his contemplative pauses. "Thank you for reminding me. I shall spread myself as much as possible before he comes—try to produce so much of my effect that I shall be safe. But what did Mr. Longdon ask him for?"

"Ah," said Nanda gaily, "what did he ask *you* for?"

"Why, for the reason you just now mentioned—that his interest in me is so uncontrollable."

"Then isn't his interest in Mitchy——"

"Of the same general order?" Vanderbank broke in. "Not in the least." He seemed to look for a way to express the distinction, which suddenly occurred to him. "He wasn't in love with Mitchy's mother."

"No"—Nanda turned it over. "Mitchy's mother, it appears, was awful. Mr. Cashmore knew her."

Vanderbank's smoke-puffs were profuse and his pauses frequent. "Awful to Mr. Cashmore? I'm glad to hear it—he must have deserved it. But I believe in her all the same. Mitchy's often awful himself," the young man rambled on. "Just so I believe in *him*."

"So do I," said Nanda—"and that's why I asked him."

"*You* asked him, my dear child? Have you the inviting?"

"Oh yes."

The eyes he turned on her seemed really to ask if she jested or were serious. "So you arranged for me too?"

She turned over again a few leaves of his book and, closing it with something of a clap, transferred it to the bench beside him—a movement in which, as if through a drop into thought, he rendered her no assistance. "What I mean is that I proposed it to Mr. Longdon, I suggested he should be asked. I've a reason for seeing him—I want to talk to him. And do you know," the girl went on, "what Mr. Longdon said?"

"Something splendid of course."

"He asked if you wouldn't perhaps dislike his being here with you."

Vanderbank, throwing back his head, laughed, smoked, jogged his foot more than ever. "Awfully nice. Dear old Mitch! How little afraid of him you are!"

Nanda wondered. "Of Mitch?"

"Yes, of the tremendous pull he really has. It's all very well to talk—he *has* it. But of course I don't mean I don't know"—and as with the effect of his nervous sociability he shifted his position. "I perfectly see that you're *not* afraid. I perfectly know what you have in your head. I should never in the least dream of accusing you—as far as *he* is concerned—of the least disposition to flirt; any more indeed," Vanderbank pleasantly pursued, "than even of any general tendency of that sort. No, my dear Nanda"—he kindly kept it up—"I *will* say for you that, though a girl, thank heaven, and awfully *much* a girl, you're really not on the whole more of a flirt than a respectable social ideal prescribes."

"Thank you most tremendously," his companion quietly replied.

Something in the tone of it made him laugh out, and the particular sound went well with all the rest, with the August day and the charming spot and the young man's lounging figure and Nanda's own little hovering hospitality. "Of course I strike you as patronising you with unconscious sublimity. Well, that's all right, for what's the most natural thing to do in these conditions but the most luxurious? Won't Mitchy be wonderful for feeling and enjoying them? I assure you I'm delighted he's coming." Then in a different tone a moment later, "Do you expect to be here long?" he asked.

It took Nanda some time to say. "As long as Mr. Longdon will keep me, I suppose—if that doesn't sound very horrible."

"Oh, he'll keep you! Only won't he himself," Vanderbank went on, "be coming up to town in the course of the autumn?"

"Well, in that case I would perfectly stay here without him."

"And leave him in London without *you*? Ah, that's not what we want: he wouldn't be at all the same thing without you. Least of all for himself!" Vanderbank declared.

Nanda again thought. "Yes, that's what makes him funny, I suppose—his curious infatuation. I set him off—what do you call it?—show him off: by his going round and round me as the acrobat on the horse in the circus goes round the clown. He has said a great deal to me of your mother," she irrelevantly added.

"Oh, everything that's kind of course, or you wouldn't mention it."

"That's what I mean," said Nanda.

"I see, I see—most charming of him." Vanderbank kept his high head thrown back as if for the view, with a bright, equal, general interest, of everything that was before them, whether talked of or seen. "Who do you think I yesterday had a letter from? An extraordinary funny one from Harold. He gave me all the family news."

"And what *is* the family news?" the girl after a minute inquired.

"Well, the first great item is that he himself——"

"Wanted," Nanda broke in, "to borrow five pounds of you? I say that," she added, "because if he wrote to you——"

"It couldn't have been in such a case for the simple pleasure of the intercourse?" Vanderbank hesitated, but continued not to look at her. "What do you know, pray, of poor Harold's borrowings?"

"Oh, I know as I know other things. Don't I know everything?"

"*Do* you? I should rather ask," the young man gaily enough replied.

"Why should I not? How should I not? You know what I know." Then as if to explain herself and attenuate a little the sudden emphasis with which she had spoken: "I remember you once telling me that I must take in things at my pores."

Her companion stared, but with his laugh again changed his posture. "That you '*must*'——?"

"That I do—and you were quite right."

"And when did I make this extraordinary charge?"

"Ah then," said Nanda, "you admit it *is* a charge. It was a long time ago—when I was a little girl. Which made it worse!" she dropped.

It made it at all events now for Vanderbank more amusing. "Ah, not worse—better!"

She thought a moment. "Because in that case I mightn't have understood? But that I do understand is just what you've always meant."

"'Always,' my dear Nanda? I feel somehow," he rejoined very kindly, "as if you overwhelmed me!"

"You 'feel' as if I did—but the reality is just that I don't. The day I overwhelm you, Mr. Van—!" She let that pass, however; there was too much to say about it and there was something else much simpler. "Girls understand now. It has got to be faced, as Tishy says."

"Oh well," Vanderbank laughed, "we don't require Tishy to point that out to us. What are we all doing most of the time but trying to face it?"

"Doing? Aren't you doing rather something very different? You're just trying to dodge it. You're trying to make believe—not perhaps to yourselves but to *us*—that it isn't so."

"But surely you don't want us to be any worse!"

She shook her head with brisk gravity. "We don't care really what you are."

His amusement now dropped to her straighter. "Your 'we' is awfully beautiful. It's charming to hear you speak for the whole lovely lot. Only you speak, you know, as if you were just the class apart that you yet complain of our—by our scruples—implying you to be."

She considered this objection with her eyes on his face. "Well then, we do care. Only——!"

"Only it's a big subject."

"Oh yes—no doubt; it's a big subject." She appeared to wish to meet him on everything reasonable. "Even Mr. Longdon admits that."

Vanderbank wondered. "You mean you talk over with him——"

"The subject of girls? Why, we scarcely discuss anything else."

"Oh, no wonder then you're not bored. But you mean," Vanderbank asked, "that he recognises the inevitable change—?"

"He can't shut his eyes to the facts. He sees we're quite a different thing."

"I dare say"—her friend was fully appreciative. "Yet the old thing—what do *you* know of it?"

"I personally? Well, I've seen some change even in *my* short life. And aren't the old books full of us? Then Mr. Longdon himself has told me."

Vanderbank smoked and smoked. "You've gone into it with him?"

"As far as a man and a woman can together."

As he took her in at this with a turn of his eye he might have had in his ears the echo of all the times it had been dropped in Buckingham Crescent that Nanda was "wonderful." She *was* indeed. "Oh, he's of course on certain sides shy."

"Awfully—too beautifully. And then there's Aggie," the girl pursued. "I mean for the real old thing."

"Yes, no doubt—if she *be* the real old thing. But what the deuce really *is* Aggie?"

"Well," said Nanda with the frankest interest, "she's a miracle. If one could be her exactly, absolutely, without the least little mite of change, one would probably do the best thing to close with it. Otherwise—except for anything *but* that—I'd rather brazen it out as myself."

There fell between them on this a silence of some minutes, after which it would probably not have been possible for either to say if their eyes had met while it lasted. This was at any rate not the case as Vanderbank at last exclaimed: "Your brass, my dear young lady, is pure gold!"

"Then it's of me, I think, that Harold ought to borrow."

"You mean therefore that mine isn't?" Vanderbank inquired.

"Well, you really haven't any natural 'cheek'—not like *some* of them. You're, in yourself, as uneasy, if anything's said and every one giggles or makes some face, as Mr. Longdon, and if Lord Petherton hadn't once told me that a man hates almost as much to be called modest as a woman does, I would say that very often in London now you must pass some bad moments."

The present might precisely have been one of them, we should doubtless have gathered, had we seen fully recorded in Vanderbank's face the degree to which this prompt response embarrassed or at least stupefied him. But he could always laugh. "I like your 'in London now'!"

"It's the tone and the current and the effect of all the others that push you along," she went on as if she had not heard him. "If such things are contagious, as every one says, you prove it perhaps as much as any one. But you don't begin"—she continued blandly enough to work it out for him; "or you can't at least originally have begun. Any one would know that now—from the terrific effect I see I produce on you by talking this way. There it is—it's all out before one knows it, isn't it, and I can't help it any more than you can, can I?" So she appeared to put it to him, with something in her lucidity that would have been infinitely touching; a strange, grave, calm consciousness of their common doom and of what in especial in it would be worst for herself. He sprang up indeed after an instant as if he had been infinitely touched; he turned away, taking just near her a few steps to and fro, gazed about the place again, but this time without the air of particularly seeing it, and then came back to her as if from a greater distance. An observer at all initiated would, at the juncture, fairly have hung on his lips, and there was in fact on Vanderbank's part quite the look of the man—though it lasted but just while we seize it—in suspense about himself. The most initiated observer of all would have been poor Mr. Longdon, who would now have been destined, however, to be also the most defeated and the sign of whose tension would have been a smothered "Ah, if he doesn't do it *now*!" Well, Vanderbank didn't do it "now," and the long, odd, irrelevant sigh that he gave out might have sufficed as the record of his recovery from a peril lasting just long enough to be measured. Had there been any measure of it meanwhile for Nanda? There was nothing at least to show either the presence or the relief of anxiety in the way in which, by a prompt transition, she left her last appeal to him simply to take care of itself. "You haven't denied that Harold does borrow."

Vanderbank gave a note as of cheer for this luckily firmer ground. "My dear child, I never lent the silly boy five pounds in my life. In fact I like the way you talk of that. I don't know quite for what you take me, but the number of persons to whom I *have* lent five pounds——"

"Is so awfully small"—she took him up on it—"as not to look so very well for you?" She held him an instant as with the fine intelligence of his meaning in this, and then, though not with sharpness, she broke out: "Why are you trying to make out that you're nasty and stingy? Why do you misrepresent——"

"My natural generosity? I don't misrepresent anything, but I take, I think, rather markedly good care of money." She had remained in her place and he was before her on the grass, his hands in his pockets and his manner perhaps a little awkward. "The way you young things talk of it!"

"Harold talks of it—but I don't think *I* do. I'm not a bit expensive—ask mother, or even ask father. I do with awfully little—for clothes and things, and I could easily do with still less. Harold's a born consumer, as Mitchy says; he says also he's one of those people who will never really want."

"Ah, for that, Mitchy himself will never let him."

"Well then, with every one helping us all round, aren't we a lovely family? I don't speak of it to tell tales, but when you mention hearing from Harold all sorts of things immediately come over me. We seem to be all living more or less on other people, all immensely 'beholden.' You can easily say of course that I'm the worst of all. The children and their people, at Bognor, are in borrowed quarters—mother got them lent her —as to which, no doubt, I'm perfectly aware that I ought to be there sharing them, taking care of my little brother and sister, instead of sitting here at Mr. Longdon's expense to expose everything and criticise. Father and mother, in Scotland, are on a programme of places—! Well"—she pulled herself up —"I'm not in *that* at any rate. Say you've lent Harold only five shillings," she went on.

Vanderbank stood smiling. "Well, say I have. I never lend any one whatever more."

"It only adds to my conviction," Nanda explained, "that he writes to Mr. Longdon."

"But if Mr. Longdon doesn't say so—?" Vanderbank objected.

"Oh, that proves nothing." She got up as she spoke. "Harold also works Granny." He only laughed out at first for this, while she went on: "You'll think I make myself out fearfully deep—I mean in the way of knowing everything without having to be told. That *is*, as you say, mamma's great accomplishment, so it must be hereditary. Besides, there seem to me only too many things one *is* told. Only Mr. Longdon has in fact said nothing."

She had looked about responsibly, as if not to leave in disorder the garden nook they had occupied, picking up a newspaper and changing the place of a cushion. "I do think that with him you're remarkable," Vanderbank observed—"putting on one side all you seem to know and on the other all he holds his tongue about. What then *does* he say?" the young man asked after a slight pause and perhaps even with a slight irritation.

Nanda glanced round again—she was folding, rather carefully, her paper. Presently her glance met their friend, who, having come out of one of the long windows that opened to the lawn, had stopped there to watch them. "He says just now that luncheon's ready."

XXV

"I've made him," Nanda said in the drawing-room to Mitchy, "make Mr. Van go with him."

Mr. Longdon, in the rain, which had come on since the morning, had betaken himself to church, and his other guest, with sufficiently marked good-humour, had borne him company. The windows of the drawing-room looked at the wet garden, all vivid and rich in the summer shower, and Mitchy, after seeing Vanderbank turn up his trousers and fling back a last answer to the not quite sincere chaff his submission had engendered, adopted freely and familiarly the prospect not only of a grateful, freshened lawn, but of a good hour in the very pick, as he called it, of his actual happy conditions. The favouring rain, the dear old place, the charming serious house, the large inimitable room, the absence of the others, the present vision of what his young friend had given him to count on—the sense of these delights was expressed in his fixed, generous glare. He was at first too pleased even to sit down; he measured the great space from end to end, admiring again everything he had admired before and protesting afresh that no modern ingenuity—not even his own, to which he did justice—could create effects of such purity. The final touch in the picture before them was just the composer's ignorance. Mr. Longdon had not made his house, he had simply lived it, and the "taste" of the place—Mitchy in certain connections abominated the word—was nothing more than the beauty of his life. Everything on every side had dropped straight from heaven, with nowhere a bargaining thumb-mark, a single sign of the shop. All this would have been a wonderful theme for discourse in Buckingham Crescent—so happy an exercise for the votaries of that temple of analysis that he repeatedly spoke of their experience of it as crying aloud for Mrs. Brook. The questions it set in motion for the perceptive mind were exactly those that, as he said, most made them feel themselves. Vanderbank's plea for his morning had been a pile of letters to work off, and Mitchy—then coming down, as he announced from the first, ready for any-thing—had gone to church with Mr. Longdon and Nanda in the finest spirit of curiosity. He now—after the girl's remark—turned away from his view of the rain, which he found differ-ent somehow from other rain, as everything else was differ-ent, and replied that he knew well enough what she could make Mr. Longdon do, but only wondered at Mr. Longdon's secret for acting on their friend. He was there before her with his hands in his pockets and appreciation winking from every yellow spot in his red necktie. "Afternoon service of a wet Sunday in a small country town is a large order. Does Van do everything the proprietor wants?"

"He may perhaps have had a suspicion of what *I* want," Nanda explained. "If I want particularly to talk to you——"

"He has got out of the way to give me a chance? Well then, he's as usual simply magnificent. How can I express the bliss of finding myself enclosed with you in this sweet old security, this really unimagined sanctity? Nothing is more charming than suddenly to come across something sharp and fresh after we've thought there was nothing more that could draw from us a groan. We've supposed we've had it all, have squeezed the last impression out of the last disappointment, penetrated to the last familiarity in the last surprise; then some fine day we find that we haven't done justice to life. There are little things that pop up and make us feel again. What *may* happen is after all in-calculable. There's just a little chuck of the dice, and for three minutes we win. These, my dear young lady, are my three min-utes. You wouldn't believe the amusement I get from them, and how can I possibly tell you? There's a faint, divine old fra-grance here in the room—or doesn't it perhaps reach you? I shan't have lived without it, but I see now I had been afraid I should. You, on your side, won't have lived without some touch of greatness. This moment is great, and you've pro-duced it. You were great when you felt all you *could* produce. Therefore," Mitchy went on, pausing once more, as he walked, before a picture, "I won't pull the whole thing down by the vulgarity of wishing that I too had a first-rate Cotman."

"Have you given up some *very* big thing to come?" Nanda inquired.

"What in the world is very big, my child, but the beauty of this hour? I haven't the least idea *what*, when I got Mr. Longdon's note, I gave up. Don't ask me for an account of anything; everything went—became imperceptible. I *will* say that for myself: I shed my badness, I do forget people, with a facility that makes me, for bits, for little patches, so far as they are concerned, cease to *be*; so that my life is spotted all over with momentary states in which I'm as the dead of whom nothing is said but good." He had strolled toward her again while she smiled at him. "I've died for this, Nanda."

"The only difficulty I see," she presently replied, "is that you ought to marry a woman really clever and that I'm not quite sure what there may be of that in Aggie."

"In Aggie?" her friend echoed very gently. "Is *that* what you've sent for me for—to talk about Aggie?"

"Didn't it occur to you it might be?"

"That it couldn't possibly, you mean, be anything else?" He looked about for the place in which it would express the deepest surrender to the scene to sit, then sank down with a beautiful prompt submission. "I've no idea of what occurred to me—nothing at least but the sense that I had occurred to *you*. The occurrence is clay in the hands of the potter. Do with me what you will."

"You appreciate everything so wonderfully," Nanda said, "that it oughtn't to be hard for you to appreciate *her*. I do dream so that you may save her; and that's why I haven't waited."

"The only thing that remains to me in life," he answered, "is a certain accessibility to the thought of what I may still do to figure a little in your eye; but that's precisely a thought you may assist to become clearer. You may for instance give me some pledge or sign that if I do figure—prance and caracole and sufficiently kick up the dust—your eye won't suffer itself to be distracted from me. I think there's no adventure I'm not ready to undertake for you; yet my passion—chastened, through all this, purified, austere—is still enough of this world not wholly to have renounced the fancy of some small reward."

"How small?" the girl asked.

She spoke as if feeling that she must take from him, in

common kindness, at least as much as she would make him take, and the serious, anxious patience such a consciousness gave to her tone was met by Mitchy with a charmed reasonableness that his habit of hyperbole did nothing to misrepresent. He glowed at her with the fullest recognition that there was something he was there to discuss with her, but with the assurance in every soft sound of him that no height to which she might lift the discussion would be too great for him to reach. His every cadence and every motion was an implication, as from one to the other, of the exquisite. Oh, he could sustain it! "Well, I mean the establishment of something between us. I mean your arranging somehow that we shall be drawn more together—know together something nobody else knows. I should like to terrifically to have a secret with you."

"Oh, if that's all you want you can be easily gratified. *Rien de plus facile*, as mamma says. I'm full of secrets—I think I'm really most secretive. I'll share almost any one of them with you—that is if it's a good one."

Mitchy hesitated. "You mean you'll choose it yourself? You won't let it be one of mine?"

Nanda wondered. "But what's the difference?"

Her companion jumped up again and for a moment pervaded the place. "When you say such things as that, you're of a beauty—! *May* it," he asked, as he stopped before her, "be one of mine—a perfectly awful one?"

She showed her clearest interest. "As I suppose the most awful secrets are the best—yes, certainiy."

"I'm hideously tempted." But he hung fire; then dropping into his chair again: "It would be too bad. I'm afraid I can't."

"Then why won't *this* do, just as it is?"

"'This'?" He looked over the big bland room. "Which?"

"Why, what you're here for?"

"My dear child, I'm here—most of all—to love you more than ever; and there's an absence of favouring mystery about *that*——"

She looked at him as if seeing what he meant and only asking to remedy it. "There's a certain amount of mystery we can now *make*—that it strikes me in fact we *must* make. Dear

Mitchy," she continued almost with eagerness, "I don't think we *can* really tell."

He had fallen back in his chair, not looking at her now and with his hands, from his supported elbows, clasped to keep himself more quiet. "Are you still talking about Aggie?"

"Why, I've scarcely begun!"

"Oh!" It was not irritation he appeared to express, but the slight strain of an effort to get into relation with the subject. Better to focus the image he closed his eyes awhile.

"You speak of something that may draw us together, and I simply reply that if you don't feel how near together we are in this I shouldn't imagine you ever would. You must have wonderful notions," she presently went on, "of the ideal state of union. I pack every one off for you—I banish everything that can interfere, and I don't in the least mind your knowing that I find the consequence delightful. *You* may talk, if you like, of what will have passed between us, but I shall never mention it to a soul; literally not to a living creature. What do you want more than that?" He opened his eyes in deference to the question, but replied only with a gaze as unassisted as if it had come through a hole in a curtain. "You say you're ready for an adventure, and it's just an adventure that I propose. If I can make you feel for yourself as I feel *for* you the beauty of your chance to go in and save her——"

"Well, if you can—?" Mitchy at last broke in. "I don't think, you know," he said after a moment, "you'll find it easy to make your two ends meet."

She thought a little longer. "One of the ends is yours, so that you'll act *with* me. If I wind you up so that you go——"

"You'll just happily sit and watch me spin? Thank you! *That* will be my reward?"

Nanda on this rose from her chair as with the impulse of protest. "Shan't you care for my gratitude, my admiration?"

"Oh yes"—Mitchy seemed to muse. "I shall care for *them*. But I don't quite see, you know, what you *owe* to Aggie. It isn't as if—!" But with this he faltered.

"As if she cared particularly for *me*? Ah, that has nothing to do with it; that's a thing without which surely it's but too possible to be exquisite. There are beautiful, quite beautiful people who don't care for me. The thing that's important to one is the thing one sees one's self, and it's quite enough if *I* see what can be made of that child. Marry her, Mitchy, and you'll see who she'll care for!"

Mitchy kept his position; he was for the moment—his image of shortly before reversed—the one who appeared to sit happily and watch. "It's too awfully pleasant your asking me anything whatever!"

"Well then, as I say, beautifully, grandly save her."

"As you say, yes"—he sympathetically inclined his head. "But without making me feel exactly what you mean by it."

"Keep her," Nanda returned, "from becoming like the Duchess."

"But she isn't a bit like the Duchess in any of her elements. She's a totally different thing."

It was only for an instant, however, that this objection seemed to count. "That's exactly why she'll be so perfect for you. You'll get her away—take her out of her aunt's life."

Mitchy met it all now in a sort of spellbound stillness. "What do you know about her aunt's life?"

"Oh, I know everything!" She spoke with her first faint shade of impatience.

It produced for a little a hush between them, at the end of which her companion said with extraordinary gentleness and tenderness: "Dear old Nanda!" Her own silence appeared consciously to continue, and the suggestion of it might have been that for intelligent ears there was nothing to add to the declaration she had just made and which Mitchy sat there taking in as with a new light. What he drew from it indeed he presently went on to show. "You're too awfully interesting. Of course—you know a lot. How shouldn't you—and why?"

"'Why'? Oh, that's another affair! But you don't imagine what I know; I'm sure it's much more than you've a notion of. That's the kind of thing now one *is*—just except the little marvel of Aggie. What on earth," the girl pursued, "do you take us for?"

"Oh, it's all right!" breathed Mitchy, divinely pacific.

"I'm sure I don't know whether it is; I shouldn't wonder if it were in fact all wrong. But what at least is certainly right is for one not to pretend anything else. There I am for you at any rate. Now the beauty of Aggie is that she knows nothing —but absolutely, utterly: not the least little tittle of anything."

It was barely visible that Mitchy hesitated, and he spoke quite gravely. "Have you tried her?"

"Oh yes. And Tishy has." His gravity had been less than Nanda's. "Nothing, nothing." The memory of some scene or some passage might have come back to her with a charm. "Ah, say what you will—it *is* the way we ought to be!"

Mitchy, after a minute of much intensity, had stopped watching her; changing his posture and with his elbows on his knees, he dropped for a while his face into his hands. Then he jerked himself to his feet. "There's something I wish awfully I could say to you. But I can't."

Nanda, after a slow head-shake, covered him with one of the dimmest of her smiles. "You needn't say it. I know perfectly which it is." She held him an instant, after which she went on: "It's simply that you wish me fully to understand that *you're* one who, in perfect sincerity, doesn't mind one straw how awful——"

"Yes, how awful?" He had kindled, as she paused, with his new eagerness.

"Well, one's knowledge may be. It doesn't shock in you a single hereditary prejudice."

"Oh, 'hereditary'—!" Mitchy ecstatically murmured.

"You even rather like me the better for it; so that one of the reasons why you couldn't have told me—though not of course, I know, the only one—is that you would have been literally almost ashamed. Because, you know," she went on, "it *is* strange."

"My lack of hereditary——?"

"Yes, discomfort in the presence of the fact I speak of. There's a kind of sense you don't possess."

His appreciation again fairly goggled at her. "Oh, you do know everything!"

"You're so good that nothing shocks you," she lucidly persisted. "There's a kind of delicacy you haven't got."

He was more and more struck. "I've only that—as it were —of the skin and the fingers?" he appealed.

"Oh, and that of the mind. And that of the soul. And some other kinds certainly. But not *the* kind."

"Yes"—he wondered—"I suppose that's the only way one can name it." It appeared to rise there before him. "*The* kind!"

"The kind that would make me painful to you. Or rather not me perhaps," she added as if to create between them the fullest possible light; "but my situation, my exposure—all the results of them that I show. Doesn't one become a sort of a little drain-pipe with everything flowing through?"

"Why don't you call it more gracefully," Mitchy asked, freshly struck, "a little æolian-harp set in the drawing-room window and vibrating in the breeze of conversation?"

"Oh, because the harp gives out a sound, and *we*—at least we try to—give out none."

"What you take, you mean, you keep?"

"Well, it sticks to us. And that's what you don't mind!"

Their eyes met long on it. "Yes—I see. I *don't* mind. I've the most extraordinary lacunæ."

"Oh, I don't know about others," Nanda replied; "I haven't noticed them. But you've that one, and it's enough."

He continued to face her with his queer mixture of assent and speculation. "Enough, my dear, for what? To have made me impossible for you because the only man you could, as they say, have 'respected' would be a man who *would* have minded?" Then as under the cool, soft pressure of the question she looked at last away from him: "The man with '*the* kind,' as you call it, happens to be just the type you *can* love? But what's the use," he persisted as she answered nothing, "in loving a person with the prejudice—hereditary or other—to which you're precisely obnoxious? Do you positively *like* to love in vain?"

It was a question, the way she turned back to him seemed to say, that deserved a responsible answer. "Yes."

But she had moved off after speaking, and Mitchy's eyes followed her to different parts of the room as, with small pretexts of present attention to it, small touches for symmetry, she slowly measured it. "What's extraordinary then is your idea of my finding any charm in Aggie's ignorance."

She immediately put down an old snuff-box. "Why, it's the one sort of thing you don't know. You can't imagine," she said as she returned to him, "the effect it will produce on you. You must get really near it and see it all come out to feel all its beauty. You'll like it, Mitchy"—and Nanda's gravity was wonderful—"better than anything you *have* known."

The clear sincerity of this, even had there been nothing else, imposed a consideration that Mitchy now flagrantly could give, and the deference of his suggestion of difficulty only grew more deep. "I'm to do then, with this happy condition of hers, what you say *you've* done—to 'try' it?" And then as her assent, so directly challenged, failed an instant: "But won't my approach to it, however cautious, be just what will break it up and spoil it?"

Nanda thought. "Why so—if mine wasn't?"

"Oh, you're not me!"

"But I'm just as bad."

"Thank you, my dear!" Mitchy rang out.

"Without," Nanda pursued, "being as good." She had on this, in a different key, her own sudden explosion. "Don't you see, Mitchy dear—for the very heart of it all—how good I *believe* you?"

She had spoken as with a flare of impatience at some justice he failed to do her, and this brought him after a startled instant close enough to her to take up her hand. She let him have it, and in mute, solemn reassurance he raised it to his lips, saying to her thus more things than he could say in any other way; which yet just after, when he had released it and a motionless pause had ensued, didn't prevent him from adding three words. "Oh, Nanda, Nanda!"

The tone of them made her again extraordinarily gentle. "Don't 'try' anything then. Take everything for granted."

He had turned away from her and walked mechanically, with his air of blind emotion, to the window, where for a minute he looked out. "It has stopped raining," he said at last; "it's going to brighten."

The place had three windows, and Nanda went to the next. "Not quite yet—but I think it will."

Mitchy soon faced back into the room, where after a brief hesitation he moved as quietly—almost as cautiously—as if on tiptoe to the seat occupied by his companion at the beginning of their talk. Here he sank down watching the girl, who stood awhile longer with her eyes on the garden. "You want me, you say, to take her out of the Duchess's life; but where am I myself, if we come to that, but even more *in* the Duchess's life than Aggie is? I'm in it by my contacts, my associations, my indifferences—all my acceptances, knowledges, amusements. I'm in it by my cynicisms—those that circumstances somehow from the first, when I began for myself to look at life and the world, committed me to and steeped me in; I'm in it by a kind of desperation that I shouldn't have felt perhaps if you had got hold of me sooner with just this touch with which you've got hold of me to-day; and I'm in it more than all—you'll yourself admit—by the very fact that her aunt desires, as you know, much more even than you do, to bring the thing about. Then we *should* be—the Duchess and I—shoulder to shoulder!"

Nanda heard him motionless to the end, taking also another minute to turn over what he had said. "What is it you like so in Lord Petherton?" she asked as she came to him.

"My dear child, if you could only tell me! It would be, wouldn't it?—it must have been—the subject of some fairy-tale, if fairy-tales were made now, or better still, of some Christmas pantomime: 'The Gnome and the Giant.'"

Nanda appeared to try—not with much success—to see it. "Do you find Lord Petherton a Gnome?"

Mitchy at first, for all reward, only glared at her. "Charming, Nanda—charming!"

"A man's giant enough for Lord Petherton," she went on, "when his fortune's gigantic. He preys upon you."

His hands in his pockets and his legs much apart, Mitchy sat there as in a posture adapted to her simplicity. "You're adorable. *You* don't. But it *is* rather horrid, isn't it?" he presently went on.

Her momentary silence would have been by itself enough of an answer. "Nothing—of all you speak of," she nevertheless returned, "will matter then. She'll so simplify your life." He remained just as he was, only with his eyes on her; and meanwhile she had turned again to her window, through which a faint sun-streak began to glimmer and play. At the sight of it she opened the casement to let in the warm freshness, "The rain *has* stopped."

"You say you want me to save her. But what you really mean," Mitchy resumed from the sofa, "isn't at all exactly that."

Nanda, without heeding the remark, took in the sunshine. "It will be charming now in the garden."

Her friend got up, found his wonderful crossbarred cap after a glance on a neighbouring chair, and with it came toward her. "Your hope is that—as I'm good enough to be worth it—she'll save *me*."

Nanda looked at him now. "She will, Mitchy—she *will*!"

They stood a moment in the recovered brightness; after which he mechanically—as with the pressure of quite another consciousness—put on his cap. "Well then, shall that hope between us be the thing——?"

"The thing?"—she just wondered.

"Why, that will have drawn us together—to hold us so, you know—this afternoon. I mean the secret we spoke of."

She put out to him on this the hand he had taken a few minutes before, and he clasped it now only with the firmness it seemed to give and to ask for. "Oh, it will do for that!" she said as they went out together.

XXVI

It had been understood that he was to take his leave on the morrow while Vanderbank was to stay another day. Mr. Longdon had for the Sunday dinner invited three or four of his neighbours to "meet" the two gentlemen from town, so that it was not till the company had departed, or in other words till near bedtime, that our four friends could again have become aware, as between themselves, of that directness of mutual relation which forms the subject of our picture. It had not, however, prevented Nanda's slipping upstairs as soon as the doctor and his wife had gone, and the manner indeed in which on the stroke of eleven Mr. Longdon kept up his tradition of appropriating a particular candle was as positive an expression of it as any other. Nothing in him was more amiable than the terms maintained between the rigour of his personal habits and his free imagination of the habits of others. He deprecated as regards the former, it might have been seen, most signs of resemblance, and no one had ever dared to learn how he would have handled a show of imitation. "The way to flatter him," Mitchy threw off five minutes later, "is not to make him think you're like him, but to let him see how different you perceive he can bear to think you. I mean of course without hating you."

"But what interest have *you*," Vanderbank asked, "in the way to flatter him?"

"My dear fellow, more than you. I haven't been here all day without arriving at conclusions on the credit he has opened to you——!"

"Do you mean the amount he'll settle?"

"You have it in your power," said Mitchy, "to make it anything you like."

"And is he then—so bloated?"

Mitchy was on his feet in the apartment in which their host had left them, and he had at first for this question but an expressive motion of the shoulders in respect to everything in the room. "See, judge, guess, feel!"

But it was as if Vanderbank, before the fire, consciously controlled his attention. "Oh, I don't care a hang!"

This passage took place in the library and as a consequence of their having confessed, as their friend faced them with his bedroom light, that a brief, discreet vigil and a box of cigarettes would fix better than anything else the fine impression of the day. Mitchy might at that moment, on the evidence of the eyes Mr. Longdon turned to them and of which his innocent candle-flame betrayed the secret, have found matter for a measure of the almost extreme allowances he wanted them to want of him. They had only to see that the greater window was fast and to turn out the library lamp. It might really have amused them to stand a moment at the open door that, apart from this, was to testify to his conception of those who were not, in the smaller hours, as *he* was. He had in fact by his retreat—and but too sensibly—left them there with a deal of midnight company. If one of these presences was the mystery he had himself mixed, the manner of our young men showed a due expectation of the others. Mitchy, on hearing how little Vanderbank "cared," only kept up a while longer that observant revolution in which he had spent much of his day, to which any fresh sense of any exhibition always promptly committed him and which, had it not been controlled by infinite tact, might have affected the nerves of those in whom enjoyment was less rotary. He was silent long enough to suggest his fearing that almost anything he might say would appear too allusive; then at last once more he took his risk. "Awfully jolly old place!"

"It is indeed," Van only said; but his posture in the large chair he had pushed toward the open window was of itself almost an opinion. The August night was hot and the air that came in charged and sweet. Vanderbank smoked with his face turned to the dusky garden and the dim stars; at the end of a few moments more of which he glanced round. "Don't you think it rather stuffy with that big lamp? As those candles on the chimney are going we might put it out."

"Like this?" The amiable Mitchy had straightway obliged his companion and he as promptly took in the effect of the diminished light on the character of the room, which he commended as if the depth of shadow produced were all this companion had sought. He might freshly have brought home to Vanderbank that a man sensitive to so many different things could never really be incommoded, though that personage presently indeed showed himself occupied with another thought.

"I think I ought to mention to you that I've told him how you and Mrs. Brook now both know. I did so this afternoon on our way back from church—I hadn't done it before. He took me a walk round to show me more of the place, and that gave me my chance. But he doesn't mind," Vanderbank continued. "The only thing is that I've thought it may possibly make him speak to you, so that it's better you should know he knows. But he told me definitely Nanda doesn't."

Mitchy took this in with an attention that spoke of his already recognising how the less tempered darkness favoured talk. "And is that all that passed between you?"

"Well, practically; except of course that I made him understand, I think, how it happened that I haven't kept my own counsel."

"Oh, but you *have*—didn't he at least feel?—or perhaps even have done better, when you've two such excellent persons to keep it *for* you? Can't he easily believe how we feel with you?"

Vanderbank appeared for a minute to leave this appeal unheeded; he continued to stare into the garden while he smoked and swung the long leg he had thrown over the arm of the chair. When he at last spoke, however, it was with some emphasis—perhaps even with some vulgarity. "Oh rot!"

Mitchy hovered without an arrest. "You mean he *can't* feel?"

"I mean it isn't true. I've no illusions about you. I know how you're both affected, though I of course perfectly trust you."

Mitchy had a short silence. "Trust us not to speak?"

"Not to speak to Nanda herself—though of course too if you spoke to others," Vanderbank went on, "they would immediately rush and tell her."

"I've spoken to no one," said Mitchy.

"I'm sure of it. And neither has Mrs. Brook."

"I'm glad you're sure of that also," Mitchy returned, "for it's only doing her justice."

"Oh, I'm quite confident of it," said Vanderbank.

"And without asking her?"

"Perfectly."

"And you're equally sure, without asking, that *I* haven't betrayed you?" After which, while, as if to let the question lie there in its folly, Vanderbank said nothing, his friend pursued: "I came, I must tell you, terribly near it to-day."

"Why must you tell me? Your coming 'near' doesn't concern me, and I take it you don't suppose I'm watching or sounding you. Mrs. Brook will have come terribly near," Vanderbank continued as if to make the matter free; "but she won't have done it either. She will have been distinctly tempted——"

"But she won't have fallen?" Mitchy broke in. "Exactly—there we are. *I* was distinctly tempted and I didn't fall. I think your certainty about Mrs. Brook," he added, "shows you do know her. She's incapable of anything deliberately nasty."

"Oh, of anything nasty in any way," Vanderbank said musingly and kindly.

"Yes; one knows on the whole what she *won't* do." After

which for a period Mitchy roamed and reflected. "But in spite of the assurance given you by Mr. Longdon—or perhaps indeed just because of your having taken it—I think I ought to mention to you my belief that Nanda does know of his offer to you. I mean by having guessed it."

"Oh!" said Vanderbank.

"There's in fact more still," his companion pursued, "that I feel I should like to mention to you."

"Oh!" Vanderbank at first only repeated. But after a moment he said: "My dear fellow, I'm much obliged."

"The thing I speak of is something I should at any rate have said, and I should have looked out for some chance if we had not had this one." Mitchy spoke as if his friend's last words were not of consequence, and he continued as Vanderbank got up and, moving rather aimlessly, came and stood with his back to the chimney. "My only hesitation would have been caused by its entailing our going down into things in a way that, face to face—given the private nature of the things —I dare say most men don't particularly enjoy. But if you don't mind——"

"Oh, I don't mind. In fact, as I tell you, I recognise an obligation to you." Vanderbank, with his shoulders against the high mantel, uttered this without a direct look; he smoked and smoked, then looked at the tip of his cigarette. "You feel convinced she knows?" he threw out.

"Well, it's my impression."

"Ah, any impression of yours—of that sort—is sure to be right. If you think I ought to have it from you I'm really grateful. Is that—a—what you wanted to say to me?" Vanderbank with a slight hesitation demanded.

Mitchy, watching him more than he watched Mitchy, shook a mildly decisive head. "No."

Vanderbank, his eyes on his smoke-puffs, seemed to wonder. "What you wanted is—something else?"

"Something else."

"Oh!" said Vanderbank for the third time.

The ejaculation had been vague, but the movement that followed it was definite; the young man, turning away, found himself again near the chair he had quitted, and resumed possession of it as a sign of being at his friend's service. This friend, however, not only hung fire but finally went back to take a shot from a quarter they might have been supposed to have left. "It strikes me as odd his imagining—awfully acute as he is—that she has *not* guessed. One wouldn't have thought he could live with her here in such an intimacy—seeing her every day and pretty much all day—and make such a mistake."

Vanderbank, his great length all of a lounge again, turned it over. "And yet I do thoroughly feel the mistake's not yours."

Mitchy had a new serenity of affirmation. "Oh, it's not mine."

"Perhaps then"—it occurred to Vanderbank—"he doesn't really believe it."

"And only says so to make you feel more easy?"

"So that one may—in fairness to one's self—keep one's head, as it were, and decide quite on one's own grounds."

"Then you *have* still to decide?"

Van took his time to answer. "I've still to decide." Mitchy became again on this, in the sociable dusk, a slow-circling, vaguely agitated element, and his friend continued: "Is your idea very generously and handsomely to help that by letting me know——"

"That I do definitely renounce"—Mitchy took him up—"any pretension and any hope? Well, I'm ready with a proof of it. I've passed my word that I'll apply elsewhere."

Vanderbank turned more round to him. "Apply to the Duchess for her niece?"

"It's practically settled."

"But since when?"

Mitchy barely faltered. "Since this afternoon."

"Ah then, not with the Duchess herself."

"With Nanda—whose plan from the first, you won't have forgotten, the thing has so charmingly been."

Vanderbank could show that his not having in the least forgotten was yet not a bar to his being now mystified. "But, my dear man, what can Nanda 'settle'?"

"My fate," Mitchy said, pausing well before him.

Vanderbank sat now a minute with raised eyes, catching the indistinctness of his friend's strange expression. "You're both beyond me!" he exclaimed at last. "I don't see what you in particular gain."

"I didn't either till she made it all out to me. One sees then, in such a matter, for one's self. And as everything's gain that isn't loss, there was nothing I *could* lose. It gets me," Mitchy further explained, "out of the way."

"Out of the way of what?"

This, Mitchy frankly showed, was more difficult to say, but he in time brought it out. "Well, of appearing to suggest to you that my existence, in a prolonged state of singleness, may ever represent for her any real alternative."

"But alternative to what?"

"Why, to being *your* wife, damn you!" Mitchy, on these words turned away again, and his companion, in the presence of his renewed dim gyrations, sat for a minute dumb. Before Van had spoken indeed he was back again. "Excuse my violence, but of course you really see."

"I'm not pretending anything," Vanderbank said—"but a man *must* understand. What I catch hold of is that you offer me—in the fact that you're thus at any rate disposed of—a proof that I at any rate shan't, if I hesitate to 'go in,' have a pretext for saying to myself that I *may* deprive her——"

"Yes, precisely," Mitchy now urbanely assented: "of something, in the shape of a man with *my* amount of money, that she may live to regret and to languish for. My amount of money, don't you see?" he very simply added, "is nothing to her."

"And you want me to be sure that—so far as I may ever have had a scruple—she has had her chance and got rid of it."

"Completely," Mitchy smiled.

"Because"—Vanderbank, with the aid of his cigarette, thoughtfully pieced it out—"that may possibly bring me to the point."

"Possibly!" Mitchy laughed.

He had stood a moment longer, almost as if to see the possibility develop before his eyes, and had even started at the next sound of his friend's voice. What Vanderbank in fact brought out, however, only made him turn his back. "Do you like so very much little Aggie?"

"Well," said Mitchy, "Nanda does. And I like Nanda."

"You're too amazing," Vanderbank mused. His musing had presently the effect of making him rise; reflection indeed possessed him after he was on his feet. "I can't help its coming over me then that on such an extraordinary system you must also rather like *me*."

"What will you have, my dear Van?" Mitchy frankly asked. "It's the sort of thing you must be most used to. For at the present moment—look!—aren't we all at you at once?"

It was as if Vanderbank had managed to appear to wonder. "'All'?"

"Nanda, Mrs. Brook, Mr. Longdon——"

"And you. I see."

"Names of distinction. And all the others," Mitchy pursued, "that I don't count."

"Oh, you're the best."

"I?"

"You're the best," Vanderbank simply repeated. "It's at all events most extraordinary," he declared. "But I make you out on the whole better than I do Mr. Longdon."

"Ah, aren't we very much the same—simple lovers of life? That is, of that finer essence of it which appeals to the consciousness——"

"The consciousness?"—his companion took up his hesitation.

"Well, enlarged and improved."

The words had made on Mitchy's lips an image by which his friend seemed for a moment to be held. "One doesn't really know quite what to say or to do."

"Oh, you must take it all quietly. You're of a special class; one of those who, as we said the other day—don't you remember? —are a source of the sacred terror. People made in such a way must take the consequences; just as people must take them," Mitchy went on, "who are made as *I* am. So cheer up!"

Mitchy, uttering this incitement, had moved to the empty chair by the window, in which he presently was sunk; and it might have been in emulation of his previous strolling and straying that Vanderbank himself now began to revolve. The meditation he next threw out, however, showed a certain resistance to Mitchy's advice. "I'm glad at any rate I don't deprive her of a fortune."

"You don't deprive her of mine of course," Mitchy answered from the chair; "but isn't her enjoyment of Mr. Longdon's at least a good deal staked after all on your action?"

Vanderbank stopped short. "It's his idea to settle it *all?*"

Mitchy gave out his glare. "I thought you didn't 'care a hang.' I haven't been here so long," he went on as his companion at first retorted nothing, "without making up my mind for myself about his means. He *is* distinctly bloated."

It sent Vanderbank off again. "Oh well, she'll no more get all in the one event than she'll get nothing in the other. She'll only get a sort of a provision. But she'll get that whatever happens."

"Oh, if you're sure—!" Mitchy simply commented.

"I'm not sure, confound it!" Then—for his voice had been irritated—Van spoke more quietly. "Only I see her here—though on his wish of course—handling things quite as if they were her own and paying him a visit without apparently any calculated end. What's that on *his* part but a pledge?"

Oh, Mitchy could show off-hand that he knew what it was. "It's a pledge, quite as much, to you. He shows you the whole thing. He likes you not a whit less than he likes her."

"Oh thunder!" Van impatiently sighed.

"It's as 'rum' as you please, but there it is," said the inexorable Mitchy.

"Then does he think I'll do it for *this?*"

"For 'this'?"

"For the place, the whole thing, as you call it, that he shows me."

Mitchy had a short silence that might have represented a change of colour. "It isn't good enough?" But he instantly took himself up. "Of course he wants—as I do—to treat you with a tact!"

"Oh, it's all right," Vanderbank immediately said. "Your 'tact'—yours and his—is marvellous, and Nanda's greatest of all."

Mitchy's momentary renewal of stillness was addressed, he somehow managed not obscurely to convey, to the last clause of his friend's speech. "If you're not sure," he presently resumed, "why can't you frankly ask him?"

Vanderbank again, as the phrase is, "mooned" about a little. "Because I don't know that it would do."

"What do you mean by 'do'?"

"Well, that it would be exactly—what do you call it?— 'square.' Or even quite delicate or decent. To take from him, in the way of an assurance so handsomely offered, so much and then to ask for more: I don't feel I can do it. Besides, I have my little conviction. To the question itself he might easily reply that it's none of my business."

"I see," Mitchy dropped. "Such an inquiry might suggest to him moreover that you're hesitating more than you perhaps really are."

"Oh, as to *that*," said Vanderbank, "I think he practically knows how much."

"And how little?" He met this however with no more form than if it had been a poor joke, so that Mitchy also smoked for a moment in silence. "It's your coming down here, you mean, for these three or four days, that will have fixed it?"

The question this time was one to which the speaker might have expected an answer, but Vanderbank's only immediate answer was to walk and walk. "I want so awfully to be kind to her," he at last said.

"I should think so!" Then with irrelevance Mitchy harked back. "Shall *I* inquire?"

But Vanderbank, with another thought, had lost the thread. "Inquire what?"

"Why, if she does get anything——!"

"If I'm not kind *enough*?"—Van had caught up again. "Dear no; I'd rather you wouldn't speak unless first spoken to."

"Well, *he* may speak—since he knows we know."

"It isn't likely, for he can't make out why I told you."

"You didn't tell *me*, you know," said Mitchy. "You told Mrs. Brook."

"Well, *she* told you, and her talking about it is the unpleasant idea. He can't get her down anyhow."

"Poor Mrs. Brook!" Mitchy meditated.

"Poor Mrs. Brook!" his companion echoed.

"But I thought you said," he went on, "that he doesn't mind."

"*Your* knowing? Well, I dare say he doesn't. But he doesn't want a lot of gossip and chatter."

"Oh!" said Mitchy with meekness.

"I may absolutely take it from you then," Vanderbank presently resumed, "that Nanda has her idea?"

"Oh, she didn't tell me so. But it's none the less my belief."

"Well," Vanderbank at last threw off, "I feel it for myself. If only because she knows everything," he pursued without looking at Mitchy. "She knows everything, everything."

"Everything, everything." Mitchy got up.

"She told me so herself yesterday," said Van.

"And she told *me* so to-day."

Vanderbank's hesitation might have shown he was struck with this. "Well, I don't think it's information that either of us required. But of course she can't help it," he added. "Everything, literally everything, in London, in the world she lives in, is in the air she breathes—so that the longer *she's* in it the more she'll know."

"The more she'll know, certainly," Mitchy acknowledged. "But she isn't in it, you see, down here."

"No. Only she appears to have come down with such accumulations. And she won't be here for ever," Vanderbank hastened to subjoin.

"Certainly not if you marry her."

"But isn't that at the same time," Vanderbank asked, "just the difficulty?"

Mitchy looked vague. "The difficulty?"

"Why, as a married woman she'll be steeped in it again."

"Surely"—oh, Mitchy could be candid! "But the difference will be that for a married woman it won't matter. It only matters for girls," he plausibly continued—"and then only for those on whom no one takes pity."

"The trouble is," said Vanderbank—but quite as if uttering only a general truth—"that it's just a thing that may sometimes operate as a bar to pity. Isn't it for the non-marrying girls that it doesn't particularly matter? For the others it's such an odd preparation."

"Oh, I don't mind it!" Mitchy declared.

Vanderbank visibly demurred. "Ah, but your choice——"

"Is such a different sort of thing?" Mitchy, for the half-hour, in the ambiguous dusk, had never looked more droll. "The young lady I named isn't my *choice.*"

"Well then, that's only a sign the more that you do these things more easily."

"Oh, 'easily'!" Mitchy murmured.

"We oughtn't, at any rate, to keep it up," said Vanderbank, who had looked at his watch. "Twelve twenty-five—good-night. Shall I blow out the candles?"

"Do, please. I'll close the window"—and Mitchy went to it. "I'll follow you—good-night." The candles after a minute were out, and his friend had gone, but Mitchy, left in darkness face to face with the vague, quiet garden, still stood there.

Tishy Grendon

XXVII

THE FOOTMAN, opening the door, mumbled his name without sincerity, and Vanderbank, passing in, found in fact—for he had caught the symptom—the chairs and tables, the lighted lamps and the flowers alone in possession. He looked at his watch, which exactly marked eight, then turned to speak again to the servant, who had however, without another sound and as if blushing for the house, already closed him in. There was nothing indeed but Mrs. Grendon's want of promptness that failed of a welcome: her drawing-room, on the January night, showed its elegance through a suffusion of pink electricity which melted, at the end of the vista, into the faintly golden glow of a retreat still more sacred. Vanderbank walked after a moment into the second room, which also proved empty and which had its little globes of white fire—discreetly limited in number—coated with lemon-coloured silk. The walls, covered with delicate French mouldings, were so fair that they seemed vaguely silvered; the low French chimney had a French fire. There was a lemon-coloured stuff on the sofa and chairs, a wonderful polish on the floor that was largely exposed, and a copy of a French novel in blue paper on one of the spindle-legged tables. Vanderbank looked about him an instant as if generally struck, then gave himself to something that had particularly caught his eye. This was simply his own name written rather large on the cover of the French book and endowed, after he had taken the volume up, with the power to hold his attention the more closely the longer he looked at it. He uttered, for a private satisfaction, before letting the matter pass, a low confused sound; after which, flinging the book down with some emphasis in another place, he moved to the chimney-piece, where his eyes for a little intently fixed the small ashy wood fire. When he raised them again it was, on the observation that the beautiful clock on the mantel was wrong, to consult once more his watch and then give a glance, in the chimney-glass, at the state of his moustache, of which he twisted for a moment with due care the ends. While so engaged he became aware of something else and, quickly facing about, recognised in the doorway of the room the other figure the glass had just reflected.

"Oh *you?*" he said, with a quick hand-shake. "Mrs. Grendon's down?" But he had already passed with Nanda, on their greeting, back into the first room, which contained only themselves, and she had mentioned that she believed Tishy to have said 8.15, which meant of course anything people liked.

"Oh then, there'll be nobody till nine. I didn't, I suppose, sufficiently study my note; which didn't mention to me, by-the-way," Vanderbank added, "that you were to be here."

"Ah, but why *should* it?" the girl candidly exclaimed. She spoke again, however, before he could reply. "I daresay that when she wrote to you she didn't know."

"Know you would come up to meet me?" Vanderbank laughed. "Jolly at any rate, thanks to my mistake, to have in this way a quiet moment with you. You came on ahead of your mother?"

"Oh no—I'm staying here."

"Oh!" said Vanderbank.

"Mr. Longdon came up with me—I came here, Friday last, straight."

"You parted at the door?" he asked with marked gaiety.

She thought a moment—she was more serious. "Yes—but only for a day or two. He's coming tonight."

"Good. How delightful!"

"He'll be glad to see you," Nanda said, looking at the flowers.

"Awfully kind of him when I've been such a brute."

"How—a brute?"

"Well, I mean not writing—nor going back."

"Oh, I see," Nanda simply returned.

It was a simplicity that, clearly enough, made her friend a little awkward. "Has he—a—minded? But he can't have complained!" he quickly added.

"Oh, he never complains."

"No, no—it isn't in him. But it's just that," said Vanderbank, "that makes one feel so base. I've been ferociously busy."

"He knows that—he likes it," Nanda returned. "He delights in your work. And I've done what I can for him."

"Ah," said her companion, "you've evidently brought him round. I mean to this lady."

"To Tishy? Oh, of course I can't leave her—with nobody."

"No"—Vanderbank became jocose again—"that's a London necessity. You can't leave anybody with nobody—exposed to everybody."

Mild as it was, however, Nanda missed the pleasantry. "Mr. Grendon's not here."

"Ah, where is he?"

"Yachting—but she doesn't know."

"Then she and you are just doing this together?"

"Well," said Nanda, "she's dreadfully frightened."

"Oh, she mustn't allow herself," he returned, "to be too much carried away by it. But we're to have your mother?"

"Yes, and papa. It's really for Mitchy and Aggie," the girl went on—"before they go abroad."

"Oh then, I see what you've come up for! Tishy and I are not in it. It's all for Mitchy."

"If you mean there's nothing I wouldn't do for him, you're quite right. He has always been of a kindness to me——"

"That culminated in marrying your friend?" Vanderbank asked. "It was charming, certainly, and I don't mean to diminish the merit of it. But Aggie herself, I gather, is of a charm now——!"

"Isn't she?"—Nanda was eager. "Hasn't she come out?"

"With a bound—into the arena. But when a young person's out with Mitchy——!"

"Oh, you musn't say anything against that. I've been out with him myself."

"Ah, but my dear child—!" Van frankly argued.

It was not, however, a thing to notice. "I knew it would be just so. It always is when they've been like that."

"Do you mean as she apparently *was*? But doesn't it make one wonder a little *if* she was?"

"Oh, she was—I know she was. And we're also to have Harold," Nanda continued—"another of Mitchy's beneficiaries. It *would* be a banquet, wouldn't it? if we were to have them all."

Vanderbank hesitated, and the look he fixed on the door might have suggested a certain open attention to the arrival of their hostess or the announcement of other guests. "If you haven't got them all, you've got, in having me, I should suppose, about the biggest."

"Ah, what has he done for you?" Nanda asked.

Again her friend hung fire. "Do you remember something you said to me down there in August?"

She looked vague but quite unembarrassed. "I remember but too well that I chattered."

"You declared to me that you knew everything."

"Oh yes—and I said to Mitchy too."

"Well, my dear child, you don't."

"Because I don't know——?"

"Yes, what makes *me* the victim of his insatiable benevolence."

"Ah well, if you've no doubt of it yourself, that's all that's required. I'm quite *glad* to hear of something I don't know," Nanda pursued. "And we're to have Harold too," she repeated.

"As a beneficiary? Then we *shall* fill up! Harold will give us a stamp."

"Won't he? I hear of nothing but his success. Mother wrote me that people are frantic for him; and," said the girl after an instant, "do you know what cousin Jane wrote me?"

"What *would* she now? I'm trying to think."

Nanda relieved him of this effort. "Why, that mother has transferred to him all the scruples that she felt—'even to excess'—in *my* time, about what we might pick up among you all that wouldn't be good for us."

"That's a neat one for *me*!" Vanderbank declared. "And I like your talk about your antediluvian 'time.'"

"Oh, it's all over."

"What exactly is it," Vanderbank presently demanded, "that you describe in that manner."

"Well, my little hour. And the danger of picking up."

"There's none of it here?"

Nanda appeared frankly to judge. "No—because really, Tishy, don't you see? is natural. We just talk."

Vanderbank showed his interest. "Whereas at your mother's——?"

"Well, you were all afraid."

Vanderbank laughed straight out. "Do you mind my telling her that?"

"Oh, she knows it. I've heard her say herself you were."

"Ah, *I* was," he concurred. "You know we've spoken of that before."

"I'm speaking now of all of you," said Nanda. "But it was she who was most so, for she tried—I know she did, she told me so—to control you. And it was when you were most controlled——"

Van's amusement took it up. "That we were most detrimental?"

"Yes, because of course what's so awfully unutterable is just what we most notice. Tishy knows that," Nanda wonderfully observed.

As the reflection of her tone might have been caught by an observer in Vanderbank's face, it was in all probability caught by his interlocutress, who superficially, however, need have recognised there—what was all she showed—but the right manner of waiting for dinner. "The better way then is to dash right in? That's what our friend here does?"

"Oh, you know what she does!" the girl replied as if with a sudden drop of interest in the question. She turned at the moment to the opening of the door.

It was Tishy who at last appeared, and her guest had his greeting ready. "We're talking of the delicate matters as to which you think it's better to dash right in; but I'm bound to say your inviting a hungry man to dinner doesn't appear to be one of them."

The sign of Tishy Grendon—as it had been often called in a society in which variety of reference had brought to high perfection, for usual safety, the sense of signs—was a retarded facial glimmer that, in respect to any subject, closed up the rear of the procession. It had been said of her indeed that when processions were at all rapid she was usually to be found, on a false impression of her whereabouts, mixed up with the next; so that now, for instance, by the time she had reached the point of saying to Vanderbank "Are you *really* hungry?" Nanda had begun to appeal to him for some praise of their hostess's appearance. This was of course with soft looks, up and down, at her clothes. "Isn't she too nice? Did you ever see anything so lovely?"

"I'm so faint with inanition," Van replied to Mrs. Grendon, "that—like the traveller in the desert, isn't it?—I only make out, as an oasis or a mirage, a sweet green rustling blur. I don't trust you."

"I don't trust *you*," Nanda said on her friend's behalf. "She isn't 'green'—men are amazing: they don't know the dearest old blue that ever was seen."

"*Is* it your '*old* blue'?" Vanderbank, monocular, very earnestly asked. "I can imagine it was 'dear,' but I should have thought——"

"It was yellow"—Nanda helped him out—"if I hadn't kindly told you." Tishy's figure showed the confidence of objects consecrated by publicity; bodily speaking a beautiful human plant, it might have taken the last November gale to account for the completeness with which, in some quarters, she had shed her leaves. Her companions could only emphasise by the direction of their eyes the nature of the responsibility with which a spectator would have seen them saddled—a choice, as to consciousness, between the effect of her being and the effect of her not being dressed. "Oh, I'm hideous—of course I know it," said Tishy. "I'm only just clean. Here's Nanda now, who's beautiful," she vaguely continued, "and Nanda——"

"Oh but, darling, Nanda's clean too!" the young lady in question interrupted; on which her fellow-guest could only laugh with her as in relief from the antithesis of which her presence of mind had averted the completion, little indeed, for the most part, as in Mrs. Grendon's talk that element of style was involved.

"There's nothing in such a matter," Vanderbank observed as if it were the least he could decently say, "like challenging inquiry; and here's Harold, precisely," he went on in the next breath, "as clear and crisp and undefiled as a fresh five-pound note."

"A fresh one?"—Harold had passed in a flash from his hostess. "A man who like me hasn't seen one for six months, could perfectly do, I assure you, with one that has lost its what-do-you call it." He kissed Nanda with a friendly peck, then, more completely aware, had a straighter apprehension for Tishy. "My dear child, *you* seem to have lost something, though I'll say for you that one doesn't miss it."

Mrs. Grendon looked from him to Nanda. "Does he mean anything very nasty? I can only understand you when Nanda explains," she returned to Harold. "In fact there's scarcely anything I understand except when Nanda explains. It's too dreadful her being away so much now with strange people, whom I'm sure she can't begin to do for what she does for me; it makes me miss her all round. And the only thing I've come across that she *can't* explain," Tishy launched straight at her friend, "is what on earth she's doing there."

"Why, she's working Mr. Longdon, like a good true girl," Harold said; "like a good true daughter, and even, though she doesn't love me nearly so much as I love *her*, I will say, like a good true sister. I'm bound to tell you, my dear Tishy," he went on, "that I think it awfully happy, with the trend of manners, for any really nice young thing to be a bit lost to sight. London, upon my honour, is quite too awful for girls, and any big house in the country is as much worse—with the promiscuities and opportunities and all that—as you know for yourselves. *I* know some places," Harold declared, "where, if I had any girls, I'd see 'em shot before I'd take 'em."

"Oh, you know too much, my dear boy!" Vanderbank remarked with commiseration.

"Ah, my brave old Van," the youth returned, "don't speak as if *you* had illusions. I know," he pursued to the ladies, "just where some of Van's must have perished, and some of the places I've in mind are just where he has left his tracks. A man must be wedded to sweet superstitions not nowadays to *have* to open his eyes. Nanda, love," he benevolently concluded, "stay where you are. So at least I shan't blush for you. That you've the good fortune to have reached your time of life with so little injury to your innocence makes you a case by yourself, of which we must recognise the claims. If Tishy can't stump you, that's nothing against you—Tishy comes of one of the few innocent English families that are left. Yes, you may all cry 'Oho!'—but I defy you to name me, say, five, or at most seven, in which some awful thing or other hasn't happened. Of course ours is one, and Tishy's is one, and Van's is one, and Mr. Longdon's is one, and that makes you, bang off, four. So there you are!" Harold gaily wound up.

"I see now why he's the rage!" Vanderbank observed to Nanda.

But Mrs. Grendon expressed to their young friend a lingering wonder. "Do you mean you go in for the adoption——?"

"Oh, Tishy!" Nanda mildly murmured.

Harold, however, had his own tact. "The dear man's taking her quite over? Not altogether unreservedly. I'm with the governor: I think we ought to *get* something. 'Oh yes, dear man, but what do you *give* us for her?'—that's what *I* should say to him. I mean, don't you know, that I don't think she's making quite the bargain she might. If he were to want *me* I don't say he mightn't have me, but I should have it on my conscience to make it in one way or another a good thing for my parents. You *are* nice, old woman"—he turned to his sister—"and one can still feel, for the flower of your youth, something of the wonderful 'reverence' that we were all brought up on. For God's sake therefore—all the more— don't really close with him till you've had another word or two with me. I'll be hanged"—he appealed to the company again—"if he shall have her for nothing!"

"See rather," Vanderbank said to Mrs. Grendon, "how little it's like your really losing her that she should be able this evening fairly to bring the dear man to you. At this rate we don't lose her—we simply get him as well."

"Ah, but is it quite the dear man's *company* we want?"— and Harold looked anxious and acute. "If that's the best arrangement Nanda can make——!"

"If he hears us talking in this way, which strikes me as very horrible," Nanda interposed very simply and gravely, "I don't think we're likely to get anything."

"Oh, Harold's talk," Vanderbank protested, "offers, I think, an extraordinary interest; only I'm bound to say it crushes me to the earth. I've to make at least, as I listen to him, a big effort to bear up. It doesn't seem long ago," he pursued to his young friend, "that I used to feel I was in it; but the way you bring home to me, dreadful youth, that I'm already *not*——!"

Harold looked earnest to understand. "The hungry generations tread you down—is that it?"

Vanderbank gave a pleasant tragic head-shake. "We speak a different language."

"Ah, but I think I perfectly understand yours!"

"That's just my anguish—and your advantage. It's awfully curious," Vanderbank went on to Nanda, "but I feel as if I must figure to him, you know, very much as Mr. Longdon figures to me. Mr. Longdon doesn't somehow get into me. Yet I do, I think, into him. But we don't matter!"

"'We'?"—Nanda, with her eyes on him, echoed it.

"Mr. Longdon and I. It can't be helped, I suppose," he went on, for Tishy, with sociable sadness, "but it *is* short innings."

Mrs. Grendon, who was clearly credulous, looked positively frightened. "Ah but, my dear, thank you! I haven't begun to *live*."

"Well, *I* have—that's just where it is," said Harold. "Thank you all the more, old Van, for the tip."

There was an announcement just now at the door, and Tishy turned to meet the Duchess, with Harold, almost as if he had been master of the house, figuring but a step behind her. "Don't mind *her*," Vanderbank immediately said to the companion with whom he was left, "but tell me, while I still have hold of you, who wrote my name on the French novel that I noticed a few minutes since in the other room?"

Nanda at first only wondered. "If it's there—didn't *you*?"

He just hesitated. "If it were here you would see if it's my hand."

Nanda faltered, and for somewhat longer. "How should I see? What do I know of your hand?"

He looked at her hard. "You *have* seen it."

"Oh—so little!" she replied with a faint smile.

"Do you mean I've not written to you for so long? Surely I did in—when was it?"

"Yes, when? But why *should* you?" she asked in quite a different tone.

He was not prepared on this with the right statement, and what he did after a moment bring out had for the occasion a little the sound of the wrong. "The beauty of *you* is that you're too good; which, for me, is but another way of saying you're too clever. You make no demands. You let things go. You don't allow in particular for the human weakness that enjoys an occasional glimpse of the weakness of others."

She had deeply attended to him. "You mean perhaps one doesn't show enough what one wants?"

"I think that must be it. You're so fiendishly proud."

She appeared again to wonder. "Not too much so, at any rate, only to want from *you*—"

"Well, what?"

"Why, what's pleasant for yourself," she simply said.

"Oh dear, that's poor bliss!" he declared. "How does it come then," he next said, "that, with this barrenness of our intercourse, I know so well *your* hand?"

A series of announcements had meanwhile been made, with guests arriving to match them, and Nanda's eyes at this moment engaged themselves with Mr. Longdon and her mother, who entered the room together. When she looked back to her companion she had had time to drop a consciousness of his question. "If I'm proud, to you, I'm not good," she said, "and if I'm good—always to you—I'm not proud. I know at all events perfectly how immensely you're occupied, what a quantity of work you get through and how every minute, for you, counts. Don't make it a crime to me that I'm reasonable."

"No, that would show, wouldn't it? that there isn't much else. But how it all comes back——!"

"Well, to what?" she asked.

"To the old story. You know how I'm occupied. You know how I work. You know how I manage my time."

"Oh, I see," said Nanda. "It *is* my knowing, after all, everything."

"Everything. The book I just mentioned is one that, months ago—I remember now—I lent to your mother."

"Oh, a thing in a blue cover? I remember then too." Nanda's face cleared up. "I had forgotten it was lying about here, but I must have brought it—in fact, I remember I did —for Tishy. And I wrote your name on it so that we might know——"

"That I hadn't lent it to either of you? It didn't occur to you to write your own?" Vanderbank went on.

"Well, but if it isn't mine? It *isn't* mine, I'm sure."

"Therefore, also, if it can't be Tishy's——"

"It's simple enough—it's mother's."

"'Simple'?" Vanderbank laughed. "I like you! And may I ask if you've read the remarkable work?"

"Oh yes." Then she wonderfully said: "For Tishy."

"Too see if it would do?"

"I've often done that," the girl returned.

"And she takes your word?"

"Generally. I think I remember she did that time."

"And read the confounded thing?"

"Oh no!" said Nanda.

He looked at her a moment longer. "You're too particular!" he rather oddly sounded, turning away with it to meet Mr. Longdon.

XXVIII

When after dinner the company was restored to the upper rooms, the Duchess was on her feet as soon as the door opened for the entrance of the gentlemen. Then it might have been seen that she had a purpose, for as soon as the elements had again, with a due amount of the usual shuffling and mismatching, been mixed, her case proved the first to have been settled. She had got Mr. Longdon beside her on a sofa that was just right for two. "I've seized you without a scruple," she frankly said, "for there are things I want to say to you as well as very particularly to ask. More than anything else of course I want again to thank you."

No collapse of Mr. Longdon's was ever incompatible with his sitting well forward. "'Again'?"

"Do you look so blank," she demanded, "because you've really forgotten the gratitude I expressed to you when you were so good as to bring Nanda up for Aggie's marriage?—or because you don't think it a matter I should trouble myself to return to? How can I help it," she went on without waiting for his answer, "if I see your hand in everything that has happened since the so interesting talk I had with you last summer at Mertle? There have been times when I've really thought of writing to you; I've even had a bold bad idea of proposing myself to you for a Sunday. Then the crisis, my momentary alarm, has struck me as blowing over, and I've felt I could wait for some luck like this, which would sooner or later come." Her companion, however, appeared to leave the luck so on her hands that she could only snatch up, to cover its nudity, the next handsomest assumption. "I see you cleverly guess that what I've been worried about is the effect on Mrs. Brook of the loss of her dear Mitchy. If you've not at all events had your own impression of this effect, isn't that only because these last months you've seen so little of her? *I've* seen," said the Duchess, "enough and to spare." She waited as if for her vision, on this, to be flashed back at her, but the only result of her speech was that her friend looked hard at somebody else. It was just this symptom indeed that perhaps sufficed her, for in a minute she was again afloat. "Things have turned out so much as *I* desire them that I should really feel wicked not to have a humble heart. There's a quarter indeed," she added with a noble unction, "to which I don't fear to say for myself that no day and no night pass without my showing it. However, you English, I know, don't like one to speak of one's religion. I'm just as simply thankful for mine—I mean with as little sense of indecency or agony about it—as I am for my health or my carriage. My point is at any rate that I say in no cruel spirit of triumph, yet do none the less very distinctly say, that Mr. Mitchett's disgusted patroness may be now to be feared." These words had the sound of a climax, and she had brought them out as if, with her duty done, to leave them; but something that took place, for her eye, in the face Mr. Longdon had half averted gave her after an instant what he might have called her second wind. "Oh, I know you think she always *has* been! But you've exaggerated—as to that; and I don't say that even at present it's anything we shan't get the better of. Only we must keep our heads. We must remember that from her own point of view she has her grievance, and we must at least look as if we trusted her. That, you know, is what you've never quite done."

Mr. Longdon gave out a murmur of discomfort which produced in him a change of position, and the sequel to the change was that he presently accepted from his cushioned angle of the sofa the definite support it could offer. If his eyes moreover had not met his companion's they had been brought by the hand he repeatedly and somewhat distressfully passed over them closer to the question of which of the alien objects presented to his choice it would cost him least to profess to handle. What he had already paid, a spectator would easily have gathered from the long, suppressed wriggle that had ended in his falling back, was some sacrifice of his habit of not privately depreciating those to whom he was publicly civil. It was plain, however, that when he presently spoke his thought had taken a stretch. "I'm sure I've fully intended to be everything that's proper. But I don't think Mr. Vanderbank cares for her."

It kindled in the Duchess an immediate light. "*Vous avez bien de l'esprit.* You put one at one's ease. I've been vaguely groping, while you're already there. It's really only for Nanda he cares?"

"Yes—really."

The Duchess hesitated. "And yet exactly how much?"

"I haven't asked him."

She had another, but a briefer pause. "Don't you think it about time you *should?*" Once more she waited, then seemed to feel that her opportunity wouldn't. "We've worked a bit together, but you don't take me into your confidence. I dare say you don't believe I'm quite straight. Don't you really see how I *must* be?" She had a pleading note which made him at last fix her. "Don't you see," she went on with the advantage of it, "that, having got all I want for myself, I haven't a motive in the world for spoiling the fun of another? I don't want in the least, I assure you, to spoil even Mrs. Brook's; for how will she get a bit less out of him—I mean than she does now —if what you desire *should* take place? Honestly, my dear man, that's quite what *I* desire, and I only want, over and above, to help you. What I feel for Nanda, believe me, is pure pity. I won't say I'm frantically grateful to her, because in the long run—one way or another—she'll have found her account. It nevertheless worries me to see her, and all the more because of this very certitude, which you've so kindly just settled for me, that our young man hasn't really with her mother——"

Whatever the certitude Mr. Longdon had kindly settled, it was in another interest that he at this moment broke in. "Is he *your* young man too?"

She was not too much amused to cast about her. "Aren't such marked ornaments of life a little the property of all who admire and enjoy them?"

"You 'enjoy' him?" Mr. Longdon asked in the same straightforward way.

"Immensely."

His silence for a little seemed the sign of a plan. "What is it he hasn't done with Mrs. Brook?"

"Well, the thing that *would* be the complication. He hasn't gone beyond a certain point. You may ask how one knows such matters, but I'm afraid I've not quite a receipt for it. A woman knows, but she can't tell. They haven't done, as it's called, anything wrong."

Mr. Longdon frowned. "It would be extremely horrid if they had."

"Ah but, for you and me who know life it isn't *that* that— if other things had made for it—would have prevented! As it happens, however, we've got off easily. She doesn't speak to him——!"

She had forms he could only take up. "'Speak' to him——?"

"Why, as much as she would have liked to be able to believe."

"Then where's the danger of which you appear to wish to warn me?"

"Just in her feeling in the case as most women would feel. You see she did what she could for her daughter. She did, I'm bound to say, as that sort of thing goes among you people, a good deal. She treasured up, she nursed along Mitchy, whom she would also, though of course not so much, have liked herself. Nanda with a word could have kept him on, becoming thereby for *your* plan so much the less accessible. That would have thoroughly obliged her mother, but your little English girls, in these altered times—oh, I know how you feel them!—don't stand on such trifles; and—even if you think it odd of me—I can't defend myself, though I've so directly profited, against a certain compassion also for Mrs. Brook's upset. As a good-natured woman I feel in short for both of them; I deplore all round what's after all rather a sad relation. Only, as I tell you, Nanda's the one, I naturally say to myself, for me now most to think of: if I don't assume too much, that is, that you don't suffer by my freedom."

Mr. Longdon put by with a mere drop of his eyes the question of his suffering: there was so clearly for him an issue more relevant. "What do you know of my 'plan'?"

"Why, my dear man, haven't I told you that ever since Mertle I've made out your hand? What on earth for other people can your action look like but an adoption?"

"Of—a—*him*?"

"You're delightful. Of—a—*her*! If it does come to the same thing for you, so much the better. That at any rate is what we're all taking it for, and Mrs. Brook herself *en tête*. She sees —through your generosity—Nanda's life, more or less, at the worst, arranged for, and that's just what gives her a good conscience."

If Mr. Longdon breathed rather hard it seemed to show at least that he followed. "What does she want of a good conscience?"

From under her high tiara an instant she almost looked down at him. "Ah, you do hate her!"

He coloured, but held his ground. "Don't you tell me yourself she's to be feared?"

"Yes, and watched. But—if possible—with amusement."

"Amusement?" Mr. Longdon faintly gasped.

"Look at her now," his friend went on with an indication that was indeed easy to embrace. Separated from them by the width of the room, Mrs. Brook was, though placed in profile, fully presented; the satisfaction with which she had lately sunk upon a light gilt chair marked itself as superficial and was moreover visibly not confirmed by the fact that Vanderbank's high-perched head, arrested before her in a general survey of opportunity, gave her eyes in conversation too prayerful a flight. Their companions were dispersed, some in the other room, and for the occupants of the Duchess's sofa they made, as a couple in communion, a picture, framed and detached, vaguely reduplicated in the high polish of the French floor. "She *is* tremendously pretty." The Duchess appeared to drop this as a plea for indulgence and to be impelled in fact by the interlocutor's silence to carry it further. "I've never at all thought, you know, that Nanda touches her."

Mr. Longdon demurred. "Do you mean for beauty?"

His friend, for his simplicity, discriminated. "Ah, they've neither of them 'beauty.' That's not a word to make free with. But the mother has grace."

"And the daughter hasn't?"

"Not a line. You answer me of course when I say *that*, with your adored Lady Julia, and will want to know what then becomes of the lucky resemblance. I quite grant you that Lady Julia must have had the thing we speak of. But that dear sweet blessed thing is very much the same lost secret as the dear sweet blessed *other* thing that went away with it— the decent leisure that, for the most part, we've also seen the last of. It's the thing at any rate that poor Nanda and all her kind have most effectually got rid of. Oh, if you'd trust me a little more you'd see that I'm quite at one with you on all the changes for the worse. I bear up, but I'm old enough to have known. All the same Mrs. Brook has something—say what you like—when she bends that little brown head. *Dieu sait comme elle se coiffe*, but what she gets out of it! Only look."

Mr. Longdon conveyed in an indescribable manner that he had retired to a great distance; yet even from this position he must have launched a glance that arrived at a middle way. "They both know you're watching them."

"And don't they know *you* are? Poor Mr. Van has a consciousness!"

"So should I if two terrible women——"

"Were admiring you both at once?" The Duchess folded the big feathered fan that had partly protected their range. "Well *she*, poor dear, can't help it. She wants him herself."

At the drop of the Duchess's fan he restored his nippers. "And he doesn't—not a bit—want *her*!"

"There it is. She has put down her money, as it were, without a return. She has given Mitchy up and got nothing instead."

There was delicacy, yet there was distinctness, in Mr. Longdon's reserve. "Do you call *me* nothing?"

The Duchess at this fairly swelled with her happy stare. "Then it *is* an adoption?" She forbore to press, however; she only went on: "It isn't a question, my dear man, of what *I* call it. *You* don't make love to her."

"Dear me," said Mr. Longdon, "what would she have had?"

"That could be more charming, you mean, than your famous 'loyalty'? Oh, *caro mio*, she wants it straighter! But I shock you," his companion quickly added.

The manner in which he firmly rose was scarce a denial; yet he stood for a moment in place. "What after all can she do?"

"She can *keep* Mr. Van."

Mr. Longdon wondered. "Where?"

"I mean till it's too late. She can work on him."

"But how?"

Covertly again the Duchess had followed the effect of her friend's perceived movement on Mrs. Brook, who also got up. She gave a rap with her fan on his leg. "Sit down—you'll see."

XXIX

He mechanically obeyed her, though it happened to lend him the air of taking Mrs. Brook's approach for a signal to resume his seat. She came over to them, Vanderbank followed, and it was without again moving, with a vague upward gape in fact from his place, that Mr. Longdon received as she stood before him a challenge of a sort to flash a point into what the Duchess had just said. "Why do you hate me so?"

Vanderbank, who, beside Mrs. Brook, looked at him with attention, might have suspected him of turning a trifle pale; though even Vanderbank, with reasons of his own for an observation of the sharpest, could scarce have read into the matter the particular dim vision that would have accounted for it —the flicker of fear of what Mrs. Brook, whether as daughter or as mother, was at last so strangely and differently to show herself.

"I should warn you, sir," the young man threw off, "that we don't consider that—in Buckingham Crescent certainly— a fair question. It isn't playing the game—it's hitting below the belt. We hate and we love—the latter especially—but to tell each other why is to break that little tacit rule of finding out for ourselves which is the delight of our lives and the source of our triumphs. You can say, you know, if you like, but you're not obliged."

Mr. Longdon transferred to him something of the same colder apprehension, looking at him manifestly harder than ever before and finding in his eyes also no doubt a consciousness more charged. He presently got up, but, without answering Vanderbank, fixed again Mrs. Brook, to whom he echoed without expression: "Hate you?"

The next moment, while he remained in presence with Vanderbank, Mrs. Brook was pointing out her meaning to him from the cushioned corner he had quitted. "Why, when you come back to town you come straight, as it were, here."

"Ah, what's that," the Duchess asked in his interest, "but to follow Nanda as closely as possible, or at any rate to keep well with her?"

Mrs. Brook however had no ear for this plea. "And when I, coming here too and thinking only of my chance to 'meet' you, do my very sweetest to catch your eye, you're entirely given up——"

"To trying of course," the Duchess broke in afresh, "to keep well with *me*!"

Mrs. Brook now had a smile for her. "Ah, that takes precautions then that *I* shall perhaps fail of if I too much interrupt your conversation."

"Isn't she nice to me," the Duchess asked of Mr. Longdon, "when I was in the very act of praising her to the skies?"

Their interlocutor's reply was not too rapid to anticipate Mrs. Brook herself. "My dear Jane, that only proves that he had reached some extravagance in the other sense that you had in mere decency to match. The truth is probably in the 'mean'—isn't that what they call it?—between you. Don't *you* now take him away," she went on to Vanderbank, who had glanced about for some better accommodation.

He immediately pushed forward the nearest chair, which happened to be by the Duchess's side of the sofa. "Will you sit here, sir?"

"If you'll stay to protect me."

"That was really what I brought him over to you for," Mrs.

Brook said while Mr. Longdon took his place and Vanderbank looked out for another seat. "But I didn't know," she observed with her sweet, free curiosity, "that he called you 'sir.'" She often made discoveries that were fairly childlike. "He has done it twice."

"Isn't that only your inevitable English surprise," the Duchess demanded, "at the civility quite the commonest in other societies?—so that one has to come here to find it regarded, in the way of ceremony, as the very end of the world!"

"Oh," Mr. Longdon remarked, "it's a word I rather like myself even to employ to others."

"I always ask here," the Duchess continued to him, "what word they've got instead. And do you know what they tell me?"

Mrs. Brook wondered, then again, before he was ready, charmingly suggested: "Our pretty manner?" Quickly too she appealed to Mr. Longdon. "Is *that* what you miss from me?"

He wondered however more than Mrs. Brook. "Your 'pretty manner'?"

"Well, these grand old forms that the Duchess is such a mistress of." Mrs. Brook had with this one of her eagerest visions. "Did mamma say 'sir' to you? Ought *I*? Do you really get it, in private, out of Nanda? *She* has such depths of discretion," she explained to the Duchess and to Vanderbank, who had come back with his chair, "that it's just the kind of illustrative anecdote she never in the world gives me."

Mr. Longdon looked across at Van, placed now, after a moment's talk with Tishy in sight of them all, by Mrs. Brook's arm of the sofa. "You haven't protected—you've only exposed me."

"Oh, there's no joy without danger"—Mrs. Brook took it up with spirit. "Perhaps one should even say there's no danger without joy."

Vanderbank's eyes had followed Mrs. Grendon after his brief passage with her, terminated by some need of her listless presence on the other side of the room. "What do you say then, on that theory, to the extraordinary gloom of our hostess? Her safety, by such a rule, must be deep."

The Duchess was this time the first to know what they said.

"The expression of Tishy's face comes precisely from our comparing it so unfavourably with that of her poor sister Carrie, who, though she isn't here to-night with the Cashmores—amazing enough even as coming *without* that!—has so often shown us that an *âme en peine*, constantly tottering, but, as Nanda guarantees us, usually recovering, may look after all as beatific as a Dutch doll."

Mrs. Brook's eyes had, on Tishy's passing away, taken the same course as Vanderbank's, whom she had visibly not neglected moreover while the pair stood there. "I give you Carrie, as you know, and I throw Mr. Cashmore in; but I'm lost in admiration to-night, as I always have been, at the way Tishy makes her ugliness serve. I should call it, if the word weren't so for ladies'-maids, the most 'elegant' thing I know."

"My dear child," the Duchess objected, "what you describe as making her ugliness serve is what I should describe as concealing none of her beauty. There's nothing the matter surely with 'elegant' as applied to Tishy save that as commonly used it refers rather to a charm that's artificial than to a state of pure nature. There should be for elegance a basis of clothing. Nanda rather stints her."

Mrs. Brook, perhaps more than usually thoughtful, just discriminated. "There *is*, I think, one little place. I'll speak to her."

"To Tishy?" Vanderbank asked.

"Oh, *that* would do no good. To Nanda. All the same," she continued, "it's an awfully superficial thing of you not to see that her dreariness—on which moreover I've set you right before—is a mere facial accident and doesn't correspond or, as they say, 'rhyme' to anything within her that might make it a little interesting. What I like it for is just that it's so funny in itself. Her low spirits are nothing more than her features. Her gloom, as you call it, is merely her broken nose."

"*Has* she a broken nose?" Mr. Longdon demanded with an accent that for some reason touched in the others the spring of laughter.

"Has Nanda never mentioned it?" Mrs. Brook inquired with this gaiety.

"That's the discretion you just spoke of," said the Duchess.

"Only I should have expected from the cause you refer to rather the comic effect."

"Mrs. Grendon's broken nose, sir," Vanderbank explained to Mr. Longdon, "is only the kinder way taken by these ladies to speak of Mrs. Grendon's broken heart. You must know all about that."

"Oh yes—*all*." Mr. Longdon spoke very simply, with the consequence this time, on the part of his companions, of a silence of some minutes, which he himself had at last to break. "Mr. Grendon doesn't like her." The addition of these words apparently made the difference—as if they constituted a fresh link with the irresistible comedy of things. That he was unexpectedly diverting was, however, no check to Mr. Longdon's delivering his full thought. "Very horrid of two sisters to be both, in their marriages, so wretched."

"Ah, but Tishy, I maintain," Mrs. Brook returned, "*isn't* wretched at all. If I were satisfied that she's really so I would never let Nanda come to her."

"That's the most extraordinary doctrine, love," the Duchess interposed. "When you're satisfied a woman's 'really' poor you never give her a crust?"

"Do you call Nanda a crust, Duchess?" Vanderbank amusedly asked.

"She's all at any rate, apparently, just now, that poor Tishy has to live on."

"You're severe then," the young man said, "on our dinner of to-night."

"Oh, Jane," Mrs. Brook declared, "is never severe: she's only uncontrollably witty. It's only Tishy moreover who gives out that her husband doesn't like her. *He*, poor man, doesn't say anything of the sort."

"Yes, but after all you know"—Vanderbank just put it to her—"where the deuce, all the while, *is* he?"

"Heaven forbid," the Duchess remarked, "that we should too indiscreetly inquire."

"There it is—exactly," Mr. Longdon subjoined.

He had once more his success of hilarity, though not indeed to the injury of the Duchess's next word. "It's Nanda, you know, who speaks, and loud enough, for Harry Grendon's dislikes."

"That's easy for her," Mrs. Brook declared, "when she herself isn't one of them."

"She isn't surely one of anybody's," Mr. Longdon gravely observed.

Mrs. Brook gazed across at him. "You *are* too dear! But I've none the less a crow to pick with you."

Mr. Longdon returned her look, but returned it somehow to Van. "You frighten me, you know, out of my wits."

"*I* do?" said Vanderbank.

Mr. Longdon just hesitated. "Yes."

"It must be the sacred terror," Mrs. Brook suggested to Van, "that Mitchy so often speaks of. *I'm* not trying with you," she went on to Mr. Longdon, "for anything of that kind, but only for the short half-hour in private that I think you won't for the world grant me. Nothing will induce you to find yourself alone with me."

"Why, what on earth," Vanderbank asked, "do you suspect him of supposing you want to do?"

"Oh, it isn't *that*," Mrs. Brook sadly said.

"It isn't what?" laughed the Duchess.

"That he fears I may want in any way to—what do you call it?—make up to him." She spoke as if she only wished it had been. "He has a deeper thought."

"Well then, what in goodness is it?"

Mr. Longdon had said nothing more, but Mrs. Brook preferred none the less to treat the question as between themselves. She *was*, as the others said, wonderful. "You can't help thinking me"—she spoke to him straight—"rather tortuous." The pause she thus momentarily produced was so intense as to give a sharpness that was almost vulgar to the little "Oh!" by which it was presently broken and the source of which neither of her three companions could afterwards in the least have named. Neither would have endeavoured to fix an indecency of which each doubtless had been but too capable. "It's only as a mother," she added, "that I want my chance."

But the Duchess at this was again in the breach. "Take it, for mercy's sake then, my dear, over Harold, who's an example to Nanda herself in the way that, behind the piano there, he's keeping it up with Lady Fanny."

If this had been a herring that, in the interest of peace, the Duchess had wished to draw across the scent, it could scarce have been more effective. Mrs. Brook, whose position had made just the difference that she lost the view of the other side of the piano, took a slight but immediate stretch. "*Is* Harold with Lady Fanny?"

"You ask it, my dear child," said the Duchess, "as if it were too grand to be believed. It's the note of eagerness," she went on for Mr. Longdon's benefit—"it's almost the note of hope: one of those that *ces messieurs*, that we all in fact delight in and find so matchless. She desires for Harold the highest advantages."

"Well then," declared Vanderbank, who had achieved a glimpse, "he's clearly having them. It brings home to one his success."

"His success is true," Mrs. Brook insisted. "How he does it I don't know."

"Oh *don't* you?" trumpeted the Duchess.

"He's amazing," Mrs. Brook pursued. "I watch—I hold my breath. But I'm bound to say also I rather admire. He somehow amuses them."

"She's as pleased as Punch," said the Duchess.

"Those great calm women—they like slighter creatures."

"The great calm whales," the Duchess laughed, "swallow the little fishes."

"Oh, my dear," Mrs. Brook returned, "Harold can be tasted, if you like——"

"If *I* like?" the Duchess parenthetically jeered. "Thank you, love!"

"But he can't, I think, be eaten. It all works out," Mrs. Brook expounded, "to the highest end. If Lady Fanny's amused she'll be quiet."

"Bless me," cried the Duchess, "of all the immoral speeches—! I put it to you, Longdon. Does she mean"—she appealed to their friend—"that if she commits murder she won't commit anything else?"

"Oh, it won't be murder," said Mrs. Brook. "I mean that if Harold, in one way and another, keeps her along, she won't get off."

"Off where?" Mr. Longdon inquired.

Vanderbank immediately informed him. "To one of the smaller Italian towns. Don't you know?"

"Oh yes. Like—who is it? I forget."

"Anna Karénine? You know about Anna?"

"Nanda," said the Duchess, "has told him. But I thought," she went on to Mrs. Brook, "that Lady Fanny, by this time, *must* have gone."

"Petherton then," Mrs. Brook returned, "doesn't keep you *au courant?*"

The Duchess blandly wondered. "I seem to remember he had positively said so. And that she had come back."

"Because this looks so like a fresh start? No. *We* know. You assume besides," Mrs. Brook asked, "that Mr. Cashmore would have received her again?"

The Duchess fixed a little that gentleman and his actual companion. "What will you have? He mightn't have noticed."

"Oh, you're out of step, Duchess," Vanderbank said. "We used all to march abreast, but we're falling to pieces. It's all, saving your presence, Mitchy's marriage."

"Ah," Mrs. Brook concurred, "how thoroughly I feel that! Oh, I knew. The spell's broken; the harp has lost a string. We're not the same thing. *He's* not the same thing."

"Frankly, my dear," the Duchess answered, "I don't think that you personally are either."

"Oh, as for that—which is what matters least—we shall perhaps see." With which Mrs. Brook turned again to Mr. Longdon. "I haven't explained to you what I meant just now. We want Nanda."

Mr. Longdon stared. "At home again?"

"In her little old nook. You must give her back."

"Do you mean altogether?"

"Ah, that will be for you in a manner to arrange. But you've had her practically these five months, and, with no desire to be unreasonable, we yet have our natural feelings."

This interchange, to which circumstances somehow gave a high effect of suddenness and strangeness, was listened to by the others in a quick silence that was like the sense of a blast of cold air, though with the difference between the spectators that Vanderbank attached his eyes hard to Mrs. Brook and that the Duchess looked as straight at Mr. Longdon, to whom clearly she wished to convey that if he had wondered a short time before how Mrs. Brook would do it he must now be quite at his ease. He indulged in fact, after this lady's last words, in a pause that might have signified some of the fulness of a new light. He only said very quietly: "I thought you liked it."

At this his neighbour broke in. "The care you take of the child? They *do*!" The Duchess as she spoke, became aware of the nearer presence of Edward Brookenham, who within a minute had come in from the other room; and the determination of her character leaped forth in her quick signal to him. "Edward will tell you." He was already before their semicircle. "*Do* you, dear," she appealed, "want Nanda back from Mr. Longdon?"

Edward plainly could be trusted to feel in his quiet way that the oracle must be a match for the priestess. "'Want' her, Jane? We wouldn't *take* her." As if knowing quite what he was about he looked at his wife only after he had spoken.

XXX

His reply had complete success, to which there could scarce have afterwards been a positive denial that some sound of amusement even from Mr. Longdon himself had in its degree contributed. Certain it was that Mrs. Brook found, as she exclaimed that her husband was always so awfully civil, just the right note of resigned understanding; whereupon he for a minute presented to them blankly enough his fine dead face. "'Civil' is just what I was afraid I wasn't. I mean, you know," he continued to Mr. Longdon, "that you really mustn't look to us to let you off——"

"From a week or a day"—Mr. Longdon took him up—"of the time to which you consider I've pledged myself? My dear sir, please don't imagine it's for *me* the Duchess appeals."

"It's from your wife, you delicious dull man," that lady elucidated. "If you wished to be stiff with our friend here you've really been so with *her*; which comes, no doubt, from the absence between you of proper preconcerted action. You spoke without your cue."

"Oh!" said Edward Brookenham.

"That's it, Jane"—Mrs. Brook continued to take it beautifully. "We dressed to-day in a hurry and hadn't time for our usual rehearsal. Edward, when we dine out, generally brings three pocket-handkerchiefs and six jokes. I leave the management of the handkerchiefs to his own taste, but we mostly try together in advance to arrange a career for the other things. It's some charming light thing of my own that's supposed to give him the sign."

"Only sometimes he confounds"—Vanderbank helped her out—"your light and your heavy!" He had got up to make room for his host of so many occasions and, having forced him into the empty chair, now moved vaguely off to the quarter of the room occupied by Nanda and Mr. Cashmore.

"That's very well," the Duchess resumed, "but it doesn't at all clear you, *cara mia*, of the misdemeanour of setting up as a felt domestic need something of which Edward proves deeply unconscious. He has put his finger on Nanda's true interest. He doesn't care a bit how it would *look* for you to want her."

"Don't you mean rather, Jane, how it looks for us *not* to want her?" Mrs. Brook inquired with a detachment now complete. "Of course, dear old friend," she continued to Mr. Longdon, "she quite puts me with my back to the wall when she helps you to see—what you otherwise mightn't guess—that Edward and I work it out between us to show off as tender parents and yet to get from you everything you'll give. I do the sentimental and he the practical; so that we, in one way and another, deck ourselves in the glory of our sacrifice without forfeiting the 'keep' of our daughter. This must appeal to you as another useful illustration of what London manners have come to; unless indeed," Mrs. Brook prattled on, "it only strikes you still more—and to a degree that blinds you to its other possible bearings—as the last proof that I'm too tortuous for you to know what I'd be at!"

Mr. Longdon faced her, across his interval, with his original terror represented now only by such a lingering flush as might have formed a natural tribute to a brilliant scene. "I haven't the glimmering of an idea of what you'd be at. But please understand," he added, "that I don't at all refuse you the private half-hour you referred to a while since."

"Are you really willing to put the child up for the rest of the year?" Edward placidly demanded, speaking as if quite unaware that anything else had been said.

His wife fixed her eyes on him. "The ingenuity of your companions, love, plays in the air like the lightning, but flashes round your head only, by good fortune, to leave it unscathed. Still, you have after all your own strange wit, and I'm not sure that any of ours ever compares with it. Only, confronted also with ours, how can poor Mr. Longdon really choose which of the two he'll meet?"

Poor Mr. Longdon now looked hard at Edward. "Oh, Mr. Brookenham's, I feel, any day. It's even with *you*, I confess," he said to him, "that I'd rather have that private half-hour."

"Done!" Mrs. Brook declared. "I'll send him to you. But we *have*, you know, as Van says, gone to pieces," she went on, twisting her pretty head and tossing it back over her shoulder to an auditor of whose approach to her from behind, though it was impossible she should have seen him, she had visibly within a minute become aware. "It's your marriage, Mitchy, that has darkened our old, bright air, changed us more than we even yet know, and most grossly and horribly, my dear man, changed *you*. You steal up in a way that gives one the creeps, whereas in the good time that's gone you always burst in with music and song. Go round where I can see you: I mayn't love you now, but at least, I suppose, I may look at you. Direct your energies," she pursued while Mitchy obeyed her, "as much as possible, please, against our uncanny chill. Pile on the fire and close up the ranks; this *was* our best hour, you know—and all the more that Tishy, I see, is getting rid of her superfluities. Here comes back old Van," she wound up, "vanquished, I judge, in the attempt to divert Nanda from her prey. Won't Nanda sit with poor *us*?" she asked of Vanderbank, who now, meeting Mitchy in range of the others, remained standing with him and as at her commands.

"I didn't of course ask her," the young man replied.

"Then what did you do?"

"I only took a little walk."

Mrs. Brook on this was woeful at Mitchy. "See then what we've come to. When did we ever 'walk' in *your* time save as a distinct part of the effect of our good things? Please return to Nanda," she said to Vanderbank, "and tell her I particularly wish her to come in for this delightful evening's end."

"She's joining us of herself now," said the Duchess, "and so is Mr. Cashmore, and so is Tishy—*voyez!*—who has kept on—bless her little bare back!—no one she oughtn't to keep. As nobody else will now arrive it would be quite cosy if she locked the door."

"But what on earth, my dear Jane," Mrs. Brook plaintively wondered, "are you proposing we should do?"

Mrs. Brook, in her apprehension, had looked expressively at their friends, but the eye of the Duchess wandered no further than Harold and Lady Fanny. "It would perhaps serve to keep that pair a little longer from escaping together."

Mrs. Brook took a pause no greater. "But wouldn't it be, as regards another pair, locking the stable door after—what do you call it? Don't Petherton and Aggie appear already to have escaped together? Mitchy, man, where in the world's your wife?"

"I quite grant you," said the Duchess gaily, "that my niece is wherever Petherton is. This I'm sure of, for *there's* a friendship, if you please, that has not been interrupted. Petherton's not gone, is he?" she asked in her turn of Mitchy.

But again, before he could speak, it was taken up. "Mitchy's silent, Mitchy's altered, Mitchy's queer!" Mrs. Brook proclaimed, while the new recruits to the circle, Tishy and Nanda and Mr. Cashmore, Lady Fanny and Harold too after a minute and on perceiving the movement of the others, ended by enlarging it, with mutual accommodation and aid, to a pleasant talkative ring in which the subject of their companion's ejaculation, on a low ottoman and glaring in his odd way in almost all directions at once, formed the conspicuous, attractive centre. Tishy was nearest Mr. Longdon, and Nanda, still flanked by Mr. Cashmore, between that gentleman and his wife, who had Harold on her other side. Edward Brookenham was neighboured by his son and by Vanderbank, who might easily have felt himself, in spite of their separation and given, as it happened, their places in the group, rather publicly confronted with Mr. Longdon. "Is his wife in the other room?" Mrs. Brook now put to Tishy.

Tishy, after a stare about, came back to consciousness to account for this guest. "Oh yes—she's playing with him."

"But with whom, dear?"

"Why, with Petherton. I thought you knew."

"Knew they're playing—?" Mrs. Brook was almost Socratic.

"The Missus is regularly wound up," her husband meanwhile, without resonance, observed to Vanderbank.

"Brilliant indeed!" Vanderbank replied.

"But she's rather naughty, you know," Edward after a pause continued.

"Oh, villainous!" his interlocutor said with a short, smothered laugh that might have represented for a spectator a sudden start at such a flash of analysis from such a quarter.

When Vanderbank's attention at any rate was free again their hostess, assisted to the transition, was describing the play, as she had called it, of the absentees. "She has hidden a book, and he's trying to find it."

"Hide and seek? Why, isn't it innocent, Mitch!" Mrs. Brook exclaimed.

Mitchy, speaking for the first time, faced her with extravagant gloom. "Do you really think so?"

"That's *her* innocence!" the Duchess laughed to him.

"And don't you suppose he has found it *yet*?" Mrs. Brook pursued earnestly to Tishy. "Isn't it something we might *all* play at if—?" On which however, abruptly checking herself, she changed her note. "Nanda, love, please go and invite them to join us."

Mitchy, at this, on his ottoman, wheeled straight round to the girl, who looked at him before speaking. "I'll go if Mitchy tells me."

"But if he does fear," said her mother, "that there may be something in it——?"

Mitchy jerked back to Mrs. Brook. "Well, you see, I don't want to give way to my fear. Suppose there *should* be something! Let me not know."

She met him tenderly. "I see. You couldn't—so soon—bear it."

"Ah but, *savez-vous*," the Duchess interposed with some majesty, "you're horrid!"

"Let them alone," Mitchy continued. "We don't want at all events a general romp."

"Oh, I thought just that," said Mrs. Brook, "was what the Duchess wished the door locked for! Perhaps moreover"—she returned to Tishy—"he has not yet found the book."

"He can't," Tishy said with simplicity.

"But why in the world——?"

"You see she's sitting on it"—Tishy felt, it was plain, the responsibility of explanation. "So that unless he pulls her off——"

"He can't compass his desperate end? Ah, I hope he won't pull her off!" Mrs. Brook wonderfully murmured. It was said in a manner that stirred the circle, and unanimous laughter seemed already to have crowned her invocation, lately uttered, to the social spirit. "But what in the world," she pursued, "is the book selected for such a position? I hope it's not a very big one."

"Oh, aren't the books that are sat upon," Mr. Cashmore freely inquired, "as a matter of course the bad ones?"

"Not a bit as a matter of course," Harold as freely replied to him. "They sit, all round, nowadays—I mean in the papers and places—on some awfully good stuff. Why, I myself read books that I couldn't—upon my honour I wouldn't risk it!—read out to you here."

"What a pity," his father dropped with the special shade of dryness that was all Edward's own, "that you haven't got one of your favourites to try on us!"

Harold looked about as if it might have been after all a happy thought. "Well, Nanda's the only girl."

"And one's sister doesn't count," said the Duchess.

"It's just because the thing's bad," Tishy resumed for Mrs. Brook's more particular benefit, "that Lord Petherton is trying to wrest it."

Mrs. Brook's pale interest deepened. "Then it's a real hand-to-hand struggle?"

"He says she shan't read it—she says she will."

"Ah, that's because—isn't it, Jane?" Mrs. Brook appealed—"he so long overlooked and advised her in those matters.

Doesn't he feel by this time—so awfully clever as he is—the extraordinary way she has come out?"

"'By this time'?" Harold echoed. "Dearest mummy, you're too sweet. It's only about ten weeks—isn't it, Mitch? You don't mind my saying that, I hope," he solicitously added.

Mitchy had his back to him and, bending it a little, sat with head dropped and knees pressing his hands together. "I don't mind any one's saying anything."

"Lord, are you already past that?" Harold sociably laughed.

"He used to vibrate to everything. My dear man, what *is* the matter?" Mrs. Brook demanded. "Does it all move too fast for you?"

"Mercy on us, what *are* you talking about? That's what *I* want to know!" Mr. Cashmore vivaciously declared.

"Well, she *has* gone at a pace—if Mitchy doesn't mind," Harold interposed in the tone of tact and taste. "But then don't they always—I mean when they're like Aggie and they once get loose—go at a pace? That's what *I* want to know. I don't suppose mother did, nor Tishy, nor the Duchess," he communicated to the rest, "but mother and Tishy and the Duchess, it strikes me, must either have been of the school that knew, don't you know? a deuce of a deal before, or of the type that takes it all more quietly after."

"I think a woman can only speak for herself. *I* took it all quietly enough both before and after," said Mrs. Brook. Then she addressed to Mr. Cashmore with a small formal nod one of her lovely wan smiles. "What I'm talking about, *s'il vous plaît*, is marriage."

"I wonder if you know," the Duchess broke out on this, "how silly you all sound! When did it ever, in any society that could call itself decently 'good,' *not* make a difference that an innocent young creature, a flower tended and guarded, should find from one day to the other her whole consciousness changed? People pull long faces and look wonderful looks and punch each other, in your English fashion, in the sides and say to each other in corners that my poor darling has 'come out.' *Je crois bien*, she has come out! I married her —I don't mind saying it now—exactly that she *should*, and I should be mightily ashamed of every one concerned if she hadn't. I didn't marry her, I give you to believe, that she should stay 'in,' and if any of you think to frighten Mitchy with it I imagine you'll do so as little as you frighten *me*. If it has taken her a very short time—as Harold so vividly puts it —to which of you did I ever pretend, I should like to know, that it would take her a very long one? I dare say there are girls it would have taken longer, just as there are certainly others who wouldn't have required so much as an hour. It surely isn't news to you that if some young persons among us all are very stupid and others very wise, *my* dear child was never either, but only perfectly bred and deliciously clever. Ah, *that*—rather! If she's so clever that you don't know what to do with her, it's scarcely *her* fault. But add to it that Mitchy's very kind, and you have the whole thing. What more do you want?"

Mrs. Brook, who looked immensely struck, replied with the promptest sympathy, yet as if there might have been an alternative. "I don't think"—and her eyes appealed to the others —"that we want *any* more, do we? than the whole thing."

"Gracious, I should hope not!" her husband remarked as privately as before to Vanderbank. "Jane—for a mixed company—does go into it."

Vanderbank, for a minute and with a special short arrest, took in the circle. "Should you call us 'mixed'? There's only *one* girl."

Edward Brookenham glanced at his daughter. "Yes, but I wish there were more."

"*Do* you?" And Vanderbank's laugh at this odd view covered, for a little, the rest of the talk. But when he again began to follow no victory had yet been snatched.

It was Mrs. Brook naturally who rattled the standard. "When you say, dearest, that we don't know what to 'do' with Aggie's cleverness, do you quite allow for the way we bow down before it and worship it? I don't quite see what else we—in here—can do with it, even though we *have* gathered that, just over there, Petherton is finding for it a different application. We can only each in our way do our best. Don't therefore succumb, Jane, to the delusive charm of a grievance. There would be nothing in it. You haven't got one. The beauty of the life that so many of us have so long led together"—and she showed that it was for Mr. Longdon she more particularly brought this out—"is precisely that nobody has ever had one. Nobody has dreamed of it—it would have been such a rough, false note, a note of violence out of all keeping. Did *you* ever hear of one, Van? Did you, my poor Mitchy? But you see for yourselves," she wound up with a sigh and before either could answer, "how inferior we've become when we have even in our defence to assert such things."

Mitchy, who for a while past had sat gazing at the floor, now raised his good natural goggles and stretched his closed mouth to its widest. "Oh, I think we're pretty good still!" he then replied.

Mrs. Brook indeed appeared, after a pause and addressing herself again to Tishy, to give a reluctant illustration of it, coming back as from an excursion of the shortest to the question momentarily dropped. "I'm bound to say, all the more you know, that I don't quite see what Aggie mayn't now read." Suddenly, however, her look at their informant took on an anxiety. "Is the book you speak of something *very* awful?"

Mrs. Grendon, with so much these past minutes to have made her so, was at last visibly more present. "That's what Lord Petherton says of it. From what he knows of the author."

"So that he wants to keep her——?"

"Well, from trying it first. I think he wants to see if it's good for her."

"That's one of the most charming cares, I think," the Duchess said, "that a gentleman may render to a young woman to whom he desires to be useful. I won't say that Petherton always knows how good a book may be, but I'd trust him any day to say how bad."

Mr. Longdon, who had sat throughout silent and still, quitted his seat at this and evidently in so doing gave Mrs. Brook as much occasion as she required. She also got up, and her movement brought to her view at the door of the further room something that drew from her a quick exclamation. "He can tell us now, then—for here they come!" Lord Petherton, arriving with animation and followed so swiftly by his young companion that she presented herself as pursuing him, shook triumphantly over his head a small volume in blue paper. There was a general movement at the sight of them, and by the time they had rejoined their friends the company, pushing back seats and causing a variety of mute expression smoothly to circulate, was pretty well on its feet. "See—he *has* pulled her off!" said Mrs. Brook.

Little Aggie, to whom plenty of pearls were singularly becoming, met it as pleasant sympathy. "Yes, and it was a *real* pull. But of course," she continued with the prettiest humour and as if Mrs. Brook would quite understand, "from the moment one has a person's nails, and almost his teeth, in one's flesh——!"

Mrs. Brook's sympathy passed, however, with no great ease from Aggie's pearls to her other charms; fixing the former indeed so markedly that Harold had a quick word about it for Lady Fanny. "When poor mummy thinks, you know, that Nanda might have had them——!"

Lady Fanny's attention, for that matter, had resisted them as little. "Well, I daresay that if I had wanted *I* might!"

"Lord—*could* you have stood him?" the young man returned. "But I believe women can stand anything!" he profoundly concluded. His mother meanwhile, recovering herself, had begun to ejaculate on the prints on Aggie's arms, and he was then diverted from the sense of what he "personally," as he would have said, couldn't have stood, by a glance at Lord Petherton's trophy, for which he made a prompt grab. "The bone of contention?" Lord Petherton had let it go, and Harold remained arrested by the cover. "Why, blest if it hasn't Van's name!"

"Van's?"—his mother was near enough to effect her own snatch, after which she swiftly faced the proprietor of the volume. "Dear man, it's the last thing you lent me! But I don't think," she added, turning to Tishy, "that I ever passed such a production on to *you*."

"It was just seeing Mr. Van's hand," Aggie conscientiously explained, "that made me think one was free——!"

"But it isn't Mr. Van's hand!"—Mrs. Brook quite smiled at the error. She thrust the book straight at Mr. Longdon. "*Is* that Mr. Van's hand?"

Holding the disputed object, which he had put on his nippers to glance at, he presently, without speaking, looked over these aids straight at Nanda, who looked as straight back at him. "It was I who wrote Mr. Van's name." The girl's eyes were on Mr. Longdon, but her words as for the company. "I brought the book here from Buckingham Crescent and left it by accident in the other room."

"By accident, my dear," her mother replied, "I do quite hope. But what on earth did you bring it for? It's too hideous."

Nanda seemed to wonder. "Is it?" she murmured.

"Then you haven't read it?"

She just hesitated. "One hardly knows now, I think, what is and what isn't."

"She brought it only for *me* to read," Tishy gravely interposed.

Mrs. Brook looked strange. "Nanda *recommended* it?"

"Oh no—the contrary." Tishy, as if scared by so much publicity, floundered a little. "She only told me——"

"The awful subject?" Mrs. Brook wailed.

There was so deepening an echo of the drollery of this last passage that it was a minute before Vanderbank could be heard saying: "The responsibility's wholly mine for setting the beastly thing in motion. Still," he added good-humouredly and as if to minimise if not the cause at least the consequence, "I think I agree with Nanda that it's no worse than anything else."

Mrs. Brook had recovered the volume from Mr. Longdon's relaxed hand and now, without another glance at it, held it behind her with an unusual air of firmness. "Oh, how can you say that, my dear man, of anything so revolting?"

The discussion kept them for the instant well face to face. "Then did *you* read it?"

She debated, then jerked the book into the nearest empty chair, where Mr. Cashmore quickly pounced upon it. "Wasn't it for that you brought it me?" she demanded. Yet before he could answer she again challenged her child. "Have you read this work, Nanda?"

"Yes, mamma."

"Oh, I say!" cried Mr. Cashmore, hilarious and turning the leaves.

Mr. Longdon had by this time ceremoniously approached Tishy. "Good-night."

Vanderbank

XXXI

"I THINK then you had better wait," Mrs. Brook said, "till I see if he has gone;" and on the arrival the next moment of the servants with the tea she was able to put her question. "Is Mr. Cashmore still with Miss Brookenham?"

"No, ma'am," the footman replied. "I let Mr. Cashmore out five minutes ago."

Vanderbank showed for the next short time by his behaviour what he felt at not yet being free to take this up; moving pointlessly about the room while the servants arranged the tea-table and taking no trouble to make, for appearance, any other talk. Mrs. Brook, on her side, took so little that the silence—which their temporary companions had all the effect of keeping up by conscious dawdling—became precisely one of those precious lights for the circle belowstairs which people fondly fancy they have not kindled when they have not spoken. But Vanderbank spoke again as soon as the door was closed. "Does he run in and out that way without even speaking to *you?*"

Mrs. Brook turned away from the fire that, late in May, was the only charm of the crude, cold afternoon. "One would like to draw the curtains, wouldn't one? and gossip in the glow of the hearth."

"Oh, 'gossip'!" Vanderbank wearily said as he came to her pretty table.

In the act of serving him she checked herself. "You wouldn't rather have it with *her?*"

He balanced a moment. "Does she have a tea of her own?"

"Do you mean to say you don't know?"—Mrs. Brook asked it with surprise. "Such ignorance of what I do for her does tell, I think, the tale of how you've lately treated us."

"In not coming for so long?"

"For more weeks, for more months than I can count. Scarcely since—when was it?—the end of January, that night of Tishy's dinner."

"Yes, that awful night."

"Awful, you call it?"

"Awful."

"Well, the time without you," Mrs. Brook returned, "has been so bad that I'm afraid I've lost the impression of anything before." Then she offered the tea to his choice. "*Will* you have it upstairs?"

He received the cup. "Yes, and here too." After which he said nothing again till, first pouring in milk to cool it, he had drunk his tea down. "That's not literally true, you know. I *have* been in."

"Yes, but always with other people—you managed it somehow; the wrong ones. It hasn't counted."

"Ah, in one way and another, I think everything counts. And you forget I've dined."

"Oh—for once!"

"The once you asked me. So don't spoil the beauty of your own behaviour by mistimed reflections. You've been, as usual, superior."

"Ah, but there has been no beauty in it. There has been nothing," Mrs. Brook went on, "but bare, bleak recognition, the curse of my hideous intelligence. We've fallen to pieces, and at least I'm not such a fool as not to have felt it in time. From the moment one did feel it why should one insist on vain forms? If *you* felt it, and were so ready to drop them, my part was what it has always been—to accept the inevitable. We shall never grow together again. The smash was too great."

Vanderbank for a little said nothing; then at last: "You ought to know how great!"

Whatever had happened her lovely look here survived it. "I?"

"The smash," he replied, "was indeed as complete, I think, as your intention. Each of the 'pieces' testifies to your success. Five minutes did it."

She appeared to wonder where he was going. "But surely not *my* minutes. Where have you discovered that I made Mitchy's marriage?"

"Mitchy's marriage has nothing to do with it."

"I see." She had the old interest at least still at their service. "You think we might have survived that." A new thought of it seemed to glimmer. "I'm bound to say Mitchy's marriage promises elements."

"You did it that night at Mrs. Grendon's." He spoke as if he had not heard her. "It was a wonderful performance. You pulled us down—just closing with each of the great columns in its turn—as Samson pulled down the temple. I was at the time more or less bruised and buried, and I didn't in the agitation and confusion fully understand what had happened. But I understand now."

"Are you very sure?" Mrs. Brook earnestly asked.

"Well, I'm stupid compared with you, but you see I've taken my time. I've puzzled it out. I've lain awake on it: all the more that I've had to do it all myself—with the Mitchys in Italy and Greece. I've missed his aid."

"You'll have it now," Mrs. Brook kindly said. "They're coming back."

"And when do they arrive?"

"Any day, I believe."

"Has he written you?"

"No," said Mrs. Brook—"there it is. That's just the way we've fallen to pieces. But you'll of course have heard something."

"Never a word."

"Ah then it's complete."

Vanderbank thought a moment. "Not quite, is it?—I mean it won't be altogether unless he hasn't written to Nanda."

"Then *has* he?"—she was keen again.

"Oh, I'm assuming. Don't *you* know?"

"How *should* I?"

This too he turned over. "Just as a consequence of your having, at Tishy's, so abruptly and wonderfully tackled the question that, a few days later as I afterwards gathered, was to be crowned with a measure of success not yet exhausted. Why, in other words—if it was to know so little about her and to get no nearer to her—did you secure Nanda's return?"

There was a clear reason, her face said, if she could only remember it. "Why did I—?" Then as catching a light: "Fancy your asking me—at this time of day!"

"Ah, you *have* noticed that I haven't asked before? However," Van promptly added, "I know well enough what you notice. Nanda hasn't mentioned to you whether or no she has heard?"

"Absolutely not. But you don't suppose, I take it, that it was to pry into her affairs that I called her in."

Vanderbank on this lighted for the first time with a laugh. "'Called her in'? How I like your expressions!"

"I do then, in spite of all," she eagerly asked, "remind you a little of the *bon temps*? Ah," she sighed, "I don't say anything good now. But of course I see Jane—though not so often either. It's from Jane I've heard of what she calls her 'young things.' It seems so odd to think of Mitchy as a young thing. He's as old as all time, and his wife, who the other day was about six, is now practically about forty. And I also saw Petherton," Mrs. Brook added, "on his return."

"His return from where?"

"Why, he was with them at Corfu, Malta, Cyprus—I don't know where; yachting, spending Mitchy's money, 'larking,' he called it—I don't know what. He was with them for weeks."

"Till Jane, you mean, called him in?"

"I think it must have been that."

"Well, that's better," said Van, "than if Mitchy had had to call him out."

"Oh, Mitchy—!" Mrs. Brook comprehensively sounded.

Her visitor quite assented. "Isn't he amazing?"

"Unique."

He had a short pause. "But what's she up to?"

It was apparently for Mrs. Brook a question of such variety of application that she brought out experimentally: "Jane?"

"Dear, no. I think we've fathomed 'Jane,' haven't we?"

"Well," mused Mrs. Brook, "I'm by no means sure that *I* have. Just of late I've had a new sense!"

"Yes, of what now?" Van amusedly put it as she held the note.

"Oh, of depths below depths. But poor Jane—of course after all she's human. She's beside herself with one thing and another, but she can't in any consistency show it. She took her stand so on having with Petherton's aid formed Aggie for a *femme charmante*——"

"That it's too late to cry out that Petherton's aid can now be dispensed with? Do you mean then that he *is* such a brute that after all Mitchy has done for him—?" Vanderbank, at the rising image, pulled up in easy disgust.

"I think him quite capable of considering with a magnificent insolence of selfishness that what Mitchy has *most* done will have been to make Aggie accessible in a way that—for decency and delicacy of course, things on which Petherton highly prides himself—she could naturally *not* be as a girl. Her marriage has simplified it."

Vanderbank took it all in. "'Accessible' is good! Then—which was what I intended just now—Aggie has already become so?"

Mrs. Brook, however, could as yet in fairness only wonder. "That's just what I'm dying to see."

Her companion smiled at it. "'Even in our ashes live their wonted fires!' But what do you make, in such a box, of poor Mitchy himself? His marriage can scarcely to such an extent have simplified *him*."

It was something, none the less, that Mrs. Brook had to weigh. "I don't know. I give it up. The thing was of a strangeness!"

Her friend also paused, and it was as if, for a little, they remained looking at each other over it and over what was unsaid between them. "It *was* 'rum'!" he at last merely dropped.

It was scarce for Mrs. Brook, all the same—she seemed to feel after a moment—to surround the matter with an excess of silence. "He did what a man does—especially in that business—when he doesn't do what he wants."

"Did you mean what somebody else wanted?"

"Well, what he himself *didn't*. And if he's unhappy," she went on, "he'll know whom to pitch into."

"Ah," said Vanderbank, "even if he is he won't be the man to what you might call 'vent' it on her. He'll seek compensations elsewhere and won't mind any ridicule——"

"Whom are you speaking of as 'her'?" Mrs. Brook asked as on feeling that something in her face had made him stop. "I wasn't referring," she explained, "to his wife."

"Oh!" said Vanderbank.

"Aggie doesn't matter," she went on.

"Oh!" he repeated. "You meant the Duchess?" he then threw off.

"Don't be silly!" she rejoined. "He *may* not become unhappy—God grant *not*!" she developed. "But if he does he'll take it out of Nanda."

Van appeared to challenge this. "'Take it out' of her?"

"Well, want to know, as some American asked me the other day of somebody, what she's 'going to do' about it."

Vanderbank, who had remained on his feet, stood still at this for a longer time than at anything yet. "But what *can* she 'do'——?"

"That's again just what I'm curious to see." Mrs. Brook then spoke with a glance at the clock. "But if you don't go up to her——"

"My notion of seeing her alone may be defeated by her coming down on learning that I'm here?" He had taken out his watch. "I'll go in a moment. But, as a light on that danger, would *you*, in the circumstances, come down?"

Mrs. Brook, however, for light could only look darkness. "Oh, you don't love *me*."

Vanderbank, still with his watch, stared then as an alternative at the fire. "You haven't yet told me, you know, if Mr. Cashmore now comes *every* day."

"My dear man, how can I say? You've just your occasion to find out."

"From *her*, you mean?"

Mrs. Brook hesitated. "Unless you prefer the footman. Must I again remind you that, with her own sitting-room and one of the men, in addition to her maid, wholly at her orders, her independence is ideal?"

Vanderbank, who appeared to have been timing himself, put up his watch. "I'm bound to say then that, with separations so established, I understand less than ever your unforgettable explosion."

"Ah, you come back to that?" she wearily asked. "And you find it, with all you've to think about, unforgettable?"

"Oh, but there was a wild light in your eye——!"

"Well," Mrs. Brook said, "you see it now quite gone out." She had spoken more sadly than sharply, but her impatience had the next moment a flicker. "I called Nanda in because I wanted to."

"Precisely; but what I don't make out, you see, is what you've since gained by it."

"You mean she only hates me the more?"

Van's impatience, in the movement with which he turned from her, had a flare still sharper. "You know I'm incapable of meaning anything of the sort."

She waited a minute while his back was presented. "I sometimes think in effect that you're incapable of anything straightforward."

Vanderbank's movement had not been to the door, but he almost reached it after giving her, on this, a hard look. He then stopped short, however, to stare an instant still more fixedly into the hat he held in his hand; the consequence of which in turn was that he the next minute stood again before her chair. "Don't you call it straightforward of me just not to have come for so long?"

She had again to take time to say. "Is that an allusion to what—by the loss of your beautiful presence—I've failed to 'gain'? I dare say at any rate"—she gave him no time to reply—"that you feel you're quite as straightforward as I and that we're neither of us creatures of mere rash impulse. There was a time in fact, wasn't there? when we rather enjoyed each other's dim depths. If I wanted to fawn upon you," she went on, "I might say that, with such a comrade in obliquity to wind and double about with, I'd risk losing myself in the mine. But why retort or recriminate? Let us not, for God's sake, be vulgar—we haven't yet, bad as it is, come to *that*. I *can* be, no doubt—I some day *must* be: I feel it looming at me out of the awful future as an inevitable fate. But let it be for when I'm old and horrible; not an hour before. I do want to live a little even yet. So you ought to let me off easily—even as I let you."

"Oh, I know," said Vanderbank handsomely, "that there are things you don't put to me! You show a tact!"

"There it is. And I like much better," Mrs. Brook went on, "our speaking of it as delicacy than as duplicity. If you understand it's so much saved."

"What I always understand more than anything else," he returned, "is the general truth that you're prodigious."

It was perhaps a little as relapse from tension that she had nothing against that. "As for instance when it *would* be so easy——"

"Yes, to take up what lies there, you yet so splendidly abstain."

"You literally press upon me my opportunity? It's *you* who are splendid!" Mrs. Brook rather strangely laughed.

"Don't you at least want to say," he went on with a slight flush, "what you *most* obviously and naturally might?"

Appealed to on the question of underlying desire, Mrs. Brook went through the decent form of appearing to try to give it the benefit of any doubt. "Don't I want, you mean, to find out before you go up what *you* want? Shall you be too disappointed," she asked, "if I say that, as I shall probably learn, as we used to be told as children, 'all in good time,' I can wait till the light comes out of itself?"

Vanderbank still lingered. "You *are* deep!"

"You've only to be deeper."

"That's easy to say. I'm afraid at any rate you won't think I am," he pursued after a pause, "if I ask you what in the world —since Harold does keep Lady Fanny so quiet—Cashmore still requires Nanda's direction for?"

"Ah, find out!" said Mrs. Brook.

"Isn't Mrs. Donner quite shelved?"

"Find out," she repeated.

Vanderbank had reached the door and had his hand on the latch, but there was still something else. "You scarce suppose, I imagine, that she has come to like him 'for himself'?"

"Find out!" And Mrs. Brook, who was now on her feet, turned away.

He watched her a moment more, then checked himself and left her.

XXXII

She remained alone for ten minutes, at the end of which her reflections—they would have been seen to be deep—were interrupted by the entrance of her husband. The interruption was indeed not so great as if the couple had not met, as they almost invariably met, in silence: she took at all events, to begin with, no more account of his presence than to hand him a cup of tea accompanied with nothing but cream and sugar. Her having no word for him, however, committed her no more to implying that he had come in only for his refreshment than it would have committed her to say: "Here it is, Edward dear—just as you like it; so take it and sit down and be quiet." No spectator worth his salt could have seen them more than a little together without feeling how everything that, under his eyes or not, she either did or omitted rested on a profound acquaintance with his ways. They formed, Edward's ways, a chapter by themselves, of which Mrs. Brook was completely mistress and in respect to which the only drawback was that a part of her credit was by the nature of the case predestined to remain obscure. So many of them were so queer that no one but she *could* know them and know thereby into what crannies her reckoning had to penetrate. It was one of them for instance that if he was often most silent when most primed with matter, so when he had nothing to say he was always silent too—a peculiarity misleading, until mastered, for a lady who could have allowed in the latter case almost any variety of remark. "What do you think," he said last, "of his turning up to-day?"

"Of old Va—"

"Oh, has he turned up?"

"Half-an-hour ago, and asking almost in his first breath for Nanda. I sent him up to her and he's with her now." If Edward had his ways she had also some of her own; one of which, in talking him, if talk it could be called, was never to produce anything till the need was marked. She had thus a card or two still to play, for it was her theory that she never knew what went, as she would have called it, one that she had not said now. I've just been with her."

"He left me up?" Mrs. Brook was immensely interested. "Know—how should I know, to do so."

"Then he went out without seeing her." Mrs. Brook took it in. "He changed his mind out there on the stairs."

"Well," said Edward, "it won't be the first mind that has been changed there. It's about the only thing a man can change."

"Do you refer particularly to *my* stairs?" she asked with her whimsical woe. But meanwhile she had taken it in. "Then whom were you speaking of?"

"Mr. Longdon's coming to tea with her. She has had a note."

"But when did he come to town?"

"Last night, I believe. The note, an hour or two ago, announced him—brought by hand and hoping she would be at home."

Mrs. Brook thought again. "I'm glad she is. He's too sweet. By hand!—it must have been so he sent them to mamma. He wouldn't for the world wire."

"Oh, Nanda has often wired to *him*," her father returned.

"Then she ought to be ashamed of herself. But how," said Mrs. Brook, "do you know?"

"Oh, I know when we're in a thing like this."

"Yet you complain of her want of intimacy with you! It turns out that you're as thick as thieves."

Edward looked at this charge as he looked at all old friends, without a sign—to call a sign—of recognition. "I don't know of whose want of intimacy with me I've ever complained. There isn't much more of it, that I can see, that any of them could put on. What do you suppose I'd have them do? If I, on my side, don't get very far, I may have added to *that*."

"Oh, but you do," Mrs. Brook declared. "You think you don't, but you get very far indeed. You always, as I said just now, bringing out something that you're somewhere."

"Yes, and seeing you flare up at it. The things I bring out is only what they tell me."

This limitation offered, however, the things p... faculty. "Ah, but it seems to me that... nowadays tell one—! What more do... while—

"Well"—and Edward from his ch... you."

"the difference must be in what the... what I give them—

"Things that are better?" ...must each do our best.

"Yes—worse. I daresay," he went on...

"Isn't as bad as what I do? Oh, ...

But when I hear from you," Mrs. Brook pursued, "that Nanda has ever permitted herself anything so dreadful as to wire to him, it comes over me afresh that *I* would have been the perfect one to deal with him if his detestation of me hadn't prevented." She was by this time also—but on her feet —before the fire, into which like her husband she gazed. "*I* would never have wired. I would have gone in for little delicacies and odd things she has never thought of."

"Oh, she doesn't go in for what you do," Edward assented.

"She's as bleak as a chimney-top when the fire's out, and if it hadn't been after all for mamma—!" And she lost herself again in the reasons of things.

Her husband's silence seemed to mark for an instant a deference to her allusion, but there was a limit even to this combination. "You make your mother, I think, keep it up pretty well. But if she *hadn't*, as you say, done so——?"

"Why, we shouldn't have been anywhere."

"Well, where are we now? That's what *I* want to know."

Following her own train, she had at first no heed for his inquiry. "Without his hatred he would have liked me." But she came back with a sigh to the actual. "No matter. We must deal with what we've got."

"What *have* we got?" Edward continued.

Again with no ear for his question his wife turned away, only however, after taking a few vague steps, to approach him with new decision. "If Mr. Longdon is due, will you do me a favour? Will you go back to Nanda—before he arrives—and let her know, though not of course as from *me*, that Van has been here half-an-hour, has had it put well before him that she's up there and at liberty, and has left the house without seeing her?"

Edward Brookenham made no motion. "You don't like b   to do it yourself?"

        'ked better," said Mrs. Brook, "I would have already
             way to make it not come from me is surely not
                  '+ to her. Besides, I want to be here to receive

                   w it afterwards?"
                     s gone? The whole point is that she
                       him know it."

Edward still communed with the fire. "And what's the point of *that*?" Her impatience, which visibly increased, carried her away again, and by the time she reached the window he had launched another question. "Are you in such a hurry she should know that Van doesn't want her?"

"What do you call a hurry when I've waited nearly a year? Nanda may know or not as she likes—may know whenever: if she doesn't know pretty well by this time she's too stupid for it to matter. My only pressure's for Mr. Longdon. She'll have it there for him when he arrives."

"You mean she'll make haste to tell him?"

Mrs. Brook, for a moment, raised her eyes to some upper immensity. "She'll mention it."

Her husband, on the other hand, with his legs outstretched, looked straight at the toes of his boots. "Are you very sure?" Then as he remained without an answer: "Why should she if he hasn't told *her*——?"

"Of the way I so long ago let you know that he had put the matter to Van? It's not out between them in words, no doubt; but I fancy that, for things to pass, they've not to dot their i's quite so much, my dear, as we two. Without a syllable said to her, she's yet aware in every fibre of her little being of what has taken place."

Edward gave a still longer space to taking this in. "Poor little thing!"

"Does she strike you as so poor," Mrs. Brook asked, "with so awfully much done for her?"

"Done by whom?"

It was as if she had not heard the question that she spoke again. "She has got what every woman, young or old, wants."

"Really?"

Edward's tone was of wonder, but she simply went on: "She has got a man of her own."

"Well, but if he's the wrong one?"

"Do you call Mr. Longdon so very wrong? I wish," she declared with a strange sigh, "that *I* had had a Mr. Longdon!"

"I wish very much you had. I wouldn't have taken it like Van."

"Oh, it took Van," Mrs. Brook replied, "to put *them* where they are."

"But where *are* they? That's exactly it. In these three months, for instance," Edward demanded, "how has their connection profited?"

Mrs. Brook turned it over. "Profited which?"

"Well, one cares most for one's child."

"Then she has become for him what we've most hoped her to be—an object of compassion still more marked."

"Is that what you've hoped her to be?"

Mrs. Brook was obviously, for herself, so lucid that her renewed expression of impatience had plenty of point. "How can you ask after seeing what I did——"

"That night at Mrs. Grendon's? Well, its the first time I *have* asked it."

Mrs. Brook had a silence more pregnant. "It's for being with *us* that he pities her."

Edward thought. "With me too?"

"Not so much—but still you help."

"I thought you thought I didn't—that night."

"At Tishy's? Oh, you didn't matter," said Mrs. Brook, "Everything, every one helps. Harold distinctly"—she seemed to figure it all out—"and even the poor children, I daresay, a little. Oh, but every one"—she warmed to the vision—"it's perfect. Jane immensely *par exemple.* Almost all the others who come to the house. Cashmore, Carrie, Tishy, Fanny—bless their hearts all!—each in their degree."

Edward Brookenham, under the influence of this demonstration, had gradually risen from his seat, and as his wife approached that part of her process which might be expected to furnish the proof he placed himself before her with his back to the fire. "And Mitchy, I suppose?"

But he was out. "No. Mitchy's different."

He wondered. "Different?"

"Not a help. Quite a drawback." Then as his face told her these *were* involutions, "You needn't understand, but you can believe me," she added. "The one who does most is of course Van himself." It was a statement by which his failure to apprehend was not diminished, and she completed her operation. "By not liking her."

Edward's gloom on this was not quite blankness, yet it was dense. "Do you like his not liking her?"

"Dear no. No better than *he* does."

"And he doesn't——?"

"Oh, he hates it."

"Of course I haven't asked him," Edward appeared to say more to himself than to his wife.

"And of course *I* haven't," she returned—not at all in this case, plainly, for herself. "But I know it. He'd like her if he could, but he can't. That," Mrs. Brook wound up, "is what makes it sure."

There was at last in Edward's gravity a positive pathos. "Sure he won't propose?".

"Sure Mr. Longdon won't now throw her over."

"Of course if it *is* sure——"

"Well?"

"Why, it is. But of course if it isn't——"

"Why, she won't have anything. Anything but *us*," he continued to reflect. "Unless, you know, you're working it on a certainty——"

"That's just what I *am* working it on. I did nothing till I knew I was safe."

"'Safe'?" he ambiguously echoed, while on this their eyes met longer.

"Safe. I knew he would stick."

"But how did you know Van wouldn't?"

"No matter 'how'—but better still. He hasn't stuck." She said it very simply, but she turned away from him.

His eyes for a little followed her. "We don't *know*, after all, the old chap's means."

"I don't know what you mean by 'we' don't. Nanda does."

"But where's the support if she doesn't tell us?"

Mrs Brook, who had faced about, again turned from him. "I hope you don't forget," she remarked with superiority, "that we don't ask her."

"*You* don't?" Edward gloomed.

"Never. But I trust her."

"Yes," he mused afresh, "one must trust one's child. Does Van?" he then inquired.

"Does he trust her?"

"Does he know anything of the general figure?"

She hesitated. "Everything. It's high."

"He has told you so?"

Mrs. Brook, supremely impatient now, seemed to demur even to the question. "We ask *him* even less."

"Then how do we know?"

She was weary of explaining. "Because that's just why he hates it."

There was no end however, apparently, to what Edward could take. "But hates what?"

"Why, not liking her."

Edward kept his back to the fire and his dead eyes on the cornice and the ceiling. "I shouldn't think it would be so difficult."

"Well, you see it isn't. Mr. Longdon can manage it."

"I don't see what the devil's the matter with her," he coldly continued.

"Ah, that may not prevent—! It's fortunately the source at any rate of half Mr. Longdon's interest."

"But what the hell *is* it?" he drearily demanded.

She faltered a little, but she brought it out. "It's *me.*"

"And what's the matter with 'you'?"

She made, at this, a movement that drew his eyes to her own, and for a moment she dimly smiled at him. "That's the nicest thing you ever said to me. But ever, *ever*, you know."

"Is it?" She had her hand on his sleeve, and he looked almost awkward.

"Quite the very nicest. Consider that fact well and even if you only said it by accident don't be funny—as you know you sometimes *can* be—and take it back. It's all right. It's charming, isn't it? when our troubles bring us more together. Now go up to her."

Edward kept a queer face, into which this succession of remarks introduced no light, but he finally moved and it was only when he had almost reached the door that he stopped again. "Of course you know he has sent her no end of books."

"Mr. Longdon—of late? Oh yes, a deluge, so that her room looks like a bookseller's back shop: and all, in the loveliest bindings, the most standard English works. I not only know it, naturally, but I know—what you don't—why."

"'Why'?" Edward echoed. "Why but that—unless he should send her money—it's about the only kindness he can show at a distance?"

Mrs. Brook hesitated; then with a little suppressed sigh: "That's it!"

But it still held him. "And perhaps he does send her money."

"No. Not now."

Edward lingered. "Then is he taking it out——?"

"In books only?" It was wonderful—with its effect on him now visible—how she possessed her subject. "Yes, that's his delicacy—for the present."

"And you're not afraid for the future——?"

"Of his considering that the books will have worked it off? No. They're thrown in."

Just perceptibly cheered, he reached the door, where, however, he had another pause. "You don't think I had better see Van?"

She stared. "What for?"

"Why, to ask what the devil he means."

"If you should do anything so hideously vulgar," she instantly replied, "I would leave your house the next hour. Do you expect," she asked, "to be able to force your child down his throat?"

He was clearly not prepared with an account of his expectations, but he had a general memory that imposed itself. "Then why in the world did he make up to us?"

"He didn't. We made up to *him*."

"But why in the world——?"

"Well," said Mrs. Brook, really to finish, "we were in love with him."

"Oh!" Edward jerked. He had by this time opened the door, and the sound was partly the effect of the disclosure of a servant preceding a visitor. His greeting of the visitor before edging past and away was, however, of the briefest and might have implied that they had met but yesterday. "How d'ye do, Mitchy?—At home? Oh, rather!"

XXXIII

Very different was Mrs. Brook's welcome of the restored wanderer, to whom, in a brief space, she addressed every expression of surprise and delight, though marking indeed at last, as a qualification of these things, her regret that he declined to partake of her tea or to allow her to make him what she called "snug for a talk" in his customary corner of her sofa. He pleaded frankly agitation and embarrassment, reminded her even that he was awfully shy and that after separations, complications, whatever might at any time happen, he was conscious of the dust that had settled on intercourse and that he couldn't blow away in a single breath. She was only, according to her nature, to indulge him if, while he walked about and changed his place, he came to the surface but in patches and pieces. There was so much he wanted to know that— well, as they had arrived only the night before, she could judge. There was knowledge, it became clear, that Mrs. Brook almost equally craved, so that it even looked at first as if, on either side, confidence might be choked by curiosity. This disaster was finally barred by the fact that the spirit of inquiry found for Mitchy material that was comparatively plastic. That was after all apparent enough when at the end of a few vain passes he brought out sociably: "Well, has he done it?"

Still indeed there was something in Mrs. Brook's face that seemed to reply "Oh come—don't rush it, you know!" and something in the movement with which she turned away that described the state of their question as by no means so simple as that. On his refusal of tea she had rung for the removal of the table, and the bell was at this moment answered by the two men. Little ensued then, for some minutes, while the servants were present; she spoke only as the butler was about to close the door. "If Mr. Longdon presently comes show him into Mr. Brookenham's room if Mr. Brookenham isn't there. If he is, show him into the dining-room, and in either case, let me immediately know."

The man waited, expressionless. "And in case of his asking for Miss Brookenham——?"

"He won't!" she replied with a sharpness before which her interlocutor retired. "He will!" she then added in quite another tone to Mitchy, "That is, you know, he perfectly *may*. But oh the subtlety of servants!" she sighed.

Mitchy was now all there. "Mr. Longdon's in town then?"

"For the first time since you went away. He's to call this afternoon."

"And you want to see him alone?"

Mrs. Brook thought. "I don't think I want to see him at all."

"Then your keeping him below——?"

"Is so that he sha'n't burst in till I know. It's *you*, my dear, I want to see."

Mitchy glared about. "Well, don't take it ill if, in return for that, I say that I myself want to see every one. I could have done even just now with a little more of Edward."

Mrs. Brook, in her own manner and with a slow head-shake, looked lovely. "*I* couldn't." Then she puzzled it out with a pause: "It even does come over me that if you don't mind——"

"What, my dear woman," said Mitchy encouragingly, "did I *ever* mind? I assure you," he laughed, "I haven't come back to begin!"

At this, suddenly dropping everything else, she laid her hand on him. "Mitchy love, *are* you happy?"

So for a moment they stood confronted. "Not perhaps as *you* would have tried to make me."

"Well, you've still *got* me, you know."

"Oh," said Mitchy, "I've got a great deal. How, if I really look at it, can a man of my peculiar nature—it *is*, you know, awfully peculiar—*not* be happy? Think, if one is driven to it for instance, of the breadth of my sympathies."

Mrs. Brook, as a result of thinking, appeared for a little to demur. "Yes—but one mustn't be too much driven to it. It's by one's sympathies that one suffers. If you should do that I couldn't bear it."

She clearly evoked for Mitchy a definite image. "It *would* be funny, wouldn't it? But you wouldn't have to. I'd go off and do it alone somewhere—in a dark room, I think, or on a desert island; at any rate where nobody should see. Where's the harm moreover," he went on, "of any suffering that doesn't bore one, as I'm sure, however much its outer aspect might amuse some others, mine wouldn't bore me? What I should do in my desert island or my dark room, I feel, would be just to dance about with the thrill of it—which is exactly the exhibition of ludicrous gambols that I would fain have arranged to spare you. I assure you, dear Mrs. Brook," he wound up, "that I'm not in the least bored now. Everything's so interesting."

"You're beautiful!" she vaguely interposed.

But he pursued without heeding: "Was it perhaps what you had in your head that *I* should see him——?"

She came back but slowly, however, to the moment. "Mr. Longdon? Well, yes. You know he can't bear *me*——"

"Yes, yes"—Mitchy was almost eager.

It had already sent her off again. "You're too lovely. You *have* come back the same. It seemed to me," she after an instant explained, "that I wanted him to be seen——"

"Without inconvenience, as it were, either to himself or to you? Then," said Mitchy, who visibly felt that he had taken her up successfully, "it strikes me that I'm absolutely your man. It's delicious to come back to a use."

But she was much more dim about it. "Oh, what you've come back to!"

"It's just what I'm trying to get at. Van is still then where I left him?"

She was just silent. "Did you really believe he would move?"

Mitchy took a few turns, speaking almost with his back presented. "Well, with all the reasons—!" After which, while she watched him, he was before her again with a question. "It is utterly off?"

"When was it ever really on?"

"Oh, I know your view, and that, I think," said Mitchy, "is the most extraordinary part of it. I can tell you it would have put *me* on."

"My view?" Mrs. Brook thought. "Have you forgotten that I had for you too a view that didn't?"

"Ah, but we didn't differ, you and I. It wasn't a defiance and a prophecy. You wanted *me*."

"I did indeed!" Mrs. Brook said simply.

"And you didn't want him. For *her*, I mean. So you risked showing it."

She looked surprised. "*Did* I?"

Again they were face to face. "Your candour's divine!"

She wondered. "Do you mean it was even then?"

Mitchy smiled at her till he was red. "It's exquisite now."

"Well," she presently returned, "I knew my Van!"

"*I* thought I knew 'yours' too," Mitchy said. Their eyes met a minute, and he added: "But I didn't." Then he exclaimed: "How you've worked it!"

She looked barely conscious. "'Worked it'?" After which, with a slightly sharper note: "How do you know—while you've been amusing yourself in places that I'd give my head to see again, but never shall—what I've been doing?"

"Well I saw, you know, that night at Tishy's, just before we left England, your wonderful start. I got a look at your attitude, as it were, and your system."

Her eyes were now far away, and she spoke after an instant without moving them. "And didn't I by the same token get a look at yours?"

"Mine?" Mitchy thought, but seemed to doubt. "My dear child, I hadn't any then."

"You mean that it has formed itself—your system—since?"

He shook his head with decision. "I assure you I'm quite at sea. I've never had, and I have as little as ever now, anything but my general philosophy, which I won't attempt at present to go into and of which moreover I think you've had, first and last, your glimpses. What I made out in you that night was a perfect policy."

Mrs. Brook had another of her infantine stares. "Every one that night seems to have made out something! All I can say is at any rate," she went on, "that in that case you were all far deeper than I was."

"It was just a blind instinct, without a programme or a scheme? Perhaps then, since it has so perfectly succeeded, the name doesn't matter. I'm lost, as I tell you," Mitchy declared, "in admiration of its success."

She looked, as before, so young, yet so grave. "What do you call its success?"

"Let me ask you rather—mayn't I?—what *you* call its failure."

Mrs. Brook, who had been standing for some minutes, seated herself at this as if to respond to his idea. But the next moment she had fallen back into thought. "Have you often heard from him?"

"Never once."

"And have you written?"

"Not a word either. I left it, you see," Mitchy smiled, "all to *you*." After which he continued: "Has he been with you much?"

She just hesitated. "As little as possible. But, as it happens, he was here just now."

Her visitor fairly flushed. "And I've only missed him?"

Her pause again was of the briefest. "You wouldn't if he *had* gone up."

"'Gone up'?"

"To Nanda, who has now her own sitting-room, as you know, for whom he immediately asked and for whose benefit, whatever you may think, I was, at the end of a quarter of an hour I assure you, perfectly ready to release him. He changed his mind, however, and went away without seeing her."

Mitchy showed the deepest interest. "And what made him change his mind?"

"Well, I'm thinking it out."

He appeared to watch this labour. "But with no light yet?"

"When it comes I'll tell you."

He hung fire, once more, but an instant. "You didn't yourself work the thing again?"

She rose at this in strange sincerity. "I think, you know, you go very far."

"Why, didn't we just now settle," he promptly replied, "that it's all instinctive and unconscious? If it was so that night at Tishy's——"

"Ah, *voyons, voyons*," she broke in, "what did I do even then?"

He laughed out at something in her tone. "You'd like it again all pictured——?"

"I'm not afraid."

"Why, you just simply—publicly—took her back."

"And where was the monstrosity of that?"

"In the one little right place. In your removal of every doubt——"

"Well, of what?" He had appeared not quite to know how to put it.

But he saw at last. "Why, of what we may still hope to do for her. Thanks to your care, there were specimens." Then as she had the look of trying vainly to focus a few, "I can't recover them one by one," he pursued, "but the whole thing was quite lurid enough to do us all credit."

She met him after a little, but at such an odd point. "Excuse me if I scarcely see how much of the credit was yours. For the first time since I've known you, you went in for decency."

Mitchy's surprise showed as real. "It struck you as decency——?"

Since he wished she thought it over. "Oh, your behaviour——"

"My behaviour was—my condition. Do you call *that* decent? No, you're quite out." He spoke, in his good-nature, with an approach to reproof. "How can I ever——?"

But it had already brought her quite round, and to a firmer earth that she clearly preferred to tread. "Are things really bad with you, Mitch?"

"Well, I'll tell you how they are. But not now."

"Some other time?—on your honour?"

"You shall have them all. Don't be afraid."

She dimly smiled. "It will be like old times."

He rather demurred. "For you perhaps. But not for me."

In spite of what he said it did hold her, and her hand again almost caressed him. "But—till you do tell me—is it very, very dreadful?"

"That's just perhaps what I may have to get you to decide."

"Then shall I help you?" she eagerly asked.

"I think it will be quite in your line."

At the thought of her line—it sounded somehow so general —she released him a little with a sigh, yet still looking round as it were for possibilities. "Jane, you know, is in a state."

"Yes, Jane's in a state. That's a comfort!"

She continued in a manner to cling to him. "But is it your only one?"

He was very kind and patient. "Not perhaps quite."

"*I'm* a little of one?"

"My dear child, as you see."

Yes, she saw, but was still launched. "And shall you have recourse——?"

"To what?" he asked as she appeared to falter.

"I don't mean to anything violent. But shall you tell Nanda?"

Mitchy wondered. "Tell her——?"

"Well, everything. I think, you know," Mrs. Brook musingly observed, "that it would really serve her right."

Mitchy's silence, which lasted a minute, seemed to take the idea, but not perhaps quite to know what to do with it. "Ah, I'm afraid I shall never really serve her right!"

Just as he spoke the butler reappeared; at the sight of whom Mrs. Brook immediately guessed. "Mr. Longdon?"

"In Mr. Brookenham's room, ma'am. Mr. Brookenham has gone out."

"And where has he gone!"

"I think, ma'am, only for some evening papers."

She had an intense look for Mitchy; then she said to the man: "Ask him to wait three minutes—I'll ring;" turning again to her visitor as soon as they were alone. "You don't know how I'm trusting you!"

"Trusting me?"

"Why, if he comes up to you."

Mitchy thought. "Hadn't I better go down?"

"No—you may have Edward back. If you see him you must see him here. If I don't myself, it's for a reason."

Mitchy again just sounded her. "His not, as you awhile ago hinted——?"

"Yes, caring for what I say." She had a pause, but she brought it out. "He doesn't believe a word——"

"Of what you tell him?" Mitchy was splendid. "I see. And you want something said to him."

"Yes, that he'll take from *you*. Only it's for you," Mrs. Brook went on, "really and honestly, and as I trust you, to give it. But the comfort of you is that you'll do so if you promise."

Mitchy was infinitely struck. "But I haven't promised, eh? Of course I can't till I know what it is."

"It's to put before him——"

"Oh, I see: the situation."

"What has happened here to-day. Van's marked retreat, and how, with the time that has passed, it makes us at last know where we are. You of course for yourself," Mrs. Brook wound up, "see that."

"Where we are?" Mitchy took a turn and came back. "But

what then did Van come for? If you speak of a retreat, there must have been an advance."

"Oh," said Mrs. Brook, "he simply wanted not to look too brutal. After so much absence he *could* come."

"Well, if he established that he wasn't brutal, where was the retreat?"

"In his not going up to Nanda. He came—frankly—to do that, but made up his mind on second thoughts that he couldn't risk even being civil to her."

Mitchy had visibly warmed to his work. "Well, and what made the difference?"

She wondered. "What difference?"

"Why, of the effect, as you say, of his second thoughts. Thoughts of what?"

"Oh," said Mrs. Brook suddenly and as if it were quite simple—"I know *that*! Suspicions."

"And of whom?"

"Why, of *you*, you goose. Of your not having done——"

"Well, what?" he persisted as she paused.

"How shall I say it? The best thing for yourself. And of Nanda's feeling that. Don't you see?"

In the effort of seeing, or perhaps indeed in the full act of it, poor Mitchy glared as never before. "Do you mean Van's *jealous* of me?"

Pressed as she was, there was something in his face that momentarily hushed her. "There it is!" she achieved however at last.

"Of *me*?" Mitchy went on.

What was in his face so suddenly and strangely was the look of rising tears—at sight of which, as from a compunction as prompt, she showed a lovely flush. "There it is, there it is," she repeated. "You ask me for a reason, and it's the only one I see. Of course if you don't care," she added, "he needn't come up. He can go straight to Nanda."

Mitchy had turned away again as with the impulse of hiding the tears that had risen and that had not wholly disappeared even by the time he faced about. "Did Nanda know he was to come?"

"Mr. Longdon?"

"No, no. Was she expecting Van——?

"My dear man," Mrs. Brook mildly wailed, "when can she have *not* been?"

Mitchy looked hard for an instant at the floor. "I mean does she know he has been and gone?"

Mrs. Brook, from where she stood and through the window, looked rather at the sky. "Her father will have told her."

"Her father?" Mitchy frankly wondered. "Is *he* in it?"

Mrs. Brook at this had a longer pause. "You assume, I suppose, Mitchy dear," she then quavered, "that I put him up——"

"Put Edward up?" he broke in.

"No—that of course. Put Van up to ideas——"

He caught it again. "About *me*—what you call his suspicions?" He seemed to weigh the charge, but it ended, while he passed his hand hard over his eyes, in weariness and in the nearest approach to coldness he had ever shown Mrs. Brook. "It doesn't matter. It's every one's fate to be in one way or another the subject of ideas. Do then," he continued, "let Mr. Longdon come up."

She instantly rang the bell. "Then I'll go to Nanda. But don't look frightened," she added as she came back, "as to what we may—Edward or I—do next. It's only to tell her that he'll be with her."

"Good. I'll tell Tatton," Mitchy replied.

Still, however, she lingered. "Shall you ever care for me more?"

He had almost the air, as he waited for her to go, of the master of the house, for she had made herself before him, as he stood with his back to the fire, as humble as a relegated visitor. "Oh, just as much. Where's the difference? Aren't our ties in fact rather multiplied?"

"That's the way *I* want to feel it. And from the moment you recognise with me——"

"Yes?"

"Well, that he never, you know, really *would*——"

He took her mercifully up. "There's no harm done?" Mitchy thought of it.

It made her still hover. "Nanda will be rich. Toward that you *can* help, and it's really, I may now tell you, what it came into my head you should see our friend here *for*."

He maintained his waiting attitude. "Thanks, thanks."

"You're our guardian angel!" she exclaimed.

At this he laughed out. "Wait till you see what Mr. Longdon does!"

But she took no notice. "I want you to see before I go that I've done nothing for myself. Van, after all—!" she mused.

"Well?"

"Only hates me. It isn't as with you," she said. "I've really lost *him*."

Mitchy for an instant, with the eyes that had shown his tears, glared away into space. "He can't very positively, you know, now like *any* of us. He misses a fortune."

"There it is!" Mrs. Brook once more observed. Then she had a comparative brightness. "I'm so glad *you* don't!" He gave another laugh, but she was already facing Mr. Tatton, who had again answered the bell. "Show Mr. Longdon up."

"I'm to tell him then it's at your request?" Mitchy asked when the butler had gone.

"That you receive him? Oh yes. He'll be the last to quarrel with that. But there's one more thing."

It was something over which of a sudden she had one of her returns of anxiety. "I've been trying for months and months to remember to find out from you——"

"Well, what?" he inquired, as she looked odd.

"Why, if Harold ever gave back to you, as he swore to me on his honour he would, that five-pound note——"

"But which, dear lady?" The sense of other incongruities than those they had been dealing with seemed to arrive now for Mitchy's aid.

"The one that, ages ago, one day when you and Van were here, we had the joke about. You produced it in sport, as a 'fine' for something, and put it on that table; after which, before I knew what you were about, before I could run after you, you had gone off and ridiculously left it. Of course the next minute—and again before I could turn round—Harold had pounced on it, and I tried in vain to recover it from him. But all I could get him to do——"

"Was to promise to restore it straight to its owner?" Mitchy had listened so much less in surprise than in amusement that he had apparently after a moment re-established the scene. "Oh, I recollect—he did settle with me. *That's* all right."

She fixed him from the door of the next room. "You got every penny?"

"Every penny. But fancy your bringing it up!"

"Ah, I always do, you know, *some* day."

"Yes, you're of a rigour—! But be at peace. Harold's quite square," he went on, "and I quite meant to have asked you about him."

Mrs. Brook promptly was all for this. "Oh, it's all right."

Mitchy came nearer. "Lady Fanny——?"

"Yes—*has* stayed for him."

"Ah," said Mitchy, "I knew you'd do it! But hush—they're coming!" On which, while she whisked away, he went back to the fire.

XXXIV

Ten minutes of talk with Mr. Longdon by Mrs. Brookenham's hearth elapsed for him without his arriving at the right moment to take up the business so richly put before him in his previous interview. No less time indeed could have sufficed to bring him into closer relation with this affair, and nothing at first could have been more marked than the earnestness of his care not to show impatience of inquiries that were, for a person of his old friend's general style, simple recognitions and decencies. There was a limit to the mere allusiveness with which, in Mr. Longdon's school of manners, a foreign tour might be treated, and Mitchy, no doubt, plentifully showed that none of his frequent returns had encountered a curiosity at once so explicit and so discreet. To belong to a circle in which most of the members might be at any moment on the other side of the globe was inevitably to fall into the habit of few questions, as well as into that of making up for their fewness by their freedom. This interlocutor in short, while Mrs. Brook's representative privately thought over all he had in hand, went at some length and very charmingly— since it was but a tribute to common courtesy—into the Virgilian associations of the Bay of Naples. Finally, however, he started, his eye on the clock. "I'm afraid that, though our hostess doesn't appear, I mustn't forget myself. I too came back but yesterday and I've an engagement—for which I'm already late—with Miss Brookenham, who has been so good as to ask me to tea."

The divided mind, the express civility, the decent "Miss Brookenham," the escape from their hostess—these were all things Mitchy could quickly take in, and they gave him in a moment his light for not missing his occasion. "I see, I see—I shall make you keep Nanda waiting. But there's something I shall ask you to take from me as quite a sufficient basis for that: which is simply that after all, you know—for I think you do know, don't you?—I'm nearly as much attached to her as you are."

Mr. Longdon had looked suddenly apprehensive and even a trifle embarrassed, but he spoke with due presence of mind. "Of course I understand that perfectly. If you hadn't liked her so much——"

"Well?" said Mitchy as he checked himself.

"I would never, last year, have gone to stay with you."

"Thank you!" Mitchy laughed.

"Though I like you also—and extremely," Mr. Longdon gravely pursued, "for yourself."

Mitchy made a sign of acknowledgment. "You like me better for *her* than you do for anybody else *but* myself."

"You put it, I think, correctly. Of course I've not seen so much of Nanda—if between my age and hers, that is, any real contact is possible—without knowing that she now regards you as one of the very best of her friends, treating you, I almost fancy, with a degree of confidence——"

Mitchy gave a laugh of interruption. "That she doesn't show even to you?"

Mr. Longdon's poised glasses faced him. "Even! I don't mind," the old man went on, "as the opportunity has come up, telling you frankly—and as from my time of life to your own—all the comfort I take in the sense that in any case of need or trouble she might look to you for whatever advice or support the affair might demand."

"She has told you she feels I'd be there?" Mitchy after an instant asked.

"I'm not sure," his friend replied, "that I ought quite to

mention anything she has 'told' me. I speak of what I've made out myself."

"Then I thank you more than I can say for your penetration. Her mother, I should let you know," Mitchy continued, "is with her just now."

Mr. Longdon took off his glasses with a jerk. "Has anything happened to her?"

"To account for the fact I refer to?" Mitchy said in amusement at his start. "She's not ill, that I know of, thank goodness, and she has not broken her leg. But something, none the less, has happened to her—that I think I may say. To tell you all in a word, it's the reason, such as it is, of my being here to meet you. Mrs. Brook asked me to wait. She'll see you herself some other time."

Mr. Longdon wondered. "And Nanda too?"

"Oh, that must be between yourselves. Only, while I keep you here——"

"She understands my delay?"

Mitchy thought. "Mrs. Brook must have explained." Then as his companion took this in silence, "But you don't like it?" he inquired.

"It only comes to me that Mrs. Brook's explanations——!"

"Are often so odd? Oh yes; but Nanda, you know, allows for that oddity. And Mrs. Brook, by the same token," Mitchy developed, "knows herself—no one better—what may frequently be thought of it. That's precisely the reason of her desire that you should have on this occasion explanations from a source that she's so good as to pronounce, for the immediate purpose, superior. As for Nanda," he wound up, "to be aware that we're here together won't strike her as so bad a sign."

"No," Mr. Longdon attentively assented; "she'll hardly fear we're plotting her ruin. But what has happened to her?" he more sharply demanded.

"Well," said Mitchy, "it's you, I think, who will have to give it a name. I know you know what I've known."

Mr. Longdon, with his nippers again placed, hesitated. "Yes, I know."

"And you've accepted it."

"How could I help it? To reckon with such cleverness——"

"Was beyond you? Ah, it wasn't my cleverness," Mitchy said. "There's a greater than mine. There's a greater even than Van's. That's the whole point," he went on while his friend looked at him hard. "You don't even like it just a little?"

Mr. Longdon wondered. "The existence of such an element——?"

"No; the existence simply of my knowledge of your idea."

"I suppose I'm bound to keep in mind in fairness the existence of my own knowledge of yours."

But Mitchy gave that the go-by. "Oh, I've so many 'ideas'! I'm always getting hold of some new one and for the most part trying it—generally to let it go as a failure. Yes, I had one six months ago. I tried that. I'm trying it still."

"Then I hope," said Mr. Longdon with a gaiety slightly strained, "that, contrary to your usual rule, it's a success."

It was a gaiety, for that matter, that Mitchy's could match. "It does promise well! But I've another idea even now, and it's just what I'm again trying."

"On me?" Mr. Longdon still somewhat extravagantly smiled.

Mitchy thought. "Well, on two or three persons, of whom you *are* the first for me to tackle. But what I must begin with is having from you that you recognise she trusts us."

"Nanda?"

Mitchy's idea after an instant had visibly gone further. "Both of them—the two women up there at present so strangely together. Mrs. Brook must too, immensely. But for that you won't care."

Mr. Longdon had relapsed into an anxiety more natural than his expression of a moment before. "It's about time! But if Nanda didn't trust us," he went on, "her case would indeed be a sorry one. She has nobody else to trust."

"Yes," Mitchy's concurrence was grave. "Only you and me."

"Only you and me."

The eyes of the two men met over it in a pause terminated at last by Mitchy's saying: "We must make it all up to her."

"Is that your idea?"

"Ah," said Mitchy gently, "don't laugh at it."

His friend's grey gloom again covered him. "But what *can*—?" Then as Mitchy showed a face that seemed to wince with a silent "What *could*?" the old man completed his objection. "Think of the magnitude of the loss."

"Oh, I don't for a moment suggest," Mitchy hastened to reply, "that it isn't immense."

"She does care for him, you know," said Mr. Longdon.

Mitchy at this gave a long wide glare. "'Know—'?" he ever so delicately murmured.

His irony had quite touched. "But of course you know! You know everything—Nanda and you."

There was a tone in it that moved a spring, and Mitchy laughed out. "I like your putting me with her! But we're all together. With Nanda," he next added, "it *is* deep."

His companion took it from him. "Deep."

"And yet somehow it isn't abject."

The old man wondered. "'Abject'?"

"I mean it isn't pitiful. In its way," Mitchy developed, "it's happy."

This too, though rather ruefully, Mr. Longdon could take from him. "Yes—in its way."

"Any passion so great, so complete," Mitchy went on, "is —satisfied or unsatisfied—a life." Mr. Longdon looked so interested that his fellow-visitor, evidently stirred by what was now an appeal and a dependence, grew still more bland, or at least more assured, for affirmation. "She's not *too* sorry for herself."

"Ah, she's so proud!"

"Yes, but that's a help."

"Oh—not for *us*!"

It arrested Mitchy, but his ingenuity could only rebound. "In *one* way: that of reducing us to feel that the desire to 'make up' to her is—well, mainly for *our* relief. If she 'trusts' us, as I said just now, it isn't for *that* she does so." As his friend appeared to wait then to hear, it was presently with positive joy that he showed he could meet the last difficulty. "What she trusts us to do"—oh, Mitchy had worked it out!— "is to let *him* off."

"Let him off?" It still left Mr. Longdon dim.

"Easily. That's all."

"But what would letting him off hard be? It seems to me he's—on any terms—already beyond us. He *is* off."

Mr. Longdon had given it a sound that suddenly made Mitchy appear to collapse under a sharper sense of the matter. "He *is* off," he moodily echoed.

His companion, again a little bewildered, watched him; then with impatience: "Do, please, tell me what has happened."

He quickly pulled himself round. "Well, he was, after a long absence, here a while since as if expressly to see her. But after spending half-an-hour he went away without it."

Mr. Longdon's watch continued. "He spent the half-hour with her mother instead?"

"Oh 'instead'—it was hardly that. He at all events dropped his idea."

"And what had it been, his idea?"

"You speak as if he had as many as I!" Mitchy replied. "In a manner indeed he has," he continued as if for himself. "But they're of a different kind," he said to Mr. Longdon.

"What had it been, his idea?" the old man, however, simply repeated.

Mitchy's confession at this seemed to explain his previous evasion. "We shall never know."

Mr. Longdon hesitated, "He won't tell *you*?"

"Me?" Mitchy had a pause. "Less than any one."

Many things they had not spoken had already passed between them, and something evidently, to the sense of each, passed during the moment that followed this. "While you were abroad," Mr. Longdon presently asked, "did you hear from him?"

"Never. And I wrote nothing."

"Like me," said Mr. Longdon. "I've neither written nor heard."

"Ah, but with you it will be different." Mr. Longdon, as if with the outbreak of an agitation hitherto controlled, had turned abruptly away and, with the usual swing of his glass, begun almost wildly to wander. "You *will* hear."

"I shall be curious."

"Oh, but what Nanda wants, you know, is that you shouldn't be too much so."

Mr. Longdon thoughtfully rambled. "Too much—?"

"To let him off, as we were saying, easily."

The elder man for a while said nothing more, but he at last came back. "She'd like me actually to give him something?"

"I dare say!"

"Money?"

Mitchy smiled. "A handsome present." They were face to face again with more mute interchange. "She doesn't want *him* to have lost——!" Mr. Longdon, however, on this once more broke off while Mitchy's eyes followed him. "Doesn't it give a sort of measure of what she may feel——?"

He had paused, working it out again with the effect of his friend's returning afresh to be fed with his light. "Doesn't what give it?"

"Why, the fact that we still like him."

Mr. Longdon stared. "Do *you* still like him?"

"If I didn't how should I mind——?" But on the utterance of it Mitchy fairly pulled up.

His companion, after another look, laid a mild hand on his shoulder. "What is it you mind?"

"From *him*? Oh, nothing!" He could trust himself again. "There are people like that—great cases of privilege."

"He *is* one!" Mr. Longdon mused.

"There it is. They go through life, somehow, guaranteed. They can't help pleasing."

"Ah," Mr. Longdon murmured, "if it hadn't been for that——!"

"They hold, they keep every one," Mitchy went on. "It's the sacred terror."

The companions for a little seemed to stand together in this element; after which the elder turned once more away and appeared to continue to walk in it. "Poor Nanda!" then, in a far-off sigh, came across from him to Mitchy. Mitchy on this turned vaguely around to the fire, into which he remained gazing till he heard again Mr. Longdon's voice. "I knew it of course after all. It was what I came up to town for. That night, before you went abroad, at Mrs. Grendon's——"

"Yes?"—Mitchy was with him again.

"Well, made me see the future. It was then already too late."

Mitchy assented with emphasis. "Too late. She was spoiled for him."

If Mr. Longdon had to take it he took it at least quietly, only saying after a time: "And her mother *isn't?*"

"Oh yes. Quite."

"And does Mrs. Brook know it?"

"Yes, but doesn't mind. She resembles you and me. She 'still likes' him."

"But what good will that do her?"

Mitchy sketched a shrug. "What good does it do *us?*"

Mr. Longdon thought. "We can at least respect ourselves."

"*Can* we?" Mitchy smiled.

"And *he* can respect us," his friend, as if not hearing him, went on.

Mitchy seemed almost to demur. "He must think we're 'rum.'"

"Well, Mrs. Brook's worse than rum. He can't respect *her.*"

"Oh, that will be perhaps," Mitchy laughed, "what she'll get just most out of!" It was the first time, however, of Mr. Longdon's showing that even after a minute he had not understood him; so that as quickly as possible he passed to another point. "If you do anything may I be in it?"

"But what can I do? If it's over it's over."

"For *him,* yes. But not for her or for you or for me."

"Oh, I'm not for long!" the old man wearily said, turning the next moment to the door, at which one of the footmen had appeared.

"Mrs. Brookenham's compliments, please sir," this messenger articulated, "and Miss Brookenham is now alone."

"Thanks—I'll come up."

The servant withdrew, and the eyes of the two visitors again met for a minute, after which Mitchy looked about for his hat. "Good-bye. I'll go."

Mr. Longdon watched him while, having found his hat, he looked about for his stick. "You want to be in *everything?*"

Mitchy, without answering, smoothed his hat down; then he replied: "You say you're not for long, but you won't abandon her."

"Oh, I mean I shan't last for ever."

"Well, since you so expressed it yourself, that's what I mean too. I assure you *I* shan't desert her. And if I can help you——"

"Help me?" Mr. Longdon interrupted, looking at him hard.

It made him a little awkward. "Help you to help her, you know——!"

"You're very wonderful," Mr. Longdon presently returned. "A year and a half ago you wanted to help me to help Mr. Vanderbank."

"Well," said Mitchy, "you can't quite say I haven't."

"But your ideas of help are of a splendour!"

"Oh, I've told you about my ideas." Mitchy was almost apologetic.

Mr. Longdon hesitated. "I suppose I'm not indiscreet then in recognising your marriage as one of them. And that, with a responsibility so great already assumed, you appear fairly eager for another——!"

"Makes me out a kind of monster of benevolence?" Mitchy looked at it with a flushed face. "The two responsibilities are very much one and the same. My marriage has brought me, as it were, only nearer to Nanda. My wife and she, don't you see? are particular friends."

Mr. Longdon, on his side, turned a trifle pale; he looked rather hard at the floor. "I see—I see." Then he raised his eyes. "But—to an old fellow like me—it's all so strange."

"It *is* strange." Mitchy spoke very kindly. "But it's all right."

Mr. Longdon gave a head-shake that was both sad and sharp. "It's all wrong. But *you're* all right!" he added in a different tone as he walked hastily away.

Nanda

XXXV

NANDA BROOKENHAM, for a fortnight after Mr. Longdon's return, had found much to think of; but the
bustle of business became, visibly for us, particularly great with
her on a certain Friday afternoon in June. She was in unusual
possession of that chamber of comfort in which so much of
her life had lately been passed, the redecorated and rededi-
cated room, upstairs, in which she had enjoyed a due measure
both of solitude and society. Passing the objects about her in
review she gave especial attention to her rather marked wealth
of books; changed repeatedly for five minutes the position of
various volumes, transferred to tables those that were on
shelves and rearranged shelves with an eye to the effect of
backs. She was flagrantly engaged throughout indeed in the
study of effect, which moreover, had the law of an extreme
freshness not inveterately prevailed there, might have been
observed to be traceable in the very detail of her own appearance. "Company" in short was in the air and expectation in
the picture. The flowers on the little tables bloomed with a
consciousness sharply taken up by the glitter of knick-knacks
and reproduced in turn in the light exuberance of cushions on
sofas and the measured drop of blinds in windows. The
friends in the photographs in particular were highly prepared,
with small intense faces each, that happened in every case to
be turned to the door. The pair of eyes most dilated perhaps
was that of old Van, present under a polished glass and in a
frame of gilt-edged morocco that spoke out, across the room,
of Piccadilly and Christmas, and visibly widening his gaze at
the opening of the door, the announcement of a name by a
footman and the entrance of a gentleman remarkably like him
save as the resemblance was on the gentleman's part flattered.
Vanderbank had not been in the room ten seconds before he
showed that he had arrived to be kind. Kindness therefore becomes for us, by a quick turn of the glass that reflects the

whole scene, the high pitch of the concert—a kindness that almost immediately filled the place, to the exclusion of everything else, with a familiar, friendly voice, a brightness of good looks and good intentions, a constant though perhaps sometimes misapplied laugh, a superabundance almost of interest, inattention and movement.

The first thing the young man said was that he was tremendously glad she had written. "I think it was most particularly nice of you." And this thought precisely seemed as he spoke a flower of the general bloom—as if the niceness he had brought in was so great that it straightway converted everything to its image. "The only thing that upset me a little," he went on, "was your saying that before writing it you had so hesitated and waited. I hope very much, you know, that you'll never do anything of that kind again. If you've ever the slightest desire to see me—for no matter what reason; if there's ever the smallest thing of any sort that I can do for you, I promise you I shan't easily forgive you if you stand on ceremony. It seems to me that when people have known each other as long as you and I there's one comfort at least they may treat themselves to. I mean of course," Van developed, "that of being easy and frank and natural. There are such a lot of relations in which one isn't, in which it doesn't pay, in which 'ease' in fact would be the greatest of troubles and 'nature' the greatest of falsities. However," he continued while he suddenly got up to change the place in which he had put his hat, "I don't really know why I'm preaching at such a rate, for I've a perfect consciousness of not myself requiring it. One does half the time preach more or less for one's self, eh? I'm not mistaken at all events, I think, about the right thing with *you*. And a hint's enough for you, I'm sure, on the right thing with me." He had been looking all round while he talked and had twice shifted his seat; so that it was quite in consonance with his general admiring notice that the next impression he broke out with should have achieved some air of relevance. "What extraordinarily lovely flowers you have and how charming you've made everything! You're always doing something—women are always changing the position of their furniture. If you happen to come in in the dark—no matter how well you know the place—you sit down on a hat or a puppy-dog. But of course you'll say one doesn't come in in the dark, or at least if one does deserves what one gets. Only you know the way some women keep their rooms. I'm bound to say *you* don't, do you?—you don't go in for flower-pots in the windows and half-a-dozen blinds. Why *should* you? You *have* got a lot to show!" He rose with this for the third time, as the better to command the scene. "What I mean is that sofa —which, by-the-way, is awfully good; you do, my dear Nanda, go it! It certainly was *here* the last time, wasn't it? and this thing was there. The last time—I mean the last time I was up here—was fearfully long ago: when, by-the-way, *was* it? But you see I *have* been and that I remember it. And you've a lot more things now. You're laying up treasure. Really the increase of luxury—! What an awfully jolly lot of books—have you read them all? Where did you learn so much about bindings?"

He continued to talk; he took things up and put them down; Nanda sat in her place, where her stillness, fixed and colourless, contrasted with his rather flushed freedom, and appeared only to wait, half in surprise, half in surrender, for the flow of his suggestiveness to run its course, so that, having herself provoked the occasion, she might do a little more to meet it. It was by no means, however, that his presence in any degree ceased to prevail; for there were minutes during which her face, the only thing in her that moved, turning with his turns and following his glances, actually had a look inconsistent with anything but submission to almost any accident. It might have expressed a desire for his talk to last and last, an acceptance of any treatment of the hour or any version, or want of version, of her act that would best suit his ease, even in fact a resigned prevision of the occurrence of something that would leave her, quenched and blank, with the appearance of having made him come simply that she might look at him. She might indeed well have been aware of an inability to look at him little enough to make it flagrant that she had appealed to him for something quite different. Keeping the situation meanwhile thus in his hands he recognised over the chimney a new alteration. "There used to be a big print—wasn't there? a thing of the fifties—we had lots of

them at home; some place or other 'in the olden time.' And
now there's that lovely French glass. So you see." He spoke
as if she had in some way gainsaid him, whereas he had not
left her time even to answer a question. But he broke out
anew on the beauty of her flowers. "You have awfully good
ones—where do you get them? Flowers and pictures and—
what are the other things people have when they're happy
and superior?—books and birds. You ought to have a bird or
two, though I dare say you think that by the noise I make I'm
as good myself as a dozen. Isn't there some girl in some story
—it isn't Scott; what is it?—who had domestic difficulties and
a cage in her window and whom one associates with chick-
weed and virtue? It isn't Esmeralda—Esmeralda had a poodle,
hadn't she?—or have I got my heroines mixed? You're up
here yourself like a heroine; you're perched in your tower or
what do you call it?—your bower. You quite hang over the
place, you know—the great wicked city, the wonderful London sky and the monuments looming through: or am I again
only muddling up my Zola? You must have the sunsets—
haven't you? No—what am I talking about? Of course you
look north. Well, they strike me as about the only thing you
haven't. At the same time it's not only because I envy you
that I feel humiliated. I ought to have sent you some flowers." He smote himself with horror, throwing back his head
with a sudden thought. "Why in goodness when I got your
note didn't I for once in my life do something really graceful?
I simply liked it and answered it. Here I am. But I've brought
nothing. I haven't even brought a box of sweets. I'm not a
man of the world."

"Most of the flowers here," Nanda at last said, "come from
Mr. Longdon. Don't you remember his garden?"

Vanderbank, in quick response, called it up. "Dear yes—
wasn't it charming? And that morning you and I spent there"
—he was so careful to be easy about it—"talking under the
trees."

"You had gone out to be quiet and read——"

"And you came out to look after me. Well, I remember,"
Van went on, "that we had some good talk."

The talk, Nanda's face implied, had become dim to her; but
there were other things. "You know he's a great gardener—I

mean really one of the greatest. His garden is like a dinner in a house where the person—the person of the house—thoroughly knows and cares."

"I see. And he sends you dishes from the table."

"Often—every week. That is, now that he's in town his gardener does it."

"Charming of them both!" Vanderbank exclaimed. "But his gardener—that extraordinarily tall fellow with the long red beard—was almost as nice as himself. I had talks with *him* too, and I remember every word he said. I remember he told me you asked questions that showed 'a deal of study.' But I thought I had never seen all round such a charming lot of people—I mean as those down there that our friend has got about him. It's an awfully good note for a man, pleasant servants, I always think, don't you? Mr. Longdon's—and quite without their saying anything; just from the sort of type and manner they had—struck me as a kind of chorus of praise. The same with Mitchy's at Mertle, I remember," Van rambled on. "Mitchy's the sort of chap who might have awful ones, but I recollect telling him that one quite felt as if it were with *them* one had come to stay. Good note, good note," he cheerfully repeated. "I'm bound to say, you know," he continued in this key, "that you've a jolly sense for getting in with people who make you comfortable. Then, by-the-way, he's still in town?"

Nanda hesitated. "Do you mean Mr. Mitchy?"

"Oh, *he* is, I know—I met them two nights ago; and by-the-way again—don't let me forget—I want to speak to you about his wife. But I've not seen, do you know? Mr. Longdon —which is really too awful. Twice, thrice I think, have I at moments like this one snatched myself from pressure; but there's no finding the old demon at any earthly hour. When do *you* go—or does he only come here? Of course I see you've got the place arranged for him. When I asked at his hotel at what hour he ever *was* in, blest if the fellow didn't say 'Very often, sir, about ten!' And when I said 'Ten P.M.?' he quite laughed at my innocence over a person of such habits. What *are* his habits then now, and what are you putting him up to? Seriously," Vanderbank pursued, "I *am* awfully sorry, and I wonder if, the first time you've a chance, you'd kindly tell him you've heard me say so and that I mean yet to run him to earth. The same really with the dear Mitchys. I didn't, somehow, the other night, in such a lot of people, get at them. But I sat opposite to Aggie all through dinner, and that puts me in mind. I should like volumes from you about Aggie, please. It's too revolting of me not to go to see her. But every one knows I'm busy. We're up to our necks!"

"I can't tell you," said Nanda, "how kind I think it of you to have found, with all you have to do, a moment for *this*. But please, without delay, let me tell you——"

Practically, however, he would let her tell him nothing; his almost aggressive friendly optimism clung so to references of short range. "Don't mention it, please. It's too charming of you to squeeze me in. To see *you* moreover does me good. Quite distinct good. And your writing me touched me—oh, but really. There were all sorts of old things in it." Then he broke out once more on her books, one of which for some minutes past he had held in his hand. "I see you go in for sets —and, my dear child, upon my word, I see, *big* sets. What's this?—'Vol. 23: The British Poets.' Vol. 23 is delightful—do tell me about Vol. 23. Are you doing much in the British Poets? But when the deuce, you wonderful being, do you find time to read? *I* don't find any—it's too hideous. One relapses in London into illiteracy and barbarism. I have to keep up a false glitter to hide in conversation my rapidly increasing ignorance: I should be so ashamed after all to see other people *not* shocked by it. But teach me, teach me!" he gaily went on.

"The British Poets," Nanda immediately answered, "were given me by Mr. Longdon, who has given me all the good books I have except a few—those in that top row—that have been given me at different times by Mr. Mitchy. Mr. Mitchy has sent me flowers too, as well as Mr. Longdon. And they're both—since we've spoken of my seeing them—coming by appointment this afternoon; not together, but Mr. Mitchy at 5:30 and Mr. Longdon at 6:30."

She had spoken as with conscious promptitude, making up for what she had not yet succeeded in saying by a quick, complete statement of her case. She was evidently also going on with more, but her actual visitor with a laugh had already taken her up. "You *are* making a day of it and you run us like railway trains!" He looked at his watch. "Have *I* then time?"

"It seems to me I should say 'Have I?' But it's not half-past four," Nanda went on, "and though I've something very particular of course to say to you it won't take long. They don't bring tea till five, and you must surely stay till that. I had already written to you when they each, for the same reason, proposed this afternoon. They go out of town to-morrow for Sunday."

"Oh, I see—and they have to see you first. What an influence you exert, you know, on people's behaviour!"

She continued as literal as her friend was facetious. "Well, it just happened so, and it didn't matter, since, on my asking you, don't you know? to choose your time, you had taken, as suiting you best, this comparatively early hour."

"Oh perfectly." But he again had his watch out. "I've a job, perversely—that was my reason—on the other side of the world; which, by-the-way, I'm afraid, won't permit me to wait for tea. My tea doesn't matter." The watch went back to his pocket. "I'm sorry to say I must be off before five. It has been delightful at all events to see you again."

He was on his feet as he spoke, and though he had been half the time on his feet his last words gave the effect of his moving almost immediately to the door. It appeared to come out with them rather clearer than before that he was embarrassed enough really to need help, and it was doubtless the measure she after an instant took of this that enabled Nanda, with a quietness all her own, to draw to herself a little more of the situation. The quietness was plainly determined for her by a quick vision of its being the best assistance she could show. Had he an inward terror that explained his superficial nervousness, the incoherence of a loquacity designed, it would seem, to check in each direction her advance? He only fed it in that case by allowing his precautionary benevolence to put him in so much deeper. Where indeed could he have supposed that she wanted to come out, and what that she could ever do for him would really be so beautiful as this present chance to smooth his confusion and add as much as possible to that refined satisfaction with himself which would proceed from his having dealt with a difficult hour in a gallant and delicate way? To force upon him an awkwardness was like forcing a disfigurement or a hurt, so that at the end of a minute, during which the expression of her face became a kind of uplifted view of her opportunity, she arrived at the appearance of having changed places with him and of their being together precisely in order that he—not she—should be let down easily.

XXXVI

"But surely you're not going already?" she asked. "Why in the world then do you suppose I appealed to you?"

"Bless me, no; I've lots of time." He dropped, laughing for very eagerness, straight into another chair. "You're too awfully interesting. Is it really an 'appeal'?" Putting the question indeed, he could scarce even yet allow her a chance to answer it. "It's only that you make me a little nervous with your account of all the people who are going to tumble in. And there's one thing more," he quickly went on; "I just want to make the point in case we should be interrupted. The whole fun is in seeing you this way alone."

"Is *that* the point?" Nanda, as he took breath, gravely asked.

"That's a part of it—I feel it, I assure you, to be charming. But what I meant—if you'd only give me time, you know, to put in a word—is what for that matter I've already told you: that it almost spoils my pleasure for you to keep reminding me that a bit of luck like this—luck for *me*: I see you coming! —is after all for you but a question of business. Hang business! Good—don't stab me with that paper-knife. I listen. What *is* the great affair?" Then as it looked for an instant as if the words she had prepared had just, in the supreme pinch of her need, fallen apart, he once more tried his advantage. "Oh, if there's any difficulty about it, let it go—we'll take it for granted. There's one thing at any rate—do let me say this— that I *should* like you to keep before me: I want before I go to make you light up for me the question of little Aggie. Oh, there are other questions too as to which I regard you as a perfect fountain of curious knowledge! However, we'll take them one by one—the next some other time. You always seem to me to hold the strings of such a lot of queer little dramas. Have something on the shelf for me when we meet again. *The* thing just now is the outlook for Mitchy's affair. One cares enough for old Mitch to fancy one may feel safer for a lead or two. In fact I want regularly to turn you on."

"Ah, but the thing I happen to have taken it into my head to say to you," Nanda now placidly enough replied, "hasn't the least bit to do, I assure you, either with Aggie or with 'old Mitch.' If you don't want to hear it—want some way of getting off—please believe *they* won't help you a bit." It was quite in fact that she felt herself at last to have found the right tone. Nothing less than a conviction of this could have made her after an instant add: "What in the world, Mr. Van, are you afraid of?"

Well, that it *was* the right tone a single little minute was sufficient to prove—a minute, I must yet haste to say, big enough in spite of its smallness to contain the longest look ever, on any occasion, exchanged between these friends. It was one of those looks—not so frequent, it must be admitted, as the muse of history, dealing at best in short cuts, is often by the conditions of her trade reduced to representing them —which after they have come and gone are felt not only to have changed relations but absolutely to have cleared the air. It certainly helped Vanderbank to find his answer. "I'm only afraid, I think, of your conscience."

He had been indeed for the space more helped than she. "My conscience?"

"Think it over—quite at your leisure—and some day you'll understand. There's no hurry," he continued—"no hurry. And when you do understand, it needn't make your existence a burden to you to fancy you must tell me." Oh he was so kind—kinder than ever now. "The thing is, you see, that *I* haven't a conscience. I only want my fun."

They had on this a second look, also decidedly comfortable, though discounted, as the phrase is, by the other, which had really in its way exhausted the possibilities of looks. "Oh, I want *my* fun too," said Nanda, "and little as it may strike you in some ways as looking like it, just this, I beg you to believe, is the real thing. What's at the bottom of it," she went on, "is a talk I had not long ago with mother."

"Oh yes," Van returned with brightly blushing interest. "The fun," he laughed, "that's to be got out of 'mother'!"

"Oh, I'm not thinking so much of that. I'm thinking of any that she herself may be still in a position to pick up. Mine now, don't you see? is in making out how I can manage for this. Of course it's rather difficult," the girl pursued, "for me to tell you exactly what I mean."

"Oh, but it isn't a bit difficult for me to understand you!" Vanderbank spoke in his geniality as if this were in fact the veriest trifle. "You've got your mother on your mind. That's very much what I mean by your conscience."

Nanda had a fresh hesitation, but evidently unaccompanied at present by any pain. "Don't you still *like* mamma?" she at any rate quite successfully brought out. "I must tell you," she quickly subjoined, "that though I've mentioned my talk with her as having finally led to my writing to you, it isn't in the least that she then suggested my putting you the question. I put it," she explained, "quite off my own bat."

The explanation, as an effect immediately produced, mani- festly for Vanderbank—and also on the spot—improved it. He sat back in his chair with a pleased—a distinctly exhilarated— sense of the combination. "You're an adorable family!"

"Well then, if mother's adorable why give her up? That I don't mind admitting she did, the day I speak of, let me see that she feels you've done; but without suggesting either— not a scrap, please believe—that I should make you any sort of scene about it. Of course in the first place she knows per- fectly that anything like a scene would be no use. You couldn't make out even if you wanted," Nanda went on, "that *this* is one. She won't hear us—will she?—smashing the furniture. I didn't think for a while that I could do anything at all, and I worried myself with that idea half to death. Then suddenly it came to me that I could do just what I'm doing now. You said a while ago that we must never be—you and I —anything but frank and natural. That's what I said to myself also—why not? Here I am for you therefore as natural as a cold in your head. I just ask you—I even press you. It's be- cause, as she said, you've practically ceased coming. Of course I know everything changes. It's the law—what is it?—'the great law' of something or other. All sorts of things happen— things come to an end. She has more or less—by his marriage —lost Mitchy. I don't want her to lose everything. Do stick to her. What I really wanted to say to you—to bring it straight out—is that I don't believe you thoroughly know how awfully she likes you. I hope my saying such a thing doesn't affect you as 'immodest.' One never knows—but I don't much care if it does. I suppose it *would* be immodest if I were to say that I verily believe she's in love with you. Not, for that matter, that father would mind—he wouldn't mind, as he says, a tuppenny rap. So—" she extraordinarily kept it up—"you're welcome to any good the information may have for you: though that, I dare say, does sound hideous. No matter—if I produce any effect on you. That's the only thing I want. When I think of her downstairs there so often nowadays practically alone I feel as if I could scarcely bear it. She's so fearfully young."

This time at least her speech, while she went from point to point, completely hushed him, though after a full glimpse of the direction it was taking he ceased to meet her eyes and only sat staring hard at the pattern of the rug. Even when at last he spoke it was without looking up. "You're indeed, as she herself used to say, the modern daughter! It takes that type to wish to make a career for her parents."

"Oh," said Nanda very simply, "it isn't a 'career' exactly, is it—keeping hold of an old friend; but it may console a little, mayn't it, for the absence of one? At all events I didn't want not to have spoken before it's too late. Of course I don't know what's the matter between you, or if anything's really the matter at all. I don't care at any rate *what* is—it can't be anything very bad. Make it up, make it up—forget it. I don't pretend that's a career for *you* any more than for her; but there it is. I know how I sound—most patronising and pushing; but nothing venture nothing have. You *can't* know how much you are to her. You're more to her, I verily believe, than any one *ever* was. I hate to have the appearance of plotting anything about her behind her back; so I'll just say it once for all. She said once, in speaking of it to a person who repeated it to me, that you had done more for her than any one, because it was you who had really brought her out. It *was*—you did. I saw it at the time myself. I was very small, but I *could* see it. You'll say I must have been a most uncanny little wretch, and I dare say I was and am keeping now the pleasant promise. That doesn't prevent one's feeling that when a person has brought a person out——"

"A person should take the consequences," Vanderbank broke in, "and see a person through?" He could meet her now perfectly and proceeded admirably to do it. "There's an immense deal in that, I admit—I admit. I'm bound to say I don't know quite what I did—one does these things, no doubt, with a fine unconsciousness: I should have thought indeed it was the other way round. But I assure you I accept all consequences and all responsibilities. If you don't know what's the matter between us I'm sure *I* don't either. It can't be much— we'll look into it. I don't mean you and I—*you* mustn't be any more worried; but she and her so unwittingly faithless one. I *haven't* been so often, I know"—Van pleasantly kept his course. "But there's a tide in the affairs of men—and of women too, and of girls and of every one. You know what I mean—you know it for yourself. The great thing is that—bless both your hearts!—one doesn't, one simply *can't* if one would, give your mother up. It's absurd to talk about it. Nobody ever did such a thing in his life. There she is, like the moon or the Marble Arch. I don't say, mind you," he candidly explained, "that every one *likes* her equally: that's another affair. But no one who ever *has* liked her can afford ever again for any long period to do without her. There are too many stupid people— there's too much dull company. That, in London, is to be had by the ton; your mother's intelligence, on the other hand, will always have its price. One can talk with her for a change. She's fine, fine, fine. So, my dear child, be quiet. She's a fixed star."

"Oh, I know she is," Nanda said. "It's *you*——"

"Who may be only the flashing meteor?" He sat and smiled at her. "I promise you then that your words have stayed me in my course. You've made me stand as still as Joshua made the sun." With which he got straight up. "'Young,' you say she is?" he, as if to make up for it, all the more sociably continued. "It's not like anything else. She's youth. She's *my* youth—she *was* mine. And if you ever have a chance," he wound up, "do put in for me that, if she wants *really* to know, she's booked for my old age. She's clever enough, you know" —and Vanderbank, laughing, went over for his hat—"to understand what you tell her."

Nanda took this in with due attention; she was also now on her feet. "And then she's so lovely."

"Awfully pretty!"

"I don't say it, as they say, you know," the girl continued, "*because* she's mother, but I often think when we're out that wherever she is——"

"There's no one that, all round, really touches her?" Vanderbank took it up with zeal. "Oh, so every one thinks, and in fact one's appreciation of the charming things that, in that way, are so intensely her own, can scarcely breathe on them all lightly enough. And then, hang it, she has perceptions—which are not things that run about the streets. She has surprises." He almost broke down for vividness. "She has little ways."

"Well, I'm glad you do like her," Nanda gravely replied.

At this again he fairly faced her, his momentary silence making it still more direct. "I like, you know, about as well as I ever like anything, this wonderful idea of yours of putting in a plea for her solitude and her youth. Don't think I do it injustice if I say—which is saying much—that it's quite as charming as it's amusing. And now good-bye."

He had put out his hand, but Nanda hesitated. "You won't wait for tea?"

"My dear child, I can't." He seemed to feel, however, that something more must be said. "We shall meet again. But it's getting on, isn't it, toward the general scatter?"

"Yes, and I hope that this year," she answered, "you'll have a good holiday."

"Oh, we shall meet before that. I shall do what I can, but upon my word I feel, you know," he laughed, "that such a tuning-up as *you*'ve given me will last me a long time. It's like the high Alps." Then with his hand out again he added: "Have you any plans yourself?"

So many, it might have seemed, that she had to take no time to think. "I daresay I shall be away a good deal."

He candidly wondered. "With Mr. Longdon?"

"Yes—with him most."

He had another pause. "Really for a long time?"

"A long, long one, I hope."

"Your mother's willing again?"

"Oh, perfectly. And you see that's why."

"Why?" She had said nothing more, and he failed to understand.

"Why you mustn't too much leave her alone. *Don't!*" Nanda brought out.

"I won't. But," he presently added, "there are one or two things."

"Well, what are they?"

He produced in some seriousness the first. "Won't she after all see the Mitchys?"

"Not so much either. That of course is now very different."

Vanderbank hesitated. "But not for *you*, I gather—is it? Don't you expect to see them?"

"Oh yes—I hope they'll come down."

He moved away a little—not straight to the door. "To Beccles? Funny place for them, a little though, isn't it?"

He had put the question as if for amusement, but Nanda took it literally. "Ah, not when they're invited so very very charmingly. Not when he wants them so."

"Mr. Longdon? Then that keeps up?"

"'That'?"—she was at a loss.

"I mean his intimacy—with Mitchy."

"So far as it *is* an intimacy."

"But didn't you, by-the-way"—and he looked again at his watch—"tell me they're just about to turn up together?"

"Oh, not so very particularly together."

"Mitchy first alone?" Vanderbank asked.

She had a smile that was dim, that was slightly strange. "Unless you'll stay for company."

"Thanks—impossible. And then Mr. Longdon alone?"

"Unless Mitchy stays."

He had another pause. "You haven't after all told me about the efflorescence of his wife."

"How can I if you don't give me time?"

"I see—of course not." He seemed to feel for an instant the return of his curiosity. "Yet it won't do, will it? to have her out before *him*? No, I must go." He came back to her, and at present she gave him a hand. "But if you do see Mr. Longdon alone will you do me a service? I mean indeed not simply to-day, but with all other good chances?"

She waited. "*Any* service. But which first?"

"Well," he returned in a moment, "let us call it a bargain. I look after your mother——"

"And I—?" She had had to wait again.

"Look after my good name. I mean for common decency to *him*. He has been of a kindness to me that, when I think of my failure to return it, makes me blush from head to foot. I've odiously neglected him—by a complication of accidents. There are things I ought to have done that I haven't. There's one in particular—but it doesn't matter. And I haven't even explained about *that*. I've been a brute and I didn't mean it and I couldn't help it. But there it is. Say a good word for me. Make out somehow or other that I'm *not* a brute. In short," the young man said, quite flushed once more with the intensity of his thought, "let us have it that you may quite trust *me* if you'll let me a little—just for my character as a gentleman—trust *you*."

"Ah, you may trust me," Nanda replied with her hand-shake.

"Good-bye then!" he called from the door.

"Good-bye," she said after he had closed it.

XXXVII

It was half-past five when Mitchy turned up; and her relapse had in the meantime known no arrest but the arrival of tea, which, however, she had left unnoticed. He expressed on entering the fear that he failed of exactitude, to which she replied by the assurance that he was on the contrary remarkably near it and by the mention of all the aid to patience she had drawn from the pleasure of half-an-hour with Mr. Van— an allusion that of course immediately provoked on Mitchy's part the liveliest interest. "He *has* risked it at last then? How tremendously exciting! And your mother?" he went on; after which, as she said nothing: "Did *she* see him, I mean, and is he perhaps with her now?"

"No; she won't have come in—unless you asked."

"I didn't ask. I asked only for you."

Nanda thought an instant. "But you will still sometimes come to see her, won't you? I mean you won't ever give her up?"

Mitchy at this laughed out. "My dear child, you're an adorable family!"

She took it placidly enough. "That's what Mr. Van said. He said I'm trying to make a career for her."

"Did he?" Her visitor, though without prejudice to his amusement, appeared struck. "You must have got in with him rather deep."

She again considered. "Well, I think I did rather. He was awfully beautiful and kind."

"Oh," Mitchy concurred, "trust him always for that!"

"He wrote me on my note," Nanda pursued, "a tremendously good answer."

Mitchy was struck afresh. "Your note? What note?"

"To ask him to come. I wrote at the beginning of the week."

"Oh—I see," Mitchy observed as if this were rather different. "He couldn't then of course have done less than come."

Yet his companion again thought. "I don't know."

"Oh come—I say: you do know," Mitchy laughed. "I should like to see him—or you either!" There would have been for a continuous spectator of these episodes an odd resemblance between the manner and all the movements that had followed his entrance and those that had accompanied the installation of his predecessor. He laid his hat, as Vanderbank had done, in three places in succession and appeared to have very much the same various views about the security of his stick and the retention in his hand of his gloves. He postponed the final selection of a seat and he looked at the objects about him while he spoke of other matters. Quite in the same fashion indeed at last these objects impressed him. "How charming you've made your room and what a lot of nice things you've got!"

"That's just what Mr. Van said too. He seemed immensely struck."

But Mitchy hereupon once more had a drop to extravagance. "Can I do nothing then but repeat him? I came, you know, to be original."

"It would be original for *you*," Nanda promptly returned, "to be at all like him. But you *won't*," she went back, "not sometimes come for mother only? You'll have plenty of chances."

This he took up with more gravity. "What do you mean by

chances? That you're going away? That *will* add to the attraction!" he exclaimed as she kept silence.

"I shall have to wait," she answered at last, "to tell you definitely what I'm to do. It's all in the air—yet I think I shall know to-day. I'm to see Mr. Longdon."

Mitchy wondered. "To-day?"

"He's coming at half-past six."

"And then you'll know?"

"Well—*he* will."

"Mr. Longdon?"

"I meant Mr. Longdon," she said after a moment.

Mitchy had his watch out. "Then shall I interfere?"

"There are quantities of time. You must have your tea. You see at any rate," the girl continued, "what I mean by your chances."

She had made him his tea, which he had taken. "You do squeeze us in!"

"Well, it's an accident your coming together—except of course that you're *not* together. I simply took the time that you each independently proposed. But it would have been all right even if you *had* met. That is, I mean," she explained, "even if you and Mr. Longdon do. Mr. Van, I confess, I did want alone."

Mitchy had been glaring at her over his tea. "You're more and more remarkable!"

"Well then, if I improve so give me your promise."

Mitchy, as he partook of refreshment, kept up his thoughtful gaze. "I shall presently want some more, please. But do you mind my asking if Van knew——"

"That Mr. Longdon's to come? Oh yes, I told him, and he left with me a message for him."

"A message? How awfully interesting!"

Nanda thought. "It *will* be awfully—to Mr. Longdon."

"Some more *now*, please," said Mitchy while she took his cup. "And to Mr. Longdon only, eh? Is that a way of saying that it's none of *my* business?"

The fact of her attending—and with a happy show of particular care—to his immediate material want added somehow, as she replied, to her effect of sincerity. "Ah, Mr. Mitchy, the business of mine that has not by this time ever so naturally become a business of yours—well, I can't think of any just now, and I wouldn't, you know, if I could!"

"I can promise you then that there's none of mine," Mitchy declared, "that hasn't made by the same token quite the same shift. Keep it well before you, please, that if ever a young woman had a grave lookout——!"

"What do you mean," she interrupted, "by a grave lookout?"

"Well, the certainty of finding herself saddled for all time to come with the affairs of a gentleman whom she can never get rid of on the specious plea that he's only her husband or her lover or her father or her son or her brother or her uncle or her cousin. There, as none of these characters, he just stands."

"Yes," Nanda kindly mused, "he's simply her Mitchy."

"Precisely. And a Mitchy, you see, is—what do you call it? —simply indissoluble. He's moreover inordinately inquisitive. He goes to the length of wondering whether Van also learned that you were expecting *me*."

"Oh yes—I told him everything."

Mitchy smiled. "Everything?"

"I told him—I told him," she replied with impatience.

Mitchy hesitated. "And did he then leave me also a message?"

"No, nothing. What I'm to do for him with Mr. Longdon," she immediately explained, "is to make practically a kind of apology."

"Ah, and for me"—Mitchy quickly took it up—"there can be no question of anything of that kind. I see. He has done me no wrong."

Nanda, with her eyes now on the window, turned it over. "I don't much think he would know even if he had."

"I see, I see. And we wouldn't tell him."

She turned with some abruptness from the outer view. "We wouldn't tell him. But he was beautiful all round," she went on. "No one could have been nicer about having for so long, for instance, come so little to the house. As if he hadn't only too many other things to do! He didn't even make them out nearly the good reasons he might. But fancy, with his important duties—all the great affairs on his hands—our making vulgar little rows about being 'neglected'! He actually made so little of what he might easily plead—speaking so, I mean, as if he were all in the wrong—that one had almost positively to *show* him his excuses. As if"—she really kept it up—"he hasn't plenty!"

"It's only people like me," Mitchy threw out, "who have none?"

"Yes—people like you. People of no use, of no occupation and no importance. Like you, you know," she pursued, "there are so many." Then it was with no transition of tone that she added: "If you're bad, Mitchy, I won't tell you anything."

"And if I'm good what will you tell me? What I want really most to *know* is why he should be, as you said just now, 'apologetic' to Mr. Longdon. What's the wrong he allows he has done *him?*"

"Oh, he has 'neglected' him—if that's any comfort to us—quite as much."

"Hasn't looked him up and that sort of thing?"

"Yes—and he mentioned some other matter."

Mitchy wondered. "Mentioned it?"

"In which," said Nanda, "he hasn't pleased him."

Mitchy after an instant risked it. "But what other matter?"

"Oh, he says that when I speak to him Mr. Longdon will know."

Mitchy gravely took this in. "And shall you speak to him?"

"For Mr. Van?" How, she seemed to ask, could he doubt it? "Why, the very first thing."

"And then will Mr. Longdon tell you?"

"What Mr. Van means?" Nanda thought. "Well—I hope not."

Mitchy followed it up. "You 'hope'——?"

"Why, if it's anything that could possibly make any one like him any less. I mean I shan't in that case in the least want to hear it."

Mitchy looked as if he could understand that and yet could also imagine something of a conflict. "But if Mr. Longdon insists——?"

"On making me know? I shan't let him insist. Would *you?*" she put to him.

"Oh, I'm not in question!"

"Yes, you are!" she quite rang out.

"Ah—!" Mitchy laughed. After which he added: "Well then, I might overbear you."

"No, you mightn't," she as positively declared again, "and you wouldn't at any rate desire to."

This he finally showed he could take from her—showed it in the silence in which for a minute their eyes met; then showed it perhaps even more in his deep exclamation: "You're complete!"

For such a proposition as well she had the same detached sense. "I don't think I am in anything but the wish to keep *you* so."

"Well—keep me, keep me! It strikes me that I'm not at all now on a footing, you know, of keeping myself. I quite give you notice in fact," Mitchy went on, "that I'm going to come to you henceforth for everything. But you're too wonderful," he wound up as she at first said nothing to this. "I don't even frighten you."

"Yes—fortunately for you."

"Ah, but I distinctly warn you that I mean to do my very best for it!"

Nanda viewed it all with as near an approach to gaiety as she often achieved. "Well, if you should ever succeed it would be a dark day for you."

"You bristle with your own guns," he pursued, "but the in-genuity of a lifetime shall be devoted to taking you on some quarter on which you're not prepared."

"And what quarter, pray, will that be?"

"Ah, I'm not such a fool as to begin by giving you a clue!" Mitchy on this turned off with an ambiguous but unmistak-ably natural sigh; he looked at photographs, he took up a book or two as Vanderbank had done, and for a couple of minutes there was silence between them. "What does stretch before me," he resumed after an interval during which clearly, in spite of his movements, he had looked at nothing—"what does stretch before me is the happy prospect of my feeling that I have found in you a friend with whom, so utterly and unreservedly, I can always go to the bottom of things. This luxury, you see now, of our freedom to look facts in the face is one of which, I promise you, I mean fully to avail myself." He stopped before her again, and again she was silent. "It's so awfully jolly, isn't it? that there's not at last a single thing that we can't take our ease about. I mean that we can't intelligibly name and comfortably challenge. We've worked through the long tunnel of artificial reserves and superstitious mysteries, and I at least shall have only to feel that in showing every confidence and dotting every 'i' I follow the example you so admirably set. You go down to the roots? Good. It's all I ask!"

He had dropped into a chair as he talked, and so long as she remained in her own they were confronted; but she presently got up and, the next moment, while he kept his place, was busy restoring order to the objects that both her visitors had disarranged. "If you weren't delightful you'd be dreadful!"

"There we are! I could easily, in other words, frighten you if I would."

She took no notice of the remark, only, after a few more scattered touches, producing an observation of her own. "He's going all the same, Mr. Van, to be charming to mother. We've settled that."

"Ah, then he *can* make time——?"

She hesitated. "For as much as *that*—yes. For as much, I mean, as may sufficiently show her that he has not given her up. So don't you recognise how much more time *you* can make?"

"Ah—see precisely—there we are again!" Mitchy promptly ejaculated.

Yet he had gone, it seemed, further than she followed. "But where?"

"Why, as I say, at the roots and in the depths of things."

"Oh!" She dropped to an indifference that was but part of her general patience for all his irony.

"It's needless to go into the question of not giving your mother up. One simply *doesn't* give her up. One can't. There she is."

"That's exactly what *he* says. There she is."

"Ah, but I don't want to say nothing but what 'he' says!" Mitchy laughed. "He can't at all events have mentioned to you any such link as the one that in my case is now almost the most sensible. *I've* got a wife, you know."

"Oh, Mitchy!" the girl protestingly though vaguely murmured.

"And my wife—did you know it?" Mitchy went on, "is pos-

itively getting thick with your mother. Of course it isn't new
to you that she's wonderful for wives. Now that our marriage
is an accomplished fact she takes the greatest interest in it—or
bids fair to, if her attention can only be thoroughly secured—
and more particularly in what I believe is generally called our
peculiar situation: for it appears, you know, that we're in the
most conspicuous manner possible *in* a peculiar situation. Aggie is therefore already, and is likely to be still more, in what's
universally recognised as your mother's regular line. Your
mother will attract her, study her, finally 'understand' her. In
fact, she'll 'help' her, as she has 'helped' so many before and
will 'help' so many still to come. With Aggie thus as a satellite
and a frequenter—in a degree" in which she never yet *has*
been," he continued, "what will the whole thing be but a
practical multiplication of our points of contact? You may remind me of Mrs. Brook's contention that if she did in her
time keep something of a saloon the saloon is now, in consequence of events, but a collection of fortuitous atoms; but
that, my dear Nanda, will become none the less to your clearer
sense but a pious echo of her momentary modesty or—call it
at the worst—her momentary despair. The generations will
come and go, and the *personnel*, as the newspapers say, of the
saloon will shift and change, but the institution itself, as resting on a deep human need, has a long course yet to run and a
good work yet to do. *We* shan't last, but your mother will, and
as Aggie is happily very young she's therefore provided for, in
the time to come, on a scale sufficiently considerable to leave
us just now at peace. Meanwhile, as you're almost as good for
husbands as Mrs. Brook is for wives, why aren't we, as a couple, we Mitchys, quite ideally arranged for, and why mayn't I
speak to you of my future as sufficiently guaranteed? The only
appreciable shadow I make out comes, for me, from the question of what may to-day be between you and Mr. Longdon.
Do I understand," Mitchy asked, "that he's presently to arrive
for an answer to something he has put to you?"

Nanda looked at him a while with a sort of solemnity of
tenderness, and her voice, when she at last spoke, trembled
with a feeling that clearly had grown in her as she listened to
the string of whimsicalities, bitter and sweet, that he had just
unrolled. "You're wild," she said simply—"you're wild."

He wonderfully glared. "Am I then already frightening you?" He shook his head rather sadly. "I'm not in the least trying yet. There's something," he added after an instant, "that I do want too awfully to ask you."

"Well, then—!" If she had not eagerness she had at least charity.

"Oh, but you see I reflect that though you show all the courage to go to the roots and depths with *me*, I'm not—I never have been—fully conscious of the nerve for doing as much with you. It's a question," Mitchy explained, "of how much—of a particular matter—you know."

She continued ever so kindly to face him. "Hasn't it come out all round now that I know everything?"

Her reply, in this form, took a minute or two to operate, but when it began to do so it fairly diffused a light. Mitchy's face turned of a colour that might have been produced by her holding close to it some lantern wonderfully glazed. "You know, you know!" he then rang out.

"Of course I know."

"You know, you know!" Mitchy repeated.

"Everything," she imperturbably went on, "but what you're talking about."

He was silent a little, with his eyes on her. "May I kiss your hand?"

"No," she answered: "that's what I call wild."

He had risen with his inquiry and after her reply he remained a moment on the spot. "See—I've frightened you. It proves as easy as that. But I only wanted to show you and to be sure for myself. Now that I've the mental certitude I shall never wish otherwise to use it." He turned away to begin again one of his absorbed revolutions. "Mr. Longdon has asked you this time for a grand public adhesion, and what he turns up for now is to receive your ultimatum? A final, irrevocable flight with him is the line he advises, and he'll be ready for it on the spot with the post-chaise and the pistols?"

The image appeared really to have for Nanda a certain vividness, and she looked at it a space without a hint of a smile. "We shan't need any pistols, whatever may be decided about the post-chaise; and any flight we may undertake together will need no cover of secrecy or night. Mother, as I've told you——"

"Won't fling herself across your reckless path? I remember," said Mitchy—"you alluded to her magnificent resignation. But father?" he oddly inquired.

Nanda thought for this a moment longer. "Well, Mr. Longdon has—off in the country—a good deal of shooting."

"So that Edward can sometimes come down with his old gun? Good then too—if it isn't, as he takes you by the way, to shoot *you*. You've got it all shipshape and arranged, in other words, and have only, if the fancy does move you, to clear out. You clear out—you make all sorts of room. It *is* interesting," Mitchy exclaimed, "arriving thus with you at the depths! I look all round and see every one squared and every one but one or two suited. Why then reflection and delay?"

"You don't, dear Mr. Mitchy," Nanda took her time to return, "know nearly as much as you think."

"But isn't my question absolutely a confession of ignorance and a renunciation of thought? I put myself from this moment forth with you," Mitchy declared, "on the footing of knowing nothing whatever and of receiving literally from your hands all information and all life. Let my continued attitude of inquiry, my dear Nanda, show it. Any hesitation you may yet feel, you imply, proceeds from a sense of duties in London not to be lightly renounced? Oh," he thoughtfully said, "I do at least know you *have* them."

She watched him with the same mildness while he vaguely circled about. "You're wild, you're wild," she insisted. "But it doesn't in the least matter. I shan't abandon you."

He stopped short. "Ah, that's what I wanted from you in so many clear-cut golden words—though I won't in the least of course pretend that I've felt I literally need it. I don't literally need the big turquoise in my neck-tie; which incidentally means, by the way, that if you should admire it you're quite welcome to it. Such words—that's my point—are like such jewels: the pride, you see, of one's heart. They're mere vanity, but they help along. You've got of course always poor Tishy," he continued.

"Will you leave it all to *me?*" Nanda said as if she had not heard him.

"And then you've got poor Carrie," he went on, "though *her* of course you rather divide with your mother."

"Will you leave it all to *me*?" the girl repeated.

"To say nothing of poor Cashmore," he pursued, "whom you take *all*, I believe, yourself?"

"Will you leave it all to *me*?" she once more repeated.

This time he pulled up, suddenly and expressively wondering. "Are you going to do anything about it at present?—I mean with our friend?"

She appeared to have a scruple of saying, but at last she produced it. "Yes—he doesn't mind now."

Mitchy again laughed out. "You *are*, as a family—!" But he had already checked himself. "Mr. Longdon will at any rate, you imply, be somehow interested——"

"In *my* interests? Of course—since he has gone so far. You expressed surprise at my wanting to wait and think; but how can I not wait and not think when so much depends on the question—now so definite—of how much further he *will* go?"

"I see," said Mitchy, profoundly impressed. "And how much does that depend on?"

She had to reflect. "On how much further I, for my part, *must*."

Mitchy's grasp was already complete. "And he's coming then to learn from you how far this is?"

"Yes—very much."

Mitchy looked about for his hat. "So that of course I see my time's about up, as you'll want to be quite alone together."

Nanda glanced at the clock. "Oh, you've a margin yet."

"But you don't want an interval for your thinking——?"

"Now that I've seen you?" Nanda was already very obviously thoughtful.

"I mean if you've an important decision to take."

"Well," she returned, "seeing you *has* helped me."

"Ah, but at the same time worried you. Therefore——" And he picked up his umbrella.

Her eyes rested on its curious handle. "If you cling to your idea that I'm frightened you'll be disappointed. It will never be given you to reassure me."

"You mean by that that I'm primarily so solid——"

"Yes, that till I see you yourself afraid——"

"Well?"

"Well, I won't admit that anything isn't exactly what I was prepared for."

Mitchy looked with interest into his hat. "Then what is it I'm to 'leave' to you?" After which, as she turned away from him with a suppressed sound and said, while he watched her, nothing else, "It's no doubt natural for you to talk," he went on, "but I do make you nervous. Good-bye—good-bye."

She had stayed him however by a fresh movement as he reached the door. "Aggie's only trying to find out——"

"Yes—what?" he asked, waiting.

"Why, what sort of a person she is. How can she ever have known? It was carefully, elaborately hidden from her—kept so obscure that she could make out nothing. She isn't now like *me*."

He wonderingly attended. "Like you?"

"Why, I get the benefit of the fact that there was never a time when I didn't know *something* or other and that I became more and more aware, as I grew older, of a hundred little chinks of daylight."

Mitchy stared. "You're stupendous, my dear!" he murmured.

Ah, but she kept it up. "*I* had my idea about Aggie."

"Oh, don't I know you had? And how you were positive about the sort of person——"

"That she didn't even suspect herself," Nanda broke in, "to be? I'm equally positive now. It's quite what I believed, only there's ever so much more of it. More *has* come—and more will yet. You see, when there has been nothing before, it all has to come with a rush. So that, if even I am surprised, of course *she* is."

"And of course *I* am!" Mitchy's interest, though even now not wholly unqualified with amusement, had visibly deepened. "You admit then," he continued, "that you *are* surprised?"

Nanda just hesitated. "At the mere scale of it. I think it's splendid. The only person whose astonishment I don't quite understand," she added, "is cousin Jane."

"Oh, cousin Jane's astonishment serves her right!"

"If she held so," Nanda pursued, "that marriage should do everything——"

"She shouldn't be in such a funk at finding what it *is*

doing? Oh no, she's the last one!" Mitchy declared. "I vow I enjoy her scare."

"But it's very bad, you know," said Nanda.

"Oh, too awful!"

"Well, of course," the girl appeared assentingly to muse, "she couldn't after all have dreamed—!" But she took herself up. "The great thing is to be helpful."

"And in what way—?" Mitchy asked with his wonderful air of inviting competitive suggestions.

"Toward Aggie's finding herself. Do you think," she immediately continued, "that Lord Petherton really is?"

Mitchy frankly considered. "Helpful? Oh, he does his best, I gather. Yes," he presently added—"Petherton's all right."

"It's you yourself, naturally," his companion threw off, "who can help most."

"Certainly, and I'm doing my best too. So that with such good assistance"—he seemed at last to have taken it all from her—"what is it, I again ask, that, as you request, I'm to leave to you?"

Nanda required, while he still waited, some time to reply. "To keep my promise."

"Your promise?"

"Not to abandon you."

"Ah," cried Mitchy, "that's better!"

"Then good-bye," she said.

"Good-bye." But he came a few steps forward. "I *mayn't* kiss your hand?"

"Never."

"Never?"

"Never."

"Oh!" he oddly sounded as he quickly went out.

XXXVIII

The interval he had represented as likely to be useful to her was in fact, however, not a little abbreviated by a punctuality of arrival on Mr. Longdon's part so extreme as to lead the first thing to a word almost of apology. "You can't say," her new visitor immediately began, "that I haven't left you alone, these many days, as much as I promised on coming up to you that afternoon when after my return to town I found Mr. Mitchett instead of your mother awaiting me in the drawing-room."

"Yes," said Nanda, "you've really done quite as I asked you."

"Well," he returned, "I felt half-an-hour ago that, near as I was to relief, I could keep it up no longer; so that though I knew it would bring me much too soon I started at six sharp for our trysting-place."

"And I've no tea, after all, to reward you!" It was but now clearly that she noticed it. "They must have removed the things without my heeding."

Her old friend looked at her with some intensity. "Were you in the room?"

"Yes—but I didn't see the man come in."

"What then were you doing?"

Nanda thought; her smile was as usual the faintest discernible outward sign. "Thinking of *you.*"

"So tremendously hard?"

"Well, of other things too and of other persons. Of everything really that in our last talk I told you, you know, it seemed to me best I should have out with myself before meeting you for what I suppose you've now in mind."

Mr. Longdon had kept his eyes on her, but at this he turned away; not, however, as an alternative, embracing her material situation with the embarrassed optimism of Vanderbank or the mitigated gloom of Mitchy. "Ah"—he took her up with some dryness—"you've been having things out with yourself?" But he went on before she answered: "I don't want any tea, thank you. I found myself, after five, in such a fidget that I went three times in the course of the hour to my club, where I have the impression that I each time had it. I dare say it wasn't there, though, that I did have it," he after an instant pursued, "for I've somehow a confused image of a shop in Oxford Street—or was it rather in Regent?—into which I gloomily wandered to beguile the moments with a liquid that if I strike you as upset I beg you to set it all down to. Do you know in fact what I've been doing for the last ten minutes? Roaming hither and thither in your beautiful Crescent till I could venture to come in."

"Then did you see Mitchy go out? But no, you wouldn't"—

Nanda corrected herself. "He has been gone longer than that."

Her visitor had dropped upon a sofa, where, propped by the back, he sat rather upright, his glasses on his nose, his hands in his pockets and his elbows much turned out. "Mitchy left you more than ten minutes ago, and yet your state on his departure remains such there could be a bustle of servants in the room without your being aware? Kindly give me some light then on the condition into which he has plunged you."

She hovered before him with her obscure smile. "You see it for yourself."

He shook his head with decision. "I don't see anything for myself, and I beg you to understand that it's not what I've come here to-day to do. Anything I may yet see which I don't already see will be only, I warn you, so far as you shall make it very clear. There—you've work cut out. And is it with Mr. Mitchett, may I ask, that you've been, as you mention, cutting it?"

Nanda looked about her as if weighing many things; after which her eyes came back to him. "Do you mind if I don't sit down?"

"I don't mind if you stand on your head—at the pass we've come to."

"I shall not try your patience," the girl good-humouredly replied, "so far as that. I only want you not to be worried if I walk about a little."

Mr. Longdon, without a movement, kept his posture. "Oh, I can't oblige you there. I *shall* be worried. I've come on purpose to be worried, and the more I surrender myself to the rack the more, I seem to feel, we shall have threshed our business out. So you may dance, if you like, on the absolutely passive thing you've made of me."

"Well, what I *have* had from Mitchy," she cheerfully responded, "is practically a lesson in dancing; by which I perhaps mean rather a lesson in sitting, myself, as I want you to do while *I* talk, as still as a mouse. They take," she declared, "while *they* talk, an amount of exercise!"

"They?" Mr. Longdon wondered. "Was his wife with him?"

"Dear no—he and Mr. Van."

"Was Mr. Van with him?"

"Oh no—before, alone. All over the place."

Mr. Longdon had a pause so rich in inquiry that when he at last spoke his question was itself like an answer. "Mr. Van has been to see you?"

"Yes. I wrote and asked him."

"Oh!" said Mr. Longdon.

"But don't get up." She raised her hand. "Don't!"

"Why should I?" He had never budged.

"He was most kind; stayed half-an-hour and, when I told him you were coming, left a good message for you."

Mr. Longdon appeared to wait for this tribute, which was not immediately produced. "What do you call a 'good' message?"

"I'm to make it all right with you."

"To make what?"

"Why, that he has not, for so long, been to see you or written to you. That he has seemed to neglect you."

Nanda's visitor looked so far about as to take the neighbourhood in general into the confidence of his surprise. "To neglect *me*?"

"Well, others too, I believe—with whom we're not concerned. He has been so taken up. But you above all."

Mr. Longdon showed on this a coldness that somehow spoke for itself as the greatest with which he had ever in his life met an act of reparation and that was infinitely confirmed by his sustained immobility. "But of what have I complained?"

"Oh, I don't think he fancies you've complained."

"And how could he have come to see me," he continued, "when for so many months past I've been so little in town?"

He was not more ready with objections, however, than his companion had by this time become with answers. "He must have been thinking of the time of your present stay. He said he hadn't seen you."

"He has quite sufficiently tried—he has left cards," Mr. Longdon returned. "What more does he want?"

Nanda looked at him with her long, grave straightness, which had often a play of light beyond any smile. "Oh you know, he does want more."

"Then it was open to him——"

"So he so strongly feels"—she quickly took him up—"that you must have felt. And therefore it is that I speak for him."

"Don't!" said Mr. Longdon.

"But I promised him I would."

"Don't!" the old man repeated.

She had kept for the time all her fine clearness turned to him; but she might on this have been taken as giving him up with a movement of obedience and a strange soft sigh. The smothered sound might even have represented to a listener at all initiated a consenting retreat before an effort greater than her reckoning—a retreat that was in so far the snap of a sharp tension. The next minute, none the less, she evidently found a fresh provocation in the sight of the pale and positively excessive rigour she had imposed, so that, though her friend was only accommodating himself to her wish, she had a sudden impulse of criticism. "You're proud about it—too proud!"

"Well, what if I am?" He looked at her with a complexity of communication that no words could have meddled with. "Pride's all right when it helps one to bear things."

"Ah," said Nanda, "but that's only when one wants to take the least from them. When one wants to take the most——"

"Well?"—he spoke, as she faltered, with a certain small hardness of interest.

She faltered, however, indeed. "Oh, I don't know how to say it." She fairly coloured with the attempt. "One must let the sense of all that I speak of—well, all come. One must rather like it. I don't know—but I suppose one must rather grovel."

Mr. Longdon, though with visible reluctance, turned it over. "That's very fine—but you're a woman."

"Yes—that must make a difference. But being a woman in such a case has then," Nanda went on, "its advantages."

On this point perhaps her friend might presently have been taken as relaxing. "It strikes me that, even at that, the advantages are mainly for others. I'm glad, God knows, that you're not also a young man."

"Then we're suited all round."

She had spoken with a promptitude that appeared again to act on him slightly as an irritant, for he met it—with more delay—by a long, derisive murmur. "Oh, *my* pride—!" But this she in no manner took up; so that he was left for a little to his thoughts. "That's what you were plotting when you told me the other day that you wanted time?"

"Ah, I wasn't plotting—though I was, I confess, trying to work things out. That particular idea of simply asking Mr. Van by letter to present himself—that particular flight of fancy hadn't in fact then at all occurred to me."

"It never occurred, I'm bound to say, to *me*," said Mr. Longdon. "I've never thought of writing to him."

"Very good. But you haven't the reasons. I wanted to attack him."

"Not about me, I hope to God!" Mr. Longdon, distinctly a little paler, rejoined.

"Don't be afraid. I think I had an instinct of how you would have taken *that*. It was about mother."

"Oh!" said her visitor.

"He has been worse to her than to you," she continued. "But he'll make it all right."

Mr. Longdon's attention retained its grimness. "If he has such a remedy for the more then, what has he for the less?"

Nanda, however, was but for an instant checked. "Oh, it's I who make it up to *you*. To mother, you see, there's no one otherwise to make it up."

This at first unmistakably sounded to him too complicated for acceptance. But his face changed as light dawned. "That puts it then that you *will* come?"

"I'll come if you'll take me as I am—which is, more than I've ever done before, what I must previously explain to you. But what *he* means by what you call his remedy is my making you feel better about himself."

The old man gazed at her. "'Your' doing it is too beautiful! And he could really come to you for the purpose of asking you?"

"Oh no," said the girl briskly, "he came simply for the purpose of doing what he *had* to do. After my letter how could he not come? Then he met most kindly what I said to him for mother and what he quite understood to be all my business with him; so that his appeal to me to plead with you for—well, for his credit—was only thrown in because he had so good a chance."

This speech brought Mr. Longdon abruptly to his feet, but

before she could warn him again of the patience she continued to need he had already, as if what she evoked for him left
him too stupefied, dropped back into submission. "The man
stood there for you to render him a service?—for you to help
him and praise him?"

"Ah, but it wasn't to go out of my way, don't you see? He
knew you were presently to be here." Her anxiety that he
should understand gave her a rare, strained smile. "I mustn't
make—as a request from him—too much of it, and I've not a
doubt that, rather than you should think any ill of him for
wishing me to say a word, he would gladly be left with whatever bad appearance he may actually happen to have." She
pulled up on these words as if with a quick sense of their
really, by their mere sound, putting her in deeper; and could
only give her friend one of the looks that expressed: "If I
could trust you not to assent even more than I want, I should
say 'You know what I mean!'" She allowed him at all events
—or tried to allow him—no time for uttered irony before
going on: "He was everything you could have wished; quite
as beautiful about *you*——"

"As about you?"—Mr. Longdon took her up.

She demurred. "As about mother." With which she turned
away as if it handsomely settled the question.

But it only left him, as she went to the window, sitting
there sombre. "I like, you know," he brought out as his eyes
followed her, "your saying you're not proud! Thank God you
are, my dear. Yes—it's better for us."

At this, after a moment in her place, she turned round to
him. "I'm glad I'm anything—whatever you may call it and
though I can't call it the same—that's good for *you*."

He said nothing more for a little, as if by such a speech
something in him were simplified and softened. "It would be
good for me—by which I mean it would be easier for me—if
you didn't quite so immensely care for him."

"Oh!" came from Nanda with an accent of attenuation at
once so precipitate and so vague that it only made her attitude at first rather awkward. "Oh!" she immediately repeated,
but with an increase of the same effect. After which, conscious, she made as if to save herself a quick addition. "Dear
Mr. Longdon, isn't it rather yourself most——?"

"It would be easier for me," he went on heedless, "if you didn't, my poor child, so wonderfully love him."

"Ah, but I don't—please believe me when I assure you I *don't*!" she broke out. It burst from her, flaring up, in a queer quaver that ended in something queerer still—in her abrupt collapse, on the spot, into the nearest chair, where she choked with a torrent of tears. Her buried face could only after a moment give way to the flood, and she sobbed in a passion as sharp and brief as the flurry of a wild thing for an instant uncaged; her old friend meantime keeping his place in the silence broken by her sound and distantly—across the room—closing his eyes to his helplessness and her shame. Thus they sat together while their trouble both conjoined and divided them. She recovered herself, however, with an effort worthy of her fall and was on her feet again as she stammeringly spoke and angrily brushed at her eyes. "What difference in the world does it make—what difference ever?" Then clearly, even with the words, her checked tears suffered her to see that it made the difference that he too had been crying; so that "I don't know why you mind!" she, on this, with extravagance, wailed.

"You don't know what I would have done for him. You don't know, you don't know!" he repeated—while she looked as if she naturally couldn't—as with a renewal of his dream of beneficence and of the soreness of his personal wound.

"Well, but *he* does you justice—he knows. So it shows, so it shows——!"

But in this direction too, unable to say what it showed, she had again broken down and again could only hold herself and let her companion sit there. "Ah, Nanda, Nanda!" he deeply murmured; and the depth of the pity was, vainly and blindly, as the depth of a reproach.

"It's I—it's I, therefore," she said as if she must then so look at it with him; "it's I who am the horrible impossible and who have covered everything else with my own impossibility. For some different person you *could* have done what you speak of, and for some different person you can do it still."

He stared at her with his barren sorrow. "A person different from him?"

"A person different from *me*."

"And what interest have I in any such person?"

"But your interest in me—you see well enough where *that* lands us."

Mr. Longdon now got to his feet and somewhat stiffly remained; after which, for all answer, "You say you *will* come then?" he asked. Then as—seemingly with her last thought— she kept silent: "You understand clearly, I take it, that this time it's never again to leave me—or to *be* left."

"I understand," she presently replied. "Never again. That," she continued, "is why I asked you for these days."

"Well then, since you've taken them——"

"Ah, but have *you?*" said Nanda. They were close to each other now, and with a tenderness of warning that was helped by their almost equal stature she laid her hand upon his shoulder. "What I did more than anything else write to him for," she had now regained her clearness enough to explain, "was that—with whatever idea you had—you should see for yourself how he could come and go."

"And what good was that to do me? *Hadn't* I seen for myself?"

"Well—you've seen once more. Here he was. I didn't care what he thought. Here I brought him. And his reasons remain."

She kept her eyes on her companion's face, but his own now and afterwards seemed to wander far. "What do I care for his reasons so long as they're not mine?"

She thought an instant, still holding him gently and as if for successful argument. "But perhaps you don't altogether understand them."

"And why the devil, altogether, *should* I?"

"Ah, because you distinctly want to," said Nanda ever so kindly. "You've admitted as much when we've talked——"

"Oh, but when *have* we talked?" he sharply interrupted.

This time he had challenged her so straight that it was her own look that strayed. "When?"

"When."

She hesitated. "When *haven't* we?"

"Well, *you* may have; if that's what you call talking—never saying a word. But I haven't. I've only to do at any rate, in the way of reasons, with my own."

"And yours too then remain? Because, you know," the girl pursued, "I *am* like that."

"Like what?"

"Like what he thinks." Then so gravely that it was almost a supplication, "Don't tell me," she added, "that you don't *know* what he thinks. You do know."

Their eyes, on that strange ground, could meet at last, and the effect of it was presently for Mr. Longdon. "I do know."

"Well?"

"Well!" He raised his hands and took her face, which he drew so close to his own that, as she gently let him, he could kiss her with solemnity on the forehead. "Come!" he then very firmly said—quite indeed as if it were a question of their moving on the spot.

It literally made her smile, which, with a certain compunction, she immediately corrected by doing for him in the pressure of her lips to his cheek what he had just done for herself. "To-day?" she more seriously asked.

He looked at his watch. "To-morrow."

She paused, but clearly for assent. "That's what I mean by your taking me as I am. It *is*, you know, for a girl—extraordinary."

"Oh, I know what it is!" he exclaimed with an odd fatigue in his tenderness.

But she continued, with the shadow of her scruple, to explain. "We're many of us, we're most of us—as you long ago saw and showed you felt—extraordinary now. We can't help it. It isn't really our fault. There's so much else that's extraordinary that if we're in it all so much *we* must naturally be." It was all obviously clearer to her than it had ever been, and her sense of it found renewed expression; so that she might have been, as she wound up, a very much older person than her friend. "Everything's different from what it used to be."

"Yes, everything," he returned with an air of final indoctrination. "That's what he ought to have recognised."

"As *you* have?" Nanda was once more—and completely now —enthroned in high justice. "Oh, he's more old-fashioned than you."

"Much more," said Mr. Longdon with a queer face.

"He tried," the girl went on—"he did his best. But he couldn't. And he's so right—for himself."

Her visitor, before meeting this, gathered in his hat and stick, which for a minute occupied his attention. "He ought to have married——"

"Little Aggie? Yes," said Nanda.

They had gained the door, where Mr. Longdon again met her eyes. "And then Mitchy——"

But she checked him with a quick gesture. "No—not even then!"

So again before he went they were for a minute confronted. "Are you anxious about Mitchy?"

She faltered, but at last brought it out. "Yes. Do you see? There I am."

"I see. There we are. Well," said Mr. Longdon—"to-morrow."

CHRONOLOGY

NOTE ON THE TEXTS

NOTES

Chronology

1843   Born April 15 at 21 Washington Place, New York City, the second child (after William, born January 11, 1842, N.Y.C.) of Henry James of Albany and Mary Robertson Walsh of New York. Father lives on inheritance of $10,000 a year, his share of litigated $3,000,000 fortune of his Albany father, William James, an Irish immigrant who came to the U.S. immediately after the Revolution.

1843–45   Accompanied by mother's sister, Catharine Walsh, and servants, the James parents take infant children to England and later to France. Reside at Windsor, where father has nervous collapse ("vastation") and experiences spiritual illumination. He becomes a Swedenborgian (May 1844), devoting his time to lecturing and religious-philosophical writings. James later claimed his earliest memory was a glimpse, during his second year, of the Place Vendôme in Paris with its Napoleonic column.

1845–47   Family returns to New York. Garth Wilkinson James (Wilky) born July 21, 1845. Family moves to Albany at 50 N. Pearl St., a few doors from grandmother Catharine Barber James. Robertson James (Bob or Rob) born August 29, 1846.

1847–55   Family moves to a large house at 58 W. 14th St., New York. Alice James born August 7, 1848. Relatives and father's friends and acquaintances—Horace Greeley, George Ripley, Charles Anderson Dana, William Cullen Bryant, Bronson Alcott, and Ralph Waldo Emerson ("I knew he was great, greater than any of our friends")—are frequent visitors. Thackeray calls during his lecture tour on the English humorists. Summers at New Brighton on Staten Island and Fort Hamilton on Long Island's south shore. On steamboat to Fort Hamilton August 1850, hears Washington Irving tell his father of Margaret Fuller's drowning in shipwreck off Fire Island. Frequently visits Barnum's American Museum on free days. Taken to art shows and theaters; writes and draws stage scenes. Described by father as "a devourer of libraries." Taught in assorted private schools and by tutors in lower Broadway and Greenwich Village. But father claims in 1848 that American schooling fails to provide "sensuous education" for his children and plans to take them to Europe.

1855–58 Family (with Aunt Kate) sails for Liverpool, June 27. James is intermittently sick with malarial fever as they travel to Paris, Lyon, and Geneva. After Swiss summer, leaves for London where Robert Thomson (later Robert Louis Stevenson's tutor) is engaged. Early summer 1856, family moves to Paris. Another tutor engaged and children attend experimental Fourierist school. Acquires fluency in French. Family goes to Boulogne-sur-mer in summer, where James contracts typhoid. Spends late October in Paris, but American crash of 1857 returns family to Boulogne where they can live more cheaply. Attends public school (fellow classmate is Coquelin, the future French actor).

1858–59 Family returns to America and settles in Newport, Rhode Island. Goes boating, fishing, and riding. Attends the Reverend W. C. Leverett's Berkeley Institute, and forms friendship with classmate Thomas Sergeant Perry. Takes long walks and sketches with the painter John La Farge.

1859–60 Father, still dissatisfied with American education, returns family to Geneva in October. James attends a pre-engineering school, Institution Rochette, because parents, with "a flattering misconception of my aptitudes," feel he might benefit from less reading and more mathematics. After a few months withdraws from all classes except French, German, and Latin, and joins William as a special student at the Academy (later the University of Geneva) where he attends lectures on literary subjects. Studies German in Bonn during summer 1860.

1860–62 Family returns to Newport in September where William studies with William Morris Hunt, and James sits in on his classes. La Farge introduces him to works of Balzac, Merimée, Musset, and Browning. Wilky and Bob attend Frank Sanborn's experimental school in Concord with children of Hawthorne and Emerson and John Brown's daughter. Early in 1861, orphaned Temple cousins come to live in Newport. Develops close friendship with cousin

Mary (Minnie) Temple. Goes on a week's walking tour in July in New Hampshire with Perry. William abandons art in autumn 1861 and enters Lawrence Scientific School at Harvard. James suffers back injury in a stable fire while serving as a volunteer fireman. Reads Hawthorne ("an American could be an artist, one of the finest").

1862–63 Enters Harvard Law School (Dane Hall). Wilky enlists in the Massachusetts 44th Regiment, and later in Colonel Robert Gould Shaw's 54th, one of the first black regiments. Summer 1863, Bob joins the Massachusetts 55th, another black regiment, under Colonel Hollowell. James withdraws from law studies to try writing. Sends unsigned stories to magazines. Wilky is badly wounded and brought home to Newport in August.

1864 Family moves from Newport to 13 Ashburton Place, Boston. First tale, "A Tragedy of Error" (unsigned), published in *Continental Monthly* (Feb. 1864). Stays in Northampton, Massachusetts, early August–November. Begins writing book reviews for *North American Review* and forms friendship with its editor, Charles Eliot Norton, and his family, including his sister Grace (with whom he maintains a long-lasting correspondence). Wilky returns to his regiment.

1865 First signed tale, "The Story of a Year," published in *Atlantic Monthly* (March 1865). Begins to write reviews for the newly founded *Nation* and publishes anonymously in it during next fifteen years. William sails on a scientific expedition with Louis Agassiz to the Amazon. During summer James vacations in the White Mountains with Minnie Temple and her family; joined by Oliver Wendell Holmes Jr. and John Chipman Gray, both recently demobilized. Father subsidizes plantation for Wilky and Bob in Florida with black hired workers. (The idealistic but impractical venture fails in 1870.)

1866–68 Continues to publish reviews and tales in Boston and New York journals. William returns from Brazil and resumes medical education. James has recurrence of back ailment and spends summer in Swampscott, Massachusetts. Begins friendship with William Dean Howells. Family moves to 20 Quincy St., Cambridge. William, suffering from nervous ailments, goes to Germany in spring 1867. "Poor Richard," James's longest story to date, published in *Atlantic Monthly* (June–Aug. 1867). William begins intermittent criticism of Henry's story-telling and style (which will continue throughout their careers). Momentary meeting with Charles Dickens at Norton's house. Vacations in Jefferson, New Hampshire, summer 1868. William returns from Europe.

1869–70   Sails in February for European tour. Visits English towns and cathedrals. Through Nortons meets Leslie Stephen, William Morris, Dante Gabriel Rossetti, Edward Burne-Jones, John Ruskin, Charles Darwin, and George Eliot (the "one marvel" of his stay in London). Goes to Paris in May, then travels in Switzerland in summer and hikes into Italy in autumn, where he stays in Milan, Venice (Sept.), Florence, and Rome (Oct. 30–Dec. 28). Returns to England to drink the waters at Malvern health spa in Worcestershire because of digestive troubles. Stays in Paris en route and has first experience of Comédie Française. Learns that his beloved cousin, Minnie Temple, has died of tuberculosis.

1870–72   Returns to Cambridge in May. Travels to Rhode Island, Vermont, and New York to write travel sketches for *The Nation*. Spends a few days with Emerson in Concord. Meets Bret Harte at Howells' home April 1871. *Watch and Ward*, his first novel, published in *Atlantic Monthly* (Aug.–Dec. 1871). Serves as occasional art reviewer for the *Atlantic* January–March 1872.

1872–74   Accompanies Aunt Kate and sister Alice on tour of England, France, Switzerland, Italy, Austria, and Germany from May through October. Writes travel sketches for *The Nation*. Spends autumn in Paris, becoming friends with James Russell Lowell. Escorts Emerson through the Louvre. (Later, on Emerson's return from Egypt, will show him the Vatican.) Goes to Florence in December and from there to Rome, where he becomes friends with actress Fanny Kemble, her daughter Sarah Butler Wister, and William Wetmore Story and his family. In Italy sees old family friend Francis Boott and his daughter Elizabeth (Lizzie), expatriates who have lived for many years in Florentine villa on Bellosguardo. Takes up horseback riding on the Campagna. Encounters Matthew Arnold in April 1873 at Story's. Moves from Rome hotel to rooms of his own. Continues writing and now earns enough to support himself. Leaves Rome in June, spends summer in Bad Homburg. In October goes to Florence, where William joins him. They also visit Rome, William returning to America in March. In Baden-Baden June–August and returns to America September 4, with *Roderick Hudson* all but finished.

1875   *Roderick Hudson* serialized in *Atlantic Monthly* from January (published by Osgood at the end of the year). First book, *A Passionate Pilgrim and Other Tales*, published January 31. Tries living and writing in New York, in rooms at 111 E. 25th Street. Earns $200 a month from novel installments and continued reviewing, but finds New York too expensive. *Transatlantic Sketches*, published in April, sells almost 1,000 copies in three months. In Cambridge in July decides to return to Europe; arranges with John Hay, assistant to the publisher, to write Paris letters for the *New York Tribune*.

1875–76   Arriving in Paris in November, he takes rooms at 29 Rue de Luxembourg (since renamed Cambon). Becomes friend of Ivan Turgenev and is introduced by him to Gustave Flaubert's Sunday parties. Meets Edmond de Goncourt, Émile Zola, G. Charpentier (the publisher), Catulle Mendès, Alphonse Daudet, Guy de Maupassant, Ernest Renan, Gustave Doré. Makes friends with Charles Sanders Peirce, who is in Paris. Reviews (unfavorably) the early Impressionists at the Durand-Ruel gallery. By midsummer has received $400 for *Tribune* pieces, but editor asks for more Parisian gossip and James resigns. Travels in France during July, visiting Normandy and the Midi, and in September crosses to San Sebastian, Spain, to see a bullfight ("I thought the bull, in any case, a finer fellow than any of his tormentors"). Moves to London in December, taking rooms at 3 Bolton Street, Piccadilly, where he will live for the next decade.

1877   *The American* published. Meets Robert Browning and George du Maurier. Leaves London in midsummer for visit to Paris and then goes to Italy. In Rome rides again in Campagna and hears of an episode that inspires "Daisy

Miller." Back in England, spends Christmas at Stratford with Fanny Kemble.

1878   Publishes first book in England, *French Poets and Novelists* (Macmillan). Appearance of "Daisy Miller" in *Cornhill Magazine*, edited by Leslie Stephen, is international success, but by publishing it abroad loses American copyright and story is pirated in U.S. *Cornhill* also prints "An International Episode." *The Europeans* is serialized in *Atlantic*. Now a celebrity, he dines out often, visits country houses, gains weight, takes long walks, fences, and does weight-lifting to reduce. Elected to Reform Club. Meets Tennyson, George Meredith, and James McNeill Whistler. William marries Alice Howe Gibbens.

1879   Immersed in London society (". . . dined out during the past winter 107 times!"). Meets Edmund Gosse and Robert Louis Stevenson, who will later become his close friends. Sees much of Henry Adams and his wife, Marian (Clover), in London and later in Paris. Takes rooms in Paris, September–December. *Confidence* is serialized in *Scribner's* and published by Chatto & Windus. *Hawthorne* appears in Macmillan's "English Men of Letters" series.

1880–81   Stays in Florence March–May to work on *The Portrait of a Lady*. Meets Constance Fenimore Woolson, American novelist and grandniece of James Fenimore Cooper. Returns to Bolton Street in June, where William visits him. *Washington Square* serialized in *Cornhill Magazine* and published in U.S. by Harper & Brothers (Dec. 1880). *The Portrait of a Lady* serialized in *Macmillan's Magazine* (Oct. 1880–Nov. 1881) and *Atlantic Monthly*, published by Macmillan and Houghton, Mifflin (Nov. 1881). Publication both in United States and in England yields him the then-large income of $500 a month, though book sales are disappointing. Leaves London in February for Paris, the south of France, the Italian Riviera, and Venice, and returns home in July. Sister Alice comes to London with her friend Katharine Loring. James goes to Scotland in September.

1881–83   In November revisits America after absence of six years. Lionized in New York. Returns to Quincy Street for Christmas and sees ailing brother Wilky for the first time in ten years. In January visits Washington and the Henry Adamses and meets President Chester A. Arthur. Summoned to Cambridge by mother's death January 29 ("the sweetest, gentlest, most beneficent human being I have ever known"). All four brothers are together for the first time in fifteen years at her funeral. Alice and father move from Cambridge to Boston. Prepares a stage version of "Daisy Miller" and returns to England in May. William, now a Harvard professor, comes to Europe in September. Proposed by Leslie Stephen, James becomes member, without the usual red tape, of the Atheneum Club. Travels in France in October to write *A Little Tour in France* (published 1884) and has last visit with Turgenev, who is dying. Returns to England in December and learns of father's illness. Sails for America but Henry James Sr. dies December 18, 1882, before his arrival. Made executor of father's will. Visits brothers Wilky and Bob in Milwaukee in January. Quarrels with William over division of property—James wants to restore Wilky's share. Macmillan publishes a collected pocket edition of James's novels and tales in fourteen volumes. *Siege of London* and *Portraits of Places* published. Returns to Bolton Street in September. Wilky dies in November. Constance Fenimore Woolson comes to London for the winter.

1884–86   Goes to Paris in February and visits Daudet, Zola, and Goncourt. Again impressed with their intense concern with "art, form, manner" but calls them "mandarins." Misses Turgenev, who had died a few months before. Meets John Singer Sargent and persuades him to settle in London. Returns to Bolton Street. Sargent introduces him to young Paul Bourget. During country visits encounters many British political and social figures, including W. E. Gladstone, John Bright, and Charles Dilke. Alice, suffering from nervous ailment, arrives in England for visit in November but is too ill to travel and settles near her brother. *Tales of Three Cities* ("The Impressions of a Cousin," "Lady Barberina," "A New England Winter") and "The Art of Fiction" published 1884. Alice goes to Bournemouth in late January. James joins her in May and becomes an intimate of Robert Louis Stevenson, who resides nearby. Spends August at Dover and is visited by Paul Bourget. Stays in Paris for the next two months. Moves into a flat at 34 De Vere Gardens in Kensington early in March 1886. Alice takes rooms in London. *The Bostonians* serialized in *Century* (Feb. 1885–Feb. 1886; published 1886), *The Princess Casamassima* serialized in *Atlantic Monthly* (Sept. 1885–Oct. 1886; published 1886).

1886–87   Leaves for Italy in December for extended stay, mainly in Florence and Venice. Sees much of Constance Fenimore Woolson and stays in her villa. Writes "The Aspern Papers" and other tales. Returns to De Vere Gardens in July and begins work on *The Tragic Muse*. Pays several country visits. Dines out less often ("I know it all—all that one sees by 'going out'—today, as if I had made it. But if I had, I would have made it better!").

1888   *The Reverberator, The Aspern Papers, Louisa Pallant, The Modern Warning*, and *Partial Portraits* published. Elizabeth Boott Duveneck dies. Robert Louis Stevenson leaves for the South Seas. Engages fencing teacher to combat "symptoms of a portentous corpulence." Goes abroad in October to Geneva (where he visits Woolson), Genoa, Monte Carlo, and Paris.

1889–90   Catharine Walsh (Aunt Kate) dies March 1889. William comes to England to visit Alice in August. James goes to Dover in September and then to Paris for five weeks. Writes account of Robert Browning's funeral in Westminster Abbey. Dramatizes *The American* for the Compton Comedy Company. Meets and becomes close friends with American journalist William Morton Fullerton and young American publisher Wolcott Balestier. Goes to Italy for the summer, staying in Venice and Florence, and takes a brief walking tour in Tuscany with W. W. Baldwin, an American physician practicing in Florence. Miss Woolson moves to Cheltenham, England, to be near James. *Atlantic Monthly* rejects his story "The Pupil," but it appears in England. Writes series of drawing-room comedies for theater. Meets Rudyard Kipling. *The Tragic Muse* serialized in *Atlantic Monthly* (Jan. 1889–May 1890; published 1890). *A London Life* (including "The Patagonia," "The Liar," "Mrs. Temperly") published 1889.

1891   *The American* produced at Southport is a success during road tour. After residence in Leamington, Alice returns to London, cared for by Katharine Loring. Doctors discover she has breast cancer. James circulates comedies (*Mrs. Vibert*, later called *Tenants*, and *Mrs. Jasper*, later named *Disengaged*) among theater managers who are cool to his work. Unimpressed at first by Ibsen, writes an appreciative review after seeing a performance of *Hedda Gabler* with Elizabeth Robins, a young Kentucky actress; persuades her to take the part of Mme. de Cintré in the London production of *The American*. Recuperates from flu in Ireland. James Russell Lowell dies. *The American* opens in London, September 26, and runs for seventy nights. Wolcott Balestier dies, and James attends his funeral in Dresden in December.

1892   Alice James dies March 6. James travels to Siena to be near the Paul Bourgets, and Venice, June–July, to visit the Daniel Curtises, then to Lausanne to meet William and his family, who have come abroad for sabbatical. Attends funeral of Tennyson at Westminster Abbey. Augustin Daly agrees to produce *Mrs. Jasper*. *The American* continues to be performed on the road by the Compton Company. *The Lesson of the Master* (with a collection of stories including "The Marriages," "The Pupil," "Brooksmith," "The Solution," and "Sir Edmund Orme") published.

1893   Fanny Kemble dies in January. Continues to write unproduced plays. In March goes to Paris for two months. Sends Edward Compton first act and scenario for *Guy Domville*. Meets William and family in Lucerne and stays a month, returning to London in June. Spends July completing *Guy Domville* in Ramsgate. George Alexander, actor-manager, agrees to produce the play. Daly stages first reading of *Mrs. Jasper*, and James withdraws it, calling the rehearsal a mockery. *The Real Thing and Other Tales* (including "The Wheel of Time," "Lord Beaupré," "The Visit") published.

1894   Constance Fenimore Woolson dies in Venice, January. Shocked and upset, James prepares to attend funeral in Rome but changes his mind on learning she is a suicide. Goes to Venice in April to help her family settle her affairs. Receives one of four copies, privately printed by Miss Loring, of Alice's diary. Finds it impressive but is concerned that so much gossip he told Alice in private has been included (later burns his copy). Robert Louis Stevenson dies in the South Pacific. *Guy Domville* goes into rehearsal. *Theatricals: Two Comedies* and *Theatricals: Second Series* published.

1895   *Guy Domville* opens January 5 at St. James's Theatre. At play's end James is greeted by a fifteen-minute roar of boos, catcalls, and applause. Horrified and depressed, abandons the theater. Play earns him $1,300 after five-week run. Feels he can salvage something useful from playwriting for his fiction ("a key that, working in the same *general* way fits the complicated chambers of *both* the dramatic and the narrative lock"). Writes scenario for *The Spoils of Poynton*. Visits Lord Wolseley and Lord Houghton in Ireland. In the summer goes to Torquay in Devonshire and stays until November while electricity is being installed in De Vere Gardens flat. Friendship with W. E. Norris, who resides at Torquay. Writes a one-act play ("Mrs. Gracedew") at request of Ellen Terry. *Terminations* (containing "The Death of the Lion," "The Coxon Fund," "The Middle Years," "The Altar of the Dead") published.

1896–97 Finishes *The Spoils of Poynton* (serialized in *Atlantic Monthly* April–Oct. 1896 as *The Old Things*; published 1897). *Embarrassments* ("The Figure in the Carpet," "Glasses," "The Next Time," "The Way It Came") published. Takes a house on Point Hill, Playden, opposite the old town of Rye, Sussex, August–September. Ford Madox Hueffer (later Ford Madox Ford) visits him. Converts play *The Other House* into novel and works on *What Maisie Knew* (published Sept. 1897). George du Maurier dies early in October. Because of increasing pain in wrist, hires stenographer William MacAlpine in February and then purchases a typewriter; soon begins direct dictation to MacAlpine at the machine. Invites Joseph Conrad to lunch at De Vere Gardens and begins their friendship. Goes to Bournemouth in July. Serves on jury in London before going to Dunwich, Suffolk, to spend time with Temple-Emmet cousins. In late September 1897 signs a twenty-one-year lease for Lamb House in Rye for £70 a year ($350). Takes on extra work to pay for setting up his house—the life of William Wetmore Story ($1,250 advance) and will furnish an "American Letter" for new magazine *Literature* (precursor of *Times Literary Supplement*) for $200 a month. Howells visits.

1898   "The Turn of the Screw" (serialized in *Collier's* Jan.–April; published with "Covering End" under the title *The Two Magics*) proves his most popular work since "Daisy Miller." Sleeps in Lamb House for first time June 28. Soon after is visited by William's son, Henry James Jr. (Harry), followed by a stream of visitors: future Justice Oliver Wendell Holmes, Mrs. J. T. Fields, Sarah Orne Jewett, the Paul Bourgets, the Edward Warrens, the Daniel Curtises, the Edmund Gosses, and Howard Sturgis. His witty friend Jonathan Sturges, a young, crippled New Yorker, stays for two months during autumn. *In the Cage* published. Meets neighbors Stephen Crane and H. G. Wells.

1899   Finishes *The Awkward Age* and plans trip to the Continent. Fire in Lamb House delays departure. To Paris in March and then visits the Paul Bourgets at Hyères. Stays with the Curtises in their Venice palazzo, where he meets and becomes friends with Jessie Allen. In Rome meets young American-Norwegian sculptor Hendrik C. Andersen; buys one of his busts. Returns to England in July and Andersen comes for three days in August. William, his wife, Alice, and daughter, Peggy, arrive at Lamb House in October. First meeting of brothers in six years. William now has confirmed heart condition. James B. Pinker becomes literary agent and for first time James's professional relations are systematically organized; he reviews copyrights, finds new publishers, and obtains better prices for work ("the germ of a new career"). Purchases Lamb House for $10,000 with an easy mortgage.

1900   Unhappy at whiteness of beard which he has worn since the Civil War, he shaves it off. Alternates between Rye and London. Works on *The Sacred Fount*. Works on and then sets aside *The Sense of the Past* (never finished). Begins *The Ambassadors*. *The Soft Side*, a collection of twelve tales, published. Niece Peggy comes to Lamb House for Christmas.

1901   Obtains permanent room at the Reform Club for London visits and spends eight weeks in town. Sees funeral of Queen Victoria. Decides to employ a typist, Mary Weld, to replace the more expensive overqualified shorthand stenographer, MacAlpine. Completes *The Ambassadors* and begins *The Wings of the Dove*. *The Sacred Fount* published.

Has meeting with George Gissing. William James, much improved, returns home after two years in Europe. Young Cambridge admirer Percy Lubbock visits. Discharges his alcoholic servants of sixteen years (the Smiths). Mrs. Paddington is new housekeeper.

1902   In London for the winter but gout and stomach disorder force him home earlier. Finishes *The Wings of the Dove* (published in August). William James Jr. (Billy) visits in October and becomes a favorite nephew. Writes "The Beast in the Jungle" and "The Birthplace."

1903   *The Ambassadors, The Better Sort* (a collection of eleven tales), and *William Wetmore Story and His Friends* published. After another spell in town, returns to Lamb House in May and begins work on *The Golden Bowl.* Meets and establishes close friendship with Dudley Jocelyn Persse, a nephew of Lady Gregory. First meeting with Edith Wharton in December.

1904–05   Completes *The Golden Bowl* (published Nov. 1904). Rents Lamb House for six months, and sails in August for America after twenty-year absence. Sees new Manhattan skyline from New Jersey on arrival and stays with Colonel George Harvey, president of Harper's, in Jersey shore house with Mark Twain as fellow guest. Goes to William's country house at Chocorua in the White Mountains, New Hampshire. Re-explores Cambridge, Boston, Salem, Newport, and Concord, where he visits brother Bob. In October stays with Edith Wharton in the Berkshires and motors with her through Massachusetts and New York. Later visits New York, Philadelphia (where he delivers lecture "The Lesson of Balzac"), and then Washington, D.C., as a guest in Henry Adams' house. Meets (and is critical of) President Theodore Roosevelt. Returns to Philadelphia to lecture at Bryn Mawr. Travels to Richmond, Charleston, Jacksonville, Palm Beach, and St. Augustine. Then lectures in St. Louis, Chicago, South Bend, Indianapolis, Los Angeles (with a short vacation at Coronado Beach near San Diego), San Francisco, Portland, and Seattle. Returns to explore New York City ("the terrible town"), May–June. Lectures on "The Question of Our Speech" at Bryn Mawr commencement. Elected to newly founded American Academy of Arts and Letters

(William declines). Returns to England in July; lectures had more than covered expenses of his trip. Begins revision of novels for the New York Edition.

1906–08 Writes "The Jolly Corner" and *The American Scene* (published 1907). Writes eighteen prefaces for the New York Edition (twenty-four volumes published 1907–09). Visits Paris and Edith Wharton in spring 1907 and motors with her in Midi. Travels to Italy for the last time, visiting Hendrik Andersen in Rome, and goes on to Florence and Venice. Engages Theodora Bosanquet as his typist in autumn. Again visits Edith Wharton in Paris, spring 1908. William comes to England to give a series of lectures at Oxford and receives an honorary Doctor of Science degree. James goes to Edinburgh in March to see a tryout by the Forbes-Robertsons of his play *The High Bid*, a rewrite in three acts of the one-act play originally written for Ellen Terry (revised earlier as the story "Covering End"). Play gets only five special matinees in London. Shocked by slim royalties from sales of the New York Edition.

1909 Growing acquaintance with young writers and artists of Bloomsbury, including Virginia and Vanessa Stephen and others. Meets and befriends young Hugh Walpole in February. Goes to Cambridge in June as guest of admiring dons and undergraduates and meets John Maynard Keynes. Feels unwell and sees doctors about what he believes may be heart trouble. They reassure him. Late in year burns forty years of his letters and papers at Rye. Suffers severe attacks of gout. *Italian Hours* published.

1910 Very ill in January ("food-loathing") and spends much time in bed. Nephew Harry comes to be with him in February. In March is examined by Sir William Osler, who finds nothing physically wrong. James begins to realize that he has had "a sort of nervous breakdown." William, in spite of now severe heart trouble, and his wife, Alice, come to England to give him support. Brothers and Alice go to Bad Nauheim for cure, then travel to Zurich, Lucerne, and Geneva, where they learn Robertson (Bob) James has died in America of heart attack. James's health begins to improve but William is failing. Sails with William and Alice for America in August. William dies at Chocorua soon after arrival, and James remains with the family for the winter. *The Finer Grain* and *The Outcry* published.

1911 Honorary degree from Harvard in spring. Visits with Howells and Grace Norton. Sails for England July 30. On return to Lamb House, decides he will be too lonely there and starts search for a London flat. Theodora Bosanquet obtains two work rooms adjoining her flat in Chelsea and he begins autobiography, *A Small Boy and Others*. Continues to reside at the Reform Club.

1912 Delivers "The Novel in *The Ring and the Book*," on the 100th anniversary of Browning's birth, to the Royal Society of Literature. Honorary Doctor of Letters from Oxford University June 26. Spends summer at Lamb House. Sees much of Edith Wharton ("the Firebird"), who spends summer in England. (She secretly arranges to have Scribner's put $8,000 into James's account.) Takes 21 Carlyle Mansions, in Cheyne Walk, Chelsea, as London quarters. Writes a long admiring letter for William Dean Howells' seventy-fifth birthday. Meets André Gide. Contracts bad case of shingles and is ill four months, much of the time not able to leave bed.

1913 Moves into Cheyne Walk flat. Two hundred and seventy friends and admirers subscribe for seventieth birthday portrait by Sargent and present also a silver-gilt Charles II porringer and dish ("golden bowl"). Sargent turns over his payment to young sculptor Derwent Wood, who does a bust of James. Autobiography *A Small Boy and Others* published. Goes with niece Peggy to Lamb House for the summer.

1914 *Notes of a Son and Brother* published. Works on "The Ivory Tower." Returns to Lamb House in July. Niece Peggy joins him. Horrified by the war ("this crash of our civilisation," "a nightmare from which there is no waking"). In London in September participates in Belgian Relief, visits wounded in St. Bartholomew's and other hospitals; feels less "finished and useless and doddering" and recalls Walt Whitman and his Civil War hospital visits. Accepts chairmanship of American Volunteer Motor Ambulance Corps in France. *Notes on Novelists* (essays on Balzac, Flaubert, Zola) published.

1915–16   Continues work with the wounded and war relief. Has
           occasional lunches with Prime Minister Asquith and fam-
           ily, and meets Winston Churchill and other war leaders.
           Discovers that he is considered an alien and has to report
           to police before going to coastal Rye. Decides to become
           a British national and asks Asquith to be one of his spon-
           sors. Receives Certificate of Naturalization on July 26.
           H. G. Wells satirizes him in *Boon* ("leviathan retrieving
           pebbles") and James, in the correspondence that follows,
           writes: "Art *makes* life, makes interest, makes importance."
           Burns more papers and photographs at Lamb House in
           autumn. Has a stroke December 2 in his flat, followed by
           another two days later. Develops pneumonia and during
           delirium gives his last confused dictation (dealing with the
           Napoleonic legend) to Theodora Bosanquet, who types it
           on the familiar typewriter. Mrs. William James arrives De-
           cember 13 to care for him. On New Year's Day, George V
           confers the Order of Merit. Dies February 28. Funeral ser-
           vices held at the Chelsea Old Church. The body is cre-
           mated and the ashes are buried in Cambridge Cemetery
           family plot.

Note on the Texts

This volume collects four novels published by Henry James between 1896 and 1899: *The Other House* (1896), *The Spoils of Poynton* (1897), *What Maisie Knew* (1897), and *The Awkward Age* (1899). Each novel was first published serially and then appeared in book form almost simultaneously in England and the United States. James later included *The Spoils of Poynton*, *What Maisie Knew*, and *The Awkward Age* in the 1907–9 New York Edition of his collected works, revised to reflect the further evolution of his style.

James first sketched out a scenario for *The Other House* in a notebook on December 26, 1893. Using the title *The Promise*, he developed it into a scenario for a three-act play, which he showed to the actor-manager Edward Compton. James eventually decided to use the material in a work of fiction, and on February 26, 1896, agreed with Clement K. Shorter, editor of the *Illustrated London News*, to write a novel in 13 installments in return for £300. (In 1908–9 James wrote a stage version of *The Other House*, which failed to find a producer; this version was first published in *The Complete Plays of Henry James*, edited by Leon Edel, in 1949.) James wrote the serial during the spring and summer of 1896, and it appeared in the *Illustrated London News* from July 4 to September 26, 1896. In July 1896 James completed arrangements for book publication of the novel in both England and America. *The Other House* was published in two volumes by William Heinemann in London on October 1, 1896. Following two impressions totaling 1,000 copies, a cheaper one-volume printing of 1,500 copies was published by Heinemann on July 17, 1897; in this printing, the spaces between the lines of standing type were reduced. There were no further printings of the novel by Heinemann. The American edition of *The Other House* was published in New York by the Macmillan Company on or about October 17, 1896, in a printing of 2,150 copies. (Its publication was announced in the *New York Journal* on October 18 in an item with the caption: "Henry James's New Novel of Immorality and Crime: The Surprising Plunge of the Great Novelist into the Field of Sensational Fiction.") There were no further printings of this edition.

Collation of the serial version against the two first editions shows that James made substantive revisions in the text of the serial version only while preparing the English edition. These revisions consisted of minor changes in wording. For example, "all the plain prettiness" became "all the dull prettiness" (9.13); "what on earth would become" was changed to "what on earth do you suppose would become" (24.31); and "he humorously inquired" was replaced by "he playfully inquired" (129.17). The English edition also has fewer commas than the serial version and the American edition, although some commas appear in the English edition that are not present in the other versions. James did not make any further revisions to the novel. This volume prints the text of the two-volume 1896 Heinemann edition of *The Other House*.

James recorded "the subject of a little tale—a little social and psychological picture" in a notebook on December 24, 1893, after being told at dinner the night before a story about a quarrel between a mother and her son over a house and its furnishings. In 1895 he worked on the story, using the title *The House Beautiful*, and gradually expanded its length until it became a novel. By early 1896 James had changed the title to *The Old Things*, and it was under this name that it appeared in the *Atlantic Monthly* between April and October 1896. The novel was then published as *The Spoils of Poynton* in London by William Heinemann on or about February 6, 1897, in a printing of 2,000 copies. There were no further printings of this edition. An American edition of *The Spoils of Poynton* was published in Boston by Houghton, Mifflin on February 13, 1897, in a first printing of 1,500 copies; there was a second printing of 500 copies in March 1897.

Collation of *The Old Things* against the English and American editions of *The Spoils of Poynton* shows that James made numerous substantive revisions in the text of the serial version that were incorporated into both editions. These revisions consisted of relatively minor changes in wording. For example, "the jollity of London was not merely a diplomatic name for the jollity of Mona Brigstock" was changed to "the jollity of London was not merely the only name his small vocabulary yielded for the jollity of Mona Brigstock" (226.31–33), and "the refutation of Mrs. Gereth was easy" became "the refutation of that boast was easy" (348.11–12). James also made similar revisions that appeared only in the English edition, such as changing "A second glance, this morning, at the young lady" to "A second glance, a sharp one, at the young lady" (214.26–27), and "more subtly discovered" to "more finely discovered" (228.27–28). The English edition contains fewer commas than the American edition, which has fewer commas than the serial version. Contractions are closed up in the English edition (i.e., "would n't" becomes "wouldn't"), and English spellings are adopted. James did not revise the novel again until he prepared it for publication in the 1907–9 New York Edition of his collected works. This volume prints the text of the 1897 William Heinemann edition of *The Spoils of Poynton*.

James described in a notebook on November 12, 1892, a story he had recently heard at dinner regarding a child of divorced parents, and he further developed the idea in an entry dated August 26, 1893. He outlined the plot of the work in detail on December 22, 1895, and had finished eight chapters by October 26, 1896, when he wrote detailed notes regarding the remainder of the novel. *What Maisie Knew* appeared serially in *The Chap-Book*, a Chicago periodical, from January 15 to August 1, 1897, and in abridged form in the *New Review*, a London magazine, between February and September 1897. The novel was published in book form in London by William Heinemann on or about September 17, 1897, in a first printing of 2,000 copies; there were two subsequent impressions. An American edition was published in Chicago by Herbert S. Stone & Co. in October 1897.

Collation of the *Chap-Book* version against the English and American editions indicates that James prepared the two editions independently of each other. Some substantive changes from the serial version, such as the replacement of "Mrs. Beale looked surprised" with "Mrs. Beale diffused surprise" (485.13) appear in both editions. Other alterations, such as changing "her gentle friend" to "her patient friend," were made only in the American edition. More often James made substantive changes that appear only in the English edition; for example, "a tenderness that would never fail her" became "a tenderness that would never give way" (414.28–29) and "an effort resisted by the third person" was changed to "an effort deprecated by their comrade" (418.25–26). In some cases, James revised a passage in the serial text differently in each of the book editions. For example, "to thrill with response to the picture" became "to thrill with relish to the picture" in the American edition and "to thrill with enjoyment of the picture" (559.16–17) in the English edition. The punctuation of the three versions varies, with the English edition having the lightest use of commas. Contractions are closed up in the English edition, and English spellings are adopted. James did not revise *What Maisie Knew* again until he prepared it for inclusion in the 1907–9 New York Edition. Because the substantive revisions James made for the English edition were equivalent in nature and greater in number than the ones he made for the American edition, this volume prints the text of the 1897 William Heinemann edition of *What Maisie Knew*.

James recorded his basic idea for *The Awkward Age* in a notebook on March 4, 1895. He originally described it as "a real little situation for a short tale," but by October 1895 he had decided that it "would fatally exceed that measure." In November 1897 James arranged with Henry Loomis Nelson, editor of *Harper's Weekly*, for the novel's serialization, and it appeared in that periodical between October 1, 1898, and January 7, 1899. *The Awkward Age* was published in London by William Heinemann on April 25, 1899, in a printing of 2,000 copies, and in New York by Harper & Brothers on May 12, 1899, in a printing of 1,000 copies. Collation of the *Harper's Weekly* version against the English and American book editions shows that James made many substantive revisions in the text of the serial version that were incorporated in both editions. These revisions consisted of relatively minor verbal changes, such as altering "perhaps a little disappointed one?" to "perhaps a little, after the warnings, let one down?" (706.7–8) and "something in Mr. What was his name's face" to "something in his entertainer's face" (730.33–34). In many cases substantive changes appeared only in the English edition. For example, "a circumstance, however, that might by no means, on occasion, have failed" was changed to "a circumstance, not withstanding, that would not in every case have failed" (861.16–18), and "He *is* distinctly rich" became "He *is* distinctly bloated" (898.8). The punctuation of the three versions varies, with the English edition having the lightest use of commas. English spellings were adopted in the Heinemann edition. James did not revise *The Awkward Age* again until he prepared it for publication in the 1907–9 New York Edition. This volume prints the text of the 1899 William Heinemann edition of *The Awkward Age*.

This volume presents the texts of the original printings chosen for inclusion here, but it does not attempt to reproduce nontextual features of their typographic design. The texts are presented without change, except for the correction of typographical errors. Spelling, punctuation, and capitalization are often expressive features and are not altered, even when inconsistent or irregular. The following is a list of typographical errors corrected, cited by page and line number: 39.34, "She; 47.16, you Dennis; 48.14, my; 63.14, keep you; 88.1, look; 108.17, returned,; 127.22, "That's; 177.10, him; 203.5, the the; 251.37, Poyton; 268.2, so,; 397.22, crest; 401.28, mono grams; 409.28, Beale; 505.6, pockethandkerchief; 505.34–35, hnsband; 565.9, drove me; 673.37, London's; 740.22, When; 747.29, of,; 747.40, reminder; 814.33, *Ella*; 929.14, Fanny [missing period].

Notes

In the notes below, the reference numbers denote page and line of this volume (the line count includes chapter headings). No note is made for material included in standard desk-reference books. Quotations from Shakespeare are keyed to *The Riverside Shakespeare*, ed. G. Blakemore Evans (Boston: Houghton Mifflin, 1974). For further background, see *Henry James Letters*, ed. Leon Edel (Cambridge: The Belknap Press of Harvard University Press, Vol. I—1843–1875 [1974]; Vol. II—1875–1883 [1975]; Vol. III—1883–1895 [1980]; Vol. IV —1895–1916 [1984]) and *The Complete Notebooks of Henry James*, ed. Leon Edel and Lyall H. Powers (New York and Oxford: Oxford University Press, 1987). For the prefaces to *The Spoils of Poynton*, *What Maisie Knew*, and *The Awkward Age* in the New York Edition, see Henry James, *Literary Criticism: French Writers, Other European Writers, The Prefaces to the New York Edition* (New York: The Library of America, 1984).

THE OTHER HOUSE

12.9   Berlin-wool]   Fine dyed wool used for embroidery.

43.7   *Voyons, voyons*]   Let's see, let's see.

75.36   fly]   A light, one-horse carriage.

101.17–18   "I seem to have uttered a *bêtise*]   I seem to have uttered something stupid.

113.35   Almanach de Gotha]   A reference book published annually from 1763 to 1944 in Gotha, Germany, that contained extensive genealogical information on European royalty as well as statistical information and a diplomatic gazetteer.

139.17   *A bientôt.*]   See you soon.

THE SPOILS OF POYNTON

213.31   *endimanchée*]   In her Sunday best.

226.3   Louis Quinze]   Louis XV (1710–74), king of France 1715–74.

234.3   the "Stores,"]   The Army and Navy Stores, a chain of department stores founded in 1872 that catered to the growing middle classes.

235.5   *n'en parlons plus*]   Let's say no more about it.

260.34   *morceaux de musée*]   Museum pieces.

264.18   Louis Seize]   Louis XVI (1754–93), king of France 1774–92.

269.3   flyman]   The driver of a one-horse hackney coach.

306.5   Universal Provider]   Popular name for William Whiteley (1831–1907), the founder of the Whiteley department store in Bayswater, north of Kensington Gardens.

311.14   Marie Antoinette in the Conciergerie]   The Conciergerie, a surviving section of a 14th-century royal palace on the Ile de la Cité in Paris, was used during the Revolution as a prison. Marie Antoinette was confined there from August 2, 1793, until her execution on October 16.

WHAT MAISIE KNEW

492.6   "Moonlight Berceuse"]   Moonlight lullaby.

495.7–10   Forest of Arden . . . Rosalind?]   Sir Claude refers to the principal characters and setting in Shakespeare's *As You Like It*.

542.8   apollinaris]   A mineral water.

552.38–39   portemonnaie]   Purse.

560.7   *plage*]   Beach.

564.17   *petits verres*]   Small glasses (of liqueur).

564.30   *déjeuner*]   Lunch.

572.22   s*alon de lecture*]   Reading room.

582.17   *haute ville*]   The upper (and generally the older) part of the town.

605.24–25   the *omelette aux rognons* and the *poulet sauté*]   The kidney omelette and the sautéed chicken.

612.37   *café complet*]   Coffee and rolls.

620.29   *patronne*]   Innkeeper.

621.4   "*Et bien soigné, n'est-ce-pas?*"]   And very elegant, right?

621.5   "*Soyez tranquille*"]   You can depend on it.

621.5–6   "*Et pour Madame?*"]   And for Madame? ("Madame" can mean "your wife.")

621.8   "*Rien encore?*"]   Nothing yet.

626.17   "*Les tartines sont là.*"]   The bread and butter is there.

626.32–33   *vous n'y êtes pas.*]   You're not even close.

635.40   *coupé*]   Carriage.

636.27   *Monsieur est placé?"*]   Does the gentleman have his seats?

636.28   *"Pas encore."*]   Not yet.

636.29   *"Et vos billets?—vous n'avez que le temps."*]   And your tickets? You have only just enough time.

636.30   *"Monsieur veut-il que je les prenne?"*]   Would the gentleman like me to get them?

636.32–33   *"Veux-tu bien qu'il en prenne?"*]   Is it all right with you if he gets tickets?

636.38   *"Prenny, prenny. Oh prenny!"*]   In childishly accented French: Get them, get them. Oh, get them!

636.39   *"Ah, si mademoiselle le veut——!"*]   Oh, if Mademoiselle wishes it——!

637.4   *"En voiture, en voiture!"*]   All aboard, all aboard!

637.5–6   *"Ah, vous n'avez plus le temps!"*]   Oh, you've run out of time!

THE AWKWARD AGE

663.13   *'caro mio.'*]   My dear.

686.13   *cara mia*]   My dear (feminine).

689.2   *des femmes bien gracieuses*]   Very graceful women.

689.5–6   *toutes ces dames*]   All these ladies.

689.15   *Voilà, ma chère.*]   There we are, my dear.

690.12   *femmes du monde*]   Women of the world.

691.29   *pourparlers*]   Negotiations.

692.22   *J'aime, moi, . . . pas d'autres.*]   For myself, I like situations that are crystal clear—I don't understand any others.

694.16   *vous autres!*]   You people!

694.17   *drôlement*]   Oddly.

707.2   *à toute épreuve*]   Foolproof.

709.37   *c'est tout dire*]   What more can one say?

710.40   *pour deux sous*]   In the least.

717.15–16   *"Je ne peux pourtant . . . cette chérie"*]   I can hardly ask the darling girl to leave the room.

719.15   *impudeur*]   Indiscretion.

721.26–27   *comme cette petite*]   Like that young woman.

721.32   *esprit de conduite*]   A sense of how to behave.

723.21–22   *"Vous avez parfois la grande beauté."*]   At times, you possess a surpassing beauty.

725.36   *Elle se les passe*—her little fancies!]   She does permit herself—her little fancies!

732.10   *qui ne court pas les rues,*]   Which you don't find on every street corner.

736.25–26   I see them, I know, with a *raccourci.*]   I see them, I know, with an abridgement, i.e., in a simplified way.

760.37   *mesquinerie*]   Pettiness.

770.17   *oncle d'Amérique,*]   An American (i.e., rich) uncle.

778.8   *c'est la moindre des choses*]   Nothing could be easier.

781.5   *Basta,*]   Enough said.

781.21   *vous me rendez la vie!*]   You've saved my life!

782.27   *la voilà*]   She's here.

792.18–20   Isn't it one crowded . . . age without a name.]   Cf. Thomas Mordaunt (1730–1809), "Verses Written During the War": "Sound, sound the clarion, fill the fife! / Throughout the sensual world proclaim, / One crowded hour of glorious life / Is worth an age without a name."

794.3   *"Intrigant!"*]   Schemer.

806.39   *le fond de ma pensée.*]   What I'm getting at.

807.2–3   Caro signore,]   My dear sir.

807.27   *A tantôt.*]   See you soon.

812.3   her *monde,*]   Her class; her social milieu.

813.31   Edward and I have a *cousinage,*]   Edward and I are cousins.

813.36   *coureur*]   A chaser after women.

813.39   *beau comme le jour,*]   Beautiful as the day.

814.33–34   *Elle l'a bien voulu,*]   She asked for it.

815.17   *doter*]   Provide a dowry for.

815.20–21   a *parti*]   A catch, i.e., someone especially eligible.

817.37   *Voyons*]   Look here.

818.3   '*Pourquoi faire?*']   What for?

818.23   *rassurez-vous bien!*]   You can rest easy!

818.30   *femme d'esprit.*]   A woman of great wit.

821.2   *mal' aria*]   Poisoned atmosphere.

836.21–22   investigating Society.]   Probably a reference to the Society for
Psychical Research, founded in England in 1882 to promote scientific investi-
gation of psychic phenomena. William James helped found an American Society in 1884 and served as its president, 1895–96.

843.1   *Comment donc?*]   How's that?

845.13   *que diable*]   Devil take it.

852.15   *béte*]   Stupid.

855.31   of a *soigné!*]   The most meticulous!

859.6   *point de répere,*]   Reference point.

859.11–12   'Our antagonist . . . from being superficial'?]   Cf. Edmund
Burke in *Reflections on the Revolution in France* (1790): "He that wrestles
with us strengthens our nerves, and sharpens our skill. Our antagonist is our
helper."

870.26   Beatrice came out to Benedick:]   Cf. Beatrice in Shakespeare's
Much Ado About Nothing, II.iii.247–48: "Against my will I am sent to bid
you come in to dinner."

883.16–17   *Rien de plus facile*]   There's nothing easier.

910.1–2   "The hungry generations tread you down]   Cf. John Keats, *Ode
to a Nightingale* (1820), stanza 7, lines 61–64: "Thou wast not born for death,
immortal Bird! / No hungry generations tread thee down; / The voice I
hear this passing night was heard / In ancient days by emperor and clown."

914.14–15   "*Vous avez bien de l'esprit.*]   You're very quick.

916.14   and Mrs. Brook herself *en téte.*]   And Mrs. Brook herself was the
first to do.

917.20–21   *Dieu sait comme elle se coiffe,*]   Heaven knows how her hair
looks.

921.5   *âme en peine,*]   A soul in pain.

924.10   *ces messieurs*]   These gentlemen.

929.6   *voyez!*]   You see!; take note.

931.1   *savez-vous*]   Do you know.

932.37   *Je crois bien,*]   I should think.

940.18   the *bon temps?*]   The good old days.

940.40   a *femme charmante*]   A charming woman.

941.16–17   'Even in our ashes live their wonted fires!']   From Thomas Gray, *Elegy Written in a Country Churchyard* (1751), lines 89–92 : "On some fond breast the parting soul relies, / Some pious drops the closing eye requires; / Even from the tomb the voice of Nature cries, / Even in our ashes live their wonted fires."

957.28   *voyons, voyons*,"]   Let's see; wait a moment.

983.15   "But there's a tide in the affairs of men]   Cf. Brutus in Shakespeare's *Julius Caesar*, IV.iii.218–21: "There is a tide in the affairs of men,/ Which taken at the flood, leads on to fortune;/ Omitted, all the voyage of their life/ Is bound in shallows and in miseries."

Library of Congress Cataloging-in-Publication Data

James, Henry, 1843–1916.
  [Novels. Selections]
  Novels, 1896–1899 / Henry James.
        p. cm.—(Library of America ; 139)
  Includes bibliographical references (p.).
      Contents: The other house—The spoils of Poynton—What Maisie knew
  —The awkward age.
  ISBN 1–931082–30–8 (alk. paper)
  I. Title.   II. Series.
PS2112 2003
813′.4—dc21

                                                      2002030167

THE LIBRARY OF AMERICA SERIES

The Library of America fosters appreciation and pride in America's literary heritage by publishing, and keeping permanently in print, authoritative editions of America's best and most significant writing. An independent nonprofit organization, it was founded in 1979 with seed money from the National Endowment for the Humanities and the Ford Foundation.

1. Herman Melville, *Typee, Omoo, Mardi* (1982)
2. Nathaniel Hawthorne, *Tales and Sketches* (1982)
3. Walt Whitman, *Poetry and Prose* (1982)
4. Harriet Beecher Stowe, *Three Novels* (1982)
5. Mark Twain, *Mississippi Writings* (1982)
6. Jack London, *Novels and Stories* (1982)
7. Jack London, *Novels and Social Writings* (1982)
8. William Dean Howells, *Novels 1875–1886* (1982)
9. Herman Melville, *Redburn, White-Jacket, Moby-Dick* (1983)
10. Nathaniel Hawthorne, *Collected Novels* (1983)
11. Francis Parkman, *France and England in North America*, vol. I (1983)
12. Francis Parkman, *France and England in North America*, vol. II (1983)
13. Henry James, *Novels 1871–1880* (1983)
14. Henry Adams, *Novels, Mont Saint Michel, The Education* (1983)
15. Ralph Waldo Emerson, *Essays and Lectures* (1983)
16. Washington Irving, *History, Tales and Sketches* (1983)
17. Thomas Jefferson, *Writings* (1984)
18. Stephen Crane, *Prose and Poetry* (1984)
19. Edgar Allan Poe, *Poetry and Tales* (1984)
20. Edgar Allan Poe, *Essays and Reviews* (1984)
21. Mark Twain, *The Innocents Abroad, Roughing It* (1984)
22. Henry James, *Literary Criticism: Essays, American & English Writers* (1984)
23. Henry James, *Literary Criticism: European Writers & The Prefaces* (1984)
24. Herman Melville, *Pierre, Israel Potter, The Confidence-Man, Tales & Billy Budd* (1985)
25. William Faulkner, *Novels 1930–1935* (1985)
26. James Fenimore Cooper, *The Leatherstocking Tales*, vol. I (1985)
27. James Fenimore Cooper, *The Leatherstocking Tales*, vol. II (1985)
28. Henry David Thoreau, *A Week, Walden, The Maine Woods, Cape Cod* (1985)
29. Henry James, *Novels 1881–1886* (1985)
30. Edith Wharton, *Novels* (1986)
31. Henry Adams, *History of the U.S. during the Administrations of Jefferson* (1986)
32. Henry Adams, *History of the U.S. during the Administrations of Madison* (1986)
33. Frank Norris, *Novels and Essays* (1986)
34. W.E.B. Du Bois, *Writings* (1986)
35. Willa Cather, *Early Novels and Stories* (1987)
36. Theodore Dreiser, *Sister Carrie, Jennie Gerhardt, Twelve Men* (1987)
37. Benjamin Franklin, *Writings* (1987)
38. William James, *Writings 1902–1910* (1987)
39. Flannery O'Connor, *Collected Works* (1988)
40. Eugene O'Neill, *Complete Plays 1913–1920* (1988)
41. Eugene O'Neill, *Complete Plays 1920–1931* (1988)
42. Eugene O'Neill, *Complete Plays 1932–1943* (1988)
43. Henry James, *Novels 1886–1890* (1989)
44. William Dean Howells, *Novels 1886–1888* (1989)
45. Abraham Lincoln, *Speeches and Writings 1832–1858* (1989)
46. Abraham Lincoln, *Speeches and Writings 1859–1865* (1989)
47. Edith Wharton, *Novellas and Other Writings* (1990)
48. William Faulkner, *Novels 1936–1940* (1990)
49. Willa Cather, *Later Novels* (1990)
50. Ulysses S. Grant, *Memoirs and Selected Letters* (1990)

This book is set in 10 point Linotron Galliard,
a face designed for photocomposition by Matthew Carter
and based on the sixteenth-century face Granjon. The paper
is acid-free Domtar Literary Opaque and meets the requirements
for permanence of the American National Standards Institute. The
binding material is Brillianta, a woven rayon cloth made by
Van Heek-Scholco Textielfabrieken, Holland. The compo-
sition is by The Clarinda Company. Printing and
binding by R.R.Donnelley & Sons Company.
Designed by Bruce Campbell.